SHADOW PEOPLE

A TOM DOHERTY
ASSOCIATES BOOK

NEW YORK

JAMES SWAIN

SHADOW PEOPLE

SHADOW PEOPLE

A Tor Book
Published by Tom Doherty Associates, LLC
175 Fifth Avenue
New York, NY 10010

www.tor-forge.com

Tor® is a registered trademark of Tom Doherty Associates, LLC.

ISBN 978-0-7653-2995-0 (hardcover)
ISBN 978-1-4299-4308-6 (e-book)

Tor books may be purchased for educational, business, or promotional use.
For information on bulk purchases, please contact Macmillan Corporate
and Premium Sales Department at 1-800-221-7945 extension 5442
or write specialmarkets@macmillan.com.

First Edition: June 2013

Printed in the United States of America

0 9 8 7 6 5 4 3 2 1

For Bob Elliott

ACKNOWLEDGMENTS

The author wishes to thank Claire Eddy, Katharine Critchlow, and Laura Swain for their generous contributions to this book.

I know that ghosts have wandered on earth. Be with me always—take any form—drive me mad! Only do not leave me in this abyss, where I cannot find you!

—Emily Brontë,
Wuthering Heights

PART I

THE WITCHING HOUR

1

Something didn't feel right.

It wasn't the setting. Milly Adams's luxurious apartment in the Dakota on New York's fashionable Upper West Side looked as magnificent as ever. Laid out like a photo spread in a glossy home furnishings magazine, each piece of antique furniture was in its proper place, as were the exquisite wall decorations and fresh-cut flowers.

Nor was it the other guests sitting at the table with Peter Warlock. In fact, the group of psychics gathered in Milly's apartment on this particular Friday evening were the young magician's most trusted friends. It consisted of Max Romeo, a retired magician who'd trained Peter in the art of legerdemain; Lester Rowe, a puckish Scotsman who gave psychic readings out of his Lower East Side apartment, and ventured north of 14th Street only to attend Milly's weekly séances; Milly's beautiful if somewhat spoiled niece Holly, a sophomore at Columbia and an aspiring witch; and the group's newest member, a blind African-American psychic named Homer, who made his living telling fortunes beneath the arch in Washington Square Park in Greenwich Village.

Everything looked the same, yet something wasn't right. Peter could feel it in his bones. He'd been leading the Friday night séances since his teens, his ability to channel the dead far greater than that of the other psychics in the room.

The clock on the mantel struck midnight. Striking a single wooden match, the young magician lit the three white candles sitting on the dining room table. "Ready for takeoff?"

"Ready," the others replied.

They clasped hands and formed a circle. Staring into the flames, Peter began to recite the mystic words that would grant him entry to the world where the spirits resided.

In darkness, I see light: in daylight, I see night.
Shadows as bright as sunshine, the blind able to see.
This is the world we wish to enter.

A movement caught his eyes, and he stopped. On the far wall, a quivering black mass danced beside the portrait of Mary Glover, an infamous Salem witch from whom Milly was directly descended. Peter had never seen anything quite like it. Without warning, the mass slipped into a crack in the wall, and vanished without a trace.

"I just saw something really strange," Peter announced.

"Was it a ghost?" Holly asked, sitting to his right.

"Not like any I've ever seen."

"What was different about it?"

"It didn't have a face."

"Come on. All ghosts have faces."

"I know they do. But this one didn't."

As everyone at the table knew, every ghost had a face, as well as a voice, and sometimes a warped personality as well. "You must be imagining things," Holly teased him.

"You're right. After all, there are no such things as ghosts, are there?"

They all laughed. Ghosts and spirits were everywhere, yet people refused to acknowledge them. Instead, they convinced themselves they were imagining things, or that their eyes were playing tricks on them.

"Whatever it was, it's gone now," Peter said. "Let's resume. Is everyone ready?"

His friends nodded in unison.

"Good. Here we go."

A séance was a ritual with a strict set of rules. Peter snuffed the three candles on the table with his fingertips, then relit them using another wooden match. They again joined hands, and he repeated the mystic words that allowed him entry to the spirit world.

A jolt of electricity went straight up his spine. His world turned dark as his spirit left his physical body and transported itself to the parallel world where the spirits dwelled. He likened the experience to falling down a mine shaft, his arms and legs flailing helplessly in the air.

Finally his fall ended, and he found himself inside a basement with a low, claustrophobic ceiling with exposed beams, a rattling furnace, and a naked bulb hanging by a cord that swung eerily back and forth. It felt like the set of a teenage slasher movie, and he took a deep breath, wondering where in God's name he was.

Every Friday night, the spirits took him on a dark journey. Sometimes, they sent him into the past, while other times, he was plunged headlong into the future. No two journeys were ever the same. Tonight's had started badly, and he hoped things would improve.

The sound of a voice caught him by surprise, and he spun around. On the other side of the basement, an overweight man wearing corduroy pants and a blazer with sandy patches on the elbows stood by a worktable. He had a neatly trimmed beard and glasses, and looked like a college professor. He was also talking to himself, and had no idea that Peter was there.

Peter found the man's appearance odd. Normally, the people he encountered on the other side were downright evil and engaged in unspeakable acts. This fellow wasn't even mildly scary, and Peter wondered if the spirits had dropped him in the wrong house.

Only the spirits didn't make mistakes. He edged up next to the man, and noted the items lying on the worktable. There was a handgun, a hunting knife, a ball of twine, nickel-plated handcuffs, a black hood, and a bottle of clear liquid. Definitely not the type of stuff most college professors carried around. He picked up the bottle of clear liquid and read the label.

Chloroform.

Looks could be deceiving. The man was either a kidnapper or a killer. Or he was both.

That must have been why the spirits had brought him here. To stop a madman.

But who was he? Where did he live? And what did he do for a living? Peter needed that one clue that would help him tip off the police. It didn't have to be much. Once he had it, the spirits would whisk him back to Milly's place, the séance would end, and the Friday night psychics would go about the task of figuring out their killer's identity. Once they did, an anonymous call would be made to Special Agent Garrison, his friend with the FBI, and the wheels would be set in motion for the killer to be brought to justice.

He looked around the basement for a meaningful clue, but came up empty. Then he had an idea. He'd memorize their killer's features, and pass them on to Garrison, who would find the man in one of the FBI's endless databases.

Peter studied the killer from head to toe. He needed to give him a name; it would make him easier to remember. Dr. Death seemed appropriate. Dr. Death it was.

Dr. Death consulted his watch and made a face. "Look at the time," he muttered, and began to place the items on the table into the various pockets of his blazer. Before putting the gun away, he checked the chamber. All six bullets were there. Dr. Death slipped the weapon into his jacket with a little smile. "Uh-oh," he said aloud. "What's this?" He pulled a pearl necklace from the same pocket, and shook his head in displeasure.

"We're getting sloppy," he scolded himself.

A dresser stood beside the worktable. Dr. Death pulled open the top drawer. It contained a woman's skirt, neatly folded, and matching blouse. Lying on the blouse was a pair of gold hoop earrings, a gold necklace, and a gold lamé purse.

"Not Mary," he said.

Dr. Death shut the drawer, and pulled open the one beneath it. Another wardrobe consisting of a pair of faded blue jeans, neatly folded, a navy sweater, gold stud earrings, a diamond necklace, and a pocketbook.

"Not Joan."

The third drawer contained another set of women's clothes, meticulously kept, along with jewelry and a small handbag.

"Not Kelly."

The fourth drawer contained similar items as the first three.

"Not Diane."

And so did the fifth.

"Not Christine."

Opening the bottom drawer, he said, "Ah, yes, these were Edie's. Such a charming girl," and laid the strand of pearls atop a pink blouse before shutting the drawer.

Peter had watched enough TV cop shows to know what he was seeing. He'd been brought to the lair of a serial killer, and the dresser was his trophy collection of his victims' personal belongings. But who were the victims? And who was Dr. Death? The spirits were mean that way; they told him next to nothing, and forced him to figure out the rest.

Dr. Death went up a creaky flight of stairs like he had bad knees. Peter followed him to the first floor, and entered a kitchen with a yellow linoleum floor and ancient appliances. The light was better here. He was as plain as a loaf of white bread. His only distinguishing feature were his eyes. They were black and utterly soulless. Dr. Death again consulted his watch. "Look at the time. I'd better hurry, or Rachael will think I've stood her up."

Was Rachael his next victim? If the items on the worktable were any indication, she was. Peter looked around the kitchen for a piece of mail, or something that might have Dr. Death's name, or his address. Lying on the counter was an upside-down copy of the *New York Times*. A label on the cover said it was the Westchester County edition, an affluent suburb north of the city. Dr. Death went out the front door, whistling under his breath.

Peter was right on his heels. A black four-door Volvo sedan sat in the drive. A full moon cast an eerie patina off the car's windshield. Volvos were practical cars, and it only confirmed Peter's suspicion that Dr. Death was indeed a doctor. Dr. Death got behind the wheel, and fired up the engine. It took several starts before coming to life.

Peter moved to the back of the vehicle, hoping to catch the license plate. To his surprise, the Volvo took off in reverse, nearly hitting him as it raced past. The vehicle braked a few yards behind him with a rubbery squeal, the headlights catching him within their twin beams. The driver's window lowered, and Dr. Death stuck his head out.

"Thought I didn't know you were there, didn't you? " he shouted.

Peter froze. Normally when he journeyed to the other side, he was invisible to everyone he came in contact with. For Dr. Death to have seen him meant only one thing—he was in league with the Devil.

"Say something, before I run you down!" Dr. Death shouted.

"Nice to meet you," Peter said lamely.

"Very funny. Who sent you?"

"The spirits. Who do you think?"

"You're not the first one they've sent. They've been after me for some time. I suppose they'd like me to stop killing their little darlings."

"What happened to the others?"

"I got rid of them, just as I'm going to get rid of you."

"What about the women?"

"What women?"

"Mary, Joan, Kelly, Diane, Christine, and Edie."

"How clever. You memorized their names."

"Will you tell me why you killed them?"

"Let's just say I enjoy spreading misery, one bad deed at a time."

"The spirits will stop you eventually. You must know that."

"They haven't so far. Do you communicate with the spirits?"

Peter said that he did.

"Tell them I said hello. You're going to be joining them very soon."

The Volvo lurched forward. Peter could just as easily perish here as in the real world, and he feinted to his left, before bolting to his right. The Volvo passed with inches to spare.

"Asshole," he yelled.

A thick hedge ran parallel to the drive. Peter leapt through it, the branches tearing at his face and hands. A steep hill awaited him on the other side. His momentum carried him forward, and he went helter-skelter down the side.

"Get me out of here," he begged the spirits.

Nothing happened. Normally, the spirits responded quickly when he needed help. He came to a hard stop at the bottom. The Volvo was racing down the hill with Dr. Death leaning out the window, aiming his pistol. He squeezed off a round, and the bullet kicked up dust at Peter's feet.

He ran for his life. Other houses lined the hill, their light casting a muted glow into the night. He'd been having a pretty decent day until now. It wasn't the first time the spirits had pulled the rug out from under him. They were rotten that way, and he sometimes wondered if they were truly his friends.

Another shot rang out. This time, he was not so lucky, and he grabbed his wounded thigh and hobbled over to the side of the road.

There was nowhere to hide. Was this the end? He'd always imagined himself old and gray when the time came. Never had he thought he'd be twenty-five and in the prime of his life.

The Volvo braked, and Dr. Death climbed out. A warped smile distorted his face.

"Get on your knees."

Peter fell to his knees. He needed to buy some time. Perhaps Dr. Death would give him a final cigarette, or let him have a last meal.

Fat chance.

"Want to say something before I shoot you?" Dr. Death asked.

"Tell me why you killed those women," Peter said.

"Why do you care?"

"I just do. Think of it as a dying request."

"How touching. Very well, I'll tell you why. I kill those who push back at the darkness. As a psychic, I'm sure you understand what that means."

Peter certainly did. The war of good versus evil was fought on many levels. Dr. Death wasn't just killing innocent women. His victims were involved in good deeds, which made them the enemies of Satan. That was what he meant by pushing back at the darkness.

The gun's warm barrel pressed against the side of his head. A jolt of electricity ran up his spine as he was pulled back to the other side.

Hurry, he thought.

Then the shot rang out.

2

P *eter!"*

How many times had Holly said his name like that? More than he could remember. Friends since childhood, she'd always been yelling his name.

Peter came back to the real world in a hurry, and found himself lying on the dining room floor in Milly's apartment, his overturned chair beside him. He lifted his head to glance at his leg. No bullet wound. That part of his trip had not come back with him. So much for small favors.

Max and Milly knelt beside him. They'd taken turns raising him after his parents had died. Most people were lucky if they had one set of parents. He'd been blessed to have two.

"How long have I been under?" he asked.

"Just a few minutes," Max replied.

"Are you all right?" Milly wanted to know.

"Yes, I think so."

"Tell us what happened," Holly said, hovering behind them.

Peter pulled himself up to a sitting position and took a deep breath. The memory was starting to fade, no different from the way a dream faded upon awakening. "I was taken to see one of Satan's disciples. I need to write down what I saw before I forget."

"Holly, please get some paper and a pen from my study," Milly said.

Her niece hurried from the room. Peter got to his feet, righted his chair, and parked himself in it. Max pulled a handkerchief from his pocket, and draped it over his palm. Whisking it away, he produced a tall glass of water, which he handed to his student.

"Drink this. It will make you feel better."

Peter sipped the water. Max had fooled him, and he would stay up late into the night wondering where the glass had been hidden, and how

Max had produced it without spilling a single drop. Max's repertoire was endless, his knowledge of all things magical unsurpassed.

"I found a new evil," Peter told his teacher. "I encountered a man who looked like a frumpy college professor, but in reality is a serial killer who's targeting innocent women."

"That describes most serial killers," Max replied. "I read in a book that most serial killers target prostitutes and runaways because they want victims no one will miss."

"These victims are missed. They were actively involved in doing good in the world, and they pushed back at the darkness," Peter said.

"Then he shouldn't be too difficult for the authorities to track down. I'd say you've hooked a live one."

"Or perhaps he hooked you," Homer said, his cane tapping the floor.

For a blind man, Homer had an uncanny way of seeing things. Peter *had* been hooked, and knew he was lucky to have escaped with his life. Holly returned with a pad and pen, and pulled up a chair. "You talk, and I'll write," she said.

Peter described his encounter with Dr. Death with Holly transcribing. Tomorrow, he would contact the FBI, and pass along the information in the hopes they'd be able to track down the serial killer. Peter's name would be kept out of it, along with the rest of the Friday night psychics. That was the deal he'd struck with Garrison after he'd helped the FBI stop a madman from releasing a canister of deadly nerve gas in Times Square. So far, the arrangement had worked pretty well.

When he was done, Holly read aloud what she'd written. It was exactly as he remembered it. Now it was his job to try and stop Dr. Death from carrying out his grim task. So far, he'd been successful in preventing many bad things from happening, but deep down, he knew that every streak came to an end. Even the best struck out sometimes.

He thought back to the copy of the *New York Times* he'd seen in Dr. Death's kitchen. The headline was a highly publicized murder trial in New York that had ended with the jury finding the defendant guilty on all counts. A photograph had shown the victim's family rejoicing outside the courthouse. Justice had been served.

"Who's been following the Crawford murder trial?" Peter asked.

"I have," Holly replied.

"When is the jury supposed to get the case?"

"Late next week after the lawyers wrap up their arguments."

"I saw a newspaper in the killer's house. It had the verdict on the cover."

"You know how the trial ends—tell me!"

"He's guilty," Peter said.

"Yea!"

"Now here's the bad news. Our killer is going to strike on the evening of the day that the verdict is announced. That doesn't give us much time."

Milly placed her hand on Peter's shoulder. "Don't tell me you're thinking of getting involved. Remember what happened last time? The CIA nearly caught you, and sent you down to that farm in Virginia where they keep psychics prisoner and force them to spy on people."

"I still need to alert the authorities," Peter said.

Peter placed his empty glass on the table. His mind was made up, and there would be no changing it.

It was Homer who spoke next. "You said this man was in league with the Devil?"

"He is one of the Devil's disciples," Peter answered.

"Then you will have to go to the FBI to make sure he doesn't kill all of them when he's captured. That is reason enough to get involved."

"Thank you," Peter said.

Homer dipped his chin. He'd been an ordinary housepainter until a car accident had stolen his sight. With the loss of vision had come a gift of prescience and clarity of thought that few people ever obtained. His advice was always heartfelt, and seldom was he wrong.

Peter stiffened. The room's temperature was dropping, a sign that a spirit was in their midst. His eyes found the quivering dark spirit hovering against the far wall. Blacker than black, it looked like a tear in the universe, and pulsated as if breathing. The rest of the group saw it as well, except for Homer, whose metal cane continued to tap the floor.

"That thing tried to kill me," Peter said under his breath.

"It looks like the work of the Devil," Lester said. "Max, do you have any idea what it is?"

"Beats me," Max confessed. "Milly, any ideas?"

"I have no earthly clue," the old witch said.

"I'm going to talk to it," Holly said out of the blue.

"Peter said it was evil. You'll do no such thing," her aunt told her.

"If it's evil, then why did it come back?" Holly asked. "I think it returned for another reason. Let's find out, shall we?"

Holly pulled a small talisman from the pocket of her faded jeans. She crossed the dining room and waved the talisman in front of the dark spirit while reciting in a soft voice.

Shadow, shadow, dark as night, explain to me your mission tonight.
Are you here to see a friend, or have you come to make amends?
If there's something you wish to say, then say it now, or go away.

It was impossible to resist a witch. The quivering mass jumped off the wall, and swirled cyclonelike over the dining room table. Out of the vortex popped the shape of a hand. It was followed by the shape of a foot, then a human head. Each shape struggled to break free, only to be pulled back inside. Suddenly, it jumped back to the wall, and was swallowed up by a large crack. Holly stood transfixed.

"Holly?" Lester asked. "Are you all right?"

No response.

The little Scotsman hurried to Holly's side. He clicked his fingers in front of Holly's eyes while repeating her name. After a few tense seconds, she snapped to.

"Oh, my," Holly said.

"What happened?" Lester asked.

"That thing was trying to take me away. It was scary."

"To where?" Peter asked.

"The basement of some creepy house."

Just like me, Peter thought.

"I hate to say I told you so," her aunt said stiffly, "but I will in this case."

Lester had taken to examining the crack in the wall into which the dark spirit had escaped. Running his forefinger across the crack, he emitted a stiff cry. "Ow!"

Peter rushed to his aid. A nasty red blister had formed on the tip of Lester's finger.

"What in God's name was that thing?" he wanted to know.

If any of the Friday night psychics knew, they were not saying.

3

The gathering soon broke up. Lester left with a Band-Aid, vowing not to stick his finger where it didn't belong. Then Max bid adieu. The old magician made the glass he'd pulled out of nowhere disappear in equally baffling fashion, and left with a smug look on his face.

Holly was next. She kissed everyone good night before departing. When it came to kissing Peter, she gazed dreamily into his face. "We need to talk. I'll call you tomorrow."

She left, leaving Peter, Homer, and Milly. Peter would have liked nothing better than to stay up trying to figure out what the dark spirit was, but tomorrow was Saturday, and he had two shows to do, a matinee in the afternoon followed by an eight o'clock show in the evening. He needed his rest if he was to be sharp. "I wish I knew what that damn thing was," he said.

"I suppose it was some form of poltergeist," Milly said. "To be forewarned is to be forearmed. Next time it comes around, fight it."

"Do you think it will return?"

The rules governing the spirit world were vague. She shrugged.

"Homer, what do you think?" Peter asked.

Homer was bundled up from head to toe, ready to brave the elements, the tip of his cane tapping the floor as he spoke. "I talk to ghosts regularly, and am visited by poltergeists. Our visitor tonight was neither. It came from the darkest of places. I heard its silent scream."

Peter had no earthly idea what Homer was talking about. "What's that?"

"A silent scream is a life force begging to be heard. I started hearing them soon after I lost my sight. There is no sound, just the pain. It cuts through the air like a sharp knife."

"How many times have you heard this?" Milly asked.

"Enough times to last a lifetime. I have a theory about their origin. I believe there is a place which exists between the spirit world and our world. A buffer zone, so to speak. These life forces exist there."

Spirits were like lightning, and rarely struck in the same place twice. Peter had seen the dark spirit twice in the same evening, which was not normal. "This thing made itself known to me twice tonight. Should I be worried?"

"To worry is to poison oneself," Homer replied. "I would advise caution. I think we should say good night before Milly throws us out."

"Perish the thought," their hostess said.

Milly walked them out of her apartment to the elevators at the hallway's end. She kissed them both affectionately on the cheek. "Be safe," she said.

"And you as well," they both replied.

Peter and Homer descended to the lobby. A uniformed attendant opened the front door for them while tipping his cap good night.

A cold wind slapped their faces as they stepped outside. Two weeks from May, and the city was still locked in winter's grasp. Peter's limo idled at the curb, his driver buried in the sports section of the *Post*. "Let me give you a lift home," he offered.

"No offense, but I'll take the subway," Homer replied.

"Are you sure? It's late."

"I realize that. There is something perversely pleasurable in the feeling of passing subways rumbling beneath my feet. Don't ask me to explain, because I can't."

"Well, then let's talk here."

"What would you like to talk about?"

"You're holding back. I want to know why."

A frown creased Homer's face. "You're right. Did you read my mind upstairs?"

"I didn't have to. Your cane gave you away."

"My cane? How so?"

"You tap your cane whenever you talk. The tapping accelerates when you start bending the truth. I've noticed it before."

"So you can hear when I'm lying."

"Afraid so."

Homer's frown became a scowl. "Well, I'll be damned. I'd throw my cane away, only then I'd be in a real bind. You should have become a detective, Peter. You're very observant."

Peter had been told this before. He caught things that other people missed. It had as much to do with his perceptive skills from being a magician as it did from his psychic ability.

"I was holding back—to use your expression—because I was sworn to secrecy by a psychic named Selena about the very thing you saw tonight," Homer explained.

Peter had heard of but had never met the legendary Selena, who was consulted by the most powerful people in the city for her celestial advice.

"You've actually met Selena?" Peter asked.

"I most certainly have. Years ago, a dark spirit visited my apartment, and scared the daylights out of my family. My family described this spirit to me in detail. It was not like any ghost I'd ever heard of. I needed help, and a mutual friend arranged a meeting."

"Was she helpful?"

"She most certainly was. Selena told me that the dark spirit that visited my apartment was a shadow person. Shadow people are evil apparitions that attach themselves to humans, and refuse to let go. They are usually seen out of the corner of the eye for a split second before disappearing. When a person sees one fully—like you did tonight—it's because the shadow person is seeking him out."

"What do they want?"

"I asked Selena that very question, and she did not reply. But she did tell me this: Shadow people can destroy your life. They'll attach themselves to you, and scare away your family, friends, and everyone else. Your existence will become a living hell."

Peter understood the gravity of what Homer was saying. Most psychics could deal with ghosts and spirits, but their friends and families could not. More than one psychic had seen his personal life destroyed by the intrusion of unwanted visitors.

"Did you rid the shadow person from your apartment?" Peter asked.

"Eventually, I did," Homer said. "At Selena's urging, I began to wear a five-pointed star to ward it off. I've worn one ever since, and so have my wife and children. I also keep them hanging on the walls. You can never be too careful about these things."

"Did the shadow person return?"

"No. My family has not seen it since."

"Did you ever wonder why it picked you?"

"Sometimes. But I quickly pushed the thought out of my mind. If I thought about it too much, I was afraid it might return."

Peter understood this as well. Often, ghosts and spirits became tuned in to a person's thought waves, and knew when their subject was thinking about them. It was at these times that a ghost often chose to pay its subject a visit.

Peter touched Homer's arm. "How about that lift home?"

"Thanks, but no. I'm looking forward to that subway ride. It's where I do some of my best thinking. If you'll point me in the right direction, I'll be on my way."

"At least let me walk you to the station."

"By all means. I would enjoy your company."

The subway station was a half block away. As they walked down the street, Peter's limo crawled behind them, its headlights turned low. Reaching the station's entrance, Peter stopped to shake the blind psychic's hand. Thank you for confiding in me," he said.

"You are more than welcome," Homer replied. "First thing tomorrow, I'm going to purchase a rubber tip for my cane. Good night, Peter. Be safe."

"And you as well."

Peter climbed into the backseat of his limo. Herbie spun the wheel and headed toward the 65th Street transverse through Central Park without being told. "Want some music?" he asked.

"I'm good," Peter said.

"That blind guy you were talking to, I've seen him before. He tells fortunes down in the Village. Why you hanging out with him?"

Herbie did not know of his employer's psychic talents. One day, Peter planned to tell his driver about his unusual talents, but it wasn't going to be today.

"We're old friends," Peter said.

"You don't say. He's a strange one, that's for sure."

"Why do you say that?"

"Another limo driver told me that guy can make himself disappear while standing beneath the arch in Washington Square Park."

"That's impossible."

"I'm just telling you what the other driver told me. He said it was some kind of trick."

"The man is blind, Herbie. He doesn't do tricks."

"I know he's blind. But that's what this driver told me. Swore on a stack of Bibles he was telling me the truth. Said he saw it with his own eyes."

"Even I can't do that."

"Maybe he can teach you."

Peter leaned back in his seat. He tried to put Homer and the shadow person out of his mind. There were more important matters to deal with, like the serial killer he'd seen during the séance. A woman named Rachael was going to die if he didn't solve this thing.

He removed Holly's notes from his pocket and reread them. Her notes were meticulous, and captured every detail of his encounter with Dr. Death. Yet it was all still terribly vague. He didn't know the killer's name or address, what he did for a living, or anything solid about him. He simply knew that the man had joined forces with the Devil, which had allowed him to know that Peter was present when he shouldn't have. That kind of thing wouldn't show up on a Google search. Finding Dr. Death would be like finding a needle in a haystack, maybe harder.

Herbie stopped to let a pair of bundled joggers run past. Central Park was an oasis in a concrete jungle, and someone was always out running. New Yorkers were like that. They didn't care about things like cold weather. Peter caught Herbie's frowning eyes in the mirror.

"What's wrong?"

"You're thinking too hard, boss. Remember what I told you. Just use Occam's razor when something's eating at you. Always worked for me."

Occam's razor was Herbie's solution to life's problems. A British philosopher, William of Occam, believed the simplest solution was usually the best solution. In this case, the simplest solution was to contact Special Agent Garrison, who knew a thing or two about solving crime. Garrison would take the clues Peter had assembled, and put together a profile of Dr. Death. Once a profile was finished, it would be only a matter of time before the FBI would figure out who the bearded man in the basement was.

Only there was a problem with contacting Garrison. Garrison was with the government, and the government, especially the CIA, was looking for him. The CIA wanted to imprison him on a farm in Virginia with his psychic buddy Nemo, where they could track down the nation's enemies and other assorted bad guys.

That was the risk he faced contacting the FBI. Garrison had sworn never to reveal his identity, but if Garrison slipped up, or betrayed him, Peter would simply disappear from the general population.

They had reached the east side of the park. Herbie's eyes found his employer in the mirror. Peter took a deep breath as if to say, *I'm still working on it.*

"You want me to drive around the block a few times?" Herbie asked.

"No. Let's go home."

Peter lived on 320 East 62nd Street, a few blocks away. His girlfriend, Liza, was up waiting for him, just like she did every Friday night, with a spread of delicious food waiting on the kitchen table. He'd grown up an orphan, and coming home to a house filled with pleasant smells and music playing on the stereo was the most wonderful thing he could ask for.

He read Holly's notes again. There really wasn't anyone else he could call besides Garrison. And if he didn't alert someone, an innocent woman would die next Friday night.

It was the simplest solution. Occam's razor had won again.

He sent an instant message to Garrison. He hoped he wasn't making a mistake.

4

Peter had grown up in New York largely on the generosity of others. His parents had left enough money behind for him to attend private school, and that was it. His parents' friends, all of whom were psychics, had rotated him between their homes a year at a time, and raised him. Milly Adams and Max Romeo had been his primary guardians, and had kept him clothed and fed. He hadn't been poor, but he hadn't been rich either.

As a boy, he'd known he was different, and he'd had few close friends. To ward off loneliness, he'd roamed the streets on afternoons and weekends, and familiarized himself with the city's rich and varied neighborhoods. He'd fallen in love with Chinatown, Little Italy, Chelsea, Hell's Kitchen, the meatpacking district, Times Square, Greenwich Village, and the Upper East and West sides. Each had possessed a special charm all its own.

Over time, he'd settled on the neighborhood which most attracted him, and a building that he wished to someday call home. His choice was an old brownstone on 62nd Street, between Second and First avenues. From the street it didn't look like much, but that was an illusion. It had three stories plus a sunroof, nine rooms with three working fireplaces, a small basement, and a private courtyard. It also had a history that he rather liked. Every previous owner had been an artist.

It had been his dream house. Someday, when he was rich, he'd buy the brownstone, and turn it into his castle.

That day had come sooner than he'd expected. At twenty-one, he'd shot a series of TV commercials for Apple that made him a household name. Overnight, his magic shows had gone from being half filled to sold out. He'd become wealthy and had saved every penny. The week he'd turned twenty-four, he'd bought the building outright without a mortgage, and moved in.

His brownstone was more than just a home. He also used it to store his ever-growing magic collection. The first floor was crammed with illusions and apparatus, the upper floors devoted to his library of first-edition magic books and his vast collection of magic wands, of which he owned one from every corner of the world. Liza claimed it was like living inside a magic store, complete with her very own demonstrator.

The limo braked at the curb. As he started to get out, he got a call on his Droid. It was Garrison. He didn't want Herbie hearing the call, and he hopped out and banged his hand on the roof. "Night, Herbie. Drive safe."

"Take care, boss. See you in the morning."

The limo drifted away. The street was quiet, the empty sidewalk a good place to talk. Peter pushed the Answer button and raised the Droid to his face. "You're up late."

"No rest for the weary," Garrison replied. "I need to ask you some questions about this text you just sent me. Can you talk?"

Peter glanced at the upper floors of the brownstone. The master bedroom was all lit up; Liza was up, watching a horror movie. Parking himself on the stoop, he zipped up his leather jacket to keep warm. "I can talk."

"In your message, you said you encountered a serial killer during a séance, and that he nearly murdered you," Garrison said. "How is that possible?"

Explaining the workings of the spirit world was tricky, and Peter chose his words carefully. "During my séance, I went forward in time, and witnessed a serial killer preparing to abduct his next victim. It seems he was also watching me. It was a trap."

"You went forward in time? How does that work?"

"Time consists of three dimensions: the past, the present, and the future. The spirits can send a person backward in time, or forward into the future, or leave him in the present. Tonight, the spirits decided to send me into the future."

"Is it scary?"

"Tonight sure was."

"What else can you tell me about this killer?"

He gave Garrison a physical description. Dr. Death was short and fat and didn't look like he could harm a fly, when in fact, he was a monster. In conclusion, he said, "Just remember that he's in league with the Devil. It was the only possible way he could have known I was present in his home. To anyone else, I would have been invisible."

"You're sure he's a devil worshiper?"

"Positive. His next victim is a woman named Rachael. He was going out to meet her when I dropped in on him."

Peter heard a noise and glanced over his shoulder. Bright light was pulsating from the master bedroom. Liza had a thing about watching horror movies with the volume on full blast, the louder and scarier the better. He resumed his conversation.

"You're looking for this guy, aren't you?" Peter asked.

"Stop doing that," Garrison said.

"Doing what?

"Reading my mind over the phone."

"I can't read your mind over the phone, just in person."

"Then how did you know the FBI was looking for this guy?"

"The way you framed your questions told me he was on your radar."

"Fine, you're right. He is on our radar."

"What do you know about him?"

"Not much. During the past two years, a killer has been sending the FBI taunting letters that contained photographs of dead women lying facedown in grassy fields. There have been six victims so far, with a promise of more to come. We don't know the victims' names, or what they look like. We haven't even found the bodies. The letters were post-marked from different locations in the Northeast, so we're assuming that's where he lives. An occult sign was burned into the grass beside each body. That's how we knew he was a devil worshiper."

Peter's breath formed a white cloud in front of his face. The FBI liked to think it knew a thing or two about the Devil and his twisted follow-ers, but they were wrong. What the Bureau knew only scratched the surface of a group whose history stretched back thousands of years.

"Describe the sign in the grass," he said.

"It was an inverted triangle balanced atop a large V with a line drawn across the top. The FBI keeps a databases of symbols used by various cults and the like, and has seen this symbol at crime scenes before."

An icy finger ran down Peter's spine, and he shivered. Garrison had just described a magical sigil. Made of complex occult symbols and geometric figures, sigils were used by psychics to make contact with the spirit world, their true meaning known only to practitioners of dark magic. The sigil in the photos sent to the FBI was the Seal of Satan, and meant Dr. Death was working directly with one of the Devil's sons. Two thousand years ago, the Devil had sent six of his sons to the earth with the purpose of causing havoc and misery. Those sons were responsible for most of the horrible events which mankind had inflicted upon itself. If Peter was right, Dr. Death had entered into a pact with one of these sons, and been given special gifts which made him more powerful than an ordinary devil worshipper.

"How close are you to finding this madman?" he asked.

"We're not. The Bureau has run out of leads. That was why I called you right back."

"Maybe this will help. His victims are women who push back against the darkness. Their names are Mary, Joan, Kelly, Diane, Christine, and Edie. His next victim's name is Rachael."

"Did he tell you that?"

"Yes. He's killing women involved in good works."

"That's something we didn't know before. How good a look did you get at him?"

"Very. I was right next to him."

"I know you want to keep your psychic powers a secret, but I need you to let a police artist draw a composite of this guy. It could help us nab him."

"No cops."

"What's wrong with the cops?"

"They're not good at keeping secrets."

"We can use an FBI artist, then. I'll set it up for tomorrow."

There was a click on the line. It was Liza, probably wondering where he was.

"I need to run," he said to Garrison.

"Don't go yet. I want you to think if there's anything you might have forgotten to tell me about your encounter with this guy. This is important, Peter."

"Can't it wait until tomorrow?"

"No. People forget things when they sleep. We have to do it right now."

Another click on the line, indicating that Liza had hung up. "There was one thing," Peter said, realizing he'd left out an important part. "I saw this strange apparition before and after the séance. It was a quivering black mass that didn't have a face. Another psychic told me it's called a shadow person. I've never seen anything like it before."

"Could it be connected to the killer?"

"I think so. This thing kidnapped me."

"What do you mean 'kidnapped'?"

"My soul."

Another click on the line. Liza again. His girlfriend wouldn't have called again unless she was pissed off. "I've got to beat it. Let's talk in the morning."

"One more thing."

"No more. Liza is going to kill me."

The sound of shattering glass sent Peter flying off the stoop. A man's dress shoe landed at his feet along with shards of glass. He picked up the shoe. It was one of his.

Turning around, he looked at the brownstone. The master bedroom window had a gaping hole in it. Loud music was streaming out, the voice of Coldplay's "Every Teardrop Is a Waterfall" ripping a hole in the still night.

He ran up the steps to his front door, fumbling with his keys. "I've got to go," he said into the phone.

"Is something wrong?"

"Yes."

"Should I send someone over?"

"Capital idea." He hit the button that let him switch calls and said, "I'm coming through the front door."

"There's a man in the bedroom," Liza screamed. "He's attacking me!"

5

Peter burst into his brownstone. Every light was turned on, and so were the CD players. He loved music, and kept a stereo system in every room. His intruder had turned them to full volume, the competing voices of Amy Winehouse and Fifty Cent filling the downstairs.

What the hell was going on? Burglars tried to keep things quiet, or at least the ones he'd heard about. He flew up the staircase while glancing into the living room. His favorite illusions had been knocked off their pedestals and lay in a gut-wrenching heap on the floor. The Flying Carpet would never fly again, and the Zig-Zag illusion that let him pull out a woman's middle was now just a pile of boards. Butch, the mechanical toy panda that predicted the future, sat on the mantel over the fireplace, banging its miniature cymbals in obvious displeasure.

Dark thoughts filled his head. Had Liza been injured? Was she okay? If the burglar had harmed her . . . he tried not to imagine it.

He reached the second-floor landing. On the walls hung promotional photos of famous magicians that had once adorned the lobby of Lou Tannen's, the greatest magic shop that had ever existed. Every frame was shattered, the photos torn to shreds. They could never be replaced.

"Liza!" he called out.

"He's in the bedroom with me," came her voice from the third floor.

"I'm coming!"

The stairs groaned beneath his feet. Many old buildings in New York were inhabited by ghosts, and he sensed that the ghost in his brownstone was trying to warn him about the danger that awaited him upstairs.

The third floor was another disaster area. Pictures yanked off the walls, illusions in the hallway turned upside down and destroyed. His intruder had targeted his collection, and everything appeared ruined.

Peter entered the master bedroom ready to confront the person who'd wrecked his home. The room had been ransacked, his prized sixty-inch plasma TV torn off the wall, its screen kicked in.

He looked around the bedroom. No sign of Liza, or of a burglar. He checked the adjoining bathroom, and also looked under the bed. Nothing but a few dust balls. The Coldplay CD was still rocking the house, and he silenced the music with the remote.

"Liza? Where are you?"

"In the closet," she replied.

The master bedroom had a spacious walk-in closet. He opened the double doors to find Liza backed into the corner with a letter opener clutched in her hands. She was trembling, and looked half scared to death. "I know this sounds stupid, but are you all right?" he asked.

"I'm freaking out. Did you see him?"

"There's no one there."

"That can't be—he was here a few moments ago."

"I just looked. He's gone. Come on out. There's nothing to be afraid of."

"That's easy for you to say. Check the fire escape. Please."

Entering the hall, he checked the fire escape. It was empty, the window locked from the inside, and he quickly returned to the bedroom.

"It's safe," he said.

She cautiously emerged from the closet and tossed the letter opener onto the bed. They embraced, and she leaned her head against his chest. "God, that was scary."

"Did he hurt you?"

"No, but he scared the shit out of me. I was lying in bed watching the remake of *Dawn of the Dead* when I heard someone on the first floor destroying things. I locked the bedroom door, and called nine one one, but got put on hold. Then he started banging on the door. I got scared and hid in the closet. Somehow he got the door open, came in here, and starting trashing the place."

"Did you dead-bolt the door?"

"Yes. Don't ask me how he opened it."

Peter checked the dead bolt. It was functioning normally, and he shook his head. Even Houdini couldn't pick a dead bolt.

"Did you get a look at him?"

"I caught a glimpse of him from the closet. He was dressed in black. I didn't see his face, just the back of his head. He almost looked like . . ."

"Like what?"

"This is so weird."

"Tell me. Please."

"He almost looked like a ghost."

The proverbial lightbulb went off in Peter's head. Now he understood how the intruder had gotten into his house, and picked the lock on the bedroom door. It was a shadow person.

"What else did you see?" he asked, just to be sure.

"He was moving really fast around the room. It was almost surreal. The stuff just flew off the walls and broke apart on the floor. He didn't seem to touch things."

Peter realized he was shivering. A cold wind was blowing through the broken window, and he went to close the curtains. A strange thought occurred to him. "Why did you throw my shoe through the window?" he asked.

"Your shoe?"

"Yes. I was outside talking to Special Agent Garrison. Next thing I knew, my shoe came through the window and hit the pavement."

"I didn't throw your shoe. Why were you talking to the FBI?"

"I saw something bad during a séance tonight. I texted Garrison, and he called me back."

"Is Garrison the agent I met? The pushy guy built like a refrigerator?"

"That's him. He's coming over right now. Maybe he'll help us clean up this mess. You should see downstairs. Everything's ruined."

"Oh, Peter, I'm so sorry."

She joined him at the window and they again embraced. They'd been living together for two years, yet only a few weeks ago had he come clean, and told her about his psychic powers, including secret things about his past. Along with his confession had come the promise that he would not keep secrets from her. It was the only way the relationship could survive.

"I need to tell you something." He took her hands in his own, and gazed into her soft brown eyes. "The intruder wasn't human. It's called a shadow person, and it's somehow connected to the bad thing I saw during the séance."

"What does it want? Besides your shoe?"

"I wish I knew."

"So what do we do? Rent a suite in the Waldorf and wait for it to leave?"

"I don't think there's any way to hide from it. But there is a way to keep it away from us. Permanently."

"I'm all for that."

Liza was getting her spirit back. That was good, because his life was filled with unexpected visitors, and he couldn't have her freaking out whenever one came calling. Entering the closet, he spun the dial on the wall safe, and opened it with a few deft turns. From its interior he removed an ornamental gold box, and brought it to his girlfriend.

"That's your mother's jewelry box," she said. "What does that have to do with this?"

"My parents used to conduct séances in our apartment with their friends. One night, I stumbled into the room, and caught them in the act. My mother was wearing an unusual piece of jewelry, which I inherited when she died. I didn't understand the significance of it until tonight."

He opened the box's lid, and his mother's jewelry sparkled up at them. He sifted through the items and removed a gold necklace with a five-pointed gold star pendant. "I want you to have this. It has a special power to ward off evil spirits. Put it on."

"Are you sure about this, Peter?"

"Yes. It's the only way I know to keep the shadow person away."

"But it's your mother's."

"She would have wanted you to have it."

Liza slipped the necklace over her head. She appraised it in the broken mirror on the dresser. The pendant rested comfortably at the base of her neck. "It's beautiful."

"The five-pointed star is a talisman, and will keep the shadow person away, along with any other evil spirits. I want you to wear it until this thing is gone."

"Do I have to give it back?"

"No, it's yours."

"You're sure about this?"

It was not the circumstances under which he would have liked to be giving her a piece of his mother's jewelry, but it would have to do. Liza brought her hand up to her mouth.

"Oh, my God. It's back."

A shadow person lurked on the other side of the bedroom. Shaped like a person but without a face, it hovered a few inches above the floor, and made no sound. Peter stepped protectively in front of Liza. Through the broken window he heard a car pull up in front of the brownstone and Garrison and his team get out. They all knew about Peter's powers, and were people he trusted. The cavalry had arrived.

"That's Garrison. I locked the front door. Better let them in."

"And leave you here with this monster?"

"I can handle him."

"No!"

Liza did not understand the danger she was in. With his body, he gently pushed her toward the door. She resisted, and pushed right back.

"I'm not leaving," she said defiantly.

Their unearthly visitor glided across the floor as it came toward them. Objects flew through the air as if weightless, while the electricity flickered on and off.

Peter stepped forward, knowing what he had to do.

6

♁

Because he'd moved around as kid, Peter hadn't had a lot of stuff. Just his clothes, his school uniforms, a worn baseball mitt, and some toys. It hadn't been much.

As a result, he did not buy things on a whim. Every purchase was carefully thought out. The tricks and illusions in his brownstone were a perfect example. They were things he'd coveted as a child, but could not afford. When he'd finally had the money to buy them, he'd taken his time, and made one purchase at a time. Each item he bought, he savored.

And now, it was all gone.

The shadow person had wrecked his home, while scaring the woman he loved. Ghosts had broken things in his home before, but it had been out of sheer clumsiness, never on purpose. The shadow person had attacked him on purpose.

Homer had said this might happen. If Peter didn't respond, the shadow person would ruin his life, and drive Liza away. And then where would he be? Alone and brokenhearted, no different from before.

Seen in that light, there was no other choice but to turn to a power within him that he feared and loathed, and summon the demon that had resided inside of him since birth. Through clenched teeth he muttered the words that would allow him to fight back.

Darkness, take my hand.
Give me the power to vanquish my enemies, and rule the world as I
   see fit.

He started to change. The feeling started like a bad case of heartburn, and grew worse, until he was burning up inside. With his heart pounding in his ears like a bass drum, he marched across the bedroom. Shooting his arm out, he struck the shadow person right in the nose, if it had had a nose. The black mass emitted a yelp, and wavered uncertainly.

"Oh, my God, you hurt it," Liza squealed.

"Score one for the good guys," he said.

Filled with confidence, he brought his fist down hard on the shadow person's shoulder, and saw it crumple. Being already dead, a spirit could not be killed. But it could be injured, and that hurt would last for an eternity. It shrunk before his eyes.

"You did it again," Liza said.

"Think I should stop?"

"No! Let the bastard have it."

Downstairs, the pounding on the front door had grown louder. If they didn't let Garrison and his team in, they'd kick the door down, and something else would be in need of repair.

"Please go downstairs, and let them in," he said more calmly than before.

"What am I supposed to tell them?"

"Don't tell them anything. Let me do the talking."

"What are you going to do to this thing?"

"Convince it not to return."

"I'm all for that. I'll be right back. I love you."

"I love you, too."

She smiled with her eyes, and left without making a sound.

Peter blinked. The shadow person was no longer standing in front of him.

"Damn it," he cursed.

He hunted for it. He could still feel its presence, and sensed it was hiding behind a piece of furniture or inside the wall. With his knuckles he rapped loudly on the plaster. Getting no response, he got on his knees, and looked beneath the furniture and the bed.

Still nothing.

He got to his feet, still burning with anger. Then he noticed something odd. None of Liza's perfume bottles sitting atop her dresser had been touched. The shadow person hadn't come here to mess with his girlfriend. *It's me he wants.*

Garrison and his team came up the stairs. How was he going to explain this? He never should have told Garrison about the shadow person in the first place. It added nothing to the situation, and led to too many other topics that he didn't want to discuss.

He decided to meet the FBI agents in the hallway, and take them back downstairs. He'd fix a pot of coffee and offer them something to eat. It would give him time to make up a story. It wasn't a perfect plan, just the best he could do given the circumstances.

He started to walk out of the bedroom when he saw his unearthly intruder inside the vanity on the dresser, hiding within the mirror's reflection. Staring at him, even though it had no eyes. He approached the dresser, shaking his fist. "Damn you for wrecking my house. I want you to leave, and never return. Do you understand?"

No response. Was it mocking him?

"I've had enough of your games," he said angrily.

He rushed the vanity, prepared to break it into a thousand pieces. The mirror turned a deathly black that expanded into the bedroom like a storm cloud spreading over the horizon. He was sucked into the void, and desperately tried to resist. Too late. He'd been trapped again.

His world changed. He was transported from his bedroom to the dirt road on the hill beside Dr. Death's house. Dr. Death was chasing him, the Volvo's headlights dancing in the darkness as the vehicle snaked down the hill. It was déjà vu all over again.

Peter ran for his life. In all the years he'd been visiting the other side, he'd never been taken back to the same place twice. Every trip was a once-in-a-lifetime experience. Not just for him, but for every other psychic he'd ever communicated with. It was always a one shot.

But the rules were different now. The shadow person had taken him back so Dr. Death could finish the job, and take Peter out of the picture. It wasn't fair, but the spirit world rarely was. In that regard, it was no different from the real world.

He looked for a landmark that might tell him where he was. In the distance, two-story houses with pitched roofs dotted the hillside. He counted four, along with a number of cars and pickup trucks parked in driveways.

The Volvo reached the bottom of the hill, and chased him. Peter looked for a tree or some bushes on the side of the road to hide behind, just to buy himself some time. He could not remember having ever felt more helpless in his entire life.

A gunshot ripped the still night air. He stopped running and clasped his leg. Blood was flowing freely out of a wound in his thigh, just like the first time. He hobbled over to the grass and tried to stop the blood by pressing on it with his palm.

The Volvo braked and Dr. Death got out with a lunatic smile distorting his face. Gun in hand, he came over to where Peter stood, and told him to kneel. The young magician complied.

"Anything you want to say before I kill you?" Dr. Death asked.

His mind raced. Dying was for quitters, and he wasn't about to quit. He was going to go back to the real world, and track this bastard down. To do that, he had to learn more about Dr. Death. Even the simplest detail would help the FBI find him.

"Who are you?" he said boldly.

"You want to know my name?"

"Yes. I have a right to know who my killer is."

"I don't think so."

"What does it matter? I'm going to die, anyway."

"I'm still not going to tell you."

"You're a doctor, aren't you?"

"That's none of your business. Now close your eyes, and I'll make this painless."

Dr. Death was being bathed in the Volvo's soft headlights. Peter gazed up into the killer's eyes, and saw Dr. Death walking into a room filled with college students taking a class. His hunch was right: Dr. Death *was* a college professor.

"Aren't you afraid of being caught?" Peter asked.

"I said, close your eyes."

"Not even by your neighbors? They must have heard your gun."

"My neighbors won't save you, and neither will anyone else in this hellhole. Now close your eyes and shut your damn mouth."

Dr. Death had just told him something important, yet Peter had no earthly idea what it meant. The FBI would, and he prayed he got to speak with Garrison again.

The gun's warm barrel pressed against his forehead. A pair of hands begin to shake him, trying to bring him back to the real world where he lived.

Then the shot rang out.

7

L iza shook him hard. "Peter, wake up."

He returned with the gunshot still ringing in his ears. Lying on his back on his own bed, the white plaster ceiling spinning in a lazy clockwise rotation. He checked the gunshot wound on his leg for the second time that night, and found that it had healed itself.

Liza's lovely face came into the picture. She looked scared out of her mind. She'd just saved his life, and didn't even realize it. "What in God's name happened?"

"I took a little trip to the other side. Thanks for bringing me back."

"Did that thing draw you over?"

"Yes. Is Garrison here?"

The FBI agent's solemn face came into the picture. Built like a pro linebacker, he wore a dark suit whose jacket's left side bulged more than its right from the gun that he carried. He was breathing hard from running up to the third floor of the brownstone.

"We're here," Garrison said. "How you doing?"

"I'm okay. Thanks for getting here so fast."

"Not fast enough, I'm afraid. Let me help you up."

Peter got out of bed on shaky legs while leaning on Garrison for support. Not seeing the rest of Garrison's team, he said, "Where's your gang?"

"Having a look around. Your place looks like a tornado hit it."

"That's one explanation. I need a cup of coffee. Want some?"

"I never say no to coffee," Garrison replied.

The kitchen was on the first floor and faced a private courtyard. It hadn't gotten much use until Liza had moved in. The miracles she produced in it were every bit as amazing as those Peter performed onstage each night. That was an exaggeration, only there was something about home-cooked food that seemed totally magical to him.

Liza served fresh coffee and reheated bagels. Garrison's team consisted of three male agents dressed in dark suits, and a droll blonde named Nan Perry.

"What just happened upstairs?" Garrison asked.

Peter took a moment to gather his thoughts. Saying too much would lead to trouble; too little, and the FBI would be no help at all. "I took another trip into the future, and saw our killer. The scene was exactly the same. I was outside his house, trying to run from him, and he shot me in the leg. He was getting ready to put a bullet in my head, when Liza shook me awake."

"That's intense," Garrison said.

"The good news is I got a hard look at him. His face will be easier for me to remember when I sit down with your artist for a composite."

"That's a plus. Did anything else stand out?"

"Well, he said something strange. Right before he was going to shoot me, I asked him if he was worried that his neighbors might hear the gunshot. He replied that his neighbors wouldn't save me. He called where he lived a hellhole."

"What do you think he meant?"

"Hard to say. He lived in a nice area. It didn't look like anything remotely resembling a hellhole."

"Maybe something happened there that made him feel that way."

"Could be."

"Why do you keep going back there?"

"Believe me, it's not by choice. An evil spirit called a shadow person is taking me."

"Did this shadow person rip your place apart?"

Peter nodded and sipped his drink.

"What's its motive? You must have some idea."

Every psychic had a spirit which looked over his shoulder and protected him. Peter guessed the same was true for people who were in league with the Devil.

"It's our serial killer's guardian angel," he said quietly.

"So those really exist," Garrison said.

"They most certainly do."

"And this serial killer has one."

"That would be my guess."

The kitchen fell silent. Peter hated when that happened. Garrison leaned forward on his elbows. He looked tired, but his eyes were sharp. "You talk with the spirits on a regular basis. Why not talk with them again, and ask them who this killer is. It can't hurt, can it?"

Peter had been communicating with spirits since boyhood. There were rules to the game, and he said, "It doesn't work like that. I can't just cross over, and start asking questions."

"Why not?"

"Because I can't. I rarely speak when I'm on the other side."

"What do you do, then?"

"I watch and listen."

"Can't you at least give it a try?"

He laughed under his breath. The other side was not gentle. Within its ever-shifting landscape of light and dark was a force that ruled with a firm, if not brutal hand. He likened it to the Old Testament: An eye for an eye, a tooth for a tooth, where wars lasted for centuries and grudges were never settled. It was not a place where you wanted to spend eternity, and those who did suffered for it, every single moment of their wretched lives.

"No," the young magician said. "You have to trust me on this."

Garrison let out an exasperated breath and put down his mug. He looked ready to call it a night. "I'll come by your theater with the artist tomorrow. What time works for you?"

"Come at four. We can do it in my dressing room between shows."

"Four o'clock it is." Garrison put his empty mug in the sink. One by one, his team filed out of the kitchen. "You need help cleaning up?" he asked at the door.

Peter stole a glance at Liza, who still looked upset. He needed to have a talk with her, and not with the FBI hanging around. "We'll manage. Thanks for the offer."

Peter walked the agents to the front door. The hallway was lined with rare magic playbills that he'd purchased at auction at Christie's. Each was one-of-a-kind, and worth a fortune. Their frames had been smashed, and Garrison pointed at the ruined glass.

"Look at that," he said. "The breaks in each frame are the same."

Peter had a look. The breaks in the glass weren't the same, they were *identical*. He wondered how that was possible. The spirits conformed to the laws of physics when visiting the real world, and the broken frames were an obvious violation of that.

"I need to take a photo of this," Garrison said.

He snapped a series of photos on his iPhone. When he was finished, Peter walked him to the door. His team waited outside on the sidewalk.

"Sure you don't need some help?" Garrison asked.

"We're good," Peter said.

He started to leave, then asked the inevitable final question. "Will it come back?"

"Probably. It hasn't gotten what it wants."

"Meaning you. I could leave two of my team to act as bodyguards."

"They'll only end up getting hurt."

"Don't be so sure. We deal with more bad stuff than you can imagine."

Garrison didn't get it. The shadow person existed in another dimension that was either light-years away, or right next door, and had the power to visit the real world whenever it chose. The FBI did not possess the means to stop it.

"We'll manage. Thanks, anyway," Peter said.

Their ride was a black GMC Terrain with needle antennas on the hood. The vehicle seemed to disappear as it drove away. Peter waved and shut the door.

"What a night. Ready to tackle this mess?"

Liza put her head on his chest and started to cry. Her evening had been one long horror show, and now he was asking her to clean up.

"I'm sorry. I didn't mean that," he said.

"No, it's probably a good idea." She sniffled. "It will take my mind off things."

"You sure?"

She answered him with a kiss, and climbed the stoop and went inside.

8

⤳

The living room had been hit the worst, so they decided to start there. Liza went to the kitchen to find a broom while he started to pick up pieces of broken illusions from the floor. A sizzling sound filled his ears. Without warning, the brownstone was plunged into darkness.

"Peter!" Liza called from the kitchen.

"I'm right here. Are you all right?"

"It's back. I saw it out of the corner of my eye."

He stumbled down the darkened hallway. "Don't move. I'm coming."

"Hurry. I'm scared."

"Me, too."

"Oh, great. Now I'm more scared."

As he reached the entrance to the kitchen, a flash of white light exploded before his eyes. It had no sound, and continued to flash on and off like heat lightning. In the kitchen he found Liza huddled by the fridge, her hair standing on end as if electrified. Clutched in her hands was a frying pan she'd grabbed off the stove. He held her protectively against his chest.

"Make it go away," she pleaded.

"Do you want me to go back to the other side?"

"No!"

"Then I can't make it go away. We need to go outside, and hope it doesn't follow us. Ghosts and spirits don't like to be seen, so we should be okay."

They headed for the front door still holding each other. Halfway down the hall, the electricity returned and the flashing stopped. In the living room, Butch was frantically clashing his cymbals. Spirits had a way of becoming attached to objects, and the shadow person had taken a liking to the automated toy panda on the mantel.

The clashing became more intense. So loud that Peter thought Butch might fall apart. Sticking his head into the living room, he gasped.

"Holy crap," he said.

Liza jerked open the front door. "Don't stop," she said.

"Come here. You have to see this."

"Peter!"

Love was based on trust. He grabbed Liza by the hand, and pulled her into the living room. She was afraid, but did not resist. She raised her hand to her mouth in utter disbelief.

"Oh, my God," she exclaimed.

Peter was rarely amazed. Tonight was one of those exceptions. His prized illusions had miraculously repaired themselves and returned to their designated spots in the living room. The Flying Carpet levitated in midair, while the Zig-Zag illusion looked ready to remove a person's middle. If he hadn't seen it with his own eyes, he wouldn't have believed it possible.

"Am I dreaming?" Liza asked, lowering her hand.

"Not at all. What you see is what you get."

"Do I have to kill you, or are you going to explain this to me?"

"Of course I'll explain it to you. Hold on for a second."

The best tricks continued to fool a person long after they were over. He stepped into the hallway to inspect his collection of rare playbills. To his delight, the shattered frames had miraculously restored themselves, the playbills untouched. But what about the other floors? As he headed up the stairs to find out, Liza crossed her arms, demanding an explanation.

"Now," she said, raising her voice.

"None of it was real," he said, stopping on a step. "I should have realized it before, when Garrison pointed out that all the breaks in the frames were identical."

"What do you mean, none of it was real? We all saw the damage, Peter."

"It was an illusion."

"Is this thing some kind of magician?"

"In a way, yes. It can distort reality, and make you see things which really don't exist. For whatever reason, it decided to trash my place without really trashing it. Come upstairs with me. I need to check something out."

She followed him upstairs to the third floor. The photos of magicians past that lined the stairway had returned to their original condition, as had the furniture in the master bedroom. Everything was normal again, except for the broken window his shoe had gone through.

"This is so flipping weird," he said.

Liza struck a defiant pose. What he was telling her, and what she'd just seen, had collided, and she no longer trusted him. He made her sit beside him on the bed.

"I don't believe this," she said.

"I can prove it was an illusion," he said.

"Show me."

He pulled up Garrison's number on his Droid. As the call went through, he put the phone on speaker so Liza could hear the conversation. Garrison answered on the first ring.

"Something wrong?" the FBI agent asked.

"Nothing's wrong. In fact, everything's just great," Peter replied, putting his hand around Liza's waist, and drawing her close. "I have a favor to ask."

"Go ahead."

"Can you look at those photos you shot in my place, and call me back?"

"What am I looking for?"

"See if the broken glass in the frames repaired itself."

"Come again?"

"The damage you saw earlier wasn't real. It was an illusion."

"No offense, but I'm not buying that for one minute."

"Make you a bet. Loser buys a steak dinner at Smith & Wollensky."

"You're on, magic man. I'll call you right back."

Peter ended the call. His shoe was lying on the floor, and he picked it up. "This is the part I don't understand," he said.

"You understand the rest of it?" Liza asked in disbelief.

"I'm beginning to. The shadow person wants my undivided attention. It pulled this stunt to get it. Now I have to figure out what it wants."

"How wonderful."

The Droid vibrated in his hand and Peter answered it on speaker. "I want my steak medium-rare with all the trimmings."

"Remind me never to make a bet with you," Garrison said.

* * *

Sleep proved elusive, and they lay in bed beneath the warm covers, trying to make sense of it all. Liza rested her head on Peter's chest, and listened to the rhythmic beat of his heart. A blanket covered the broken window, muting the street noise.

"Is this what it's going to be like living with you?" she asked.

Kaboom, Peter thought. He chose his words with extra care.

"Normally, my life is pretty dull."

"You talk to the dead every Friday night with your friends. That's not normal."

"It's only once a week."

"Be serious, Peter."

"Sorry."

"You promised me that you'd stop keeping secrets from me. It's the one thing I can't stand about living with you. You're always *hiding* something."

It was true. He kept his darkest secrets from Liza, and the rest of his friends as well. Secrets about his past, his parents, and the genetic code they'd passed on to him which extended his powers far beyond anything a normal psychic could do. Liza couldn't stand not knowing these things about him, and wanted him to level with her. If he didn't, they both knew what the outcome would be. She'd pack up and leave and he'd be alone again. It was his greatest fear, and he was ready to tell her everything about his life, only a voice inside his head said not yet.

"Let me ask you a question," she said. "You nearly died during the séance at your friend's apartment. Were you planning to tell me? Be truthful."

"No. I didn't want to alarm you."

"That's not fair. You had this absolutely horrible thing happen to you, and you internalize it, and don't let your emotions out. I'm more than just your lover, Peter. I'm your friend. You have to confide in me, and share your feelings."

"I'm sorry."

She grabbed his chin and gave his head a shake. "Stop saying that."

He started to say "I'm sorry," and stopped himself. Liza fell back onto her pillows, and for the longest time stared at the ceiling.

"I want us to see a counselor. We're running in circles," she said.

"But I like chasing you."

No response, not even a giggle. They'd discussed seeing a counselor before. He turned on his side, and rested his head on the palm of his hand. "Okay, I'm game."

"Do you really mean that?"

"Yes. We'll go see a pro, and talk this out. I don't want you angry with me."

"You have a problem, Peter. You realize that, don't you?"

"I'm different. So were my parents. They taught me to hide my gifts. So did the people who raised me after they died. I'm not making excuses. It's how I was brought up."

"But you can't hide things from me. Not if we're going to live together."

"I understand that. You have to be patient. This isn't easy for me."

He gently stroked her hair, and elicited a faint smile. The first time he'd laid eyes on Liza at the Beacon Theatre during a performance by Cirque du Soleil had been like something out of a dream. He'd taken a date, buying front-row seats. The show was filled with gymnasts able to turn their elastic bodies into pretzels, and it would have been nothing more than a fun night out until a troupe of Chinese aerialists called the Lings took the stage. Mom and dad, a pair of muscle-bound twin brothers, and two drop-dead beautiful girls, Liza and her sister Kim.

The Lings had flown through space as if they had wings. They looked like angels, and Peter's heart had caught in his throat as Liza had twirled overhead while hanging on to a bright red sash with one hand. He'd never believed in love at first sight, but that night had changed his notions about romance and physical attraction. He had wanted her not just physically, but also emotionally. This was the woman he was meant to be with; this was the partner he'd longed to have in his life, and he hadn't even known her name.

His feelings had been impossible to conceal. When the act was over, he'd jumped from up his seat and applauded wildly while his date stormed out of the theater.

That had been two years ago. Liza had entered his life, and become his lover, while her younger sister had replaced her in the family troupe. He had showered Liza with everything she could have asked for, and treated her like a princess. A perfect arrangement, except he'd hidden his psychic abilities from her, fearful that she'd think he was a freak, and run away. He knew now it had been a mistake, one that he must fix.

"Do you have someone in mind?" he asked, breaking the silence.

"I did some research on the Internet. One name kept popping up. A professor at NYU Medical School named Dr. Raul Sierra. He's written several highly regarded books on relationship counseling. He teaches partners how to communicate with each other."

"You want to go see him?"

"Uh-huh."

"How much do I have to tell him about myself?"

"Enough for him to understand you."

"You mean everything."

"If that's what it takes, yes."

"You're serious."

"I've never been more serious in my life. It's now or never, Peter."

They shared a brief silence. It carried in it an unstated answer that he didn't want to hear, and it went like this: *If we don't fix this relationship, I'll go back to the circus with my family.* But he'd never told anyone *everything.* His life was filled with secrets that he'd expected to take with him to his grave, and maybe beyond. Yet at the same time, if he didn't come clean with Liza, she'd walk out on him, and his heart would be forever broken.

"Okay," he mumbled halfheartedly.

"You mean that?"

"Uh-huh."

She kissed him on the lips in the darkness. The fear and anxiety of the past few hours went away, and he felt whole again. Just a single kiss had done it.

"Thank you," she said.

"When do you want to go see him?"

"Monday morning, nine thirty. I booked a session a week ago. For me. But you can come, too."

"You were going to see a shrink?"

"I had to do something. I don't know how to deal with this."

He suddenly felt like a shit. Liza had been agonizing for days, and he hadn't noticed. Too busy with the show and his Friday night séances to be paying attention to her needs. He vowed to change that, too. His Droid vibrated on the night table, and he lifted the phone to his face. "The FBI never sleeps," he said.

"Garrison?"

"The one and only."

"It must be something important for him to be calling this late."

"Your intuitive skills are amazing, Dr. Watson."

"Answer it, smart-ass."

He answered the call. "Hello, Special Agent Garrison. What a pleasant surprise."

"Sorry for the intrusion, but I thought you'd want to hear this," Garrison said. "The pattern in your broken frames struck a nerve. I was sure I'd seen it somewhere before, so I sketched it from memory, scanned it into my computer, and ran it through a database of symbols the FBI has found at different crime scenes. I got a hit."

"From where?"

"Westchester County a decade ago. He killed five homeless men, and dumped their bodies in a field. The bodies were laid out in this strange pattern, like an upside-down cross. It was the same pattern that I saw in your broken frames."

"Then it's him."

"Has to be. The FBI did up a profile. He's a white male in his late forties, lives by himself, is smart, and has no social life."

Peter groaned. In all the excitement, he'd forgotten to tell Garrison that he'd glimpsed into the killer's mind, and seen him entering a room of students. "He's a college professor. I forgot to tell you."

"Are you sure about this?"

"I read his mind right before he tried to shoot me. There can't be that many college professors who fit that physical description in Westchester. Your haystack just got smaller."

"It sure did. See you tomorrow."

"Still want that composite?"

"Damn straight I do."

Garrison was a hunter, and his prey was in his sights. This was good news, because once Dr. Death was behind bars, the shadow person would lose its sponsor, and return to wherever it came from. He returned the Droid to the night table, feeling better than he had a minute ago.

Liza's cool breath tickled his skin. "Good news?" she asked.

"Getting better," he said.

9

〜

Holly was being a bad girl. After coming home from the séance, she'd lit candles inside her studio apartment, put on some classical music, and drawn the shades. When she'd deemed the mood was just right, she'd filled a round vase with tap water, added a mixture of magic herbs, and begun to scry on Peter, the man she loved.

Holly knew that playing voyeur cam with Peter's private life was wrong. Witches had a dreadful reputation for snooping, and she was only making it worse. But she couldn't help it. She had loved Peter since she was a child. For the longest time, she'd kept these feelings bottled up, and her emotions in check.

No more.

She'd had an epiphany. Life was fleeting, and terribly short. Peter had nearly died, and she'd never gotten to express her true feelings to him. That was about to change.

Water, water, oh so clear, show me the boy that I hold so dear.
I love him with all my heart, and feel terrible when we're apart.

The water in the vase grew cloudy, then cleared. The image of Peter at his brownstone on the East Side appeared. For a while, Peter sat on the stoop talking on his cell phone. Then a shoe came through an upper window, and landed at his feet. Peter raced inside in alarm.

She should have ended things right there. But instead, she recited the mystic words that let her follow Peter inside.

Oh spirits from above, take me inside the house of the man that I
    love.

Let me see what's happening to dear Peter, so that I may help him and
*   be near him.*

It wasn't the best rhyme she'd come up with, but it would do. The image inside the vase changed, and she saw Peter bound upstairs and run down a hallway to the master bedroom. She'd visited Peter's brownstone during her supernatural visits before, but never ventured inside his bedroom. It had not seemed the right thing to do

She now followed him, hoping she might help. A dark spirit waited in Peter's bedroom, and it snatched Peter's soul away to the spirit world, while his body lay motionless on the floor. Every few moments, one of his arms or legs twitched, signaling he was still alive.

Every time that happened, Holly's heart skipped a beat.

Peter's beautiful girlfriend, Liza, and a gang of stern-faced FBI agents appeared. Holly knew they were FBI because of the badges clipped to their chests. Seeing Peter on the floor, Liza had tried to shake him awake. She was crying, her face flush.

Holly cried as well. If Peter died . . . she tried not to imagine it.

Finally, Peter's eyes opened and he returned to the real world. Holly yelped for joy. The sound had a strange effect, and the water in the vase grew cloudy, ending the session.

"Damn it," she cursed.

Vase in hand, she crossed the studio and dumped the water into the sink. She tried to look on the bright side. The danger had passed and Peter was now safe. But she could not avoid seeing the dark side. Her beloved was still with Liza, and not with her. That wasn't fair, was it? Liza didn't have any powers, and she could never love Peter like Holly did. She was going to go crazy if that situation didn't change soon. Sometimes, she felt like she already had.

Holly lived in Morningside Heights, not far from Columbia. The space was small, but the view of the Hudson River made it feel big. On the walls hung her witch's things: astrological charts along with those devoted to numerology, plus shelves lined with jelly jars filled with magical herbs, rainbow powders, and bone-white charms. She lived by herself, which was depressing in a city as large as New York. She'd considered getting a roommate, but it couldn't be *any* roommate. It would have to be a person with an open mind, one who'd tolerate her strange habits. Like talking to ghosts and seeing into the future, for one thing.

She was a direct descendant of Mary Glover, who'd been hanged in Boston during the Salem witch trials. She bore a striking resemblance to the late great witch, right down to the cute dimple on her chin. A witch's powers were many: clairvoyance, casting spells, and the ability to hold sway over farm animals and domesticated beasts. But these powers came with a price, and she had few close friends.

It was hard being a young woman living in New York by yourself, even if you weren't a witch. Harder still when you belonged to a two-person club that included you and your aunt. Sometimes, it was all she could do not to feel sorry for herself. Holly told herself to get over it.

There had been a boy once. A drop-dead gorgeous foreign exchange student named Jean-Claude. One night at the restaurant where she worked as a hostess, he'd come in, and started to chat. One thing had led to another, and Jean-Claude had ended up in her apartment, sharing a bottle of wine. It had turned physical. As they'd made their way to her bed, she'd read his thoughts, and seen him preparing an exit strategy. She'd thrown him out, along with any notion that she could have a relationship with a normal boy.

She thought back to Peter. He was safe, but for how long? He'd been kidnapped twice tonight, and it could happen again. He was not going to win this fight without some help. As a rule, the Friday night psychics did not get involved in each other's personal lives, but this was different. This had started during a séance, when all of them were together. It was as much an attack on the group as it was on Peter, and the group needed to fight back.

She dug out her iPhone. The digital clock on the face said 3 A.M. What some people called the witching hour.

She rang her aunt, knowing she'd be up.

W hat are you doing awake at this ungodly hour?" Milly asked by way of greeting.

"Peter needs our help," Holly replied, getting to the heart of the matter.

"Is he there with you?"

"No, he's at home, and I'm at my studio."

"Have you been talking to him?"

"No."

"Then how do you know Peter needs us, unless you've been scrying on him."

The words were not a question, but a statement of fact. Witches often spoke in such a manner to each other. It made small talk all but out of the question. "Come to mention it, I have been scrying on him," Holly replied, deciding to meet her aunt's charge head on. "I love Peter, although you already know that. I watch him sometimes. Actually, I watch him a lot."

"Shame on you, Holly. That's wrong."

"Tell me you haven't done the same thing, and I'll apologize."

Her aunt went mute. Of course she'd done the same thing. Holly had spent part of her childhood at her aunt's place, learning the art of witchcraft. Many times when she was supposed to be practicing, she'd snuck into her aunt's study, and had seen Milly scrying on an unsuspecting person. Holly had never questioned it, and did not want her aunt questioning her now.

"Tell me why Peter needs our help," her aunt said, breaking the silence.

"He came home to find that black thing from the séance in his house. It pulled him back to the other side. That's two times in one night. When he came to, he looked shaken up."

"We cannot fight Peter's battles for him," Milly said.

"This thing appeared at our séance. It's a battle against all of us."

"It's called a shadow person, and it has an interest in Peter. Peter must deal with this."

"You're not going to help him?" Holly's voice rose indignantly.

"Peter is the son I never had, and I love him with all my heart. But there are some things which a psychic must experience on his own, without the interference of others. It is part and parcel of the learning process we all go through. Someday, you will go through it yourself."

"He nearly died," Holly said, not hearing a word her aunt just said.

"So?

"What do you mean, so?"

"Did I not teach you anything when you were growing up? Our lives are not days at the beach. The trials and tribulations that a psychic must endure are far greater than those of a normal person. It is the price we must pay for these dark gifts."

"Have you paid such a price?"

"I most certainly have. So have Max, Lester, and Homer, who was struck by a car and left blind. Every psychic goes through a trial of some kind. May yours not be so harsh."

"We still must help him," Holly said. "If not for Peter, then for ourselves."

"What do you mean?"

"The FBI were in Peter's place when this happened."

"How did the FBI get involved?"

"Peter contacted them. Instead of calling one of us for help, he called them. Do you see my point now?"

The sharp intake of Milly's breath sounded like a gun going off. Next to the Devil, the police were their worst enemy, and capable of ruining their lives. "Yes, I do," her aunt said. "I will call the others in the morning, and seek their opinions. I don't like you interfering in Peter's life, but in this you are right. We must help Peter deal with this."

Holly was relieved. Milly was as stubborn as a mule, and so was she. The difference was age. It was rare for Holly to come out on the winning side of an argument, and she chalked this one up as a major victory.

"May I make a suggestion?" her aunt said.

"Of course."

"Instead of scrying on Peter, why not scry on the killer Peter saw during the séance? Once he's caught, this thing will be over."

"But I don't know who the killer is. I need a name to work with."

"Why not use the name that Peter gave him—Dr. Death?"

"Will that work?"

"It should. Peter gave you the man's physical description, and said that he lives in Westchester County and is a college professor. How much more information do you need?"

"I've always had a name before."

"It's time for the training wheels to come off. You can do it."

"I'll most certainly try. Good night, Aunt Milly."

"Good night, dear child."

* * *

olly ended the call. Milly was right. Her time was better spent finding Dr. Death than spying on Peter and his girlfriend. And if she did happen to find the killer, then wouldn't Peter be thrilled? It would put their relationship on a whole new level.

Drawing the shades, she relit the candles, filled the vase with tap water, mixed in the magic herbs, and pulled up a chair. Into the vase she stared.

> *Oh, spirit from above, help me find a twisted college professor,*
> *Who's trying to kill the man I love.*
> *This man is small and somewhat fat, with a thick beard, and eyes like*
> *   a rat.*
> *He lives in a county called Westchester, where he kills women for his*
> *   pleasure.*
> *His name is unknown, so we've given him one, all our own.*
> *We call him Dr. Death, and so should you.*
> *For Death is his calling card, and the thing he shall always do.*

The water became the color of mushroom soup. As it cleared, Holly saw the image of a man sleeping on a bar in a smokey tavern. A cigarette burned in an ashtray while a movie played on an old TV with bad color. Was this Dr. Death? The man looked more like a drunk than a serial killer. The bartender tried to shake him awake. The man stirred, and raised his head off the bar. He looked directly at Holly, and she froze.

Evil had a face. It was mean and cruel and lacked a soul. It could be seen in the faces of evil dictators and ruthless madmen as they stood at podiums and made hateful proclamations. The man sleeping on the bar had such a face. His expression was ugly and harsh, and lacked compassion for other human beings. No wonder Peter had christened him Dr. Death.

Dr. Death continued to look right at her.

Then he spoke. "Fuck off."

The water grew cloudy, and he vanished.

"Damn it!" Holly said.

10

❧

The serial killer in Holly's vase of water was named Harold Munns, "Doc" to those who knew him. Forty-five, never married, he lived in the town of Pelham in Westchester County where he'd grown up. He had no friends except the bottle of whiskey on the bar.

"Last call," the bartender announced. "Come on, Doc. Don't make me toss you again."

Munns lifted his head off the bar. "Fuck off."

"Watch your language."

"Gimme some coffee."

A steaming cup was set in front of him. Munns sucked it down, felt himself come around. The bar was clearing out. He settled his tab and followed the others outside. Someone asked him if he had the time.

"Three A.M.," he replied.

Munns wondered if the others understood the significance of the hour. Christ had died on the cross at three o'clock in the afternoon, so it had been decided by Satan that his disciples would be most active twelve hours later.

Three A.M. Some called it the witching hour, others the Devil's hour. It really didn't matter: More bad things happened at three A.M. than at any other time of the day. That was a fact, and had been for two thousand years. Munns, and people like him, made sure of that.

"This town sucks," Munns said hoarsely.

The late-night crew laughed. To them, Munns was a fat, chronically shy townie who worked at the local college and liked to get drunk on cheap whiskey, and that was all he was. If the police ever caught Munns and his crimes became known, his friends would be sure to say, "But he seemed like a decent guy." because that was how he acted around them.

The late-night crew got in their cars and spun their tires in the loose gravel. Soon Munns was all by himself. He sucked on a cigarette.

"I hate this fucking place," he shouted.

He'd lived in Pelham his whole life. The town had redbrick streets and gaslight replicas on every corner. It sold itself as a great place to raise a family, but that was a lie. A child could be locked in a dungeon here, and no one would care.

Soon, he was driving his Volvo through town. The streets were deserted, and he could have broken the sound barrier and not gotten a ticket. But that wasn't his style. He never broke the law or drew suspicion to himself. The trick to being a killer was to stay off the police's radar. His friend Ray had taught him that, along with many other useful things. If not for Ray, he'd probably be doing life in prison right now.

He passed the railroad station where the town's homeless lived. Ten years ago, he'd used it as his laboratory. With the promise of a warm meal, he'd had lured homeless men to his car, strangled them, and dumped their bodies en masse in a field. He'd read in a book that when the homeless died, no one cared. The book had been right. No one *had* cared.

He pulled into a seedy strip mall, his destination a tattoo parlor called the Blue Devil. A blue neon sign in the window said CLOSED. Munns knew better and got out.

His legs felt like rubber. Booze was his weakness, but that was okay; the town was filled with drunks, and he fit right in. He banged on the front door with his palm. Ray, the owner, came through a beaded curtain and unchained the door. A self-proclaimed body artist, Ray had decorated himself in tattoos which covered ninety percent of his skin. Every tattooist had something he did particularly well. Ray's specialty was ghoulish skeletons, flesh-eating zombies, and the assorted demons and serpents that guarded the gates of hell.

"How's it going?" Ray asked.

"I'm hungry," Munns said, shaking off the cold.

"It's been too long, hasn't it?"

"Yes, over nine months."

"Is there someone in the wings?"

"You're very perceptive."

"Give me a name. It will help me visualize her."

"Her name is Rachael."

"Age?"

"Thirty-two. Single. Tall and trim. A runner. Tight ass."

"You've seen pictures?"

"Google Images."

"Is she coming here?"

Munns smiled and nodded.

"When?"

"Friday night on a train from New York. I'll be picking her up at the station. She thinks she's been invited to do an internship at the college. Won't she be surprised when I take her to my house, and lock her in the basement."

"Sounds like you've thought everything out."

Ray headed toward the back of the parlor. Munns fell in line behind him.

Just thinking about Rachael's arrival got Munns excited. Like most serial killers, his killing fell into cycles, which could be represented by the hands of a clock. Each time he killed, he felt satiated and very happy. That was the first three hours on the clock. The happiness faded away, and he would fall into a depression, hardly able to come out of his house and function. Those were the next three hours. This depression led to a manic stage, where he would begin to plot to secure his next victim. Often, he would stay up for days at a time, and was filled with unbridled energy. The next three hours. Finally, he would reach the countdown, where his next victim was about to step into his web. During this phase, he drank heavily, and felt like he was having a nervous breakdown. Those were the last three hours on the clock.

"I have a surprise for you," Ray said.

"What's that?"

"A new tattoo. I've been working on it all day."

"For me?"

"Yes. Just for you."

They entered Ray's studio with its black walls and a space heater that faced a barber chair hex-bolted to the floor. Munns stripped down to his trousers. He was shaped like a bowling pin, with all his weight centered around the middle. His upper body was covered in tattoos, but not as spectacularly as Ray's. There was still much work to be done.

"Where's this new tattoo going to go?" Munns asked.

"On your right arm," Ray said. "I want you to look at it every single day. It will serve as a reminder. Now take a seat, and we'll get started."

Munns sat in the barber chair and tried to get comfortable. He'd been physically abused as a child, his body used like a punching bag by his parents, and the prospect of having a hot needle stuck into his skin was not appealing. But there was no getting around it. Ray's tattoos had been his salvation; each time he got one, he became a new man.

Ray snapped on a pair of rubber gloves like a surgeon. He removed the needles from the sterilized autoclave bag, fitted them into his tattoo machine, and turned on the power by stepping on a foot pedal. Coils sent an electric current through the machine, causing the needles to move up and down at a rapid pace. His unblinking eyes searched for the virgin skin on Munns's arm. Finding his target, he pounced.

Munns settled in for the ride. It seemed like only yesterday that he'd gotten a flyer in the mail containing samples of Ray's work. Looking at the grisly images, he'd known that Ray was someone he should meet. Up until that point, Munns's killings had been poorly organized, more to satisfy a dark craving than any life calling. Meeting Ray had changed that. Ray had gone over to the dark side long ago. A convicted rapist and murderer, Ray had spent twenty years in prison, where he'd become a member of a group of devil worshipers called the Order of Astrum.

The first time they'd gotten together, Ray had convinced Munns to join the Order. Ray had shown him that the taking of innocent life was part of the Order's master plan, and that if he subscribed to that plan, his ability to cause suffering would only grow.

Munns had liked Ray, and had decided to sign up.

Part of the process required that his body be covered in tattoos, just like Ray's. It had all been done in secret, with the sessions taking place late at night in the Blue Devil's back room. Thirty-three sessions so far, his pasty white skin gradually being replaced.

New skin, new attitude.

One day, in the not too distant future, he'd be done, and everything but his hands and face would be covered with images of death and despair. And when that day happened, the Devil would own him, just as he owned Ray.

"Can I see the new tattoo?" Munns asked.

"Not until I'm done," Ray replied. "Now, tell me about Friday night. Who is this woman? How did you find her?"

"She e-mailed the college about an internship that was posted online. I intercepted the e-mail, and made contact. She sent me a résumé, and it fit all the requirements. Young, brilliant, filled with ambition. She thinks she can change the world."

"Does she push back at the darkness?"

The vibrating needle touched a nerve in Munns's arm. He silenced the scream coming out of his mouth. "Yes," he gasped. "She pushes back at the darkness."

"How?"

"Cancer research. She told me she was on the verge of a huge discovery, but it was going to take more time before she could publish her findings."

"Our Father will be pleased."

"My only desire is to make him happy."

"And mine as well. Will her disappearance be noticed?"

"She has no family, and recently moved to New York, and has no friends. I spoke with her several times and gained her confidence. She believes I've arranged living accommodations for her on campus, and even the use of a car. She will step off the train on Friday night into my trap, and will never be seen or heard from again."

"Won't the people she works with miss her?"

"She works part time at a college when she's not doing research. She told me she was planning to resign her post this week. Friday will be her last day."

"A perfect victim. There, I'm done."

Munns's right arm felt like it was burning. Never before had a tattoo hurt like this. Ray picked up a mirror, and held it in front of his latest creation. In its reflection was a red-eyed demon holding a decapitated human head.

"What is that thing?" Munns asked.

"Surtr," Ray replied. "According to Norse mythology, Surtr is a member of a race that is as strong as the gods. He looks small, yet can spring up at any time, and become a Jotunn, or a giant. At the end of the world, Surtr will wage war with the gods, and ravage the world with fire."

No wonder his arm felt like it was burning. "Whose head is he holding?"

"Don't you recognize him? He's famous."

The decapitated head belonged to a handsome young man with dark spiked hair and an expressive face. He looked vaguely familiar, and Munns tried to place him.

"I feel like I know him," he said.

"He's a professional magician named Peter Warlock, who's also a psychic," Ray replied. "Warlock will come to Pelham, and try to stop you from killing Rachael. Your job will be to kill Warlock. If you succeed, you'll become one of the Order's chosen few. Does that sound appealing to you?"

The breath caught in Munns's throat. Becoming a member of the Order had given his life purpose, and made him strong. He could only imagine what his new role would be like.

"I won't let you down," Munns promised.

"Glad to hear it," the body artist said.

11

It was a damp and dreary Saturday afternoon. But that hadn't stopped six hundred happy kids from Fort Apache, the Bronx, from showing up for today's matinee. The kids came from poor families, and could not have afforded the price of a ticket, much less the cost of a bus ride and box lunch. Nor did they have to. Peter picked up the tab.

It was a practice he'd started when he'd first opened his theater. Performing for adults paid the bills, but performing for kids was what he loved. There were a lot of kids in New York who couldn't afford to come to his show. So every Saturday, he opened his doors, and invited a group of them in.

He couldn't have pulled it off without Liza's help. His show was staged in an old sausage plant in the meatpacking district, the building cold and a little spooky. That was fine for adults who came to his evening shows, but not for the little ones. To make the place more appealing, Liza strung papier-mâché streamers on the walls and cheerful orange rugs on the cold tile floors. She also changed the preshow music from a moody piano concerto to a cheerful song by the Muppets. Upon entering the theater, the kids were greeted by a pair of old-fashioned popcorn machines, and carts filled with free drinks.

The show Peter performed on Saturday afternoons was also different. Gone were his mind-boggling illusions and baffling mind-reading stunts. Instead, he did his kid show, and performed the Multiplying Bottles, Sucker Die Box, the Professor's Nightmare, Eggs from the Mouth, Rabbit out of the Hat, and a dozen other timeless routines. They were tricks designed to make kids scream with delight. That was what his Saturday show was all about.

Peter was in his dressing room getting ready. He wore a tailored Italian jacket, the pockets of which he now checked. The two normal pockets on the outside contained a deck of cards and a set of multiplying billiard balls, while the four secret pockets sewn into the lining contained a reel, a thumb tip, a hand flasher that sent a burst of flash paper into the air, and a trick scarf that changed colors just by flicking it in the air. Everything was where it should be, and he turned to his guest.

"You done yet?" he asked.

"I'm getting there," the FBI artist replied, sketching away.

"I don't mean to be rude, but I have a show to do."

"One minute."

"One minute I can do."

Special Agent Roe had come to the theater by himself, and set up shop in the dressing room with his sketch pad and charcoal pencils. Garrison was not present, and Peter guessed the FBI agent had been pulled away on another assignment.

"Here, tell me what you think." Roe turned his pad around for Peter to see the composite of Dr. Death he'd drawn. It was good, but not good enough.

"Wow," Peter said.

"You like it?"

"It's great, but it's missing something."

"What's that?"

"His inner rage."

Roe frowned. "You said he was the quiet type. That's what I drew."

"He's carrying around a lot of anger. The volcano inside of him could erupt at any moment." Peter snapped his fingers for effect. "Just like that."

"What are you, a profiler?"

The truth be known, he could have been a detective or maybe even a profiler; his ability to look at people and gauge their feelings was as good as his ability to read minds.

"I'm open to suggestions," Roe said, breaking the silence.

"Can I take a closer look?"

Roe handed him the sketch pad. Dr. Death had the kind of face that was easily lost in a crowd. If Roe didn't capture his inner rage, there was a chance the killer would continue to elude the FBI, and an innocent woman named Rachael would perish this Friday night. Peter couldn't let that happen. He was going to open up with Roe, and decided the trade was worth it.

"Our killer has entered into a pact with the Devil. You need to capture that in your drawing."

"Are you serious?"

"Dead serious. Pardon the pun."

"But how could you possibly know that?"

"How much did Garrison tell you about me?"

"He said you did magic, and that if I wasn't careful, you'd read my mind. I assumed he was pulling my leg." Roe paused. "Can you read minds?"

"I sure can. I read the killer's mind. That's how I know these things about him."

Roe chuckled under his breath. It was how most people reacted when confronted by something out of the realm of their comprehension. Only this situation wasn't humorous, and Peter realized he needed to make Roe understand.

Peter stared into the FBI agent's eyes, and plumbed his thoughts. He saw Roe enjoying a candlelight dinner with an elegant young woman. The restaurant had polished wood floors and smokey etched glass that separated the tables. It looked like the Grotta Azzurra in Little Italy.

"What if I told you what you're having for dinner tonight?" Peter asked. "Would you believe me then?"

Roe stopped laughing. "That's impossible."

"Then you won't mind if I do it."

"Go ahead."

"You're going to have the same thing you always have, the signature dish Lobster Fra Diavlo, while your date will order the gluten-free Spaghetti Carbonara, which takes extra time to prepare. You'll also order a whole bottle of wine instead of by the glass, which is what you normally do."

"Jesus Christ. How'd you do that?"

"I just told you. I'm psychic. You can call me Peter."

Roe's face changed from a nonbeliever to a believer in no time flat. He turned the pad around on his lap, and sketched while he spoke. "My grandmother was psychic. She used to tell me what the rest of my family was thinking when I was a little kid. My parents thought she was nuts, but I knew better. How long have you had the gift?"

Peter chose his words carefully, not wanting to tell Roe any more about himself than he'd already told Garrison. "We're all born with psychic ability. Some of us realize it early, while others never do. I realized mine when I was a kid. I've been honing it ever since."

"You're saying that everyone can read minds?" Roe asked, not looking up.

"To a certain degree. It's one of the ways people communicated before language was invented. Then people started talking, and stopped using their psychic powers. As a result, their abilities began to wane."

"But yours didn't."

"I'm a little different. Both of my parents were psychics, and they passed it on to me. Mine is stronger than most people's."

Roe nodded as he drew. Peter had told him just enough to make him a believer, but not enough to turn him into a threat. He stole another glimpse into Roe's head. Tonight over dinner, Roe would tell his date that he'd met someone who could read minds, and she'd smile and laugh, and it would be forgotten by the time dessert was served.

Perfect.

Finished, Rose spun his pad around. Dr. Death no longer looked like an everyman. His nostrils were now flared, and his eyes had taken on a predator's glint, and become narrow and suspicious. The corners of his mouth were turned down in a frown. Seething out of every pore on his body was a palpable rage. The madman was lurking right below the surface.

"That's a winner," Peter said.

Roe acted pleased. He gathered up his pencils, and Peter walked him to the door. They shook hands, and the artist flashed a smile. "Your secret's safe with me," he said.

Peter tried to put Dr. Death out of his mind, and concentrate on how he was going to make a theater full of kids happy.

"Hey, Peter, can you talk?" a voice asked. It was Liza, speaking to him through the inner-canal earpiece that let his staff secretly communicate with him during the show.

"Sure can," he said. "How's it looking out there?"

"Looking good. The kids are in their seats. I don't mean to freak you out, but I'm a little nervous. What if that thing from last night comes back? What should we do?"

"It's called a shadow person, and I've already taken care of it," Peter said.

"You have? How?"

"Shadow people are like ghosts, and prefer darkness. If the shadow person appears during my show, I'll give Snoop a signal to turn on the house lights, and flood the stage. That should make it go away."

"What if it doesn't? What if it takes you to the other side again?"

"Then you'll have to finish the show. Still remember how to do Miser's Dream?"

"Come on. I'm being serious."

"I've taken other precautions. I went through a box containing my father's things this morning. Sure enough, he had a five-pointed star, similar to the one that belonged to my mother. My father's is hanging around my neck, along with a string of garlic."

"You have a string of garlic hanging around your neck?"

"Yeah. It really smells."

"Quit farting around. I got frightened half to death last night. You're not helping."

Liza was stressed. He wished he could have been in the same room with her, and not having this conversation with his collar. "I texted my psychic friends, and told them I was having problems. They're going to get together and try to help."

"Help how?"

"Lester Rowe will gaze into his crystal ball, Max will read his tea leaves, and Milly and Holly will mix magic potions into a vase of water. They'll talk to the spirits, and see if they can get to the bottom of what's going on."

"Is this another joke? I'm not laughing."

"No joke. It's what my friends do. Come on, don't be mad. It works."

"All I want to know is that I'm safe. I don't feel that way right now."

He swallowed the formidable lump in his throat. "Please don't be afraid."

"Give me one good reason why I shouldn't be."

"I can stop this thing, if I have to."

"You can? How?"

The answer was complicated. Lurking inside him was a person far different from the man Liza knew. He liked to think of it as his alter ego, but in fact it was a demon that he'd been born with, courtesy of his parents' peculiar genetic makeup. He could summon that demon if he chose, but there was a price to pay if he did.

"I have to go through a change," he said. "The source of my psychic power is buried deep within me. If I really need to I can summon it to deal with this thing. But there are consequences."

"Such as?"

"I can scare people, and I don't want to do that."

"But you'll go back to being yourself eventually."

Peter hesitated. He'd summoned the demon only as a last resort, and each time it had stayed around longer than he would have liked. Maybe one day the demon would not go back. That was the other reason he kept it suppressed, only he was not going to tell Liza that.

"Of course. Now please stop worrying."

"I can't help it. I'm sorry."

A buzzer rang backstage, signaling that the show was about to start. He headed for the door when her voice stopped him in his tracks.

"How will you stop it?" Liza asked. "Pistols at twenty paces?"

"With my hands. I'll grab it and shake it until it stops moving. Then it will fade away, and the threat will be gone. Okay?"

"You'll kill it?" Her voice had taken on a chill.

"This thing isn't alive. Its soul left this earth, and only a small portion remains in the form you saw last night. If I get my hands on it, I can shake that small piece out of it, and it will go join the rest of its spirit. I know it sounds weird, but that's how it works."

"So you're not killing it?"

"You can't kill something that's already dead. But I can make it go away."

"That makes me feel a lot better."

The fear had left her voice. For now, she was good with things. He supposed that was the best he could hope for.

He walked down a narrow hall and up a staircase that led to the back of the stage. He could hear the faint voices of children, chattering away. He didn't have to read their minds to know what each of them was thinking. They wanted to see some magic, and be transported to the world of make-believe.

He was not about to disappoint them.

12

Most magicians hated working for kids. They were little monsters, unruly and disruptive, and became distracted at the drop of a hat. In the world of magic, there was nothing lower than doing a kid show.

Peter felt differently about performing for children. Maybe it was because he'd never stopped being a kid himself.

Children of a certain age still believed in magic. The tricks they loved could be found on the shelves of any well-stocked magic shop, and would make a kid scream with delight if properly done. Pull a rabbit out of a hat, or a flapping dove from a scarf; make a pitcher of milk disappear in a newspaper; cause a silver ball to float mysteriously beneath a foulard; pluck fans of cards out of nothing, make billiard balls appear at your fingertips. Do these things right, and kids beg to see more. Their happiness will become your happiness, and it will last a long time.

Peter's kid show contained twenty tricks. Some could fit in his pocket, while others required a prop. None was more than four minutes long. Each had a definite beginning, middle, and end. Classics, they had withstood the test of time, and thousands of performances. He could have performed each in his sleep.

"Hello, boys and girls, and welcome to a very special afternoon of fun and magic," Liza's cheerful voice boomed over the PA. "Before we start, please remember, no flash photography or recording is permitted during the show, and cell phones must be turned off. Thank you, and have fun."

Over the PA came recorded music, followed by a drum roll. When it ended, the curtains parted, and Peter stepped out of a white puff of smoke onto a bare stage. Six hundred wide-eyed children stared up at him in awe.

Peter smiled. It was one of Max's rules. Every show began with a smile. If you weren't happy to be there, then why should your audience be? Displaying empty palms, he plucked a red scarf out of the air. As if creating life, a white dove appeared in its folds. The bird flew out of his hands, and landed in a lacquered box on an ornamental table. In the moment it had taken for the bird to appear, the stage had become filled with beautiful props.

From the children's mouths came a collective gasp.

Bang! Peter thought.

He hit them hard at the start, and made three more doves appear, placing them in the small lacquered box with the first. Firing a cap pistol at the box, he broke it apart, showing each piece as he did, and tossing them into Liza's waiting hands.

"Say good-bye to the birds," he told the children.

The kids applauded and stomped their feet. As the applause died down, he took stock of the crowd. He owned them.

For the next hour and twenty minutes, he worked his magic while spinning stories about the world of make-believe. In that imaginary world, no child felt hurt, or abandoned, or lonely, and every tale had a happy ending. It was a place where everybody got along, and there was at least one hour of sunshine, every single day. It was a world where anything was possible.

All good things must come to an end, his show no exception. He stepped to the foot of the stage, and the stage lights dimmed. He could no longer see the kids' faces, but he could hear their breathing, and smell the popcorn on their breath.

"Want to see one more?" he asked.

A cheer rose up. Liza wheeled an oversized dollhouse onto the stage. The prop was three feet wide by three feet high, with a pitched roof and matching front doors that opened at the center. He parted the doors to reveal an interior painted like a child's bedroom.

"What do you see inside this dollhouse?" he asked.

"Nothing," the kids replied.

"Good. Now, watch closely. Is everyone ready?"

"Yes," his fans chorused.

Liza sat on the edge of the dollhouse, curled herself into a ball, and gracefully wiggled her body inside. Shutting the doors, Peter spun the dollhouse around on its wheels.

"Everyone say 'Abracadabra!'" the young magician said.

"Abracadabra!" the kids shouted back.

"I can't hear you."

"*Abracadabra!*"

There was a shifting inside the dollhouse as Liza slipped into the crawl space hidden in the base of the prop. The trick's clever construction made it appear that there was no place for her to hide, when in fact, there was more than enough room.

"Ready?" he whispered.

"Ready," she whispered back.

He pressed a button on the roof, and the front doors sprung open. A small white terrier named Norman was supposed to leap out. A circus dog, Norman never missed a cue.

Only today there was no Norman. In his place, a shadow person oozed out of the prop, and hovered a few inches above the stage like a hologram. Peter touched the five-pointed star underneath his shirt. The shadow person could not kidnap him and take him to the other side. A small comfort, for the dark spirit was about to wreck his show.

"That's cool!" a kid called out.

"Totally awesome," another kid shouted.

The kids were on their feet, staring in awestruck wonder. No trick he'd performed this entire afternoon had elicited this much excitement. He'd been upstaged by a rogue spirit.

"Peter, help me," said Liza in his earpiece.

Poor Liza was stuffed inside the dollhouse's floor, breathing through the air holes drilled into the wood. "Hold on," he whispered into the speaker in his collar.

"I can't."

"What do you mean?"

"He's chasing me."

"What are you talking about?"

"Your killer."

"*What?*"

"That thing took me over to the other side. At least, that's where I think I am." She sounded terrified, and was breathing hard. "I'm running down a gravel driveway on the side of a steep hill. A guy in a Volvo is chasing me. Oh, my God, he's leaning out of his window—he's pointing a gun at me!"

It was the same nightmare he'd experienced. Liza had been taken to Dr. Death's house, and was being chased down a rural road by the serial killer in his Swedish-made car. A gunshot ripped through his earpiece. Peter's heart skipped a beat.

"Keep running," he whispered.

"This maniac is shooting at me! Bring me back!"

Onstage, the shadow person was going in convulsions. Forms appeared from within. A hand pushed at the spirit's lining, as if trying to break free. It was both fascinating and horrifying to watch. The kids in the audience appeared hypnotized. Maybe part of the process was a form of hypnosis that prepared your soul to be whisked to another place. If that was the case, then a large number of kids from Fort Apache were not going to make it home this afternoon.

One of the oldest rules in show business was never to turn your back on your audience. Peter broke that rule, and turned his back while stepping in front of the convulsing spirit. The moment he did, he let the anger festering inside of him come out. The anger had been there for as long as he could remember. He'd been raised to keep a lid on it, even if it meant biting his tongue, or turning the other cheek, or any of the other passive things that civilized people did.

His anger changed him. His psychic powers grew, and so did his physical strength. Overall, the effect was extraordinary. But it came with a price, as the evil side to his personality came out as well. It wasn't pretty, and certainly not suitable for kids to see.

With his back turned, he plunged his fist into the shadow person's midsection. The evil spirit emitted a painful sound, and appeared to shrink in size.

"Peter!" Liza screamed.

"I'm coming! Hold on!"

Another shot rang out, this one closer than the first.

"Oh, my God, he shot me in the leg!" Liza said.

Peter struck the shadow person several times. It shrunk in size, until it was no bigger than a beach ball. He shoved it back inside the dollhouse, and pressed the secret mechanism which let Liza escape from her hiding place. His girlfriend poured out of the illusion into his waiting arms, her eyes firmly shut. He looked at her leg, and did not see a bullet wound. So much for small favors. He kissed her, and she snapped awake.

"You're going to be okay," he said.

"What took you so long?" she whispered.

"We need to finish the show."

She slipped out of his arms. Clasping hands, they bowed to the audience, and were showered with applause. Peter looked at the crowd, and saw a sea of smiles. And the huge false one planted on Liza's face that was there to reassure the children.

13

⤴

Peter sat on the couch in his dressing room, holding Liza in his arms. Entering the spirit world was a harrowing experience, and Liza had not completely fallen back to earth, her mind still wandering in the shallow space somewhere in between.

"Drink this," he said.

The water bottle touched her lips. Eyes still faraway, she sipped. "Explain what just happened to me."

"The shadow person sent you forward in time to a house in Westchester where a serial killer lives. That killer was getting ready to pick up his next victim, a woman named Rachael, when you dropped in on him."

"Was he the same guy from your séance last night?"

"Yes. I nicknamed him Dr. Death. He has a beard, and dresses like a college professor."

"That's the guy I saw. How many people has he killed?"

"Nearly a dozen, according to the FBI."

She took another sip. "Why did the shadow person send me to see him? To get to you?"

"I guess." He stared at Liza's bare neck. His face grew into a deep frown. "You took off my mother's five-pointed star. I asked you not to do that."

"It was scratching my neck, so I took it off for the show. Big mistake."

"Promise me you won't do that again until this is over."

"I promise."

He kissed her on the forehead. It had a calming effect on her, and she rested her head on his shoulder and closed her eyes. An eerie scratching sound at the door made them both jump. Peter jumped up and sprang open the door. A white ball of fur came bounding in.

"Norman! Oh, my God, we forgot all about you," Liza said.

Norman was panting hard. They took turns stroking his fur until he calmed down.

"I wonder where he was," Peter said.

"He was with me," Liza said. "He was running down the road with me, barking at Dr. Death. Dr. Death started yelling at him, and tried to run him over with his car. It had to be the most cruel thing I've ever seen. What kind of person would run over a lovable dog like this?"

"An evil one. What happened then?"

"Norman ran between the car's tires, and somehow escaped." She petted Norman's furry head. "Can you imagine what's going through his little brain?"

Peter could hardly understand what was going through his own head, much less the poor dog's. Rising from the couch, he walked down the hall to Liza's dressing room, removed his mother's five-pointed star from the pewter jewelry dish, and returned to his own dressing room with it dangling from his finger. "Please put this back on."

Liza fitted the star around her neck, and tucked it beneath her collar. "I won't take it off, even if it rips my throat."

They played with the dog for a while. Peter had taught Norman how to walk on his hind legs while balancing a red rubber ball on the tip of his nose. He had used animals in his magic show since he was kid. Back then, his doves had lived in a drawer of his dresser, while he'd kept a Dutch dwarf rabbit in a cardboard box in his closet. These days, his pets lived in large pens with plenty of sunlight, and were showered with daily attention by himself and his staff.

"So, how are we going to catch this guy?" Liza asked.

Her words caught him by surprise. They were not what he'd expected her to say, and it took a moment for them to sink in. "Did you say *we*?" he asked, just to be sure.

"Yes. I want to stop him from killing Rachael. So do you."

"But you're putting yourself at risk."

"So are you."

"I have powers. I can fight back."

"Then I'll make sure to stand right next to you."

"I don't want you doing this."

Liza stopped playing with the dog. "I have to. I heard her voice."

"You mean Rachael's?"

"Yes, Rachael's. As Dr. Death got out of his car, his cell phone rang, and he answered it. I heard the caller. It was Rachael calling to say that her train was running late because of a delay out of Grand Central Station. She sounded like a good person."

"You're sure about this."

"Positive. I'd like to think she'd do the same for me."

Liza had connected with a woman in the future she didn't know, and now wanted to prevent her from perishing. It was an emotion he knew all too well, for it was one which consumed him also. Rachael with no last name was a life that needed saving.

"You're probably right," he said.

"So you're okay with it?"

"I appreciate and support your position."

"Thank you, counsel."

"What else do you remember about your experience? Any little detail might help the FBI to figure out who Dr. Death is."

Liza stopped petting the dog, her face a study in concentration. "It was dark. I didn't see all that much. The interior of his house was kind of drab. Judging by the decorations, I'd say he's a bachelor, doesn't have any lady friends. The car he was driving stuck out. It was an older make of Volvo my parents drove when I was a kid. My father always complained about the suspension."

"How old?"

"Twelve–thirteen years."

"This is great. Keep going."

"Do you think we can really catch him?"

"The FBI has a profile. If we give them enough clues, they'll find him."

She shut her eyes and tried to bring the rest of it back. "He had a really bad vibe. Like he was carrying around a huge chip on his shoulder."

Dr. Death had called the town he lived in a hellhole, and Peter guessed something traumatic had happened to him growing up. His soul had been seared, so he sought revenge against those who had wronged him. It was as good an explanation as any for what he was.

"That's all I remember," Liza said. "Does it help?"

"Everything helps."

There was a tap on the door. Snoop stuck his head into the dressing room. Snoop was Peter's stage manager, and one of his closest friends.

Snoop wore his blond locks combed over his eyes, and looked like Norman's older brother. Snoop had seen a lot of unusual things, and never said much about it. He was cool with the strange comings and goings in Peter's life.

"You two lovebirds okay?" Snoop asked.

"We're doing fine," Peter said.

"I've got a question. Is that black thing that came out of the dollhouse going to be a permanent part of the show? That was one heck of a trick."

"I don't think so," Peter said.

"You're not going to do it again? Why not?"

Snoop got his name because he enjoyed prying into other people's business. Lying to him was pointless because he'd eventually figure out the truth. Better to level with him up front, and be done with it, Peter decided.

"The thing you saw wasn't part of the show," Peter said.

"Then what was it?"

"An unwanted guest."

"You mean a ghost?"

"Ghosts are friendly. That thing wasn't. It's called a shadow person."

"That's heavy. I'm glad I got it on tape. Wait until I post it on You-Tube."

"You taped the show?"

"You betcha."

Peter sometimes filmed his shows so he could later critique himself. The Saturday matinee hadn't been filmed in a while, and it was a stroke of luck that Snoop had chosen to film today. Ghosts and spirits did not like to be captured on film. When watched frame by frame, their true identities often revealed themselves. Perhaps Snoop's film of the shadow person would reveal its true identity, and lead them to Dr. Death.

"You're a genius," Peter told him.

"Glad you finally noticed," his assistant replied.

14

⌘

Garrison arrived at the theater after the evening show let out, and gathered with Peter, Liza, and Snoop in Peter's dressing room. Peter kept a TV in the room, and it was on this that they watched the video Snoop had shot of the shadow person during the matinee.

The video's resolution along with the bright stage lighting gave remarkable clarity to a presence that was normally viewed in a fleeting glance before disappearing. About five feet tall, it was shaped like a woman, but could have easily been a man. They watched Peter stuff it into the Dollhouse illusion, and make the lovely Liza reappear, her body falling into his arms. It was here that the video ended.

"Let me make sure I've got this straight," Garrison said to Liza. "While that thing was on stage, you were hidden in a secret compartment in the bottom of the illusion, but your spirit was whisked away to the future, where you encountered Dr. Death."

Liza had changed into a pair of gray sweats. The strain of two shows and her nerve-racking trip had taken its toll, and she looked exhausted. "That's right."

"What do you remember about him? Think hard."

"He tried to run over a little dog in the road. He has to be the most rotten person I've ever met. I mean, who runs over little dogs?"

"That's a very helpful piece of information," Garrison said.

She brightened. "It is? Why?"

"People who are really angry with the world run over dogs and cats, and leave them in the road for other motorists to see. The FBI has seen this before in serial killers. I can think of three off the top of my head."

"Will it help you catch him?" Liza asked.

"It just might. The three serial killers I'm thinking of all shared something else in common. They'd all gone berserk in public, and been arrested. They all had records which detailed what they'd done. If we're lucky, our serial killer in Westchester will have a record, and that will make it easier to find him."

Liza smiled. She was a person who searched for meaning in just about every situation. She'd been searching for the meaning of her harrowing trip, and Garrison had just served it to her. The FBI was one step closer to catching Dr. Death. "Thank you for sharing that. I'm going to think about what happened some more. If anything else pops up, I'd like to call you."

Garrison handed her a business card. "Call me anytime."

She slipped the card into her pocket. Her world was back on keel. It occurred to Peter that this was an important moment in their relationship. She had not run. His other girlfriends had all done that at some point. His psychic gifts had scared them, and they'd gone from being lovers to Facebook friends in a New York minute. Not Liza. She was in it for the long haul. No girlfriend had ever done that for him before. Somehow, he would find a way to thank her.

"Let's see the video again," Garrison said.

Snoop punched the remote, and the shadow person danced across the screen. The FBI agent brought his face close to study the unearthly presence.

"You'll go blind doing that," Snoop said. "My mother told me that, so I thought it was worth passing along."

"Shut up," Garrison said.

Snoop and Garrison were not friends. One of the agents in Garrison's team had arrested Snoop in college for hacking government computers, and Garrison had made it clear that he thought the public would be well served if Snoop was locked up in prison. Snoop knew of these feelings, and made it a point to needle the FBI agent whenever they were together.

The video ended, and Garrison twirled his finger. "Play it again."

"Only if you say please."

"Don't push your luck, son."

The tape played again, and Garrison went back into his pose. He resembled a baseball umpire crouching behind home plate, his face scrunched up in anticipation of a hundred-mile-per-hour fastball ready to fly into the catcher's mitt. His eyes squinted, and then he smiled.

"Isn't that something," he said.

Peter assumed a similar pose beside him. Whatever Garrison was seeing was invisible to his untrained eye. "What did you see?"

"Your spook is dancing in front of those kids," Garrison said. "Look how it sways back and forth while shrugging its shoulders. That's modern dance."

Liza made it a threesome, also staring. "Oh, my God, you're right. You can see how it moves across the stage in rhythm to the music. How weird is that."

This was not how evil spirits acted. Usually, they did scary things around kids, whom they liked to torture. It was a part of being evil that Peter had never quite understood. Hurting adults was something he could vaguely understand, but how could someone hurt a child?

Certainly not the shadow person. It seemed more intent on entertaining the crowd of kids than scaring the daylights out of them. But Peter was letting his imagination run away with him. This was an evil spirit they were looking at. Perhaps the dance was a preamble of what was about to come, and the shadow person was preparing to enter the audience, and kidnap the spirits of several kids in the front row.

It could happen. Peter had heard stories about evil spirits abducting children. They'd always ended badly. The poor kids had come back traumatized, and were never the same.

He'd been justified in hurting this thing, and stuffing it back in the box. In hindsight, he should have hurt it more when he'd had the chance. Only he hadn't wanted the kids to see the full force of his rage. It would have scared them as badly, so he'd held back.

"I need to take this tape, and have the forensic boys analyze it," Garrison said.

"It's yours," Peter told him. "Make sure they study the face. Ghosts and evil spirits are ashamed to have been left behind, so they hide their faces, and avoid the light."

"Sounds like some girls I've dated," Snoop said.

"Skip the commentary, and get me the tape," Garrison said.

Snoop produced the video. He'd burned it onto a CD, which he dutifully handed over. He started to raise his arm, and give the infamous middle finger salute. Peter caught his assistant's attention eye, and shook his head. Snoop lowered his arm dejectedly.

"We've got until Friday to catch this madman," Garrison said. "We're off to a good start because of your efforts. Call me if you remember anything else."

"Will do," Peter said.

Peter and Liza walked Garrison to the back alley where the agent's SUV was parked. The temperature had dropped, with the promise of another bitterly cold night. Garrison produced his keys and hit a button that unlocked the doors and killed the security system.

"I heard her voice," Liza said.

"Whose voice?" Garrison asked.

"Rachael, his next victim. It was over the phone. Dr. Death was setting the trap."

"What can you tell me about her?"

"I didn't see her—I just heard her voice."

"You formed a mental image of Rachael while listening to her speak. It's something we all subconsciously do. Describe that image to me."

Liza tried to remember and shook her head. "I'm sorry."

Garrison did not seem discouraged. He was a family man, with a wife and kids out in a small town on Long Island. He could have been home with them right now, but instead he was here, trying to solve a difficult case. Peter decided to help him.

"Let me find it," the young magician said.

"How are you going to do that?" Garrison asked.

"If Liza will let me, I'll find the memory buried in her subconscious."

"All right. Just don't go snooping where you don't belong," she said.

Peter put his hands onto Liza's shoulders and gazed into her eyes. Of all his gifts, mind reading was the one he had the most control over. It was like crossing his eyes, only the crossing took place inside his head. It took but a second, and allowed him to peer into another person's head, and mine his or her innermost thoughts and memories.

He hunted for Liza's trip to the other side. The memory was vivid, with Liza running for her life as Dr. Death tried to run her down. The faces of Liza's mother, father, and her three siblings appeared. *She thought she was going to die.*

Another face appeared, buried deep away. Faint, so he had to stare.

A dark-haired woman, late thirties, with Irish features and a strong chin. Was this Rachael, the woman Liza had imagined when she'd heard the voice over the killer's phone?

"I think I've got her. Rachael is Irish, with a pleasant face and a strong disposition."

Liza clapped her hands excitedly. "That's the woman I imagined."

"Define strong disposition," Garrison said.

"Strong willed. When I look at her, I think doctor, or nurse," Peter said.

"You nailed her," Liza said. "Her voice reminded me of a doctor's voice. She was very precise in the way she spoke, like she was used to telling people what to do."

"Good going," Garrison said. "Now we can work the case from both ends. If we can't find the killer, hopefully we can find his victim before she leaves town."

The best days were the ones that ended well. Garrison got into his car. The driver's window came down, and he stuck his head out, his breath turning into vapor.

"One more question," he said.

Why did Garrison always have one more question? Why couldn't he just fade away into the sunset like lawmen were supposed to do?

"What's that?" Peter asked.

"The thing you two just did, does it have a name?"

Peter squeezed Liza's hand. "It's called teamwork."

15

Sixty-five blocks away, on the fifth floor of the ultra-exclusive Dakota, Milly Adams sat at her dining room table with Max Romeo, Lester Rowe, the blind psychic Homer, and her niece Holly. The purpose of their gathering was to use their psychic powers to decode why a shadow person had attached itself to their beloved Peter. They had yet to begin, and the men sat at the far end of the table, eating pretzels while listening to one of Max's fanciful stories.

"Have I ever told you about the Great Chesto? He was far and away the most amazing novelty act I've ever seen," the old magician said.

"Can't say that you have," Lester replied.

"I think I would have remembered that name. What exactly did he do?" Homer asked.

"Chesto billed himself as the Man Who Felt No Pain. He would place a concrete block on his chest, then invite a muscular young man from the audience to pick up a sledgehammer, and hit the block as hard as he could."

"He did this more than once?" Lester asked.

"It was how he made his livelihood."

"Astonishing."

Max bit into his pretzel while staring wistfully into space. "A long time ago, I was part of a traveling road show. There was a drunk plate spinner, a Barbra Streisand look-alike with a voice like a feral cat, a musical group that couldn't carry a tune, and myself. We were working the corn belt, traveling in a pair of broken-down vans. I don't mean to wax nostalgic, but it was one of the most enjoyable experiences I've ever had.

"One day, we entered a town where a county fair was taking place. Since our show wasn't until that night, I bought a ticket. At first I was disappointed. The fair was more a livestock exhibition, with smelly cows being judged by men in coveralls missing most of their front teeth. The spectators were the biggest people I've ever seen, and every piece of food they were eating was fried or dripping with barbecue sauce. There was an auction going on, with the prize animals being sold off for slaughter. Having spent my formative years on the Lower East Side, I can tell you the experience was nothing less than a shock to my frail system."

"Max, we need to get started," Holly said impatiently. "How long is this going to take?"

"I'm nearing the finish line," the old magician said.

"Sorry."

"So where was I? Oh, yes, I was at the fair, debating whether I should try a corn dog or a pulled-pork sandwich, when over the loudspeaker came an announcement that the Great Chesto was about to perform a death-defying feat, so please gather round. This piqued my curiosity, and I followed the rest of the crowd to a makeshift dirt arena.

"The Great Chesto awaited us. He was rather stout, as big around the middle as he was tall. He addressed the crowd over a microphone to build up his trick. It was the only thing he did, so he had to draw it out. When the preamble was over, Chesto asked a man from the crowd to assist him. A big farm boy stepped forward. I was standing next to the fellow, and got a good look at his face. The expression "dumb as a fence post" came to mind.

"Chesto didn't notice. If he had, I'm sure he would have selected someone else. He lay down on a blanket, and picked up a concrete block lying on the ground, which he balanced on his chest. He instructed the farm boy to pick up a sledgehammer, which lay beside him. The farm boy did as told. Then Chesto said, 'When I nod my head, I want you to hit it as hard as you can. Got it?' The farm boy said yes. The Great Chesto nodded his head, and that was the end of him!"

Lester and Homer slapped their hands on the table and howled with laughter.

"Max, that's a terrible story, and not the way we wish to start our evening," Milly scolded him, trying not to grin. "Let's get down to the business at hand, shall we?"

Max nodded compliance, as did Lester and Homer. Milly passed the baton to her niece.

"Go ahead, my dear," she said.

"Yesterday, Peter texted us, and asked for our help figuring out the mystery of the shadow person," Holly began. "But Peter left out something very important. Last night, after Peter left our séance, the shadow person followed him home, where Peter was again taken to the other side and nearly perished. I'm fearful for his safety, and want us to collectively figure out how to prevent this from happening again."

"Did Peter tell you about this second trip?" Max asked.

Holly swallowed hard. "No, not exactly."

"I didn't think so, because he usually comes to me first with that kind of information, and I never heard a peep out of him. So how did you know?"

"If you must know, I was scrying on him."

"Did you say you were spying on him?"

"No, I was scrying on him."

"Same difference, I suppose. You were watching Peter when you weren't supposed to. We're not allowed to do such things, Holly. It's against the rules."

"I was afraid for him," she said, her lower lip trembling. "Don't you remember what happened during our séance? He nearly died."

"But he got out of it," Max said.

"Barely."

"But he did. And I'm guessing he got out of it the second time as well. Which means he has the situation under control, and we should not meddle in his affairs. The shadow person is visiting him for a reason, and it's Peter's responsibility, not ours, to find out what it is."

Max rolled a shiny silver dollar across his knuckles as he spoke. Holly slapped the table in anger, and the coin jumped from Max's hand to the floor.

"Our responsibility is to help each other whenever possible," she said, the rage boiling over in her voice. "Peter needs help, the rules be damned. If you won't come to his aid, I'll go it alone. I'm not going to abandon him."

"I didn't say that," the old magician said defensively.

"You most certainly did. Peter thinks of you as his father, and yet you refuse to help him. How can you be so thoughtless?"

Max looked to Milly for help. "Please explain to your niece what I'm trying to say."

"I thought you were doing a perfectly miserable job of it yourself," Milly told him. To Holly she said, "What Max is trying to say is this. Peter seems to need our help, but he may not need our help. This may simply be some kind of test Peter must endure. I know I agreed with you earlier that we must help Peter, but now I'm not so sure. All psychics go through learning phases during their lives when the spirit world makes contact with them for reasons that are never quite clear. Peter is now in one of those phases."

"A learning phase? How quaint. When have any of you ever had a gun put to the side of your head during a séance?" Holly crossed her arms and awaited a response. "I'm waiting."

The ticking grandfather clock in the corner kept time to their silence. Holly had challenged them, and drawn an imaginary line in the sand. Who would cross it first?

"Peter's different," Lester said quietly. "We are all psychics, but Peter is special. You must accept that, Holly."

"You don't think he could have been killed?"

Lester thought about it, and shook his head. "No," he said for emphasis.

"For God's sake, I saw him writhing around on the floor in his bedroom. If his girlfriend hadn't shaken him awake, he'd have died."

"Hooray for his girlfriend," Lester said.

"That's not funny."

"I'm not trying to be funny," the Scottish psychic said. "Peter beat the Devil, and has learned from the experience. These are lessons we must not deny him."

"Are you telling me that this is some kind of master plan?" Holly asked.

"Our fate is bestowed upon us the day we're born," Lester explained. "This is Peter's fate. You must stop interfering. For your own sake, and his as well."

"Here, here," Max said. "Do you agree, Homer?"

"I do. We must let Peter fend for himself."

Holly could not believe how poorly they were acting. Peter had come to their aid so many times she'd lost count. Yet now they refused to help him during his time of need.

"Do you agree with this nonsense?" she asked her aunt.

"I'm afraid that after some consideration I do, my dear," Milly said.

"We must not interfere. If Peter feels he needs our help, we're but a phone call away. We can stand on the sidelines and watch, but we must not jump in. In the psychic world, there is no room for the uninvited."

Holly had heard the term before. The uninvited were psychics who didn't play by the rules, and upset the natural balance of the universe. They were pariahs, and shunned by their peers. It should have been enough to stop her, only this was Peter they were talking about, the boy who'd lit the candle in her heart. She suddenly realized that the object of the meeting tonight wasn't about helping Peter but getting Holly to stop interfering in his life. She rose from her seat. "Thank you for granting me an audience tonight. I am sure this is not the first time we'll disagree. But in the end, we will all remain friends, and that's the most important thing. Now if you'll excuse me, I must go home."

Her aunt's apartment was thirty-six hundred square feet. That was bigger than many houses in New York. Holly's footsteps followed her down the hallway to the coat closet. She pulled her winter coat off a hanger and felt a presence behind her.

"Let me help you with that."

Max helped her into her coat. He seemed embarrassed by what had happened, as well he should. Holly had turned twenty-one only a short time ago. She was old enough to drink and vote, and did not appreciate being treated like a child.

"You're angry with me," Max said.

"Whatever gave you that idea, Max?" She removed the scarf from her pocket and tied it around her neck. "I asked you to help, and you said no. Why should I be angry?"

"You don't understand the gravity of this."

"Stop talking to me like I'm still in diapers."

"I'm closer to that than you are."

"I'm in no mood for jokes, Max. What don't I understand?"

"Peter is different than we are."

"I know that. But does that make the rules different as well?"

"I'm afraid it does."

"I'm not buying that for one minute, Max. I think you're all scared of that evil thing we saw last night, and want nothing more to do with it, Peter's safety be damned."

Max started to speak, then thought better of it. The expression on his face said it all. There was something he wanted to tell her, yet chose to hold back instead. It was all Holly could do not to scream. She headed for the front door, ready to go home.

"Wait."

Max made a conciliatory gesture with his hands. From out of nowhere appeared two beautiful bouquets of red and gold feather flowers. Max's flower trick was one of Holly's favorites, the bouquets' hiding place on the old magician's clothing still a mystery. Tonight, the trick had the opposite effect on her, and she grabbed the bouquets from his hands, and angrily shook them in his face. Tears streamed down her cheeks, and before she knew it, she was crying.

"Oh, Holly, I'm so sorry," he said.

He put his arms around her, and let Holly cry on his shoulder.

16

*

eter loved Mondays. His theater was dark, and with Liza glued to his side, he'd set about to explore the city's hundreds of different ethnic neighborhoods. Finding them was a challenge, and part of the fun. Many of the smaller ones weren't on any map, nor did any of the guidebooks list them, except for the obvious spots like Chinatown and Little Italy. Liza had a cool trick that usually worked. They'd walk into a restaurant and read all the items on the menu. If half the stuff sounded foreign, they knew they'd found another.

Only this particular Monday was different. He'd woken up in a dark mood, and Liza had shoved him out of bed with the words, "You promised, Peter. Today's the day."

He'd put on nice clothes while she'd taken a shower. Instead of a leisurely breakfast, they'd noshed on bagels and sucked down coffee. Then out the door they went into the chilly morning. As Peter's feet hit the sidewalk, he nearly turned around. Why he'd ever agreed to see a relationship counselor, he had no idea. A moment of weakness, he supposed. Men said stupid things when they were in love.

But there was more to it than that. He was going because he didn't want Liza to pack up and leave, which was how his other relationships had ended. That was a good reason, and he should have been okay with it, only he wasn't. Spilling his guts to a stranger just seemed wrong, and he hoped the whole thing didn't blow up in his face.

r. Raul Sierra worked out of a somber building the color of ash. Across the street was NYU's Medical Center, which his practice was affiliated with. According to his online profile, Sierra was an authority on guiding couples through difficult periods in their lives. The photo on his Web site showed a rather frail little man with an unruly mop of black hair that resembled a bird's nest. He looked harmless, but looks were deceiving. Sierra hadn't gotten to be one of the world's foremost authorities on relationships without being a good interrogator, and Peter guessed he was in for a long morning.

Monday was also Herbie's day off, and they cabbed it, arriving a few minutes before their appointment. As they waited to be buzzed in, a cold wind whipped off the East River that knifed through their clothes and made them both shiver. Peter said, "Let's go find a restaurant and get a nice hot chocolate."

"Not on your life," Liza replied.

They were let in, and took an elevator to the top floor. Sierra's waiting room was small and dreary. A receptionist sat at a computer and appeared hypnotized by its screen.

"Good morning. We're here to see Dr. Sierra," Liza said.

"He's waiting for you. Go right in," she replied without looking up.

They passed into an office whose walls sagged under the weight of thick medical books. Sierra stood at a window that faced onto the street with a faraway expression on his face. He had aged since his photo, his hair now gray. Turning, he said, "Is it already nine thirty?"

It was a strange way to begin a counseling session. Peter acknowledged that it was while helping Liza remove her coat. Dr. Sierra crossed the room and politely shook hands. "I must have lost track of the time. Please make yourselves comfortable."

The doctor motioned toward a leather couch in the room's center. On the side table was an open box of Kleenex. Sierra pulled up a chair so he was sitting directly in front of them.

"Excuse me for acting so distracted when you came in," he said. "I'm afraid I was daydreaming."

"It must have been some daydream," Liza said.

"A strange case that was never resolved to my satisfaction. But that was a long time ago. Please tell me about yourselves, and why you've come to see me. My receptionist said you were vague over the phone as to the nature of your problems."

Liza cupped her hands in her lap and gazed at the floor. "God, I don't know where to start. It's so complicated. And so . . . well, weird."

"Is the problem sexual in nature?" Sierra gently asked.

"Our sex life is terrific. Peter is a wonderful lover."

Sierra glanced at Peter and dipped his chin approvingly. It was hard not to like the guy, but Peter wasn't taking the plunge just yet. He made eye contact with Liza.

"You're wonderful, too."

"Well, we're off to a good start," Sierra said, clapping his hands enthusiastically. "You are both in love, and enjoy each other's company in bed. Is your problem financial?"

"Peter makes a very good living," Liza said, still doing floor patrol.

"Is it religious in nature?"

"Sorry."

"That leaves family. Are your families interfering in your lives?"

"Peter's family is gone, and mine isn't a problem," Liza said.

"Well, this hardly sounds like a bad situation. Unless of course I'm missing something."

Liza squirmed uncomfortably. Peter felt like he was in a cab stuck in traffic with the meter running. He reached across the couch and took Liza's hands in his own, then cleared his throat. "Okay, here's the deal. The problem with our relationship is me. I'm a psychic. I can read minds, see into the future, and communicate with the dead. Liza and I have been living together for two years. I kept this hidden from her until recently. It's causing us a lot of problems."

Sierra's face had gone blank, and Peter wondered if it was too much information for him to absorb. After a moment, the good doctor spoke.

"You look familiar. Aren't you a professional magician?" Sierra asked.

"That's right. I have a show downtown."

"And you're telling me that the tricks you do are real?"

"Some of them."

"But not all."

"Correct."

"If you don't mind my saying so, I'm finding this rather hard to believe."

Sierra had a bemused look on his face, and Peter felt himself grow flush. He hated when people laughed at him, and he felt his inner demon about to rear its ugly head. He didn't want that to happen in the presence of a stranger, and forced himself to calm down.

"Perhaps you could give me a demonstration," Sierra said.

"You want me to read your mind?"

"Could you? That would be splendid."

"Give me your hand."

With a twinkle in his eye, Sierra placed his hand onto Peter's out-stretched palm. As their skin touched, the doctor jumped in his chair. "Your hands are ice-cold," Sierra said.

"I have a demon inside of me. When it starts to come out, my skin turns cold."

"Oh, come on, you can't be serious."

"Dead serious. Now, think of something in your past. Anything at all."

Sierra looked at Liza for help. "Is your boyfriend on the level?"

"Everything he says is true," Liza said.

"Including this demon?"

"Including the demon."

"This must have come as a great shock to you."

"Well, it's definitely taken some getting used to."

Sierra shifted his attention back to Peter, who had not let go of his hand. "Most people think I was born in Havana, because that is what it says on my passport. In fact, I was born in a small village in the mountains of Cuba that is not on any map. Tell me about it."

"Are you thinking about this village right now?" Peter asked.

"I most certainly am."

Peter gazed into the depths of Sierra's eyes and went searching. The doctor's head was a library of information, and it took an extended moment before he found the images he was looking for. The rural village where Sierra had been born and raised held a special place, and Peter treaded carefully on the older man's memories. "You were born in a farming village in the Sierra Maestra mountains in the western region of Cuba. Your family has lived there for six generations, raising sheep and cattle. On the outskirts of the village is a primitive cemetery where many of your relatives are buried. Your older brother rests there: He perished after being thrown by a horse. He was your best friend, and it broke your heart the day it happened.

"You left the village at the age of twelve to attend a school for gifted students in Havana. When you were a teenager, you escaped Cuba with a group of friends on a makeshift raft made of tires, and landed on a small island off Key West. You later relocated to New York, where you worked three jobs to put yourself through college and, later, medical school. You have not been back to your birthplace in forty years, and long for the day you can return safely, without fear of retribution from the government."

Sierra's eyes welled with tears. "Astonishing. How long have you had this . . . gift?"

"Ever since I could remember. At first, I thought everyone could do these things. But then I learned that only certain people can."

Sierra adjusted himself in his chair and ran his fingers through his hair. He seemed to be having a hard time coming to grips with what Peter had just done. There was a name for this: seeing but not believing. The brain did not accept what the eyes had seen, and that caused the mind to wrestle with reality. It was not a fun process, but in the end, re- ality usually won out.

"You said that you did not tell your girlfriend about your gifts until recently, yet you've been living together for two years," Sierra said, the professional tone returning to his voice. "The obvious question would be, did you read her mind during that time, and not tell her?"

Peter looked at Liza as he replied. "No, I didn't."

"Why not? Most men would."

"I wanted our relationship to work. If I started to read Liza's mind, it would make things off balance."

"Not even once?"

"No, sir."

Sierra addressed Liza. "Do you believe him?"

"Yes, I believe him," she said.

"Then I would say you are off to a wonderful start. Now, tell me more about this demon inside of you. I'm curious to hear how this came about."

"Why is that important?" Peter asked.

"You cannot simply tell Liza you have a monster inside of you, and then expect her to accept it, and move on. That is not fair to her, or to you."

"I didn't say it was a monster. It's a demon, and I have it under control."

"What triggers it?"

"The demon comes out whenever Peter blows his top," Liza inter- jected. "A dark cloud comes over his face, and his nostrils flare, and he starts to look like a total maniac. The demon also has powers that Peter doesn't."

"So you've seen this firsthand," Sierra said.

Liza started to reply, but nodded instead. Not long ago, she'd seen Peter kill a man who'd been intent on murdering her and Snoop. Peter had killed him with a screwdriver with a dull point. It had been like watching a macabre magic trick. One moment the screwdriver was in Peter's hand, the next it was embedded in their attacker's heart.

What had bothered her most was the transformation Peter had gone through. One moment he was gentle, fun-loving Peter, the next a snarling Mr. Hyde. The transformation had been painful to watch and, thankfully, had not lasted very long.

"Your anger brings it to the surface?" Sierra asked Peter.

"That's right," Peter said.

"How long does the demon stay?"

"A couple of minutes at the most."

"When it finally leaves, how do you feel?"

"Pretty awful. Especially if I've hurt someone. I suffer for weeks."

"Were you ever tempted to see a psychiatrist?" Sierra asked.

He shook his head. "I was raised not to talk about these things."

"Raised not to talk about these things by who?"

"My mother and father."

"Your parents knew about this demon? How did they deal with it?"

Sierra was on the edge of his seat, and had the unmistakable gleam in his eye of someone stumbling upon something of great value. The look bothered Peter. What was the good doctor planning to do with the information? Write about it in a prominent medical journal? Or sell it to Hollywood one day? These things had happened to psychics who'd made the mistake of baring their soul to strangers, and Peter didn't want it happening to him. "Before I answer your question, I want you to promise me that you'll never reveal what I'm about to say to you to anyone else."

"Your secrets are safe," Sierra assured him. "Nothing you say will leave this office."

"Is that a promise?"

"Yes, it's a promise."

"All right. I inherited this demon from my mother and father. They were trapped by one of the Devil's sons when they were children, and forced to become his disciples. They grew up, got married, had me, and I got this demon. They raised me in a loving household, and taught me not to lose my temper. I can still hear my mother saying, 'Don't get angry—you'll just tempt the Devil.' I didn't realize she was telling me the truth."

"Your parents were trapped—how?"

"They lived in a small village in the south of England. One day they were playing with their friends, and saw an injured black cat on a frozen lake. When they went to rescue it, the ice broke under their weight. One of the Devil's sons was waiting on the bottom of the lake for them. He converted them, so to speak, and the children became his disciples."

"The Devil has children?"

"He has six sons. They're responsible for most of the horrible things that have happened to mankind in the past two thousand years."

"What kind of people were your parents?"

"They were wonderful people. Even though they knew they were possessed by an evil spirit, they still choose to be good. It was a struggle, but they won out."

"How extraordinary. Where are they now?"

"They're dead. They were murdered when I was a boy."

"Where? In England?"

"Here in New York. We moved here when I was small, and lived in an apartment in Murray Hill. They were abducted and killed by a gang of evil psychics after seeing a show in Times Square. I was with them."

Sierra's head bobbed up and down, drinking in every word. "The night your parents died—how did you react? Did the demon come out then? Did you go berserk?" he asked.

The words hit Peter like an invisible punch. He had cried and cried that night, just like any normal kid would do. What did Sierra think he was? A freak?

"What kind of question is that?" Peter snapped.

"I'm sorry. That didn't come out right."

"It sure didn't."

"Please don't get angry," Sierra said, trying to sooth him. "It was a slip of the tongue."

"No, it wasn't. You asked a deliberate question that took deliberate thought. Now here's my answer. I'm not Linda Blair in *The Exorcist*. I don't piss on rugs and spin my head and say crude things to party guests. I can control myself. I do control myself."

"Of course you do," Sierra said.

"I don't like the way you're looking at me," Peter said.

"And how is that?"

"Like a lab rat that's grown two heads."

"Oh, Peter," Liza said, knowing what was coming next.

"You are a patient, and I am a doctor. That is how I'm looking at you," Sierra said.

"You've got something else on your mind."

"I'm sorry, but you're wrong."

"I'm never wrong about stuff like that. You're a snake, and you're going to betray me." Peter rose from the couch and glanced down at Liza. "I'm leaving. You're welcome to stay, if you'd like. I'll meet you back at the house."

"No, I'm coming, too," Liza said.

She rose and clasped Peter's hand. She could find the good in just about anything, even a disaster like this. To Sierra she said, "Thank you for taking the time to see us. We really appreciate it."

"But we're not done," the doctor said.

"Yes, we are," Peter replied, and pulled Liza toward the door.

17

Sierra chased the young couple into the reception area. His receptionist's desk was empty. "I'm sorry I offended you. I meant no harm."

Peter gave Sierra the evil eye. The look came straight from the depths of his troubled soul. Liza clutched his hand while staring discreetly at the floor.

"You asked if the demon came out the night my parents died. What exactly did you mean by that?" Peter asked.

Sierra felt Peter's eyes burning a hole in him. He did not want the young magician reading his mind, and shifted his gaze to the clutter of paperwork on his receptionist's desk.

"I don't know. It was a slip of the tongue," he said.

"You're lying."

"Peter!" Liza said.

"He's lying," Peter repeated. "One moment, he's being all nice and friendly, the next he's asking me if the demon came out the night my parents died. He knows something."

Sierra cursed under his breath. He had handled this all wrong. He should have told Peter the truth the moment Peter had told him that his parents had moved from London to New York when he was a boy. Had he told him the truth, none of this would be happening now.

He tried to repair the damage as best he could. "You are a troubled young man. I can help you and your girlfriend, if you'll let me. Please give me another chance."

"Up yours," Peter said.

"Peter—that's so rude!" Liza scolded.

"I don't trust him," he said, not caring anymore. "He's got something else on his mind—you can see it in his face. The moment I told him my

parents were murdered, his whole demeanor changed. I don't know what
this clown is up to, and I'm not about to find out."

"I'm not a clown," Sierra said indignantly.

Peter wagged a finger in Sierra's face. A simple gesture that carried an
implied threat. This young man was capable of causing him great harm
if he chose to, and Sierra listened carefully to what he had to say.

"If one word of what was said here today gets out, there will be hell to
pay," Peter said. "Do you understand that? None of this can ever be repeated, or written down in a journal or a diary, or passed on to another
doctor in a conversation. It stays here. Got it?"

"I understand," Sierra repeated.

"Look me in the eyes when you say that."

Sierra swallowed hard. The image of Peter's mother and father sitting
in his office burned vividly in the theater of his mind. They'd been a nice
couple, except for the terrible secret they'd carried with them. He'd tried
to help them, and when that had failed, he'd gone to a higher source.

Sierra repressed the memory, fearful Peter would see it. He locked eyes
with the young magician. "You have my word. I will not repeat anything
you said here today."

Satisfied Sierra was telling the truth, Peter ushered Liza out and
slammed the door behind him, causing the walls to shake.

"Damn it," Sierra said under his breath.

Sierra began to shiver. A gust of cold wind swept through the office,
even though the window facing the street was shut tight. This was
Peter's doing. He had not trusted Sierra, so part of him had stayed behind
as a warning, in case Sierra had second thoughts about the promises he'd
been sworn to keep.

His receptionist returned, reeking of cigarette smoke. "Are you okay,
Dr. Sierra?"

"Do I not look okay?"

"Come to mention it, you look like you've seen a ghost."

Back in his office with the door shut, he tried to decide his best
course of action. His eyes fell upon the thick volumes of psychiatric journals filling the bookshelf behind his desk. One of the journals inched
out of its space and fell to the floor, landing on its spine with a dull thud.

As he bent down to retrieve it, another journal crept out of its place, and fell on top of his head, then another and another, until all eleven volumes in the series were raining down upon him. It could have been much worse, and he returned the books to their spots.

The greatest fear was of those things we did not understand. Sierra sat down at his desk, and tried to regain his composure. His heart was racing, and adrenaline was coursing through his veins. His professional career had been filled with challenges, but one had stood out above all the rest. It had never been resolved, and he'd accepted that it probably never would. Each morning he'd stood at his office window, remembering the sunny fall morning twenty years past when a charming British couple named Henry and Claire Warren had paid him a visit to discuss their unusual problem. He'd seen them only once, yet the effect they'd had on him had been so profound that he'd never forgotten them.

He rummaged through his desk drawers. In the bottom drawer was an ancient Rolodex, and he flipped through it, quickly finding the card he was looking for. The pencil markings had grown faint, and he had to hold it beneath the lamp on his desk.

Hunsinger
555-1259

That was all. Just a last name and a phone number.

Sierra could not help the Warrens, so he'd put them in touch with Hunsinger, who had tried to help them with their problem. Hunsinger had failed, just as Sierra had failed. Had Hunsinger's curiosity been eating at him ever since? Did he also stare through a window each day, pondering life's unexplainable mysteries? Sierra guessed that it had. Situations like this happened once in a lifetime.

Picking up the phone, he punched in the number on the card, and heard the call go through. Three rings, four rings, five. Sierra expected voice mail or an answering machine to pick up, but instead heard the unhealthy sound of a man's raspy cough.

"Hello?"

"Good morning. I hope I have the right number," Sierra said.

"I've had this number for forty years. I think you do," the voice replied.

The receiver grew tight in Sierra's hand. "This is Dr. Raul Sierra. We met many years ago."

"I remember you, Dr. Sierra. How have you been?"

"I'm well. How about yourself?"

"My health is not what it used to be. So to what do I owe the pleasure of this call?"

Sierra hesitated. Ten minutes ago, he'd made a promise that he was now about to break, and he hoped it would not come back to haunt him. "Do you remember a British couple I sent to see you named Claire and Henry Warren?"

"How could I have forgotten, even after all this time? Is this about them?"

"No, it's about their son."

"You mean Peter."

"Yes, Peter."

"I always wondered what happened to him. I read in the newspapers that his parents had been killed, and I tried to track Peter down. He disappeared, you know. I assumed he was sent back to England to live with his relatives. I think about him often."

"He's here in New York."

"Really. May I ask how you came about this information?"

"Peter and his girlfriend just left my office. They are having issues and needed counseling. A strange twist of fate that he would seek me out."

"Everything happens for a reason, Dr. Sierra. Please tell me, how is Peter coping?"

"Not well. He's battling with his demons, so to speak."

"Did you talk to him about his past?"

"No."

"You didn't tell him what happened?"

"The situation was not right. That's why I contacted you. I thought we could do it together, being that we were both involved. It might . . ."

"Lessen the blow?"

"Yes."

"Give me an hour. I still remember your address," Hunsinger said.

18

New York was constantly reinventing itself. The neighborhood around Sierra's office was a perfect example. It was known as Kips Bay, yet most New Yorkers now called it Curry Hill for the many authentic Indian restaurants that had opened there. Saravana Bhavan was Peter and Liza's favorite of the bunch, and it specialized in South Indian fare of dosas and vegetarian plates.

The owner greeted them cheerfully at the front door. It was a family operation, with his wife behind the register, his son working the kitchen. He escorted them to a table in the back.

"Menus? Or are we having the usual?" the owner asked.

"The usual," Peter replied.

The breakfast crowd had thinned out, and the restaurant was quiet. Soon the owner served them crispy lentil doughnuts with sambar and chutney, and cups of steaming Madras coffee. Liza munched silently on a doughnut.

"Aren't you going to eat?" she asked.

"I'm not hungry," Peter replied.

"You're always hungry. Eat something. It will make you feel better."

He bit into a doughnut. It was deliciously warm and melted in his mouth. Liza sipped her coffee before speaking again. "What happened back there at the doctor's office?"

"I don't know," he answered truthfully.

"It was ugly."

"How ugly is ugly?"

"On a scale of one to ten, it was a nine."

"With a ten being my throwing Sierra out the window?"

"I sure hope not. Why did you act like that?"

He stared at his reflection in his plate. Sierra's question about the demon coming out after his parents had died had hit a nerve. It was as if Sierra had known about the demon, and was baiting him. But how could that be? He'd never met Sierra until this morning. Except for the Friday night psychics and Liza, no one knew about his special powers or his past, and he planned to keep it that way. The only reason he told the doctor was because of the doctor/patient oath, and he was already regretting that he had done so.

"You cry in your sleep a lot," Liza said. "Did you know that?"

What an icebreaker. He shook his head.

"What do you dream about?" she asked.

"Can we talk about this some other time?"

"No more running away. I want to know."

"I dream about the night I lost my parents."

"Were you traumatized?"

There are events in a person's life which change everything. The night of his parents' deaths was such an event. His life had been one thing before, another thing ever since. Not a fair thing to do to a seven-year-old, but life was hardly fair. He'd accepted that hard fact long ago.

"Yes," he said.

"Is the dream always the same?"

"Pretty much. Three men whisk my parents down an alley in the theater district. I start to run after them, fall down, and rip my pants. When I look up, my mother and father are being hustled into the back of a waiting car. My mother looks over her shoulder at me. Her face tells me everything. I'm never going to see her or my father alive again."

"Your mother knew she was going to die?"

"People were chasing them. They left England and came to New York. She knew."

"You were seven. You're twenty-five now, and still having nightmares. Don't you think you should talk to Sierra about this?"

"I'm not going back there. Sierra's no good."

"He's a highly respected expert in his field. You're just making excuses."

One doughnut remained on the plate. Peter tore it in half, and munched on his piece. He was not going to let Dr. Sierra peel back the layers of his soul. Not in this lifetime.

"Is that a no?" Liza asked.

"Let's find someone else," he suggested.

"And start over? You think I want a repeat of this? No, thanks."

He wiped his mouth on a napkin and looked across the table at Liza. "Why are you stuck on this guy? Do you like seeing me getting hurt?"

"That was low," she said.

"Do you?"

"Stop it."

"Why are you the only one that gets to ask the tough questions?"

"I'm going outside. Come out when you have something nice to say."

"Can I have the other half of the doughnut?"

"Is that supposed to be a joke? You're not funny."

Peter stuffed the remaining piece of doughnut into his mouth as Liza walked out the front door. He hadn't told her the whole story about his nightmares. The pain of his parents' passing had eased over time. What hadn't gone away was the helplessness he'd felt as they were abducted. The pained expression on his mother's face was one he'd never forget. *Help us*, her eyes had cried out. *Help us*.

But by the time he'd reached the street, the car was gone.

He'd failed her and his father.

That was why he wept in his sleep at night.

The key to dealing with tragedy was to avoid thinking about it. But that wasn't always possible. When Peter thought about the night he'd lost his parents, it made him grow angry, and the demon reared its ugly head.

"Help!" a voice cried out.

The owner raced out of the kitchen, followed by his son. Both men had their arms in the air and were moving fast. The owner grabbed his wife from behind the cash register, and the family fled to the street.

The restaurant was filling with smoke. Rising from his chair, Peter pushed open the swinging kitchen door to see what the problem was. A grease fire on the stove had jumped onto a wall and was burning out of control. The demon inside of him was like that. It was capable of creating havoc and destruction with little regard for the consequences. It had no conscience, or sense of right and wrong.

He looked straight up. The kitchen ceiling had turned transparent. In the apartment above the restaurant, an older Italian couple was eating a late breakfast. In the apartment next door, four women were playing gin rummy while chatting away. Next door to them, a young mother was nursing a newborn. The building's other apartment units were also occupied. So was the apartment building next door. It was filled with people, maybe fifty in all.

They were all about to die.

Within moments, the fire would be as hot as a nova, and eat through the structure with the speed of a runaway train. Once that happened, there would be no stopping it. It would race up the walls of both buildings, becoming so hot that the bricks would catch fire. The occupants of both buildings would hear a loud *whoosh!* like the sound of wind passing through a tunnel. That would be the last thing they heard. No a soul would be spared.

The fire trucks would come, and the city's bravest would give battle to the roaring flames, but it would be too little, too late. The block between 26th and 27th streets would be destroyed, the street's foundation buckling from the heat. Before it was eventually contained, the fire would destroy tens of millions of dollars in real estate and ruin countless lives.

And Peter knew in his bones that it was no mere accident, that it had been his temper that had started the fire.

But Peter also knew that the things he started he could stop. It wasn't easy, but he could do it. He walked into kitchen and faced the burning wall. The fire had eaten through the plaster, and was heading to the second floor. He had a few seconds at most to stop it.

He had to make the demon leave. There was only one way to do that—through his mind. He thought back to when he was a kid, and the Sunday afternoons he'd spent with his father going to see the Yankees play in the Bronx. His father had showered him with attention, and bought him baseball caps and hot dogs and anything else his heart had desired. They were his fondest childhood memories, and he could not help but smile.

The demon began to recede into the deepest regions of his soul. It was like pushing back a boulder, and took all his strength. As it did, the flames rolled down the wall and returned to the frying pan on the stove. The heat vanished, and the choking smoke evaporated like fog being burned off by the sun. The room returned to normal in the blink of an eye.

Even Peter had to marvel at the illusion.

Liza stood at the open door with her hand over her mouth.

"Holy shit," she said. "Did you do that?"

"I sure did," he said.

He heard voices. The owner and his son were coming back. Peter couldn't explain what he'd just done without exposing his psychic powers to them.

"Stall them," he told her.

"What?"

"You heard me. Stall them. Please."

Liza turned around and blocked the owner and his son and from entering. Peter found a fire extinguisher hanging on the wall, and he quickly doused the room with white foam until the interior looked as if a snowstorm had hit it.

"All clear," he called out.

Liza stepped away from the doorway, and they rushed in. The owner clapped his hands together joyously, and embraced the young magician.

"Thank you for saving my restaurant," he exclaimed.

The police were the first to show up, followed by a fire truck and an ambulance, then more police, followed by a gaggle of onlookers. Peter had wanted to bolt, but did not want to raise eyebrows. So he gave a statement to a uniformed cop, and asked if he could leave. The cop said okay, and they headed up Lexington Avenue with their heads bowed to the punishing wind.

"Did you cause that fire to happen?" Liza asked, her hands tucked in her pockets.

"I think so. I was mad."

"Bad things happen when you get angry."

"I've never burned down a building before. I know that sounds juvenile, but it's true."

"I believe you. But there could always be a first time."

"You want me to go back and see Sierra, don't you?"

"He was trying to help us. Why can't you see that?"

"It didn't feel like help. It felt like torture."

"Just give it a shot. That's all I'm asking."

"How many times is a shot?"

"Just one more."

Peter could deal with that, and said okay. Liza said she would contact Sierra's office and schedule another session. They stopped and kissed and things were good again. He felt like a regular human being whenever he was with her, and wondered if the trick to having a normal life was to never let her out of his sight. *Not a bad solution.*

They decided to walk home. It was a long hike, and would let them clear their heads. They headed up Lex with the city's thrum in their ears. Buses rumbled, horns honked, and a car alarm wailed like a colicky baby. A racket to some, they were the noises Peter had known his entire life, and sounded like music. It was not hard for him to imagine Gershwin in the sound of garbage cans being thrown, or a symphony in the roar of a subway. By the time they reached the brownstone, the morning's bad events had faded into the past.

Walking up the front steps, Peter had his keys out when he heard a car door slam. The sound was not friendly, and he spun around to see Garrison climb out of his parked SUV. The look on the FBI agent's face was nothing but trouble.

"Just the man I was looking for," Garrison said.

PART II

SHADOW PEOPLE

19

Special Agent Garrison was a man of simple tastes. His wardrobe ran from blazers and dark trousers to sweatshirts and blue jeans. Today, he wore faded denims and a charcoal gray cardigan.

"You need to start keeping your cell phone on," the FBI agent said. "I've been looking for you all morning."

Not on Mondays. On Mondays, Peter's cell phone was turned off while he and Liza roamed the city's neighborhoods.

"Peter put out a fire at a restaurant in Kips Bay this morning," Liza jumped in. "He was a hero."

Peter squeezed Liza's hand. She hadn't told Garrison the whole story of how he'd lost his temper and accidentally set the restaurant's kitchen fire, and it made him love her that much more. Garrison acted impressed and slapped him on the shoulder. "Nice going. I realize this is your day off, but I've got a situation on my hands and I need your help. Do you mind coming downtown with me for a little while?"

Peter tried to help the law whenever possible. He also tried to have a life with Liza. Right now, the two were colliding. "Where to?"

"Grand Central Station. The police caught a shadow person running through the terminal on a surveillance camera. I want you to have a look, see what you think."

Peter instinctively touched his shirt, and felt the five-pointed star around his neck. Liza did the same. Their recent encounter with the shadow person was still fresh in their minds.

"What do you think?" he asked Liza.

"By all means, go. Maybe you can catch this thing."

"You're welcome to come along."

She shook her head. They got only one day a week off. Liza used some of that time to talk with her family, whom she regularly stayed in touch with. "I need to talk to CiCi. She's been having difficulty with one of the routines in the act."

Liza's younger sister CiCi had replaced Liza in the family troupe, and Liza continued to coach her whenever possible.

"Tell her I said hi," Peter said.

"I will. Please be careful. Don't let that thing kidnap you again."

They kissed and Liza went inside the brownstone. Garrison tapped his shoulder, and Peter climbed into the passenger seat of the SUV without a word. As he was strapping himself in, the vehicle lurched away from the curb like a wild animal jumping out of a cage.

The fluid human dance of Grand Central was best viewed from the main concourse. A mammoth space framed by high windows, glittering constellations in the ceiling, and a double staircase at either end, it was here that a person could observe the complex patterns made by arriving and departing passengers on the Connecticut and Westchester railroads. During rush hour, it was one of the busiest areas of the city, and one of the loudest. That changed once rush hour ended and the commuters cleared out. Then it became a tourist site, with group tours and lots of pictures being snapped of the famous architecture. Garrison hurried up the staircase on the west side with Peter glued to his side.

"I analyzed the film of the shadow person your smart-mouthed assistant shot," Garrison said. "You're not going to believe what I found."

"His name is Snoop, and he's my best friend," Peter said.

"He's got a bad attitude and is a threat to national security."

"Just because he can hack your computers doesn't make him a threat."

"I'll be the judge of that."

They hurried down a marble hallway. With multiple exits and doors leading to multiple train platforms, it was easy to get lost, and Peter realized he didn't know where he was.

"I examined the video of the shadow person frame by frame like you suggested," Garrison went on. "I was able to make out a face."

"Man or woman?"

"It looks like a woman, but that's just a guess."

They stopped at a door marked NYPD—NO ENTRANCE at the hallway's end, and Garrison rapped loudly.

"I told you—no cops," Peter said in alarm.

"There aren't any cops here right now. You're safe."

"Then what are we doing here?"

"I sent the video to the NYPD, and asked them to run it against their database of collected images from the past thirty days. The cops have thousands of surveillance cameras in the city, and I figured one of them might have spotted your ghost. Sure enough, I was right. The Grand Central team found the shadow person on a tape, and alerted me."

"You gave the police the video?" Peter asked. "I'm on it, for Christ's sake. And so is Liza."

"I didn't tell them anything about your involvement, and neither did anyone on my team."

"The police aren't stupid. They'll make the connection."

"Which is what? That you were visited by a ghost? If they contact you, play dumb."

There were times when Peter wished he'd never struck a deal with Garrison. The FBI agent didn't know how to keep a secret, and might someday blow Peter's cover, and mistakenly tell the world who the young magician really was.

The door swung in, and Special Agent Nan Perry ushered them into a windowless room lined with video screens monitoring the ebb and flow of the terminal concourse. The lighting was muted, and the images popped off the screens. As promised, there were no cops.

Garrison's team sat at desks facing the screens. Each agent was at a keyboard with an odd-looking joystick. Peter had seen those joysticks before. Back when he was breaking in his act, he'd worked at one of Trump's lavish casinos in Atlantic City, and had been given a private tour of the casino's surveillance room, where he'd been shown how cheaters were caught trying to scam the games. The cheaters' moves were invisible to the naked eye, but they weren't invisible to the cameras, and they all got caught.

"This looks like a Pelco DX system," Peter said.

"Who told you about Pelco?" Garrison asked.

"A casino I once worked at. Pelco can search thirty days of video images in a minute. When it comes to catching bad guys, this system is state-of-the-art."

"I'm impressed," Garrison said.

"Thanks. So, what did you find?"

Garrison got onto a keyboard and typed in a command.

"Over the past thirty days, the shadow person has been filmed on four different occasions running across Grand Central's main concourse. I'll show you the first video we found. Look at screen number three."

His eyes found screen three on the wall of monitors. A surveillance video began to play. On it, a shadow person ran through the main concourse. It looked like a puff of smoke, and hovered inches above the floor. It moved quickly before disappearing through a street exit. Several people in the concourse saw it pass, shook their heads, and went back to whatever they had been doing, which was how people usually reacted when confronted by a ghost.

The video was short, barely five seconds long. Peter stared at the screen long after it had stopped playing. The shadow person had appeared to be in a hurry. Why?

He shook his head in frustration. He had no earthly idea what any of this meant. The time stamp on the corner of the video caught his eye. It had been shot on Friday night at 11:50.

He shuddered.

The shadow person had been hurrying to reach the Friday night séance at Milly's apartment on the other side of town, where it had appeared ten minutes later.

"What's outside the exit I just saw?" he asked.

"A taxi stand," Garrison replied.

That made sense. The shadow person had taken a taxi. Not in the traditional sense. It had simply hung on the roof and bummed a ride. Ghosts did it all the time.

"May I see the other videos?" Peter said.

Garrison worked his magic on the keyboard. Three videos appeared in rapid succession, shot on the floor of the main concourse. In each, a shadow person could be seen fleeing past. Peter read the time stamps on each video.

The first had been recorded at 1 A.M. on Saturday morning, right around the time the shadow person had invaded his brownstone. The second was from Saturday afternoon, right before the shadow person had disrupted his matinee. The third was from this morning. In each video, the shadow person ran past a newspaper kiosk in the concourse. With the kiosk as a point of reference, the differences were clear.

"There's more than one of them," he said.

"What? Are you sure?"

"I compared the images on the videos. They're different sizes. They're traveling into the city on the Westchester railroad. Once they arrive at Grand Central, they run across the concourse to get outside, and go searching for me."

"I thought these things could slip through walls," Garrison said.

"They can slip into cracks in walls in the same way ghosts can. But they can't pass through solid walls. No spirit can. That forces them to make a mad dash in order to reach the street. From there, they're hitching cab rides to their final destinations."

"You're kidding me."

"Happens all the time. I need to go."

"But you just got here."

Peter had encountered all of the shadow people who'd traveled to New York, except the last one, which had arrived this morning. Was another of his friends about to be kidnapped, like poor Liza? He couldn't let that happen, and he brushed past Garrison on his way to the door.

"Something urgent's come up," he said. "I'll call you when I'm done."

G rand Central was like a small city, and had over a hundred shops and restaurants, and contained everything a visitor could desire. Peter hurried to a jewelry store called Forever Silver inside the Lexington Avenue Passageway that sold hand-crafted necklaces and bracelets.

Peter was in luck. There was a jewelry maker on duty. He was babysitting his young son, a dark-haired boy sitting on the counter, watching the world go by. Peter offered to do tricks for the boy if the jewelry maker would fill his order right away.

"Good luck. He's got a short attention span," the jewelry maker said.

"What's his name?" Peter asked.

"Anthony."

Peter did his best to entertain Anthony while his father went to work. Peter waved his hands magically in front of Anthony's face, and pulled a shiny half-dollar out of the boy's ear, which he split into two. The coins jumped from hand to hand not once but several times. For a finale, he rubbed them together, and they turned into a silver dollar.

Anthony giggled and clapped his hands enthusiastically.

"Want to see some more?" Peter asked.

It was the magician's first rule. Wait for them to ask for more.

"Yes," the boy said.

"Anthony," his father said.

"Please," the boy added.

Peter continued the show. He removed a piece of string from his pocket, and began to tear it into tiny pieces. Anthony's eyes did not leave his hands.

"How many necklaces did you say you wanted?" the jewelry maker asked.

"Five," Peter said. "Each needs to have a five-pointed star hanging from it. Make sure the star has five points."

"I've got some really beautiful diamond pendants on sale," the jewelry maker said. "They're our best sellers. The women love them."

Peter rolled the pieces of string into a ball, and had Anthony blow on them.

"Just a five-pointed star."

"Do you mind my asking what they're for? I'm not being nosy. Just curious."

Peter grabbed the ends of the string and pulled it apart. It had magically restored itself, and Anthony squealed with delight. The jeweler probably dealt with a hundred customers a day. Five-pointed stars weren't an item that people requested. Peter could have told him that Grand Central was being visited by evil spirits that were trying to kill him and hurt his friends, and that the stars were needed to ward them off, only that would have ruined the man's day, and he didn't want to do that.

"It's a long story," the young magician said. "How much longer will you be?"

"Ten minutes, tops."

Peter went back to entertaining Anthony. The boy looked no more than seven, the same age he'd been when he'd lost his parents. He'd often wondered how his life would have turned out had his parents not been taken away from him at such a tender age. Would he still have become a magician, or would his life have taken another path, and sent him on a different journey then the one he was on now? And would he have met Liza and fallen in love, or would another woman have claimed his heart? There was no way to know; even his psychic powers would not let him look back into past and see what might have been.

The trick ended, and Anthony clapped his hands and giggled with laughter. Ever since Peter could remember, he'd wanted to have a family of his own, and a child he could pass down his magic to. Knowing what he did now about himself, he wondered if he'd dare even try.

"All done. Cash or credit card?" the jewelry maker asked.

Peter paid the jeweler cash and took the gift bag off the counter.

"Sure I can't interest you in those diamond pendants?"

"Maybe some other time," Peter said.

20

Leaving Grand Central, Peter hailed a cab from the taxi stand on Lexington Avenue. He needed to hunt down Milly, Holly, Max, Lester, and Snoop, and present them with the five-pointed-star necklaces. It was the only way he could ensure that the newly arrived shadow person would not harm his friends.

He gave the driver an address in the Village, and the vehicle headed downtown. Of all his friends, he considered his teacher to be the most at risk. Max had lost his wife a year ago, and now spent his days traveling between restaurants and taverns in the city, doing magic to keep himself busy. He often acted like he was walking around in a fog, and would be an easy target.

Peter decided to call Max, and tell him of his impending arrival. As he pulled out his Droid, the phone vibrated as if alive. Caller ID said it was Garrison.

"You're a pain in the ass," he said to the phone.

Then Peter answered the call. "Special Agent Garrison, what a pleasant surprise," he said.

"Where are you?" the FBI agent barked.

"In a cab, heading downtown."

"Can you get back to Grand Central? I need your help."

Peter's priorities would always be to his friends and loved ones, and he said, "I'm sort of busy at the moment. What's going on?"

"About an hour ago, a surveillance camera at a train station in Westchester picked up a shadow person climbing onto the roof of a New York–bound train. It will be arriving soon, and I'm trying to figure out what to do. That's why I called you."

Another shadow person was coming into the city? It was starting to feel like an invasion.

"I was thinking of having a team of agents board at one of the stops, and see if they can root this thing out," Garrison went on. "Is that practical?"

Peter sat up straight in his seat. "I would advise you not to do that."

"Look, my men are trained professionals. They've seen everything there is to see."

"Don't do it."

"So what do I do?"

"Nothing."

"They don't pay me to do nothing. Come on, think of something."

Ordinary people who engaged with the spirits often spent the rest of their lives regretting it. As a result of their unearthly encounters, ghosts visited them regularly, and they were plagued by otherworldly voices in their dreams. Their nerves became frayed, and they walked around perpetually scared. Garrison had no idea of the danger he was placing his agents in.

"The best thing you can do is to leave it alone," Peter said.

"Some help you are. Don't tell me there isn't a way to fight these things."

So that was it. Garrison wanted to fight. He was stubborn that way, and would probably try to capture the shadow person no matter what Peter told him. And then there'd be hell to pay for Garrison and his team. "You can't fight a shadow person. But you can catch it the same way you capture a ghost. Promise me you'll do exactly as I say."

"You have my word."

"Here's what's going to happen. The train will pull into the terminal, and the shadow person will stay on the roof until the passengers have departed and the platform is quiet. Then it will get off and creep up the stairs to the exit, and hang by the door. Once it sees an opening in the terminal, it will bolt toward an exit. That's when you have a chance to catch it."

"How? With a butterfly net?"

"Turn on the lights inside the terminal to their brightest wattage. It will freeze the thing in its tracks."

"It's that simple?"

"Yes. Whatever you do, make sure you don't touch it."

"How am I going to move it?"

"You don't. Unless you want to cause great harm to yourself and your team."

"What? And leave it there for everyone to see? Are you nuts?"

The taxi had reached its destination, and the driver raised the flag on the meter.

"Call me if you catch it," Peter said, "and I'll tell you what to do."

Max had made a living doing magic for half a decade. Unlike most stage performers, who lugged around lots of bulky props, his act fit into a small suitcase. The Egg Bag, Linking Rings, Floating Ball, Rising Cards, and an occasional mind-reading stunt made up his repertoire. In his hands, each trick was a masterpiece of deception tempered by delicious patter and funny stories. Max the Magnificent, One of the Better Cheaper Acts.

These days, Max limited his act by performing close-up tricks that fit into his pockets. On Mondays he could be found entertaining the lunch crowd at a Bleecker Street landmark called the Peculier Pub that featured hundreds of imported beers and ales and a menu of traditional British fare. The pub had a low tin ceiling, which magnified the sound of the diners and folks lining the bar, and Max often had to shout to be heard.

The room was mobbed, and Peter sifted his way to the back, where he found his teacher doing a card trick for a group of businessmen having lunch at a table. The deck was not cooperating, and Max kept getting the wrong card, much to the men's' delight.

Max pulled an ace of hearts from beneath his collar. "Is this your selected card?"

"Nope," said a businessman drinking beer.

"Rats! How about this one?" From behind his knee, Max made the king of hearts magically appear, and waited expectantly.

"Wrong again." The businessman snorted derisively.

"Godfrey Daniels! Give me one more chance. I'll give you a prize if I don't succeed."

"What kind of prize?" the businessman asked.

"A very valuable one, worth lots of money."

"You're on."

The businessman tapped his knife against a water glass. A hush fell over the pub, with all eyes glued to the old magician with shoulder-length white hair and frayed tuxedo. Max cuffed his sleeves and displayed his empty palms. His hands were soft and supple. When his fingers danced, it was with the lightness of butterfly wings. A playing card materialized out of thin air.

"Wow," someone at the bar gasped.

"Name your card," Max said triumphantly.

"It was the nine of spades," the businessman declared.

Max spun the card around to reveal the three of diamonds.

A groan went through the tavern.

"You lose," the businessman roared. "Pay up!"

Max acted disgusted with himself. Reaching into his pocket, he removed the businessman's wallet, and presented it to him. Next followed the man's wristwatch, car keys, cigarette lighter, and reading glasses. The businessman grabbed helplessly at his empty pockets while the pub roared with laughter. It was a staple of many tricks to turn failure into triumph. No one did it better than Max, and sustained applause followed.

Max hadn't lost his touch. The great ones never did. As Peter approached him, he sensed an otherworldly presence in the room. Had the shadow person beaten him here?

"Why, hello, Peter, how are you?" Max asked. "Enjoy the show?"

"It was great. You killed them. I need to get you out of here."

"But I'm just getting warmed up."

Peter looked around to make sure no one was listening, then brought his mouth up to Max's ear. "There's a shadow person in the room. You're not safe."

"No, there's not. Sit down and have some lunch. The corned beef is very good."

"I felt it, Max. Come outside with me."

Peter pulled his teacher toward the front door. Max waved to the crowd on his way out.

"Be back in sixty," he called out.

The feeling of an evil spirit disappeared the moment Peter stepped onto the sidewalk outside the pub. Max grinned at him the way an older man smiles at a child.

"See? I told you it wasn't a shadow person," his teacher said.

"But I felt something strange in there."

"And so did I. A feeling of anxiety, yes?"

"That's right. Do you know what it was?"

"I most certainly do. It's called electromagnetic hypersensitivity. Ghost hunters often mistake electromagnetic hypersensitivity for ghosts, when it fact it comes from refrigerators."

"I got spooked by a refrigerator?"

"Afraid so. The owner lets me set up my show in the kitchen. I noticed that a refrigerator had been moved so it backed up onto a wall of the pub. As the refrigerator's cooling settings cycled on, the electromagnetic field it emitted passed through the wall. That's what you felt."

Peter lowered his eyes in embarrassment. "Sorry."

"You know what they say. There's a paddle for everyone's behind, and yours just got paddled. Now if you'll excuse me, I need to finish my show."

"Hold on. I have a present for you."

Peter presented a small jewelry box to his teacher. Max opened it, and examined the five-pointed star. As a rule, psychics did not interfere with the lives of other psychics, or offer them help or counsel. On those rare times that a psychic did reach out, it was for a good cause, and the offer was rarely refused. Without a word, Max slipped the necklace on, and tucked it under his shirt. He nodded appreciatively.

"Thank you, Peter."

"You're welcome, Max."

"I see other gifts in your bag. Who are they for?"

"One of my assistants, and the rest of the Friday night group."

"Will you be presenting one to Holly?"

"Yes, she's on the list. Why do you ask?"

Max's eyes narrowed and he dropped his voice. "Someone was going to have to tell you, so I suppose it should be me. Holly has been scrying on you. She admitted it to me and the rest of the group the other night. I told her to stop, and she got quite upset with me. She thinks the present predicament you're in with the shadow people gives her the right to play voyeur cam with your life. It's not right, and I wanted you to know."

"That doesn't sound like Holly. What's come over her?"

"I'm afraid she's changed, and not for the better. Her crush on you is out of control. The poor girl is head over heels in love."

Peter rocked back on his heels. He'd known Holly since she was five. He'd babysat her as a teenager, and watched her grow up. How could he have missed this?

"I also sense that Holly thinks you're in love with her," Max went on. "Are you?"

"In love with Holly? I have feelings for her, but not like that."

"Are you?"

"Max, come on. Be serious. This is Holly we're talking about."

"Are you?"

"What do you think?"

"I think you're avoiding the question."

The door to the pub swung open and a comely red-headed waitress stuck her head out. "Hey, Max, your adoring fans await you. Are you going to finish your show?"

"Of course I'm going to finish my show," Max said.

"Then hurry. The natives are getting restless."

She went back inside. Max sprung his deck of cards playfully between his hands like an accordion. He threw back his shoulders and glanced at his pupil. "Yes or no?"

"I care for the girl, but I am not in love with Holly," Peter said matter-of-factly. "She's the little sister that I never had, which is why I have feelings for her."

Max did several deft one-handed cuts without looking at the cards. "Those feelings have been misinterpreted. You must be careful. Witches are dangerous creatures when their passions become inflamed. Take my advice, and stay away from her. She's not the young woman you think she is. I must go. Be safe."

"And you as well."

Max entered the pub to a healthy round of applause, leaving Peter to contemplate this new wrinkle in his personal life. He wasn't big on confronting his problems, preferring to run away whenever possible, but this situation had to be addressed. He was in love with Liza, and that wasn't about to change anytime soon.

He should have left right then, and warned his other friends. Instead, he went to the pub's window, and peered through the smokey glass. It was the one great lesson that he'd learned from losing his parents at such a tender age. Nothing in this world lasts forever. The people and things that you love and cherish will one day be stolen away from you, never to be returned. It was the natural order of the universe, and could not be changed. The only question was, when would this happen? When would you lose those things that you loved? He'd always believed that day was sooner rather than later. If he didn't enjoy the special things in his life right now, they'd be gone in a blink of an eye, and he'd forever regret not experiencing them one last time.

That was why he stayed at the window and watched Max entertain the crowd.

21

⁓

Munns rose late, took a hot shower, did all the usual things. Naked and clean, he stood before the full-length mirror attached to the bathroom door, and gazed at the freakish assortment of tattoos on his body. He looked like a walking billboard for the Devil.

Munns often wondered what would happen if he decided to change his ways, and revert back to his old life. Would the Devil let him? Or would the tattoos spring to life, jump off his skin, and tear every limb from his body, and when they were done torturing him, kill him and bury his torso? Once, during a feverish dream, he'd seen that very thing, and had no doubt that it was a sign from below of what happened to traitors.

The silver tattoo on his neck was shimmering like a dull neon sign. It often did that, and he didn't quite understand why. He'd asked Ray what it meant, and the body artist had replied that it was the sign that the Devil was paying him a visit. Munns was not fond of the silver tattoo and wished he could figure out a way to turn the damn thing off.

He drew closer to the mirror. His latest tattoo was already his favorite. The mighty Surtr holding a bloody sword in one hand, the head of Peter Warlock in the other. Ray had predicted that Munns would become Surtr one day, and do away with the young magician. Munns had tried to imagine what that transformation would be like. Would he grow in size and become stronger? And what about his face? Would it turn as hideous as Surtr's?

Munns had never heard of Surtr so he'd done a search on the Internet. During the time of the Norse gods, Surtr had single-handedly guarded the gates of hell. He resembled Yoda from *Star Wars*, and did not look fierce enough to fight off a teenager. But when enemies approached,

Surtr grew into a horrifying monster with horns on his head and eye-popping muscles. As part of this transformation, the knife on his belt grew into a flaming sword, which he used to chop off the heads of his enemies. Munns had liked the sound of that, and had started to carry a Swiss Army knife with him wherever he went.

His cell phone vibrated on the counter, the word UNKNOWN lighting up the screen. Munns had no friends, and he couldn't remember the last time someone had called him. Perhaps it was Rachael calling to say that she wouldn't be coming on Friday night. The very notion filled him with dread, and he snatched up the phone. "Yes?"

"Is this Doc Munns?" an older man's gruff voice asked.

It was not Rachael calling to cancel, and he instantly relaxed.

"That's me. Who am I speaking to?"

"Name's Clyde Jucko. I own EZ Storage, where you rent a unit."

The Jucko clan were longtime residents and could trace their lineage back to the first Dutch families that had settled in the area. Clyde Jucko, the family patriarch, was a local slumlord and a tough customer. Locals often turned the J in his name into an F when describing him.

"What can I do for you, Mr. Jucko?" Munns asked, wrapping himself in a towel. "Did you not get my rent check?"

"I got the check. There's something not right with your unit."

"Excuse me?"

"I said, there's something not right with your unit. There's a big gaping hole torn in the roof. I was up on a ladder doing some repairs to the gutters when I spotted it. It looks like someone tore a hole in the roof of your unit from the inside. You wouldn't by chance happen to know how something like that could happen, would you?"

"I have no earthly idea what you're talking about," Munns stammered.

"You don't have someone illegally living in the unit, do you?"

"No." This time, Munns choked on the word.

"Then how the hell did a flipping hole get in the roof?"

"I have no idea. You have to believe me."

"I think you're lying, son. Matter of fact, I'm sure of it."

"You're not going to call the police . . ."

"I was considering it."

Munns thought he might pass out. He grabbed the sink edge to steady himself and filled his lungs with air. Like most serial killers, his killings followed a specific pattern that included taking his victims to a rental unit at EZ Storage, where he put their plastic-shrouded bodies in metal footlockers stacked inside. There the bodies stayed, locked away from the world. Ray had taught him this little trick. Without the bodies, the police had no evidence to play with, and the crime was reduced to a question mark which faded over time.

Only now something had happened inside his unit. Munns couldn't imagine how a hole had appeared in the roof, not that it really mattered. His landlord was suspicious, and Munns needed to deal with him before things got out of control.

"I'm sure we can work this out," Munns said.

"Hah," the old man laughed derisively.

"I'll pay you to keep quiet."

"Think you can bribe me, huh?"

"Isn't that why you called?"

"Don't be a wiseass, son." Jucko paused. "Give me a range."

"How about two thousand dollars?"

"That's chickenshit. Make it five grand, cash, and you've got yourself a deal."

"You're on. Give me a half hour to get the money. I'll come by and give it to you."

"Bring another three hundred to fix the roof."

"Whatever you say. I'll see you soon."

"Don't hang up. There's one more thing that's bothering me. I want to know what you've been keeping in that unit. Was it a man, a woman, a boy, or a girl? Was it an illegal alien, or some kind of sex slave? Or was it something else? I want to know what it was."

"That's none of your business," Munns said.

"It is now. You don't tell me, I'm calling the police."

Munns's cheeks burned. Jucko had gone from being a problem to being a threat. He needed to stall him so he could figure out what to do, and he said, "I can't tell you over the phone. I'll tell you later, when I bring the money."

"You *have* been keeping someone in there," Jucko said.

"I'll explain everything later."

"I'm going to hold you to that."

Jucko hung up on him. Munns went into the bedroom and sat down on the very edge of the bed. His head was pounding, his heart beating out of control. If he didn't deal with this right now, Jucko would start talking, and he'd be doomed.

He pulled up Ray's number on his cell phone. Ray would know what to do in a situation like this. Ray was street smart and he knew all the angles. Several rings later, the tattoo artist answered, his voice thick with sleep.

"I need your help. Clyde Jucko's onto me," Munns said breathlessly.

"Leave a message, and I'll call you back," an automated voice replied.

Munns let out a string of profanities. A beeping sound filled his ear.

"Meet me at EZ Storage," he said into the phone.

Then he threw on his clothes, grabbed his keys, and ran out of the house.

22

～

eter's next stop was Lester Rowe's shabby fortune-telling parlor on the Lower East Side. The small reception area was filled with clients, and he didn't stay long.

Then he headed uptown to pay Milly a visit at the Dakota. The old witch met him at the door of her apartment wearing a flowing black robe and a mystical gold pendant hanging around her neck. Milly also told fortunes, but to a much wealthier clientele, and he guessed by her wardrobe that she was working. He passed the five-pointed star through the door.

"Please put this on right away," he said.

"Am I in danger?" Milly asked.

"Yes. The shadow people are going after my friends."

Milly thanked him with her eyes and shut the door.

His last stop was Holly. Max's warning was still ringing in his ears, and he wondered what to do. Should he tell Holly that he couldn't see her anymore? That would mean one of them would have to leave the Friday night psychics, and he didn't see that happening. No, he was going to act like an adult, and sit down with her and have a talk. He couldn't think of anything more unpleasant, except perhaps going to see Dr. Sierra again.

As his cab neared Holly's place, his cell phone started to crawl out of his pocket as if alive. Only one person he knew could do that, and he flipped the phone open.

"Hey, Nemo, how you been?" he asked.

"Great for a guy doing life in prison," the Puerto Rican psychic said. "We need to talk. Give me your coordinates."

The CIA kept Nemo on a farm in Virginia where they used him to travel across time and space to see what fiendish plots the nation's enemies were hatching. It was a lousy existence, and the reason Peter didn't trust people in law enforcement. He glanced out the window at the approaching intersection. "I'm in a cab at the corner of Ninetieth and Central Park West, right next to Central Park."

"Look in the eastern sky. Do you see any clouds?"

"I see a few."

"Excellent. Get out of the cab, and stare at them. I'll be right there."

"You're going to visit me in person?"

"Yeah, aren't you excited?"

The line went dead. Nemo hadn't told him what was going on. But it wasn't like Nemo to bother him with trivial things, and Peter told the driver to pull over. The cab's tires kissed the curb, and he passed a twenty through the partition and hopped out. Walking over to the stone wall that surrounded the park, he located a formation of puffy clouds in the otherwise flawless sky, and stared. The outline of Nemo's face gradually appeared.

"Aren't we special," Peter said.

"Yes we are," his friend replied.

Nemo was a street kid from Spanish Harlem whom Peter had knocked around with as a teenager. Each psychic had a special gift. Nemo's was astral projection. He could project himself anywhere in the world if he set his mind to it. That was why the CIA found him so valuable. He was like a drone that didn't need gas, and couldn't be shot down.

Out-of-body experiences were nothing new in the psychic world. Psychics had been projecting themselves across the globe since the beginning of time. When people saw human faces in the clouds, or appearing on oil slicks on the road, or in rock formations on the sides of mountains, it was often a psychic projecting himself. The psychic never stayed for very long, but sometimes the image lingered behind, causing people to get excited, and even build shrines.

"How's life on the funny farm?" Peter asked.

"They're treating me like a king," Nemo replied. "Great food, beautiful accommodations, premium cable. The only problem is, they won't let me out."

"We're going to have to work on that. How did you call me? Don't tell me they gave you a cell phone."

"I wish. I stole my one of handlers' cell phones."

"That's going to come back and bite you."

"I stole his credit card, too. Amex silver, no less."

"Aren't you afraid of what they'll do when they find out?"

"What are they going to do? Arrest me? Then they'd have to acknowledge that they're holding me, and that's not going to happen. You should see all the stuff I bought on his card. Trips, hotel rooms, airline tickets, the works."

"For who?"

"My cousin and her little kid. She lost her job, and has been living on welfare. They needed a vacation, so I sent them down to Disney World. First class, all the way."

"How much did you charge on his card?"

"Enough to piss him off."

"You're my hero."

Nemo laughed in the clouds. His face was starting to fade, as was his voice. Out-of-body experiences never lasted more than a few minutes, and Peter strained to hear him.

"I had a strange thing happen to me that I wanted to warn you about," Nemo said. "My handlers routinely give me files of dangerous people they're trying to catch, and ask me to find them. This morning, I was given a composite of a serial killer in Westchester County called Dr. Death. My handlers asked me to project myself to Friday night, and see if I could find Dr. Death, so I did."

"What happened?"

"I found him. I also found someone else."

"Who?"

"You."

"Me? What was I doing in Westchester?"

"That's the million-dollar question. I projected myself to Friday night in Westchester County, and floated around for a few minutes. After a while, I felt your aura. It was really strong, and I spotted you standing in the parking lot of a train station on the outskirts of town."

"Was I by myself?"

"No. You were with a hulking black guy who acted like a cop."

"Special Agent Garrison, FBI."

"You're hanging out with the FBI? That's dangerous stuff, Peter."

"Tell me about it. Now, what did you see?"

"Garrison drove you to a house on a hill that reminded me of the house on the hill in *Psycho*. It had faded shingles and a gravel driveway surrounded by a thick hedge. You and Garrison went inside the house, where a really terrified woman was being held in the living room. She was tied to a chair, and was totally freaking out. Dr. Death was also in the living room. He's an overweight guy, dressed like a nerd, didn't look scary at all. At first I thought, what's going on here? Then things got freaky."

"How so?"

"Dr. Death's body started to change until he looked like a gargoyle on steroids. The guy grew horns and his hands turned into claws. It was like watching a bad horror flick. You guys started fighting to the death."

People who entered into pacts with the Devil often lost their human qualities, and became like their master. Monsters in every sense of the word, they deserved no place on this earth.

Peter had never fought one of these people, and had no idea how his powers would stack up. He supposed there was a first time for everything.

"You've got me on the edge of my seat. What happened then?" Peter asked.

"I woke up," Nemo said.

"You suck, you know that?"

"Hey, nobody's perfect."

Nemo's face was now an afterimage, his voice barely a faint whisper. In a few seconds he would be gone, leaving Peter to wonder when they'd again hook up.

"Be careful, Peter. Whatever this guy is, it isn't human," his friend said.

Peter started to thank him for the warning. But by then, Nemo had disappeared in the clouds, leaving nothing but a pair of gulls circling overhead.

23

*C*lyde Jucko had the disposition of a junkyard dog and a face to match. He was waiting outside EZ Storage as Munns pulled into the parking lot, and climbed out of his car. A big man, he cast a long, menacing shadow that stretched halfway across the lot.

Munns approached Jucko cautiously. Jucko was holding what looked like bolt cutters in his hand. Munns's eyes fell on the broken padlock lying on the ground.

"You went into my unit without my permission," Munns said.

"It's my unit. You just rent it from me," Jucko corrected him.

"You had no right to do that, or to touch my things."

"I didn't touch your goddamn things. I just wanted to see what you've been up to. You bring the money?"

"I got it."

"Give it to me right now."

Munns pulled an envelope stuffed with hundreds from his pocket and tossed it to the older man. As Jucko counted the money, Munns glanced in both directions. The other units were empty and they were alone. Except for the steady hiss of cars on the nearby highway, the air was still. Munns knew that the best course of action was to shoot Jucko in the head at point-blank range, and throw his body in the trunk of his car. A single gunshot would carry through the woods and trail off like a lonely clap of thunder. It would go unnoticed, and Jucko would join the list of people who'd come in contact with Munns and disappeared.

Only there was a problem with that scenario. Jucko was pointing the bolt cutters like he was planning to cut Munns's balls off. He looked ready for a fight, and drawing a gun on him at this moment seemed out of the question.

"All here," Jucko said, pocketing the cash. "Okay, now I want you to tell me what's been going on. Who's been living in that unit?"

"No one," Munns said.

"That's a bunch of bull. I had a look. Someone's been living in there."

"I don't know what you're talking about."

"No? Have a look, see for yourself."

Jucko had not lowered the bolt cutters, and Munns stepped around him while keeping his distance. He brought his face to the open door of his unit, and gazed into the darkened interior. Inside were six stainless-steel footlockers stored on the rack of a metal shelving unit. Inside each footlocker was the body of one of his victims. One of the footlockers had fallen from its spot, and lay broken on the concrete floor. Light streamed down from the gaping hole in the ceiling. Jucko had been correct in his assumption that the hole had been created from within. But by who? Or what? Munns couldn't be sure. He started to slide the door shut and felt a hand on his arm.

"What the hell are you keeping in those footlockers?" Jucko demanded.

"That's none of your business," Munns said.

"Everything's my business."

Jucko pushed him to the side before Munns could reply. Sliding back the door, he entered the unit, and flipped over the broken footlocker lying on the floor. A corpse wrapped in plastic tumbled out, and Jucko used the bolt cutters to cut away the plastic shroud. A skeletal face stared up at him. It was Edie, Munns's last victim. She had cursed Munns as he strangled her to death, and the invective was slow to leave her face.

"It's a dead woman," Jucko said in horror. "What kind of monster are you?"

Munns's gun was tucked in his belt behind his back. As he reached for it, Jucko swung the bolt cutters up from the floor and their blades brushed his face. Warm blood ran down Munns's cheek and his vision blurred. His hands covered the bleeding wound.

Jucko reached behind Munns's back, and relieved him of his gun. Dropping it in his pocket, he triumphantly rested the bolt cutters on his shoulder. "I should kill you. Save the state the trouble of locking you up. Now get on your knees, or I'll bust your head open."

"I thought we had a deal," Munns blurted out.

"I ain't making no deals with the Devil. On your knees."

Munns's neck began to burn. The sensation started at the shimmering tattoo, and spread straight up his neck and into his brain like so much bad poison sent from below.

"No," Munns said.

"What did you say?" Jucko declared.

"I'm not kneeling to you, or anyone else."

For reasons Munns could not explain, he no longer felt afraid of Jucko. In his mind, he saw himself taking Jucko outside the shed and dismembering him in the parking lot, the old man's blood staining the pavement and spoiling an otherwise perfect day.

Munns's hands were burning as well. He brought them up to his face to have a look. The skin was turning a sickening black, and his fingernails had grown into talons. A sound escaped his lips that was not human.

"Jesus H. Christ. What in God's name are you?" Jucko whispered.

The bolt cutters hit the floor. Jucko looked like he might cry. The presence of the Devil did that to some people. Munns backed Jucko into the corner, put his hands around Jucko's throat, and lifted him clean off the floor. Then he carried him outside into the parking lot.

Jucko begged for mercy, and Munns squeezed the words as they came out of his throat. Munns had been tortured as a child, and every person in town knew it, including Clyde Jucko. Mercy was the last thing on his mind.

Munns drew the Swiss Army knife from his pocket, and flicked open the blade. Before his eyes, it grew into a gleaming sword. He released his grasp on Jucko, and let him stand on his own. In one swift motion, he cut off the old man's head. One quick slice was all it took, and the disembodied corpse hit the pavement with a sickening thud.

Jucko's head rolled for several yards before coming to a stop. The old man's eyes were blinking wildly, like he didn't know he was dead yet. A screech of brakes shattered the stillness. Ray's black van pulled into the parking lot, and the tattoo artist jumped out. Ray started to approach, saw Munns, and started backing up, as if he didn't know who Munns was.

"Doc, is that you?" he asked.

"Who do you think it is?" Munns barked.

Ray opened his mouth, but no words came out. He looked terrified. In all their time together, Ray had never shown fear. It was not a quality he seemed to possess, until now.

"Why are you staring at me like that?" Munns demanded.

"You don't know?" Ray asked.

"No. Tell me what's going on."

Ray went to the van and bent the side mirror so Munns could see his own reflection. The image staring back did not look real. Munns's clothes were shreds, and he'd been transformed into a hulking demon with horns coming out of his skull, rapierlike fangs, and a ridge of spikes running the length of his spine. The most recent tattoo Ray had inked on his skin had come to life, and now stood ready to do battle with whichever enemies stood in his way.

A coarse laugh escaped Munns's lips. Surtr had risen.

24

Peter got out of the cab in front of Holly's apartment wondering what a gargoyle on steroids looked like. Not the kind of date to spend Friday night with, that was for sure. At least he'd have Garrison backing him up when he confronted the thing.

He entered the lobby, and searched for Holly's name on the intercom. He had always envied Holly for making it into Columbia. It was New York's best school, and one of the finest in the country. His own college experience had consisted of a single semester at CCNY, where he'd majored in not falling asleep in class before being thrown out.

He sometimes wondered what his life would have been like if he'd stayed in school, and gotten a degree. Perhaps he would have become a doctor or a lawyer. He would have made a hell of an attorney, especially during a cross-examination. No one was going to keep any secrets from him! But that was just an idle daydream. He'd wanted to be a magician for as long he could remember. It was his calling, as strange as that sounded.

Right as he found Holly's listing, he got a call from Liza. How strange that she'd call just as he entered Holly's building.

"When are you coming home?" she asked.

"Soon. I've been running some errands," he replied.

"You could have called, you know."

"I thought you wanted to have a quiet afternoon by yourself."

"You leave in the company of an FBI agent. Then I don't hear from you for three whole hours. You could be a little more considerate."

"Sorry."

"How did it go with Garrison?"

"It was a strange morning. It appears there's more than one shadow person in the city. The FBI has tapes of them inside Grand Central Terminal. It's like an invasion."

"Eeek! What do the shadow people want?"

"Me."

"Don't say that. You're scaring me."

"All right. They want you."

"You're not funny. So, where are you now? Can you talk for a minute?"

It did not seem the right time to be telling his girlfriend that he was about to enter another woman's apartment to give her a piece of jewelry. He stepped out of the lobby onto the sidewalk, and cupped his hand over his ear to block out the street noise. "I can talk."

"I called Dr. Sierra," Liza said. "He's very disturbed by what you told him this morning. He's afraid you could hurt yourself when you go into one of your states. He wants to help you."

"Hurt myself how?"

"By doing something awful, and then later being held accountable for it."

"Like nearly burning down the restaurant this morning."

"Exactly."

"Did you tell him what happened?"

"No. I was going to let you do that."

Peter swallowed the lump in his throat. The moment of truth had finally arrived. "You think I should tell him what happened at the restaurant?" he asked.

"Yes, I do. Dr. Sierra said he could fit us in tomorrow morning."

"That soon, huh?"

"He wants us to meet a colleague of his named Hunsinger. Dr. Sierra said that Hunsinger has dealt with people who have problems just like yours. Dr. Sierra put in a call to Hunsinger, and he's agreed to meet with us."

"He spoke with Hunsinger before you called?"

"Yes. Why?"

Something inside of him snapped. It must have shown in his face, for a man walking toward him on the sidewalk stepped into the gutter and immediately crossed the street.

"Dr. Sierra promised not to talk to anyone about us. Remember?"

"You're losing your temper. Calm down," Liza said.

The demon lurking inside of him never truly went to sleep. It was always simmering just below the surface, ready to attack like a vicious watchdog. "He betrayed me."

"Dr. Sierra consulted Hunsinger for advice," she said. "He's trying to help, and you're putting handcuffs on him."

"He deserves a lot worse than handcuffs."

"That's not funny. Stop talking like that."

Betrayals were the Devil's playthings. They started wars, ruined marriages, and brought out the worst in mankind. A betrayal had taken his parents' lives, and forever altered his own. He would make Sierra pay for this indiscretion, even with Liza in the room. Looking up into the sky, he let the warm sunlight bathe his face, and felt his anger recede, if only a little.

"I'll do whatever you want," he said.

"Will you go see him tomorrow?"

"Yes. I'll go see him."

"Thank you for doing this. Are you mad?"

"Not at all."

"You sound mad. Please don't be. It's for the best."

He loved Liza more than anything in the world. Yet there were times when she made him so angry, he wanted to scream. Saying good-bye, he ended the call.

H olly was in her apartment. She sounded happy to hear his voice, and buzzed him in.

He took a creaky elevator to the ninth floor. Once upon a time, he'd loved Mondays. It was the day he used to escape his problems. Now it seemed like all he was doing was confronting them. The elevator rumbled to a stop. He got out, and walked down a narrow hallway to a door painted a muted black.

Holly lived by herself. Most psychics did. He was one of the lucky ones, although he wasn't sure how long that was going to last. He and Liza seemed to be growing further apart with every conversation. It was like slipping down a cliff.

He tapped lightly. No answer. He tapped a little harder. To his surprise, the door opened by itself. People didn't leave their doors unlocked in New York, not even in the best apartment buildings. He stuck his head in. "Holly?"

Nothing. He entered and shut the door behind him. Holly lived in a large studio with a sweeping westerly view of the Hudson River. The walls and ceilings were painted black, while thick white candles decorated the bookshelf and coffee table. A haunting violin solo played over the music system. He looked around the room, not seeing her.

"It's Peter. Come out, come out, wherever you are."

Growing up, Holly had loved to play hide-and-seek. She'd make herself disappear in her aunt's vast apartment, and Peter would have to search for her. She'd always squealed when he'd discovered her hiding in the closet, or under a bed. That had been the best part of the game.

A voice shattered the stillness. "Who's that?"

"Where are you?"

"Here."

He walked around the couch. Holly lay on the cushions, her eyes half open, as if in a daze. She wore jeans and a tight T-shirt that exposed her midriff and accentuated her breasts. Her dark hair lay seductively on a pillow, and her lips were painted a hot pink. He didn't think he'd ever seen her dressed like that before. She did not look like the woman he knew.

"Are you okay?"

Her eyelids fluttered. "I think so."

"You didn't get visited by a shadow person, did you?"

"I think I would have known that. I'm just a little light-headed. Get me some water, would you? I'm dying of thirst."

The kitchen was the size of a phone booth. He ran the tap until the water was chilled, then filled a glass and brought it to her. She was sitting up and smiling.

"Are you all right?"

She nodded and sipped the water. He sat down on the edge of the couch so they were a few feet apart. He noticed a large vase of water sitting on the coffee table. Beside it, a pouch of magic herbs. "You've been scrying on me again, haven't you?" he said bluntly.

"Yes, I have," she admitted without a hint of shame. "I got scared on Friday night during the séance. You were lying there on the floor in my aunt's apartment, twitching your legs, and I realized that I might never see you again. It nearly broke my heart. So I started to watch you."

"What did scrying on me accomplish?"

"I wanted to help you. I was scared for you."

He looked away and stared into space. "How much have you seen?"

"Everything."

"Everything?"

"Yes. I saw you at the doctor's office this morning, and at the Indian restaurant which you nearly burned down, and later at Grand Central Station with the FBI agent, where you watched the videotapes of the shadow people running across the terminal floor."

"Did you see me talking to Max?"

"Yes."

"Did you hear what Max said about you?"

"Yes. Max is angry with me. I already knew that."

"Did you see me talking to Nemo?"

"Was that the face in the clouds? I didn't recognize him. You shouldn't be talking out in public like that to Nemo. People will become suspicious. Next time, stick a Bluetooth in your ear, and they'll think you're on a cell phone."

"That's not fair, Holly."

"Do you think I'm abusing my powers?"

"Yes—don't you?"

She moved closer to him on the couch. "I only planned to watch you after you left my aunt's apartment Friday night to make sure you were safe. But once I started watching you, I couldn't stop. I guess you could say it's become an addiction."

This was bad. Holly could make his life far more complicated than it already was and there wasn't an earthly thing he could do to stop her except get on his knees and plead with her. Only that would probably be taken the wrong way. Damn it, what was he supposed to do?

"Please stop this," he begged her. "Please."

"I'll try." She paused. "But I won't make any promises."

"Not even to me?"

She put her hand on his knee and left it there. "Not even to you. Want to know why?"

"Why?"

"Because I know who you are, and what you are. That's why. You're not normal, and neither am I. But we pretend to be. That's the lie we have to live in order to fit in. But it doesn't work all the time. Like you're learning now."

"You mean with Liza."

"Especially with Liza. She can't change you, no matter how hard she tries."

Holly was making it sound like his relationship with Liza was doomed, and would end like every other relationship he'd ever had. He shook his head in disagreement.

"It's not like that between us," he said. "Liza's trying to help me."

"Peter."

"What?"

"Look at me."

Holly pulled herself close, and moved her hand to his stomach, where she rested her palm. Her eyes danced across his face. Every inch of her skin looked radiant. Before his eyes she had changed from a girl into a ravishing young woman. Or had she been that way for a while, and he just hadn't noticed? He did not resist as she climbed into his lap.

Witches were strange creatures. Their powers were linked to their imaginations much differently than other psychics. If they imagined something vividly enough, it would become their reality, as well as the reality of those in their presence. They were dangerous that way.

The candles sparked to life. As they did, the walls expanded like a movie set, and the apartment was transformed into a high-ceilinged boudoir with a four-poster bed in its center. Over the sound system, the violin solo turned into a romantic ballad.

Holly climbed off his lap. She motioned for him to rise, and he did. She offered him her hand, and he took it. They started across the room together toward the bed. He tried to pull away, but it was too late. She had cast a spell on him, and there was nothing he could do.

They stopped in front of the bed. She put her hands on his shoulders, and gazed longingly into his eyes. This couldn't be happening, but it was. He had to escape.

"No," he said, the word taking all his strength to utter.

"No?" She acted amused. "Don't tell me you never considered it."

Of course he'd considered it. Holly was beautiful, and the thought of having sex with her had entered his mind more than once. Each time it had, his conscience had shouted it down.

"It's not right," he whispered.

"What's not right? Our falling in love?"

He nodded stiffly.

"I beg to differ. You've had plenty of girlfriends, and they've all left you, and broken your heart. We were meant for each other, Peter. You have to know that."

"Let me out of this spell."

"Not on your life."

She unbuttoned his shirt and ran her fingertips across his hairless chest. He could not deny the powerful effect it had on him. He was becoming aroused, and would soon be lying in bed with Holly. But if he let that happen, his life would never be the same. He'd lose Liza, and start down a road with Holly whose ending was totally unclear. He was not ready for either of those things to happen. Somehow, someway, he had to make her stop.

Holly leaned in close, and kissed him on the mouth. A painful spark jumped between their lips. The boudoir disappeared, and Holly's student furnishings returned. Around the room, the candles spouted flames that caused the textbooks and magazines on the coffee table to catch fire. Peter stamped them out on the floor.

"Check to see if anything else is on fire," he said.

Holly was in a daze. She checked the kitchen and the bathroom.

"All clear?" he asked.

She nodded dumbly. He hated to be a party pooper, but it was time to go. He removed the five-pointed star from the gift bag he'd brought, and made her put it on.

"Don't take that off until I tell you to, okay?"

Utterly embarrassed, Holly stared at the floor. He wanted things to go back to the way they used to be, and gave her a hug.

"Can't we just be friends?" he asked.

She started to cry. He hated when she did that. He got a paper towel from the kitchen, and wiped away the tears. She looked vulnerable now and more than a little afraid. He grabbed the bag with the remaining necklace and went to the front door. She followed him as if blind.

"Good-bye. I'll call you in a few days," he said.

"Aren't you going to explain?" she blurted out.

"Explain what?"

"You were under a spell."

He waited, certain there was more.

"No one can break a witch's spell. It's not possible."

"I guess there's a first time for everything."

"Be serious, Peter. How did you do that?"

There were certain things that even Peter didn't understand about himself. Like how he moved objects with his mind or set off car alarms or made cups of coffee boil or flames jump off kitchen stoves. At the most unexpected of times these things just happened, and he never knew why. His temper was partially responsible, but there was another reason, and he had yet to fathom its meaning. Now he had another strange power to add to the list. He could not be kept under a witch's spell. It pleased him to know that Holly could not make him her prisoner, and he hugged her before going out the door.

25

Ray was freaking out.

What if someone came, and saw Jucko's headless body lying on the ground? They'd most certainly call the police, and he and Doc Munns would be arrested and sent to jail. He could not let that happen, not unless he wished to anger the Order of Astrum.

Ray was more afraid of the elders of the Order than he was of the police, or of going to jail, or just about anything else he could think of. He'd seen the kind of horror the elders were capable of wreaking upon people in their service who did not perform up to their standards. They were brutal, and he had made it a point to never make them angry.

Ray made Munns get into the passenger side of the van. Munns had calmed down and was reverting back to his old self. The transformation was as startling as it was remarkable One moment, he was the embodiment of a beast that had guarded the gates of hell for over two thousand years; the next, he was a pudgy slob, and easily the world's biggest loser.

"Stay here," Ray said.

"What's going on? What happened?" Munns asked, sounding bewildered.

"You don't know?"

"No. Did I kill Jucko?"

"You cut his head off. I'll tell you about it later."

Ray went about cleaning up the mess. He dragged Jucko's body into Munns's storage unit, near the footlockers that contained Munns's previous victims. Then he threw in Jucko's head. Keeping the victims in airtight footlockers had seemed like a good idea, until now. The bodies were a liability, and Ray wasn't sure what he was going to do with them, or with Jucko. He'd think of something, it was just going to take a little time.

Ray had known that Munns had problems when he'd first recruited him. Men who killed had troubled pasts, which was why they killed. It was sweet revenge for all the terrible things that had happened to them growing up.

Munns's childhood had been a living hell. Ray had heard the stories from the people in town. Munns's parents were no-good drunks who'd taken turns torturing him. One day his father was beating the snot out of him while his mother looked on; the very next, Mom was giving him the belt while Dad smoked a butt and watched. Beating their son had been a sick sport that had lasted for many years. It had stunted Munns's growth and left psychological scars that no amount of time would ever heal.

That was Munns's story, at least part of it. There was another sordid chapter, although Ray had never gotten the details. Something had happened when Munns was a teenager that had been the icing on the cake. It was so ugly, that at times Munns lost control, and did crazy things, like try to run over townspeople's dogs.

Ray had known all these things about Munns, yet still had recruited him into the Order. In hindsight, it now seemed a mistake. Munns was too imperfect for the job, too flawed. The Order did not tolerate mistakes, and Ray would pay for his lack of judgment.

As Ray started to leave the unit, the sliding metal door clanged shut in his face, throwing the interior into darkness. The door wouldn't budge. Was Munns playing a trick on him?

"Let me out!" he said, banging on the door with his palm.

A scraping sound made him jump. Something was crawling across the floor. He dug out his lighter and flicked it on.

He gasped. Jucko's severed head was rolling across the floor by itself. Coming to its own body, it stopped. Before Ray's disbelieving eyes, the tendons and sinew rejoined in perfect union, and the dismembered corpse became whole again.

Jucko stood up. His face was lifeless, his eyes unblinking. Ray had thought he knew evil. But now, he realized he didn't know evil at all. The evil he knew was clever and sly and played wicked tricks on the world. The evil standing before him was different. It was pure, and came straight from the depths of hell.

"Give me your lighter," came a ghostly voice out of Jucko's mouth.

Ray hesitated. He did not want the room to return to darkness. Then his imagination would take over, and he'd lose his sanity.

"No," he squeaked.

"Do as I say. It's for your own good," the voice said.

The voice of reason, coming out of a dead man's mouth. Ray reluctantly handed over the lighter. In the dead man's hand, it turned into a torch, which illuminated the entire room.

The lid to one of the footlockers popped open, and a female corpse climbed out. It was no longer shrouded in plastic, but wore stylish city clothes and had a skeletal face. The lid to a second footlocker popped open, and a second victim emerged, this one dressed like a much older woman. The dead women stared at Ray with hollow eyes.

Their number gave them away. It was the elders, come to pay him a visit. Ray had never felt more afraid in his life. "Guess I screwed up, huh?" he said.

The unholy trio did not reply.

"I can do better," Ray promised them. "I swear I can."

"To who do you swear?" came a voice out of Jucko's mouth.

"To Satan and everything he stands for."

"Forever and ever?"

"Yes, forever and ever."

"Good. There has been a change in plans. We need you to speed up the process. Munns needs to bring the woman named Rachael out on the train sooner. Munns must call this woman, and convince her to come out right away."

"But everything's in place for Friday night," Ray protested. "She'll become suspicious and start questioning him."

"Help Munns deal with her suspicions. Work with him."

"Munns is a basket case. He'll screw up," Ray said, speaking his mind.

"We're giving you another chance," said the voice. "Make the most of it."

"You're crazy," Ray said under his breath.

"Deal with him," said the voice.

The two dead women charged across the shed, and pinned Ray against the door. Their bony fingers gripped his arms and held his struggling body in place. The one to his left bit into his cheek and held the flesh between her teeth; the one on his right clamped her teeth down on his earlobe, and tugged on the skin. At any moment, he expected to be eaten alive.

"Care to reconsider?" asked the voice.

Ray took a deep breath, expecting it to be his last. Not once had the elders asked him his opinion. They didn't care what he thought. He was just a slave.

"All right," he said.

"You'll work with Munns and make the girl come out?" the voice asked.

"I'll try."

"That's not good enough!"

The dead women began to tear away at Ray's flesh.

"I'll do it!" Ray screamed.

They stopped eating him. Ray shut his eyes, and tried to wish this nightmare away. Opening them a moment later, he found that nothing had changed.

"Is that a promise?" the voice asked.

"On my mother's grave," Ray said.

"We're going to hold you to that."

"I said I'd do it," Ray said. "Why is this woman so important to you? Is there a reason?"

Jucko brought his face within inches of Ray's. His breath reeked of the rotted architecture of an evil man's soul. "The woman is meaningless. It's Peter Warlock we're after. Warlock is trying to save Rachael, and will travel from New York to come to her aid. That is predestinated, and there's no changing it. When Warlock arrives in your little town, he will have an FBI agent with him. That is predestined as well. The agent will arrest Munns, and you as well if you're not careful. Your job at that point will be to stay out of the way. Understood?"

"Why? What will happen?"

"What do you think will happen, you stupid little man?"

Ray shook his head, his thoughts clouded by fear. The teeth of one of the dead women began to gobble his ear and he shrieked in agony. "Please! Spare me!"

His ear was being torn from his head. The other dead woman tried to rip a hunk of flesh out of his cheek. He screamed and struggled but could not free himself from their bony grasp. The dead man standing in front of him lowered the torch onto the top of Ray's head. Ray felt his hair catch fire, and knew that this was the end.

As if by magic, the torch extinguished itself, throwing the shed into darkness. The dead women stopped eating his face. They seemed to just melt away, and Ray brought his hand up to touch his unscathed head. Behind him, the sliding door slid open on its own accord and filled the shed with sunlight. Jucko's headless body lay on the floor, his head a few feet away, while the footlockers were propped against the wall, the corpses of Munns's victims still inside.

None of it had been real.

It didn't matter. Ray was still terrified. The elders had tapped his innermost fears. They knew what scared him, and had used those fears to turn his soul inside out. Locking the sliding door behind him, he hurried across the parking lot to his van. Munns sat in the passenger seat, listening to a Marilyn Manson CD on the sound system.

"Where you been?" Munns asked.

"Shut the hell up."

Ray stared through the windshield at the road, thinking hard. He would have to concoct some reason to draw Rachael from New York. He'd always been good at making up stories, and supposed it wouldn't be too hard to come up with a convincing lie. The hard part would be to get Munns to call Rachael, and make her believe him.

Ray glanced at his passenger. Munns was humming along to the music. He did not appear the least bit upset by what he'd done. Munns rolled up his sleeve and began to scratch the skin around the tattoo of Surtr holding the severed head of Peter Warlock. It was one of Ray's best creations, the colors so vivid it almost looked alive.

"The skin is burning," Munns explained.

Of course it was burning. The skin always burned for the new recruits entering into hell. The hard part was that it never stopped burning.

"Change of plans," Ray said. "We're going to get Rachael to come out sooner. We need to come up with a story that she'll believe."

"Why? What's going on?" Munns asked.

Ray hesitated. How did he explain what had just happened in the storage shed? The words had not been invented. Even if they had, he was not sure he would have uttered them.

"It's a long story," the tattoo artist said.

26

Peter cabbed it back downtown. He'd dodged a bullet, but had a feeling that this was not the end of things between him and Holly in the romance department. Holly was in love and she was also a witch. That was a recipe for disaster if there ever was one.

The last person on his list was Snoop, never the easiest person to track down. Once Peter found his assistant and gave him the five-pointed-star necklace, he'd go home to Liza and apologize for not calling. Perhaps a quiet dinner, or a foreign movie at an Upper East Side art house would do the trick.

He sent his assistant a text, and told him they needed to meet up. Snoop wrote back to say that he was setting up a pop-up club at Jobee, a Taiwanese restaurant on Howard Street. Did Peter want to join him? Peter wrote back that he did, and gave the cabdriver the address.

Pop-up clubs were the latest rage. All across the city, party promoters were setting up velvet ropes and plugging in turntables in dim sum parlors, Midtown office spaces, strip clubs, school playgrounds, even Laundromats. At midnight, these unassuming spaces were transformed into trendy nightclubs, complete with snarling bouncers and a line of party-goers stretched halfway around the block hoping to get in.

Snoop liked to work pop-up clubs because they were great places to meet women. The fact that the clubs weren't legal added to the thrill. Jobee, his newest venue, was located just north of the fake handbag district on Canal Street. The cab pulled up to the door, and Peter hopped out.

Jobee's front door had a paper menu taped to it, and the house specialty, Taiwanese Oyster Pancake, caught his eye. It was the only restaurant in the city that served the dish, and he decided to take some home to Liza as a surprise.

He went in. The restaurant's interior looked like a cyclone had hit it. A waiter was shouting into a cell phone, asking the police to hurry. Tables and chairs were turned upside down, the kitschy paper lanterns swung wildly from the ceiling. He cursed under his breath, knowing he was too late.

He hurried to the back of the restaurant. There, he found Snoop slumped in a chair. His assistant's head sagged on his chest, and his eyes were tightly shut. The only thing moving were his legs, both of which twitched uncontrollably. The restaurant's owner and a cook knelt beside Snoop, trying to rouse him. Behind the chair stood the party promoter, a Russian named Boris from the Williamsburg section of Brooklyn. Boris was telling the waiter not to call the police, and the waiter was ignoring him. It was not a pretty scene.

Peter took the last five-pointed star from his bag, and fitted it around his assistant's neck. He had no idea if this would do any good, but he gave it a try. Snoop's lips started to move. Peter leaned over and put his ear up next to his assistant's mouth, listening hard.

"Peter, is that you?" Snoop asked.

"Yeah," Peter said. "Did that thing take you away?"

"Oh, man, this is crazy. One minute I'm in the club, the next I'm at some crazy guy's house on the side of the hill, and he's trying to run me down with his car."

"Are you still there?"

"I ran away from him. Trying to find my way to town, wherever the hell that is."

"I need to get you out of there."

"Can you do that?"

"I'm going to try."

"Great. Here he comes in his car. He's got a gun—he's trying to shoot me!"

Snoop's feet began to tap the floor as he attempted to run away from Dr. Death. Only Snoop wasn't going to succeed, just as Liza hadn't gotten away, nor Peter himself. Dr. Death had a home field advantage, and was going to shoot Snoop if Peter didn't act quickly. Rising, he quickly hustled the owner, cook, waiter, and Russian promoter out the front door.

"What do you think you're doing?" the owner asked him.

"My friend needs help. Please stand here, and keep the police out."

"What is wrong with your friend?" the owner asked. "Is he on drugs?"

"That's none of your business."

With that, Peter went back into the restaurant and locked the door behind him. He didn't want an audience to witness Snoop coming around, and hearing what he had to say. As a psychic he was sworn to keep secrets and not talk about his dealings with the other side. It was a hard promise to keep, but he did his best. He grabbed Snoop by the shoulders and attempted to shake him awake. His eyelids fluttered.

"He's shooting at me!" Snoop said desperately.

"Wake up! Wake up!" Peter implored him.

"Oww! Something hit my leg. Oh, my God, it's bleeding. He winged me!"

"Snoop, you've got to open your eyes!"

"I can't. This is so crazy. Get me out of here, will you!"

Peter stopped shaking his assistant. Something was keeping Snoop from returning. He let his eyes canvass the room. In the back of the restaurant was a darkened space with several booths. His eyes locked on the shadow person hovering over a table. The last times hadn't worked, so the shadow person had decided to hang around, and make sure it did this time.

Peter did not remember moving across the restaurant toward the booths. Nor did he remember raising his arm. Just the sound of his fist striking the shadow person in the space that should have been its head. The evil spirit emitted a groan, and shrank into itself. Two more blows produced similar effects. He was hurting it, and making it smaller. The third blow did the trick, and the shadow person became the size of a beach ball before disappearing, the sound coming out of its mouth a pitiful cry.

He hurried back to Snoop. His assistant had woken up, and was examining his leg where he'd been shot by Dr. Death. He was in a daze, having a hard time grasping that his trip hadn't been real. Peter helped him out of his chair.

"You're my hero," Snoop said.

"Let's get out of here before the police come. This is one trip you can't talk to anyone about."

"What's this thing around my neck, anyway? It's not my color."

"Leave it on. It will protect you from being kidnapped again."

He pushed Snoop into the kitchen and looked for an exit. Snoop pilfered a vegetarian egg roll out of a pan sitting on the stove, and started to eat it. "Is that what happened to me? I was kidnapped by that weird black thing?"

"It's called a shadow person, and it's an evil spirit. It kidnapped your soul, and took you to the home of a serial killer. Don't ask me why, because I haven't figured out that part yet."

"Could I have died?"

"It was a distinct possibility. I need to pick your brain. We have to catch this guy."

Snoop chewed contemplatively. "I'm game."

27

〜

Opening Ceremony was the most daring clothing boutique in the city, and a few short blocks away. Snoop suggested they get a window seat at the Starbucks across the street from it. Girl watching was his passion.

They both got the house roast and a toasted sesame bagel. A window table opened up and they grabbed it. Peter sipped his drink, realizing how lucky it was Snoop was still alive. Either he was going to have to give every person he knew a five-pointed star, or he'd have to come up with another way to deal with this problem. Snoop leaned forward on his elbows and spoke in a whisper. "I heard you beating that thing in the restaurant. Did you kill it?"

Peter shook his head and sipped his drink.

"If you don't mind my asking, how did you do that?"

Another moment of truth. There should have been a law that a person didn't have to deal with more than one of those a day. Should he tell Snoop who he was, or continue to lie to his best friend? He decided to tell the truth.

"It's called dark magic," Peter explained, his voice barely audible. "It's a special gift that I was born with. I can read minds, see into the future, and when I set my mind to it, move objects around by telekinesis. I also conduct séances with some of my psychic friends."

"Do you talk to dead people?"

"Sometimes."

"Are there really such things as ghosts?"

"Yes, and they're everywhere."

Snoop chewed on his bagel. He did not seem terribly surprised by Peter's admission. Perhaps he'd known all along that Peter was psychic, and because they were tight, had never let on. A better friend he'd never had.

"What about the magic tricks? Are they your cover?" Snoop asked.

"I guess you could call them that," Peter said. "If I slip up, I tell people it's a trick, and no one's the wiser. I've been doing it all my life, and never been caught."

"Which makes you a very interesting guy. Does Liza know?"

"I told her a few weeks ago. The shock is starting to settle in."

"That bad?"

"We went to see a shrink this morning. It didn't go well."

Snoop put down his half-eaten bagel. A knowing look spread across his face.

"Was the shrink's name Dr. Sierra?" his assistant asked.

Peter's coffee cup hit the table hard. "How did you know that?"

"Oh, wow, I fooled you. That's a first. Let's write this down and get it notarized."

"Come on, tell me."

Snoop took out his Droid. He carried the same model that Peter did, and was resisting turning it in for an upgrade, just as Peter was. They were alike in many ways, and often joked that they were twins separated at birth. Snoop punched an app, and a live shot of a surveillance camera outside Peter's theater appeared on the tiny screen. He hit another button, and a live shot from the camera in the alley came on. Pushing more buttons, he revealed shots from the surveillance cameras inside the theater that ran 24/7.

"I didn't know that was possible with a Droid," Peter said.

"They don't call me Snoop for nothing. The system also has a memory. Take a look at this video that was shot earlier."

Snoop pushed another button. On the screen appeared a video showing a man standing outside the theater, banging on the front door. It was Dr. Sierra, wearing a hat and coat. With him was a second man, quite sickly in appearance, who carried a wooden cane. The second man wore a solemn expression on his face.

"I like to check on the theater and make sure everything's okay," Snoop explained. "I caught Dr. Sierra and his friend banging on the door this afternoon. He was there for a while. Then he went across the street to get a sandwich with his friend. Something told me I should call this guy, and find out what he wanted. So I called the restaurant, and asked to speak with him."

"He must have been surprised," Peter said, enjoying his assistant's ingenuity.

"He was. He said he urgently needed to speak with you. I thought he was a kook, and asked him who his friend was. That's when he clammed up."

"He wouldn't tell you who the other person was?"

"No, and I asked him a few times. It bothered me that he wouldn't give me the other guy's name or anything."

Was this Hunsinger, the colleague Dr. Sierra had mentioned to Liza? If so, why had Sierra dragged him out on a Monday afternoon and brought him to Peter's theater? Sierra had betrayed him in so many ways that it made Peter angry thinking about it.

At the next table, a college-aged girl enjoying a latte let out a yelp. Her cup was boiling over, the brown liquid singeing her manicured fingers. She looked bewildered, which was how most people reacted when confronted by the paranormal. Peter forced himself to calm down, and the drink went back to its normal state.

Peter glanced at Snoop. His assistant mouthed the word "Wow!"

"Can you teach me that?" Snoop asked under his breath.

It comes with a heavy price tag, Peter nearly told him.

"Afraid not," he said instead. "What else did Dr. Sierra say?"

"He asked for your phone number. I told him it was private, and not something I could hand out. He got insistent, and I told him to have a nice day."

"He wouldn't tell you what he wanted, huh?"

"No. If you ask me, this guy is trouble."

"Why do you say that?"

"You're a public person. People don't just come banging on your door unannounced every day, do they? This guy Sierra is unhinged. Take my advice, and stay away from him."

"I've got another session with him tomorrow morning."

"Cancel it."

"I promised Liza."

"Excuse me, but aren't you Peter Warlock the magician?" the college girl at the next table asked. "Why, yes, you are. I saw your show with my girlfriend last year. We had the best time. Will you do that trick for me again? I'm just dying to know how it's done."

She held out her cup of latte, as if expecting Peter to make it boil again. Snoop pulled back in his chair. He was laughing under his breath and enjoying himself at his boss's expense. Peter gave him the eye. It wasn't funny, but Snoop kept laughing.

"What's your name?" Peter asked.

"Sheri," she replied.

Peter borrowed one of Sheri's rings and made it magically pass through a coffee stirrer. The ring was put into a paper napkin and made to disappear. Peter then asked Sheri to pick a packet of sugar from the dish on the table. Sheri chose a yellow packet of Splenda. Tearing the packet open, he produced the ring and slipped it on her finger. Sheri squealed with delight, and seemed to have forgotten about the boiling latte. He stole a peek inside her head just to be sure. The memory was on a back shelf, never to be used. He breathed a sigh of relief.

"Is it safe?" Snoop asked under his breath.

"Yes, it's safe."

Peter's Droid vibrated. Garrison calling. He took the call in the street.

"We caught one," the FBI agent said.

28
∾

Y ou caught a shadow person," Peter said breathlessly.

"Caught it dead in its tracks," Garrison replied. "We spotted it coming out the Westchester train platform and watched it run across the main concourse. There were people in the concourse, so we waited until it ran upstairs into a hallway by the west-side exits. That's when we hit the lights. You'd be amazed at how bright they can make them."

"How did it react?"

"It screamed so loud I heard it upstairs. Then it turned to stone. We cordoned off the area, and are keeping people away. My boss wants it moved out of here. He's telling me to take it to an empty hangar at Kennedy Airport so a bunch of pointy-headed scientists can stick needles in it. I didn't like the sound of that, so I decided to call you. Is that a wise idea?"

Peter panicked. Violating a ghost or spirit would upset the psychic balance of the universe. Innocent people would perish as a result, not just here, but in other parts of the world as well. "That's a bad idea. Lots of people will die in ways that you cannot possibly imagine."

"How about if we just move it down the hall to a room?"

"Don't. It will burn you. The scars will never heal."

"Well, I can't just leave it here. Too many people will see it."

"You want my help?"

"I didn't call to hear the sound of your voice. Of course I want your help."

It was not uncommon for a spirit to become trapped in this world. When that happened, psychics often rushed to the spirit's aid, and built makeshift walls around it to hide it from peering eyes. Those walls, along with a few well-placed sawhorses, usually did the trick.

"Build a wall around it using plywood and sheets of translucent plastic," Peter said. "The plastic will keep the public from seeing it. At the same time, the plastic will allow the light to filter through, which will keep the shadow person frozen."

"I want you to take a look at this thing. You game?"

"I'm game."

A cab crawled down the street looking for a fare and Peter waved the driver down. He glanced over his shoulder and saw Snoop inside the coffee shop, chatting away with Sheri. Snoop was doing a magic trick where it appeared he removed his thumb, and then made it whole. Sheri seemed absolutely enthralled. Peter waved good-bye before hopping into the backseat.

"Whatever you do, don't throw a blanket over it," Peter said. "The darkness will allow it to become unfrozen, and it will escape."

The cabbie turned around in his seat, his dreadlocks bouncing on his shoulders. "You talking to me, mon?"

"No, I wasn't. Grand Central Terminal."

The cab lurched ahead. Peter went back to his conversation. "I would also advise you not to stare at it very long, either. It will give you nightmares that will last a long time."

"I've got enough of those," Garrison said. "How soon can you get here?"

"As fast as my cabbie can drive."

Peter put away his phone. So much for taking Liza out to the movies. It was stuff like this that ruined relationships, yet he wasn't sure how to stop it.

"You're that magic guy I heard about," the driver said, spinning the wheel.

"That's me," Peter replied.

"Are you the devil? I've talked to passengers who've seen your show. They say you do weird shit, like move things with your mind, and know what people are thinking. I've heard enough of them talking to know that something ain't right."

Peter's face burned. "It's all a bunch of tricks."

"Is that so?" The cabbie took a corner at Canal and headed uptown. "I heard other drivers talking. Their passengers told them the same things. The stuff you do defies imagination and cannot be explained. If enough people believe something, it's usually true. At least in my experience it is."

Peter tried to imagine the other cabbies the driver worked with. They probably all got together after their shift was over, and had a cold beer. Peter needed this Jamaican telling those drivers that he was an ordinary guy who was adept at fooling people, and that was all he was.

The cab braked at a light. Peter said, "I want to show you something." Taking a flesh-colored hollow thumb from his pants pocket, he passed it through the partition. "This handy little device is called a thumb tip. You can buy one in any magic store. They'll actually help you mold it so it fits perfectly onto your thumb. Put it on."

It was not every day that a passenger was carrying a hollow thumb. The driver inspected it closely before slipping it onto his thumb. The plastic jarred with his dark skin.

"Now move your hand around," Peter said.

The driver waved his hand, and the thumb tip did not fall off.

"I use that to make small objects disappear," Peter said.

The driver passed the gimmick back. The light changed, and he hit the gas. "What's all this supposed to mean?" he asked.

"Do you honestly think that if I had supernatural powers that I'd carry that stupid thing around in my pocket all day long? Do you?"

The driver burst into laughter. "No, I guess not."

"Thank you."

"You really can't read minds?"

"I wish."

"Or move things around by thought control?"

"Give me a break, will you?"

"You're not in league with the Devil?"

"No, but I once dated his sister."

The driver's eyes danced in his mirror, and he slapped the wheel. He had been won over, but how many more were there like him out there? A hundred? A thousand? For all Peter knew, half the population of New York thought he had supernatural powers, and were whispering behind his back. Or maybe it was just this driver and the guys he hung out with. There was no way of knowing for sure. One day, his whole world might fall apart, and there was nothing he could do about it. It gave him an idea. Again he stuck his head through the partition.

"Change of plans," Peter said. "Take me to 320 East 62nd. I need to pick someone up."

29

The driver parked at the curb and left the meter running. Peter bounded inside. He found Liza in the living room sitting cross-legged on the Flying Carpet illusion and floating three feet above the floor. Her dark hair tied in a ponytail, eyes tightly shut, she looked like a genie that had just popped out of a bottle.

"Hey, beautiful."

Her eyes opened in surprise. "You startled me."

"Sorry. Grab your jacket. The FBI caught a shadow person running through Grand Central Terminal. Garrison wants me to have a look at it. I want you there with me."

Her face grew concerned. "But those things terrify me."

"And doctors' offices scare me."

"This is different. Shadow people are dangerous."

"So is Dr. Sierra. I need you to come along. Please do this for me."

She chewed her lip. "What if I say no?"

"I'll cry."

"Be serious, Peter."

He touched Liza's arm. "The reason we're having problems is that I keep secrets from you. If I include you in the psychic part of my life, then there won't be any secrets. You'll know everything there is to know about me."

"Will you still go to see Sierra?"

"There's a problem with Sierra. He came to the theater this afternoon with another man and started banging on the door. Snoop caught him on a surveillance camera, and called him at a restaurant across the street. Sierra told Snoop he needed to see me. He made it sound like it was life or death. What kind of doctor does that?"

"He came to the theater? That's ridiculous."

"Now do you understand why I don't trust him?"

"Who was the other man?"

"Snoop didn't get his name. Snoop played the surveillance film on his phone for me. He was an older man and walked with a cane. I think it was Hunsinger."

"You think Sierra brought his colleague to the theater?"

"That's what it looked like. It sort of scared me."

Liza shook her head in bewilderment. "His Web site sure read well. What if I pick another counselor?"

"I'll do whatever you want."

"Is that a promise? No backing out at the last minute."

"I promise."

"If I go with you now, will you protect me?"

"With my life."

They kissed on the lips, sealing the deal. Liza hopped off the flying carpet and went to the hall closet, grabbing a cashmere scarf and gloves along with a leather jacket. As they headed out the door, Peter said, "There's a cab waiting outside. Be careful what you say around the driver. He thinks I'm some kind of demon."

"Your secret's safe with me," she said.

They held hands during the cab ride to Grand Central. Liza looked happier than she had in a long time. All it had taken was a little compromise. He needed to remember that. Despite his powers, he couldn't always have things his way.

The cab dropped them off at the south entrance and they went inside. It was rush hour, with commuters dashing toward train platforms with the vigor of Olympic athletes. Garrison stood at the foot of a marble stairway leading to the second floor with a scowl on his face.

"Sorry it took us so long to get here," Peter said.

"So am I," Garrison replied. "My boss just left. I'm afraid I've got some bad news. My boss nixed your idea of keeping the shadow person under wraps. He thinks it's too dangerous, and wants the thing moved."

"Didn't you tell your boss what would happen? Didn't you warn him?"

"I tried. He doesn't get the paranormal stuff, thinks it's all a bunch of hooey."

Peter turned to Liza. "Lesson number one: No one ever listens to the psychic until it's too late."

"What's going to happen?" she asked.

"Fire and brimstone with the earth tilting on its axis. Real wrath of God stuff."

"Be serious, Peter."

"I *am* being serious. You don't mess with the spirits in any capacity." He addressed Garrison. "Where is the shadow person right now?"

"Follow me."

Garrison hurried up the marble stairs with Peter and Liza on his heels. Reaching the top, the FBI agent went down a hallway only to abruptly halt. Peter and Liza nearly crashed into him.

"What the hell," he said.

Twenty feet away, his team stood with the frozen shadow person. The team also appeared frozen, with mouths agape and arms locked at their sides, and looked like empty shells.

"Nan, Fred, Johnny," Garrison called to them.

The team did not respond.

Garrison shoved his hand into his jacket. He was going for his side-arm. Why did cops think that shooting something you didn't understand was the best alternative?

"Put your gun away," Peter said. "You'll only make it angry."

"Is that so?" Garrison said.

"Let me deal with this. I've had experience with these things."

"Peter beat one up at the theater yesterday," Liza said. "He can hurt them."

"Yeah? Well, you have my permission to hurt this one, too."

Peter started down the hall. Garrison hadn't heard a word Peter had said, and started to follow him. "Stay back," Peter said.

"I don't take orders from you. My people are in danger."

"You're in a foreign land. Act like a tourist. Okay?"

"Don't talk to me like that."

"I don't want to call your wife later, and tell her you're dead. Stay put."

"You've got a lot of nerve."

"You asked me here, didn't you?"

Garrison didn't have a good answer for that.

Peter turned to Liza. "Lesson number two: The FBI is never wrong."

"Very funny," Garrison snorted.

Liza smiled with her eyes. Peter realized how much he liked having her with him. It gave him a sense of confidence that he had not experienced before. He went down the hall toward the shadow person and cluster of FBI agents. This time, Garrison did not follow him.

He drew close to the gathering. The shadow person was smaller than its predecessors, and stood about five feet tall. Small in stature, it could not have weighed much when it was alive. The bright overhead lights had captured it in an awkward pose, and it hovered in fear against the wall. There was nothing threatening about its presence at all.

He studied Garrison's team. To his relief, their spirits were still inside Grand Central. Their frozen expressions and rigid bodies were the product of something else.

Shock.

Shock was not uncommon when dealing with the supernatural. Seeing things that did not compute could cause a mental meltdown. Even Peter dealt with it sometimes. Garrison's team needed to be brought back to earth. He started with Nan Perry, whom he knew the best.

"Did anyone ever tell you that you'd make a really good mime?" Peter asked.

Perry continued to stare straight ahead. "It's alive," she whispered.

"Excuse me?"

"This thing's alive."

"No, it's not. It's deader than dead."

"Take a look."

He followed her gaze. There was a spot on the shadow person's neck no larger than a coin. Its color was dark blue. It looked like the corner of a lapel to a shirt.

"What is that?"

"It's a piece of a blouse," Perry said. "There's more. Look at its face."

Peter got closer to the dark spirit and stared at where its face should have been. His heart leapt into his throat. A woman's eye stared back at him. It was a murky brown and filled with everlasting dread. Was this the last facial expression the shadow person had experienced before passing into the great beyond? Something told him that it was. He was look-ing death in the face, and it shook him to the core.

"That's creepy," he said under his breath.

There was more. The tip of an ear was also showing. And a finger. The middle finger, to be exact. A black substance was oozing out of it. He bent over to get a better look. The fingernail was torn, the flesh bleeding. Evil spirits were bad people who went to hell when they died. The Devil was a cruel host, and relegated his subjects to suffering and indignation. This shadow person was clearly being punished for past sins.

Then Peter noticed something else. The shadow person's wristwatch was bleeding through the darkness. An art deco Cartier. Whoever she was, she'd had good taste.

"Do you know what's going on?" Perry asked.

"Well, for starters, it isn't alive," Peter said. "What you're seeing are remnant memories and emotions that stayed behind. Think of them as leftovers."

"Of a person."

"That's right. We shed a lot when we die."

"It's not a zombie, then."

"Nope. It won't eat you."

Perry breathed a sigh of relief, and visibly relaxed. So did the other agents. The threat had passed. Or so everyone thought.

"Let's move this thing," Perry said.

"Don't touch it," Peter warned.

Perry stuck out her hand and made contact with the shadow person. Humans and spirits were not meant to physically interact, and many bad things could have happened at that moment. Perry's hand could have caught fire and been burned to a crisp, or it could have melted, with the fingers falling off like icicles. Her hand could have also disappeared, never to be seen again. This was what happened to people who touched things they weren't supposed to.

But Perry got lucky. Nothing happened to her hand. Instead, she was given an invisible shove, and sent flying down the hall. Now unfrozen, the shadow person raced up the wall, and disappeared inside an ornate light fixture. Moments later, the hallway was thrown into darkness.

"It's going to get away," Peter called out. "Call someone, and tell them to turn the light back on."

"Are you all right, Peter?" Liza called out.

"I'm fine. We're all fine."

Garrison got on his cell phone and began barking out orders. Peter could feel the shadow person's unearthly presence lurking overhead. At any moment, it could leap down, and kidnap Perry or the other FBI agents in the hall. He whispered to Perry and the others, and they formed a tight circle around him. "It won't attack you if you're standing close to me," he said.

"Attack us how?" one of the agents asked.

"You don't want to know."

The hallway light flickered to life. The shadow person had done something to the bulb, and it burned only half as brightly as before. Peter looked straight up. So did the others. *Like a bunch of tourists visiting the city for the first time,* he thought. It was almost funny.

What they saw was not meant for any tourist's eyes. The shadow person was stuck to the ceiling like a giant spider, and appeared to be gazing down at them, as if sizing up its next meal. Peter stuck his hand down into his shirt and pulled out the five-pointed star. He held the star so it was pointing directly at the evil spirit that seemed intent on harming them.

"Leave us alone," he said.

The shadow person pulled back. Peter held the star up higher and raised his voice. "Go back to where you came from. Leave us alone."

"I think it's leaving," Perry said under her breath. "Way to go."

It was a little-known fact that human beings were capable of chasing away ghosts and evil spirits. Bathing them in bright light was one way to do it. Another was to hold up a mirror and expose them to their own reflection. But the best way was with a talisman. All of these methods had been used by ghost hunters to rid dwellings of evil spirits for hundreds of years.

The five-pointed star was as powerful a talisman as you will find. The shadow person slid down the wall and slithered across the floor, passing so close to Peter's feet that he could have touched it with his shoe, had he wanted to.

"Can you brighten the lights?" Peter called to Garrison.

"We're trying to, but it's not working," Garrison called back.

The shadow person continued down the hall toward where Garrison and Liza stood at the top of the stairway leading to the main floor, its movements like a giant stingray gliding across the ocean floor. Liza stood perfectly motionless, as did Garrison. The shadow person slipped past them and disappeared down the stairs.

The eye was strange. It often saw only what it wanted to see. For the first time, Peter noticed a third person in the picture. A woman in her late twenties, with a shock of blond hair, painted eyebrows, dressed in black. She stood behind Liza and Garrison, using their bodies as a shield. In her hands was an iPhone that she was using to record what was taking place.

Was she a reporter? Or just some person who liked to film stuff and post it on YouTube? Whoever she was, she was a problem, and Peter needed to talk with her.

"Excuse me, miss? Can I speak with you for a second?"

She lowered the camera. She wore a bemused expression, like a cat that's just eaten a canary. Definitely trouble. She ran down the marble stairs without responding.

"Hey, hold on," Peter called out.

He raced down the stairs in pursuit. The young woman had reached the main floor and was running hard, her footsteps pounding the marble.

"I said stop!" Peter shouted.

At the exit, she paused to glance over her shoulder. Their eyes met, and Peter read her thoughts. Her name was Maddison O'Brien Jones, MJ to her friends, and she was a freelance journalist and a blogger. She was working on a piece that would expose Peter's psychic powers that she planned to sell to one of the New York tabloids. If they didn't bite, she'd post the story on her Web site, of which she had several thousand followers. The video was the final piece of her story, and would prove that Peter did indeed communicate with the spirit world.

MJ ran outside. Peter was five seconds behind. The sidewalks were mobbed and she was nowhere to be seen. A sinking feeling came over him. His psychic powers were about to be revealed, and his world turned upside down. He'd never be able to lead a normal life again.

He had to find MJ, and talk her out of this. He had an idea, and looked to the sky.

"Call me," he said to the clouds.

30

is cell phone vibrated. It was Holly, calling on the landline from her apartment. He pressed the icon on the screen that let him answer the call.

"Need some help?" the young witch asked.

Liza burst through the exit and ran toward him. While Peter was willing to share things with Liza, there were some things about his life that he wasn't yet ready to talk about; his strained relationship with Holly was one of them. "I'm going to have to call you back," he said.

"I see lovely Liza has joined you," Holly said. "Why don't I start texting?"

He ended the call. Liza grabbed his arm, looking panicked. "Who was that blonde, and why was she filming you inside Grand Central?"

"Her name is MJ, and she's a blogger writing an exposé on my psychic abilities. She was shooting a video of me with the shadow person, which she plans to put on her Web site."

"Oh, my God, Peter, what are you going to do?"

"Move to the country and grow vegetables."

"You have to stop her."

Peter wasn't quite sure how to accomplish that. It was a free country, and MJ could publish anything on her blog she wanted about him. There were many amazing things that he could do with his psychic powers, but making people do his bidding was not one of them. His cell phone vibrated and an icon appeared on the screen indicating that he had a text message.

"Let me see who this is," he said.

It was Holly. No one was better at finding people than a witch. She'd tracked MJ to the bar of a trendy Mexican joint called Zengo on Third Avenue a few blocks away. MJ had gotten settled into a booth and was reading the bar's long list of exotic tequilas available for sampling. *She's going to have a victory drink on me,* Peter thought.

"Anything important?" Liza asked.

"Just Snoop checking in. I need to think this through. Let's go get something to eat."

"You're hungry?"

"Starving."

Liza acted puzzled. Food was the last thing on her mind right now. Peter took her arm and headed down the sidewalk. Reaching the corner of 42nd Street, he took a left, and went east.

"You're acting weird, Peter," Liza said.

He pretended not to hear her. They came to Third Avenue and walked south to Zengo's on the west side of the street. He'd read about the restaurant but never eaten there. One of the partners was the famous opera singer Placido Domingo, which seemed unusual, considering the menu was Mexican.

They went inside, and Peter canvassed the restaurant. He did not spot MJ sitting at any of the booths or up at the bar. Had Holly made a mistake?

He approached the hostess stand. A pair of female eyes looked up from a seating chart filled with Xs and Os. "Table for two?" the hostess asked.

"Do you have a bar?" Peter asked.

"La Biblioteca is our house bar, and is on the lower level."

"Does it serve tequila?"

"It's their specialty. It has over four hundred brands on the menu."

"Sounds like our kind of place. Thanks for the help."

"Are you going to tell me what's going on?" Liza asked as they walked away. "And you hate tequila. It makes you puke."

"Only when I eat the worm in the bottom of the bottle," Peter said.

Liza reluctantly followed him down the winding stairway to the bar. It was a cavernous space filled with polished dark wood, the walls lined with display cabinets featuring expensive agave drinks. Peter searched for MJ among the booths. She was in the back of the room, working on a drink while reading a menu. Liza tugged on his sleeve.

"Tell me what's going on," she demanded.

"Our snooping reporter friend is here," he said.

"Where?"

"In the back corner in a booth. She's sitting by herself, getting ready to order."

Liza had a look. "You're right—she's over there. How did you find her?"

Peter could not tell Liza that this was Holly's doing while their relationship was having so many problems. So he told a lie instead. He hoped it was the last one he told her.

"My psychic powers sometimes let me do things that I normally could never do. Like find people who are running away from me," he explained. "MJ left a psychic trail, and I just followed it. I'd explain it to you, but I don't understand it myself."

"Wow. That's some power to have."

"Well, let's just say that I'm probably never going to lose my car keys. Now comes the hard part. We need to convince MJ that I'm not really a psychic."

"How are we going to do that?"

"Easy. Just follow my lead."

The snooping blogger did not look up from her menu as they approached. She'd already polished off her drink and was ready for another. In his best waiter voice, Peter said, "May I get you a refill?"

"Please," she said. "Wait a minute—you're not my waiter."

"No, I'm not. This is my girlfriend, Liza. May we join you?"

Peter and Liza sat down, effectively blocking MJ into the booth. Her eyes darted back and forth liked a caged animal's. In a trembling voice she said, "How did you find me so fast?"

Peter's mind had been racing since they'd entered the restaurant. He needed to tell MJ a yarn, and it needed to be convincing enough for her to buy on the spot. That was going to take some doing, and he was glad he had Liza alongside to back up his fabricated story.

"One of my assistants was standing outside Grand Central when you ran out," he explained. "He decided to follow you, and told me you were here."

"Your assistant?" MJ asked suspiciously. "You don't work Mondays."

MJ had done her homework, and he wondered how much more she knew. Holly was scrying on him and MJ was spying on him. He wasn't sure which was worse, and he said, "You're right. My theater is dark on Mondays, which is when I rehearse new material. I've been working on an hour-long special for HBO that features illusions that I perform around New York. I was inside Grand Central with my team practicing a new illusion when you caught us in the act."

"That black thing I saw was a trick?" MJ said. "Gimme me a break. That thing was real. You're into dark magic, and have these amazing powers. Admit it."

Peter gently kicked Liza beneath the table, and she picked up without missing a beat.

"What you saw inside Grand Central was a hologram," Liza said in a matter-of-fact tone. "It's a brand-new illusion in Peter's show, and he was trying to see if it would work outside the theater. Unfortunately, there are still some kinks to be worked out."

MJ leaned across the table to stare at Liza. "Are you into dark magic, too?"

"Not at all," Liza said with a frozen smile.

"Then why are you lying for him?"

"What you saw is a trick," Liza said, not backing down. "If you publish a story that says Peter has some kind of weird powers you're going to look like a fool."

"Is that so."

MJ's face flushed. Peter tried to read her mind but found her thoughts blocked off. The young blogger dug an iPhone from her purse and punched a command into it. She showed them the screen. "I've been collecting videos of you. I took this one at your theater on Saturday when that black thing jumped out of the Dollhouse trick. Take a look."

On the small screen appeared a video of Peter striking the shadow person during Saturday's matinee. How had MJ gotten into the theater without Snoop spotting her?

"Here's another one of you doing real mind reading," MJ said.

On the screen appeared another video taken inside the theater of Peter reading the mind of a woman from the audience. It was followed by an interview of the woman outside the theater on the sidewalk. The woman told the camera how Peter had known things about her past that not a single living person knew, and how could he not be a psychic?

"Want to see some more?" MJ asked when the video was over.

"How did you get inside my theater on Saturday?" Peter asked.

"Trade secret."

"I could have you arrested for trespassing."

"I wasn't trespassing."

"Taking videos is strictly prohibited during the show," Liza jumped in.

"So sue me."

"I just might do that," Peter said.

"There's more," MJ said with a smirk. "I interviewed your classmates from private school and several of your teachers. They said you seemed to know the answers to questions before they were asked. One of your class-mates said he once heard you talking to a ghost."

"Are you going to put that on your blog as well?" Peter asked.

"It's all going in," MJ said.

Against one accusation Peter knew he had a fighting chance. But against a whole slew of accusations dating back to childhood he had little chance. MJ hadn't just gone digging into his private life, she'd used an earth mover, and gathered enough secret information to expose him to the public and ruin whatever semblance of a normal life he enjoyed.

He started to laugh. It was the only way to respond without caving in. He nudged Liza with his toe, and she started to laugh as well.

"You don't fool me," MJ told them.

Peter rose from the table. MJ had resumed reading the menu while sipping her drink. She'd won this round, and she knew it.

"I'll be right back," he said.

He found the restroom and splashed cold water on his face. Drying himself with a paper towel, he stared long and hard at his reflection in the mirror above the sink.

"Mirror, mirror on the wall, tell me what the hell to do."

His cell phone vibrated. He knew who it was without having to look at the face.

"I'm listening," he said.

"Why don't I cast a spell on her, and wipe her memory out?" Holly suggested. "I've gotten rather good at that, you know."

"Will it harm her?" Peter asked.

"Of course. She'll be a blathering idiot for the rest of her life."

Peter groaned into the cell phone.

"All right, how about if I just make her blind?" Holly said.

"You're not helping."

"Spoilsport."

"Any other ideas? Come on, I'm in a real bind."

"Sorry, but I'm afraid that's all I can offer you. The thing I don't understand is, how did she get into your theater? Your security is awfully tight."

Peter had been wondering that very thing himself. His security was so good that it had caught Dr. Sierra knocking on the front door that morning. So how had MJ snuck in and filmed him so many times without being spotted? After a moment the answer hit him. She'd had help.

"I've got to go," he said.

Ending the call, he pulled up Snoop's number. His assistant answered with dance music playing in the background. He was back at the pop-up club getting ready for tonight.

"How long have you and MJ been an item?" Peter asked his assistant.

"Who told you I was dating MJ?" Snoop said.

"I found out the hard way. Your girlfriend is writing an exposé about me. She used you to get into the theater. She's going to tell the world that I'm a psychic, and ruin everything."

"What? MJ's a reporter?"

"Afraid so. You once told me that there wasn't a computer that you couldn't hack. Does that hold true for private computers as well?"

"Sure. They're the easiest to get into. All you need is the person's e-mail address."

"Then do it."

"Do what?"

"Do I have to spell it out for you in black and white?"

The line went silent. Then Snoop said, "But that's a crime."

"Like you haven't committed crimes before? Call me when you're done."

Peter ended the call and headed back to the booth. MJ had gotten another tequila drink and had a sly smile on her face. *Just you wait*, he thought as he sat down.

He picked up a menu and studied the array of tasty appetizers. MJ was a formidable opponent, and he felt certain that this wasn't the last time their paths would cross. To be forewarned was to be forearmed, and he pulled out his cell phone, and placed it on the table.

A minute later, it vibrated. Snoop calling. He answered it by saying, "All done?"

"Yup," Snoop replied.

"What about backup?"

"That's gone, too."

"See you tomorrow."

"Do I still have my job?"

"Of course. Just next time be more careful."

Peter put his phone away. MJ was watching him. The smile had left her face. She was smart enough to know that something had gone down that wasn't in her favor. He wondered how long it would take her to figure out what it was. He would have liked to have been there when that happened, but he had more important things to do, and he rose from the table.

"Time to get out of Dodge," he said.

Liza rose as well. Without a word to MJ, they walked out of the bar. Under her breath, Liza said, "Are you just going to leave? She's going to ruin you."

"Not today," he whispered back.

"What do you mean? What did you do?"

"She can't hurt me anymore. I'll explain in the cab."

Peter gave MJ a parting look. The young blogger was on her iPhone trying to retrieve the clandestine videos she'd shot of him. She'd spent a great deal of time composing her exposé, and it seemed a shame that it had all been erased in the amount of time it took to strike a keyboard. She slapped the table in anger and looked across the room. Their eyes locked. If looks could have killed, he would have been six feet under pushing up daisies.

He waved pleasantly and headed up the stairs.

31

〜

Lying in bed that night, Liza asked, "Is your life always this exciting?"

"Hardly," Peter murmured, his eyelids heavy.

"Will it go back to normal soon?"

"Boy, I sure hope so."

"Can you look into the future, and make sure? My heart beat's still racing."

"Ask me tomorrow, okay?"

Liza rested her head on his chest and stared at the grisly images on the flat-screen TV. They were halfway through season two of *The Walking Dead*, one of the better zombie shows in recent years. They had come to the series late, and rented the episodes from Netflix. They were both hooked on the show, only Liza didn't like the fact that in the first season the zombies had staggered around with wooden legs, while in the second they ran like deer. She was thinking of going online to post a negative comment about it.

The episode ended with a zombie getting its head shot off, just like all the other episodes had. Peter started to ask Liza if she wanted to watch the next episode, when he realized she was fast asleep. She looked like an angel, and he kissed her forehead.

"Thanks for not running away," he whispered.

He killed the TV and the picture was reduced to a tiny blip, which hung there for a while before vanishing. The bedroom fell dark. The day had started out lousy but ended well. While he hadn't stopped the shadow people or found Dr. Death, he'd reunited with Liza, and that was all that mattered. Alone, there was only so much he could accomplish. But with Liza by his side, just about anything seemed possible.

He didn't really understand it. He'd had plenty of girlfriends before

Liza, but none of the relationships had been this deep. She was more than just his lover and soul mate. She was also his assistant, and with him almost every waking moment of every day. His previous assistants had found him too demanding, and had all quit. Not Liza. She'd embraced the challenge of performing on stage every night. It was hard work, and to her credit, she'd never once screwed up a trick.

He did eight shows a week, fifty-one weeks a year, along with a few dozen private events sprinkled into his schedule. Liza had been with him for two years, and not made a single mistake. Had she ever dropped a prop or forgotten a cue? Had she ever not floated perfectly in midair, or not magically jumped out of an empty box when she was supposed to?

He couldn't remember a single time when she hadn't been perfect. Not one. But that was impossible. Everyone who performed magic made mistakes. It was part of the business, and there was no getting around it. It was how you learned, and grew.

Yet Liza didn't make mistakes. Not any that he'd been aware of. The matinee this past Saturday was a perfect example. She'd been hidden inside the secret compartment of the Dollhouse illusion when the shadow person had kidnapped her spirit and taken her into the future. It had been a hair-raising experience that would have sent anyone else to the hospital. Not Liza. Not only had she escaped from Dr. Death, she'd also ended the trick correctly, and taken her bow beside him.

He decided that he was being irrational. Liza made mistakes just like everyone else, and he just wasn't catching them. Love was blind that way.

A noise from downstairs lifted his head. A tinny clanging sound. His hand instinctively touched the five-pointed star hanging around his neck. Then he checked for the star around Liza's neck. It was there as well. They were both protected.

He slipped out of bed and into his bathrobe. The floor was cold to his bare feet. Down the stairs he went to the first floor, the noise growing louder with each step. His destination was the living room, where Butch sat on the mantel banging his toy cymbals. He touched the hidden switch behind the panda's neck and the music stopped.

The main keypad for the security system resided in the foyer. He checked it. The place was locked up tight. No intruders had slipped in. At least, not any human intruders.

He inspected the downstairs rooms, expecting to see his favorite things smashed to bits, or at least the illusion of that. But that wasn't the case. Each room was how he'd left it before going to bed. In his study the computer was turned on, the screen saver of Harry Houdini hanging upside down in a straitjacket lighting up the darkened room.

His last stop was the kitchen. The pantry doors were wide open. He stuck his head in to see if any food items were missing. He clearly remembered closing the pantry doors before coming to bed. Had the shadow person reopened them?

If so, why?

He knew a thing or two about ghosts and spirits. The longer they remained stuck on earth, the more cranky and mean they became. If a ghost or spirit stayed too long, it turned into a destructive force, capable of all sorts of mayhem. The shadow people had impressed him as these very types of destructive forces. Yet their behavior was also strange. One had thrown a shoe out the window at him, while another had raided his kitchen pantry.

Cold air danced around his bare legs. Icy, invisible fingers touched his skin. He felt himself drawn to the other side of the kitchen and stood at the window facing the courtyard. The courtyard was his private sanctuary, and contained a wrought-iron table and two wrought-iron chairs. When the weather was warmer, he and Liza ate breakfast there and split the newspaper. His breath fogged the window. Liza's chair was now occupied by a shadow person. A piece of its face was visible, and a piece of its hand. It was the same evil spirit he'd encountered in Grand Central.

The shadow person lifted its hand in a macabre salute. Peter felt his blood start to boil. How many times were these damn things going to invade his home? The only solution was to destroy every last one of them, and he was more than ready to do that.

The back door had a variety of locks. He opened each of them and stepped outside. From the foyer, the security system started to wail. He decided that was a good thing. Liza didn't need to be sleeping while a shadow person was lurking around.

The shadow person floated out of the chair, its body a quivering mass. It almost seemed frightened of him. A psychic could get rid of an otherworldly spirit through physical force. It wasn't pretty, but dealings with the dead seldom were. As he grabbed it with his hands, its essence turned to a vaporlike substance, and slipped out of his grasp as if melting away.

"No, you don't." With the tips of his fingers, Peter pinched the visible piece of flesh on the shadow person's face, and held it tight. It felt like worn leather.

"How do you like that?" he said triumphantly.

The shadow person wiggled and squirmed, but could not escape. He made his other hand into a fist. The shadow person let out a tortured sound as if begging for mercy. Could it be reasoned with? He was willing to give it a try. He spoke where its ear should have been.

"Leave me and my friends alone. If you don't go away, I'll destroy you. Do you understand?"

"Peter, who are you talking to? What's going on? Why is the alarm ringing?"

Liza stood in the doorway with a sleepy expression on her face. She wore one of his dress shirts and her favorite Garfield slippers. She stepped outside.

"What is that you're holding?" she asked.

"I caught one of them," he replied. "Please stay back."

"Oh, my God, you really did. This is so creepy. What is that thing on its face?"

"Skin."

"Ecch. Why are you holding it?"

"It was the only way I could stop it from escaping. Want to touch it? I dare you."

"You're not funny, Peter. That thing is dangerous. Please get rid of it."

The shadow person had shrunk in size, and did not seem the least bit harmful now. That was another illusion, courtesy of the dark world which it inhabited, and he twisted the piece of skin as if to rip it from its face. It screamed and began to corkscrew into the ground.

"You're hurting it," Liza said in alarm.

"And your point is?"

"No, Peter. I can't let you do that. No matter how evil it is."

He disagreed, but was not going to have an argument over it. He'd shown the shadow person he meant business, and maybe that was all he really needed to do. He released the piece of skin and watched the shadow person float straight up into the night sky. It sailed higher and higher into the night like a lost balloon. Stars shone down, their light passing straight through it.

The threat had passed, and Peter felt himself relax.

A glimmer of light caught his eye. From far above, a tiny object began to fall noiselessly through space. As the object entered the courtyard, Liza let out a shriek.

"Watch out!"

Peter jumped in front of Liza and stuck his hand into the air. The object landed in his palm and he wondered if the flesh would burn off or his fingers might explode. But neither of those things happened. All he felt was a slight stinging sensation.

He brought his hand down and stared. Liza let out a gasp. His own sharp intake of breath was equally loud. Not a meteor or a falling star, but a lady's art deco Cartier watch. It was the same watch the shadow person in Grand Central had been wearing. Its face was cracked, the hands of time stopped at ten minutes of ten.

"What does it mean?" Liza asked.

Peter wasn't sure. The world was filled with the Devil's playthings. If the watch was such an object, it would have a simmering aura around it, which was in fact the Devil's fingerprints.

The watch had no such aura. It was a perfectly normal timepiece, as far as he could tell. Had the shadow person dropped it during her ascent into space? Or had it purposely fallen from her wrist? There was no way to be certain why it now rested in his hand.

He knew only one thing for certain. He was freezing to death. He grabbed Liza by the arm, and pulled her inside.

PART III

THE
LITTLE DEMON

32

Central Park was a lush oasis within the city's concrete jungle. Here, joggers ran at all times of the day and night, dogs were walked, lovers sought refuge, and horse-drawn carriages clip-clopped on twisting roads designed to slow motorists down.

Milly Adams was a woman of rituals. Each morning, she awoke at the crack of dawn, fixed herself a poached egg over toast, ate it while reading the morning paper, and when she was done, left her apartment and journeyed across the street to a well-worn bench that sat beside one of the park's most popular footpaths, where she stayed for the next hour or so depending upon the weather and her mood, talking to no one, enjoying the sights.

It was here that Peter found Milly at eight o'clock the next morning. The park was filled with joggers huffing and puffing their way into shape, and Milly was watching them pass by with a keen eye, as if she knew their futures with just a casual glance. Peter asked if he could join her.

"Of course." Milly patted the spot beside her. "Sit down right here."

Peter took the spot. Milly had helped raise him, and was the closest thing to a mother that he had. He hated spoiling her morning, but didn't see that he had any other choice. Holly was out of control, and Milly needed to rein her niece in before Holly ruined his life.

"I need to talk to you about Holly," he said.

"You sound terribly solemn. Is she still scrying on you?"

"Yes, yes, and yes. I made the mistake of encouraging her yesterday when I discovered a reporter spying on me. Now she keeps texting me every five minutes."

"But she's love in with you, and says you have feelings for her."

"Of course I have feelings for Holly. I also have feelings for you. But that doesn't make us in love, does it?"

Milly laughed under her breath. "I suppose not. But Holly is young and infatuated. You need to go gently with her. Let her down easy, as they say."

Milly did not understand the gravity of what was taking place. Holly had held him against his will in her apartment through the use of a spell. She was also using her powers to stalk him, and that didn't feel like any kind of love he'd experienced before.

"Holly won't listen to me," he said in a quiet but firm voice. "I have enough problems in my life right now, and she's only making them worse. Please talk to her, Milly."

Milly drew back, clearly alarmed. "I suppose I could call her."

"I would be forever in your debt."

"What exactly would you like me to say?"

"Ask her to stop intruding. Order her, if you have to. Just make her do it."

They fell silent. On the other side of the path, a dozen feisty black crows lined the limb of an oak tree. They were the jackdaw variety, and perched in a militarylike formation. They'd migrated with Milly from the town of Ipswich, Massachusetts, decades ago, and had taken up residence in the park across the street from her apartment. Witches had many unusual powers, including the ability to hold sway over dogs, cats, and birds. The crows were Milly's pets, and would have done anything their master asked.

"Are you implying that Holly can't be reasoned with?" Milly asked.

"Holly is out of control. She's messing with my life, and refuses to stop. I'm afraid if I talk with her, I'll lose my temper, and ruin whatever's left of our friendship."

"So you still care for her."

"How could I not?"

"But she's making you miserable."

"That's the understatement of the year."

"A truer definition of love I've never heard."

Peter gritted his teeth. Milly was letting her feelings for her niece cloud her judgment. It was understandable considering that they were both witches, and that Milly had trained Holly to cast spells, scry, and perform other strange rituals that made up the witch's playbook. Milly would side with Holly no matter what her niece had done, and he rose from the bench.

"I need to go. Thanks for listening."

"Ever since you were a child, you've run away from your troubles," Milly said. "It's a defense mechanism, I suppose. Well, dear Peter, you can't run away from this. You've been in love with Holly since she was a little girl. I saw it one night when you were babysitting for her, after I'd come home from the theater. The way you looked at her told her you were in love. But since she was much younger than you, and you were a proper young gentleman, you did not act on your impulses. Admit it."

"That was a long time ago," he said defensively.

"Love never dies."

Milly was right. He still had strong feelings for Holly. If he hadn't, he'd have found some nasty way to blow her off. But he couldn't do that to Holly. He cared about her too much to cause her pain. Maybe Milly was right, maybe he loved Holly more than he realized.

"Yes, I love Holly," he said, "but I love Liza more. We live together, for Christ's sake, and she's my best friend. Why can't you see that?"

"You love Liza more *now*," Milly said. "But that might change. Liza is normal, and you are not. I hate to be the bearer of bad news, but relationships with nonpsychics don't work out, at least none that I've ever heard about. Don't throw away your feelings for Holly just yet."

"Liza and I are doing great," he said. "We're a team."

"How long have you and Liza been together?"

"Two years."

"And how long has she known you're different?"

"I told her last month. It wasn't easy, but we're working it out."

"How much does she know?"

"Enough."

"Everything?"

"No, not everything."

"So you haven't told her the true origin of your parents' powers, or yours."

Peter felt the air escape from his lungs. "Not yet."

"Still keeping secrets from her? That will never work in a million years."

"I'm going to tell her. I just have to find the right time and place to do it."

"Oh, no, here he comes," Milly said under her breath.

Milly's eyes shifted their focus as an elderly fellow wearing gray sweats and a sweatshirt tied around his waist came jogging down the path. He was downright handsome for his age, with a mane of snow-white hair and a runner's lean physique. A smile lit up his face at the sight of Milly. Cupid's arrow had struck, Peter guessed.

"You didn't tell me you had a boyfriend," Peter said. "He's cute."

"The man is practically stalking me. I can't stand him."

"You've been out with him?"

"Just once. Dinner and a movie. It was a terrible mistake."

"You made it through dinner and a movie? I'd say you're doing great. Introduce me."

"I'll do no such thing."

"Come on. Love never dies."

"Be still."

Milly's beau was veering toward their bench, ready to strike up a conversation. Milly was having none of it, and raised a crooked finger to ward him off. In all the world, there was no greater force than a witch's crooked finger, at least not that he knew of. With that single finger, oceans could be parted and skies made to darken. It was a power not to be used lightly, and he was surprised that Milly used it now. From the oak trees a single kamikaze crow exploded in a beeline for the elderly gentleman's perfectly coifed head. He saw the bird coming in time to halt his forward progress and raise his hands in self-defense, exactly what Milly had intended.

"Go away," the man said.

The bird did the opposite, and continued to buzz his head, while doing arcing somersaults befitting an aerial show. Peter could not help but laugh under his breath.

"You think this is funny?" Milly scolded him.

"I was thinking of filming it, putting it on YouTube."

"You'll do no such thing!"

Love is blind. It was also stupid, deaf, and incredibly dumb. Milly's beau would not give up, his feelings for the old witch too great. He came toward them while continuing to do battle with the crow, his arms flailing like a crazy man just released from an asylum. Milly raised her crooked finger again. More crows exploded out of the trees and added to the first bird's aerial assault, forming a cloud of black around the poor man.

"Have them pluck his eyes out," Peter suggested. "That will do the trick."

"Don't think I haven't considered it," Milly said with a stern face. "I made the mistake of giving him my phone number. He won't stop calling me."

"You gave him your phone number? This sounds serious."

"A moment of weakness."

Milly's beau continued to inch toward the bench. There was no doubt in Peter's mind that this man was truly in love with Milly. There was also no doubt that Milly had found him attractive. So why was she trying to scare the fellow half to death?

Milly raised her crooked finger a third time. A barking dog ran down the path trailing a leash. Dogs in New York came in three sizes: large, medium, and symbolic. The dog belonged to the third category, and could have fit comfortably in a lady's handbag.

The barking mutt nipped at Milly's beau's ankles. Canines were clearly his weakness, and he began to head back the way he'd come, but not before glancing over his shoulder and waving good-bye. He'd be back tomorrow, Peter was sure of it.

The crows returned to the trees and quieted down. Taking a tissue from her purse, Milly blew her nose. Her eyes were wet with tears.

"What's wrong?" Peter asked.

She took a moment to gather herself. When she spoke, her voice was filled with pain. "Back when I lived in Ipswich, I knew a man named Henry Quinton. Henry was decent and strong and a perfectly normal fellow, and I absolutely adored him. He was a banker, and made a nice living, had a boat and a membership at a country club. We dated for a while, then one day out of the blue, he got down on his knee, and popped the big question.

"I wanted so desperately to say yes! Having a normal life seemed terribly attractive to me. But for it to work, I knew that Henry had to know who I was. That trust had to be established from the start. It was the only way a marriage could possibly work.

"So I sat dear Henry down and told him the whole story. It wasn't easy, but I did it. I even did a little demonstration for him, and persuaded a stray cat to do tricks for us. Henry was stunned, to say the least." She paused to wipe her eyes. "A few days later he broke it off. No reason was offered, nor did I need to hear one. The act itself spoke volumes. I moved to New York City soon after, and have never been home since."

"I'm so sorry, Milly."

She put her hand on his arm. "I didn't tell you this story for sympathy, but as a warning. What happened to me can happen to you and Liza. And if she breaks your heart, your life will never be the same." Milly glanced at her watch and shook her head. "I must be gone. Think about what I've told you. Don't break things off with Holly just yet. You might regret it one day."

Milly rose from her spot on the bench and Peter did as well. She offered a peck on the cheek and the faintest of smiles. She was in his corner, he realized, and always would be.

"Good-bye, Milly. Be safe," he said.

"And you as well, dear boy," she replied.

33

Peter escorted Milly out of the park, and watched her cross the street to the Dakota. Only after she'd gone inside the building did he hunt for his limo. Herbie had parked in a striped No Parking zone at the corner of Columbus and 72nd Street. Limos were status symbols in New York, and drivers could park just about anywhere, and not get towed.

Peter climbed in and made himself comfortable in the backseat. His driver looked preoccupied, with an open textbook in his lap. The partition slid back.

"Where to, boss?" Herbie asked.

"Let's go home. What are you reading?"

"A book on accounting. I'm taking some night classes at CCNY. I'm studying entertainment management."

"They really have classes devoted to that?"

"Sure do. Most entertainers are bad businesspeople, present company excluded."

"How do you know that I'm not a bad businessperson?"

"Well, you're not broke."

The truth be known, he still didn't know how to balance a checkbook, and relied on Liza to take care of the household finances while a team of well-paid accountants kept track of the money he made at the theater. They were soon gliding down Broadway. There were many people like Herbie in the city. They worked long days, yet still managed to pursue other careers during their off-hours. New York was a city of dreams, and everyone had a dream he or she was chasing. Not so long ago he'd been one of those dreamers, and knew how powerful the urge could be.

His cell phone vibrated. He sometimes thought of his cell phone as a little pet that clawed his leg whenever it craved attention. It was Liza. Despite what Milly had said, he believed their relationship really did have a chance. Psychics could have relationships with nonpsychics. It just took a lot of work, no different from any other relationship he'd ever had.

"I'm on my way home," he said by way of greeting.

"Good. You need to get here soon," Liza said.

"What's wrong? You sound stressed out."

"I *am* stressed out. We have company."

He and Liza rarely entertained at home, preferring the solitude of the brownstone after the labors of performing the show each night. He didn't like the sound of this, and sat up in his seat. "And who might that be?"

"Dr. Sierra and his friend Hunsinger are here."

"You can't be serious. What are they doing there in my home?"

"You're losing your temper. Please calm down."

"What did you expect me to do? Break out in song?"

"Peter, control yourself."

"I'm sorry. Now tell me, what are they doing there?"

"I forgot to cancel our session this morning. Dr. Sierra had asked Hunsinger to come to his office and meet with us. When we didn't show, they decided to come here. I stupidly gave Dr. Sierra's receptionist our address when I booked our session."

"Why didn't you just slam the door in his face?"

"I couldn't. Dr. Sierra begged me to let him in. He made it sound like life and death."

Peter's blood started to boil like so much bad poison. His brownstone was his sanctuary where he went to escape from the world. Sierra and Hunsinger had no right to be there. In the mirror he caught Herbie giving him an eyeful. He twirled a finger, and the limo accelerated.

"Where are they now?" he asked through clenched teeth.

"Sitting at the kitchen table. I made them a pot of coffee."

"That was nice of you. Maybe they'd like some pancakes."

"Please don't be angry. I went with my heart, and my heart said let them in."

"Why not tell them to go to a restaurant? I would have met them there. Why let them in?"

"Hunsinger is very frail and he can hardly breathe. I think he may be dying."

"So?"

"Peter, this isn't like you. These men want to speak with you, that's all. Why are you so afraid of talking to them? What harm can it cause?"

Since he was a kid, he'd lived in other people's homes, a year in one apartment, the next year in another apartment. He never had his own room or furniture that was his. He'd longed for those things, and for a special place to call home. The brownstone was that place, and he didn't want men like Sierra or his friend to step foot inside.

Liza broke the silence. "Do you want me to throw them out?"

"No, let me," he said.

Sometimes, mind reading was easy. Herbie knew exactly what was on his employer's mind as he pulled to the curb in front of the brownstone. Throwing the limo into Park, he hopped out and stood on the sidewalk with his arms outstretched. As Peter climbed out, Herbie grabbed him in a bear hug. Herbie was a big man, and made Peter his prisoner.

"Boss, calm down. You act like you're gonna hurt someone," his driver said.

"I just might."

"Ain't worth it. Trust me, I know."

As a teen, Herbie had run with a gang and had shot a man. He had done hard time in a maximum security prison called Sing Sing, and had come out a changed man. He spoke from experience, and Peter took a deep breath, and forced himself to calm down. His driver smiled sheepishly and released him.

"Feel better?" Herbie asked.

"Come to mention it, yes. You're a great hugger."

"Thanks, boss. Not mad at me, are you?"

"No. Thanks for doing that."

Peter headed up the front steps. He had a temper, no doubt about it, and he was fortunate to have people like Herbie there to stop him when his emotions got the best of him. The door opened and Liza came out wearing drab workout clothes.

"You okay?" she asked.

"I'm managing."

She led him down the hallway to the kitchen, where his two un-wanted guests sat at the table sipping java. Both looked up as if startled out of a daydream. Sierra was the first to rise and seemed apprehensive and more than a little nervous about being here.

"I'm sorry to come barging into your home like this," Sierra said.

"It must be important," Peter heard himself say.

"It is. Please let me introduce my friend. This is Richard Hunsinger."

The second man slowly came out of his chair. He was little more than skin and bones, and wore a black shirt buttoned to his neck, and black slacks that hung loosely around his waist. His hair was flecked with spots of white that looked like snowflakes, his eyes sallow and pale.

"Hello," Peter said stiffly.

"Hello, Peter," his guest replied. "Do you remember me?"

"No. Should I?"

"We met long ago. You and your parents came to see me. Think hard."

"Is this a quiz?"

"It will be easier this way. Please," Hunsinger said.

"How long ago was this?"

"You had just celebrated your seventh birthday."

Peter tried to imagine a younger version of Hunsinger. After a few moments, it dawned on him who this person was. Hunsinger was the bogeyman he'd been seeing in his dreams since he was a kid, the strange man in black who'd made him cry.

In his dream, Peter was in a study with a scary painting of Jesus Christ hanging on the cross. Jesus's face was filled with so much pain that he'd avoided staring at it. Beneath the painting sat a man wearing black clothing and the gravest of expressions. The man motioned for Peter to step forward, only Peter wouldn't budge. The man gently took Peter by the hand, and pulled the boy toward him. Peter had started to cry. His parents were standing nearby, and he looked to them for help. His mother was crying as well. But she would not help him.

A strange dream, for sure. But now the young magician knew other-wise. It had actually happened. Hunsinger was real, and had known his parents. For that reason alone, Peter needed to hear what the man had to say. Maybe then the dream would go away, and be replaced by some other unexplained mystery from his youth.

"I remember you now," Peter said. "My parents brought me to see you, although to be honest, I have no earthly idea why. Did I do something wrong?"

Hunsinger picked up his coffee cup as if to take a drink. Instead, he stared into its depths as if it held the secret to the universe. He had the kind of honest face that Peter associated with people with a clean conscience. He'd not met many people he could say that about.

Hunsinger looked up. "Do you remember anything that happened?"

"All I have left are dreams."

"I hope your dreams are not painful."

"Actually, they are. You made me cry."

"It was a difficult time. Dr. Sierra met with your parents on several occasions, and he referred them to me. Your parents brought you to me, and I examined you and gave them my opinion." His voice had gone weak, and he paused to catch his breath. "Dr. Sierra and I always wondered what became of you. When Dr. Sierra called to tell me that he'd found you, I asked him to arrange a meeting. I hope you don't mind."

"At first I did mind, but now I'm glad you came," Peter said. "Now, would you please tell me who you are, and what this is about? The suspense is killing me."

"Of course. You see, I'm a priest."

34

Peter could not have been more confused. His mother and father weren't Catholic. Why on earth had they taken him to see a priest? "Why did my parents come to see you? Were they thinking of converting to Catholicism?"

Hunsinger stole a glance at Sierra. *Where to begin?* his facial expression seemed to say. After a moment his eyes returned to Peter's face. "If you don't mind, I need to sit down. My body is frail, and I am unable to stand for long periods of time."

The priest lowered himself into his chair. He was sickly and moved in slow motion. The fact that he'd ventured out in such poor health to meet Peter was not lost on the young magician.

"Can I interest either of you gentlemen in more coffee?" Peter asked.

The offer brought a smile to both their faces, Liza's also.

"Another cup of your delicious coffee would be splendid," the priest replied.

"I would love another cup as well," Sierra said.

"Me, too," Liza chimed in.

Peter fixed a fresh pot and served his guests and Liza, then pulled up a chair to the table. His heart was racing and he could hear a bass line pounding in his ears. Life was filled with unexplained mysteries which we carried with us to our graves. One of those mysteries was about to be explained to him. Liza sat on the windowsill overlooking the courtyard, content to listen as Peter's past unfolded.

"Perhaps I should go first, since it was me your parents first came to see," Sierra began. "As you and Liza know, I am a marriage counselor by profession, and I specialize in dealing with relationship issues. One day, your parents appeared in my office, and said they were having problems, which is nothing new in my line of work. They were both rather vague about the situation, and seemed to be having difficulty coming out in the open and discussing it. Whatever this problem was, I could tell it was affecting them deeply, and harming their marriage. As our session wound down, I bluntly asked them to tell me what was going on. If they were unwilling to do this, I said, then there was no point in their coming back, since I couldn't help people who couldn't be honest with themselves."

Peter stared at the table. It sounded like an echo of his own problems with Liza. "Did they finally tell you what was going on?"

"Your mother broke the spell and explained the situation," Sierra said. The problem, it seems, was you."

Peter drew back in his chair. "Was I causing problems?"

"I'm afraid so. Your parents were beside themselves as to what to do. It was tearing them apart, so they decided to come and see me."

"How bad were the things I was doing?"

"Very bad, I'm afraid."

"Did they spell them out?"

"No, but they alluded to them. Don't you remember?"

"Not at all. I must have repressed the memories."

"That is not uncommon in violent children," Sierra said.

The kitchen fell quiet. A sense of enormous guilt came over Peter. To think that he'd done things that had nearly ruined his parents' marriage was unconscionable, and he felt the overwhelming urge to bolt from the room. Milly had accused him of running away from his problems, and he forced himself to sit tight and face the music.

"You must have some idea of what I was doing," he said. "Was I hurting other kids at school? I had a rough time when I first came to the United States. I was small, and my British accent made me stand out. I got into a fight with a bully at school who was picking on me. Was that what they were talking about?"

"No, it was not," Sierra said. "Your parents told me that you had a demon inside of you. They said that you were born with this demon, and that when it showed its face, it was capable of all sorts of horrible acts. At first, I thought they were exaggerating, and blowing the problem out of proportion. After all, you were only seven, and how much trouble could a child that age cause? It was at that point that your father decided to show me the photos."

"What photos?"

"Your father took photos of the things you'd done. I'm not exactly sure why. Perhaps he needed evidence to convince men like myself what you were capable of. I still have them."

"Are they *bad?*" Peter choked on the word.

"Yes, I'm afraid they are."

He glanced at Liza. She nodded as if to say it was okay.

"Show them to me," he said.

Sierra produced a faded envelope from his jacket pocket, pulled back the flap, and removed a stack of photos. "I want you to know something. Up until now, I've shown these photographs to no one except Richard. I protected your family's privacy, and will continue to do so. Your family's secrets are safe with me, despite what you might think."

"Thank you," Peter said.

The stack was handed to him. Taken on a Kodak Instamatic, the color had faded but not enough to hide the horror of the images. The top photo showed Peter's bedroom in the family's apartment in Murray Hill. They had lived in a third-floor walk-up with rattling pipes and noisy neighbors. In the photo, there was shattered glass on the floor that appeared to be swimming in a substance that resembled catsup.

He stared hard. Not catsup. Blood. And there was a lot of it. Had someone died in his bedroom, and he'd not heard about it? It didn't seem possible, yet the photo said otherwise.

His eyes shifted to the broken window in the photograph. There was a hole in the glass big enough for a man to slip through. The hole led to a fire escape outside.

"I don't understand," Peter said. "What happened?"

"Look at the rest of them," Sierra said.

Peter laid the photos in a row on the table, and let his eyes drift over the disturbing images. After the bedroom came the narrow hallway, where bloody handprints covered the walls. Next was the kitchen, where the furniture had been turned upside down, leaving more bloodstains. Then came the study, where his parents held séances with their psychic friends and talked with the dead. This photo was the most troubling of all. In it, Peter sat in his father's chair dressed in his Batman pj's. His eyes were half open as if in a trance, his mouth twisted in a menacing snarl. The front of his shirt was soaked in blood, as were his hands. He looked more animal than human.

Peter looked across the kitchen at Liza. If she saw these photographs, things between them would never be the same. But if she didn't see them, things wouldn't be the same either. Whatever was left of his relationship with Liza was about to go up in flames.

Stacking the photos, he went to her, and placed them in her hands. "Here."

Then he poured himself more coffee.

35

Liza shocked him. After she'd finished studying the photos—which she spent over a minute doing—she dragged a chair up to the kitchen table, sat down beside Peter, and placed her hand on top of his, clasping it in the process. She was going to go down this road with him, no matter where it took them both. What was the expression from the country-and-western song? "Stand By Your Man." He wanted to hug her.

"Who did I kill?" Peter asked his two guests in the calmest of voices.

It was Sierra who replied. "You didn't kill anyone. At least your parents didn't think so."

"But I hurt someone pretty badly."

Sierra nodded gravely. No wonder he'd asked Peter if the demon inside of him had come out the night his parents had been murdered in Times Square. Sierra had already seen the demon, and knew the carnage it could wreak.

"Any idea who it was?" Peter asked.

"Your father said that the apartment house where you lived had been burglarized several times," Sierra replied. "Late one night, a burglar broke the window in your bedroom, and tried to enter. That was when the burglar encountered you. He managed to get away, but only barely. Your father said there was a great deal of blood on the fire escape and also in the alley below."

"Did I stab him?"

"You used the sharp edge of one of your toys."

"Wow. Talk about a little demon."

No one laughed. Peter picked up his mug and drained it.

"Your parents were torn over what to do," Sierra went on. "Your mother was fearful that your demon was out of control and might strike again. The night of the burglary, your parents went over to a neighbor's for a few minutes to see her new baby. This was when the burglar chose to enter your apartment. When your parents returned, it was your mother who found you."

"Did seeing me covered in blood scare her?" Peter asked.

"Very much. She told me that she had this same demon inside of her, and explained how difficult it had been for her to keep it contained all her life. It upset her that the demon had come out in you at such a tender age. She was fearful it might take control of your soul."

"Is that what she said?"

"In so many words, yes."

But it hadn't taken control of my soul, Peter thought. The demon went back to its dark hiding place, and he'd gotten on with his life. End of story.

"Your father viewed the matter differently," Sierra continued. "He was fearful that if doctors started examining you, the demon would be unleashed, and never go away. He wanted to treat you with tender loving care, which he said was the only cure."

"Who won out?" Peter asked.

"I did, actually," Sierra said.

"How so?"

"Your parents brought you in, and I examined you. I tested your reflexes to make sure you didn't have any neurological damage, which is not uncommon in violent children. You know when a doctor hits a patient in the knee with a rubber hammer? Well, I struck you in the knee with my hammer, and the next thing I knew, I was lying on the floor in a pool of blood."

"I hit you?" Peter asked incredulously.

"Knocked me right across the room. I never saw the blow. To be honest, I'm not certain you actually threw one. You did it with your mind. That's when I convinced your parents that Richard needed to be brought in."

Peter looked across the table at the sickly man dressed in black. "You're an exorcist."

"I am a priest who on occasion practices exorcisms," Hunsinger replied.

"Same difference. Did you perform an exorcism on me?"

"Yes, I did."

Peter took a deep breath. "And?"

"Nothing happened," the priest confessed. "We performed the exorcism in my chambers at the church. You lay on a couch with your parents sitting to either side of you. I wore an alb, a purple stole, as prescribed in the Old Testament. I made the sign of the cross over you, doused your body with holy water, and invoked the words '*Ecce crucem Domini! Fugite, partes adversae*' while placing my right hand on your forehead in the same manner in which Jesus healed the sick. I followed the procedure exactly as it was written."

"How did I react?"

"You looked up at me and let out a little laugh."

"I laughed?"

"Yes."

"Was it demonic?"

"Not at all. It was a little boy's laugh. The demon inside of you had receded. I don't know if I sent it away, or if it left on its own accord, but it was gone. What remained was a precious seven-year-old boy."

Liza squeezed his hand as this last sentence was spoken. It made Peter feel like there was still hope. "Thanks," he whispered.

"Anytime," she whispered back.

"Now you understand why Dr. Sierra and I wanted to see you," Hunsinger said. "We wanted to know what had become of you. To see how you turned out, if you will."

"You wanted to know what had happened to my demon," Peter said.

"That, too," the priest admitted.

"Yes, that, too," Sierra echoed.

Peter drummed the table. The phrase "troubled childhood" was taking on a whole new meaning. But he still wasn't sure why Sierra and Hunsinger had gone to such great pains to seek him out. Both men had seen scores of troubled people during their careers. So why had they worried about him? Because he was a child when this had occurred? That was one explanation, although he was quite certain both men had seen scores of troubled children during their careers. There had to be another reason.

His drumming grew louder. So loud that he could hardly hear himself think. Out of frustration, he attempted to read both men's brains to see what they were up to.

It didn't work. Both men were cutting him off by thinking about the lunch they'd shared a few hours ago. It was almost as if they'd planned it.

He gave Liza a look and whispered, "We need to talk." She rose from her chair the same time he did, said, "Please excuse us," and followed Peter out of the room.

Huddled in the hallway, Peter spoke in a hushed tone. "They know something they're not telling me."

Liza gave him a quizzical look. "What more is there to know?"

"That's a good question. I keep thinking back to Sierra asking me if the demon had come out the night my parents died. I think he already knew the answer and just wanted confirmation that it had."

"How would he have known if it had?"

"My parents' murders made the front page of the New York newspapers. Maybe I did something horrible that night that also made the newspapers, and Sierra and Hunsinger read about it, and made the connection."

"Did you?" Liza asked.

"Not that I remember."

"But you don't remember hurting the burglar in your apartment either."

Liza was right. Was this dark spirit inside of him so powerful that he couldn't control it, much less remember when it took over his body? It scared him to think it might be true. Grabbing his leather jacket off a peg, he gave Liza a kiss.

"I need to talk to the police. They'll know what happened that night," he said.

"What about Dr. Sierra and Hunsinger? What should I tell them?"

That was a good question. Sierra and Hunsinger had opened Pandora's box, and Peter didn't think he'd ever get it closed. But why had they done that? Out of an insatiable curiosity, or was something else in play here? Peter was determined to find out the answer.

"Thank them for dropping by," he said, and flew out the door.

36

He hurried uptown.

Soon he was standing outside the 19th Precinct on East 67th Street. Did he really want to know the truth about himself? Could he handle the truth? He was about to find out.

He went inside. The lobby reminded him of the Port Authority bus terminal and was just as noisy. He sifted through the crowd, picking up people's thoughts. When he was under stress, his psychic powers got the better of him, and he heard things without meaning to.

He waited dutifully in line to talk to the female desk sergeant working reception. In front of him, a Puerto Rican man was trying to determine how he was going to tell his brother—who'd beat up someone over a girl—that he didn't have the money to bail him out of jail. Behind him, a distraught mother was wondering if the police had any fresh information about her runaway teenage daughter. Their thoughts were incredibly loud, as most stressful thoughts were, and bounced around him like so many echoes.

Finally his turn came, and he approached the desk.

"Hey, magic man, long time no see," the desk sergeant said. "How's tricks?"

He'd helped the police solve a murder not long ago, and was surprised she remembered him. "I've been good. I'd like to see Detective Schoch."

"Do some magic first. I want to be amazed."

He searched his pockets for something to fool her with. He'd left the house without so much as a deck of cards. Normally in situations like this, he would have read her mind, but the desk sergeant was one of those rare birds whose minds could not be read. He pointed at the notepad lying on the desk.

"Pick up that pad and draw something on it. Don't let me see it," he said.

"You gonna read my mind?"

"I'm going to try."

"Cool." The desk sergeant picked up the pad and a pencil. "Turn around, I don't trust you."

"Come on, I'm one of the good guys."

"I still don't trust you. Now turn around."

Peter obeyed, and found himself staring at a scummy-looking character standing where the distraught mother had been. Day-old stubble, rheumy eyes, and lifeless blond hair made up the picture. The man's dark thoughts invaded Peter's head. He was a cold-blooded murderer.

"Something wrong?" the scummy-looking man asked, picking up his vibe.

"There was a woman standing behind me," Peter explained.

"She left."

"I'm finished," the desk sergeant said loudly.

"Nice meeting you," Peter said.

"Right."

Peter turned back around. The man's crime was running through his head like a trailer to a movie. Friday night, a rough bar in Hell's Kitchen, the man and a drinking buddy left the bar together, walked into a dark alley, where the scummy-looking man robbed his friend and shot him for good measure. He was a stone-cold killer.

"So tell me what I drew," the desk sergeant said.

Peter had absolutely no idea what the desk sergeant had drawn while his back was turned. But he was about to find out without his subject being the wiser. "Please tear off what you drew, and hide the drawing," he replied.

The desk sergeant tore off the drawing and hid it under her desk. Peter wondered how was he going to tell her about the killer without tipping her off that he was a psychic. He decided to finish the trick, hoping a solution would come to him.

"May I please have the pad and your pencil," he said.

"So polite. I like that in a man."

She winked at him while handing over the items. Peter held the pad up close to his chest. Using the edge of the pencil, he lightly shaded the page, and the impression of what she'd just drawn popped to life. There were only ten objects that people ever drew. Peter pegged the desk sergeant for a house, and glanced down at the page. Sure enough, she'd drawn a house. But not just any house. This one had a winding driveway, a mailbox at the road, and a front lawn. Had she drawn the house out in the suburbs where she lived?

"You drew something very dear to you, a special place."

The desk sergeant lit up like a Christmas tree.

"Boy, you're good," she said.

"It's a house in the suburbs."

"Right again."

"Is it the house where you live?"

"I'll be damned. You're amazing."

Behind the desk appeared an attractive brunette wearing a sidearm strapped to her side. Detective Colleen Schoch, the very person he'd come to the precinct to see.

"Hello, Peter. How have you been?" she asked.

"I'm okay. I need to speak with you. In private."

"May I ask what this is about? I'm kind of busy right now."

"The night my parents were killed."

Schoch did not know what to say. She'd been the first officer on the scene the night his parents had died, and had taken Peter to the station house and taken care of him. Schoch was a friend, and one of the few people outside of his Friday night group who knew of his powers.

Schoch motioned him to come around the desk, and they walked to a bank of elevators and waited for a car to come. She brought her face up close to his. Their eyes locked.

"What's going on?" Schoch asked.

First things first, Peter thought. "The creepy guy behind me on line is a killer."

"You're kidding me."

"I read his mind. He shot a guy in Hell's Kitchen Friday night. His victim was left lying in an alley. If you don't grab him now, he's going to escape."

"You're sure about this?"

"Positive. I saw the whole thing clearly."

"How do I prove this?"

"He stole his victim's wallet. He's still carrying it."

"Wait here. I'm going to go arrest the son of a bitch."

M ost criminals were stupid. The man in line was no exception. His victim's ID was still in his wallet when Schoch arrested him.

Schoch was beaming as they sat in her tiny cubicle in Homicide. Her desk was as neat as a pin, which could not be said of the desks around her. She offered him a soft drink.

"No, thanks. Let me tell you why I'm here," Peter said. "I've been having some problems lately, and I think they stem from the night my parents were murdered. I'd like to ask you a couple of questions, if you don't mind. It will help me sort things out."

Schoch leaned back in her chair. "What kind of problems?"

"Anger issues."

"That's not uncommon for victims of violent crimes."

"These are extreme."

"You're becoming violent?"

"Close enough. Will you help me? Please?"

Her face softened, if just a little bit. "All right, fire away. What do you want to know?"

"Did I become violent the night my parents died?"

"No. You cried a lot at the station house, but that was it."

He thought back to what he knew about his demon. It came out right at the moment he became angry, like a spark turning to a flame. "I mean at the scene of the crime. Did I do anything out of the ordinary?"

"I honestly don't know," Schoch replied.

"But you were the first responder. You would have seen how I was acting. Try to remember. It's very important to me."

"I don't know if I ever told you this, but when I first got to the scene, you weren't there," Schoch said. "I was a foot cop working Times Square with my partner. A call came in that a man and his wife had been abducted in an alley beside the Shubert Theatre. We got to the scene as fast as we could, and discovered there were plenty of eyewitnesses. We took their statements, and every single one of them said there had been a little boy. Well, there was no little boy."

"I wasn't there?"

"No, and we looked high and low for you. You vanished."

"Then how did I show up at the station house?"

"A man brought you. I remember him quite clearly. He had snow-white hair and was theatrical looking. I pegged him for an actor. He said he'd found you wandering the streets."

"Did you get his name?"

"No. It was weird. He came into the lobby and handed you off to me. You were in a state of shock and not communicating. While I was watching you, he disappeared."

He disappeared? Peter felt the invisible stab to his heart. The physical description matched that of Max, his teacher. He took a deep breath before continuing. "How long I was gone?"

Schoch had to think. "The call came in at ten o'clock at night, and you showed up at the station house at around three A.M."

Five whole hours. That was a long time. Yet it made sense, the pieces of the puzzle falling together, the empty holes filling in. Right as his parents were abducted, he'd looked into his mother's eyes, and had known that he was never going to see her or his beloved father again. *He'd known his parents were about to die, just as they'd known.* A shared truth had never been more painful. And with that terrible knowledge had come an anger so great that the little boy in pajamas who'd maimed a burglar had gone on a rampage that had lasted into the small hours of the night. Once the rampage was over, he'd somehow ended up with Max, his parents' dearest friend.

There was no doubt in his mind this is what had happened that awful night. The only question was, how much damage had he caused?

37

∞

P eter sat on the edge of the detective's desk and tried to act calm, even though his heart was racing out of control. "I have another question. I know this is going to sound strange."

"I'm sure it isn't anything I haven't heard before," Schoch replied.

"The night my parents died, were there other deaths in the city that you didn't solve?"

"Deaths? Do you mean murders?"

He swallowed the lump in his throat and nodded.

"That's a strange question," she conceded. "Why do you want to know that?"

The detective wouldn't have believed him if he'd told her, so he said instead, "I've been having some weird dreams lately that concern that night. I've been wondering if the things I'm seeing in my dreams might have actually happened."

"Fair enough. Let's ask Dag. He'll know."

Schoch told Peter that her toothpick-chewing partner, Dag, had recently been assigned to work on a slew of cold cases from that year, and he'd be the person to ask. She called Dag on her intercom. "You busy? I need a favor."

"What's going on," Dag replied over the squawk box.

"Peter Warlock is here. He needs our help."

Moments later, Detective Sal Dagastino, known as Dag to his friends, entered the cubicle and pumped Peter's hand. "How's life in the fast lane?" he asked.

"Traveling at the speed of sound," Peter replied.

"I need to score four tickets for Saturday night's show," Dag said without missing a beat. "My in-laws are coming to town, and I want to show them a good time."

"Consider it done. You can pick them up at Will Call. Will third row center do the trick?"

"Perfect. Now it's my turn. What do you need?"

"I was wondering if there were any unsolved murders or violent crimes which took place the night my parents died. Detective Schoch said you've been working cold cases lately."

"Peter was roaming the city that night and might have seen something," Schoch explained.

As a rule, cops did not share information about open investigations. But Peter had helped Dag and Schoch solve a difficult murder case not long ago, and gained their trust. The toothpick twirled between Dag's teeth as he considered their visitor's request.

"There were several violent killings in the city that night that were never solved," Dag said. "We recently reopened them because of a new DNA test called 'scraping.' Scraping lets us test for DNA in places we weren't able to test before."

Peter swallowed hard. *Several violent killings.* Were they his doing?

"Were the cases linked?" he asked.

"They sure were. All our victims had skin underneath their fingernails which wasn't theirs," Dag said. "With scraping, we were able to find DNA, and compare it. The same assailant was responsible, and might be a serial killer. Kind of scary to think this person has been roaming around the city for the past eighteen years and we didn't know it."

Pools of black opened up before Peter's eyes, and he would have liked nothing better than to jump through one of them, and disappear. He felt the weight of Dag's stare, and realized the detective was waiting for a response. If the police shared information with you, they expected you to give something in return, and he said, "The memories from that night have recently been coming back to me. Maybe while I was roaming the city I came across your killer."

"Would you remember him?"

"I might."

"How about his victims? Would you remember them?"

He took a deep breath. "I don't know."

The toothpick did another slow twirl. Going to the next cubicle, Dag grabbed a manila folder off the top of a pile, and dropped it in Peter's lap upon his return.

"That's them," Dag said.

"You mean the victims?"

"That's right. The photos aren't pretty."

The file felt heavy. "How many unsolved cases were there that night?"

"Six."

Peter thought he was going to be sick. Possessed little boy runs amok in city, killing six innocent people. It sounded like the plot to a low-budget horror film.

"Not that any of them were going to be missed," Dag went on. "Whoever took those guys out was doing the good citizens of New York a favor, and deserves a medal."

"You're starting to sound like a vigilante, Dag," Schoch said.

"Just speaking my mind," her partner said.

"Were the victims bad people?" Peter asked.

"Scum of the earth," Dag said. "I say good riddance."

Peter went through the file. It contained six Homicide reports that had been written back in the day when cops used typewriters. Each report had its own collection of gruesome crime-scene photographs. Each victim had died in a pool of his own blood. He thought back to the snapshot of him in his Batman pajamas. The front of his pj's had been blood soaked. No doubt the shedding of blood was something the demon found appealing.

38

An approximate time of death was printed on each report. All the victims had died during the five hours he'd been roaming the city. All had also been found within a twenty-block radius of the Shubert Theatre in Times Square, where his parents had been abducted.

The cases had other similarities as well. Each victim had a lengthy criminal record, and was wanted by the law. One rapist, an armed robber, three men wanted for murder, and a drug dealer known for selling poisonous drugs to his clients. In keeping with the theme of his rampage, they had died brutally, with their necks broken and skulls crushed in, their bodies left in alleyways to be discovered a few hours later.

He closed the file. He was going to have to find a way to deal with this; he just didn't know how. When he spoke, his voice sounded like a recording. "Did anyone see who did this?"

"There was one eyewitness," Dag said. "A woman walking her dog saw our killer kneeling over one of the victims, strangling the crap out of him."

I killed them with my bare hands, he thought. *How lovely.*

"Did she give you a physical description?"

"Witness said he was a little guy, if you can believe that."

He started to tremble. For the first time, he realized what a huge risk he'd taken coming here. If he wasn't careful, Dag and Schoch would realize that he was the little guy the eyewitness had seen, and they'd take a sample of his DNA, compare it to the victims' samples, and then they'd have to arrest him.

Dag wore a blank look, and wasn't making the connection. Schoch hadn't made the connection yet, either. So far so good, but what about later on? They were smart cops, and their brains worked like filters. Eventually, it would dawn on them why Peter had come to see them.

He needed to stop that from happening, and decided to blur their memories. Magicians were masters at blurring their audiences' memories, and he would do the same with the detectives.

He asked Dag what several notations he'd seen in the homicide reports referred to. Dag obliged him, and spent five minutes explaining the notations. When Dag was done, Peter asked Schoch to explain the coroner's reports in the files. Schoch obliged him as well, and five more minutes were spent. Getting the detectives talking served an important purpose. Instead of asking questions, they were now having to answer questions. This made them switch gears, and use a different part of their brains.

The second thing it did was kill time. The further away they moved from the thing Peter didn't want them to remember, the less in focus the memory became. If he killed enough time, the memory would become blurred with the things he was now asking them. Magicians called this stalling technique time delay. During a magic show, things happened onstage which the magician did not want the audience to remember. By creating a time delay, the audience often forgot the very thing which allowed the trick to work.

Peter worked his magic on the detectives. Soon they looked bored, and ready to go back to work. "Thanks for talking to me. I'll let you know if I remember anything from that night."

The phone on the desk lit up. Schoch snatched the receiver and waved good-bye. Dag walked him to the elevators and punched the button.

"I'll e-mail you about those tickets," the detective said.

"I won't forget," Peter promised.

Riding down in the elevator, Peter hugged himself and shut his eyes. How could he have murdered six men with his bare hands and not remember the act? It just didn't seem possible.

Perhaps someone else was responsible, a madman maybe, or another poor soul possessed by a demon. Those were logical explanations, and he was willing to accept them, except he still couldn't understand how he'd managed to end up with Max.

Stepping outside the 19th Precinct, he texted Liza that he'd be home in a few hours, then hailed a cab and headed downtown to the Village.

39

Long ago, a freight rail line had run high above the streets of Manhattan on the West Side. One day the trains had stopped running, and the elevated line had fallen into disrepair, with weeds and garbage strewing the tracks. The city had planned to tear down the constant eyesore along with all the memories.

Only this was New York, where everything old became new again. A vocal group of residents had banded together with the goal of preserving the tracks. Calling themselves Friends of the High Line, they'd begun the arduous process of convincing the city's leaders to change their minds. In the end, they had won, and the tracks were saved.

Today, the tracks served as a pedestrian walkway that stretched from Gansevoort to 34th Street, and was filled with well-tended gardens, dozens of pieces of modern sculpture, and comfy places to curl up with a book, which many people did when the weather was pleasant.

Because this was New York, the High Line had plenty of rules. No smoking, biking, skateboarding, picking flowers, climbing, throwing objects, littering, filming movies, or blasting boom boxes were allowed. And there were no street performers of any kind.

Except for one.

One performer was allowed to hold court on the High Line and entertain the masses, and his name was Max Romeo.

Max had lived in New York most of his life, and knew everybody. He'd pulled some strings, and had gotten the city to issue him a permit to perform magic on the High Line whenever the mood suited him. In Peter's opinion, it was the greatest gig in the city.

Tuesday afternoon, bright and sunny, Peter found his teacher near the West 20th Street entrance. Max was plucking shiny silver dollars out of a young boy's ears and nose, the coins landing into a metal pail with a loud *clunk!* The appreciative crowd laughed and applauded.

"Stand up straight, my boy," Max commanded with a playful air.

More coins appeared and were tossed in. Soon the pail grew heavy in Max's hand. The old magician shook the coins while casting a suspicious gaze at the crowd. There was no tougher crowd than a bunch of New Yorkers. Yet Max had them in the palm of his hand.

"On the count of three, I will perform a miracle," Max proclaimed. "Please count along. Are you ready? Here we go. One."

"One!" the crowd echoed.

"Two."

"Two!"

Max started to say "Three" and dumped the bucket into the crowd. Silver-colored confetti floated to the sidewalk, the coins miraculously gone. Max gave a matadorlike bow.

It was all about the applause. Shakespeare had said that, and he'd been right. The crowd rewarded Max generously. When the applause subsided, several members of the crowd tried to give Max tips. The old magician politely but firmly refused. Only when the crowd had dispersed did he address his student.

"Why, Peter, it's good to see you," Max said.

"Why didn't you tell me I was a murderer?" Peter asked.

They sat on a bench with their backs to the gloomy Hudson. Max treaded softly.

"You look troubled," Max said. "Have the shadow people visited you again? I saw one earlier when I stepped out of my apartment." He patted the five-pointed star resting beneath his shirt. "Thank God you gave me this."

"I didn't come here to talk about the shadow people," Peter said.

"Milly saw one, too," Max said, as if not hearing him. "So did Lester, and Homer called to tell me that his wife believes one was floating outside their apartment window this morning around breakfast time. Have you figured out what they want?"

"That's simple. They want me."

"But why? Still no clue? I would have thought they would have made their intentions known by now. The spirits aren't ones to beat around the bush, you know."

Peter shook his head. He had three days left to save Rachael from walking into Dr. Death's trap. Right now, though, he needed to deal with his own issues, and uncover the truth, as ugly as it might be. "I want to talk to you about the night my parents perished. I learned today that I was roaming around the city for five hours, and that a kindly old man who bore a striking resemblance to you deposited me at the police station house at three o'clock in the morning."

Max lowered his eyes. "Is that so," he mumbled.

"Was it you? Please be honest with me about this."

"I believe it was."

"Thank you. So here's the question I want to ask you, Max. When you found me that night, were my hands covered in blood?"

His teacher's head snapped, and he locked eyes with his student. "Who told you that?"

"Does it matter?"

"Yes, it most certainly does."

"Will you tell me the truth?"

"Tell you the truth about what?"

"Me."

"You want to know the truth about you?"

"Yes, Max. Something tells me you know exactly who I am."

Max placed his arm around Peter's shoulders, and pulled him close to his chest. With his other hand, he ran his knuckles across his hair. Max hadn't done that to him in a long time, and it brought a long-forgotten smile to Peter's face.

"I'll tell you who you are," Max said. "You are one of the most caring and generous people I have ever known. That's who you are, and I'm proud to have helped raise you. Is that good enough for you?"

"No. I want to know if there was blood on my hands."

Max scowled and released him. "How much do you remember from that night?"

"Nothing. It's all a blank."

"There's your answer. There wasn't any blood."

"But that's not true," he said, hearing the fear in his voice. "I went on a rampage that night, and killed six men in the city. The police confirmed it. I saw the cold case file with photographs of my victims. It was awful. "

Max winced like he'd been kicked. A deck of cards appeared in his hands. He fanned and cut them one-handed without being disrespectful. "So you know."

"Yes. Now tell me the rest."

"If you insist. At the exact moment your mother and father were abducted, Milly Adams was taking a hot bath. Milly had a vision, and saw your parents being shoved into a car at gunpoint. She knew your parents were doomed, but held out hope for you."

"Did Milly see me in her vision?"

"Yes. She said you changed."

"Into a monster?"

"She said you turned into a little demon. Milly alerted her psychic friends, and asked us to look for you. I owned a car at the time, and was given an area to search. I looked for hours, and finally found you on Ninth Avenue."

"What was I doing?"

At first, Max did not respond. The pools of black reappeared and Peter felt all the more ready to step into one. "Please, Max. Tell me."

"You were in the act of interrupting a serious crime," Max said solemnly. "A mugger was robbing an elderly man and kicking him. You jumped in, and got your hands around the mugger's throat. You were four and a half feet tall and weighed seventy pounds. The mugger was a brute, and four times your size, yet he didn't stand a chance."

"Did I kill him?"

"You snapped his neck like it was a bread stick. But it was for a good cause. As were the others, I'm sure."

Dag had made a similar comment, as if the six killings were justifiable. Peter didn't believe there was ever a good reason to take a human life. The truth was, he'd gone berserk that night, and become a killing machine. How he was going to live with that, he had no idea.

"What happened then?"

"I took you home, where I cleaned you up, while Anna fixed you something to eat," Max replied. "You remember how my wife always wanted to feed everyone. Anyway, you'd calmed down by then, and gone back to being a little boy. A very frightened little boy, I might add. It was Anna's idea to take you to the police in the hopes you might identify the men who'd stolen your parents away. Which was exactly what I did."

The cards were snapped in a fan. They had shrunk to half their size. Another fan, and they shrunk to the size of a matchbook. Then, like a puff of smoke, they were gone.

"But why did you do that, Max?" he asked pleadingly. "Didn't the fact that I'd killed six men weigh on your decision? I was a dangerous little boy. Shouldn't you have taken me to a hospital instead?"

Max opened his hands and the deck of cards miraculously reappeared. Seeing them made Peter swallow hard. The cards had been there all along, perhaps up Max's sleeve, or someplace else, but hiding in plain sight nonetheless. So simple, yet it had fooled him.

"You had killed before, you do know that," Max said.

"The burglar at our apartment. He died?"

"Of course he died. I mean, before that."

Someone could have knocked him over with a feather.

"I don't know what you're talking about," he stammered.

"So you don't know the truth, then."

The truth. Peter had been waiting a long time to hear the truth. Max rose from the bench and motioned for Peter to rise as well.

"Let's take a walk," he said.

40

∿

D own at street level they went to a hidden Italian eatery called Pepe Giallo, its motto, "Feeding the Starving Artists since 1997." For a restaurant in New York to be Italian, it not only had to serve authentic Italian fare, but had to be run by Italians with accents and rude manners. Pepe Giallo had all those things. A host led them to a small courtyard in the back with rustic redbrick walls and a murky skylight. Tossing a pair of menus on the table, he walked away.

"I'm not hungry. Let's go someplace else," Peter said.

"Nonsense, you're always hungry, even though you manage to never gain weight," Max said. "Food will make you feel better. Try the roasted eggplant. It's wonderful."

An indifferent waiter took their drink orders. When he was gone, Max glanced at a couple sitting nearby. Deciding they were not a threat, he leaned forward and said, "I once read a quote by Ernest Hemingway that stayed with me. Hemingway said that memoirs are fiction. People reinvent their pasts to suit them. We take out the things we don't want repeated, and embellish the things we do. When it comes to the past, there is no such thing as the truth."

"Is my past fiction?" Peter asked.

"Yes. Part of your family's past is fiction."

"So this includes my parents."

"I'm afraid so."

"How bad is it?"

"I never planned to tell you, if that's what you mean."

Peter removed a bread stick from the basket, broke off a piece. Did he really want to hear dark things about his family's past? Milly's accusation that he ran away from his problems didn't seem such a bad idea right now.

"Go ahead," he said.

Max wiped his hands with a cloth napkin. Bunching the napkin up, he extracted a full glass of water, complete with ice cubes and a slice of lemon, which he triumphantly placed in front of his bug-eyed student. *Fooled again,* Peter thought.

"You flashed. Do it again," Peter said.

"I did no such thing," Max thundered. "Admit you're fooled!"

"All right, you fooled me. Bravo."

A thin smile crossed Max's face. "Listen carefully to what I have to say. This will be upsetting at first. Once I explain certain things, I think you'll understand. Okay?"

"Sure, Max."

"All right, here we go. You were raised to believe that your mother and father left London and came to New York because they were being threatened by the group of evil psychics called the Order of Astrum. Correct?"

"Correct."

"That is not the actual reason your parents left England. The real reason they left is that their precious son killed a man in Hyde Park, and they were running from the law."

"I did *what?*"

"Please let me tell my story without interruption."

Peter could feel the blood draining from his head. "Sure, Max, whatever you say."

"Thank you. Here's what happened. Your parents lived in London and taught at a small college. Each Sunday when the weather was favorable, they packed a picnic and went to Hyde Park, where they allowed you to play while they read books. It was one of their favorite things to do. One Sunday in the early spring, your parents were going about their usual routine when your father realized you had disappeared. He grew alarmed, and went searching for you. Several minutes passed before he found you behind a thick hedge a hundred yards from where your parents had been sitting. You were in a daze, and barely speaking. Lying on the ground was a man with blood pouring out of his nose and mouth. The man's neck was broken and he was dead. Your father gathered you in his arms, and asked you what had happened. And you said, 'I killed him, Father. He was going to hurt us.'"

"Who was he?"

"Please, don't make me get ahead of myself."

"Sorry."

"On the ground beside the dead man was a lead pipe. Your father couldn't be sure if the man had been holding the pipe, or if it had been lying there. Your father rushed you home, where your mother gave you a bath, and wiped the blood away."

"Why didn't they call the police?"

"Your parents knew you were different in many ways, and did not always understand the things you did. That night, after you were put to bed, your parents talked it over. They couldn't imagine why anyone would want to harm them. After all, they were college professors, and led dull, uneventful lives. If the man in the bushes had wanted to rob them, he wouldn't have gotten much money. And if he'd wanted to hurt them, why?

"The next day, the story hit every newspaper in London. Scotland Yard was looking for you, and claimed to have a rather vague description of what you looked like provided by an old woman who'd been bird-watching in the park. Your father saw the newspapers and panicked. If the police found you, he was afraid they would have stuck you into a mental institution. He had to protect you, and convinced your mother that they needed to leave London, and quickly."

"So they left because of me."

"That's right. Your father knew there was more to the story, and felt certain he'd figure out the rest eventually. Your parents came to New York, where they took jobs at Hunter College and went about their lives. Then the unthinkable happened."

"I killed again."

Max nodded gravely. "Six months to the day, to be exact. It happened at night. You were in bed, and your parents went to see a newborn in a neighbor's apartment. When they returned, your mother went to check on you, and found you covered in blood."

Peter stared at the table, thinking he might be sick.

Max squeezed his arm. "It gets better," he said.

"How can this story possibly get better?" he half whispered.

"Because now you're going to hear the truth."

His head snapped. "Which is what?"

"While your mother tended to you, your father went onto the fire escape outside your bedroom. Finding more blood, he followed it down to an alley. It was there that he found your victim, who'd been beaten around the face and had died from loss of blood."

"How awful."

"Stop flogging yourself. I said it got better, didn't I?"

"Sorry."

"The man in the alley reminded your father of your victim in Hyde Park. Both men were physically large, in their early thirties, and rough looking. That bothered your father, yet he was still unable to make the connection. He decided to move the body before someone discovered it, and called me for help."

"Because you had a car."

Max nodded.

"Had he told you what I'd done in Hyde Park?"

"Yes, he had. Like him, I believed there was more to the story than met the eye. Mind you, Peter, I'd gotten to know you during my visits to your family's apartment, and you impressed me as a fine fellow and not some little serial killer in waiting. Anyway, I rushed over with my car, and your father and I loaded the dead man in the trunk. We hauled him to a vacant lot in Brooklyn, where we planned to dump him."

Peter found himself shaking his head. Max and his father were the two most important men in his life. The idea that they'd dumped a dead man in a lot in order to save him from the police brought out an emotion that he could not describe. He took a deep breath.

"Wow."

"Wow is right. And that was when I had a eureka moment," Max said triumphantly.

"Your victim was wearing a turtleneck sweater. As we dragged him out of the trunk, it got pulled down, and I spied a shimmering silver tattoo on his neck."

Peter gasped. "He was a member of the Order of Astrum."

"Indeed he was. He wasn't a burglar, as your parents originally thought, but an assassin who had been sent to kill them." Max paused again. "And you stopped him."

"You think I knew who he was?"

"Of course you did—why else would you have killed him?"

Peter wrestled with what Max was telling him. Why couldn't a few memories of these events have remained? It would have made it so much easier for him to deal with this. But the memories had been erased along with the violent emotions that had gone with them.

"So these killings weren't random acts of violence, but served a purpose," Peter said.

"That was the conclusion your father and I came to," Max replied. "As you know, your parents were founding members of the Order. They left the organization in their teens, got married, and moved to London. One day, the three remaining members of the Order paid them a visit, and asked them to rejoin. Your parents said no, and they threatened them. Your father said he hadn't taken the threats seriously. Now he did."

"What about the man in Hyde Park? Was he an assassin as well?"

"Excellent deduction. Yes, he was."

"How can you be certain?"

"I have a friend in London whose brother is with Scotland Yard. I called my friend, and asked him to ask his brother to check the autopsy report of the dead man to see if he had a shimmering tattoo on his neck. Not surprisingly, the man did."

"So the man in Hyde Park was sent to kill my parents. When he failed, a second assassin was sent to New York, and he failed as well. Is that what you're telling me?"

"You're stealing my thunder."

"Finally, the Order got fed up, and the other members came to New York to do the job themselves," Peter said. "Only this time, I wasn't able to protect my parents, and they were stolen out from under me. I went into a rage, and ran around New York killing bad men in retaliation. Is that the deal?"

"You make it sound like you were a monster," Max said. "That was not the case."

"From what you've just told me, I killed eight men before I turned eight years old. What would you call it?"

"They were bad men, and got the fate they deserved."

"I was a child. Children are not supposed to kill. It was wrong. Please don't justify it."

"But they were trying to kill your parents."

"Why didn't my parents stop them? They were both psychic. How could they have been so blind to the danger they were in?"

Max shook his head, clearly frustrated. "Your mother and father left the Order of Astrum because they wanted to lead normal lives. They were psychics, but it was a small part of who they were. They kept their powers turned off most of the time, so to speak. That was why they didn't see the danger."

But their seven-year-old son *had* seen the danger. Unlike his loving parents, Peter had not turned off his psychic powers, and when danger had come calling, the demon inside of him responded in a way that was so horrible that the memories had been repressed.

His chair made a harsh scraping sound. Standing, Peter tossed his napkin onto his plate. Why couldn't Max's story have been different? Something easy for him to digest and come to grips with? He could have accepted just about anything, except this.

Max looked into his student's face, and saw his pain. "What's wrong?"

"I want to have a normal life, too," Peter said, and walked out of the restaurant.

41

Peter got out of the cab at the Centre Street entrance to the Brooklyn Bridge.

"Keep the change."

The driver smiled at his good fortune and pulled away. It was not every day that a passenger gave him a hundred bucks for a twelve-dollar fare.

Peter zipped up his leather jacket and climbed the stairway to the elevated pedestrian walkway that ran the length of the bridge. Day or night, rain or shine, freezing cold or unbearably hot, there was always a mob of people walking and jogging and enjoying the sights from the bridge. And then there were poor souls like him, who needed to clear dark thoughts from their heads.

It was a half mile to the bridge's center. Upon reaching it, he gazed up at the main tower, which was as tall as a skyscraper. Many times, he'd imagined climbing over the railing, crawling on a beam to the tower, taking the stairs to the top, ripping off his clothes, and diving into murky depths of the East River. Not to kill himself, but simply as a way to change, believing that the Peter who came out of the water would be different from the Peter who'd jumped in.

But he hadn't done it. In the end, something had always held him back. He gripped the railing with both hands and gazed at the water. He'd read once that everyone desired to be someone else. For him, that person was someone totally ordinary. He yearned for a morning when he'd wake up and not have had a vision the night before which foretold the future, or step into an old building and not be confronted by a ghost. He wanted a life with the normal daily ups and downs, happiness and pain. Was that too much to ask for?

"There you are."

He released the railing and spun around. Liza came toward him wearing stone-washed jeans and a wool sweater, looking as radiant as the day he'd first laid eyes on her.

"How did you know I was here?"

"Because this is where you come when you're in the dumps. Did you get my texts?"

He took out his Droid and saw the message icon flashing in the upper corner of the screen. Had his cell phone buzzed in his pocket and he'd not noticed? That was no excuse, and he said, "I haven't been myself today. What happened to Sierra and his friend?"

"They left right after you did." Liza saw something she didn't like, and placed her hand beneath his chin so she could stare fully into his eyes. "You look despondent. Please tell me what's going on. I want to help."

Where to begin? *Start by how you feel and take it from there.* "I used to think that the day my parents died was the worst day of my life. I was wrong. Today is the worst day of my life."

"Because of what Dr. Sierra and Hunsinger told you this morning."

"That was just the beginning."

He edged up to the railing and resumed looking at the river. Liza clasped his hand and stood beside him. They shared the same view, but he doubted they were seeing the same things, and he found himself wishing that Liza could read minds, for he would have given anything not to repeat the things that Max had told him.

"Sierra and Hunsinger were the tip of the iceberg. I killed eight different people when I was a little kid."

"Oh, my God, Peter. Are you sure?"

"Max confirmed it. He saw me strangling a mugger the night my parents died. Said the guy deserved it, not that it made me feel any better."

"Who were the others?"

"Two of them were assassins trying to do away with my parents; the other six came after my parents died. My demon did a 'Death Wish' on all the bad guys roaming the city that night."

"So you only killed bad people. Well, I guess that's some consolation. Isn't it?"

When confronted by the forces of evil, most people turned away, or made excuses, or tried to ignore the facts staring them in the face. It was how they coped with evil in its purest form, and Liza was no exception. He fell silent.

"So what are you going to do?" she asked.

He struggled to reply. In the back of his mind he saw himself taking the plunge into the river and emerging a different person, or not. That was one way out.

"I remember the first time you brought me here," she said. "We had just started dating, and you took me out to dinner, and then brought me here. We stood right in this spot, and you explained to me that there were sixteen bridges that connected the island of Manhattan to the different boroughs, and then you named them. There was the Brooklyn Bridge, the George Washington Bridge, the Triborough Bridge, and I can't remember the others. Then you told me how you grew up believing the bridges were anchors that kept the city from floating away. Remember?"

He nodded.

"Is that why you came here? Because you feel like you're floating away?"

It was as good an analogy as Peter could think of, and he nodded again.

"Are you afraid your demon will come out again, and go on a rampage?"

Growing up, his parents and later his parents' friends had taught him to control his anger, and it allowed him to control the demon as well. So far, he'd been able to keep the monster under control, but who knew what the future held?

"That's part of it," he said.

"So tell me the rest. Please, Peter, I want to know. Say what's on your mind."

"I lost my dream. I've always known I was different. I talked to my mother about it, and she told me not to worry. She told me that one day I'd grow up, and everything would work out. I took that to mean that when I became an adult, I'd meet a special person, get married, have a couple of kids, and lead a normal life. I'd get to shed being a psychic just like a soldier gets out of the army, you know? Sure, I'd still have gifts, but I wouldn't have to use them unless I wanted to. That was my dream, and I've held on to it for all this time. But now I know that isn't true. This evil inside of me will always be there, and I'll always need to keep a lid on it. Because if I don't, it will come out, and there will literally be hell to pay. I won't get to retire, ever. I'm stuck being who I am."

"But I love who you are," Liza said.

"What about the demon? Do you love him as well?"

"I love you, warts and all."

He laughed silently to himself. He had a lot more than warts to deal with.

"We can deal with this," Liza said. "We'll work on it day by day, just like other couples that are having problems. We just have to believe in each other, that's all. Isn't that what your parents did?" She glanced at her watch and her eyes grew wide. "Oh, my God, look at the time. We've got a show in a few hours. Come on!"

Liza grabbed his hand. She was not giving up on him. That was good, because Peter didn't see how he could deal with this by himself. He stole a final glance at the river, the idea of jumping not far from his thoughts.

Together, they ran across the bridge.

42

⁓

illy was telling fortunes for three wealthy widows in her apartment when her cell phone rang. It had been Holly's idea to buy her a ringtone, and the recorded cat's meow sounded like the poor animal was being mutilated.

"So sorry." Milly muted the phone without bothering to check caller ID. Cell phones were like traffic lights. Necessary, but terribly annoying. "Now, where were we?"

The widows sat at a round table draped in black felt covered in astrological signs in the center of Milly's living room. Every Tuesday at five o'clock, they assembled in Milly's apartment, where they drank tea, ate cookies, and had their futures told. The widows paid Milly enough money to maintain a lifestyle that most psychics only dreamed about.

"Who'd like to go first?" Milly asked.

"Let me start," the widow Miller said. "I want to know what's going to happen with my oldest son. He's been causing me all sorts of trouble lately."

"I see. Please give me your cup of tea and we'll begin."

The cup was passed across the table. Milly swirled the remaining liquid so the tea leaves were distributed, drained the liquid onto a paper napkin, then gazed into the cup. The key to reading tea leaves was the ability to interpret the symbols suggested by the leaves, of which there were over a hundred, each with different meanings. If the leaves looked like a stone, it meant there was work to be done. If they resembled a house, it meant that prosperity was in the future, while a mountain meant an arduous journey was ahead.

The symbol in the widow's cup was a snake, a bad sign. But Milly wasn't going to tell her guest that. Bad news was bad for business.

Instead, she said, "Your son will continue to make questionable choices. He means well, but his decisions do not always reflect this."

"Will he ever get a real job?" the widow asked.

Snakes did not work. They hung around all day, sleeping, and were the laziest of creatures. The widow's son was no different.

"I don't see a job in his immediate future," Milly replied truthfully.

"Someday?"

"Perhaps."

"Can you be more specific? He's thirty years old and I'm still supporting him!"

Milly studied the leaves some more. The snake appeared to be well fed. The widow's son wasn't going to leave home until his mother stopped babying him. "Your son has the potential to do many useful things with his life. Whether or not he does is up to you."

"Up to me? So what do I do?"

"Take a long trip. I hear a cruise to Alaska is nice this time of year."

"Seriously? What about my son? Should I take him along?"

"Leave him behind."

"But I've never done that before. Will he be all right?"

Milly again consulted the leaves. The snake had sprouted wings and resembled a butterfly, a symbol of growth and change. "He'll be fine," she assured her.

A telephone rang in the study down the hall. Milly's home number was unlisted, and hardly everyone ever called her.

"Did you need to get that?" the widow asked.

"They can leave a message," Milly replied.

The phone continued to ring. Like most witches, Milly was a private person, and hated intrusions. An annoying telemarketing firm had found out the hard way, and she'd cast a spell over them when they wouldn't stop harassing her. Only after they'd gone out of business had the company's operators gotten their voices back.

The phone would not stop ringing.

"Let me get that," Milly said. "Please, help yourselves to more tea."

She went to her study to take the call. She'd already decided that her caller would wake up tomorrow with an ugly mole on their nose with black hairs sprouting out of it. That would make them think twice about calling her again. She snatched up the receiver.

"Who is this, and what do you want?" she demanded.

"Good afternoon, Ms. Adams, this is Joe, the building's head of security," a man's deep voice said. "I'm sorry to bother you, but you have a visitor."

"I'm busy, Joe," she said icily.

"I know you are, Ms. Adams. I told your visitor that you had guests and were not to be disturbed, but she insisted that I ring you."

Joe was a decent fellow, and always helped her bring in her groceries. Milly quickly undid the spell that she'd just cast over him, then reminded herself to look at Joe's nose tomorrow morning to be sure he was all right.

"Does this visitor have a name?" Milly asked.

"It's your niece, Holly."

So that was who'd called her cell phone. And when Milly hadn't answered, Holly had rushed over to see her. Something told Milly this was about Peter, and could wait.

"Tell her that I'm busy, and will call her later," Milly said.

"She says it's a matter of life and death, and that she must see you now," Joe said.

"Really. Well, I guess you'd better send her right up."

"Will do."

Milly hung up the phone. This sounded serious. She returned to the living room to check on her guests. Their teacups were full, their conversation light and pleasant.

"I'll just be a few more minutes," she promised them.

A witch's life was filled with drama and suspense. It was part of the job description, and there was no getting around it. A light tapping on the door announced Holly's arrival. Milly ushered her niece into the foyer with a finger to her lips and shut the door behind her.

"There are clients in the living room. What's wrong?"

Holly pulled the wool cap from her head and shook out her hair. Her cheeks were without color, her eyes glassy from crying. She struggled for a proper reply.

"This is about Peter, isn't it? Don't tell me you've been scrying on the poor boy again. I see it clearly in your face. You must leave Peter alone!"

"But I can't," Holly said, the tears rolling down her cheeks. "Peter wants to kill himself."

"What? Are you sure?"

"He nearly jumped off the Brooklyn Bridge this afternoon. I was scrying on him, and I saw the whole thing. He would have done it, but his girlfriend Liza came to the rescue. I'm so worried about him, Aunt Milly."

"Lower your voice," Milly said, glancing at the living room. "Tell me something. Why do you assume Peter was going to jump? He might have just been out for an afternoon walk."

"Peter gets depressed sometimes. He wants his life to be different. Sometimes he can't handle it. He told me once that he imagined himself jumping off the Brooklyn Bridge, and coming out of the water a different person. I told him that if he jumped off the bridge, he'd surely die. He said, 'If that's what it takes . . . ' and his voice trailed off."

Milly squeezed her niece's arm. "Why didn't you ever tell me this?"

"Peter swore me to secrecy."

"You still should have told me. I would have talked to him."

"It won't make it any better. Trust me, I've tried."

Milly wanted to grab her niece by the shoulders, and shake some common sense into her. Milly understood who Peter was, and what he was, better than anyone else, except maybe Max. If anyone could talk the boy off a ledge, it was her. Not that she could convince Holly of that.

"My powers of persuasion are far greater than yours," Milly said. "I will go see Peter tomorrow, and talk some sense into him. He'll listen to me."

Holly shook her head and stared at the floor. A tiny sob escaped her lips. "It's too late. Max told Peter about some horrible things he did when he was a little boy. I heard the whole thing. Peter ran out of the restaurant with the most horrible expression on his face."

"You mean Max told Peter about the killings," Milly said matter-of-factly.

"You know about them?"

"Of course I know about them. Come on, dear girl, I helped raise Peter." A noise from the other room caught Milly's ear; her guests were growing restless. If she wasn't careful, the subtle spell she'd cast over them would evaporate like a puff of smoke, and they'd seek out another psychic in the city to look into their futures and soothe their fears. "I must get back to my guests. Come back later, and we'll go have dinner and talk this through some more."

Holly shook her head, still miserable.

"What is it now?" her aunt said stiffly.

"Peter's going to do harm to himself. I can feel it in my bones," Holly declared.

A feeling in the bones was the window to a witch's soul, and could not be denied.

"And what do you propose we do?" Milly asked.

"We must protect Peter," Holly said.

Her niece didn't understand. Milly didn't have the time or the patience to explain it to her. Holly would have to learn on her own about Peter, just as Milly had done. She opened the front door and gently but firmly pushed her niece into the hall. Nearly fifty years separated them in age, but sometimes it felt more like hundreds, the different between them was so great.

"What are you doing?" Holly said, sounding hurt.

"Showing you out, my dear."

"But why—what have I done?"

"You don't understand what's going on. Because if you did, you wouldn't have raced across town, and barged in on me like this."

A hurt look crossed Holly's face. "I don't understand what you're saying to me."

Milly stuck her head through the open door. "You and I were not put on this earth to protect Peter. Peter was put here to protect us. Now go home. I'll call you later."

Holly looked stunned, the words slow to sink in. Milly shut the door firmly in her niece's face, and returned to her guests in the living room.

PART IV

DANTE

43

*C*all her," Ray said.

Early Wednesday morning, the sun was barely up. Munns stared at the cell phone lying on his kitchen table. It was a clamshell Motorola, ancient by today's standards. He would have bought a newer model if he'd had friends to talk to. But Munns had no friends. Few serial killers did.

"Come on, call her," Ray implored him. "You need to set this thing up."

Munns lifted his eyes to stare at the tattoo artist leaning against the sink. He didn't like the tone of Ray's voice, or that Ray had driven to Munns's house so early in the morning, and banged on his front door like an irate bill collector.

"It already is set up," Munns said irritably. "Rachael is coming out on the train Friday night. If I call her now and tell her to come early, she'll get suspicious and stop trusting me."

"You're not going to do it? Not even for me?"

"Nope, not even for you."

"Don't you trust me?"

Munns's silence was his answer. He knew how to draw victims into his web, and did not appreciate Ray's interference into the one thing he did rather well.

Ray pulled up a chair and sat backward in it. Whenever he could, he liked to show off the demonic-inspired tattoos that covered his arms. Like wild reptiles moving across the jungle floor, they slithered across his skin in perfect synchronicity. "I had a dream last night. Rachael came out on the Friday night train, and she had a pair of detectives with her. Something happened on Friday morning that made her suspicious, and she decided to call the cops."

"You saw this in your dream," Munns said.

"I sure as hell did. The detectives busted you and searched your car," Ray said, not missing a beat. "They found rope and handcuffs and a bottle of chloroform. Then they came here, and tore your house apart. They found your trophy collection of clothing and jewelry of the women you've killed. They threw your ass in the county lockup, and the judge refused to grant you bail. You know what that means, don't you?"

Munns shuddered, and drew his bathrobe tightly around him. When a judge didn't grant bail, it meant the system thought you were guilty, and was not going to let you back into society no matter how fancy your lawyer was.

"I know," Munns whispered.

"Then call Rachael right now, and get her to come out on the train tonight. You know how to talk to women. You told me so yourself."

"But why tonight? Why so soon?"

"Because she still isn't suspicious. I saw that in my dream, too."

Munns understood the power of dreams. He'd started having them right after Ray had stamped the shimmering silver tattoo on his neck. They'd given him glimpses into the future, and he'd watched himself kill several of his victims before it had actually happened. He'd seen these dreams as gifts, for it had allowed him to watch himself and hone his skills. But they had not come without a price. Each time he'd had one, he'd awakened in sweat-soaked sheets and he knew that he had ceded another chunk of his soul to the Devil.

Finally, he gave in. "All right."

Ray seemed relieved. From the fridge he grabbed a long-neck beer. Perhaps he'd seen himself going down on Friday night as well. No doubt he had some skin in the game.

"You gonna stand there and listen to me?" Munns asked.

"What—I make you nervous?"

"Everything makes me nervous. Go in the living room."

"Whatever you say, Doc."

Ray walked out of the kitchen, and Munns pulled up Rachael's number from his cell's directory. He'd talked to her many times, knew her schedule by heart. She worked at a cancer research center in New

York affiliated with one of the universities, and got to work by seven thirty each morning so she could feed the rats that she used in her experiments and would one day have to inject with pink juice and put to sleep. She'd told Munns this was the most difficult part of her job, and always made her cry. Munns hadn't understood how anyone could feel compassion for a rodent, but had pretended he did, just to make her happy.

The call went through. Munns quickly made up a story. Rachael lived by herself on the Upper East Side and had no close friends or social life. A single woman living in New York who didn't get out much or have any attention showered upon her. It gave him an idea.

"Hello?" she answered, sounding out of breath.

"Rachael? This is Doc Munns. How are you? I sure hope didn't catch you at a bad time. I have some wonderful news to share with you."

"Not at all. I just came through the door and was pulling off my coat. It sure is cold for April. And I'd love to hear some good news."

"The dean of the college called me last night, and said he wanted to hold a party at his house tonight so he can introduce you to the faculty. I thought it was a great idea, so I said yes. I hope you don't mind."

"Tonight? But I'm not coming out until Friday night."

"I know. But I didn't think you'd want to pass up this opportunity. Kevin and Bob and Marty and Roland will all be there, and I know they want to meet you. Roland's a long-distance runner, just like you. If I'm not mistaken, Kevin attended the same college you did. And Marty and Bob are both great guys. They were all thrilled to hear they'll be having a nice young lady in their ranks."

He heard the hesitation in her voice. Four single men, one single women. Those were a lot better odds than she was going to find in some stinky bar in the city.

"But I have to work tomorrow," she said rather lamely.

"I realize that. Here's what I'd like to suggest. When the party's over, I'll drive you back to the city in my car. The trip won't take more than an hour and a half. It will be a late night, but I think it will be worth it. You game?"

"You sure it's no trouble?" she asked.

Munns smiled into the phone. "Not at all."

"But I don't have anything to wear. This is too sudden. No."

He frowned. "The party is strictly casual, jeans and sweaters. No one will be dressed up."

"Casual is different between men and women. You know what they say. You only get one chance to make a good first impression."

"Trust me, you won't make a bad impression."

"You sound awfully determined to get me out there. Is there something else going on here I should know about?"

Rachael's intuition was kicking in, and intuition was the messenger of fear. If Munns didn't put this fire out now, she would not enter his trap. "Of course not," he said in his smoothest tone. "It's just that I already told the dean that you'd come, and his wife is making a special dessert to serve the guests. They'll both be terribly disappointed if you cancel."

"Oh, God, now I'm backed into a corner," Rachael said. "I really wish you hadn't committed for me. That wasn't fair."

"I didn't feel comfortable saying no," Munns replied. "The dean's my boss, you know."

"Oh, that's right. I forgot."

"Do you want me to cancel for you? I can, you know."

Rachael hesitated. It was at that moment that Munns knew she was coming.

"I'll call him the moment we hang up," he threw in for good measure.

"No, I want to come," his next victim said.

"You sure?"

"Yes. It sounds like a good time."

"That's wonderful. You'll love the dean, and everyone else, too."

"I'm sure I will. I'll finish up my work early, and grab a late afternoon train out of Grand Central. I'll text you when I know my arrival time."

"That works for me. I'll see you at the station. I'm looking forward to meeting you."

"Same here. Good-bye, Doc."

Munns ended the call. That hadn't been nearly as difficult as he'd thought. A woman's greatest weakness was her desire to be loved. It blinded them to so many things.

"All done," he called into the next room.

44

Ray skillfully maneuvered down the twisting gravel driveway outside Munns's house. He hadn't liked setting Munns up, and hoped it did not come back to haunt him.

At the bottom of the hill, the road turned smooth. The lassitude of highway driving took over, and he fired up a cigarette and settled in for the ride back to town. Tonight was going to be the end of the line for Munns. The elders of the Order of Astrum had said as much, and they were never wrong.

Ray took a deep drag on the cigarette. He needed to get out of town. He didn't like leaving on such short notice, but had no other choice. There would be bloodshed tonight, and he needed to distance himself from the carnage.

But where would he go? To the hinterlands of upstate New York? The wilds of Maine? Or to a remote town in Vermont? They were good places to hide, with plenty of farms and wide open spaces. He'd grab a map when he got back to the tattoo parlor and make his decision.

Music came out of his radio's speakers like a funeral dirge played extra slow. As the noise grew louder, he fiddled with the dial to make it go away. Instead, the sound became deafening, and the interior of his car turned black.

He hit the brakes, fearful of hitting something in the road. When the lights returned, he found himself sitting in a deserted theater, dead center with the stage. The strange music he'd heard was coming from the orchestra pit, where a quartet of skeletons plucked discordant notes on violins and blew savagely on wind instruments. Had he died, and gone to hell?

"Hello, Ray," a voice said.

Three men wearing black robes appeared. One sat to his left, the second to his right, the third directly in front of him, positioned backward in his seat. Ray was trapped. Were these the elders? He had to think so. They were handsome devils, with strong facial features and good teeth, and appeared to be in their late twenties, although Ray knew the elders were much older, having been granted eternal youth as part of their pact with Satan. It was not a bad deal, only the spark of humanity that colored all human beings was missing, and they looked like ghouls.

"You're the elders of the Order of Astrum," Ray said respectfully.

"We thought it was time we had a chat with you," the elder facing him said. "You've been an outstanding recruiter, the best we've ever had. You've done such a good job, we decided you deserved to be rewarded. Would you like that, Ray?"

Ray started to get excited. He'd become a member of the Order in prison after hearing stories about members gaining mystical powers as rewards for pleasing their masters.

"Are you going to give me special powers?" he asked.

"We can. Is there something in particular you'd like?"

"I know this is going to sound stupid, but I've always wanted to bend silverware with my mind. You know, like spoons. I always thought that was really cool."

The elder facing him smiled like a department store mannequin. The elder didn't possess a soul, and it showed through in everything he said and did. Ray imagined himself as an elder one day, immortal and able to wreak havoc on the world whenever it suited him.

"Consider it done," the elder said.

"Cool," the tattoo artist said.

"There's something else we'd like to give you as well."

"What's that?"

"Call it the gift of knowledge. It's time for you to be enlightened."

Enlightened. That was a strange word for the elder to use, and Ray nearly laughed.

"I'm game."

"Good," the elder to his right chimed in. "You see, we have a master plan which involves the good citizens of New York being exposed to something that will forever change their lives. A portentous event designed to alter their souls, so to speak. We cannot put this plan into motion with Peter Warlock in the picture. Warlock must be erased."

"I thought that was Munns's job," Ray said, uncertain where this was going.

"You must make sure that Munns does not fail."

"Whoa. I was going to leave town."

"You cannot leave," the elder facing him said sternly. "You must stay, and make sure that Munns does away with Warlock."

Ray shifted uncomfortably in his plush velvet seat. He didn't like when plans got changed at the last moment. Yet at the same time, he understood the elders' concern. Munns was erratic, and could very well screw up. If Peter Warlock was going to be taken out of the picture, it would probably be better if Ray hung around and made sure the job got done correctly.

"If I say yes, will I become like you?" Ray asked.

"You will be given the opportunity to become like us," the elder facing him replied. "The process takes time. First, your old self will fall away, then your new self will be born. With your new self will come new responsibilities. You will become one of Dante's disciples."

"Who's Dante?"

"Dante is the anti-conjuror. For the past thousand years, he's performed his magic for the delight of Satan and his guests. Satan has decided that it's time to unleash him, and is sending Dante to New York. You will have the honor to be one of his assistants."

"Will this make me like you guys?"

"Yes. It will bring you one step closer. Would you care to meet Dante?"

Ray had always wanted to join the inner sanctum of the Order, for he knew that one day it would lead to him standing at Satan's side and becoming immortal. Whoever Dante was, he was sure he could find a way to get along with him.

"Bring him on," Ray said, unable to hide his excitement.

"Splendid. Enjoy the show."

The elders vanished, and Ray found himself sitting alone in the theater, shuddering from a burst of cold air. He could no longer remember what the elders looked like, their memory having been erased. He would have given anything to be so powerful.

The house lights dimmed. The curtains parted to reveal a darkened stage. A single spotlight shone down, its beam so bright it reminded Ray of a light coming out of a flying saucer in a Spielberg movie. Smoke filled the stage, followed by a flash of light, from which stepped a wild-looking young man wearing a flowing purple robe. This had to be Dante, his new boss. The guy was a trip, with spiked purple hair, pierced eyebrows, lips, and nose, and Gothic designs smeared across his face. He moved in a slight crouch while staring sinisterly from side to side, and looked like a jackal that had learned to walk on its hind legs. Plucking two black scarves out of the air, the anti-conjuror bunched them together, and made a screaming vulture appear.

The vulture was released into the theater, and flew in a lazy circle over Ray's head. More vultures appeared from the same scarves, and were also set loose. The birds weren't hidden in Dante's coat or stuffed up his sleeves, but were molded to life right before his disbelieving eyes. Ray had once seen a magician at a birthday party, and thought the whole thing was a bunch of crap, the tricks obvious if you looked hard enough. Dante's magic was different. It looked real, and something told him it probably was.

Ray started to applaud, figuring he'd better make his new boss happy. The hollow sound echoed throughout the theater. Dante silenced him with a menacing glare. Clearly, he did not like interruptions.

A final vulture was brought to life, and sent airborne to join the flock. Ray kept one eye overhead, noticing that the vultures had positioned themselves directly over his chair.

"What's your name?" Dante's voice was high-pitched, like a woman's.

"Ray," he replied. "Nice to meet you."

"Do you know what the purpose of magic is, Ray? Magic is supposed is to reveal the secrets of the universe and life itself. Magic is not supposed to create illusion, it's supposed to strip illusion away. It's about finding eternal truth."

Ray didn't know what the hell Dante was talking about but nodded anyway.

"Here. Let me show you." Dante cupped his empty palms together while his eyes bored a hole into Ray's soul. "Think of a thing which truly frightens you. Don't tell me, just think of it."

That was easy. The one thing that truly frightened Ray were rats. One had bitten him in the foot as a kid, and he'd never shaken the experience.

From Dante's cupped hands appeared a rat with a curled tail. It leapt to the stage, and was quickly followed by another. Soon, rats were pouring out of Dante's cupped hands in such great numbers that they flooded the stage, and began to pour into the audience.

Ray had seen enough, and jumped out of his seat in fear. Too late. A rat was attached to his pant leg, tearing at the fabric. Several more jumped on his shoe, their weight dragging him down. Within seconds he was covered in furry rodents whose sole intent was to scare him to death. Then the vultures swooped down, attaching their beaks to the tattoo artist's shirt, and lifted him into the air with the rats still clinging to his body.

"Don't do this to me," Ray cried.

Dante stepped to the foot of the stage to appraise his handiwork. He had peeled back the darkest layer of his subject's soul, and seemed pleased with himself. "You now work for me, Ray. Do as I say, and you'll do fine. But if you disobey me, my furry friends will skin you alive. Do I make myself clear?"

"Yes. Please make them go away," he begged.

"When your job is finished here, you will join me in the city. We're starting rehearsals soon, and I want you to be there. Does that sound good, Ray?"

"Yes. They're biting me!"

Dante howled with laughter and lifted his arms into the air. The vultures released their grip on his clothes, and Ray let out a blood-curdling scream as he fell into the audience.

A car horn's blast brought Ray back to the real world of Westchester County. A delivery truck idled behind him at an intersection, the driver fuming. Ray could still feel the rats on his body, and tried to swipe the invisible creatures away. The delivery truck passed, firing its horn.

Ray pulled off the road and started to cry. Dante had made him want to die. He'd never felt that way before, and his fear was tearing him apart. This was not what he'd bargained for, and he told himself there was still time to escape to Maine or upstate New York and get out with his soul. He would live in the woods if he had to. He was ready to do just about anything to get away from this madness.

A shadow fell over his van. It was a perfectly sunny day, without a cloud in the sky. Rolling down his window, he stuck his head out. A mob of vultures hung directly overhead. Try to run, they dared him, and see what happens. He wiped away his tears, knowing he was doomed to serve a master far darker than any he'd known before.

45

E very day began with the promise of a new beginning. Peter had read that in a book while growing up. The message had stayed, and had helped him get through the dark times.

Wednesday morning was a perfect example. Sunlight flooded through his bedroom window and delicious breakfast smells floated up from the kitchen. It was enough to make him forget what a nightmare the previous few days had been, if just for a little while.

He tossed on a bathrobe and bounded downstairs. The brownstone had been sold to him with a warning. The previous tenant had fallen down the stairs, and broken his ankle. The staircase was treacherous, and not using the handrail was a serious mistake.

Soon after moving in, Peter had learned that the staircase wasn't treacherous at all. The problem was a cantankerous ghost named Zachary Nathaniel Harrison who'd inhabited the brownstone for over a century, and occupied the spacious guest bedroom on the second floor. Zack, as he liked to be called, was a light sleeper, and punished those who woke him up by tripping them during their stair runs.

Ghosts could be reasoned with. Peter had conducted a séance in the bedroom, and summoned Zack to the table. The old ghost had obliged him, and they'd sat and talked and eventually worked out a deal. When the sun was up, Peter was free to run the stairs as much as he wished. When it was down, there would be no running. They had shaken hands on it, which had felt strange, since there had been nothing there to physically shake.

The kitchen greeted him with a spread of food fit for a king and Liza at the counter squeezing fresh oranges. It still amazed him that she'd not packed her bags and split after yesterday's revelations. The expression "love was blind" had taken on a whole new meaning.

"If it isn't Sleeping Beauty," she said.

"What's the special occasion?" he asked.

"I just thought you needed a fresh start after yesterday."

"Why? What happened yesterday?"

She wiped her hands on a paper towel and wrapped her arms around Peter's thin waist. "We have a lot of talking to do, you know."

"I'm ready when you are."

"Good. How about later this afternoon?"

He kissed the tip of her nose. "I'm game."

They sat down at the kitchen table and dug in. Liza had hit the nail on the head. A fresh start was exactly what the doctor ordered. He couldn't change the horrific things he'd done as a child, but he could make sure they never happened again. He was an adult now, and his own boss. He would stop the demon inside of him from controlling his actions.

Finished, they stood at the sink with Liza washing the dishes and Peter drying and putting them away. "Do you remember that antique wristwatch that fell out of the sky while we were standing in the court-yard the other night?" she asked.

Peter remembered the watch well. Made by Cartier, it had belonged to the shadow person he'd confronted in the lobby of Grand Central Station. He'd never understood its significance, and wondered if Liza had plumbed it secret.

"I may have found its owner," Liza went on. "I noticed it wasn't working properly, so I found a store online that repairs antique watches, and sent them an e-mail along with a photo I shot on my iPhone. The manager e-mailed me right back. Come to find out, he thinks he's repaired the watch before. His shop is called Time After Time, and is in the West Village. He asked me to come by this morning, and show the watch to him so he could confirm it."

"Did he say who the owner was?"

"No. The manager's name is Walter, and he was very mysterious about the whole thing. Maybe he can tell us who the owner is, and that will lead to figuring out what the shadow people want. It's a stretch, but who knows."

Peter hung the dish towel on the hook next to the fridge. The other world was a difficult place to understand, the motives of the spirits never fully clear. Liza was reacting the same way he usually did, which was to plunge ahead, and hope for the best.

"I'm game," he said. "Let's go talk to Walter."

"I'll go change," Liza said.

Peter took out his cell phone and called Herbie. "Be at the brownstone in half an hour," he told him. "We're going on a fishing expedition."

The West Village was old New York, its streets twisting and narrow. Time After Time sat in a dusty storefront filled with grandfather clocks and rare timepieces in glass display cabinets.

Peter told Herbie to circle the block, and entered the shop with Liza.

The cramped interior was a mess. Any more than a handful of customers, and the place would have felt crowded. An eccentric-looking manager with a halo of curly white hair stood behind the counter, and nodded courteously as they entered .

"You must be Walter," Liza said. "I'm Liza. We spoke yesterday on the phone."

Walter said nothing. He probably got a hundred phone calls a day. Or he didn't get any phone calls, and was playing stupid. From her purse, Liza removed the antique woman's watch that had fallen from the sky, and placed it on a felt mat on the counter. Walter stuck a loupe in his eye and studied the exquisite timepiece. "This is an original Cartier, special limited edition, very rare to find these days. May I ask where you came upon this?"

"Is that important?" Liza asked.

"I just would like to know, that's all."

"My boyfriend and I found it."

Walter studied Peter briefly, then looked back at Liza. "May I ask where?"

"I'm sorry, but that's none of your business."

They'd been in the store less than a minute, and Walter was already giving them the third degree. Something wasn't right with this picture, and Peter scanned the store's interior. Not one, but three surveillance cameras were trained upon them, two from the ceiling, the third bolted to the wall behind the counter. The wall camera was a recent addition as evidenced by the sales sticker glued to the side. And there was a large rottweiler lying at Walter's feet behind the counter. The dog was panting and its tail wasn't wagging. Dogs fed off their owner's emotions, and Walter was subliminally telling the dog to be on alert.

Peter thought he knew what was going on. The watch was hot, and on a list of stolen items that the police sent to store owners in the city. Walter had recognized it from Liza's photo, and had decided to set a trap. *Better start telling the truth,* he thought.

"Look, we know that this watch belongs to someone else," Peter interrupted. "How we came upon it doesn't matter. What's important is that we return it to its rightful owner. Right, dear?"

The corners of Liza's mouth turned up in a smile. He'd never called her dear before, and she seemed to like it.

"We just want to do the right thing," Liza continued. "Yesterday when we spoke, you indicated you knew who the owner might be. If you'll tell us, we'll return it to her right away. Or you can do it. Whatever you think is best."

Walter looked perplexed and let out a deep breath. "Oh, my," he said.

"Is something wrong?" Peter asked.

"You're not thieves. I can tell by listening to you. Thieves come into my store often, and try to sell me hot timepieces. You're not like them."

"Of course we're not thieves," Liza said with a little laugh.

"Well, I'm deeply sorry, then. Truly, I am."

The shopkeeper took a deliberate step away from the counter. As he did, a black sedan pulled up in front of the store, and double-parked in the street. Four plainclothes detectives wearing silver NYPD detective shields pinned to their jackets piled out, and rushed through the front door. Each had a gun drawn. At the same time, a door behind the front counter parted, and two more gun-toting detectives appeared.

"Don't tell them anything," Peter said under his breath.

46

Peter had lived on TV cop shows as a kid, and knew what was about to happen. The detectives would separate him and Liza, and grill them. They would ask each of them a series of questions, and write down their answers in spiral pads. Then the detectives would reconvene, and compare notes. If the detectives caught either of them lying, the drilling process would continue until they got to the truth.

Liza was sent to the back room of the store while Peter remained in front. As she was led away, she winked at him. She didn't appear the least bit nervous or afraid. She'd been through a lot lately, certainly a lot more than any of his other girlfriends had ever put up with. He winked back.

"Cut the crap," the detective in charge barked.

The detective's name was Velasco. Short and balding, his most prominent feature was his beach ball stomach. *Who needs a six-pack when you can have a keg?* Peter thought.

Velasco pulled a stool out from behind the counter, and made Peter sit on it. The detective towered over him while another detective covered Peter's back. A third detective stood by the locked front door. The shades had been pulled over the window for privacy.

"What's your name?" Velasco asked.

"Peter Warlock."

"Very funny. Your real name."

"Peter Warren. Warlock's my stage name."

"You some kind of performer?"

"I'm a magician. I have a show in town, *Anything's Possible*."

Velasco nodded like he'd heard of him. Early in his career, Peter had performed a number of stunts around the city to gather much-needed publicity for his show. As a result, there were a lot of people who had heard his name but who'd never seen him perform.

"All right, Mr. Magic, tell me where you got the antique watch," Velasco said.

"I found it," Peter replied.

"Be a little more specific."

"Do you know who the owner is? I've been trying to locate her."

"I'm the one asking the questions, pal. Now tell me about the watch."

"It fell out of the sky," Peter replied truthfully.

"Oh, boy, a regular comedian. How do you think it's going to look if I run you and your girlfriend in? Think that kind of publicity is going to help ticket sales?"

"Are you going to arrest us?"

"I will if you don't come clean with me. That watch doesn't belong to you."

"That doesn't mean we stole it. You don't have a case, Detective. Let us go, and I'll be happy to explain to you how the watch came into our possession."

Velasco didn't like being told how to run his investigation, and wagged a finger in his suspect's face. "Keep up the banter, and I'll throw your skinny ass in jail."

"Which jail?" Peter wanted to know.

"MCC. Ever been there?"

MCC was the Metropolitan Correctional Center on Park Row behind the U.S. Federal Courthouse. Peter knew the facility like the back of his hand, and said, "Matter of fact, I have. I was locked up in a cellblock in the basement that the warden claimed was inescapable. I managed to escape in four minutes flat, and beat Houdini's record by thirty seconds. There's a video on my Web site if you don't believe me."

"I remember that stunt," the detective guarding the door said. "You moved all the other inmates in the block into different cells. That took a lot of nerve."

"Thanks," Peter said.

"Shut up," Velasco told both of them. Looking his suspect in the eye, he said, "I think you're hiding something. I'm hauling you in."

"On what charges?"

"I'll think of something. Get up."

Peter gazed into Velasco's eyes and read his mind. The detective was having a bad day. He'd started his morning by having a knock-down, drag-out argument with his teenage daughter. Then the battery on his car had been dead when he'd tried to start it. Now this wiseass magician was giving him a hard time. Peter and his girlfriend were going to spend the rest of the day in jail if Peter didn't think of something quick.

Velasco pulled open his sports jacket and removed a pair of nickel-plated handcuffs from his belt. Peter wanted to tell Velasco that he could escape from those, too, but didn't think the detective would appreciate the humor.

"I'll tell you about the watch, but first you need to call a friend of mine," Peter said.

Velasco eyed him suspiciously. "Who's that?"

"His card's in my wallet. You'll understand when I show it to you."

"All right, show it to me."

Peter pulled Special Agent Garrison's business card from his billfold and handed it to the detective. Velasco stared at the embossed lettering on the white card.

"The FBI? What do they have to do with this?"

"Just call him," Peter said.

G arrison barged into the watch shop with his badge pinned to the lapel of his sports jacket and a disgruntled look on his face. Peter wondered what pressing matter he'd pulled the FBI agent away from. New York was the greatest city on earth, but there were plenty of bad people here as well, and the life of a law enforcement agent was nothing but a challenge.

"Thanks for getting here so fast," Peter told him.

"Who are these guys?" Garrison asked.

"This is Detective Velasco. He wants to arrest me."

"What for? You tell him one of your jokes?"

"Possession of stolen property," Velasco said. "You know this smart-ass?"

"He does consulting work for me. Now, tell me what he did," Garrison said.

"He was caught with a stolen wristwatch whose owner has been missing for over a year," Velasco replied. "When I tried to question him, he started talking in riddles."

"Peter's a psychic, he does that sometimes," Garrison said.

Velasco's jaw dropped open. "Cut it out."

"I'm dead serious. Don't tell me you've never worked with psychics before."

"Tried to. They were worthless."

"They were probably fakes. Peter's the real deal."

"I'm having a hard time believing this." Velasco spoke to Peter, "So read my mind."

Peter was boxed into a corner. He tried to avoid public displays of mind reading whenever possible. When mind reading was performed onstage, all sorts of explanations were possible; when done in person, there was only one explanation—the person doing the mind reading was a psychic. He lowered his voice so the other detectives would not hear. "At breakfast this morning, you had words with your daughter over her choice of boyfriends. Then your car's battery died, and you had to carpool with a cop you can't stand. When you got to work, the coffeepot was empty. That good enough for you?"

"Jesus H. Christ," Velasco said.

"I told you he was real," Garrison said smugly.

The antique Cartier that had brought them together lay on the counter. The watch was a mystery, along with most of the events of the past several days. If Peter could plumb the watch's secrets, then perhaps the rest of the puzzles would solve themselves.

"What can you tell me about the watch's owner?" Peter asked.

"What do you want to know?"

"Everything."

"Her name is Barbara Metcalf," Velasco replied. "Single woman, early fifties, lived alone, got a couple of PhDs, is one of the top brass at the CDC. Went missing about a year ago and hasn't been heard from. We suspect foul play, but don't have a suspect or a motive. Metcalf had a nice collection of antique jewelry. This watch was one of her favorite pieces, which she often wore. When she went missing, so did several pieces of her jewelry, including this watch. We asked every jewelry store in town to be on the lookout for it.

"Yesterday, your girlfriend e-mailed the manager of this store a photo of Metcalf's watch, asking if he could repair it. Walter immediately recognized the watch, and contacted the police. We laid a trap for you, and you walked into it. That's it in a nutshell."

Peter felt numb. The story wasn't what he'd expected to hear at all. He'd assumed the shadow person he'd confronted in Grand Central Station was a thoroughly evil spirit whose human life had been filled with crimes against society, as well as humanity. A person wicked through and through, and in league with the Devil.

"What's does CDC stand for?" Peter asked.

"Centers for Disease Control," Velasco explained. "Metcalf ran their research department. She was responsible for finding cures for things like bubonic plague and anthrax."

"So she was a good person," the young magician said.

"That's what Walter told us," Velasco said.

"The shop manager knew her personally?"

"Yes. They were friends."

"I need to speak with him."

Walter was led into the front of the store. There was nothing more powerful than the truth, and Peter's head was still spinning from the things Velasco had told him. If Barbara Metcalf had been a good person on this earth, then it was not possible that she'd turned into an evil spirit in the afterlife. That was not how things worked. Which meant that there had been a black mark in her background which Velasco didn't know about. It was the only explanation he could think of, and now he needed to hear the shop manager confirm it.

"What can you tell me about the owner of this watch?" Peter asked.

Walter's face softened as he was overcome with memories. Peter took a look inside Walter's head, and saw the woman he had known. Short and rather petite, her clothing suggested a person who appreciated the finer things in life, while the way she carried herself indicated she was used to getting her way. The description strong willed came to mind.

"How do I describe Barbara?" Walter scratched his chin. "Brilliant, headstrong, filled with passion about her work, demanding at times. She had quite a temper. I remember one time, this is going to sound funny, but once I promised to repair her watch, only I stuck the watch in a drawer, and forgot about it. You should have seen the look on her face when she found out."

"Did she get mad?" Peter asked.

"Mad was not the word. She became furious. She started to stomp out, and then she turned around, oh, I shouldn't be telling this, not with her missing for so long."

"Please. It's important you tell me everything."

"Very well. Barbara went to the front door like she was going to leave. Then she spun around in a huff, lifted her foot, and pulled off her shoe. She threw it across the store at me!"

"Her shoe," Peter said in shock.

"That's right. Of course she immediately apologized. I later learned from a mutual friend that Barbara had done this before."

"She threw a shoe at someone," Peter said.

"Yes. It happened in the lab where she worked. Another doctor made a mistake, and ruined a week's worth of work. Barbara pulled off a shoe and tossed it at him. She had a boiling point. When she got mad, she threw shoes at people."

Peter thought back to Friday night, standing on his front stoop talking to Garrison, when a shoe had come flying through the bedroom window, and landed at his feet. Was this Metcalf's not-so-subtle way of telling him that she was angry at him? If that was the case, then he'd gotten this whole thing terribly, terribly wrong.

He broke out of his thought. Liza had returned to the front of the store with two of the detectives. The look on her startled face said she'd heard every word Walter had said, and was thinking the same thoughts that he was thinking.

"Oh, my God, Peter," she exclaimed. "Oh, my God."

47

I need to talk to Peter in private," Garrison said to Velasco. "Do you mind?"

The FBI had jurisdiction over the NYPD, and Garrison didn't need to be asking Velasco's permission for anything. Velasco appreciated the gesture, however, and said, "Be my guest. Be careful. He's a slippery one."

"That's one way to describe him," Garrison said with a laugh.

Peter and Garrison walked outside. It was bitter cold and blowing hard. Peter's limo was parked across the street by the curb.

"Want to talk in my limo?" Peter asked.

"Beats freezing to death," Garrison replied.

They crossed and climbed into the backseat. Herbie looked up from the sports section. Peter shook his head and his driver went back to his reading. The interior was toasty and they spent a moment getting comfortable. Peter handed his guest a bottled water.

"Thanks. Now tell me what's going on," Garrison said.

"Up until now, I thought the shadow people were trying to lure me over to the other side to have me killed," Peter said. "Now I'm not so sure."

"Then what's their purpose?"

"Your guess is as good as mine. Maybe they're trying to show me something."

"In a good way?"

"I think so."

"Hold on a second. You told me the other night that you were taken into the future, where Dr. Death shot you in the leg, and was just about to put a final bullet in your head when you returned to the present. That doesn't sound very good to me."

"Perhaps something else was going on."

"Like what?"

Peter had journeyed to the other side many times, yet still could not fathom much of what he saw. He'd always assumed that as he grew older and more mature, the unexplained would untangle itself, and the truth would become clear. So far that hadn't happened, leaving him to wonder if the other side would ever be fully explained. "I don't know what the shadow people are up to, but I plan to find out. There's a psychic in town named Selena who communicates with the shadow people on a regular basis. I need to track her down, and have a chat."

"Think she'll talk? You psychics are a cagey bunch."

Garrison was right about that—psychics were as secretive with each other as they were with the general public. It came from a lifetime of secrecy, born out of growing up knowing you were different, and also knowing how that difference would be perceived. Getting Selena to talk wouldn't be easy, but he didn't see that he had any other choice. She was a keeper of secrets, and he needed to gain her trust.

"I'm willing to give it a shot," Peter said.

"You and your girlfriend are free to go. I'll deal with the cops. Call me if you learn something."

"I'll do that. Would you mind giving me another of your business cards? Detective Velasco kept the one I gave him."

"What for? You've got my number in your cell, don't you?"

"It's my Get out of Jail Free card."

Garrison pulled a dozen cards from his wallet and stuck them in Peter's hand. "Take 'em all. Something tells me you're going to need them."

Garrison went back inside the watch shop. Moments later Liza came out the front door, and was soon snuggled up beside Peter. She had not enjoyed being detained by the detectives, even if just for a little while. Peter told Herbie to head to Washington Square Park, then pulled a club soda out of the minirefrigerator, twisted off the top, and handed it to Liza. She took a long swallow.

"Are psychics lives always this eventful?" she asked.

"Most psychics lead pretty normal lives," he admitted.

"What makes you so special?"

That was a good question. Of late, there never seemed to be a dull moment. Perhaps one day he'd find out why, along with the other unanswered mysteries which consumed his life.

"I wish I knew," he said.

The blind held a special place in most New Yorkers' hearts. They rode the subways and walked the sidewalks with their Seeing Eye dogs without a worry in the world, their calm demeanor in sharp contrast to madness swirling around them.

Homer, the blind psychic, spent his days beneath the Washington Square Park's famed marble arch. Built two centuries ago, the arch resembled an ancient Roman artifact, and dwarfed everything around it. Long ago, the police had run off the fortune-telling gypsies who'd held court at the arch, but out of kindness, had allowed Homer to stay.

Homer sat on a folding metal stool and told people's fortunes. Part of his charm was that he dressed in a similar fashion to the professors at nearby New York University. Today he wore a brown cashmere sweater, a navy scarf, and brown corduroy pants. Unlike most fortune-tellers, he did not have a plate or tin cup for donations. If someone wanted to give him money, it was tucked into Homer's breast pocket. If not, he did not complain.

Peter's limo pulled up to the northern entrance to the park, and the partition slid back.

"Tell him to do his trick for you," Herbie called from the front.

"What trick?" Peter asked.

"Homer can make himself invisible," his driver said.

"Cut it out."

"No joke. I heard a bunch of other limo drivers talking about it. One minute Homer is standing there, the next minute, poof! he's gone. I hear it's a real mindblower."

"I'll be sure to ask him."

Peter and Liza got out and entered the park. The arch acted as a gateway to Greenwich Village, and was a favorite meeting spot. During the arch's construction, a perfect set of human remains had been found in a spot directly below where the park's only hanging had taken place. Rumors claimed the arch was haunted, and that the ghost of the dead man, a convicted ax murderer named Witten, ventured out at night to dance in the park's enormous fountain. Peter had never confronted Witten, or his ax, and had assumed that it was only a matter of time before they became acquainted.

Homer was in his usual spot. As they approached, his head bobbed up and down.

"Hello, Homer," Peter said. "It's Peter Warlock."

"Hello, Peter. What a pleasant surprise."

"I brought a friend. Her name is Liza. Liza, meet my friend Homer."

"Hello, Homer," Liza said.

"Hello to you as well," Homer said. "You picked a chilly day to visit the park. A group of classical musicians are warming up near the south entrance. You might want to hear them. They're quite good."

"Perhaps some other time," Peter said. "I need to talk to Selena about the shadow people. You told me the other night that you knew her. Please tell me how to contact her."

Homer scowled. "You know the rules, Peter."

"Yes, I do."

"Yet you ask me to break them."

"This is urgent, a matter of life or death."

"That does not change how the game is played."

"It doesn't?"

Homer shook his head. "No."

"What rules? What are you two talking about?" Liza asked.

"Psychics play by certain rules," Homer explained. "We are not supposed to ask each other questions about the mysteries of the universe for fear that one question will lead to another and then another until the end of time. The answers to these questions must be answered through self-discovery and inner examination. Then the truth will be revealed."

"But a woman's life is at stake," Liza said.

"Do you know this woman?" Homer asked.

"I heard her voice on the phone. Her name is Rachael."

"Well, then go find her, and save her," the blind psychic said.

"But I don't know who she is. Why won't you help us?"

"Because it's not allowed."

Homer rose from his stool. The sun had come out and it was warming up. He removed his scarf, and Peter stared at the open neck of his sweater. Homer was not wearing the five-pointed star that he'd told Peter he wore to ward away the shadow people. Without thinking, Peter blurted out, "Damn it! Why didn't you tell me that the shadow people weren't a threat?"

"Because I'm not supposed to," Homer replied. "If you'll excuse me, I must be going."

"You're leaving?" Liza said. "What kind of friend are you?"

"I'm Peter's friend, and always will be," Homer said stiffly.

"You're not acting like a friend."

"You're not one of us, are you?"

"What's that supposed to mean?"

"You're not a psychic."

"Afraid not."

"An ancient Chinese philosopher once said, 'A secret is no longer a secret by the time it gets to you.'"

"Come on, Homer," Peter implored. "A woman is going to get murdered if I don't figure this thing out."

Homer started to reply, but pursed his lips instead. People lived and people died, but the rules that governed a psychic's existence remained constant, and to break them was unthinkable. Picking up his metal stool, he folded it with a snap of the wrist.

"Would you mind hailing me a cab?" Homer asked.

There was usually a taxi or two parked at the park's northern entrance, ready to whisk people uptown. Peter and Liza both turned around. Today, there were none.

"I'm afraid you're out of luck," Peter said.

When they both turned back around, Homer was gone.

48

here did he go?" Liza said in disbelief.

Peter scanned the area beneath the arch where Homer had just stood. It was not entirely impossible for psychics to make themselves invisible to the naked eye. Peter had seen it done, and hoped someday to master the art himself. Had Homer just made himself invisible?

The answer was immediately obvious. Homer had not.

Psychics could make themselves invisible, but they could not make inanimate objects invisible. And Homer's folding stool was gone as well. Which meant the blind psychic had tricked them in the brief instant it had taken them to turn around to hail a cab.

"He's somewhere nearby," Peter said. "Start looking."

"How do you know he's nearby?"

"Because blind people don't move very fast. Check the bushes."

Liza scoured the nearby bushes while also checking a number of homeless men sleeping on benches. None proved to be Homer. Peter walked around the arch, looking for a hiding place that Homer might have ducked into. Liza joined him a moment later.

"So where is he?" she asked.

"Like I said, he's nearby."

"Peter, he's gone. I looked everywhere."

The greatest lie is the one which we tell ourselves. The lie Liza was telling herself was that Homer had slipped away and could not be found. But what if Homer was still right here, hiding in plain sight? That was a more likely explanation, even if the evidence did not support it.

He examined the spot where Homer had stood. His eyes drifted to the arch. Had the blind psychic somehow managed to get inside of it? And if so, how?

A door was usually the way people entered things. Peter went to the arch and ran his fingertips across the smooth marble. The original arch had been made of wood in celebration of George Washington's birthday. It had been such a hit that a permanent marble arch had been commissioned and built. He ran his forefinger across a break in the marble, and saw that it was the outline to a hidden door. He'd passed beneath the arch countless times in his life and never imagined that it had a door that went inside. He felt Liza's breath on his neck and glanced over his shoulder into her unblinking eyes.

"You are so smart," she said. "Should we knock?"

"Let's surprise him."

"How are you going to get in?"

"Watch."

Peter didn't think Homer had locked the door behind him. Most people in a hurry usually didn't. Kneeling, he slipped his fingers beneath the door's sill and pulled. It popped open, revealing a darkened space inside. He entered while Liza hesitated.

"There's no light," she said.

Taking out his Droid, he went onto the Internet, which caused the screen to light up. It was as good as having a flashlight, and he pointed it into the darkness. "You coming?"

She entered and they ventured ahead. The air was dank and chilly and very still. Just to be sure he was in the right place, Peter pointed his Droid at the floor, and saw a fresh set of footprints in the dust. So this was how Homer made himself disappear.

They came to a spiral staircase. With his Droid, he looked up the twisting stairs. The staircase went to the very top of the arch. There were fresh footprints on the steps as well.

"I'll flip you to see who goes first," Peter said.

"Very funny. You sure you want to go up there? It's awfully dark."

Peter had never been afraid of the dark. Not even as a child had it bothered him. He wondered what that said about his personality as he headed up the stairs.

They were breathing hard by the time they reached the top. Peter checked out their new surroundings with his Droid, and found himself standing inside a vaulted room with an ornate tiled ceiling. He would never have imagined such a room existed on top of the Washington Square Arch. Tucked away in the basement perhaps, but not at the very top. Several windows were blackened by dust and age, and a smattering of light seeped through them.

"Who's that?" Homer's voice called out.

"It's Peter and Liza. We found your hiding place."

"Why won't you leave me alone?"

"I won't let an innocent woman die. Now, are you going to help us, or not?"

Homer let out a pronounced sigh. "Only if you promise never to ask again."

"I promise never to ask you again. Where are you, anyway?"

"Sitting against the far wall. Whatever you do, don't turn on the light."

"There's a light in here?" Peter asked.

"Long ago, this room was the park manager's office, if you can imagine him climbing those stairs every day. The room has electricity and running water. It's quite comfy."

"Why don't you want me to turn on the light?"

"Because it will anger my guests," Homer replied.

"What's he talking about?" Liza whispered.

"Beats me," Peter replied.

Peter made Liza stand behind him. With the light of his Droid, he located Homer on the far wall, parked on his folding stool. Behind him stood a mob of angry ghosts hovering just off the floor. Judging from the forlorn expressions on their sunken faces, they had suffered heavily during their previous lives. One member stood out. Tall and thin, with a pinched face and a scowl, he had a bloodstained ax clutched in his hands. The infamous Witten.

Peter wondered how fast he and Liza could make it down the stairs. Probably not fast enough. "Aren't you going to introduce us to your friends?" he asked.

"These are the ghosts of the park. I'm sure you've heard of them," Homer said.

"I've heard of Witten, but not the others. Who are they?"

"Remember, you only get to ask me one question."

"I know who they are," Liza interrupted. "Before Washington Square Park was built, this area of land was a potter's field where the city's poor and homeless were buried. I read it in a book. Those ghosts are people who are buried right here. Right?"

"There's more to it," Homer said.

Peter again studied the ghosts with his Droid. One held a bloody butcher's knife, while another clutched a thick lead pipe. Their necks were badly discolored and pulled to one side. The city's criminals were buried here as well, he realized.

"These ghosts are criminals, and were hanged for their crimes," he said.

"Eek," Liza said under her breath.

Homer nodded approvingly. This was how the game was supposed to be played. Peter noticed that the ghosts stood behind Homer instead of in front. Clearly, they sensed danger.

But from who?

Certainly not Liza. That left only one other choice.

They were afraid of him.

It didn't seem possible. They'd all died long before he was born, and nothing in his life had ever touched them. He decided to find out, and took a step forward.

"Where are you going?" Liza said under her breath.

"Just wait," he whispered.

The ghosts retreated into the wall, making them half visible, half gone. The fear factor was real. It had never been that way before. In the past, ghosts had been his friends, and he'd confided in many of them while growing up. Some deep spiritual change had caused his physical presence to be feared by even the most dangerous of spirits.

"Tell me how to find Selena," Peter said.

"Selena can be found at the corner of Forty-second Street and Seventh Avenue," Homer replied. "She will explain to you the meaning of the shadow people. Go now, or you will miss her."

Forty-second Street and Seventh Avenue was in the heart of Times Square, and some of the most expensive real estate in the city. No fortune-tellers or psychics could afford to work out of storefronts there. Was Selena a street person?

"Are you sure that's where she is?" Peter asked.

"Positive. Tell her I said hello."

"I'll do that. Thanks for the help. Say good-bye to your friends for me."

"Have a nice day," Homer said.

Peter took a last look at the ghosts with his Droid. They had pulled out of the wall, and seemed relieved that he and Liza were leaving. *That makes two of us*, he thought.

49

Liza sat in the backseat of the limo with her head resting against Peter's chest. Peter could not remember her ever looking so vulnerable.

"That was scary," she said. "What were those things going to do to us?"

"Something unthinkable," he replied.

"So why didn't they?"

"I'm not sure. Ghosts are strange. They have the ability to see through things. You know, like when a person lies or tries to pull a fast one, a ghost will know it in a second. The ghosts inside the arch saw something inside of me they didn't like, and got frightened."

"Have ghosts ever acted that way before?"

What had happened inside the arch was a brand-new experience. Had his demon come so close to the surface that Homer's otherworldly friends had wanted nothing to do with him?

"No," he said. "Never."

Liza clasped his hand and gave it a healthy squeeze. "Remind me to bring you along the next time I visit a haunted house."

They rode the rest of the way uptown in silence. Liza still hadn't run away from him. If anything, she seemed even more committed to making their relationship work. That was good, because he had a sneaking suspicion that there were plenty of other surprises still in store. The limo braked at the corner of 42nd Street and Seventh Avenue, and the driver's partition slid back.

"No place to park around here, unless I go into a garage, and they'll charge me thirty bucks an hour," Herbie said. "How about I circle around until you need me."

"Sounds like a plan." Limo drivers knew the city's streets like the back of their hands, and Peter wondered if Herbie had ever encountered

Selena. "Have you ever seen a female fortune-teller working this corner? She goes by the name Selena."

"Can't say that I have," Herbie replied.

"You sound pretty sure about that."

"Cops ran all the mimes and musicians off. Fortune-tellers, too."

Peter felt defeated even before he started. Perhaps Selena was inside one of the many office buildings in the area. It would only take about a year to check all of those. He climbed out of the backseat along with Liza. His driver's window lowered.

"Check down below," Herbie suggested.

"The subway?"

"Yeah. A lot of street performers work down there. Transit cops leave them alone."

"Got it."

The Times Square subway entrance was about as wide a city street. They went down the stairs and entered the city's noisy underworld. The station was the linking point for five different lines, and contained five different sets of platforms. It was another needle in a haystack, and he approached a pair of transit cops flipping their nightsticks.

"Excuse me, but I'm looking for a female fortune-teller named Selena."

"Describe her," one of the cops said.

How was he supposed to describe someone he'd never met?

"She's wise beyond her years," he replied.

The cop pointed straight ahead. "I think I know her. She sits by the platform for the Number Three train. Take the escalator down. You can't miss her."

They bought Metrocards and followed the arrows to the Number 3. An escalator took them down to the lower level. Beneath a ripped poster for a rap artist sat a sixtyish woman wearing a black dress that could have belonged to a nun, no makeup, her gray hair tied in a bun. The contours of her face said Russian, perhaps Ukrainian. Two empty folding chairs were positioned to either side. Had she known they were coming?

"You must be Selena," Peter said.

"And you must be Peter Warlock and Liza," she said, without a hint of an accent. "I was reading a man's fortune earlier, and you both popped up. Make yourself comfortable. I hope you don't mind the noise."

They sat to either side of her. A train pulled in and disgorged people wearing business attire. A particularly well-dressed man carrying a leather briefcase dropped several bills into Selena's dented tin cup. They were big bills, a fifty and two hundreds.

"He a regular?" Peter asked.

"Hedge fund manager. I saved him a billion dollars last year," Selena said.

"Holy cow," Liza said.

"Got him on retainer?" Peter asked with a smile.

"Come to mention it, I do. His partners as well. Does that seem vulgar to you?"

"You have a right to make a living as much as anyone else."

"Good answer."

Selena fished the money out of her cup and stuffed it into the pocket of her dress. It was not easy making a living telling fortunes. There were so many fakes in the city, it was hard for a real psychic to get by. Selena had obviously found a gold mine inside the subway station, and Peter guessed her drab appearance was more costume than real.

"So tell me why you're here," Selena said. "It's not often that another psychic seeks out my counsel."

"I'm having a problem with a shadow person," Peter explained. "Actually, several of them. They keep kidnapping me and my friends, and taking us into the future where we nearly die at the hands of a serial killer. I just learned that one of them was the victim of this same serial killer. I'm having a hard time understanding all this. Will you help me?"

"Does your boyfriend always talk so fast?" Selena asked Liza.

"Only when he's on edge," Liza replied.

She addressed Peter. "The answer is obvious. You're just not seeing it."

"Will you tell us?" Peter asked.

"Bad question. Try again."

"Will you guide us?" Peter asked.

Another businessman stepped up and dropped big bills into the dented tin cup.

"Investment banker," she said as the man departed.

"Did you save him a bundle?" Peter asked.

"Just his bank. You don't need me, Peter. You already know the answer."

"Thanks. That makes me feel much better."

"Repeat the words you said to me a moment ago. Dissect them one by one. One of those words holds the key to your mystery. Do it, and see if I'm right."

Peter played back to himself what he'd just told Selena. While he did, a third man deposited more good tidings in Selena's cup. Not a gold mine, but a mint.

"He runs a foreign embassy," she said.

"Friend or foe?" Peter asked.

"Friend, of course. The only information I'd sell to a foe would be bad information. Have you got it yet?"

"I think so. The word *nearly*."

Selena nodded approvingly. "That is correct. You said the shadow people were taking you and your friends into the future, and that you nearly died at the hands of a serial killer. But none of you have died. You're assuming you will die, but that may not be the case."

"I was taken into the future, and the serial killer put a gun to my head," Liza jumped in. "He pulled the trigger right as I was yanked back into the real world. I would have died."

"But you didn't," Selena said forcefully.

"I got lucky."

Selena's eyes laughed, and the corners of her mouth turned up ever so slightly.

"Why is that funny?" Liza asked.

"No one gets lucky," Selena said.

"Sure they do. Haven't you heard of Lady Luck smiling down on you?"

"Tell her," Selena said to Peter.

"Luck is controlled by the spirits, and they only dole it out to babies and drunks," Peter explained. "Everything else that happens in life is a role of the dice."

"Next you'll be telling me there isn't a Santa Claus," Liza said.

"Come to mention it . . ."

"What about you and Snoop? You were both taken to the future, and escaped before you were shot in the head," Liza said. "Isn't that luck?"

"No, that was fate. There's a big difference."

"Now I'm really confused."

Selena's eyes were still laughing. She rose from her chair and headed for the escalators. They followed and were soon standing in bustling

Times Square. Down 42nd Street they went to one of the area's many overpriced parking garages. The afternoon light was beginning to fade, and Peter realized he needed to get to his theater and prepare for tonight's show. Selena's day might be over, but his had just begun. Selena handed a parking attendant a stub, and the uniformed man hustled away.

"You don't take the subway?" Peter asked.

"No. I live outside the city," Selena said.

She removed a giant wad of cash from the pocket of her dress and began to count it. Her take for the day was well into the thousands of dollars.

"I think I've figured out what's going on," Peter said. "Will you hear me out?"

"Go ahead," she said, still counting.

He spent a moment collecting his thoughts. When he finally spoke, it was with the conviction of someone who'd finally found a truth that had been evading him for the longest of times. "I was wrong from the start. The shadow people aren't trying to hurt me, and in fact, aren't evil spirits at all. They're victims who are taking me into the future to reveal things that will help me stop the killer from claiming his next victim."

Selena's face was a blank. A shiny black Mercedes with New Jersey license plates came out of the garage. Selena tipped the attendant handsomely, then nodded good-bye to Peter and Liza as she climbed in.

"At least tell me if I'm getting warm," Peter said.

She looked at him before shutting the driver's door.

"You're on fire," she said.

50

eter's limo raced downtown. In less than two hours, he would be performing a full-evening magic show for a packed house. Solving crimes was important, but so was satisfying the people who paid to see him perform.

Liza fidgeted uncomfortably in her seat. It was rare to see her so unsettled. He was tempted to read her thoughts, but fought back the urge. Their relationship was never going to work if he kept stealing looks inside her head, and he told himself the practice had to stop.

"What are you going to do?" she asked.

"I guess I'm going to be taking a trip to the other side."

"You mean you're going to let the shadow people kidnap you again? Don't you remember what happened the two previous times? If you go back again, that crazy serial killer will shoot you."

Liza was wrong. This time would be different. This time, he was going to figure out who Dr. Death was, and bring him to justice. "The shadow people aren't trying to harm me. They're trying to show me something that will help me figure out who Dr. Death really is. I need to go back."

"The shadow people may not be trying to hurt you, but Dr. Death is. You think you can escape from him? I couldn't, and neither could Snoop. I know you have special powers, but do they work on the other side?"

Peter shook his head. When he was in the spirit world, his psychic gifts were weak at best.

"Then how can you stop him from killing you?" Liza asked.

He didn't know the answer to that question. Dr. Death had come close to putting a bullet in his head the two previous times he'd paid him a visit. Going back a third time was a definite risk, but he needed to discover what it was the shadow people wanted him to see.

"I'll find out when I get there," he said.

Liza became angry with him and stared out the window. "What if I say no?"

"No, as in, don't go?"

"Uh-huh."

"Then I won't go," he replied.

"You won't?"

"We're a team, remember? If this upsets you, then no, I won't do it."

She faced him. "Thank you. That means a lot to me."

"Now let me ask you a question. What about Rachael? If I do nothing, she's probably going to die."

"You don't know that. The police or the FBI might still find Dr. Death."

"Maybe so. But it might not be in time to save her. She's going out to see Dr. Death on Friday night, and he's going to kill her, just like he did his other victims. And you and I will have to live with that for the rest of our lives."

"Why do you say that?"

"Because we know what's going to happen. That's the curse of knowing the future. If we don't do anything to prevent the horrible things we know from happening, our consciences will eat at us, and we'll walk around feeling like shits because we didn't act."

"Has that ever happened to you?"

He nodded stiffly, the memory still fresh. "About ten years ago. We did a séance one Friday night, and I got pulled over to the other side. I found myself standing outside an Italian restaurant in the neighborhood where I used to live. The owner was a nice old guy who got along with everybody. Two punks went in and tried to rob the place. The owner pulled a gun and ran them off. I was standing outside when the punks ran out with the owner chasing after them. I thought it was funny as hell. When the séance was over, I told the psychics in our group what had happened. They told me that I had to warn him. I didn't see the point."

"Did you warn him?"

"No. And it still eats at me."

"Why?"

"The owner got robbed two days later. It played out just like I'd seen it. Except there was one thing I didn't see during my séance. The owner chased the punks down the street and around the corner. Then he had a heart attack and dropped dead."

"Oh, Peter, I'm sorry. If he had a bad heart, he probably would have had a heart attack eventually."

"I still should have gone to see him. It was my responsibility, and I let him down."

"How often do you think about it?"

"Every single day."

The back of the limo fell silent. Being a psychic was a gift, and it was also a curse, and sometimes, quite strangely, it was a little bit of both.

"So the moral of the story is, we have to let the shadow people take you over to the other side if we're going to save Rachael," Liza said.

"Only if we want to live with ourselves."

She shook her head. "I don't know, Peter. I just don't know."

A magic show took as long to prepare as it did to perform. Every prop that Peter used in his act needed to be tested to ensure it was working properly. Musicians and comics could have things go wrong and still salvage a show, but that wasn't true with magic. If a trick went haywire during a performance, the mystical illusion of wonderment that Peter had worked so hard to create would be shattered, and the audience's evening ruined.

Each night before his show he did a prop check, a light check, a sound check, and a music check. Only after those were completed to his satisfaction did he retire to his dressing room, and change into his performance clothes.

He took his time dressing. He got nervous before going on, and dressing helped calm him down. Soon, his fans would begin lining the sidewalk in front of the theater with tickets clutched in their hands. Mostly families with kids, but lots of couples as well, and plenty of squealing teenage girls. The front doors would open, and they'd file in. Sometimes, he'd peek out the window to the street to glimpse their expectant faces. They came from all over, yet shared one thing in common: They loved to be fooled.

He stood in front of a mirror as he dressed. A strange motion in the reflection caught his eye, and he watched a shadow person seep out of a crack in the wall, and stand directly behind him, hovering a few inches off the floor. He turned around, and faced his unwanted guest.

"Leave me alone. I have a show to do!"

It made no sound, and continued to hover. From the same crack seeped a second shadow person, followed by a third and a fourth, until six otherworldly spirits were crammed into his tiny dressing room. He tried to reason with them.

"I know what you want. Come back later, and I'll go over to the other side with you, and you can show me whatever it is you want to show me. But not now. I have a show to do."

His guests didn't budge. That was a problem, because he wasn't going to back down. He shook a finger in what would have been their faces, if they'd had them.

"I'm not kidding. Get out of here."

The wall of black closed around him. He heard a sharp scraping sound as a chair was pulled across the floor, and his body was forced into it. The lapels of his jacket were tugged back, the front of his shirt unbuttoned. He roared his disapproval.

"Damn you!" he shouted.

His buttons popped as his shirt was pulled open. A black hand grabbed the five-pointed star hanging around his neck, and yanked on it.

"Stop that!"

There was a loud banging on the door. He jerked his head, fearful a stranger might step into his dressing room and see this insane scene. "Yes?"

"Peter, what's wrong?" Liza said fearfully through the door.

"The shadow people are here. They're trying to take me away."

"Hold on—I'll help you!"

Liza started kicking the door. He tried to summon the demon within, wondering how it would fare against a band of spirits. Before he could find out, the black hand ripped the five-pointed star from his neck, and tossed it to the floor.

He entered the next world still fighting.

51

It was déjà vu all over again.

Peter was transported from his dressing room to the snaking dirt road on the hill beside Dr. Death's house in Westchester County. As before, Dr. Death was chasing him, the Volvo's headlights dancing in the darkness as the vehicle raced down the hill.

Damn the shadow people! Peter thought as he ran for his life. Why couldn't they just come out and tell him who Dr. Death was? Or at least point him in the right direction? Why did each visit have to be a hair-raising experience that made his heart beat so hard that he could hardly breathe?

At the bottom of the hill he took a hard left, sprinting ahead. Something felt different from his two previous visits. The air was noticeably cooler, the sky not nearly as dark. He'd been brought back to the same place, but it was not at the same time in the future.

The Volvo's wheels skidded as Dr. Death took the turn and goosed the accelerator. Peter knew what came next. Dr. Death would stick his handgun out his window, take aim, and shoot him in the leg, delivering a nasty flesh wound. The beginning of the end, unless he did something drastically different from the two previous times.

He bolted to his right. Maybe he could change the outcome of this. At the edge of the road he tried to jump into the forest, only it was as dense as a jungle, and there was nowhere to escape to.

"Damn it," he swore.

He wondered if the shadow people heard him, or if they cared. Ghosts and spirits were bad that way. Divorced from human feelings, they often forgot what it was like to suffer.

A gunshot ripped the still night air. He groaned and grabbed his thigh. Blood was pouring down his leg, and he pressed his hand against the gaping wound to stop the flow. The Volvo parked in the road, and Dr. Death climbed out. The serial killer wore the same college professor clothes and the same lunatic smile. Gun in hand, he told Peter to kneel. The young magician complied.

"Want to say something before you die?" Dr. Death asked.

Peter told himself that he was going to somehow escape, and that he must learn who Dr. Death was before he was sent back to the real world.

"What day is it?" he asked.

"What kind of stupid question is that?" Dr. Death replied.

"I was brought here against my will. I want to know."

"Very well. It's Wednesday evening. Happy now?"

Today was Wednesday. The shadow people hadn't taken him to Westchester County on Friday night like the previous times. Instead, they'd transported him to a Westchester County in the present. Had Rachael's encounter with Dr. Death been moved up two days?

"Close your eyes, and I'll make this painless," the serial killer said.

Dr. Death glanced at his watch as he spoke. Was he going to meet someone? Then it hit Peter why the shadow people had brought him here.

"Rachael is coming out tonight instead of Friday, isn't she?" Peter said. "You're going to the train station to pick her up, aren't you?"

Dr. Death blinked. Peter had nailed it.

"You know too much," Dr. Death said. "Shut your eyes, and I'll get this over with."

"I don't think so."

"What did you say?"

"You heard me. I'm not shutting my eyes."

Dr. Death shoved the barrel of the gun against his temple, its muzzle still warm. "I'll splatter your brains across the road."

"You don't have the guts."

"I didn't have the guts. But I do now. Let me show you why."

Reaching up with his free hand, Dr. Death undid his necktie, unbuttoned the top button of his shirt, and jerked back the collar. Tattooed to his neck was the shimmering symbol of the Order of Astrum. The tattoo looked alive, and glowed mysteriously in the dark. "I have the Order of Astrum on my side," he said with a sick smile. "Now say good-bye. I have a train to meet."

He's really going to shoot me this time. The expression "three strikes and you're out" came to mind, and he prayed for Liza to pull him back to the other side.

Then the shot rang out.

Peter had always wondered what it felt like when you died. He'd imagined the sensation would be similar to hurtling at the speed of light through the universe with no idea of his final destination, if there even was a final destination. A journey that would be both amazingly beautiful and terribly frightening at the same time.

Wrong.

The afterlife felt surprisingly like this life. In fact, it felt exactly like it. He was still kneeling on the side of the road, with blood streaming down his leg. Dr. Death had not moved either, and was still holding the gun to his temple.

Nothing had changed.

Except the look on Dr. Death's face. The sick smile had been replaced by a mask of fear. His eyes were trained on the forest directly behind them.

"Munns—let him go!" a woman's shrill voice called out.

Peter turned his head to see a rather small woman in hiking clothes burst through a dense wall of shrubs. In one hand was a flashlight, in another a smoking handgun. Moments later a panting chocolate Labrador with a huge stick clenched in its mouth came through behind her.

"Gladys Hadden," Dr. Death said in surprise. "What are you doing here?"

"Taking my evening constitutional with Brewster, just like I do every night." She stopped a few yards from where they stood, her gun pointed at the ground. "Oh, my God, you shot him."

"He was breaking into my house," Munns said defensively.

"You don't say. Do you know who he is?"

"I think he's a drug addict. He was going through my things when I caught him," Dr. Death lied, his gun still pressed to Peter's temple. "He ran away, and I got into my car and chased him. I was just about to shoot him when you fired your gun."

"Why were you going to shoot him, Doc?"

"I just told you, he was robbing me."

"That doesn't give you the right to shoot him. I'd suggest you call nine one one, and let the police deal with this. I'll call them myself if you like."

Gladys Hadden was talking down to Munns like he was a child. Munns acted confused, and didn't seem to know what to do. His cell phone rang. He jerked it from his pocket to stare at the face.

"I need to take this," he said, and stepped away.

"Thanks for saving my life," Peter mumbled under his breath.

"You're not a drug addict, are you?" Gladys Hadden asked. "You certainly don't dress like one."

"It's a long story. I'm helping the FBI catch your neighbor."

"Really? What did Doc do?"

"His name's Doc? Is he a doctor?"

"No, it's just his nickname. He likes to pretend he's one. He's really the janitor over at the local college, has been for God knows how long. Now, tell me what he's done."

"He's a serial killer," Peter whispered. "He brings women to his house, and kills them."

Gladys Hadden gasped. "No."

"Yes."

Munns was talking excitedly into his cell phone. They heard him say, "Your train is running ahead of schedule? I'm glad you called to let me know. Yes, I can be at the station when you pull in. I'm sure the dean won't mind if we show up for dinner a little early."

"Who's that?" Gladys Hadden asked in a whisper.

"His next victim," Peter replied.

"Oh, my Lord. What should we do?"

"Shoot him."

"You want me to shoot him?"

"Yes. Otherwise, he's going to kill her."

"You're certain about this?"

"On my parents' graves."

Flipping his cell phone shut, Munns stared at Peter and his neighbor. The glint in his eyes said a decision was being made. Peter didn't have to use his psychic powers to know what that decision was. Munns was going to shoot them in cold blood, and deal with the consequences later. Rachael was drawing closer, and he could practically taste his next kill.

Munns stepped forward, prepared to gun them down.

Brewster stopped him.

The Lab had been lying in the grass gnawing on his stick. Sensing that his owner was in danger, Brewster jumped up and tried to bite Munns's hand off. He jumped back in fear. Brewster kept barking, and Munns started backing up.

"He's getting away," Peter said.

Gladys Hadden aimed her gun. "Stay right where you are."

"Gladys, you can't shoot me," Munns begged her.

"I'm calling the police, Doc. Don't you dare move."

Munns turned his back and ran to his car. He pulled away in a swirl of rubber and raced down the twisting hill. Gladys Hadden lowered her gun to her side, and sadly shook her head. She was a good person, and good people did not shoot their neighbors.

Peter felt an invisible tug on his shoulder. Liza was pulling him back to the other side. He resisted, knowing he must stop Munns from picking up Rachael at the train station. He was dealing with real time now, and every second counted.

"Call nine one one," he said.

"What do I tell them?" Gladys asked. "I don't even know your name."

"Tell the police that Munns is a serial killer. If they call Special Agent Garrison with the FBI in New York City, Garrison will confirm it."

"The police will think I'm a nut."

"Do it anyway. Please."

"Where are you going?"

"I'm leaving."

"But you're wounded. You need to get help."

She punched three numbers into her phone. An operator came on, and she said that a man had been shot, and requested an ambulance. She gave her address and Peter memorized it. His world started to change, the image of his dressing room taking soft focus.

"Do you walk your dog every night?" Peter asked.

"Why yes, I do," she replied. "Why do you ask?"

It explained everything. The shadow people had brought him here twice, and both times it had seemed that Munns was about to shoot him in the head right before he was pulled back. But that hadn't been the situation at all; the gunshot he'd heard each time had come from Gladys Hadden's gun, and had been meant to stop Munns from killing him. His life had never been in danger at all.

He began to slip away. He wished he had a camera to take a photo of the startled look on Gladys Hadden's face as he disappeared. Brewster would not stop barking.

52

Washed in cold sweat, Peter awoke lying on the couch in his dressing room. Liza sat beside him, forcefully shaking his shoulders. "How long have I been out?" he asked.

"Too long," she replied. "The curtains go up in ten minutes. Can you go on?"

"I don't know. Let me check."

He pushed himself up to a sitting position. The bullet wound in his right thigh had miraculously healed itself, and he felt no worse for wear. Garrison leaned against the far wall with a grave look on his face.

"Have a nice trip?" the FBI agent asked.

"Come to mention it, I did," Peter replied. "How did you get here so fast?"

"I was in the neighborhood."

Liza brought a water bottle to his lips. "Here. Drink this."

Peter took a long swallow. His dressing room was void of spirits. He had expected the shadow people to follow him back, but they'd chosen to remain with Munns. Perhaps they were hoping to stop Munns from claiming his next victim. They hadn't succeeded in the past, and were going to need some help. "I know who our killer is."

Garrison pushed himself off the wall. "Start talking."

"His name is Doc Munns, only he isn't really a doctor. He lives in a town called Pelham, and is a janitor at a local college."

Garrison produced a notepad and started scribbling.

"You need to call the Westchester police immediately," he went on. "I saw Munns in real time. His next victim is coming out on a train tonight, not on Friday like I originally thought. When I left, Munns was racing to the train station to pick her up."

"You're sure about all of this?"

Peter nodded and drained the water bottle.

"Do you have any proof?" Garrison asked.

"What do you mean? I was just with him."

"I can't tell the Westchester police that. I mean I can, but they won't buy it."

"Why not?"

"Because they're not going to take the word of a psychic and detain someone. It's not how the law works. I need to offer up some proof to what you're saying."

Peter felt stymied. He'd *seen it,* hadn't he?

"Can't the police at least detain him?" the young magician asked.

"Not without a good solid reason."

"Tell them to make one up."

"The police won't do that."

"This is crazy. A women's life is hanging in the balance. Isn't that enough reason?"

Garrison flipped the notepad shut. "We have to work within the law. This isn't the Wild West. We can't just go grab someone because you think he's a killer."

"It has nothing to do with what I think. Munns *is* a serial killer."

"You don't know that for certain."

Peter threw the empty water bottle at the trash can in anger. When he visited the other side, there were no illusions, subtleties, or nuanced shades of gray. It was all black and white. Munns was their killer, and needed to be stopped. "You're a fool," he said.

"Peter," Liza said.

"Watch your mouth." Garrison simmered.

"I just risked my life to go to the other side, and now you're disputing what I'm saying," Peter said, not calming down. "I should throw you out of here."

"Peter!" Liza said.

A loud rap on the dressing room door snapped their heads. The door opened a foot, and Snoop stuck his shaggy head in. "Why, Detective Garrison, fancy seeing you here. What a pleasant surprise."

"It's Special Agent Garrison, wiseass," Garrison said.

"Sorry. Do you mind if I talk with my boss for a second?" Snoop asked.

"Be my guest."

"Are we going on?" Snoop asked.

"How much time do I have?" Peter asked.

"Five minutes. I can get on the PA, and say we're running late."

Peter wore many hats. The biggest hat was that of a professional magician, and there were rules which he needed to follow. Starting the show on time was one of them. He'd never been late before, and wasn't going to start now. "No, I'm going on right now."

"Beautiful. I'll be up in the booth," Snoop said. "Nice seeing you, Detective."

"You're pushing it," Garrison said.

S oon, the three of them were walking down the hallway toward the back of the stage. Peter's usual nervousness started to set in, just like it did every night before he went on.

"There has to be some solution here," Peter implored the FBI agent.

"I'll call the Westchester police and ask them to send a cruiser to the train station, if you think it will do any good," Garrison said.

"You can't pull Munns in for questioning?"

"I need tangible proof. It's how the law works."

Peter came to a short stairwell that led to the stage. Through the back of the stage he could hear the crowd's murmuring. They were ready to see a magic show, but was he ready to put one on for them? No, he wasn't, and he realized that he had to get Munns out of his mind. That sounded easy to do, only there was an unsuspecting woman named Rachael whose life he was supposed to be saving. He thought back to his encounter with Munns on the hillside. Munns had been carrying a loaded firearm. That was illegal in the state of New York without a concealed weapons permit, and he had a feeling that Munns didn't possess one of those.

"I'm going to get ready," Liza said. "Good luck."

"Thanks for being there for me," he told her.

"Always," she said.

They kissed and Liza hurried away.

"Munns is carrying a loaded gun," he said. "If you told the Westchester police that you had reason to believe he was a dangerous person, would they haul him in?"

"Of course," Garrison said.

"Then please do it. Right now."

"You're sure he's carrying a loaded gun?"

"He shot me with it."

"That's not what I'm asking. Are you certain he's carrying it right now? If not, the police will have to release him, and Munns will know we're on to him."

Peter didn't know if Munns still had his gun. Maybe he'd thrown it out the window of his car after his encounter with Gladys Hadden. But Peter felt certain that Munns still had his kill kit, which had contained a rope, handcuffs, and a bottle of chloroform.

"Munns has a leather bag filled with the stuff he uses to capture his victims," Peter said. "Tell the police to look for it."

"You're sure about this?" Garrison said.

"I saw the bag in his house."

Garrison hesitated. Something was clearly wrong, and Peter gazed into the FBI agent's eyes and read his thoughts. If the Westchester police blew this, Munns would go home and destroy evidence linking him to his crimes. The FBI would be back to square one with the case, and Garrison would have to sleep at night knowing that a dangerous killer was roaming free.

That was a bad scenario, but Peter's was much worse. A woman who pushed back at the darkness was going to die tonight if Munns wasn't arrested. The shadow people had chosen to save Rachael because she was someone who made a difference in the world. Peter was going to save her, the law be damned.

"Promise me you'll talk the police into arresting Munns," Peter said.

"I'll do my best," Garrison replied.

"That's not good enough."

"What did you say?"

"Munns's next victim isn't an ordinary person. She's going to do something extraordinary in her life that will make a tremendous difference in the world. That's why the dark side wants her dead. Do you understand what I'm saying?"

"Is this woman some kind of saint?"

Peter nodded, and a look of recognition spread across the FBI agent's face, along with the weight of knowing that if he didn't act fast, he'd be responsible for her demise as well.

"Then I'll order the police to arrest him," Garrison said.

"Can you do that?"

"Yes. I'm putting my ass on the line, but I'm willing to take that chance."

"Thank you. You won't regret it."

Peter climbed the steps to the back of the stage as Garrison began to make the call. The music had already started, his other life about to begin. He cleared his head, and prepared himself to enter the world of make-believe.

53

The parking lot of the Pelham train station was deserted as Munns parked and killed his headlights. During the day, there was not a space to be found, and cars often parked illegally on the street. Nighttime was a different story, and most of the spaces were empty.

Munns lowered his window. The sound of the northbound train from New York could often be heard a mile or more away as it lumbered into the station. Each of Munns's six victims had come on the train to Pelham, where Munns had picked them up with the promise of a nice job at the local college but instead had taken them to the basement of his house where he'd tied them up, laid them out on a long table, and ended their miserable lives in whatever fashion struck his fancy. He never decided ahead of time, preferring to follow his impulses and go with the flow. Rachael would be no different.

The train's whistle caught his ear. It was time. On the passenger seat sat his kill kit. From it, he took the bottle of chloroform, which he put into his left jacket pocket. Next he removed a folded handkerchief, which went into his right jacket pocket. The kill kit was moved to the floor of the backseat. He climbed out of the car.

He waited on the platform. He was not alone. A woman had come to pick up her husband, and was chatting on a cell phone while holding an infant in her arm. That was the extent of his worries.

He glanced at his reflection in the window of the station house, fixed his necktie, and patted down his lapels. If Rachael stepped off the train and got a bad vibe, she wouldn't get in his car. He had to win her over right from the start.

The ground shook as the train pulled in, and a handful of passengers disembarked. Dark suits and ties for the men, power suits and fancy shoes for the women. One passenger stood out. A tall, sallow women with prematurely gray hair and a slightly lost expression. His heart skipped a beat at the sight of her.

"Rachael?" he called out expectantly.

She smiled and came toward him. Not too fast, not too slow. Sizing him up like any intelligent woman would do. Munns stepped forward and opened his arms in welcome.

"It's so good to finally meet you. Welcome to Pelham," he said.

"You must be Doc Munns." She stuck out her hand. "It's nice to meet you, too."

Her handshake was firm but also friendly. He waved to his parked car. "Your chariot awaits. The dean is expecting us. I'm told his wife has cooked up a wonderful meal with all the trimmings. I hope you brought your appetite."

"Matter of fact, I did. I've been so looking forward to this," she said.

They continued to chat as they walked to Munns's car. Out of the corner of his eye, Munns saw the woman with the kid drive away with her husband. The other passengers were piling into cars and heading home. No one was paying them the slightest bit of attention. Munns opened the passenger door for his guest.

"Such a gentleman. I like that in a man," Rachael said.

"My pleasure," the serial killer said.

The routine that Munns used to abduct his victims never varied. Like a short one-act play, he'd memorized the lines that he would say, and had choreographed the individual steps that led to his victims being knocked unconscious in the passenger seat of his car. He had performed his play in the railroad station parking lot, and in the supermarket parking lot down the street where he'd taken several of his victims after picking them up. It had seemed bold at first to perform the abduction in public, but time had proved it a smart tactic. His victims did not think anything could happen to them while in a public place, and let their guards down. As a result, none of them had seen it coming. He did not anticipate Rachael being any different.

He fastened his seat belt and requested that his passenger do the same.

"Sorry," Rachael said, buckling up. "I hardly take car rides anymore."

"How do you get around in the city?" he asked.

"Mostly by the subway, sometimes when I'm late I'll take a cab."

"You don't own a car?"

"On my salary? You're funny."

No one had ever called him funny before, and he grinned. He found himself liking her, but that feeling would soon fade. It always did when he brought his victims to his house and carried them downstairs to the basement. Each step down the creaky staircase was a painful journey back in time. By the time he reached the basement, he was ready to kill.

He fired up the ignition and threw the car into reverse. Then he started to wheeze and cough. It was an ugly sound, and he pounded his chest with his fist.

"Is something wrong?" she asked in alarm.

He threw the car back into Park. More pounding on the chest and heavy breathing followed. Pointing at the glove compartment, he said, "If you don't mind. I need my pills."

"Is this serious? Do I need to call nine one one?"

"Not at all. I just forgot to take them, that's all."

"Do you have any water?"

"No," he gasped.

"Have no fear." She produced a water bottle from her purse and stuck it into the cup holder jutting out of the dashboard. Then she turned her attention to the glove compartment. The latch was tricky, and she fumbled opening it. She rummaged through maps and car junk.

"I'm not seeing any pills," she said.

"They should be there," he wheezed. "Keep looking."

She obeyed, paying him no attention. Sticking his hand into his left pocket, he unscrewed the chloroform bottle with a quick twist. His right hand removed the handkerchief, which he doused liberally. He kept his face turned to avoid knocking himself out with fumes.

"I'll still not seeing them," Rachael said.

"Do you know what it's like to be beaten as a child?" he asked in a normal voice.

The words caught her off guard. Rachael turned her head, and Munns placed the handkerchief over her nose and mouth. It was important to get his victim to turn into the chloroform, and not shove it into her face. Her eyes rolled into her head, and she slumped into her seat.

* * *

The hard part over, Munns felt himself relax. As he started to back
out of his spot, a police cruiser rolled into the lot and pulled up behind him, its headlights bathing his vehicle.

"Shit," he swore.

In his mirror he spied a grim-faced cop at the wheel. Before the
economy had taken a dump, the Pelham Police Department had employed pairs of officers for its nightly patrols. Budget cuts had changed
that, and officers now rode solo at night.

Munns strained to make out the officer's face. He'd gone through school
with many of the cops in town and knew most of them by first name.

The cop was someone new. A clean-cut rookie with a square jaw and
straw-blond hair. Munns decided to have a talk with him. He had talked
his way out of tight jams before, and felt confident he could handle this
rookie. Opening his door, he placed his foot on the ground.

"Stay in your car," the officer barked over a bullhorn.

Munns pulled himself back in, and slammed the door.

"Hands on the wheel," the officer commanded.

Munns placed his hands on the wheel. He wondered if was going to
have to kill a police officer tonight. He couldn't hide a dead cop the way
he'd hidden his other victims, and would have to figure out a clever way
to dump the body. Perhaps he'd cut it up first, and dispose of the pieces in
Dumpsters behind different restaurants. The rotted food would hide the
smell perfectly.

A flashlight's beam touched the back of his head. Munns turned in
his seat to glare at the officer.

"Look straight ahead," the officer barked.

Munns turned around. The flashlight beam traveled to the passenger
seat, and rested on Rachael's slumping profile.

"Who's that in the car with you?" the officer demanded.

Munns rolled down his window and stuck his head out. "Look, can't
we talk?"

"Answer the question!"

"My wife. She just got off work."

"What's wrong with her?"

"She fell asleep. She's had a long day. May I ask what this is about?"

"Be quiet, and turn your head around."

"But I've done nothing wrong."

"Do it!"

Munns turned back around. Killing the police officer seemed a certainty. No other real choice. His gun was in his kill kit and not handy. He would have to use his hands, like he had with Clyde Jucko at the storage facility, and tear the officer apart limb from limb. Thinking about it brought a faint smile to his lips. Tonight was going to be a two-bagger.

He devised a plan. He'd let the officer come up to his window and ask for his ID. He would stick his driver's license out the window. When the officer took it, he'd grab his arm, pull him into the car, and tear his head off. Easy as pie.

He tapped his fingers on the wheel. When the officer did not come, he glanced into his mirror. The officer was talking on his car radio to a dispatcher. He tried to lip-read what the officer was saying. He caught a couple of key words, and realized the officer was calling for backup like he'd just apprehended a dangerous criminal.

It was time to make his move. Opening the driver's door, he hopped out, and marched toward the cruiser with his arms outstretched in a placating manner.

"Get back in your car!" roared the officer over the bullhorn.

Stopping, he struck a neutral pose. "Please. Tell me what's wrong."

"Back up!"

"Have I broken any laws? Is my tag expired?"

"*Do it!*"

"Why won't you talk to me?"

The officer reached for his gun. The look in his eyes bordered on pure panic. Pelham was a sleepy place, and the officer had probably never dealt with a situation like this before. Munns decided that was in his favor, and took a giant step forward.

"Son, you're overreacting."

"Listen to me!" the officer shouted.

Munns raised his arms in mock surrender. "What are you afraid of? Do I scare you?"

"Son of a bitch," the officer swore.

Squealing rubber tore a hole in the still night air. A black van had entered the parking lot and was flying. Its headlights flashed and the driver mouthed the words, "Get out of the way!"

It was Ray.

Ray plowed into the back of the cruiser without hitting his brakes. The impact sounded like a bomb going off, and the officer flew through the windshield like a human cannonball, his body landing on the rear of the Volvo with a sickening thud.

Munns pulled himself off the pavement. He was covered with broken glass, but otherwise unharmed. Ray jumped out of the van and joined him. Together they stared at the officer's crumpled body. The surprised look on his face said he'd never known what had hit him.

"Did you get Rachael?" the tattoo artist asked.

"She's passed out in the car."

"Get her out of here. I'll deal with this guy."

Ray pulled the dead cop off the trunk and dragged him to the van. For a skinny guy, Ray was strong, and Munns felt certain he would figure out a way to dispose of the body.

Munns drove away knowing he was in good hands.

54

Fight or flight.

Ray had never understood the meaning of the expression, until now.

He had murdered a cop. If that wasn't bad enough, the cop's broken body was lying on the floor of his van, bleeding on the carpet. He had to dispose of the body, and then he had to run. Ray didn't know where he was going to go, and he supposed it really didn't matter.

Just run.

Hanging around Pelham was a bad idea. The police would haul him and Munns in, and question them. Munns would squeal like a fat boy in a candy store, and point the finger at Ray. No fancy lawyer could save him. Ray would spend the rest of his life in the slammer.

Ray cursed the Order of Astrum. They had sent him down this path, and told him to make sure Munns got the girl no matter what. When Ray had driven past the train station and seen the cop about to arrest Munns, he'd lost his head, and crashed his van into the cruiser. Looking back, the smart thing would have been to let Munns take the fall, and not get involved. Ray knew that now, not that it was going to do him any good.

He navigated Pelham's narrow roads while trying to keep to the speed limit. More criminals got busted speeding away from the scene of their crimes than just about anything else. So he kept it under thirty and fought to stay calm.

He thought about the places he might escape to. Canada seemed like a wise choice, or perhaps a remote town in Mexico. Let Munns take the heat for the dead cop.

He drove down a dead-end street on the outskirts of town. Pulled down a dirt road that was part of a wooded lot where nobody lived.

Parked and got out to look around. Didn't see a soul or hear anything that would suggest people nearby. A perfect spot to dump a corpse.

He lit a cigarette and filled his lungs with smoke. This whole damn thing was crazy. He'd let the elders kidnap his soul, and make him do things that he'd never dream of doing on his own. Before joining the Order of Astrum, he'd placed limits on the crimes he would commit. Not anymore. There were no limits to the depravity and suffering he'd been asked to be a part of.

He finished the cigarette and ground the butt into the dirt. Walked back to the van and saw a figure sitting in the passenger seat, waiting for him. Was it Munns? It was too dark to tell, and he fired up his lighter and held it with his arm outstretched.

It was the dead cop, come back to life.

Ray let out a savage yell.

The dead cop rolled down the passenger window and stuck his bloody head out. It was said that the eyes were the last thing to die. The dead cop's eyes had died long ago, and all that was left now was the shell of the man inhabited by the most evil of spirits.

"Get in the van, Ray," the dead cop said.

The dead cop's voice had a British accent. One of the elders had inhabited his body.

"Nothing doing," the tattoo artist stammered.

"Do as I say. There's nowhere for you to run. Canada is terribly cold this time of year, Mexico is too far, and the police will eventually track you down. You need to stay here and finish the job. You made a promise, which we plan to hold you to. Get in the van."

Ray thought he was going to lose it. Killing the cop had been bad enough. Talking to his dead corpse was worse. And he couldn't imagine sitting next to it. Not on his life.

"I ain't getting in that van with you," he said.

The passenger door swung open and the dead cop piled out. His broken neck left his head sitting on his shoulder blade like a bowling ball, and Ray recoiled at the sight of him. He stood in front of Ray with his arms hanging limply at his sides.

"Do I repulse you?" the dead cop asked.

"That's one way to put it," Ray said.

"This is nothing, Ray. I can show you things that will twist your soul inside out, and make you wish that you had never been born. Would you like that?"

"No thanks."

"Glad to hear it. Now, let me explain to you what the future holds. Munns is going back to his house with Rachael. The police will soon follow. Not long after that, a black FBI agent and Peter Warlock will appear. Warlock and Munns will square off, and fight to the death. We need the police and the FBI agent kept out of the way. That's where you come in."

"Me?"

"You own a hunting rifle with a telescopic lens, yes? Go get it, and perch yourself on the neighboring hill. Keep the police and the FBI at bay, while Munns and Warlock do battle. That doesn't sound too hard, does it?"

"You're nuts."

"Are you afraid of being caught? Don't be. We will whisk you away and give you a new life. You will become one of Dante's disciples, and have powers beyond your wildest dreams. Doesn't that sound good to you?"

"What kind of powers?"

"Prescience, incredible strength, the ability to live forever. Do those things excite you?"

Ray nodded, even though he didn't know what prescience was.

"Would you like a taste?" the dead cop asked.

Ray nodded again, this time more enthusiastically.

"Step forward so I can touch you."

Ray moved closer to the man he'd killed a short while ago. The dead cop lifted his arm and stuck his cold palm against Ray's forehead. A sharp current passed between them, and Ray gasped as a bolt of white light illuminated the theater of his mind. The dead cop removed his palm and pointed at the forest. "Look. See for yourself."

Ray gazed into the dense forest. Despite the darkness and abundance of trees, he was able to see a deer sleeping on the ground a hundred yards from where he stood. A raccoon came into the picture, followed by squirrels, chipmunks, and an overly large owl. The animals had been there all this time, only Ray hadn't been able to see them, until now.

"You gave me night vision," he said under his breath.

"Do you like it?" the dead cop asked.

"It's way cool. Yeah, I like it a lot."

"Good. Now go. There is more work to be done."

The dead cop staggered into the forest. Ray nearly told him to stop. What was he supposed to do after Munns killed Warlock? And how was he supposed to meet up with Dante? The dead cop read his thoughts, and turned stiffly around.

"Everything will be revealed to you. Trust me."

That was good enough for Ray. He watched the dead cop walk to a clearing. His body shuddered, and he dropped like a stone as the elder inhabiting his body abandoned him. Ray looked to the sky, imagining he could see the evil spirit floating overhead.

Then he went home to get his hunting rifle.

55

There was no such thing as a perfect show.

Every night, something went wrong in Peter's performance of *Anything's Possible*. Usually it was minor, like a cue being missed, or a prop malfunctioning. Rarely did it interfere with the audience's enjoyment of the act. Most of the time, they hardly noticed.

But those mishaps rankled Peter no end. Details made perfection, but perfection was no detail, just a goal that could never be reached, only strived for.

Tonight's mishap had taken place during the show's opening. A puff of smoke had filled the center of the empty stage from which the young magician emerged. Stepping to the footlights, he engaged the audience with a brief introduction. When he finished, the lights were raised to reveal a stage filled with gorgeous props that had materialized out of no-where. The trick never failed to garner a gasp of astonishment, followed by a sustained burst of applause.

Except tonight.

Tonight, there had been no gasp, and the applause had been polite. The audience had been given a clue to how the trick worked, just enough to spoil the illusion.

The trick's secret was based upon the lazy Susan principle. The stage was actually two stages. One of these stages was bare, the other filled with props. The stages were secretly rotated while Peter gave his opening speech, which was enough of a distraction to keep the audience in the dark. Only tonight a squeaky gear beneath the stage had given the secret away. It had told the audience that something was going on, and spoiled the illusion.

Peter was furious. At the show's end, he went beneath the stage to fix the squeaky gear. Liza held a flashlight while he squirted WD-40 lubricant onto the culprit.

He heard footsteps too large to be Snoop. Liza heard them, too.

"Who's that?" she whispered.

"Beats me. Can I help you?"

"Garrison, FBI," a familiar voice called out. "I need to talk with you."

They crawled out from beneath the stage to find Garrison by the stairwell. He was smiling, always a good sign. "We found the son of a bitch," he announced.

Liza squealed with delight and hugged Peter. The news made everything Peter had gone through the past few days through seem bearable. Now the shadow people would stop harassing him and his friends, and he could get on with his life.

"Your information was all good. His name is Harold Munns, and he lives in the village of Pelham where he works as a janitor at the local community college, " Garrison went on. "I spoke to the Pelham police chief, and he knew exactly who I was talking about. The chief said Munns had a history of problems dating back to childhood. The things I told him weren't a surprise."

"Have the police arrested him?" Peter asked.

"They're scouring the town for him. Sent a pair of cruisers to his house, and another cruiser to the train station to see if he was there."

"So they're all over it."

"They most certainly are. Now here's the funny part. I explained to the chief how we used a psychic to track Munns down. The chief didn't sound terribly surprised. Seems he used a psychic to find a missing kid, and the case had a happy ending."

"So he's a believer."

"A true-blue believer. He expects to catch Munns tonight and haul him in. He asked if you'd drive up to Pelham with me, and feed him any details about the case that you uncovered during your trips to the other side. He really wants your help."

The exhaustion of the past few days had caught up to Peter, and he wanted nothing more than to go home with Liza, share a hot bath, and watch a scary zombie flick. Sensing his hesitation, Garrison put his hand on the young magician's shoulder.

"You don't have to come, but it would be a huge help if you did."

"Right now?" Peter asked wearily.

"Afraid so. I'll drive. You can sit in the passenger seat and sleep on the way up."

Peter looked at Liza. "You cool with going home by yourself?"

"Not really. How about I come with you?" she said.

"You sure?"

"Positive. We're a team, remember?"

His whole life he'd been facing the unknown by himself. He hadn't minded, but it had gotten lonely at times. Having Liza by his side was going to make his life a lot nicer. To Garrison he said, "Give me five minutes to get out of these clothes."

"I'll be waiting outside in the car," the FBI agent replied.

Peter went to change. Opening the door to his dressing room, a cry escaped his lips. The room was trashed, his props and clothing scattered across the floor.

He'd been burglarized. It happened all the time in New York. The question was, how had the burglar gotten in? Certainly not through any of the theater's entrances. There were only two, the front and the back, and they were watched 24/7 by surveillance cameras.

That left the window in his dressing room. It would have been hard, considering the room was on the second floor and there was no fire escape, but burglars were a resourceful lot, and would go to any means to enter a building if there was something worth stealing.

He went to the window to check the latch. To his surprise, it hadn't been touched. So how had the burglar gotten in? He pulled out his cell phone, planning to call Snoop and ask him to check the surveillance videos, when a movement stopped him cold. A curling wisp of black smoke was seeping out of a crack plaster in the wall. Before his eyes it took shape. He had seen the shadow people enough times to differentiate them by their sizes. It was the same shadow person who'd dropped her antique watch into his hands a few nights ago, Barbara Metcalf.

"What have I done to upset you now?" he asked.

No response.

"You know that I'm trying to help you, don't you?"

Nothing.

"I'm going to Pelham to track down Munns. That's what you want from me, isn't it? To stop this crazy guy before he kills Rachael."

Still nothing.

"I'm getting tired of you messing with me," he blurted out.

She made an angry squeal. Across the room, five black wisps came out of their hiding place to join her. They swarmed around Peter like a hive of angry bees, threw him into the chair in front of his dressing table, and held him down.

"Cut it out!" he protested.

A pair of scissors on his dressing table were crawling toward him, its blades snapping like an alligator's jaws. His left hand was pinned to the table; as he watched, the shadow person that was Barbara Metcalf began to snip off the tip of his left forefinger.

"Not my hand," he howled.

The scissors were dull, and it took tremendous effort to break the skin and cut into the bone. Before his disbelieving eyes, the tip of his finger fell to the table. Bright red blood spurted from the wound, and he struggled not to pass out.

"Peter, let me in," Liza shouted through the door.

"They're back," he gasped.

"What are they doing to you?"

"Bad stuff."

"Tell me!"

"Cutting off my finger . . ."

Metcalf wasn't done with him. Grabbing his hand, she brought his bleeding finger up to the three-way mirror on his dressing table, and used his blood to write a message. Peter thought he would be sick, and shut his eyes. The next thing he knew, Liza was standing beside him, shaking his arm with both his hands.

"Peter—don't let them kidnap you!"

His eyes snapped open. The dressing room was back to normal, all the broken furniture and scattered things returned to their rightful places. It had all been a trick of the mind.

He stared at his severed finger. It had miraculously healed itself. No blood, no missing tip, he flexed it several times, found it in good working order.

Liza knelt beside him. "Oh, God, are you okay?"

"I think so."

One thing hadn't gone away. His dressing mirror was smeared with blood. He leaned forward to make out the single word left behind as a memento:

HURRY

Grabbing Liza by the arm, he ran from the dressing room.

PART V

PELHAM

56

Witches were not supposed to fall in love. Nor were they supposed to get married and become soccer moms. It was not how being a witch worked.

It wasn't written down anywhere. Most of the rules which dictated a witch's life were not written down anywhere at all. But they were passed down to each generation of young women who were born into the coven of spells and sorcery. And those rules were clear.

True love and witches simply did not mix.

Of course, they could have partners, and engage in sex, and be all things that women could and should be. There were no laws against that. But they were not allowed to lose themselves with a partner and forget who they were, which was what happened to most people who fell in love. They forgot who they were, and became someone else for a while. Witches were not supposed to do that. They had to remain true to themselves throughout their lives, and never forget who they were. It made relationships with the opposite sex tricky, to say the least.

Perhaps this was Holly's problem. She had gotten crazy over Peter before the rules of the game had been properly explained to her. By the time Milly had gotten down to spelling out the rules, Cupid's arrow had pierced her heart, and nothing would ever be the same.

Peter had been such a logical choice. Cute, clever, with one foot stuck in the dark side, what more could she want from a boy? They had grown up together, and always been fond of each other. Falling in love had been a natural progression, and Holly didn't think the world would fall off its axis because of it.

She poured the magic herbs into the water-filled vase sitting on the coffee table. The water grew cloudy, with lifelike forms swirling about.

Oh spirits from above, show me Peter, the boy I love.

The water grew clear, and there Peter was, slumped in a chair in his dressing room while lovely Liza shook his arm. Clearly, something was amiss, which seemed almost routine for poor Peter these days. He'd become a poster boy for the problems that came from being psychic.

Peter woke up. Soon he and Liza were in a car racing out of the city. At the wheel was a grim-faced man whom Holly recognized as an FBI agent of Peter's acquaintance. The FBI agent was driving one-handed while talking on a cell phone and to Peter at the same time. It was like watching a silent movie, and Holly tried to make out what they were saying.

"Holly!" a familiar voice called out.

Holly looked up in alarm. The voice had come out of nowhere. "Aunt Milly, is that you?"

"Who do you think it is, the Girl Scouts of America?"

"You have no right scrying on me, if that's what you're doing."

"*Au contraire,* I have every right to be scrying on you. You must leave Peter alone."

"Why should I? I'm in love with him."

"I fully understand that. But love doesn't give you the right to invade his privacy. Peter must not be disturbed. Do you understand me?"

Holly glanced at the vase of water at the object of her desire. "Certainly."

"You're not listening to me. Peter is not like us. He's different."

"I know."

"Much different."

"I'll agree to that."

"Damn it, Holly."

A framed photograph fell off the wall and crashed to the floor.

"Please stop destroying my things," Holly said.

"Not until you do as I say."

Holly had never won an argument with her aunt, and doubted she ever would. Clicking her fingers three times, she made the water grow cloudy and the images disappear. Rising from the floor, she found her aunt's ghostly image in the oval mirror over her water bed.

Holly crossed her arms defiantly. Her aunt countered with a frown.

"What do you want, Aunt Milly?"

"Peter has enough on his plate these days. Stop pestering him."

"Who said I was pestering him? And when did this become your business? I'm a grown woman living in my own apartment. I can do whatever I please, thank you very much."

Her aunt started to argue, but stopped herself. The wisdom of old age was knowing when silence was more powerful than words. Her face softened. "You're right. You are no longer a child, and I have no right to treat you that way. So consider this a warning, instead."

"A warning about what?"

"Be careful with Peter."

"How so?"

"Be discreet. Respect his privacy. Know when to look away."

An icy finger ran the length of Holly's spine. Was there a side to Peter that she didn't know? If that was the case, then her aunt had every right to be checking up on her, and Holly suddenly felt bad about the way she was acting.

"I'm sorry I'm acting like such a turd," she said.

"No need to apologize my dear. I wasn't very tactful."

"How will I know?"

"About Peter? You will see the change. It will not be pleasant to watch."

"You mean he'll grow ugly like he does when he gets angry?"

"This will be more severe. He will physically alter himself. It will not be pretty, to say the least."

Holly brought her hand up to her mouth. "Have you seen him do this?"

"Yes, when Peter was a little boy. It occurred the night his parents died. The demon inside of him fully took over. It was like he turned himself inside out."

"Did it affect your relationship with Peter?"

"It most certainly did. And it will change your relationship with him as well."

Holly swallowed hard. "How can you be so certain?"

Her aunt smiled the way adults do when they're talking to children. Her image in the mirror began to fade and turned a foggy whitish color. Just wait, her eyes seem to say.

"Do as I say for once," Milly said, and then was gone.

*   *   *

Holly parted the blinds and gazed at the city's canopy of blinking lights. Had she fallen in love with a monster? Or just someone who was frightfully different? Better to know what she was getting into right now, she supposed, than to get surprised down the road.

She had talked herself into it. She would scry on Peter and discover his terrible secret, her aunt's warning be damned.

57

⁓

Like many New Yorkers, Peter's sense of direction was useless once he stepped off the island of Manhattan, and he paid scant attention as Garrison followed the signs for the Cross Bronx Expressway and West 178th Street as he drove up the West Side Highway. Liza sat in the backseat, studying a traffic app on her iPhone. "This doesn't clear up until the George Washington Bridge. We're never going to get there."

Garrison slapped a flashing red light on the dashboard and punched his horn. The lines of cars in front of them parted like the Red Sea, and the FBI agent began to weave between lanes with the skill of a NASCAR driver.

"That's more like it," Garrison said.

Peter rode shotgun and stared at the highway. His hands had grown sweaty and he felt nervous in anticipation of finally meeting Munns in the flesh. The greatest mass murderers in history were all associated with the Devil in some way, and there was no question in his mind that Munns would put up a terrible fight when the police tried to arrest him.

"You scared?" Garrison asked.

"A little," he said. "Aren't you?"

"Not really. I've dealt with serial killers before."

The hairs on the back of Peter's neck stood up. Hadn't he warned Garrison about the dangers that Munns posed? Munns was capable of causing more harm than Garrison could possibly imagine. "If you're not careful, he'll kill every cop in Pelham, and you and me as well."

"Come on. Doc Munns is an angry little man. Most serial killers are."

"What do you know about him?" Peter asked.

Garrison stopped talking long enough to merge onto the I-95 Lower Level North/George Washington Bridge exit out of the city. The sound of the bridge's metal grating beneath their wheels was oddly soothing. "The chief of the Pelham Police Department said Munns was a troubled soul. His parents were alcoholics who abused their son. They made him live in the basement and didn't let him eat with them. They also made him work around the house and do a lot of manual labor. He went to school in dirty clothes without lunch money."

"Sounds like they tortured him," Liza said from the backseat.

"That came later," Garrison said.

"His childhood got worse?"

"Yes, unfortunately. When Munns was a teenager, his father got laid off work, and started hitting the bottle. He and his wife used to sit around the house all day, collect welfare checks, and get blistered. They convinced Munns to quit high school, and get a full-time job so they could pay their bills and support themselves in the lifestyle to which they'd become accustomed. It was a crummy thing to do, but that's what kind of people they were.

"At first, Munns wouldn't do it. He had dreams of going to college and being a medical doctor. One day, he came to school with a black eye and a busted front tooth. Everyone knew who had given it to him."

"His father," Liza said.

"That's right, his father. Munns dropped out of high school, and took a job driving a truck. The money wasn't good, and the family barely scraped by. On weekends, the police were often called to the house to settle domestic arguments. Munns's father was beating up his son pretty regularly, and should have gone to jail, only Munns wouldn't play ball with the cops."

"So he was loyal," Peter said.

"That he was," Garrison said. "But that all changed one day. Munns got a phone call from a lady with the Social Security office in Washington. A woman claiming to be Munns's birth mother was looking for him. Did Munns want to talk with her?"

"Wait a second," Liza said, leaning through the seats. "The people who were torturing and treating him like a slave weren't really his parents?"

"No, they weren't. His biological mother gave Munns up for adoption when he was two years old. The torturers were his adoptive parents."

"That's so sick. What did Munns do?"

"That's the strange part. He did nothing to his parents, and in fact, continued to care for them when they became sick and eventually died. The people he took his anger out with were his neighbors and other people who lived in Pelham."

"Why? They weren't responsible."

"That's not how Munns saw it. The townspeople knew he was being abused, and they also knew that his parents weren't really his parents, yet they turned their backs and didn't step in. Munns held that against them. Still does."

"How old is he?" Peter asked.

"Munns is forty-eight years old. Is that important?"

Munns had been carrying his anger around for a long time. It had corrupted his soul and erased any semblance of decency. His joining the Order of Astrum and taking his anger out on the world by killing innocent women was yet another chapter in his sick life. But were those women the people Munns was really after? Peter didn't think so. It was the citizens of Pelham he wanted to pay back, every last one of them. By joining the Order, Munns had been given the means to accomplish his grisly task, and one day he eventually would. Had that day arrived?

"You need to drive faster," Peter implored.

"I'm already doing seventy-five," the FBI agent replied.

"Faster."

Garrison floored the accelerator and the vehicle lurched ahead. Peter watched the exit signs as they flashed by, praying they were not too late.

The exit for Mt. Vernon/Pelham appeared just as Garrison's cell phone let out a sonic blast. He yanked it from his pocket and took the call. He listened for several seconds and made an ugly face. "What? When did this happen?"

Peter could have waited for Garrison to hang up and explain what was going on, or he could plumb the agent's thoughts and find out himself. Liza's hand came up and squeezed his arm. "What's going on?" she whispered.

"A rookie cop in Pelham spotted Munns at the train station," he whispered back. "He was asking a dispatcher for backup when he got cut off. Munns may have gotten away."

"Ugh," Liza said.

Garrison finished his call. "Quit reading my mind. I don't like it."

"Sorry. Just trying to save time."

"What about Rachael? Did anyone see her come into the station?" Liza asked.

"The cop who called in the license told the dispatcher there was a second person passed out in Munns's car," Peter said. "That was probably her."

"So Munns abducted her."

"It sure looks that way."

Liza fell back in her seat and shut her eyes. Traffic had thinned out since leaving the city, and Garrison took the exit with his tires squealing.

"Go ahead. Tell her the rest," Garrison said.

"There's more?" Liza said.

"The Pelham police chief sent several of his officers to the next town to help with an apartment house fire," Peter explained. "As a result, he's short staffed, and only has a handful of available officers to deal with Munns."

"You can't be serious," Liza said.

"It's a small town. The force isn't that big to begin with."

"Does he realize how dangerous Munns is? Or that he's in league with the Devil?" Liza asked.

"The chief's a small-town cop. He's never dealt with anything this serious before. He sent two cruisers to Munns's house earlier, but hasn't spoken to them. We're meeting the chief at the train station, and then we're all going to Munns's place together."

"Does this man know what he's doing?" Liza asked.

Peter glanced across the seat at Garrison, who was thinking the same thing. The Pelham police chief was going to blow this if they didn't hurry.

The two-lane road leading into Pelham twisted and turned across the hilly landscape, forcing Garrison to ease up on the gas. They began to crawl, and Peter felt his anxiety grow. Devil worshippers did not go quietly when caught. Often, they went on rampages, intent on taking down as many innocent lives as possible before being taken down themselves. This was the great threat that Munns posed to the people of Pelham.

Ten minutes later, they arrived in a quaint town with artificial gaslights lining the streets and an array of enticing storefronts. The railroad tracks ran next to the town. Signs warned people not to play on the tracks or risk electrocution.

Garrison followed the tracks to the station. A police cruiser with a flashing red light waited in the parking lot. Beside it was a second cruiser, which had been rear-ended and had a shattered windshield. Garrison parked beside the first cruiser, and they got out.

Peter checked out the damaged cruiser. The gaping hole in the windshield suggested a body had been thrown through it. On the ground he found glass and a dark black stain.

"Is this blood?"

Garrison studied the stain. "Sure looks like it."

Peter had helped the police with difficult cases, and was adept at reconstructing a crime scene. There was no doubt that someone had died here. What he did not understand was how. The officer was calling in Munns's license when he was rammed from behind, and the call was cut off. That didn't make sense, unless Munns had a partner.

"Where is everybody?" Liza asked.

"Beats me. Anybody home?" Garrison called out.

"In here," replied a man's voice.

The voice had come from inside the station house. The front door was ajar, and Peter entered a small waiting room lined with wooden benches. Another open door led to the ticket office with a desk and a chair. A uniformed cop in his fifties greeted him with a glare.

"Who are you?" the cop asked gruffly.

"Peter Warlock. I'm helping Special Agent Garrison track down Munns."

"Are you the psychic he's using?"

"Yes, he is." Garrison followed Peter into the office. "You must be Chief Burns. I'm Special Agent Garrison. This young lady behind me is Liza. She's also helping."

"Welcome to Pelham," Burns said. "It was a quiet little town, up until a little while ago."

"Can you tell me what happened outside?" Garrison asked.

"I'm about to find out."

A video monitor sat on the desk. Burns punched a button on a remote, and a grainy surveillance tape began to play on the small screen.

Taken by a camera attached to the station house roof, it had a date and time stamped in the corner. It had been recorded twenty-two minutes ago, and showed a train pulling into the station and a group of passengers disembarking and going to their cars or rides. One nicely dressed woman remained on the platform. She looked nervous, and glanced from side to side as if looking for someone.

"That's Rachael," Liza said.

"How can you be sure?" Garrison asked.

"I don't know. I just am."

"Who's Rachael?" Chief Burns wanted to know.

"Munns's next victim," Liza said.

Munns appeared in the frame, and warmly greeted the woman. Together, they walked off the platform to Munns's Volvo. Rachael got into the car, and they watched Munns put a handkerchief over her face, and knock her out. Liza let out a shriek, and momentarily averted her eyes.

Munns began to back out of his spot just as a police cruiser pulled into the lot, and blocked him from leaving. The cop in the cruiser exchanged words with Munns, and began to call in his license to a dispatcher. From out of nowhere a black van appeared, and rammed the cruiser from behind. The officer was propelled through the windshield and landed on the trunk of the Volvo, his head flopped to one side. Liza turned away again. Chief Burns swore.

The driver of the van hopped out. He wore a sinister Fu Manchu and his arms and neck were covered in tattoos. Peter had been right. Munns was working with a partner.

"Any idea who that guy is?" Garrison asked.

"Never seen the bastard before," Burns swore.

Burns's cell phone vibrated, and he yanked it off his belt. Looking at its face, he said, "It's about time they called me back. I need to take this outside. Reception's bad in here."

Everyone went outside. Burns stepped away and took the call. It was from the cops he'd sent to Munns's house. Judging by the expression on the chief's face, the news was not good.

Peter peeked inside the chief's head to find out what the problem was. And saw it clearly.

Munns was holed up inside his house with his latest victim. Burns's men had peeked through the front windows, and seen Rachael tied to a chair in the living room. She was conscious, and trying to reason with her abductor. Munns was also in the living room but not visible, and the cops couldn't pinpoint his location.

The cops had stepped back from the house. One of them had called Burns to find out what to do. Break down the front door and save Rachael, or stay outside and wait for backup?

Burns hemmed and hawed. He was a small-town police chief, and dealt with domestic situations and lost dogs. This was new to him.

"Tell your men not to go in," Peter told him.

"Hold on a second," Burns said into the phone. "What did you say?"

"Don't let your men go in. Munns will kill them."

"You think so?"

"Yes. Then he'll go into town, and kill as many people as he can."

"How do you know this?"

"That isn't important. Let me deal with Munns. I can stop him. It's why I'm here. Don't ask me to explain any more, because I can't. You have to trust me."

Burns looked to Garrison for confirmation. The FBI agent nodded. That was good enough for Burns, and he passed the instructions to the man on the line before ending the call.

"I hope you know what you're doing," the chief said.

58

Garrison followed Burns's cruiser out of the parking lot and into Pelham. Soon the town ended, and they drove down a two-lane road with signs for crossing deer.

"How are you going to deal with Munns?" Liza asked from the backseat.

Peter had promised not to keep secrets from Liza, but there were times when he would have preferred not to give her a straight answer. It would have made things so much easier.

"I'd like to hear the answer to that question myself," Garrison said.

"I have a friend who's a witch," Peter explained. "I'm going to call her right now, and ask her to cast a spell on Munns that will incapacitate him so I can get into the house, and free Rachael. The spell should also let me subdue him."

"A spell?" Garrison said, sounding incredulous.

"Yes. It's one of a witch's more potent powers."

"What will it do to him?" Liza asked.

"That's up to my friend. Some spells can set their subjects on fire. Others make a person blind, or incontinent. My friend will know which one to pick."

"Is this witch someone I know?"

Liza did not sound pleased. It was not the time to be discussing this, and Peter glanced into the backseat. "Her name's Holly Adams, and she's a student at Columbia University. I told you about her, remember? We grew up together."

"I seem to recall the name. Maybe I should meet her one day."

He decided to let that one go. They started to climb a steep hill. The scenery looked terribly familiar, and Peter realized that it was here that Munns had tried to end his life on three different occasions. It was a memory that he would just as soon forget.

"I've got a question," Garrison said, eyes glued to the road. "This spell your friend Holly is going to cast on Munns, will it wear off?"

"Eventually, yes. A spell is never permanent," Peter replied.

"How quickly?"

"It all depends on how strong the spell is, and if Munns is able to ward it off."

"Can he do that?"

"He might. Members of the Order of Astrum have special powers as well."

"That's not the news I wanted to hear. If the spell doesn't work, do you have a Plan B?"

Peter hadn't thought that far ahead, and shook his head. "Afraid not," he added for emphasis.

"Well, think of one."

Peter stared out his window and gave it some thought. The night held the answer to many of life's mysteries, and after a moment he knew what he must do. He'd enter Munns's house and summon the demon inside him. The demon would destroy Munns, just like it had destroyed the criminals the night his parents had perished, and the assassin who'd entered their apartment, and the assassin in Hyde Park. His victims had been evil people, and it was because of their evil that the demon had done away with them. Munns would be no different.

That was his Plan B.

But how to tell Garrison? The demon was at the top of the list of things he was never going to discuss with the FBI agent. Only he had to tell Garrison *something* . . .

A gunshot interrupted his thoughts.

The car lurched to a stop, and Garrison rolled down his window. The night had grown still again. "That sounded like a high-powered hunting rifle," he said.

"Do people around here hunt at night?" Liza asked.

"Not animals, they don't."

Climbing out, Garrison drew his gun. He motioned for them to stay put, and started up the road. Peter opened his door and felt Liza's hand come through the seats and grab his arm.

"We're supposed to stay here," she said.

"I was brought here for a reason," he reminded her. "I have to go."

"Oh, God, Peter, this is scary. Please be careful."

"Remember, I've got some powers of my own."

He slipped out of the car, and headed down the road after Garrison. Pieces of glass crunched beneath his feet. Rounding a curve, he saw a police cruiser lying in a ditch, its warning lights flashing. Garrison stood next to the ditch, shaking his head in dismay.

Burns had taken the hit.

The bullet hole in the cruiser's windshield was the size of a man's fist. Garrison opened the driver's door and the interior light came on. Still strapped in, the chief of the Pelham Police Department stared straight ahead with his hands clutching the steering wheel. The bullet had cut him in half, his lower torso drenched in blood.

"Didn't see that coming," Burns whispered.

"I'm calling nine one one," Garrison said, grabbing for his cell phone.

"Too late for that. Tell my kids . . ." His voice trailed off.

"Tell them what?"

"That their father . . ."

Burns stopped talking and licked his lips. He blinked, and then he blinked again. Peter gently pushed Garrison to one side. Crouching down, he pried the chief's hand off the wheel, and clasped it with both of his own.

"Let your thoughts go. It will make things easier," Peter said.

Burns nodded and seemed to relax. Peter looked into his head, and saw that the chief had a lot on his mind. Some of it was meaningless, but most of it not. He owed five dollars to another officer that he'd been meaning to pay back; the dry cleaning had to be picked up; the upstairs bathroom still needed painting. Then there was the important stuff, his family. On the hard drive of his computer was a letter to his son stationed in Afghanistan that he had yet to send. He'd been meaning to tell his wife how he appreciated her waiting up for him at night, but never gotten around to it. To his teenage daughter, a simple I love you was all he'd wanted to say. Those were the things that were on his mind. And how much he was going to miss them.

Peter squeezed the dying man's hand. "I'll tell them for you."

Burns's eyelids fluttered. The look on his face was skeptical.

"I'll make sure your son gets his letter, and I'll tell your wife how important her staying up was to you," he said. "And I'll tell your daughter that she was the apple of her father's eye."

Burns let out a deep breath, satisfied.

"Anything else?" Peter asked.

Burns looked like he was drifting on a cloud. Then he was gone. Garrison reached in, and shut the dead man's eyes.

Another gunshot ripped the still night air.

59

eter!" It was Liza, calling out in the darkness.

"I'm here," he said.

"I heard another gunshot. Are you all right?"

"Get back in the car," Garrison said. "You're not safe."

"Not until I know Peter's okay," she said.

Peter thought he was all right. But then again, maybe he wasn't. Maybe the bullet he'd just heard had gone straight through his heart, and what was now standing here was a ghost instead. It was entirely possible. He ran his hands up and down himself, feeling flesh and bone.

"I'm not hurt," he said.

"Please be careful," Liza said.

Peter listened to her walk away. Then he looked up the hill. Munns's house sat at the top, bathed in the bright moonlight. A two-story shingle box with a pitched roof and sagging gutters, it reflected years of neglect and disrepair. Back when Munns's parents had owned it, it had probably been nice. But evil had a way of corrupting everything it came in contact with, even the exterior of houses.

He started up the hill. He wondered who the shooter was. Was it the man in the van who'd killed the first police officer? It really didn't matter. Whoever it was had to be stopped.

"Get back here," Garrison ordered.

Peter ignored him, and kept walking. He dug out his cell phone and pulled up Holly's number. The call went through, and Holly picked up on the second ring.

"Get down before you get shot," Holly warned.

He fell into a crouch. "You watching me?"

"Yes. You're going to get killed if you're not careful."

"Where's the shooter hiding?"

"His name is Ray, and he's hiding behind an old oak tree on the same hill as the serial killer's house. Ray's got a hunting rifle with a telescopic sight, and somehow is able to see in the dark. He must be a devil worshipper."

"Make him stop shooting at us. I need to get inside the house."

"And fast. I looked in there, too."

"What did you see?"

"There's a woman tied to a chair. Your serial killer is about to strangle her to death."

"Stop him, please."

"I tried, but he shrugged off my spell."

"You're slipping."

"This was a strong spell. He was just stronger."

Another rifle shot rang out and kicked up dirt around Peter's feet. "Help me."

"Stay tuned."

His Droid made a funny beep as Holly ended the call. It would have been nice if she'd bothered to tell him if he was supposed to lie on the ground, or go hide behind a particular tree. Witches were peculiar in that regard: They gave only so much of themselves.

He scrunched down. The smaller a target he was, the better. His eyes had adjusted to the darkness, and he tried to find the shooter, only there were too many trees. It occurred to him that if the shooter fired another round, he'd see the bullet as it left the barrel of the rifle, and that was the probably the last thing he'd ever see. He glanced over his shoulder to see Garrison lying on the ground.

"Didn't I tell you to stay put?" he scolded.

"Get ready," Peter said.

"For what?"

"The shooter is about to be taken out of the picture."

"How are you going to do that?"

"I told you, I have a friend who's a witch, and she's going to cast a spell on him."

"I'll believe it when I see it."

Peter shifted his gaze straight ahead. "Keep watching."

A witch's powers were derived from nature and employed all of its destructive elements. Wind, earth, fire, and rain were all part of a witch's repertoire, along with the ability to hold sway over wild animals. Which of these powers Holly would use was anyone's guess. If Peter had been a betting man, he would have put his money on an owl swooping down out of a tree, and ripping the shooter's face clean off.

He would have lost the bet. A menacing black storm cloud formed overhead. A bolt of lightning sprang out of its belly and pointed a crooked finger at a large oak tree in Peter's line of vision. The oak tree burst into bright orange flames. Not ordinary flames, but ones of incredible heat. The shooter hiding behind the tree emitted a blood-curdling scream.

Bull's-eye, Peter thought.

The shooter ran out from his hiding spot with his clothes on fire. Garrison came crablike up the hill.

Peter pointed at the burning man. "There's your shooter."

"Tell your witch I said thanks." Garrison rose to a full standing position and took careful aim. Several shots rang out as he tried to take the shooter out. "Damn," he swore.

"Keep firing at him." Peter rose from his crouch, and started up the hill.

"Where are you going?"

"Guess."

"I'm ordering you to stay here."

"Sorry, I don't answer to you."

"You don't know what's up there. This may all be an elaborate trap."

The words struck Peter as being prophetic. Since Friday night, he'd known that he would meet up with a serial killer who'd do everything in his power to kill him. The whole thing was a trap, courtesy of the Order of Astrum, and he was about to step right into the thick of it. To be forewarned was to be forearmed, and he felt ready for the dangers that lay in store.

"I'm ready," Peter said.

He ran up the hill as fast as his legs would carry him.

60

~

The scene at the top of the hill was reminiscent of a war movie. Two police cruisers were parked on the gravel driveway in front of Munns's house with their windshields shot out and their front tires deflated. Each had sunk into the ground like a wounded animal.

Both cruisers had contained a single uniformed officer. Both officers now lay on the driveway with bloodied legs, tending to their wounds while aiming their guns at the front door of the house. Seeing Peter approach, they cautioned him to get down.

"Are you guys going to be okay?" Peter asked.

They gritted their teeth and nodded. Their faces were filled with pain compounded by the anguish that they hadn't stopped Munns.

"Who are you?" one of the officers asked.

"I'm working with the FBI. I just took out the guy with the hunting rifle who was shooting at you."

Peter looked toward the house. "Is Munns still in there?"

"Yeah, he's in there, and so is the woman he's holding hostage," the second officer replied. "We just heard her begging him not to kill her."

Rachael was still alive. But for how long? Light was streaming through the downstairs windows, and Peter tried to place where the living room was located. He decided that it was off to the left of the front door. He imagined Rachael bound to a chair and Munns about to end her life. He hadn't come all this way to let that happen.

I'm going in," he said. "Wish me luck."

The officers did not protest. They knew that something had to be done. He cautiously approached the front door. He supposed he could have grabbed one of the officers' guns, but he'd never shot a gun before, and didn't think now was a good time to start.

Not that he needed a gun. He had a weapon far more powerful. He thought back to the night his parents had perished. Rage filled his body like so much poison, the demon boiling up from within. His shoulder hit the door. The hinges gave way, and his momentum carried him into the foyer. He made a hard stop and looked into the room where he'd guessed Rachael was being held prisoner. His guess was on the money. She was there, bound to a chair.

So was Munns. He'd wrapped a thick piece of rope around her throat, and was pulling it taut, causing her eyes to grotesquely bulge out. Those same eyes were begging for mercy.

Evil did not know mercy. Nor did it know kindness, or love. Munns spun around to glare at his intruder. "I know you. Your name is Peter Warlock, and you were sent here to stop me."

Peter wasn't the only one who'd been warned. "That's right. Let her go."

"Not on your life."

Munns pulled the rope tighter while grinning sadistically. Rachael was jerked out of her chair as the life began to leave her body. Her eyes shifted to Peter for the first time.

Save me, they said.

A yell came out of the young magician's mouth. It did not resemble any sound that had ever come out of his mouth before. He charged across the living room, having decided to tear Munns apart and throw his limbs out the front door for the wounded cops to see.

His fist crashed into Munns's jaw and snapped the serial killer's head. He'd never been much of a fighter growing up, preferring to talk his way out of tight spots. Now the opposite was true, and he wanted nothing more than to beat Munns to a bloody pulp.

The rope dropped from Munns's hand. Kicking it away, Peter struck Munns again. The sound of Munns's nose breaking was loud and sharp. Blood poured from his nostrils like they were wide-open spigots. He started to lose his balance, and appeared ready to fall.

Peter should have stopped there, but the demon was having none of it. He struck Munns with all his might, the blow sending him across the living room and sprawling onto a couch. Munns lay on his back and stared at the ceiling. He looked dazed, and gasped for breath as Peter came forward, prepared to finish him off.

"Stop," Rachael said.

Peter raised a fist. One more blow was all it would take to end Munns's miserable life.

"I said stop," she said.

"I'm not done with him."

"He's taken enough punishment. Please don't hurt him any more."

"I was planning on killing him," he heard himself say.

She let out a gasp. "No—don't do that."

"You want him to live? Come on. He was going to kill you."

"That's not what I said. I'd love nothing more than if that horrible man was dead. But that still doesn't give you the right to beat him to death. No one has that right."

There was no rage in her voice or sense of outrage over what Munns had done to her.

"You're not angry at him?" he asked.

"Of course I am. But my anger doesn't justify taking another life. Would you mind untying me? The ropes are cutting off the circulation in my arms."

Peter was impressed that she could be thinking so clearly. As he started to untie her, Garrison rushed in through the front door, gun clasped in both hands. He zeroed in on Munns. He was still lying on the couch and had shut his eyes. Garrison aimed at his chest.

"Get up," he said.

No response. Garrison pulled back an eyelid. Satisfied that Munns was no longer a threat, he holstered his weapon and crossed the room to where Rachael sat. "I'm Special Agent Garrison with the FBI. How are you feeling?"

"Hello, Mr. Garrison," Rachael said politely. "All things considered, I'm doing fairly well, thanks to our friend here."

"Peter does good work, doesn't he?"

"I would say so."

"There's an ambulance coming to tend to a pair of wounded police officers outside," Garrison said. "I'll have them take you to the hospital as well."

"Do you think that's necessary?" she asked.

"It's always smart. You know, as a precaution."

Her arms free, Rachael touched her rescuer. "This is going to sound funny, but I had a dream about you the other night. Isn't that amazing?"

So the spirits had talked to Rachael as well. Peter undid the last of the knots and offered her his hand. She stood up too quickly, and fell back into the chair. He pulled her upright.

"Be careful," he said.

She thanked him with a smile. "I've never had a guardian angel before."

"Is that what I am?"

"I think so."

"I'll feel better when you're safely out of this house."

Peter spied movement on the other side of the living room. Munns had woken up, and was going through a terrifying transformation, his body tearing out of its clothes. His fingers grew into talons, and lizardlike scales appeared on the back of his hands. He didn't look human anymore. Grabbing Rachael, Peter pushed her out the front door.

Garrison went next, loudly complaining.

Peter slammed the door in the FBI agent's face, locking it.

"Stay outside, and don't look through the windows," he warned.

"What's going on?" Garrison said through the door.

"I'll tell you later."

He returned to the living room. The transformation was complete. The bearded faux college professor was nothing but a memory; in his place, a monster served straight up from the depths of hell. In his hand was a Swiss Army knife, which turned into a gleaming sword.

Now I know what a gargoyle on steroids looks like, Peter thought.

61

The water in the vase on Holly's coffee table had turned a dreamy whitish color. Like a storm cloud, the water twirled and danced. Holly recited the magical words that would let her once again spy on her beloved Peter. The water cleared, and she leaned forward, filled with anticipation.

She gasped. Peter was inside a strange house, fighting to the death with a hideous giant reptile. The reptile looked half human, half alligator, with a head shaped like a monkey's, and talons instead of fingertips. Incredibly strong, it was tossing poor Peter around like a rag doll.

To his credit, Peter was fighting back. He'd never been much of a scrapper, not that Holly had ever seen. But now he was using his fists with real skill, and landing solid blows against his opponent's skull. It thrilled her to see him in this mode.

Only there was a problem. Peter's blows were having little to no effect, and seemed to be making the giant reptile even more enraged. Throwing Peter to the floor, the thing began to stomp on Peter's chest.

Holly shrieked.

Witches weren't supposed to do that. Nor were they supposed to cry, or fall madly and hopelessly in love. But Holly *had* fallen in love, and now her emotions were on full display.

A loud banging on her front door caught her by surprise.

"Yes? Who is it?"

Her next-door neighbor, asking her if she was all right.

"I'm fine, Mrs. Burt," Holly said.

Mrs. Burt asked if she should call the police.

Holly jumped off the couch. The last thing she wanted was the police in her apartment and seeing her wall of potions and herbs. There was no law against being a witch, but it could still lead to unpleasantness with the landlord and even eviction if she was not careful. In the vase, Peter was back on his feet, whacking the thing with a poker he'd pulled from the fireplace.

"Come on, Peter, smash its head in," she urged.

"Is someone in there with you?" Mrs. Burt asked through the door.

Holly threw the dead bolt, and cracked the door. Mrs. Burt stood in the hallway wearing a pink bathrobe and curlers, cell phone at the ready.

"Is someone hurting you?" her neighbor asked.

"No, Mrs. Burt, no one's hurting me. In fact, I'm by myself."

Mrs. Burt stuck one eye to the door. "Why, isn't that amazing! You have a movie playing inside a bowl of water! How on earth is that possible?"

Closing the door in her neighbor's face was not the proper response, and Holly had to think fast. "It's the latest technology, Mrs. Burt. I bought it online."

"The figures inside the water are so lifelike! When I was growing up, the big thing was owning a color TV. Times have certainly changed. What do they call it?"

"Water movies."

"What will they think of next?"

"Good night, Mrs. Burt. Thanks for checking up on me."

"I'm here if you need me."

Her neighbor shuffled off to her apartment. Holly shut the door, threw the dead bolt, and returned to the couch. Peter and the thing were still doing battle. They had destroyed the room they were in, the furniture in splinters on the floor. Peter's face was a bloody mess and he was favoring his left arm. The thing had definitely hurt him. Holly had naturally assumed that Peter would win simply because Peter managed to somehow always come out on top.

But what if she was wrong? What if Peter had met his match, and was about to lose? The very thought threw her into a tailspin. Her aunt had warned her against interfering in Peter's affairs, and Holly put the warning right out of her mind.

Water shiny and oh so bright, do my bidding this darkest night,
Give the strength to the boy I love, so that he may vanquish . . .

Her cell phone slithered across the coffee table. Caller ID said Milly. She decided not to answer it, and continued.

. . . this thing that would end his life.
Let him fight with the strength of . . .

Her cell phone flipped off the table into her lap. It had enough force behind it to tell Holly that if she didn't answer it right now, there would be hell to pay down the road. Flipping it open, she politely said, "Well, hello, Aunt Milly, how are you?"

"Leave Peter alone," her aunt replied sternly.

"I will do no such thing. Peter needs our help."

"Stay out of it, damn it!"

Holly could not remember her aunt ever cursing at her. Not that Holly had been an angel growing up—few witches were—but harsh words had rarely passed between them. She had crossed over an invisible line, yet refused to back down. "Give me one good reason why I should."

"Because you're going to royally fuck things up," Milly said.

Holly nearly fell off the couch. The f bomb? From her aunt?

"I'm just trying to help," she stammered.

"For the thousandth time, Peter does not need our help."

Her aunt could not have been more wrong. The giant reptile had put its slimy hands around Peter's throat, and was choking the life out of him. Peter's knees had buckled, and his face lost its color. He began to sink into the earth one excruciating inch at a time.

"He's going to die," she whispered into the phone.

"No, he's not."

"Are you seeing the same thing I'm seeing?"

"I most certainly am. And so are the others. Max, Homer, and Lester are here with me."

"You're scrying on Peter *and* me?"

"That's right. As they say, two vases are better than one."

"You all see the peril that Peter's in, don't you?"

"He's not in any peril."

"Aunt Milly, are you blind?"

"For once in your life, stop questioning me."

"What about the others? What do they say?"

"They agree with me. Peter will be all right."

Holly started to cry. Peter was dying before her eyes, and her aunt was forbidding her from doing anything to prevent it.

Her aunt spoke again. "There's one more thing you must do, my dear child. You must stop watching. Something is about to happen which you are not supposed to see."

"Stop treating me like a child."

"Listen to me. It's for your own good."

"Good-bye, Aunt Milly."

The cell phone hit the wall and shattered. She'd been wanting to get a new one anyway. Kneeling on the floor, she pressed her face against the vase as Peter was pushed farther into the floor. She would have watched even if it had turned her blind, her love for him was so great.

62

As Surtr squeezed the life out of Peter's body, the young magician began to slip away to the next world. The experience was peaceful, almost serene. Not dead yet, but getting close.

His eyes snapped open. He stood in a black forest filled with dense smoke. Hanging from the trees were corpses of men who had not pleased their master and now hung there for eternity. From the distance came the battle cries between the forces of good and evil that had been taking place since the beginning of mankind.

It was dusk, and it took a moment for his eyes to adjust. When they did, he found himself staring at a throne made of human skulls on which sat a man well over seven feet tall. Dressed in a black hooded robe, the man's once handsome face had been grotesquely melted on one side like a worn-down candle.

Peter had two fathers. One biological and one . . . demonic. The black forest was residence to the second, whom he knew simply as the wicked one. Two thousand years ago, the Devil and his counterpart in heaven had struck a deal, with each of them sending six of his sons to earth to see which would prevail, the forces of evil or the forces of good. Lucifer had cheated, and made his six sons immortal. The earth had never been the same since.

"Hello, Peter," the wicked one said.

Peter grunted a coarse greeting under his breath.

"Not happy to see me, are you?" the wicked one asked.

"Our meetings never end well," Peter replied.

"You are a stubborn young man."

"Do I get that from you?"

A wind whipped through the clearing, causing the hanging men to twirl from their ropes.

"You're losing," the wicked one said. "That's unacceptable."

"He's much stronger than me, whatever the hell he is."

"His name is Surtr, and he's the eternal guardian at the gates of hell. The Order of Astrum sent him to earth to do away with you, once and for all. The fair-haired girl was nothing more than bait."

"What threat do I pose to the Order?"

"The elders of the Order are sending one of their disciples to New York in the hopes that he will attract more converts to their cause. Only one thing stands in their way. You."

"Who said I wanted to get involved?"

"I'm afraid you do not have a choice."

Peter shook his head at these words. His life was becoming a dark, uncharted journey where he had no say in the matter. The wicked one rose from his throne and stepped toward him. "Give me your hand, and I will give you the strength to do battle with Surtr."

"I don't want your fingers digging into my flesh," Peter told him.

"Do it. Before he kills you."

Peter saw himself jumping off the Brooklyn Bridge and emerging from the waters a changed person. Perhaps if he died at Surtr's hand, the same thing might happen.

"What if I say no?"

"Have it your way."

The wicked one clicked his fingers. Peter's body went stiff and his left arm rose on its own accord. The wicked one grabbed his wrist as his fingers turned into venomous snakes whose fangs tore into Peter's flesh and sent their poison coursing through his bloodstream. Peter bit his lip and tried not to scream. He could feel himself growing stronger, but at what cost?

"I'll be watching," the wicked one said.

Like a switch being thrown, Peter returned to the living room of Munns's house. The room had been wrecked by their battle, and Surtr still had his hands around Peter's throat, and was choking the last breath of life from his body. Nothing had changed.

Except, of course, him. He had been infused with an evil that had wreaked havoc upon mankind since the beginning of time, an evil that came straight from the source. Breaking free of Surtr's grasp, he clutched the thing's head and twisted it violently to the left, then violently to the right, hearing the bones in his neck crack like so many empty peanut shells.

"Uhhh," the thing from hell groaned.

Surtr released him, and staggered around the room with its arms flailing, mortally wounded. Peter rose from the floor. He should have stopped right then. But he was no longer himself, and wondered if he ever would be again.

He crossed the living room and gave Surtr's head another series of violent twists, and felt its neck grow looser. He found himself thinking about the three elders of the Order of Astrum, whom he felt certain were watching. It was time to send them a message.

He spun Surtr's head clear around its body like it was attached by a string. Then he released his enemy. Surtr's broken body hit the floor with a resounding thud. In the blink of an eye, he reverted back to being Doc Munns, whose head was now turned in the wrong direction.

"Peter, are you all right?" Garrison shouted from the front lawn.

Peter didn't know if he was all right or not. He certainly didn't feel the same. A piece of him had been stripped away during his journey, another layer of his soul lost.

An antique mirror hung over the fireplace. In its reflection, he saw what he had become.

He nearly cried.

He no longer looked human. His face was narrow as a wolf's, his nostrils flared, his mouth set in a permanent snarl. The pupils of his eyes were tinged a savage red, and darted wickedly from side to side.

Covering his face, he begged the evil thing he'd become to go away.

Garrison started banging on the front door. Finally, he'd had enough, and took the door down with his shoulder, and came inside. He looked at Munns lying dead on the floor.

"For the love of Christ, you nearly tore his head off."

"Guess I don't know my own strength," Peter whispered.

"That's brutal, man. Did he hurt you?"

"No. How's Rachael?"

"She's fine. The woman's amazing."

"You still need to take her to a hospital."

"I plan to. And you as well. Now stand aside for a minute. I need to record this." Garrison memorialized the crime scene through photos snapped on his cell phone.

Lowering his hands, Peter took another look in the mirror. He had become his old self again.

"I need to get some fresh air," he said.

"Be my guest. I'll be done in a minute," Garrison replied.

Outside, Peter stood in the gravel driveway and sucked down the chilly night air. Rachael was gone, and so were the pair of wounded officers, the ambulance's siren carrying across the hills as they were taken to the local hospital.

He took out his cell phone to call Liza, and found a text waiting for him. **U OK?** she asked. **THINK SO**, he wrote back, then added, **SAVED RACHAEL**. That got a dozen exclamation points in reply. He found it in him to smile. Something good had come out of this.

Garrison came out of the house holding a promotional mailer in his hand. He shoved it into Peter's face and said, "Take a look at this. I found it on the dining room table."

Peter held the mailer up to the light coming from the house. It was for a tattoo parlor called the Blue Devil, and featured glossy photos of various tattoos that you could have inked onto your body for a nominal fee. The tattoos were routinely hideous and featured snakes and demons. One tattoo in particular caught his eye: the shimmering symbol of the Order of the Astrum. He flipped the mailer over. On the postage side was a photo of the owner, a biker type with a ponytail. Only his surname was given: Ray.

"This is the same guy with the hunting rifle who killed Chief Burns, and rammed the police cruiser at the train station," Peter said. "He's part of the Order as well."

Garrison took the mailer and studied the address. "We need to run this character down before he skips town. Let's move."

"What about Munns?"

"You afraid of him coming back to life? Trust me, he's dead."

Garrison walked down the hill toward his car. Peter started to follow, then went in the opposite direction, and returned to the house. Munns had not moved from his spot on the living room floor. He looked dead, but looks could be deceiving. Peter wanted a sign, just to be sure.

"Show me," he said aloud. "I have a right to know."

In the oval mirror over the fireplace appeared a swirling form. Munns falling down an endless black hole as a silent scream came out of his mouth. It was fair punishment for all the terrible things he'd done, and Peter left the house believing there was still justice in the world.

63

Peter sat in the backseat with Liza while Garrison drove into town under the guidance of his GPS system. In a voice that was barely a whisper, Liza said, "What happened up there?"

"I really don't want to talk about it," he whispered back.

"Come on. No secrets."

He had taken no pleasure in killing Munns, and wouldn't sleep for the next few nights because of it. Talking about it would only make how he felt worse.

"Was it bad?" she asked, refusing to let go.

"On a scale of one to ten, it was a fifteen."

"Ugh. Will you tell me later?"

He didn't know if he could. Better to bury the memory and act like it had never happened. Just like all those times he'd killed as child. Just forget about it, and move on. The silence troubled her, and she squeezed his hand. "Is that a yes or a no?"

"How about, I don't know?"

"You aren't the same. The rage is boiling right below the surface. I can feel it."

She was right. The rage had not gone away like it had the other times. The demon was lurking in the shadows of his soul, ready to rise up and kill again. He needed to get his emotions under in check, and he said, "I just killed somebody, okay?"

She fell back in her seat. Looked out her window at the two-story shingle houses that lined the road at the bottom of the hill. "You've changed. I can see it in your face and hear it in your voice. You look scary."

"Do you want to get away from me?"

"No. Not yet, anyway."

"But you might."

"I will if I don't get some answers."

Garrison was doing a fine job of chauffeuring, and Peter guessed the FBI agent had overheard every word they'd said. Placing his mouth against Liza's ear, he said, "I'll tell you everything that happened, just not here."

She mouthed the word "When?"

"Later tonight. At home." And nearly added, "Lying in bed in the darkness."

"Is that a promise?"

"Uh-huh."

"Come on, say it."

"It's a promise."

His answer seemed to satisfy her. They held each other and kissed, and it all felt good again. His whole life, he'd been holding back his innermost feelings. Not since he'd lost his parents had he truly confided in anyone. That had changed when he'd fallen in love with Liza. Yet even with her, he'd held back certain things. Somehow, that was going to have to change.

"I also want to hear about your friend Holly," Liza said. "She sounds like someone I should get to know."

The words hit him like an invisible punch and he winced in the darkness.

"She actually kind of dull," he said.

"I'll be the judge of that," she replied.

The Blue Devil was located in a half-ugly strip mall on the outskirts of Pelham. In the parlor's front window was a blue neon sign of a smiling devil wielding a pitchfork. Beneath it, a second blue neon sign said CLOSED. A pair of police cruisers had taken the parking spaces in front of the store. Garrison said, "Stay put," and hopped out of the car.

Staring at the neon devil in the window, Peter had an unpleasant thought. Ray, the store's owner, had sent a mailer to people in town, shopping for clients. Each of the tattoos in the mailer had a demonic theme, and would attract a certain type of clientele. Munns had taken the bait, paid Ray a visit, and gotten an Order of Astrum tattoo stamped on his neck and become their slave. That meant Ray was a recruiter for the Order, and knew how things worked. Perhaps Ray could lead him to the elders, and he could pay them back for murdering his parents. Just thinking about it ignited a hot wire in his blood, and he threw open his door.

"Didn't you hear what Garrison just said?" Liza asked. "He meant it this time."

"Was he talking to me?"

"You're not funny. Please stay here."

"I need to talk to the man who owns this place. He knows things."

"You have that look in your eye again."

"You mean the suave and debonair look?"

"No, the evil one. No more bloodshed. I mean it, Peter."

Her voice had a finality that he could not ignore.

"Okay," he said.

Inside the Blue Devil, he felt a drop in temperature that chilled him to the bone. The reception area had a pair of cheap folding chairs and a counter with brochures strewn across it, the walls covered in posters of naked men and women whose bodies were tattoo canvases. A beaded curtain led to a cluttered back room with a low ceiling and jet-black walls. A barber chair sat in the room's center. It was here that customers got their tattoos inked onto their bodies while listening to music coming out of a boom box on the floor. Ray, the owner, sat in the barber chair, his wrist handcuffed to the arm. He reeked of smoke and was covered in bandages. There was no doubt this was the person who'd been shooting at them with the hunting rifle.

Garrison and the local cops stood nearby, exchanging information. Garrison's back was turned, and Peter drew up next to Ray, who shrank in his chair.

"Something the matter?" Peter asked.

"You're the guy that Doc Munns was supposed to kill," the tattoo artist said.

"Didn't work out that way."

"Is Munns dead?"

"Yes. I killed him."

"But he was possessed by Surtr."

"I still killed him." Peter let the words sink in and dropped his voice. "I want you to tell me what you know about the elders of the Order of Astrum."

Ray shook his head fearfully. "I do that, they'll snuff me for sure."

"You need to cooperate with the police. It's the only chance you've got."

"Right," Ray said.

One of the cops said, "Son of a bitch was going to pour kerosene on the walls right when we came into the store, probably planning to burn the place down, destroy evidence."

"What did you find in the van?" Garrison asked.

"We found a hunting rifle with a telescopic scope lying on the back-seat, along with a box of ammo," the same cop said. "We think it's the same rifle that killed Chief Burns."

"Then let's charge him. We've got a long night ahead of us."

Once the cops charged Ray, they'd take him to the station to be pro-cessed, and Peter would lose his chance to question him. He drew closer to the barber chair, and Ray cowered like a frightened dog. "You had to know you'd get caught," Peter told him. "What did the elders do? Make you an offer you couldn't refuse?"

"You know about the elders?" Ray squeaked.

"We're old friends. Now what did they offer you?"

"I'm not talking to you."

"Tell me, damn it."

Ray clamped his mouth shut. Peter was not planning to leave empty-handed, and he stole a look inside Ray's mind. It was filled with troubling images, but one in particular stood out. A sinister figure wearing dark flowing robes covered in astrological signs commanded a stage not un-like the one in his own theater. His spiked hair and dark fright makeup were pure Gothic. Plucking a succession of black silks out of the air, he bunched them together, and made a half dozen screaming vultures mag-ically appear. With a mad explosion of feathers, the carnivorous crea-tures flew into the theater to pluck at the faces of the unlucky patrons sitting in the first row.

"Who is he?" Peter asked.

"I don't know what you're talking about," the tattoo artist said.

"The man on the stage with spiked hair and the vultures. I want to know who he is."

Ray gulped. "You know about Dante?"

"Is that his name? Dante?"

Peter felt a hand come down on his arm, and he spun around. Garrison pulled him away from the barber chair to the other side of the room.

"I told you to stay in the car," Garrison said angrily.

"Just give me another minute with him," Peter pleaded.

"That's out of the question. We have an investigation to finish. Now go outside, or you'll end up getting in trouble."

"There's something else going on here, and this guy knows what it is."

"You heard me. Leave. Right now."

Peter bit the words about to come out of his mouth. The expression "devil got your tongue" took on a whole new meaning. He pointed an accusing finger at Ray. "You've got to make him talk."

"We'll do that. Now vamoose."

He started to leave and heard an odd popping sound. The noise reminded him of a soda can being punctured and the air escaping. Against the wall, the five-gallon kerosene tanks that Ray had intended to torch his studio with had mysteriously punctured themselves. The smelly liquid was pouring out, and racing across the concrete floor, where it puddled at the base of the barber chair, and climbed up its sides. Ray was talking to one of the cops, not having a clue.

"Get away from the chair," Peter said.

The Pelham cops looked at him, not understanding.

"Why should we?" Garrison asked.

"Because it's going to explode."

"Is he serious?" one of the cops asked.

The rules of physics did not hold in the psychic world. An ashtray with a dead cigarette sat on the table where Ray kept his tattoo needles. The cigarette sparked to life, rolled out of the ashtray, and landed on the floor in a stream of kerosene. The stream caught flame, and did a mad dash toward the barber chair. In a split second, the chair was engulfed in flames along with the man chained to the arm. It was like watching a bomb go off.

Ray screamed.

The cops ran for the door.

Peter rushed toward Garrison. The arm of Garrison's sports jacket had caught fire, and he pulled the FBI agent out of the building, found a patch of grass, and rolled him around until the flames were extinguished. The cops stood in the parking lot coughing and hacking but otherwise no worse for wear. The elders had spared them. It was Ray they wanted silenced.

The Blue Devil burned like a tinderbox, the flames licking the sky by the time the fire trucks and ambulance pulled in. As the building's walls started to crumble, Ray's final screams could be heard above the wailing sirens. The elders had kept him alive so they could torture him. It was the price you paid for striking a deal with the Devil.

Peter drew closer to the burning building and strained to hear Ray's last words. He was trying to say something before he died, his voice rising above the din.

"Dante . . . will . . . kill you all . . ."

Peter still had no idea who Dante was. Only Ray knew the answer to that question, and as the fiery building collapsed, he guessed the secret would follow the tattoo artist to his grave.

64

You can go upstairs, Ms. Adams," the uniformed guard said.

Holly crossed the lobby and punched the elevator button. She had been coming to the Dakota for so many years that security knew her by name, yet the guards still called her aunt before allowing her to go upstairs.

She rode the elevator wishing she'd heeded her aunt's warning. Milly had told her not to scry on Peter any longer, that she would end up getting hurt if she did. There were rules to being a psychic, and she'd broken every one of them. What an awful mistake she'd made.

The elevator doors parted and she walked down a hallway to Milly's apartment. She wiped away her tears before pressing the buzzer. The image of Peter twisting the head of the serial killer from side to side would not go away. He had not seemed human.

She raised her hand to knock on the door. Before she could, it opened wide, revealing her aunt in the foyer along with Max, Lester, and Homer. Their collective faces were filled with sorrow. Had they continued to scry on her while she scryed on Peter? Something told her that they had. She entered the apartment, and the door was shut behind her.

"I'm sorry I disobeyed you," Holly said to the group, her voice cracking.

"Peter is not like us—you understand that now," her aunt said.

"He's a monster. How could I have not seen that before?"

Milly gripped her niece by the shoulders and looked her in the eye. "Peter is *not* a monster. He is of both worlds, both good and evil. He can make choices, which purely evil people cannot. Do you understand the difference?"

Holly shook her head. All she understood was that there were two Peters: the one she loved, and the inhuman one she'd seen in the vase that terrified her. She had no idea how to deal with her feelings, so she'd run to her aunt's apartment for help.

A tiny sob escaped her lips. Milly put her arms around her niece, and gave her a hug. Max, Lester, and Homer circled around her, and placed their hands consolingly on her as well. It made her feel better, and she told herself that somehow, she'd get through this.

Garrison was taken to the ER of the nearby Lawrence Hospital Center to be checked out.

A sign on the wall boasted that the hospital had over four hundred doctors. Judging from the activity inside the ER, most of them were on duty tonight.

Peter and Liza stood in a curtained room with Garrison, waiting for a doctor to see him. The agent sat on a table wearing slacks and an undershirt. He kept looking at his arms, shocked that the skin had not been burned. To Peter he said, "Why was I spared?"

"It's complicated," Peter said.

"Go ahead. I'm not going anywhere."

"The Order was in retreat mode. Munns was dead, and the police were about to arrest Ray and start interrogating him. Ray was a recruiter and had direct contact with the three elders that call the shots. The elders needed to silence Ray before he started talking. That was their sole objective, and they succeeded."

"Why didn't they kill the rest of us as well?" Garrison asked.

"The elders don't kill innocent civilians, if they can avoid it. They let their underlings do that."

"And by not killing civilians, the police don't pursue them. Makes sense. Looks like we've got company."

Rachael came through the curtains. Except for a square bandage covering a scrape on her forehead, she looked no worse for wear, and she gave Peter's arm a squeeze. "There you are. I was hoping to see you before I blew out of here."

"You're leaving?" Peter asked.

"I gave my statement to the police, and really don't see any reason to hang around," she said. "I think a good night's sleep in my own bed is just what the doctor ordered."

Liza stepped forward. "You must be Rachael. I'm Liza. It's great to finally meet you. I heard you on the phone a few days ago."

"You heard me on the phone?" Rachael said, sounding confused.

"It's a long story," Peter explained. "Maybe someday we can get together, and Liza and I will explain it to you."

"That would be very nice. There's an awful lot of what's happened here that I still don't completely understand. One of the policemen told me about the fire at the tattoo parlor. I hope no one was injured who didn't deserve to be."

"The good guys came out unscathed," Garrison replied.

"How wonderful is that?" Rachael broke into a smile. It was the first time she'd done that, and it made her look radiant. To Peter she said, "May I steal you away from your friends for a couple of minutes? I have a question that I think only you can answer."

Peter looked at Liza and saw her nod. Pulling aside the curtain, he allowed Rachael to leave first, then turned to his friends. "I'll be right back."

He followed Rachael outside the hospital to the parking lot. A yellow cab idled by the front entrance. Peter guessed this was Rachael's ride back to the city. She would go home tonight and, hopefully, return to a normal life. He wished he could be so lucky.

"Can you please tell me what those things are?" she asked.

A darkish cloud hung over the taxi. Peter had thought it was the taxi's dirty exhaust, but upon closer inspection, realized it was the shadow people, all clustered together. He'd assumed the shadow people would go back to wherever they came from once Munns was dead, and the threat to Rachael had passed.

Wrong.

The shadow people were not going anywhere until Rachael was back in New York, safe and sound. Their sole purpose for being was to protect Rachael. It had never been about him, or Munns, or the Order of Astrum. Their skin in the game was to keep Rachael unharmed, and they had succeeded.

"Can you make them go away?" she asked. "They're scaring me."

"You don't want them to go away," Peter said. "Those are your other guardian angels. They're going to hang around for a while, and make sure you get home okay."

She shuddered from an invisible chill. "I guess I can deal with that. But what are they? Ghosts? Or are they something else? I really want to know."

Peter wanted to tell her to forget about them. She had escaped from the forces of evil, and that was all that really mattered. Asking questions would only lead to more questions and soon she'd be bogged down by the horrible weight of it all. He chose his words carefully.

"Think of them as friends from the other side."

"Like fairies?"

He laughed to himself. That was one way to describe them. "Call them what you want. Don't be afraid if you catch them hanging around. They're just trying to protect you. Now, let me ask you a question. What do you do for a living?"

"Why is that important?" she asked.

Rachael had been targeted because she made a difference in the world, and Peter wanted to know what that difference was. "I'm just curious."

"Very well. I'm a research scientist. It's boring work. Endless hours in the lab staring through a microscope at tiny molecules. I specialize in molecular biology in the hopes it will one day lead to a breakthrough in cancer research."

Peter had his answer. He smiled. "That's wonderful."

"Actually, no. I was looking forward to taking a break. I've had a rough couple of days."

"May I ask why?"

She impressed him as a private person, and she gazed at the ground as she spoke. "Most of my experiments are done with lab rats. They are much nicer animals than you'd imagine. This past week, I had to put down six of my favorites. I gave them names, which made it that much more painful. It put me in a terrible depression. I hate killing animals."

"But you keep doing it."

She lifted her eyes. "You make that sound like a crime."

"It makes you feel bad, doesn't it?"

"It's supposed to make me feel bad. But that doesn't make it wrong. A long time ago I realized that some of us were put on this earth to kill in the hopes that it might better mankind. I know that sounds very noble, but I happen to think it's true. Soldiers kill so that we may have peace, policeman kill to stop criminals from hurting innocent people, and I euthanize some unlucky lab rats in the hope I'll discover a cure for cancer. It's hard, but there's no other way."

Peter thought about the killing he'd done in his life. Had those bloody acts left the world a better place? He supposed they had, for the men he'd killed were the personification of evil, and had victimized countless innocent people. It was one way to rationalize the things he'd done, and the things that he'd no doubt do someday in the future.

"Well, it was nice meeting you," he said.

"Am I safe to go home?" she asked.

"I think so."

"How do I thank you for saving my life?"

"No need to. I'm glad I was in time."

She gave him a hug. The best things in life were the good deeds we did for strangers. Someone a lot smarter than him had said that, and it felt very true right now. He went to the cab and held open the door for her. The shadow people continued to hover above the vehicle like a storm cloud. "I have a question," he said. "You said before that you saw me in a dream. Do you remember what was I doing?"

She stopped before getting in the cab. "It was so strange. You were standing on stage doing your magic. I was in the front row watching. When your trick was done, a single person in the audience started to clap. The sound had a hollow ring, and it caused me to turn around in my seat to see what was going on. To my surprise, the seats behind me were empty."

"Who was doing the clapping?"

"A dark figure standing in the very back row. He wore hideous stage makeup and a flowing black Gothic robe. There was a black bird perched on his shoulder that looked like a vulture. He asked me if I wanted to join him."

"Join him in what?"

"I honestly don't know. He spoke to me by name. It was so strange."

"What happened then?"

"I told him no thanks. Then I woke up, and found myself covered in sweat." She paused. "I have no idea what the dream meant. Do you?"

Ray the tattoo artist had been thinking of a magician who made vultures appear from scarves as well. Was the man in Rachael's dream the same person?

"No, I don't," Peter said.

"Well, I sure hope he doesn't come back. Good night. Thanks again for saving my life."

The taxi pulled out with the dark cloud still hovering above it. It occurred to Peter that he didn't even know Rachael's last name. He would have to ask one of the cops what it was. That way, he'd be able to Google her, and find out how her research was going. Something told him that before long, her name would be in the newspapers, and for all the right reasons.

He headed back inside. Through the glass doors he spied Liza standing in the lobby. She had a cell phone pressed to her ear, and was waving frantically to him.

He rushed inside.

65

It's Dr. Sierra. He needs to speak with you," Liza said, handing him her cell phone.

Sierra was the last person Peter wanted to be talking to right now, and he pressed the cell phone to his ear. "Hello, Dr. Sierra. What a pleasant surprise."

"I'm sorry to be calling at such a late hour," Sierra said. "Hunsinger is dying. I'm with him at his apartment. The doctor just left, and said he only has a few hours left. It was Hunsinger who asked me to call you. He wishes to speak with you before he passes."

A dying man's last request was hard to turn down, only Hunsinger had already told him enough bad things about his childhood to last a lifetime, and Peter didn't want to hear any more horror stories tonight. "I'm sorry your friend is dying, Dr. Sierra, but I'm going to take a pass. I'm already having a hard enough time dealing with what he told me the other day."

"This concerns your parents," Sierra said as if not hearing him. "It seems that your father confided in Hunsinger about certain events which had happened during your parents' childhoods. Hunsinger wishes to share these things with you."

"I already know about my parents' childhoods. Good night."

"Please don't hang up. You don't know about these things."

"What are you talking about?"

"Hunsinger said your mother was the reason it all happened in the first place."

"My mother? What is that supposed to mean?"

"He said your mother was the prize."

"The prize for what?"

"I'm sorry, but I have no idea what any of this means. I would suggest that you speak to Hunsinger yourself. And hurry. The clock is running out for my friend."

Peter cursed under his breath. If he didn't rush back to the city to see Hunsinger, he'd never know what the old priest was talking about. The words would haunt him for the rest of his life, and he had no doubt this was why Hunsinger had uttered them to Sierra.

"Where does he live?" Peter asked.

Sierra gave him the street address and apartment number. Peter memorized it and ended the call. He felt like throwing the cell phone against the wall, only it happened to belong to Liza. "We need to go back to the city," he said.

"Right now?" Liza said.

"Yes. Right now."

They sat in a pair of middle seats on the midnight train back to New York, facing each other. The car was otherwise empty.

"That was rude to leave and not say good-bye," Liza said.

Peter had sent Garrison a text, explaining that he had to go see a dying friend. He'd also asked Garrison to contact Chief Burns's family, and pass along those things which Burns had communicated to him a few moments before he died.

"Hunsinger is on his deathbed, and has asked to speak with me," Peter explained. "He knows a secret about my mother that he wants to tell me. I couldn't say no."

Liza had run out of patience, and she gazed out the window at the passing scenery. "When are things ever going back to normal? I feel like a puppet being jerked around on a string. First I get yanked one way, then another. This isn't right, Peter."

"Our lives used to be dull, You even complained about it once."

She frowned at him. "Our lives are out of control, I don't know what normal is anymore. You're going to have to make a decision."

"I am?"

"Yes. Do you want to be a psychic who runs around helping the FBI solve crimes, or do you want to be in love with me? You can't have both."

"I can't?"

"No. I've reached my limit."

It was his turn to stare at the scenery. Being a psychic was a reward for all it enabled him to achieve and punishment for all the lies it forced him to tell. That was his destiny, and there was no getting around it. But was it fair to Liza? He was pulling her into a world where she had no control. If he was going to keep her, he would have to change, even if it meant never sitting down to another Friday night séance with his psychic friends and talking with the dead. He had to stop it if he truly loved the woman sitting across from him.

And he had to do it right now.

"I want to be in love with you," he said. "It's the only thing I've ever really wanted. I'll stop the psychic stuff. No more talking to ghosts, or helping the FBI."

The words hit her hard, and it took a moment for her to compose herself.

"Is that a promise?"

"Yes, it's a promise."

Liza switched seats, and snuggled up beside him. They held hands and kissed, and he saw how incredibly happy she was. That alone told him he'd made the right decision. That hadn't been so hard. All he'd ever wanted was to have a normal life. By walking away from being a psychic, he could have one. It was as simple as that.

He resumed looking out the window. The train route was lined with billboards for theatrical shows playing in the city. There were musicals, revivals, and plenty of serious dramas, reminders that New York was the theater capital of the world.

One billboard caught his eye. It was for a magic show, the performer someone he'd never heard of. Peter tried to stay up on any magicians who played New York, if for no other reason than to know who his competition was.

He brought his face up to the glass for a better look. The billboard showed a dark figure wearing a flowing black robe, his face painted in fright makeup, his hypnotic eyes daring you to enter his world. Perched on his shoulder was vulture with a bunny rabbit in its mouth. Bold lettering announced his show at a theater in Times Square.

Dante—The Anti-Conjuror
Prepare to have your imagination turned inside out,
and your emotions stripped bare.
Call now for tickets

It was the same dark magician that Ray the tattoo artist had been thinking of before he died, the same evil character who'd invaded Rachael's dreams as well.

Peter fell back in his seat. Anti-conjurors were the Devil's entertainers, and were sent to earth during times of turmoil and strife, their sole purpose to recruit more disciples to the Devil's unholy cause. Dante was about to unleash his dark magic on the unsuspecting populace of New York. If unstopped, the city would never be the same.

He had to act. He could not sit by, and let the city he loved be harmed. But how was he going to tell Liza that? Hadn't he just promised to stop being a psychic? She was not going to let him off the hook this time. If he didn't stop, she would leave him for good.

The train hit a bump in the tracks. The lights inside the car went off, plunging him into darkness. It helped him think, and by the time they'd reached their destination, Peter knew exactly what he must do.

STATISTICS AND STYLE

MATHEMATICAL LINGUISTICS
AND AUTOMATIC LANGUAGE PROCESSING

A Group of Monographs and Textbooks

General Editor: David G. Hays, State University of New York at Buffalo

Already Published:

1. David G. Hays (Ed.)
   Readings in Automatic Language Processing, 1966

2. David G. Hays
   Introduction to Computational Linguistics, 1967

3. Ferenc Kiefer
   Mathematical Linguistics in Eastern Europe, 1968

4. Henry Kučera and George K. Monroe
   A Comparative Quantitative Phonology of Russian, Czech, and German, 1968

5. Robert R. Freeman, Alfred Pietrzyk, and A. Hood Roberts (Eds.)
   Information in the Language Sciences: Proceedings of the Conference held at Airlie House, Warrenton, Virginia, March 4–6, 1966, under the Sponsorship of the Center for Applied Linguistics, 1968

6. Lubomír Doležel and Richard W. Bailey (Eds.)
   Statistics and Style, 1969

In Preparation:

7. Petr Sgall, Ladislav Nebeský, Ala Goralčíková, and Eva Hajičová
   A Functional Approach to Syntax: A New Type of Generative Description of Language, 1969

Statistics and Style

Edited by

LUBOMÍR DOLEŽEL

Academy of Sciences, Prague

and

RICHARD W. BAILEY

The University of Michigan, Ann Arbor

1969

AMERICAN ELSEVIER PUBLISHING COMPANY, INC.

NEW YORK

April, 1970

AMERICAN ELSEVIER PUBLISHING COMPANY, INC.
52 Vanderbilt Avenue, New York, N.Y. 10017

ELSEVIER PUBLISHING CO. LTD.
Barking, Essex, England

ELSEVIER PUBLISHING COMPANY
335 Jan Van Galenstraat, P.O. Box 211, Amsterdam, The Netherlands

Standard Book Number 444-00039-9
Library of Congress Card Number 69-11151

PRINTED IN THE UNITED STATES OF AMERICA

PREFACE

Many fields in the humanities have not only survived but profited from the application of mathematical models and techniques; not the least among these is the study of the creative use of language. Stylistics and the study of texts have become a crossroads for the interests of literary scholars and critics, linguists, psychologists, sociologists, and mathematicians. The mathematician finds in the study of texts a body of material to use for testing and refining distributional and discriminatory formulas. The sociologist is interested in the text as it reflects social forces and developments in the history of ideas. The psychologist investigates the text as a product of the highest and most distinctive capacity of the human mind. The linguist studies the text structure in order to discover patterns and variability both in language system and the uses of language. Finally, the literary scholar and critic finds in the text the focus of his professional interest in artistic language. It is no wonder that this startling variety of approaches to the text and its style leads to widely disparate results.

The statistical investigation of texts and text styles can serve all of the specialists just mentioned. But at the same time, it is most directly concerned with the description and explanation of the features inherent in the text, their organization and variability. Nevertheless, statistical stylistics has not yet acquired the scientific authority that it deserves, and certainly one of the principal reasons for this state of affairs can be traced to the communication barriers that separate the scholars at work in the field. Though a scholar may be highly competent in his own area, he is often very much an amateur in one or more of the disciplines that find their meeting ground in statistical stylistics. Yet without extraordinary competence in all of them—mathematics, linguistics, sociology, psychology, and criticism—the scholar's work may be misunderstood and even maligned. Another such barrier to communication in the field results from the multiplicity of styles and the variety of languages that have been scrutinized by statistical methods. Without the native speaker's sensitivity to stylistic nuance, the scholar may be unable to profit from the insights of his colleagues working in other languages.

In preparing the collection that follows, we have tried to overcome these communication barriers. We have chosen what seems to us the best efforts of statisticians, psychologists, linguists, and literary scholars and at the same time have tried to illustrate both the questions asked and the techniques used in answering them. The range of these questions is surveyed by Bailey in the concluding article of the collection; as a glance at the table of contents will show, the essays are topically arranged in an attempt to reveal the unity and variety of the field. In addition to those essays originally written in English, we have selected and translated major contributions from French, Russian, and German. But in selecting the essays in whatever language, we have attempted to illustrate matters of general interest to all scholars concerned with style.

It is our hope that the collection demonstrates the general agreement between contemporary theories of language and literature and the statistical study of texts. A generative system of language description and a structuralist conception of literature underlie many of the essays gathered here. This fact illustrates our belief that the statistical study of texts and styles is an integral component of modern theories of language and literature; the relative neglect of statistical matters in both disciplines seems to us largely due to a misunderstanding of the aims and methods of statistical work—a misunderstanding that we hope will be at least partly remedied by this collection.

Our book is likewise intended to show the present state of the discipline. The essays collected here are mostly of recent origin and many of them are published here for the first time. But our focus on recent efforts should not be interpreted as a denial of the merits of such classic work as that of Zipf, Yule, Herdan, Guiraud, Mandelbrot, Fucks, Tomaševskij, Kolmogorov, and others. As many of the essays in this book show, the pioneer work of these men in formulating the problems and defining the techniques of statistical stylistics is a continuing stimulus to further efforts. A reader of this collection can expect to be informed about the most topical problems of the discipline and can, we hope, find material that will touch on his own interests, whatever his area of study and whatever his experience of the field. A textbook that will serve as a meeting ground for scholars of various backgrounds has long been needed; we feel that the collection of essays that follows will begin to fill this need.

We are grateful for the cooperation of the authors and publishers of the essays reprinted here and for the patience and perseverance of those who have written original essays for this collection. We would also like to thank Dr. Mark E. Suino, Mr. Karl Ortseifen, and Miss Angela McCourt for their help in making the translations and Mrs. Margaret Bailey for her work in preparing the manuscript. Finally, we acknowledge the encouragement and advice given by Dr. David G. Hays, the general editor of this series.

March, 1968

L.D.
R.W.B.

TABLE OF CONTENTS

I
THE THEORY OF
STATISTICAL STYLISTICS

STYLES AS DIALECTS

WERNER WINTER

From a linguist's point of view, references to style as commonly found in literary analyses of texts are often too intuitive and impressionistic to carry much weight. A random example may be cited for an illustration: If a Soviet scholar, D. S. Likhačev, states in a recent edition of Russian diplomatic reports of the 16th and 17th cent. (*Putešestvija russkikh poslov XVI–XVII vv.*, Izd. AN SSSR, M.-L., 1954) that the language of these documents contains a blend of the "bookish" and the "colloquial," and that it is "factual" language, then such statements may well sum up our first reactions to the material before us; still, we will feel that the use of such labels is not legitimate unless we can describe in an accurate, objective way what constitutes "bookish," "colloquial," or "factual," language.

The following is a discussion of some recent attempts to discover distinctive properties of certain groups of texts by means of statistical evaluation. The methods used were originally developed for work on German; a presentation of procedures and results has been offered in *Phonetica*, 7 (1962), 193–216. Later on, one of my graduate students, Ludek A. Kozlik, applied the same approach to Russian; his findings are included in his master's thesis, *Some frequency characteristics of Russian styles*, Univ. of Texas (Austin, Texas, 1962). My work has been supported most generously by the U. S. Army Signal Corps project in mechanical translation at the University of Texas.

A style may be said to be characterized by a pattern of recurrent selections from the inventory of optional features of a language. Various types of selection can be found: complete exclusion of an optional element, obligatory inclusion of a feature optional elsewhere, varying degrees of inclusion of a specific variant without complete elimination of competing features.

In these properties, styles agree with dialects, in particular with social dialects; it may even be claimed that styles can be considered special types of social dialects.

The identification of different styles can be undertaken in much the same way as the identification of different dialects of a language: a boundary between two styles can be established on the basis of a bundle of isoglosses. Style boundaries may or may not coincide with boundaries of idiolects; one has the general impression that any speaker of a given language is free to make use of different styles depending very much on circumstances and on choice. However, it seems that there is a certain correlation between, on the one hand, what one might call (rather inadequately) "erudition" and, on the

This essay was delivered to the Ninth International Congress of Linguists (1960) and printed in the *Proceedings* (The Hague, 1964), pp. 324–330. It is reprinted here by permission of the author and Mouton & Company.

3

other, versatility in the use of different styles (or of what we suspect to be identifiable as different styles); use of "poetic" language, for one, seems to presuppose at least previous exposure to this type of diction, use of "scientific" language generally appears to depend on appropriate training.

A complete characterization of a style would require the previous recognition of all distinctive properties of an entire class of utterances. It is not wise to hope and wait for such recognition as we know only too well that exhaustive descriptions of much less complex facets of language still remain desiderata; for all practical purposes it will be sufficient to base a proposed identification on the establishment of some characteristic isoglosses. Any one of the selection types mentioned above can be the source of a differentiation reflected by such an isogloss; only one of them, however, yielded data readily usable in our kind of investigation.

As is the case with other forms of dialect, a section of a language for which we want to use the term "style" cannot be determined by an a-priori decision or even on the basis of comparative evidence. The fact that a special style is used in language A for scientific discourse does not mean that in language B a special style has to exist for the same purpose; the fact that poetic forms are used in a given language and at a given time does not by itself mean that we can postulate the existence of a special poetic style for this language. We have to depend entirely on the discovery of combinations of distinctive properties in any particular section of a language. While this is true, we have to take note of the fact that the native or near-native analyst of spoken and written materials in a given language usually has at least certain rather specific intuitive feelings about "stylistic" properties of his materials and about contrasting styles found in them, just as a native speaker of a language often has a fairly good prescientific notion about dialect distribution.

Ideally of course the identification of contrasting styles should be made without recourse to native reactions (just as one may ideally insist on a phonemic analysis without reference made to meaning); in practice, to heed the common-sense assessment (which after all reflects a thorough exposure to the language and all the reaction conditioning that goes with it) means considerable gains in the efficiency of one's investigations: to pay due attention to native opinion means being kept out of numerous blind alleys. This does not imply that the native speaker is always right: it goes without saying that every conclusion drawn by him from intuitive reaction must be verified by exact checks.

The two approaches, the ideal and the practical, may be briefly illustrated here:

We are interested in the question of word length in Russian (needless to say that our interest was aroused by certain things we observed, and that we have a hunch that we may come upon something significant).

Ideally we would now follow a procedure and a chain of arguments as follows: We decide to check the distribution of long words; by trial and error we detect that a definition of "long word" as a word of nine or more letters yields reasonably clear results. Finite verb forms we exclude from our investigation since their occurrence is conditioned by obligatory rules throughout the entire language, so that they cannot possibly be used in the determination of styles. We take samples of text, one thousand words each (the sample size has been found appropriate in previous work), from fifty different sources, all by writers of the last two centuries. Wherever possible, we select dialogue passages marked by special punctuation features in our printed texts. (We also search non-dialogue passages occurring alongside dialogue in the same text, but we do not include them in our first set of data.) We find: In 20 of the 50 samples, long words occur with a relative frequency of more than 15%; in 30 samples, this frequency amounts to less than 9%. All instances of low relative frequency occur in dialogue passages. A check of the texts with high relative frequency of long words shows that all are from journalistic and scientific prose (the terms used here to refer to content categories). We conclude that we can use the feature of relative frequency of long words for the purpose of characterizing (in part, to be sure) two forms of speech that are found in dialogue and in argumentative prose, respectively. If the difference found here is confirmed by further independent data, we will revise this statement to say that low frequency of long words is one distinctive property of (simulated) oral style or, once the evidence from fictional narrative is brought in, a distinctive property of non-argumentative prose. If we find the last formulation too involved, we may decide to use its converse, namely, that high relative frequency of long words is one distinctive property of argumentative prose—"long word" here being defined as a word of nine or more letters, "high relative frequency" as a frequency of more than 15%.

The second approach would reflect more closely the actual discovery process: We have noticed that what might be called argumentative prose is full of rather long words: we read the dialogue of stage plays and of novels and find that such is not the case there; we set out to verify our impressions, using the same definition of "long word" as given before. Our impressions are confirmed, but—and this is of course decisive and will offset all inherent weakness of the second approach—the mere impressions are replaced in the process by statements of data, which we now can use with confidence. Even though we did not pretend to start without any notion as to what we would find, our final results are as valid as those obtained by the first approach.

Various aspects of linguistic form are utilized in the identification of dialects: lexicon, phonology, morphology, syntax may all contribute valuable isoglosses. Literary stylistic analysis relies heavily on features of the vocabulary and their distribution.

In our own work, it soon became clear that lexical items, though they may well be distinctive features of specific styles, could not be used for our particular type of investigation. We were interested in determining frequency characteristics of our texts by the evaluation of random selections of constant size, selections which we considered to be representative of the entire text they had been taken from. All but a few (and generally non-optional) features of the lexicon have too low a frequency to draw conclusions from the absence of a particular feature in a given sample or set of samples; conversely, its occurrence within these samples cannot be taken to reflect similar distribution in the remainder of the text. Conclusions based on lexical items will have to be derived from the entire corpus studied, and typically (as exemplified in the procedures of literary analysis) the fact of the occurrence of a given item is not as significant as the determination under what circumstances it is used. Our analysis provides only for quantitative findings, not for qualitative evaluation; we therefore had to forgo any consideration of lexical units found in our materials.

Instead, we concentrated in our investigation on phenomena of sufficient generality to assure recurrence in our selected data. Thus, we were interested in the relative complexity of word, phrase, clause, sentence; we studied problems of the order of parts of sentences; we considered the question of paratactic versus hypotactic construction within our sentences.

The principal consideration observed in the choice and development of search techniques was that of simplicity. Only through the greatest possible simplicity in our procedures could we hope to be able to cover a rather large sample of text in a moderate amount of time (for a set of questions concerning order of sentence parts in German, 63,093 sentences from 30 different sources were examined); only through simplicity could we assure that our procedures could easily be repeated by other people interested in our problems. Thus, as seen above, the question of word complexity was reduced to a question of word length, and this word length was to be measured in letters, not in phonemes. One may justly label such approach crude; but only by being so unsophisticated we could hope that anybody setting out to check our results with the same texts would arrive at exactly the same figures we had obtained (barring only outright adding mistakes). For practical purposes, the much more refined technique advocated by Greenberg in his typological investigations must be called a failure; neither does it seem possible to arrive at identical results once a group of investigators sets out to duplicate Greenberg's morph count of a sample of words in a language well known, like English, nor is the technique, tedious as it is, feasible for work with really representative bodies of data.

Similarly, to handle a problem like that of clause length in a refined way would have required a great deal of skill and, just as important, a very great amount of time. Again we decided to use a simplified, though indirect and somewhat imprecise, approach to this matter. Taking cognizance of the fact that a finite verb is an obligatory constituent of a clause, and disregarding the fact that some clauses can be joined so that either the verbal or the nonverbal element can become multiple, and finally disregarding the special case (not rare in Russian) that the verb "to be" may be zeroed out, we decided to use the finite verb as an index of clause length: if 10% of all words in a sample were finite verb forms, we interpreted this as indicating an average clause length of ten words. This procedure turned out to be fast and reliable, and it provided simple criteria for the description of such elusive an entity as "nominal style."

What could be studied effectively varied from language to language. In German, the opener of a main clause could be determined at high speed since it involved only the classification of preverbal material assignable to one part of the sentence. In Russian, the fact that the verb position is not as rigidly fixed as in German created such plotting problems that a study of the clause openers was not made part of the pilot projects included in Mr. Kozlik's work, even though extensive exploratory checks indicated that results not too different from those had in German could be obtained. The distinction between main and subordinate clauses could be made very fast in German, again because of contrastive verb position; in English, a similar search requires a much higher degree of sophistication in text analysis.

In conclusion a brief résumé of our findings will be presented.

In German, the relative frequency of subject in first position in main clauses was studied. A significant contrast was detected between (simulated) spoken language (of stage plays) and the language of scientific treatises: all samples of the first category had a subject frequency in the upper part (73.6–79.2%) of the total frequency range (54.2–82.2%); all samples of the second category had a low subject frequency (54.2–63.5%)

Conversely, scientific texts showed high frequency of adverbial in first position (30.9–39.7%), while stage dialogue had low frequency values here (15.4–18.6%); the total frequency range for the initial adverbial in main clauses was 15.4–39.7%, so that the two types of language contrasted appear at opposite ends of the scale.

The measurable difference between stage dialogue and scientific prose is noteworthy also in the case of the relative frequency of finite verb forms, our index, as will be remembered, of relative clause length. Here the total range of frequency of finite verb forms per hundred words is 7.4–17.1%; the range for scientific treatises alone is 7.4–11.3%, for stage dialogue, 13.6–15.0%. At this point, values were also obtained for the dialogue passages in fictional prose; here the range was 12.3–17.1%, so that here too we find scientific and dialogue prose at opposite ends of the spectrum.

Not so clear-cut was the distinction when we studied the question of parataxis and hypotaxis in German prose sentences. The stage dialogue showed a strong preponderance of paratactic constructions: in eight out of nine texts studied, 73.6–84.9% of all verbs were found in main clauses; in contrast to this, 18 of 19 scientific texts analyzed belonged to a frequency range of 46.5–68.5%. However, one each of the texts showed the range characteristics of the other group: one stage play had a main verb frequency of only 60.3%, one scientific book, a frequency of 77.0%. Dialogue from novels covers almost the entire frequency range: we find values from 50.8 to 83.1%. If in the previous examples we can say that we are dealing with indications of what we may call a genre style, we must take note here of strong interference with the same genre style; in other discussions of these data (note reference above) I have tried to explain this interference as due to the effects of choice on the part of an author.

We may sum up our findings for German and state that the frequency properties of scientific prose contrast strongly with those of simulated dialogue. If we take the latter as an approximation of the spoken language, then we can say that scientific German shows marked and measurable deviations from the patterns of the spoken language. Once the values obtained for fictional prose are taken into consideration, we find that this type of language provides a transition between the extremes, not by occupying a well-defined area in the middle between the two, but by covering the entire scale of which the other two form the extremes. This means that, when dialogue style resembles oral German and scientific style represents written German par excellence, fictional German can be made to resemble either more the spoken or more the argumentative style of the language, apparently very much in accordance with the intentions of a writer.

If we come to note a smooth transition from fictional to argumentative German, there is strong evidence for a sharp break between the two genres in Russian.

Reference has been made before to an investigation of the occurrence of long words. In argumentative prose, 15.8–36.6% of all words fell into this category; in dialogue from stage plays and fiction, the range was 2.9–8.9%. The values obtained for fictional narrative were 7.4–15.1%.

Strikingly similar were the findings for a syntactic feature, the use of adnominal genitives. In argumentative prose, 23.4–35.4% of all noun forms were adnominal genitives; in dialogue, the frequencies were 1.2–8.4%. Fictional narrative covered a range of 4.6–17.0%.

The same general pattern is repeated in the figures for clause length. The average number of words per clause (computed on the basis of the frequency of finite verb forms, as pointed out above) is 12.4–20.0 in argumentative prose, 5.8–9.3 in dialogue, and 5.7–9.1 in fictional narrative.

Fictional narrative patterns with argumentative prose only in one of our counts (in another, concerned with the frequency of adjectives, fictional narrative provides for a transition between dialogue and scientific discourse, similar to what was found in German): the average number of words per sentence in dialogue is 4.3–8.4, in argumentative prose, 11.5–21.6, and in fictional narrative, 7.9–19.1. A comparison of the values in the last two counts indicates that the internal structure of a sentence in fictional prose tends to be radically different from that of a sentence in scientific prose; it seems warranted to assume that mere sentence length is not as significant a distinctive feature as clause length is.

In contrast to German, the prose of Russian fictional narrative shows great affinity to the prose of the dialogue. If we again assume that the latter can be considered simulated spoken Russian, we note that there is no severe break between spoken and literary Russian, but that a radical difference exists between literary and scientific Russian. This appraisal of the nature of literary Russian seems to agree well with facts of its history: the importance of the spoken language for its development seems very much greater than that of spoken German for the language of a great many eminent writers, witness in particular Goethe.

What has been presented here, are first findings in a field of rather vast scope. The frequency values discussed may eventually turn out not to furnish the most important isoglosses between the style dialects they help define; this is a risk that had to be taken. All findings presented appear to be based on sufficiently broad data (the number of samples used is 76 in Russian, between 30 and 57 in German; the size of the sample usually is 1,000 or 2,000 of the entities evaluated: words, clauses, sentences, depending somewhat on the limitations imposed by the size of the texts); it is therefore likely that the results obtained are representative.

A FRAMEWORK FOR THE STATISTICAL
ANALYSIS OF STYLE

Lubomír Doležel

The foundations of the statistical theory of style can be summarized in a simple statement: *style is a probabilistic concept*. A probabilistic concept has two fundamental features: (1) In a probabilistic "world," the occurrence of phenomenon A is not unequivocally predetermined by the existence of condition X. Under condition X, the phenomenon A will occur with a certain probability only—$P_X(A)$; with a probability $P_X(B)$, phenomenon B can occur; with the probability $P_X(C)$, phenomenon C, and so on. Even if the probability of A under condition X is high—that is, when $P_X(A)$ approximates 1—the possibility of non-occurrence of A, or the possibility of occurrence of B, C . . . cannot be excluded. The expectancy of each phenomenon of the set A, B, C . . . under the condition X is given by the *probability distribution* $P_X(A), P_X(B), P_X(C) \ldots$.

(2) The probability distribution describes the expectancy of phenomena A, B, C . . . in a complete or ideal ensemble of occurrences—in the so-called population. Empirically, however, phenomena A, B, C . . . occur or can be observed in rather limited and not-ideal ensembles, in the so-called samples. In samples, values of the probability distribution are liable to random fluctuations. In other words, one cannot expect that the values $P_X(A)$, $P_X(B)$, $P_X(C)$ . . . will be stable (identical) in various samples; rather, probability distribution is reflected in sample *frequency distributions:* $p^{(1)}{}_X(A)$, $p^{(1)}{}_X(B)$, $p^{(1)}{}_X(C)$ . . .; $p^{(2)}{}_X(A)$, $p^{(2)}{}_X(B)$, $p^{(2)}{}_X(C)$ . . . (the index numbers 1, 2 . . . symbolize various samples). The values of the frequencies—$p^{(i)}{}_X(A)$ . . .—fluctuate in a certain admissible (statistically insignificant) interval around the values of probabilities $P_X(A) \ldots$.

There is strong evidence that style properties of texts display both features of a probabilistic concept. To make our argument more easily understandable, let us consider a rather popular statistical style indicator—sentence-length.[1]

Let us suppose that the style of author X_1 is characterized by use of a short sentence (on the average), whereas the style of author X_2 is distinguished by use of a long sentence (on the average). It is obvious, however, that this stylistic regularity does not prohibit author X_1 from using longer (or even quite long) sentences in certain cases; author X_2, in turn, is not deprived of the possibility of using short sentences at any time. In other words, sentence-length is not a fixed value determined unequivocally by an author's habits; it is rather a *tendency* that can be described by probability distributions of the individual sentence-lengths. In this way, a probabilistic conception enables us to describe style not as a fixed habit, but rather as a preference for one or another mode of expression. The overall character of a style is called forth by

10

the *degree* of presence (or absence) of a certain mode of expression, rather than by its exclusive use (or complete suppression). Thus, a probabilistic approach reveals the flexible character of stylistic features; these features resist any description in terms of necessity or in terms of strict rules and prohibitions.

Since stylistic features are apparently consciously controlled to only a limited degree, an author cannot be expected to exhibit identical values of sentence-length distribution in all samples of his style (i.e., in all his texts). Values of the sample frequency distributions—as well as the value of the average sentence-length—in various texts by the same author will fluctuate within certain intervals around the stable values of the probability distribution.[2] A probabilistic approach reveals *the stylistic stability* (i.e., the stable probability distribution) *behind the variability of concrete manifestations* (i.e., the fluctuations of frequency distributions). By using specific statistical procedures—tests—the student of style is able to distinguish between insignificant fluctuations which do not affect the basic character of a style and significant fluctuations which signal differences in styles or stylistic change.

If we accept the assumption that (a) style features are *tendencies* toward certain modes of expression and (b) the variety of concrete manifestations represents an underlying stylistic stability, then the probabilistic conception is to be considered an *adequate theory of style*, rather than a secondary aspect of stylistic theory or a mere descriptive technique.[3] However, there is a long way from the acceptance of this assumption to the formulation of an adequate probabilistic theory of style. The empiricism that has hitherto predominated in statistical stylistics can only be overcome by the combined efforts of linguists, statisticians, and literary scholars in developing theoretical models and schemes. Our outline of a theoretical framework for statistical stylistics is an attempt to move in that direction.

THE STYLE-FORMING PROCESS

A stylistic theory can only be said to account for stylistic differences between texts and to provide a framework for a taxonomy of styles if it offers a description of the origins and underlying factors responsible for the variety of styles. I am convinced that contemporary linguistics provides a suitable general background for explaining stylistic variety in the distinction of linguistic competence and linguistic performance.[4] Style-forming processes are to be considered a fundamental component of linguistic performance: style originates in the process of producing (encoding) a text (a discourse) by a certain speaker.[5] Therefore, stylistic theory is a substantial part of the theory of linguistic performance.

It is well known that the theory of performance and its relation to the theory of competence lacks the degree of elaboration that is characteristic of contemporary theories of linguistic competence.[6] Nevertheless, it seems possible to formulate at least some preliminary conclusions that are relevant to the theory of style.

(1) The theory of linguistic competence is a necessary background for any theory of style. The theory of competence (in its syntactic component) provides definitions of "grammaticality," "syntactic ambiguity," and "syntactic similarity between sentences."[7] These terms of the theory of competence correspond precisely to the fundamental terms of the theory of style: grammaticality corresponds to *stylistic deviance;* ambiguity corresponds to the *stylistic effect of ambiguity;* and similarity corresponds to *stylistic choice.*

(2) While stressing the importance of the theory of competence for the theory of style, we must at the same time acknowledge that the theory of competence cannot supplant a theory of style, just as it cannot replace a theory of performance in general.[8] The theory of performance has to account for all components of verbal behavior and therefore is not "a repetition of grammatical theory under the guise of a performance theory."[9] Unfortunately, many contemporary schemes of linguistic performance prefer to iterate substantial components of a theory of competence rather than to concentrate on the specific processes of verbal behavior.

(3) From the viewpoint of stylistics, extant theories of linguistic performance reveal the following principal shortcomings:

(a) Performance schemes are strongly biased in the direction of representing the process of text recognition (i.e., the hearer's behavior) rather than the process of text production (the speaker's behavior).[10] The style of a text, however, seems to be entirely a product of the speaker's behavior; variables that operate on *the input of the process of communication* seem to be responsible for the variety of styles.[11] It can be assumed, therefore, that models of the "generation situation" will be much more relevant for the theory of style than will models of the "recognition situation."[12]

(b) The extant performance schemes fail to represent pragmatic features of performance. This deficiency can easily be discovered, for example, in the scheme proposed by R. J. Wales and J. C. Marshall; it is the more surprising because of the following claim made by these authors: "Complete performance theories will need to go beyond semantic studies and will have to systematize various 'pragmatic rules' that select utterances which are not merely well formed but also 'appropriate to the situation'."[13]

(c) Because of their apragmatic nature, performance schemes usually lack a selectional component, that is, they do not provide a description of the processes that the speaker employs in selecting the one most appropriate mode of expression from a set of alternatives.[14] It is well known from the history of stylistics that the notion of selection (choice) is crucial for many modern theories of style.[15] In some cases, especially in poetic texts, the selective process seems to be controlled consciously; the production of a text (poem) is then described by the poet as a succession of choices that are optimal from the viewpoint of the realization of a text "design."[16]

Our criticism of the extant performance schemes already reveals what we must expect from such a scheme: a complete performance scheme has to account for (a) the pragmatic features of verbal behavior and (b) the substantial differences in verbal products (texts). In other words, a performance scheme has to describe the *style-forming process* that, on the one hand, reflects the impact of pragmatic features, and, on the other, is responsible for stylistic differences between texts.

In this essay, we concentrate on the description of the selective process that is considered to be the basic component of the style-forming process.[17] In a preliminary way, the selective process can be outlined as follows: at every step of text production, the speaker selects one mode of expression from a set of alternatives—$A = \{a, b \ldots n\}$—offered by his linguistic competence. In the simplest case, a set of alternatives consists of two members only; for example, $A = \{$active construction, passive construction$\}$. In producing a sentence, the speaker decides whether it will remain in the active form, or whether the passive transformation will be applied. In a more complicated case, set A consists of more than two alternatives. Thus, for example, when deciding about the length of the produced sentence, the speaker is offered a wide range of possibilities, from a one-word sentence to a sentence of several hundred words. Selective operation on the set A is repeated whenever this set is presented to the speaker. In both the examples just mentioned, the selective operation on the pertinent sets of alternatives will be repeated in the production of each sentence. In other cases, selective operation on the set A does not take place in the production of each sentence. Thus, for example, in the selection from a set of synonyms (*man, guy, fellow* . . .), the choice will be repeated only when the sentence produced requires the content expressed by the given set of synonyms.

In every case, the repeated selective operation will result in the arrangement of the set A into a probability distribution: $P\{A\} = P(a), P(b) \ldots P(n)$. Each of the alternatives will be assigned a certain probability of occurrence in the produced population of texts. In our simplest example, as a result of repeated selections between the active form and the passive transformation, active phrases will occur in the produced text population with a probability $P(a)$ and passive phrases with a probability $P(b)$.

We assume that the selection process is controlled by factors of a pragmatic nature. Every speaker shapes his text in accordance with his individual idea of efficiency, on the one hand, and in accordance with the requirements of the context (in the broadest sense) on the other. Those qualities of the speaker that are relevant for the selection process (verbal preferences, mental type, stylistic skills, etc.) represent the *subjective factor* of selection. Context Q_j can be designated as the *objective factor* of selection; it is independent of the speaker, though it exercises its influence through him. Context is represented by such factors of verbal communication as the form of language (written or oral), the form of discourse (dialogue or monologue), the genre, the function of the text, and so on.

To make the selection process easier to understand, let us draw a simple scheme of its components and their relationships:

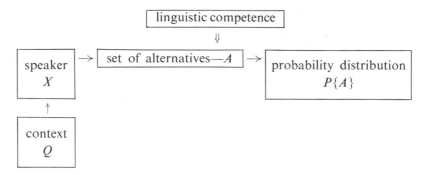

Pragmatic factors, both subjective and objective, are always present when a text is produced. (Our pragmatic classification of texts is based on this fact— see p. 18.) However, the impact of these factors on the style-forming process varies, and our whole theory is based on the assumption that the impact of one or another class of factors can be weakened or even completely eliminated. Theoretically, three basic possibilities arise:

(1) Two speakers, X_1 and X_2, when selecting from the set of alternatives A, are controlled solely by their personal preferences and habits; the impact of context Q is fully eliminated. Under such circumstances, our speakers will generate probability distributions $P_{X_1}\{A\}$ and $P_{X_2}\{A\}$, which will not change under changing contexts, Q_j. The following scheme gives a representation of this situation:

SCHEME 1

	Q_1		Q_2	
	X_1	X_2	X_1	X_2
a	$P_{X_1}(a)$	$P_{X_2}(a)$	$P_{X_1}(a)$	$P_{X_2}(a)$
b	$P_{X_1}(b)$	$P_{X_2}(b)$	$P_{X_1}(b)$	$P_{X_2}(b)$
.	.	.	.	.
.	.	.	.	.
.	.	.	.	.
n	$P_{X_1}(n)$	$P_{X_2}(n)$	$P_{X_1}(n)$	$P_{X_2}(n)$
$\{A\}$	$P_{X_1}\{A\}$	$P_{X_2}\{A\}$	$P_{X_1}\{A\}$	$P_{X_2}\{A\}$

A speaker whose selection behavior is described by scheme 1 will be called a *context-free speaker*. Empirically, this type could be represented by a poet who imposes his highly personal style on all texts he produces, regardless of differences in genres or forms. The model of the context-free speaker is rather common in the theory of style: it is assumed that style features indicate (or discriminate) always and solely particular authors (speakers). Much empirical data, however, seems to indicate that this model has no universal validity; rather, its adequacy is limited to exceptional cases.[18]

(2) Let us assume that speakers X_1 and X_2 have completely suppressed their personal preferences and habits and are entirely subject to the impact of context when selecting from the set of alternatives $\{A\}$. In other words, let us now observe a selective process which is controlled by only the objective factors and not at all by the subjective ones. The resulting distributions of $\{A\}$ will depend on the changes of Q_j only and will remain the same when the speaker changes. Scheme 2 represents this situation:

SCHEME 2

	Q_1		Q_2	
	X_1	X_2	X_1	X_2
a	$P_{Q_1}(a)$	$P_{Q_1}(a)$	$P_{Q_2}(a)$	$P_{Q_2}(a)$
b	$P_{Q_1}(b)$	$P_{Q_1}(b)$	$P_{Q_2}(b)$	$P_{Q_2}(b)$
.	.	.	.	.
.	.	.	.	.
.	.	.	.	.
n	$P_{Q_1}(n)$	$P_{Q_1}(n)$	$P_{Q_2}(n)$	$P_{Q_2}(n)$
$\{A\}$	$P_{Q_1}\{A\}$	$P_{Q_1}\{A\}$	$P_{Q_2}\{A\}$	$P_{Q_2}\{A\}$

A speaker whose selective behavior can be described by scheme 2 will be called *context-bound*. Bureaucrats can be taken as empirical examples of context-bound speakers; they produce their official messages in a standardized style in which any personality features are absent and even undesirable.[19] From the viewpoint of a universal stylistic theory, texts of context-bound speakers are not deprived of style; their style, however, does not reflect the individuality of the speaker but supra-individual conditions and functions of context.

(3) Let us now consider the third possibility, that of a speaker who adjusts his choices to the requirements of the supra-individual context and at the same time preserves the individuality and idiosyncrasy that distinguishes him from other speakers. We suggest calling such a speaker *context-sensitive*. The

selective behavior of the context-sensitive speaker is governed by both objective and subjective factors. The representation of his selective behavior is a more complicated task than the representation of the two previous cases. Scheme 3 is a preliminary outline of such a representation:

SCHEME 3

	Q_1		Q_2	
	X_1	X_2	X_1	X_2
a	$P_{X_1Q_1}(a)$	$P_{X_2Q_1}(a)$	$P_{X_2Q_2}(a)$	$P_{X_2Q_2}(a)$
b	$P_{X_1Q_1}(b)$	$P_{X_2Q_1}(b)$	$P_{X_1Q_2}(b)$	$P_{X_2Q_2}(b)$
.	.	.	.	.
.	.	.	.	.
.	.	.	.	.
n	$P_{X_1Q_1}(n)$	$P_{X_2Q_1}(n)$	$P_{X_1Q_2}(n)$	$P_{X_2Q_2}(n)$
{A}	$P_{X_1Q_1}\{A\}$	$P_{X_2Q_1}\{A\}$	$P_{X_1Q_2}\{A\}$	$P_{X_2Q_2}\{A\}$

The impact of subjective factors differentiates the generated distributions $P_{X_1Qj}\{A\}$ and $P_{X_2Qj}\{A\}$; at the same time, objective factors are responsible for the difference between $P_{XjQ_1}\{A\}$ and $P_{XjQ_2}\{A\}$. We can say that the Q factors delimit zones within which the distributions of the particular speakers are spread.

In my opinion, the selective behavior described by the scheme of the context-sensitive speaker is the most frequent of all possible cases. Empirically, it is manifested in the selective behavior of a "common" speaker, who preserves his individual style but at the same time differentiates the style of his written and spoken texts, of his public speeches and private correspondence, of his professional writings and poetic essays, and so on.

It has to be stressed that the terms *context-free, context-bound,* and *context-sensitive* are terms of the abstract model and not empirical ones. Our examples (poet, bureaucrat, common speaker) were used for the sake of entertainment only. Our theory presupposes that every actual (empirical) speaker can display a variable nature in terms of the model: at one time, he can behave as the context-free speaker; at another, as the context-bound speaker; and at another—perhaps most frequently the case—his texts can be produced in accordance with the scheme of the context-sensitive speaker. This variability can be explained by considering the two classes of pragmatic factors (subjective and objective) as two forces aimed in opposite directions and striving to dominate the communication "space" of the natural language.

In the central zone of the communication space, the influence of the two factors is balanced; here, the speaker is subject to the control of both subjective and objective factors and behaves as a context-sensitive speaker. On the peripheries of the communication space, either subjective or objective factors dominate, minimizing or even completely eliminating the influence of the opposite class of factors. A speaker producing texts in these communication zones finds himself under the control of one class of factors only and behaves either as a context-free or as a context-bound speaker.[20] A specification of the communication zones and the degree of control over them by the two competing classes of factors could constitute, in my opinion, an important step in the development of the pragmatics of language communication.

THE STATISTICAL STRUCTURE OF TEXTS

The representation of the selective process just discussed was intended as a framework for explaining the origins and variability of text styles. It is now necessary to turn to the study of variable features inherent in texts that are responsible for the variety of text structures and styles.

Natural language texts can be measured in various aspects or on various levels of their structure: phonemic, morphological, syntactic, lexical, suprasyntactic, etc. Some text measures are already well established in the statistical study of texts: phonemic (or graphemic) entropy, word-length distribution (e.g., Fucks's distribution), ratios based on various word classes (e.g., Busemann's coefficient), various measures of the "richness" of vocabulary (e.g., Yule's characteristic), distribution of sentence-lengths, ratios of various phrases or clauses, etc. Most of these measures are discussed in the contributions to this collection, especially in sections II and III and in Bailey's historical survey (section VI).

Each text can be represented by a set of measurable, statistical characteristics: $T = \{C_1, C_2 \ldots C_z\}$, in which C_i symbolizes text characteristics. In other words, each text can be described in a multidimensional space, with the values of C_i representing individual vectors. By this formula the statistical structure of a text is represented in a very abstract and unspecified manner; therefore, this formula will be called the *elementary text formula*.

The elementary text formula is deficient because it does not express one essential empirical fact, namely that text characteristics are variable in their statistical properties, and therefore do not form a homogeneous class. The variability of statistical properties of characteristics represents the fundamental problem of statistical text analysis; at the same time, because of their variability, statistical characteristics qualify as sensible and effective discriminators of text styles.

The specification of text characteristics that will be attempted in the following paragraphs requires the establishment of a pragmatic classification of texts. A pragmatic classification is based on the existence of pragmatic factors of text production, factors which have been outlined in the previous section of this essay.[21] In terms of these factors, the set of texts of a language—$T(L)$—

can be classified in two dimensions: (a) according to the subjective factors—a classification yielding classes $T(X_i)$, that is, classes of texts produced by a certain speaker, X_i; and (b) according to the objective factors—a classification yielding classes $T(Q_j)$, that is classes of texts produced in a certain context, Q_j. Because the two criteria are independent, they can be applied in combination to yield the specified classification represented in the following matrix:

	Q_1	Q_2 . . .	Q_m	
X_1	$T(X_1Q_1)$	$T(X_1Q_2)$ . . .	$T(X_1Q_m)$	$T(X_1)$
X_2	$T(X_2Q_1)$	$T(X_2Q_2)$ . . .	$T(X_2Q_m)$	$T(X_2)$
.	.	. . . .	.	.
.	.	. . . .	.	.
.	.	. . . .	.	.
X_n	$T(X_nQ_1)$	$T(X_nQ_2)$ . . .	$T(X_nQ_m)$	$T(X_n)$
	$T(Q_1)$	$T(Q_2)$ . . .	$T(Q_m)$	$T(L)$

Classes $T(X_iQ_j)$ represent text sets produced by a certain speaker in a certain context. Since some speakers do not produce texts in all possible contexts, we should assume that some sets $T(X_iQ_j)$ will be empty.

The subjective and objective factors of texts can be determined empirically. Therefore, a pragmatic classification represents an empirical framework for the statistical analysis of texts; any text corpus can be classified according to the pragmatic criteria before we know anything about the statistical structure of the corpus. This circumstance has an essential bearing on the further development of our framework: the particular text classes, defined on the basis of pragmatic criteria, can be interpreted as "populations" and can be used for determining the statistical properties of text characteristics. This is the direction in which we will proceed when seeking a specification of text characteristics.

Let us first consider two aspects of this problem:

(1) We assume that some text characteristics will prove to be statistically stable (homogeneous) in the set $T(L)$, that is, in all the texts of a synchronous state of language L. This means, of course, that these characteristics have no discriminatory power for the study of styles in the text set $T(L)$. We can say that such characteristics have a supra-stylistic nature; they will be called *L-characteristics* (*L-C*). *L*-characteristics represent a background for the stylistic differentiation of texts, but they are otherwise irrelevant for the stylistic theory.

There are good reasons for regarding the distribution of phonemes (graphemes) and phoneme (grapheme) entropy as an L-characteristic.[22] Even if the hypothesis about the L-nature of phoneme (grapheme) distribution should be refuted, the existence of L-characteristics has to be taken into account by the theory.

(2) Empirical evidence indicates that some characteristics are non-stationary in a text T and some are statistically unstable in the text class $T(X_iQ_j)$. The problem of the stationary character of style measures is as old as the statistical study of texts.[23] Nevertheless, it has not been solved in a satisfactory way. We can suppose that in most cases characteristics are stationary throughout the text; there is, however, strong evidence—especially in the data obtained from poetic texts—that in exceptional cases a characteristic may prove to be non-stationary.[24]

As far as the statistical instability of a characteristic in $T(X_iQ_j)$ is concerned, we can cite here Busemann's observation: the verb-adjective ratio was observed to fluctuate significantly in some texts by the same author and produced in the same context. This fluctuation is apparently due to the "disturbing" influence of occasional, transient factors of the speaker's mental or physiological state.[25]

It is obvious that both the non-stationarity within a text T and the significant fluctuation within the class $T(X_iQ_j)$ are to be explained by the impact of some pragmatic factors which have not been accounted for in our theory. In other words, characteristics with these properties are unaccountable and undescribable within our framework. From our viewpoint, these characteristics will be treated as *sub-stylistic features*. Their existence represents a serious challenge to the statistical theory of style; their description and explanation, however, require a special approach.

We are now able to specify the scope of our theory by eliminating both supra-stylistic and sub-stylistic characteristics from the elementary text formula. After this step, the text formula will contain a set of style characteristics proper: $T = \{C_1{}^s, C_2{}^s \ldots C_r{}^s\}$. This new formula will be designated the *elementary text-style formula*.[26]

Before we proceed further in the specification of text characteristics, let us suggest another refinement in the text-style formula: the number of style characteristics can be reduced by examining their correlations. If two characteristics—C_i and C_j—prove to be highly correlated, then the elementary text-style formula can be said to contain a certain redundancy. This redundancy can be eliminated by omitting dependent characteristics and leaving only the independent ones. As we know, the correlation procedures themselves do not indicate the direction of dependency; therefore, our decision as to which characteristics are independent and which dependent will be largely determined by the aim of the investigation.[27]

My own data indicate that there exists a correlation between average sentence-length and average word-length in a corpus of texts in contemporary standard Czech (excluding poetic texts). The coefficient of correlation is rather high, $r=0.90$. However, an examination of the linear correlation by the method of "least squares" did not lead to a satisfactory result.[28]

After eliminating dependent characteristics from the formula, we obtain the *reduced text-style formula*: $T=\{C_1, C_2 \ldots C_n\}$, with $n<r$, where C_i are independent style characteristics.[29]

Let us now proceed further in specifying the style characteristics on the basis of their statistical properties. The basic populations for testing these properties will be the text classes $T(X_iQ_j)$, that is, sets of texts produced by one speaker with a fixed context.[30] The sum total of the text sets $T(X_iQ_j)$ is the set $T(Q_j)$, which will be considered our basic corpus. When testing the statistical homogeneity of a characteristic, C_i, with regard to the populations, $T(X_iQ_j)$, we can obtain two contrary results:

(1) The values of C_i in various populations, $T(X_iQ_j)$, of the corpus $T(Q_j)$ will prove to be significantly different. In other words, C_i is statistically stable in texts of a certain speaker—here the stability is given by definition (see p. 19)—but it shows significantly different values in text sets of different speakers.[31] Such a characteristic can be assumed to express individual style features of a speaker and will therefore be called the *subjective style characteristic (S-C_i)*.

(2) The values of C_i in various populations, $T(X_iQ_j)$, of the corpus $T(Q_j)$ will prove to fluctuate, but within statistically insignificant limits. In other words, C_i is homogeneous in the corpus $T(Q_j)$. In this case, the characteristic can be considered to express the supra-individual (objective) style features; it will be called the *objective style characteristic (O-C_i)*.

A third result of the test can be theoretically assumed: the characteristic C_i will prove to be homogeneous for only a group of speakers (two, for example) for the same Q_j, whereas for the majority of speakers it will prove to be statistically unhomogeneous. This case I would prefer to interpret as an expression of stylistic similarity between two (or more) speakers with regard to the characteristic C_i rather than an indication of the presence of objective stylistic features.[32] It is obvious that this possibility brings further complications into the study of style characteristics; it does not, however, alter our basic scheme.

Subjective style characteristics (S-C_i) will be subject to a second test that aims at determining the range of their (significant) fluctuation. This step of testing presupposes a comparison of at least two corpuses, $T(Q_j)$ and $T(Q_k)$. Two possible tests can be suggested:

(1) Let us test the hypothesis that the fluctuation of S-C_i in the corpus $T(Q_j)$ falls within the interval $<a;k>$, whereas its fluctuation in the corpus $T(Q_k)$ is confined to the interval $<l;z>$. The two intervals are, of course, not overlapping.

(2) Let us test the hypothesis that the average value (mathematical expectation) of S-C_i in $T(Q_j)$ is significantly different from its average value in $T(Q_k)$.

If the result of either of these tests is positive, we can conclude that the S-C_i

of the corpus $T(Q_j)$ fluctuates within a certain range which is different from that of another corpus, $T(Q_k)$. The tested characteristic thus apparently expresses both a subjective style feature (by its significant fluctuation within the corpus) and an objective style feature (by the demarcated range of fluctuation). In our framework, the characteristics that satisfy the requirements of the suggested tests will be called *subjective-objective* $(SO\text{-}C_i)$; those which will not meet these requirements will form the class of *subjective* characteristics $(S\text{-}C_i)$ proper.[33]

The two steps of testing thus lead to a specification of style characteristics into three classes: subjective, subjective-objective, and objective. Introducing this specification into our formula, we obtain a *specified text-style formula* of the general form: $T = \{S\text{-}C_1, \ S\text{-}C_2 \ \ldots \ S\text{-}C_k; \ SO\text{-}C_{k+1}, \ SO\text{-}C_{k+2} \ \ldots \ SO\text{-}C_m; \ O\text{-}C_{m+1}, \ O\text{-}C_{m+2} \ \ldots \ O\text{-}C_n\}$. It can be said that the specified text style formula is a formal representation of the text style by the set of its independent and variable components. It expresses the degree of participation of subjective and objective components and their specific balance; it displays the text style as a complex statistical structure. The specified characteristics can be treated as "elementary quanta"—as "distinctive features" of style—that are practically unlimited in their combinatorial possibilities. We believe that the breaking down of style into a limited number of specified, exactly measurable style components represents the most important contribution of the statistical conception to the theory of style.

It is time now to return to our conclusions in the first section of this essay in order to find connections between the style-forming process and the nature of the specified style characteristics. We assume that S-characteristics are under the control of subjective factors of the selective process, that O-characteristics are under the control of contextual factors, and that SO-characteristics are under the simultaneous control of both the subjective and contextual factors. However, as we stated on p. 16, the share of subjective and contextual factors in the control of the selective process varies. This variability will of course be reflected in the share of the particular classes of characteristics in the specified formula. If all the stages of the selective process (i.e., with regard to all possible sets, A) are controlled solely by subjective factors (one of the extreme cases), then texts will be produced that will be represented by the formula: $T = \{S\text{-}C_1, S\text{-}C_2 \ldots S\text{-}C_n\}$; all the characteristics will be S-characteristics. If, on the contrary, the selective process is controlled in all its stages solely by factors of context (another extreme case), then all of the characteristics of the produced text will be O-characteristics; such a text will be represented by the formula: $T = \{O\text{-}C_1, O\text{-}C_2 \ldots O\text{-}C_n\}$. If the text is produced in that zone of the communicative space where all the stages of the selective process are controlled by both subjective and contextual factors (always in combination), then the texts produced will be characterized by the formula: $T = \{SO\text{-}C_1, SO\text{-}C_2 \ldots SO\text{-}C_n\}$. These cases of "homogeneous" texts seem to be rather exceptional. Most texts, we can assume, will combine in their style all the three classes of specified characteristics with varying shares of each and will be represented by the "mixed" formula, which, in its abstract form, is given on p. 21.

Our consideration of the control of the selective process as well as our observations about the nature of style characteristics lead to the following general conclusion: the specific statistical nature of a style characteristic is not determined by its linguistic character, but by the pragmatic factors by which the generation of the characteristic is controlled. Because alternations of factors controlling the same characteristic are possible (and, apparently, quite common), *the statistical nature of a linguistically identical characteristic is subject to change in various texts (or text classes)*. Thus, for example, sentence-length distribution can be shown to be statistically unhomogeneous for one text or one text class; in terms of our framework, it is therefore to be considered an *S-characteristic*. For another text (or text class), sentence-length distribution can assume the property of statistical homogeneity and become an *O*-characteristic. In still another text (or text class), sentence-length can show properties of an *SO*-characteristic. It is obvious that sentence-length distribution can serve as an indicator (or discriminator) of individual styles only in the cases in which it behaves as an *S*-characteristic. If it behaves as an *O*-characteristic, it is totally unfit to be used for discriminating individual styles. If it becomes an *SO*-characteristic, it is able to discriminate individual styles only in a limited zone, that is, in the zone of the same (fixed) context.

The unstable statistical nature of style characteristics represents the most difficult, but at the same time the most important problem of statistical stylistics. It seems to me that the statistical study of styles has hitherto almost completely neglected this essential problem.[34] Some of the surprising contradictions in the various interpretations of style characteristics can be explained by this deficiency in theory.

At the same time, it must be stressed that deficiencies in theory are only partly responsible for the common uncertainties and contradictions in the existing results of statistical stylistics. One must be aware that any interpretation of statistical data has a highly hypothetical character. As in other areas of applied statistics, empirical data are mostly obtained from samples, not from populations. Moreover, in statistical stylistics, the evaluation of the accuracy of the data is relatively more difficult because of the complicated relationship between "text sample" and "text population." A satisfactory delimitation of the text population (or populations) is a complicated task because for all practical purposes text populations are open sets (uncountable).[35]

Therefore, all conclusions about the properties and nature of style characteristics, about the speaker type and text types, and about stylistic differences are to be considered hypotheses that will be confirmed or refuted by the accumulation of vast empirical material in the future. Nevertheless, it seems obvious that the accumulation of large bodies of data (now made possible by the use of computers) is only one path toward progress in statistical stylistics; another no less important one concerns the development of theoretical schemes and models that can serve as a basis for the taxonomy of styles and for the explanation of stylistic differences. In view of the substantial lack of a theory of statistical stylistics, it seems necessary to concentrate our efforts in that direction in order to accelerate the development of the statistical study of style into a modern scientific discipline.

REFERENCES

1. Sentence-length distribution is generally considered to be an elementary style indicator; see, for example, the essays by Williams (pp. 69–75) and Buch (pp. 76–79) in this volume.
2. For simplicity's sake, we suppose here that texts of a certain author represent a homogeneous population.
3. Even in those conceptions of style that avoid statistical terminology, the notion of "preference" is present in an intuitive form. See, for example, Richard Ohmann's suggestion that style is a "preferred way of organizing experience" ("Generative Grammars and the Concept of Literary Style," Word, XX [1964], 434).
4. A new formulation of this crucial problem in linguistic theory is to be attributed to Noam Chomsky; see especially his Aspects of the Theory of Syntax (Cambridge, Mass., 1965).
5. Compare: "Stylistic analysis . . . is the study of patterns formed in the process of the linguistic encoding of information" (Sally Yeates Sedelow and Walter A. Sedelow, Jr., "A Preface to Computational Stylistics," in The Computer and Literary Style, ed. Jacob Leed [Kent, Ohio, 1966], p. 1).
6. For a recent discussion of these matters, see Psycholinguistics Papers, eds. J. Lyons and R. J. Wales (Edinburgh, 1966).
7. J. Fodor and M. Garrett, "Some Reflections on Competence and Performance," in Psycholinguistics Papers, p. 142.
8. "Competence and performance are not simply two sides of one coin; competence is only one of many systematic factors that determine observable performance. Also contributing to performance are the structure of memory, the nature of attention, the mechanisms of perception, and the psycho-motor skills. More explicit and fundamental mechanisms for language behavior may yet be identified" (A. L. Blumenthal in Psycholinguistics Papers, pp. 81–82).
9. Blumenthal, p. 82.
10. The general assumption that models of the speaker will be equivalent to models of the hearer seems not to be sufficiently substantiated.
11. In some cases, the speaker can "control the style" with respect to the receiver; see Michael Riffaterre, "Criteria for Style Analysis," Word, XV (1959); reprinted in Essays on the Language of Literature, eds. Seymour Chatman and Samuel R. Levin (Boston, 1967); nevertheless, even this factor operates on the input of the communication process, that is, it influences the speaker's behavior.
12. Terminology used here in the sense employed by John Morton in "A Preliminary Functional Model for Language Behavior," International Audiology, III, ii (1964).
13. Psycholinguistics Papers, p. 76.
14. The "selection mechanism" introduced by Morton has a quite different, purely physiological function.
15. Compare: "A style may be said to be characterized by a pattern of recurrent selections from the inventory of optional features of a language" (Werner Winter, "Styles as Dialects," see p. 3 of this volume).
16. For example, Edgar Allan Poe's The Philosophy of Composition (1846), and V. V. Majakovskij's Kak delat' stikhi [How to Make Verse] (1926).
17. While concentrating on the selective process, I do not intend to deny the importance of the other components of the style-forming process. There is no doubt that a kind of synthesizing process takes place in the formation of style. However, a more general

discussion of the components and hierarchies of the style-forming process does not belong in the framework of this essay.

18. Compare: "Only a part of the variance within texts of the same author is due to personality factors. . . . This variance needs to be split into a part which is due to transient and specific attitudes and a part which is due to more stable habits of expression" (H. H. Somers, "Statistical Methods in Literary Analysis," in *The Computer and Literary Style*, p. 129)

19. Scheme 2 does not account for the case in which the context-bound speaker is insensitive even to the alternations of *Q*. This case would be manifested by a bureaucrat who produces not only his official messages, but also his speeches, his private correspondence, and perhaps even his poems in the standard bureaucratic style. This phenomenon should be described as a stylistic anomaly, as a transposition of an objective style into an inappropriate context. The effect of the "actualization" that arises in such a case proves the anomaly of this transposition (consider Franz Kafka's style).

20. See my "Russian and Prague School Functional Stylistics," *Style*, II (1968), 143–158.

21. Let us recall that, according to our theory, pragmatic factors are *always present* when a text is produced; their *influence* on the style of the text produced, however, varies, as was demonstrated in the first section of this essay.

22. See my investigation reported in "Předběžný odhad entropie a redundance psané češtiny" [A Preliminary Estimate of the Entropy and Redundancy of Written Czech], *Slovo a slovesnost*, XXIV (1963), 165–175; see also I. Fónagy, "Communication in Poetry," *Word*, XXVII (1961), 199ff.

23. The problem was already formulated by L. A. Sherman. See "Some Observations upon the Sentence-Length in English Prose," *University of Nebraska Studies*, I (1888), 118–130, and "On Certain Facts and Principles in the Development of Form in Literature," *ibid.*, I (1892), 337–366.

24. See my article, "The Prague School and the Statistical Theory of Poetic Language," in *Prague Studies in Mathematical Linguistics*, II (Prague, 1967), 102.

25. F. Busemann, *Die Sprache der Jugend als Ausdruck der Entwicklungsrhythmik* (Jena, 1925), esp. pp. 74–86.

26. In the discussion that follows, the symbol C^s is replaced by the symbol C for the sake of simplicity; C should henceforth be read "style characteristic."

27. The elimination of redundant information from the text style formula does not mean that this information is irrelevant for stylistic interpretations. It is well known that any information obtained from texts is relevant for stylistics; if it seems irrelevant in a certain aspect, it will certainly prove relevant in another.

28. Comp. also: H. Arens, "Verborgene Ordnung (Die Beziehung zwischen Satzlänge und Wortlänge in deutscher Erzählprosa vom Barock bis heute)," *Wirkendes Wort – Beihefte*, XI (1965). It is of course possible that some correlations of style characteristics will be non-linear, a fact that was recognized in the early work of R. E. Moritz, "On a Quantitative Relation Governing Certain Linguistic Phenomena," *Modern Language Notes*, XXIV (1909), 234–241.

29. A radical reduction of the data in the formula could be attained by a method which reduces a large number of statistical variables to a very limited number of factors (the so-called factor analysis). The application of factor analysis in statistical stylistics seems to be very promising. See, for instance, Carroll's essay in this volume (pp. 147–155); Josephine Miles and Hannan C. Selvin, "A Factor Analysis of the Vocabulary of Poetry in the Seventeenth Century," in *The Computer and Literary Style*, pp. 116–127; and J. Kraus and J. Polák, "Text Factors and Characteristics," in *Prague Studies in Mathematical Linguistics*, II, 155–171.

30. The notion of "speaker," as well as that of "individual style," is to be understood in a strictly synchronous sense. If there are reasons to believe that a speaker's style underwent changes in time, it is necessary to limit the pertinent set, $T(X_i Q_j)$, to a stable section. Compare the result of Buch's test on p. 79 of this volume and the discussion of "Chronology Problems and Diachronic Stylistics" in Bailey's essay (pp. 227–230).

31. In other words, with such a characteristic, "we should expect non-significant differences in successive samples from the same author and significant differences when one author is tested against another" (J. J. Dreher and E. L. Young, p. 159 of this volume).

32. Compare the non-significant difference between the "late Kuo" distribution of segment lengths and that of Chao Yu-pei determined by Dreher and Young (p. 163 of this volume).

33. Limits of intervals are used by Werner Winter (see pp. 3–9 of this volume). A specified form of test two was used by the Brown University Research Group; see M. L. Marckworth and L. M. Bell, "Sentence-Length Distribution in the Corpus," in *Computational Analysis of Present-Day American English*, eds. Henry Kučera and W. Nelson Francis (Providence, R. I., 1967), pp. 374ff. The significance of the differences between texts of individual speakers was not tested in the work at Brown. Therefore, in terms of our framework, it cannot be decided whether sentence-length in the corpus is an O-characteristic or an SO-characteristic.

    It would also be possible to test the difference of values of O-C_i in $T(Q_j)$ and $T(Q_k)$. If the test—against expectations—resulted in a statistically insignificant difference, we would interpret it as similarity of two objective styles (with regard to the tested characteristic). On the other hand, it is possible that such testing could result in discovering certain more general classes of objective styles.

34. As far as I know, this variability has been partly accounted for only by F. Antosch (pp. 62–65 of this volume).

35. In our framework, "text population" is a relative term changing with the aim of the investigation. All the text classes defined in the pragmatic classification—$T(X_i Q_j)$, $T(X_i)$, $T(Q_j)$—can serve as populations.

II

VOCABULARY MEASURES

THE STATISTICAL MEASUREMENT OF A STYLISTIC TRAIT IN *JULIUS CAESAR* AND *AS YOU LIKE IT*

PAUL E. BENNETT

Underlying most discussions of the authorship of Elizabethan plays of anonymous and disputed authorship is the assumption that the styles of the various playwrights are individual enough to permit differentiation of their works.[1] But this is a very large assumption and has not always been examined with the rigor that its importance demands. One of the main reasons why the truth or falsity of the assumption has not been firmly and thoroughly established is that scholars have lacked a method of measuring objectively any significant aspect of literary style. In the absence of a valid, reliable, and objective measure of any significant stylistic trait, a host of conflicting subjective "tests" for this or that playwright's hand has sprung up. The state of affairs has not changed greatly since fifty years ago, when Sir Edmund Chambers wrote of those scholars who were then heatedly debating the authorship of *Titus Andronicus:* "They frame such an hypothesis as . . . sentiment may suggest to them; and proceed to support it with that combination of rhetorical appeal and unconscious manipulation of evidence which the theologians have elaborated into a system under the title of apologetics. Meanwhile the inductive method, of which it is of the very essence that it is disinterested and leaves the hypothesis to be suggested by the facts themselves, is neglected, or is regarded as an instrument belonging to the natural sciences and somewhat beneath the dignity of literature."[2]

But an instrument for the precise and objective measurement of a significant trait of literary style has recently been fashioned for us by the well-known British statistician G. Udny Yule and is fully explained in his book, *The Statistical Study of Literary Vocabulary* (Cambridge University Press, 1944). As students of literature we have been very slow to use Yule's instrument.[3] Our hesitation to use it seems lamentable to me, though understandable, for the statistical theory behind Yule's measure is admittedly difficult. But the measure itself is quite simple to use; it can be used in much the same fashion that one uses a calculating machine, without bothering one's head about the mechanics or the theory of the machine.

The purpose of this article is to explain as simply as possible what Yule's measure is, what it measures, how to apply it to a given work, and what to do with it after it has been obtained. By way of illustration I should like to set

This essay originally appeared in *Shakespeare Quarterly*, VIII (1957), 33–50; it is reprinted here by permission of the author and of the editor of the journal. We have omitted an appendix in which Professor Bennett lists all the nouns appearing two or more times in the two plays.

forth applications of Yule's measure to *Julius Caesar* and *As You Like It*, with the results obtained and their interpretation.

Yule termed the measure that he developed the *characteristic*. It is expressed as a simple numerical value, such as 10.6, or 88.0, or 125.3. What the characteristic measures is the repetitiveness of the vocabulary of a given literary work, which is certainly a significant stylistic trait. We have all noticed how one writer will hammer away at certain words and employ them again and again, where another writer may scrupulously avoid exact repetition of the same words. No one can read the Gospel according to St. John, for instance, without being struck by the constant repetition of certain words, such as *bread* and *world*. Yule computed the characteristic of St. John's Gospel and found it to be 177.9. At the opposite extreme is a writer like Thomas Babington Macaulay, four of whose essays Yule computed the characteristics of, finding them to be 17.9, 21.8, 27.2, and 34.1, very low in comparison with the characteristic of St. John's Gospel. Between these extremes was John Bunyan, four of whose works Yule also computed the characteristics of, finding them to be 56.5, 66.9, 80.6, and 88.0. It seems almost unnecessary to comment on the significance of the fact that Yule was able to measure a significant aspect of literary style, something which had never been done before.

Yule's characteristic is computed from certain data arranged in what the statistician calls a frequency-distribution, which we are familiar with in terms of "how many students got A, how many got B, C, D," etc., or "how many people made $10,000 in 1954, how many made $9,000," and so on. In computing the characteristic what we have to know is *how many common nouns occurred* (were used) *once, how many occurred twice, thrice,* and so on. Once we have obtained those figures—and obtaining them is the most tedious part of computing the characteristic—we simply insert them in Yule's formula for the characteristic, do a little multiplication, addition, subtraction, and division, and we have the characteristic.

It might be asked why the characteristic should be based on common nouns and whether this is necessarily so. The characteristic need not be based on common nouns, but Yule worked from common nouns and I did so as well, partly in order to make meaningful comparisons with his results. No one, I believe, would wish to base his work on a writer's use of pronouns or prepositions or conjunctions. Verbs or adjectives or adverbs might equally well have been chosen and anyone who wishes to compute the "verb characteristic" or the "adjective characteristic" for *Julius Caesar* or *As You Like It* is welcome to try. I had a sufficiently difficult time deciding, with the assistance of the *O.E.D.*, just which words were nouns, especially in regard to the substantives used attributively and the quasi-substantives. In fact it is possible that there may be some disagreement about my decisions, and that is why I have appended a list of the nouns used twice, thrice and so on, in *Julius Caesar* and *As You Like It.*

Something must be said about the choice of those two plays as subjects for the application of Yule's measure. The reader may well ask, why those two plays? Why not more plays, some by Shakespeare, some by Jonson, some by Greene, Marlowe, Peele, and so on? I began with the assumption that Yule's method was valid, objective, and reliable. It would tell me or anyone else who employed it what the characteristic of any play is. The first thing to do, it seemed to me, was to compare Shakespeare to himself. Is he alike—as measured objectively by the characteristic—in different plays? If he is, then it may be rewarding to go on and compare him with another playwright. But if he is not alike in different plays, then perhaps the contention is true that style—or at least that aspect of style measured by the characteristic—was not very individual among the Elizabethan playwrights. The most logical starting-place seemed to be the comparison of two quite different plays unquestionably by the same writer. *Julius Caesar* is a tragedy, without sub-plots, primarily in blank verse; *As You Like It* is a comedy, largely in prose, abounding in sub-plots, and there are other differences between the plays as well. Moreover, the First Folio offered the same sole textual authority for both plays, both of which are relatively free from editorial cruxes.

As to why I have not gone on and compared many plays, the answer is very simple: Yule *longa, vita brevis*. In order to find out how many common nouns occur once, how many occur twice, thrice, and so on, it is necessary to go through the play and note each occurrence of every common noun on a separate 3″ by 5″ card. Alphabetizing these cards brings all the occurrences of the same nouns (disregarding inflectional forms) together, and they can be sorted into stacks, the once-occurring stack, the twice-occurring stack, etc., and then counted. Wishing to be sure of my count, I checked my results against Bartlett's *Concordance* and found to my dismay that Bartlett had inexplicably omitted dozens of occurrences. Anyone wishing to check my work would use Bartlett and infallibly conclude that I could not count. I decided that the discrepancies between my count and Bartlett's would have to be noted. The work of checking words in the *O.E.D.* was also laborious. To make a long story short, one lifetime will not suffice to compute the characteristics of the extant Elizabethan plays. That being the case, it seemed wise to publish what I had and attempt to interest other students in the method.

Two things remain to be said before turning to *Julius Caesar* and *As You Like It*. First, Yule worked out and used a method of *sampling* the vocabulary of the very lengthy works whose characteristics he computed. I should like it to be clearly understood that I have *not* sampled the vocabulary of the two plays whose characteristics I have computed. My figures are based on the entire vocabulary: I counted, within the limits of human fallibility, every occurrence of every common noun, and then checked my count against Bartlett's *Concordance* to be on the safe side. Yule's method of sampling is perfectly justified in computing the characteristic of a lengthy work (I should not, for instance, care to count every occurrence of all the common nouns in *The Anatomy of Melancholy*), but there is no reason to sample the vocabulary of a play which will not yield a total of more than two or three thousand occurrences of nouns. The second point is that Yule's characteristic *is indepen-dent of the length* of the literary work. This very important feature of the characteristic enables one to compare works of different length in regard to their repetitiveness as measured by the characteristic. There are, for instance, 2,919 occurrences of nouns in *Julius Caesar*, as against 3,609 occurrences in *As You Like It*, but this difference in no way affects the characteristic. The reader with sufficient interest in the purely statistical side of Yule's measure to pursue this question further is referred to Chapters 3 and 4 in Yule's book.

The following table will be used to illustrate the computation of the charac-teristic of Act I of *Julius Caesar*. Column 1, labeled X, lists the occurrence categories, that is, once-occurring, twice-occurring, thrice-occurring, and so on. Column 2, labeled f_x, which is an abbreviation of "frequency of X," lists the number of words occurring once, twice, thrice, etc.

TABLE 1

Act I of *Julius Caesar*

1	2	3	4	5
X	f_x	f_xX	f_xX^2	X^2
1	272	272	272	1
2	63	126	252	4
3	18	54	162	9
4	5	20	80	16
5	4	20	100	25
6	7	42	252	36
7	2	14	98	49
8	2	16	128	64
9	1	9	81	81
10	3	30	300	100
11	1	11	121	121
12	1	12	144	144
37	1	37	1,369	1,369
Total	—	$S_1=663$	$S_2=3,359$	—

In Table 1, cols. 1 and 2 simply tabulate the data in the form of a frequency-distribution. They state, in convenient form, that there are 272 once-occurring nouns in Act I of *Julius Caesar*, 63 twice-occurring nouns, 18 thrice-occurring nouns, and so on.

The figures in col. 3 are obtained by multiplying the X-values in col. 1 by the corresponding f_x-values in col. 2. One times 272 is 272; 2 times 63 is 126, and so on. The figures in col. 3 are added together, and their total or summa-tion (S_1) is an important ingredient of the characteristic.

The figures in col. 4 are obtained by multiplying the X^2-values in col. 5 (omitted from subsequent tables, but included here for the sake of clarity and completeness) by the corresponding f_x-values in col. 2. The first figure in col.

4 is obtained by multiplying 1^2 by 272; the second figure, 252, is 2^2 times 63, and so on. The total or summation of the figures in col. 4 (S_2) is the second important ingredient of the characteristic.

Yule's formula[4] for the characteristic (K) is:

$$K = 10,000 \frac{S_2 - S_1}{(S_1)^2},$$

where the number 10,000 is introduced simply to avoid the inconvenience of handling very small decimals. Substituting in Yule's formula the values S_1 and S_2 found from Table 1, we obtain:

$$K = 10,000 \frac{(3359 - 663)}{(663)^2} = 61.3$$

as the value of the characteristic for Act I of *Julius Caesar*.

TABLE 2

Act II of *Julius Caesar*

1	2	3	4
X	f_x	$f_x X$	$f_x X^2$
1	260	260	260
2	50	100	200
3	21	63	189
4	10	40	160
5	5	25	125
6	7	42	252
7	8	56	392
8	2	16	128
9	1	9	81
10	1	10	100
26	1	26	676
Total	—	$S_1 = 647$	$S_2 = 2,563$

The characteristic of Act II of *Julius Caesar* is 45.7.

Even though we have computed the characteristics of the individual acts, we are not yet in a position to compute the characteristic of the play as a whole. The reason why we cannot derive the characteristic of the whole play from the characteristics of its acts by any additive or averaging process is that a word used once in Act I may be used twice in Act II and thus become a thrice-occurring word for the whole play. The word *man* (disregarding in-flectional forms), for instance, occurs 37 times in Act I, 26 times in Act II, 36 times in Act III, 14 times in Act IV, and 12 times in Act V, so that for the whole play it becomes a 125-times-occurring word. The characteristic of the

TABLE 3
Act III of *Julius Caesar*

1	2	3	4
X	f_x	$f_x X$	$f_x X^2$
1	210	210	210
2	53	106	212
3	30	90	270
4	7	28	112
5	10	50	250
6	6	36	216
7	5	35	245
8	2	16	128
11	1	11	121
12	1	12	144
15	1	15	225
16	1	16	256
20	1	20	400
21	1	21	441
36	1	36	1,296
Total	—	$S_1 = 702$	$S_2 = 4,526$

The characteristic of Act III of *Julius Caesar* is 77.5.

TABLE 4
Act IV of *Julius Caesar*

1	2	3	4
X	f_x	$f_x X$	$f_x X^2$
1	180	180	180
2	45	90	180
3	22	66	198
4	8	32	128
5	7	35	175
6	2	12	72
7	1	7	49
8	1	8	64
9	2	18	162
14	1	14	196
15	1	15	225
Total	—	$S_1 = 477$	$S_2 = 1,629$

The characteristic of Act IV of *Julius Caesar* is 50.6.

TABLE 5

Act V of *Julius Caesar*

1	2	3	4
X	f_x	f_xX	f_xX^2
1	149	149	149
2	42	84	168
3	13	39	117
4	6	24	96
5	3	15	75
7	6	42	294
8	1	8	64
10	2	20	200
11	1	11	121
12	2	24	288
14	1	14	196
Total	—	$S_1 = 430$	$S_2 = 1,768$

The characteristic of Act V of *Julius Caesar* is 72.3.

whole play will be computed from the data in Table 6 following. There were two reasons why the computation of the characteristics of the individual acts was carried through. The first reason was that doing so provides an excellent check on the accuracy of the work, namely, that the sum of the occurrences of nouns in the acts (S_1 of Act I plus S_1 of Act II and so on) must equal the sum of the occurences for the play as a whole (S_1 of the whole play). The second reason was simply to find out if the acts differed greatly among themselves. And they did: $K_I = 61.3$; $K_{II} = 45.7$; $K_{III} = 77.5$; $K_{IV} = 50.6$; $K_V = 72.3$. This is perhaps not the place to go into the significance of the variations among the acts, but some remarks may be made in passing. First the highest act characteristic, 77.5, is that for Act III, which is surely the most concentrated act in *Julius Caesar*, all the action centering around Caesar's assassination. There are only two scenes in Act III, and Caesar, living and dead, is the sole focus of the act, almost, one might say, the sole topic of conversation, with consequent concentration of the vocabulary and a high characteristic due to the high degree of repetitiveness. The lowest characteristic is that for Act II, 45.7, because Act II sprawls over four scenes, involves a variety of different people doing different things, and therefore lacks concentration and repetitiveness. In Scene 1, for instance, Brutus talks to Lucius, to himself, to Lucius again, to the conspirators about several subjects, to Portia, and to Ligarius. Scene 2 shows us Caesar and Calpurnia talking about omens and portents and whether Caesar shall go to the senate-house. Scenes 3 and 4 contribute still further to the dispersion of the vocabulary. All in all, the characteristic reveals some interesting things about the variations in concentration among the acts, and further investigation would seem to promise rewards.

TABLE 6

Julius Caesar as a whole

1	2	3	4
X	f_x	$f_x X$	$f_x X^2$
1	534	534	534
2	173	346	692
3	66	198	594
4	52	208	832
5	37	185	925
6	22	132	792
7	18	126	882
8	6	48	384
9	6	54	486
10	4	40	400
11	6	66	726
12	3	36	432
13	4	52	676
14	7	98	1,372
15	2	30	450
16	4	64	1,024
17	1	17	289
18	2	36	648
20	1	20	400
23	2	46	1,058
24	1	24	576
25	2	50	1,250
28	2	56	1,568
31	2	62	1,922
32	2	64	2,048
33	1	33	1,089
39	2	78	3,042
44	1	44	1,936
47	1	47	2,209
125	1	125	15,625
Total	—	$S_1 = 2,919$	$S_2 = 44,861$

The characteristic of *Julius Caesar* as a whole is 49.2.

The meaning of the characteristic of *Julius Caesar* as a whole will be discussed after the computation of the characteristic of *As You Like It*, to which we now proceed (see Tables 7–12).

We have seen that the characteristic of *Julius Caesar* is 49.2 and that the characteristic of *As You Like It* is 40.5. What valid conclusions can we draw from the data? We can, I believe, warrantedly conclude that in regard to the aspect of style which we have measured objectively in the two plays, Shakespeare is very similar to himself. Comparison with the results Yule obtained for Macaulay and Bunyan will bear out this conclusion. Macaulay's essays

TABLE 7

Act I of *As You Like It*

1	2	3	4
X	f_x	$f_x X$	$f_x X^2$
1	229	229	229
2	48	96	192
3	27	81	243
4	11	44	176
5	7	35	175
6	5	30	180
7	3	21	147
8	4	32	256
9	2	18	162
10	2	20	200
11	1	11	121
12	1	12	144
13	1	13	169
16	1	16	256
20	2	40	800
21	1	21	441
38	1	38	1,444
Total	—	$S_1 = 757$	$S_2 = 5,335$

The characteristic of Act I of *As You Like It* is 79.9.

TABLE 8

Act II of *As You Like It*

1	2	3	4
X	f_x	$f_x X$	$f_x X^2$
1	333	333	333
2	49	98	196
3	26	78	234
4	16	64	256
5	6	30	150
6	4	24	144
7	3	21	147
8	2	16	128
9	2	18	162
10	1	10	100
11	1	11	121
24	2	48	1,152
Total	—	$S_1 = 751$	$S_2 = 3,123$

The characteristic of Act II of *As You Like It* is 42.0.

TABLE 9

Act III of *As You Like It*

1	2	3	4
X	f_x	$f_x X$	$f_x X^2$
1	373	373	373
2	77	154	308
3	28	84	252
4	10	40	160
5	10	50	250
6	9	54	324
7	5	35	245
8	3	24	192
9	1	9	81
10	1	10	100
11	3	33	363
14	2	28	392
16	1	16	256
17	1	17	289
32	1	32	1,024
41	1	41	1,681
Total	—	$S_1 = 1,000$	$S_2 = 6,290$

The characteristic of Act III of *As You Like It* is 52.9.

TABLE 10

Act IV of *As You Like It*

1	2	3	4
X	f_x	$f_x X$	$f_x X^2$
1	206	206	206
2	38	76	152
3	25	75	225
4	4	16	64
5	5	25	125
6	3	18	108
7	1	7	49
8	4	32	256
9	1	9	81
10	1	10	100
16	1	16	256
17	1	17	289
Total	—	$S_1 = 507$	$S_2 = 1,911$

The characteristic of Act IV of *As You Like It* is 54.6.

TABLE 11

Act V and the epilogue of *As You Like It*

1	2	3	4
X	f_x	$f_x X$	$f_x X^2$
1	211	211	211
2	44	88	176
3	18	54	162
4	14	56	224
5	7	35	175
6	4	24	144
7	5	35	245
8	3	24	192
9	1	9	81
10	1	10	100
11	1	11	121
15	1	15	225
22	1	22	484
Total	—	$S_1 = 594$	$S_2 = 2,540$

The characteristic of Act V and the epilogue of *As You Like It* is 55.2.

had characteristics of 17.9, 21.8, 27.2, and 34.1 respectively. The difference between Essay A and Essay B is 1.9; between A and C the difference is 9.3, and the difference between A and D is 16.2. The difference between *Julius Caesar* and *As You Like It* is 8.7, a greater difference than that between two of Macaulay's essays and a smaller difference than that between the other two pairs. With regard to Bunyan, the comparison is more striking. The differences among his works are all greater than that between *Julius Caesar* and *As You Like It*. And since we deliberately chose, as a test case, so to speak, two quite dissimilar plays by Shakespeare, the close agreement between their characteristics warrants our concluding that his style is similar—in the trait measured—in these two plays. Whether that similarity is exhibited by his other works is, of course, still to be ascertained. Comparison of two more plays, one very early play and one late one, should throw further light on the question, and I hope next to undertake just that investigation.

I believe that students of literature must master and employ Yule's method if they are to go on comparing and contrasting the styles of various Elizabethan playwrights in the hope of attributing the plays correctly. Indeed, Yule's method is only one step in the direction that research must take, for it cannot be overemphasized that Yule's method measures only *one* aspect of style, namely, repetitiveness. There certainly must be other significant aspects of style which scholars can devise means of measuring. And it is desirable that they should do so, for repetitiveness is influenced not only by the individuality of the author but also, as we have seen from variations in the

TABLE 12
As You Like It as a whole

1	2	3	4
X	f_x	$f_x X$	$f_x X^2$
1	729	729	729
2	214	428	856
3	100	300	900
4	46	184	736
5	27	135	675
6	25	150	900
7	17	119	833
8	13	104	832
9	4	36	324
10	3	30	300
11	14	154	1,694
12	7	84	1,008
13	4	52	676
14	4	56	784
15	1	15	225
16	2	32	512
17	4	68	1,156
18	2	36	648
19	2	38	722
20	1	20	400
21	1	21	441
23	2	46	1,058
24	2	48	1,152
25	1	25	625
26	1	26	676
27	1	27	729
28	2	56	1,568
29	1	29	841
32	1	32	1,024
33	1	33	1,089
35	1	35	1,225
39	1	39	1,521
40	1	40	1,600
46	2	92	4,232
48	1	48	2,304
54	1	54	2,916
75	1	75	5,625
113	1	113	12,769
Total	—	$S_1 = 3,609$	$S_2 = 56,305$

The characteristic of *As You Like It* as a whole is 40.5.

characteristic among the different acts of *Julius Caesar* and *As You Like It*, by the subject matter. I should not care to suggest that the characteristic is going to provide an infallible test of authorship, for it may well turn out that some of

Shakespeare's plays will have the same characteristic as some, say, of Jonson's plays, whereas other of his plays might yield the same characteristic as, perhaps, one of Marlowe's. The real desideratum is to develop objective measures of several different significant aspects of style; authorship might then confidently be ascribed when two or three or four of these measures were in substantial agreement. All that is claimed for Yule's characteristic is that it provides an objective measurement of one significant aspect of literary style.

REFERENCES

1. The only explicit denial of this assumption I know of was expressed in passing by W. L. Renwick, in his edition of *John of Bordeaux* (Oxford, 1936, p. xi), on the attribution of the play to Greene. "Arguments from style require a firm basis," Renwick wrote validly enough; "style was not very individual at that period." How do we know that it was not?

2. *Shakespeare: A Survey* (London, 1925), p. 33. These prefaces to the plays are reprinted from the Red Letter Shakespeare (London, 1904–1908).

3. I know of no studies of vocabulary or style which have employed Yule's method other than those of Yule himself. Harold G. McCurdy uses some of Yule's data about Bunyan and Macaulay in his *The Personality of Shakespeare* (New Haven, 1953, pp. 64–65) but does not use Yule's method. [The reader should recall that Bennett's article appeared in 1957. Eds.]

4. Yule consistently writes $S_1{}^2$ where I write $(S_1)^2$ as being somewhat more readily comprehensible and as less liable to just the sort of typographical error which occurs on p. 53. There Yule says: "As written in (3.18) the characteristic is a very small decimal, for S_1 [*sic*] is large compared with S_2. . . ." In Yule's ms. this must have read "for $S_1{}^2$ is large compared with S_2," because S_1 cannot possibly be larger than S_2.

LEXICAL DISTRIBUTION RECONSIDERED: THE WARING-HERDAN FORMULA

Charles Muller

Gustav Herdan's latest book, *Quantitative Linguistics* (which we have reviewed elsewhere), presents an interesting innovation in the field of lexical statistics.[1] It concerns the application to linguistic phenomena of a distribution hitherto unknown to linguists as far as I know: the Waring distribution. We have been in the habit of concluding the lexical description of a text with a comparison of the observed numerical data with the theoretical values obtained by applying "Zipf's law" in order to ascertain once again that the agreement between the two series was unsatisfactory and only furnished a gross approximation.[2] It seems that we must now turn our attention to another model and that this time our approach comes closer to linguistic reality, for it is now a problem—and Herdan insists on this fact—of a purely empirical procedure and not a translation into a formula of some theory of memory or of information.[3]

Let us give a brief account of the problem in question. When one considers the list of lexical units (dictionary entries) that appear in a text of a given length,[4] it is seen that the number of words that are used once is greater than that of words used twice, that the latter are more numerous than those appearing three times, and so on (the pages that follow furnish numerous examples of this phenomenon). As long as the number of words in a class is great enough, the decrease is constant. The problem is to determine if this decrease obeys a law and to predict the numerical agreement which is established between the frequency classes thus constituted.

Herdan reviews the previous attempts to deal with this problem. He cites Zipf, whose law we now know will not provide any worthwhile prediction and which only holds for mean frequencies, and then cites Yule, who demonstrated the inadequacy of Zipf's data and claimed that the phenomenon follows Poisson's law. But Yule's efforts to construct a model to account for the facts ended in failure. The same goes for Herdan's own attempt to apply a lognormal law and also for the procedures proposed by Simon.[5]

Herdan has since returned to the problem in a purely "exploratory" way. He examined various laws of theoretical probabilities to discover one that, converging towards unity, would account for the pattern by which the size of the class decreases. He discovered one such law, defined by Waring as early as the eighteenth century and recently reintroduced by J. O. Irwin in describing biological phenomena.[6] This law predicts the development of an

This essay originally appeared in *Cahiers de Lexicologie*, VI (1965), 35–53; we wish to thank the author for granting us permission to reprint. We are grateful to Miss Angela McCourt for her help with the translation.

expression $1/(x-a)$ in which $0 < a < x$. By multiplying by $(x-a)$ the expression itself on the one hand, and the series which is obtained by its expansion, on the other, we obtain unity for the former and a decreasing series for the latter:

$$\frac{x-a}{x} + \frac{(x-a)a}{x(x+1)} + \frac{(x-a)a(a+1)}{x(x+1)(x+2)} \ldots + \frac{(x-a)a(a+1)\ldots(a+n-2)}{x(x+1)(x+2)\ldots(x+n-1)} \ldots$$

of which the sum is 1. The hypothesis is that the term of rank n represents the probability of a lexical item appearing n times in the text. This term is then defined by the equation:

$$p_n = \frac{(x-a)a(a+1)\ldots(a+n-2)}{x(x+1)(x+2)\ldots(x+n-1)}$$

The x and a parameters must then characterize the length of the text, the extent of its vocabulary, and—most difficult of all—the dispersion or the richness of its vocabulary.

The solution proposed by Herdan consists of taking account of the following three parameters:

the number of units (occurrences) which form the text: N
the number of (lexical) units which form the vocabulary: V
the number of lexical units which appear only once: V_1

It must follow that $V_1 \leq V$ and that $V \leq N$; the difference between these values increases as N increases, that is, as the text grows longer. Therefore, it follows that the ratios V/N and V_1/N decrease from 1 (in a text of a few words) to 0; this limit for V_1/V would be reached in a text in which all the lexical units are used at least twice (a case that has never been found!).

From these data, one can deduce two further ratios:

1. the mean frequency in the text of the words which form its vocabulary:

$$\bar{x} = N/V$$

This value, the inverse of V/N, becomes greater than one when a word is repeated; it increases without limit as N increases. When the text lengths are equal, it is smaller as the vocabulary is more varied (a characteristic of style).

2. the probability that a certain word of the vocabulary has *one* occurrence in the text. This probability is estimated by the relation between words employed only once and the number of words of whatever frequency used in the text:

$$p_1 = V_1/V$$

We have seen that this probability decreases from 1 towards 0 when the text becomes longer. When texts are equal in length, it becomes greater as the vocabulary is more varied. This variation is inverse to the variation of $\bar{x}$; its value is less than 1 while $\bar{x}$ is, by definition, equal to or greater than 1.

We can then calculate the a and x parameters:

$$a = \frac{1}{\dfrac{1}{(1-p_1)} - \dfrac{1}{x} - 1}$$

$$x = \frac{a}{(1-p_1)}$$

The expression $(1-p_1)$ is the complement of p_1 to one. It represents the contrary probability, that is, the chance that a lexical item will appear more than once in the text. p_1 and $(1-p_1)$ are necessarily less than 1, and it follows that x will be greater than a.

Let us make an experiment. We know that the conversations recorded in the investigation of Basic French[7] comprise a total of 312,135 occurrences, among which were found 7,995 different words. Of these, 2,700 appeared only once. From these figures, we can try to calculate how many words of the vocabulary should appear, for example, five times.

We will find that the mean frequency ($\bar{x} = 312{,}135/7{,}995$) equals 39.04, and the proportion of words of a frequency of one ($p_1 = 2{,}700/7{,}995$) is 0.338. By applying the formula given above, we find:

$$a = \frac{1}{1.51 - 0.0256 - 1} = 2.064 \text{ and } x = \frac{2.064}{0.662} = 3.116$$

We can then calculate p_5, the probability of an item of the vocabulary (V) appearing with a frequency equal to 5:

$$p_5 = \frac{1.052 \times 2.064 \times 3.064 \times 4.064 \times 5.064}{3.116 \times 4.116 \times 5.116 \times 6.116 \times 7.116} = 0.0479$$

Given that there are 7,995 different words, we can find for a frequency of 5 a theoretical value:

$$V_5 = p_5 V = 0.479 \times 7{,}995 = 383 \text{ words}$$

In fact, in the count of Basic French, there are 237 words employed five times.

*   *   *

While this experiment has illustrated the calculation procedure, the result is not very good. We can calculate (using the chi-square test) that the observed difference has scarcely one chance in a thousand of having been caused by chance, suggesting the conclusion that the Waring formula does not describe this frequency distribution. But it would be imprudent to reject the hypothesis on the basis of a single trial.

In order to appreciate the efficiency of the formula, it is clear that we must begin by investigating not just a comparison for one of the frequency classes, but for an entire series. This calculation becomes very tedious. Herdan provides some easily consulted tables in which all the values from p_2 to p_{50} are given when two figures are known: the mean frequency ($\bar{x}$) and the proportion of words appearing only once in the vocabulary (p_1). It is no longer necessary to calculate the *a* and *x* parameters, but only to multiply *V* (the vocabulary of the text) by the values found in the tables.

On the basis of the procedure just described, let us see how it can be applied.

Herdan himself has made an experiment in which his precision puts the results beyond suspicion. He took the figures from Josselson's *Russian Word Count*,[8] which were obtained on the basis of the 30,000 occurrences in Puškin's short story, "The Captain's Daughter." I only reprint here the first rows of his results in order to give an idea of the precision achieved:

$$N = 29,581 \qquad \bar{x} = 5.97$$
$$V = 4,783 \qquad p_1 = 0.498$$
$$V_1 = 2,384$$

Word Frequency	Number of Words		Difference
	Calculated	Observed	
1	(2,384)	2,384	—
2	845.0	847	+ 2
3	422.3	433	+10.7
4	250.5	238	−12.5
5	164.4	146	−18.5
6	115.5	114	− 1.5
7	85.3	82	− 3.3
8	65.3	79	+13.7
9	51.5	41	+10.5
10	41.6	39	+ 2.6 etc.

There are certainly some differences between observed and calculated values, but they are inevitable. If there is a law governing the distribution of frequencies, it would not be capable of determining the use of words with exact precision.

The author nevertheless pursues the investigation up to the mean frequency (40), where the decrease in the number of words is no longer regular. He then finds excessive differences, but we can assume that he has been too demanding in his expectations, as we will shortly see.

What I have preferred to do is put this new formula to the test by applying it to several texts. Here is what I obtained for the vocabulary of Pierre Corneille's *l'Illusion Comique*:

$$N = 16,586 \qquad V_1 = 345$$
$$V = 1,906 \qquad p_1 = 0.443*$$

By applying Pearson's test to these differences, we find a χ^2 value of 20.95. How are we to evaluate this figure? We worked on 21 classes, but the calculated and observed distributions are not independent of each other:

*See table on p.46.

| Word Frequency | Number of Words | | Difference |
	Calculated	Observed	
1	(845)	845	—
2	341.7	318	−23.7
3	182.6	165	−17.6
4	112.5	118	+ 5.5
5	75.7	70	− 5.7
6	54.3	58	+ 3.7
7	40.6	50	+ 9.4
8	31.4	31	− 0.4
9	25.0	31	+ 6.0
10	20.4	23	+ 2.6
11	16.8	17	+ 0.2
12	14.1	14	− 0.1
13	12.0	10	− 2.0
14	10.3	8	− 2.3
15	9.0	11	+ 2.0
16	7.8	12	+ 4.2
17	6.9	5	− 1.9
18	6.1	4	− 2.1
19	5.5	4	− 1.5
20	5.0	4	− 1.0
≥21	83.3	108	+24.7
	1,906.0	1,906	

a) The V_1 parameter imposes on both distributions the same number of words for the frequency of one.

b) The V parameter imposes upon them an identical total and this means that the figure 83.3 (theoretical calculation for frequencies of 21 and above) is determined by those that precede.

c) Finally, the value of the variable is determined by N, which is contained in the $\bar{x}$ parameter, that is, N/V.

Therefore, to estimate the degrees of freedom, we must subtract 3 from the number of classes—we estimate it at 18. Pearson's tables indicate, for 18 degrees of freedom, that a significance level of 5% is attained for a χ^2 of 28.87. We are far from that value. The value that we have obtained is reached or surpassed—by the effect of chance alone—with a probability of about 0.30, which is about once in three. The empirical data are thus very favorable to the hypothesis that the Waring-Herdan formula describes the frequency distribution of our text, at least up to the frequency of 20.[9]

I applied the same methods to the three major divisions of this play (the Comedy, the Tragedy, and the Prologue),[10] and at the same time to the speeches of the three major characters: Matamore, Isabelle (omitting her monologue), and Alcandre. Here are the values obtained:

	N	V	V_1	$\bar{x}$	p_1
Comedy	10,010	1,477	718	6.78	0.485
Tragedy	3,399	751	404	4.52	0.538
Prologue	3,177	808	488	3.93	0.603
Matamore	2,438	690	425	3.52	0.616
Isabelle	1,752	494	302	3.54	0.611
Alcandre	1,629	534	366	3.05	0.685

The differences obtained can be tested as follows:

	χ^2	Degrees of Freedom	Probability
Comedy	19.14	14	0.15
Tragedy	9.80	8	0.30
Prologue	7.53	8	0.50
Matamore	1.58	6	0.95
Isabelle	5.75	6	0.45
Alcandre	2.11	5	0.80

The results are very satisfactory. The probability level of 0.05, below which the hypothesis is no longer admissible, is neither attained nor approached by any of these examples.

Frequency	COMEDY calc.	COMEDY obs.	COMEDY diff.	TRAGEDY calc.	TRAGEDY obs.	TRAGEDY diff.	PROLOGUE calc.	PROLOGUE obs.	PROLOGUE diff.
1	(718)	718	—	(404)	404	—	(488)	488	—
2	262.2	248	− 14.2	130.0	144	+ 14	129.3	132	+ 2.7
3	134.0	132	− 2.0	62.2	52	− 10.2	58.2	56	− 2.2
4	80.3	91	+ 10.7	35.8	34	− 1.8	32.6	32	− 0.6
5	53.2	45	− 8.2	23.0	18	− 5.0	20.6	24	+ 3.4
6	37.7	35	− 2.7	16.0	20	+ 4.0	14.1	6	− 8.1
7	27.9	32	− 4.1	11.6	8	− 3.6	10.2	8	− 2.2
8	21.4	20	− 1.4	8.9	10	+ 1.1	7.6	8	+ 0.4
9	17.0	12	− 5.0	6.9	6	− 0.0	6.0	5	− 1.0
10	13.7	10	− 3.7	5.6	2	− 3.6	4.8	5	+ 0.2
11	11.4	13	+ 1.6						
12	9.5	13	+ 3.5						
13	8.0	3	− 5.0						
14	6.9	10	+ 3.1	47.0	53	+ 6.0	36.6	44	+ 7.4
15	5.9	5	− 0.9						
16	5.2	8	+ 2.8						
≧17	64.7	82	+ 17.3						
	1,477.0	1,477		751.0	751		808.0	808	

MATAMORE				ISABELLE				ALCANDRE		
Frequency	calc.	obs.	diff.	calc.	obs.	diff.	calc.	obs.	diff.
1	(425)	425	—	(302)	302	—	(366)	366	—
2	108.2	110	+1.8	78.2	79	+0.8	72.8	71	−1.8
3	47.8	45	−2.8	34.7	30	−4.7	30.2	28	−2.2
4	26.1	28	+1.9	19.3	17	−2.3	16.3	15	−1.3
5	16.7	15	−1.7	12.2	17	+4.8	10.1	12	+1.9
6	11.3	11	−0.3	8.3	5	−3.3	6.8	5	−1.8
7	8.2	10	+1.8	6.1	5	−1.1	4.9	5	+0.1
8	6.2	8	+1.8	4.5	4	−0.5	}26.9	32	+5.1
≧9	40.5	38	−2.5	28.7	35	+6.3			
	690.0	690		494.0	494		534.0	534	

We turn now to a study of a text in Old French, the chantefable of *Aucassin et Nicolette*, for which the data are provided by a recent thesis:[11]

$N = 9{,}870$ $\bar{x} = 9.2$
$V = 1{,}073$ $p_1 = 0.450$
$V_1 = 483$

Word Frequency	Number of Words		Difference
	Calculated	Observed	
1	(483)	483	—
2	191.2	173	− 18.2
3	100.8	95	− 5.8
4	61.9	59	− 2.9
5	41.5	39	− 2.5
6	29.6	27	− 2.6
7	22.2	20	− 2.2
8	17.2	22	+ 4.8
9	13.6	14	+ 0.4
10	11.1	8	− 3.1
11	9.2	9	− 0.2
12	7.7	13	+ 5.3
13	6.5	12	+ 5.5
14	5.6	7	+ 1.4
≧15	71.9	92	+ 20.1
	1,073.0	1,073	

The χ^2 is 19.29. For 12 degrees of freedom, the probability lies within the generally admissible limits of 0.10 and 0.05. The discrepancy between the model and the actual distribution is not proved, but the result is somewhat less favorable. It is nevertheless encouraging, for we are dealing here with a text having two alternating styles with sharply marked differences in the frequency distribution between the verse parts and the passages in prose.

From this example, we turn to two Latin texts analyzed by the *Laboratoire d'analyse statistique* at Liège, the two *Consolations* of Seneca.[12]

Frequency	CONSOLATION A POLYBE $N = 5,688 \quad \bar{x} = 3.97$ $V = 1,430 \quad p_1 = 0.575$ $V_1 = 822$			CONSOLATION A HELVIA $N = 6,775 \quad \bar{x} = 3.65$ $V = 1,856 \quad p_1 = 0.563$ $V_1 = 1,045$		
	calculated	*observed*	*difference*	*calculated*	*observed*	*difference*
1	(822)	822	—	(1,045)	1,045	—
2	237.8	229	− 8.8	317.9	301	−16.9
3	109.7	91	−18.7	148.8	158	+ 9.2
4	62.1	78	+15.9	84.6	91	+ 6.4
5	39.6	41	+ 1.4	53.8	40	−13.8
6	27.2	24	− 3.2	36.9	32	− 4.9
7	19.6	17	− 2.6	26.7	42	+15.3
8	14.9	16	+ 1.1	20.2	24	+ 3.8
9	11.6	13	+ 1.4	15.8	14	− 1.8
10	9.3	7	− 2.3	12.4	11	− 1.4
11	7.6	9	+ 1.4	10.2	13	+ 2.8
12	6.3	4	− 2.3	8.4	6	− 2.4
13	5.3	11	+ 5.7	7.1	10	+ 2.9
14	4.6	4	− 0.6	5.2	5	− 0.2
≧15	52.4	64	+11.6	63.0	64	+ 1.0
	1,430.0	1,430		1,856.0	1,856	

The comparison yields a χ^2 for the first text of 19.14 and of 18.64 for the second. The number of degrees of freedom is the same as that for the Old French text; the range of the differences and the probability of their random character are thus comparable. But the allocation of negative and positive differences is more regular in the Latin examples. For *Aucassin*, it seems that the use of this method of calculation gave too high an estimate of the number of words in the lower frequencies, a correct estimate for the frequencies near the mean, and too low a figure for the high frequencies. Nothing of this sort is apparent in the Latin texts, except for the figure for words having a frequency of 2.

Now let us take the statistics for the Greek texts of the gospel of St. Mark and the epistles of St. Paul.[13]

	SAINT MARK			SAINT PAUL		
	N = 11,229 x̄ = 9.2			N = 32,303 x̄ = 12.2		
	V = 1,345 p_1 = 0.450			V = 2,648 p_1 = 0.435		
	V_1 = 634			V_1 = 1,140		
Frequency	calculated	observed	difference	calculated	observed	difference
1	(634)	634	—	(1,140)	1,140	—
2	237.8	219	−18.8	468.2	442	−26.2
3	122.8	108	—14.8	249.7	230	−19.7
4	74.2	71	− 3.2	154.1	143	−11.1
5	49.5	52	+ 2.5	104.3	123	+18.7
6	35.1	36	+ 0.9	74.9	62	−12.9
7	26.2	18	− 8.2	56.4	58	+ 1.6
8	20.2	23	+ 2.8	43.7	50	+ 6.3
9	16.1	16	− 0.1	35.0	35	0
10	13.0	15	+ 2.0	28.6	30	+ 1.4
11	10.1	12	+ 1.9	23.6	17	− 6.6
12	9.0	16	+ 7.0	19.9	22	+ 2.1
13	7.7	5	− 2.7	16.9	15	− 1.9
14	6.6	3	− 3.6	14.6	27	+12.4
15	5.7	12	+ 6.3	12.7	15	+ 2.3
16				11.1	15	+ 3.9
17				9.8	14	+ 4.2
18				8.7	11	+ 2.3
19				7.9	8	+ 0.1
20	77.0	105	+28.0	7.2	7	− 0.2
21				6.4	10	+ 3.6
22				5.8	5	− 0.8
23				5.3	8	+ 2.7
24				4.8	5	+ 0.2
≧25				138.4	156	+17.6
	1,345.0	1,345		2,648.0	2,648	

The χ^2 is 32.67 for the first text. At 13 degrees of freedom, the probability of these differences is scarcely 0.001 (one chance in a thousand). Thus, the disagreement between the two distributions is too great to be attributed to chance. In the second, the χ^2 is 33.18. For 22 degrees of freedom, it approaches the 5% level—the limit of decision usually allowed.

*   *   *

After these several applications—which might easily be expanded to include other texts—I should like to present some considerations, albeit of a very provisional nature, that other experiments may well refine or correct.

The first conclusion is self-evident. A table of frequencies and the number of words assigned to them begins, as we have seen, with a constant decrease in the number of words. As the frequency increases, the number of words is equal to or greater than the size of the preceding classes. Then the size of some classes drops to zero (or, if you like, some frequencies are not represented). Finally, we arrive at an area in which only certain frequencies further and further apart are represented, with a number of words generally equal to 1. Is it legitimate to apply the "Waring distribution" to these "tails"? That is too much to expect of it.

In fact, when we apply the distribution to biological problems, as Irwin did, or to social or demographic problems, etc., the material upon which we operate has generally been classified by decreasing magnitude. But that does not hold for our applications where the order is determined not by the magnitude of the classes analyzed, but by that of the corresponding frequencies where there is an additional cause of fluctuation.

It seems, therefore, that we must, as I have done, stop the class-by-class comparison either at the level where the theoretical values fall to 5 (a rule generally observed in the use of Pearson's test), or at the point at which the irregularities begin to appear in the observed values. Then we should condense the remainder of the distribution into a single figure. If we are to study distributions "with very long tails," as Irwin did, it is probably convenient either to make use of the method of moving averages—I have made the attempt on the Puškin material—or to examine the average frequencies by grouping them by five, then by ten, etc., as Herdan has done for the frequencies from 31 to 40.

When we find an excessive disagreement between the calculated distribution and that derived from the text, there are two causes which must be distinguished. The first is linguistic: after a certain point, the size of the classes no longer decreases without irregularities. No formula can account for fluctuations of this sort. The other cause derives from the model employed: there will be a disagreement between the model and reality that will give for one zone of the distribution differences which are either all positive or all negative. The theoretical curve, instead of intersecting the broken line of the actual data, will deviate for a long stretch. This second shortcoming—again leading to discrepancy—will be the more serious, though we find few examples of it in our investigations.

The following example would seem to prove that the recorded differences may be attributed to the fundamental irregularities inherent in the distributions rather than to a deficiency in the proposed model. Next to the frequency tables for l'Illusion Comique and its subdivisions, I have arranged the "theoretical distributions" calculated by the computer for each of the three parts of the play, based on frequencies from the text and applying a formula derived from the binomial law.[14] I have compared these distributions with those given by the Waring-Herdan formula for the same parts based on the values of N', V', and V_1' of my theoretical distributions. We note that the binomial model that I have used does not exclude the irregularities, but that in general it moderates them and smoothes the curve. But it should be made very clear here that it is not a matter of comparing the two competing procedures for establishing a theoretical distribution. The binomial calculation that I propose calls for knowledge of the actual distribution of the whole and is applicable only to a part of that whole. On the other hand, the Waring-Herdan formula can be applied to the whole or to any part of it, using the three parameters—N, V, and V_1—of the whole or of the part under consideration. Suppose for a moment that this formula accounts for linguistic reality just as Newton's binomial applies to coin tossing—that is, that it expresses perfectly the average occurrence of heads or tails, each departing from the model only by random deviation. From this hypothesis, the frequency distributions in the text I examined at the outset (the whole play) obeys the Waring formula, with the exception of those irregularities caused by chance. Our test (given on p. 48) allows this conclusion, and the same holds for the several parts (pp. 47–48). The theoretical distribution that I calculated by adjusting it to the length of one of the parts cannot differ from the corresponding actual distribution except:

(1) by the elimination or attenuation of "irregularities," that is, the random differences;

(2) by the effect of fundamental stylistic differences between the whole and the parts (which holds for the Tragedy and the Prologue, though not for the Comedy).

It is then predictable that, if our hypothesis holds, the theoretical distribution must be closer to the Waring-Herdan formula than to the actual distribution.

I next made the attempt to apply this procedure to the sections of Tragedy and Prologue:

	TRAGEDY			PROLOGUE		
Frequency	*W.–H.*	*binomial*	*difference*	*W.–H.*	*binomial*	*difference*
1	(499)	499	—	(484)	484	—
2	134.9	141	+6.1	129.3	135	+5.7
3	60.7	61	+0.3	58.2	57	−1.2
4	34.0	32	−2.0	32.6	30	−2.6
5	21.5	20	−1.5	20.6	18	−2.6
6	14.8	13	−1.8	14.1	13	−1.1
7	10.6	10	−0.6	10.2	9	−1.2
8	8.0	8	0	7.7	7	−0.7
9	6.2	6	−0.2	6.0	5	−1.0
10	5.0	5	0	4.8	4	−0.8
≧11	48.3	48	−0.3	40.5	46	+5.5
	843.0	843		808.0	808	

It would be difficult to obtain a better fit; the differences still occur, partly because in one of these operations but not in the other the results are rounded off to units. The χ^2 values are 0.755 and 2.144 respectively, which indicates a probability greater than 99 % in the first case and about 98 % in the second.

Encouraged by this precision, I applied the same procedure to the Comedy, including this time the frequencies below 5:

		COMEDY					
Frequency	*W.–H.*	*binomial*	*difference*		*W.–H.*	*binomial*	*difference*
1	(735)	735	—	14	6.8	6	−0.8
2	267.6	258	−9.6	15	5.9	6	+0.1
3	135.8	135	−0.8	16	5.2	5	−0.2
4	81.1	84	+2.9	17	4.6	5	+0.4
5	53.5	56	+2.5	18	4.0	4	0
6	37.7	39	+1.3	19	3.6	4	+0.4
7	28.0	28	0	20	3.2	4	+0.8
8	21.4	20	−1.4	21	2.9	3	+0.1
9	18.1	15	−3.1	22	2.6	3	+0.4
10	13.7	12	−1.7	23	2.4	3	+0.6
11	11.2	10	−1.2	24	2.2	2	−0.2
12	9.5	8	−1.5	≥25	44.1	56	+11.9
13	7.9	7	−0.9				
					1,508.0	1,508	

The χ^2 value is only 5.343. For 22 degrees of freedom, the effect of chance alone produces 99 out of 100 differences with a value of 9.542. One can then say that the two calculated distributions correspond remarkably, and both adapt themselves very well to the two actual distributions given above.

The second remark is rather a question. If the formula is good, can it be applied to any text whatsoever, whatever its length may be, and above all, whatever its language or style?

With regard to length, it is well to ignore very short texts (for example, where $N < 1,000$), where, in virtue of what we have already said, the prediction only holds for two or three frequency classes. With lengthy texts ($N > 100,000$), it seems likely that the Waring distribution would no longer be successful in giving a clear account. The relative failure that I have encountered when dealing with the data for Basic French[15] has probably no other source; I had thought of attributing it to an abnormal dispersion of the lexicon, caused by the fundamental disparity of this corpus. In fact, the results have been similarly disappointing in a study of a homogeneous literary whole of comparable length, the vocabulary of Cervantes' *Don Quixote*.[16] In an investigation of the vocabulary of the New Testament ($N = 137,238$), considerable differences emerged at the outset, though, as we have seen, the parts of this text deviate less obviously from the model. It seems, then, at first sight, that a bias must be foreseen when the text is very long.

From the diversity of languages (not to mention that of counting techniques), we can predict some differences in the adaptation to the model. It is surprising enough that the most obvious differences are not found in Latin texts, which however have a profoundly different lexical system (the relative rarity of grammatical words) from that of Greek and above all from those of the modern languages cited here. On the other hand, the Greek of the Evangelists responds rather badly to our techniques. But it is premature to speculate in this area. We will be content to note that the best fits have been obtained for the Corneille texts, followed fairly closely by those for the Russian short story, followed by the samples of Latin prose and by the chantefable.

Are stylistic differences detrimental to the application of the model? I really do not know. In the example of the two very clearly differentiated sections of *l'Illusion*, it seems that they are not. On the other hand, a tentative study of a piece of prose by Flaubert yielded some results that are downright bad, with a considerable underestimate for frequency classes greater than 2.

*   *   *

[We have omitted here a discussion of a proposed alteration in Herdan's tables (mentioned on p. 44). A reader who plans to make use of these tables should see Muller's discussion of their bias and the consequent effects on the theoretical distributions derived from them. Eds.]

*   *   *

It would be naïve to hope that the Waring-Herdan formula can account for all possible lexical distributions. But its success over a large range of data is striking and cannot simply be attributed to a series of happy coincidences. Above all, its value lies in its simplicity, since it only employs unmodified data (N, V, and V_1) without either a coefficient or an arbitrary correction factor. N and V are basic characteristics of all vocabulary. V_1 has always been considered a very significant value,[17] and its role in the formula confirms its importance. In order to obtain a dynamic image of what is called the vocabulary of a text, we must consider the transition of "langue" into "discours," of lexicon into vocabulary. For each element in discourse (occurrence) an element of the mental lexicon is actualized; if many elements of the lexicon are put to work, low frequency classes will have many members, and particularly the lowest, the class of the frequency of 1: whence the importance of the "hapax" to the text. In the static pattern that constitutes a text, the proportion of hapax reveals the rhythm by which the vocabulary is augmented—a phenomena that gives us a glimpse of the extent of the lexicon at work. Stopping after a certain length of text (N), observing the number of words that appear only once in it (V_1), and comparing it to the number of words already used (V) is the same as photographing the movement of the lexical units that come to constitute the vocabulary in order to capture in a single frame the movement of the lexicon. Experience shows that Herdan was right in his estimate that this indicator, provided that it is related to N, will roughly determine the continuation of the distribution.

The conclusion that Herdan draws from this discovery is that the distribution of words in discourse obeys two laws: one is the law of chance—expressed from the mathematical viewpoint as the "normal" law, of which the binomial formula is only one application. The other, which he calls the "law of solidarity" and which is expressed mathematically in Waring's formula, is a reflection of the fact that, as Ferdinand de Saussure said, "la langue est un système où tout se tient." In consequence, the frequency scale consists of interdependent elements and not of figures drawn at random.

The uses of this formula will be interesting to explore. Favorable or not, they must reveal stylistic peculiarities and illustrate typological differences. They can only enrich our still limited knowledge of the processes which transform the elements of our mental lexicon into vocabulary in action.

REFERENCES

1. London, 1964. The review appeared in *Etudes de Linguistique Appliquée*, no. 4 (1966), 181–184.
2. See especially, G. Herdan, "Mathematical Models of Linguistic Distribution Functions," *Etudes de Linguistique Appliquée*, no. 2 (1964), 47–48.
3. Herdan, *op. cit.*, p. 85.
4. Since the lexicon is not infinite (though its limits can only be speculated about), the point must come where, if the text is very long, the introduction of a new word becomes exceptional. In the long run, there should be more words of the frequency class 2 than of frequency class 1. This phenomena, if in fact it can occur, has never been observed. It is most unlikely that it would occur except in a very long text (on the order of more than a million words).
5. Herdan, *op. cit.*, p. 85; for the bibliography, see p. 93.
6. J. O. Irwin, "The Place of Mathematics in the Medical and Biological Sciences," *Journal of the Royal Statistical Society*, Series A, CXXVI (1963), 1–41.
7. G. Gougenheim, R. Michéa, P. Rivenc, and A. Sauvageot, *Elaboration du Français Fondamental* (Paris, 1964). The distribution of frequency classes is given on pp. 127–134.
8. H. H. Josselson, *The Russian Word Count* (Detroit, 1953).
9. For the Puškin text, which was treated as the others (i.e., stopping at the theoretical number 5 which corresponds to a frequency of 24), I found a χ^2 of 27.48, or a probability of 0.20. The result is thus almost as good as for the investigations of Corneille, and better than that for the others.
10. For the explanation and justification of this selection, see my *Essai de Statistique Lexicale* (Paris, 1964), pp. 7ff. The numerical data given above, as well as that for the other roles, are on p. 88.
11. Simone Monsonégo, "Etude stylo-statistique du vocabulaire de la chantefable d'*Aucassin et Nicolette*" (typed thesis, Strasbourg, 1965; published, Paris, 1966).
12. Louis Delatte and Eugène Évrard, *Sénèque: Consolation à Polybe: Index Verborum, Relevés Statistiques* (The Hague, 1962) and *Consolation à Helvia...* (1963).
13. Robert Morgenthaler, *Statistik des Neutestamentlichen Wortschatzes* (Zürich and Frankfurt, 1958).
14. For an explanation and justification of this procedure, see "Calcul des probabilités et calcul d'un vocabulaire," *Travaux de linguistique et de littérature*, II, i (1964). For some applications of it, see *Essai de Statistique Lexicale*, pp. 93ff. and 143ff.
15. Here are the results for the first frequency classes (the observed figures are in parentheses):

2	1,353.9	(1,170)
3	810.9	(694)
4	538.8	(450)
5	383.4	(327)
6	286.4	(260)

16. Carlos Fernandez Gomez, *Vocabulario de Cervantes* (Madrid, 1962). The statistical material given in this work is unfortunately incomplete and inconveniently arranged.
17. See, for example, Pierre Guiraud, *Problèmes et méthodes de la statistique linguistique* (Paris, 1954), pp. 86–89: "This relation is by far the simplest and most accurate of all those I have had occasion to examine." We could quote many other statements of this sort. The nuisance is that in non-exhaustive statistical surveys, and even in *indices verborum*, attention is generally concentrated on the most frequently occurring words, while those that appear only once are passed over without comment.

THE DIAGNOSIS OF LITERARY STYLE WITH THE VERB-ADJECTIVE RATIO

FRIEDERIKE ANTOSCH

In 1925, A. Busemann[1] published a new method of specifying the exact relation of the "active" and "qualitative" aspects of a literary text. Busemann established a formula

$$\frac{\text{Active Statements}}{\text{Qualitative Statements}}$$

and called it the *Aktionsquotient*. Active statements are statements on activities and are expressed in words that "imply action"; qualitative statements are statements expressing properties, that is, "quality in the ordinary sense and quantity." But the identification of these two kinds of statement in specific cases depends largely on intuition, and it is often difficult to distinguish precisely between them. V. Neubauer and A. Schlismann of Innsbruck[2] considerably simplified the method by restricting "active statements" to verbs and "qualitative statements" to adjectives and adjective-modifiers. Thus the formula for the ratio was altered to a simplified form:

$$\text{Verb-Adjective Ratio (VAR)} = \frac{\text{Number of Verbs}}{\text{Number of Adjectives}}.$$

All verbal forms (with the exception of the auxiliary verbs *haben, sein,* and *werden*) are counted as verbs; all adjectives attributed to a noun and such intensifiers as *sehr, ausgesprochen,* etc., are counted as adjectives.

The original aim of this paper was to answer the question: "Is the difference between spoken and written language reflected in the verb-adjective ratio?" But during the investigation, further questions arose: "Is the VAR influenced by the theme?" and "Are there any other exterior factors which help to determine the VAR?"

In his various investigations, Busemann found that the VAR is higher in the spoken language. He attributes this result to the slower speed of writing as compared to the speed of speech; the intervals between the reproduction of the individual words can lead to the elaboration of "substantival" ideas and result in a greater number of qualifiers. From this explanation, he draws the further conclusion that qualitative style is generally brought about by the speed of the inner voice when writing. In his later work, "Stil und Charakter,"[3] however, Busemann claims that, despite the increase of the VAR in speech, an individual style remains constant. What influence must be ascribed to speed will be discussed later in the exposition of my own investigations.

This essay originally appeared as "Stildiagnostische Literaturuntersuchungen mit dem Aktionsquotienten" in *Wiener Archiv für Psychologie, Psychiatrie und Neurologie*, III (1953), 65–73. We are grateful to Mr. Karl Ortseifen for his help in making the translation.

In the later work, Busemann abandons his original claim that theme has no influence on the VAR and admits that his further experiments (reported in "Stil und Charakter") show that the impact of theme grows more dominant as the personal style of an individual is less elaborate and more open to influence. He attributes this openness to theme to immaturity in the individual's personality. A. Schlismann also discovered a relation between the VAR and theme, but she did not define it in detail.

INVESTIGATIONS IN LITERATURE

The problem of the difference between written language and spoken language implies the question: "What is the position of the drama?" We suppose that drama should occupy an intermediate position. The following examples— based on passages of about 500 to 700 syllables in length—show that the VAR values from drama are indeed higher than those from non-dramatic writing (i.e., epic and theoretical writing of any kind):

Grillparzer:

145 passages from 19 plays: VAR=4.05 (range[4]=13.21).

74 passages from non-dramatic works: VAR=1.69 (range=8.68).

Goethe:

153 passages from 9 plays: VAR=3.33 (range=15.66).

166 passages from 11 non-dramatic works: VAR=2.44 (range= 13.15).

Anzengruber:

269 passages from 13 plays: VAR=6.20 (range=42.49).

171 passages from 22 stories and novels: VAR=3.39 (range=23.03).

Moreover, the question arises as to whether prose plays—which are closer to natural speech than verse plays—have a higher VAR. In Grillparzer's works, the VAR in 15 verse plays is 4.11, and in four fragments of prose plays it is 3.60. The reason for this apparent contradiction can be found in a comparison of these works: Grillparzer's prose plays are fragments hardly comparable to his great poetic plays, and they are written in a language that is by no means the "natural" language we expect in prose.

An analogous comparison in Goethe's works—where verse plays are equal in quality to those in prose—may serve as proof of our expectation. The VAR calculated from five prose plays is 4.23, but in five verse plays it amounts to only 2.94.

Plays written in dialect come even closer to the spoken language. This supposition is confirmed by a comparison of the VAR values in Anzengruber's works. The average VAR of 11 plays in dialect (235 passages) is 6.52; the average VAR of two plays in the standard language (34 passages) is only 4.57.

In the plays of Grillparzer and particularly in those of Anzengruber, we frequently found a great range of VAR values. Spirited short speeches between characters seem to have higher VAR values than do monologues or

longer speeches. This conjecture is verified by a closer examination of Anzengruber's plays:

  11 plays in dialect:
      VAR=6.84 for dialogue.
      VAR=4.56 for monologue.[5]
  2 plays in standard language:
      VAR=4.88 for dialogue.
      VAR=3.71 for monologue.

The only exception in his works is the play *Der Pfarrer von Kirchfeld*, with a
VAR of 4.97 in dialogue and 5.17 in monologue. We shall provide an explanation for this disparity later in this paper.

The mode of presentation, however, does not only influence the drama but
also the novel. We can distinguish four modes of presentation in Anzengruber's novels: (1) genuine dialogue of the kind found in plays, (2) monologues, (3) purely narrative or descriptive writing, and (4) speeches interspersed in the narrative portions of the text. In the following table, we present
our results for the two novels *Der Sternsteinhof* and *Der Schandflek*.

MODE:	1	2	3	4	Total Text
Der Sternsteinhof:	5.51	3.80	2.05	3.80	3.01
Der Schandflek:	7.83	4.61	2.04	4.53	3.53
Average for the novels:	6.58	4.16	2.05	4.17	3.26
Average for the plays:	6.56	4.34			

We observe in these figures a gradual decline from the VAR of the dialogue
(which is closer to the spoken language) to the monologues, and finally to the
"written language" of the narrative passages. The speeches interspersed in the
narration, as we would expect, have an intermediate position. That the respective VAR values of the plays correspond almost exactly to those of the
novels shows that the VAR is dependent upon the mode of presentation.

In examining a variety of works by several authors, we found that the VAR
discriminated not only dramatic and non-dramatic works but also subclasses in the non-dramatic texts. In these texts, we distinguished narratives
of a personal sort (stories, novels, diaries, etc.) and theoretical works of a
factual kind (a type often called *Vermischte Schriften*). In Grillparzer's works,
the average VAR for the first class is 2.00 and for the second 1.43; in texts
by Stifter, the values are 2.36 and 1.44 respectively. These observations
suggest that the VAR is related to the theme of the text. On the basis of these
findings, we attempted to distinguish various literary genres without regard to
the authors of the individual works.

Let us first compare novels and stories to scientific works. From a random
selection of 521 passages from novels and stories by 25 different authors, we

calculated an average VAR of 2.42. But in scientific and critical works from 21 different authors (105 passages) the average VAR was 1.10. On the basis of this study, the contrast suggested by the Grillparzer and Stifter calculations was confirmed. Furthermore, another literary genre—the fairy tale—can be included in the comparison. The average VAR of 35 fairy tales was 4.11, much *higher* than the corresponding figure for novels and stories (2.42). In considering the values for the fairy tales more closely, we soon discovered that the folk tale has a higher VAR than the literary tale. Literary tales thus come closer to the category of novels and stories.

We turn next to a comparison of poems and ballads. Preliminary examination of several poets (Grillparzer, Goethe, and Eichendorff) revealed an ascending scale of VAR values: low values were found for the ode and the elegy, higher ones for lyric poetry, higher ones still for the ballad, and the highest for epigrams and (in Grillparzer) "political" poetry. This examination was followed by a contrastive analysis of ballads and lyric poetry by various poets. The selection—again made by random sampling—showed the following values:

Ballads by 16 different poets	4.08
15 folk ballads	4.18
Love lyrics (selected from 9 poets)	2.89
Reflective lyrics (selected from 15 poets)	3.02

Such a comparison of various literary genres shows clearly that the VAR is dependent upon the theme of the work. Uniform results did not appear from a more delicate subdivision of the lyrics into reflective and amatory subclasses. In a similar attempt, not discussed here, to classify epic prose into classic and modern categories and to subdivide scientific writing by discipline, we found a similar inconclusiveness. The reason for the indeterminacy of these studies lies partly in the fact that the VAR examines only one component of style; works which differ in other stylistic features may still have the same VAR. But the analysis of plays eventually revealed the nature and power of the influences we have already mentioned.

We next considered the characters in several plays and determined the VAR of the characters' speeches. An examination of Goethe's *Faust* yielded the following results: the VAR of the whole play is 3.06, the VAR for Part I is 3.40, and for Part II, 2.80.

	Part I	*Part II*	*In the Whole Play*
Faust	2.79	2.54	2.60
Mephistopheles	3.66	2.70	3.08
Wagner	4.23	3.75	4.04
Gretchen	5.43	—	(5.43)

First of all, the differences between the two parts of *Faust* must be discussed. An examination of Goethe's works in chronological order showed that the difference between his early and late styles is also reflected in the VAR, though no such influence of age was found in Stifter's letters. There is no distinction between an early and a late style in Stifter. Examining the VAR values for Goethe's *Faust*, we can see that there is a decrease in the total values from Part I to Part II; and, by considering the values in the table, we can see that this decrease extends to all the characters. We find an overall shift in the values, though each character retains his rank relative to the others. This observation allows us to conclude that the VAR values of the several characters are not accidental but are a function of the character's personality.

The plays of Anzengruber suggest the idea of considering the characters as individuals, since the diction of the clergy and the people is so conspicuously distinct. A good example is provided by *Der Pfarrer von Kirchfeld*. In this play, the main characters are young Parson Hell; his antagonist Count Finsterberg; Annerl, who is at the heart of the dramatic conflict; and Wurzelsepp, who violently opposes Hell at first and then sides with him with the same zeal.

	VAR	*Number of Passages*
Finsterberg	3.77	5
Hell	5.53	12
Annerl	4.76	6
Wurzelsepp	9.34	7
The whole play	5.02	

As we expected, different VAR values for each of the main characters in *Der Pfarrer von Kirchfeld* were obtained. In this instance, we shall attempt an interpretation of the characters by relating the VAR values to personality type. But we must not draw definite conclusions from the VAR values alone as an indication of personality, and we shall not attempt to do so here. Bearing in mind what we have already said both about the mode of presentation and the relations of dialect and standard language, we are puzzled at first by the apparent contradictions in the values obtained for Anzengruber's play. Although Hell speaks standard German and is given several monologues and long speeches, the VAR for his language is above average. Wurzelsepp's language shows the highest VAR values—far above the average—even though he speaks in dialect and is given many monologues. Yet the value for Annerl is below average, though she too speaks in dialect and is given only one monologue (a speech yielding a VAR that is by no means the lowest). The lowest VAR is that of Finsterberg, even though he is given virtually no monologues.

But these four VAR values take on significance when they are considered from another point of view. Parson Hell's high VAR reflects his youth and his passionate and sensitive character. Wurzelsepp is rough and boisterous—he is very much one of the people—and is violent both in good and bad; the high VAR for his language fits these attributes exactly. Annerl is best described in Hell's own words: "[beautiful], decorous, and intelligent"; her low VAR is thus explained. Finsterberg is well characterized by his low VAR value, for he is first didactic and later cold and ironic. Incidentally, the climax of his scene with Hell is reflected in the increase of the VAR of his speeches: $2.30 \rightarrow 5.87, 4.45$.

The contradictions of our first approach become even more evident in another detail of *Der Pfarrer von Kirchfeld*. The average VAR of the dialogue (4.97) is lower than that for monologues (5.17), and this exception to our general observation needs explanation. What can have disturbed the relation between the mode of presentation and the VAR? As an aid to the reader's understanding, let us first outline some terms and concepts, and then answer this question.

The VAR of a literary work—particularly that of a play—can either be determined by "form" or by "content" (*Gehalt*). What we have considered as "exterior influences" up to this point can be designated "form" or "formal tendencies." We have considered some of them already, such as mode of presentation, prose as opposed to verse, dialect as opposed to standard language, and theme. Each of these tendencies consists either of two contrary components—one tending toward a high VAR and the other toward a low VAR—or of only one trend tending toward either high or low values. For example, in the case of the binary tendencies, we have shown that for mode of presentation, monologues tend toward low values and dialogues toward high ones. Verse tends toward low values, prose toward high. Literary language tends toward low values, and dialect toward high ones. On the other hand, theme is unidirectional. Scientific works tend to have low values and folk tales tend to have high values. Both tendencies are tied to "form," though they differ in strength.

Let us turn again to the play *Der Pfarrer von Kirchfeld*. Parson Hell speaks standard German—tendency toward a low VAR; his role contains a comparatively large number of monologues—likewise a tendency to low VAR. These are formal tendencies in Hell's language that should reinforce each other and lead to a low VAR. It might be argued that there is a third formal tendency at work—prose—having a tendency toward high values. This argument is justified, but we must remember that the VAR of the whole play is affected by this formal tendency, since it is written entirely in prose. Therefore the tendency toward high values in prose affects all the characters equally and will only result in increasing the VAR level for the whole play.

In Finsterberg's language, two formal tendencies work against each other. He speaks standard German—low VAR—but his role contains almost no monologues—high VAR. In Wurzelsepp's language, we find just the contrary situation. He speaks in dialect—high VAR—but is given many monologues—

low VAR. In Annerl's language, there is no such conflict of formal tendencies; she too speaks in dialect—high VAR—but a virtual balance of monologues and dialogues neutralizes the formal influence of mode of presentation. Thus we find that formal tendencies can push in the same direction (Hell); or they can pull in opposite directions (Finsterberg, Wurzelsepp); or finally there are tendencies that remain neutral because high and low components cancel each other (as shown in Annerl's modes of presentation).

Our example, however, has also demonstrated that these tendencies imposed by form may have no effect at all on the VAR. Therefore, there must be other tendencies that override the formal ones and eventually determine the VAR scale. They are the "tendencies of content." These are likewise directed forces and submit to the same laws as the formal tendencies. When aimed in the same direction, they are cumulative in their effect; or they can obstruct each other or cancel each other. There can also be binary tendencies consisting of a high and a low component. There is, for instance, age: youth—high; maturity—low. Within childhood and adolescence there are: active phases—high; qualitative phases—low (see Busemann's *Sprache der Jugend*). But there are also cases where the factor of age has no effect and the components cancel each other—that is, when the age level is neutral in relation to the VAR. Another bidirectional tendency is sex: female—high; male—low. This opposition will be proved in the experimental portion of our investigation. Apart from the binary tendencies, there are also tendencies of content whose number we cannot yet specify exactly. Directed either high or low, they are the various character qualities. It is their influence that is decisive in *Der Pfarrer von Kirchfeld*, as our attempts at interpretation show. Thus, it is not surprising that the average values of the VAR are higher in monologue than they are in dialogue. The formal tendencies have no effect since the main characters are determined by content. The inner dynamism of the play is so strong that it breaks through the barriers of form. And what is the personality of the poet behind the play? Here are the facts: Anzengruber was then thirty years old—the play was his first masterpiece—and he had chosen a highly topical problem. But our analysis of three more plays by Anzengruber (*Der Meineidbauer, Das vierte Gebot*, and *Der Fleck auf der Ehr*) revealed that form had a prominent effect in them.

An increase in the force of formal tendencies, however, need not lead to an insipid play with faintly drawn characters. Grillparzer's *Ahnfrau* may illustrate this point. It is the work of a twenty-five-year-old playwright, and was composed in only sixteen days. The play is written in rhymed trochaic tetrameter. It has a tremendously dynamic effect and the tension is maintained from the first scene to the last. Yet the play is wholly determined by form. The characters are indeed faintly drawn, for *Die Ahnfrau* is not a drama of character but a drama of fate. The dramatic energy and the consequent effectiveness on the stage are brought about by the action, the situation, and the dynamic meter. Therefore, to say that a play is "determined by form" or "determined by content" is by no means a value judgment. Franz Theodor

Csokor's play, *Kalypso*, is likewise determined wholly by form, but it is a profound play and makes use of very melodic language.

A comparison of the VAR values of the individual characters in corresponding scenes of Anzengruber's *Das vierte Gebot* and Grillparzer's *Des Meeres und der Liebe Wellen* gives further credence to our treatment of literary characters as real persons. In the same circumstances, the VAR values for the characters are different.

The degree of emotional engagement—highly involved or detached—of a given character in a scene is also reflected in the character's VAR value for that scene. The observation that a character's VAR increases in moments of high emotional involvement leads us to suppose that the climax of the action will be marked by an increase in the VAR. This supposition may be illustrated by examining three contemporary plays that differ from each other in every respect. Let us contrast the opening scenes with two scenes of great dramatic intensity in each of these plays.

1. Bertold Brecht's *Der gute Mensch von Sezuan* (a play virtually determined by content):
   Average VAR = 6.32.
   Scene I: VAR = 6.60 (the water seller's monologue).
   Scene IX: VAR = 6.16 (Shui Ta-Sun loses her fortune; Sun shows his true character).
   Scene XVIII: VAR = 4.37 (confession of Shui-Ta in court).

Here the climaxes have somewhat lower VAR values! Despite the precision in characterization, there is no marked increase leading to a climax. The play develops in epic broadness, a conclusion already indicated by the fact that the play is a loosely organized sequence of eighteen episodes.

2. Ödon von Horvath's *Der jüngste Tag* (predominantly determined by content):
   Average VAR = 9.92.
   Scene I: VAR = 2.00 (passengers waiting for a train).
   Scene IV: VAR = 12.66 (decisive dialogue between Anna and Hudetz).

Der jüngste Tag is dramatic in the literal sense. Climactic scenes have a strikingly higher VAR value.

3. Franz Theodor Csokor's *Kalypso* (completely determined by form):
   Average VAR = 11.56.
   Scene I: VAR = 12.00 (conversation between Kalypso, Hermes, and the bard).
   Scene V: VAR = 30.00 (the ghost of Agamemnon calls on Odysseus to leave Kalypso).
   Scene VI: VAR = 30.00 (Kalypso lets Odysseus go).

Taking into consideration the enormous range of the VAR values and the composition of these three ($V/A = 24/2$, $30/1$, $30/1$), we find that the increase in the VAR at the points of climax must be considered as really quite small. But we must remember that these scenes are not at all "dramatic"—few of the scenes in *Kalypso* are really dramatic. Instead we are dealing with turning points in the action that are stylistically submerged in the unvarying melody of the language.

Even though there is insufficient evidence from the material just examined to convince us that opening scenes have the lowest VAR values and climactic ones the highest, we may be satisfied with a negative hypothesis: if a play lacks rising action leading to climaxes and lacks turning points in the plot, it will be difficult to find maximal VAR values except in outbursts of emotion or in those passages that are determined by formal tendencies.

REFERENCES

1. A. Busemann. *Die Sprache der Jugend als Ausdruck der Entwicklungsrhythmik*. Jena: Fischer, 1925. [Busemann's work is discussed by George A. Miller in *Language and Communication* (New York, 1951), pp. 127–130; and his quotient is included in the list of style measures employed by Charles E. Osgood in his study, "Some Effects of Motivation on Style of Encoding," in *Style in Language*, ed. Thomas A. Sebeok (Cambridge, Mass., and New York, 1960), pp. 293–306. A more extensive use of the *Aktionsquotient* is to be found in David P. Boder's "The Adjective-Verb Quotient: A Contribution to the Psychology of Language," *Psychological Record*, III (1940), 309–343. Eds.]
2. A. Schlismann, "Sprach– und Stilanalyse mit einem vereinfachten Aktionsquotienten," *Wiener Zeitschrift für Philosophie, Psychologie, und Pädagogik*, II, ii (1948), 42 *et seq.*
3. A. Busemann. *Stil und Charakter: Untersuchungen zur Psychologie der individuellen Redeform*. Meisenheim/Glan: Westkulturverlag Anton Hain, 1948.
4. The difference between the highest and the lowest VAR values.
5. The number of monologues examined depends upon the number of monologues in the whole play.

III

SENTENCE-LEVEL

MEASURES

A NOTE ON THE STATISTICAL ANALYSIS OF SENTENCE-LENGTH AS A CRITERION OF LITERARY STYLE

C. B. WILLIAMS

Some years ago I made a number of calculations of the frequency distribution of words of different length in different books to see to what extent authors kept to a definite distribution and so perhaps might be identified by such a method. The results obtained, however, were not striking and the work was put at one side.

Mr. Udny Yule (1939), however, has attacked the problem of authorship from the angle of the variation in sentence-length, and this appears to be a much more fertile method of approach.

Mr. Yule shows that the frequency distribution of sentence-length (i.e., number of words between successive full stops) is of the skew type and by comparing in two different manuscripts, the mean, the median, quartiles, and deciles he is able to produce convincing mathematical evidence on the identity or otherwise of their authorship.

Mr. Yule does not comment on the skew distribution further than to state (p. 371) "they are not of the Poisson type, but of the type in which the square of the standard deviation largely exceeds the mean."

When I converted some of Yule's tables into diagrams I was struck by their general resemblance to certain skew distributions with which I have recently been dealing in some entomological problems, and which distributions, I found, became normal and symmetrical if the logarithm of the number was taken as a basis for subdivision into groups instead of the number itself (see Williams, 1937).

I was unable to test this transformation on Yule's figures as he unfortunately does not give the original data, but only the word-length of sentences in groups of five; so it was necessary to obtain some new data.

These I obtained by counting the number of words in each of 600 sentences from the following three books:

(1) G. K. Chesterton, *A Short History of England*, 1917.
(2) H. G. Wells, *The Work, Wealth and Happiness of Mankind*.
(3) G. Bernard Shaw, *An Intelligent Woman's Guide to Socialism*.

All three works deal with the exposition of somewhat similar sociological subjects and none of them are in the "conversational" style.

The selection of the sentences was randomized as follows. Each of the books is divided up into chapters, sections, or both. In Chesterton's book the first 30 sentences were counted in each of the first 20 chapters. In Wells's book the

Except for the last section, this essay appeared in *Biometrika*, XXXI (1939–1940), 356–361; it is reprinted here by permission of the author and the Biometrika Trustees.

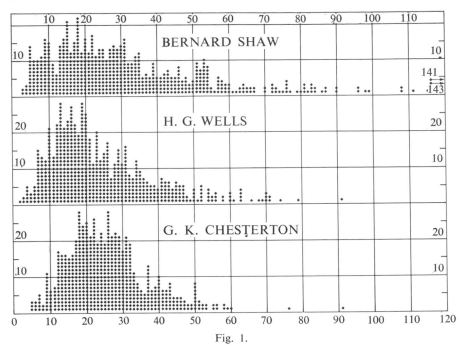

Fig. 1.

first 10 sentences were counted in each chapter subdivision up to chapter VII, division 11. In Shaw's book the first 15 sentences in each of sections 1–40 were taken. In each case the greater part of the book was covered.

The original data thus obtained are shown diagrammatically in Fig. 1. Each of the distributions is of the typical skew type obtained by Yule: Shaw is the most extreme and varies from 3 words to 143; Wells is less skew and ranges from 3 to 91; while the Chesterton curve is the least skew and varies from 5 to 91 with only two values over 60.

From Table I it will be seen that the arithmetic mean number of words per sentence is 25.87 for Chesterton, 24.11 for Wells, and 31.23 for Shaw. The medians are also different and presumably the quartiles and deciles, but these latter were not calculated.

If, however, instead of taking the frequency distribution of the actual number of words per sentence we take that of the logarithm of the number we get the distributions shown in Figs. 2–4. They undoubtedly show a very close resemblance to the "normal distribution." The mean log and standard deviation for Chesterton is 1.37 $\pm$0.20; for Wells 1.31 $\pm$0.24; and for Shaw 1.39 $\pm$0.29. The standard error of the mean is, owing to the large number of observations, in all cases very small and approximately $\pm$0.01.

On each of the three figures is superimposed a normal curve of the same area, mean, and standard deviation; and it will be seen how closely it fits the observed values.

Fig. 2.

Fig. 3.

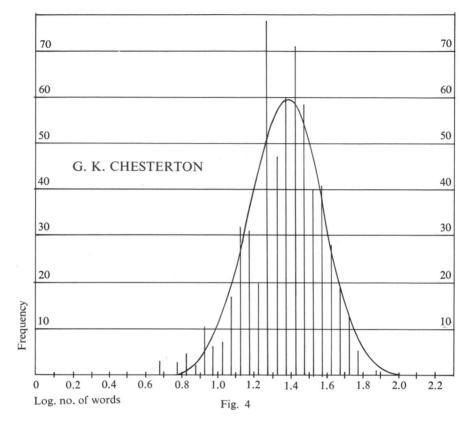

Fig. 4

TABLE I

Frequency Constants of the Distribution of Sentence-length

	Chesterton	*Wells*	*Shaw*
Number of sentences	600	600	600
Number of words	15,521	14,463	18,735
Arithmetic mean no. of words	25.87	24.11	31.23
Median no. of words	25.3	20.8	26.0
Mean log no. of words	1.37	1.31	1.39
Geometrical mean no. of words	23.5	20.5	24.5
Standard deviation of mean log	0.200	0.237	0.290
Standard error of mean log	0.0080	0.0095	0.0112

The following comments may, however, be made:

(1) The greater irregularity of the observed values in the lower portion of the distribution is due to the irregular distribution of the logarithms of

integers when grouped in small artificial divisions as in the present case. Thus there is no logarithm of an integer between 0.01 and 0.25; none between 0.61 and 0.65 and between 0.71 and 0.75. On the other hand, there are two between 1.11 and 1.15; two between 1.16 and 1.20; only one between 1.21 and 1.25; and three between 1.26 and 1.30. Thus in all three diagrams the frequency of 1.21–1.25 is well down and that of 1.26–1.30 is far up. Some process of smoothing would undoubtedly eliminate these irregularities, but it was thought better to leave the data in their original form and draw attention to the sources of irregularity.

(2) There appears to be on all three diagrams a slight shortage of high values and a slight excess of low ones. On the latter I have no comment but it appears possible that the small deficit in the longer sentences might easily be due to a biased effect introduced by the habit that many writers have of cutting up unusually long sentences into their component parts when reading over their manuscript or proofs.

On the assumption that the normal curve is a sound representation of the frequency distribution of the log number of words in sentences, Fig. 5 has

Fig. 5.

been prepared which shows the means and normal curves for the three books superimposed on one another. The means are close together but the distributions are very different.

The difference in means between Shaw and Wells is 0.09 and the standard error of the difference is only 0.015. Thus the difference is six times the standard error and hence certainly significant. Between Shaw and Chesterton the difference of the means is barely significant but that between the standard deviations is quite striking.

If the above reasoning is correct, it is unnecessary for the comparison between two documents to compare arithmetic means, medians, quartiles, and deciles, but only the log mean and the log standard deviation; all other comparisons are included in these.

It follows also that Mr. Bernard Shaw, while undoubtedly under the impression that he was punctuating at his own free will, was for this particular book hidebound within the limits of

$$Z = \frac{1}{0.29\sqrt{(2\pi)}} \exp\left[\frac{(1.4 - \chi)^2}{2(0.29)^2}\right]$$

while similarly Mr. Wells was writing under the restricting influence of

$$Z = \frac{1}{0.24\sqrt{(2\pi)}} \exp\left[\frac{(1.3 - \chi)^2}{2(0.24)^2}\right]$$

where Z is the frequency and χ the logarithm of the number of words per sentence.

Perhaps something might be added on the meaning in words of the above mathematical transformation. If the log distribution is normal we can infer that the extent to which a sentence in the process of writing is likely to vary is at any level proportional to the length of the sentence. Thus when he is thinking in short sentences of about ten words an author is likely to vary say from 8 to 12 words; when he is thinking in longer sentences of say 100 words he will vary from 80 to 120. In other words the variations are proportional or geometric and do not merely involve the addition or subtraction of words at all levels. Further, if the geometric mean is taken as a basis, sentences between this and half its length are as frequent as those between it and twice its length; sentences down to one-quarter its length are as likely to occur as sentences up to four times its length; and so on.

If the arithmetic mean were the true basis, then sentences of ten words more than the arithmetic mean would be as likely to occur as sentences of ten words less, and it is easy to see that this is not the case.

Before the whole theory of the use of such distribution for separating works of different authorships can be fully accepted it will of course be necessary to study the results obtained from many different works by the same author, in different styles, on different subjects, and at different periods of his life. From these it may be possible to find what variation can occur "within authors" as compared with "between authors." This note is not meant to deal with this basic problem but only to draw attention to the simplification of the method of approach to such a problem by the use of a transformation which produces a normal instead of a skew distribution.

*   *   *

The article reprinted above was written in 1940, after the publication of Yule's work on sentence-length (which appeared in 1939), but before his much more important work on vocabulary studies (1944). It was also before my discovery of Mendenhall's early and extensive work on the frequency distribution of word-lengths (see my 1956 article).

I still believe that the ideas put forward in it are sound, and particularly my insistence on the fact that, within a single author, variation of sentence-length is geometric about the geometric mean, and *not* arithmetic about the arithmetic mean. The median is always very close to the geometric mean and well below the arithmetic mean. The acceptance of this premise considerably alters the statistical approach; failure to recognize it may lead to entirely false conclusions.

The same basic principle has since been shown to apply to the frequency of words of different lengths, and to the frequency of usage of different vocabulary words.

I have developed the ideas contained in the article reprinted here in various subsequent publications: in *Nature* (1946) and *Biometrika* (1956), from a technical point of view; in *Science News* (1952), *The Listener* (1964), and *The New Scientist* (1967) for a more popular audience. My forthcoming book, *Literary Style and Vocabulary* will contain a more detailed account of these matters. Discussion of the basic problems from a wider biological aspect (which has been my main work) will be found in my *Patterns in the Balance of Nature* (London and New York, 1964).

REFERENCES

Williams, C. B. "The Use of Logarithm in the Interpretation of Certain Entomological Problems," *Annals of Applied Biology*, XXIV (1937), 404–414.

————. "Yule's 'Characteristic' and the 'Index of Diversity,' " *Nature*, CLVII (1946), 482.

————. "Statistics as an Aid to Literary Studies," *Science News*, XXIV (1952), 99–106.

————. "Studies in the History of Probability and Statistics IV. A Note on an Early Statistical Study of Literary Style," *Biometrika*, XLIII (1956), 248–256.

————. "Literature and Statistics," *The Listener*, LXXI (1964), 960–961.

————. "Writers, Readers and Arithmetic," *The New Scientist*, XXXV (1967), 88–91.

————. *Literary Style and Vocabulary: Numerical Studies* (London: Charles Griffin & Co., forthcoming).

Yule, G. Udny. "On Sentence-Length as a Statistical Characteristic of Style in Prose, with Application to Two Cases of Disputed Authorship," *Biometrika*. XXX (1938–1939), 363–390.

A NOTE ON SENTENCE-LENGTH AS RANDOM VARIABLE

Kai Rander Buch

In a paper entitled "A Note on the Statistical Analysis of Sentence-Length as a Criterion of Literary Style" C. B. Williams has contributed to the discussion on the interesting problem of how far it is possible to characterize the works of an author by means of statistics.[1] To be precise we can put the question in the following way: Is it possible with *nearly absolute certainty* to decide that a work was *not* written by a certain author? Williams, however, does not go into this last question in the paper mentioned above, but the author calls attention to the fact that this is really the chief question.

For his investigation Williams has counted the number of words in 600 sentences taken from one work by each of the following authors: G. K. Chesterton, G. B. Shaw, and H. G. Wells. Works of nearly the same character have been chosen, and the conversation style has been avoided.

If we do not take the sentence-length z, but *the logarithm of the sentence-length* $x = \log z$ as random variable, all three distributions get a certain likeness to the normal distribution having the probability density

$$y = \frac{1}{\sqrt{2\pi}\,\sigma}\, e^{-\frac{(x-\mu)^2}{2\sigma^2}}$$

which consequently seems to be a characteristic feature of literary style, first noticed by Williams.

In the Table I is given a comparison of certain of the constants found by Williams (on condition that the hypothesis mentioned is valid).

None of the usual tests, however, has been made to investigate whether the hypothesis of normal distribution is acceptable or not. Likewise only little is said about the fact whether the three samples can be thought to belong to the same category or not, which must be regarded as a question of greatest importance.

TABLE I

	Chesterton	Shaw	Wells
Number of sentences	600	600	600
Number of words	15,521	18,735	14,463
Arithmetic mean of words	25.87	31.23	24.11
μ	1.37	1.39	1.31
σ	0.200	0.290	0.237

This essay was presented to the eleventh Skandinaviske Matematiker-kongress, August 1949, and printed in the proceedings of that congress (Oslo, 1952); it is reprinted here by permission of the author.

Before we can consider such mutual comparisons between authors to be right we must (as also Williams remarks) first investigate the works of the authors thoroughly, that is, primarily *through all his periods*. If in the course of time his style undergoes important alterations, the question of the usefulness of statistical methods will naturally be extremely uncertain.

As a small contribution to the solution of this question we have here chosen two works of the Danish author Johannes V. Jensen, published with an interval of about 20 years, viz.: *Den lange Rejse*, which appeared during the years 1908–1922 and is here quoted (1915) and *Myter*, vol. 8 (1940). From either of the two works have been chosen arbitrarily 600 sentences, and the number of words in each of these has been counted. A mention of how the selection of sentences has been made is of no importance in this connection.[2]

Based on the raw material found, with the logarithm of sentence-length as a variable and under the hypothesis of normal distribution the constants of Table II have been found.

TABLE II

	(1915)	(1940)
Number of sentences	600	600
Number of words	21,821	17,802
Arithmetic mean of words	36.37	29.67
μ	1.417	1.358
σ	0.383	0.342

Accordingly the theoretical probability densities should be

(1915)
$$y = \frac{1}{\sqrt{2\pi}\,0.383}\, e^{-\frac{(x-1.417)^2}{2(0.383)^2}}$$

(1940)
$$y = \frac{1}{\sqrt{2\pi}\,0.342}\, e^{-\frac{(x-1.358)^2}{2(0.342)^2}}$$

In the figure these curves have been drawn in the same coordinate system (Fig. 1).

We have, after division into classes, on one of the two sets of material, namely (1915), applied the χ^2-test, and have, corresponding to 16 degrees of freedom found a value — $\chi^2 \sim 45$ — which does not make the correctness of the hypothesis plausible, but naturally does not discard it either. Consequently Fisher's t-test, which supposes normal distribution, is not particularly suitable for comparison of the two sets of material.

Therefore, we have chosen another method, proposed by Smirnoff,[3] which can be applied *independent of the kind of distribution*.

The problem is to investigate whether two samples

$$x_1^{(1)} \leq x_2^{(1)} \leq \cdots \leq x_n^{(1)}$$
$$x_1^{(2)} \leq x_2^{(2)} \leq \cdots \leq x_n^{(2)}$$

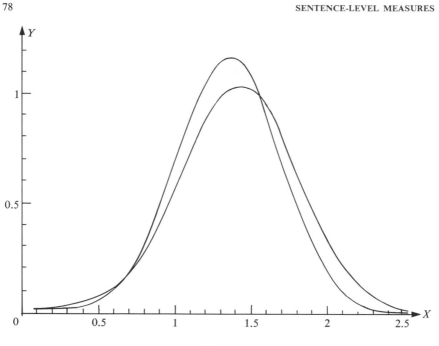

Fig. 1.

belong to the same category or not. For this purpose Smirnoff defines two staircase-lines, $S_{n_1}(x)$, defined by

$$S_{n_1}(x) = \begin{cases} 0 \text{ for } x < x_1^{(1)} \\ \dfrac{k}{n_1} \text{ for } x_k^{(1)} \leqq x < x_{k+1}^{(1)} \\ 1 \text{ for } x_n^{(1)} < x \end{cases}$$

and a corresponding one for $S_{n_2}(x)$. If we introduce the quantity

$$D(n_1, n_2) = \lim_{-\infty < x < \infty} \sup |S_{n_1}(x) - S_{n_2}(x)|$$

it is, on condition that the samples belong to the same category, valid that

$$\text{Prob.}\left\{ D(n_1, n_2) \leqq \lambda \sqrt{\frac{1}{n_1} + \frac{1}{n_2}} \right\} \to \phi(\lambda), \qquad (1)$$

where

$$\phi(\lambda) = \sum_{k=-\infty}^{+\infty} (-1)^k e^{-2k^2\lambda^2},$$

if n_1 and n_2 go to infinity in such a way that their proportion remains constant.

And this is valid *independent* of what distribution the category has.

Our material gives

$$D(600, 600) = 0.107.$$

In a former treatise by Kolmogorov[4] the function $\phi(\lambda)$ has already been investigated, a. o. is found

$$\phi(1.4) = 0.9603.$$

If in the formula (1) we put. $\lambda = 1.4$, $n_1 = n_2 = 600$, we find

$$\text{Prob. } \{D(600, 600) \leq 0.08\} \sim 0.96.$$

Thus it must in this case be said that the author's style in the course of time has undergone so great alterations that no proof can with any certainty be established to the effect that the two samples belong to the same category.

REFERENCES

1. Reprinted in this volume, pp. 69–75.
2. This point is discussed at length by Henning Spang-Hanssen, "Sentence-Length and Statistical Linguistics," in *Structures and Quanta* (New York, 1963), pp. 58–73. Eds.
3. N. Smirnoff, "On the Estimation of the Discrepancy between Empirical Curves of Distribution for Two Independent Samples," *Bulletin Mathématiques de l'université de Moscou, Série Internationale*, II, ii (1939), 1–16.
4. A. Kolmogorov, "Sulla determinazione empirica di una legge di distribuzione," *Giornali dell'Instituto Italiano degli Attuari*, IV (1933), 83–91.

A STUDY IN PROSE STYLES:
EDWARD GIBBON AND ERNEST HEMINGWAY

CURTIS W. HAYES

INTRODUCTION

This paper is in part an exercise in the analysis of prose style and in part an abstract of a larger study that I made on the prose style of Edward Gibbon.[1] In that study I pointed out that sensitive readers of literature have certain stylistic "intuitions" that enable them to identify certain familiar authors. For instance, if two extracts from the authors chosen for this study, Edward Gibbon and Ernest Hemingway, were given to these readers they would have little difficulty in determining their authorship. This intuitive ability may not, I believe, be adequately accounted for by the more familiar approaches to stylistic analysis. By "more familiar" I mean the school of literary criticism that attaches impressionistic labels to prose styles. For example, Hemingway's style in the more familiar stylistic analysis has been described as "simple," "direct," and sometimes "linear." Gibbon's style, which is intuitively more complex than Hemingway's, has been labeled as "grand" and "majestic."

These labels, however, do not describe style, but rather mirror an impression one receives when reading extracts from these two authors. The analysis must go beyond the mere tagging of impressionistic labels to prose styles. It is the analyst's job to account for these subjective impressions. I believe that recent developments in linguistic science, particularly the development of the transformational/generative concept of syntax, is an invaluable aid in formalizing the notion of what one means when he attaches descriptive labels to prose styles.

Generative grammarians have in recent publications stated the inherent advantages of a generative/transformational model for representing syntax.[2] In particular they maintain that a generative grammar following the Chomskian model would have the ability to generate (a better term would be enumerate) all the well-formed sentences of a language and would be able, further, to provide a deep structural description for each. Since in great part the impression that a sensitive reader perceives from a given work rests upon the types of syntactical processes that an author uses, it would seem that the theory and methods of generative grammarians might lend themselves to the explication of literary style. The following study is thus an experiment in the applied use of generative grammar and reflects the thesis, already implicitly stated, that such a grammar is a "powerful" and valuable tool in analyzing literary style.[3]

For the purpose of this paper style may be defined as a characteristic,

This essay is reprinted slightly abridged from *Texas Studies in Literature and Language*, VII (1966), 371–386, by permission of the author and the editor of the journal.

habitual, and recurrent use of the transformational apparatus of language. Whatever is "characteristic, habitual, and recurrent" must be, moreover, amenable to statistical measurement. There are certain transformations (statistical attributes) in Gibbon's style, for example, that can be measured and these transformations can be compared to those of another writer. In this sense, the study of style is a study of the complexity of sentences.

The basic unit of description in this paper is the textual sentence. Here defined, a textual sentence corresponds to the "institutionalized" sentence: that is, any body of material occurring between one period or question mark and the following one. Textual sentences are not always simple or kernel sentences, but are often complex sentences, which have been generated from two or more underlying source sentences. It is best to consider the ultimate textual sentence (the one which appears after the final transformation) a composite of two types of source sentences. The matrix (independent) sentence forms the overall pattern, the frame, of the ultimate sentence. Those sentences which are embedded, nested, or added to the matrix sentence are the constituent (dependent) sentences. This view of matrix and constituent sentence, Robert B. Lees says, "makes essential use of the notion that part of the syntactic structure of a sentence is the set of underlying, sometimes very abstract, representatives of the simple sentences from which it may be said to be derived by explicit grammatical rules called transformations."4

Textual sentence: The boy who is wearing the cap is my brother.
Matrix: The boy is my brother.
Constituent: The boy is wearing the cap.

The constituent sentence, *the boy is wearing the cap*, is embedded in the matrix sentence by the use of an "explicit grammatical rule," the relative-clause transformation.

TRANSFORMATIONS

The following transformational rules (one-string and two-string), though not complete, provide the descriptive framework for describing an author's style. The rules in pure form are complex, but for the purpose of this paper I have simplified them.5

A. The passive transformation takes an active sentence and transforms it into the passive voice:

Nom+X-Vtr-Nom'-Y→Nom'+be+En-Vtr-by-Nom
    Nom=Nominal
    Vtr=any transitive verb
    En=past participle inflection
    X, Y=symbols included to cover material which may appear after Nom, Nom', such as post-nominal modifiers
    ──→="rewrite" (convert the left-hand symbol into the right-hand representation of that symbol)

Sentence: Mary called Joy $\longrightarrow$ Joy was called by Mary.
The agent *by Mary* can be optionally deleted:
Sentence: Joy was called by Mary $\longrightarrow$ Joy was called.

B. Certain transformations called *Generalized Transformations* involve the manipulation of two or more strings (sentences). The *Nominalizing Transformation* is just one type of generalized transformation.

Nominalizing transformation T_{to} (Infinitive)
Nominalizing transformation T_{ing} (Gerund)

These rules convert a sentence having the structure $NP+VP$ into a noun phrase of the form $to+VP$ or $ing+VP$. These "crippled" sentences may then be embedded into the nominal slot of the matrix sentence.

-ing+VP (Gerundive Nominal)
Textual sentence: John enjoys playing the piano.

$$\overset{1}{}\qquad\overset{2}{}$$
Matrix: (John enjoys)+(Nominal:it)

$$\overset{3}{}\qquad\overset{4}{}$$
Constituent: (John+Tns+Be:) (-ing+play the piano).

Transformation: $\left.\begin{array}{c} 1+2 \\ \\ 3+4 \end{array}\right\} \longrightarrow 1+4 \longrightarrow$ John enjoys playing the
$$\text{piano.}$$

to+VP (Infinitival Nominal)
Textual sentence: I asked him to play the piano.

$$\overset{1}{}$$
Matrix: (I asked him)

$$\overset{2}{}\qquad\overset{3}{}$$
Constituent: (He+Tns)+(play the piano).

Transformation: $\left.\begin{array}{c} 1 \\ \\ 2+3 \end{array}\right\} \longrightarrow 1+\text{to-}3 \longrightarrow$ I asked him to play the
$$\text{piano.}$$

The final Nominalizing Transformation to be explicated is the *Factive Nominal*. The rules which generate factive nominals will handle the following constructions.

Subject: that clause

$$\overset{1}{}\qquad\overset{2}{}$$
(Nominal:it)+(was evident)

$$\overset{3}{}$$
(He did it)

Transformation: $\left.\begin{array}{c} 1+2 \\ \\ 3 \end{array}\right\} \longrightarrow \text{that-}3+2 \longrightarrow$ *That he did it*
$$\text{was evident.}$$

Subject: question-word clause

        1   2
    (Nominal)+(was a surprise)
        3   4
    (He went)+(there)
      Transformation: 1+2⎤
                          ⎬——→ where-3+2 ——→ *Where he went*
                       3+4⎦   was a surprise.

"Non-Action" Verb Object

        1   2
    (I know)+(Nominal: it)
        3
    (He did it)
      Transformation: 1+2⎤
                          ⎬——→ 1+that-3——→ I know *that he did it.*
                       3⎦

A sentence (NP+VP) may fill an adverb slot and the process is known as "adverbialization." For example, in the sentence, *he killed the man*+(*Adv*), the *Adv* slot may be filled by either a single lexical item, a phrase, or by a clause (a "crippled" sentence):

He killed the man+(quickly)
He killed the man+(in the dark)
He killed the man+(while the city burned)

The constituent sentence which fills the *Adv* slot in sentence three is embedded through these operations:

              1   2
Matrix: (He killed the man)+(Adv)
Constituent: (the city burned).
      Transformation: 1+2⎤
                          ⎬——→1+while-3 (Right-branching)
                       3⎦

The constituent sentence and its slot may be optionally permuted to sentence-initial position (left-branching):

While the city burned, he killed the man.

Or the construction may be self-embedded.

He, *while the city burned*, killed the man.

The *Relative Clause Transformation* is an adjective-transformation. Some linguists believe that prenominal adjectivals are ultimately derived from the reduction of the relative-clause construction. The *red* of *the red house*, they posit, can be derived in the following way:

the house is red $\longrightarrow$ the house which is red $\longrightarrow$ the house red $\longrightarrow$ the red house.

Other linguists, who combine the transformational and tagmemic approaches, would not hold to the notion that a phrase such as *the red house* may be derived from any kind of sentence in which the word *red* appears in predicate position. Archibald A. Hill, for example, points out that the two approaches—tagmemic and transformational—seem to be falling together, in that the transformational grammarians are accepting the notion of slots for modifiers which can occur before the noun. This avoids the necessity of assuming (at least in this paper) that *the red house was burned down* is anything more than a slot with a filler in it, whereas *the house was burned down* has the same slot but has left it empty.[6] In this paper adjectives will not be considered as being derived from the reduction of relative clauses.

The relative-clause transformation involves these processes:

$$1 \qquad\qquad 2$$
Matrix: (The boy)+(is my brother)

$$3 \qquad\qquad 4$$
Constituent: (The boy)+(is here)

$$\text{Transformation:} \quad \left.\begin{array}{c}1+2\\[1em]3+4\end{array}\right\} \longrightarrow 1+\text{WH-}4+2$$

$$5 \qquad\qquad 6 \qquad\qquad 7$$
Result: (The boy)+(who is)+(here is my brother)
Deletion (ellipsis): $5+6+7 \longrightarrow 5+7 \longrightarrow$ The boy here is my brother.

The additive process (in essence, a transformational expansion) is signaled by a coordinate conjunction. The entire process may be called *addition: expansion of X slot*. There are various types of slot expansions that a speaker or a writer may perform: he may conjoin sentences:

$$\left.\begin{array}{c}S^1\\[1em]S^2\end{array}\right\} \longrightarrow S^1+\text{conjunction: and/but/or}+S^2$$

There are other possibilities of slot expansions. For instance, one may do as Gibbon habitually does and employ the following transformational expansions:

$$\left.\begin{array}{c}N\\[1em]N\end{array}\right\} \longrightarrow N+\text{conj}+N$$

$$\left.\begin{array}{l} \text{NP} \\ \text{NP} \end{array}\right\} \longrightarrow \text{NP} + \text{conj.} + \text{NP}$$

$$\left.\begin{array}{l} \text{V} \\ \text{V} \end{array}\right\} \longrightarrow \text{V} + \text{conj.} + \text{V}$$

$$\left.\begin{array}{l} \text{VP} \\ \text{VP} \end{array}\right\} \longrightarrow \text{VP} + \text{conj} + \text{VP}$$

$$\left.\begin{array}{l} \text{Prep Phrase} \\ \text{Prep Phrase} \end{array}\right\} \longrightarrow \text{PP} + \text{conj} + \text{PP}$$

If the expansion includes only two lexical items (e.g., Caesarea was *plundered and burnt* by the licentious barbarians), then the constituents which fill the slot are referred to by the generic name, *doublet*.

STATISTICAL METHODS

A linguist when selecting a corpus of linguististic material for analysis takes from that corpus a sample that he hopes will be typical and representative. He does this because a corpus is often too large for individual analysis. Sampling is an economical procedure and it is particularly necessary in this paper, since it would be uneconomical to analyze each sentence in *The Decline and Fall*. Each sample should be tested for reliability. To test for reliability a linguist employs the following statistical formula:[7]

A. *Reliability:* Standard Error $=\sqrt{PQ/N}$

P equals the proportion (frequency) of one of the items being counted; Q equals the absence of that item. $P+Q=100\%$. N is the total number of items counted. For example, assume that 70 sentences contain a given stylistic device, while 30 sentences do not. In that event,

$$SE = \sqrt{\frac{.70 \times .30}{100}}$$
$$= \sqrt{.21}$$
$$= 4.5\%$$

If the *SE* should exceed 5%, more items must be selected to reduce the error.

Earlier I posited that style is in part a habitual and characteristic use of the transformational apparatus of one's language. To determine whether a defined stylistic device (transformation) is characteristic of one author in comparison to another author, a linguist must test for statistical significance. In a randomly chosen sample suppose he finds that in author X 70 sentences out of 100 contain doublets, while in author Y the doublet is found in only 60 sentences. He wants to determine whether these two proportions (frequencies) can be said to belong to the same population (*no* statistical significance) or to belong to different populations (statistical significance). To test for significance, a linguist employs these formulas:

B. *Significance:* $P = \dfrac{N_1 P_1 + N_2 P_2}{N_1 + N_2}$

The value P is simply the proportion for the two samples combined. That is, 130 of the 200 sentences contain doublets.

$$P = \frac{100 \times .60 + 100 \times .70}{100 + 100}$$
$$= 130/200$$
$$= .65$$

With the above information the sampling variance (the Standard Error of the difference between two proportions) may be calculated:

$$\sigma P_1 \text{-} P_2 = \sqrt{\frac{PQ + PQ}{N_1 + N_2}}$$
$$= \sqrt{\frac{.65 \times .35 + .65 \times .35}{100 + 100}}$$
$$= \sqrt{.00455}$$

= .675 (Standard Error of the Difference between two proportions)

The *actual* difference between the two proportions is .10 (.70 − .60 = .10).

$$\text{Significance in Standard Errors} = \frac{\text{Actual difference}}{\text{SE difference between two proportions}}$$
$$= \frac{.10}{.675}$$
$$= 1.48 \text{ Standard Errors}$$

Consultation of a probability table shows that deviations of this size (1.48) are expected to occur by chance alone in 13.88% of the samples. The difference between the proportions is, therefore, not significant. A percentage of probability above 5.0% is usually taken by statisticians to denote a *chance* deviation; a factor other than chance is responsible if the percentage of probability is below 5.0%; e.g., if the SE is 1.96 or more, the difference between the proportions is significant at the 5.0% level. Anything less than 1.96 denotes that the Standard Error is non-significant.

RESULTS OF ANALYSIS AND STATISTICAL COMPARISON

What follow are the result of this analysis and a comparison of the types of transformations that Gibbon and Hemingway employ. This is done in an effort to determine whether statistical significance exists in Gibbon's use of a specific transformation compared to Hemingway's use of the same transformation. The attributes (transformations) are in the left-hand column, the frequency of the transformation is in the center column, and significance is noted in the right-hand column.

ATTRIBUTE	Gibbon	Hemingway	Standard Errors
Transformations per sentence	4.3	1.3	— —
Sentences undergone GT	98%	60%	SE= 6.5
Passive	68%	2%	9.48
Doublet	68%	8%	9.0
Sentences containing only one doublet	40%	8%	—
Sentences containing 2 doublets	18%	0%	—
Sentences containing 3 doublets	7%	0%	—
Sentences containing 4 doublets	1%	0%	—
Sentences containing 5 doublets	2%	0%	—
Total # of doublets	111	8	—
#N doublets	64	4	—
# Adj doublets	33	4	—
# V doublets	13	0	—
# Adv doublets	1	0	—
NP expansions	16%	0%	—
VP expansions	14%	28%	SE= 2.6
PP expansions	7%	2%	1.7
Factive Nominal Expansions	2	0	—
% of S which have doublet expansions	79%	36%	SE= 6.0
Triplet	14%	4%	2.5
# N expansions (triplet)	4	2	—
# NP expansions	2	0	—
# V expansions	2	0	—
# VP expansions	3	0	—
# Adj expansions	0	2	—
# PP expansions	2	0	—
# Factive Nominal expansions	1	0	—
Quadruplet	3	0	—
# N expansions	1	0	—
# NP expansions	1	0	—
# Factive Nominal expansions	1	0	—
Nominalizations	49%	22%	SE= 4.0
Infinitival Nominal	31%	9%	3.9
Total Number	37	10	—
S containing 1 Infinitival	25	8	—
S containing 2 Infinitivals	6	1	—
Gerundive Nominal	16%	4%	— 2.8
Factive Nominal	19%	13%	1.17
Embedding			
# S which have embedded elements	64%	20%	6.3
Total # of embedded structures	105	24	—
# S containing 1 embedded structure	36	16	—

(continued)

ATTRIBUTE	Gibbon	Hemingway	Standard Errors
# S containing 2 embedded structures	18	4	—
# S containing 3 embedded structures	7	0	—
# S containing 4 embedded structures	3	0	—
S having Rel. Cl. structures	51%	8%	7.0
Total # of RC structures	77	10	
S having 1 RC	30	6	—
S having 2 RC	16	2	—
S having 3 RC	5	0	—
Types of Branching			
Right Branching	26	4	—
Deleted Right Branching	14	4	—
Self Embedded	19	0	—
Deleted Self Embedded	17	2	—
S having *Adv Clause* structures	23%	12%	2.0
Total # Adv Clauses	28	14	—
S containing 1 AC	19	10	—
S containing 2 AC	3	2	—
S containing 3 AC	1	0	—
Types of Branching			
Right Branching	9	8	—
Deleted Right Branching	2	0	—
Left Branching	12	4	—
Deleted Left Branching	1	2	—
Self Embedded	4	2	—
Additive Process: Expansion of S Slot			
% of S which are expansions	68%	32%	5.1
S having 2 conjoined S	41	30	—
S having 3 conjoined S	18	1	—
S having 4 conjoined S	9	0	—

The table indicates what we already knew intuitively, that the styles of Gibbon and Hemingway are different—that the style of Gibbon is "grand," "majestic," "complex," and that the style of Hemingway in comparison is "simple." The importance of the tables, however, is that they offer us an objective measure to "capture" this intuition. In other words, we may use the table as a tool to show the reasons behind our intuition. Instead of basing our analysis on subjective impressions and using opaque terminology to describe these impressions, we may say exactly how two styles differ. Generative grammar is important to the literary analyst for that reason: it offers him a device through which objective statements can be made about style. For instance, he can say that the style of Gibbon is more complex than that of Hemingway, since the number of transformations per sentence is an indication of that complexity. This is further indicated by the number of sentences having embedded structures (relative clauses, adverbial clauses), nested structures (nominalizations), and expanded structures within them. Rarely are there transformational expansions or embedded structures within Hemingway's sentences.

It is traditional to say that Gibbon's style is characteristically balanced. The table shows the degree of this parallelism. Not only can we say that Gibbon uses a high degree of parallel structures, we can also say something about the kinds of parallel structures. We can say that the number of doublet expansions in Gibbon far exceeds those found in Hemingway; and that there are other types of balanced structures in addition to the two-membered balanced entity (for example, the balanced noun phrases, verb phrases, and prepositional phrases). In sum, the table enables us to make exact descriptions of each author's style.

The following is a statistical summation of the transformations counted. The list is graded from most significant (the passive) to least significant (adverbial clause) to non-significant.

	Significance in Standard Errors
Passive Transformation	9.48
Doublet	9.0
Infinitival Nominal	8.9
Relative-clause transformation	7.0
S having undergone transformation	6.5
% of S having embedded structures	6.3
% of S having doublet expansions	6.0
S which are additive	5.1
% of S having Nominalizations	4.0
Gerundive Nominal	2.8
VP expansion	2.6
S having 3 conjoined S	2.5
Adverbial Clause	2.0
Transformations which did not show statistical significance (below 1.96)	
Prepositional Phrase Expansion	1.7
Factive Nominal	1.17

CONCLUSION

Explicit in this paper has been the hypothesis that a generative/transformational grammar based upon the Chomskian model is an extremely effective and useful tool in capturing the notion of style; and, further, that the transformations which an author employs to express content is a significant part of what a reader perceives as literary style. This hypothesis stems from the notion that speakers (and thus writers) may employ various and different models (sentence types) to express relatively the same content. That is, an author theoretically has an option at each linguistic situation. Whether an author, for example, generates *John hit the ball* or *the ball was hit by John* is a linguistic choice. To be more specific, whether an author habitually generates sentences in the passive voice, as Gibbon does, or whether he prefers the active voice, as Hemingway does, is an alternative which the language provides. Notice that a choice in this sense is not a lexical choice but a choice of a transformational rule.

In brief, a transformational/generative grammar has the power to differentiate different styles. As transformationalists are fond of saying, their grammar formalizes the notion of how complex sentences are produced and the manner in which complex sentences are related to simple source sentences. The amount of complexity, it follows, is an indication of how an author employs the rules of his language; and by breaking down ("rewriting") sentences into their kernel components and by specifying the types of grammatical transformations used to construct the ultimate textual sentence, one may arrive at the degree of complexity, which, I have maintained, is one indication of an author's style.

Since complexity is only one indication of style, the complexity in Gibbon's sentences may not differ from the complexity in the sentences of similar authors, say Samuel Johnson and David Hume. In that case, if one may hypothesize, the difference, if there is any, may exist on other levels (imagery, metaphor, etc.).

After making these strong claims for the efficacy of a transformational model in literary analysis, it is perhaps self-defeating to point out that this method is not a panacea for correcting the ills of past stylistic analyses. With this in mind, it would be perhaps helpful to state what this study has accomplished and what the limitations of such a study are. First, the study as presented is an attempt toward capturing the elusive notion of literary style. Yet, as pointed out, style exists at all levels, not merely at the syntactical level; and certainly style exists beyond the sentence, say in the realm of imagery. This study in other words, has not exhausted the possibilities of discovering the inherent differences in Hemingway's and Gibbon's styles. Nothing, for example, has been said about their respective vocabularies. Certainly Gibbon's vocabulary is more latinate than Hemingway's; and this is a distinctive difference. Moreover, a transformational study could be deeper in some respects: for example, in pointing to the position of adjectives. Gibbon's adjectives, which usually occur in attributive position, could be compared to Hemingway's adjectives, which normally occur in predicate position. To conclude, the importance of this type of analysis is that the intuitively felt differences between two differing styles can at least be explained by the types (and frequencies) of transformations that each author exploys in constructing his sentences.

REFERENCES

1. See my study, "A Linguistic Analysis of the Prose Style of Edward Gibbon," unpublished dissertation (University of Texas, 1964).
2. For example, see Paul Postal, "Constituent Structure: A Study of Contemporary Models of Syntactic Description," *International Journal of American Linguistics*, XXX, Part 3 (January, 1964), 1 ff.

3. The motivation for such a study has been clearly stated by Richard Ohmann, "Generative Grammars and the Concept of Literary Style," *Word*, XX (December, 1964), 423–439. See also James P. Thorne, "Stylistics and Generative Grammars," *Journal of Linguistics*, I (April, 1965), 49–59.

4. "The Promise of Transformational Grammar," *English Journal*, LII (1963), 330.

5. The reader may wish to examine the formal and more detailed rules of transformational grammar. I suggest that he consult the works of Noam Chomsky, especially *Syntactic Structures* ('s–Gravenhage, 1957) and *Aspects of the Theory of Syntax* (Cambridge, Mass. 1965); Robert B. Lees, especially his "Grammar of English Nominalizations," *International Journal of American Linguistics*, XXVI, Part 2 (1960; revised, March, 1961); and Carlotta A. Smith, "A Class of Complex Modifiers in English," *Language*, XXXVII (July–September, 1961), 342–365, and "Determiners and Relative Clauses in a Generative Grammar of English," *Language*, XXXX (January–March, 1964), 37–52.

6. Professor Archibald Hill made this suggestion in a paper delivered before the Linguistic Society of America, December, 1964.

7. A complete account of the statistical methods incorporated in this paper can be found in publications by David W. Reed. See his "The History of Inflectional *n* in English Verbs before 1500," *University of California Publications in English*, VII, iv (1950), especially pp. 172–180, and "A Statistical Approach to Quantitative Linguistic Analysis," *Word*, V (December, 1949), 235–247.

IV
POETICS

MATHEMATICAL ASPECTS OF THE THEORY OF VERSE

Jiří Levý

When we meet in life or in art a complex of elements in which the individual elements or the relationships among them occur more frequently than they would at random, we begin to consider this ordering a *tendency toward style* and the complex itself a *structure*. If we find four trees standing in a row, we consider this line an unexpected, non-random order of the elements in the plane; four such lines arranged in the form of a square would be an even greater deviation from a random order: we have now not an *element* of an ornament, but a simple ornamental *figure* before us. When examining a structure, we try—no matter whether consciously or unconsciously—to find the complex of the simplest elements and to compare their arrangement (i.e., their *frequency and distribution*) with the non-artistic order of this complex.

Therefore, it is not surprising to find the first systematic application of mathematical methods in those schools that made the first radical attempt to analyze formal structures in literature: those of the Russian *formalists* and the Czech (and Polish) *structuralists*. Because of this development—whose further cultural and historical aspects cannot be discussed here—it is especially in the more or less secluded area of some Slavonic literatures, which are not particularly well known in Western Europe, where the mathematical analysis of verse has a tradition richest in theory and material.

The development of the mathematical analysis of verse began in 1910 with the book of the Russian poet and critic, A. Belyj, *Symbolism* (*Simvolizm*, Moskva, 1910). In this book, the program of a systematic, statistical examination of the structure of verse was formulated. It is necessary "to compile tables: (1) of the meters of the individual poets, (2) of their rhythmic peculiarities, (3) of their rhymes, assonances, alliterations, etc., (4) of their punctuation, (5) of their verse forms, and (6) of their figures of speech."[1] Belyj's statistical investigations inspired a whole group of verse statisticians, the so-called circle. (The idea of a research team studying statistical data in comparative Slavonic prosody was recently reintroduced by a group of Czech and Polish prosodists.) But even the first detailed application of mathematics in the analysis of verse unfortunately led to various fantastic deductions in the interpretation of the objective data. For instance, Belyj connected phonologically unrealized metrical stresses in successive lines to construct various geometrical ornaments (triangles, rhombs, etc.). In his book, *Rhythm as*

From *Mathematik und Dichtung: Versuche zur Frage einer exakten Literaturwissenschaft*, edited by Helmut Kreuzer and Rul Gunzenhäuser and published by Nymphenburger Verlagshandlung GmbH., München (second edition, 1967). The essay is reprinted here by permission of the publisher; we wish to thank Mr. Karl Ortseifen for his help in making the translation.

95

Dialectics (*Ritm kak dialektika*, Moskva, 1929), this playing with figures reached its highpoint.

But as early as 1923, two fundamental works by Russian formalists on the mathematical analysis of verse appeared. In his book *Treatise on Verse* (*Traktat o stikhe*, Moskva-Petrograd, 1923), Georgij Šengeli published statistical data on the frequency of Russian word classes and the rhythmical variations of verse, as well as numerous statistics on the vocabulary of the individual metrical forms. In his treatise *The Technique of Verse* (*Tekhnika stikha*, Moskva, 1960), he investigated the possible rhythmic combinations that can be established from this material. In the book *Iambic Pentameter in Puškin* (*Pjatistopnyj jam Puškina*, Berlin, 1923), Boris Tomaševskij gave a brilliant example of an interpretation of rhythmic statistics in the restricted field of Puškin's iambic pentameter. Moreover, it was the first comprehensive calculation of the combinatory possibilities of the stanza, of rhyme, of the probability of the succession of like rhythmic variants, etc. It is surprising that his calculations of verse combinations and the transitional probabilities did not have a successor for almost forty years. Only in recent years have the group around the Soviet mathematician A. N. Kolmogorov—in particular, A. Kondratov in *Mathematics and Poetry* (*Matematika i poezija*, Moskva, 1962)—continued investigations of that kind.

Using the statistical method developed by Belyj and Tomaševskij, the Yugoslav scientist Kiril Taranovski examined the development of Russian iambic and trochaic verse (*Ruski dvodelni ritmovi* I–II, Beograd, 1953). A specific variant of the statistical method was developed by the Czech structuralists and applied to research in the history of Old Czech verse (Roman Jakobson), of Modern Czech verse (Jan Mukařovský), of Slovak verse (Mikuláš Bakoš), and of the comparative characteristics of Czech and Polish verse (Josef Hrabák), etc. The Czech structuralists did not develop new mathematical methods, but they deserve great praise for the phonological and aesthetic interpretation of the statistical results—as had been already demonstrated by the Russian formalist, Roman Jakobson (who had moved to Czechoslovakia, and then, on the eve of World War II, found refuge in the U.S.A., where he initiated further developments in quantitative linguistics at the Massachusetts Institute of Technology). With their concept of marked and unmarked features in linguistics and of "actualization" in aesthetics, the Czech structuralists came close to the stochastic view of the problems of style. Let us quote an impartial observer: "The work of the Prague School on stylistics bears certain resemblances to the view that style is connected with frequency-distribution and transitional probabilities. According to Havránek and Mukařovský, linguistic elements in ordinary communicative messages are, as a rule, automatized, whereas in poetry they are deautomatized, or foregrounded. . . . We can thus say that automatized linguistic elements are elements that occur with high-order probability and are hence to that extent redundant. Foregrounding is thus a function of transitional probability, one in which the linguistic element is of a low-order probability in its occurrence in the particular sentence. Notice that foregrounding implies a comparison with automatized messages."[2]

Today, comprehensive statistical data and the experience in interpretation gained by Slavic scientists are available for evaluation with modern mathematical methods. This is particularly valuable, since after all the starting point of every mathematical calculation of structures and processes is in the empirically and statistically established frequency of the elements of language (phonemes, rhythmic work types, etc.). But we do not have this material for many languages, and therefore we must rely in this study on non-German material from time to time.

In my opinion, the mathematical examination of verse is of particular cognitive importance. We have to deal in verse with apparently discrete units (sounds, syllables, etc.), with a limited number of qualities (long, short, positional length; stressed, unstressed, secondary stress). Therefore, a mathematical calculation of structure is quite possible, and it is to be expected that we shall soon be in a position to describe the literary structure of poetry through exact methods and to explain its aesthetic effect by means of a psychological experiment. Because of this expectation, we now want to make some remarks on the quantitative investigation of verse.

THE SOUND STRUCTURE OF VERSE

The elementary units of human speech are the phonemes. When they appear in a non-random order—that is, when some of them are repeated more frequently than the average frequency in common speech indicates— *sequential sound effects* are created:

Muse ruft zu Bach und Tal

From an examination of the sound sequence, a geometrical pattern seems to offer itself. We see a scheme of two pairs of vowels symmetrically divided by the caesura (the two unstressed *u*-sounds can be considered as connecting links of the two pairs):

$$u \quad u \quad / \quad a \quad a$$
$$u \qquad\qquad u$$

But in reality, the literary critic is a victim of an optical illusion. The sound structure of the line—unlike the optical figure—does not have an effect as a whole, but as a temporal sequence of phonemes and prosodic (supra-segmental) qualities. What we perceive is the cyclical repetition of the same relationship among several layers of this complex language stream: u+stress—another configuration—u+stress—another configuration—a+stress—another configuration—a+stress. The effect of this sound sequence resides in the following phenomenon: (a) the *frequency* of the vowels u and a is higher than was to be anticipated statistically (their combined frequency in these six syllables should be about 25% and not 100%), (b) their *distribution* is not random (we would expect them to be irregularly distributed among stressed and unstressed syllables). The euphonic effect of this sound sequence is conditioned (at least partially) by the relationship of the frequency and the distribution of its language elements to the "normal," stochastic frequency and distribution.

It was determined that the "euphonic quality of a certain sound is not only dependent on the number of repetitions, but also on its relative frequency in comparison to its normal frequency."[3] Since the g-sound in German is less frequent than the s-sound (5.70% and 3.15%), it is to be expected that the alliteration in the second half of the following line is more striking than the first:

Wir singen und sagen vom Grafen so gern

However, one must consider that relative frequency is only one of the factors that influence the expressiveness of a sound sequence, as the following example shows:

Über allen Gipfeln
Ist Ruh,
In allen Wipfeln
Spürest du
Kaum einen Hauch.

Although *ü*, *a*, and *u* each occur twice, the repetition of *ü* and *u* is more expressive for several qualitative and quantitative reasons:

(a) the *a*-sound in German is 10 times more frequent (6.08%) than *ü* (0.64%) and is also more frequent than *u* (4.04%).

(b) *ü* and *u* are more striking phonetically than *a* (at least in some respects).

(c) *ü* and *u* appear here more frequently in prominent positions (*ü* stands emphatically at the beginning of the line, and *u* appears in the end-rhyme). For these reasons, the vowels *e* and *i* are the least expressive components in the vowel instrumentation of these lines, though they do occur most frequently.[4]

At this point in our consideration of the quantitative conditioning of the aesthetic function of linguistic elements, we must emphasize the fact that this conditioning remains valid only within certain limits that are mainly determined by *memory*. We can hardly claim that there are any effects if, for instance, in a sequence of sounds, the *f*-sound is repeated in every twenty-fifth position, or if it is distributed in odd-numbered positions, or organized after the prime numbers, although all these causes would mean a striking deviation from the normal distribution. On the other hand, it is likely that even in a stochastically organized text two words with initial *b* will occur within one phrase, for example, among the thousands of words in *Thus Spake Zarathustra*, "Baum und Berg." This combination is nevertheless understood as alliteration, that is, a stylistic arrangement. *Thus Spake Zarathustra* is not acoustically present as a whole in the memory of the reader. In the realm of sound instrumentation, the extent of the segments most intensely felt to be wholes reaches from a word to a phrase. In the realm of stylistic syntactic phenomena (parallelism, etc.), the extent of these segments ranges to several paragraphs. Only motifs, plot development, etc., find their function in the work as a whole. The proper application of statistical methods then demands —besides the necessary statistical data—an investigation into the *structure of literary perception*, but above all, it demands a determination of the *maximal and minimal psychically realizable complexes.*

The common methods in literary criticism can only determine the conspicuous repetitions of sounds. But the general organization of all sounds contained in a text likewise contributes to the euphony or cacaphony of a poem. As a rule, there are two extreme cases of "normal" or "average" distribution of language (and other) elements possible in a literary work:

(A) regular distribution of the elements at intervals which come close to the median value (abababababab).

(B) irregular distribution whose average interval can be the same as in (A), but whose actual intervals show great variety (abbaaababbb).

The arrangement of type A is idealized; the tendency toward such an arrangement could be the reason for some verses flowing "fluently" or "melodically," although there is no organization of a sound sequence perceivable at first glance. These two extremes, by the way, also have a more general cognitive importance. The idealization of reality against its naturalistic imitation, the Aristotelian conception of probability against the non-Aristotelian, etc.

Modern mathematics can measure the extent to which the organization of sound tends toward type A or type B by means of Shannon's formula for *entropy*:[5]

(a) the greater the difference between the frequencies of the individual phonemes, the smaller the entropy of the first order (H_1);

(b) the farther the phoneme distribution deviates from type A, the smaller is the limit entropy ($H\infty$).

According to the calculation of L. Doležel,[6] we find the following entropy values in Czech texts:

	Verse	Prose
H_1	4.5722	4.5919–4.7044
$H\infty$	1.9115	0.7034–1.7126

I. Fónagy[7] found analogous results for Hungarian. Corresponding results in calculating entropy for several languages lead us to such general conclusions as the following: The small entropy of the first order suggests that rare sounds (letters) are even rarer in poetry than in prose and that the dominance of the most frequent sounds becomes even more striking in verse. Verse makes more use of the typical sounds of a given language and suppresses the rare ones.

Even in the relatively simple field of the phonetic structure of verse, mathematical calculations have been made recently whose importance for the study of literature and their aesthetic relevance will eventually reveal their full impact, particularly once whole structures have been calculated instead of just isolated components.

RHYME

Mathematical considerations are particularly useful in the theory of rhyme. The quantitative principle of rhyme is conspicuous. If, for instance, lines like

> Und doch versagt mir der Entschluss
> Sie anzugehen mit meinem Gruss,

were in prose, the second line could theoretically end with any masculine or neuter noun, or any adjective or other word class—thousands of German words. The semantic context limits this selection, but still, a large number of possibilities remains. But since we are dealing with the end of an iambic line, the possibilities are limited to monosyllabic words—the frequency or probability of which is 0.5% in the German vocabulary. And since furthermore we have to do with rhyming lines, the respective word has to end with -*us*—that is, it must be one of the words in the rhyme group *Gruss, Kuss, Nuss, Schluss, Schuss*, etc. This limiting pressure of form—and the meaning for form lies in the *limitation of choice*—can be expressed in mathematical terms. The fragment of the vocabulary that is at the poet's disposal equals the product of three factors: probability of occurrence of the permissible word class, probability of a monosyllabic word, and probability of the like-sound -*us*. In Czech, where we have pertinent statistical material,[8] the calculation for a monosyllabic masculine noun ending with -*us*[9] has this result:

$$0.28 \quad \cdot \quad 0.47 \quad \cdot \quad 0.26 \quad \cdot \quad 0.0015 = 0.00007 \text{ of the vocabulary}$$
$$\text{noun} \qquad \text{masc.} \qquad \text{monosyllable} \qquad \textit{-us}$$

In German this limitation will scarcely differ in order, and it is therefore natural that only the word *Gruss* and some others can stand in the position discussed.

From the aspect of rhyme, the vocabulary of every language is divisible into a certain number (*n*) of rhyme groups, which differ in every language:

SCHEME A

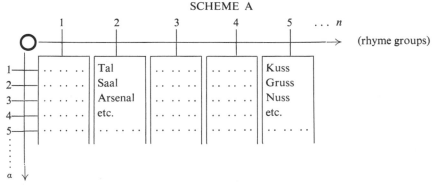

members of the rhyme groups

The number of *lexical units* is equal to the number of entry words in a complete dictionary of the respective language, and their number is 10^4 to 10^5 in the European languages. The number of monosyllabic rhyme groups (n) is equal to the number of phonetically different ending syllables in the respective language; in English it is about 400, in German and French about 600, in Czech it is more than 700 (for monosyllabic rhymes). The number of the members (a) of the individual rhyme groups is different and varies between one (in the case of words that cannot rhyme—J. Minor, for instance, names the words *Apfel, Mensch, Tochter* as non-rhyming words in German) and several thousand words (French rhyming dictionaries list thousands of rhymes with -*er*, about 1,200 rhymes with -*ment*; Peregrinus Syntax lists about 5,000 German rhymes with -*er*).

Moreover, not only the basic forms of the lexical units can rhyme, but also the inflected forms of the words: *Grusses, Grusse, Grüsse, Grüssen*. Therefore, we likewise find rhyme connections between those words which belong to different rhyme groups in their basic forms:

SCHEME B

↑	↑					
Wüste	Verlust	*Gruss* →	*Grusse*	→	*Grüsse* →	
↑	↑	↓	↓		↓	
müsste←	musst ←	muss	Russe →	Russen	süsse →	süsses →
↓	↓	↓	↓	↓	↓	

In an analytic language like English, the rhyming vocabulary is almost exclusively arranged in terms of scheme A—that is, the English rhyming word can, as a rule, rhyme with a limited number of words which end with the same syllable in their basic form, which at the same time is their only form (*elm, helm, realm, whelm, overwhelm*). The rhyme vocabulary is divided into a fixed number of rhyme groups (i.e., into discrete sub-sets) with fixed numbers of elements.

In a synthetic language like Czech or Russian, the words of the fundamental grammatical categories (nouns, verbs, adjectives) assume during their inflection numerous phonetically different endings and can in their inflected forms rhyme with words whose basic forms have very different terminations. The rhyme vocabulary in these languages is arranged in terms of scheme B—that is, it is not divided into fixed groups, but is continuous. German is a transitional type in this respect: it has fixed rhyme groups, which—due to the large number of inflected forms (particularly of the verb)—are frequently transgressed and linked.

Thanks to its discrete character, the analytical rhyme vocabulary is open to mathematical characterization. Even the simple statistics of *the number of elements in the rhyme groups* gives a useful guide to the knowledge of the rhyme possibilities that are available to the poet. In English,[10] for instance, it becomes clear that with regard to acoustically exact rhymes, the groups with

2–9 elements are most frequent and that the groups with 2–15 elements constitute about 60 % of the rhyme repertoire. If we also take eye and conventional rhyme into consideration, the number of groups with 2–7 elements is reduced, but even then the groups with 2–15 elements make up more than 50 % of the rhyme repertoire. Grammatical rhymes can be used in 50 rhyme groups; therefore the number of groups with 2–15 elements diminishes to 40 %. Even with very liberal demands on rhyme, the English poet has very limited possibilities for most of his rhymes in the choice of the rhymed counterpart.

As to the rhyme vocabulary of a synthetic language, such as Czech, for instance, no simple frequency table can be compiled, since the limits of the rhyme groups fluctuate and the individual groups overlap. It can be roughly presumed that the groups with more than 100 elements are most frequent. The total number of units in the rhyme vocabulary is several times higher, too, because most lexical units in it are represented with several forms of the word (the instance of the 300,000 German rhymes in the dictionary of Peregrinus Syntax, as against the 60,000 in Hübner's lexicon and the 15,000 in Steputat, can be partly explained in that in Peregrinus Syntax the inflected forms are also included). Just as the number of lexical units is an indicator of the expressiveness of a language, so too is the number of word forms an indicator of its richness in rhymes.

The different quantitative organization of the rhyme vocabulary in an analytic and synthetic language naturally creates different conditions for the technique of rhyme in the two literatures and has certain direct aesthetic consequences:

(a) The repetition of the same sound harmony in rhyme is sometimes difficult in English. At times it is even impossible. While an Italian poet has several thousand rhyming words for *amare*, as does the Czech poet for the inflected forms of the word *láska*, an English poet has only three words that rhyme with *love* (*dove, glove, above*). If he wants to repeat the same rhymes in complicated stanzas four to six times, he cannot employ about one half of the rhyme groups. For these reasons, the rhyme scheme of the octet of the Italian sonnet *abba abba* became common in English literature in the form *abab cdcd*.

(b) Since the English rhyme groups are closed and the number of their elements is small, the same rhyme combinations are repeated again and again (*love-dove, helm-realm, womb-tomb*). The English rhyme combinations are generally more worn out or automatized than the Italian, German, or Czech combinations—under these circumstances the repetition of the same rhyme is not only difficult, but aesthetically disadvantageous.

After having indicated how differently the mechanism of rhyme functions in individual languages regarding the different organization of their rhyme repertoire, we can proceed to *characterize quantitatively the function of any given word in rhyme*. Words of the same rhyme group are not equivalent in this respect. Some are less frequent and therefore more surprising. The degree of surprise of a rhyme combination can be quantitatively expressed as the product of the probability of occurrence of these words. We give an example from Czech (since we possess Czech data on the frequency of individual words). In the group of Czech monosyllabic words, some words show the following average frequencies;[11]

jen (6477 · 1.6 · 10⁻⁶), *den* (2257 · 1.6 · 10⁻⁶), *sen* (731 · ...), *kmen* (143 · ...), *ven* (187 · ...), *len* (12 · ...), *plen* (5 · ...), *sten* (4 ·...).

Disregarding the semantic combinations, the contemporary style and so forth, the probability of occurrence of the rhyme pair *kmen-len* is:

$$143 \cdot 1.6 \cdot 10^{-6} \cdot 12 \cdot 1.6 \cdot 10^{-6},$$

the probability of occurrence of the rhyme pair *plen-sten* is:

$$5 \cdot 1.6 \cdot 10^{-6} \cdot 4 \cdot 1.6 \cdot 10^{-6},$$

which is 86 times smaller than the first. The degree of surprise of a rhyme word depends at the same time on the rhyme group to which it belongs. It can be said generally that the larger a rhyme group is, the smaller is the probability that we can predict which word is to stand at the end of the respective line. The word *Freude* can only rhyme with a few words and its predictability comes close to 100%; the word *Jahr* can rhyme with dozens of other words, and the degree of its predictability is only a few percent (disregarding context). The degree of surprise, I (amount of information), of a rhyme word is directly proportional to the number of elements of a rhyme group (F_g), but is indirectly proportional to the relative frequency of the respective lexical unit (F_l):

$$I = \text{constant} \cdot \frac{F_g}{F_l}$$

These mathematical premises can be confirmed by psychological tests employing the so-called Cloze procedure.[12]

The terms *probability* and *degree of surprise*, or degree of expectation—to use both mathematical and psychological terms—stand side by side in our considerations. The less frequent, the less probable an element is, the more surprising—*ceteris paribus*—it is. But it is doubtful, on the other hand, whether rarity and surprise are directly proportional, whether a ten times less frequent element is at the same time ten times more surprising. Some results suggest that the degree of surprise is rather a logarithmic function of rarity; these problems cannot be answered for the time being, since we do not possess a direct measure for the degree of surprise. The calculation of frequency must here substitute for this measure; we must not forget, however, that its results will only be reflected in an attenuated form in the psychological sphere.

Apart from the aspect of probability, the aspects of *combination* play a role in rhyme, for each harmony of sound in rhyme is a combination of elemental phonetic units—the sounds.

The number of rhyme groups depends on how many different sound groups the given language has. In English, for instance, which has 42 phonemes, the number of theoretically possible variations of only two phonemes is $42^2 = 1764$; in reality, however, the number of rhyme groups is hardly 400. In his *Neuhochdeutsche Metrik*, J. Minor has calculated that German, having 5 vowels, 3 umlaut vowels, and 3 dipthongs, possesses 11 types of monosyllabic and $11^2 = 121$ types of bisyllabic assonances. The magnitude of these groups is different, of course: those types of bisyllabic assonances which have an *e* in their second syllable have a much higher frequency than the others. (Spanish has a very large number of types of assonances, since it has 21 vowels and diphthongs.) The monosyllabic rhyme, as a matter of fact, has more types than the bisyllabic assonance (about 400–800 in the main languages of Europe). The number of different bisyllabic rhymes should theoretically be equal to the square of the number of monosyllabic rhymes, which would be 360,000 in German! Even though the larger part of these theoretically possible bisyllabic variations do not exist in the language, the variability of bisyllabic rhymes is considerably higher. But the possibilities of rhyme-word choice are limited by that fact: the German poet can choose from many thousands of words for the *a*–assonance, for the *a*–*e*–assonance there are only a few thousands left, and for the bisyllabic sound harmony for *Adel*, there are only a few possibilities for rhyme left (*Nadel*, *Tadel*, and some few others). When the poet chooses a fairly complex sound harmony which is at the same time rare, this usage is surprising from the phonetic point of view (one single permutation out of hundreds of thousands). But since at the same time the possibilities of lexical choice are limited, a conspicuous automatization arises from the semantic point of view. Phonetic and semantic originality here are indirectly proportional. As we know, the refined and complicated form often compels attention at the expense of content. In this very simple situation, we have a clear opportunity to compute the relationship of dominance between "form" and "content."

It has been mathematically determined how difficult the formation of rhyming pairs is in different languages. The probability of two *arbitrarily* selected Russian words rhyming is, as A. N. Kolmogorov determined,[13] about 0.005. Since 190 word pairs can be compiled from 20 words, it is to be expected that one rhyming pair occurs among 20 words. Taking *n* as the number of words and M_2 as the number of rhyming pairs, the following formula holds:

$$M_2 = \frac{n^2 - n}{2} \cdot 0.005 = \frac{n^2 - n}{400}$$

Kolmogorov also determined the probability of triple and quadruple rhymes (M_3, M_4, etc.):

n	number of pairs	M_2	M_3	M_4	M_5	M_{10}
10	45	0.25				
20	190	1	0.05	0.088		
50	1,225	6.25	0.52	0.032		
100	4,995	25	4.17	0.52	0.052	
200	19,900	100	33.3	8.3	1.67	0.00022
500	124,750	625	520	325	162	7

On the basis of these findings, we can estimate the relative difficulty of rhyme schemes with multiple repetition of rhymes. Approximately 60 *different* words are needed to form 7 rhyme pairs, which is only slightly greater than the number of words contained in the 14 lines of a sonnet. To form a quadruple rhyme, the poet needs approximately 350 different words, which is a vocabulary only to be expected in a relatively long poem.

In a similar way, P. Guiraud[14] has calculated for French that n words theoretically make $37 \cdot \left(\dfrac{n}{100}\right)^2$ rhymes possible. It is remarkable that his data come close to those established by Kolmogorov for the Russian rhyme:

number of words	number of rhyming pairs	
	Russian	French
10	0.25	0.37
100	25	37
500	625	925

The calculation of the possibilities of rhyme in the various languages will certainly have important implications for the comparative theory of rhyme.

RHYTHM

It is not the determination of the metrical scheme of a poem that is a problem for the literary critic, but the determination of its rhythmic individuality. The problem is in specifying objectively the relationship between two aspects, namely the sequence of accented and unaccented syllables of a metrical scheme (e.g., ∪−∪−∪−∪−∪− in blank verse) and the sequence of phonologically stressed and unstressed syllables (e.g., x x́ x x x x́ x x́ x x́) by which the given meter is realized:

Und also, fuhr der Richter fort, wenn ihr   x x́ x x́ x x́ x x́ x x

Nicht meinen Rat, statt meines Spruches wollt: x x́ x x́ x x́ x x́ x x́

Geht nun!—Mein Rat ist aber der: ihr nehmt   x́ x x x́ x x́ x x́ x x́

Die Sache völlig wie sie liegt. Hat von   x x́ x x́ x x́ x x́ x x

Lessing, Nathan the Wise

Lessing's blank verse cannot be represented through the variant that seems subjectively most common or is most frequent. What is characteristic of blank verse is both the relationship of all possible types— that is, the dominance of some of them and complete absence of others—and their sequence, which again is frequency and distribution. To determine the *typical* does not mean that the multiplicity of phenomena is reduced to the most frequent one among them; rather, it is a matter of determining the system of frequency and distribution patterns.

The *statistics of the frequency of rhythm* of a poet can be examined by two statistical methods:

(a) *vertically*: The stressed syllables in lines are added in vertical columns, and the results in percentages then indicate the relative frequency of the accent from the first to the nth syllable of the line. Consequently, it can be seen how the meter is realized in various places of the line.

(b) *horizontally*: The frequency of type one—with phonological stresses in all metrically stressed positions (2, 4, 6, 8, 10)—of type two, with an "omitted" accent on the first ictus (4, 6, 8, 10), and so on, is determined.

We shall now demonstrate both types of the statistics with the iambic decasyllabics in Lessing's *Nathan the Wise*. For the sake of clarity, we limit the vertical statistics to metrically stressed, even-numbered syllables, and in the horizontal statistics, we omit those types whose frequency does not reach 2%.

Horizontal Statistics (sum of the variants)		*Vertical Statistics* (matrix of phonological stresses)				
		2	4	6	8	10
2, 4, 6, 8, 10	36	36	36	36	36	36
— 4, 6, 8, 10,	2	—	2	2	2	2
2, — 6, 8, 10	10	10	—	10	10	10
2, 4, — 8, 10	10	10	10	—	10	10
2, 4, 6, — 10	12	12	12	12	—	12
2, 4, 6, 8, —	16	16	16	16	16	—
2, — 6, 8, —	4	4	—	4	4	—
2, 4, — 8, —	8	8	8	—	8	—
	100%	96	86	82	88	70%

As can be seen from the horizontal statistics, the regular type with five stresses is most frequent:

So *kam* nun *die*ser *Ring* von *Sohn* zu *Sohn*

In the types with four and three stresses, the frequency decreases proportionately to the distance of the phonologically unrealized stress from the end of the line. The type 2, 4, 6, 8, –, is most frequent:

Wie kann ich meinen Vater weniger

then the type 2, 4, 6, –, 10:

Der einen Ring von unschätzbarem Wert.

and so on. This indicates that Lessing's lines most frequently begin with the energetic rhythm carried by rather short words, while the rhythm at the end of the verse is weakened by longer words. Vertical statistics shows a remarkable difference between the first and last ictus in this respect. The lines examined have in almost all cases (96%) a completely realized iambic beginning, but they frequently end (30%) with a falling cadence of several syllables (... x́ x x). In the same way, the most conspicuous peculiarity of Lessing's verse—his system of pauses—can be characterized statistically.

The discovery of *vertical* statistics was of similar importance to prosody as the invention of the microscope was for optics—it is actually based on the same principle: inconspicuous phenomena are made perceptible by enlargement. Vertical statistics is particularly advantageous when we compare the progression of several layers of linguistic phenomena and it becomes very clear when we present the results graphically. As an example, we now present a comparison of the statistics of stresses and the word boundaries in the octosyllabic and hexasyllabic lines of Coleridge's *Rime of the Ancient Mariner* (in English, stress and word boundaries are relatively independent of each other):

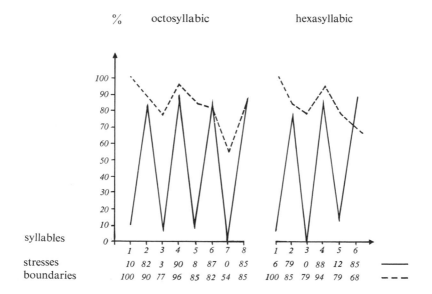

		octo	osyllabic						hexasyllabic				
syllables	1	2	3	4	5	6	7	8	1	2	3	4	5	6
stresses	10	82	3	90	8	87	0	85	6	79	0	88	12	85
boundaries	100	90	77	96	85	82	54	85	100	85	79	94	79	68

The hexasyllabic line of Coleridge's ballad has the same structure as the first six syllables of the octosyllabic line. That 94% to 96% of the word boundaries appear before the fourth syllable suggests a strong tendency toward a caesura in this place in the line (which is sometimes emphasized by internal rhyme, but sometimes concealed by the syntactic structure). The first half-line shows a very striking rising-falling pattern (x x́ x), while the second begins with a falling one (x́ x x). The curve falling at the sixth syllable indicates that there is remarkably often a polysyllabic rising word at the point of the fifth or sixth syllable. The hexasyllabic line ends with this word, while the octosyllabic line continues with a longer word into the seventh syllable and is emphasized by an accentuated monosyllabic word. After the rhythmic parallelism of the first six syllables in both meters, we have a contrasting cadence: the octosyllabic line ends almost obligatorily with a monosyllabic word, while we often find a rising polysyllabic word at the end of a hexasyllabic line:

> In mist or cloud, on mast or shroud,
> It perched for vespers nine.
> Whiles all the night, through fog-smoke white,
> Glimmered the white moon-shine.

If we expanded vertical statistics to further components of the language of the poetic text, we could find out, for instance, that in Coleridge's poem there is not only a parallelism in the distribution of stresses and long vowels (which is natural in an English text), but also one in stresses and positional lengths, that is, from accumulations of consonants, etc. (which is not usual in other English poems).

The value of vertical statistics for historical poetics is highly significant. It has been discovered that the rhythmic shape of a line is at least in some languages a stylistic constant, which characterizes the rhythmic tendencies of whole groups and generations of poets. These statistics enable us to discover both the tendencies in the development of rhythmic sensibility in the given literature and the historical changes in the rhythmic shape of a certain meter. The statistics of the distribution of sentence endings in the individual lines of a stanza can reveal the individualistic tendencies of a composition. Finally, the determination of the tendencies in the distribution of the grammatical categories in verse can be a first step toward a statistical model of the semantic structure of the poem.[15]

Horizontal statistics of rhythm seems especially useful for discussing lines with a varying number of syllables. Therefore it is particularly common in English, German, and Russian prosody. In recent years it has also been preferred for theoretical reasons, for it also takes into account the linear character of the message.

Each of the rhythmic variants of the meter—with which the horizontal statistics deals—has a *probability of occurrence* that is determined as the product of the average frequency of all words contained in that word sequence. The basic form of the Czech trochaic tetrameter of the type 1, 3, –, 7 is x́ x / x́ x x x / x́ x—that is, a bisyllabic (average frequency 0.319), a tetra-syllabic (0.136), and a bisyllabic word (0.319).[16] The presumed probability of occurrence of this variant is

$$0.319 \cdot 0.136 \cdot 0.319 = 0.013$$

That is, it is probable that in a line of 1,000 randomly organized Czech words, approximately thirteen rhythmic figures of that type occur. After the average probability of the individual rhythmic variants has been determined, their unmarked (normal) frequency can be calculated in poems written in the given language.

This method leaves much to be desired if a genuine and not illusory accuracy is to be achieved: (1) The results which are based on 1,000 words should be converted to a basis of 1,000 lines of poetry. (2) This demand becomes even more necessary, since some variants can be realized by several combinations that consist of different numbers of words (e.g., x́ x / x́ x x x / x́ x or x́ x / x́ x x x / x / x́ x or x́ x / x́ x / x / x / x́ x—i.e., three to five words); the calculated probabilities therefore are horizontally comparable only when they consist of the same number of words. (3) We suppose that the ordering of the words in a text is stochastic—which is apparently not entirely the case. Moreover, we have to define the relevant units of verse: Are they words or word groups? And what are the transitional probabilities within or between the phonetically defined word groups? For these reasons, the theoretical calculations must be considered as only approximate. Therefore, some proso-dists (for instance, J. Woronczak, M. Červenka, et al.) prefer to base their comparison on empirically (statistically) calculated frequences of the dif-ferent word combinations in prose.

The results of the horizontal statistics can be interpreted with reference to the neutral background of the theoretically calculated values: "If the cal-culated 'automatized' random frequency agrees with the actual frequencies in the verse of the poet analyzed, this means that . . . the poet tried his best to exploit the possibilities of expression in the framework of the meter he employs. . . . If the actual frequencies are different from the 'calculated' values, this means that the poet tried to give his verse—consciously or unconsciously —a certain rhythmic individuality. . . . The verses of major poets mostly show a tendency toward an individual rhythmic pattern."[17]

By a comparatively time-consuming procedure, whose details we shall not develop here, the limiting influence of meter on the poet's choice of words at any place in the line can be calculated,[18] that is, the percentage of words or groups of words which cannot be employed in the first to the nth syllable of the line if a new word begins on that syllable. We present the curve for the impact of form on word choice in the Czech and English iambic decasyllabic line:

	1	2	3	4	5	6	7	8	9	10
English	21.5	20.0	21.5	10.0	21.5	10.0	21.5	13.0	25.8	30.7
Czech	73.7	24.6	98.2	19.4	73.6	19.4	73.6	43.8	93.0	73.6

It becomes evident that the constraint of the line-end not only works deeply back into the line, but that under certain conditions, its influence increases across several syllables (see the third and ninth syllable of the Czech line).

Thanks to mathematics, we can expect to learn something about the constraining and determining circumstances of the poet's work and about the aesthetic experience of the reader, though we are not yet able to explain its qualitative character in terms of mathematics. This point of view is also relevant in retrospect for the interpretation of mathematically obtained data: they express dimensions of literary texts and of reality, but not their essence. They explain some conditions and causes, but not always the reasons. They explain some consequences, but not always the effects.

STANZA STRUCTURES

The stanza is a *system of systems*: the rhyme scheme and its realization by various types of rhyme, the combination of meters and their realization in rhythm, the relationship between syntax and line, the syntactically determined intonation scheme of the stanza, and so on. Each of these systems in the given stanza is in one of x possible states. The variability of a stanza depends on the *number of the possible states* of the individual systems (the number of the possible combinations of the elements). The expressiveness of the selected variant depends among other things on surprise, on the low *relative frequency* of the chosen states of the individual systems. Let us mention only two factors for an elementary demonstration: (a) the rhyme scheme, (b) the rhythmic variants of the meter.

(a) *The number of possible rhyme combinations* rapidly increases with the growing number of lines in the stanza. The theoretical possibilities of stanza variants were determined by G. Šengeli[19] in his *Treatise on Verse*. Under the condition that there are an even number of lines in a stanza and that each line has only one rhyming counterpart (i.e., that only two lines and not three rhyme with each other), we determine the number of variants by the formula

$$V = 1 \ \cdot \ 3 \ \cdot \ 5 \ ...(n-1)$$

A couplet has only one possibility (aa), a quatrain has three stanzaic variants (aabb, abab, abba), a sextet has 15, an octet has 105, a sonnet stanza has 135,135 possible combinations of seven rhyme pairs. Comparing the theoretical possibilities with the actual list of existing stanzas, it becomes obvious that in couplets and quatrains, all possible types are very frequent, while in stanzas with more lines the percentage of the number of patterns actually used decreases rapidly. The English sonnet (ababcdcdefefgg) is only one of the 135,135 possibilities. When we consider the rhyming of not only two, but also three and four lines, as in the Italian sonnet, the number of theoretical possibilities increases considerably. The greater number of them, however, is inapplicable for aesthetic reasons, such as too great distances between rhyming lines.

(b) An even more powerful means of variation is the alternation of several *rhythmic variants*. From the number of variants of a certain meter, the possibilities of combinations in the stanza with *m* lines of the same meter can be calculated. According to the matrix of the probable frequencies of the individual variants, the degree of surprise of multiple repetition in succession of the same variant can be determined.

The number (N_n) of the possibilities of variations in the vocabulary in iambic verse with *n* feet was determined as early as 1923 by Tomaševskij in his examination of Puškin's iambic pentameter:

$$N_n = 4N_{n-1} - N_{n-2}$$

This number represents only a tiny fraction of all possible combinations of word types in a prose segment of equivalent length. For linguistic reasons, only a part of this supply of possibilities, reduced by the demands of the iambic rhythm, actually occurs in verse:

	4 syll.	*6 syll.*	*8 syll.*	*10 syll.*
theoretical possibilities of the iambic lines	2	15	56	209
employed variants	2	4	8	16

The probability that a given variant is repeated *n* times successively was calculated by Tomaševskij with the formula:

$$P_n = p^n \cdot (1-p)^n$$

where *p* is the average frequency of the variant concerned. For Puškin's *Boris Godunov* and for *The House in Kolomna* Tomaševskij calculated the probabilities of repetition of all rhythmic variants for $n=1$, $n=2$, etc. The number of repetitions theoretically determined and that were actually found were surprisingly congruent—proof that the sequence of rhythmic variants in Puškin is not unconventional. The table shows the following data for lines of the type 2, 4, 6, 10:

	once	*twice*	*3 times*	*4 times*	*5 times*	*6 times and more frequently*
Theoretical	236	69	20	6	2	0
Observed	234	68	19	9	1	0

For the number of possible variants in a stanza of *m* lines, we then have the formula $K_m = N_n^m$. If we assume the possibility of 6 rhythmic variants for the iambic tetrameter, then $6^4 = 1,296$ different rhythmic variants are possible in the quatrain.

G. Šengeli[20] examined several Russian poets to determine statistically the portion of the 1,296 theoretically possible variants of the quatrain which actually occur in 250 stanzas of that type. He found to his surprise that the rhythmic variability has no direct relationship to the merits of the poetry examined. In the 250 quatrains Jazykov showed 95, Puškin 115, Majkov 118, Blok 123, Nekrasov 133, Brjusov 138, Fet 142, Bunin 146, and Severjanin 163 variants.

On the basis of the average frequency of individual stanza variants, the probable "normal number" of the variants in 250 verses could be determined. After this "normal value" was calculated, one could discover the extent to which given authors deviate from the average. We are thus led to the mathematical determination of the objective limit between two tendencies of style: the direction toward the classical, "regular" form or, in contrast, the direction that denies regularity, norm, and "style." These two quantitatively different principles of style are evident as historical factors in the most widely differing areas of literature and art. When the term "style" is used—as it sometimes is—to express the constant, repeated, and, therefore, fixed means of expression, then we have to deal with *anti-style* in those instances where variability is greater than normal. Most democratizations of vocabulary, the expansions of morphology, and the possibilities of literature were wholly anti-styles at first from the point of view of average probabilities. Similarly the negation of the form of the novel, the anti-novel, is only an expansion of the means of form and presentation.

REFERENCES

1. Andrej Belyj, *Simvolizm* (Moskva, 1910), p. 399.
2. Samuel R. Levin, *Linguistic Structures in Poetry* ('s–Gravenhage, 1962), p. 17.
3. Jan Mukařovský, *Kapitoly z české poetiky*, II (Praha, 1948), p. 76.
4. We quote the phoneme statistics from Gustav Herdan's *Language as Choice and Chance* (Groningen, 1956), p. 134.
5. See C. E. Shannon and W. Weaver, *The Mathematical Theory of Communication* (Urbana, 1949).
6. Lubomír Doležel, "Předběžný odhad entropie a redundance psané češtiny," *Slovo a slovesnost*, XXIV (1963), 173.
7. "Informationsgehalt von Wort und Laut in der Dichtung," *Poetics* (Warszawa, 1961), pp. 590–605.
8. The frequency of Czech word categories has been obtained from J. Jelínek, J. V. Bečka, and M. Těšitelová, *Frekvence slov, slovních druhů a tvarů v českém jazyce* (Praha, 1961).
9. The frequency of Czech digraphs has been obtained from L. Doležel, *op. cit.*
10. See the detailed statistics in Jiří Levý, "Matematický a experimentální rozbor verše," *Česká literatura*, XII (1964), 199.
11. The frequency of Czech words has been obtained from J. Jelínek, *et al., op. cit.*
12. See J. Levý, *op. cit.*
13. *Strukturno-tipologičeskije issledovania* (Moskva, 1962), p. 288.
14. Pierre Guiraud, *Language et versification* (Paris, 1953), pp. 108–109.
15. See J. Levý, "Předběžné poznámky k informační analýze verše," *Slovenská literatura*, XI (1964), 34ff.
16. A. Kondratov, *Matematika i poezija* (Moskva, 1962), pp. 18ff. G. Šengeli, *Tekhnika stikha* (Moskva, 1960), p. 252, similarly determined the probability of occurrence of the individual rhythmic variants.
17. A. Kondratov, *op. cit.*
18. For more details, see J. Levý, "Matematický a experimentální rozbor verše," 191ff.
19. See G. Šengeli, *Tekhnika stikha.*
20. *Ibid.*, p. 111.

INFORMATION THEORY AND POETICS:
THE ENTROPY OF RUSSIAN SPEECH RHYTHM

A. M. KONDRATOV

Statistical investigations of language as a code with probability constraints have made it possible to introduce precise numerical evaluations into linguistics. Such an approach may also be applied in poetics, inasmuch as the material of poetry is language with all of its statistical regularities. The present essay is devoted to an examination of rhythmic regularities in Russian speech and to the variability in the degree of uncertainty (entropy) depending on the requirements of various types of texts, ranging from scientific and expository prose to classical verse meters.

RHYTHM AS A STOCHASTIC PROCESS

The rhythm of Russian speech may be described as a sequence in which stressed and unstressed syllables alternate in a word and in a sentence (intonation is not considered here). In contrast to many other Indo-European languages, stress in the Russian language may fall on any syllable of a "content" word. Such "content" words having a mandatory stress are nouns, adjectives, verbs, numerals, adverbs, and many pronouns. Particles, conjunctions, and, frequently, pronouns are joined to the "content" words and form, together with them, a single rhythmic word.

Such a view was used by Tomaševskij to segment texts into rhythmic word types—this is confirmed by the fact that his data are very close to the findings in Table 1 of this article. There is also another method of segmenting texts into independent (stressed) words. This is the method of Šengeli and it consists of a more scrupulous division into words, with only prepositions, conjunctions, and particles remaining unstressed. This latter method is used by A. N. Kolmogorov and N. G. Ryčkova in their formal analyses of verse. The Tomaševskij method—the standard adopted in this essay—is here illustrated in the text: "I on skazal im: Perestanete vy ili net? Oni zamolčali. Stalo očen' tikho, tak tikho, čto slyšno bylo mukhu, žužžavšuju za steklom." ["And he said to them: Will you stop or not? They fell silent. It became very quiet, so quiet that a fly was heard buzzing behind the windowpane."] In applying that method, we find that there is one monosyllabic word (the remainder have merged with neighboring words), while by Šengeli's method, we find five such words. The divergence in the number of one-syllable words reached considerable proportions in their analyses of "The Queen of Spades." In Tomaševskij, one-syllable words comprise about 7% of the text, while in Šengeli, the figure is over 15%!

This essay originally appeared in *Problemy kibernetiki*, no. 9 (1963), 279–286; we wish to thank Mark E. Suino for his help in making the translation.

In the present essay, we used the system of transcription suggested by Čudovskij and Tomaševskij: every "content" word is transcribed, not dia-critically,[1] which would complicate the calculation of rhythmic word types, but as a combination of figures: the base indicates the number of syllables in the word, and the exponent indicates the position of the stressed syllable (counting from the beginning of the word). Thus the passage cited above is written as:

$$2^2 \quad 3^2 \quad 5^3 \quad 1^1 \quad 3^3. \qquad 2^2 \quad 4^3. \qquad 2^1 \quad 2^1 \quad 2^1 \quad 3^2 \quad 3^2 \quad 2^1 \quad 2^1 \quad 4^2 \quad 3^3.$$

Any Russian text which is broken down into rhythmic word types will be represented by a sequence of numbers, and the occurrence of each sequence will have its own entropy. Constraints imposed by various texts on the rhythm of Russian speech concern not only the use of individual rhythmic word types, but also combinations of these types. These constraints reduce the overall entropy of rhythm, which, in turn, is a component of the overall entropy of speech.

The intent of this article is to obtain a numerical value for the entropy of rhythm. Eight texts with varying rhythmic organization were selected: scientific prose, expository prose, prose fiction, conversational speech, accen-tual verse, and the iambic tetrameters of Blok, Lomonosov, and Puškin. One thousand content words were selected. The probability of occurrence (more precisely, the statistical frequency) of each rhythmic word type was computed (see Table 1). Finally, by applying Shannon's formula,[2]

$$H_1 = c(-p_1 \log p_1 - p_2 \log p_2 - \ldots - p_N \log p_N)$$

we found the entropy (the degree of uncertainty) of the rhythm of each of the eight texts (see Table 1 and the Summary Table). For scientific prose, a sample of 1,000 words was taken from the article "Teorija informacii i lingvistika" ["Information Theory and Linguistics"] by R. L. Dobrušin, A. M. Jaglom, and I. M. Jaglom.[3] The sample of expository prose was taken from the catalog of an exhibition of Krymov's paintings; the conversation from Čekhov's play, "The Cherry Orchard"; the accentual verse from Maja-kovskij's "A Cloud in Trousers," "At the Top of My Voice," and his poems from 1925–1929. Samples of 100 words each were taken from the works of ten authors of prose fiction. Further, 1,000-word samples were taken from the iambic pentameter of Blok, Puškin, and Lomonosov.

The rhythmic entropy per syllable was found by dividing the entropy per word by the average word-length (in syllables). The entropy value diminished successively from scientific prose—which had the highest rhythmic entropy per word—to the iambs of Lomonosov, whose verse demonstrated the smallest degree of rhythmical uncertainty both for the word and the syllable. The low entropy value per syllable in scientific prose—an exception to the general tendency—is apparently to be explained by the vocabulary of the text. The average word-length is greater in the scientific text than in the "literary language" (see Table 1).

TABLE 1
Statistical Frequencies of Rhythmic Word Types in Various Texts

Word Types		Types of Texts							
							IAMBICS		
numeric symbol	graphic symbol	conver-sation	scien-tific prose	exposi-tory prose	artis-tic prose	accen-tual verse	Blok	Puškin	Lomo-nosov
1¹	´	063	048	083	074	078	105	068	066
2¹	´◡	158	130	139	163	158	175	127	110
2²	◡´	180	085	101	167	123	194	249	255
3¹	´◡◡	103	071	088	059	063	037	049	035
3²	◡´◡	165	125	169	167	221	282	300	321
3³	◡◡´	109	077	063	084	057	053	040	055
4¹	´◡◡◡	004	008	024	012	008	003	003	001
4²	◡´◡◡	041	087	083	063	067	062	047	056
4³	◡◡´◡	077	094	090	097	105	056	052	063
4⁴	◡◡◡´	012	012	022	016	014	030	020	026
5¹	´◡◡◡◡	001	003	001	000	000	000	000	000
5²	◡´◡◡◡	004	022	026	008	012	007	009	003
5³	◡◡´◡◡	040	088	038	025	035	004	000	000
5⁴	◡◡◡´◡	019	037	015	029	019	029	016	009
5⁵	◡◡◡◡´	001	009	004	008	000	000	000	000
6¹	´◡◡◡◡◡	000	002	002	001	000	000	000	000
6²	◡´◡◡◡◡	001	010	006	002	001	000	000	000
6³	◡◡´◡◡◡	006	015	007	005	000	000	000	000
6⁴	◡◡◡´◡◡	010	028	020	009	013	014	008	000
6⁵	◡◡◡◡´◡	005	009	002	003	005	002	000	000
6⁶	◡◡◡◡◡´	001	003	002	000	000	004	000	000
7²	◡´◡◡◡◡◡	000	000	002	000	000	000	000	000
7³	◡◡´◡◡◡◡	000	003	001	001	000	000	000	000
7⁴	◡◡◡´◡◡◡	000	013	006	003	002	000	001	000
7⁵	◡◡◡◡´◡◡	000	014	004	001	001	001	001	000
7⁶	◡◡◡◡◡´◡	000	001	001	000	001	000	000	000
8³	◡◡´◡◡◡◡◡	000	001	000	000	000	000	000	000
8⁴	◡◡◡´◡◡◡◡	000	001	000	000	000	000	000	000
8⁵	◡◡◡◡´◡◡◡	000	001	000	000	000	000	000	000
8⁶	◡◡◡◡◡´◡◡	000	002	001	003	000	000	000	000
9⁷	◡◡◡◡◡◡´◡◡	000	001	000	000	000	000	000	000
Entropy per word		3.25	3.94	3.72	3.47	3.27	3.10	2.82	2.75
Entropy per syllable		1.13	1.11	1.18	1.18	1.11	1.13	1.05	1.03
Average word length		2.87	3.56	3.16	2.95	2.95	2.75	2.68	2.67

Other rhythmic word types do not occur in the texts.

DETERMINATION OF RHYTHMIC ENTROPY REGARDLESS OF WORD BOUNDARIES

In order to determine the value of H_2, which describes the constraints imposed by the text on the combinations of two rhythmic word types, we must determine the statistical frequencies of all the pairs and calculate, according to Shannon's formula—

$$H_2 = Ha_2(a_1) = H(a_1a_2) - H(a_1)$$

the value for each text. By a like procedure, computing the frequencies of all possible combinations of three, four, etc. adjacent rhythmic word types, we could find the values H_3, H_4, etc., up to H_∞. The value of H_∞—the limit value of rhythmic entropy—describes the reduction in degree of rhythmic uncertainty of speech that results from the rhythmic requirements imposed on a text.

The practical determination of high order entropy, however, involves considerable difficulty. Thus, for example, in finding the value of H_2, it would be necessary to count no fewer than 400 (of the most frequently used) combinations of two rhythmic word types in material involving several thousand pairs. Therefore, it is advisable to simplify the counting procedure and to count, not the combinations of various rhythmic word types, but rather the number of unstressed syllables between stresses regardless of word boundaries. This yields an approximate value for H_2 (see Table 2).

TABLE 2
Statistical Frequencies of the Number of Unstressed Syllables between Stresses

Number of syllables (unstressed intervals)	scientific	expository	artistic	conversational	Turgenev	Čekhov	Leskov	Dostoevskij	Puškin	accentual verse	iambic verse
0	056	064	056	085	060	117	087	064	103	006	013
1	164	249	330	359	288	350	325	284	298	494	771
2	327	303	359	352	314	330	332	330	321	321	004
3	265	215	163	145	194	156	179	189	197	149	208
4	131	117	069	053	103	046	063	084	068	018	000
5	038	035	018	006	028	010	012	038	008	011	004
6	013	012	002	000	009	001	002	010	005	001	000
7	006	005	001	000	004	000	000	001	000	000	000
entropy H_2	2.38	2.40	2.12	2.04	2.32	2.12	2.15	2.31	2.21	1.67	0.91
$H_1 - H_2$	1.56	1.32	1.35	1.21	–	–	–	–	–	1.60	1.95

In this type of count, the text is transcribed as a sequence of figures which expresses the number of unstressed syllables between the stressed syllables. Thus the text which we introduced above is transcribed as follows:

1 1 3 2 2.   1 2.   1 1 1 2 2 1 1 2 4.

If the two stressed syllables occur in adjacent positions, the figure "0" will appear in the transcription.

For the calculation of H_3, we determined the frequencies of pairs of unstressed intervals (see Table 3).

TABLE 3
Statistical Frequencies of Pairs of Unstressed Intervals

intervals	scientific	expository	artistic	conversational	Turgenev	Čekhov	Leskov	Dostoevskij	accentual verse	iambic verse
0 0	02	02	03	02	06	16	16	05	01	01
0 1	13	20	12	24	07	57	28	23	03	03
0 2	21	16	40	49	24	36	33	19	02	04
0 3	12	13	10	04	17	07	10	13	00	05
0 4	07	11	05	06	06	05	06	01	00	00
0 5	01	02	04	00	00	01	04	03	00	00
1 0	12	22	22	29	20	42	30	17	03	01
1 1	18	65	115	147	85	121	104	87	245	569
1 2	54	78	103	112	70	117	114	89	137	00
1 3	41	46	59	52	66	54	52	59	100	200
1 4	32	28	26	12	31	07	24	20	05	00
1 5	05	06	05	07	14	02	01	07	04	04
1 6	02	03	02	00	02	01	00	05	00	00
1 7	00	01	00	00	00	00	00	00	00	00
2 0	13	17	33	33	19	39	38	18	03	00
2 1	73	76	119	137	94	123	108	95	169	00
2 2	100	93	126	120	85	110	109	111	88	00
2 3	86	69	54	52	64	35	64	65	43	00
2 4	44	28	20	16	35	17	08	28	12	00
2 5	08	13	07	04	14	06	02	11	05	00
2 6	03	05	00	00	03	00	02	01	01	00
2 7	00	02	00	00	00	00	00	01	00	00
3 0	15	14	10	13	06	23	11	14	00	02
3 1	54	58	46	56	59	50	54	55	92	180
3 2	91	63	57	39	70	43	56	64	26	00
3 3	58	50	36	22	35	23	42	35	28	30
3 4	29	16	12	13	21	15	14	13	01	00
3 5	12	10	02	02	04	02	02	07	02	00
3 6	04	03	00	00	01	00	00	01	00	00
3 7	02	01	00	00	00	00	00	00	00	00

TABLE 3 (continued)
Statistical Frequencies of Pairs of Unstressed Intervals

intervals	scientific	expository	artistic	conversational	Turgenev	Čekhov	Leskov	Dostoevskij	accentual verse	iambic verse
4 0	04	04	01	02	02	09	04	05	00	00
4 1	14	20	30	13	38	11	26	18	06	00
4 2	35	34	25	22	34	19	14	29	06	00
4 3	36	27	07	12	11	05	10	13	05	00
4 4	26	21	04	04	14	02	09	13	01	00
4 5	10	08	01	00	04	00	00	05	00	00
4 6	04	02	00	00	00	00	00	01	00	00
4 7	03	01	01	00	00	00	00	00	00	00
5 0	01	01	00	00	02	00	01	01	00	00
5 1	06	04	06	04	04	03	05	07	07	01
5 2	14	17	07	01	12	04	04	13	03	00
5 3	07	08	03	01	04	01	02	08	01	00
5 4	05	03	02	00	06	02	00	05	00	00
5 5	02	01	00	00	00	00	00	03	00	00
5 6	02	01	00	00	00	00	00	01	00	00
5 7	01	00	00	00	00	00	00	00	00	00
6 0	02	01	00	00	01	10	00	00	00	00
6 1	01	02	01	00	02	00	00	02	00	00
6 2	05	04	01	00	02	00	00	06	01	00
6 3	02	03	00	00	01	01	01	02	00	00
6 4	02	02	00	00	02	00	01	00	00	00
6 5	01	00	00	00	01	00	00	00	00	00
7 0	00	00	00	00	00	00	00	01	00	00
7 1	01	01	00	00	00	00	00	00	00	00
7 2	02	01	00	00	02	00	00	00	00	00
7 3	01	02	00	00	01	00	00	00	00	00
7 4	02	01	01	00	01	00	00	00	00	00
entropy H_3	2.36	2.31	2.12	2.00	2.31	2.12	2.08	2.25	1.65	0.79

No other combinations occurred.

To our 1,000-word selections, we added selections from the prose of Leskov (*Ledi Makbet Mcenskogo uezda* [*The Lady Macbeth of the Mtsensk District*]), Turgenev (*Stuk, stuk, stuk* [*Tap, Tap, Tap*]), Čekhov (*Nevesta* [*The Betrothed*]), and Dostoevskij (*Prestuplenie i nakazanie* [*Crime and Punishment*]). In addition, using Tomaševskij's data (from his book *Jazyk i stikh* [*Language and Verse*]), we found the value of H_2 for Puškin's "Pikovaja dama'' ["The Queen of Spades"]. The iambic tetrameters of Puškin, Blok, and Lomonosov were united into one 1,000-word sample, taking roughly 300–350 words from each poet.

The entropy H_2 of all texts diminished considerably from the values of H_1. The reduction was greatest in the accentual verse and iambic tetrameters (see Summary Table). The decrease of H_3 compared to H_2 was less. The entropy of prose remained virtually undiminished, if we consider the limitations of precision imposed by a 1,000-word sample. On the basis of the data from Table 2 and Table 3, we may conclude that the rhythmic requirements of prose are insignificantly small and impose almost no constraints on a text.

SUMMARY TABLE

text type	av. word length	H_{word}	$H_{syll.}$	H_2	H_3	$H_1 - H_2$	$H_2 - H_3$
Scientific prose	3.56	3.94	1.11	2.38	2.36	1.56	0.02
Expository prose	3.16	3.72	1.18	2.40	2.31	1.32	0.09
Artistic prose	2.95	3.47	1.18	2.12	2.12	1.35	0.00
Turgenev				2.32	2.31		0.01
Dostoevskij				2.31	2.25		0.06
Čekhov				2.12	2.08		0.04
Leskov				2.15	2.08		0.07
Conversational speech	2.87	3.25	1.13	2.04	2.00	1.21	0.04
Accentual verse	2.95	3.27	1.11	1.67	1.65	1.60	0.02
Iambic verse	2.70	2.86		0.91	0.79	1.95	0.12
Blok	2.75	3.10	1.13				
Puškin	2.68	2.82	1.05				
Lomonosov	2.67	2.75	1.03				

Rhythmic word types in prose occur as almost independent events, subject only to the task of conveying the *content*, although a very small part of the overall entropy is dissipated when a phrase is given rhythmic "polish" (especially at the beginning and the end of a sentence).

The rhythm of artistic prose did not differ significantly from that of expository and scientific prose. It appears that the distinctions between these stylistically different types do not lie in the area of rhythm (as long as we are not dealing with a "prose poem"), but rather in the system of imagery in artistic prose. On the other hand, the difference between verse and prose is quite evident in the data in Tables 1—3 and in the Summary Table. The slight reduction in the value of H_3 as compared to H_2 in accentual verse is probably to be explained by the fact that the counting of pairs of intervals was "continuous," that is, it ignored stanza patterns. When the latter were accounted for, the entropy of accentual verse decreased not by 0.02 but by approximately 0.25.

RHYTHMIC ENTROPY OF VERSE

Any meaningful text, whether it be a scientific article or a piece of poetry, is a product of the language system in which that text is written. The system of the Russian language, just as that of any other language, imposes constraints on the possible combinations of letters, words, syllables, and sentences. These constraints influence the rhythmical regularity of speech since rhythm is composed of:

(1) primary rhythmic units—syllables—consisting of one vowel and $0, 1, 2 \ldots N$ consonants.

(2) "content" words, each of which consists of one stressed syllable and $0, 1, 2 \ldots N$ unstressed syllables. Since it is impossible to imagine the "longest word in the Russian language," there may theoretically be any number of different rhythmic word types.

(3) combinations of "content" words into sentences or lines of poetry. Unlike ordinary speech, versification is a system of text construction in which the constraints are not probabilistic but *fixed*.

The number of "content" words whose combinations constitute rhythm depends entirely on the number of words necessary to transmit meaning in prose, while in verse this number of "content" words and, hence, the number of stresses is strictly controlled. A rhythmic unit in ordinary speech (a sentence) is not an exact equivalent of a rhythmical unit of poetry (poetic line and stanza). Constraints on verse involve both the use of individual words and their combinations into groups of two, three, etc. For example, in iambic tetrameter it is "forbidden" to use such rhythmic word types as 9^1 or 9^3 (see Table 1), or such combinations as 5^1, 5^3, etc. In accentual verse, these restrictions are less rigorous, but nevertheless even here it is highly unlikely that we will encounter such rhythmic word types as 12^7 or the combination $9^3 7^7$. These prohibitions make it possible to assign exact quantitative properties to each type of poetic meter (on the basis of word boundaries) and to compute $H\infty$ (the limit entropy) for each individual meter. The value of H_2 for prose is close to the value of H_∞, while for each poetic meter, H_∞ is approximately equal to the value of the entropy per line, since the rhythmic connections of successive lines (within a stanza) are weak and are subject, as almost independent events, to the formulas of probability multiplication.

CONCLUSION

In concluding we would like to make some remarks concerning the application of mathematical methods and, in particular, information theory to such a manifestly "humanistic" science as poetics. At its present level, information theory only permits the evaluation of "code" information, ignoring its content and its social value. Even more difficult problems are raised in evaluating information contained in a work of art, where transmission of information involves the presence of a series of parameters: stylistic, semantic, etc. In the present essay, only rhythm was investigated. Information theory makes possible the introduction of exact quantitative measurements into poetics. Mathematical methods, following the course already taken by linguistics, have also found application in the study of the specific language that is called art.

REFERENCES

1. In a diacritic transcription, a stressed syllable is indicated by $\prime$ and an unstressed syllable by $\smile$. A word boundary is shown as $|$; for example, the word *grafičeski* is transcribed as " $|\smile \prime \smile\smile|$ ".
2. Here, H_1 is the entropy of an experiment having N possible outcomes (rhythmic word types); c is the coefficient of proportionality, depending on the logarithmic base (for the binary logarithms used here, it equals unity, or one bit [roughly 3.32 of a decimal unit]), and $p_1, p_2 \ldots p_N$ are the probabilities (statistical frequencies) of each rythmic word type.
3. In *Voprosy jazykoznanija*, no. 1 (1960).

TONALITY STRUCTURE IN RUSSIAN VERSE

Lawrence Gaylord Jones

INTRODUCTION

This study presents an exploratory analysis of the distribution and patterning of one distinctive feature through the stressed vowels of several examples of nineteenth- and twentieth-century Russian verse. The calculations and measurements are simple and attention is centered on the contour of the feature throughout the entire text, although details are pointed out wherever appropriate.

It is assumed that in the poetic text all linguistic elements potentially have autonomous value and may interact with one another in various ways and on various levels since the main characteristic of the poetic function of language is a focus "on the message for its own sake . . . promoting the palpability of signs."[1] Phonemes, syllables, morphemes, syntactic constructions, in short, all structural elements of the language may take on independent value, occurring in a great number of statable patterned relationships.

On the level of sound texture alone, the tendency towards patterning has often been noted. Osip Brik in his analysis of sound repetitions in Russian verse concluded that the poetic text is "a single, undivided composition for which not only the separate central harmonies (*sozvučija*) are vitally important, but also the whole aggregate of the sound material."[2] Examining the total sound texture of several Russian poems, Kušner discovered a symmetrical distribution of consonants throughout entire poems.[3]

In his discussion of the sound texture of verse Boris Ejkhenbaum pointed out that every work of art is an intricate complex of elements and that:

It is not the finished word (*gotovoe slovo*) which serves as the organizing basis of lyrical verse but an intricate complex of rhythm and speech acoustics, often with certain elements dominating others. This complex is the first point in the realization of the abstract artistic representation. In this sense of the word, the sounds of verse (speech representations—acoustic and articulatory) have *autonomous value* and are *self-significant*. They do not "accompany" and do not simply "correspond."[4]

Now that it has become possible to analyze phonemes into bundles of distinctive features, the sound texture of verse can be considered in even greater detail than it has previously, and it is possible now to pursue relationships through entire verse structures which had hitherto remained unnoticed.

Analyzing verse into distinctive features, however, adds even more items to an already extremely complex structure of linguistic elements. Consider, for instance, the first three words of Puškin's *Ja vas ljubil*:[5]

This essay is reprinted in a slightly abridged form from the *International Journal of Slavic Linguistics and Poetics*, IX (1965), 125–151, by permission of the author and Mouton & Company.

TABLE I

	/j	a	v	a	s	u	ḅ	i	1/6
Vocalic	−	+	−	+	−	+	+	−	+
Consonontal	−	−	+	−	+	+	−	+	−
Diffuse	O	−	O	−	O	O	+	O	+
Compact	O	+	−	+	−	O	O	−	O
High Tonality	O	O	−	O	+	O	−	−	+
Strident	O	O	+	O	+	O	O	−	O
Nasal	O	O	O	O	O	O	O	−	O
Continuous	O	O	O	O	+	+	O	O	+
Voiced	O	O	+	O	−	O	O	+	O
Sharped	O	O	−	O	−	+	O	+	O
Accented	O	−	O	+	O	O	−	O	+

When such an "intricate complex" of elements is approached from the view-point of poetics, it must be organized in terms of the underlying metrical structure. "All strictly regulated metric systems are founded on syllabification, existing on the physiological, physical, and psychological levels of speech transmission,"[7] according to Lotz, who goes on to point out that the terms "syllable," "vowel," and "consonant" are among the most obscure in phonemic theory.[8] To analyze simultaneously the entire phonemic text (whether in terms of distinctive features or in any other system of relations) one requires a system of weighting to correspond to the syllabic and hence metrical system of the text. But because of the vagueness of the basic terms such a system of weighting can only be done in a very arbitrary way. That is not to say that it cannot or should not be done, but that as an initial step in an analysis of the sound texture of verse, it can be a very dangerous step. There-fore, in the present study, only the vowels, and the (metrically) stressed vowels in particular, have been chosen for analysis.

The reason for choosing the vowels is that they are the "peaks," "centers," "nuclei" of syllables, the obligatory members of syllables, and from the view-point of Russian prosody, the bearers of the metrical rhythm. To analyze all of the vowels in such a prosodic system would lead again to the problem of weighting, and to such arbitrary decisions as whether to consider the stressed vowels twice or three times as important as unstressed vowels. Restriction of analysis to only those stressed vowels which occur in metrically stressed position is related to the syllabo-tonic Russian metrical system in which all of the examined texts are written.

With few exceptions, the poems discussed below are written in binary meters (iambic or trochaic). As is well known, in Russian prosody of the nineteenth and twentieth centuries, not all of the metrically stressed positions need be filled by a stressed syllable.[9] Except for the final stressed position in the line, which is obligatory, the pattern of stressed vowels can be quite irregular in a poem written in such a system. The result of this situation is that the metrically stressed vowels serve as markers of the poetic rhythm, and hence can be considered as the most predominant phonemes in the text.

This concentration on the metrically stressed vowels obviates the necessity for any kind of weighting factors at all and eliminates a large number of variables which are difficult to control. The system of procedure outlined above and the method of analysis presented below can be looked upon as the first step in the analysis of the "whole aggregate of the sound material." It is true that it concentrates on what Brik would probably call the "central harmonies," but at the same time, it is highly probable, that in any weighting system which would have to be applied as more and more elements of the sound texture were to be analyzed, the metrically stressed vowels would have to be assigned the greatest weighting factor and would thus tend to dominate the sound patterning.

THE TONALITY FEATURE

The five stressed vowel phonemes of Russian are distinguished from one another by the following distribution of three distinctive features:

TABLE II

	/i	e	a	o	u/[10]
Compact	—	—	+	—	—
Diffuse	+	—	—	—	+
High Tonality	+	÷	O	—	—

Of these three features, the High Tonality feature appears to be the best one with which to begin an analysis of the sound texture of verse, for reasons to be presently given. This feature, which in acoustic terms refers to a high second formant (+) as opposed to a low second formant (−), and in articulatory terms opposes unrounded (+) to rounded (−) lip position, divides the vowels into three groups: (+): /i/, /e/; (O): /a/; and (−): /o/, /u/. One of the reasons for choosing this feature to begin the analysis, is that from a statistical point of view, as pointed out in detail in the next section, there appear to be fewer constraints in the distribution of the members of this opposition both in prose and in poetry.

From the viewpoint of poetics, however, the main reason for choosing this feature is that it is the High Tonality feature which is most frequently, although usually unconsciously, referred to in commentaries on the "phonetic" or "sound effects" of verse. For instance, in discussing the "instrumentation" of Annenskij' *Toska mimoletnosti*, Setchkarev notes that in the last stanza "the č in the first line combined with the contrasting e and o corresponds to the e–o and i–u sequences of the second. . . ."[11] Thus high and low tonality are in "contrast" and sequences of high-low tonality "correspond." When Močul'skij points out, in a comparison of two poems which he considers to be otherwise quite similar, that Fet's *Opavšij list* ends with a "cheerful 'morale' in a major key" as opposed to Blok's *Medlitel'noj čredoj niskhodit den' osennij*, which he feels has a very gloomy ending[12] the difference can be shown in terms of the tonalities of the stressed vowels in the final lines of both poems.

In synaesthetic reactions to vowels, moreover, it is evidently this feature which operates most clearly,[13] high tonality being associated with lightness, happiness, low tonality with darkness, sadness. The great eighteenth-century Russian scientist and poet Lomonosov in his *Short Handbook of Eloquence* attributes to certain "vowel" letters of the alphabet the abilities to express particular moods and concepts. Assuming these letters to have had approximately the same sound correspondences in his day as at the present time, his classification closely follows the division into high and low tonality: /i/ and /e/ express tenderness, endearment, /o/ and /u/ express anger, envy, etc. The neutral /a/ expresses magnificence, spaciousness, etc.[14]

Finally, it should be noted, that in analyzing the vowels into high, neutral, and low tonalities, the distinctive feature of compactness is also reflected in the data: (+): /a/ as opposed to the remaining (−): /i/, /e/, /o/, /u/. Thus, in the data presented below, a preponderance of the vowel /a/ indicates a strong compact orientation in the text. Articulatorily this is the opposition of open *vs.* close and acoustically it is associated with greater *vs.* lesser amplitude.[15] Synaesthetically it is often associated with largeness as opposed to smallness as in the example from Lomonosov given above.[16]

STATISTICAL PERSPECTIVE

To show the distribution of the members of the three distinctive features of the Russian vowel phonemes, several counts were made of the stressed vowels as they occur in prose and poetical texts. To these was added an existing count of the stressed vowels as they occur in conversation. The prose[17] and poetical[18] texts each represent a count of 1,000 consecutive stressed vowels and the conversational data represent a count of 10,000 "sounds."[19] Tables III and IV give the distribution of these quantities in percentages.

TABLE III

Percentage frequency of occurrence of individual vowels

	/i/	/e/	/a/	/o/	/u/
Conversation	.1466	.2070	.3252	.2287	.0923
Prose	.1723	.1704	.3190	.2333	.1047
Poetry	.1794	.2015	.2634	.2484	.1069

TABLE IV

Percentage frequency of occurrence of members of high tonality feature

	High (+) (/i/ + /e/)	Neutral (O) (/a/)	Low (−) (/o/ + /u/)
Conversation	.3536	.3252	.3210
Prose	.3428	.3190	.3380
Poetry	.3810	.2634	.3554

TABLE V

Percentage frequency of occurrence of the compact and diffuse distinctive features

	Compact		Diffuse	
	+ (/a/)	− (/i/ + /e/ + /o/ + /u/)	+ (/i/ + /u/)	− (/e/ + /a/ + /o/)
Conversation	.3252	.6746	.2389	.7609
Prose	.3190	.6809	.2771	.7228
Poetry	.2634	.7365	.2864	.7135

Table III indicates little difference among all three types of linguistic behavior. For each vowel, at least two of the types differ by less than one percent. Differences higher than one percent are not consistent with linguistic behavior. For instance, the percentage for conversation differs from the other two for the vowel /i/, but for the vowel /e/ it is the percentage for prose which differs from the other two percentages. The only possibly significant figure in this table is for the poetical sample for the vowel /a/ (.2634), which differs by at least .05 from either of the other percentages for this vowel. This fact might be due to the manipulation of the tonality feature in most of the poetry samples. That is, if the poet consciously or unconsciously strives for a pattern of high or low tonality, he may suppress the vowel /a/, since it is neutral for this feature.

Tables IV and V show the same data arranged according to the three distinctive features of the vowels. Again the percentages across language type do not appear to be significant.

One fact, however, stands out quite sharply concerning the high tonality feature as opposed to the other two features: the percentages for the high (+) and low (−) members of the high tonality feature are very close as opposed to the (+) and (−) values for either of the other two features. In general, the three members of the high tonality feature are about equally distributed in frequency of occurrence, as opposed to the other two features in which one member of the opposition occurs at least .50 more frequently than the other member.

If these statistics are valid, then they lead to two conclusions relevant to the present study: (1) A statistical sample of this type is inappropriate for distinguishing between poetic language and other types of linguistic behavior.[20] (2) Since the three members of the high tonality feature occur with roughly the same frequency in all types of linguistic behavior, and since therefore, in terms of information theory, there are fewer constraints on their occurrence, if a poet consciously or unconsciously wishes to manipulate the sound texture of his verse through the stressed vowels, he has a greater chance of success if he does this by treating them as classified according to the high tonality feature.

In addition to these two points, these facts indicate that in dealing with the distribution of the members of the high tonality feature in specific texts it is not necessary to weight the individual members according to frequency of occurrence in order to discover their relative predominance, since their frequency of occurrence across large samples of linguistic behavior is evenly distributed among the three of them.[21]

CHOICE OF TEXTS

For this study more than twenty-five poems were analyzed, all of them relatively short lyrics with one or two exceptions. All of them have a clear metrical substructure which could be determined statistically by counting the word stresses according to syllabic (or vowel) position in the line and summing these accents over the whole poem.[22]

With the exception of Pasternak's *Roždestvenskaja zvezda* and his *Belaja noč'*, all of the poems have a binary metrical structure (iambic or trochaic), the line and stanza length of each poem also are constant.

Puškin's *Čto v imeni tebe mojem* and his *Ja vas ljubil* were chosen to determine whether or not the tonality structure could be related to Jakobson's grammatical analyses of these poems.[23] Several other poems of identical length and metrical substructure were chosen to compare with these poems. Pasternak's *Gamlet* was also chosen as a focus of attention and Akhmatova's *Stal mne reže snit'sja slava Bogu*, identical in length and metrical substructure, compared with it.[24] Lermontov's *Kazač'ja kolybel'naja pesnja* was chosen for comparison of parodies on it written by N. A. Nekrasov[25] and O. N. Čjumina.[26]

For the remaining poems, the only principle of choice was curiosity.

METHODS AND MEASUREMENTS

For the sake of convenience and to avoid ambiguity, the high tonality feature will henceforth be referred to merely as the tonality feature. The three members of the feature will be called *high* ($+$), *neutral* ($\bigcirc$), and *low* ($-$).

Table VI, which presents an analysis of Puškin's *Čto v imeni tebe mojem*, will serve as an illustration for the explanation of the methods and measurements of tonality.

The following principle was followed rigorously in accepting or rejecting a vowel in a poem: Except for prepositions, conjunctions, and particles, if the vowel of a monosyllabic word, or the stressed vowel of a polysyllabic word occurred in a metrically stressed position, it was included in the data.[27] Thus in I.1 (stanza I, line 1) of the Puškin poem, the vowel in the word *Čto* was not included in the data because it is not in a metrically stressed position; but the vowel of the same word is included in the data for Pasternak's *Gamlet* (Table IX: I.4) since it occurs there in a metrically stressed position.

In Table VI the accepted vowels are listed according to syllable position in the line in the column labelled *Stressed Syll.* In the next column, *TS* (tonality sequence) the same data are translated into the members of the tonality feature. In line I.1, for instance, /i/ and /e/ are both listed as (+) and /o/ as (−). The following columns contain various measurements on the *TS* data.

1. *Quantities* (*Q*). This is the sum of a given member for a certain portion of the text. The table lists the line and stanza values, for example, in line I.1, there are two highs, no neutrals, and one low; the first stanza has an accumulation of 4 highs, 2 neutrals, and 9 lows. All of the subsequent measurements are derived from these figures.

2. *Tonal Balance* (*TB*). This measurement disregards the neutrals and sums the highs (treated as positive values) and lows (treated as negative values). It measures the predominance of one member of the feature over the other. If there is an equal number of highs and lows in a line, then the value is zero, as in II.1, and IV.2. *TB* values are given for line (*TBl*) and stanza (*TBs*).

3. *Tonal Difference* (*TD*). This measurement, based on the *TB* values, is the difference between successive pairs of *TB* values. In the table the line (*TDl*) and stanza (*TDs*) values are given, for example, the *TDl* for lines I.1 and 2 is 4; the *TDs* between I and II is 3. Tonal difference values are useful in noting the patterning properties over the extent of a whole poem or stanza and also in noting the tonal "shift" from one line or stanza to another.

4. *Tonal Symmetry.* The curious phenomenon of tonal symmetry is treated in detail below. As a measurement, it is derived from the *TD* values and represents a tendency for the terminal *TD* values to be the same, or to differ by only a figure of 1. That is, in the table, the first and last *TDs* values are both 3. When the terminal values are smaller than the central values, this will be called terminal symmetry as in the table: *TDs*: 3–5–3; when the terminal values are greater than the central values, the sequence will be called centralized symmetry as in *Gamlet*: *TDs*: 6–1–8.

A NOTE ON INTERPRETATION

As is pointed out below, the tonality structure of a poem often coincides with aspects of its grammatical, lexical, or semantic organization. The question of conscious (or unconscious) manipulation of the sound material by the poet to bring about such coincidence cannot be answered except by the poet himself (if it is a conscious act).[28] The interesting fact is that such coincidences can be found.

In contrast to this situation is the question of private interpretation, wherein the assumption of some fact about the poem is related to the sound texture. For instance, in Akhmatova's "*Stal mne reže . . .* ," if one of the monks who passes by had been the lyricist's lover, then it is an interesting fact that the tonality structure of the stanza in which the monk appears is significantly different from that of the remaining stanzas. But this, unlike the coincidences mentioned above, is a conditional, but plausible juxtaposition of facts, not an ostensible coincidence of elements.

PUŠKIN: *ČTO V IMENI TEBE MOJEM*

At the beginning of his remarks on the grammatical structure of this poem[29] Jakobson notes its obvious division into two parts, each part introduced by a question. In the tonality structure of the poem, this division is reflected in the equal tonal differences between stanzas I–II and III–IV. The *TDs* of each pair is 3. The fact that the other *TDs* (between II–III) is 5 could be interpreted as showing a close tonal connection between each question and its answer, but a great difference between pairs of questions and answers.

Jakobson also points to the grammatical oppositions between the first and fourth stanzas, the latter replacing the adjectival forms of the former by nouns: I: *pečal'nyj*, IV: *pečal'*; I: *nočnoj*, IV: *noč'*. There is further the semantic opposition of noise to silence between the two stanzas: I: *šum volny*, IV: *v tišine*.[30] These stanzas are also the farthest apart tonally: there is a tonal difference of 11 between them, the first having the lowest tonality balance and the fourth the highest tonality balance.

Jakobson further mentions the fact that the diffuse vowels (/i/ and /u/) accrue in the first and fourth stanzas, and that the "dark" (rounded) vowels are maximal in the first stanza and minimal in the final stanza.[31] The *TB* figures for this poem in Table VI show a gradual rise in tonality from low (−5) in the first stanza to high (+6) in the last stanza. Returning to the division of the poem into questions and answers, one notes that the tonality of each answer is higher than the tonality of its question.

The tonal contour of this poem considered in and of itself is quite unusual, in two ways. First of all, the gradual rise of the tonal balance of the stanzas. In a sample of several poems of this type alone, an alternation from stanza to stanza would be more typical. The second peculiarity is the terminal symmetry of the tonal differences for the stanzas: *TD* 3–5–3. Although there is a strong tendency among the Russian poems analyzed for this study for the terminal *TD* figures to be close in value, it is not often that they are identical.

Table VII lists the *TB* and *TD* values for several poems with a metrical substructure, line, and stanza length as *Čto v imeni. . . .* The first one, *Ne poj krasavica . . .*, was chosen because the last stanza is a word for word repetition of the first. Although such a structure rules out the possibility of a continuously rising tonal balance, it does not rule out a symmetrical disposition of

TABLE VI

	Stressed Syllable				TS				Q			TB	TD	
	MS: 2	4	6	8	2	4	6	8	+	O	−		1	s
Что в имени тебе моем?	/i		e	o	+		+	−	2	0	1	+1		
Оно умрет, как шум печальный	o	o	u	a	−	−	−	O	0	1	3	−3	4	
Волны, плеснувшей в берег дальный,	i	u	e	a	+	−	+	O	2	1	1	+1	4	
Как звук ночной в лесу глухом.	u	o	u	o	−	−	−	−	0	0	4	−4	5	
									4	2	9	−5		3
Оно на памятном листке	o	a		e	−	O		+	1	1	1	0		
Оставит мертвый след, подобный	a	o	e	o	O	−	+	−	1	1	2	−1	1	
Узору надписи надгробной	o	a		o	−	O		−	0	1	2	−2	1	
На непонятном языке.		a		e		O		+	1	1	0	+1	3	
									3	4	5	−2		5
Что в нем? Забытое давно	o	i		o	−	+		−	1	0	2	−1		
В волненьях новых и мятежных,	e	o		e	+	−		+	2	0	1	+1	2	
Твоей душе не даст оно	e	e	a	o	+	+	O	−	2	1	1	+1	0	
Воспоминаний чистых, нежных.		a	i	e		O	+	+	2	1	0	+2	1	
									7	2	4	+3		3
Но в день печали, в тишине,	e	a		e	+	O		+	2	1	0	+2		
Произнеси его тоскуя;			i	u			+	−	1	0	1	0	2	
Скажи: есть память обо мне,	i	a		e	+	O		+	2	1	0	+2	2	
Есть в мире сердце, где живу я.	i	e	e	u/	+	+	+	−	3	0	1	+2	0	
									8	2	2	+6		

TD values, but the terminal *TD* values are not identical as in the analyzed poem.

Puškin's *Vo glubine sibirskikh rud* has alternating *TB* values and no *TD* symmetry. It is interesting to note in passing, however, that the preponderance of negative *TB* values may reflect synaesthetically the gloom of the poem.

The only other poem in Table VII which has absolute *TD* symmetry is a light satiric poem by Dobroljubov. Although there is no necessary connection between the two points, the symmetry is accompanied by a gradual fall in *TB* values from first to last stanza. In the poem itself there are no clear grammatical or thematic features which coincide with the sound structure. The closest one can come to a criterion for dividing the first two from the last two stanzas is that the verbs in the first two stanzas have the same subject, *moralist*, whereas the verbs in the other stanzas do not share this characteris-

tic. Possibly the thematic material of the poem could be associated synaesthetically with the falling *TB* values, since the first stanza tells of the moralist
speaking eloquently about the poor and justice, and the last stanza points out
that two poor old women who tried to listen to him at the window were
driven away.

TABLE VII

		I		II		III		IV
Puškin, *Ne poj, krasavica, pri mne*	TB:	+3		+7		−1		+3
	TD:		4		8		5	
Puškin, *Vo glubine sibirskikh rud*	TB:	−2		+1		−8		−3
	TD:		3		9		5	
Pasternak, *Pakhota*	TB:	+4		+1		+3		+3
	TD:		3		2		0	
Akhmatova, *Večerom*	TB:	−6		−1		−3		+4
	TD:		5		2		7	
Dobroljubov, *Sila slova*	TB:	+6		+4		+1		−1
	TD:		2		3		2	
Tjutčev, *Ne raz ty slyšala priznan'e*	TB:	+3		−1		−1		+4
	TD:		4		0		5	

Finally, the Tjutčev example has almost symmetrical *TB* and *TD* stanza
sequences, but grammatical or thematic coincidence with this tonal structure
is not clear.

The problem of symmetry is taken up in detail below.

PUŠKIN: *JA VAS LJUBIL*

In his analysis of this poem Jakobson points out that in it fourteen (almost
half) of the words are pronouns, ten of the words are verbs.[32] For a discussion
of the tonality structure of the poem, it is necessary to add that the first verb
form, *ljubil* occurs three times in the poem and is clearly a "key"[33] or thematic
word in the text. (The root *ljub-* occurs in addition, in two other formations
in the poem.) Furthermore, regarding the pronouns *ja* and *vy* (the latter of
which occurs only in the dative and accusative) it should be noted that the
vowels all have neutral tonality (*ja, vas, vam*), whereas the pronoun *drugoj*,
occurring as *drugim*, not only has high and low tonality, but has the same
tonality sequence in its vowels and the same stress pattern as *ljubil*, that is

	/ļ u b̦ i l/	/d r u g i m/
Tonality	− +	− +
Accented	− +	− +

These two words are also the respectively first and last bisyllabic words in
the poem.

This low-to-high tonality sequence is repeated in the rhyme vowels of the first four lines. (See Table VIII. Although usually printed without a break, the poem here has been divided into two parts according to its rhyme pattern, and so that the stanza Q and TB values could be recorded conveniently.) From a purely *phonetic* point of view, one could also say that the rhyme scheme of the second four lines also follows the low-to-high tonality sequence, since phonetically /e/ is lower in tonality than /i/. Finally, in regard to the rhyme, it is interesting to note that it is an alternation of feminine and masculine, so that the low tonality vowel in the rhyme schemes is in non-final position, and the high tonality vowel in final position, just as they are in the words *ljubil* and *drugim*.

TABLE VIII

						TS				Q	TB		TD	
						MS:				+ O −			1	s
						2	4	6	8	10				
Я вас любил: любовь еще быть может,						O	+	−	−	−	1 1 3	−2			
В душе моей угасла не совсем;						+	+	O		+	3 1 0	+3		5	
Но пусть она вас больше не тревожит;						−	O	−		−	0 1 3	−3		6	
Я не хочу печалить вас ничем.							−	O	O	+	1 2 1	0		3	
											5 5 7	−2			9
Я вас любил безмолвно, безнадежно,						O	+	−		+	2 1 1	+1			
То робостью, то ревностью томим;						−		+		+	2 0 1	+1		0	
Я вас любил так искренно, так нежно,						O	+	+		+	3 1 0	+3		2	
Как дай вам Бог любимой быть другим.						O	−	+	+	+	3 1 1	+2		1	
											10 3 3	+7			

The pattern of low-to-high tonality again occurs in the tonal balance figures for the first four lines. (See Table VIII TB values. As can be verified from the Q values, this alternation would obtain even if the rhyme vowels were omitted from the count.)

The low-to-high tonality pattern occurs once again in the TB values for the two quatrains, the first having a value of −2 and the second +7.

Statements such as the above cannot be made for Puškin's *Tri ključa*, chosen for comparison because of its identical meter and length. The TB values drop from 7 to 0 between the first and second quatrains, possibly reflecting synaesthetically the theme of transition from youth to age.

Concerning symmetry as noted above in the other Puškin poem, it is obvious that in a two part poem, the TD stanza value would have to be 0 (or 1 if this degree of freedom were admitted). The TD values of both are far from symmetrical.

PASTERNAK: *GAMLET*

This poem, which is analyzed in Table IX, differs metrically from the Puškin examples above in that it is in trochaic pentameter. It also differs from them in that it has no clearly definable "key" word. Nevertheless the two middle stanzas are unified by an item of grammatical structure: both stanzas end with an imperative addressed to God, who is referred to directly in II as *Avva Otče* and indirectly as the addressee of the imperative in III. (To these may be added the pronominal adjective *Tvoj* in III.1). Reference to God does not occur in the other two stanzas, nor do any imperative forms.

While the TD stanza sequence is not strictly symmetrical: *TD*: 6–1–8, the first and last values are close and the middle value is low. It is thus the reverse of the sequence for *Čto v imeni tebe mojem* (*TD*: 3–5–3). Where the latter showed a parallel in tonality and the division of the stanzas into pairs (I–II and III–IV), the grammatical characteristics mentioned above and the *TD* sequence shows *Gamlet* divided into three groups (I, II–III, and IV), the second and third stanzas being tonally united by a small *TD*, as was the case for I–II and III–IV in the Puškin poem.

Just as the tonality sequence of the vowels in the key words in *Ja vas ljubil* were reflected in the rhymes and stanza tonalities, so in *Gamlet* the tonality sequence of the opening sentence is repeated:

	/g u l	z a ṭ i x/
Tonality	—	O ' +

This low-neutral-high sequence can be said to occur in the rhyme scheme, which is entirely low in tonalities in stanza I, alternates between high and low in II, between neutral and low in III, and is entirely high in IV. The sequence is again reflected in the *TB* stanza values which range from −7 in stanza I, are relatively neutral in II and III, and rise to +6 in IV.

If the last line of I is accepted as a question ("What is happening in my age") with its answering comment in IV.4 ("Life has to be lived out—it's not a field you cross"), then the low-to-high tonality pattern for question and answer found in Puškin's *Čto v imeni tebe mojem* occurs here in *Gamlet* also.

There are many curious details in the tonality structure of the second and third stanzas of *Gamlet*, apparently related to other levels of organization. For instance the *TD* values for the lines of II (3–4–6) are strikingly different from the line *TD* values for any other stanza, and especially different from stanza III (1–1–1). As pointed out above, in the section on "Methods and Measurements," the tonal difference measurement should be a good indication of tonal "shift" from one point to another in the structure, a lack of balance from one point to another. It may occur also as an indication of tension. The highest line *TD* value in stanza II is between the last two lines of the stanza. This is semantically connected with the quotation of Christ's words in the Garden of Gethsemane, "If it is only possible, Abba, Father, Take this cup from me."

TABLE IX

	TS					Q			TB	TD	
	MS:					+	O	−		l	s
	1	3	5	7	9						
Гул затих. Я вышел на подмостки.	−	+	+		−	2	0	2	0		
Прислонясь к дверному косяку,		O	−		−	0	1	2	−2	2	
Я ловлю в далеком отголоске,	O	−	−		−	0	1	3	−3	1	
Что случится на моем веку.	−	+		−	−	1	0	3	−2	1	
						3	2	10	−7		
На меня наставлен сумрак ночи		O	O	−	−	0	2	2	−2		
Тысячью биноклей на оси.	+		−		+	2	0	1	+1	3	
Если только можно, Авва Отче,		−	−	O	−	0	1	3	−3	4	
Чашу эту мимо пронеси.	O	+	+		+	3	1	0	+3	6	
						5	4	6	−1		
											6
Я люблю Твой замысел упрямый	O	−	O		O	0	3	1	−1		
И играть согласен эту роль.		O	O	+	−	1	2	1	0	1	
Но сейчас идет другая драма,	O	−	O	O		0	3	1	−1	1	
И на этот раз меня уволь.	+	O	O	−		1	2	1	0	1	
						2	10	4	−2		
											1
Но продуман распорядок действий,			−	O	+	1	1	1	0		
И не отвратим конец пути.			+	+	+	3	0	0	+3	3	
Я один, все тонет в фарисействе.	O	+	−		+	2	1	1	+1	2	
Жизнь прожить – не поле перейти.	+	+	−		+	3	0	1	+2	1	
						9	2	3	+6		8

The third stanza not only has low and identical *TD* values which oppose it to all other stanzas, but also a repetitive *TB* sequence, alternating between −1 and 0. These values are counterbalanced by the *Q* value for the neutral vowel /a/, which reaches its maximum of 10 in stanza III. Since this vowel is compact in opposition to the remaining vowels (see section 1 above), the *Q* sequence represents a kind of crescendo from its low value of 2 in stanza I, which is also the value it returns to in the last stanza.

Finally, there is one other instance of patterning in stanza III, which does not appear to be related to patterning on any other level. The tonal sequence (*TS*) is identical for lines 1 and 3, although the vowels of both lines are not in the same metrically stressed positions: O − O O. This is not true for any other pair of lines in any other stanza in this poem.

It may be added parenthetically that stanzas II and III are also united by a symmetrical distribution of the archiphoneme $/R/$ (the phonemes $/r/$ and $/ŗ/$). The numbers of occurrence by line are:

Line	1	2	3	4
II	1	0	0	1
III	1	2	2	1

This situation does not obtain for either of the other stanzas, nor for any other consonant examined, although each of the archiphonemes $/R/$ and $/L/$ separately shows a symmetrical distribution according to syllabic position in the line:

	Syllable Sequence								
Occurrences of	1	2	3	4	5	6	7	8	9
$/L/$	1	5	2	0	2	4	1	(0	3)
$/R/$	1	2	1	2	2	1	2	(3	3)

(The symmetry is centered about the 4th syllable for $/L/$ and between the 4th and 5th for $/R/$, and the pattern goes only as far as the 7th.)[34]

Anna Akhmatova's *Stal mne reže snit'sja, slava Bogu*, analyzed in Table X, like *Gamlet* is written in trochaic pentameter and contains four four-line stanzas. There do not appear to be any grammatical characteristics which clearly give pattern to the poem, but the middle stanzas are united by rhyme and by semantic content. In both II and III the rhymes end in $/-Ni/$ and $/-ĺ'i/$. Semantically these stanzas deal with the particular events: all day the bells have not been silent; two monks pass by. On the other hand the first and fourth stanzas describe a general situation, the *status quo*: "I rarely dream of him any more, thank God"; "The King of Heaven has healed me with the icy calm of non-love."

Unlike *Gamlet*, however, this unity is not reflected by low *TD* values between II and III. The *TD* sequence has a terminally oriented distribution: 3–9–5. Unlike most of the poems analyzed, the *TB* value of the last stanza is very close to that of the first. Hence both *TD* and *TB* values are close to being symmetrical for the first and last stanzas.

The tonal balance reaches a peak (+9) in the third stanza. This cannot be associated with any grammatical or other linguistic patterning in this stanza. Given a certain "private" interpretation (see above, "A Note on Interpretation"), this peak coincides with a kind of climax in the poem. That is, the theme of the poem has to do with the lyricist's lover about whom she "no longer dreams." In the third stanza, while she is pruning the lilacs, two monks pass by. (It should be noted, incidentally, that the word *podstrigaju* which begins this stanza, in this context, is highly charged semantically.) If one of the monks is her former lover, then this stanza can easily be considered the climax, or dominant stanza of the poem.

But the most interesting tonal characteristics of this poem, wherein it differs not only from *Gamlet*, but from all other poems examined for this study, lie in the tonal balance of the lines and in the pattern of the line tonal differences.

TABLE X

	TS					Q			TB	TD	
	MS:					+	O	−		l	s
	1	3	5	7	9						
Стал мне реже сниться, слава Богу,	O	+	+	O	−	2	2	1	+1		
Больше не мерещится везде,	−		+		+	2	0	1	+1	0	
Лёг туман на белую дорогу,	−	O	+		−	1	1	2	−1	2	
Тени побежали по воде.	+		O		+	2	1	0	+2	3	
						7	4	4	+3		
И весь день не замолкали звоны		+		O	−	1	1	1	0		
Над простором вспаханной земли,		−	O		+	1	1	1	0	0	
Здесь всего сильнее от Ионы	+	−	+		−	2	0	2	0	0	
Колокольни Лаврские вдали.		−	O		+	1	1	1	0	0	
						5	3	5	0		3
Подстригаю на кустах сирени		O		O	+	1	2	0	+1		
Ветки те, что нынче отцвели;	+	+	+		+	4	0	0	+4	3	
По валам старинных укреплений		O	+		+	2	1	0	+2	2	
Два монаха медленно прошли.	O	O	+		+	2	2	0	+2	0	
						9	5	0	+9		9
Мир родной понятный и телесный	+	−	O		+	2	1	1	+1		
Для меня незрячей оживи.		O	O		+	1	2	0	+1	0	
Исцелил мне душу Царь Небесный	+	−		O	+	2	1	1	+1	0	
Ледяным покоем нелюбви.	+	−			+	2	0	1	+1	0	
						7	4	3	+4		5

Within the stanza, the *TB* values of each line is the same in II (*TBl*: 0) and IV (*TBl*+1). This of course results in the fact that the *TDl* values for these stanzas are all zero. In addition to this, the *TDl* values of the other two stanzas are reverse images one of the other:

$$\text{I:} \quad 0 \quad 2 \quad 3$$
$$\text{IV:} \quad 3 \quad 2 \quad 0$$

This patterning does not appear to be connected with any other characteristic of the poem.

Finally, in comparing this poem with *Gamlet* two relatively minor points should be mentioned. First of all, as in *Gamlet*, the vowel /a/ reaches its highest frequency of occurrence in stanza III, but actually, the *Q* values for the other stanzas are so close that this fact appears to have little significance. The other point is the curious fact that in both poems, God is referred to in two stanzas, and in all cases the *TD* values are lower for these stanzas than for the other stanzas (Pasternak II–III; Akhmatova I–IV).

A NOTE ON TONAL SYMMETRY

As pointed out above in the section on "Methods and Measurements," the term symmetry has been used here to refer to the case where the first and last stanzas of a poem have the same or very close *TD*, or sometimes *TB* values. Although it is rare that these terminal values are identical, such as is the case in Puškin's *Čto v imeni tebe mojem*, about a third of the poems examined have *TD* sequences in which the values for the first and last stanzas differ by only 1 or 2. This phenomenon is very difficult to evaluate and requires separate study. It will be sufficient here to outline the phenomenon and the problems involved.

As is very frequently the case with poetic language, it is difficult to assess this phenomenon statistically, since we are dealing with texts all of which may have been consciously or unconsciously manipulated by their creators to bring out just such tonal effects. Therefore, to say that terminal symmetry occurs about a third of the time in poetical texts is to say very little except that it does not always occur.

There is still the possibility, of course, that it is merely a chance phenomenon and it is this possibility which needs special treatment. To do this it will be necessary to show that there is some restraint on the values involved. For instance, if there is a strong tendency for particular *TD* values to recur, then the probability of such symmetry increases. Given the fact that the *TD* values must be either *a* or *b* and a sequence of three values, in a list of permutations of only those sequences where both *a* and *b* are present, a third of the sequences have terminal symmetry (*a–b–a* and *b–a–b*).

A survey of the data for this study does not show this restriction to occur. For instance, in just the four-stanza iambic tetrameter poems listed in Table VII, eight different *TD* values are represented, three of which occur more than three times, and of the two poems which show "absolute" symmetry (Puškin's *Čto v imeni* . . . and Dobroljubov's *Sila slova*) only the latter involves one of these values.

For the sake of comparison with prose structure, the following experiment was made. The line sequence of stressed vowels of Puškin's *Čto v imeni tebe mojem* was used as a matrix and was filled with the stressed vowels from prose selections:[35]

Matrix for Stanza II				Vowels from Čekhov story			
2	4	6	8	2	4	6	8
	V	V	V		/i	o	i
V	V	V	V	o	a	a	e
	V	V	V		u	o	e
		V	V			a	i/

(The effect of rhyme was incorporated by repeating the vowel of the last syllable appropriately.) Several such "random" sets of values showed no tendency towards symmetry. Random lines from Puškin's *Mednyj Vsadnik* were organized as four-line stanzas and groups of four "stanzas" analyzed. Again there was no tonal symmetry. If such experiments are capable of proving anything, they should be carried out on a larger scale.

A very interesting example of the phenomenon of tonal symmetry is found by comparing Lermontov's *Kazač'ja kolybel'naja pesnja*, with two parodies of it, one by Nekrasov and one by Čjumina.[36] In such a case we have poems which not only have the same metrical substructure, but also share a certain amount of vocabulary. In certain cases, the parodies reverse the tonalities of the original: where Lermontov has *tikho smotrit mesjac* . . ., Nekrasov has *tusklo smotrit mesjac* . . ., a change from high to low tonality. The *TD* values for the three poems are as follows (Čjumina's parody has only five stanzas):

TABLE XI

Stanza		I	II	III	IV	V	VI
Lermontov	TD:	8	0	1	5	9	
Nekrasov	TD:	0	11	13	13	4	
Čjumina	TD:	2	3	8	15	—	

Of the three poems, the original comes closest to terminal symmetry with values of 8 and 9. Relatively, but to a much smaller degree Nekrasov's parody tends towards symmetry in that the first and last *TD* values are closer to one another than they are to any of the others, which in turn are all close. Čjumina's parody shows no symmetry whatsoever, but rather an increase of values from one pair of stanzas to the next. In respect to these values, it is interesting to note the place of these poets in Russian literature. The first two are usually considered major poets, but although Čjumina's verse frequently occurs in anthologies, she is never considered to be a major poet.

If this tendency towards symmetry is something other than chance in Russian poetry, the phenomenon is at least plausible. Although it has been pointed out *ad nauseam* that analogies between arts are dangerous, it is at least safe to indicate that both poetry and music, as opposed to the graphic and plastic arts, share the phenomenon of unfolding in time, the music is played, the poem read or recited. Therefore, the setting up of a pattern and a return to it in the form of parallelism or symmetry can give a sense of cohesion. This type of symmetry is found in music in the obvious repetition of parts of movements, such as the *ABA* structure of the sonata form.[37] Exact repetition, such as the first and last stanzas of Puškin's *Ne poj, krasavica* . . . is relatively rare and is usually given over to the repetition with variation which we call rhyme.[38] It is entirely plausible, that consciously or unconsciously the poet organizes the tonalities of the poem in such a way that shifts in content, or an indication of return or finality is indicated by the differences in these tonalities in certain parts of the poem. It must be remembered that all of the values for tonal balance and tonal difference presented above represent, with very few exceptions, at least a whole line of poetry, and more often than not an entire stanza. In other words, the discussion has centered on fairly long stretches of vowels and not on detailed patterns of individual vowels. To return to the analogy with music, the tonal structures discussed above are comparable either to large divisions such as the phrase or movement on the one hand or to modulations from one key to another on the other hand. They are in no way comparable to such detailed structures as melody.[39]

SOME SPECULATIONS

The above discussions of tonality structures in examples of Russian verse center mainly on the contours of entire texts. Some attention should be given to such details of tonal structure as exemplified in Puškin's *Ja vas ljubil*, although one wonders if such detailed structures are really worthwhile pursuing, without treating poets as nothing more than crossword puzzle experts, attempting to form interesting patterns of individual sounds. On the other hand, the tonalities of all phonemes, including consonants, can often be utilized as a commentary on parts of poems. For instance, in *Razluka*, one of Pasternak's *Živago* poems, it is an interesting fact that the last two syllables, (*vtikho*)*molku*, of this very sad poem, contain no high tonalities in either vowels or consonants, and also they coincide with the final intonation fall in the poem. For comments on such isolated examples, the tonalities of the whole phonemic system can be used with or without reference to the relation between stressed and unstressed vowels, vowels and consonants, etc.

In proceeding with further analysis of the tonality contours of entire texts, the next step, presumably, would be to add the unstressed vowels. Brief excursions in this direction have indicated that, if the unstressed vowels are given half the value of the stressed vowels, the tonal contours tend to remain substantially the same. One exception seems to be Pasternak's *Zimnjaja noč'*. When the unstressed vowels were added, the Q values show an interesting alternation between high tonality and the neutral /a/ through the stanzas of the poem.

If it is true that in a valid system of weighting, the addition of tonality values for other phonemes does not materially disturb the tonal pattern of the stressed vowels, then these latter indeed could be considered the central harmonies of the poem, or to use an analogy with the visual arts, the basic composition of the picture which is modified through shading and highlighting, but which remains the central geometrical disposition of elements.

REFERENCES

1. Roman Jakobson, "Linguistics and Poetics," *Style in Language*, Thomas E. Sebeok, ed. (New York, 1960), p. 356. (In further references this volume will be designated as *SIL*.)

A similar statement was made by Jan Mukařovský in "La dénomination poétique et la fonction esthétique de la langue," *Actes du Quatrième Congrès International de Linguistes, Copenhagen, 1938*, p. 104: "Les fonctions pratiques de la langue, qui sont la représentation, l'expression et l'appel, se trouvent, dans la poésie, subordonnées à la fonction esthétique qui attire l'attention sur le signe même. . . ." In his essay "Ob izučenii jazyka literaturnykh proizvedenij," G. O. Vinokur in a related fashion remarks that the rhythm and harmonies (*sozvučija*) of verse can have their own sense (*smysl*) and thus "take part in the transmission of poetic meaning" (*Izbrannye raboty po russkomu jazyku*, Moscow, 1959, pp. 252). In his discussion of a probabilistic approach to the theory of literary style, L. Doležel takes it as an axiomatic principle that "the literary work is the central part of the communication process . . . and can be scientifically interpreted only in a system of connections which characterize this communicative process" ("Vercjatnostnyj podkhod k teorii khudožestvennogo stilja," *Voprosy jazykoznanija*, 1964, 2, p. 19).

2. Osip Brik, "Zvukovye povtory," *Poètika, sborniki po teorii poètičeskogo jazyka* (Petrograd, 1919), p. 98.

3. B. A. Kušner, "O zvukovoj sisteme poètičeskcj reči," *Sborniki po teorii poètičeskogo jazyka*, I (Petrograd, 1916), pp. 42–49. Except for a puzzling analysis of Puškin's *Prorok*, his analysis of consonantal symmetry is quite convincing. This phenomenon is taken up below in discussing Pasternak's *Gamlet*.

4. B. M. Ejkhenbaum, *Skvoz' literaturu* (Leningrad, 1926); photomechanic reprint (*Slavistic Printings and Reprintings*, XXVI) (The Hague, 1962), p. 206. Interesting speculations on the sound texture of verse from a linguistic point of view can be found in J. Vendryes' "La phonologie et la langue poétique," *Choix d'études linguistiques et celtiques* (Paris, 1952), pp. 51–63, and also in Jan Mukařovský's "La phonologie et la poétique," *Travaux du Cercle Linguistique de Prague*, 4 (1931), pp. 278–288.

5. Transliterations from the Cyrillic alphabets are given in italics, phonemic transcriptions are enclosed in slanted lines.

6. The phonemic analysis and its resolution into distinctive features followed in this study is that presented by Morris Halle in his *Sound Pattern of Russian* (The Hague, 1959). The distinctive feature "code" is there given, p. 45. For the sake of arithmetical isomorphism, the present study changes the designation of Halle's "Low Tonality" to "High Tonality" and reverses the plus and minus symbols throughout. (More detail is given below in footnotes 10 and 15.)

7. John Lotz, "Metric Typology," *SIL*, p. 138.

8. Lotz, *loc. cit.*, footnote 7.

9. For a formulation of stress structure in Russian binary meters see Jakobson, *op. cit.*, pp. 361–363. Russian binary meters have been exhaustively studied by K. Taranovski in his *Ruski dvodelni ritmovi* (Belgrade, 1955). Boris Tomaševskij in his *Stilistika i stikhosloženie* (Leningrad, 1959), p. 358, states that the average length of the Russian word is three syllables. This illustrates the difficulties involved in placing a stressed vowel in every metrically stressed position. This situation may also play a role in the peculiarities of stress in Russian poetic vocabulary noted by V. A. Nikonov in his "Mesto udaren'ja v russkom slove," *International Journal of Slavic Linguistics and Poetics*, VI (1963), pp. 1–8.

10. The feature of High Tonality listed here is the same as Halle's Low Tonality, but with the plus and minus symbols interchanged. In general terms it is the same feature as Grave/Acute or Flat/Plain listed in R. Jakobson, G. Fant, and M. Halle, *Preliminaries to Speech Analysis* (= *M.I.T. Acoustics Laboratory Technical Report*, no. 13, May 1952) and R. Jakobson, and M. Halle, *Fundamentals of Language* (=*Janua linguarum*, I) (The Hague, 1956). Concerning this feature in the vowels Halle remarks, *op. cit.*, p. 53: "It was suggested in *Preliminaries*, and the suggestion is followed here, that flat *vs.* natural, the only distinctive tonality feature for the vowels be considered in complementary distribution with grave *vs.* acute, the primary tonality feature of the consonants."

11. Vsevolod Setchkarev, *Studies in the Life and Work of Innokentij Annenskij* (The Hague, 1963), p. 111.
12. K. Močul'skij, *Aleksandr Blok* (Paris, 1948), pp. 37–38.
13. Cf. R. Jakobson, "Kindersprache, Aphasie und allgemeine Lautgesetze," *Selected Writings*, I (1962), 387: ". . . überhaupt sind die Zuordnungen zu den dunkeln Vokalen anscheinend zwangsmässiger und fester als diejenigen zu den hellen, und wiederum die Zuordnungen zur 'U-I-Linie' fester als die zur 'A-Linie'." Cf. also his remarks in "Linguistics and Poetics," *op. cit.*, pp. 372–373: "Sound symbolism is an undeniable objective relation founded on a phenomenal connection between different sensory modes, in particular between the visual and auditory experience. . . . Particularly from the linguistic point of view the picture has often been distorted by lack of attention to the phonological aspect of speech sounds or by inevitably vain operations with complex phonemic units instead of with their ultimate components."
14. *Polnoe sobranie sočinenij*, Vol. 7, p. 241. The problem of sound symbolism is treated in detail by Ivan Fònagy in his *Die Metaphern in der Phonetik* (=*Janua linguarum*, series minor, XXV) (The Hague, 1963). Interesting conjectures from a historical and anthropological point of view can be found in Chapter 2 of Ernst Cassirer's *The Philosophy of Symbolic Forms*, Vol. I (New Haven, 1953).
15. Cf. Jakobson and Halle, *op. cit.*, p. 29.
16. Concerning the synaesthetic value of the vowels of German Junker relates how Rudolph Bindung, on the basis of the phoneme /a/ in the German word "Wahrheit" considered the form closer to the concept of "truth" than the French "vérité" (H. Junker, "Die Bedeutung der Vokale," *Archiv für Vergleichende Phonetik*, Vol. II, p. 231).
17. The prose count consisted of the stressed vowels in a section of Čekhov's *Zloj Mal'čik* taken as accented by H. G. Lunt in his *Kniga dlja čtenija* (The Hague, 1957), pp. 47–48; two other samples, one from Tolstoy's *Anna Karenina* and one from Dostoevsky's *Mal'čik u Khrista na jelke* were taken from Harry Josselson and Fan Parker, *From Puškin to Pasternak* (Englewood Cliffs, 1963), pp. 5–6 and 14–15. In addition to the accents given by Josselson and Parker, appropriate monosyllabic words were accented in these two samples to bring the data into consistency with the other samples.
18. The poetry data consisted of all the poems discussed or mentioned in this study with the exception of Pasternak's *Roždestvenskaja zvezda*, because of its length, plus poems by Jesenin, Majakovskij, and several others. In all, the number of vowels was over 1000.
19. From A. Peškovskij's "Desjat' tysjač zvukov russkogo jazyka," as represented in Table C, p. 41 of E. Colin Cherry, Morris Halle, and Roman Jakobson, "Toward the Logical Description of Languages in their Phonemic Aspect," *Language*, 29 (1953), pp. 34–46.
20. Cf. also Dell Hymes, "Phonological Aspects of Style: Some English Sonnets," *SIL*, p. 115: ". . . frequency and its associated statistical analysis is probably relatively insensitive, a vague mirror, when the focus is on the individual poem. It may well be that the sheer data, usefully arranged, are about as good a kind of statistics as we can get." These sober words have influenced the presentation of the data in the present study.
21. There is no great advantage gained in eliminating such a weighting factor, except its presence as an arithmetical nuisance, since it is not arbitrarily determined.
22. Or according to the system presented by John Lotz in "A Notation for the Germanic Verse Line," *Lingua*, 6, pp. 1–7.
23. Roman Jakobson, "Poèzija grammatiki i grammatika poèzii," *Poetics. Poetyka. Poètika* (The Hague, 1961), pp. 397–417.
24. Most of the poems discussed below can be found in *The Penguin Book of Russian Verse* edited by Dimitri Obolensky (Baltimore, 1962), or in other easily accessible anthologies. Only the sources for relatively obscure poems will be indicated.
25. N. A. Nekrasov, *Sočinenija v trekh tomakh*, Vol. I (Moscow, 1959), p. 16.
26. L. A. Plotkin and N.I. Totubalin, eds., *Russkaja satira* (Moscow, 1960), pp. 425–426.

27. This is roughly the approach of Tomaševskij as opposed to that of Šengeli. A short but interesting discussion of the two methods is given by A. M. Kondratov in "Teorija informacii i poètika," *Problemy kibernetiki*, 9 (Moscow, 1963), pp. 279–286. See pp. 113-121 in this volume.

28. It is relatively easy to find statements by poets regarding their feelings regarding sound texture, but rare that they speak in detail about specific poems. For instance, Aleksandr Blok, in his essay on Puškin ("O naznačenii poèta"), speaks of "waves of sound" at the "bottomless depths of the soul" where a person ceases to be a person, existing at depths "unattainable for the state and society . . . there proceed rhythmic oscillations, similar to the processes which form mountains, winds, sea currents, flora and fauna" (*Sobranie sočinenij v vos'mi tomakh*, Vol. 6, 1962, p. 163). He also spoke of the "mathematics of the word (like the mathematics of all other arts) especially in verse" (*op. cit.*, Vol. 7, 1963, p. 434) but such statements say nothing about individual poems. Sievers quotes a similar statement by Schiller: "Das Musikalische eines Gedichtes schwebt mir weit öfter vor der Seele, wenn ich mich hinsetze, es zu machen, als der klare Begriff vom Inhalt, über den ich kaum mit mir einig bin" (Eduard Sievers, *Rhythmisch-Melodische Studien*, Heidelberg, 1912, p. 59).

29. Jakobson, *op. cit.*, pp. 410–417.

30. *Op. cit.*, p. 413.

31. *Op. cit.*, pp. 414–415.

32. *Op. cit.*, p. 405.

33. As used herein, "key" word simply means a word which clearly indicates the theme of the poem. As such, it fulfills only the second of Hymes' three criteria for a "key" word. (Hymes, *op. cit.*, p. 118). The general idea of a "key" word is best avoided in analyzing poetry because not every poem can be shown to have such words. It would be extremely difficult, for example, to find a single "key" word in Pasternak's *Gamlet*, analyzed below.

34. Many of Kušner's patterns are made up of sonorants (Kušner, *op. cit.*). See also L. Jakubinskij, "Skoplenie odinakovykh plavnykh v praktičeskom i poètičeskom jazykakh," *Poètika, sbornik po teorii poètičeskogo jazyka* (Petrograd, 1919), pp. 50–57.

35. Stressed vowels from several pages in Lunt, *op. cit.;* Puškin's *Pikovaja dama*, p. 5; Čekhov's "Lev i solnce," p. 60.

36. The sources of these two poems are given above in footnotes 24 and 25.

37. An excellent treatment of symmetry in music, comparing it with visual symmetry is given in C. Chavez, *Musical Thought* (Cambridge, Mass., 1961), especially Chapter III. Allusions to musical symmetry can also be found in Walter Piston, *Harmony* (New York, 1941), pp. 56, 215; and in K. Liepmann, *The Language of Music* (New York, 1953), especially p. 287 ff. Probably the best general treatment of symmetry is Herman Weyl, *Symmetry* (Princeton, 1952). Weyl, however, centers most of his attention on visual symmetry.

38. Certain rhyme schemes are symmetrical in the sense of the term used here, for example, *A b b A*. It is interesting to note that "parallelism" can be described as the inverse of rhyme: where rhyme represents the repetition of a vowel and supporting consonants at the end of a line, parallelism represents a repetition of entire portions of the line. For a study of parallelism in poetry and music see R. Austerlitz, "Parallelismus," *Poetics. Poetyka. Poètika* (The Hague, 1961), pp. 439–443.

   Two excellent examples of such parallelism in Russian verse are Marina Cvetaeva's "V lob celovat'—zabotu steret' "—which is "terminally symmetrical" in that the last two lines are a repetition (except for the second half of the next to the last line) of the first two lines, and there is no rhyme as such (cf. B. Filippova, ed., *Sovetskaja potajennaja muza*, Munich, 1961, p. 19) and V. Khlebnikov's "Kogda umirajut koni—dišat" (*Stikhotvorenija i poèmy*, Leningrad, 1960, p. 86).

39. In discussing the structure of Puškin's *Eugene Onegin* Vladimir Nabokov points out that "Its eight chapters form an elegant colonnade. The first and the last are linked up by a system of sub-themes responding to each other in a pleasing interplay of built-in

echoes. The St. Petersburg of Chapter One is antiphonally doubled by the St. Petersburg of Chapter Eight . . . . The Moscow theme. . . in Chapter Two, is developed in Chapter Seven . . .," *Eugene Onegin*, 4 vols. (New York, 1964), Vol. 1, pp. 16–17. This can easily be taken as terminal symmetry on yet another level of structure.

V
INDIVIDUAL STYLES

VECTORS OF PROSE STYLE

John B. Carroll

The very concept of style implies variation. It takes little argument or evidence to secure agreement that there are different manners of writing, and that these differ among themselves not only by virtue of the content or the subject matter treated but also by virtue of a host of "stylistic" elements which are present in varying degrees in samples of prose. But what, exactly, are these stylistic elements? Ever since man discovered the pleasure of commenting upon his own and others' oral and written compositions, he has been seeking a useful set of pigeonholes for classifying style. The tendency has been for the classifications to proliferate without design or system. Literary criticism today does not have any well and sharply defined set of elements by which a sample of prose may readily be characterized.

In 1935, the renowned psychologist L. L. Thurstone[1] published a book in which he presented the technique of what is generally known as *factor analysis* —a statistical procedure for identifying and measuring the fundamental dimensions ("vectors") that account for the variation to be observed in any set of phenomena. Since then factor analysis has been a tool widely used by psychologists in studying intelligence, personality, interests, emotions, rates of learning, and even word meanings, but the technique has never heretofore been applied to the study of literary style. If we can study the "personalities" of people by factor analysis, we should be able to study the "personalities" of samples of prose. In the simplest possible terms, factor analysis enables the investigator to apply a large number of measurement procedures to a sample of objects and find out to what extent these measures overlap with each other.

Although the objective study of literary style by means of statistical analysis is not a completely novel endeavor, none of the scholars who have engaged in such study has ventured to ask the question raised here: What are the basic dimensions in which style varies? In contrast to previous statistical studies of style, each of which has fixed attention on one or a small number of the possible ways of measuring style, this investigation examines the relations among a large number of indices of style and attempts to identify the most salient ways of describing stylistic variation in prose.

The notion of attempting to quantify aspects of literary style will be repulsive to many literary critics and outright ridiculous to others. The writer must confess that even he, after completing the study, remains skeptical whether the dimensions identified here adequately represent the aspects of style that truly make the difference between great literature and the not so great, or even the

This essay was delivered to the Conference on Style held at Indiana University in 1958 and first printed in *Style in Language*, ed. Thomas A. Sebeok (Cambridge, Mass., and New York, 1960), pp. 283–292. It is reprinted here by permission of The Massachusetts Institute of Technology Press and the author.

aspects that serve to differentiate some of the recognized styles of writing. Nevertheless, some of the hopes in which the study was undertaken seem to have been realized: the study points to some of the more obvious characteristics of prose which have to be observed, mentioned, and duly noted before the literary critic can really go to work. It injects a semblance of order into the study of "readability" and suggests certain bases for guiding the teaching of English composition in schools. Further it provides leads toward the psycholinguistic study of the "encoding" processes by which the individual translates nonverbal prelinguistic states of behavior into linguistically encoded output. It lends some support to the notion that certain factors of literary style correspond to predispositional "sets" which govern the emission of large classes of verbal responses—personal pronouns, for example.

PROCEDURES

There are two distinct kinds of problems to be faced in designing any study that seeks to identify the major dimensions of a set of phenomena: (1) how can we obtain a sufficiently heterogeneous sample of the things we want to study, and (2) what measurements shall we take in order to sample all the significant ways in which the phenomena vary? Practical considerations set certain limits in both of these problems.

The sample of objects studied here consisted of 150 passages from various sources and styles of English prose. Each passage was chosen so as to be more or less self-contained within a little more than 300 words. By selecting passages according to categories—novels (both British and American, both nineteenth and twentieth centuries), essays, newspaper features and editorials, biographies, scientific papers, textbooks, speeches, legal documents, personal letters, and sermons were among the categories used—we hoped to include the widest possible assortment of subject matters and styles. The sample even included several relatively low-grade high-school English compositions.

The measures taken on these 150 passages fell into two classes: subjective and objective. The objective measures involved various counts, indices, and ratios based on the enumeration of certain classes of words, clauses, sentences and other linguistic entities and included some of the measures used in previous statistical studies of style. Subjective measures were secured partly to help in the interpretation of results for the objective measures, partly to provide bench marks for certain characteristics of style which the objective measures could hardly be expected to describe. It was of intrinsic interest, also, to study the extent to which a group of competent judges could agree in assigning ratings, and to determine the totality of ways they could find for characterizing the passages. In order to make the rating task as simple as possible, 29 adjectival scales were chosen with a view to covering the major qualities and traits of style as far as they could be determined *a priori*, and 8 expert judges—all with interest and training in English literature—were secured to rate each of the 150 passages on each of the 29 scales, the form of which may be illustrated as follows:

meaningless   :   :   :   :   :   :   meaningful
_____ _____ _____ _____ _____ _____ _____

The 8 judgments obtained for each passage on each scale were then averaged.

In all, 68 scores were obtained for each of the 150 passages: the 29 averaged ratings of the 8 judges, and 39 objective measures. The names of the measures are listed in the first column of Table 1; unfortunately, space does not permit a full description of the procedures for obtaining the objective measures. The resulting 68×150 scores formed the basis for the ensuing statistical analysis. The correlation of each measure with each other measure was determined— the results being exhibited in a very large table with 68 rows and 68 columns. This *correlation matrix* was then subjected to a factor analysis in order to determine how many fundamental dimensions would be needed, at a minimum, to account for all the interrelations among the 68 measures.[2]

RESULTS

The formidable appearance and size of Table 1 are due simply to the desire to compress a maximum of the essential results of the study into a single table: the reader is invited to examine it carefully. It contains information bearing on two kinds of questions about the 68 measures. (1) How "reliable" are the measurements? In the case of the 29 subjective measures, this question relates to the extent to which the judges agreed in their ratings. A reliability coefficient of 1.00 would denote perfect agreement, and a coefficient of .00 would denote purely random agreement. In the case of the 39 objective measures, the coefficients given in Table 1 (where they are present at all) refer to the extent to which each measure gives consistent results from the first half of a 300-word sample to the second half. (2) What general trait or traits does each variable measure and to what extent? The data relevant to this question are the coefficients found in the last six columns of the table. All coefficients larger than about .25 in absolute magnitude may be regarded as significant for purposes of interpretation.

The reliability coefficients (in the first data column of Table 1) for the 29 averaged subjective ratings range from .64 for the scale *weak-strong*, to .92 for the scale *humorous-serious*, with a median at .80. Although the figures are high enough to suggest that each measure is sufficiently reliable to give meaningful results, the lack of perfect agreement is particularly noticeable for some scales. Some scales, such as *meaningful-meaningless* and *ordered-chaotic*, have low reliability because, we may guess, judges differ in their conceptions of how these terms apply to prose passages. It is of more than passing interest that scales which (as will be seen later) denote general stylistic evaluation, such as *good-bad, pleasant-unpleasant, strong-weak, interesting-boring, graceful-awkward, varied-monotonous, clear-hazy*, have uniformly low reliabilities, whereas such scales as *serious-humorous, abstract-concrete, emotional-rational, opinionated-impartial, earnest-flippant, intimate-remote,* and *personal-impersonal*, all of which refer to specific and relatively non-evaluative qualities of style, have high reliabilities. Judges can often agree in making descriptive

TABLE 1

Results for 68 Measures of Prose Style; Reliability Coefficients and Loadings on Six Dimensions (Factors) of Prose Style

Variable	Variable Number	Reliability	General Stylistic Evaluation A	Personal Affect B	Ornamentation C	Abstractness D	Seriousness E	Characterization F
*Subjective Ratings**								
Profound-superficial	1	.84	.43	−.11	.06	.53	.41	.15
Subtle-obvious	2	.81	.20	−.17	.09	.72	−.09	.15
Abstract-concrete	3	.90	.02	−.01	.18	.64	.11	.16
Meaningful-meaningless	4	.70	.70	−.11	−.04	.04	.41	.03
Succinct-wordy	5	.78	.51	−.15	−.65	−.15	.14	−.01
Graceful-awkward	6	.73	.84	−.01	.07	.17	.08	.12
Vigorous-placid	7	.80	.26	.63	.17	−.06	−.21	−.10
Lush-austere	8	.80	−.01	.43	.55	.07	−.29	.17
Earnest-flippant	9	.87	.06	−.05	−.01	.05	.71	.13
Intimate-remote	10	.87	.10	.82	.02	−.33	.03	−.01
Elegant-uncouth	11	.82	.33	−.29	.44	.40	−.11	.02
Natural-affected	12	.80	.49	.06	−.51	−.26	.29	.08
Clear-hazy	13	.78	.72	.16	−.09	−.45	.10	−.17
Interesting-boring	14	.78	.84	.25	−.04	.12	.01	.06
Strong-weak	15	.64	.88	.21	.13	.00	.11	−.07
Opinionated-impartial	16	.89	−.01	.53	.36	.01	.07	.02
Original-trite	17	.77	.54	−.08	.04	.44	−.20	.15
Ordered-chaotic	18	.69	.65	−.29	−.04	−.15	.06	−.09
Vivid-pale	19	.80	.61	.54	.07	−.09	−.05	−.01
Personal-impersonal	20	.86	.03	.83	.14	−.26	.00	−.01
Precise-vague	21	.71	.64	.00	.10	−.47	.03	−.17
Masculine-feminine	22	.85	.22	.06	.08	−.08	.58	−.09
Varied-monotonous	23	.75	.75	.22	.04	.20	−.10	.15
Emotional-rational	24	.90	−.05	.77	.22	−.12	−.02	.09
Complex-simple	25	.82	−.09	−.18	.48	.51	−.07	.04
Pleasant-unpleasant	26	.75	.88	.15	−.03	.07	−.11	.08
Serious-humorous	27	.92	.01	−.12	.00	.13	.70	.08
Florid-plain	28	.82	−.08	.33	.66	.16	−.28	.11
Good-bad	29	.74	.95	.01	−.02	.12	−.05	.02

*The positive pole of the adjectival scales is represented by the *first* of the two adjectives specified.

Objective measures (All based on 300 words)	No.							
No. paragraphs	30	-.03	-.23	-.02	-.50	-.13	-.09	—
No. syllables	31	-.23	.09	.05	.30	-.58	-.10	.86
No. sentences	32	.05	-.18	.13	-.61	-.03	.05	.85
Standard deviation sentence length	33	-.01	.12	.00	.54	.25	.11	.17
No. clauses	34	.04	.22	.26	.60	.28	.01	.78
Clause complexity index	35	-.15	.18	.02	.39	.18	-.08	.60
% noun clauses	36	-.25	.13	.45	.22	.01	-.02	—
% adjectival clauses	37	.34	.05	-.21	.19	-.07	-.13	—
% adverbial clauses	38	.06	-.17	-.20	.04	.09	.11	—
% parenthetical clauses	39	-.29	-.02	-.01	.08	.04	-.01	.76
% "action" verbs	40	-.01	-.23	-.17	-.40	.11	.06	.58
% "cognitive" verbs	41	-.06	.05	.12	.07	.46	.06	.33
% transitive verbs	42	.63	.03	-.15	.03	-.06	.01	.26
% intransitive verbs	43	.32	-.17	-.05	-.09	.14	-.14	.44
% copulative verbs	44	.43	.12	.18	-.06	-.04	.04	.44
% Latin-derived verbs	45	-.25	.10	.12	.20	-.33	-.06	.57
% passive verbs	46	.12	.16	-.07	.15	-.45	-.06	.49
Mean tense	47	.04	-.01	-.02	.11	-.15	-.12	.88
Entropy of tense	48	-.29	-.04	.06	-.02	.07	-.16	.42
No. infinitives	49	-.02	.05	-.01	-.14	.16	.04	—
No. participles	50	-.15	-.07	-.31	.17	-.08	.08	—
No. gerunds	51	-.15	-.04	.08	-.03	-.20	.13	—
No. proper nouns	52	-.38	-.01	.01	-.03	.01	-.04	.83
No. common nouns	53	.13	-.11	-.22	.18	-.49	-.01	.74
% unmodified common nouns preceded by "the"	54	.18	.03	.10	-.50	.07	.07	.45
% nouns with Latin suffixes	55	-.22	.20	.22	.42	-.22	-.06	.69
No. articles	56	.20	.04	.01	-.11	-.28	.18	.52
% indefinite articles	57	.01	-.48	-.01	-.10	-.09	.07	.48
No. personal pronouns	58	-.09	-.10	.20	-.23	.60	.11	.84
No. possessive pronouns	59	-.14	-.21	.08	.09	.30	-.07	.64
No. indefinite pronouns	60	.27	.21	.14	-.18	.28	.01	.43
No. indefinite and quantitative determiners	61	.20	.35	-.24	.11	-.09	-.10	.27
No. demonstrative pronouns	62	.13	.22	.05	-.05	.11	-.18	.44
No. numerical expressions	63	-.02	-.06	-.49	-.09	-.07	-.01	.67
No. prepositions	64	-.01	.09	-.01	.35	-.34	-.01	.58
No. pronouns	65	-.13	-.14	.18	-.26	.58	-.01	.83
No. determiners	66	.25	.34	-.45	.00	.01	-.19	.52
No. descriptive adjectives	67	.20	-.10	.09	.38	-.18	.11	.66
No. participial modifiers	68	-.01	-.13	.01	.33	-.05	.09	.38

classifications of prose passages but they agree less often in making general evaluations of style. Perhaps this is what makes literary criticism exciting.

Concerning the reliabilities of the objective measures, we shall only comment that the figures indicate the extent to which a writer is likely to hold certain formal characteristics of his style constant within relatively short stretches.

We come now to the main findings of the study, the findings that give a provisional answer to the question of what are the dimensions of literary style. Although *seven* dimensions were indicated by the factor analysis technique, it appeared that only six of these could be given meaningful interpretation, and thus the data for the seventh are omitted from Table 1. The order in which the six remaining factors are discussed is actually immaterial, but they are listed in Table 1 as factors *A*, *B*, *C*, *D*, *E*, and *F*, in order of their apparent interest, importance, and relevance in connection with the study of literary style.

The variables having high coefficients in column *A* of Table 1 are in every case subjective ratings. In order of the magnitude of their "loadings" (as the coefficients are often called) they are the scales *good-bad* (29), *pleasant-unpleasant* (26), *strong-weak* (15), *interesting-boring* (14), *graceful-awkward* (6), *varied-monotonous* (23), *clear-hazy* (13), *meaningful-meaningless* (4), *ordered-chaotic* (18), *precise-vague* (21), *vivid-pale* (19), *original-trite* (17), *succinct-wordy* (5), *natural-affected* (12), *profound-superficial* (1), *elegant-uncouth* (11), and *vigorous-placid* (7). All these scales, in differing degrees, denote overall positive or negative evaluation of a prose passage. We are therefore inclined to identify this factor by the name General Stylistic Evaluation. Notice, however, that some of the scales have significant loadings on certain other factors. Only the first six scales mentioned are unequivocal measures of stylistic evaluation alone. It is cheering to note that not a single objective measure shows any significant loading on factor *A*, General Stylistic Evaluation. Although the style of literary passages can be indexed in certain ways mechanically, it cannot be *evaluated* mechanically!

The key to the interpretation of factor *B* seems to be the presence of the subjective scales *personal-impersonal* (20), *intimate-remote* (10), *emotional-rational* (24), *vigorous-placid* (7), and to a lesser extent *vivid-pale* (19) and *opinionated-impartial* (16). Let us call this dimension Personal Affect. It is also indexed by a number of objective measures, such as number of personal pronouns (58), number of pronouns (65), and (negatively) number of syllables (31). (The negative loading of number of syllables is to be interpreted as indicating that passages with high Personal Affect have a relatively small number of syllables in 300 words, that is, the words tend to be short.) The dimension of Personal Affect is unrelated to General Stylistic Evaluation: it refers simply to the extent to which a passage uses personal references, emotive terms, and similar devices, without necessarily making for "good" style or for "bad" style, either, for that matter.

Let us proceed to column *C* in Table 1. If the reader will run his finger down this column he will find high loadings for the following subjective scales:

florid-plain (28), *wordy-succinct* (5) [reversing the polarity of the scale makes the loading positive], *lush-austere* (8), *affected-natural* (12), *complex-simple* (25), and *elegant-uncouth* (11). The factor is also indexed by long sentences (measure 32), long clauses (34), wide variation in sentence length (33), a relatively high proportion of common nouns which are preceded by adjectival or participial modifiers (54), long paragraphs (30), a high proportion of nouns with Latin suffixes (55), a low proportion of verbs denoting physical action (40), a high degree of use of dependent clauses of various orders (35), and a high number of descriptive adjectives (67). "Ornamentation" (as opposed to "plainness") is clearly a suitable name for this dimension.

The subjective scales having high loadings on factor *D* are *subtle-obvious* (2), *abstract-concrete* (3), *profound-superficial* (1), *complex-simple* (25), *hazy-clear* (13), *original-trite* (17), *elegant-uncouth* (11), and *remote-intimate* (10). The common element in these scales seems to be a generalized notion of abstractness and obscurity as opposed to concreteness, precision, and per-spicuity; for convenience let us call this dimension Abstractness. Like factors *B* (Personal Affect) and *C* (Ornamentation), it is independent of factor *A* (General Stylistic Evaluation); that is, abstractness versus concreteness, the use of personal references versus the failure to use them, and ornamentation versus plainness have nothing to do with whether a prose passage is favorably thought of or with each other. Factor *D* (Abstractness) can be fairly well measured by several objective indicators: by a low proportion of numerical expressions (63), a low number of determining adjectives and pronouns like "this," "each," etc. (66), a high proportion of noun clauses (36), and a low number of participles (50).

Factor *E* we call Seriousness. The two subjective scales measuring this factor best are *earnest-flippant* (9) and *serious-humorous* (27). We are some-what surprised to find, however, that the scale *masculine-feminine* (22) also relates to this factor. Evidently the term "masculine" as applied to literary style connotes earnestness and seriousness, whereas flippancy and humor are associated with femininity. Other scales measuring seriousness are *meaningful-meaningless* (4) and *profound-superficial* (1), and the factor can be indexed objectively by a low proportion of indefinite articles (57), a high proportion of indefinite and quantifying determining adjectives (61), and a high number of determiners (66). Whether these objective measures are intrinsically related to seriousness, or whether the findings are simply a reflection of the particular sample of literary passages used, we do not know.

Factor *F* in Table 1 is measured exclusively by objective measures: a low proportion of transitive verbs (42), a high proportion of copulative verbs relative to all verbs (44), a low number of proper nouns (52), a high propor-tion of adjective clauses (37), and a high proportion of intransitive verbs (43). We can make only a tentative interpretation of the underlying significance of this dimension; the evidence seems to point to a dimension of Characteriza-tion versus Narration. We would expect passages with high scores on this factor to be those that are more concerned with the "characterization" of entities—

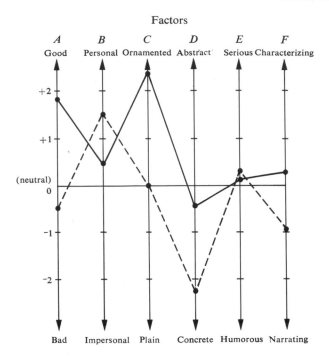

Figure 1. Style profiles of two prose passages: (———) a selection from F. Scott Fitzgerald's *A Diamond as Big as the Ritz*; (– – – –) a selection from Mickey Spillane's *Vengeance is Mine*.

either by equating them with other entities through the use of copulative verbs or by describing them through the use of adjective clauses. Passages with low scores on this factor are more likely to be concerned with the reporting of action, most frequently the action of persons; they would thus be found to have a high proportion of transitive verbs and proper nouns.

These, then, are the six independent dimensions of "style" which have been identified in this study: General Stylistic Evaluation, Personal Affect, Ornamentation, Abstractness, Seriousness, and Characterization versus Narration. Just to intimate the possibility of using these dimensions as the basis for a typology of style, we present in Figure 1 the "profiles" of two of the passages measured in the study. One was a selection from F. Scott Fitzgerald's short story *A Diamond as Big as the Ritz*, in which the author paints a vivid picture of the impressions of the hero and his companion as they wander through the diamond palace. The other is a passage from a very different sort of writing, that of Mickey Spillane.

Two questions may have harassed the reader: are all these dimensions really of "style"—are not some of them rather a matter of the content of a passage? And are not some of these "dimensions" merely dimensions of the *meaning* of adjectives, not necessarily dimensions truly inherent in samples of prose? With respect to the first question, we must reply that there is no hard and fast distinction between style and content. Try as we may to define style as the *manner* of treating subject matter, the type of subject matter will in general impose constraints upon the possible kinds of stylistic treatment. In the present study a vain attempt was made to have judges differentiate between content and style: *content* was to be rated with scales 1 through 4, and *style* was to be rated with scales 5 through 29. The results make it abundantly clear that the judges did not differentiate content and style, at least not in their ratings.

With respect to the second question, it must be insisted that even though somewhat comparable results might be obtained by asking raters simply to judge adjectives for similarity of meaning in the abstract, the dimensions of meaning themselves cannot exist without some support in the real world to which the adjectives presumably refer. The reality and substantiality of these dimensions is further attested to by the abundant instances of correlation between subjective ratings and completely objective, quantitative indices which derive meaning only when applied to actual samples of prose.

ACKNOWLEDGMENTS

The research reported herein was performed pursuant to a contract with the United States Office of Education, Department of Health, Education, and Welfare. Reproduction in whole or in part is permitted for any purpose of the United States Government. I am indebted to the eight raters used in the study, Zita Gray, Grace Kestenman, Don McCaull, R. Dale Painter, Mrs. Newton Press, Dr. E. H. Sauer, Mrs. Mary G. Seifel, and Mary Alice Tomkins, and to Marilyn Brachman, Mrs. Mary S. Carroll, Arthur S. Couch, Marjorie Morse, Frederic Weinfeld, and Mrs. Marcia Wideman for their help in various aspects of analysis. The statistical computations were performed by means of facilities made available at the Littauer Statistical Laboratory of Harvard University, the Computation Center of Massachusetts Institute of Technology, and the John Hancock Life Insurance Company, and thanks are hereby tendered to each of these organizations.

REFERENCES

1. L. L. Thurstone, *The Vectors of Mind; Multiple-Factor Analysis for the Isolation of Primary Traits* (Chicago, 1935).
2. Of possible technical interest to some readers is the fact that the initial factor analysis was performed by means of Thurstone's centroid method, after which the factors were "rotated" to oblique simple structure by the writer's so-called *normal biquartimin* (see J. B. Carroll, "Biquartimin Criterion for Rotation to Oblique Simple Structure in Factor Analysis," *Science*, CXXVI (1957), 1114–1115). All these computations were performed with the aid of high-speed electronic computing machines.

CHINESE AUTHOR IDENTIFICATION BY SEGMENT DISTRIBUTION

JOHN J. DREHER AND ELAINE L. YOUNG

Our original intention in this study was to find a statistical technique for the identification of Chinese authors.[1] Although we feel the evidence presented here does actually do this (at least for all cases we have examined), an equally fascinating study of a personality also emerges. Because this technique should focus upon style, regardless of subject matter or when it was written, our selection of a test author was a man who wrote over a period of decades and upon many diverse subjects—Kuo Mo-jo, the grand old man of contemporary Chinese letters.

Described by biographers[2] as a poet, playwright, novelist, essayist, translator, historian, paleographer, art critic, and propagandist, Kuo Mo-jo was equally eloquent in a romantic poem, a vitriolic attack on a fellow politician, or the translation of a Russian novel. Certainly an identification technique confronting such versatility would be put to a rigorous test.

Accordingly, various works by this man were obtained from the archives of the Hoover Institution, Stanford, California, for examination. These works included stories, poems, essays, and that most subjective of literary forms, the personal letter (see references 7–18). Also selected for analysis were speech texts of Mao Tse-tung (ref. 3), Sun Yat-sen (ref. 4), and Chao Yu-p'ei (ref. 5), an educational writer now living in Taiwan. The last named had generously supplied us with personal copies of his publications in 1966.

METHODOLOGY AND DISCUSSION

As in any other pattern discrimination problem, one of the critical elements in literary identification concerns the criterion measure. Viewed from afar, two bottles may be indistinguishable to the naked eye, while at the other end of the continuum a microscopic examination of their surface might also fail to give us usable differences. In the first instance, our criteria were too gross; in the second, too fine. Just so in literary style—somewhere between the level of the individual word and the entire collection of a man's works should lie some areas that bear his unmistakable stamp and separate his expression from others.

Because writing style can be represented as a complex vector-space, the particular dimension or set of dimensions we choose to examine represents a very large set of measuring tools. If we elect a set of concepts, or specific word usages, or grammatical constructs, or whatever, it quickly becomes apparent that considerable expertise in any particular set is called for, with categoriza-

The work presented herein was conducted by the Douglas Advanced Research Laboratories under company-sponsored Independent Research and Development funds.

tion of an author heavily dependent upon the sophistication of the analyst. Furthermore, where our style-measuring device is subject to conscious control of the author (e.g., word choice), the risk of misclassification grows when that author wishes to adopt the earmarks of another. Ideally, the yardstick of most use should meet the following constraints:

1. It should be simple enough for the relatively untrained reader to isolate.
2. Its occurrence should follow as a natural consequence of a writer's habits or physiological rhythms.
3. It should identify an author irrespective of subject matter.
4. It should separate his works from others.

At this point, having set down some *a priori* ground rules, the most obvious search begins with some kind of single measure, hopefully one which will eventually contribute heavily to a limited set constituting an unequivocal proof of authorship.

Because the phrasal digram approach (ref. 1) had shown promise of possible usefulness, it was decided that some other aspect of "phrase," or, more accurately, "segment" length usage of a writer might contain a clue.

After several digram matrices of Kuo Mo-jo's works had been made, it became apparent that most of his segments (and sequences of segments) were contained in an area bounded by one to sixteen characters. This was his habitual range, and therefore it appeared logical to look first at distributions in this area.

As the reader may have noted, the sample of Kuo's output included several literary forms extending over approximately forty years. This allows us to examine two hypotheses: first, that his metric behavior might be specific to the kind of vehicle he was writing (letter, essay, etc.); and second, that this metric usage might show some systematic change as a function of time, a factor that might correlate with other influences that could be verified.

We should, at this point, raise an intuitive objection to the proposed analysis, an objection posed by many—namely, the changes wrought by editing. No man's published work, the argument goes, is his own—it always is subject to the editor's hand. A closer look at this thesis, however, brings out some doubts about the objection itself. In the first place, while the statement may literally be true, the crux of the argument lies in the *extent* to which an editor changes a writer's style. Actual experience on the part of all of us has indicated that editors can, indeed, change the course of a text. For the most part, however, those changes are not customarily monumental, nor are they always effected in the exact style of the editor himself, the writer usually assuming the burden of rework. If not, successive samples of different publications (presumably with different editors) should reveal distinctly different usages, providing the measure has any merit at all.

The first decision in the choice of measure was the use of some kind of non-parametric statistical treatment, since the texts offer several areas for counting techniques. The second decision was some application of the segment. The segment (or "phrase") is defined as the number of separate characters appearing between two elements of "pause" punctuation—period, commas, semicolons, colons, question marks, exclamation marks, and dashes—in any combination. Individual characters are specified as the counting unit because of their unambiguous definition, without the involvement of what constitutes a word, compound term, and so on.

The procedure here makes the assumption that frequency distributions of phrases become asymptotic to some stable value at an N of something over 500. Consequently, to achieve sample sizes of 700 or 800 or more, several specimen texts of a certain kind from a certain era were sometimes considered as a representative sample. To put it another way, let us say that we are dealing with personal letters to friends. Normally these are not extensive literary efforts, and therefore to get "letter style," several letters written about the same time were pooled to get the necessary number of phrases to operate upon. This is simply to say we were attempting to stabilize the sample and render it less sensitive to capricious fluctuation.

Two questions are immediately of interest: (1) does a man change his distribution of phrase lengths as he grows older? and (2) does he use a different mix of phrase lengths when he writes different vehicles? If he does not, then it makes some sense to talk of his "style." If changes are noted, then our observation must be qualified by "style of the 30's," "story style," and so on.

The statistical techniques used here are simplicity itself—the $(2 \times k)$ and $(n \times k)$ chi-square tests of separate samples, and the Kolmogorov-Smirnov Cumulative Frequency Distribution Test, all of which are described in reference 6. For those readers who do not customarily use these statistics or for those who have no need for a detailed explanation, we briefly summarize what they accomplish.

If we observe certain categories of things that occur a given number of times, we can, in some cases, formulate an educated guess about how often they can be expected to happen. In short, we sometimes may assume an *a priori* distribution of these happenings, as in the case of coin tossing or dice throwing. Because these last are relatively simple events, they lend themselves to simple mathematical modeling on a probability basis. In such cases, the chi-square test, given an expected (or assumed) frequency of how often things should happen, we can estimate whether a series of observed events obeys the basic rule that it has been given.

In the case of literary segment usage, however, the picture is not so simple. To begin with, we have no prior knowledge of how often a man uses phrases of a certain length. Indeed we cannot even assume that he does have a habitual pattern. We can, however, expect some help from our statistic by using it in one of its slightly modified forms. Let us suppose we have counted characters in the marked-off segments of two essays. These segments we now distribute according to their lengths, from one to sixteen characters, noting how often we have tabulated each particular length. We thus wind up with two separate distributions, one for each essay.

Using the $(2 \times k)$ test, we may now compare the two tabulations, and the result will be an estimate of the probability that the two samples could have come from the (previously unknown) same parent population of segment usage. In other words, the two samples, although different in size and even in the proportions assigned to their different categories, may fall within some limits of variation such that it is highly probable (or not probable at all) that they are possible random drawings from a large stable distribution. This is all the mathematics tells us. Any inference over and above that single result is extra-statistical, and depends upon why we did the operation in the first place, that is, the experimental hypothesis we were testing.

Let us continue this last aspect further. Suppose the two essays we know had been written by the same author. If our chi-square result failed to indicate a statistical difference (in this study a level of 0.05, or chance occurrence of five in a hundred), we assume that his style is consistent—or that he has *a* style. If the results go the other way and a difference is indicated, we must assume the samples could not reasonably be isolated examples of a single style, but actually (not probably) represent really different usages. In short, the frequencies of segment occurrence noted are not merely chance occurrences of those in a single style.

Under conditions where we know beforehand that there really are two different authors, a non-significant difference would indicate like (or "same") usages; a significant difference would mean just that—the authors were different, which in this case tells us what we knew to start with.

To make such a test useful, we should expect non-significant differences in successive samples from the same author and significant differences when one author is tested against another. In dealing with Kuo Mo-jo we have the opportunity to compare different literary forms within time periods and across periods, as well as the opportunity of comparing his many works with those of the other available authors. In the following pages we shall attempt to do just this.

PROCEDURE

We started off our comparisons of Kuo's output with a few basic assumptions:

1. If his style were constant over a given ten-year period, it would be more likely to be detected in a single kind of vehicle (e.g., stories) than in a variety of literary forms.

2. If this consistency could be demonstrated, the possibility existed that this style persevered in other vehicles (e.g., essays, letters, etc.) within that same time period.

3. If style were constant over the given decade regardless of the purpose of writing (e.g., expression as in letters, instruction as in essays, etc.), this phrase usage distribution might persevere through time.

4. If a change were detected as a function of time, this change might appear in all vehicles of the period in which the new style was detected.

Any one or combination of these alternatives might occur, and the explanation thereof would imply a spectrum of causes that might be inferred from Kuo's activities or political involvement at the time. Of course, to be completely useful as a fingerprint, any detected style should be statistically differentiable from that of other writers.

This is to say, if our chi-square value is sufficiently large to reach the 0.05 level, we are content to assume a real difference in styles for the samples compared.

STABILITY TESTS OF KUO MO-JO'S STYLE

As indicated earlier, Kuo offers a good testing ground for our experimental measures. Phrase lengths from one to sixteen characters were taken as criterion. Several kinds of comparisons—vertical (in time) and cross (different vehicles)—were performed to examine style changes as a function of era and subject matter.

STORIES

Selections of three decades of stories were taken from refs. 7 through 11. These consisted of "The End of Spring" (1922), "Kung's Dinner," and "Meng's Wife" (1935), "At the Foot of Golden Hill," and "My Good Friend" (1945). Our question here involved two parts: did Kuo change his style from story to story within a decade? and did he show an overall change within the 33-year period?

In view of the diversity of subject matter, involving autobiography, biography, and light fantasy, such a gamut of writing would seem to be a reasonably good test of stylistic differences. Our interest here, of course, is focused only on phrase-length usage.

The first comparison dealt with the 1922 autobiography and the two "fantasy" tales of 1935. A chi-square value of 17.26 (15 degrees of freedom) establishes a probability level of 0.30, assuring us that the two proportions of phrase-lengths appearing in the two works are not significantly different—in other words, they cannot be assumed to come from different parent populations. Once this result was noted, we were able to stabilize our sample by combining the frequencies of both decades and testing them against those of the 1945 story, "At the Foot of Golden Hill."

Again, we note a non-significant difference, this time with a chi-square of 11.07 ($p=0.80$). Thus, on the basis of this evidence, we may say that Kuo's "meter" remained the same for these literary expressions, regardless of the different kinds of subject matter or era of his output.

STORIES VERSUS LETTERS

Because of the style homogeneity of the story, we were now at liberty to use any or all of the stories tested in subsequent comparisons. Consequently, a phrase-length distribution of letters during 1936 and 1937 (ref. 12) was tested against that of the 1945 "At the Foot of Golden Hill," and we still note a non-significant chi-square of 10.25 (with 30.58 required for a difference). Story and letter style, therefore, are non-different at a level of $p=0.80$. This rather startling agreement in such nominally different vehicles may be observed in the plots of Figure 1, where we compare his letter style of the 30's with all his specimen stories over a two-decade period.

STORIES AND LETTERS VERSUS ESSAYS

As our evidence increased that Kuo's metric style remains stable with time, we widened our inquiry to another literary form—the essay. For this test we used six essays from 1937 (refs. 13 and 14) and our combined non-different frequencies from the stories and letters. The result was again a non-significant chi-square (0.70 for 30 df), establishing a stable usage among three literary forms. Although not shown, the same is true for dispatches (ref. 15). On the basis of the evidence shown graphically in Figure 2, we can conclude that for a period of some thirty years Kuo Mo-jo consistently employed a homogeneous metric prose style. Because, as we shall see below, some influence or other became clearly apparent with the advent of the Communist regime, this usage of his earlier period will be referred to as "Early Kuo."

STYLE OF THE 1950's

Ever the romanticist and idealist, Kuo continued into the Communist era, prolific as ever. Now a disciple of Mao's thought, Kuo produced, as before, on a wide range of topics, but with new overtones. "Be first Red, then a technician," goes his line, exhorting his readers to put first things first and political doctrine above all. We might inquire if the "new" Kuo was able to follow his own advice—to write like Mao, as well as hold his thoughts. Since phrase-length usage appears to be a sort of "biological timeclock," an imitation of another's style to this extent might indeed show a powerful influence that reaches below the surface of conscious expression.

Amazingly enough, Kuo does indeed show a changed style in those writings after 1950 which we have analyzed so far. To begin with, the phrase distribution in a series of discourses on Communist thought (ref. 16) from 1957 and 1958 were compared with phrase distribution in six essays from 1937 (refs. 13 and 14). A violent change is noted by a highly significant chi-square value of 85.17, far beyond that needed to show a difference at the 0.01 level. In short, in these works we can no longer detect the former well-defined meter of Kuo Mo-jo, with most of the change involving far heavier usage of four-, five-, and six-character segments (see Figure 3). A new alter ego has apparently emerged.

The extent and effects of this new style can be observed by the significantly different distributions shown in Figure 4. Here we have taken a collection of discourses from propaganda efforts (ref. 17) and compared them with artistic essays (ref. 18), all written during the post-1949 era.

From these curves one thing is immediately apparent—the propaganda material makes greater use of short, punchy phrases (heavy usage of four and six characters), while the artistic works show evidence of extensive use of the longer seven-character phrase that moved his earlier style. The points of similarity, however, between these 1950 productions may be seen in the bimodal nature of both curves. Something has changed, but one curve shows more influence of the old style.

Even more interesting is the statistical instability of the propaganda meter. Figure 5 compares political discourses of 1957 and 1958 (ref. 16) with those of 1959 (ref. 17). A significant difference in phrase exceeding the 0.01 level is indicated by a chi-square of 34.00, where only 30.58 is necessary for statistical separation. Despite this mathematical judgment, the marked 4/6 lengths are quite apparent, and because of this we have portrayed this feature (albeit a bit illegally) as a single representative curve, the Late Kuo. This is contrasted with Early Kuo in Figure 6. As we shall see later, the magnitude of difference from his previous style makes it immaterial whether we consider Late Kuo as one single curve or a somewhat unstable family of curves.

KUO VERSUS MAO TSE-TUNG

The relation of Kuo's Pauline style change to "the thinking of Mao" was clearly enunciated in one of his discourses of 1959 (ref. 17). According to this pronouncement, "People had better read and reread the works of Mao and put all his ideas into action." Further, "Mao's own writing style is highly representative of his credo," that is, in clarity, freshness, and descriptiveness. According to Kuo Mo-jo, one of the rules for "Mao-like" writing is: "Do not use long sentences."

Certainly Kuo has taken his own advice here. It is quite clear from the Late Kuo curve of Figure 6 that after 1950 he has definitely shifted to shorter segments, and much of this correlates positively with sentence length. It must be observed, however, that his master apparently does not feel the same constraint, for an analysis of over thirty years of Mao's output (ref. 3) results in the curve shown in Figure 7 plotted against Late Kuo style.

The chi-square value of 88.0 (only 27.7 required for 0.01 difference) is highly significant and tells us the segment-length usage of the two men is radically different. The continuity of Mao's style is demonstrated by results of the Kolmogorov-Smirnov cumulative frequency distribution test (ref. 6), which indicated no difference in Mao's segment usage from 1926 to 1949. We leave to literary analysts the determination of those other respects in which Kuo and Mao agree or differ.

KUO VERSUS SUN YAT-SEN

To continue the comparisons, we shall now examine Kuo's meter with that of Sun Yat-sen. For the latter data we analyzed a collection of Sun's speech manuscripts contained in reference 4. Their normalized occurrence frequencies of segment-length usage appear in Figure 8, and a highly significant chi-square of 93.5 (27.7 required for 0.01 difference) identifies Early Kuo as distinctive. An even greater difference separates Sun from Late Kuo, where chi-square reaches a value of 120.8 (curve not shown).

KUO VERSUS CHAO YU-P'EI

Figure 9 contrasts Early Kuo with the writings of Chao Yu-p'ei, a contemporary Taiwan educator. Several of Chao's current writings (ref. 5) served as the basis of comparison here. Again we note a significant chi-square value of 65.98, contrasted with 29.14 necessary for an 0.01 confidence level for the appropriate degrees of freedom.

The Late Kuo distribution, however, is a different matter, and here we note our only failure of the method. A chi-square of 18.82 ($p=0.20$) indicates that the probability of a different source for the two styles is only a four-out-of-five situation. We could therefore not separate the two writings on the basis of this test alone. Here, for instance, is a case where we would be forced to the more sensitive digram probability (ref. 1).

CHAO VERSUS MAO AND SUN

Predictably, Chao's writings are distinguishable from those of Mao and Sun. Their contrasting curves are shown in Figures 10 and 11, with chi-squares of 118.82 and 66.5, respectively.

CONCLUSION

From the investigations conducted, segment distribution appears to be a promising and reasonably powerful tool in differentiating authors of Chinese texts. Intuitively we would not expect all authors to be unique in this respect alone. One might, by using larger matrixes (i.e., using more comparison cells), pinpoint the differences with greater sensitivity. Offshoots of this method could further strengthen the validity of identification, promising extensive possibilities in this area of research.

REFERENCES

1. See Dreher, J. J., "Author Identification by Digram Probabilities," *DARL Research Communication*, no. 36 (Douglas Advanced Research Laboratories, Huntington Beach, California).
2. Boorman, H. L. (ed.), *Biographical Dictionary of Republican China* (New York and London, 1967).
3. *Selected Works of Mao Tse-tung* (Shanghai: Jen Ming Publishing Company, 1964).
4. Sun Yat-sen, *Selected Essays* (Stanford, Calif.: Hoover Library, Chinese Language Research Center).
5. Chao Yu-p'ei, *A Guide to Mandarin Language and Literature* (Taipei, Taiwan, 1964).
6. Siegel, S., *Nonparametric Statistics for the Behavioral Sciences* (New York, 1956).
7. Kuo Mo-jo, "The End of Spring," from *Selected Works of Kuo Mo-jo* (Hong Kong: Hsueh Publishing Company, 1964).
8. ———, "Kung's Dinner," from *Selected Works*.
9. ———, "Meng's Wife," from *Selected Works*.
10. ———, "At the Foot of Golden Hill," from *Selected Works*.

11. ———, "My Good Friend," from *My Good Friend* (Shanghai: Liang You Library, 1946).
12. ———, *Collection of Letters* (Shanghai: Hwa Tung Publishing Company, 1937).
13. ———, Selections from *A Little Collection of Essays from the War against Japan* (Shanghai: Ta Shih Tai Publishing Company, 1937).
14. ———, Selections from *Collection of Dispatches* (Shanghai: Chun Yueh Publishing Company, 1947).
15. ———, *Collection of Dispatches* (Shanghai: Chun Yueh Publishing Company, 1947).
16. ———, *Collection of Discourses Concerning Literature and History* (Peking: Jen Ming Publishing Company, 1961).
17. ———, Selection from *Collection of Discourses*.
18. ———, Artistic Critiques from *Collection of Discourses*.

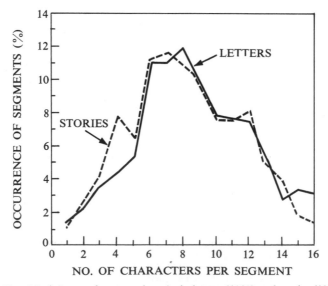

Figure 1.   Kuo Mo-jo's use of segment lengths in letters (1937) and stories (1922-1945)

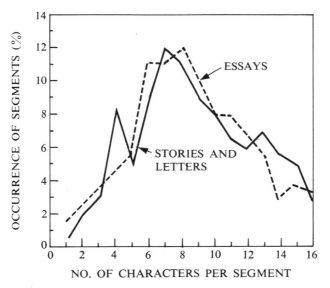

Figure 2.   Comparison of Kuo Mo-jo's style in letters and stories versus essays (1922-1945)

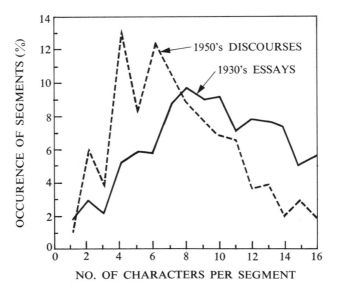

Figure 3.   Comparison of Kuo Mo-jo's style in essays of the 1930's versus discourses of the 1950's

Figure 4. Comparison of Kuo Mo-jo's styles in propaganda versus
artistic subjects in discourses of the 1950's

Figure 5. Comparison of Kuo Mo-jo's styles in political and artistic
discourses of the late 1950's

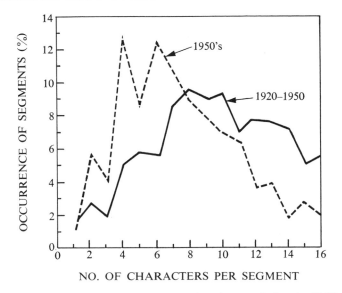

Figure 6. Change in Kuo Mo-jo's segment-length usage during the 1950's

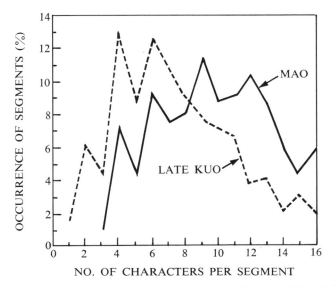

Figure 7. Comparison of segment-length usage of Mao Tse-tung (1929–1949)
and Kuo Mo-jo (1950's)

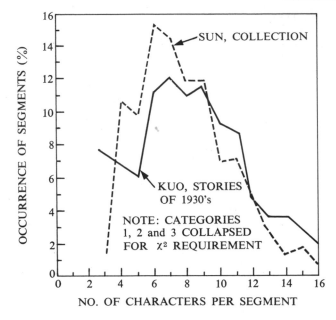

Figure 8. Comparison of styles of Kuo Mo-jo and Sun Yat-sen

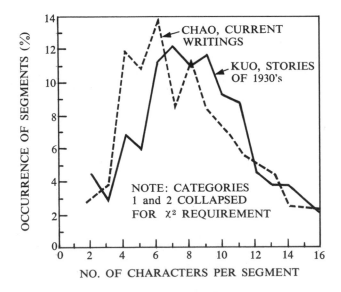

Figure 9. Comparison of styles of Kuo Mo-jo and Chao Yu-p'ei

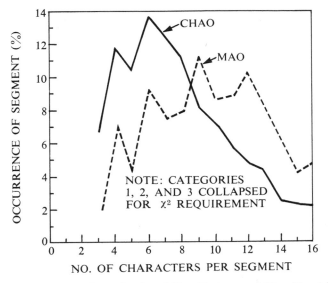

Figure 10. Comparison of styles of Mao Tse-tung and Chao Yu-p'ei

Figure 11. Comparison of styles of Sun Yat-sen and Chao Yu-p'ei

THE QUANTIFICATION OF METAPHORIC LANGUAGE IN THE VERSE OF WILFRED OWEN[1]

George M. Landon

PURPOSE

This essay is concerned with the type of metaphoric language which can be said to arise from the violation of constraints on lexical co-occurrence in the sentences of a language. More specifically, it reports an attempt to establish a method for describing both the amount and variety of this kind of metaphoric language in a corpus of English verse. Finally, it presents a body of data on metaphoric usage in the verse of Wilfred Owen and highlights three problems for the field of stylistics which are suggested by these data.

METHODOLOGICAL BACKGROUNDS

Quite obviously, if one wants to say how much metaphoric language there is in some text, one must be able to view that text as a finite set of domains within each of which the language may be judged to be metaphoric, normal, or undecidable. In addition, if one wants to describe the variety of metaphoric language in that text, one must have available an explicit taxonomy of metaphor. This section is devoted to these two matters.

Let us begin a discussion of the former requirement by considering a stanza from the poem "Miners" by Wilfred Owen:[2]

> But the coals were murmuring of their mine,
>   And moans down there
> Of boys that slept wry sleep, and men
>   Writhing for air.

By means of a procedure which is here termed "kernelization,"[3] the stanza given above, or in principle, any language sample, may be re-represented in the form of a set of simple sentences:

1. The coals were murmuring of their mine.
2. The coals were murmuring of moans.
3. Boys moan down there.
4. Boys slept sleep.
5. The sleep is wry.
6. The coals were murmuring of men.
7. The men were writhing for air.

Let us now extract from the simple sentences given above those pairs of constituents between which certain functional relationships—subject, object, or attribute—may be said to obtain. Let us call each of these pairs of constituents a collocation. Thus, a subject collocation will contain a verb and the

170

noun phrase which serves as its subject; an object collocation will contain a verb and the noun phrase which serves as its object; an attribute collocation will contain a noun and an adjective which modifies the noun:

Subject	Object	Attribute
1. *coals murmur of	murmur of mine	
2. *coals murmur of	murmur of moans	
3. boys moan		
4. boys sleep	sleep sleep	
5.		*sleep wry
6. *coals murmur of	murmur of men	
7. men writhe for	writhe for air	

*metaphoric collocations

Clearly, as illustrated here, a re-representation of the text as a set of collocations defines for that text a set of domains within each of which the metaphorical status of the language may be judged. But the question arises: Do collocations defined on the subject, object, and attribute relations alone provide an ample basis for exhaustively quantifying the metaphoric expression contained in some text? The answer, of course, is that these three relations are not a sufficient basis. Linguists recognize many other functional relationships.[4] If one is to approach an exhaustive quantification of the metaphoric language in some text, one must base the quantification upon a set of collocations which, in turn, have been defined on an exhaustive set of functional relationships. A study such as this one, which is ultimately based upon only three functional relationships, must be regarded as illustrative.

Let us now turn to the second requirement mentioned above: that if one wants to describe the variety of metaphoric expressions in a text, one must have available an explicit taxonomy of metaphor. The bases for such a taxonomy are contained in the so-called base component of a generative transformational grammar.[5] Here, among other things, nouns and nominals are specified in terms of a set of properties which are described as inherent in the entities which the nouns and nominals designate. Some of these properties are, for example, abstract, concrete, animate, and human. Verbs and adjectives, on the other hand, are specified in terms of properties which determine with just which nouns and nominals they may compatibly stand in some functional relationship in a given sentence. When, for a given sentence, the nouns, nominals, verbs, and adjectives standing in various functional relationships with one another are all appropriately compatible, the sentence will not exhibit any metaphorical language; that is, it will not exhibit any metaphorical collocations. Conversely, when for a given sentence, the lexical items in one or more collocations are incompatible with respect to one or more semantic properties, then metaphorical collocations result; that is, the sentence will exhibit metaphorical language.

Thus, for example, among the collocations listed above, those containing the lexical items *coals* and *murmur* are metaphoric. *Murmur* is a verb which is specified for compatibility with grammatical subjects which, in turn, are specified as human. Instead, *coals* is specified as concrete. The explanation of the metaphor lies in this incompatibility and in the apparent attribution of the various properties of humanness to *coals* by the lexical item *murmur*.[6]

The four properties named above—abstract, concrete, animate, and human—are sufficient to provide a basis for characterizing three types of metaphoric expression. These types correspond fairly closely to figures which have traditionally borne the names *reification, animation*, and *personification*. In the terms set out just above, reification is exhibited by a collocation containing one lexical item specified as concrete, the other as abstract; animation is exhibited where one lexical item is marked as animate, the other as concrete or abstract; personification is exhibited where one form is marked human, the other animate, concrete, or abstract.

Given the three types of functional relationship, the three types of metaphoric expression, and judgments on the metaphoric status of collocations, it is possible to distinguish eighteen types of collocation of which nine can be metaphoric as illustrated below (Table I) with examples from the verse of Wilfred Owen.[7]

TABLE I

Nine Types of Metaphoric Collocation

Types of Metaphor	Functional Relationship		
	Subject	Object	Attribute
Reification	time drains trouble spills	breathe happiness drink sorrow	crimson slaughter blue courage
Animation	dawn peered misery swelters	wake clay tease hunger	sly twilight frantic shell
Personification	the bough sighs retreat sings	thrill the word groin granite	sad dawn brave drum

Clearly, as illustrated here, a taxonomy of metaphoric collocations provides a useful basis for determining the amount and variety of metaphoric expression in some text. But again, the question arises: Does a taxonomy which recognizes only three types of metaphor provide an ample basis for exhaustively quantifying the variety of metaphoric expression in a text? The answer, of course, is that these three types of metaphor are not a sufficient basis. Linguists recognize that there is an indefinite number of semantic properties in terms of which lexical incompatiblities may be displayed—in terms of which metaphor may be explained.[8] Again, a study such as this one, which is ultimately based upon only three types of metaphor, must be regarded as illustrative.

THE DENSITY OF METAPHORICAL COLLOCATIONS IN THE VERSE OF WILFRED OWEN

The methodology described in the preceding section was applied to a corpus of English verse, *The Poems of Wilfred Owen*.[9] This corpus contained 59 poems ranging in length from approximately 50 to approximately 400 words. There was a total of 9,244 words or approximately 1,209 lines of verse. In re-represented form, the corpus contained 3,102 collocations. Of these, 318 were judged to be metaphoric. Thus, if collocations are judged to be those points in a text where metaphor may find expression, granting the methodological limitations set out in the preceding section, the corpus is 10.25 percent metaphorical.

Considering the 59 poems individually, the density of metaphorical collocations ranges from 0 (zero) to 33 percent, exhibiting the distribution shown in Table II.

TABLE II

The Density of Metaphorical Collocations in the Poems of Wilfred Owen

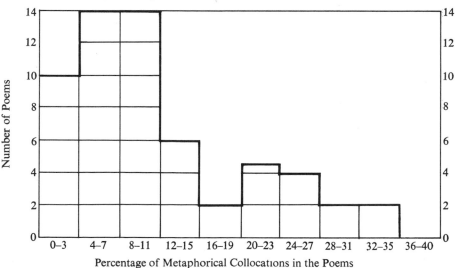

Percentage of Metaphorical Collocations in the Poems

Since the corpus of verse contained poems of various sorts on various topics, one might suppose that the density of metaphorical collocations varied with the topic or subject matter of the poem. But this was simply not the case in Owen's verse. There, one finds poems which both Owen and literary critics claim to be on the same topic; but of these, some have very similar amounts of metaphorical expression; others have widely different amounts. For an example of the former case, see the poems "A Terre (Being the Philosophy of Many Soldiers)" and "Wild with All Regrets (Another Version of 'A Terre')," which yielded the density figures 5.6 and 4.9 percent respectively. For an example of the latter case, see the poems "Arms and the Boy" and "Sonnet (On Seeing a Piece of Artillery Brought into Action)," which yielded the density figures 25.6 and 9.5 percent respectively.[10] Similarly, one finds poems which both Owen and critics take to be on different topics; and of these, some have very similar amounts of metaphoric expression, others have very different amounts. For an example of the former case, see the poems "Anthem for Doomed Youth" and "Song of Songs," which yielded 24.3 and 23.5 percent metaphorical collocations respectively. Ultimately, the amount of metaphor in a poem appears to have been determined not so much by the topic as by the way in which Owen chose to "talk about" the topic.

Let us consider the distribution of collocations over the types of functional relationship (Table III).

TABLE III
The Distribution of Collocations over the Types of Functional Relationship

Functional Relation	Total Collocations		Metaphoric Collocations		Reifications		Animations		Person- ifications	
	no.	%	no.	%	no.	%	no.	%	no.	%
Subject	1,495	48	218	68	57	51+	79	82	82	74
Object	660	21	50	16	36	32+	7	7	7	6
Attribute	947	31	50	16	18	16+	10	11	22	20
Totals	3,102	100	318	100	111	100	96	100	111	100

First, it is not surprising that, of the total number of collocations, 48 percent are subjects, 21 percent are objects, and 31 percent are attributes: intransitive verbs and constituents derived from them outnumber transitive verbs and constituents derived from them in many kinds of English text. But second, when one considers that 14.58 percent of the subject collocations, 7.57 percent of the object collocations, and 5.27 percent of the attribute collocations are metaphorical, one sees that the subject collocation is obviously the favored point for the expression of metaphor in this corpus. This fact invites further investigation: Is it characteristic of Owen, of English verse, or of poetry in general?

Let us now consider the distribution of collocations over the types of metaphor (Table IV).

TABLE IV

The Distribution of Collocations over the Types of Metaphor

Type of Metaphor	Metaphoric Collocations		Subject		Object		Attribute	
	no.	%	no.	%	no.	%	no.	%
Reification	111	35	57	26	36	72	18	36
Animation	96	30	79	36	7	14	10	20
Personification	111	35	82	38	7	14	22	44
Totals	318	100	218	100	50	100	50	100

First, notice that the metaphorical collocations as a whole are distributed rather evenly over the types of metaphor. But second, notice that for the object relation, reification is strongly favored over animation and personification for the expression of metaphor. This fact also invites further investigation: it does not appear to correlate with any other quantitatively known property of English texts.

If one were to examine sets of frequency tables corresponding to III and IV above, but compiled on each of the poems individually, one would notice a variety of distribution patterns. Some poems show rather even distribution over the nine types of metaphorical collocation; others favor metaphoric expression in one or another functional relationship with rather even distribution over the types of metaphor; still others favor one or another type of metaphor with rather even distribution over the types of functional relationship; and finally, some favor one or another of the nine types of metaphorical collocation. But where poems are short and the absolute frequency of metaphorical collocations very small, it is not safe to make much of these various skewed distribution patterns.

CONCLUSIONS

At this point, one must ask about the significance of these data. In particular, is the general configuration of metaphorical usage displayed by these data a unique characteristic of Wilfred Owen's verse, that is, a distinguishing feature of his style? Or is it a property common to most English verse of Owen's period, or to English verse, or to poetry in general? The same questions arise with respect to certain figures contained within the body of data. Exactly what is the status of the general favoring of subject collocations in the expression of metaphor? Exactly what is the status of favoring of reification in the expression of metaphor in object collocations? Table V highlights these questions.

TABLE V

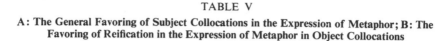

A: The General Favoring of Subject Collocations in the Expression of Metaphor; B: The Favoring of Reification in the Expression of Metaphor in Object Collocations

KEY

A		B	
TC	= % of Total no. of Collocations	MC	= %of Metaphoric Collocations
MC	= % of Metaphoric Collocations	A	= % of metaphor in Attribute relation
A	= % of Animations	O	= % of metaphor in Object relation
P	= % of Personifications	S	= % of metaphor in Subject relation
R	= % of Reifications		
(values are from Table III)		(values are from Table IV)	

But lacking comparable data based upon other poets' works, these displays and these questions must be construed as an invitation to further study. And in the case of the favoring of reification in object collocations, not only are comparable frequency data needed, but also careful examination of the words used in metaphorical object collocations. It is hoped that the methods are sufficiently unproblematic to encourage others to help with the answers to questions set out here.

REFERENCES

1. This article is based upon two sections (the methods and conclusions) of one part of "The Contribution of Grammar to the Poetic Style of Wilfred Owen," unpublished doctoral dissertation by the author, presented to Indiana University, July, 1964. The dissertation itself is a pilot study; procedures for extending the scope of the study presented here are being explored.
2. Edmund Blunden (ed.), *The Poems of Wilfred Owen* (London, 1963), p. 98.

3. For background and further discussion, see Noam Chomsky, *Aspects of the Theory of Syntax* (Cambridge, Mass., 1965).

4. For background and further discussion, see Charles J. Fillmore, "The Case for Case," to appear in Emmon Bach and Robert Harms, eds., *Universals in Linguistic Theory* (New York: Holt, Rinehart and Winston).

5. For background and further discussion, see Noam Chomsky, *op. cit.*

6. For other recent linguistically oriented accounts of metaphor, see for example Noam Chomsky, "Some Methodological Remarks on Generative Grammar," *Word*, XVII (1961), 219-239, but especially section five; Samuel Levin, "Internal and External Deviation in Poetry," *Word*, XXII (1965), 225-237; and Sol Saporta, "The Application of Linguistics to the Study of Poetic Language," in *Style in Language*, ed. Thomas A. Sebeok (Cambridge, Mass., and New York, 1960), pp. 82-93. For works with a more literary orientation, see also Morton Bloomfield, "A Grammatical Approach to Personification Allegory," *Modern Philology*, LX (1962-63), 161-171; and Christine Brooke Rose, *A Grammar of Metaphor* (London, 1958).

7. *Op. cit.*

8. For background and further discussion, see James D. McCawley, "Concerning the Base Component of a Transformational Grammar," distributed by the Program for Exchange of Generative Studies, The Department of Linguistics, The University of Chicago, 1966.

9. *Op. cit.*

10. For further discussion of the subject matter and thematic relatedness of these poems, see *The Poems of Wilfred Owen*, especially Owen's preface and table of contents, as reproduced in Edmund Blunden's memoir, pp. 40-41; also D. S. R. Welland, *Wilfred Owen: A Critical Study* (London, 1960), p. 130.

STYLISTIC CONTINUITY AND CHANGE IN THE PROSE OF THOMAS CARLYLE

FREDERICK L. BURWICK

In a recent statistical study, I endeavored to demonstrate the relationship between associationist rhetoric and Scottish prose style in the early part of the nineteenth century.[1] Among the twelve passages analyzed were two from the works of Thomas Carlyle: one passage from the *Life of Schiller* and another from "The Diamond Necklace." Comparing these two texts, I noted that Carlyle persisted in using the figures of syntax favored by the associational rhetoricians, but with an increased frequency. In the later text, Carlyle gave greater attention to alliterative and assonant effects and took greater liberties with sentence structure. Among the figures of order, he used three times as many inversions and twice the number of parentheses and appositions; among the figures of omission, he curtailed the random ellipses and turned to the condensed clausal patterns of *zeugma* and *diazeugma*, omitting the verbs in a sequence of clauses three times as often, and omitting the subjects more than twice as often; the figures of repetition, too, were more profuse. By contrast, the periodic and balanced sentences of the Ciceronian tradition almost disappeared from his prose. These changes seemed to indicate that Carlyle's style was becoming more exuberantly associational.

Perhaps "The Diamond Necklace" was merely an anomaly, not truly indicative of the trend of Carlyle's development as a prose stylist. Only a more extensive sampling could give adequate evidence of the aspects of continuity or divergence in his prose. To determine quantitatively the various manipulations of his syntax, and then to interpret the quantitative data in terms of rhetorical significance, are the tasks I shall assume here, and I shall endeavor to explain my methods as cogently as possible, step by step.

The first problem in pursuing statistical analysis is adequate and representative sampling. The independent unit considered in this study is the word; the dependent unit is the sentence. Further, the word (W) is classified in an array of twelve basic functions ($w_1, w_2, \ldots w_{12}$), and the sentence (S) in an array of eight basic patterns ($s_1, s_2, \ldots s_8$):

WORD CLASSIFICATION

w_1 structural noun

subject
predicate noun
direct object
object complement
indirect object

178

w_2	semi-structural noun	object of preposition object of verbal address/apostrophe apposition
w_3	intransitive verb; transitive active verb	
w_4	transitive passive verb	
w_5	verbal modifier	
w_6	structural modifier	predicate modifier object complement
w_7	semi-structural modifier	
w_8	coordinating conjunction	
w_9	subordinating conjunction	
w_{10}	non-syntactic (interjection, exclamation)	
w_{11}	alliteration / assonance	
w_{12}	repetition[2]	

SENTENCE CLASSIFICATION

Examples

		Verb Class	*Sentence*
s_1	N V	w_3	Dogs bark.
		w_4	Postmen are frightened.
s_2	N V M	w_3	Dogs are noisy.
		w_4	Dogs are considered vicious.
s_3	N V N	w_3	Dogs are animals.
		w_4	Dogs are considered enemies.
s_4	N V N	w_3	Dogs frighten postmen.
		w_4	Postmen are given a fright. A fright is given postmen.
s_5	N V N M	w_3	Postmen consider dogs vicious.
s_6	N V N N	w_3	Postmen consider dogs enemies.
s_7	N V N N	w_3	Dogs give postmen a fright.
s_8	variant[3]		

The word-sentence relationships are presumed finite (either in terms of the available corpus or in terms of syntactic possibilities). The multiple of factors squared determines the sample size of the independent factor. Since the purpose is to sample occurrences and estimate their frequency and distribution for a given text, the formula for a word-sample representative of word-sentence relationships is $(W \cdot S)^2 = (12 \cdot 8)^2 = 9,216$. For convenience, the size of the samples has been rounded and approximated: the termination of the sentence closest to 10,000 words.

The sampling, however, remains biased, for it assumed a static corpus. The corpus of Carlyle's published prose comprises approximately 3,052,800 words (with an average of 32.7 words per sentence), spanning some sixty years. In the effort to study aspects of continuity and change in greater detail, I have added to the two texts originally analyzed, four more passages, representing various periods in Carlyle's career:

I.   *Life of Schiller* (1821; published 1823–24)
II. *Sartor Resartus* (1830–31; published 1833–34)
III. "The Diamond Necklace" (1837)
IV. *Past and Present* (1843)
V.   *Frederick the Great* (started 1852; published 1858–65)
VI. *Early Kings of Norway* (1875).[4]

Each of the 10,000-word texts from the above sources has been analyzed with the mechanical assistance of the computer. The program (see Overall Flow-chart) operates in two phases: the first phase parses the text, which has been punched on cards, the second phase tabulates all syntactic patterns as well as the occurrence of specific figures of syntax. In interpreting the significance of syntactic patterns and rhetorical figures, three kinds of statistical measures are used:

(a) conditional probability measures—first and second order entropy to determine pattern manipulation;
(b) parametric measures—mean and standard deviation to determine the distribution of patterns;
(c) correlative measures—correlation coefficients to determine common traits and persistent syntactic characteristics in all the sampled passages.

Since all language is repetitive, all acts of speaking or writing can be ana-lyzed probabilistically—indicating the various language components and their frequency of repetition. In considering the probabilities of word-sentence relationships, words (w_1, w_2, ... w_{12}) are treated initially as events occurring in sequence (Q_2, Q_3, ... Q_n). Sequence is an arbitrary but necessary conven-tion, for sentence-length is variable and unpredictable. A sequence may or may not constitute a sentence; for example, a sequence of two words (Q_2) may be either "dogs vicious" or "dogs bark." The probability of an occur-rence, w_1, in a given sequence, Q, is the limit of the relative frequency of occurrences (the number of occurrences of w_1 divided by the number of sequences); the conditional probability for a particular word type, i, given an occurrence of word j, may be expressed:

$$P(w_i/w_j) = \frac{P(w_i\, w_j)}{P(w_j)}$$

where $P(w_i\, w_j)$ is the probability of the two words occurring together. This formula may be extended for larger sequences and need not be modified for

PACKAGE A.   OVERALL FLOWCHART

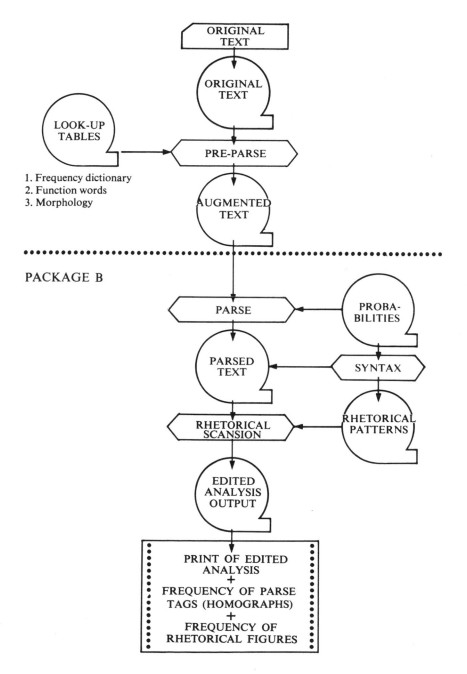

w_{11} and w_{12}, which are treated as probabilistically independent even though they are practically (linguistically) dependent.

Style also represents, in part, individual habits of repetition; therefore entropic measurement may aid stylistic analysis. Entropic measurement provides a means of determining the variation in the number of specific ways the larger patterns can be realized. The measure of entropy is generally defined by the formula:

$$H = - \Sigma P(i) \log_2 P(i),$$

where H is the entropy of a syntactic system which has events i, the probabilities of which are $P(i)$. Conditional entropy of the second order expresses the variation in a syntactic relationship in which the probability of the outcome of one specific occurrence is conditioned by another set of occurrences:

$$H_2 = - \Sigma P(ij) \log_2 P(ij) + \Sigma P(i) \log_2 P(i)$$

The significance of these measures is based on the principle (adapted from thermodynamics) that the entropy decreases with an increase in internal structure and increases only with an increase in randomness.

With computer assistance, I have established the critical proportions, conditional and relative entropies, and conditional probabilities for sequences Q_2, Q_3, Q_4, and Q_5 in the six texts from Carlyle.[5] I will limit discussion here to Q_5 sequences. Since Q_5 recognizes classes w_1 through w_{12} in sequences of five, the sequential possibilities are $12^5 = 248,832$. This is a mathematical statement of possibilities, not a linguistic statement. How many of these 248,832 sequences might be impossible, I do not know; nor do I know of any way to determine which patterns could not occur. A sequence of five coordinate conjunctions may seem unlikely; still Carlyle does find a use for "But—, but—, but—, but—, but—."[6] In Table I, I have listed the total number of sequences, the number of different patterns, and the conditional and relative entropies; in Table II, I have listed the most frequent patterns (critical proportion of 0.13% or greater). The total of Q_5 types, as noted in Table I, ranges from a high of 2111 in the earliest text to a low of 1570 in the latest; with all six texts

TABLE I

Five-word sequences

Text:	I. 1821	II. 1831	III. 1837	IV. 1843	V. 1865	VI. 1875
Total sequences	6685	5707	6550	6685	7525	7722
Total types	2111	1706	1978	2047	1608	1570
Conditional entropy	2.01710	1.99040	2.02877	2.02729	2.00551	1.03011
Correct frequency of predictors with relative entropy	.5579	.5649	.5716	.5850	.5597	.5563

TABLE II

Five-word sequences

Most frequent patterns with critical proportions

Text: I. 1821	Text: II. 1831	Text: III. 1837	Text: IV. 1843	Text: V. 1865	Text: VI. 1875
12137 = .13 %	11327 = .13 %	13172 = .18 %	13166 = .13 %	11366 = .14 %	11327 = .15 %
12722 = .16 %	11352 = .13 %	13631 = .18 %	13172 = .16 %	13172 = .27 %	11352 = .15 %
13172 = .28 %	13172 = .27 %	13672 = .15 %	13652 = .13 %	13631 = .13 %	12527 = .15 %
13177 = .13 %	13666 = .16 %	13712 = .15 %	13712 = .16 %	13712 = .18 %	13172 = .22 %
13666 = .16 %	13672 = .14 %	13713 = .18 %	13716 = .18 %	13716 = .13 %	13527 = .18 %
13712 = .20 %	13712 = .18 %	13771 = .15 %	13717 = .16 %	13717 = .13 %	13672 = .15 %
13717 = .16 %	13771 = .16 %	16312 = .15 %	13752 = .21 %	13722 = .14 %	13712 = .15 %
17728 = .14 %	17131 = .14 %	17131 = .15 %	13772 = .19 %	13772 = .21 %	13713 = .29 %
21317 = .16 %	17272 = .18 %	17213 = .15 %	13775 = .13 %	13913 = .18 %	13771 = .15 %
21371 = .27 %	17352 = .13 %	17728 = .15 %	13913 = .21 %	17272 = .18 %	13913 = .15 %
21372 = .19 %	21321 = .13 %	21363 = .15 %	13937 = .14 %	21317 = .16 %	21371 = .18 %
22131 = .19 %	21352 = .21 %	21371 = .21 %	17131 = .13 %	21371 = .19 %	21372 = .18 %
22282 = .13 %	21371 = .18 %	21372 = .15 %	17272 = .19 %	21372 = .14 %	21375 = .15 %
22772 = .13 %	21372 = .21 %	22722 = .18 %	17383 = .16 %	21377 = .16 %	22771 = .18 %
22913 = .20 %	22131 = .13 %	22771 = .15 %	21317 = .14 %	21393 = .14 %	22772 = .21 %
27213 = .19 %	22132 = .16 %	23631 = .15 %	21352 = .19 %	22132 = .16 %	23631 = .18 %
27728 = .16 %	22772 = .13 %	27272 = .15 %	21377 = .18 %	22136 = .16 %	27272 = .18 %
28213 = .14 %	22913 = .21 %	27722 = .26 %	22132 = .13 %	23771 = .13 %	27577 = .15 %
28272 = .17 %	27213 = .18 %	28036 = .15 %	22136 = .13 %	25712 = .14 %	28272 = .18 %
29136 = .20 %	27272 = .13 %	28272 = .15 %	23752 = .19 %	27213 = .16 %	29131 = .21 %
31728 = .16 %	31728 = .16 %	28772 = .18 %	23771 = .14 %	27272 = .18 %	31752 = .21 %
31772 = .14 %	31772 = .14 %	29131 = .15 %	25712 = .16 %	27721 = .16 %	31772 = .15 %
37172 = .28 %	31975 = .14 %	29132 = .21 %	25727 = .18 %	27722 = .18 %	37132 = .21 %
52772 = .13 %	37172 = .27 %	31631 = .15 %	27213 = .21 %	27772 = .14 %	52522 = .18 %
71282 = .14 %	52827 = .22 %	36272 = .15 %	27222 = .18 %	28613 = .13 %	52527 = .18 %
71312 = .13 %	57722 = .16 %	36316 = .15 %	27722 = .16 %	28727 = .18 %	52872 = .24 %
71366 = .13 %	71137 = .16 %	37152 = .15 %	28727 = .13 %	31572 = .13 %	71231 = .18 %
71367 = .13 %	71231 = .18 %	52913 = .18 %	29131 = .21 %	32772 = .13 %	71772 = .15 %
71472 = .14 %	71772 = .21 %	71137 = .15 %	31572 = .16 %	52872 = .27 %	72137 = .26 %
71728 = .16 %	72172 = .16 %	71231 = .18 %	31728 = .16 %	71282 = .13 %	72252 = .18 %
71913 = .14 %	72272 = .22 %	71772 = .18 %	32772 = .13 %	71371 = .16 %	72272 = .26 %
72131 = .13 %	72872 = .22 %	72137 = .15 %	37152 = .16 %	71728 = .16 %	72913 = .26 %
72136 = .13 %	72913 = .22 %	72172 = .15 %	37172 = .16 %	72136 = .21 %	75213 = .21 %
72137 = .19 %	77131 = .16 %	72272 = .29 %	38372 = .13 %	72137 = .22 %	77272 = .22 %
72722 = .14 %	77277 = .13 %	72282 = .21 %	52872 = .18 %	72213 = .14 %	77282 = .18 %
72727 = .19 %	77572 = .18 %	72367 = .15 %	52522 = .16 %	72252 = .19 %	78722 = .15 %
72728 = .17 %	77872 = .14 %	72772 = .15 %	52527 = .16 %	72272 = .22 %	79135 = .15 %
72772 = .20 %	79135 = .14 %	72872 = .18 %	55772 = .13 %	72572 = .13 %	87152 = .15 %
72813 = .16 %	87172 = .14 %	72913 = .24 %	71371 = .16 %	72717 = .14 %	87172 = .15 %
72827 = .13 %	87213 = .16 %	77222 = .15 %	71723 = .16 %	72721 = .13 %	91315 = .18 %
72872 = .16 %	91315 = .18 %	77227 = .18 %	72137 = .21 %	72772 = .29 %	91371 = .21 %
72913 = .14 %	91365 = .16 %	77714 = .15 %	72272 = .22 %	72872 = .18 %	
77131 = .17 %	91371 = .16 %	77872 = .15 %	72722 = .21 %	72913 = .18 %	———
77213 = .14 %	91372 = .13 %	91310 = .21 %	72752 = .22 %	75213 = .18 %	7.60 %
77272 = .19 %			72913 = .21 %	77227 = .14 %	
77272 = .14 %	———	———	77222 = .13 %	77272 = .16 %	
77872 = .13 %	7.43 %	7.48 %	77227 = .18 %	77275 = .13 %	
78722 = .16 %			77713 = .13 %	77277 = .16 %	
87172 = .14 %			79135 = .19 %	87213 = .14 %	
91371 = .13 %			85213 = .16 %	91363 = .16 %	
			87152 = .18 %	91371 = .14 %	
———			91315 = .16 %		
8.11 %			91371 = .16 %	———	
				8.42 %	
			———		
			8.82 %		

considered as a single corpus, the total of different Q_5 types is 2357. Carlyle, then, uses 10.2% of the total mathematical possibilities; an average for the six texts of 7.6%; a common core (1368 sequences) of 5.5%.

In terms of the most frequent patterns in Carlyle's prose, we can make a few general observations on his stylistic techniques. The most obvious and dominant characteristic is Carlyle's preference for subordinated modification. The six combinations of w_2 and w_7 among the three-word sequences (Q_3: 227, 272, 277, 722, 727, 772) constitute a critical proportion of 8% of all the three-word sequences; among the two-word sequences, 72 appears more often than any other pair in each and every one of the texts, again with a critical proportion of 8%. The critical proportions for individual occurrences, in order of frequency, are: w_1 (18.13%), w_2 (17.68%), w_7 (17.41%), w_3 (12.18%), w_6 (11.33%), w_8 (6.05%), w_5 (5.43%), w_9 (4.51%), w_4 (2.41%), w_{12} (1.62%), w_{11} (0.58%), and w_{10} (0.29%). The nouns dominate, but Carlyle characteristically lets the subject or object stand by itself, not buried under a heap of adjectives. The conditional probability for a modifier following a structural noun is 0.1539, for a modifier preceding, 0.2802; but for a modifier following a semi-structural noun, the conditional probability increases to 0.2008 and to 0.3794 for a modifier preceding. Clearly, Carlyle delights in the descriptive, in the rhetorical vivacity and logical subtlety attained through judicious modification of terms: yet this he prefers to accomplish within apposition or parenthesis, within verbal or prepositional phrase. Carlyle's manner of subordinated modification can be observed in this account of Teufelsdröckh's grave appearance:

> His look, as we mentioned, is probably the gravest ever seen: yet it is not of that cast-iron gravity frequent enough among our own Chancery suitors; but rather the gravity as of some silent, high-encircled mountain-pool, perhaps the crater of an extinct volcano; into whose black deeps you fear to gaze: those eyes, those lights that sparkle in it, may indeed be reflexes of the heavenly Stars, but perhaps also glances from the region of Nether Fire. (Text II)

The description, by contrast and by comparison, suggests and associates images, but it is restricted to the prepositional and appositional phrases; aloof from the outset, separated by parenthesis, the subject, "His look," stands gravely alone.

The most frequent patterns listed in Table II also give supporting evidence of the general uniformity of Carlyle's syntactic predilections; the lists are surprisingly similar—the patterns favored by Carlyle in 1821 continue to dominate in the prose of 1875, with but little variation in between. Even the distribution of patterns remains relatively the same in all six texts. It would be tedious to give examples for all the patterns of high frequency, but to see how Carlyle makes use of a few of them is informative. I note that 13172, 21371, 52872, and 72913 appear with a generally high frequency; here is how they look in practice:

13172: "They are cherishing destruction in their bosom" (Text IV)

"Death has no victory over the valiant hero" (Text IV)

"You have wedged them at the four inches" (Text V)

21371: "As for historians, they shroud, gloomily, all hope" (Text III)

"By fits, his faculties find, strangely enough, glimmers of truth" (Text III)

52872: "gaining money and more folly" (Text V)

"drawing sword and popular contempt" (Text V)

72913: "of the sacrificial festival, which Hakon abhorred" (Text VI)

"with this wonderful proposal that we should renounce" (Text VI)

"of huge peril, because they were" (Text IV)

"for every hour, that they continue" (Text IV)

Patterns 13172 and 72913 are standard and would have a fairly high frequency in most modern English prose; pattern 21371 reveals a syntax more peculiarly Carlyle's; pattern 52872 is interesting in the above examples for the ironic pairing of verbal objects. Several patterns with lower critical proportions, but still present in the list of the most frequent, reveal syntactic junctures that strike me as being typically, if not exclusively, Carlysian:

75213: "Unarchaic, disciplined at all points, you might" (Text V)

"Foolish, bedraggled mortal, the Ministers knew" (Text V)

79135: "Already, as we slept, putting" (Text II)

"Never, because he desired, pausing" (Text II)

Although many of the same patterns occur most frequently in all six texts, there are a few variations. Passive verbs (w_4) are used more in the *Life of Schiller* and *Frederick the Great*, but it seems likely that such alternation might have been prompted by Carlyle's concern with the causes acting upon the man or the state. The conditional proportion of w_5 rises from 4.35% in Text I to a high of 5.88% in Text IV; it is 5.43% for the six texts combined. This increase in verbal patterns can be related to what has already been said in regard to the habits of subordinate modification: verbal phrases implement the vigor of the clausal predication and provide additional modification. As Carlyle comes to rely more and more on the rhetorical patterns of omission, the verbal phrases often stand in place of predication. There is a steady increase in the conditional proportions for w_{11} and w_{12}: occurrences of alliteration, assonance, and repetition rise from the lowest frequency in the *Life of Schiller* to the highest in *Past and Present*, then decline slightly in *Frederick the Great* and *Early Kings of Norway*. The increased use of repetition is related, in part, to the associational rhetoric of Carlyle's prose; but the increased use of repetition, assonance, and alliteration in Texts II, III, and IV may also be explained as part of the sharpened tonal acuity of Carlyle's polemical prose. Consider the tonal effects of this passage from *Past and Present*:

> On the poor workers such fiat falls first, in its rudest shape; but on the rich master-workers too it falls; neither can the rich master-idlers, nor any richest or highest man escape, but all are like to be brought low with it, all made "poor" enough, in the money sense or a far fataler one. (Text IV)

The alliterating "fiat falls first" at the opening, the "far fataler" at the close, provide an emphatic frame for Carlyle's statement; and the repetition underscores his successive contrasts between "poor workers," "rich master-workers," and "rich master-idlers." The sound itself becomes part of the argument, calling attention to essential similarities among things that appear different, so that when "poor" is echoed at the close, it embraces both the "money sense" and the "far fataler one."

Before discussing the rhetorical figures governing Carlyle's sentences, we may well consider some of the peculiarities of the sentences themselves. The eight basic patterns (s_1, s_2, . . . s_8) do not, in fact, provide a restrictive definition of the sentence because the variant s_8 admits any sequence marked off by terminal punctuation. For many authors, this would be but a minor point; for Carlyle, it becomes major. He frequently ignores terminal boundaries, and he characteristically treats commas, dashes, semicolons, and periods as rhetorical rather than as grammatical devices. Carlyle's manner of rhetorical punctuation is apparent in the following passage:

> Generation after generation, hundreds of them or thousands of them, from the unknown Beginning, so loud, so stormful-busy, rushing torrent-wise, thundering down, down; and falling all silent,—nothing but some feeble re-echo, which grew ever feebler, struggling up; and Oblivion swallowed them *all*. Thousands more, to the unknown Ending, will follow: and *thou* here, of this present one, hangest as a drop, still sun-gilt, on the giddy edge; one moment, while the Darkness has not yet engulfed thee. O brother, is *that* what thou callest prosaic; of small interest? Of small interest and for *thee*? Awake, poor troubled sleeper: shake off thy torpid nightmare-dream; look, see, behold it, the Flame-image; splendours high as Heaven, terrors deep as Hell. (Text III)

> No more success: mere sham-success, for a day and days; rising ever higher,—towards its Tarpeian Rock. Alas, how, in thy soft-hung Longacre vehicle, of polished leather to the bodily eye, of red-tape philosophy, of expediencies, club-room moralities, Parliamentary majorities to the mind's eye, thou beautifully rollest: but knowest thou whither? It is towards the *road's end*. Old use-and-wont; established methods, habitudes, *once* true and wise; man's noblest tendency, his perseverance, and man's ignoblest, his inertia; whatsoever of noble and ignoble Conservatism there is in men and Nations, strongest always in the strongest men and Nations: all this is as

a road to thee, paved smooth through the abyss,—till all this end. Till man's bitter necessity can endure thee no more. Till Nature's patience with thee is done; and there is no road or footing any farther, and the abyss yawns sheer! (Text IV)

In the first sentence above, Carlyle omits almost all predication: a series of nouns and modifiers, participles ("rushing," "thundering," "falling," "struggling"), and a subordinate clause ("which grew ever feebler"—N V M); the single independent clause occurs after the last semicolon ("and Oblivion swallowed them *all*"—N V N). The fourth sentence ("Of small interest and for thee?") echoes the conclusion of the third, but is set apart for emphasis, even though it is without predication. The verbless style of the first part of this passage is called *scesis onomaton*, a kind of rhetorical condensation relying heavily on nouns and modifiers. That Carlyle relies regularly on this kind of sentence structure accounts for the high frequency of extended sequences of w_7 and w_2. The last sentence of the first passage exhibits a different sort of condensation, *diazeugma*, relying heavily on the verbs ("Awake," "shake off," "look, see, behold"). The second passage begins with *scesis onomaton*; then the second sentence creates a periodic effect with a series of prepositional phrases interrupting the exclamation "how . . . beautifully thou rollest." The exclamational impact is suspended, for Carlyle adds a colon and turns from exclamation to question. A punctuational turn is evident again in the series of "till" clauses at the end of the passage, the first divided by a dash from the preceding statement, the second and third set off more emphatically with periods; the metaphorical unity, however, is sustained across the terminal barriers by repetition of the key terms: "*road's end* . . . road . . . abyss . . . *end* . . . no road . . . abyss."

Carlyle frequently catalogs noun after noun, verb after verb, modifier after modifier, a whole series of appositions; the effect is plethoric fullness, not simple wordiness but logical precision where the appositions qualify and define, rhetorical power where they echo and reverberate. His use of punctuation to mark rhetorical units often sets a modifier apart from the sentence to which it may be syntactically related, creating a fairly high frequency of s_8 variants. The same habit is also responsible for long and lumbering sentences in which numerous clauses are tied together by semicolons. These sequences may be analyzed in terms of the relative frequencies of the patterns $(s_1, s_2 \ldots s_8)$ in each of the sequential positions $(n_1, n_2 \ldots$ etc.) and computed as follows:

$$f = \frac{s_1}{\sum_{i=1}^{i=8} s_i}$$

Example: s_1 in the first position (Text I):

$$f = \frac{95}{\underset{s_1 \quad s_2 \quad s_3 \quad s_4 \quad s_5 \quad s_6 \quad s_7 \quad s_8}{95+47+36+102+3+3+3+2}} = 0.32646$$

Each pattern may also be considered as a predictor for a following pattern, and sequence may be analyzed in terms of conditional probabilities, just as the sequences of w were analyzed above. The interesting factor here is that alternation of the two major patterns, s_1 and s_4, is almost as probable in Carlyle's style as a parallel of patterns:

$s_1 \ s_1 \ P=0.3027$	$s_4 \ s_1 \ P=0.2802$
$s_1 \ s_2 \ P=0.1113$	$s_4 \ s_2 \ P=0.1695$
$s_1 \ s_3 \ P=0.1016$	$s_4 \ s_3 \ P=0.1021$
$s_1 \ s_4 \ P=0.2998$	$s_4 \ s_4 \ P=0.3794$
$s_1 \ s_5 \ P=0.0155$	$s_4 \ s_5 \ P=0.0121$
$s_1 \ s_6 \ P=0.0132$	$s_4 \ s_6 \ P=0.0119$
$s_1 \ s_7 \ P=0.0141$	$s_4 \ s_7 \ P=0.0202$
$s_1 \ s_8 \ P=0.0040$	$s_4 \ s_8 \ P=0.0040$

Subordination and condensation of patterns, of course, renders the analysis of clausal sequences more complex, but Carlyle typically relies on parallelism or repetition to clarify the logic of the sequence. The following sentence has a sequence of s_4, s_4, s_7, and subordinate s_3 (N V N: N V N-N: N V N N-N/ $\overparen{\text{N V N}}$/.):

> Midas had misjudged the celestial music-tones; Midas had insulted Apollo and the gods: the gods gave him his wish, and a pair of long ears, which were a good appendage to it. (Text IV)

The technique here is incremental: the second clause parallels the first but adds a compound object; the third clause takes the second object of the second sentence as its subject and adds an indirect object as well as a compound direct object; the second object of the third clause is then modified by a subordinate clause with a predicate noun. In patterns of clausal condensation, the sequences become smaller rather than larger; this technique is apparent in the following sentence, in which Carlyle urges the importance of calculating the laws of style:

> On the whole, Genius has privileges of its own; it selects an orbit for itself; and be this never so eccentric, if it is indeed a celestial orbit, we mere star-gazers must at last compose ourselves; must cease to cavil at it, and begin to observe it, and calculate its laws.[7]

The structure again relies on parallelism and repetition, but the basic s_4 pattern is condensed step by step; with "we mere star-gazers" as subject, the structure is:

subject+modal aux.+verb+object;
   modal aux.+verb+(infinitive+object),
      verb+(infinitive+object),
        (infinitive+object).

Many of these structural techniques are related to the principles of associationist rhetoric which prevailed in Scotland during Carlyle's school years, and they are best explained in terms of the rhetorical manner.

John Luxton's *Rhetoric* was the text at Annan Grammar School during the years that Carlyle studied there (1806–1809); Luxton's book was based on the theory of rhetoric formulated by George Campbell in *The Philosophy of Rhetoric*. The assumption of this rhetorical theory is that the mind operates through the "association of ideas" and that the most effective style is that which conforms to the natural associational sequence; this theory confirmed the notion that language and ideas were disparate factors, that grammar was not necessarily confluent with the sequences of thought and therefore often hindered thought. Ideas are associated in the mind by relations of causality, contiguity, similitude, or contrariety. A coterie of ideas typically has a node—that is, attendant ideas cluster or coalesce about a central or key idea. Stylistically, that key idea should be given prominence, and the "chain of ideas" associated with it should follow in natural sequence; therefore associationist rhetoric justified various figures of syntactic manipulation—inversion, parenthesis, apposition, repetition, omission—that would allow ideas to be presented associationally, rather than regimented by the usual syntactic order.

The various figures of syntax in Carlyle's prose, their frequency and variation, I have tabulated for each of the six texts. The computer dictionary of rhetorical figures was derived from the Scottish rhetoricians of the late eighteenth and early nineteenth centuries,[8] with the figures translated into the same notation used in the parsing phase. In Table III, I have divided the rhetorical figures into five categories, according to the type of syntactic manipulation involved, and have listed occurrences for each of the texts. Because some figures may occur many times per sentence (e.g., parenthesis) and others only once (e.g., periodicity), I have found it useful to express in raw count the frequency of individual figures in each 10,000-word sample.

The style of the *Life of Schiller*, in contrast to the rhetorical pyrotechnics of Carlyle's later polemical prose, seems bland and conservative; formal and fluent, not stiff but not vibrant either. The syntax is not often varied, and the clausal patterns do not alternate as often as in the later texts: parallelism is the rule. Among the rhetorical figures of syntax, many of the figures frequent in the later prose are used, but less exuberantly, almost mechanically. A short passage will provide an illustration:

> He felt it hard enough to be driven from the enchantments of poetry by the dull realities of duty; but it was intolerable and degrading to be hemmed in still farther by the caprices of severe and formal pedagogues. Schiller brooded gloomily over the constraints and hardships of his situation. Many plans he formed for deliverance. Sometimes he would escape in secret to catch a glimpse of the free and busy world to him forbidden: sometimes he laid schemes for utterly abandoning a place which he abhorred, and trusting to fortune for the rest. Often the sight of his class-books and school-

TABLE III

Rhetorical figures of syntax

	I. 1821	II. 1831	III. 1837	IV. 1843	V. 1865	VI. 1875
I. Syntactic order:	*130*	*221*	*260*	*202*	*210*	*227*
inversion	46	83	129	76	73	79
parenthesis	42	80	80	52	58	67
apposition	26	43	40	41	41	51
hysterologia	1	4	2	5	6	7
hypallage	1	2	2		1	2
periodic	14	9	7	28	31	21
II. Syntactic omission:	*102*	*132*	*176*	*178*	*172*	*166*
ellipsis	20	11	4	2	3	12
zeugma	10	31	36	29	28	26
syllepsis	3	3		8	10	6
scesis onomaton		5	3	22	20	21
diazeugma	46	59	111	85	79	78
brachylogia	15	13	14	18	13	11
asyndeton	8	10	8	14	19	12
III. Syntactic repetition:	*17*	*30*	*38*	*175*	*166*	*148*
hypozeuxis	1	3	9	9	8	4
epizeuxis		1		4	4	4
diacope		3		46	51	40
anaphora	1	7	8	60	58	44
epistrophe		1	7	4	5	6
symploce				3	1	4
epanalepsis				3	2	4
antimetabole				2	1	3
anadiplosis	1		2	6	3	5
gradatio				2	1	1
ploce	14	15	12	36	32	33
IV. Syntactic balance:	*122*	*93*	*89*	*81*	*70*	*66*
isocolon	16	4	1	5	4	3
parison	90	79	82	28	30	33
paromoion	1	2		4	4	2
homoioteleuton	14	5	2	18	17	12
antithesis			1	12	3	6
paradiastole	1		3	.	1	1
polysyndeton		3		14	11	9
V. Syntactic exchange:	*6*	*6*	*3*	*20*	*23*	*29*
enallage	4	1		6	4	4
hendiadys						
anthimeria						
polypteton	2	5	3	14	19	25

apparatus became irksome beyond endurance; he would feign sickness, that he might be left to his own chamber to write poetry and pursue his darling studies without hindrance. (Text I)

With the exception of the inversion in "many plans he formed . . .," the syntax here is regular and forward-pacing. The rhythm, too, is regular but fairly monotonous, for it relies almost exclusively on balance; the doublets become tedious in their frequency:

intolerable and degrading
severe and formal
constraints and hardships
free and busy
class-books and school-apparatus
to write poetry and pursue his darling studies

One gets the impression that Carlyle is determined to express everything in pairs. Of course, he is not restricting his style to the teeter-totter rhythm of balances quite so severely as did Lyly and his "euphuistic" imitators, but the devices are the same: *isocolon* (syllabic balance), *parison* (syntactic balance), *paromoion* (echoic balance), and *homoioteleuton* (rhyme endings). These devices Carlyle often employs with skill; in the parallel adverbial phrases in the first sentence, for example, the like syntax and like endings sharpen the contrast:

to be driven from the enchantments of poetry
by the dull realities of duty.

Anaphora (repetition of the first word) tightens the clausal relation in the third sentence ("Sometimes . . .; sometimes . . .") and contributes to the transition to the fourth sentence ("Often . . ."). The entire account of Schiller's planning is linked together by *homoioteleuton:* "deliverance," "endurance," "hindrance."

How very different is the style of *Sartor Resartus.* The euphuistic balancing and chiming are still present, although used less frequently and more judiciously. Cataloguing and condensation abounds, and the causes are no longer parallel in regular rhythm. His caprices of rhetorical punctuation are now evident. Carlyle is well aware of these stylistic devices, calling attention to the "circumlocutions, repetitions," and "quaint tricksy turns" of Teufelsdröckh's prose:

On the whole, Professor Teufelsdröckh is not a cultivated writer. Of his sentences perhaps not more than nine-tenths stand straight on their legs; the remainder are in quite angular attitudes, buttressed up by props (or parentheses and dashes), and even with this or the other tagrag hanging from them; a few even sprawl out helplessly on all sides, quite broken-backed and dismembered. (Text II)

The description is accurate, for it is in *Sartor Resartus* that Carlyle begins using those verbless sentences of nouns and modifiers, and here, too, he increments—doubles—his use of inversions, parentheses, and appositions, rhetorically dismembering his syntax. The doublets now alternate with single modifiers and with triplets; the balances are sparse and seldom symmetrical; the casual repetitions provide natural links to the logic, and the studied repetitions contribute an almost epigrammatic tone; the chiming appears to be reserved for humorous or ironic touches, as in such wordplay as "hum of real Humor" or "echo of mere Insanity and Inanity."

In the opening paragraph of this essay, I called attention to the significant contrasts between the *Life of Schiller* and "The Diamond Necklace." Now, with the perspective provided by the addition of four other texts, it can be seen that a major transition was taking place in Carlyle's style. The tendency toward inversion evidently reached a peak in the late 1830's, for in none of the later samplings does it occur quite so often; nevertheless, it remains a marked feature of his style and he continues to invert approximately one-tenth of his clauses. The huge increase in the number of clausal sequences with the subjects omitted (*diazeugma*), as may be noted in Table III, distorts what was apparently a general trend in Carlyle's prose: *diazeugma* continues to be used often, yet not quite so often as the sample from "The Diamond Necklace" would indicate. The character sketches and descriptive settings in "The Diamond Necklace" are given in a deft and bold sequence of apocopated clauses, as in this little sketch of the heroic Roland, in which Carlyle argues against the romantic conception:

Roland of Roncesvalles too, we see well in thinking of it, found rainy weather as well as sunny; knew what it was to have hose need darning; got tough beef to chew, or even went dinnerless; was saddle-sick, calumniated, constipated (as his madness too clearly indicates); and oftenest felt, I doubt not, that this was a very Devil's world, and he, Roland himself, one of the sorriest caitiffs there. (Text III)

In the passage on Teufelsdröckh's grave appearance, discussed above, I called attention to Carlyle's manner of placing the subject prominently at the head of the sentence, then setting it off with a parenthetical phrase; the device occurs again here, but with an added effect—the predicate, also standing apart, establishes a pattern that is echoed over and over—emphasizing here the petty and relentless torments of life. The omission of the subject in the successive clauses permits the verbs to strike with full vigor; then Carlyle concludes with a repetition so emphatic—"he, Roland himself"—that the reader cannot possibly forget that there is a subject involved with all these verbs.

In *Past and Present*, several new aspects of stylistic change become apparent: the figures of order and omission are still present with high frequency, but that frequency is almost matched by the figures of repetition, which now play a major part in Carlyle's style. Among the figures of balance, the once favored *parison* (syntactic balance) has diminished, but many other figures of balance are being used more. In short, Carlyle has extended his rhetorical range; he is using more figures of syntax—more in quantity, more in variety. The periodic sentences, which had become less and less frequent since the *Life of Schiller*, are revived here: twice as many as in Text I, three times as many as in Text II, four times as many as in Text III. These periodic sentences, however, are not the sweeping Ciceronians that Carlyle sought to create in the *Life of Schiller;* they are typically terse and draw full force from the climactic verb:

> Not in sharp fever-fits, but in chronic gangrene of this kind is Scotland suffering. (Text IV)

With effective periodicity, too, Carlyle places the whole weight of the sentence on a brief predication, as here on the tight opposition of direct object and object complement (s_6):

> Oceans of horse-hair, continents of parchment, and learned-serjeant eloquence, were it continued till the learned tongue wore itself small in the indefatigable learned mouth, cannot make unjust just. (Text IV)

Table III shows that in *Sartor Resartus* and "The Diamond Necklace," Carlyle gradually increased his use of the figures of repetition; in *Past and Present* they more than quadruple, and this seems to be the plateau, if the sampling is reliable, for the later texts exhibit approximately the same number. These figures have both an associational and a polemical function in Carlyle's prose: repetition may indicate the link between one idea and another; repetition, as Carlyle also uses it, may underscore angry invective or urgent appeal. A few examples of the figures in Text IV will serve to illustrate the range and variety of his rhetorical repetition. Although the definitions here are from a source familiar to Carlyle,[9] no hyper-sophistication is being suggested: the rhetorical terms were originally used to describe what is effective in language; Carlyle employs the figures out of an awareness of what is effective, whether he recalled the classical terms or not.

hypozeuxis (complete subject and predicate in parallel clauses):
> "the work they have done, the fruit they have realized"

epizeuxis (repetition of words with none in between):
> "Away, Away!" "Sinking, Sinking"

diacope (repetition of words with one or few in between):
> "A Poor-law, any and every Poor-law"

anaphora (repetition of first word in a series of phrases or clauses):
> "Midas had misjudged the celestial music-tones; Midas had insulted Apollo and the gods"
> "Foolish men cannot answer it aright! Foolish men mistake . . ."

epistrophe (repetition of last word in a series of phrases or clauses):
> "There will a radical alteration of your regimen and way of life take place; there will a most agonizing divorce between you and your chimeras, luxuries and falsities, take place; a most toilsome, all but

'impossible' return to Nature, and her veracities and her integrities, take place: . . . . Either death, or else all this will take place."

symploce (repetition of first and last word in a series of phrases or clauses): "We have more riches than any nation ever had before; we have less good of them than any nation ever had before."

epanalepsis (first word of one clause repeated as the last of the following clause):
"A Poor-law, any and every Poor-law, it may be observed, is but a temporary measure; an anodyne, not a remedy: Rich and Poor, when once the naked facts of their condition have come into collision, cannot long subsist together on a mere Poor-law."

antimetabole (repetition of words in converse order):
"Do they look with satisfaction on more things and human faces in this God's-Earth; do more things and human faces look with satisfaction on them?"

anadiplosis (last word of one clause repeated as first of following clause):
"Midas had insulted Apollo and the gods: the gods gave him his wish, and a pair of long ears."

"Had they known Nature's right truth, Nature's right truth would have made them free."

climax (repetition in a causally linked series of phrases or clauses):
"The use of spun shirts is but to cover human backs, human backs to labor, labor to plough or spin and weave, and that to yield shirts for fair wages."

The style of *Frederick the Great* appears less strenuous syntactically than the polemical prose of *Past and Present*; however, it builds upon the same figures and the same sequential patterns. The difference is in the tighter predication and briefer subordinated modification, which creates a style more generally curt:

But wise or unwise, how great are his Britannic Majesty's activities in this Pragmatic Business! We may say, they are prodigious, incessant, ubiquitous. They are forgotten now, fallen wholly to the spiders and dust-bins;— though Friedrich himself was not a busier King in those days, if perhaps better directed. It is a thing wonderful to us, but sorrowful and undeniable. We perceive the Britannic Majesty's own little mind pulsing with this Pragmatic Matter, as the biggest volcano would do;—shooting forth dust and smoke (subsidies, diplomatic emissaries, treaties, offers of treaty, plans, foolish futile exertions), at an immense rate. (Text V)

The figures of order, omission, and repetition are operative here, as well as some balancing and chiming (note such rhymes as "prodigious" and "ubiquitous" in the triad, or "subsidies, . . . emissaries, treaties" in the catalog). The omission of conjunctions between words and clauses (*brachylogia* and *asyndeton*) is relatively frequent in Texts III and IV. Carlyle tends to leave out subordinating conjunctions (*which, that*), and seldom links clauses with any coordinate other than *but*; in his catalogs and triadic modifiers ("prodigious, incessant, ubiquitous"; "subsidies, diplomatic emissaries . . .") he usually omits the coordinating conjunction, but he retains it in his doublets ("wise or unwise," "sorrowful and undeniable," "dust and smoke").

Precisely the same characteristics are observable in the *Early Kings of Norway*, and the style is even more apocopated, almost staccato, because of the frequent syntactic intrusions and numerous omissions:

> Hakon Jarl, such the style he took, had engaged to pay some kind of tribute to King Blue-tooth, "if he could"; but he never did pay any, pleading always the necessity of his own affairs; with which excuse, joined to Hakon's readiness in things less important, King Blue-tooth managed to content himself, Hakon being always his good neighbour, at least, and the two mutually dependent. In Norway, Hakon, without the title of king, did in a strong-handed, steadfast, and at length successful way, the office of one; governed Norway (some count) for above twenty years; and, both at home and abroad, had much consideration through most of that time; specially amongst the heathen, fixed in his mind against these chimerical Christian innovations and unsalutary changes of creed, and would have gladly trampled out all traces of what the last two kings (for Greyfell, also, was an English Christian after his sort) had done in this respect. (Text VI)

Such sentences as these, with their intensive use of the figures of order and omission are representative of Carlyle's style during the last decades of his career. In comparing the early prose with the late, it becomes obvious that Carlyle came to favor syntactic fragmentation in the presentation of ideas. Further, it is a style that grew out of his active career as a public speaker; at the podium, Carlyle learned the persuasiveness of compact phrasing, and learned, too, the cadences and pauses which he represented in his prose with various punctuational tricks.

The rhetorical principles of Carlyle's prose style have been discussed here in accordance with those of the Scottish associationists. In *The Philosophy of Rhetoric*, Campbell assumes as first principle that grammar has "a close connexion with understanding, and the theory of the association of ideas," and as second that "there is no art whatever that has so close a connexion with all the faculties and powers of the mind, as eloquence, or the art of speaking." With this intimacy between rhetoric and syntax and the mind, the devices of order, omission, and repetition are defined as psychologically natural and logically necessary. As Campbell explains, "we are apt to consider the customary arrangement as the most consonant to nature, in consequence of which notion we brand every departure from it as a transgression of the natural order"; yet it is false to dismiss every departure from the customary arrangement "as a transgression," for the nature of thought and passion may well justify syntactic manipulation; "whatever strongly impresses the fancy or awakens the passions, is sufficient to a certain degree to authorize the violation."[10]

Carlyle developed a style based on this logic: ideas are arranged as they strike the mind—in association with the ideas that stimulated them. The mind associates things and appearances, actions and consequences; at the same time, the mind evaluates intellectually or responds emotionally to these associations. Since all the factors that occur simultaneously in the mind cannot be expressed simultaneously in language, Carlyle simply intrudes and omits in order to present ideas in close juxtaposition. The repetition maintains a fluent association of ideas, even though the syntax itself is disrupted.

Carlyle once called attention to the distinction between the "Orator," who "persuades and carries all with him, he knows not how," and the "Rhetorician," who can merely demonstrate how and why.[11] The counting and calculating of figures and patterns is a trivial task if it does not bring us closer to understanding the intellectual and literary performance in language. Again Carlyle's comment: "On the whole, Genius has privileges of its own; it selects an orbit for itself; and be this never so eccentric, if it is indeed a celestial orbit, we mere star-gazers must at last compose ourselves; must cease to cavil at it, and begin to observe it, and calculate its laws."

REFERENCES

1. "Associationist Rhetoric and Scottish Prose Style," *Speech Monographs*, XXXIV (1967), 21–34.
2. Word classes w_{10}, w_{11}, and w_{12} are recognized in computer scansion by the symbols O, −, and + respectively. Alliteration, assonance, or repetition are marked by a − or + tag following the word.
3. Sentence classes s_1 through s_7 are recognized as basic predication patterns and include such regular variations as split predicates and interrogative inversions. s_8 is the class which includes all other variants: in the Carlyle texts, 95% of the s_8 variants are sentence fragments with no finite predication.
4. *Complete Works of Thomas Carlyle* (New York, 1901). For computer analysis, a 10,000-word text was taken from each of the following: *Life of Schiller*, XX, 14–41; *Sartor Resartus*, I, 3–30; "The Diamond Necklace," XV, 226–254; *Past and Present*, XII, 3–31; *Frederick the Great*, Book 13, VIII, 3–35; *Early Kings of Norway*, XIX, 393–421.
5. I have used here the "STRING" program developed by Dr. Walter S. Stolz of the Department of Psychology of the University of Texas, assisted by Mr. Fred Carstensen of the Department of Mass Communications, The University of Wisconsin. The parsing phase of the rhetorical scansion program is based on their "WISSYN" program.
6. Carlyle, XII, 26 (Text IV).
7. Carlyle, XIII, 21; from the essay "Jean Paul Friedrich Richter" (1827).
8. Henry Home, Lord Kames, *Elements of Criticism* (Edinburgh, 1762); George Campbell, *The Philosophy of Rhetoric* (Edinburgh, 1776); Hugh Blair, *Lectures on Rhetoric and Belles Lettres*, 2 vols. (Edinburgh, 1783); James Burnett, Lord Monboddo, *Of the Origin and Progress of Language*, 6 vols. (Edinburgh, 1772–1792).
9. These definitions are all drawn from Lord Monboddo's chapters on composition and syntax: *Of the Origin and Progress of Language*, III (Edinburgh, 1786), Ch. 6, "Of the Figures of Syntax," 65–105; VI (Edinburgh, 1792), Ch. 3, "Composition," 113–128.
10. Campbell, pp. xlviii–xlix, and 355–356.
11. Carlyle, XIV, 349; from the essay "Characteristics" (1831).

PERILS OF QUANTIFICATION: THE EXEMPLARY CASE OF JANE AUSTEN'S *EMMA*

KARL KROEBER

For some time I have been engaged in analyses of fiction in an effort to establish quantitative measures of nineteenth-century novelists' styles. To anyone seeking systematic and relatively objective methods for describing style in fiction the attraction of vocabulary analysis is strong. Words appear to be definite, countable items whose organization can be defined unsubjectively. Unfortunately, there is no *necessary* relationship between the frequency with which a specific word is used and its aesthetic significance. Prepositions, which are useful if one is trying to solve a problem of attribution, occur with great frequency in all novels. But study of "in" or "of" or "to" does not provide much insight into the artistic design of a novel. A word used only once may be very significant, or it may be exceedingly trivial.[1] The aesthetic significance of word-choice depends upon a patterning of qualities which is not readily identifiable through the discrimination and classification of words treated as quantities.

If raw frequencies of vocabulary (such as the lists provided by concordances) are not so helpful as one could wish, it would nevertheless seem possible that preferences for specific groups of words ought to be identifiable and important. But how does one decide upon the proper grouping? The vocabulary of any given piece of writing is largely determined by its subject-matter. One wouldn't look for words related to automobiles in nineteenth-century novels, as one might in twentieth-century novels.

Because novels always have characters, it seemed to me a useful cluster would be one of the words referring to parts of the body and to bodily movements. I therefore scanned some novels for nouns referring to parts of the body and verbs descriptive of bodily movements. Because there are few concordances or word-lists for novels and novelists, I used a sampling system. It is not at all improbable, of course, that ten pages from a novel will have special vocabulary characteristics not typical of the novel as a whole (or of the novelist's predominant usage), but a series of such samples should have some validity.

Although there is considerable variation between samples from different novels by the same author in Table 1, the general pattern of the table is clear: *relatively* Jane Austen uses fewer substantives referring to parts of the body than do Eliot, Dickens, or Brontë; and the latter two use *relatively* more than does Eliot. Verbs follow the same pattern, suggesting that in this case syntactic preferences are of minor importance. That the four novelists together may be part of a larger "nineteenth-century" configuration, part, that is, of a persistent tendency in British fiction, is suggested by analogous figures derived from two eighteenth-century and two twentieth-century novels (Table 1), but

TABLE 1

Column 1 Novel	Column 2 Total no. nouns in sample	Column 3 No. nouns referring to parts of body	Column 4 Column 3 ÷ Column 2
Northanger Abbey	539	28	.05
Sense and Sensibility	267	2	.01
Mansfield Park	198	12	.06
Emma	591	18	.03
Persuasion	791	19	.02
AUSTEN Totals	2,386	79	.03
Oliver Twist	591	53	.09
David Copperfield	425	69	.16
Bleak House	171	19	.11
Great Expectations	412	91	.22
Our Mutual Friend	237	35	.15
DICKENS Totals	1,836	267	.15
The Professor	169	25	.15
Jane Eyre	124	32	.26
Shirley	252	28	.11
Villette	447	52	.12
BRONTË Totals	992	137	.14
Adam Bede	443	19	.04
Mill on the Floss	363	39	.11
Silas Marner	506	48	.09
Romola	214	22	.10
Middlemarch	397	10	.03
Daniel Deronda	348	41	.12
ELIOT Totals	2,271	179	.08
* *	*	*	*
Novelist	Total no. verbs in sample	No. verbs of bodily movement	Column 3 ÷ Column 2
Austen—five novels	2,032	13	.006
Dickens—five novels	3,106	78	.025
Brontë—four novels	1,487	30	.020
Eliot—seven novels	2,537	38	.015
* *	*	*	*
Novel	Total no. nouns in sample	No. nouns referring to parts of body	Column 3 ÷ Column 2
Pamela	285	11	.04
Tom Jones	454	17	.04
Sons and Lovers	460	68	.15
Jacob's Room	991	106	.11

such a conclusion must await the collection and evaluation of more data, and, as I suggest below, efforts to establish any general norm may be misguided.

The figures in Table 1 verify rather than reveal. Most readers recognize that Jane Austen devotes little attention to physical description or to the narration of physical actions. But the counting technique might be used for discovery; if, that is, we concentrate upon carefully discriminating between the characteristics of related authors' vocabularies, we may be able to arrive at stylistic definitions based not on some absolute norm but, instead, on simple differentia. By gradually collecting such differentia we may, finally, be able to establish inductively stylistic norms for periods, genres, and so on. In any case, the figures in Table 1 provide not absolute frequency (obtainable only by analysis of all the works of each novelist, that is, by the creation of complete concordances) but relative frequency, that is, preference for one word-cluster of one novelist vis-à-vis another. Such relative frequencies become more illuminating as more word-clusters are tested.

A refinement of this method is illustrated in Tables 2 through 4. The vocabulary of each sample is first divided according to conventional parts of speech. Then some high-frequency words are eliminated from each part-of-speech group. Then a further, arbitrary classification is made: descriptive adjectives of "measure," or verbs denoting "psychic action," or adverbs answering the question "how?" and ending in "-ly" are singled out. These sub-clusters are further screened by the elimination of words which never appear more than once in a single sample and of words which, however frequently they may appear in one or two samples, do not occur in at least fifty percent of the samples tested. The purpose of the latter screening is to reduce the vocabulary resulting solely from a particular subject-concentration. The purpose of the first screening is to highlight slightly unusual vocabulary somewhat emphasized by repetition. I do not specially commend this technique. It is meant merely to illustrate the kind of operation which may be helpful in discovering characteristics of word-choice.

One should remember that the figures in Table 2, for example, do not show which words of the particular group are used most often by each of the novelists but indicate only relative emphasis. Nonetheless, some statistical balance has to be kept. Results from a sample of 100,000 words from one novelist are not strictly comparable with a sample of 1000 words from another. In Table 2, then, we can most properly compare Eliot to Austen, and, less effectively, Dickens to Brontë. It is worth noting, however, that reductions of the samples from Austen, Eliot, and Dickens which bring their total number of nouns down to the Brontë total of 1300 leave a substantially longer list of nouns for each of the novelists.

Although Dickens' "pool" of nouns is larger than Brontë's, the noun "love" does not pass through the screens for his samples as it does for Brontë (and Austen and Eliot). The point deserves attention because Dickens favors the *verb* "love." Here, for whatever reason, a distinction between parts of speech points up a difference in usage.

TABLE 2

"Abstract" Nouns

Jane Austen: samples from seven novels; total no. nouns = 2,427
Charles Dickens: samples from five novels; total no. nouns = 1,673
Charlotte Brontë: samples from five* novels; total no. nouns = 1,270
George Eliot: samples from seven novels; total no. nouns = 2,327

Word	No. of samples in which word occurs	No. of occurrences
AUSTEN		
feelings	7	26
love	7	24
spirits	7	23
happiness	7	17
manners	7	17
visit	6	13
attention	6	12
pleasure	6	10
account	6	9
connection	6	7
sensibility	6	7
beauty	5	7
journey	5	7
		179
DICKENS		
manner	4	9
look	4	8
influence	4	6
course	3	7
death	3	7
nothing	3	5
point	3	4
matter	3	4
silence	3	4
		54
BRONTË		
love	3	12
nature	3	8
degree	3	7
taste	3	5
		32
ELIOT		
sense	7	17
feelings	6	14
love	6	13
pleasure	5	15
opinion	5	14
presence	5	11
experience	5	10
consciousness	5	9
		103

*Including the juvenile story "The Spell."

Austen apparently operates with a smaller "abstract" noun vocabulary than Eliot. Austen repeats her favoured abstract nouns more than Eliot does. The leading nouns for both refer to complex psycho-physical conditions involving rationality as well as emotion. But for Austen these occur in a context of specifically social actions and interactions: "visit," "journey," "manners," "attention." Eliot's nouns point toward the more modern concern with "consciousness" of personal "experience."

The relative sombreness of Dickens' list, especially in contrast to Austen's, may be due to the rather "dark" nature of the five novels sampled. But the two words which top his list in Table 2 make one recall his relatively high proportion of nouns referring to bodily parts. Dickens undoubtedly emphasizes "manner" in contrast to Austen's stress on "manners."

TABLE 3
"Psychic Action" Verbs

No. of novelists using word	Word	Austen	Eliot	Dickens	Brontë
all four	believe	5/11	3/8	4/7	3/7
three	hope	5/13	4/5		3/4
	know	4/8		4/6	3/4
	like	3/7	4/12	4/9	
two	mean	3/9	3/6		
one	mind		3/4		
	love			5/16	
	learn			3/4	
	wonder			3/4	
	forget			3/4	
	care				3/6
	dare				3/4
	desire				3/4
	doubt				3/4
	suffer				3/4

Results of the same kind of test for verbs representing "psychic" action I present in a slightly different form in Table 3, since in this case I work from a common base of approximately 350 words from five samples for each novelist. In Table 3, the number before the slash indicates the number of samples in which the word occurs and the number after the slash indicates the total number of occurrences. The most striking feature of Table 3 is the small number of occurrences of a small list of words. With the exception of Dickens' "love" there is no verb which appears frequently enough to be outstanding. Although Austen has only five words which pass through the screens, these five account for nearly twenty percent of her total "pool" of 350. Eliot's five words account for only about ten percent of her pool. Again we observe Austen repeating more than Eliot. Again, too, we notice Austen's predilection for "common" words: all her words in Table 3 are shared with at least one other novelist sampled. While I would be loath to base any interpretation on these figures, they do seem to me to point toward Jane Austen's tendency to manipulate a small, unspecialized vocabulary so as to clarify subtle shadings of meaning within conventional and often rather generalized terms. Dickens and Brontë use verbs not so characteristic of the other two novelists: the five words unique to Brontë seem remarkably close to the special kind of action she favors in her fiction.

With both adjectives (Table 4) and adverbs (Table 5) it is not worthwhile to establish consistent pools of words. In Table 4, for example, the figures for Austen are drawn from a total pool of more than twice the size of either Brontë's or Dickens', yet for Austen (as for Eliot) only six words pass through the screens, whereas for Brontë ten pass through and for Dickens, eighteen.

The lists for Dickens and Brontë would be longer if derived from pools as large as that used for Austen, but the difference in the variety of adjectives would be only slightly accentuated since it is already impressive. As contrasted to Austen, Dickens and Brontë prefer to repeat less frequently a greater number of adjectives yet, leaving aside the difference in the meanings of the adjectives favored, Dickens is distinguishable from Brontë. Her ten words passing through the screens account for about eight percent of her pool—close to Austen's seven percent for six words. Dickens' eighteen words account for thirteen percent of his pool. (Eliot's preference for non-repetition of adjectives is highlighted, incidentally, by the fact that her six words account for only some three percent of her pool.)

In Table 4, as in Table 3, one can observe a patterning which associates Dickens and Brontë as opposed to Eliot and Austen. This patterning may be trivial, but it is at least conceivable that it reflects some differences in larger form, a difference, for example, between "novels" and "romances." At any rate, the adverb table (Table 5) reinforces this patterning, even though, in terms of the number of words passing through the screens, it reverses the proportions of the adjective table.

Although a larger pool would presumably lengthen the Brontë and Dickens lists in Table 5, it would be unlikely to bring them anywhere near the length of Austen's, because in this test multiple occurrences were not required—only the second screen was applied. This table alone is enough to suggest that for Austen the adverb plays a special role. Whereas repetition of modifiers in Dickens and Brontë is found more amongst adjectives than adverbs, Austen's tendency is in the opposite direction—Eliot being nearly balanced. Among her repeated adverbs which are not colorless, Austen favors cheerful ones such as "happily," "heartily," "comfortably," "easily," "warmly," and it is worth remembering the appearance of "happy" on her adjective list and of "happiness" on her noun list.

I have been trying to point up the potential rewards of quantitative analyses of fictional vocabularies. The techniques I have used are not in themselves particularly valuable: they only suggest that more sophisticated methods of

TABLE 4
Descriptive Adjectives

Word	No. of samples occurs in	Total no. of occurrences

AUSTEN: eight samples; total number of descriptive adjectives = 2,084

Word	No. of samples occurs in	Total no. of occurrences
dear	7	38
sure	7	35
happy	7	33
handsome	6	16
agreeable	6	11
amiable	6	9
		142

DICKENS: five samples; total number of descriptive adjectives = 1,035

Word	No. of samples occurs in	Total no. of occurrences
strong	5	11
dark	5	9
sure	4	11
hard	4	9
open	4	7
general	4	7
blue	4	7
usual	4	7
cold	4	6
quiet	4	6
afraid	4	6
dear	3	9
beautiful	3	7
different	3	6
heavy	3	6
mysterious	3	6
natural	3	6
pale	3	6
		132

BRONTË: five samples; total number of descriptive adjectives = 885

Word	No. of samples occurs in	Total no. of occurrences
human	5	11
strange	5	9
true	5	7
white	5	6
calm	4	6
strong	4	6
quiet	4	5
cold	3	7
dim	3	7
wild	3	6
		70

ELIOT: seven samples; total number of descriptive adjectives = 1,747

Word	No. of samples occurs in	Total no. of occurrences
strong	5	11
painful	5	10
fine	4	12
ready	4	10
true	4	8
human	4	7
		58

TABLE 5

Simple Adverbs Ending in "-ly" Answering the Question "How?"

Austen: five samples; 741 adverbs.
Dickens: five samples; 716 adverbs.
Brontë: five samples; 417 adverbs.
Eliot: six samples; 587 adverbs.

Word	No. of samples occurs in	Total no. of occurrences
AUSTEN		
hardly	4	9
entirely	4	6
merely	4	4
scarcely	3	8
directly	3	7
equally	3	7
perfectly	3	7
happily	3	5
heartily	3	5
particularly	3	4
properly	3	4
absolutely	3	3
comfortably	3	3
easily	3	3
evidently	3	3
exceedingly	3	3
instantly	3	3
nearly	3	3
separately	3	3
warmly	3	3
		93
DICKENS		
suddenly	4	7
slowly	4	6
		13

Note: "scarcely" appears five times in two samples and "faintly" four times in two samples; all other adverbs appear in one sample only.

Word	No. of samples occurs in	Total no. of occurrences
BRONTË		
wildly	3	6
		6

Note: "hardly" appears five times in two samples, "especially" and "nearly" three times in two samples; all other adverbs appear in one sample only.

Word	No. of samples occurs in	Total no. of occurrences
ELIOT		
simply	5	5
hardly	3	7
gradually	3	4
quickly	3	4
alternately	3	3
chiefly	3	3
evidently	3	3
thoroughly	3	3
		32

measurement might help us to understand better the aesthetic characteristics of fiction.[2] But there appear to me to be severe limitatio:1s to the effectiveness of *any* such quantitative analyses. Although, as I have suggested, my technique points toward an inductively-derived definition of stylistic characteristics (a kind of definition likely to be more viable than abstract, normative ones), it seems possible that any quantitative analysis of literature destroys in the very process of analysis the literary qualities it seeks to describe. To make the same point a little less violently, I shall propose that such analysis tends to obscure precisely what is most significant in a novelist's selection and disposition of his words. I shall try to substantiate the proposal by examining the opening paragraph of Chapter Three of *Emma*, a fair sample of Jane Austen's mature prose.

Mr. Woodhouse was fond of society in his own way. He liked very much to have his friends come and see him; and from various united causes, from his long residence at Hartfield, and his good nature, from his fortune, his house, and his daughter, he could command the visits of his own little circle, in a great measure as he liked. He had not much intercourse with any families beyond that circle; his horror of late hours and large dinner-parties made him unfit for any acquaintance, but such as would visit him on his own terms. Fortunately for him, Highbury, including Randalls in the same parish, and Donwell Abbey in the parish adjoining, the seat of Mr. Knightley, comprehended many such. Not unfrequently, through Emma's persuasion, he had some of the chosen and best to dine with him, but evening-parties were what he preferred, and, unless he fancied himself at any time unequal to company, there was scarcely an evening in the week in which Emma could not make up a card-table for him.[3]

Analysis of this paragraph of apparently straightforward expository narration reveals astonishing subtlety in its graciously low-toned representation of the tyranny of dependence. The key is provided by the first sentence: "Mr. Woodhouse was fond . . . in his own way." Everything turns on *him*. "He liked . . . his friends . . . see him . . . his long residence . . . his good nature . . . his fortune, his house, and his daughter, he could command . . . his own circle . . . he liked . . . his horror . . . made him unfit . . . visit him on his own terms . . . he preferred . . . he fancied . . . a card-table for him." Jane Austen likes to use proper names. By my count one out of five of her nouns is a proper one, a proportion greater than that of any other novelist I have studied.[4] But in this paragraph she uses pronouns exclusively after the opening sentence. The pronoun enables her to maintain a subterraneous emphasis on Mr. Woodhouse's egocentrism. The pronouns permit unobtrusive repetition because the different cases of the third person differ in form. In the paragraph all three forms occur frequently, highlighting the fact that subject, object, and possessor are all but different aspects of one all-encompassing ego.

In the paragraph, moreover, is embodied one of the essential motifs of the novel, tyranny, the exploitation of one human being by another, in the guise of love, affection, and so forth. Mr. Woodhouse exploits his dependence upon Emma so as to tyrannize over her. He determines her life in much the same way that an infant determines its mother's life, as in fact Emma's sister Isabella's children determine her life. Emma's befriending of Harriet Smith is virtually a compensatory exploitation and tyranny, Miss Taylor having escaped her loving control. In a different fashion Frank Churchill exploits both Emma and Jane Fairfax—and he in turn is tyrannized by Mrs. Churchill. One need not pursue the point further, except to observe that because Jane Austen represents this exploitation in subtle forms her apparently simple and straightforward manner of writing is appropriate. What she describes are not crude or overt exploitations. Today we would call Mr. Woodhouse's and Emma's tyrannies "unconscious." They are that, of course, but they are also unconscious operations of very civilized people. To put it another way, the unconscious motives run counter to conscious motivations that are every bit as real and strong. Mr. Woodhouse *is* fond of Emma, who genuinely *does* befriend Harriet. Jane Austen does not oversimplify: Mr. Woodhouse is a gentle, kindly, lovable monster.

Just as Mr. Woodhouse's egocentricity is "concealed" beneath the easy lucidness and conventional expositoriness—even the formal "correctness"— of the paragraph, so what Jane Austen commends to us as properly civilized relations between human beings depends upon recognition of the inevitability of such discrepancies. For Jane Austen civility means exploiting others as little as possible but graciously submitting to some tyranny by others less rationally and imaginatively sympathetic than oneself. Mr. Knightley criticizes Emma for not submitting to the tyranny of Miss Bate's foolishness; and it is noteworthy that she, recognizing the justice of his criticism, tries to soothe her conscience by determining not to fail in her duty to her father. This is no subterfuge: Emma's loyal kindness to the father who victimizes her is one of her most redeeming traits. In other words, what is most important to the style of the paragraph I have discussed lies in its special reinforcement in miniature of the formal order of the novel as a whole. What is true of this paragraph is, *mutatis mutandis*, true of all subordinate parts of the novel.

I doubt, therefore, that any quantitative analysis of vocabulary could point up what is essential to the form and meaning of the paragraph discussed, because such analysis begins by destroying the *relationship* between "microscopic" and "macroscopic" elements in the novel. It is in that relationship that fictional style exists. One can, perhaps, extend this hypothesis to illuminate the problem of "analysis" of literature generally. Analysis presupposes that the part analyzed is somehow in itself significant. In a work of fiction, parts have virtually no significance except insofar as they contribute to the whole. I suspect that many of the "quantities" in fiction, words, for example, are in fact qualities. Hence the limited usefulness of even such handy tools as concordances, which take apart what the artist has put together. It is the togetherness that makes the art.

When we speak of a novelist's choice of words we are referring to something different from mere language, just as when we speak of language we refer to something different from mere sound. Just as language is made out of sounds, so literature is made out of language, but to reduce the "higher" system to elements of the "lower" material of which it is composed is to obscure the difference which we wish to define. Quantitative analysis tends to make this fatal reduction; by discriminating parts it blurs the qualitative relationship of part to whole which in fact defines the essential nature of the part. Useful analysis of literary works requires methods which might be called those of qualitative dissection. These would discriminate elements (and their inter-relationships) defined by the *form* of the work itself. The elements would not be defined by the materials—the "mere language"—out of which literature is made.

The paragraph is both too indefinite and too arbitrary a unit to be used for establishing the relationship of vocabulary to total form in fiction. But since I have used a paragraph from *Emma* to illustrate some aspects of word-choice, I shall use paragraphs as a means of illustrating how aesthetic function of vocabulary in fiction must be defined in terms of its relationship to the design of the novel as a whole, how, in other words, even individual words in a novel are less units of language than they are units of fictional form.

The opening paragraph of each of the early chapters in *Emma* is function-ally analogous to the chapter opening I have already discussed. The first, one-sentence paragraph of the novel, for example, pivots on the colorless word "seemed," which suggests unobtrusively a potential discrepancy between the superficial reality of Emma's situation and another reality beneath it, a dis-crepancy from which will arise the circumstances which "distress" and "vex" her.

The initial paragraph of Chapter Two, an exposition of Mr. Weston's history, centers on his "independence"—which is presented in terms of his "active cheerful mind and social temper," engaged with and obligated to the demands both of "gentility" in general and of a "respectable family" in particular. By Chapter Four we have entered into the immediate action with which the novel is concerned, and Emma's tyranny over her friend is explicitly portrayed: Harriet is "useful" to Emma; although Emma's designs for Harriet are "kind," "*a* Harriet Smith" is "a valuable addition to her privi-leges." Mr. Knightley's observation to Mrs. Weston opening Chapter Five is a direct moral judgment upon this relation. Both the basis and the accuracy of his condemnation are conveyed in the opening of Chapter Six, where, moving more deeply into the realm of subjective impression, we find that the manipulation of Harriet and Mr. Elton is "agreeable" to Emma; she is without "scruple"; she enjoys the "gratitude" of Harriet's "young vanity," and she is "confident," "without a doubt" about her control of people. One must again stress the complex balance that is essential to Jane Austen's art: Mr. Knightley will finally admit, without condoning Emma's earlier practices, that she would have chosen better for Mr. Elton than he chooses for himself.

All these chapter openings are directed toward problems of dependence and independence, although in all of them the problem slips in unobtrusively. Jane Austen's art consists in presenting subtle complexities (which give her novels their abiding interest) in a simple, lucid, even conventionalized manner. All these chapters, except the fifth, in which dialogue momentarily delays the appearance of Mr. Knightley's name, open with the name of a character. The very names seem commonplace; they do not at first strike one as containing special connotations.

If we turn to the paragraphs which open the final chapters of *Emma*, however, we encounter interesting differences. Independence-dependence is no longer the focus, which is now feelings. There is no longer much discrepancy between lucid, formalized surface and complex depths. The first paragraph of Chapter Fourteen (Volume III) stresses Emma's "happiness" in contrast to her preceding hope for mere "respite from suffering." The beginning of the next chapter tells how Frank's letter makes "its way to Emma's feelings," despite her "determination" to think harshly of Frank: "though it was impossible not to feel that he had been wrong, yet . . . he had suffered and was very sorry . . . so grateful . . . so much in love . . . and she was so happy . . . there was no being severe."[5] In Chapter Sixteen we are first told of Emma's "relief" at escaping a "painful" meeting with Harriet, and in Chapter Seventeen of the general happiness at Mrs. Weston's "safety." The penultimate chapter begins with possibilities of "an alarming change" and events "to agitate and grieve" Emma, although with Mr. Knightley's entrance "distressing thoughts" are succeeded by "pleasure," the succession foreshadowing the effect of his news about Harriet. The first paragraph of the novel's last chapter moves from Emma's "anxious feelings" to her becoming "perfectly satisfied."

In the second set of opening paragraphs, then, we find uneasy or conflicting emotions being resolved happily. The resolutions reflect the design of the novel as a whole, in which the anxieties of misunderstanding and unawareness are transformed into the pleasures of self-understanding and consciousness of the respect due others.

One way to understand the working-out of this design (which includes the gradual adjusting of the original "discrepancies" into harmonies) is to recognize its involvement with the novel's time structure. In the first chapters a past "outside" the novel's plot becomes the "present," which in its development forms the main body of the book. In the last chapters this present shades off into a future outside the novel, a future which must be at least relatively doubtful and conditional, as the past is certain.[6] This temporal evolution is certainly not unusual in fiction; indeed, it is conventional. By manipulating the conventions of her form Jane Austen attains the special excellence of her particular fictional design, just as by manipulating the language of her conventionalized description of Mr. Woodhouse she dramatizes the tyranny he exercises through his dependence. The final chapters of *Emma*—conventionally—resolve complications initiated in the first chapters. But the resolutions are more complicated than the original difficulties. In the opening chapters, for example, simple Harriet is merely "useful" to Emma. At the close of the novel Emma does not wish to "use" Harriet, one reason being that Emma has come to recognize Harriet's simplicity as "unaccountable." One thing Emma learns is that to sophistication naïveté is, if not unintelligible, at least difficult to understand and judge. The "lesson" contributes to the emphasis on "pleasure," "satisfaction," and "happiness" recorded in the second set of paragraphs. These are founded upon Emma's deepened awareness of both the hazards and rewards of the intensified self-understanding which should accompany charity of thought and feeling toward others.

The resolutions of *Emma* are not the simplifications which conclude second-rate fictions. Instead, the resolutions extend a central meaning of the novel, the relevation of how apparently trivial matters of ordinary life are in fact intricate, difficult, and significant. The conventional happy ending of *Emma* satisfies aesthetically because it symbolizes a profound truth gradually unfolded in the course of the novel: happy relationships are good. They are good because they depend upon a balance between our need for (necessarily selfish) pleasures and our need to recognize the claims and necessities of others. Each of the first set of paragraphs I have discussed describes or implies an individual's denial, in a more-or-less public context, of the "claims" of others. Each of the second set of paragraphs depicts an individual's charitable awareness of others in a moment of private satisfaction and pleasure. So it is no accident that only in the last paragraph of the first set is the point of view within Emma's mind, while all of the final set are at least partially (four paragraphs totally) organized around this point of view. A gradually emerging theme, the virtue of overcoming selfishness and self-centeredness, is counterpointed by a structural movement into more and more intensive representation of the internal processes of the mind.

Without denying the uniqueness of *Emma*, I would propose that these characteristics point up a central feature of overarching fictional form. If the stylistic characteristics of the subordinate parts of a novel have to be defined in terms of their relationship to the form of that novel as a whole, we must *begin* with at least a hypothesis as to the nature of the total, or overarching, fictional form. I propose that we should initiate the study of fictional style not at the level of the word or the sentence but at the level of the work of fiction as a total artistic entity.

The form of a tragedy such as *King Lear* or *Oedipus* is to some degree overt. The spectators' consciousness of a design in the action is part of their aesthetic satisfaction in the experience of the tragedy. Even in comedy overtness of form contributes to the spectators' appreciation of the drama. The novel, read alone and silently and usually not at one sitting, requires a different *kind* of structuring. One element of this structuring is manifested in the tendency of novels to be "realistic," that is, to represent commonplace and mundane events; to present the objects and circumstances of familiar daily life; and to narrate original, that is, non-mythic and non-legendary, stories. Thus an intrinsic characteristic of fictional form is its *apparent formlessness*.

This functional concealment, or the illusion of formlessness, I believe, is necessarily reflected in the detailed use of language within each subordinate part of the novel. Stylistic analyses of fiction, therefore, must be of the "concealed" functions of fictional language. This means that syntactic or vocabulary analyses founded upon ordinary definitions of what sentences and words are probably will fail. Stylistic analysis of fiction has to commence with redefinitions of syntax and vocabulary. A fictional sentence looks like a "non-fictional" sentence but is in reality significantly different, because its function is significantly different, just as—I have tried to demonstrate—the function of a fictional word differs significantly from the function of that word in a nonfictional context.

To repeat my earlier statement, then, stylistic analysis of a literary text should begin with characterization of total form. And it seems to me that in fiction a fundamental characteristic of total form (not merely subject-matter) is pointed up by Camus' observation that fiction possesses the capacity to hold our attention with unfamiliar narratives of trivial people and actions. A better illustration of the point than *Emma* might be hard to find, not only because of the obviously "trivial" nature of the novel's events, but also because the truly significant design of the novel is, as I have tried to show, so adroitly disguised by the simplicity and conventionality of its superficial form.

The use of conventional form as a concealment of true form is no mere trick.[7] The conventional form orients us and provides a bridge between separate readings. The conventional form gives us a sense of knowing the whole novel even when we have read only a fraction of it. Simultaneously, its very superficiality is unsatisfying. We are, as Forster says, curious—but we want to know not so much what happens next as how it will happen.[8] A large part of our curiosity is provoked by a developing awareness of the systematic discrepancy between superficial and concealed design. I have pointed out how the simplicity, lucidity, and even the formal "correctness" of Jane Austen's language can overlie a deeper complexity of meaning contained within it. I have tried to make clear that the existence of both surface and depth are essential to the aesthetic significance of *Emma*, which, among other matters, teaches us how important are the trivia of ordinary life because the "simple" facts of commonplace existence are in reality complex. The nature and function of Jane Austen's language, even in its smallest details, reflect the form of her novel as an aesthetic whole.

I do not claim that all fiction has exactly the same form as *Emma*, but I do propose that most novels have an equivalent form. At root all novelists face the same problems that Jane Austen faced, how to make an unfamiliar story interesting, how to reveal the significance of commonplace events to a quiet, solitary reader who is unlikely to peruse an entire volume at one sitting. In most novels some kind of discrepancy between "surface" and "depth" is used as a partial solution to this problem. In most novels what words are used and what these words "mean" is determined predominantly by their role in establishing an evolving discrepancy between surface and depth which defines the basic form of the novel as an aesthetic unity.

If the language of fiction possesses this primary function, there will be serious drawbacks to any criticism originating in quantitative analyses based on systematizations derived from studies of non-fictional language. To illustrate this hypothesis I might cite the two sets of paragraphs from *Emma* discussed above, because they contain approximately the same number of words and sentences and so lend themselves to statistical comparison. The differences—such as the fact that the first set contains twice as many preposed descriptive adjectives as the second—and the likenesses—each set contains approximately the same number of conjunctions "and" (although there are notably more occurrences of "but" in the first set)—do not point unequivocably to the different functions of the language in the two parts of the novel. While it is probably true that in the first set of paragraphs the chief weight of meaning is carried by substantives and modifiers (there are proportionately more adverbs as well as adjectives in the first set) and that in the second set relatively complex verb structures are emphasized, these distinctions, even when correlated with the "semantic" emphasis on emotions—particularly happy ones—in the second set, suggest only the conventionalized nature of the opening and conclusion of *Emma* without alerting one to the dynamic complexity of Austen's language manipulation.

The hypothesis, however, does not exclude the possibility that quantitative analyses might be founded on systematic description of the *aesthetic* functions of language in fiction. My current research, for example, leads me to believe that one can discriminate quantitatively between the sentence forms used by different novelists defined not as linguists customarily define them but "fictionally." Thus one can distinguish among "mixed" sentences (containing both dialogue and narrative) four predominant patterns in nineteenth-century novels: (1) dialogue-narrative ("I'll do it," he said); (2) narrative-dialogue (He said: "I'll do it."); (3) dialogue-narrative-dialogue ("I'll do it," he said, "tomorrow for sure."); (4) narrative-dialogue-narrative (He remarked casually, "I'll do it," when he turned his face from the light.) I have found

TABLE 6

Percent of total number of pages of novel on which one character only appears, two characters appear, four or more characters appear:

Austen	1	2	4+	Eliot	1	2	4+
Persuasion	6	30	57	Daniel Deronda	11	46	21
Emma	5	31	41	Middlemarch	14	40	24
Mansfield Park	5	26	45	Felix Holt	15	46	17
Pride and Prejudice	6	23	54	Silas Marner	19	51	22
Sense and Sensibility	3	41	38	Mill on Floss	12	48	22
Northanger Abbey	12	22	34	Adam Bede	19	43	29

Percent of total number "mixed" sentences in 10,000-word passages:

Novel	Form 1	Form 2	Form 3	Form 4
Emma	22	19	59	0
Middlemarch	11	72	16	1

Sentences from six novels containing dialogue:

Author	Number sentences	Number—% dialogue only		Number—% "mixed"	
Austen	927	760	82%	167	18%
Eliot	820	545	70%	245	30%

that a novelist's preference for one of these forms may correlate both with his preferred "character-grouping" patterns (the frequency with which one character only is "present," two characters are "present," etc.) and with his preferred "character-movement" patterns (the frequency with which the characters "appear" and "depart"). It can be demonstrated (to cite a single specific instance) that there is more character-grouping and more character-movement in *Emma* than in George Eliot's *Middlemarch*.[9] And I have some evidence that Austen's densest character-groupings and most active character-movements correlate with a high incidence of Form 3 "mixed" sentences, although overall Austen uses proportionately fewer mixed sentences of all forms than does Eliot. This correlation may be a quantitatively definable indicator of the relationship existing between the functional form of *Emma* as a whole and the functional form of the sentence patternings of the novel's language. To the degree that one can substantiate such findings, link them to analogous discoveries, and contrast them with diverse practices of other novelists, one can measure patterns of interrelationship between the details of a novelist's language and the total form of his fiction. Only such measurements, I propose, will finally provide viable means of describing fictional prose styles.

REFERENCES

1. Sometimes it is difficult to decide whether usage is casual or subtle. Jane Austen seldom uses color words. Early in *Pride and Prejudice*, however, the Bennett girls are lightly mocked when, by peeping out of an upstairs window at Mr. Bingley, they discover only that "he wore a blue coat and rode a black horse." Much later in the novel Lydia displays her moral idiocy by reporting her concern as to whether or not Wickham would be married to her in his "blue coat."
2. A study of Iris Murdoch's *The Unicorn* by Mr. Gary Goshgarian, who has been assisting me in my research, provides the best illustration I know of the potential reward of

sophisticated statistical analysis of fictional material. Aside from Goshgarian's discoveries about word patterning in Murdoch's novel and that patterning's relationship to the structuring of the novel around the famous "Unicorn" tapestries, his study deserves circulation for its demonstration that more than rudimentary statistical methods can be used to elucidate *critical* problems in a fashion comprehensible to a literary scholar unfamiliar with statistical procedures.

3. Jane Austen, *Emma* (New York, 1957), Riverside Edition, ed. Lionel Trilling, p.13. The text is that established by R. W. Chapman. All quotations in this paper are from this edition.

4. The research upon which this essay is based includes considerably more material than is suggested by the tables. The potential interest of the data may be suggested by the following listing of the percent of total nouns which are proper nouns for several authors. Asterisks indicate novelists for whom the total number of nouns counted is probably too small to be a reliable indicator of consistent practice.

	%		%
Defoe*	1	C. Brontë	6
Richardson*	4	Trollope*	11
Fielding	6	Eliot	6
Austen	20	Hardy	7
Dickens	8	Lawrence	7
Thackeray	8	Woolf	10

5. The underlying consistency of Jane Austen's style and perhaps the fundamental goodness of Miss Bates is dramatized by this mode of citation: by the introduction of ellipses at the proper places one can make many of Emma's speeches sound like Miss Bates's.

6. This in part explains why the verbs in the two sets of paragraphs differ so strikingly, those in the first set tending to be simple, active, and declarative; those in the second tending to be more complicated and conditional.

7. As it may appear to be in intricate fictions of commentary such as *Tristram Shandy* and *Pale Fire*, parodies such as *Joseph Andrews* and Hemingway's *Torrents of Spring*, and elaborately "recessive" narratives such as *Don Quixote* and *Wuthering Heights*. In all these the common principle of formal structure is concealment.

8. E. M. Forster, *Aspects of the Novel* (New York, 1927), especially Chapters Two and Five. Simon Lesser, *Fiction and the Unconscious* (New York, 1957) contains the best study I know of the psychological processes involved in reading fiction and includes some brilliant insights into the nature of fictional forms.

9. Table 6 provides a rough indication of some differences between Jane Austen's and George Eliot's character-groupings and illustrates distinctions between their preferences for different forms of mixed sentences as they appear in 10,000-word passages surrounding the mathematical center of *Emma* (Chapters 9–12, Volume II) and of *Middlemarch* (Chapters 40–42, the final three chapters of Book IV).

VI
HISTORY

STATISTICS AND STYLE: A HISTORICAL SURVEY

Richard W. Bailey

The history of modern statistical stylistics apparently begins in 1851 with the informal suggestion by one Augustus de Morgan that word-length might well prove to be a distinctive trait of a writer's style. "I should expect to find," de Morgan wrote, "that one man writing on two different subjects agrees more nearly with himself than two different men writing on the same subject. Some of these days spurious writings will be detected by this test. Mind, I told you so" (quoted by Lord [1958], p. 282). De Morgan's prescient suggestion stimulated T. C. Mendenhall, an American geophysicist; Mendenhall's 1887 report in *Science* reveals an attempt to test De Morgan's hypothesis in a comparison of a variety of authors, including Dickens, Thackeray, and Mill. Mendenhall was inspired by his work in spectrographic analysis, and he believed that a word-length "spectrogram" would be as distinctively revealing of an individual style as the metallurgical one is of the composition of inorganic substance. Where De Morgan seems to have thought that a simple mean word-length statistic would have the desired distinctive power, Mendenhall realized that a graphic display of the relative frequencies of word-lengths in a whole text would give a more sophisticated representation of a writer's habitual stylistic practices. Like so many who have followed him, Mendenhall felt the indeterminacy of his study and called for a more "thorough test" in which samples of at least 100,000 words would be employed. Were this test to be undertaken, he said, such interesting authorship problems as those posed by Shakespeare's plays and the letters of Junius might well be solved. The virtues of the proposed method would stem from its objectivity; thus Mendenhall revealed his attraction to the heady scientism that so often besets workers in statistical stylistics.

Mendenhall's claims did not go long unchallenged, and his essay was soon followed by three letters to the same journal. Though inconsequential in themselves, these letters reveal the problems confronted by much of the twentieth-century work in the field.

In the first of them, the author repeats Mendenhall's interest in questions of disputed authorship, but goes on to speculate about the relations of psychology and style in terms reminiscent of De Saussure's notion of *langue*, Sapir's *inner form*, and Chomsky's *competence*: "The mental machine (so to speak) which, for example, turns out the long parenthetical sentences of Gladstone, must be very different in design from that which yields the simple and direct utterances of John Bright" (A. B. M. [1889], p. 226). Though he makes no attempt to verify his speculation, this writer does suggest that another measure of style might prove even more revealing of an author's habits than the word-length measure suggested by De Morgan and Mendenhall. Sentence-length distribution is the measure he proposes, and to illustrate its use he plots the absolute frequency of sentences falling into each decile for 300-sentence samples of the prose of Carlyle, De Quincey, and Johnson. Though disavowing any particular interpretation of his data, he does suggest that "should any reader have the time and patience to pursue the inquiry further, he might find his labors not without some useful results." But an immediate response from H. A. Parker put the whole matter further in doubt. Parker reported his attempt to apply the sentence-length method to two works by Carlyle; his examination of the first 300 sentences of *A History of the French Revolution* was consonant with A. B. M.'s curve for Carlyle, but a like examination of *Sartor Resartus* yielded a "pretty close" fit to that for Dr. Johnson! "This goes to show, if it does not prove," Parker concluded, "that for detective purposes the method is valueless" (Parker [1889], p. 246). The third correspondent took issue with Parker; like Mendenhall (who may, indeed, have written the initialed letter), he raised the familiar cry for more data. Such studies, he wrote, are only valid when applied to large samples, and the spectre of counting "not less than one hundred words *or sentences*" was raised (M. [1889], p. 269; my emphasis).

This early dispute points to the issues that continue to occupy the field, including such problems as: (1) the formulation of a hypothesis to be proved, (2) the difficulties of selecting a sample of the appropriate size, (3) the question of the stylistic measure to be examined, and (4) the problem of testing results and verifying hypotheses.

Yet one further episode in this pioneer phase of statistical stylistics ought to be mentioned. Thanks to the patronage of Mr. Augustus Heminway of Boston, Mendenhall was able to carry out an extensive project involving word-length counts for some two million words from several periods of English literature. In doing so, he introduced what is perhaps the first machine to be applied to literary questions, a simple tabulating device that produced reels of paper tape imprinted with the raw word-length data. The principal hypothesis under scrutiny in this work was based on the prevailing view that no unlettered Stratfordian could have written the plays attributed to Shakespeare. As it was then fashionable to assume, Francis Bacon *must* have been the author, but, Mendenhall reported, "samples of Bacon's writing were examined and proved markedly different from the Shakespeare samples" (Mendenhall [1901], p. 103). As is so often the case, the disappointed hypothesizers were reluctant to abandon their basic premise. If Bacon could not have written the plays, Mr. Heminway said confidently, "the question still remains, who did?" (quoted by Mendenhall [1901], p. 104).

THEORETICAL PRESUPPOSITIONS

For whatever reasons—C. P. Snow would credit the bifurcation of our culture —the history of statistics and style shows few cases in which genuine expertise in language, literature, and statistics have been combined in one investigator. Limitations in one or another of these fields are sometimes admitted (see

Yule [1944], p. 7), but all too often are treated as if they were of marginal importance to the main goals of a given study. The work in the Slavic countries reveals a willingness to confront all the varied problems posed by statistical stylistics—as Professor Levý notes in the essay reprinted in this volume. But it is only recently that investigators in Western Europe and America have begun to recognize the need for competence in the three fields and, often, to attack these problems through the collective efforts of specialists in each discipline.

Various surveys of the field of statistical stylistics have appeared from time to time (e.g., Posner [1963], Thavenius [1966], and the several textbooks of quantitative linguistics by Herdan), and informal outlines of its scope have been written (e.g., Vincent [1955] and Paisley [1964]). In most such works the authors point out the poverty of experimental design in the efforts surveyed. P. J. Wexler of the University of Manchester, for instance, has recently given a succinct statement of the inadequacy of much past scholarship from the linguist's point of view. "In much of the work that comes under the heading of computational linguistics," he says, "we are struck (as I am sure others are too) by the contrast between, on the one hand, the apparent sophistication of the statistical techniques (or at least the vigour of the arguments they give rise to), and on the other hand the unfathomable naïveté, from the linguistic point of view, of the units being counted—for example, the 'word.' It is true that one has to simplify in order to quantify, but the complexity thus provisionally sacrificed cannot be restored unless this restoration is seen to be the essential and permanent target from the very beginning" (Wexler [1966], p. 122).

Considering the present state of the art from the statistician's point of view, critics find an equally lamentable state of affairs. Too often the linguist's or literary critic's attempts stop short of genuine statistical methodology. Many studies provide an enumeration of various linguistic items or structures in the text, but fail to indicate the possible influence of sampling techniques on data collection (see Spang-Hanssen [1963]) or to apply statistical significance tests to the apparent differences between samples. Such failures stem from the widespread ignorance of statistical methods characteristic of most linguistic or literary scholars, but it cannot be too often emphasized that simple enumeration or the calculation of relative frequencies is not sufficient to give real significance to what purport to be objective studies of language and literature.

But raising the level of linguistic or statistical sophistication is not the only problem faced by the field. An explicit characterization of the variables that influence the production of texts must be made, such as that provided by Doležel in his essay in this volume and elsewhere (1965a, 1965b, and 1967). Yet such a characterization depends likewise on the specification of the mechanism of linguistic creativity that underlies the data itself—a specification, as Chomsky has recently written, of a mathematical model that comprehends "the study of highly abstract principles and structures that determine the character of human mental processes "(Chomsky [1968], p.63).

INDIVIDUAL STYLES

Perhaps the best known attempt to define a statistical law underlying linguistic data is that made by G. K. Zipf for the frequency distribution of words. It was Zipf's claim—following Estoup (1916) —that a list of word-types from a large body of text ranked in order of frequency will show a *constant* decrease in the frequency with which they appear (with the exception of the most common words). This "rank-frequency" law has been the subject of considerable dispute (e.g., Herdan [1966a], p. 88) and explication; the reader should consult the essays by Condon (1928); Carroll (1938); Mandelbrot (1954); Parker-Rhodes and Joyce (1956); Bosanquet (1957); Good (1957); Miller and Newman (1958); Miller, Newman, and Friedman (1958); Wagner and Guiraud (1959); Somers (1959); and Cherry (1966) listed in the bibliography following this essay. The attempt to specify laws of this kind should be mentioned since the statistical laws of language must be taken into account in the discussion of individual or period styles, though work of this kind is perhaps more properly in the domain of statistical linguistics. Once the patterning of the lexicon defined by such laws has been established, the critic is ready to focus on the achievement of an individual style against its background.

Attempts to specify the size of the lexicon from which a writer draws his vocabulary in a particular work have been made by a variety of scholars including Thomson and Thompson (1915) for Dickens, and Carroll (1938) for Santayana and Joyce. Carroll's formulation of a "diversity index" is parallel to the attempts of Yule (1944) and Bennett (in the essay in this volume) to specify the richness of a writer's vocabulary. But vocabulary size is only one aspect of the problem; the distribution of word frequencies is likewise a means by which an individual expresses his personality (as Baker [1951] shows in his study of a paranoid schizophrenic). Both distribution and diversity of vocabulary have commonly been studied by reference to a word-frequency list compiled from some large corpus, though such lists tend to contain an implicit bias and should therefore be used with some caution: see Bull (1949), Nisbet (1960), Muller (1965), and Card and McDavid (1966). Compilations of frequency data of various sorts continue to appear (Roberts [1965], Kučera and Francis [1967], and Kučera and Monroe [1968] are recent examples); properly used they are valuable tools for statistical stylistics.

The discovery of laws underlying the distribution of vocabulary (see Muller's essay in this collection) and the attempt to illustrate an author's vocabulary development through time (Hart [1943]) both lead to significant discoveries about an author's style. Such work may direct attention to the psychological factors that influence lexical habits (see Johnson [1944], Fairbanks [1944], Mann [1944], and Chotlos [1944]), or to literary and cultural influences on a writer's behavior. But the history of this aspect of statistical stylistics illustrates the general theoretical inadequacy of most notions employed in the study of language behavior and its relation to language system. Only through the full specification of a theory of style can we expect to begin to discriminate the causes inherent in the patterns of a literary work; as Doležel points out in his contribution to this volume, we must distinguish contextual influences on style (see Bodson [1966]) and discriminate the structure of the language from the patterning imposed by the individual upon it.

In addition to studies of the distribution and variety of word-types in a writer's vocabulary, word-length has also been considered as a stylistic trait in the patterning of style (e.g., Krishnamurti [1950], Brinegar [1963], and Muller [1964]). Perhaps the most elaborate of these attempts is that first reported by Fucks (1952) and subsequently applied to texts in several languages (Fucks and Lauter [1965]). Fucks calculates (1) the relative frequencies of i-syllabled words, (2) their distribution in the text (i.e., the length of the gaps between i-syllabled words), and (3) the entropy of the syllable structure of the test. Though such stylistic shaping of the text is evidently beyond the conscious control of an author, the results of Fucks's calculations nevertheless may reveal certain distinctive traits of an author that deviate from the patterns inherent in the language.

Other aspects of diction have also been considered from a statistical point of view: the mixture of "native" and "borrowed" words in the Towneley Plays (Anttila [1963], in Bunyan and Macaulay (Yule [1944], Chap. 8, and Herdan [1966b]), and in Milton (Boone [1953]); the incidence of consciously archaic words in Spenser (R. E. Parker [1925]); and the use of words with "oriental" associations in a translation and an imitation of *The Arabian Nights* (Dufrenoy [1946]). For such studies to lead to the elucidation of individual styles, the scholar must depend upon statistical information concerning the history of words (such as that provided by Kent [1932]) as well as upon detailed information concerning the denotation and connotation of words. Much of this information is to be found in scholarly dictionaries and other resources, but the studies just mentioned illustrate the need for a deeper understanding of the structure of the lexicon in the language under consideration if such work is to achieve clear-cut results.

Syntactic properties of individual styles have generally been approached in statistical studies of word-class distribution. Milic (1967), for example, parsed texts of eighteenth-century English writers by assigning each word to the part-of-speech category established by Fries. On the basis of comparative data from a variety of writers, he was able to specify the favored sequences in Swift's prose and to construct a "Swift profile" based on the frequency and distribution of these patterns. Thanks to this profile, he was able to specify Swift's predilection for seriation and sentence-initial connectives and to show the affinity of a disputed work to the Swiftian canon. Similar techniques based on word-class distribution are discussed in Burwick's essay in this volume, and the statistical examination of syntax (employing various parsing techniques) is a major concern of Taylor (1918), Chandler (1928), Barber (1962), Keleman (1964), and Kroeber (1967).

The examination of structures beyond the sentence by statistical means is represented by only a few studies in the history of statistical stylistics, doubt-less because of the relative difficulty of quantifying structures of discourse and theme. Winburne (1964) has sketched the outlines of quantitative method of discourse analysis in an examination of the "Gettysburg Address," and Świeczkowski (1961) has studied inter-sentence connection in an attempt to show variations in cohesiveness in different types of prose. Thematic analysis of texts has been carried out with the General Inquirer dictionary, and early work with this technique suggests that the quantitative study of *leitmotifs* may soon be possible on a large scale (see Ellis [1964] and Ellis and Favat [1966]). In addition, the theoretical argument formulated by Kroeber in his contribution to this volume suggests several lines that such investigations of both individual and genre styles might take. In considering structures of dis-course and theme, the scholar will doubtless be led to think about not only the frequency with which various thematic elements appear but also their dis-persion and density in the texts studied, perhaps in terms of the method pro-posed by Spang-Hanssen (1956).

ATTRIBUTION STUDIES

The questions of statistical stylistics most often treated by statistical methods concern cases of disputed authorship, though of course such problems reflect only one application of the methods of this discipline. The most primitive technique in dealing with authorship problems concerns the identification of linguistic peculiarities shared by the unknown text and the known writings of the authorship candidate. But the enumeration of such similarities in text fails to account for the possibility of chance or of conscious imitation. In an investigation of the authorship of the Parliamentary Debates published in the eighteenth-century *Gentleman's Magazine*, for example, Sherbo found that an examination of linguistic predilections failed to distinguish the work of Dr. Johnson from Hawkesworth's imitations of Johnson's style (reported by Herdan [1966a], pp. 171–172). Without some rigorous definition of style and a notion of the factors that influence it, the critic will find that even the most sophisticated extraction of verbal parallels may fail to produce the desired discrimination of authorship. Where the evidence is slight, as in the case of the Homeric epics (see Bolling [1937]), or in the case of joint-authorship of a work (see Maxwell [1950] on the contributions of Peele and Shakespeare to *Titus Andronicus*), such studies are likely to have indeterminate or even mis-leading results.

What is wanted, of course, is a litmus test by which the critic can decide whether or not two given texts were written by the same author. Though some attempts have been made to formulate such a test, they have been almost wholly unsuccessful. Brinegar (1963), following the work by Mendenhall already mentioned, used word-length distribution to compare the works of Mark Twain and some unknown texts; Kuraskiewicz (1961) examined word-frequency lists in a study of Andrzej Trzeçieski and the anonymous biography, *Życiorys*; Grayston and Herdan (1959–1960) used a measure of homogeneity of vocabulary to determine the similarity of I Timothy and the pastoral letters usually ascribed to St. Paul, a technique similar to that used by R. B. Steele (1925) in analyzing the poems of the *Vergilian Appendix*. But on the whole, it must be said that attempts to ascribe some unknown text to a particular author have been indeterminate at best in those cases where only one candidate has been considered. Of all the measures so far employed, none can be used with the assurance that the results will settle such questions unless all the possible authors of the unknown text can be considered.

When a particular list of candidates has been determined, the chances that each one wrote the disputed text can be calculated and the problem of authorship is put on surer ground. A pioneering instance of such a problem is Yule's study of the disputed authorship of *The Imitation of Christ*, now commonly attributed to Thomas à Kempis but thought by some to have been written by Jean Charlier de Gerson, Chancellor of the University of Paris. Given these two established candidates, Yule (1938) first attempted to test the known writings of both men against the *Imitation* by an analysis of sentence-length, a technique discussed by Williams and Buch in their essays reprinted in this volume. Yule concluded that sentence-length statistics are not a wholly reliable indicator in matters of this sort, but he did raise several important questions concerning the definition of "word" and "sentence" for statistical work and the bias inherent in various sampling techniques. Not content with the sentence-length measure, Yule (1944) devised his well-known "Characteristic K," a measure of vocabulary richness illustrated in Bennett's essay in this collection. In Yule's original formulation, K was based on the assumption that the occurrence of a given word is based on chance and can be regarded as a Poisson distribution. The notion that words come out of a "treasure chest" in something like the same way that colored balls emerge from a container in the classical instance of randomness was attacked by Ross (1950) and led to a reformulation of K. This new definition, given by Herdan (1955), makes K "the coefficient of variation of a mean, or the relative fluctuation of a mean" (Herdan [1955], p. 333; also Herdan [1966a], pp. 101–104). When this technique is applied to texts, a measure of the uniformity and diversity of vocabulary is provided which may be applied to authorship questions or other literary problems of the kind illustrated in Muller's essay in this volume (see also Muller [1964]).

Despite the limitations of his method, Yule was nevertheless able to argue effectively on purely statistical grounds that à Kempis is much more likely to have written the *Imitation* than Gerson, a decision subjectively indicated by Gerson's penchant for scholastic argument and vocabulary and à Kempis' love of personal expressions of religious conviction like those in the *Imitation*. Yule's calculations led to the following values for K:

De Imitatione Christi	84.2
First set of samples from Thomas à Kempis	73.8
Whole set of samples from Thomas à Kempis	59.7
Whole set of samples from Gerson	35.9

With characteristic caution, Yule restricted himself to the conclusion that à Kempis "in some of his works yields a characteristic fairly close to that of the *Imitation*: Gerson's characteristic, taking his work as a whole, is much lower than that of Thomas. The facts seem all in favour of Thomas as against Gerson" (Yule [1944], p. 238). It should be noticed that Yule has *not* said that à Kempis wrote the disputed work; he has only calculated the likelihood of this event. From this example, it should be clear that authorship problems are "solved" only insofar as the attribution of the given work to one candidate is so likely that no other candidate's claim can reasonably be admitted.

Other measures and techniques have been applied to questions of disputed authorship. Ellegård ([1962a], pp. 10–11) suggests that Yule's technique does not have sufficient discriminating power to deal with a fairly consistent style— for example, the mid-eighteenth-century Addisonian essay—in which genre norms strongly influence stylistic choices. Though he gives no empirical support for that suggestion, Ellegård does point out that a sample containing at least 2,000 nouns (i.e., about 10,000 words of running text) is necessary for an accurate calculation of Yule's *K*. Nevertheless, Ellegård did not shy away from taking substantial samples of text, and some 1,604,800 words figured in his attempts to "solve" the Junius question. Since Ellegård gave full considera- tion to both the historical and biographical backgrounds of the various candi- dates (discussed in 1962b) and to the writings of a hundred writers active in the period, his work deserves to be discussed in some detail as a model for authorship investigations.

Ellegård began with a subjectively selected list of words that struck him as appearing quite often in the Junian texts ("plus words") and of words that seemed to appear less often in those texts than in the other writings examined. He then tested his intuitions by calculating a "distinctiveness ratio" for each of these words; this ratio is calculated by the following formula:

$$\text{distinctiveness} = \frac{\text{relative frequency of the word in Junius}}{\substack{\text{relative frequency of the word in a million-word sample of} \\ \text{non-Junian writings}}}$$

Thus, the relative frequency of *uniform* (adj.) in Junius is found to be 0.000280 and in the million-word sample of non-Junian writings it is only 0.000065 (Ellegård [1962a], p. 15):

$$\text{distinctiveness} = \frac{0.000280}{0.000065} = 4.3$$

Uniform is therefore a good "plus word" and the distinctiveness ratio indicates that this usage is more than four times as common in Junius' writings as in the writings of his contemporaries. But the compilation of a list of plus and minus words may reflect sampling bias or the tendency of a writer to employ a given word in clusters. To eliminate such variables, Ellegård gathered his original list of 458 expressions into seventeen distinctiveness groups. On the basis of this list—supplemented by an examination of 51 pairs or triplets of approximate synonyms in the writings examined (*burden-burthen, doubt that-doubt but,* etc.)—Ellegård was able to calculate the characteristics shared by Junius and each of the candidates on the list of possible authors. The combined probabilities of the "alternatives test" (synonym groups) and the plus-minus word test give a discriminating power of 0.000033 or only about one chance in thirty thousand that another writer would match the Junian parameters. But even though the writings of Sir Philip Francis are in remarkable accord with the Junius letters, Ellegård shows that we can only be 99% confident that Francis did write the letters if we assume that no more than 300 possible candidates can be admitted to the putative Junian population (see [1962a], pp. 60–63). In this case, such a restriction is by no means difficult since the internal evidence of the letters—references to events at which Junius was present—show that the Junian population is certainly less than 300. "The statement that Sir Philip Francis was Junius," Ellegård can safely conclude, "may henceforth be allowed to stand without a question-mark" ([1962b], p. 119).

Another illustration of statistical methods applied to authorship disputes— the work of Mosteller and Wallace on the disputed *Federalist* essays—should be considered, though full reports of the study are generally available (Mosteller-Wallace [1963 and 1964]) and a semipopular account has likewise appeared (Francis [1966]). In contrast to the Junius problem, only two candidates need to be considered—Madison and Hamilton—but, as in the Junius dispute, the investigators were able to draw on a large body of scholarship in which the historical and biographical aspects of the question had been thoroughly discussed.

Ellegård measured Junian habits against the background of a large body of the language of the period before turning to the examination of the writings of the various candidates. Mosteller and Wallace, on the other hand, looked for shared characteristics between the disputed papers and the known writings of the two candidates. The variables selected, they reasoned, should be independent of the content of the text and should occur often if the relatively short texts of the disputed papers were to be examined. Evidently enough, the function words of the language—for example, *of, a, all, also,* etc.—are both frequent and generally independent of content. A selection of such words was divided into "calibrating sets" and assigned values that reflect the stylistic preferences in the known essays of the two authors. Thus the investigators found that a frequent use of the word *by* generally indicates Hamilton's and not Madison's authorship, while *to* appearing in greater numbers is distinctive of Madison. From several thousand function and content words considered for inclusion in the calibrating set, the authors found some 28 words with strong discriminatory power; the following brief table (based on Francis [1966], p. 51) shows the number of papers by the two authors in which the given word appears:

	no. of Hamilton papers	no. of Madison papers
enough	14	0
commonly	9	1
whilst	0	13
language	2	10

Up to this point, the techniques employed by Mosteller and Wallace clearly resemble those used by Ellegård in determining plus and minus words.

The differences between the Ellegård and Mosteller-Wallace methods lie in the use of more powerful statistical methods by the latter, who see their work as one application of statistical discrimination methods rather than as a means of settling the *Federalist* dispute as an end in itself. Therefore, they first consider the Poisson model as a means of predicting the occurrence of a given event in samples (*m*) when the distribution of the event in the whole population (*n*) is known. In other words, if a word appears twenty times in a text of a thousand words, the Poisson model will predict the number (0, 1, 2, . . . *n*) of instances of that word in sub-samples of, say, one hundred words. This model illustrates the fact that even rare events are not haphazard, a fact constantly asserted by statisticians but seldom appreciated by the layman. In fact, the Poisson model has been shown to have a high predictive power for the distribution of such apparently random events as the dispersion of flying bombs over an area; when the total number of bombs that fell is known (*n*), the model predicts how many city blocks will be hit with 0, 1, 2, . . . *r* bombs (see Yule and Kendall [1965], pp. 193–194).

Nevertheless, Mosteller and Wallace show that, as Ross (1950) had already argued, linguistic events do not consistently follow the Poisson model. The Poisson estimates of *an, any*, and *upon* are generally consonant with the observed figures for Hamilton's known papers, but the estimates do not accord with the observed distribution of *may* and *his*. For this reason, the authors reject the Poisson model in favor of a related function, the negative binomial, by which the theoretical values closely resemble the observed distributions. But neither the Poisson nor the negative binomial functions are considered sufficient in themselves for authorship problems by Mosteller and Wallace; they are only interesting as they play a role in Bayes's Theorem, the technique actually applied to settle the Federalist dispute. Thanks to the calculated theoretical values obtained from the Poisson or negative binomial model, the investigators were able to move through the sub-sets of the population, revising the estimate of the likelihood of a given event in the next sub-set of the population from knowledge of what had already been observed. For example, if it is known that a word occurs *n* times in the population, Bayes's Theorem allows the calculation of the probability of its occurring in the next sub-set of the population when it has already appeared *p* times. Thus, the theoretical estimate is revised as each piece of text is examined to give a more accurate prediction for the next piece. In the case of an authorship question, we consider each new piece of text examined as being of unknown authorship and calculate the odds that each of the candidates might have written it. When a considerable body of known writings is considered, we have the opportunity to give a precise formulation of the odds in favor of one of the candidates when the unknown texts are approached. Thus, the odds are about 800 to 1 in favor of Madison's authorship of disputed paper number 56—and this is one of the weaker predictions in the authors' opinion. For most of the other papers in question, the odds are found to be even greater in Madison's favor. Mosteller and Wallace are therefore able to conclude beyond any reasonable doubt that Madison was the author of the twelve disputed papers.

The technique developed in the studies of Ellegård and Mosteller-Wallace can be taken as models for authorship-discrimination tests, and, by extension, for other statistical investigations in which characteristic traits of style need to be determined. Subjective judgments about the stylistic qualities of a text, as Ellegård found, are not always borne out by empirical tests; a good many of the proposed "Junian" plus-minus words that were initially selected turned out to be only weakly discriminatory or even generally typical of the usage of the period (i.e., they yielded a distinctiveness ratio close to one). In addition, the stylistic properties of a text can be accurately determined only when a substantial body of comparative material is at hand. As we have seen, Ellegård made use of more than a million and a half words of text, while even in the more restricted population of the *Federalist*, over 200,000 words were involved in the study. Finally, abundant historical evidence must be combined with the stylistic investigations if really safe predictions are to be made. Thus, given the present state of the art, it seems unlikely that the disputed Pauline epistles or such anonymous texts as *My Secret Life* can be ascribed to a particular author since the historical evidence is weak and the list of candidates is necessarily very large.

CHRONOLOGY PROBLEMS AND DIACHRONIC STYLISTICS

Closely related to the issues raised by unknown authorship are the problems connected with specifying the order of composition of the works of a given author. Stylistic traits, evidently enough, do not always remain stable and critics frequently speak of the "early" or "late" styles of an author. But in those cases in which the sequence of composition is unknown, scholars may look for developmental trends that will enable them to place undated works. Just as simplistic notions about the invariance of an author's style may vex authorship attribution (as Buch points out in his essay in this volume), so too the direction of an author's development as reflected in certain aspects of style may be the subject of rather vague or simplistic formulation. Much of the statistical work on chronology problems unfortunately reflects rather poorly justified assumptions about an author's development.

Cox and Brandwood (1959), for example, speculate that a meaningful chronology of Plato's works may be obtained by specifying the degree of similarity between the *Republic* and the other works. To this end, they examined the distribution of vowel quantity over the sentence-endings in all the texts and ranked them in order of their affinity with the *Republic*. A work with a distribution of sentence-ending types that is similar to that of the *Republic* is deemed to have been written at about the same time. The least similar work must have been written last. But they offer no argument to support their assumption that "Plato's change in literary style was monotone in time" (p. 195) and the critic is therefore justified in his skepticism about their conclusions.

A similar assumption underlies Padelford's (1930) work on Spenser's *Cantos of Mutabilitie*. In attempting to place the time of composition of these fragments, he relies on the proportion of run-on to end-stopped lines and the ratio of masculine and feminine rhymes in the *Faerie Queene* as a whole (see Langworthy [1931] for a similar treatment of Shakespeare's plays). Padelford believes that Spenser's style shows a constant development toward greater flexibility and variation in verse and therefore supposes that a simple ranking of the books of the *Faerie Queene* in terms of line and rhyme type will produce the desired chronology. Studies of an author's development (e.g., Taylor [1918]) indicate that certain traits do show a relatively constant change through time *within specifiable limits*. But the degree of significant variation in the development of these traits must be specified before any firm answers can be given to chronology questions.

In the last decades of the nineteenth century, Professor L. A. Sherman of the University of Nebraska raised another sort of chronology question, concerned not with an individual author but with the whole body of English literature. Sherman's work reflects the same sort of evolutionary perfectionism apparent in Jespersen's theory of "progress in grammar" that appeared at about the same time. Sherman tended to see the development of English prose as a reflection of cultural evolution: "The influence of classical learning had the effect of fastening a heavy unoral diction upon the English literary world. From that the race has been slowly but effectually liberating itself; so that we are to-day almost emancipated from mediaevalism in literature as in all things else" (Sherman [1892], p. 363). To illustrate this emancipation, Sherman and his assistants collected extensive data on sentence-length from the principal authors from Chaucer to their own day. This material, Sherman claimed, shows an almost unequivocal trend toward shorter sentences, a tendency he associated with progressively clearer and more "natural" thinking.

In the first exposition of his thesis, Sherman claimed that a 300-sentence sample "will generally reveal the sentence-rhythm of any writer who has achieved a style" (Sherman [1888], p. 130), and on the basis of such samples he calculated the average sentence-length for a variety of authors. In his second discussion, he considered the validity of this assumption by examining large texts by several nineteenth-century authors. Though he made no attempt to specify formally the dispersion of sentence-lengths around the mean, he concluded that "some kind of sentence-sense" operates in writers and that its essence is captured in the average sentence-length figure: "the style keeps to its orbit." This discovery led him to quite extravagant conclusions about his results: "Here, then, in this 23.43 was the resultant of the forces which had made Macaulay's literary character" (Sherman [1892], p. 353).

Sherman was not content with the simplicity of the average sentence-length measure and encouraged his student, G. W. Gerwig, to investigate related syntactic phenomena. The results of their investigation—reported by Sherman (1892 and 1893 [esp. chap. 25]), Gerwig (1894), and Moritz (1909)— were interpreted as a clear verification of their thesis concerning the evolution of English style. Not only did sentence-length decrease through time, but the proportion of simple sentences and the number of predictions in each sentence likewise showed a development toward an "unburdening" of the means of expression. A similar attempt to illustrate the thesis was carried out by Aurner (1923)—apparently without knowledge of the earlier work—and Manczak (1961) achieved similar results in his computation of the ratio of active verbs to other parts of speech in sentences from French writers of the eighteenth and nineteenth centuries. Though contemporary linguists may be unwilling to accept the thesis on the development of prose style so enthusiastically adopted by Sherman and his followers, it is only recently that a detailed examination of the syntactic predilections of writers from various literary periods have been considered in projects approximating the size of those undertaken by these early writers (see Winter [1961 and his essay reprinted here]).

Certainly better known than the work on the history of style just discussed is that of Josephine Miles. In a series of publications spread over the last three decades, Miss Miles has considered the typical diction and favored sentence patterns of each of the major periods of English and American literature. As she notes in her most recent publication (Miles [1967]), the English language offers three principal "modes" of sentence-making; "the predicative, the connective-subordinative, and the adjectival" (p. 4). The history of literature, she finds, indicates not the simple unilinear development found by Sherman, but a rising and falling pattern as the simple predicative mode loses favor at the end of the Renaissance and gains it again in modern times. The following diagram—adapted from Miles (1964), p. 7—summarizes her findings for poetry:

Soon after the results of the investigation summarized in the table first appeared, A. L. Kroeber (1958) subjected Miles's techniques and conclusions to further examination. Kroeber considered the influence of the state of the language in each period, the poetic form employed by the poets examined, and other factors that might have influenced the historical pattern Miles had found. His conclusions generally supported those reached by Miles concerning the history of style while a recent study (Baker [1967]) shows that similar methods bear fruit when applied to the favored poetic syntax of a single poetic era.

Miles's work on poetic diction is likewise of considerable interest from both synchronic and diachronic perspectives. Her technique for specifying the "major words" of a poet has taken several forms, but her continuing method has been to extract those words that appear several (about ten) times per thousand words in the texts examined. Such a technique is more properly called *enumerative* than *statistical,* and in general her procedures show a greater emphasis on the interpretation of data than on the elaboration of experimental methods, though one of her recent studies explores the use of factor analysis to distinguish significant "clusters" of favored words in an era (Miles and Selvin [1966]). Nevertheless, it is thanks to the influence of Miles and her students that statistical approaches to literary questions are sympathetically regarded in American literary criticism. Her influence on the study of literary history is widely felt and is likely to become even more important as the use of electronic data-processing machines makes the examination of large bodies of data less wearying to the scholar.

POETICS

The statistical examination of poetic devices by scholars in England and America is not nearly as extensive as is the research carried out by Slavic investigators that is described by Levý in the essay translated and reprinted in this volume. Alliteration and sound patterning were scrutinized by Skinner in his study of Shakespeare's sonnets (Skinner [1939]) and of Swinburne's poems (Skinner [1941]). But Skinner's conclusion that Shakespeare's sonnets show no greater attention to this aspect of verse structure than might be expected through chance alone apparently aroused not only immediate disbelief (see Stoll [1940]), but also a deep skepticism that appeared in print as late as a quarter century after Skinner's study had appeared (see Goldsmith [1950] and Sherbo [1966]). Skinner's response to the early criticism by Stoll, his attempt to consider alliterative patterns in structures larger than the line, and his formulation of a "coefficient of alliteration" (see Skinner [1941]) have gone virtually unnoticed in literary criticism. A few other scholars have considered the problem of alliteration in verse from a statistical point of view (see Sebeok and Zeps [1959] and Govaerts [1966]); but, given the relative ease of quantifying alliterative patterns, it is surprising that this aspect of poetry has been so little studied.

In 1953, Lynch proposed a technique for determining the dominant sound types in poems. As refined by Hymes (1960), this method involves ranking the vowels and consonants in a poem according to their weighted frequencies and examining the poem for "summative words" that act as a nexus of sound and sense. Hymes studied several sonnets by Wordsworth and Keats and concluded that the technique could point to valuable observations about the intersection of form and meaning in particular poems. Although some theoretical objections have been raised against this method (see Householder [1960]), it certainly has some value in the examination of the sound texture of poems. Now that extensive statistical material is available for the distribution of English sounds (see Roberts [1965]), the "foregrounding" of the literary work against the background of the language can be more explicitly studied. Furthermore, sound modulation within the poem—the subject of Jones's essay in this collection—can also be considered in more detail than has hitherto been possible thanks to recent developments in phonology.

Surprisingly enough, the metrical structure of English poems has seldom been studied from the statistical point of view. Much effort has of course been devoted to the enumeration of metrical types (see, for example, Propst [1932]), but few studies have been devoted to the calculation of the conditional probabilities of stress patterning in lines of poetry and the entropy of metrical types in English verse has seldom been calculated. Statistical studies of line and stanza patterns are common in Europe and are illustrated in the essays by Kondratov and Levý in this volume and in the work of Guiraud (1953), Gasparov (1963), and Fónagy (1965), to mention three representative examples. But the statistical measurement of English poetry at levels of structure higher than that of sound segments has not often been undertaken.

During the 1930's, considerable scholarly effort was focused on the enumeration and quantification of images and metaphors in poetry. Edith Rickert's introduction in 1927 to the problem of imagery—among other aspects of poetry—derived, she says, from the methods of crypto-analysis developed during World War I. Though the statistical techniques employed in this work were simple, they were applied with great ingenuity to a variety of literary problems and her book still repays close study. Perhaps even more influential was the study of Shakespeare's imagery published in 1935 by Caroline Spurgeon. Miss Spurgeon was mainly interested in unveiling Shakespeare's personality through an examination of the patterns of association revealed in his images: he must have possessed "sensitiveness, poise, courage, humour, and wholesomeness" (p. 206). Though she did discuss the role of imagery in the plays themselves, it was left for Brooks (1947) to show how the data she had collected could be used for a penetrating literary interpretation of the plays.

CONCLUSION

A variety of cultural and academic trends have combined to inhibit the development of statistical stylistics. As has already been mentioned, educational curricula seldom foster the development of the individual who is both "numerate" and "literate," despite the evident similarity in these two aptitudes. Furthermore, fashions in literary criticism in modern times have turned attention from the "large appearances" of "general nature" so praised by Dr. Johnson in literary works to a consideration of minute particulars in language and literature. Statistical methods, on the other hand, concern themselves with the broad tendencies and general characteristics in the data to which they are applied. Moreover, such techniques require a degree of explicitness in assumptions and procedures that is not highly valued in a discipline in which subjective and intuitive judgments are prized. Yet despite these apparent objections, statistical stylistics—illustrated both in the works mentioned in this historical sketch and in the essays in this collection—deals with questions that are of particular interest to the literary critic: Who wrote the work? In what directions did this writer develop? What are the constraints imposed on the writer by his language? How does the selection of the mode of presentation influence the shape of this work? How well do critics agree in their judgment of a piece of writing? Certainly these are all significant questions of vital interest to the literary scholar, and statistical methods can help him to provide answers to them. The virtues of the techniques arise from their generality and their explicitness; through their intelligent application, the critic can come closer to the matters of judgment that lie at the heart of his endeavor. "Certainly we shall never learn the secrets of style by merely mooning over them or by ejaculating admiration," wrote John Matthews Manly. "Every artist who has ever learned a lesson in technique from his predecessors has done so by a more or less incomplete analysis of its elements, by focusing attention upon the manner and means by which individual technical difficulties were overcome and technical successes achieved."

BIBLIOGRAPHY

Anttila, Raimo. "Loanwords and Statistical Measures of Style in the Towneley Plays," *Statistical Methods in Linguistics*, no. 2 (1963), 73–93.

Aurner, Robert Ray. "The History of Certain Aspects of the Structure of the English Sentence," *Philological Quarterly*, II (1923), 187–208.

Baker, Sidney J. "Ontogenetic Evidence of a Correlation between the Form and Frequency of Use of Words," *The Journal of General Psychology*, XLIV (1951), 235–251.

Baker, William E. *Syntax in English Poetry, 1870–1930*. Berkeley and Los Angeles, 1967.

Barber, C. L. "Some Measurable Characteristics of Modern Scientific Prose," in *Contributions to English Syntax and Philology*, ed. Frank Behre. Gothenburg, 1962. Pp. 21–43.

Bodson, Arthur. "Analyse quantitative dans l'étude littéraire de l'Énéide," in *Statistique et Analyse Linguistique*. Paris, 1966. Pp. 79–83.

Bolling, George Melville. "Statistics of the Homeric Language and a Queer Bit of Criticism," *Language*, XIII (1937), 238–240.

Boone, Lalia Phipps. "The Language of Book VI, *Paradise Lost*," in *South Atlantic Modern Language Association Studies in Milton*, ed. J. Max Patrick. Gainesville, Florida, 1953. Pp. 114–127.

Bosanquet, C. H. "Distribution of Word Frequencies," *Nature*, CLXXIX, no. 4559 (March 16, 1957), 596.

Brinegar, Claude S. "Mark Twain and the Quintus Curtius Snodgrass Letters: A Statistical Test of Authorship," *Journal of the American Statistical Association*, LVIII (1963), 85–96.

Brooks, Cleanth. "The Naked Babe and the Cloak of Manliness," in *The Well-Wrought Urn: Studies in the Structure of Poetry*. New York, 1947. Pp. 22–49.

Bull, William E. "Natural Frequency and Word Counts," *Classical Journal*, XLIV (1949), 469–484.

Card, William, and Virginia McDavid. "English Words of Very High Frequency," *College English*, XXVII (1966), 596–604.

Carroll, John B. "Diversity of Vocabulary and the Harmonic Series Law of Word-Frequency Distribution," *The Psychological Record*, II (1938), 379–386.

Chandler, Zilpha E. *An Analysis of the Stylistic Techniques of Addison, Johnson, Hazlitt, and Pater*. University of Iowa Humanistic Studies, vol. IV, no. 3. Iowa City, 1928.

Cherry, Colin. *On Human Communication*. 2nd edition. Cambridge, Mass., 1966.

Chomsky, Noam. *Language and Mind*. New York, 1968.

Chotlos, J. W. "A Statistical and Comparative Analysis of Individual Written Language Samples," *Psychological Monographs*, LVI (1944), 75–111.

Condon, E. U. "Statistics of Vocabulary," *Science*, LXVII, no. 1733 (1928), 300.

Cox, D. R., and L. Brandwood. "On a Discriminatory Problem Connected with the Works of Plato," *Journal of the Royal Statistical Society*, Series B, XXI (1959), 195–200.

Doležel, Lubomír. (1965a) "Un Modèle statistique de codage linguistique," *Etudes de linguistique appliquée*, III (1965), 51–63.

———. (1965b) "Zur statistischen Theorie der Dichtersprache," in *Mathematik und Dichtung*, eds. Helmut Kreuzer and Rul Gunzenhäuser. Munich, 1965. Pp. 275–293.

———. "The Prague School and the Statistical Theory of Poetic Language," *Prague Studies in Mathematical Linguistics*, II (1967), 97–104.

Dufrénoy, Marie-Louise. "Analyse statistique du langage," *Journal de la Société de Statistique de Paris*, LXXXVII (1946), 208–219.

Ellegård, Alvar. (1962a) *A Statistical Method for Determining Authorship: The Junius Letters, 1769–1772*. Gothenburg Studies in English, no. 13. Gothenburg, 1962.

———. (1962b) *Who was Junius?* Stockholm, 1962.

Ellis, Allan B. "The Computer and Character Analysis," *English Journal*, LIII (1964), 522–527.

———, and F. André Favat. "From Computer to Criticism: An Application of Automatic Content Analysis to Literature," in *The General Inquirer: A Computer Approach to Content Analysis*, by Philip J. Stone, *et al.* Cambridge, Mass., and London, 1966. Pp. 628–637.

Estoup, J. B. *Gammes stenographiques*. 4th edition. Paris, 1916.

Fairbanks, Helen. "The Quantitative Differentiation of Samples of Spoken English," *Psychological Monographs*, LVI (1944), 19–38.

Fónagy, Ivan. "Der Ausdruck als Inhalt: Ansätze zu einer funktionellen Poetik," in *Mathematik und Dichtung*, eds. Helmut Kreuzer and Rul Gunzenhäuser. München, 1965. Pp. 243–274.

Francis, Ivor S. "An Exposition of a Statistical Approach to the Federalist Dispute," in *The Computer and Literary Style*, ed. Jacob Leed. Kent, Ohio, 1966. Pp. 38–78.

Fucks, Wilhelm. "On the Mathematical Analysis of Style," *Biometrika*, XXXIX (1952), 122–129.

———, and Josef Lauter. "Mathematische Analyse des literarischen Stils," in *Mathematik und Dichtung*, eds. Helmut Kreuzer and Rul Gunzenhäuser. Munich, 1965. Pp. 107–122.

Gasparov, M. L. "Statistical Investigation of Russian 'Dolnik' Trimeter" (tr. from the Russian by D. Lieberman), *Probability Theory and Its Applications*, VIII, i (1963), 96–102.

Gerwig, G. W. "On the Decrease of Predication and of Sentence Weight in English Prose," *University of Nebraska Studies*, II, i (1894), 17–28.

Goldsmith, U. K. " 'Words out of a Hat?': Alliteration and Assonance in Shakespeare's Sonnets," *Journal of English and Germanic Philology*, XLIX (1950), 33–48.

Good, I. J. "Distribution of Word Frequencies," *Nature*, CLXXIX., no. 4559 (March 16, 1957), 595.

Govaerts, Suzanne. "Les initiales de vers chez Lucrèce et Virgile," in *Statistique et Analyse Linguistique*. Paris, 1966. Pp. 41–49.

Grayston, K., and G. Herdan. "The Authorship of the Pastorals in the Light of Statistical Linguistics," *New Testament Studies*, VI (1959–1960), 1–15.

Guiraud, Pierre. *Langage et versification d'après l'œuvre de Paul Valéry*. Paris, 1953.

Hart, Alfred. "The Growth of Shakespeare's Vocabulary," *Review of English Studies*, XIX (1943), 242–254.

Herdan, Gustav. "A New Derivation and Interpretation of Yule's 'Characteristic' K," *Journal of Applied Mathematics and Physics (ZAMP)*, VI (1955), 332–334.

———. (1966a) *The Advanced Theory of Language as Choice and Chance*. New York, 1966.

———. (1966b) "How Can Quantitative Methods Contribute to Our Understanding of Language Mixture and Language Borrowing?" in *Statistique et Analyse Linguistique*. Paris, 1966. Pp. 17–36.

Householder, Fred W., Jr. "Opening Statement: From the Viewpoint of Linguistics," in *Style in Language*, ed. Thomas A. Sebeok. Cambridge, Mass., and New York, 1960. Pp. 339–349.

Hymes, Dell H. "Phonological Aspects of Style: Some English Sonnets," in *Style in Language*, ed. Thomas A. Sebeok. Cambridge, Mass., and New York, 1960. Pp. 109–131.

Johnson, Wendell. "A Program of Research," *Psychological Monographs*, LVI (1944), 1–15.

Keleman, Bela. "A propos des caractéristiques des styles de la langue à la lumière de la statistique linguistique," *Revue Roumaine de Linguistique*, IX (1964), 621–624.

Kent, Roland Grubb. *Language and Philology*. New York, 1932.

Krishnamurti, S. "Dr. Johnson's Use of Monosyllabic Words," *Journal of the University of Bombay*, XIX (1950), 1–12.

Kroeber, A. L. "Parts of Speech in Periods of Poetry," *Publications of the Modern Language Association*, LXXIII (1958), 309–314.

Kroeber, Karl. "Computers and Research in Literary Analysis," in *Computers in Humanistic Research*, ed. Edmund A. Bowles. Englewood Cliffs, N. J., 1967. Pp. 143–152.

Kučera, Henry, and W. Nelson Francis. *Computational Analysis of Present-Day American English*. Providence, R. I., 1967.

Kučera, Henry, and George K. Monroe. *A Comparative Quantitative Phonology of Russian, Czech, and German*. New York, 1968.

Kuraszkiewicz, Władysław. "Etude de la paternité des textes anonymes d'après la méthode de la statistique linguistique," in *Poetics*. Warszawa, 1961. Pp. 625–633.

Langworthy, Charles A. "A Verse-Sentence Analysis of Shakespeare's Plays," *Publications of the Modern Language Association*, XLVI (1931), 738–751.

Lord, R. D. "Studies in the History of Probability and Statistics VIII: De Morgan and the Statistical Study of Literary Style," *Biometrika*, XLV (1958), 282.

Lynch, J. J. "The Tonality of Lyric Poetry: An Experiment in Method," *Word*, IX (1953), 211–224.

M. "Curves of Literary Style," *Science*, XII, no. 322 (April, 1889), 269.

M., A. B. "Curves of Literary Style," *Science*, XII, no. 320 (March, 1889), 226.

Manczak, Witold. "La longueur de la proposition comme facteur stylistique," in *Langue et Littérature: Actes du VIIIe Congrès de la Fédération Internationale des Langues et Littératures Modernes*. Paris, 1961, Pp. 401–403.

Mandelbrot, B. "Structure formelle des textes et communication: deux études," *Word*, X (1954), 1–27.

Manly, John Matthews. "Introduction" to Rickert (1927).

Mann, Mary B. "The Quantitative Differentiation of Samples of Written Language," *Psychological Monographs*, LVI (1944), 41–74.

Maxwell, J. C. "Peele and Shakespeare: A Stylometric Test," *Journal of English and Germanic Philology*, XLIX (1950), 557–561.

Mendenhall, T. C. "The Characteristic Curves of Composition," *Science*, IX, no. 214 (March, 1887), 237–249.

———. "A Mechanical Solution of a Literary Problem," *The Popular Science Monthly*, LXX, vii (December, 1901), 97–105.

Miles, Josephine. *Eras & Modes in English Poetry*. 2nd edition. Berkeley and Los Angeles, 1964.

———, and Hanan C. Selvin. "A Factor Analysis of the Vocabulary of Poetry in the Seventeenth Century," in *The Computer and Literary Style*, ed. Jacob Leed. Kent, Ohio, 1966. Pp. 116–127.

Miles, Josephine. *Style and Proportion: The Language of Prose and Poetry*. Boston, 1967.

Milic, Louis T. *A Quantitative Approach to the Style of Jonathan Swift*. The Hague, 1967.

Miller, G. A., and E. B. Newman. "Tests of a Statistical Explanation of the Rank-Frequency Relation for Words in Written English," *American Journal of Psychology*, LXXI (1958), 209–218

Miller, G. A., E. B. Newman, and E. A. Friedman. "Length-Frequency Statistics for Written English," *Information and Control*, I (1958), 370–389.

Moritz, Robert E. "On a Quantitative Relation Governing Certain Linguistic Phenomena," *Modern Language Notes*, XXIV (1909), 234–241.

Mosteller, Frederick, and David L. Wallace. "Inference in an Authorship Problem," *Journal of the American Statistical Association*, LVIII (1963), 275–309.

———. *Inference and Disputed Authorship: The Federalist*. Reading, Mass., 1964.

Muller, Charles. "La longueur moyenne du mot dans le théatre classique," *Cahiers de Lexicologie*, no. 5 (1964), 29–44.

———. *Essai de Statistique Lexicale*. Paris, 1964.

———. "Fréquence, dispersion et usage: à propos des dictionnaires de fréquence," *Cahiers de Lexicologie*, no. 7 (1965), 33–42.

Nisbet, J. D. "Frequency Counts and Their Uses," *Educational Research*, III (1960), 51–64.

Padelford, Frederick M. "The *Cantos of Mutabilitie*: Further Considerations Bearing on the Date," *Publications of the Modern Language Association*, XLV (1930), 704–711.

Paisley, William J. "Identifying the Unknown Communicator in Painting, Literature, and Music: The Significance of Minor Encoding Habits," *The Journal of Communication*, XIV (1964), 219–237.

Parker, H. A. "Curves of Literary Style," *Science*, XIII, no. 321 (March, 1889), 246.

Parker, R. E. "Spenser's Language and the Pastoral Tradition," *Language*, I (1925), 80–87.

Parker-Rhodes, A. F., and T. Joyce. "Distribution of Word Frequencies," *Nature*, CLXXVIII, no. 1308 (1956), 178.

Posner, Rebecca. "The Use and Abuse of Stylistic Statistics," *Archivum Linguisticum*, XV (1963), 111–139.

Propst, Louise. *An Analytical Study of Shelley's Versification*. University of Iowa Humanistic Studies, Vol. V, no. 3. Iowa City, 1932.

Rickert, Edith. *New Methods for the Study of Literature*. Chicago, 1927.

Roberts, A. Hood. *A Statistical Linguistic Analysis of American English*. The Hague, 1965.

Ross, A. S. C. "Philological Probability Problems," *Journal of the Royal Statistical Society*, Series B, XII (1950), 19–59.

Sebeok, Thomas A., and Valdis J. Zeps. "On Non-Random Distribution of Initial Phonemes in Cheremis Verse," *Lingua*, VIII (1959), 370–384.

Sherbo, Arthur. Comment following the paper by Govaerts (*q.v.*) at a conference held in 1964; printed in *Statistique et Analyse Linguistique* (Paris, 1966), p. 49.

Sherman, L. A. "Some Observations upon the Sentence-Length in English Prose," *University of Nebraska Studies*, I, ii (1888), 119–130.

———. "On Certain Facts and Principles in the Development of Form in Literature," *University of Nebraska Studies*, I, iv (1892), 337–366.

————. *Analytics of Literature: A Manual for the Objective Study of English Prose and Poetry*. Boston, 1893.

Skinner, B. F. "The Alliteration in Shakespeare's Sonnets: A Study in Literary Behavior," *The Psychological Record*, III (1939), 186–192; reprinted in his *Cumulative Record* (New York, 1961), pp. 286–292.

————. "A Quantitative Estimate of Certain Types of Sound-Patterning in Poetry," *The American Journal of Psychology*, LIV (1941), 64–79; reprinted in his *Cumulative Record* (New York, 1961), pp. 292–307.

Somers, H. H. *Analyse mathématique du langage: lois générales et mesures statistiques*. Louvain, 1959.

Spang-Hanssen, Hening. "The Study of Gaps between Repetitions," in *For Roman Jakobson*, ed. Morris Halle, *et al*. The Hague, 1956. Pp. 492–502.

————. "Sentence Length and Statistical Linguistics," in *Structures and Quanta: Three Essays on Linguistic Description*. New York, 1963. Pp. 58–72.

Spurgeon, Caroline F. E. *Shakespeare's Imagery and What It Tells Us*. Cambridge, 1935.

Steele, R. B. "Non-Recurrence of Vocabulary as a Test of Authorship," *Philological Quarterly*, IV (1925), 267–280.

Stoll, Elmer Edgar. "Poetic Alliteration," *Modern Language Notes*, LV (1940), 388–390.

Świeczkowski, Walerian. "On the Margin of Syntax and Style (A Quantitative Study)," in *Poetics*. Warszawa, 1961. Pp. 463–469.

Taylor, Warner. "The Prose Style of Johnson," *University of Wisconsin Studies in Language and Literature*, II (1918), 22–56.

Thavenius, Jan. "Kvantitativa metoder i stilistiken" [Quantitative Methods in Stylistics], in *Litteraturvetenskap: nya mål och metoder*. Stockholm: *Natur och Kultur*, 1966. Pp. 37–62.

Thomson, Godfrey H., and J. Ridley Thompson. "Outlines of a Method for the Quantitative Analysis of Writing Vocabularies," *British Journal of Psychology*, VIII (1915), 52–69.

Vincent, E. R. "Mechanical Aids for the Study of Literature and Style," in *Literature and Science: Proceedings of the Sixth Triennial Congress of the International Federation for Modern Languages and Literatures*. Oxford, 1955. Pp. 56–60.

Wagner, Robert-Léon, and Pierre Guiraud. "La méthode statistique en lexicologie," *Revue d'Enseignement Supérieur*, I (1959), 154–159.

Wexler, P. J. Comment following A. J. Greimas' "Les aspects quantitifs en linguistique diachronique" at a conference in 1964; printed in *Statistique et Analyse Linguistique* (Paris, 1966), p. 122.

Winburne, John Newton. "Sentence Sequence in Discourse," in *Proceedings of the Ninth International Congress of Linguists*, ed. Horace G. Lunt. The Hague, 1964. Pp. 1094–1098.

Winter, Werner. "Relative Häufigkeit syntaktischer Erscheinungen als Mittel zur Abgrenzung von Stilarten, " *Phonetica*, VII (1961), 193–216.

Yule, G. Udny. "On Sentence-Length as a Statistical Characteristic of Style in Prose, with Application to Two Cases of Disputed Authorship," *Biometrika*, XXX (1938), 363–390.

————. *The Statistical Study of Literary Vocabulary*. Cambridge, 1944.

————, and M. G. Kendall. *An Introduction to the Theory of Statistics*. London, 1965.

Zipf, G. K. *Selected Studies of the Principle of Relative Frequency in Language*. Cambridge, Mass , 1932.

NOTES ON THE CONTRIBUTORS

FRIEDERIKE ANTOSCH received her Ph.D. from the University of Vienna, where she worked under Professor Hubert Rohracher at the Psychologisches Institut. She is currently a practicing psychologist.

RICHARD W. BAILEY completed his Ph.D. dissertation, "The Public and Private Styles of the Earl of Chesterfield," in 1965 at the University of Connecticut. At present, he is an Assistant Professor of English at The University of Michigan and an associate editor of *Style*. With D. M. Burton he is the compiler of *English Stylistics: A Bibliography* (Cambridge, Mass., 1968); he is the author of "Current Trends in the Analysis of Style," *Style*, I (1967), 1–14, and "Language to Literature: A Rejoinder," *ibid.*, 221–224. His interests include general linguistics, stylistics, and computational lexicography.

PAUL E. BENNETT received his Ph.D from the University of Pennsylvania in 1952 and was an Instructor in the English Department of that university at the time the essay reprinted here first appeared. Since then, he has held teaching positions at Glassboro State College and at Phoenix College in Arizona.

KAI RANDER BUCH holds academic degrees from the University of Copenhagen and is currently Professor of Engineering Mechanics at the Technical University of Denmark (since 1959). His main interests include engineering mechanics, probability theory, and operational research. He is co-author of a recent textbook on elementary probability theory (in Danish, 1967) and of *Introduction to the Theory of Probability* (with Niels Arley), a work first published in Danish and subsequently translated into English and Russian. Among his numerous publications are essays on measure theory in abstract space.

FREDERICK L. BURWICK is an Assistant Professor of English at the University of California at Los Angeles. He has studied literature and philology at the Universities of Göttingen and Würzburg and has worked at the Universities of Wisconsin and California in the computer analysis of rhetorical techniques in prose style. He is the editor of *Selected Essays on Rhetoric by Thomas De Quincey* (Carbondale, Ill., 1967) and the author of *The Rhetoric and Aesthetic of Thomas De Quincey* (The Hague, forthcoming) and numerous articles on Anglo-German relations. He is currently engaged in a computer study of Romantic prose style.

JOHN B. CARROLL received his Ph.D. from the University of Minnesota in 1941, where he developed his continuing interest in the psychology of language and quantitative linguistics. He has taught at Mt. Holyoke, Indiana, and at Chicago, and from 1949 to 1967 was on the faculty of the Graduate School of Education at Harvard. Since 1967 he has been Senior Research Psychologist at the Center for Psychological Studies of the Educational Testing Service. Among his many contributions to psychology and linguistics is his edition of *Language, Thought, and Reality* (1956), the selected papers of his friend, Benjamin Lee Whorf.

LUBOMÍR DOLEŽEL is a Research Fellow of the Institute for the Czech Language and is Associate Professor at the Charles University in Prague, Czechoslovakia. From 1965 to 1968 he was a visiting professor at the University of Michigan. His main areas of interest are the structure of fiction, stylistics and poetics, and mathematical linguistics. Among his principal publications are *On the Style of Modern Czech Prose* (in Czech; Prague, 1960); "A Preliminary Estimate of the Entropy and Redundancy of Written Czech" (in Czech), *Slovo a slovesnost* (1963); "Vers la stylistique structurale," *Travaux linguistique de Prague*, I (1964); "A Statistical Law of Grapheme Combinations" (with J. Prácha), *Prague Studies in Mathematical Linguistics*, I (1966); "The Prague School and the Statistical Theory of Poetic Language," *ibid.*, II (1967); "The Typology of the Narrator: Point of View in Fiction," in *To Honor Roman Jakobson* (The Hague, 1967), Vol. I; "Russian and Prague Functional Stylistics," *Style*, II (1968).

JOHN J. DREHER is a research scientist at the Douglas Advanced Research Laboratories, McDonnell Douglas Corporation, where he is currently investigating the physical and statistical aspects of both oral and written language. From the time of his service with the Chinese 5th Field Artillery Regiment, Dr. Dreher's research has involved various aspects of the Chinese language as well as international language investigations for the U.S. Air Force Communications directorate. Coming to Douglas from physics research at Lockheed, where he directed acoustics studies, he has published extensively in related fields, including acoustical holography.

CURTIS W. HAYES is an Assistant Professor of English at the University of Nebraska; in 1968 he was Fulbright Professor of English and Linguistics at Kumamoto University, Japan. In addition to the essay reprinted in this collection, he is the author of "A Transformational-Generative Approach to Style: Samuel Johnson and Edward Gibbon," *Language and Style*, I (Winter, 1968) and of a presentation over the Voice of America in the series "Linguistics Today." His main interests include stylistics and literary criticism of eighteenth-century England; he is currently preparing a monograph on the style of Edward Gibbon.

LAWRENCE GAYLORD JONES is Professor of Linguistics and Slavic languages at Boston College, where he is also in charge of the Slavic Studies Program. He took his B.A. in English literature at Lafayette College (1943), his M.A. at

Columbia University (1948), and his Ph.D. in Russian linguistics at Harvard University (1952). Before coming to Boston College, he spent eight years teaching in the Linguistics Department at Harvard University. His publications cover topics ranging from the acoustic structure of Russian and English vowels to grammatical patterns in English and Russian verse. In addition to his speciality in acoustic phonetics, his research interests include problems in mathematical linguistics, generative grammar, and all aspects of the application of linguistic analysis to literary material.

A. M. KONDRATOV has been associated with the group of statisticians in Moscow led by A. N. Kolmogorov who are interested in applying statistics, probability theory, and information theory to the study of language and literature. Kondratov has held a teaching position at the University of Kujbyshev in Central Russia. His works include several articles on the statistical analysis of poetry that have appeared in *Voprosy jazykoznanija* and *Problemy kibernetiki;* he is the author of *Matematika i poezija* ["Mathematics and Poetry"] (Moskva, 1962).

KARL KROEBER received his Ph.D. from Columbia in 1956 and was appointed Instructor of English at the University of Wisconsin in the same year. He held the position of Associate Dean of the Graduate School at that institution from 1963 to 1965 and became a full professor in 1963. His publications include *Romantic Narrative Art* (1960), *The Artifice of Reality* (1964), *Studying Poetry* (1965), and *Backgrounds to British Romantic Literature* (1968).

GEORGE M. LANDON completed his Ph.D. in linguistics at Indiana University in 1964 and is currently an Assistant Professor of linguistics at Ohio State University. He is particularly interested in poetic language and in 1967 delivered a paper to the winter meeting of the Linguistic Society of America entitled "The Grammatical Description of Poetic Word Order in English Verse."

JIRÍ LEVY (1926–1967) was Professor of the Theory of Literature at the University of Brno, Czechoslovakia. His main areas of interest were the theory of translation, the mathematical theory of poetry, and prosody. Among his principal publications are *The Art of Translation* (in Czech; Prague, 1963); "On the Relation of Language and Stanza Pattern in the English Sonnet," in *Worte und Werte: Bruno Markwardt zum 60. Geburtstag* (Berlin, 1961), pp. 214–231; "Rhythmical Ambivalence in the Poetry of T. S. Eliot," *Anglia*, LXVII (1949), 54–64; "A Contribution to the Typology of Accentual-Syllabic Versifications," *Poetics* (Warszawa, 1961), pp. 177–188; and "Some Preliminary Remarks on the Informational Analysis of Verse" (in Czech), *Slovenská literatura*, XI (1964), 15–37.

CHARLES MULLER did his graduate work in French, Latin, and Greek at the University of Strasbourg and taught in a lycée until 1944. After the war, he held a post in the French Cultural Service in Germany. At present, he is Professor of French Philology at the University of Strasbourg. He has published widely in the field of the history of the French language and on lexicology and lexicography. Since 1960, he has given particular attention to statistical linguistics; among his contributions to this field are *Essai de statistique lexicale: l'Illusion Comique de P. Corneille* (Paris, 1964); *Etude de statistique lexicale: le vocabulaire du théâtre de P. Corneille* (Paris, 1967); and *Initiation à statistique linguistique* (Paris, 1968).

C. B. WILLIAMS, Sc.D. (Cantab.), is a Fellow of the Royal Society of London and has worked for many years on problems of biological statistics, particularly on the balance in animal populations in relation to weather and on the relative abundance of species in mixed wild populations. He became interested in literary statistics on discovering that many of the frequency distributions useful in animal population studies were also applicable to "populations" of words as represented in writings of different authors.

WERNER WINTER received his Ph.D. from the University of Bern, Switzerland, in 1949, and has held academic positions in German and Russian at the Universities of Hamburg, Kansas, and Texas. He is currently Professor of Comparative Linguistics, Indogermanisches Seminar, Universität Kiel. In addition to his work in Indo-European studies, he has published articles on the use of statistics in historical linguistics and stylistics.

ELAINE L. YOUNG is a research associate at the Douglas Advanced Research Laboratories, McDonnell Douglas Corporation, where she has pursued her interests in author-identification procedures for Chinese literary and political texts and in the identification of speakers. Her present research involves analysis of styles of some thirty authors of Chinese fiction from the period of the 1930's and co-operation in the development of computer programming techniques for authorship identification.

INDEX

Readings for Diversity and Social Justice

Third Edition

Readings for Diversity and Social Justice

Third Edition

Edited by

Maurianne Adams, Warren J. Blumenfeld,
Carmelita (Rosie) Castañeda,
Heather W. Hackman, Madeline L. Peters,
and Ximena Zúñiga

Routledge
Taylor & Francis Group

NEW YORK AND LONDON

Third edition published 2013
by Routledge
711 Third Avenue, New York, NY 10017

Simultaneously published in the UK
by Routledge
2 Park Square, Milton Park, Abingdon, Oxon OX14 4RN

Routledge is an imprint of the Taylor & Francis Group, an informa business

© 2013 Taylor & Francis

First edition published 2000 by Routledge

Second edition published 2010 by Routledge

Library of Congress Cataloging in Publication Data
Readings for diversity and social justice / [edited] by Maurianne Adams,
Warren J. Blumenfeld, Carmelita (Rosie) Castañeda, Heather W. Hackman,
Madeline L. Peters, and Ximena Zúñiga.—Third edition.
   pages cm
   Includes bibliographical references and index.
   1. Prejudices—United States. 2. Racism—United States.
   3. United States—Race relations. 4. United States—Ethnic relations.
   5. Minorities—United States. 6. Social justice—United States.
   I. Adams, Maurianne, editor of compilation.
   E184.A1R386 2013
   305.800973—dc23
   2012037595

ISBN: 978-0-415-89293-3 (hbk)
ISBN: 978-0-415-89294-0 (pbk)

Typeset in Swiss 721 and Classical Garamond
by Swales & Willis Ltd, Exeter, Devon

Printed and bound in the United States of America by Sheridan Books, Inc. (a Sheridan Group Company).

Contents

Next Steps

Table of Intersections

The tables on the following pages will enable readers to see at a glance the multiple issues that are taken up in each one of the selections. This Table of Intersections follows the sequence of the Table of Contents, but it is laid out to show the multiple interconnections discussed in each of the selections. Column indicators are as follows:

R	Racism
Cl	Classism
RO	Religious Oppression
S	Sexism
H	Heterosexism
TG	Transgender Oppression
Ab	Ableism
A&A	Ageism and Adultism
Global Issues	Discussion of issues outside of U.S. borders
Language Issues	Non-English or English as second language speakers, or use of American Sign Language rather than vocal speech

Selection number	Author and title	R	CI	RO	S	H	TG	Ab	A&A	Global Issues	Language Issues
	CONCEPTUAL FRAMEWORKS										
1	Tatum, "The complexity of identity"	X									
2	Kirk and Okazawa-Rey, "Identities and social locations"	X	X						X		X
3	Johnson, "The social construction of difference"	X			X	X		X			
4	Bell, "Theoretical foundations" / Hardiman, Jackson, Griffin, "Conceptual foundations"	X X	X X		X X						
5	Young, "Five faces of oppression"	X	X		X	X		X	X		
6	Harro, "The cycle of socialization"	X	X	X	X	X		X	X		
7	Young, "Structure as the subject of justice"		X		X					X	
	RACISM										
	CONTEXT										
8	Tatum, "Defining racism"		X	X	X	X			X		
9	Takaki, "A different mirror"		X	X						X	
10	Roppolo, "Symbolic racism, history, and reality . . . mascots"		X								
11	Lipsitz, "The possessive investment in whiteness"		X								
12	Smith, "Heteropatriarchy and the three pillars of white supremacy"		X		X	X				X	
13	Anzaldúa, *"La conciencia de la mestiza"*		X		X	X					X
14	Dalmage, "Patrolling racial borders"		X	X	X				X		X
15	National Network for Immigrant and Refugee Rights, "Injustice for all"		X	X	X	X		X			
	VOICES										
16	Chung, "Finding my eye-dentity"				X						
17	Gansworth, "Identification pleas"										
18	Fayad, "The Arab woman and I"				X						
19	Aviles, "My tongue is divided into two"										X
20	Williams, "The emperor's new clothes"										
21	Arminio, "Waking up white"										X

Selection number	Author and title	R	CI	RO	S	H	TG	Ab	A&A	Global Issues	Language Issues
	NEXT STEPS										
22	Ayvazian and Tatum, "Women, race, and racism"			X	X	X					
23	Castañeda, "FLEXing cross-cultural communication"										
24	Smith, "The personal is political"		X		X	X				X	
	CLASSISM										
	CONTEXT										
25	Mantsios, "Class in America—2006"	X									
26	Collins and Yeskel, "The dangerous consequences of growing inequality"				X				X		
27	Oliver and Shapiro, "Race, wealth, and equality"	X									
28	Williams, "What's debt got to do with it?"	X									
29	Schmidt, "At the elite colleges"	X									
30	Jaffe, "Is the near-trillion-dollar student loan bubble about to pop?"										
31	Wolanin, "Students with disabilities: Financial aid . . ."							X			
32	U.S. Dept of State, "Trafficking in Persons Report 2011"	X			X				X	X	X
33	Kochhar, Fry, Taylor, for the Pew Research Center, "Wealth gaps rise to record highs . . ."	X							X	X	X
	VOICES										
34	Romero, "Bonds of sisterhood—Bonds of oppression"	X			X						
35	hooks, "White poverty . . . invisibility"	X			X						
36	Saint, "Why can't everybody fear me like that?"	X							X		
37	Pittelman and Resource Generation, "Classified"	X			X					X	
38	Morgenson, "The debt trap"				X			X			
	NEXT STEPS										
39	van Gelder, "How Occupy Wall Street changes everything"										
40	Leondar-Wright, "Classism from our mouths" and "Tips from working-class activists"	X			X					X	
41	Pittelman and Resource Generation, "Deep thoughts about class privilege"										
42	Giecek, "Distributing income"							X			

Selection number	Author and title	R	CI	RO	S	H	TG	Ab	A&A	Global Issues	Language Issues
	RELIGIOUS OPPRESSION										
	CONTEXT										
43	Lippy, "Christian nation or pluralistic culture"	X								X	
44	Schlosser, "Christian privilege: Breaking a sacred taboo"	X									
45	Blumenfeld, "Christian privilege . . . in public schooling"	X									
46	Joshi, "Religious oppression"	X									
47	Hilberg, "Precedents"	X									
48	Gilbert, "Maps—History of anti-Semitism"	X								X	
49	Eck, "Working it out" and "See you in court"	X									
50	Echo-Hawk, "Native American religious liberty"	X									
51	Grinde Jr., "Taking the Indian out of the Indian"	X									
52	Williams, "From Pearl Harbor to 9/11"	X								X	
53	Semple, "A Somali influx unsettles Latino meatpackers"	X	X							X	
	VOICES										
54	Kaye/Kantrowitz, "Jews in the U.S."	X	X		X					X	
55	Ahmad, "Oral history of Adam Fattah"	X			X						
	Zawam, "Oral history of Hagar Omran"	X			X						
56	Nowicki, "Modesto-area atheists speak up, seek tolerance"	X									
	Goodnough, "Student faces town's wrath in protest against a prayer"										
	NEXT STEPS										
57	Nasir and Al-Amin, "Creating identity-safe spaces on college campuses for Muslim students"	X			X						
58	Whittaker, Salend, and Elhoweris, "Religious diversity in schools"	X									
59	Bernards, "Pioneers in dialogue"	X			X					X	
	SEXISM										
	CONTEXT										
60	Lorber, "Social construction of gender"					X	X				
61	Kimmel, "Masculinity as homophobia"					X	X				

Selection number	Author and title	R	CI	RO	S	H	TG	Ab	A&A	Global Issues	Language Issues
62	Johnson, "Patriarchy"										
63	hooks, "Feminism"	X									
64	Katz, "Violence against women is a men's issue"					X					
65	Heldman, "Out-of-body image"		X					X			
66	Bernstein, "Women's pay"		X								
	VOICES										
67	Chernik, "The body politic"							X			
68	Morgan, "Connect: A web of words"		X								X
69	Kirk and Okazawa-Rey, "He works, she works"		X								X
	NEXT STEPS										
70	Neely, "Promises made"		X								
71	Walker, "To stop the violence against women"	X									X
72	National Latina Institute for Reproductive Health, "Statement on healthcare for all"	X								X	
73	Hurdis, "Heartbroken: Women of color feminism"	X	X								
74	Russo and Spatz, "Stop the false race/gender divide"	X	X								
75	LaDuke, "Grassroots: Introduction"	X									
76	Maathai, "Unbowed"									X	

HETEROSEXISM

Selection number	Author and title	R	CI	RO	S	H	TG	Ab	A&A	Global Issues	Language Issues
	CONTEXT										
77	Blumenfeld, "How homophobia hurts everyone"	X			X						
78	Gokhale, "The interSEXion: A vision for a queer progressive agenda"	X	X		X		X				
79	Carbado, "Privilege"	X			X						
80	Griffin, "Sport: Where men are men and women are trespassers"				X		X				
	VOICES										
81	Blow, "Real men and pink suits"			X	X						
82	Quindlen, "The loving decision"	X			X						
83	Solis y Martinez, "Mestiza/o gender"	X			X		X			X	X

Selection number	Author and title	R	CI	RO	S	H	TG	Ab	A&A	Global Issues	Language Issues
	NEXT STEPS										
84	Evans and Washington, "Becoming an ally"	X			X		X				
85	Clinton, "United Nations address on global LGBT rights"	X		X	X		X	X	X	X	
	TRANSGENDER OPPRESSION										
	CONTEXT										
86	Meyerowitz, "Introduction—How sex changed"				X	X					
87	Stryker, "Transgender liberation"	X	X								
88	Spade, "Mutilating gender"		X		X			X	X		
89	Serano, "Trans woman manifesto"				X						
90	Ware, "The impact of juvenile court on queer . . . youth"	X	X			X			X		
	VOICES										
91	Lie, "Passing realities"										
92	Green, "Look! No, don't! The invisibility dilemma . . . "				X						
	NEXT STEPS										
93	Taylor, "Cisgender privilege"	X			X	X		X			
94	Chess, Kafer, Quizar, and Richardson, "Calling all restroom revolutionaries!"				X			X			
	ABLEISM										
	CONTEXT										
95	Bryan, "Struggle for freedom"	X			X						
96	Cerney, "Historical and cultural influences in deaf education"										X
97	Pliner and Johnson, "Historical, theoretical and foundational principles of UID in higher education"										
98	Wendell, "The social construction of disability"		X		X				X		
99	Davis, "Go to the margins of the class: Disability and hate crimes"	X	X		X	X					
100	Colligan, "Why the intersexed shouldn't be fixed"		X		X	X			X		

Selection number	Author and title	R	CI	RO	S	H	TG	Ab	A&A	Global Issues	Language Issues
101	Grossman, "Mass psychiatric casualties"										
102	Erevelles, "Disability in the New World Order"	X	X						X	X	
	VOICES										
103	Clare, "Gawking, gaping, staring"	X			X						
104	Murphy, "Post-traumatic stress disorder leaves scars . . ."		X		X	X	X			X	
105	Watsky, "On the spectrum, looking out"								X		
106	Ashley and Deborah, "How to curse in sign language"			X					X		
107	Kingsley, "What I'd tell that doctor"								X		
108	Pelkey, "In the LD bubble"					X			X		
	NEXT STEPS										
109	Hehir, "Toward ending ableism in education"	X									
110	Oesterreich and Knight, "Facilitating transitions to college for students from culturally and linguistically diverse backgrounds"	X	X							X	X
111	Howland and Gibavic, "Learning disability identity development and social construct"	X			X						
112	Invisible Disabilities Advocate, "Creating a fragrance-free zone"										
113	Peters, Castañeda, Hopkins, and McCants, "Recognizing ableist beliefs and practices and taking action as an ally"	X	X								
	AGEISM AND ADULTISM										
	CONTEXT										
114	Bell, "Understanding adultism"										
115	Dohrn, "'Look out kid, it's something you did'"	X	X								
116	Durkin, "Police make life hell for youth of color"	X	X								
117	Butler, "Ageism: Another form of bigotry"							X			
118	Sheets, "Ageing with disabilities: Ageism and more"							X			
119	Center on Aging Studies, University of Missouri—Kansas City, "Black elderly"	X									
	VOICES										
120	Huber, "There is nothing wrong with you: For teens"										

Selection number	Author and title	R	CI	RO	S	H	TG	Ab	A&A	Global Issues	Language Issues
121	Larabee, "Elder liberation draft policy statement"										
122	Curry, "People of color over fifty"	X									
	NEXT STEPS										
123	Haga, "Chicago's peace warriors"	X	X								
124	Sazama, "Allies to young people: Tips and guidelines"										
125	Gullette, "Taking a stand against ageism at all ages"				X			X			
126	Markee, "What allies of elders can do"										

WORKING FOR SOCIAL JUSTICE: VISIONS AND STRATEGIES FOR CHANGE

CONTEXT

Selection number	Author and title	R	CI	RO	S	H	TG	Ab	A&A	Global Issues	Language Issues
127	Pharr, "Reflections on liberation"	X	X		X	X		X	X		
128	Love, "Developing a liberatory consciousness"	X	X		X						
129	Collins, "Toward a new vision: Race, class, and gender"	X	X		X	X		X			
130	Johnson, "What can we do?"	X	X		X	X		X			
131	Harro, "The cycle of liberation"	X			X	X					

VOICES

Selection number	Author and title	R	CI	RO	S	H	TG	Ab	A&A	Global Issues	Language Issues
132	West, "Courage"	X	X		X	X					
133	Anzaldúa, "Allies"	X	X		X	X				X	X

NEXT STEPS

Selection number	Author and title	R	CI	RO	S	H	TG	Ab	A&A	Global Issues	Language Issues
134	Smith, "Social struggle"	X	X		X	X				X	
135	Zúñiga, "Bridging differences through intergroup dialogue"	X			X						
136	Martínez, "Unite and rebel! . . . Building alliances"	X	X	X	X	X		X		X	
137	WireTap, "Top youth activism victories of 2009"	X	X		X				X	X	

Acknowledgements

The editing team for this third edition of *Readings for Diversity and Social Justice* brings together multiple and intersecting social perspectives on the social justice issues presented in this book—we are male, female, transgender, and genderqueer; gay, lesbian, bisexual, heterosexual, and queer; African American, Latina, and White; Jewish, Hindu, Christian, and atheist; U.S.-born and born outside the United States, with a wide range of immigrant generations and statuses. Some of us have learning disabilities and physical disabilities; are young adults, middle-aged, and elders; were born poor, working class, and middle class. Our academic specializations include ableism, ageism and adultism, anti-semitism, classism, heterosexism, racism, religious oppression, sexism, and transgender oppression. We include college faculty, current doctoral students, and Social Justice Education alums who have, cumulatively among the twelve of us, many decades of experience teaching middle and high school, college undergraduates and graduate students, professional development and community courses, seminars and workshops on all of these social justice issues, whether in single, multiple, and/or intersecting and interacting social justice contexts.

We have worked together through each of these three editions as a collaborative editorial team, valuing the different gifts and perspectives each one of us brings to this work, and moving from dialogue to consensus on the overall scope, organization, and content of this volume. We continue to struggle, as a collegial writing team, with the tendency of libraries, reviewers, and scholars who cite our work to name the first author only. This practice discourages collaborative work in academe, insofar as academe most values those authors most cited, and presumes incorrectly that such authors are senior or primary. We search for ways to accurately represent the collaborative interactions within a writing team, the synergistic emergence of ideas and sharing of resources, since any line of names, however arranged, suggests a ranking order. The possibility of linking our names in a circle, while intriguing and eye-catching, remains overly challenging for typesetters and production teams. We regret that we have not yet found a manageable alternative to the convention of alphabetical order in listing editors and contributors, an ordering that affirms equity if only because it is "merely" alphabetical. As a step in the direction we want to move, however, we place a statement at the beginning of each multiply-authored section that honors the nature and value of our collaborative work with a request that people who cite us include the full names of *all* listed authors. We have followed our own preferred practice by including *all* names listed in the works we cite within our sections.

Although working as a collaborative editorial team, we have at the same time delegated specific areas of primary section responsibility. The editors whose names are identified in the Table of Contents, and each section-introduction title page with a specific section, have primary responsibility for selecting section content, writing section introductions, and developing section websites, based upon our primary areas of expertise and experience.

Decisions and agreement were not always easy—especially as we communicated by email, telephone conference calls, computer-supported conferences, and videoconferences—but this process has only increased our mutual respect and appreciation for the knowledge and insight, the dedication, energy, and goodwill that each of us has brought to this project. For all of us as co-editors—both those of us who have been with this project as editors from the first edition on and those who have joined our team to provide such excellent newly framed sections for the second and third editions—the time and attention we have all, together, devoted to the process of coordinating our perspectives has been indispensable to the integrity of this volume.

It is especially important for us to acknowledge the contributions of our many generous, knowledgeable, and supportive colleagues, families, friends, and students. We have drawn upon suggestions made by Social Justice Education course instructors and colleagues at the University of Massachusetts, Amherst—Nina Brand, Elaine Brigham, Mirangela Buggs, Stephanie Burrell, Jen Daigle-Matos, Andrea (Dre) Domingue, Michael Funk, Maru Gonzalez, Eric Hamako, Nini Hayes, Molly Keehn, Taj Valdivia Smith, Luis Valdiviezo, Marjorie Valdivia, Rani Varghese, Teeomm Williams, all doctoral students in SJE who teach undergraduate courses dealing with social justice. (Chase Catalano, Keri DeJong, and Larissa Hopkins, who migrated to the role of section co-editors, were originally members of this group.)

We consider ourselves tremendously fortunate to have worked closely with Catherine Bernard, our editor at Routledge, and her gracious, expert team, Allison Bush and Madeleine Hamlin. This new edition has benefited immeasurably from Catherine's unwavering commitment, her support and enthusiasm for this project, her careful reading of many iterations of the text, her knowledge of the literature of social justice, her expert and helpful judgment calls on numerous challenges of substance and logistics in preparing this volume, and her tactful but firm guidance in helping us make hard choices.

Two important members of the second editorial team, not active with the third edition, have our thanks for their enduring contributions. Lee Anne Bell helped shape the two racism sections in the second edition and her perspective, insight, and knowledge remain visible to us in this third edition. We remain in Elaine Whitlock's debt for her infinite patience, resourcefulness, flexibility, and tireless ingenuity in gaining the majority of permissions that continue from the second to the third edition.

We received feedback, insights, resources, and support from valued colleagues in our home and professional communities, friends and family, who suggested references, provided logistical support, and encouraged our demanding work during these past two years: John and Kedhar Bartlett, Beth Berila, Linnea Edstrom, Hanna Eslinger, Allie (Al) Forbes, John A. Hunt, Valerie Jiggetts, Michael W. Krupp, Brenda Lindgren, Aquila Ayana McCants, Jane Mildred, Susan Raffo, Shelley Roberts, Neha Singhal, Jacoba, Jasmine, and Nico Stauffer, Alina Torres-Zickler, and Riki Wilchins. Each of you will understand how much we value and appreciate your many and different generosities and contributions, when you see your name.

Fifteen years ago we were together in Amherst, Massachusetts. We were a group of faculty colleagues and advanced doctoral students, preparing the first edition of this book of readings in Maurianne's living room. But this time around we are far-flung, in various professional roles and geographical locations, relying for communication on teleconference and videoconference from various points in California, Iowa, Massachusetts, Minnesota, New York, Wyoming, and Santiago, Chile. We thank Chris Golas, James Goodrich, Jeremy Kellem, Russell Pidsosny, and David Williams for easing our virtual face-to-face conversations and feedback through university-sponsored videoconferences across these enormous distances. We felt as if we were still in the same room—well, almost.

We appreciate and acknowledge the many ways in which our long-time Social Justice Education colleagues Pat Griffin, Rita Hardiman, Bailey Jackson, Linda Marchesani, and Matt Ouellett, together with generations of social diversity and Social Justice Education course instructors and workshop facilitators from the 1970s through to the present day, have enriched the vision of social justice education that underpins this volume, the range of readings, and each other's instructional practice in the growing community of Social Justice Education students and teachers.

We especially need to thank the many authors of pedagogical designs, activities, and resources—some already published in the book text and CD for *Teaching for Diversity and Social Justice, second edition*—whose work we are drawing upon for the book's website.

Maurianne Adams, Warren J. Blumenfeld, Carmelita (Rosie) Castañeda,
Chase Catalano, Keri DeJong, Heather W. Hackman, Larissa E. Hopkins,
Khyati Y. Joshi, Barbara J. Love, Madeline L. Peters, Davey Shlasko, Ximena Zúñiga
September 2012

Readings for Diversity and Social Justice

A General Introduction

OUR APPROACH TO TOPICS AND ISSUES OF SOCIAL JUSTICE

This third edition of *Readings for Diversity and Social Justice* reflects our approach to social justice education. This approach explores the dynamics of privilege and disadvantage rooted in racism, sexism, classism, and other forms of systemic oppression, and notes their historical roots, intergenerational legacies, within-group differences, and local as well as global manifestations. We explore contemporary inequality, social hierarchy, and systemic oppression, and we also note examples of people taking action together for empowerment, equity, liberation, and sustained social change. We pay attention to the ways in which marginalized social groups contest their social inequality by renaming themselves and work together (often in alliance with privileged groups) to reshape their situations in equitable and empowering ways.

The editors who wrote the introductions and selected the readings for this new edition share an approach based on our awareness that social identities are derived from specific social groups and reflect unequal social locations or position relative to each other (that is, one group's privileges as directly related to other groups' disadvantages). The readings in this volume were selected as building blocks to enable readers both to appreciate social and cultural differences, and also to understand the ways in which these social and cultural differences have been used to justify systemic inequalities. Although we understand social and cultural *difference* to be important in its own right, we want to emphasize how it also often serves as the basis for *inequality,* especially when differences rationalize access to privilege for social groups associated with social "norms"—and when those norms are assumed to be available to everybody, but in practice are not available to marginalized or disadvantaged social groups. The overarching social system that maintains and reproduces these inequities is the system we call *oppression* and throughout this volume we present different yet compatible explorations of these dynamics, whether focused on personal experience, or analysis of social institutions and the overarching social and cultural system.

Our approach to social difference, social identity, social location, and social inequity calls for appreciation of the multiple, complex, fluid, and cross-cutting aspects of social identities, and awareness that the inequities experienced by any and all disadvantaged groups warrant our attention and our collective efforts at remedy. The statement that "There is no hierarchy of oppressions" (Audre Lorde, 1983) does not mean that different forms of oppression do not affect people in different ways, or vary in their intensity or virulence across different historical periods or various geographies, or that their duration and impact on whole populations does not differ. Despite this caveat, nonetheless, we take a "both/and" approach that acknowledges the obvious differences in experiences of oppression, and at the same time recognizes that all forms of oppression are harmful, that they interact with each other in the lives of individuals and

groups in complex ways, and that a fair, equitable, and just society requires an end to all forms of oppression. It is not useful to argue competitive victim status or to ask who has suffered more or longer. It is far more useful to understand all of the dynamics of social oppression as they affect all of us, although in different ways and to different degrees. This point is made in various ways by authors throughout this volume.

DISTINCTIVE FEATURES OF THIS THIRD EDITION

This third edition of *Readings for Diversity and Social Justice* conveys changes that have taken place during the past few years since the first and second editions—new approaches and complexities within our understanding of racism, sexism, or ableism, for example; new writing on ageism and adultism, immigration, religious oppression, and transgender oppression; and new writings that address some dramatic consequences of the recent economic recession and that emphasize the urgent need for change.

Like the first and second editions, this volume is organized in sections around specific issues of identity and oppression (such as sexuality and heterosexism, or disability and ableism) but it foregrounds the many intersections among these social group identities and their experiences of privilege and disadvantage. We pay attention to the privileges assumed by advantaged social groups but unavailable to disadvantaged social groups, and take the view that systemic oppression is characterized by unequal relationships between those who are privileged or advantaged by the social system, relative to those who are targeted or disadvantaged. We offer instances of resistance to oppression, whether through individual action, coalition, or organized social movements to create lasting change. We root our work in the social movements of the late 1950s through 1980s, and the social change and classroom pedagogies that emerged from those transformative movements.

We have learned a great deal since the publication of our earlier editions of readings some years ago. Our understanding of racism has become more nuanced and contextualized as we learn about the different histories and geographies of U.S. racism (as experienced by Native Americans, Africans, Mexicans, and peoples from throughout the Americas and Asia) and Anglo-based nativism toward immigrant European peoples (Irish, Italians, Jews). The current controversies concerning immigration and re-emergence of American-born "nativism" have helped to reframe our discussions of historical and contemporary racism(s), ethnocentrism, nationalism, and the intersections among them. Our analysis of class and classism has focused on the current global economic crisis of capitalism that is rooted in global economic interconnectedness, as well as the links between classism and other social oppressions (racism and sexism). Our increased attention to global religious oppressions has made it urgent that we focus on the experiences of marginalized, non-Christian communities of faith within the United States, as well as the vicious stereotyping of atheists. Further, the global historical approach we have taken to anti-semitism within European Christianity led us to focus more clearly on the U.S. Christian domination experienced by Native peoples (outlawed religious practices, forced relocations, forced mission schooling), as well as Hindus, Muslims, Jews, atheists—all who are outside the hegemonic Protestant-Christian U.S. mainstream. The claims for religious orthodoxy in current-day politics informs some of the emphasis and selections in the "Religious Oppression" section, especially our emphasis on the importance of "teaching about religion" as distinct from "teaching religion."

Recent writing on transgender oppression has complicated and enriched our understanding of gender, sexism, and heterosexism. The writing on transgender oppression challenges widely held assumptions about sex and gender binaries. It also highlights the role of

medical science—and science more generally—in constructing "normal" human identities and pathologizing marginalized identities and experiences. Explorations of ageism and adultism have reshaped our approach to all forms of oppression as experienced across the lifespan and suggest a living template for the intersectional experiences of multiple oppressions. We have gained new appreciation for the ways in which various forms of privilege or disadvantage—classed, raced, gendered—intersect and complicate each other in local as well as global settings and life experiences. These new understandings inform this third edition of *Readings for Diversity and Social Justice,* having already reshaped our approach to the second edition of *Teaching for Diversity and Social Justice* (2007).

Readers of our earlier work will be aware that we combine attention to the historically situated experiences of social identity groups with appreciation of the ways in which all peoples have been multiply raced, gendered, classed, able or disabled, with different age statuses. In this new edition, we have selected readings to maximize the interconnections between a "foreground" focus on the subjects of each section with a "background" of intersecting identities and forms of oppression. These intersections are highlighted in a Table of Intersections, located immediately following the more conventional Table of Contents. This Table of Intersections enables readers to identify all selections that treat issues of race, religion, gender, sexuality, disability, class, and age, beyond those in designated topical sections.

Not only has our approach to each social justice issue grown more intersectional and less unitary over the years; we have also learned to take a more global, less U.S.-centric approach. The economy is global, as are issues of class and classism, and race, racism, immigration and language, youth and age. Given the multiple zigzag diasporas of peoples crossing oceans and moving across national boundaries, it is no longer useful (if it ever was) to think in terms of domestic as distinct from "foreign" international racial or ethnic identities, especially as communities of color in the United States and elsewhere frame their own racial, ethnic, national self-awareness on current and/or more distant racial, ethnic, national, or religious legacies. Examination of religious oppression in the United States, to offer another example, brings us face to face with peoples who may be first-generation U.S. citizens and also the progeny of intergenerational diasporas, so that in this case as well, domestic and international dimensions of religious difference or conflict cannot be neatly separated from each other, or distinguished from class-based or ethnic/race-based group conflicts. The internet creates instantaneous networks and propels social movements across thousands of miles.

As section editors, we were faced with significant space constraints as we worked to create a manageable book covering eight distinct manifestations of oppression book-ended by conceptual frameworks and steps toward liberation. We do not presume to be exhaustive either in the number of social justice topics we present, or in the depth of our inquiry into each of the social justice topics. We are confident that the additional resources and further thoughts offered on the website for each of our sections will complement the reading selections for those readers seeking greater depth. Most notably, we've included short classroom-friendly videos geared to each of the section topics that provide additional perspectives or model approaches to change.

Section editors worked together to coordinate their approaches to sexism, heterosexism, and transgender oppression, and to clarify the distinctions as well as the parallels that shape experiences of gender role, gender identity, gender presentation, birth sex, sex presentation, sexual orientation, transsexual, transgender, and queer identities. The three sections on sexism, heterosexism, and transgender oppression are more closely linked than other chapters in the volume, although all editors have collaborated closely in selecting readings that maximize intersections—as with, for example, racism, classism, and religious oppression. The sections on racism and religious oppression complement each other by

incorporating the different histories and legacies of racism(s) and religious oppression experienced by Native Americans, African Americans, Mexican Americans, and Latinos/as from the diasporas within the Americas, and peoples from Asia and South Asia. We note the distinctiveness in the experiences of racism by displaced, enslaved, or colonized peoples as well as some of the overarching patterns of similarity in their oppressions. Similarly, the section on religious oppression brings together the marginalization of several different faith traditions—Hindus, Jews, Muslims, Native Americans—within U.S. Christian hegemony.

Given the enormity of the questions taken up in these and the other sections, there was no satisfactory way to maintain symmetry among equally pressing but distinctive social justice issues (in keeping with our belief that "There is no hierarchy of oppressions") while also representing and doing justice to the complexity and nuance within each of those "isms." We use section websites to extend our discussions and provide further resources.

OUR USE OF TERMINOLOGY AND LANGUAGE

We capitalize but do not hyphenate specific ethnicities (African American, Asian American) and capitalize, racial designations only when used as proper nouns and adjectives (Blacks, Latinos/as, Whites). We note that racial designations such as Black, Latino/a, Native American, Asian/Pacific Islander, White are not really parallel terms, in that they conflate race, ethnicity, and pan-ethnicity from different historical, geographical, and diasporic legacies. When we move to discussions of global diasporas, race-based or ethnic or religious descriptors become even more problematic. Whenever possible, we use terms that refer to national/geographic origin (people of South Asian descent, for example). We capitalize religions as we do names (Christians, Muslims, Jews) but we do not capitalize anti-semitism. We encourage the use of gender neutral pronouns (hir, ze) as a way of acknowledging identities that have been erased by gender binaries, as pronouns for people who state that they prefer those pronouns. The authors of each section of readings address other considerations of language usage as appropriate to the issues raised in their respective sections.

We want to notice how the terms used to describe the roles people play within the dynamics of oppression can be problematic. We propose terms which signal a focus, not on individual actors so much as on the structured roles and outcomes of an oppressive system. The binary terms "oppressor" and "oppressed," for example, do not reflect the complex and nuanced intersections of privilege or disadvantage across different identities and different social locations or positions. We continue to struggle to frame language that doesn't trivialize the power or the damage from the oppressive system we want to expose. We use various terms to emphasize different dimensions of the binaries—terms such as privileged and targeted or marginalized, advantaged and disadvantaged, dominant and subordinate—to convey the relative positions of groups of people within a system of oppression based on social hierarchy.

However much the editors share a general approach, it will be clear that not all of the editors or authors of selected readings agree on terminology. Readers will notice different terms in the section introductions and in reading selections. Our guiding principle is to adopt terms preferred by people from targeted groups who have named themselves: "people of color" rather than "nonwhite"; "gay, lesbian, bisexual" rather than "homosexual"; "people with disabilities" rather than "handicapped." Some of the reading selections will also draw on language used by targeted communities to reclaim previously negative terms such as "queer," "crip," "girl," "tranny," as terms that reframe slurs into terms of pride and ownership. We know that naming is a necessarily fluid, sometimes context-bound, and at times contradictory and confusing process, in which peoples/groups/communities rightly

insist on defining themselves rather than acquiescing to names imposed by others. We encourage people to recognize that such terms will continue to evolve and change and to appreciate the significance of the power to name oneself as an important aspect of group identity and resistance.

As already noted in the Acknowledgements, we have also struggled over many years—and now in this new edition—to find ways to publicly reflect our own collaboration in a way that does not play into the dynamics of academic power and privilege fostered by the tendency of libraries, reviewers, booksellers, and scholars to cite multiply-authored work by the first author "et al." We want to acknowledge our own collaborative work and encourage that of others in ways that do not play into the presumed seniority and power dynamics accorded the first name listed. We have searched for ways of naming all of the authors in our collaborative work in order to contest assumptions of greater or lesser professional power or relative status that follow from the listing of names. We are well aware that our strictly alphabetical approach is also unsatisfactory, in that any line of names, however arranged, suggests a ranking order—and we hope that alphabetizing our names levels the playing field and sends a clear message that we present ourselves and each other as having equivalent authority, expertise, and status.

To emphasize our shared authority, we intentionally place a statement at the beginning of each section to honor the nature and value of our collaborative work with a request that people who cite us *always* include the full names of *all* authors named as responsible for a given section, a practice we also followed in *Teaching for Diversity and Social Justice* (second edition, 2007) where we used the following footnote: "We ask that those who cite this work always acknowledge by name all of the authors listed rather than either only citing the first author or using 'et al.' to indicate coauthors. All authors listed on a section collaborated equitably on the conceptualization, development, and writing of this section." We have followed our own preferred practice by including all names in the works we cite within our own section introductions and permissions citations. The importance we attach to this challenge to professional practice is clear from the fact that we have already made this point in the Acknowledgements, repeat it here in the General Introduction and again in the footnotes to all of our multiply-authored sections.

SUGGESTIONS ON HOW TO USE THIS BOOK

This volume attempts to reflect the many dimensions of theoretical and historical content, application, and action that have emerged in the new field of social justice education. In our own practice on our own campuses we link the readings in this volume with a social justice practice that is experiential, student-centered, interactive, dialogic, question-probing rather than answer-providing—an approach that is suggested on the website that accompanies this volume, but is more fully described and spelled out in our companion volume for teachers, facilitators, and everyone interested in the pedagogical process: *Teaching for Diversity and Social Justice* (second edition, 2007).

Our focus is on specific manifestations of oppression (racism, classism, religious oppression, for example) as experienced by specific social identity groups, those privileged as well as those disadvantaged by racism, classism, or religious and other manifestations of oppression. The key themes and principles are illustrated by selections in Section 1 on "Conceptual Frameworks," a section that readers should use to help theorize and shed light on the readings in specific topic sections. We combine a section-by-section focus on specific topics of social diversity and oppression, yet we also call attention to the intersections among social identities and experiences of oppression. Each section introduction highlights

these intersections, and the Table of Intersections identifies all selections that shed light on these topics, wherever they may be located in the volume. We urge that all readers use the conceptual frameworks section as well as the relevant section introductions for key definitions, historical contexts, and current topics for each of the social justice topics, as well as an overview of the goals served by each section's reading selections. We encourage course instructors to assign these introductions along with selected readings. We also urge that all readers use the Table of Intersections to extend their readings about specific social justice topics across a number of sections and to note the complexity in single social justice topics afforded by these across-selection intersections.

Our approach to social diversity and oppression also shapes the overall organization for each separate topic section into the three areas of Context, Voices, Next Steps. All of the topical sections coordinate examples of the social system that sustains oppression with personal voices that attest to the everyday experience. Each topical section starts with Contexts that offer historical background and overviews of relevant issues, followed by personal descriptions or narratives in the Voices. The Next Steps emphasize the extraordinary efforts that individuals and groups of people have made, and continue to make, to challenge privilege and disadvantage in order to create social change. Thus each section concludes with selections that describe pathways for empowerment, action, and change at the individual, institutional, and systemic levels. The many opportunities for change, envisioned in the Next Steps part of each section, lead to a final section on "Working for Social Justice: Visions and Strategies for Change," which serves as a book-end to the opening section's analyses of social diversity and oppression in "'Conceptual Frameworks.'"

The selections in the final section, "Working for Social Justice: Visions and Strategies for Change," build on the ideas and actions described in the Next Steps part of each section. We want to encourage readers to be hopeful about the prospects of social change and to express that hope through individual and everyday actions, or through community, grassroots, or national coalitions and organizations, all of them smaller or larger steps toward positive social change. As educators, we believe that if we are to present information about systemic inequities, disadvantage, and oppression—and to expect that we become responsible for these inequities once we know about them—then as educators we must also present pathways of hope by acknowledging the role of social movements in U.S. history and the many contemporary opportunities to participate in social change.

A further innovation in this edition is the website, which provides additional resources, such as videos for classroom or supplementary use, curricula and discussion questions, and ideas for action and application for each of the sections. The website suggests further avenues for exploring a number of related topics. Organized by section, each section has five subheaders: Video (includes curated selections to complement printed readings); Discussion Questions (thematic questions to spark further engagement); Activities (materials and handouts to foster an interactive approach to course pedagogy); Next Steps (examples of action projects being taken nationally by coalitions and action groups; internet links to organizations engaged in social action); and Further Resources (print, internet, film, and video resource lists). The section website for "Conceptual Frameworks" provides a video that can be used as an overview, with examples of review questions and exam rubrics that we can recommend for instructional use. And for instructors, especially, who want to know more about the interactive, experiential, dialogic pedagogies used by the editors of this volume in our classrooms throughout the United States, we recommend *Teaching for Diversity and Social Justice* (second edition, 2007) as a resource. We have incorporated some of the resources and pedagogical activities from this book and its accompanying CD onto a number of the section websites.

The alphabetically organized Permission Acknowledgements and Citations at the rear of the book is the only bibliographical citation provided for all of the reading selections.

Readers wanting to track citations, notes and references that were cut from the reading selections, due to space constraints, will be able to use this to enable them to follow up on the readings.

We offer this book for use by different readers in many settings and situations. We use these readings in our own general education and graduate diversity classes and in graduate and undergraduate weekend seminars, in teacher education classes, and in multicultural education classes on our own campuses and communities in California, Iowa, Massachusetts, Minnesota, New Jersey, New York, and Wyoming. We know that the earlier editions have been used in many other settings—in ethnic and women's studies, history, social studies, sociology, and psychology courses, in social work and management, and in centers for teaching excellence—wherever there is an interest in the broad range of human experiences that have been shaped by social difference and by privilege or disadvantage. We anticipate that these reading selections will be understood differently, as readers themselves have had similar or dissimilar experiences. Our intention and hope is that they will provide opportunities for personal thought and reflection, empathy, connection, and discussion.

References

Adams, M., Bell, L. A., Griffin, P. (eds). (2007). *Teaching for Diversity and Social Justice* (2nd edition). New York: Routledge.

Lorde, A. (1983). There is no hierarchy of oppressions. *Interracial Books for Children Bulletin* 14 (3–4), 9.

SECTION 1

CONCEPTUAL FRAMEWORKS

Introduction

Maurianne Adams

Social diversity and *social justice* are often used interchangeably to refer to *social differences* as well as to *social inequality.* These two terms are closely related but not interchangeable. When we refer to *social diversity*, we have in mind differences between social identity groups based on social categories such as race, gender, sexuality, class, and others. These differences are reflected in a group's traditions, language, style of dress, cultural practices, religious beliefs and rituals. These are usually termed "differences" in that they are understood to differ from some larger societal norm that may be taken for granted by the majority group, and which is, therefore, socially privileged. If one thinks of oneself as a "normal" member of one's larger society, it becomes difficult to perceive oneself, one's family and group traditions, language, style of dress as part of a larger pattern of overall *diversity.* Rather, it is the norm that shapes one's notion of the "differences" of *others*, who are marginalized precisely because they are different. In this sense, it is clear why *diversity* ("difference") profoundly shapes the advantages of some groups (those who are part of the norm) relative to the disadvantages of others (because they are "othered"), which maintains *social inequalities* that are rationalized on the basis of these divergences from social norms. We also use terms such as *oppression* and *social justice* to emphasize our focus on inequality as a social form that shapes life changes for people in ways that are more profound (more "unequal") than simply different.

Thus, although these terms are not interchangeable, they are inextricably linked in everyday discourse, in that *diversity* is too often used to provide an excuse or justification for *inequality.* It's much more comfortable to talk about *diversity* than *inequality*, although clearly we need to understand both. We need to affirm and value social and cultural differences if we are to envision a society that acknowledges and appreciates such differences, by questioning what we had previously accepted as "norms." At the same time, the appreciation of social diversity is a necessary but not sufficient step toward understanding the inequalities experienced by peoples who are seen as belonging to marginalized social groups. It is necessary to understand injustice if we are ever to dismantle the institutions and policies that maintain injustice and to reconstruct institutions and policies based on fairness, equity, and justice. As Young suggests (in selection 5), our challenge is to appreciate social diversity while working to dismantle social inequality.

Several key assumptions inform our perspective throughout this volume, and we identify them in this section as a cluster of four interrelated conceptual frameworks. Our core assumptions are

presented in the General Introduction, and include our awareness that social identity groups occupy unequal social locations or positions relative to each other (that is, one group's privileges are directly related to another group's disadvantages). This awareness leads us to the following four concepts: (1) *social group identities* (such as racial and gender identities) have been used historically to justify and perpetuate the advantages of privileged groups relative to the disadvantages of marginalized groups; (2) these social identities, together with their relatively different "positions" resulting in their inequality, have been *socially constructed within specific historical conditions*, although these social constructions are often rationalized as being derived from the "facts of nature" or sustained by unquestioned religious beliefs; (3) the pervasive historical legacies of inequality require a *theory of oppression* to account for the complex levels and types of privilege and disadvantage that play out at various levels of human society; and (4) a theory of oppression also calls for *frameworks that envision opportunities for empowerment* and that help us to explain the success of past and present for social movements.

(1) SOCIAL IDENTITY IS BASED ON SOCIAL IDENTITY GROUPS IN ADVANTAGED OR DISADVANTAGED SOCIAL LOCATIONS OR POSITIONS

The first conceptual framework presented in this section examines social diversity based on differences in social identity and social location. Tatum (selection 1) defines social identity in a complex, multifaceted way that captures the tensions between dominant and subordinate identities (those privileged or disadvantaged on the basis of social group memberships) and gives examples of the tensions between them in everyday interactions. She explores the development of social identity in the context of identity development more generally, and describes the ways in which one's identity comes about through the interaction between one's internal sense of who one is (based upon one's social groupings) and the views of oneself and one's group that are reflected back by others in the broader society.

Kirk and Okazawa-Rey (selection 2) note how social identity combines self-perception with personal reactions to attribution by others, so that different contexts may highlight different dimensions of identity (such as racial identity in one context, gender or sexual or class identity in another). They also consider social identity at different levels of social interaction—at the *micro* level (between individuals), at the *meso* level (within communities or social institutions), and at the *macro* level (the overarching society and culture). Similarly, but without using the same terminology, Harro's "The Cycle of Socialization" (selection 6) walks the reader through specific *micro*, *meso*, and *macro* contexts within which social identities and social roles are learned from early childhood and reinforced during adulthood within trusted and familiar contexts—in families, schools, playgrounds, neighborhoods, the workplace, and the media.

Both Tatum, and Kirk and Okazawa-Rey, situate social identity within specific social contexts, in that "social" refers to this individual/societal interaction. Both offer numerous examples of how one's social identities build upon one's social group expectations of privilege or disadvantage, based upon cumulative, historical legacies of group privilege or disadvantage. The connections between privilege/disadvantage and the experience of social identity are the focus for selection 3, in which Johnson explores a number of everyday examples of historically rooted, socially constructed inequalities based on race, gender, sexuality, and disability. His approach, if not his specific examples, is applicable to other forms of oppression treated in this book (such as religious oppression, transgender oppression, or ageism and adultism). Many selections throughout the different sections in this book point out the role of identity and positionality in our experiences of privilege and disadvantage. They also point out the many ways in which these identities intersect, and these intersections are highlighted in the Table of Intersections, which calls attention

to specific selections dealing with race and gender, or class and disability, or many other ways in which our experiences sometimes combine privileged identities with disadvantaged identities, sometimes in the same moment.

(2) THE SOCIAL CONSTRUCTION OF PRIVILEGE AND OPPRESSION WITHIN SPECIFIC HISTORICAL CONTEXTS

A second conceptual framework involves an explanation of how social group differences are *socially constructed* in specific historical situations in which their social meanings justify inequality and oppression. In this way, social identities are understood as social creations— and the assumptions of superiority or inferiority, related to privilege and disadvantage, are also understood as social creations. As Johnson explains (selection 3), most of what we experience in personal and social life is itself a social creation—and the social differences we consider so significant, so "natural," or so theologically sanctioned, are in fact based on unexamined cultural constructions and not on essential qualities of groups or persons. The implication of this is momentous, for if we understand how specific historical and cultural conditions have given rise to privilege and to disadvantage, we can also understand that these inequities can be changed. Freire helps us grasp how important it is for people to locate conditions of oppression within history, rather than fatalistically as inevitable—that "humans, in their permanent relations with reality, produce not only material goods . . . but also social institutions, ideas, and concepts . . . create history and become historical-social beings" (1994, p. 82). Freire recommends a problem-posing approach to education that takes "the people's historicity as their starting point" (1994, p. 65).

It can be challenging to discover that skin color, accented speech, perceived gender or sexual orientation, or the presence or absence of a physical or mental disability, are themselves socially constructed categories and are, therefore, useless as indicators of talent, character, intelligence, or morality. The readings throughout all the sections in this volume locate the stereotypes we have been led to believe about "others" within their specific historical and cultural contexts, emphasizing the fact that our assumptions about what it means to be female or male or transgender; gay or straight or queer; White, Latino, or Black; young or old; learning disabled or able-bodied; Christian or atheist or Jewish, Hindu, or Muslim, have been constructed within historical conditions with cultural presuppositions (examples include selections 10, 57, 66, 91, 111, 112, 129, and 132). Harro points out (selection 6) how we unconsciously absorb stereotypes and prejudices as an unconscious part of our socialization from the people who surround us and whom we trust to know what is right and correct.

The following sections have reading selections that refer explicitly to the historical roots of specific patterns of advantage and disadvantage, and the stereotypes associated with them. Lipsitz (selection 11) and Oliver and Shapiro (selection 27) point to specific moments in history that account for the persistence of racism and classism in the present. Roppolo (selection 10), Hilberg (selection 47), Echo-Hawk (selection 50), Lorber (selection 60) and Cerney (selection 96) demonstrate the value of historical analyses of patriarchy, Christian hegemony in Europe and in the United States, or culturally sanctioned assumptions about age, gender, sexuality, and disability. Understanding that we have inherited stereotypes as well as our own group's privilege or disadvantage as part of our intergenerational legacy helps to demystify them, and makes them seem less inevitable and more susceptible to education and change. The understanding of historical legacies of privilege and disadvantage is important if we are also to learn about social resistance movements in the past that also are our legacy and that inspire us to continue working toward change.

(3) FRAMEWORKS FOR ANALYSIS OF OPPRESSION

Social justice needs a theory of *oppression* in order to make sense of the sources and persistence of social inequality in a pluralistic U.S. society that was founded on concepts of equality of opportunity and fairness in life's rewards. Thus, the third conceptual framework presented in this section involves our moving beyond the individual (or "micro") level of the socialization process, to analyze how oppression is enacted and reproduced at the institutional level ("meso") and the societal/cultural ("macro") level. Even though most of the examples in Tatum (selection 1), Johnson (selection 3) and Harro (selection 6) focus on the individual ("micro") level of privilege and disadvantage, it is clear that our everyday personal experiences take place in larger institutional contexts such as extended families, neighborhoods, schools, places of worship, and that our experiences of privilege or disadvantage in these social institutions are reinforced by the societal and cultural messages we simultaneously pick up from the media and understand to be part of our normative culture.

In selection 4, Bell itemizes the defining features of oppression and presents an inclusive approach to the many different forms of oppression—such as racism, classism, sexism—that also highlights their complex intersections in everyday life. This approach is reinforced and developed by Hardiman, Jackson, and Griffin (selection 4) as the interplay of *levels* of oppression—the individual, the institutional, the societal levels—as well as *types* of oppression—the conscious and the unconscious. These authors define key terminology and analyze the complex and overlapping ways by which interpersonal, institutional, and societal/cultural dimensions of oppression reinforce each other. They are explicit about several underlying assumptions, namely that there is no hierarchy of oppression, that all forms of oppression are interconnected, and that confronting oppression benefits everyone.

There is more than one way to analyze such a complex societal phenomenon as oppression and this section presents at least three approaches. The first can be called a *psychological* approach in that it locates the psychological processes of socialization within the institutions and broader culture of a society (for example, Tatum in selection 1, Kirk and Okazawa-Rey in selection 2, and Harro in selection 6). The second can be called a *sociological* approach in that it focuses on the structural dimensions of oppression as a social phenomenon, and is presented here by Bell, Hardiman, Jackson, and Griffin (selection 4) (Hardiman, Jackson, and Griffin, 2007). The third, presented here by Young (selection 5), is located within a *philosophical* and *political* discourse about theories of social justice, and focuses on *social* justice as distinct from *distributive economic* justice, or legal, political, or remedial justice (Young, 1990, 2001). In selection 5, Young analyzes the dynamics of oppression—as do Bell, Griffin, Hardiman, and Jackson—but seen by her as five "faces" or facets that interchangeably describe how oppression is experienced by those who are disadvantaged on the basis of social identity groups—namely through their exploitation, powerlessness, and marginalization by those in dominant social positions, or their experience of cultural imperialism and violence. A second selection by Young (selection 7), coordinates the individual or personal focus of the psychological approach with the systemic focus of the sociological approach. In selection 7, Young presents the systemic forces that constrain a young homeless woman's individual choices of residence and work, in the context of the choices made by other actors in terms of other constraints, such as a landlord who is sorry to sell her rental and the real estate economy that leads him to sell, the employers who do not hire her, the schools that did not educate her, the city managers who did not provide transportation from rental properties to workplaces. The constraints and social forces described by Young in this selection (such as market forces and educational opportunities) are themselves made up of people who often mean well, are not acting in malice, who feel "blameless" for the situation of a homeless woman, and yet whose actions taken together lead to "circumstances beyond her control." Young's repersonalization of "shared [social] responsibility" helps readers grasp their personal role in decisions that affect others, and their position in causal networks that leads to

justice for some, injustice for others. This insight, that enables us to coordinate our own personal actions with systemic consequences often far removed from those actions, sets the stage for the sections that follow—the Next Steps proposed in each of the sections—and the emphasis in the concluding section on ways that readers can take responsibility for the immediate as well as the more long-range consequences of their actions.

These three approaches to the systemic dimension of oppression—and the way they are linked in Young's "Structure as the Subject of Justice" selection (selection 7)—are compatible and mutually illuminating, while at the same time focusing on different dimensions of complex social phenomena. And they can be used as analytic frameworks for many readings through-out this volume. In selections 45 and 46, for example, Blumenfeld and Joshi explicitly take one or another of these conceptual frameworks to theorize historical and contemporary religious oppression and Christian privilege.

(4) FRAMEWORKS FOR ENVISIONING EMPOWERMENT AND SOCIAL CHANGE

All approaches to oppression have implications for a view of society that might conceivably be characterized instead by fairness and justice. In reading selections 3–5, one can instead imagine what a non-oppressive society might look like, in the absence of each and all five faces of oppres-sion (selection 5), or the reversal of the examples and dynamics of oppression as described in selections 3 and 4. How one might actually describe actions or plan projects toward social change in order to achieve relationships, institutions, and an overarching social system and culture that do not enforce or reproduce oppression is a more challenging question and a chal-lenge that this volume accepts. Each one of the individual topic sections that follow concludes with selections describing Next Steps that people have taken or can imagine taking to transform the specific forms of oppression into empowering relationships and just, equitable social institu-tions. The volume concludes with a full section describing such steps. So this entire section on conceptual frameworks can be understood as a prelude to these discussions. Harro's "The Cycle of Liberation" (selection 131), a companion piece to her "The Cycle of Socialization" (selection 6), is presented in the final section of this volume. In it, Harro describes personal behaviors that anyone can engage in, to challenge and to transform individual behavior at the personal level. Other selections throughout this volume and in the final section add collaborative institutional and societal/cultural change projects to the repertoire of possibilities available for concerted, effective social change.

See Companion Website for Additional Resources and Material

References

Freire, P. (1994, 1970). *Pedagogy of the Oppressed* (new revised edition). New York: Continuum.

Hardiman, R., Jackson, B., Griffin, P. (2007). Conceptual foundations for social justice education. In M. Adams, L. A. Bell, P. Griffin (eds), *Teaching for Diversity and Social Justice* (2nd edition, pp. 35–66). New York: Routledge.

Young, I. M. (1990). Introduction, displacing the distributive paradigm, five faces of oppression. In *Justice and the Politics of Difference* (pp. 3–65). Princeton, NJ: Princeton University Press.

Young, I. M. (2001). Equality of whom? Social groups and judgments of injustice. *The Journal of Political Philosophy* 9 (1), 1–18.

1

The Complexity of Identity

"Who Am I?"

Beverly Daniel Tatum

The concept of identity is a complex one, shaped by individual characteristics, family dynamics, historical factors, and social and political contexts. Who am I? The answer depends in large part on who the world around me says I am. Who do my parents say I am? Who do my peers say I am? What message is reflected back to me in the faces and voices of my teachers, my neighbors, store clerks? What do I learn from the media about myself? How am I represented in the cultural images around me? Or am I missing from the picture altogether? . . . What has my social context been? Was I surrounded by people like myself, or was I part of a minority in my community? Did I grow up speaking standard English at home or another language or dialect? Did I live in a rural county, an urban neighborhood, a sprawling suburb, or on a reservation?

Who I am (or say I am) is a product of these and many other factors. Erik Erikson, the psychoanalytic theorist who coined the term *identity crisis*, introduced the notion that the social, cultural, and historical context is the ground in which individual identity is embedded. Acknowledging the complexity of identity as a concept, Erikson writes,

> We deal with a process "located" *in the core of the individual* and yet also *in the core of his communal culture*. . . . In psychological terms, identity formation employs a process of simultaneous reflection and observation, a process taking place on all levels of mental functioning, by which the individual judges himself in the light of what he perceives to be the way in which others judge him in comparison to themselves and to a typology significant to them.

. . .

WHO AM I? MULTIPLE IDENTITIES

Integrating one's past, present, and future into a cohesive, unified sense of self is a complex task that begins in adolescence and continues for a lifetime. . . . The salience of particular aspects of our identity varies at different moments in our lives. The process of integrating the component parts of our self-definition is indeed a lifelong journey.

Which parts of our identity capture our attention first? While there are surely idiosyncratic responses to this question, a classroom exercise I regularly use with my psychology students reveals a telling pattern. I ask my students to complete the sentence, "I am _____," using as many descriptors as they can think of in sixty seconds. All kinds of trait descriptions are used—friendly, shy, assertive, intelligent, honest, and so on—but over the years I have noticed something else. Students of color usually mention their racial or ethnic group: for instance, I am Black, Puerto Rican, Korean American. White students

who have grown up in strong ethnic enclaves occasionally mention being Irish or Italian. But in general, White students rarely mention being White. When I use this exercise in coeducational settings, I notice a similar pattern in terms of gender, religion, and sexuality. Women usually mention being female, while men don't usually mention their maleness. Jewish students often say they are Jews, while mainline Protestants rarely mention their religious identification. A student who is comfortable revealing it publicly may mention being gay, lesbian, or bisexual. Though I know most of my students are heterosexual, it is very unusual for anyone to include their heterosexuality on their list.

Common across these examples is that in the areas where a person is a member of the dominant or advantaged social group, the category is usually not mentioned. That element of their identity is so taken for granted by them that it goes without comment. It is taken for granted by them because it is taken for granted by the dominant culture. In Eriksonian terms, their inner experience and outer circumstance are in harmony with one another, and the image reflected by others is similar to the image within. In the absence of dissonance, this dimension of identity escapes conscious attention.

The parts of our identity that *do* capture our attention are those that other people notice, and that reflect back to us. The aspect of identity that is the target of others' attention, and subsequently of our own, often is that which sets us apart as exceptional or "other" in their eyes. In my life I have been perceived as both. A precocious child who began to read at age three, I stood out among my peers because of my reading ability. This "gifted" dimension of my identity was regularly commented upon by teachers and classmates alike, and quickly became part of my self-definition. But I was also distinguished by being the only Black student in the class, an "other," a fact I grew increasingly aware of as I got older.

While there may be countless ways one might be defined as exceptional, there are at least seven categories of "otherness" commonly experienced in U.S. society. People are commonly defined as other on the basis of race or ethnicity, gender, religion, sexual orientation, socioeconomic status, age, and physical or mental ability. Each of these categories has a form of oppression associated with it: racism, sexism, religious oppression/anti-Semitism, heterosexism, classism, ageism, and ableism, respectively. In each case, there is a group considered dominant (systematically advantaged by the society because of group membership) and a group considered subordinate or targeted (systematically disadvantaged). When we think about our multiple identities, most of us will find that we are both dominant and targeted at the same time. But it is the targeted identities that hold our attention and the dominant identities that often go unexamined.

. . .

DOMINATION AND SUBORDINATION

. . .

Dominant groups, by definition, set the parameters within which the subordinates operate. The dominant group holds the power and authority in society relative to the subordinates and determines how that power and authority may be acceptably used. Whether it is reflected in determining who gets the best jobs, whose history will be taught in school, or whose relationships will be validated by society, the dominant group has the greatest influence in determining the structure of the society.

The relationship of the dominants to the subordinates is often one in which the targeted group is labeled as defective or substandard in significant ways. For example, Blacks have historically been characterized as less intelligent than Whites, and women have been viewed as less emotionally stable than men. The dominant group assigns roles to the subordinate

that reflect the latter's devalued status, reserving the most highly valued roles in the society for themselves. Subordinates are usually said to be innately incapable of performing the preferred roles. To the extent that those in the target group internalize the images that the dominant group reflects back to them, they may find it difficult to believe in their own ability.

. . .

The dominant group is seen as the norm for humanity. . . . Consequently, it remains perfectly acceptable in many circles to tell jokes that denigrate a particular group, to exclude subordinates from one's neighborhood or work setting, or to oppose initiatives that might change the power balance.

. . .

The truth is that the dominants do not really know what the experience of the subordinates is. In contrast, the subordinates are very well informed about the dominants. Even when firsthand experience is limited by social segregation, the number and variety of images of the dominant group available through television, magazines, books, and newspapers provide subordinates with plenty of information about the dominants. The dominant worldview has saturated the culture for all to learn. Even the Black or Latino child living in a segregated community can enter White homes of many kinds daily via the media. However, dominant access to information about the subordinates is often limited to stereotypical depictions of the "other." For example, there are many images of heterosexual relations on television, but very few images of gay or lesbian domestic partnerships beyond the caricatures of comedy shows. There are many images of White men and women in all forms of media, but relatively few portrayals of people of color.

. . .

In a situation of unequal power, a subordinate group has to focus on survival. It becomes very important for subordinates to become highly attuned to the dominants as a way of protecting themselves. For example, women who have been battered by men often talk about the heightened sensitivity they develop to their partners' moods. Being able to anticipate and avoid the men's rage is important to survival.

Survival sometimes means not responding to oppressive behavior directly. To do so could result in physical harm to oneself, even death. . . .

The use of either strategy, attending very closely to the dominants or not attending at all, is costly to members of the targeted group. "Not-learning" may mean there are needed skills that are not acquired. Attending closely to the dominant group may leave little time or energy to attend to one's self. Worse yet, the negative messages of the dominant group about the subordinates may be internalized, leading to self-doubt or, in its extreme form, self-hate. There are many examples of subordinates attempting to make themselves over in the image of the dominant group—Jewish people who want to change the Semitic look of their noses, Asians who have cosmetic surgery to alter the shapes of their eyes, Blacks who seek to lighten their skin with bleaching creams, women who want to smoke and drink "like a man." Whether one succumbs to the devaluing pressures of the dominant culture or successfully resists them, the fact is that dealing with oppressive systems from the underside, regardless of the strategy, is physically and psychologically taxing.

. . .

The history of subordinate groups is filled with so-called troublemakers, yet their names are often unknown. Preserving the record of those subordinates and their dominant allies who have challenged the status quo is usually of little interest to the dominant culture, but it is of great interest to subordinates who search for an empowering reflection in the societal mirror.

Many of us are both dominant and subordinate. As Audre Lorde said, from her vantage point as a Black lesbian, "There is no hierarchy of oppressions." The thread and threat of

violence runs through all of the isms. There is a need to acknowledge each other's pain, even as we attend to our own.

For those readers who are in the dominant racial category, it may sometimes be difficult to take in what is being said by and about those who are targeted by racism. When the perspective of the subordinate is shared directly, an image is reflected to members of the dominant group that is disconcerting. To the extent that one can draw on one's own experience of subordination—as a young person, as a person with a disability, as someone who grew up poor, as a woman—it may be easier to make meaning of another targeted group's experience. For those readers who are targeted by racism and are angered by the obliviousness of Whites, it may be useful to attend to your experience of dominance where you may find it—as a heterosexual, as an able-bodied person, as a Christian, as a man—and consider what systems of privilege you may be overlooking. The task of resisting our own oppression does not relieve us of the responsibility of acknowledging our complicity in the oppression of others.

Our ongoing examination of who we are in our full humanity, embracing all of our identities, creates the possibility of building alliances that may ultimately free us all.

2

Identities and Social Locations

Who Am I? Who Are My People?

Gwyn Kirk and Margo Okazawa-Rey

. . .

Identity formation is the result of a complex interplay among individual decisions and choices, particular life events, community recognition and expectations, and societal categorization, classification, and socialization. It is an ongoing process that involves several key questions:

Who am I? Who do I want to be?
Who do others think I am and want me to be?
Who and what do societal and community institutions, such as schools, religious institutions, the media, and the law, say I am?
Where/what/who are my "home" and "community"?
Which social group(s) do I want to affiliate with?
Who decides the answers to these questions, and on what basis?

Answers to these questions form the core of our existence. . . .

The *American Heritage Dictionary* (1993) defines *identity* as

the collective aspect of the set of characteristics by which a thing is definitely known or recognizable;

a set of behavioral or personal characteristics by which an individual is recognizable as a
   member of a group;

   . . .

   The same dictionary defines *to identify* as "to associate or affiliate (oneself) closely with
a person or group; to establish an identification with another or others."

   These definitions point to the connections between us as individuals and how we are
perceived by other people and classified by societal institutions. They also involve a sense
of individual agency and choice regarding affiliations with others. Gender, race, ethnicity,
class, nationality, sexual orientation, age, religion, disability, and language are all significant
social categories by which people are recognized by others. Indeed, on the basis of these
categories alone, others often think they know who we are and how we should behave.
Personal decisions about our affiliations and loyalties to specific groups are also shaped
by these categories. For example, in many communities of color women struggle over the
question of race versus gender. Is race a more important factor than gender in shaping
their lives? If a Latina speaks out publicly about sexism within the Latino community, is
she betraying her people? This separation of categories, mirrored by our segregated social
lives, tends to set up false dichotomies in which people often feel that they have to choose
one aspect of their identity over another. It also presents difficulties for mixed-race or
bisexual people, who do not fit neatly into such narrow categories.

   . . .

BEING MYSELF: THE MICRO LEVEL

At the micro level, individuals usually feel the most comfortable as themselves. Here one
can say, for example, "I am a woman, heterosexual, middle class, with a movement disability; but I am also much more than those categories." At this level we define ourselves and
structure our daily activities according to our own preferences. At the micro level we can
best feel and experience the process of identity formation, which includes naming specific
forces and events that shape our identities. At this level we also seem to have more control
of the process, although there are always interconnections between events and experiences
at this level and the other levels.

   Critical life events, such as entering kindergarten, losing a parent through death, separation, or divorce, or the onset of puberty, may all serve as catalysts for a shift in how we
think about ourselves. A five-year-old Vietnamese American child from a traditional home
and community may experience the first challenge to her sense of identity when her kindergarten teacher admonishes her to speak only in English. A White, middle-class professional woman who thinks of herself as "a person" and a "competent attorney" may begin
to see the significance of gender and "the glass ceiling" for women when she witnesses
younger, less experienced male colleagues in her law office passing her by for promotions.
A woman who has been raped who attends her first meeting of a campus group organizing
against date rape feels the power of connection with other rape survivors and their allies.
An eighty-year-old woman, whose partner of fifty years has just died, must face the reality
of having lost her lifetime companion, friend, and lover. Such experiences shape each
person's ongoing formulation of self, whether or not the process is conscious, deliberate,
reflective, or even voluntary.

   Identity formation is a lifelong endeavor that includes discovery of the new; recovery of
the old, forgotten, or appropriated; and synthesis of the new and old, as illustrated by several writers in this chapter who reflect on how their sense of identity has developed over the

course of their lives. At especially important junctures during the process, individuals mark an identity change in tangible ways. An African American woman may change her name from the anglicized Susan to Aisha, with roots in African culture. A Chinese Vietnamese immigrant woman, on the other hand, may adopt an anglicized name, exchanging Nu Lu for Yvonne Lu as part of becoming a U.S. citizen. Another way of marking and effecting a shift in identity is by altering your physical appearance: changing your wardrobe or makeup; cutting your hair very short, wearing it natural rather than permed or pressed, dyeing it purple, or letting the gray show after years of using hair coloring. . . .

COMMUNITY RECOGNITION, EXPECTATIONS, AND INTERACTIONS: THE MESO LEVEL

It is at the meso level—at school, in the workplace, or on the street—that people most frequently ask "Who are you?" or "Where are you from?" in an attempt to categorize us and determine their relationship to us. Moreover, it is here that people experience the complexities, conflicts, and contradictions of multiple identities, which we consider later.

The single most visible signifier of identity is physical appearance. . . . Questions such as "Where do you come from?" and questioning behaviors, such as feeling the texture of your hair or asking if you speak a particular language, are commonly used to interrogate people whose physical appearances especially, but also behaviors, do not match the characteristics designated as belonging to established categories. At root, we are being asked, "Are you one of us or not?" These questioners usually expect singular and simplistic answers, assuming that everyone will fit existing social categories, which are conceived of as undifferentiated and unambiguous. Among people with disabilities, for example, people wanting to identify each other may expect to hear details of another's disability rather than the fact that the person being questioned also identifies equally strongly as, say, a woman who is White, working class, and bisexual.

Community, like home, may be geographic and emotional, or both, and provides a way for people to express group affiliations. "Where are you from?" is a commonplace question in the United States among strangers, a way to break the ice and start a conversation, expecting answers like "I'm from Tallahassee, Florida," or "I'm from the Bronx." Community might also be an organized group like Alcoholics Anonymous, a religious group, or a political organization like the African American civil rights organization, the National Association for the Advancement of Colored People (NAACP). Community may be something much more abstract, as in "the women's community" or "the queer community," where there is presumed to be an identifiable group. In all of these examples there is an assumption of some kind of shared values, goals, interests, culture, or language.

At the community level, individual identities and needs meet group standards, expectations, obligations, responsibilities, and demands. You compare yourself with others and are subtly compared. Others size up your clothing, accent, personal style, and knowledge of the group's history and culture. You may be challenged directly, "You say you're Latina. How come you don't speak Spanish?" "You say you're working class. What are you doing in a professional job?" These experiences may both affirm our identities and create or highlight inconsistencies, incongruities, and contradictions in who we believe we are, how we are viewed by others, our role and status in the community, and our sense of belonging.

. . .

SOCIAL CATEGORIES, CLASSIFICATIONS, AND STRUCTURAL INEQUALITY: MACRO AND GLOBAL LEVELS

Classifying and labeling human beings, often according to real or assumed physical, biological, or genetic differences, is a way to distinguish who is included and who is excluded from a group, to ascribe particular characteristics, to prescribe social roles, and to assign status, power, and privilege. People are to know their places. Thus social categories such as gender, race, and class are used to establish and maintain a particular kind of social order. The classifications and their specific features, meanings, and significance are socially constructed through history, politics, and culture. The specific meanings and significance were often imputed to justify the conquest, colonization, domination, and exploitation of entire groups of people, and although the specifics may have changed over time, this system of categorizing and classifying remains intact. For example, Native American people were described as brutal, uncivilized, and ungovernable savages in the writings of early colonizers on this continent. This justified the genocide of Native Americans by White settlers and the U.S. military and public officials, as well as the breaking of treaties between the U.S. government and Native American tribes. Today, Native Americans are no longer called savages but are often thought of as a vanishing species, or a non-existent people, already wiped out, thereby rationalizing their neglect by the dominant culture and erasing their long-standing and continuing resistance. . . .

These social categories are at the foundation of the structural inequalities present in our society. In each category there is one group of people deemed superior, legitimate, dominant, and privileged while others are relegated—whether explicitly or implicitly—to the position of inferior, illegitimate, subordinate, and disadvantaged.

Category	Dominant	Subordinate
Gender	Men	Women, transgender people
Race	White	Peoples of color
Class	Middle and upper class	Poor, working class
Nation	U.S./First World	Second, Third Worlds
Ethnicity	European	All other ethnicities
Sexual orientation	Heterosexual	Lesbian, gay, bisexual, transgender
Religion	Christian	All other religions
Physical ability	Able-bodied	Persons with disabilities
Age	Youth	Elderly persons
Language	English	All other languages

This hierarchy of advantage and disadvantage has meant that the preponderance of analytical writing about identity has been done by those in subordinate positions: women of color, lesbians, bisexual women, and working-class women. . . . For White people descended from European immigrants to this country, the advantages of being White are not always fully recognized or acknowledged. . . . As a result, White people in the United States tend to think of all identities as equal: "I'm Italian American, you're Polish American. I'm Irish American, you're African American." This assumed equivalence ignores the very big differences between an individualist symbolic identity and a socially enforced and imposed racial identity. . . .

MAINTAINING SYSTEMS OF STRUCTURAL INEQUALITY

Maintaining this system of inequality requires the objectification and dehumanization of subordinated peoples. Appropriating their identities is a particularly effective method of doing this, for it defines who the subordinated group/person is or ought to be. This happens in several ways:

Using the values, characteristics, features of the dominant group as the supposedly neutral standard against which all others should be evaluated. For example, men are generally physically larger and stronger than women. Many of the clinical trials for new pharmaceutical drugs are conducted using men's bodies and activities as the standard. The results, however, are applied equally to both men and women. Women are often prescribed the same dosage of a medication as men are even though their physical makeup is not the same. Thus women, as a distinct group, do not exist in this research.

Using terms that distinguish the subordinate from the dominant group. Terms such as "non-White" and "minority" connote a relationship to another group, White in the former case and majority in the latter. A non-White person is the negative of the White person; a minority person is less than a majority person. Neither has an identity on her or his own terms.

Stereotyping. Stereotyping involves making a simple generalization about a group and claiming that all members of the group conform to this generalization. Stereotypes are behavioral and psychological attributes; they are commonly held beliefs about groups rather than individual beliefs about individuals; and they persist in spite of contradictory evidence. Lesbians hate men. Latinas are dominated by macho Latinos. Women with physical disabilities are asexual. Fat women are good-humored but not healthy. As Andre asserts, "A 'stereotype' is pejorative; there is always something objectionable in the beliefs and images to which the word refers."

Exoticizing and romanticizing. These two forms of appropriation are particularly insidious because on the surface there is an appearance of appreciation. For example, Asian American women are described as personifying the "mysterious orient," Native American women as "earth mothers" and the epitome of spirituality, and Black women as perpetual towers of strength. In all three cases, seemingly positive traits and cultural practices are identified and exalted. This "positive" stereotyping prevents people from seeing the truth and complexity of who these women are.

. . .

Given the significance of identity appropriation as an aspect of oppression, it is not surprising that many liberation struggles have included projects and efforts aimed at changing identities and taking control of the process of positive identity formation and representation. Before liberation struggles, oppressed people often use the same terminology to name themselves as the dominant group uses to label them. One crucial aspect of liberation struggles is to get rid of pejorative labels and use names that express, in their own terms, who people are in all their humanity. Thus the name a group uses for itself gradually takes on more of an insider perspective that fits the evolving consciousness growing out of the political movement.

As with individual identity, naming ourselves collectively is an important act of empowerment. One example of this is the evolution of the names African Americans have used to identify themselves, moving from Colored, to Negro, to Black to Afro-American, and African American. Similarly, Chinese Americans gradually rejected the derogatory label "Chink," preferring to be called Orientals and now Chinese Americans or Asians. These terms are used unevenly, sometimes according to the age and political orientation of the person or the geographic region, where one usage may be more popular than another.

Among the very diverse group of people connected historically, culturally, and linguistically to Spain, Portugal, and their former colonies (parts of the United States, Mexico, the Caribbean, and Central and South America), some use more inclusive terms such as Latino or Hispanic; others prefer more specific names such as Chicano, Puerto Rican, Nicaraguan, Cuban, and so on. . . .

COLONIZATION, IMMIGRATION, AND THE U.S. LANDSCAPE OF RACE AND CLASS

Other macro-level factors affecting people's identities include colonization and immigration. . . . This ideology that the United States is "a land of immigrants" obscures several important issues excluded from much mainstream debate about immigration: Not all Americans came to this country voluntarily. Native American peoples and Mexicans were already here on this continent, but the former experienced near-genocide and the latter were made foreigners in their own land. African peoples were captured, enslaved, and forcibly imported to this country to be laborers. All were brutally exploited and violated—physically, psychologically, culturally, and spiritually—to serve the interests of those in power. The relationships between these groups and this nation and their experiences in the United States are fundamentally different from the experiences of those who chose to immigrate here, though this is not to negate the hardships the latter may have faced. These differences profoundly shaped the social, cultural, political, and economic realities faced by these groups throughout history and continue to do so today.

. . . Early in the history of this country, for example, the Naturalization Law of 1790 (which was repealed as recently as 1952) prohibited peoples of color from becoming U.S. citizens, and the Slave Codes restricted every aspect of life for enslaved African peoples. These laws made race into an indelible line that separated "insiders" from "outsiders." White people were designated insiders and granted many privileges while all others were confined to systematic disadvantage. As Mary C. Waters points out, the stories that White Americans learn of how their grandparents and great-grandparents triumphed in the United States "are usually told in terms of their individual efforts." The role of labor unions, community organizations, and political parties, as well as the crucial importance of racism, is usually left out of these accounts, which emphasize individual effort and hard work.

. . .

On coming to the United States, immigrants are drawn into the racial landscape of this country. In media debates and official statistics, this is still dominated by a Black/White polarization in which everyone is assumed to fit into one of these two groups. Demographically, the situation is much more complex and diverse, but people of color, who comprise the more inclusive group, are still set off against White people, the dominant group. Immigrants identify themselves according to nationality—for example, as Cambodian or Guatemalan. Once in the United States they learn the significance of racial divisions in this country and may adopt the term *people of color* as an aspect of their identity here. . . .

This emphasis on race tends to mask differences based on class, another important distinction among immigrant groups. For example, the Chinese and Japanese people who came in the nineteenth century and early twentieth century to work on plantations in Hawai'i, as loggers in Oregon, or building roads and railroads in several western states were poor and from rural areas of China and Japan. The 1965 immigration law made way for "the second wave" of Asian immigration. It set preferences for professionals, highly skilled workers, and members of the middle and upper-middle classes, making this group "the most highly skilled of any immigrant group our country has ever had." The first wave of Vietnamese refugees who immigrated between the mid-1970s and 1980 were from the

middle and upper classes, and many were professionals; by contrast, the second wave of immigrants from Vietnam was composed of poor and rural people. The class backgrounds of immigrants affect not only their sense of themselves and their expectations but also how they can succeed as strangers in a foreign land. For example, a poor woman who arrives with no literacy skills in her own language will have a more difficult time learning to become literate in English than one who has several years of formal schooling in her country of origin that may have included basic English.

MULTIPLE IDENTITIES, SOCIAL LOCATION, AND CONTRADICTIONS

The social features of one's identity incorporate individual, community, societal, and global factors. The point where all the features embodied in a person overlap is called social location. Imagine a diagram made up of overlapping circles, with a circle representing one specific feature of identity such as gender, class, ability, age, and so on. A person's social location is the point at which a part of each circle touches all others—where all elements are present simultaneously. Social location is a way of expressing the core of a person's existence in the social and political world. It places us in particular relationships to others, to the dominant culture of the United States, and to the rest of the world. It determines the kinds of power and privilege we have access to and can exercise, as well as situations in which we have less power and privilege.

Because social location is where all the aspects of one's identity meet, our experience of our own complex identities is sometimes contradictory, conflictual, and paradoxical. We live with multiple identities that can be both enriching and contradictory and that push us to confront questions of loyalty to individuals and groups. . . .

3

The Social Construction of Difference

Allan G. Johnson

The late African American novelist James Baldwin once offered the provocative idea that there is no such thing as whiteness or, for that matter, blackness or, more generally, race. "No one is white before he/she came to America," he wrote. "It took generations and a vast amount of coercion, before this became a white country."

. . .

Baldwin isn't denying the reality that skin pigmentation varies from one person to another. What he is saying is that unless you live in a culture that recognizes such differences as significant, they are socially irrelevant and therefore, in a way, do not exist. A "black woman" in Africa, therefore, who has not experienced white racism, does not *think* of herself as black or experience herself as black, nor do the people around her. African, yes, a woman, yes. But not a *black* woman.

When she comes to the United States, however, where privilege is organized according to race, suddenly she becomes black because people assign her to a social category that bears that name, and they treat her differently as a result. . . .

So Baldwin is telling us that race and all its categories have no significance outside systems of privilege and oppression in which they were created in the first place. This is what sociologists call the "social construction" of reality.

. . .

The same is true with the definition of what is considered "normal." While it may come as a surprise to many who think of themselves as nondisabled, disability and nondisability are socially constructed. This doesn't mean that the difference between having or not having full use of your legs is somehow "made up" without any objective reality. It does mean, however, that how people notice and label and think about such differences and how they treat other people as a result depend entirely on ideas contained in a system's culture.

Human beings, for example, come in a variety of heights, and many of those considered "normal" are unable to reach high places such as kitchen shelves without the assistance of physical aids—chairs and step-stools. In spite of their inability to do this simple task without special aids, they are not defined as disabled. Nor are the roughly 100 million people in the United States who cannot see properly without the aid of eyeglasses. . . .

Disability and nondisability are . . . constructed through the language used to describe people. When someone who cannot see is labeled a "blind person," for example, it creates the impression that not being able to see sums up the entire person. In other words, blind becomes what they *are*. The same thing happens when people are described as "brain damaged" or "crippled" or "retarded" or "deaf"—the person becomes the disability and nothing more. Reducing people to a single dimension of who they are separates and excludes them, marks them as "other," as different from "normal" (white, heterosexual, male, nondisabled) people and therefore as inferior. . . .

There is a world of difference between using a wheelchair and being treated as a normal human being (who happens to use a wheelchair to get around) and using a wheelchair and being treated as invisible, inferior, unintelligent, asexual, frightening, passive, dependent, and nothing more than your disability. And that difference is not a matter of the disability itself but of how it is constructed in society and how we then make use of that construction in our minds to shape how we think about ourselves and other people and how we treat them as a result.

What makes socially constructed reality so powerful is that we rarely if ever experience it as that. We think the way our culture defines something like race or gender is simply the way things are in some objective sense. . . . In the 19th century, for example, U.S. law identified those having *any* African ancestry as black, a standard known as the "one-drop rule," which defined "white" as a state of absolute purity in relation to "black." Native American status, in contrast, required at *least* one-eighth Native American ancestry in order to qualify. Why the different standards? . . . Native Americans could claim financial benefits from the federal government, making it to whites' advantage to make it hard for anyone to be considered Native American. Designating someone as black, however, took *away* power and *denied* the right to make claims against whites, including white families of origin. In both cases, racial classification has had little to do with objective characteristics and everything to do with preserving white power and wealth.

This fact has also been true of the use of race to tag various ethnic groups. When the Chinese were imported as cheap laborers during the 19th century, the California Supreme Court declared them not white. Mexicans, however, many of whom owned large amounts of land in California and did business with whites, were considered white. Today, as Paul Kivel points out, Mexicans are no longer considered white and the Chinese are "conditionally white at times."

. . .

WHAT IS PRIVILEGE?

No matter what privileged group you belong to, if you want to understand the problem of privilege and difference, the first stumbling block is usually the idea of privilege itself. When people hear that they belong to a privileged group or benefit from something like "white privilege" or "male privilege," they don't get it, or they feel angry and defensive about what they do get. *Privilege* has become one of those loaded words we need to reclaim so that we can use it to name and illuminate the truth. . . .

Privilege exists when one group has something of value that is denied to others simply because of the groups they belong to, rather than because of anything they've done or failed to do. If people take me more seriously when I give a speech than they would someone of color saying the same things in the same way, then I'm benefiting from white privilege. That a heterosexual black woman can feel free to talk about her life in ways that reveal the fact that she's married to a man is a form of heterosexual privilege because lesbians and gay men cannot casually reveal their sexual orientation without putting themselves at risk.

. . .

WHAT PRIVILEGE LOOKS LIKE IN EVERYDAY LIFE

. . . Privilege shows up in the daily details of people's lives in almost every social setting. Consider the following examples of race privilege. . . .

- Whites are less likely than blacks to be arrested; once arrested, they are less likely to be convicted and, once convicted, less likely to go to prison, regardless of the crime or circumstances. Whites, for example, constitute 85 percent of those who use illegal drugs, but less than half of those in prison on drug-use charges are white.
. . .
- Whites are more likely than comparable blacks to have loan applications approved and less likely to be given poor information or the runaround during the application process.
- Whites are charged lower prices for new and used cars than are people of color, and residential segregation gives whites access to higher-quality goods of all kinds at cheaper prices.
. . .
- Whites are more likely to control conversations and be allowed to get away with it and to have their ideas and contributions taken seriously, including those that were suggested previously by a person of color and ignored or dismissed.
- Whites can usually assume that national heroes, success models, and other figures held up for general admiration will be of their race.
. . .
- Whites can assume that when they go shopping, they'll be treated as serious customers not as potential shoplifters or people without the money to make a purchase. When they try to cash a check or use a credit card, they can assume they won't be hassled for additional identification and will be given the benefit of the doubt.
. . .
- Most whites are not segregated into communities that isolate them from the best job opportunities, schools, and community services.
- Whites have greater access to quality education and health care.
. . .
- Whites can succeed without other people being surprised.

- Whites don't have to deal with an endless and exhausting stream of attention to their race. They can simply take their race for granted as unremarkable to the extent of experiencing themselves as not even having a race. Unlike some of my African American students, for example, I don't have people coming up to me and treating me as if I were some exotic "other," gushing about how "cool" or different I am, wanting to know where I'm "from," and reaching out to touch my hair.
- Whites don't find themselves slotted into occupations identified with their race, as blacks are often slotted into support positions or Asians into technical jobs.

. . .

- Whites can reasonably expect that if they work hard and "play by the rules," they'll get what they deserve, and they feel justified in complaining if they don't. It is something other racial groups cannot realistically expect.

In the following list for male privilege, note how some items repeat from the list on race but other items do not.

- In most professions and upper-level occupations, men are held to a lower standard than women. It is easier for a "good but not great" male lawyer to make partner than it is for a comparable woman.
- Men are charged lower prices for new and used cars.
- If men do poorly at something or make a mistake or commit a crime, they can generally assume that people won't attribute the failure to their gender. The kids who shoot teachers and schoolmates are almost always boys, but rarely is the fact that all this violence is being done by males raised as an important issue.

. . .

- Men can generally assume that when they go out in public, they won't be sexually harassed or assaulted just because they're male, and if they are victimized, they won't be asked to explain what they were doing there.
- Male representation in government and the ruling circles of corporations and other organizations is disproportionately high.

. . .

- Men are more likely than women are to control conversations and be allowed to get away with it and to have their ideas and contributions taken seriously, even those that were suggested previously by a woman and dismissed or ignored.
- Most men can assume that their gender won't be used to determine whether they'll fit in at work or whether teammates will feel comfortable working with them.
- Men can succeed without other people being surprised.
- Men don't have to deal with an endless and exhausting stream of attention drawn to their gender (for example, to how sexually attractive they are).
- Men don't find themselves slotted into a narrow range of occupations identified with their gender as women are slotted into community relations, human resources, social work, elementary school teaching, librarianship, nursing, and clerical, and secretarial positions.

. . .

- The standards used to evaluate men as *men* are consistent with the standards used to evaluate them in other roles such as occupations. Standards used to evaluate women as women are often different from those used to evaluate them in other roles. For example, a man can be both a "real man" and a successful and aggressive lawyer, while an aggressive woman lawyer may succeed as a lawyer but be judged as not measuring up as a woman.

In the following list regarding sexual orientation, note again items in common with the other two lists and items peculiar to this form of privilege.

- Heterosexuals are free to reveal and live their intimate relationships openly—by referring to their partners by name, recounting experiences, going out in public together, displaying pictures on their desks at work—without being accused of "flaunting" their sexuality or risking discrimination.
- Heterosexuals can marry as a way to commit to long-term relationships that are socially recognized, supported, and legitimated. This fact confers basic rights such as spousal health benefits, the ability to adopt children, inheritance, joint filing of income tax returns, and the power to make decisions for a spouse who is incapacitated in a medical emergency.

. . .

- Heterosexuals can move about in public without fear of being harassed or physically attacked because of their sexual orientation.
- Heterosexuals don't run the risk of being reduced to a single aspect of their lives, as if being heterosexual summed up the kind of person they are. Instead, they can be viewed and treated as complex human beings who happen to be heterosexual.
- Heterosexuals can usually assume that national heroes, success models, and other figures held up for general admiration will be assumed to be heterosexual.
- Most heterosexuals can assume that their sexual orientation won't be used to determine whether they'll fit in at work or whether teammates will feel comfortable working with them.
- Heterosexuals don't have to worry that their sexual orientation will be used as a weapon against them, to undermine their achievements or power.

. . .

- Heterosexuals can live where they want without having to worry about neighbors who disapprove of their sexual orientation.
- Heterosexuals can live in the comfort of knowing that other people's assumptions about their sexual orientation are correct.

In the following list regarding disability status, note again items in common with the other lists and items peculiar to this form of privilege.

- Nondisabled people can choose whether to be conscious of their disability status or to ignore it and regard themselves simply as human beings.
- Nondisabled people can live secure in other people's assumption that they are sexual beings capable of an active sex life, including the potential to have children and be parents.

. . .

- Nondisabled people can assume that they will fit in at work and in other settings without having to worry about being evaluated and judged according to preconceived notions and stereotypes about people with disabilities.

. . .

- Nondisabled people don't have to deal with an endless and exhausting stream of attention to their disability status. They can simply take their disability status for granted as unremarkable to the extent of experiencing themselves as not even having one.
- Nondisabled people can ask for help without having to worry that people will assume they need help with everything.
- Nondisabled people can succeed without people being surprised because of low expectations of their ability to contribute to society.

- Nondisabled people can expect to pay lower prices for cars because they are assumed to be mentally unimpaired and less likely to allow themselves to be misled and exploited.

. . .

- Nondisabled people are more likely to control conversations and be allowed to get away with it and have their ideas and contributions taken seriously, including those that were suggested before by a person with disabilities and then dismissed or ignored.
- Nondisabled people can assume that national heroes, success models, and other figures held up for general admiration will share their disability status.

. . .

- Nondisabled people can generally assume that when they go out in public, they won't be looked at as odd or out of place or not belonging. They can also assume that most buildings and other structures will not be designed in ways that limit their access.
- Nondisabled people can assume that when they need to travel from one place to another, they will have access to buses, trains, airplanes, and other means of transportation.
- Nondisabled people can count on being taken seriously and not treated as children.
- Nondisabled people are less likely to be segregated into living situations—such as nursing homes and special schools and sports programs—that isolate them from job opportunities, schools, community services, and the everyday workings of life in a society.

. . .

Regardless of which group we're talking about, privilege generally allows people to assume a certain level of acceptance, inclusion, and respect in the world, to operate within a relatively wide comfort zone. Privilege increases the odds of having things your own way, of being able to set the agenda in a social situation and determine the rules and standards and how they're applied. Privilege grants the cultural authority to make judgments about others and to have those judgements stick. It allows people to define reality and to have prevailing definitions of reality fit their experience. Privilege means being able to decide who gets taken seriously, who receives attention, who is accountable to whom and for what. And it grants a presumption of superiority and social permission to act on that presumption without having to worry about being challenged.

To have privilege is to be allowed to move through your life without being marked in ways that identify you as an outsider, as exceptional or "other" to be excluded, or to be included but always with conditions. . . .

OPPRESSION: THE FLIP SIDE OF PRIVILEGE

For every social category that is privileged, one or more other categories are oppressed in relation to it. . . . Just as privilege tends to open doors of opportunity, oppression tends to slam them shut.

Like privilege, oppression results from the social relationship between privileged and oppressed categories, which makes it possible for individuals to vary in their personal experience of being oppressed ("I've never been oppressed as a woman"). This also means, however, that in order to have the experience of being oppressed, it is necessary to belong to an oppressed category. In other words, men cannot be oppressed *as men*, just as whites cannot be oppressed as whites or heterosexuals as heterosexuals, because a group can be oppressed only if there exists another group with the power to oppress them.

As we saw earlier, people in privileged categories can certainly feel bad in ways that can feel oppressive. Men, for example, can feel burdened by what they take to be their responsibility to provide for their families. Or they can feel limited and even damaged by the

requirement that "real men" must avoid expressing feelings other than anger. But although access to privilege costs them something that may *feel* oppressive, to call it oppression distorts the nature of what is happening to them and why.

. . .

The complexity of systems of privilege makes it possible, of course, for men to experience oppression if they also happen to be of color or gay or disabled or in a lower social class, but not simply because they are male. In the same way, whites can experience oppression for many reasons, but not because they're white.

. . .

Finally, being in a privileged category that has an oppressive relationship with another isn't the same as being an oppressive *person* who behaves in oppressive ways. That males as a social category oppress females as a social category, for example, is a social fact. That doesn't, however, tell us how a particular man thinks or feels about particular women or behaves toward them. This can be a subtle distinction to hang on to, but hang on to it we must if we're going to maintain a clear idea of what oppression is and how it works in defense of privilege.

. . .

4

Theoretical Foundations

Lee Anne Bell

WHAT IS SOCIAL JUSTICE?

We believe that social justice is both a process and a goal. The goal of social justice is full and equal participation of all groups in a society that is mutually shaped to meet their needs. Social justice includes a vision of society in which the distribution of resources is equitable and all members are physically and psychologically safe and secure. We envision a society in which individuals are both self-determining (able to develop their full capacities) and interdependent (capable of interacting democratically with others). Social justice involves social actors who have a sense of their own agency as well as a sense of social responsibility toward and with others, their society, and the broader world in which we live. These are conditions we wish not only for our own society but also for every society in our interdependent global community.

. . .

We realize that developing a social justice process in a society and world steeped in oppression is no simple feat. For this reason, we need clear ways to define and analyze oppression so that we can understand how it operates at individual, cultural, and institutional levels, historically and in the present. Although inevitably an oversimplification of a complex social phenomenon, we believe that the conceptual frameworks presented here can help us make sense of and, hopefully, act more effectively against oppressive circumstances as these arise in our teaching and activism.

WHY SOCIAL JUSTICE EDUCATION NEEDS A THEORY OF OPPRESSION

Practice is always shaped by theory, whether formal or informal, tacit or expressed. How we approach social justice education, the problems we identify as needing remedy, the solutions we entertain as viable, and the methods we choose as appropriate for reaching those solutions are all theoretical as well as practical questions. Theory and practice intertwine as parts of the interactive and historical process that Freire calls "praxis."

DEFINING FEATURES OF OPPRESSION

PERVASIVE

We use the term *oppression* rather than discrimination, bias, prejudice, or bigotry to emphasize the pervasive nature of social inequality woven throughout social institutions as well as embedded within individual consciousness. The term *oppression* encapsulates the fusion of institutional and systemic discrimination, personal bias, bigotry, and social prejudice in a complex web of relationships and structures that shade most aspects of life in our society. . . . Woven together through time and reinforced in the present, these patterns provide an example of the pervasive of oppression.

RESTRICTIVE

On the most general level, oppression denotes structural and material constraints that significantly shape a person's life chances and sense of possibility. Oppression restricts both self-development and self-determination. It delimits who one can imagine becoming and the power to act in support of one's rights and aspirations. A girl-child in the United States in 2006, for example, especially if she is poor or of color, is still unlikely to imagine herself as president since, unlike many other countries, we have yet to elect a woman to this high office. 140 years after the abolition of slavery, African Americans as a group have still not achieved full equality and cannot even rely on their government for basic human treatment and aid in a time of crisis, as in the recent scandalous government desertion of the victims of Hurricane Katrina. Despite rhetoric that anyone can get ahead if they work hard enough, a father's economic status continues to be the best predictor of the status of his offspring, a situation that worsens as economic inequality grows and the possibilities for social mobility steadily decline.

HIERARCHICAL

Oppression signifies a hierarchical relationship in which dominant or privileged groups reap advantage, often in unconscious ways, from the disempowerment of targeted groups. Whites, for example, gain privilege as a dominant group because they benefit from access to social power and privilege, not equally available to people of color. As a group, Whites earn more money and accumulate more assets than other racial groups, hold the majority of positions of power and influence, and command the controlling institutions in society. White-dominated institutions restrict the life expectancy, infant mortality, income, housing, employment, and educational opportunities of people of color.

COMPLEX, MULTIPLE, CROSS-CUTTING RELATIONSHIPS

Power and privilege are relative, however, because individuals hold multiple complex and cross-cutting social group memberships that confer relative privilege or disadvantage differently in different contexts. Identity is not simply additive but multiplicative. An upper-class professional man who is African American, for example (still a very small percentage of African Americans overall), may enjoy economic success and professional status conferred through male, class, and perhaps dominant language and citizenship privilege as an English-speaking native-born citizen, yet face limitations not endured by white, male and female, or foreign national coworkers. Despite economic and professional status and success, he may be threatened by police, be unable to hail a taxi, and endure hateful epithets as he walks down the street. The constellation of identities that shape his consciousness and experience as an African American man, and his varying access to privilege, may fluctuate depending upon whether he is light or dark skinned, Ivy League-educated or a high school dropout, incarcerated, unemployed, or a tourist in South Africa, Brazil, or Europe.

INTERNALIZED

Oppression not only resides in external social institutions and norms but lodges in the human psyche as well. Oppressive beliefs are internalized by victims as well as perpetrators. The idea that poor people somehow deserve and are responsible for poverty, rather than the economic system that structures and requires it, is learned by poor and affluent alike. Homophobia, the deep fear and hatred of homosexuality, is internalized by both straight and gay people. Jews as well as Gentiles absorb antisemitic stereotypes.

. . .

SHARED AND DISTINCTIVE CHARACTERISTICS OF "ISMS"

In grappling with these questions, we have come to believe in the explanatory and political value of identifying both the particular histories and characteristics of specific forms of oppression such as ableism or classism, as well as the patterns that connect and mutually reinforce different oppressions in a system that is inclusive and pervasive. In this book we examine the unique ways in which oppression is manifested through racism, white privilege, and immigrant status; sexism, heterosexism, and transgender experiences; religious oppression and antisemitism; and classism, ableism, and ageism/adultism.

We look at the dimensions of experience that connect these "isms" in an overarching system of domination. For example, we examine the roles of a dominant or advantaged group and (a) subordinated or targeted group(s) in each form of oppression and the differentials of power and privilege that are dynamic features of oppression, whatever its particular form. At the same time, we try to highlight the distinctive qualities and appreciate the historical and social contingencies that distinguish one form of oppression from another. In this model, diversity and the appreciation of differences are inextricably tied to social justice and the unequal ways that power and privilege construct difference in our society.

From our perspective, no one form of oppression is the base for all others, yet all are connected within a system that makes them possible. We align with theorists such as Young who describe distinctive ingredients of oppression without prioritizing one over another. We also share with Young the view that eradicating oppression ultimately requires struggle against all its forms, and that coalitions among diverse people offer the most promising strategies for challenging oppression systematically. Therefore, we highlight theory and practice that demonstrate interconnections among different forms of oppression and suggest common strategies to oppose it collectively.

. . .

CONSTRUCTING AN INCLUSIVE THEORY OF OPPRESSION

We touch on concepts from writing and activism in the Civil Rights, New Left, and women's liberation movements of the 1960s and 1970s, and from more recent movements for equality and social change, to discern lessons about oppression that provide a conceptual framework for understanding its operations. Tracking the history of ideas developed in these movements grounds our theoretical understanding in lived experience and highlights the contradictions and conflicts in different approaches to oppression and social justice as these are lived out in practice over time and place. Here, we highlight broad themes drawn from rich and well-developed academic and social movement traditions to which we are indebted.

RACISM

The social science literature on racism and insights about racism that emerged from the Civil Rights movement of the late 1950s and early 1960s profoundly shaped the way scholars and activists have come to understand oppression and its other manifestations. The Civil Rights movement fired the imagination of millions of Americans, who applied its lessons to an understanding of their particular situations and adapted its analyses and tactics to their own struggles for equality. For example, Native American, Chicano, and Puerto Rican youth styled themselves after the African American youth in the Student Nonviolent Coordinating Committee (SNCC) and Black Panther Party. The predominantly white student antiwar movement drew directly from the experiences of the black freedom struggles to shape their goals and strategies. Early women's liberation groups were spawned within SNCC itself, as black and white women applied the analyses of racial inequality to their own positions as women, as did Latinas within the Puerto Rican Youth. The gay liberation and disability rights movements credit the Civil Rights movement as a model for their organizing and activism, and poor people's and welfare rights movements likewise drew upon this heritage as do immigrant and youth activists today.

Of the many valuable legacies of the Civil Rights movement and the academic traditions focusing on racism, we highlight here two key themes. One is the awareness that racism is a system of oppression that not only stigmatizes and violates the targeted group, but also does psychic and ethical violence to the dominator group as well. The idea that oppression affects, albeit in different ways, both those advantaged and those targeted by oppression has been useful to many other groups as a way to make sense of their experiences of oppression.

The second broad theme is that racism functions not only through overt, conscious prejudice and discrimination but also through the unconscious attitudes and behaviors of a society that presumes an unacknowledged but pervasive white cultural norm. Racial images and ideas are embedded in language and cultural practices promoted as neutral and inclusive. However, the alleged neutrality of social patterns, behaviors, and assumptions in fact define and reinforce a form of cultural imperialism that supports white supremacy. Identifying unmarked and unacknowledged norms that bolster the power position of advantaged groups is an important strategy for examining other forms of oppression as well. Feminists, for example, use the idea to examine practices of male supremacy and patriarchy, and gay and lesbian rights activists use it to analyze heterosexual privilege.

The concept of racial formation has become an important analytic tool. This concept is useful for thinking about the ways in which racism is constructed and reconstructed in different contexts and periods. It works against the tendency to essentialize current social relations as given and encourages ideas about alternative ways to frame and understand human relations against systems of oppression. Critical race theory, Lat Crit theory, and

Whiteness studies offer other important tools for analyzing oppression through the use of story to represent how racism operates and to invent alternative scenarios of possibility. . . .

CLASSISM

The New Left movements of the late 1960s and early 1970s espoused ideals of political democracy and personal liberty and applied their political energy to make power socially accountable. New Left critiques of power built on Marxist theory to examine issues of domination and exploitation and to focus on the structural rather than individual factors that maintain oppressive economic and social relations. They also exposed and critiqued normative assumptions that conflate democracy with capitalism and its role in suppressing the exploration of alternative economic and social arrangements.

New Left analyses examine how power operates through normalizing relations of domination and systematizing ideas and practices that are then taken as given. These analyses remind us to continually ask the question "In whose interest do prevailing systems operate?" The question of power and the interests it serves has been a useful analytic tool for examining oppression in all of its multiple forms. Asking who benefits and who pays for prevailing practices helps to expose the hierarchical relationships as well as the hidden advantages and penalties embedded in a purportedly fair and neutral system.

Postcolonial scholars and activists have extended these questions to an analysis of the power dynamics within global relations of transnational capital and their impact on labor, migration, gender and ethnic relations, environmental issues, and national development around the globe. These analyses of how power circulates alert us to the evershifting ways in which power maintains itself in support of the status quo and to the flexibility and persistence necessary to continually challenge its operations.

SEXISM

The women's liberation movement developed important theoretical and analytic tools for a general theory of oppression and liberation. Through consciousness-raising groups, women collectively uncovered and deconstructed the ways that the system of patriarchy is reproduced inside women's consciousness as well as in external social institutions, and challenged conventional assumptions about human nature, sexuality, family life, and gender roles and relations. Consciousness-raising groups developed a process for naming how members of targeted groups can collude in maintaining an unequal system, identifying the psychological as well as social factors that contribute to internalizing oppressive beliefs, and exploring how to raise consciousness to resist and challenge such systems both inside our own consciousness and externally in the world. Feminist practice also sought to create and enact new, more liberated ways of thinking and behaving. Insights from feminist theory and practice have been fruitfully used by other groups to raise consciousness, develop analyses of psychological and social assumptions and practices of their group(s) as these collude in maintaining oppression, and experiment with alternative practices.

MULTIPLE ISSUES

Women of color, lesbians, Jewish feminists, and poor and working-class women brought forth critiques from within the women's movement to critique unitary theories of feminism, stressing the multiple and diverse perspectives, needs, and goals of women from different social groups. These challenges have been used to critique unitary theories of class, race, and gender and to generate a range of analyses and ideas about oppression(s) that take into account both the multiple identities people hold and the range of experiences of oppression lived within any given group. Women of color who are lesbian and poor, for example, experience oppression in multiple and distinctive ways that demand more complex analyses of the mechanisms of oppression in the lives of diverse groups of people. Global feminism and global critical race feminism both critique and add to the strategies and theories developed by previous feminists, highlighting the leadership of women at the margins, building transnational consciousness of shared and distinctive problems women face under postcolonial systems and U.S. imperialism, and developing strategies and solutions locally to address the particularities of their national contexts.

Postcolonial studies and postmodern theories, and ongoing discussions among people in various social movements, continue to challenge binary categorization such as black/white, heterosexual/homosexual, male/female, and notions that essentialize, or treat as innately given, the groupings created within an oppressive social order. The inadequacy of defining the experience of individuals and groups in simplistic binary terms is reflected through challenges within the gay and lesbian movement raised by bisexual, transsexual, and transgender people. The range of experiences of people holding multiple identities and diverse social group memberships poses continuing challenges that theories of oppression account for their experiences.

. . .

4 (CONTINUED)

Conceptual Foundations

Rita Hardiman, Bailey W. Jackson, and Pat Griffin

. . .

CHOICE OF LABELS FOR OPPRESSOR AND OPPRESSED GROUPS

There are currently many terms that are used to describe oppressed and oppressor groups and the individual members of those groups. Oppressed groups are variously referred to as *targets, the targeted, victims, disadvantaged, subordinates,* or *the subordinated.* Oppressor groups are often referred to as *advantaged, dominants, agents,* and *privileged.* The reasons for choosing one term over another vary depending on a number of theoretical, political, pedagogical, and strategic considerations. Indeed, none of these terms is universally

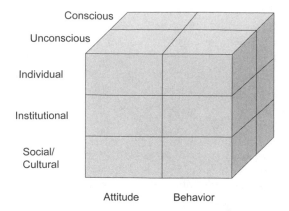

Figure 4.1 Multiple Dimensions of Oppression

accepted. As educators, we must be careful, however, not to trivialize the effects of oppression by the terms that we use in describing this serious social condition and the roles individual people play in the maintenance of this social system. . . .

OPPRESSION OPERATES ON MULTIPLE DIMENSIONS

Oppression is an interlocking, multileveled system that consolidates social power to the benefit of members of privileged groups and is maintained and operationalized on three dimensions: (a) contextual dimension, (b) conscious/unconscious dimension, and (c) applied dimension (see Figure 4.1).

The contextual dimension consists of three levels: (a) individual, (b) institutional, and (c) social/cultural. The conscious/unconscious dimension describes how oppression is both intentional and unintentional. The applied dimension describes how oppression is manifested at the individual (attitudes and behaviors), institutional (policies, practices, and norms), and societal/cultural (values, beliefs, and customs) levels. The conscious/unconscious and the applied dimensions will be discussed further within the descriptions of each of the three contextual levels below:

INDIVIDUAL LEVEL

Oppression is maintained at the individual level by attitudes or behaviors of individual persons. These attitudes and behaviors can be conscious or unconscious, but their effects are equally destructive. Examples of individual actions or attitudes include the belief that women are not as capable of making reasonable, rational decisions as men are (conscious attitude); a male employer making unwanted sexual comments to a female employee in the workplace (conscious behavior); a white person automatically taking extra care to protect personal belongings when in the presence of black or Latino people (unconscious attitude); or a temporarily able-bodied person speaking loudly or slowly and using simple terms when addressing a physically disabled person (unconscious behavior).

INSTITUTIONAL LEVEL

Social institutions such as the family, government, business and industry, education, the legal system, and religious organizations are major participants in a system of oppression.

Social institutions codify oppression in laws, policies, practices, and norms. As with behaviors and attitudes at the individual level, institutional policies and practices that maintain and enforce oppression are both intentional and unintentional. Examples of the less visible systems include the structural inequality of school funding in the United States, or tax benefits, health care benefits, and similar privileges that are available only to heterosexual couples through the institution of marriage. Other examples of institutional attitudes include the following: lack of an exit interview policy with faculty persons of color who take positions elsewhere to determine how a university can improve its ability to retain faculty of color in a predominantly white university (unconscious institutional norm), a business that decides not to provide bereavement leave to a lesbian employee whose partner dies (conscious institutional policy), and a state legislature that passes a law barring illegal immigrants from accessing public services (conscious institutional law).

Institutions fail to address discrimination and inequality or fail to see the discriminatory consequences of their policies and practices as often as they intentionally act to support, maintain, or advocate social oppression: for example, failing to enforce existing sexual harassment policies or deciding to hold an organizational social event in an inaccessible space without thinking that this decision might preclude the participation of members with mobility impairments.

SOCIETAL/CULTURAL LEVEL

Society's cultural norms and patterns perpetuate implicit and explicit values that bind institutions and individuals. In an oppressive society, the cultural perspective of dominant groups is imposed on institutions by individuals and on individuals by institutions. These cultural norms include philosophies of life, definitions of good and evil, beauty, normal, health, deviance, sickness, and perspectives on time, just to name a few. Cultural norms often serve the primary function of providing individuals and institutions with the justification for social oppression. Examples of these cultural beliefs or norms that influence the perspective of individual and institutional actions and attitudes include the assumption that the definition of a family is a heterosexual nuclear family (can be either conscious or unconscious norm) and the belief that anyone can achieve economic stability in the United States if they are willing to work hard and take personal responsibility for their own achievements (conscious norm).

WE ARE SOCIALIZED TO ACCEPT SYSTEMS OF OPPRESSION AS NORMAL

We are socialized into a system of social oppression through interactions with individuals, institutions, and culture. We learn to accept systems of oppression as normal through interactions with parents, peers, teachers, and other influential individuals in our lives as they, intentionally or unintentionally, pass on to us their beliefs about oppressor and oppressed groups. We also learn to accept oppression as normal through our experiences in schools and religious organizations, and our encounters with health care, criminal justice systems, and other institutions that affect our daily lives. We may not recognize how our embeddedness in particular cultural norms and values affects our views of oppressor and oppressed groups because of the pervasive presence of oppressor ideology. When viewed as a whole, our socialization into acceptance of oppressive systems, through our interactions with individuals, institutions, and cultural norms and values, constitutes a cycle of business as usual until we are able to interrupt it with information or experiences that call into question the truth of what we have learned about the power relationships among different social groups and our own position vis-à-vis these dynamics. At this point, we can choose to interrupt our socialization, to step out of the cycle of socialization with new awareness, information, and action.

THE SYSTEM OF SOCIAL OPPRESSION CO-OPTS THE SOCIAL CATEGORIES USED TO DESCRIBE THE DIFFERENCES AMONG AND BETWEEN SOCIAL GROUPS

. . .

We all have memberships in multiple social identity groups. That is to say, we can be described by our sex, race, sexual orientation, gender, religion, class, age, and ability. Naming our social group memberships/differences serves as a means of naming/describing our social/cultural groupings. They are primarily a way to describe our social group differences. . . . Though we experience our social group memberships as material, tangible identities (for example, woman, Black, heterosexual), we also inherit status associated with these identities in a system of oppression. In this way, oppression co-opts identities by attaching meaning and status to them that support the system of social oppression. The pervasive and systematic nature of oppression normalizes the redefined nature of the differences associated with social identity and transforms them into oppressed and oppressor social group identities at the expense of more neutral or alternative conceptions of identities and status (see Figure 4.2).

Members of oppressed groups are often more acutely aware of their membership because they experience the daily effects of oppression. Members of oppressor groups, on the other hand, are often unaware of themselves as members of a privileged group because the system of oppression enables and encourages them to view the accomplishments and achievements of their group members as deserved, the result of hard work, virtue, or natural superiority. At the same time, members of oppressor groups often blame the struggles, failures, and anger of members of oppressed groups on their inability, deficiency, or refusal to accept things as they are.

We are born into some of our social identities (e.g., race and ethnicity), and others either can be present at birth or can change or be acquired during our lifetime (e.g., age, class, religion, or physical/development ability). For some social group memberships, such as sexual orientation, the debate over whether we are born into or choose our sexual orientation has political consequences for the struggle for gay, lesbian, and bisexual rights. Opponents of gay rights in part base their arguments on the belief that homosexuality and bisexuality are sinful, immoral, and psychologically disturbed behavior choices. Many, but not all, gay rights proponents insist that sexual orientation is not a choice, but a characteristic with which we are born. Similarly, the transgender rights movement has challenged

Examples of Manifestations of Social Oppression	Examples of Oppressor Groups (US-Based)	Examples of Oppressed Groups (US-Based)
Classism	Owning Class, Upper Middle Class, Middle Class	Working Class, Poor
Heterosexism	Heterosexuals	Lesbians, Bisexuals, Gay Men
Ableism	Physical/Developmentally/ Psychologically Able-Bodied People	Physically/Developmentally/ Psychologically Disabled People
Racism	Whites	African American; Asian American; Latina/o; Native American; Multi-Racial People
Religious Oppression	Christians	Jews, Hindus, Buddhists, Muslims, Atheists
Sexism	Men	Women

Figure 4.2 Examples of Multiple Manifestations and Oppressor and Oppressed Groups

beliefs about the immutability of sex and gender assigned at birth, calling for a more fluid, nonbinary conception of gender and sex.

Most of us have social identities that are disadvantaged by some forms of oppression and privileged by others. Because our membership in oppressor or oppressed groups can change during our lifetime, our relative status in relationship to our multiple identities is not static. For example, a white man who becomes disabled, a Latina with working-class roots who becomes the CEO of a large corporation, or any of us as we grow old and experience changes in our status associated with aging, declining economic status, or disability, experience changes in social status related to group memberships.

Some forms of oppression are closely correlated; thus . . . if one is poor in the United States, whether destitute or among the working poor or chronically unemployed, one is more likely to experience illness and impairments that lead to disability due to the lack of access to health care. Similarly, acquiring a disability is closely correlated with being unemployed, being underemployed, or otherwise living on the economic margins of society without adequate access to health care.

The paradigm of "intersectionality," emerging from the fields of sociology, cultural studies, and critical race theory, informs our understanding of the complexities of how people experience privilege and disadvantage based on their social group memberships. Intersectionality suggests that markers of difference do not act independent of one another. Instead, our various social identities interrelate to negate the possibility of a unitary or universal experience of any one manifestation of oppression. An Asian or Latino gay man experiences the privilege of sexism in different ways than a white European heterosexual man because his experience of male privilege is muted by his identity as a man of color in a racist society and a gay man in a homophobic society.

. . .

The list of possible social identities is necessarily incomplete as our understanding of systems of oppression and liberation continues to evolve. Because the list of categories of social groups and the descriptions and types of social group change and expand over time with the heightening of our social consciousness, it is necessary that we acknowledge the limitations of current conceptualizations. For example, sexual orientation (gay, lesbian, bisexual, or heterosexual) was not a distinct identity until the late 19th century. Likewise, transgender and intersex identities as well as many emergent associated identities like "genderqueer" have only entered the lexicon of oppression in the last 15 years.

BORDER IDENTITIES

No attempt to describe the complex dynamics of oppression can be completely all-encompassing of lived experience. Some social identities do not clearly fit into a binary model of oppressed/targeted or oppressor/advantaged. We acknowledge this limitation with the designation *border identities*. Examples of border identities include people of mixed racial backgrounds, and persons who are bicultural by virtue of being born or raised in one country or culture and moving to a new country and cultural milieu. Adopted children of one race who are raised by persons of a different race may also occupy bordered space. Some social identities that could at one time be characterized as targeted identities have, over time, migrated to the advantaged side of the binary or at least moved out of the targeted category as oppressors rename and redefine targeted groups for their own benefit. For example, Roman Catholics were historically subjected to discrimination and violence, but are now integrated into the fabric of mainstream religions in the United States with considerable political power.

Some individuals with border identities may experience both privilege and disadvantage due to their status. For instance a bisexual man who is in a heterosexual marriage is both privileged by having access to rights only enjoyed by heterosexuals, and also potentially targeted by his identity as a bisexual in a binary system of sexual orientation. A transgender or transsexual man may intentionally or unintentionally benefit from male privilege after transitioning yet still be discriminated against by health care, criminal justice, or other social institutions because he is transgender. Similarly, children of color who are adopted by white families may have access to both race or class privilege from their parents, but are also targeted by racism due to their appearance and cultural characteristics.

DISADVANTAGED BY ASSOCIATION

Another group that does not fit within the binary notion of oppressor/advantaged or oppressed/targeted are those who occupy an intermediary or gray space due to their relationship to family members or significant others in their lives. These persons might include parents, spouses/partners, or family members of people with disabilities; parents or siblings of lesbians, gays, bisexual, or transgender people; or white people who are married or partnered to people of color, or have children of color. For example, able-bodied parents of a disabled child may have privilege as nondisabled people, yet their life circumstances are profoundly affected by their relationship to a disabled individual—their child. Their child's targeted status affects the family's income, housing, ability to travel, employment, and social interactions in their community. They may have to deal with the stereotypes or stigma attached to their child or other family member.

Similarly, a white member of a mixed-race couple or a white parent of mixed-race children is affected by racism in a secondary way and has less clear access to systems that advantage Whites in a racist society, due to this relationship. The mixed-race family's ability to find housing, social acceptance, employment, and safety is affected by racism, and this therefore has an impact on the white member of the family as well as the family members who are people of color. People in these situations are "disadvantaged by association" and live a dual existence: having access to privilege and resources in some capacities due to their personal dominant status, but also being a target of discrimination and other manifestations of oppression due to their family status. Individuals who are disadvantaged by association, however, do not automatically become allies. Many individuals in these relationships continue to support or participate in the system of oppression to which their loved one, and indeed they, are subjected by encouraging assimilation or other strategies that collude with oppression.

RELATIONSHIPS AMONG AND BETWEEN OPPRESSOR AND
OPPRESSED GROUPS IN A SYSTEM OF OPPRESSION

. . .

INTERNALIZED SUBORDINATION AND DOMINATION

Oppressive systems work most effectively when both advantaged and targeted group members internalize their roles and accept their positions in the hierarchical relationship between them.

Internalized subordination refers to ways in which the oppressed collude with their own oppression. Targeted social groups can live within a system of oppression that injures them or deprives them of certain rights without having the language or consciousness. Freire used the term *conscientization* to name their understanding of their situation as an effect of oppression rather than the natural order of things. Memmi described this process as *psychological colonization* when disadvantaged groups internalize their oppressed condition and collude with the oppressive ideology and social system. Freire refers to this process as oppressed groups playing host to the oppressor.

People who have been socialized in an oppressive environment, and who internalize the dominant group's ideology about their group, have learned to accept a definition of themselves that is hurtful and limiting. They think, feel, and act in ways that demonstrate the devaluation of their group and accept themselves as members of an inferior group. For example, internalized subordination is operating when oppressed group members question the credentials or abilities of members of their own social group without cause, yet unquestioningly accept that members of the oppressor group are qualified, talented, and deserving of their credentials. Internalized subordination also operates when target group members curry favor with dominant group members and distance themselves from their own group.

Conscious collusion occurs when oppressed group members knowingly, but not necessarily voluntarily, go along with their own mistreatment to survive or to maintain some status, livelihood, or other benefit, as when a person of color silently endures racist jokes told by a boss. Such collusion is often seen by the targeted group member as necessary to "live to fight another day." The more insidious form of collusion is unconscious, not knowing that one is collaborating with one's own dehumanization: for example, when a woman blames herself for the actions of her rapist or batterer or when gay and lesbian people, in order to gain acceptance from heterosexuals, exclude members of their community who look or act "too gay."

Internalized domination refers to the behaviors, thoughts, and feelings of oppressor group members who, through their socialization as members of the dominant group, learn to think and act in ways that express internalized notions of entitlement and privilege. Members of oppressor groups are socialized to internalize their dominant status so that it is not seen as privileged, but is experienced as the natural order of things, as rights, rather than as a consequence of systems that provide them with advantages not readily available to other groups.

Examples of internalized domination include men talking over and interrupting women in conversation, while simultaneously labeling women as chatty. Privileged groups learn to expect to be treated well and to be accommodated, as when English-only-speaking people in the United States get irritated when English language learners speak English with an accent. Extreme examples include the "erasure" of targeted group members by failing to acknowledge their existence or importance. For example, historical presentations that Columbus discovered America erase the existence of native peoples who preceded him by several thousand years.

. . .

INDIVIDUAL AND SOCIAL CHANGE

Now that we have described the characteristics of social oppression and the dynamics that serve to maintain oppressive systems, we turn our attention to an equally important topic in our courses: fostering individual and social change. . . . To be able to envision oneself as a change agent, it is necessary to have language that describes this role. We use the terms

ally for advantaged group members and *empowered targeted group members* to refer to these change agent roles.

ALLIES

Allies are members of the advantaged group who act against the oppression(s) from which they derive power, privilege, and acceptance. Individuals who choose to ally themselves with people who are targeted by oppression may have different motivations for their actions. Some allies may be motivated by an understanding that their privileges come at a cost, and working against oppression can be in one's self-interest. For example, understanding how eliminating architectural barriers that limit people with disabilities' access to buildings can also benefit temporarily able-bodied people as they themselves age or become disabled. Other allies may be motivated to act by altruistic feelings or by a moral or spiritual belief that oppression is wrong. Another source of motivation may come from one's experience as a person who is "disadvantaged by association" with people who are targeted. For example, having a child who is disabled or having a family member "come out" as lesbian or gay can spur family members to become allies against the oppression that is targeting their loved ones, and themselves by extension. Whatever the motivation for allies, their role as change agents, working with other privileged group members or in coalition with targeted group members to challenge systems of oppression, is an essential aspect of eliminating inequality.

EMPOWERED TARGETED GROUP MEMBERS

Empowered targeted group members reject the inferior status assigned to them in a system of oppression. They work to overcome the internalized aspects of oppression they were socialized to accept. They have pride in their group identity and enjoy a sense of community with others from their social identity group. Feminist conscious-raising groups and gay pride marches are two examples of these efforts. Most importantly, they develop a liberatory consciousness that leads them to become actively involved in efforts to eliminate oppression. These efforts include working in coalition with allies or working with other targeted group members. Finally, empowered targeted group members understand the interconnections among different manifestations of oppression and the importance of challenging them all, not only the ones that affect them most directly.

. . .

UNDERLYING ASSUMPTIONS

Several underlying assumptions create a philosophical foundation for our social justice education practice.

IT IS NOT USEFUL TO ARGUE ABOUT A HIERARCHY OF OPPRESSIONS

We believe that little is gained in debating which forms of oppression are more damaging or which one is the root out of which all others grow. Though we acknowledge that some

participants believe that there is an urgent need to address one form of oppression over others, we present the perspective that each form of oppression is destructive to the human spirit. We do, however, identify ways in which specific forms of oppression are similar or different, but do not rank the differences identified. Our courses are based on the belief that even if we could eliminate one form of oppression, the continued existence of the others would still affect us all.

ALL FORMS OF OPPRESSION ARE INTERCONNECTED

In addition to our use of an underlying conceptual framework to understand the dynamics of all the forms of oppression, we also recognize that each participant in our courses is a collage of many social identities. Even though a course is focused on sexism, for example, each participant's race, class, religion, sexual orientation, ability, and gender affect how that participant experiences sexism. We encourage participants to explore the intersections of their different social group memberships and also to understand the similarities in the dynamics of different forms of oppression.

CONFRONTING OPPRESSION WILL BENEFIT EVERYONE

Most people can understand how confronting sexism will benefit women or how addressing ableism will benefit people with disabilities. We also believe that men and non-disabled people will benefit from the elimination of sexism and ableism. Unfortunately, some participants react to social justice education as if engaged in a conflict in which one group wins and another loses. However, when people are subjected to oppression whatever their social group membership, their talents and potential achievements are lost and we all suffer from this loss. Moreover, we all have spheres of influence and connections that link us to people who are directly affected by oppression. Even if we are not members of a particular disadvantaged social group, we have friends, coworkers, or family members who are. In addition, we might become members of disadvantaged social groups in the future if, for example, we become disabled or have a change in economic circumstances. Another way we are hurt by oppression is that many people who are members of groups that benefit from oppression live with a burden of guilt, shame, and helplessness and are never sure whether their individual accomplishments are earned or the result of advantages received due to their social group membership. Confronting oppression can free members of all social groups to take action toward social justice. The goal in eliminating oppression is an equitable redistribution of social power and resources among all social groups at all levels (individual, institutional, and societal/cultural). The goal is not to reverse the current power inequity by simply interchanging the groups in power positions.

FIXING BLAME HELPS NO ONE; TAKING RESPONSIBILITY HELPS EVERYONE

We present the perspective that there is little to be gained from fixing blame for our heritage of social injustice. We are each born into a social system in which we are taught to accept things as they are. Nothing is gained by feeling shame about what our ancestors did or what our contemporaries do to different groups of people out of fear, ignorance, or malice. Taking responsibility, in contrast, means acting to address oppression. Rather than becoming lost in a sense of helplessness, our goal is to enable participants to understand how they can choose to take responsibility in their everyday lives for confronting social injustice.

CONFRONTING SOCIAL INJUSTICE IS PAINFUL AND JOYFUL

Most participants do not want to believe that they harbor prejudices about groups of people. Confronting these prejudices in themselves and others is difficult. Participants need to open themselves to the discomfort and uncertainty of questioning what is familiar, comfortable, and unquestioned. Facing the contradictions between what participants have been taught to believe about social justice and the realities of the experiences of different social groups is complex. Participants learn that some of what they were taught is inaccurate. Some necessary information was not part of their education. Participants need to be assisted through this process with hope and care. At the same time, we believe that understanding social oppression and taking action against it can be a joyful and liberating experience. Some participants' lives are changed in exciting and life-affirming ways as a result of their experiences in social justice education courses. They find ways to act on their beliefs and make changes in their personal lives that profoundly affect their personal and professional relationships.

. . .

5

Five Faces of Oppression

Iris Marion Young

. . .

In this chapter I offer some explanation of the concept of oppression as I understand its use by new social movements in the United States since the 1960s. My starting point is reflection on the conditions of the groups said by these movements to be oppressed: among others, women, Blacks, Chicanos, Puerto Ricans and other Spanish-speaking Americans, American Indians, Jews, lesbians and gay men, Arabs, Asians, old people, working-class people, and the physically and mentally disabled. I aim to systematize the meaning of the concept of oppression as used by these diverse political movements, and to provide normative argument to clarify the wrongs the term names.

Obviously the above-named groups are not oppressed to the same extent or in the same ways. In the most general sense, all oppressed people suffer some inhibition of their ability to develop and exercise their capacities and express their needs, thoughts, and feelings. In that abstract sense all oppressed people face a common condition. Beyond that, in any more specific sense, it is not possible to define a single set of criteria that describe the condition of oppression of the above groups. Consequently, attempts by theorists and activists to discover a common description or the essential causes of the oppression of all these groups have frequently led to fruitless disputes about whose oppression is more fundamental or more grave. The contexts in which members of these groups use the term *oppression* to describe the injustices of their situation suggest that oppression names in fact a family of concepts and conditions, which I divide into five categories: exploitation, marginalization, powerlessness, cultural imperialism, and violence.

. . .

OPPRESSION AS A STRUCTURAL CONCEPT

. . . In its traditional usage, oppression means the exercise of tyranny by a ruling group. Oppression also traditionally carries a strong connotation of conquest and colonial domination. The Hebrews were oppressed in Egypt, and many uses of the term oppression in the West invoke this paradigm. . . . New left social movements of the 1960s and 1970s, however, shifted the meaning of the concept of oppression. In its new usage, oppression designates the disadvantage and injustice some people suffer not because a tyrannical power coerces them, but because of the everyday practices of a well-intentioned liberal society. . . .

. . . Oppression in this sense is structural, rather than the result of a few people's choices or policies. Its causes are embedded in unquestioned norms, habits, and symbols, in the assumptions underlying institutional rules and the collective consequences of following those rules. . . . In this extended structural sense, oppression refers to the vast and deep injustices some groups suffer as a consequence of often unconscious assumptions and reactions of well meaning people in ordinary interactions, media and cultural stereotypes, and structural features of bureaucratic hierarchies and market mechanisms—in short, the normal processes of everyday life. . . .

I do not mean to suggest that within a system of oppression individual persons do not intentionally harm others in oppressed groups. The raped woman, the beaten Black youth, the locked-out worker, the gay man harassed on the street, are victims of intentional actions by identifiable agents. I also do not mean to deny that specific groups are beneficiaries of the oppression of other groups, and thus have an interest in their continued oppression. Indeed, for every oppressed group there is a group that is privileged in relation to that group. . . .

Racism, sexism, ageism, homophobia, some social movements asserted, are distinct forms of oppression with their own dynamics apart from those of class, even though they may interact with class oppression. From often heated discussions among socialists, feminists, and antiracism activists in the last ten years, a consensus is emerging that many different groups must be said to be oppressed in our society, and that no single form of oppression can be assigned causal or moral primacy. The same discussion has also led to the recognition that group differences cut across individual lines in a multiplicity of ways that can entail privilege and oppression for the same person in different respects. Only a plural explication of the concept of oppression can adequately capture these insights.

Accordingly, I offer below an explication of five faces of oppression as a useful set of categories and distinctions which I believe is comprehensive in the sense that it covers all the groups said by new left social movements to be oppressed, and all the ways they are oppressed. I derive the five faces of oppression from reflection on the condition of these groups. Because different factors, or combinations of factors, constitute the oppression of different groups, making their oppression irreducible, I believe it is not possible to give one essential definition of oppression. The five categories articulated in this chapter, however, are adequate to describe the oppression of any group, as well as its similarities with and differences from the oppression of other groups. But first we must ask what a "group" is.

THE CONCEPT OF A SOCIAL GROUP

. . . A social group is a collective of persons differentiated from at least one other group by cultural forms, practices, or way of life. Members of a group have a specific affinity with

one another because of their similar experience (or way of life), which prompts them to associate with one another more than with those not identified with the group. Groups are an expression of social relations; a group exists only in relation to at least one other group. . . .

A social group is defined not primarily by a set of shared attributes, but by a sense of identity. What defines Black Americans as a social group is not primarily their skin color; some persons whose skin color is fairly light, for example, identify themselves as black. Though sometimes objective attributes are a necessary condition for classifying oneself or others as belonging to a certain social group, it is identification with a certain social status, the common history that social status produces, and self-identification that define the group as a group. . . .

Groups constitute individuals. A person's particular sense of history, affinity, and separateness—even the person's mode of reasoning, evaluating, and expressing feeling—are constituted partly by her or his group affinities. This does not mean that persons have no individual styles, or are unable to transcend or reject a group identity. Nor does it preclude persons from having many aspects that are independent of these group identities. . . .

While I agree that individuals should be free to pursue life plans in their own ways, it is foolish to deny the reality of groups. . . . Even when they belong to oppressed groups, people's group identifications are often important to them, and they often feel a special affinity for others in their group. I believe that group differentiation is both an inevitable and a desirable aspect of modern social processes. Social justice requires not the melting away of differences, but institutions that promote reproduction of and respect for group differences without oppression.

. . .

THE FACES OF OPPRESSION

EXPLOITATION

The central insight expressed in the concept of exploitation is that this oppression occurs through a steady process of the transfer of the results of the labor of one social group to benefit another. The injustice of class division does not consist only in the distributive fact that some people have great wealth while most people have little. Exploitation enacts a structural relation between social groups. Social rules about what work is, who does what for whom, how work is compensated, and the social processes by which the results of work are appropriated operate to enact relations of power and inequality. These relations are produced and reproduced through a systematic process in which the energies of the have-nots are continuously expended to maintain and augment the power, status, and wealth of the haves. . . .

Feminists have had little difficulty showing that women's oppression consists partly in a systematic and unreciprocated transfer of powers from women to men. Women's oppression consists not merely in an inequality of status, power, and wealth resulting from men's excluding them from privileged activities. The freedom, power, status, and self-realization of men is possible precisely because women work for them. Gender exploitation has two aspects: transfer of the fruits of material labor to men, and the transfer of nurturing and sexual energies to men. . . . Thus, for example, in most systems of agriculture production in the world, men take to market the goods women have produced, and more often than not men receive the status and often the entire income from this labor.

... Women provide men and children with emotional care and provide men with sexual satisfaction, and as a group receive relatively little of either from men. The gender socialization of women makes us tend to be more attentive to interactive dynamics than men, and makes women good at providing empathy and support for people's feelings and at smoothing over interactive tensions. Both men and women look to women as nurturers of their personal lives, and women frequently complain that when they look to men for emotional support they do not receive it. The norms of heterosexuality, moreover, are oriented around male pleasure, and consequently, many women receive little satisfaction from their sexual interactions with men.

. . .

Is it possible to conceptualize a form of exploitation that is racially specific on analogy with the gender-specific forms just discussed? I suggest that the category of *menial* labor might supply a means for such conceptualization. In its derivation, "menial" designates the labor of servants. Wherever there is racism, there is the assumption, more or less enforced, that members of the oppressed racial groups are or ought to be servants of those, or some of those, in the privileged group. In most white racist societies this means that many white people have dark- or yellow-skinned domestic servants, and in the United States today there remains significant racial structuring of private household service. But in the United States today much service labor has gone public: anyone who goes to a good hotel or a good restaurant can have servants. Servants often attend the daily—and nightly—activities of business executives, government officials, and other high-status professionals. In our society there remains strong cultural pressure to fill servant jobs—bellhop, porter, chambermaid, busboy, and so on—with Black and Latino workers. These jobs entail a transfer of energies whereby the servers enhance the status of the served.

Menial labor usually refers not only to service, however, but also to any servile, unskilled, low-paying work lacking in autonomy, in which a person is subject to taking orders from many people. Menial work tends to be auxiliary work, instrumental to the work of others, where those others receive primary recognition for doing the job. Laborers on a construction site, for example, are at the beck and call of welders, electricians, carpenters, and other skilled workers, who receive recognition for the job done. In the United States explicit racial discrimination once reserved menial work for Blacks, Chicanos, American Indians, and Chinese, and menial work still tends to be linked to Black and Latino workers. I offer this category of menial labor as a form of racially specific exploitation, as a provisional category in need of exploration. . . .

The injustice of exploitation consists in social processes that bring about a transfer of energies from one group to another to produce unequal distributions, and in the way in which social institutions enable a few to accumulate while they constrain many more. The injustices of exploitation cannot be eliminated by the redistribution of goods, for as long as institutionalized practices and structural relations remain unaltered, the process of transfer will re-create an unequal distribution of benefits. Bringing about justice where there is exploitation requires reorganization of institutions and practices of decision making, alteration of the division of labor, and similar measures of institutional, structural, and cultural change.

MARGINALIZATION

Increasingly in the United States, racial oppression occurs in the form of marginalization rather than exploitation. *Marginals* are people the system of labor cannot or will not use. Not only in Third World capitalist countries, but also in most Western capitalist societies, there is a growing underclass of people permanently confined to lives of social marginality, most of whom are racially marked—Blacks or Indians in Latin America, and Blacks, East Indians, Eastern Europeans, or North Africans in Europe.

Marginalization is by no means the fate only of racially marked groups, however. In the United States a shamefully large proportion of the population is marginal: old people, and increasingly people who are not very old but get laid off from their jobs and cannot find new work; young people, especially Black or Latino, who cannot find first or second jobs; many single mothers and their children; other people involuntarily unemployed; many mentally and physically disabled people; American Indians (especially those on reservations).

Marginalization is perhaps the most dangerous form of oppression. A whole category of people is expelled from useful participation in social life and thus potentially subjected to severe material deprivation and even extermination. The material deprivation marginalization often causes is certainly unjust, especially in a society where others have plenty. Contemporary advanced capitalist societies have in principle acknowledged the injustice of material deprivation caused by marginalization, and have taken some steps to address it by providing welfare payments and services. The continuance of this welfare state is by no means assured, and in most welfare state societies, especially the United States, welfare redistributions do not eliminate large-scale suffering and deprivation.

Material deprivation, which can be addressed by redistributive social policies, is not, however, the extent of the harm caused by marginalization. Two categories of injustice beyond distribution are associated with marginality in advanced capitalist societies. First, the provision of welfare itself produces new injustice by depriving those dependent on it of rights and freedoms that others have. Second, even when material deprivation is somewhat mitigated by the welfare state, marginalization is unjust because it blocks the opportunity to exercise capacities in socially defined and recognized ways. I shall explicate each of these in turn.

. . .

Today the exclusion of dependent persons from equal citizenship rights is only barely hidden beneath the surface. Because they depend on bureaucratic institutions for support or services, the old, the poor, and the mentally or physically disabled are subject to patronizing, punitive, demeaning, and arbitrary treatment by the policies and people associated with welfare bureaucracies. Being a "dependent" in our society implies being legitimately subject to the often arbitrary and invasive authority of social service providers and other public and private administrators who enforce rules with which the marginal must comply, and otherwise exercise power over the conditions of their lives. In meeting the needs of the marginalized, often with the aid of social scientific disciplines, welfare agencies also construct the needs themselves. Medical and social service professionals know what is good for those they serve, and the marginals and dependents themselves do not have the right to claim to know what is good for them. Dependency in our society thus implies, as it has in all liberal societies, a sufficient warrant to suspend basic rights to privacy, respect, and individual choice.

Although dependency produces conditions of injustice in our society, dependency in itself need not be oppressive. One cannot imagine a society in which some people would not need to be dependent on others at least some of the time: children, sick people, women recovering from childbirth, old people who have become frail, depressed or otherwise emotionally needy persons have the moral right to depend on others for subsistence and support.

An important contribution of feminist moral theory has been to question the deeply held assumption that moral agency and full citizenship require that a person be autonomous and independent. Feminists have exposed this assumption as inappropriately individualistic and derived from a specifically male experience of social relations, which values competition and solitary achievement. Female experience of social relations, arising both from women's typical domestic care responsibilities and from the kinds of paid work that many

women do, tends to recognize dependence as a basic human condition. Whereas on the autonomy model a just society would, as much as possible, give people the opportunity to be independent, the feminist model envisions justice as according respect and participation in decision making to those who are dependent as well as to those who are independent. Dependency should not be a reason to be deprived of choice and respect, and much of the oppression many marginals experience would be lessened if a less individualistic model of rights prevailed.

Marginalization does not cease to be oppressive when one has shelter and food. Many old people, for example, have sufficient means to live comfortably but remain oppressed in their marginal status. Even if marginals were provided a comfortable material life within institutions that respected their freedom and dignity, injustices of marginality would remain in the form of uselessness, boredom, and lack of self-respect. Most of our society's productive and recognized activities take place in contexts of organized social cooperation, and social structures and processes that close persons out of such social cooperation are unjust. . . .

POWERLESSNESS

As I have indicated, the Marxist idea of class is important because it helps reveal the structure of exploitation: that some people have their power and wealth because they profit from the labor of others. For this reason I reject the claim some make that a traditional class exploitation model fails to capture the structure of contemporary society. It remains the case that the labor of most people in the society augments the power of relatively few. Despite their differences from nonprofessional workers, most professional workers are still not members of the capitalist class. Professional labor either involves exploitative transfers to capitalists or supplies important conditions for such transfers. Professional workers are in an ambiguous class position, it is true, because they also benefit from the exploitation of nonprofessional workers.

While it is false to claim that a division between capitalist and working classes no longer describes our society, it is also false to say that class relations have remained unaltered since the nineteenth century. An adequate conception of oppression cannot ignore the experience of social division reflected in the colloquial distinction between the "middle class" and the "working class," a division structured by the social division of labor between professionals and nonprofessionals. Professionals are privileged in relation to nonprofessionals by virtue of their position in the division of labor and the status it carries. Nonprofessionals suffer a form of oppression in addition to exploitation, which I call *powerlessness*.

. . . [D]omination in modern society is enacted through the widely dispersed powers of many agents mediating the decisions of others. To that extent many people have some power in relation to others, even though they lack the power to decide policies or results. The powerless are those who lack authority or power even in this mediated sense, those over whom power is exercised without their exercising it; the powerless are situated so that they must take orders and rarely have the right to give them. Powerlessness also designates a position in the division of labor and the concomitant social position that allows persons little opportunity to develop and exercise skills. The powerless have little or no work autonomy; exercise little creativity or judgment in their work; have no technical expertise or authority; express themselves awkwardly, especially in public or bureaucratic settings; and do not command respect. Powerlessness names the oppressive situations Sennett and Cobb describe in their famous study of working-class men.

This powerless status is perhaps best described negatively: the powerless lack the authority, status, and sense of self that professionals tend to have. The status privilege of professionals has three aspects, the lack of which produces oppression for nonprofessionals.

First, acquiring and practicing a profession has an expansive, progressive character. Being professional usually requires a college education and the acquisition of a specialized knowledge that entails working with symbols and concepts. Professionals experience progress first in acquiring the expertise, and then in the course of professional advancement and rise in status. The life of the nonprofessional by comparison is powerless in the sense that it lacks this orientation toward the progressive development of capacities and avenues for recognition.

Second, while many professionals have supervisors and cannot directly influence many decisions or the actions of many people, most nevertheless have considerable day-to-day work autonomy. Professionals usually have some authority over others, moreover—either over workers they supervise, or over auxiliaries or clients. Nonprofessionals, on the other hand, lack autonomy, and in both their working and their consumer/client lives often stand under the authority of professionals.

Though based on a division of labor between "mental" and "manual" work, the distinction between "middle class" and "working class" designates a division not only in working life, but also in nearly all aspects of social life. Professionals and nonprofessionals belong to different cultures in the United States. The two groups tend to live in segregated neighborhoods or even different towns, a process itself mediated by planners, zoning officials, and real estate people. The groups tend to have different tastes in food, decor, clothes, music, and vacations, and often different health and educational needs. Members of each group socialize for the most part with others in the same status group. While there is some intergroup mobility between generations, for the most part the children of professionals become professionals and the children of nonprofessionals do not.

Thus, the privileges of the professional extend beyond the workplace to a whole way of life. I call this way of life *respectability*. To treat people with respect is to be prepared to listen to what they have to say or to do what they request because they have some authority, expertise, or influence. The norms of respectability in our society are associated specifically with professional culture. Professional dress, speech, tastes, demeanor all connote respectability. Generally professionals expect and receive respect from others. In restaurants, banks, hotels, real estate offices, and many other such public places, as well as in the media, professionals typically receive more respectful treatment than nonprofessionals. For this reason nonprofessionals seeking a loan or a job, or to buy a house or a car, will often try to look "professional" and "respectable" in those settings.

The privilege of this professional respectability appears starkly in the dynamics of racism and sexism. In daily interchange, women and men of color must prove their respectability. At first they are often not treated by strangers with respectful distance or deference. Once people discover that this woman or that Puerto Rican man is a college teacher or a business executive, however, they often behave more respectfully toward her or him. . . .

CULTURAL IMPERIALISM

Exploitation, marginalization, and powerlessness all refer to relations of power and oppression that occur by virtue of the social division of labor—who works for whom, who does not work, and how the content of work defines one institutional position relative to others. These three categories refer to structural and institutional relations that delimit people's material lives, including but not restricted to the resources they have access to and the concrete opportunities they have or do not have to develop and exercise their capacities. These kinds of oppression are a matter of concrete power in relation to others—of who benefits from whom, and who is dispensable.

Recent theorists of movements of group liberation, notably feminist and Black liberation theorists, have also given prominence to a rather different form of oppression, which

following Lugones and Spelman I shall call *cultural imperialism*. To experience cultural imperialism means to experience how the dominant meanings of a society render the particular perspective of one's own group invisible at the same time as they stereotype one's group and mark it as the Other.

Cultural imperialism involves the universalization of a dominant group's experience and culture, and its establishment as the norm. . . . Often without noticing they do so, dominant groups project their own experience as representative of humanity as such. Cultural products also express the dominant group's perspective on and interpretation of events and elements in the society, including other groups in the society, insofar as they attain cultural status at all.

An encounter with other groups, however, can challenge the dominant group's claim to universality. The dominant group reinforces its position by bringing the other groups under the measure of its dominant norms. Consequently, the difference of women from men, American Indians or Africans from Europeans, Jews from Christians, homosexuals from heterosexuals, workers from professionals becomes reconstructed largely as deviance and inferiority. Since only the dominant group's cultural expressions receive wide dissemination, their cultural expressions become the normal, or the universal, and thereby the unremarkable. Given the normality of its own cultural expressions and identity, the dominant group constructs the differences which some groups exhibit as lack and negation. These groups become marked as Other.

The culturally dominated undergo a paradoxical oppression in that they are both marked out by stereotypes and at the same time rendered invisible. As remarkable, deviant beings, the culturally imperialized are stamped with an essence. The stereotypes confine them to a nature which is often attached in some way to their bodies, and which thus cannot easily be denied. These stereotypes so permeate the society that they are not noticed as contestable. Just as everyone knows that the earth goes around the sun, so everyone knows that gay people are promiscuous, that American Indians are alcoholics, and that women are good with children. White males, on the other hand, insofar as they escape group marking, can be individuals.

Those living under cultural imperialism find themselves defined from the outside, positioned, placed, by a network of dominant meanings they experience as arising from elsewhere, from those with whom they do not identify and who do not identify with them. Consequently, the dominant culture's stereotyped and inferiorized images of the group must be internalized by group members at least to the extent that they are forced to react to the behavior of others influenced by those images. This creates for the culturally oppressed the experience that W. E. B. Du Bois called "double consciousness"—"this sense of always looking at one's self through the eyes of others, of measuring one's soul by the tape of a world that looks on in amused contempt and pity." Double consciousness arises when the oppressed subject refuses to coincide with these devalued, objectified, stereotyped visions of herself or himself. While the subject desires recognition as human—capable of activity, full of hope and possibility—she receives from the dominant culture only the judgment that she is different, marked, or inferior.

The group defined by the dominant culture as deviant, as a stereotyped Other, is culturally different from the dominant group, because the status of Otherness creates specific experiences not shared by the dominant group, and because culturally oppressed groups also are often socially segregated and occupy specific positions in the social division of labor. Members of such groups express their specific group experiences and interpretations of the world to one another, developing and perpetuating their own culture. Double consciousness, then, occurs because one finds one's being defined by two cultures: a dominant and a subordinate culture. Because they can affirm and recognize one another as sharing

similar experiences and perspectives on social life, people in culturally imperialized groups can often maintain a sense of positive subjectivity.

Cultural imperialism involves the paradox of experiencing oneself as invisible at the same time that one is marked out as different. The invisibility comes about when dominant groups fail to recognize the perspective embodied in their cultural expressions as a perspective. These dominant cultural expressions often simply have little place for the experience of other groups, at most only mentioning or referring to them in stereotyped or marginalized ways. This, then, is the injustice of cultural imperialism: that the oppressed group's own experience and interpretation of social life finds little expression that touches the dominant culture, while that same culture imposes on the oppressed group its experience and interpretation of social life. . . .

VIOLENCE

Finally, many groups suffer the oppression of systematic violence. Members of some groups live with the knowledge that they must fear random, unprovoked attacks on their persons or property, which have no motive but to damage, humiliate, or destroy the person. In American society women, Blacks, Asians, Arabs, gay men, and lesbians live under such threats of violence, and in at least some regions Jews, Puerto Ricans, Chicanos, and other Spanish-speaking Americans must fear such violence as well. Physical violence against these groups is shockingly frequent. Rape crisis center networks estimate that more than one-third of all American women experience an attempted or successful sexual assault in their lifetimes. Manning Marable catalogs a large number of incidents of racist violence and terror against Blacks in the United States between 1980 and 1982. He cites dozens of incidents of the severe beating, killing, or rape of Blacks by police officers on duty, in which the police involved were acquitted of any wrongdoing. In 1981, moreover, there were at least five hundred documented cases of random white teenage violence against Blacks. Violence against gay men and lesbians is not only common, but has been increasing. While the frequency of physical attack on members of these and other racially or sexually marked groups is very disturbing. I also include in this category less severe incidents of harassment, intimidation, or ridicule simply for the purpose of degrading, humiliating, or stigmatizing group members.

. . .

What makes violence a face of oppression is less the particular acts themselves—though these are often utterly horrible—than the social context surrounding them, which makes them possible and even acceptable. What makes violence a phenomenon of social injustice, and not merely an individual moral wrong, is its systemic character, its existence as a social practice.

Violence is systemic because it is directed at members of a group simply because they are members of that group. Any woman, for example, has a reason to fear rape. Regardless of what a Black man has done to escape the oppressions of marginality or powerlessness, he lives knowing he is subject to attack or harassment. The oppression of violence consists not only in direct victimization, but in the daily knowledge shared by all members of oppressed groups that they are *liable* to violation, solely on account of their group identity. Just living under such a threat of attack on oneself or family or friends deprives the oppressed of freedom and dignity, and needlessly expends their energy.

Violence is a social practice. It is a social given that everyone knows happens and will happen again. It is always at the horizon of social imagination, even for those who do not perpetrate it. According to the prevailing social logic, some circumstances make such violence more "called for" than others. The idea of rape will occur to many men who pick up a hitch-hiking woman; the idea of hounding or teasing a gay man on their dorm floor

will occur to many straight male college students. Often several persons inflict the violence together, especially in all-male groupings. Sometimes violators set out looking for people to beat up, rape, or taunt. This rule-bound, social, and often premeditated character makes violence against groups a social practice.

Group violence approaches legitimacy, moreover, in the sense that it is tolerated. Often, third parties find it unsurprising because it happens frequently and lies as a constant possibility at the horizon of the social imagination. Even when they are caught, those who perpetrate acts of group-directed violence or harassment often receive light or no punishment. To that extent society renders their acts acceptable.

. . .

[T]he violation of rape, beating, killing, and harassment of women, people of color, gays, and other marked groups is motivated by fear or hatred of those groups. Sometimes the motive may be a simple will to power, to victimize those marked as vulnerable by the very social fact that they are subject to violence. If so, this motive is secondary in the sense that it depends on a social practice of group violence. Violence-causing fear or hatred of the other at least partly involves insecurities on the part of the violators; its irrationality suggests that unconscious processes are at work.

Cultural imperialism, moreover, itself intersects with violence. The culturally imperialized may reject the dominant meanings and attempt to assert their own subjectivity, or the fact of the cultural difference may put the lie to the dominant culture's implicit claim to universality. The dissonance generated by such a challenge to the hegemonic cultural meanings can also be a source of irrational violence.

. . . I have argued that group-directed violence is institutionalized and systemic. To the degree that institutions and social practices encourage, tolerate, or enable the perpetration of violence against members of specific groups, those institutions and practices are unjust and should be reformed. Such reform may require the redistribution of resources or positions, but in large part can come only through a change in cultural images, stereotypes, and the mundane reproduction of relations of dominance and aversion in the gestures of everyday life.

APPLYING THE CRITERIA

. . .

I have arrived at the five faces of oppression—exploitation, marginalization, powerlessness, cultural imperialism, and violence—as the best way to avoid such exclusions and reductions. They function as criteria for determining whether individuals and groups are oppressed, rather than as a full theory of oppression. I believe that these criteria are objective. They provide a means of refuting some people's beliefs that their group is oppressed when it is not, as well as a means of persuading others that a group is oppressed when they doubt it. Each criterion can be operationalized; each can be applied through the assessment of observable behavior, status relationships, distributions, texts, and other cultural artifacts. I have no illusions that such assessments can be value-neutral. But these criteria can nevertheless serve as means of evaluating claims that a group is oppressed, or adjudicating disputes about whether or how a group is oppressed.

The presence of any of these five conditions is sufficient for calling a group oppressed. But different group oppressions exhibit different combinations of these forms, as do different individuals in the groups. Nearly all, if not all, groups said by contemporary social movements to be oppressed suffer cultural imperialism. The other oppressions they experience vary. Working-class people are exploited and powerless, for example, but if employed

and white do not experience marginalization and violence. Gay men, on the other hand, are not qua gay exploited or powerless, but they experience severe cultural imperialism and violence. Similarly, Jews and Arabs as groups are victims of cultural imperialism and violence, though many members of these groups also suffer exploitation or powerlessness. Old people are oppressed by marginalization and cultural imperialism, and this is also true of physically and mentally disabled people. As a group, women are subject to gender-based exploitation, powerlessness, cultural imperialism, and violence. Racism in the United States condemns many Blacks and Latinos to marginalization, and puts many more at risk, even though many members of these groups escape that condition; members of these groups often suffer all five forms of oppression.

Applying these five criteria to the situation of groups makes it possible to compare the oppressions without reducing them to a common essence or claiming that one is more fundamental than another. One can compare the ways in which a particular form of oppression appears in different groups. For example, while the operations of cultural imperialism are often experienced in similar fashion by different groups, there are also important differences. One can compare the combinations of oppressions groups experience, or the intensity of those oppressions. . . .

6

The Cycle of Socialization

Bobbie Harro

INTRODUCTION AND CONTEXT

Often, when people begin to study the phenomenon of oppression, they start with recognizing that human beings are different from each other in many ways based upon gender, ethnicity, skin color, first language, age, ability status, religion, sexual orientation, and economic class. The obvious first leap that people make is the assumption that if we just began to *appreciate differences*, and *treat each other with respect*, then everything would be all right, and there would be no oppression. This view is represented beautifully by the now famous quote from Rodney King in response to the riots following his beating and the release of the police officers who were filmed beating him: "Why can't we all just get along?" It should be that simple, but it isn't.

Instead, we are each born into a specific set of *social identities*, related to the categories of difference mentioned above, and these social identities predispose us to unequal *roles* in the dynamic system of oppression. We are then socialized by powerful sources in our worlds to play the roles prescribed by an inequitable social system. This socialization process is *pervasive* (coming from all sides and sources), *consistent* (patterned and predictable), *circular* (self-supporting), *self-perpetuating* (intradependent) and often *invisible* (unconscious and unnamed). All of these characteristics will be clarified in the description of the *cycle of socialization* that follows.

In struggling to understand what roles we have been socialized to play, how we are affected by issues of oppression in our lives, and how we participate in maintaining them,

we must begin by making an inventory of our own social identities with relationship to each issue of oppression. An excellent first learning activity is to make a personal inventory of our various social identities relating to the categories listed above—gender, race, age, sexual orientation, religion, economic class, and ability/disability status. The results of this inventory make up the mosaic of social identities (our *social identity profile*) that shape(s) our socialization.

We get systematic training in "how to be" each of our social identities throughout our lives. The cycle of socialization that follows is one way of representing how the socialization process happens, from what sources it comes, how it affects our lives, and how it perpetuates itself. The "Directions for Change" that conclude this chapter suggest ways for interrupting the cycle of socialization and taking charge of our own lives. For purposes of learning, it is often useful to choose only *one* of our social identities, and trace it through

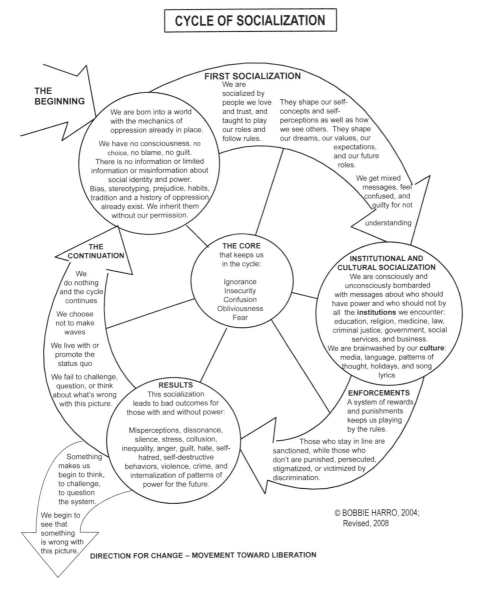

Figure 6.1 The Cycle of Socialization

the cycle of socialization, since it can be quite overwhelming to explore seven identities at once.

THE BEGINNING (CIRCLE NO. 1)

Our socialization begins before we are born, with no choice on our part. No one brings us a survey, in the womb, inquiring into which gender, class, religion, sexual orientation, cultural group, ability status, or age we might want to be born. These identities are ascribed to us at birth through no effort or decision or choice of our own; there is, therefore, no reason to blame each other or hold each other responsible for the identities we have. This first step in the socialization process is outside our control. In addition to having no choice, we also have no initial consciousness about who we are. We don't question our identities at this point. We just *are* who we are.

On top of these givens, we are born into a world where all of the mechanics, assumptions, rules, roles, and structures of oppression are already in place and functioning; we have had nothing to do with constructing them. There is no reason for any of us to feel guilty or responsible for the world into which we are born. We are innocents, falling into an already established system.

The characteristics of this system were built long before we existed, based upon history, habit, tradition, patterns of belief, prejudices, stereotypes, and myths. *Dominant* or *agent* groups are considered the "norm" around which assumptions are built, and these groups receive attention and recognition. Agents have relatively more social power, and can "name" others. They are privileged at birth, and ascribed access to options and opportunities, often without realizing it. We are "lucky" to be born into these groups and rarely question it. Agent groups include men, white people, middle- and upper-class people, abled people, middle-aged people, heterosexuals, and gentiles.

On the other hand, there are many social identity groups about which little or nothing is known because they have not been considered important enough to study. These are referred to as *subordinate* groups or *target* groups. Some target groups are virtually invisible while others are defined by misinformation or very limited information. Targets are disenfranchised, exploited, and victimized by prejudice, discrimination, and other structural obstacles. Target groups include women; racially oppressed groups; gay, lesbian, bisexual and transgendered people; disabled people; Jews; elders; youth; and people living in poverty. We are "unlucky" to be born into target groups and therefore devalued by the existing society. Both groups are dehumanized by being socialized into prescribed roles without consciousness or permission.

FIRST SOCIALIZATION (ARROW NO. 1)

Immediately upon our births we begin to be socialized by the people we love and trust the most, our families or the adults who are raising us. They shape our self-concepts and self-perceptions, the norms and rules we must follow, the roles we are taught to play, our expectations for the future, and our dreams. These people serve as role models for us, and they teach us how to behave. This socialization happens both intrapersonally (how we think about ourselves), and interpersonally (how we relate to others). We are told things like, "Boys don't cry"; "You shouldn't trust white people"; "They're better than we are. Stay in your place"; "Don't worry if you break the toy. We can always buy another one"; "Christianity is the true religion"; "Children should be seen and not heard"; "Don't tell anyone that your aunt is mentally retarded. It's embarrassing"; and "Don't kiss other girls. You're supposed to like boys." These messages are an automatic part of our early socialization, and we don't initially question them. We are too dependent on our parents

or those raising us, and we haven't yet developed the ability to think for ourselves, so we unconsciously conform to their views.

It is important to observe that they, too, are not to be blamed. They are doing the best they can to raise us, and they only have their own backgrounds from which to draw. They may not have thought critically about what they are teaching us, and may be unconsciously passing on what was taught to them. Some of us may have been raised by parents who *have* thought critically about the messages that they are giving us, but they are still not in the majority. This could be good or bad, as well, depending on what their views are. A consciously racist parent may intentionally pass on racist beliefs to his children, and a consciously feminist parent may intentionally pass on non-stereotypical roles to her children, so it can go either way.

Regardless of the content of the teaching, we have been exposed, without initial question, to a strong set of rules, roles, and assumptions that cannot help but shape our sense of ourselves and the world. They influence what we take with us when we venture out of our protected family units into the larger world of other institutions.

A powerful way to check out the accuracy of these assertions is to choose one of our social identities and write down at least ten examples of what we learned about being that identity. It's helpful to consider whether we chose an agent or a target identity. We may find that we have thought more about our target identities, and therefore they are easier to inventory. Gender rules are sometimes the easiest, so we might start there. We might also consider doing it for an agent group identity, like males, white people, heterosexuals, gentiles, adults, middle-class people, able-bodied or able-minded people. Most likely, we will find it easier to list learnings for targeted groups than for agent groups.

INSTITUTIONAL AND CULTURAL SOCIALIZATION (CIRCLE NO. 2)

Once we begin to attend school, go to a place of worship, visit a medical facility, play on a sports team, work with a social worker, seek services or products from a business, or learn about laws and the legal system, our socialization sources are rapidly multiplied based on how many institutions with which we have contact. Most of the messages we receive about how to be, whom to "look up to" and "look down on," what rules to follow, what roles to play, what assumptions to make, what to believe, and what to think will probably reinforce or contradict what we have learned at home.

We might learn at school that girls shouldn't be interested in a woodworking shop class, that only white students go out for the tennis team, that kids who learn differently or think independently get put in special education, that it's okay for wealthy kids to miss classes for a family vacation, that it's okay to harass the boy who walks and talks like a girl, that most of the kids who drop out are from the south side of town, that "jocks" don't have to do the same work that "nerds" do to pass, or that kids who belong to another religious group are "weird." We learn who gets preferential treatment and who gets picked on. We are exposed to rules, roles, and assumptions that are not fair to everyone.

If we are members of the groups that benefit from the rules, we may not notice that they aren't fair. If we are members of the groups that are penalized by the rules, we may have a constant feeling of discomfort. We learn that these rules, roles, and assumptions are part of a structure that is larger than just our families. We get consistent similar messages from religion, the family doctor, the social worker, the local store, or the police officer, and so it is hard to not believe what we are learning. We learn that black people are more likely to steal, so store detectives follow them in stores. Boys are expected to fight and use violence, so they are encouraged to learn how. We shouldn't stare at or ask questions about disabled people; it isn't polite. Gay and lesbian people are sick and perverted. Kids who live in certain sections of town are probably on welfare, taking our hard-earned tax dollars.

Money talks. White means good; black means bad. Girls are responsible for birth control. It's a man's world. Jews are cheap. Arabs are terrorists. And so on.

We are inundated with unquestioned and stereotypical messages that shape how we think and what we believe about ourselves and others. What makes this "brainwashing" even more insidious is the fact that it is woven into every structural thread of the fabric of our culture. The media (television, the Internet, advertising, newspapers, and radio), our language patterns, the lyrics to songs, our cultural practices and holidays, and the very assumptions on which our society is built all contribute to the reinforcement of the biased messages and stereotypes we receive. Think about Howard Stern, Jerry Springer, *Married with Children*, beer and car advertising, talk radio, *girl* vs. *man*, Christmas vacation, the Rolling Stones' "Under My Thumb," the "old boy's network," and websites that foster hate. We could identify thousands of examples to illustrate the oppressive messages that bombard us daily from various institutions and aspects of our culture, reinforcing our divisions and "justifying" discrimination and prejudice.

ENFORCEMENTS (ARROW NO. 2)

It might seem logical to ask why people don't just begin to think independently if they don't like what they are seeing around them. Why don't we ignore these messages if we are uncomfortable with them, or if they are hurting us? Largely, we don't ignore the messages, rules, roles, structures, and assumptions because there are enforcements in place to maintain them. People who try to contradict the "norm" pay a price for their independent thinking, and people who conform (consciously or unconsciously) minimally receive the benefit of being left alone for not making waves, such as acceptance in their designated roles, being considered normal or "a team player," or being allowed to stay in their places. Maximally, they receive rewards and privileges for maintaining the status quo such as access to higher places; attention and recognition for having "made it" or being the model member of their group; or the privilege that brings them money, connections, or power.

People who go against the grain of conventional societal messages are accused of being troublemakers, of making waves, or of being "the cause of the problem." If they are members of target groups, they are held up as examples of why this group is inferior to the agent group. Examples of this include the significantly higher numbers of people of color who are targeted by the criminal justice system. Although the number of white people who are committing crimes is just as high, those whites are much less likely to be arrested, charged, tried, convicted, or sentenced to jail than are people of color. Do different laws apply depending on a person's skin color? Battering statistics are rising as more women assert their equal rights with men, and the number one suspect for the murder of women in the United States is the husband or boyfriend. Should women who try to be equal with men be killed? The rationale given by some racists for the burning of black churches was that "they were getting too strong." Does religious freedom and the freedom to assemble apply only to white citizens? Two men walking together in a southeastern U.S. city were beaten, and one died, because "they were walking so close, they must be gay." Are two men who refuse to abide by the "keep your distance" rule for men so threatening that they must be attacked and killed? These examples of differential punishment being given to members or *perceived* members of target groups are only half of the picture.

If members of agent groups break the rules, they too are punished. White people who support their colleagues of color may be called "n—— lover." Heterosexual men who take on primary child-care responsibilities, cry easily, or hug their male friends are accused of being dominated by their spouses, of being "sissies," or being gay. Middle-class people who work as advocates on economic issues are accused of being do-gooders or self-righteous liberals. Heterosexuals who work for the rights of gay, lesbian, bisexual, or transgendered people are immediately suspected of being "in the closet" themselves.

RESULTS (CIRCLE NO. 3)

It is not surprising that the results of this systematic learning are devastating to all involved. If we are examining our target identities, we may experience anger, a sense of being silenced, dissonance between what the United States stands for and what we experience, low self-esteem, high levels of stress, a sense of hopelessness and disempowerment that can lead to crime and self-destructive behavior, frustration, mistrust, and dehumanization. By participating in our roles as targets we reinforce stereotypes, collude in our own demise, and perpetuate the system of oppression. This learned helplessness is often called *internalized oppression* because we have learned to become our own oppressors from within.

If we are examining our agent identities, we may experience guilt from unearned privilege or oppressive acts, fear of payback, tendency to collude in the system to be self-protective, high levels of stress, ignorance of and loss of contact with the target groups, a sense of distorted reality about how the world is, fear of rising crime and violence levels, limited worldview, obliviousness to the damage we do, and dehumanization. By participating in our roles as agents, and remaining unconscious of or being unwilling to interrupt the cycle, we perpetuate the system of oppression.

These results are often cited as the problems facing our society today: high drop-out rates, crime, poverty, drugs, and so on. Ironically, the root causes of them are inherent in the very assumptions on which the society is built: dualism, hierarchy, competition, individualism, domination, colonialism, and the scarcity principle. To the extent that we fail to interrupt this cycle we keep the assumptions, the problems, and the oppression alive.

A way that we might personally explore this model is to take one of the societal problems and trace its root causes back through the cycle to the core belief systems or patterns in U.S. society that feed and play host to it. It is not a coincidence that the United States is suffering from these results today; rather, it is a logical outcome of our embracing the status quo, without thinking or challenging.

ACTIONS (ARROW NO. 3)

When we arrive at the results of this terrible cycle, we face the decision of what to do next. It is easiest to do nothing, and simply to allow the perpetuation of the status quo. We may choose not to make waves, to stay in our familiar patterns. We may say, "Oh well, it's been that way for hundreds of years. What can I do to change it? It is a huge phenomenon, and my small efforts won't count for much." Many of us choose to do nothing because it is (for a while) easier to stay with what is familiar. Besides, it is frightening to try to interrupt something so large. "What does it have to do with me, anyway?" say many agents. "This isn't my problem. I am above this." We fail to realize that we have become participants just by doing nothing. This cycle has a life of its own. It doesn't need our active support because it has its own centrifugal force. It goes on, and unless we choose to interrupt it, it will continue to go on. Our silence is consent. Until our discomfort becomes larger than our comfort, we will probably stay in this cycle.

Some of us who are targets have been so beaten down by the relentless messages of the cycle that we have given up and resigned ourselves to survive it or to self-destruct. We are the victims of the cycle, and are playing our roles as victims to keep the cycle alive. We will probably go around a few more times before we die. It hurts too much to fight such a big cycle. We need the help of our brothers and sisters and our agent allies to try for change.

. . .

THE CORE OF THE CYCLE

As we begin to examine this decision, we may ask, "What has kept me in this cycle for so long?" Most answers are related to the themes listed in the core of the cycle: fear, ignorance, confusion, insecurity, power or powerlessness.

Fear—For targets, fear of interrupting the system reminds us of what happens to targets who challenge the existing power structure: being labeled as "trouble-makers," experiencing discrimination, being deported, raped, beaten, institutionalized, imprisoned, or killed. There are far too many examples like these. Some targets may decide not to take the risk.

For agents, the fear of interrupting the system is different. We fear losing our privilege if we interrupt the status quo. Will I be targeted with the targets? Will I have to face my own guilt for the years when I did nothing? Will I experience "pay-back" from targets if I acknowledge my role as an agent? Agent privilege sometimes allows us to avoid action, and the cycle continues.

Ignorance—For both targets and agents, lack of understanding about how oppression and socialization work makes it difficult to initiate change. Agents struggle more from our ignorance because we have not been forced to examine our roles. Because most of us have some agent and some target identities, we may be able to transfer what we learned in our target identities to educate ourselves in our agent identities. For example, a white lesbian may be able to translate her own experiences as a woman and a lesbian to understanding racism. This inability to see the connections may prevent us from interrupting the system.

Targets and agents both struggle with not seeing the big picture, and in our target identities, we may get caught in our own pain to the point that we cannot see the connections to other "isms." For example, a Black man may have experienced so much racism that he cannot identify with gay people or women in the U.S. This may prevent him from interrupting the systems of heterosexism and sexism.

Confusion—Oppression is very complex. It is difficult to know how to interrupt the system. That confusion sometimes prevents both targets and agents from taking action. "What if I use the wrong word when taking a stand on ableism? What if I don't know what to say when someone tells an offensive joke? What if I think I know more than I actually do?" Will I do more harm than good? Targets may know how to deal with their own category of oppression, but not categories in which they are agents. It's easy to make a mistake, and that confusion often prevents action.

Insecurity—Rarely have we been prepared for interrupting oppression, unless we went to a progressive school or worked in a progressive organization that has provided skill-building sessions. Most targets and agents feel somewhat insecure about taking a stand against oppression.

Power or Powerlessness—People with power have gained it through the existing system. It is difficult to risk losing it by challenging that same system. People without power may think they can't make a difference. As long as we are "living" in the Cycle of Socialization with the core themes holding us there, it will be difficult to break out of it, but people do it every day.

CHOOSING THE DIRECTION FOR CHANGE

How do people make the decision to interrupt the cycle and stand up for change? Sometimes the decision is triggered by a critical incident that makes oppression impossible to ignore. Perhaps a loved one is affected by some type of injustice or inequity, and we become motivated to speak out. Heterosexual parents of gay and lesbian children report that they became activists when they saw what their children were experiencing.

Perhaps we have a "last straw" experience, where things have become so intolerable that one last incident pushes us into action. Our discomfort becomes more powerful than

our fear or insecurity, and we are compelled to take some action. Women who file sex discrimination suits after years of being overlooked professionally report this example; so do women who leave abusive relationships once and for all.

Sometimes it might be some new awareness or consciousness that we gain. Perhaps a friend from a different identity group shows us a different perspective, or we read a book that makes us think differently, or we enroll in a course that introduces new possibilities. We begin to see the big picture—that groups all over the world are working on these same issues. Change movements are filled with people who made decisions to interrupt the cycle of socialization and the system of oppression. Once you know something, you can't *not* know it anymore, and knowing it eventually translates into action.

These people often share qualities that have developed as a result of uniting for change. They share a sense of hope and optimism that we can dismantle oppression. They share a sense of their own efficacy—that they can make a difference in the world. They empower themselves and they support each other. They share an authentic human connection across their differences rather than fear because of their differences. They are humanized through action; not dehumanized by oppression. They listen to one another. They take one another's perspectives. They learn to love and trust each other. This is how the world changes.

7

Structure as the Subject of Justice

Iris Marion Young

A developer has bought the central-city apartment building where Sandy, a single mother, has been living with her two children; he plans to convert it into condominiums. The building was falling apart and poorly maintained, and she thought the rent was too high anyway, so she seizes the opportunity to locate a better place. Sandy works as a sales clerk in a suburban mall, to which she has had to take two buses from her current residence, for a total of three hours commuting time each day. So she decides to look for an apartment closer to where she works, but she still needs to be on a bus line.

She looks in the newspaper and online for apartment rental advertisements, and she is shocked at the rents for one- and two-bedroom apartments. One of the agents at an apartment finding service listens to her situation and preferences, diligently looks through rental listings, and goes out of his way to arrange meetings with Sandy.

Sandy learns that there are few rental apartments close to her workplace—most of the residential property near the mall is single-family houses. The few apartments nearby are very expensive. Most suburban apartments in her price range are located on the other side of the city from her job; there are also some in the city but few that she can afford which she judges decent and in a neighborhood where she feels her children will be safe. In either case, the bus transportation to work is long and arduous, so she decides that she must devote some of the money she hoped would pay the rent to make car payments. She applies for a housing subsidy program and is told that the waiting time is about two years.

Sandy searches for two months, with the eviction deadline looming over her. Finally she settles for a one-bedroom apartment a forty-five-minute drive from her job—except

when traffic is heavy. The apartment is smaller than she hoped she would have to settle for; the two children will sleep together in the bedroom and she will sleep on a foldout bed in the living room. There are no amenities such as a washer and dryer in the building or a playground for the children. Sandy sees no other option but to take the apartment, and then faces one final hurdle: she needs to deposit three months' rent to secure the apartment. She has used all her savings for a down payment on the car, however. So she cannot rent the apartment, and having learned that this is a typical landlord policy, she now faces the prospect of homelessness.

This mundane story can be repeated with minor variations for hundreds of thousands of people in the United States. The median asking rent for a two-bedroom apartment in 2004 was $974, far out of reach of the 40 percent of renters with incomes less than $20,000. Only one in eighty subsidized apartment units is located in an area with strong job growth, and one-fifth are located in areas whose employment opportunities are declining.

. . .

WHAT IS STRUCTURAL INJUSTICE?

Most people react to a situation like Sandy's with the intuition that something is *wrong*. But what is the wrong, and who is responsible for it?

. . .

She is largely a victim of circumstances beyond her control—the landlord's decision to sell the apartment building, a sex-segregated labor market that makes low-wage service jobs the primary work opportunity for women without college or technical training, the "spatial mismatch" that locates those jobs far from most affordable housing, and so on.

For the judgment that Sandy suffers injustice refers not to her particular life history, but rather to the *position* she is in. Sandy's situation is similar to that of many others. She and they stand in a position of being *vulnerable to homelessness* or *housing deprived*. This position, being vulnerable to homelessness, is a social-structural position. Persons in this position differ from persons differently situated in the range of options available to them and in the nature of the constraints on their action. Whether persons occupying the social-structural position of being vulnerable to homelessness actually become homeless will depend partly on their own actions, partly on luck, and partly on the actions of others. Those in a different structural position might act in similar ways, however, and not risk becoming homeless. The issue of social justice raised by this story is whether it is right that *anyone* should be in a *position* of housing insecurity, especially in an affluent society.

. . .

All the individuals with whom Sandy deals about her housing issues are decent and respectful toward her. Some, such as the apartment hunting agent, go beyond what can be expected of them morally, taking extra time with Sandy at some inconvenience to themselves.

. . .

What about the landlord who has sold the building from which Sandy has been displaced? Let us imagine, however, that this landlord owns several buildings and that his financial situation makes it increasingly difficult for him to maintain them all to the standards he should. He decides to sell this building, from his point of view, in order that he can maintain the others without raising the rents in them very much. Thus he says that he is doing the best thing considering the constraints under which he operates.

What about the rental agent who tells Sandy that she needs three months' rent to secure the apartment she has found? Is she personally responsible for the harm Sandy suffers?

This agent would likely say that she is just doing her job, that she herself does not set the policy, and that the policy is standard and reasonable. It is plausible, that is, to find that Sandy suffers injustice but that no particular agent she encounters has done her a specific wrong.

. . .

The wrong that most people would agree has happened to Sandy and to others in a similar position, I submit, is attributable neither to individual fault nor to specifically unjust policy. Its causes are not so immediate as the persons with whom the wrong sufferer interacts, and not so focused as a single policy. The sources of the generalized circumstance of being vulnerable to homelessness are multiple, large scale, and relatively long term. Many policies, both public and private, and the actions of thousands of individuals acting according to normal rules and accepted practices contribute to producing these circumstances.

Just what are these practices and processes that prevent a large number of people from accessing decent affordable housing? A simple answer is this: many people earn wages insufficient to pay the rents or mortgages landlords and banks require. Indeed, the bottom fifth of renter households have seen little rise in their real incomes since 1993. As a result, the proportion of their income that many people pay for housing in the United States has increased significantly. More than 22 percent of renters, or 7.5 million people, pay more than half their incomes for housing. A large number of these people live in structurally inadequate buildings. The processes that account for poor earning, then, also help account for housing insecurity.

To understand housing insecurity as a consequence of social-structural processes, however, it is helpful also to consider the specificity of the housing industry and housing markets. In the United States, as in most of the rest of the world, housing is primarily a commodity. Unlike most other consumer commodities, however, its production is expensive, and investors often wait a considerable period of time to obtain a return on their investment. Maintaining existing buildings at a decent level of habitation is also expensive and has become more expensive in recent years.

. . .

Housing production is tied to land, for example, which is in short supply. Land price appreciation accounts for three-quarters of the inflation-adjusted increase in housing construction costs in the United States in the last ten years. As a consequence, developers cannot obtain a return on investment in newly constructed affordable housing without subsidy. Furthermore, housing markets are greatly influenced by financial markets. In recent years there has been a serious increase in trade on secondary mortgages, for example, from which speculators and developers benefit the most.

. . .

Individuals experience social structures as constraining, objectified, thing-like. Even relatively privileged individuals will often say that they "have no choice" about doing or not doing certain things because of the way that they experience structural processes. The landlord in my scenario might plausibly say that he is "forced" to sell the apartment building because his maintenance costs are rising and the offer on it is advantageous. He would be in bad faith, of course, to believe that he literally has no alternatives. It is not false, however, for him to believe, considered in isolation from the ways he might cooperate with others in the structures to change the way they constrain, and even though he is in a position of relative privilege in those structural processes, that he faces a limited set of options that are objectively given. It is easy for individuals to take the attitude that social facts are things, independent of human agency as such. Labor markets, for example, operate in their mysterious ways, and we treat large-scale unemployment like a fact of nature.

HISTORY OF RACISM: A BRIEF SNAPSHOT

The history of racism in the United States reaches back to before our origins as a nation—through the colonization and attempted extermination of the Native peoples whose land was stolen by conquest, broken treaties, and deception; the enslavement first of Native Americans and then kidnapped Africans to provide coerced and unpaid labor to develop agricultural and capital wealth for the early European settlers; the displacement of Mexican and Native American people, appropriation of their land, and redefining them as "foreign," as borders moved through war and conquest. It continued with the recruitment and then abuse and exploitation of Chinese, Japanese, and Filipino laborers who worked the mines and built the railroads that enabled the expansion of U.S. wealth and power to other parts of the globe (Takaki, 1993). Rationalized by Manifest Destiny and a "civilizing" mission, people of European Christian descent determined early on who could attain citizenship and its corresponding benefits in the U.S. (Haney-Lopez, 1997).

Migrants racialized as "white" in the context of the United States expanded and then consolidated a system of racial advantages based on "whiteness" to eventually include successive waves of European immigrants. Some northern Europeans were absorbed easily while others considered "not quite white" (e.g. Italians, Irish, Jews) took longer but were assimilated as "white" over time (Brodkin Sacks, 1994; Gaultieri, 2001; Guglielmo, 2003; Roediger, 1991). In so doing, those who could claim whiteness reaped the benefits of an economic and political system consolidated under white supremacy. Other advantages flowed from the attainment of citizenship and incorporation as Whites, such as property and voting rights, that enabled them to further accumulate wealth and to control the political system as well as write a version of history that glorified and normalized their dominance as legitimate and natural. This "colonization of the mind" enabled a writing of history that portrayed Latinos/as and indigenous peoples as "immigrants" and "foreigners" with no claim to the Americas, while "European Americans were constructed as the natural owners and inheritors of these lands" (Villenas and Deyhle, 1999, p. 421). Non-elite Whites illustrated another form of colonization of the mind—trading the potential of cross-race class alliances against elite Whites for the benefits of belonging to the "superior" white group, often against their own economic interests.

Nativism, supporting the interests of "native-born" people over "foreign-born" people, combined with racial animus toward (mainly non-Protestant) migrants of color to shape restrictive anti-immigration laws and populist white sentiments (Spickard, 2007). Immigration laws of the 1800s restricted immigration as rising nativist sentiments combined racism with the traditional hostility of U.S.-born, white, Anglo-Saxon Protestants toward newer immigrants from Catholic Ireland and Catholic Southern Europe, and East European Jews. Immigration laws tightly restricted immigration from China, Japan, the Philippines, and other parts of the world. Nativism intermingled with race, religion, and class interests to sustain the dominance of white, Anglo-Saxon, and Protestant elites while restricting access for other groups. These policies continued to shape political and social life across the United States and to entrench and increase white economic and political advantage until the Immigration Acts of 1965 relaxed barriers to immigration and the Civil Rights Acts of the same era opened up political and civil rights to people of African, Asian, Latino/a and Native American descent. Over the past few years, legislators have exploited a general anti-immigrant public sentiment to propose and pass anti-immigration laws in a number of states, including Alabama, Arizona, Georgia, Indiana, South Carolina, and Utah. Arizona's prototypical legislation, SB 1070, was passed in 2010. This law mandates police officers to stop and question people about immigration status if they suspect they may be in this country illegally, criminalizes undocumented workers who do not possess an "alien registration document," allows U.S. citizens to file suits against government agencies that do not enforce the law, and criminalizes employers who transport or hire undocumented workers (Sinha and Faithful, 2012). More recently, the governor of Arizona banned the public schools from teaching

ethnic studies classes, particularly the teaching of the Mexican American studies program in Tucson's public schools (Arizona Ethnic Studies Network, 2012; Sleeter, 2012).

RACIAL IDENTITIES, RACIAL HIERARCHIES, AND WHITE SUPREMACY

White supremacy and racism rationalize inequality (as natural and given) and homogenize experience by compressing social diversity into binaries and dividing racialized groups into artificial hierarchies. For example, the one-drop rule that defined as "Black" any person with blood quantum of a certain percentage (that varied by state and region) exemplifies this binary system. Established during the period of legal slavery, the one-drop rule ensured that anyone who had a remote relative of African descent, even if this heritage was not visible, could be kept in slavery (and later segregated under Jim Crow laws). This not only protected the interests of a small group of propertied Whites who reaped the benefits of the system but created a relatively large pool of self-reproducing cheap labor. Conversely, federal standards for who could be considered Native American used "blood quantum" rules to eliminate most "mixed-bloods" from tribal nationality rolls as a device to decrease Indians' claims for tribal land rights. In both cases, the goal was to perpetuate a system of advantages benefiting white wealth and ownership.

The realities of people's lives under this system are far more complex than a racialized binary suggests. We can see the contradictions in the widely varying ways that people describe President Barack Obama, a man whose ancestry includes Kenyan, Irish, German, and Native American. In his autobiography, he identifies himself as black, as do many other dark-skinned people of varying heritages, to acknowledge that they are and have historically been viewed and treated as Black by the larger society and to proudly claim and affirm that identity as an act of resistance to white supremacy. Others insist on naming Obama as biracial or multiracial, challenging a black/white binary that renders invisible other ethnic, national, tribal identities and heritages. The fact that people read Obama's "racial" identity in varying ways based on acceptance or resistance to racial binaries illustrates social construction of race in action.

The braided nature of race, class, gender, sexuality, ethnicity, ability, age, and other social categories further complicates our understanding of social identity. As members of multiple social identity groups, experiences of privilege and oppression are also mediated by cross-cutting issues of status, rank, power, and value linked to class, gender, sexuality, and age. Social identities are not themselves oppressive; they are often sources of self-understanding, pride, and sustenance. Rather, systemic practices of racism, sexism, classism, ableism, heterosexism, adultism/ageism, transgender, and religious oppression create hierarchies that devalue people based on social group membership.

CONTEMPORARY AND INTERSECTING MANIFESTATIONS
OF RACISM AND WHITE SUPREMACY

Certainly, there have been periods in the history of the United States when progress on racial issues has seemed to reduce prejudice and discrimination. Many would like to think that institutionalized racism suffered its demise with the civil rights movements of the mid-1960s and the laws passed in their wake. Yet, almost 250 years since the abolition of slavery and more than 50 years since the end of legalized segregation in the United States—although important changes have taken place—racist practices endure. The legacies of racism continue through entrenched and continuing economic, political, and social disparities. For instance, racist practices are reproduced

through pervasive gaps in wealth and income between Whites as a group and groups of color (see, for example, Oliver and Shapiro, selection 27). Racism, sexism, and classism intersect to create huge health disparities for women and their children (see "National Latina Institute for Reproductive Health Statement on Healthcare for All," selection 72). Racism combines with religious oppression to suppress the cultural expression of indigenous groups' religious beliefs and practices (see Echo-Hawk, selection 50, and Grinde, selection 51, in the "Religious Oppression" section).

Contemporary manifestations of racism and nativism are seen in the relentless criminalization of immigration status and use of incarceration, particularly in border communities and in how immigration policing continues to impact women, children and youth, Indigenous, Mexican, African, and South Asian communities and workers (see NNIRR, selection 15). It is alive in the incarceration without evidence or legal warrant (under the Patriot Act) of Arab Americans following the terrorist attacks of September 11, 2001. Racism is at work in racial and religious profiling of immigrants from Africa, Asia, Latin America and the Middle East, in the widespread immigrant raids in homes and workplaces, particularly, of immigrants from Latin America, and the poor working conditions of undocumented workers that labor in rural and urban centers. Recognition of the unique and multifaceted ways that individuals encounter racism simultaneously with gender, class, national origin, religion, and other forms of discrimination is necessary for understanding how diverse individuals and groups experience, resist, and organize to dismantle systems of oppression.

While the election of President Obama offered some hope for racial justice, it has become apparent that we cannot relax our efforts to push for change in a system that has institutionally embedded racism in all areas of social life, be it immigration, job opportunities, health-care practices, housing, or education. Racism impacts the quality of all our lives because it resides within all significant structures of society. Hence, by no measure are we in a *post-racial* era as many news and political commentators assert.

Pervasive historical legacies and deeply entrenched economic, political, and social factors continue to shape the experiences of people of color from diverse racial/ethnic groups in both shared and unique ways, as the readings in this section delineate. We hope this introduction and the selected readings that follow will encourage students to develop a sophisticated and complex understanding of race and racism to enable readers to build strong, multiracial coalitions for change. It is up to us to transform historical legacies and current manifestations of racism and white supremacy to create a society with justice for all.

CONTEXTS

The authors in our Context readings help conceptualize and trace some of the enduring features of racism over time and how racism functions on multiple levels and in different ways for diverse racial groups. In the first essay, Beverly Daniel Tatum (selection 8) provides a definition of racism as a phenomenon rooted in a system of advantage. Tatum explores how white privilege conveys social influence and power to Whites as a group and corollary disadvantage to people of color, even as it is mediated by socioeconomic status, gender, age, religious affiliation, and mental and physical ability. She also highlights the price we pay for inequality and injustice.

Ronald Takaki (selection 9) reveals the complexity of the racialization process, describing the historical trajectories, similarities, and differences in the experiences of Native Americans, African Americans, Chicanos/as, and Asian Americans as the nation developed. He also explores the divergent experiences of immigrants, such as the Irish and Jews, whose assimilation as white over time allowed them entrance into the advantaged white group.

Kimberly Roppolo (selection 10) takes a different slant, focusing on the "dysconcious," symbolic racism toward American Indians that is reflected in the continuing use of Indian mascots. She traces the roots of such stereotypes to a refusal to acknowledge the ongoing psychological

and physical violence toward Native peoples and our national legacy of theft, genocide, and dispossession.

George Lipsitz (selection 11) further unpacks the unacknowledged but ever-present "possessive investment in whiteness" that shapes public and private life in our society. He explores how white hegemony has been developed and preserved over the course of our history, influenced by the legacies of slavery and segregation, Native American extermination and immigrant restriction, conquest, and colonialism. He argues that only an explicitly anti-racist, interethnic movement that acknowledges and challenges the power of white supremacy will be powerful enough to break the hold of the possessive investment in whiteness.

Such a movement requires the kind of sophisticated thinking and analysis offered by Andrea Smith in her piece on the three pillars of white supremacy (selection 12): one based on the logic of slavery; a second, on the logic of genocide and colonialism; and a third, on the logic of Orientalism and war. Understanding these pillars, Smith argues, helps explain the divergent experiences of African Americans, Native Americans, Asian Americans, Latino Americans, and Arab Americans, all of whom experience racism but not in quite the same ways.

Next, Gloria Anzaldúa (selection 13) develops her concept of "*mestiza* consciousness," one that embraces the complexity of multiple perspectives, learns to tolerate ambiguities, and breaks down dualistic paradigms so as to be able to imagine a new way of thinking about the intersections of race, culture, language, and identity. She argues that *mestiza* consciousness provides a way to value the complex racial experiences of our hybrid nation and more creatively address the individual and collective challenges we face. Next, Heather Dalmage (selection 14) discusses how questions of citizenship and resource distribution impacted the development of binary racial thinking in the United States, which was in turn reinforced by anti-miscegenation laws that discriminated and marginalized multiracial families and individuals at the cultural, institutional, and interpersonal level. While the civil rights movement paved the way for the legal acceptance of multiraciality, she argues, the racial policing practices of individuals, groups, and institutions that believe that racial borders are static continue to push multiracial families, youth, and children to claim only one race using various "border enforcing" methods.

Finally, a report by the National Network for Immigrant and Refugee Rights (NNIRR) (selection 15) illustrates how the U.S. government, over the last 10 years, has put in place a relentless policing system to patrol national borders and to criminalize immigrants. These policies and practices increasingly support the criminalization of undocumented immigrants, normalizing the separation of families regardless of their immigration history or status, and the destabilization of border, rural, and urban communities. The rise of this policing regime propagates widespread human rights violations and contributes to the increase of racial discrimination and hate crimes against immigrants, particularly immigrants of color, who are perceived to be foreign born or "illegal." Taken together, the readings in this section help us think about racism systematically and analytically so that we will be prepared for new forms it may take as white supremacy, as it has in the past, shape-shifts to maintain its hold on society.

VOICES

The Voices selections recognize that reading and learning from the personal experiences of individuals who belong to different social identity groups can be a powerful and often transformative experience. Olivia Chung in "Finding My Eye-dentity" (selection 16) remembers her struggle as an Asian American female in trying to let go of white dominant definitions of beauty and physical appearance; she comes to embrace a broader definition of beauty and to see herself as beautiful.

In "Identification Pleas," Eric Gansworth (selection 17), a Native American, describes his experience when the U.S. border patrol, mistakenly assuming he was Latino, rejected his tribal

ID card as valid U.S. identification. History shows how the erasure of individual and group experience through stereotyping deprives people of their humanity and can help justify colonization, exploitation, marginalization, and discrimination. Mona Fayad (selection 18), in "The Arab Woman and I," describes the impact of stereotyping on her life as an Arab woman, showing how misinformation and ignorance lead many Westerners to render her faceless, powerless, passive, and seductive. (Other examples of the experiences of Arab American women can be found in selections 55 and 57.)

Quique Aviles (selection 19) came to Washington, DC from El Salvador during a period of political unrest. In "My Tongue is Divided into Two," he describes his journey of learning the English language and using it as a source of empowerment and liberation.

The danger of the popular notion that race or skin color no longer matters is addressed in the next selection (selection 20). In "The Emperor's New Clothes," Patricia Williams shows how the professed "color blindness" of her son's white teachers led them to ignore the very real victimization he experienced as the only black child on the playground. She shows how "color blindness" can become a rationale for the denial of racism, making it more difficult to address the many ways race and white supremacy pervades our individual lives and institutions.

Finally, Jan Arminio's "Waking Up White" (selection 21) describes the process by which white people learn to realize that being white is both a social category and a racial identity. She invites Whites to recognize the historical legacies that shape their social status in society and consciously decide what role they want to play as white individuals in a racist society.

NEXT STEPS

In Next Steps, we highlight concrete action steps we can take to challenge the causes and effects of racism and white supremacy and to work toward transforming historical legacies through individual actions, dialogues across racial divides, and multiracial coalitions for change. For example in the first selection, Andrea Ayvazian and Beverly Daniel Tatum (selection 22) illustrate the power of sustained dialogue to explore, validate, and critically examine people's experiences and perspectives across race and other social identities to foster deeper understanding and a strong sense of relational connection, even in the midst of conflict in order to forge strong ally relations.

The FLEX model developed by Carmelita (Rosie) Castañeda (selection 23) supports communication across racial, ethnic, and linguistic groups and provides concrete steps for improving intercultural communication in diverse classrooms, cross-racial/ethnic dialogues, and community-based coalitions.

We close with Chip Smith's "The Personal is Political." This selection (24) helps us think about how we each can strengthen our engagement in the struggle against white supremacy through becoming aware of privilege and internalized oppression; building intentional relationships based on equality; studying the history of people of color; questioning and challenging the evidence of white supremacy at work, schools, and communities; taking inventory of activism in one's community; and examining other aspects of one's community that may bring people together to actively address racial inequality.

See Companion Website for Additional Resources and Material

Notes

1 We ask that those who cite this work always acknowledge by name both of the authors listed rather than only citing the first author or using "et al." to indicate coauthors. Both collaborated equitably on the conceptualization, development, and writing of this section.

2 We want to acknowledge the valuable contributions made to the 2nd edition of this introduction and chapter selections by Lee Anne Bell. Her contributions remain apparent in this third edition as well.

References

The Achievement Gap Initiative at Harvard University (2011). *The Facts on the Gap*. Retrieved from http://www.agi.harvard.edu/projects/thegap.php

Alexander, M. (2012). *The New Jim Crow: Mass Incarceration in the Age of Colorblindness*. New York: The New Press.

Arizona Ethnic Studies Network (March 15, 2012). Why Ethnic Studies matter. Retrieved from http://thefeministwire.com/2012/03/why-ethnic-studies-matters/

Brodkin-Sacks, K. (1994). How did Jews become white folks? In S. Gregory and R. Sanjek (eds), *Race* (pp. 78-102). New Brunswick, NJ: Rutgers University Press.

Delpit, L. (2012). *"Multiplication is for White People." Raising Expectations for Other People's Children*. New York: The New Press.

Education Week (July 7, 2011). Achievement gap. Retrieved from http://www.edweek.org/ew/issues/achievement-gap/

Gaultieri, S. (2001). Becoming "White": Race, religion and the foundations of Syrian/Lebanese ethnicity in the United States. *Journal of American Ethnic History* 20 (4), 29–59.

Gándara, P. (2010). *The Latino Education Crisis*. Cambridge, MA: Harvard University Press.

Guglielmo, T. A. (2003). Rethinking whiteness historiography: The case of Italians in Chicago, 1890–1945. In A. W. Doane, E. Bonilla-Silva (eds), *White Out: The Continuing Significance of Racism* (pp. 49–61). New York, NY: Routledge.

Haney-Lopez, I. F. (1997). *White by Law*. New York, NY: New York University Press.

Haney-Lopez, I. F. (2010). Post-racial racism: Racial stratification and mass incarceration in the age of Obama. *California Law Review* 98, 1023–1073

Madrid, M. E. (2011). The Latino achievement gap. *Multicultural Education* 19 (3), 7–12.

Obama, B. (2008). *A More Perfect Union.* Presidential campaign speech delivered on March 18, 2008, at Convention Hall, Philadelphia, PA. Retrieved September 19, 2009, from http://my.barackobama.com/page/content/hisownwords.

Roediger, D. R. (1991). The prehistory of the white worker: Settler colonialism, race and republicanism before 1800. In *The Wages of Whiteness: Race and the Making of the American Working Class* (revised edition, pp. 19–40) London: Verso.

Sinha, A., Faithful, R. (February, 2012). State battles over immigration: The forecast for 2012. Retrieved from http://www.advancementproject.org/sites/default/files/publications/Immigrant%20Rights%202012%20Legislative%20Battles_FINAL%20Feb%201%202012_0.pdf

Sleeter, C. (February 15, 2012). Ethnic Studies and the struggle in Tucson. Retrieved from http://www.edweek.org/ew/articles/2012/02/15/21sleeter.h31.html

Spickard, P. (2007). *Almost All Aliens: Immigration, Race and Colonialism in American History and Identity*. New York, NY: Routledge.

Takaki, R. (1993). *A Different Mirror: A History of Multicultural America*. Boston, MA: Little, Brown.

U.S. Bureau of Labor Statistics (October 5, 2012). Unemployment rates by race and ethnicity, 2010. Retrieved from http://www.bls.gov/opub/ted/2011/ted_20111005.htm

Villenas, S., Deyhle, D. (1999). Critical race theory and ethnographies challenging stereotypes: Latino families, schooling, resilience and resistance. *Curriculum Inquiry* 29, 413–445.

Wise, T. (2012). *Dear White America: Letter to a New Minority*. San Francisco, CA: City Lights Books.

8

Defining Racism

"Can We Talk?"

Beverly Daniel Tatum

. . .

The impact of racism begins early. Even in our preschool years, we are exposed to misinformation about people different from ourselves. Many of us grew up in neighborhoods where we had limited opportunities to interact with people different from our own families. When I ask my college students, "How many of you grew up in neighborhoods where most of the people were from the same racial group as your own?" almost every hand goes up. There is still a great deal of social segregation in our communities. Consequently, most of the early information we receive about "others"—people racially, religiously, or socioeconomically different from ourselves—does not come as the result of firsthand experience. The secondhand information we do receive has often been distorted, shaped by cultural stereotypes, and left incomplete.

. . .

Sometimes the assumptions we make about others come not from what we have been told or what we have seen on television or in books, but rather from what we have *not* been told. The distortion of historical information about people of color leads young people (and older people, too) to make assumptions that may go unchallenged for a long time. . . .

. . .

Omitted information can have similar effects. For example, another young woman, preparing to be a high school English teacher, expressed her dismay that she had never learned about any Black authors in any of her English courses. How was she to teach about them to her future students when she hadn't learned about them herself? A White male student in the class responded to this discussion with frustration in his response journal, writing "It's not my fault that Blacks don't write books." Had one of his elementary, high school, or college teachers ever told him that there were no Black writers? Probably not. Yet because he had never been exposed to Black authors, he had drawn his own conclusion that there were none.

Stereotypes, omissions, and distortions all contribute to the development of prejudice. *Prejudice* is a preconceived judgment or opinion, usually based on limited information. I assume that we all have prejudices, not because we want them, but simply because we are so continually exposed to misinformation about others. Though I have often heard students or workshop participants describe someone as not having "a prejudiced bone in his body," I usually suggest that they look again. Prejudice is one of the inescapable consequences of living in a racist society. Cultural racism—the cultural images and messages that affirm the assumed superiority of Whites and the assumed inferiority of people of color—is like smog in the air. Sometimes it is so thick it is visible, other times it is less apparent, but always, day in and day out, we are breathing it in. None of us would introduce ourselves as "smog-breathers" (and most of us don't want to be described as prejudiced), but if we live in a smoggy place, how can we avoid breathing the air? If we live in an environment in which we are bombarded with stereotypical images in the media, are frequently exposed to the ethnic jokes of friends and family members, and are rarely informed of

CONTEXT

the accomplishments of oppressed groups, we will develop the negative categorizations of those groups that form the basis of prejudice.

People of color as well as Whites develop these categorizations. Even a member of the stereotyped group may internalize the stereotypical categories about his or her own group to some degree. In fact, this process happens so frequently that it has a name, *internalized oppression.* . . .

. . .

To say that it is not our fault does not relieve us of responsibility, however. We may not have polluted the air, but we need to take responsibility, along with others, for cleaning it up. Each of us needs to look at our own behavior. Am I perpetuating and reinforcing the negative messages so pervasive in our culture, or am I seeking to challenge them? If I have not been exposed to positive images of marginalized groups, am I seeking them out, expanding my own knowledge base for myself and my children? Am I acknowledging and examining my own prejudices, my own rigid categorizations of others, thereby minimizing the adverse impact they might have on my interactions with those I have categorized? Unless we engage in these and other conscious acts of reflection and reeducation, we easily repeat the process with our children. We teach what we were taught. The unexamined prejudices of the parents are passed on to the children. It is not our fault, but it is our responsibility to interrupt this cycle.

RACISM: A SYSTEM OF ADVANTAGE BASED ON RACE

Many people use the terms *prejudice* and *racism* interchangeably. I do not, and I think it is important to make a distinction. In his book *Portraits of White Racism*, David Wellman argues convincingly that limiting our understanding of racism to prejudice does not offer a sufficient explanation for the persistence of racism. He defines racism as a system of advantage based on race. In illustrating this definition, he provides example after example of how Whites defend their racial advantage—access to better schools, housing, jobs—even when they do not embrace overtly prejudicial thinking. Racism cannot be fully explained as an expression of prejudice alone.

This definition of racism is useful because it allows us to see that racism, like other forms of oppression, is not only a personal ideology based on racial prejudice, but a *system* involving cultural messages and institutional policies and practices as well as the beliefs and actions of individuals. In the context of the United States, this system clearly operates to the advantage of Whites and to the disadvantage of people of color. Another related definition of racism, commonly used by antiracist educators and consultants, is "prejudice plus power." Racial prejudice when combined with social power—access to social, cultural, and economic resources and decision-making—leads to the institutionalization of racist policies and practices. While I think this definition also captures the idea that racism is more than individual beliefs and attitudes, I prefer Wellman's definition because the idea of systematic advantage and disadvantage is critical to an understanding of how racism operates in American society.

. . .

The systematic advantages of being White are often referred to as White privilege. In a now well-known article, "White Privilege: Unpacking the Invisible Knapsack," Peggy McIntosh, a White feminist scholar, identified a long list of societal privileges that she received simply because she was White. She did not ask for them, and it is important to note that she hadn't always noticed that she was receiving them. They included major and minor advantages. Of course she enjoyed greater access to jobs and housing. But she also

was able to shop in department stores without being followed by suspicious sales-people and could always find appropriate hair care products and makeup in any drugstore. She could send her child to school confident that the teacher would not discriminate against him on the basis of race. She could also be late for meetings, and talk with her mouth full, fairly confident that these behaviors would not be attributed to the fact that she was White. She could express an opinion in a meeting or in print and not have it labeled the "White" viewpoint. In other words, she was more often than not viewed as an individual, rather than as a member of a racial group.

. . .

Understanding racism as a system of advantage based on race is antithetical to traditional notions of an American meritocracy. For those who have internalized this myth, this definition generates considerable discomfort. It is more comfortable simply to think of racism as a particular form of prejudice. Notions of power or privilege do not have to be addressed when our understanding of racism is constructed in that way.

. . .

RACISM: FOR WHITES ONLY?

. . .

I sometimes visualize the ongoing cycle of racism as a moving walkway at the airport. Active racist behavior is equivalent to walking fast on the conveyor belt. The person engaged in active racist behavior has identified with the ideology of White supremacy and is moving with it. Passive racist behavior is equivalent to standing still on the walkway. No overt effort is being made, but the conveyor belt moves the bystanders along to the same destination as those who are actively walking. Some of the bystanders may feel the motion of the conveyor belt, see the active racists ahead of them, and choose to turn around, unwilling to go to the same destination as the White supremacists. But unless they are walking actively in the opposite direction at a speed faster than the conveyor belt—unless they are actively antiracist—they will find themselves carried along with the others.

. . .

It is important to acknowledge that while all Whites benefit from racism, they do not all benefit equally. Other factors, such as socio-economic status, gender, age, religious affiliation, sexual orientation, mental and physical ability, also play a role in our access to social influence and power. A White woman on welfare is not privileged to the same extent as a wealthy White heterosexual man. In her case, the systematic disadvantages of sexism and classism intersect with her White privilege, but the privilege is still there. This point was brought home to me in a 1994 study conducted by a Mount Holyoke graduate student, Phyllis Wentworth. Wentworth interviewed a group of female college students, who were both older than their peers and were the first members of their families to attend college, about the pathways that led them to college. All of the women interviewed were White, from working-class backgrounds, from families where women were expected to graduate from high school and get married or get a job. Several had experienced abusive relationships and other personal difficulties prior to coming to college. Yet their experiences were punctuated by "good luck" stories of apartments obtained without a deposit, good jobs offered without experience or extensive reference checks, and encouragement provided by willing mentors. While the women acknowledged their good fortune, none of them discussed their Whiteness. They had not considered the possibility that being White had worked in their favor and helped give them the benefit of the doubt at critical junctures.

This study clearly showed that even under difficult circumstances, White privilege was still operating.

It is also true that not all people of color are equally targeted by racism. We all have multiple identities that shape our experience. I can describe myself as a light-skinned, well-educated, heterosexual, able-bodied, Christian African American woman raised in a middle-class suburb. As an African American woman, I am systematically disadvantaged by race and by gender, but I systematically receive benefits in the other categories, which then mediate my experience of racism and sexism. When one is targeted by multiple isms—racism, sexism, classism, heterosexism, ableism, anti-Semitism, ageism—in whatever combination, the effect is intensified. The particular combination of racism and classism in many communities of color is life-threatening. Nonetheless, when I, the middle-class Black mother of two sons, read another story about a Black man's unlucky encounter with a White police officer's deadly force, I am reminded that racism by itself can kill.

THE COST OF RACISM

. . . Why should Whites who are advantaged by racism *want* to end that system of advantage? What are the *costs* of that system to them?

A *Money* magazine article called "Race and Money" chronicled the many ways the American economy was hindered by institutional racism. Whether one looks at productivity lowered by racial tensions in the workplace, or real estate equity lost through housing discrimination, or the tax revenue lost in underemployed communities of color, or the high cost of warehousing human talent in prison, the economic costs of racism are real and measurable.

As a psychologist, I often hear about the less easily measured costs. When I ask White men and women how racism hurts them, they frequently talk about their fears of people of color, the social incompetence they feel in racially mixed situations, the alienation they have experienced between parents and children when a child marries into a family of color, and the interracial friendships they had as children that were lost in adolescence or young adulthood without their ever understanding why. White people are paying a significant price for the system of advantage. The cost is not as high for Whites as it is for people of color, but a price is being paid. . . .

The dismantling of racism is in the best interests of everyone.

. . .

9

A Different Mirror

Ronald Takaki

I had flown from San Francisco to Norfolk and was riding in a taxi to my hotel to attend a conference on multiculturalism. Hundreds of educators from across the country were

meeting to discuss the need for greater cultural diversity in the curriculum. My driver and I chatted about the weather and the tourists. The sky was cloudy, and Virginia Beach was twenty minutes away. The rearview mirror reflected a white man in his forties. "How long have you been in this country?" he asked. "All my life," I replied, wincing. "I was born in the United States." With a strong southern drawl, he remarked: "I was wondering because your English is excellent!" Then, as I had many times before, I explained: "My grandfather came here from Japan in the 1880s. My family has been here, in America, for over a hundred years." He glanced at me in the mirror. Somehow I did not look "American" to him; my eyes and complexion looked foreign.

. . .

Questions like the one my taxi driver asked me are always jarring, but I can understand why he could not see me as American. He had a narrow but widely shared sense of the past—a history that has viewed American as European in ancestry. "Race," Toni Morrison explained, has functioned as a "metaphor" necessary to the "construction of Americanness": in the creation of our national identity, "American" has been defined as "white."

. . .

But how should "we" be defined? Who are the people "stuck here" in America? One of the lessons of the Los Angeles explosion is the recognition of the fact that we are a multiracial society and that race can no longer be defined in the binary terms of white and black. "We" will have to include Hispanics and Asians. While blacks currently constitute 13 percent of the Los Angeles population, Hispanics represent 40 percent. The 1990 census revealed that South Central Los Angeles, which was predominantly black in 1965 when the Watts rebellion occurred, is now 45 percent Hispanic. A majority of the first 5,438 people arrested were Hispanic, while 37 percent were black. Of the fifty-eight people who died in the riot, more than a third were Hispanic, and about 40 percent of the businesses destroyed were Hispanic-owned. Most of the other shops and stores were Korean-owned. The dreams of many Korean immigrants went up in smoke during the riot: two thousand Korean-owned businesses were damaged or demolished, totaling about $400 million in losses. There is evidence indicating they were targeted. "After all," explained a black gang member, "we didn't burn our community, just *their* stores."

. . .

African Americans have been the central minority throughout our country's history. They were initially brought here on a slave ship in 1619. Actually, these first twenty Africans might not have been slaves; rather, like most of the white laborers, they were probably indentured servants. The transformation of Africans into slaves is the story of the "hidden" origins of slavery. How and when was it decided to institute a system of bonded black labor? What happened, while freighted with racial significance, was actually conditioned by class conflicts within white society. Once established, the "peculiar institution" would have consequences for centuries to come. During the nineteenth century, the political storm over slavery almost destroyed the nation. Since the Civil War and emancipation, race has continued to be largely defined in relation to African Americans—segregation, civil rights, the underclass, and affirmative action. Constituting the largest minority group in our society, they have been at the cutting edge of the Civil Rights Movement. Indeed, their struggle has been a constant reminder of America's moral vision as a country committed to the principle of liberty. Martin Luther King clearly understood this truth when he wrote from a jail cell: "We will reach the goal of freedom in Birmingham and all over the nation, because the goal of America is freedom. Abused and scorned though we may be, our destiny is tied up with America's destiny."

Asian Americans have been here for over one hundred and fifty years, before many European immigrant groups. But as "strangers" coming from a "different shore," they have been stereotyped as "heathen," exotic, and unassimilable. Seeking "Gold Mountain,"

the Chinese arrived first, and what happened to them influenced the reception of the Japanese, Koreans, Filipinos, and Asian Indians as well as the Southeast Asian refugees like the Vietnamese and the Hmong. The 1882 Chinese Exclusion Act was the first law that prohibited the entry of immigrants on the basis of nationality. The Chinese condemned this restriction as racist and tyrannical. "They call us 'Chink,'" complained a Chinese immigrant, cursing the "white demons." "They think we no good! America cuts us off. No more come now, too bad!" This precedent later provided a basis for the restriction of European immigrant groups such as Italians, Russians, Poles, and Greeks. The Japanese painfully discovered that their accomplishments in America did not lead to acceptance, for during World War II, unlike Italian Americans and German Americans, they were placed in internment camps. Two-thirds of them were citizens by birth. "How could I as a 6-month-old child born in this country," asked Congressman Robert Matsui years later, "be declared by my own Government to be an enemy alien?" Today, Asian Americans represent the fastest-growing ethnic group. They have also become the focus of much mass media attention as "the Model Minority" not only for blacks and Chicanos, but also for whites on welfare and even middle-class whites experiencing economic difficulties.

Chicanos represent the largest group among the Hispanic population, which is projected to outnumber African Americans. They have been in the United States for a long time, initially incorporated by the war against Mexico. The treaty had moved the border between the two countries, and the people of "occupied" Mexico suddenly found themselves "foreigners" in their "native land." As historian Albert Camarillo pointed out, the Chicano past is an integral part of America's westward expansion, also known as "manifest destiny." But while the early Chicanos were a colonized people, most of them today have immigrant roots. Many began the trek to El Norte in the early twentieth century. "As I had heard a lot about the United States," Jesus Garza recalled, "it was my dream to come here." "We came to know families from Chihuahua, Sonora, Jalisco, and Durango," stated Ernesto Galarza. "Like ourselves, our Mexican neighbors had come this far moving step by step, working and waiting, as if they were feeling their way up a ladder." Nevertheless, the Chicano experience has been unique, for most of them have lived close to their homeland—a proximity that has helped reinforce their language, identity, and culture. This migration to El Norte has continued to the present. Los Angeles has more people of Mexican origin than any other city in the world, except Mexico City. A mostly mestizo people of Indian as well as African and Spanish ancestries, Chicanos currently represent the largest minority group in the Southwest, where they have been visibly transforming culture and society.

The Irish came here in greater numbers than most immigrant groups. Their history has been tied to America's past from the very beginning. Ireland represented the earliest English frontier: the conquest of Ireland occurred before the colonization of America, and the Irish were the first group that the English called "savages." In this context, the Irish past foreshadowed the Indian future. During the nineteenth century, the Irish, like the Chinese, were victims of British colonialism. While the Chinese fled from the ravages of the Opium Wars, the Irish were pushed from their homeland by "English tyranny." Here they became construction workers and factory operatives as well as the "maids" of America. Representing a Catholic group seeking to settle in a fiercely Protestant society, the Irish immigrants were targets of American nativist hostility. They were also what historian Lawrence J. McCaffrey called "the pioneers of the American urban ghetto," "previewing" experiences that would later be shared by the Italians, Poles, and other groups from southern and eastern Europe. Furthermore, they offer contrast to the immigrants from Asia. The Irish came about the same time as the Chinese, but they had a distinct advantage: the Naturalization Law of 1790 had reserved citizenship for "whites" only. Their compatible complexion allowed them to assimilate by blending into American society. In making their journey successfully into the mainstream, however, these immigrants from Erin pursued

an Irish "ethnic" strategy: they promoted "Irish" solidarity in order to gain political power and also to dominate the skilled blue-collar occupations, often at the expense of the Chinese and blacks.

Fleeing pogroms and religious persecution in Russia, the Jews were driven from what John Cuddihy described as the "Middle Ages into the Anglo-American world of the *goyim* 'beyond the pale.'" To them, America represented the Promised Land. This vision led Jews to struggle not only for themselves but also for other oppressed groups, especially blacks. After the 1917 East St. Louis race riot, the Yiddish *Forward* of New York compared this anti-black violence to a 1903 pogrom in Russia: "Kishinev and St. Louis—the same soil, the same people." Jews cheered when Jackie Robinson broke into the Brooklyn Dodgers in 1947. "He was adopted as the surrogate hero by many of us growing up at the time," recalled Jack Greenberg of the NAACP Legal Defense Fund. "He was the way we saw ourselves triumphing against the forces of bigotry and ignorance." Jews stood shoulder to shoulder with blacks in the Civil Rights Movement: two-thirds of the white volunteers who went south during the 1964 Freedom Summer were Jewish. Today Jews are considered a highly successful "ethnic" group. How did they make such great socioeconomic strides? This question is often reframed by neoconservative intellectuals like Irving Kristol and Nathan Glazer to read: if Jewish immigrants were able to lift themselves from poverty into the mainstream through self-help and education without welfare and affirmative action, why can't blacks? But what this thinking overlooks is the unique history of Jewish immigrants, especially the initial advantages of many of them as literate and skilled. Moreover, it minimizes the virulence of racial prejudice rooted in American slavery.

Indians represent a critical contrast, for theirs was not an immigrant experience. The Wampanoags were on the shore as the first English strangers arrived in what would be called "New England." The encounters between Indians and whites not only shaped the course of race relations, but also influenced the very culture and identity of the general society. The architect of Indian removal, President Andrew Jackson told Congress: "Our conduct toward these people is deeply interesting to the national character." Frederick Jackson Turner understood the meaning of this observation when he identified the frontier as our transforming crucible. At first, the European newcomers had to wear Indian moccasins and shout the war cry. "Little by little," as they subdued the wilderness, the pioneers became "a new product" that was "American." But Indians have had a different view of this entire process. "The white man," Luther Standing Bear of the Sioux explained, "does not understand the Indian for the reason that he does not understand American." Continuing to be "troubled with primitive fears," he has "in his consciousness the perils of this frontier continent. . . . The man from Europe is still a foreigner and an alien. And he still hates the man who questioned his path across the continent." Indians questioned what Jackson and Turner trumpeted as "progress." For them, the frontier had a different "significance": their history was how the West was lost. But their story has also been one of resistance. As Vine Deloria declared, "Custer died for your sins."

By looking at these groups from a multicultural perspective, we can comparatively analyze their experiences in order to develop an understanding of their differences and similarities. Race, we will see, has been a social construction that has historically set apart racial minorities from European immigrant groups. Contrary to the notions of scholars like Nathan Glazer and Thomas Sowell, race in America has not been the same as ethnicity. A broad comparative focus also allows us to see how the varied experiences of different racial and ethnic groups occurred within shared contexts.

During the nineteenth century, for example, the Market Revolution employed Irish immigrant laborers in New England factories as it expanded cotton fields worked by enslaved blacks across Indian lands toward Mexico. Like blacks, the Irish newcomers were stereotyped as "savages," ruled by passions rather than "civilized" virtues such as

self-control and hard work. The Irish saw themselves as the "slaves" of British oppressors, and during a visit to Ireland in the 1840s, Frederick Douglass found that the "wailing notes" of the Irish ballads reminded him of the "wild notes" of slave songs. The United States annexation of California, while incorporating Mexicans, led to trade with Asia and the migration of "strangers" from Pacific shores. In 1870, Chinese immigrant laborers were transported to Massachusetts as scabs to break an Irish immigrant strike; in response, the Irish recognized the need for interethnic working-class solidarity and tried to organize a Chinese lodge of the Knights of St. Crispin. After the Civil War, Mississippi planters recruited Chinese immigrants to discipline the newly freed blacks. During the debate over an immigration exclusion bill in 1882, a senator asked: If Indians could be located on reservations, why not the Chinese?

Other instances of our connectedness abound. In 1903, Mexican and Japanese farm laborers went on strike together in California: their union officers had names like Yamaguchi and Lizarras, and strike meetings were conducted in Japanese and Spanish. The Mexican strikers declared that they were standing in solidarity with their "Japanese brothers" because the two groups had toiled together in the fields and were now fighting together for a fair wage. Speaking in impassioned Yiddish during the 1909 "uprising of twenty thousand" strikers in New York, the charismatic Clara Lemlich compared the abuse of Jewish female garment workers to the experience of blacks: "[The bosses] yell at the girls and 'call them down' even worse than I imagine the Negro slaves were in the South." During the 1920s, elite universities like Harvard worried about the increasing numbers of Jewish students, and new admissions criteria were instituted to curb their enrollment. Jewish students were scorned for their studiousness and criticized for their "clannishness." Recently, Asian-American students have been the targets of similar complaints: they have been called "nerds" and told there are "too many" of them on campus.

Indians were already here, while blacks were forcibly transported to America, and Mexicans were initially enclosed by America's expanding border. The other groups came here as immigrants: for them, America represented liminality—a new world where they could pursue extravagant urges and do things they had thought beyond their capabilities. Like the land itself, they found themselves "betwixt and between all fixed points of classification." No longer fastened as fiercely to their old countries, they felt a stirring to become new people in a society still being defined and formed.

. . .

. . . Through their stories, the people who have lived America's history can help all of us, including my taxi driver, understand that Americans originated from many shores, and that all of us are entitled to dignity. "I hope this survey do a lot of good for Chinese people," an immigrant told an interviewer from Stanford University in the 1920s. "Make American people realize that Chinese people are humans. I think very few American people really know anything about Chinese." But the remembering is also for the sake of the children. "This story is dedicated to the descendants of Lazar and Goldie Glauberman," Jewish immigrant Minnie Miller wrote in her autobiography. "My history is bound up in their history and the generations that follow should know where they came from to know better who they are." Similarly, Tomo Shoji, an elderly Nisei woman, urged Asian Americans to learn more about their roots: "We got such good, fantastic stories to tell. All our stories are different." Seeking to know how they fit into America, many young people have become listeners; they are eager to learn about the hardships and humiliations experienced by their parents and grandparents. They want to hear their stories, unwilling to remain ignorant or ashamed of their identity and past.

. . .

Through their narratives about their lives and circumstances, the people of America's diverse groups are able to see themselves and each other in our common past. They

celebrate what Ishmael Reed has described as a society "unique" in the world because "the world is here"—a place "where the cultures of the world crisscross." Much of America's past, they point out, has been riddled with racism. At the same time, these people offer hope, affirming the struggle for equality as a central theme in our country's history. At its conception, our nation was dedicated to the proposition of equality. What has given concreteness to this powerful national principle has been our coming together in the creation of a new society. "Stuck here" together, workers of different backgrounds have attempted to get along with each other.

> *People harvesting*
> *Work together unaware*
> *Of racial problems,*

wrote a Japanese immigrant describing a lesson learned by Mexican and Asian farm laborers in California.

. . .

10

Symbolic Racism, History, and Reality

The Real Problem with Indian Mascots

Kimberly Roppolo

The stadium lights starburst above the misty football field. The band blares and pounds out the school's fight song like only a hometown high school band can do. Blond, perky cheerleaders clap as they hop from foot to foot, rousing the fans to a controlled roar. Two of them hold a huge sign, painted painstakingly while sprawled across a dusty, linoleum-lined corridor. The men of the hour prepare to enter the arena of combat. They begin a slow trot, then burst through the paper to shouting cheerleaders—"Kill the Indians!" they scream.

Many people would say I am overreacting to be offended by this scenario. After all, what's more American than high school football? What could be a more wholesome activity for young people in today's age, when so many more dangerous temptations beset them at every side—drugs, alcohol, unprotected sex, and gang activity? I think the danger of this situation is that it is so precisely American. Americans in general see the Indian mascot controversy as "silly," and there are admittedly American Indians who see it the same way. . . . However, I think the danger of this use is more than just its potential to offend. It is representative of an endemic problem: racism against America's First Peoples. Despite the fact that racial problems still exist in our country, for the most part we are in a day and age where racial tolerance and tolerance for all kinds of diversity has increased. But this is not the case with racism against American Indians, largely because racism against American Indians is so ingrained in the American consciousness that it is invisible.

Dr. Cornell Pewewardy of the University of Kansas calls this kind of racism "dyscon-scious racism," or, in other words, racism that the people themselves who exhibit it are unaware of. The use of American Indian mascots falls under this category. The grossly exaggerated features of the Cleveland Indian, the cartooned vicious savages decorating high school spirit ribbons, the painted, dancing, fake-buckskin-clad white kids running down the sideline doing tomahawk chops, are all unintentionally stereotypical and aren't even perceived by most Americans as negative. They fall in the same category as rock singer Ted Nugent's ridiculous stage antics in a fluorescent mockery of a Plains chief's headdress. They fall under the same category as cigar store Indians topping car dealerships. They fall under the same category as words like "squaw," "papoose," "wagon burner," and "Indian giver." They fall under the same category as Disney's painted bombshell Pocahontas and the 36–24–36 asking-for-it Aztec seductress from *El Dorado* or her grotesquely depicted male counterparts. . . . The average American engages in this behavior without ever being aware of it, much less realizing that it is racism.

Every semester I ask my students what is in the front foyer of Applebee's restaurant. None of them, not even if they work there, are ever able to tell me there is a statue of an Indian man, in nonspecific tribal attire, often with a "special of the day" sign around his neck. Applebee's claims this statue "points to the next nearest Applebee's"; I guarantee that if a major restaurant chain placed a statue of an African American man in supposed tribal dress in the front of each of its restaurants pointing to the next nearest one, people would realize these statues were inappropriate. In the same way, as many others have pointed out, if we had sports teams named the New York Niggers or the Jersey Jigaboos, Americans would know this was wrong. The average American, who would clearly perceive the Louisville Lynched Porch Monkeys as a problematic name for a team doesn't even realize the Washington Redskins emerges from a history of the literal bloody skins of American Indian men, women, and children being worth British Crown bounty money—no one's skin is red. American Indian skin is brown, at least when it is on our bodies and not stripped from us in the name of profit and expansionism. African Americans, thank God, have raised the consciousness of Americans enough through the civil rights movement to keep the more obvious forms of racism usually hidden, though it took publicly armed Black Panthers, the burning of Chicago, and even the riots of Los Angeles to get this point across. American Indians are frankly so used to being literally shot down if we stick our heads up, we aren't nearly as likely to do so. In fact, from our own civil rights movement with AIM, we still have Indians like Leonard Peltier, who stuck their heads up although incarcerated for over twenty years when even the FBI admits its evidence was fabricated.

Racism against American Indians is so intrinsically part of America's political mythol-ogy, . . . that without it this country would have to do something it is has never done: face colonial guilt. Everything we see around us was made from stolen American Indian resources, resources raped from this Earth that we consider sacred, an Earth in danger of global disaster from imbalanced greed. We live like no people in the history of the world have ever lived. Our poorest are rich in comparison to the world's average citizen. We all—Indian, Euro American, Asian American, African American, or Chicano—have benefited at least in some material way from the murders of an estimated one hundred million people, crimes that are still going on in this hemisphere, in Mexico, in Argentina, in Oklahoma, in South Dakota, in New Mexico, Arizona, Montana, and more. These acts, along with innumerable rapes, along with untold numbers of sterilizations of women even up to the past few decades, along with the removal of children without cause from their parents' homes, from their cultures, along with the destruction of language, with the outlawing of religious freedom up until 1978, constitute what is defined as genocide under the United Nations Convention on Genocide's definition, a document never signed by the United States, because under it, that very government owes restitution to both American

Indians and to African Americans, an estimated forty to sixty million of whom were killed during the slave trade before they ever reached the shores of the "New World."

An estimated six million Jews died in the atrocities committed in Nazi Germany, being treated before and after death in ways the world will never forgive—starved, herded naked like cattle, poisoned to an excruciating death, made into curios—lampshades, little collectibles for the Nazi elite. But this we recognize as inhuman, not the kind of behavior we as people can tolerate. We see the sins of Germany and the sins of Bosnia, where former students report seeing little girls with dolls still in their arms, dead with open eyes in mass graves, for what they are. But unlike the rest of the world, we as Americans cannot see our own. We are not taught in school that Columbus's men smashed babies' heads on rocks in front of their mothers. We are not taught that they sliced people in two for fun, in bets over whose sword was the sharpest. We are not taught they tied men up after slaving in silver mines all day, threw them under their hammocks, and raped their wives above them. We aren't taught that the Pilgrims were called the "cut-throat people" by the Indians, who taught them survival and feasted with them because, at one meal the good Christians invited them to, those very Christians took their knives and slit them from ear to ear. We aren't taught that our "forefathers" roasted Pequot men, women, and children alive in their beds. We aren't taught that Thomas Jefferson promoted miscegenation as a means of eradicating the "Indian problem." We are not taught that American soldiers collected labia and breasts and penises for curios after slaughtering women, children, and old men on what must be considered, when we look at the primary evidence of American history, a routine basis. The list goes on and on. We aren't, indeed, taught a lot of things. And we aren't taught them for a good reason. . . .

American Indian Nations are the only sovereign nations the United States government has ever broken over five hundred treaties with, violations that Russell Means rightly suggests gives these nations the legal justification to issue one huge eviction notice to the United States, the only nations whose citizens are owed . . . billions of dollars in money that was held in "trust" for Indians thought incapable of being responsible for it, billions of dollars that same United States government has lost. Despite this, American Indians serve this country in its military forces in higher numbers per capita than any other ethnic group—and have in every war since the American Revolution. Despite this, American Indians on the whole maintain a huge amount of respect for this country and the flag that flies above it.

The real problem with the kind of dysconscious, symbolic, abstract racism that is perpetuated today by sports mascots and the kind of historical, intentionally inculcated, politically motivated racism that enabled the near total genocide of American Indian peoples is that it enables very real, very concrete, and very conscious acts of violent racism that American Indian people still face in this country and this hemisphere on a daily basis. It is our conceptualization of people that dictates our behavior toward them. Most Americans don't come into contact with Indians on a daily basis because of that very genocide, or when they do, because of the campaign of rape and encouraged miscegenation through intermarriage, they don't realize they do. To most Americans, American Indians themselves are invisible. . . . But for Americans who live near or on reservations or tribally controlled lands and for our neighbors to the south, who very much still realize an Indian presence in "their" countries, . . . and because of the atmosphere of hatred that the dysconsious racism of the rest of the country allows and even promotes, violence abounds.

This is not to say that no other group in America is still subject to prejudice-induced violence. There are occasionally still unspeakable acts against African Americans like the one in Jasper, Texas. There are also unfortunately incidents of violent bigotry against homosexuals, like the one in Laramie, Wyoming, that led to the creation of federal hate-crime legislation. But the fact is that American Indian women are twice as likely as black men to

die of homicide. White males commit most of these murders; most involve alcohol sold by white proprietors on reservation borders; many are never prosecuted. Like the murders in the 1970s that instigated the American Indian movement to begin with and the rash of Indian killings that followed it, these murders go largely unnoticed by mainstream America. So do the beatings. So do the rapes. If "real" Indians don't exist in the American mind, then hate crimes against them have no room in the American imagination of possibility. And the media, the same media that descends from that which actively promoted the extermination of Indians through the early 1900s, don't cover that continued extermination now because of their early effectiveness in our erasure.

. . .

Perpetuators of conscious racism in more Indian-populated regions of this country will justify their behavior with accusations that Indians themselves act in such a way that it encourages the negative stereotype—we are all unemployed, government-money-grubbing drunks. Yes, as well as having a higher rate of homicides, American Indians have a higher rate of every cultural malaise that can be imagined—a higher rate of unemployment, a higher rate of high school dropouts, a higher suicide rate, a higher rate of drug abuse, a higher rate of alcoholism, a higher rate of teen pregnancy, a higher rate of infant mortality . . . but one must consider the kind of low self-esteem that both conscious historical racism and dysconscious contemporary racism in the form of things like sports mascots brings about. Not only do Indian people have to deal with the fallout of being "conquered" people, the "survivor guilt" from being alive and suckered in by colonialist capitalism when so many were butchered in its creation, the shame of being men who descended from those unable to protect our women and children in the face of a demonic killing machine we could have never envisioned in our traditional cultures, the shame of being women who descended from those raped and tortured, or those who married or enconcubined themselves to European men as a means of survival. We have to deal with images of ourselves that do not match who we are—human beings. Moreover, Indian people *themselves* sometimes unconsciously internalize the stereotypical images projected on them by mainstream culture—"of course I can't succeed, I'm an Indian. I ought to either be dead or dead drunk." In comparison, the noble-savage ideal promoted by those who claim to be honoring Indians by using mascots based on Native peoples seems complimentary. No wonder some Indians find no problem with racially based mascots. American Indians are *not* all stereotypical unemployed drunks. Most are hardworking struggling, long-suffering individuals who despite the rarity of opportunity for mainstream success fight daily to keep alive what proud cultural and spiritual traditions we have remaining after the near extermination of our peoples, fight daily to minimize the risks of the negative impact of colonization on our children and promote education for them both in our traditional ways and in the mainstream ways that will ensure their success in both of the worlds in which they must live. No, we are not all dead. Neither are our extremely diverse cultures. And far from being the beneficiaries of government welfare, the average American Indian lives far below poverty level—if you have never visited a reservation like the Northern Cheyenne live on in Lame Deer or that Lakota people live on in Pine Ridge or Rosebud, then you have never seen what poverty in this country really is, not even if you have lived in the poorest of poor urban ghettos. . . . [G]overnment "handouts" like commodity cheese, the far-below-standard medical treatment dispensed by the Indian Health Service, or money distributed to the tribe for housing or other needs is dispensed, it falls way short of the government's promises to Indian peoples—that our ancestors and their descendants (us, even those of us with the lowest blood quantums) would be provided for in perpetuity in exchange for our means of providing for ourselves: our lands, the lands that we cultivated for agricultural products, the lands we obtained our game from, the lands our ancestors

lived on for centuries and our cultures are tied to, the lands our ancestors rest in. We are more than aware of what we have lost—and cartoonish depictions that make light of both those very losses and us do nothing to encourage mainstream "achievement" among our peoples. And though money from casinos has recently created an influx of capital that some tribes are using to promote economic development, it has by no means enriched the average Indian, and the existence of the casinos themselves, which the tribes as sovereign nations under the United States Constitution have the right to legally create on their own ever-shrinking land bases, is continually under attack from the states, which have no legal jurisdiction over the tribes or their lands.

Sports mascots might indeed seem to be a small issue in light of all of this. And while, admittedly, American Indians have much greater problems to worry about, I would contend that the mascots are both symptomatic of racism and promote it. Some contend that other mascots, like Notre Dame's Fighting Irish, are based on racial identity and that no other group has raised issue with this. However, I would suggest that this is because the creation of "white" as an ethnicity in America's great melting pot has both cooked off cultural identification and a strong sense of heritage for the descendants of late immigrants and early indentured servants and erased colonial guilt for the still-at-the-top-of-the-heap descendants of those who actually engaged in active genocide. The descendants of Irish American immigrants—me included, as some of my ancestors were Irish, along with those who were Cherokee, Choctaw, Creek, German, and Welsh—aren't offended by the Fighting Irish because they don't have a great stake in Irish identity, unlike those who live in Dublin and deal daily with what being Irish, much less Catholic Irish or Protestant Irish, entails. . . .

. . .

After all of the offenses our peoples have suffered throughout the history of Europeans in the Americas and in light of the kind of racism to which American Indians are still subject, it seems a small thing to me that some of us ask that sports mascots that depict American Indians be eliminated. After all, it is not that we are asking for what we will never receive—we aren't asking for a return of our stolen lands or even payment for them, we aren't asking that all of the broken treaties be honored or that the United States pay full restitution to us under the United Nations Convention on Genocide. We aren't even asking for a formal apology by a United States president for the atrocities our ancestors suffered. We are simply asking for the same respect that other ethnic groups receive in this country. We are simply asking to be recognized as people, not as television images, not as cartoons.

11

The Possessive Investment in Whiteness

George Lipsitz

. . .

Whiteness is everywhere in U.S. culture, but it is very hard to see. As Richard Dyer suggests, "[W]hite power secures its dominance by seeming not to be anything in particular." As the unmarked category against which difference is constructed, whiteness never has

to speak its name, never has to acknowledge its role as an organizing principle in social and cultural relations. To identify, analyze, and oppose the destructive consequences of whiteness, . . . requires an understanding of the existence and the destructive consequences of the possessive investment in whiteness that surreptitiously shapes so much of our public and private lives.

Race is a cultural construct, but one with sinister structural causes and consequences. Conscious and deliberate actions have institutionalized group identity in the United States, not just through the dissemination of cultural stories, but also through systematic efforts from colonial times to the present to create economic advantages through a possessive investment in whiteness for European Americans. Studies of culture too far removed from studies of social structure leave us with inadequate explanations for understanding racism and inadequate remedies for combating it.

Desire for slave labor encouraged European settlers in North America to view, first, Native Americans and, later, African Americans as racially inferior people suited "by nature" for the humiliating subordination of involuntary servitude. The long history of the possessive investment in whiteness stems in no small measure from the fact that all subsequent immigrants to North America have come to an already racialized society. From the start, European settlers in North America established structures encouraging a possessive investment in whiteness. The colonial and early national legal systems authorized attacks on Native Americans and encouraged the appropriation of their lands. They legitimated racialized chattel slavery, limited naturalized citizenship to "white" immigrants, identified Asian immigrants as expressly unwelcome (through legislation aimed at immigrants from China in 1882, from India in 1917, from Japan in 1924, and from the Philippines in 1934), and provided pretexts for restricting the voting, exploiting the labor, and seizing the property of Asian Americans, Mexican Americans, Native Americans, and African Americans.

The possessive investment in whiteness is not a simple matter of black and white; all racialized minority groups have suffered from it, albeit to different degrees and in different ways. The African slave trade began in earnest only after large-scale Native American slavery proved impractical in North America. The abolition of slavery led to the importation of low-wage labor from Asia. Legislation banning immigration from Asia set the stage for the recruitment of low-wage labor from Mexico. The new racial categories that emerged in each of these eras all revolved around applying racial labels to "nonwhite" groups in order to stigmatize and exploit them while at the same time preserving the value of whiteness.

Although reproduced in new form in every era, the possessive investment in whiteness has always been influenced by its origins in the racialized history of the United States—by its legacy of slavery and segregation, of "Indian" extermination and immigrant restriction, of conquest and colonialism. Although slavery has existed in many countries without any particular racial dimensions to it, the slave system that emerged in North America soon took on distinctly racial forms. Africans enslaved in North America faced a racialized system of power that reserved permanent, hereditary, chattel slavery for black people. White settlers institutionalized a possessive investment in whiteness by making blackness synonymous with slavery and whiteness synonymous with freedom, but also by pitting people of color against one another. Fearful of alliances between Native Americans and African Americans that might challenge the prerogatives of whiteness, white settlers prohibited slaves and free blacks from traveling in "Indian country." European Americans used diplomacy and force to compel Native Americans to return runaway slaves to their white masters. During the Stono Rebellion of 1739, colonial authorities offered Native Americans a bounty for every rebellious slave they captured or killed. At the same time, British settlers recruited black slaves to fight against Native Americans within colonial militias. The power of whiteness depended not only on white hegemony over separate racialized groups, but also on manipulating racial outsiders to fight against one another, to compete with each other for

white approval, and to seek the rewards and privileges of whiteness for themselves at the expense of other racialized populations.

. . .

Yet today the possessive investment is not simply the residue of conquest and colonialism, of slavery and segregation, of immigrant exclusion and "Indian" extermination. Contemporary whiteness and its rewards have been created and recreated by policies adopted long after the emancipation of slaves in the 1860s and even after the outlawing of *de jure* segregation in the 1960s. There has always been racism in the United States, but it has not always been the same racism. Political and cultural struggles over power have shaped the contours and dimensions of racism differently in different eras. Antiracist mobilizations during the Civil War and civil rights eras meaningfully curtailed the reach and scope of white supremacy, but in each case reactionary forces engineered a renewal of racism, albeit in new forms, during succeeding decades. Racism has changed over time, taking on different forms and serving different social purposes in each time period.

Contemporary racism has been created anew in many ways over the past five decades, but most dramatically by the putatively race-neutral, liberal, social democratic reforms of the New Deal Era and by the more overtly race-conscious neoconservative reactions against liberalism since the Nixon years. It is a mistake to posit a gradual and inevitable trajectory of evolutionary progress in race relations; on the contrary, our history shows that battles won at one moment can later be lost. Despite hard-fought battles for change that secured important concessions during the 1960s in the form of civil rights legislation, the racialized nature of social policy in the United States since the Great Depression has actually increased the possessive investment in whiteness among European Americans over the past half century.

During the New Deal Era of the 1930s and 1940s, both the Wagner Act and the Social Security Act excluded farm workers and domestics from coverage, effectively denying those disproportionately minority sectors of the work force protections and benefits routinely afforded whites. The Federal Housing Act of 1934 brought home ownership within reach of millions of citizens by placing the credit of the federal government behind private lending to home buyers, but overtly racist categories in the Federal Housing Agency's (FHA) "confidential" city surveys and appraisers' manuals channeled almost all of the loan money toward whites and away from communities of color. In the post-World War II era, trade unions negotiated contract provisions giving private medical insurance, pensions, and job security largely to the white workers who formed the overwhelming majority of the unionized work force in mass production industries, rather than fighting for full employment, medical care, and old-age pensions for all, or even for an end to discriminatory hiring and promotion practices by employers in those industries.

Each of these policies widened the gap between the resources available to whites and those available to aggrieved racial communities. Federal housing policy offers an important illustration of the broader principles at work in the possessive investment in whiteness. By channeling loans away from older inner-city neighborhoods and toward white home buyers moving into segregated suburbs, the FHA and private lenders after World War II aided and abetted segregation in U.S. residential neighborhoods. . . .

The federal government has played a major role in augmenting the possessive investment in whiteness. For years, the General Services Administration routinely channeled the government's own rental and leasing business to realtors who engaged in racial discrimination, while federally subsidized urban renewal plans reduced the already limited supply of housing for communities of color through "slum clearance" programs. In concert with FHA support for segregation in the suburbs, federal and state tax monies routinely funded the construction of water supplies and sewage facilities for racially exclusive suburban communities in the 1940s and 1950s. . . .

At the same time that FHA loans and federal highway building projects subsidized the growth of segregated suburbs, urban renewal programs in cities throughout the country devastated minority neighborhoods. During the 1950s and 1960s, federally assisted urban renewal projects destroyed 20 percent of the central-city housing units occupied by blacks, as opposed to only 10 percent of those inhabited by whites. More than 60 percent of those displaced by urban renewal were African Americans, Puerto Ricans, Mexican Americans, or members of other minority racial groups. The Federal Housing Administration and the Veterans Administration financed more than $120 billion worth of new housing between 1934 and 1962, but less than 2 percent of this real estate was available to nonwhite families—and most of that small amount was located in segregated areas.

Even in the 1970s, after most major urban renewal programs had been completed, black central-city residents continued to lose housing units at a rate equal to 80 percent of what had been lost in the 1960s. Yet white displacement declined to the relatively low levels of the 1950s. In addition, the refusal first to pass, then to enforce, fair housing laws has enabled realtors, buyers, and sellers to profit from racist collusion against minorities largely without fear of legal retribution. During the decades following World War II, urban renewal helped construct a new "white" identity in the suburbs by helping to destroy ethnically specific European American urban inner-city neighborhoods. Wrecking balls and bulldozers eliminated some of these sites, while others were transformed by an influx of minority residents desperately competing for a declining supply of affordable housing units. As increasing numbers of racial minorities moved into cities, increasing numbers of European American ethnics moved out. Consequently, ethnic differences among whites became a less important dividing line in U.S. culture, while race became more important. The suburbs helped turn Euro-Americans into "whites" who could live near each other and intermarry with relatively little difficulty. But this "white" unity rested on residential segregation, on shared access to housing and life chances largely unavailable to communities of color.

. . .

In 1968, lobbyists for the banking industry helped draft the Housing and Urban Development Act, which allowed private lenders to shift the risks of financing low-income housing to the government, creating a lucrative and thoroughly unregulated market for themselves. One section of the 1968 bill authorized FHA mortgages for inner-city areas that did not meet the usual eligibility criteria, and another section subsidized interest payments by low-income families. If administered wisely, these provisions might have promoted fair housing goals, but FHA administrators deployed them in ways that actually promoted segregation in order to provide banks, brokers, lenders, developers, realtors, and speculators with windfall profits. As a U.S. Commission on Civil Rights investigation later revealed, FHA officials collaborated with blockbusters in financing the flight of low-income whites out of inner-city neighborhoods, and then aided unscrupulous realtors and speculators by arranging purchases of substandard housing by minorities desperate to own their own homes. The resulting sales and mortgage foreclosures brought great profits to lenders (almost all of them white), but their actions led to price fixing and a subsequent inflation of housing costs in the inner city by more than 200 percent between 1968 and 1972. Bankers then foreclosed on the mortgages of thousands of these uninspected and substandard homes, ruining many inner-city neighborhoods. In response, the Department of Housing and Urban Development essentially red-lined inner cities, making them ineligible for future loans, a decision that destroyed the value of inner-city housing for generations to come.

Federally funded highways designed to connect suburban commuters with downtown places of employment also destroyed already scarce housing in minority communities and often disrupted neighborhood life as well. Construction of the Harbor Freeway in Los

Angeles, the Gulf Freeway in Houston, and the Mark Twain Freeway in St. Louis displaced thousands of residents and bisected neighborhoods, shopping districts, and political precincts. The processes of urban renewal and highway construction set in motion a vicious cycle: population loss led to decreased political power, which made minority neighborhoods more vulnerable to further urban renewal and freeway construction, not to mention more susceptible to the placement of prisons, incinerators, toxic waste dumps, and other projects that further depopulated these areas.

. . .

Minorities are less likely than whites to receive preventive medical care or costly operations from Medicare. Eligible members of minority communities are also less likely than European Americans to apply for food stamps. The labor of migrant farm workers from aggrieved racialized groups plays a vital role in providing adequate nutrition for others, but the farm workers and their children suffer disproportionately from health disorders caused by malnutrition. In her important research on health policy and ethnic diversity, Linda Wray concludes that "the lower life expectancies for many ethnic minority groups and subgroups stem largely from their disproportionately higher rates of poverty, malnutrition, and poor health care."

Just as residential segregation and urban renewal make minority communities disproportionately susceptible to health hazards, their physical and social location gives these communities a different relationship to the criminal justice system. A 1990 study by the National Institute on Drug Abuse revealed that while only 15 percent of the thirteen million habitual drug users in the United States were black and 77 percent were white, African Americans were four times more likely to be arrested on drug charges than whites in the nation as a whole, and seven to nine times more likely in Pennsylvania, Michigan, Illinois, Florida, Massachusetts, and New Jersey. A 1989 study by the Parents' Resource Institute for Drug Education discovered that African American high school students consistently showed lower levels of drug and alcohol use than their European American counterparts, even in high schools populated by residents of low-income housing projects. Yet, while comprising about 12 percent of the U.S. population, blacks accounted for 10 percent of drug arrests in 1984, 40 percent in 1988, and 42 percent in 1990. In addition, white drug defendants receive considerably shorter average prison terms than African Americans convicted of comparable crimes. A U.S. Sentencing Commission study found in 1992 that half of the federal court districts that handled cases involving crack cocaine prosecuted minority defendants *exclusively*. A *Los Angeles Times* article in 1995 revealed that "black and Latino crack dealers are hammered with 10-year mandatory federal sentences while whites prosecuted in state court face a minimum of five years and often receive no more than a year in jail." Alexander Lichtenstein and Michael A. Kroll point out that sentences for African Americans in the federal prison system are 20 percent longer than those given to whites who commit the same crimes. They observe that if blacks received the same sentences as whites for these offenses, the federal prison system would require three thousand fewer prison cells, enough to close completely six of the new five-hundred bed institutions.

Racial animus on the part of police officers, prosecutors, and judges accounts for only a small portion of the distinctive experience that racial minorities have with the criminal justice system. Economic devastation makes the drug trade appealing to some people in the inner city, while the dearth of capital in minority neighborhoods curtails opportunities for other kinds of employment. Deindustrialization, unemployment, and lack of intergenerational transfers of wealth undermine parental and adult authority in many neighborhoods. The complex factors that cause people to turn to drugs are no more prevalent in minority communities than elsewhere, but these communities and their inhabitants face more stress while having fewer opportunities to receive private counseling and treatment for their problems.

The structural weaknesses of minority neighborhoods caused by discrimination in housing, education, and hiring also play a crucial role in relations between inner-city residents and the criminal justice system. Cocaine dealing, which initially skyrocketed among white suburban residents, was driven into the inner city by escalating enforcement pressures in wealthy white communities. Ghettos and barrios became distribution centers for the sale of drugs to white suburbanites. Former New York and Houston police commissioner Lee Brown, head of the federal government's antidrug efforts during the early years of the Clinton presidency and later mayor of Houston, noted, "There are those who bring drugs into the country. That's not the black community. Then you have wholesalers, those who distribute them once they get here, and as a rule that's not the black community. Where you find the blacks is in the street dealing."

You also find blacks and other minorities in prison. Police officers in large cities, pressured to show results in the drive against drugs, lack the resources to effectively enforce the law everywhere (in part because of the social costs of deindustrialization and the tax limitation initiatives designed to shrink the size of government). These officers know that it is easier to make arrests and to secure convictions by confronting drug users in areas that have conspicuous street corner sales, that have more people out on the street with no place to go, and that have residents more likely to plead guilty and less likely to secure the services of attorneys who can get the charges against them dropped, reduced, or wiped off the books with subsequent successful counseling and rehabilitation. In addition, politicians supported by the public relations efforts of neoconservative foundations often portray themselves to suburban voters as opponents of the "dangerous classes" in the inner cities.

Minority disadvantages craft advantages for others. Urban renewal failed to provide new housing for the poor, but it played an important role in transforming the U.S. urban economy from one that relied on factory production to one driven by producer services. Urban renewal projects subsidized the development of downtown office centers on previously residential land, and they frequently created buffer zones of empty blocks dividing poor neighborhoods from new shopping centers designed for affluent commuters. To help cities compete for corporate investment by making them appealing to high-level executives, federal urban aid favored construction of luxury housing units and cultural centers like symphony halls and art museums over affordable housing for workers. Tax abatements granted to these producer services centers further aggravated the fiscal crisis that cities faced, leading to tax increases on existing industries, businesses, and residences.

. . .

When housing prices increased dramatically during the 1970s, white homeowners who had been able to take advantage of discriminatory FHA financing policies in the past realized increased equity in their homes, while those excluded from the housing market by earlier policies found themselves facing even higher costs of entry into the market in addition to the traditional obstacles presented by the discriminatory practices of sellers, realtors, and lenders. The contrast between European Americans and African Americans is instructive in this regard. Because whites have access to broader housing choices than blacks, whites pay 15 percent less than blacks for similar housing in the same neighborhood. White neighborhoods typically experience housing costs 25 percent lower than would be the case if the residents were black.

. . .

When confronted with evidence of systematic racial bias in home lending, defenders of the possessive investment in whiteness argue that the disproportionate share of loan denials to members of minority groups stems not from discrimination, but from the low net worth of minority applicants, even those who have high incomes. This might seem a reasonable position, but net worth is almost totally determined by past opportunities for asset accumulation, and therefore is the one figure most likely to reflect the history of

discrimination. Minorities are told, in essence, "We can't give you a loan today because we've discriminated against members of your race so effectively in the past that you have not been able to accumulate any equity from housing and to pass it down through the generations."

Most white families have acquired their net worth from the appreciation of property that they secured under conditions of special privilege in a discriminatory housing market. In their prize-winning book *Black Wealth/White Wealth*, Melvin Oliver and Thomas Shapiro demonstrate how the history of housing discrimination makes white parents more able to borrow funds for their children's college education or to loan money to their children to enter the housing market. In addition, much discrimination in home lending is not based on considerations of net worth; it stems from decisions made by white banking officials based on their stereotypes about minority communities. The Federal Reserve Bank of Boston study showed that black and Latino mortgage applicants are 60 percent more likely to be turned down for loans than whites, even after controlling for employment, financial, and neighborhood characteristics. . . .

Yet bankers also make money from the ways in which discrimination creates artificial scarcities in the market. Minorities have to pay more for housing because much of the market is off limits to them. Blockbusters profit from exploiting white fears and provoking them into panic selling. Minority home owners denied loans in mainstream banks often turn to exploitative lenders who make "low end" loans at enormously high interest rates. If they fail to pay back these loans, regular banks can acquire the property cheaply and charge someone else exorbitant interest for a loan on the same property.

. . .

The policies of neoconservatives in the Reagan and Bush administrations during the 1980s and 1990s greatly exacerbated the racialized aspects of more than fifty years of these social welfare policies. Regressive policies that cut federal aid to education and refused to challenge segregated education, housing, and hiring, as well as the cynical cultivation of an antiblack consensus through attacks on affirmative action and voting rights legislation clearly reinforced possessive investments in whiteness. In the U.S. economy, where 86 percent of available jobs do not appear in classified ads and where personal connections prove the most important factor in securing employment, attacks on affirmative action guarantee that whites will be rewarded for their historical advantage in the labor market rather than for their individual abilities or efforts.

. . .

Yet even seemingly race-neutral policies supported by both neoconservatives and liberals in the 1980s and 1990s have increased the absolute value of being white. In the 1980s, changes in federal tax laws decreased the value of wage income and increased the value of investment income—a move harmful to minorities, who suffer from a gap between their total wealth and that of whites even greater than the disparity between their income and white income. The failure to raise the minimum wage between 1981 and 1989 and the decline of more than one-third in the value of Aid to Families with Dependent Children (AFDC) payments injured all poor people, but they exacted special costs on nonwhites, who faced even more constricted markets for employment, housing, and education than poor whites.

Similarly, the "tax reforms" of the 1980s made the effective rate of taxation higher on investment in actual goods and services than on profits from speculative enterprises. This change encouraged the flight of capital from industrial production with its many employment opportunities toward investments that can be turned over quickly to allow the greatest possible tax write-offs. Government policies thus discouraged investments that might produce high-paying jobs and encouraged investors to strip companies of their assets to make rapid short-term profits. These policies hurt almost all workers,

but they fell particularly heavily on minority workers, who because of employment discrimination in the retail and small business sectors were overrepresented in blue-collar industrial jobs.

. . .

Subsidies to the private sector by government agencies also tend to enhance the rewards of past discrimination. Throughout the country, tax increment financing for redevelopment programs offers tax-free and low-interest loans to developers whose projects use public services, often without having to pay taxes to local school boards or country governments. In St. Louis, for example, tax abatements for wealthy corporations deprive the city's schools (and their majority African American population) of $17 million a year. Even if these redevelopment projects eventually succeed in increasing municipal revenues through sales and earnings taxes, their proceeds go to funds that pay for the increased services these developments demand (fire and police protection, roads, sewers, electricity, lighting, etc.) rather than to school funds, which are dependent upon property tax revenues. Nationwide, industrial development bonds resulted in a $7.4 billion tax loss in 1983, which ordinary taxpayers had to make up through increased payroll taxes. Compared to white Americans, people of color, more likely to be poor or working class, suffer disproportionately from these changes as taxpayers, as workers, and as tenants. A study by the Citizens for Tax Justice found that wealthy Californians spend less than eleven cents in taxes for every dollar earned, while poor residents of the state pay fourteen cents out of every dollar in taxes. As groups overrepresented among the poor, minorities have been forced to subsidize the tax breaks given to the wealthy. While holding property tax assessments for businesses and some home owners to about half of their market value, California's Proposition 13 deprived cities and counties of $13 billion a year in taxes. Businesses alone avoided $3.3 billion to $8.6 billion in taxes per year under this statute.

Because they are ignorant of even the recent history of the possessive investment in whiteness—generated by slavery and segregation, immigrant exclusion and Native American policy, conquest and colonialism, but augmented by liberal and conservative social policies as well—Americans produce largely cultural explanations for structural social problems. The increased possessive investment in whiteness generated by disinvestment in U.S. cities, factories, and schools since the 1970s disguises as *racial* problems the general social problems posed by deindustrialization, economic restructuring, and neoconservative attacks on the welfare state. It fuels a discourse that demonizes people of color for being victimized by these changes, while hiding the privileges of whiteness by attributing the economic advantages enjoyed by whites to their family values, faith in fatherhood, and foresight—rather than to the favoritism they enjoy through their possessive investment in whiteness.

. . .

Yet public opinion polls of white Americans reflect little recognition of these devastating changes. Seventy percent of whites in one poll said that African Americans "have the same opportunities to live a middle-class life as whites," and nearly three-fourths of white respondents to a 1989 poll believed that opportunities for blacks had improved under Reagan. If such optimism about the opportunities available to African Americans does not demonstrate ignorance of the dire conditions facing black communities, it indicates that many whites believe that blacks suffer deservedly, because they do not take advantage of the opportunities offered them. In opinion polls, favorable assessments of black chances for success often accompanied extremely negative judgments about the abilities, work habits, and character of black people. A National Opinion Research Report in 1990 disclosed that more than 50 percent of U.S. whites viewed blacks as innately lazy and less intelligent and less patriotic than whites. More than 60 percent said that they believed that blacks suffer from poor housing and employment opportunities because of their own lack of will power. Some 56.3 percent said that blacks preferred welfare to employment, while

44.6 percent contended that blacks tended toward laziness. Even more important, research by Mary Edsall and Thomas Byrne Edsall indicates that many whites structure nearly all of their decisions about housing, education, and politics in response to their aversions to black people.

. . .

. . . As long as we define social life as the sum total of conscious and deliberative individual activities, we will be able to discern as racist only *individual* manifestations of personal prejudice and hostility. Systemic, collective, and coordinated group behavior consequently drops out of sight. Collective exercises of power that relentlessly channel rewards, resources, and opportunities from one group to another will not appear "racist" from this perspective, because they rarely announce their intention to discriminate against individuals. Yet they nonetheless give racial identities their sinister social meaning by giving people from different races vastly different life chances.

The gap between white perception and minority experience can have explosive consequences. Little more than a year after the 1992 Los Angeles rebellion, a sixteen-year-old high school junior shared her opinions with a reporter from the *Los Angeles Times*. "I don't think white people owe anything to black people," she explained. "We didn't sell them into slavery, it was our ancestors. What they did was wrong, but we've done our best to make up for it." A seventeen-year-old senior echoed those comments, telling the reporter, "I feel we spend more time in my history class talking about what whites owe blacks than just about anything else when the issue of slavery comes up. I often received dirty looks. This seems strange given that I wasn't even alive then. And the few members of my family from that time didn't have the luxury of owning much, let alone slaves. So why, I ask you, am I constantly made to feel guilty?"

More ominously, after pleading guilty to bombing two homes and one car, vandalizing a synagogue, and attempting to start a race war by planning the murder of Rodney King and the bombing of Los Angeles's First African Methodist Episcopal Church, twenty-year-old Christopher David Fisher explained that "sometimes whites were picked on because of the color of their skin. . . . Maybe we're blamed for slavery." Fisher's actions were certainly extreme, but his justification of them drew knowingly and precisely on a broadly shared narrative about the victimization of "innocent" whites by irrational and ungrateful minorities.

The comments and questions raised about the legacy of slavery by these young whites illuminate broader currents in our culture, with enormous implications for understanding the enduring significance of race in our country. These young people associate black grievances solely with slavery, and they express irritation at what they perceive as efforts to make them feel guilty or unduly privileged because of things that happened in the distant past. The claim that one's own family did not own any slaves is frequently voiced in our culture. It is almost never followed with a statement to the effect that of course some people's families did own slaves and we will not rest until we track them down and make them pay reparations. This view never acknowledges how the existence of slavery and the exploitation of black labor after emancipation created opportunities from which immigrants and others benefited, even if they did not personally own slaves. Rather, it seems to hold that, because not all white people owned slaves, no white people can be held accountable or inconvenienced by the legacy of slavery. More important, having dispensed with slavery, they feel no need to address the histories of Jim Crow segregation, racialized social policies, urban renewal, or the revived racism of contemporary neoconservatism. On the contrary, Fisher felt that his discomfort with being "picked on" and "blamed" for slavery gave him good reason to bomb homes, deface synagogues, and plot to kill black people.

Unfortunately for our society, these young whites accurately reflect the logic of the language of liberal individualism and its ideological predispositions in discussions of race.

In their apparent ignorance of the disciplined, systemic, and collective *group* activity that has structured white identities in U.S. history, they are in good company. In a 1979 law journal article, future Supreme Court justice Antonin Scalia argued that affirmative action "is based upon concepts of racial indebtedness and racial entitlement rather than individual worth and individual need" and is thus "racist." Yet liberal individualism is not completely color-blind on this issue. As Cheryl I. Harris demonstrates, the legacy of liberal individualism has not prevented the Supreme Court from recognizing and protecting the group interests of *whites* in the Bakke, Croson, and Wygant cases. In each case, the Court nullified affirmative action programs because they judged efforts to help blacks as harmful to whites: to white expectations of entitlement, expectations based on the possessive investment in whiteness they held as members of a group. In the Bakke case, for instance, where the plaintiff argued that medical school affirmative action programs disadvantaged white applicants like himself, neither Bakke nor the Court contested the legitimacy of medical school admissions standards that reserved five seats in each class for children of wealthy donors to the university or that penalized Bakke for being older than most of the other applicants. . . . But they did challenge and reject a policy designed to offset the effects of past and present discrimination when they could construe the medical school admission policies as detrimental to the interests of whites as a group—and as a consequence they applied the "strict scrutiny" standard to protect whites while denying that protection to people of color. In this case, as in so many others, the language of liberal individualism serves as a cover for co-ordinated collective group interests.

. . .

. . . But an explicitly antiracist interethnic movement that acknowledges the existence and power of whiteness might make some important changes. Antiracist coalitions also have a long history in the United States—in the political activism of John Brown, Sojourner Truth, and the Magon brothers among others, but also in our rich cultural tradition of interethnic antiracism connected to civil rights activism. . . . These all too infrequent but nonetheless important efforts by whites to fight racism, not out of sympathy for someone else but out of a sense of self-respect and simple justice, have never completely disappeared; they remain available as models for the present.

. . .

12

Heteropatriarchy and the Three Pillars of White Supremacy

Rethinking Women of Color Organizing

Andrea Smith

Scenario #1
A group of women of color come together to organize. An argument ensues about whether or not Arab women should be included. Some argue that Arab women are "white" since

they have been classified as such in the US census. Another argument erupts over whether or not Latinas qualify as "women of color," since some may be classified as "white" in their Latin American countries of origin and/or "pass" as white in the United States.

Scenario #2
In a discussion on racism, some people argue that Native peoples suffer from less racism than other people of color because they generally do not reside in segregated neighborhoods within the United States. In addition, some argue that since tribes now have gaming, Native peoples are no longer "oppressed."

Scenario #3
A multiracial campaign develops involving diverse communities of color in which some participants charge that we must stop the black/white binary, and end Black hegemony over people of color politics to develop a more "multicultural" framework. However, this campaign continues to rely on strategies and cultural motifs developed by the Black Civil Rights struggle in the United States.

These incidents, which happen quite frequently in "women of color" or "people of color" political organizing struggles, are often explained as a consequence of "oppression olympics." . . . In this essay, I want to argue that these incidents are not so much the result of "oppression olympics" but are more about how we have inadequately framed "women of color" or "people of color" politics. . . . [T]he premise behind much "women of color" organizing is that women from communities victimized by white supremacy should unite together around their shared oppression. . . .

This framework has proven to be limited for women of color and people of color organizing. First, it tends to presume that our communities have been impacted by white supremacy in the same way. Consequently, we often assume that all of our communities will share similar strategies for liberation. In fact, however, our strategies often run into conflict. For example, one strategy that many people in US-born communities of color adopt, in order to advance economically out of impoverished communities, is to join the military. We then become complicit in oppressing and colonizing communities from other countries. Meanwhile, people from other countries often adopt the strategy of moving to the United States to advance economically, without considering their complicity in settling on the lands of indigenous peoples that are being colonized by the United States.

Consequently, it may be more helpful to adopt an alternative framework for women of color and people of color organizing. I call one such framework the "Three Pillars of White Supremacy." This framework does not assume that racism and white supremacy is enacted in a singular fashion; rather, white supremacy is constituted by separate and distinct, but still interrelated, logics. . . .

SLAVERY/CAPITALISM

One pillar of white supremacy is the logic of slavery. As Sora Han, Jared Sexton, and Angela P. Harris note, this logic renders Black people as inherently slaveable—as nothing more than property. That is, in this logic of white supremacy Blackness becomes equated with slaveability. The forms of slavery may change—whether it is through the formal system of slavery, sharecropping, or through the current prison industrial complex—but the logic itself has remained consistent.

CONTEXT

This logic is the anchor of capitalism. . . . To keep this capitalist system in place—which ultimately commodifies most people—the logic of slavery applies a racial hierarchy to this system. . . . This helps people who are not Black to accept their lot in life, because they can feel that at least they are not at the very bottom of the racial hierarchy—at least they are not property; at least they are not slaveable.

The logic of slavery can be seen clearly in the current prison industrial complex (PIC). While the PIC generally incarcerates communities of color, it seems to be structured primarily on an anti-Black racism. . . . [P]rior to the Civil War, most people in prison were white. However, after the thirteenth amendment was passed—which banned slavery, except for those in prison—Black people previously enslaved through the slavery system were reenslaved through the prison system. Black people who had been the property of slave owners became state property, through the . . . [convict] leasing system. Thus, we can actually look at the criminalization of Blackness as a logical extension of Blackness as property.

GENOCIDE/COLONIALISM

A second pillar of white supremacy is the logic of genocide. This logic holds that indigenous peoples must disappear. In fact, they must *always* be disappearing, in order to allow non-indigenous peoples rightful claim over this land. Through this logic of genocide, non-Native peoples then become the rightful inheritors of all that was indigenous—land, resources, indigenous spirituality, or culture. As Kare Shanley notes, Native peoples are a permanent "present absence" in the US colonial imagination, an "absence" that reinforces, at every turn, the conviction that Native peoples are indeed vanishing and that the conquest of Native lands is justified. Ella Shoat and Robert Stam describe this absence as "an ambivalently repressive mechanism [which] dispels the anxiety in the face of the Indian, whose very presence is a reminder of the initially precarious grounding of the American nation state itself. . . . In a temporal paradox, living Indians were induced to 'play dead,' as it were, in order to perform a narrative of manifest destiny in which their role, ultimately, was to disappear."

Rayna Green further elaborates . . . "The living performance of 'playing Indian' by non-Indian peoples depends upon the physical and psychological removal, even the death, of real Indians. In that sense, the performance, purportedly often done out of a stated and implicit love for Indians, is really the obverse of another well-known cultural phenomenon, 'Indian hating,' as most often expressed in another, deadly performance genre called 'genocide'" (Green, 1988). After all, why would non-Native peoples need to play Indian—which often includes acts of spiritual appropriation and land theft—if they thought Indians were still alive and perfectly capable of being Indian themselves? The pillar of genocide serves as the anchor for colonialism—it is what allows non-Native peoples to feel they can rightfully own indigenous peoples' land. It is okay to take land from indigenous peoples, because indigenous peoples have disappeared.

ORIETALISM/WAR

A third pillar of white supremacy is the logic of Orientalism. Orientalism was defined by Edward Said as the process of the West defining itself as a superior civilization by constructing itself in opposition to an "exotic" but inferior "Orient." . . . The logic of Orientalism

marks certain peoples or nations as inferior and as posing a constant threat to the well-being of empire. These peoples are still seen as "civilizations"—they are not property or "disappeared"—however, they will always be imaged as permanent foreign threats to empire. This logic is evident in the anti-immigration movements within the United States that target immigrants of color. It does not matter how long immigrants of color reside in the United States, they generally become targeted as foreign threats, particularly during war time. Consequently, Orientalism serves as the anchor for war, because it allows the United States to justify being in a constant state of war to protect itself from its enemies.

For example, the United States feels entitled to use Orientalist logic to justify racial profiling of Arab Americans so that it can be strong enough to fight the "war on terror." Orientalism also allows the United States to defend the logics of slavery and genocide, as these practices enable the United States to stay "strong enough" to fight these constant wars. . . . For the system of white supremacy to stay in place, the United States must always be at war.

Because we are situated within different logics of white supremacy, we may misunderstand a racial dynamic if we simplistically try to explain one logic of white supremacy with another logic. For instance, think about the first scenario that opens this essay: if we simply dismiss Latino/as or Arab peoples as "white," we fail to understand how a racial logic of Orientalism is in operation. . . . Latino/as and Arabs are often situated in a racial hierarchy that privileges them over Black people. However, while Orientalist logic may bestow them some racial privilege, they are still cast as inferior yet threatening "civilizations" in the United States. Their privilege is not a signal that they will be assimilated, but that they will be marked as perpetual foreign threats to the US world order.

ORGANIZING IMPLICATIONS

Under the old but still potent and dominant model, people of color organizing was based on the notion of organizing around shared victimhood. In this model, however, we see that we are victims of white supremacy, but complicit in it as well. Our survival strategies and resistance to white supremacy are set by the system of white supremacy itself. What keeps us trapped within our particular pillars of white supremacy is that we are seduced with the prospect of being able to participate in the other pillars. For example, all non-Native peoples are promised the ability to join in the colonial project of settling indigenous lands. All non-Black peoples are promised that if they comply, they will not be at the bottom of the racial hierarchy. And Black, Native, Latino, and Asian peoples are promised that they will economically and politically advance if they join US wars to spread "democracy." Thus, people of color organizing must be premised on making strategic alliances with each other, based on where we are situated within the larger political economy. . . . [F]or example, Native peoples who are organizing against the colonial and genocidal practices committed by the US government will be more effective in their struggle if they also organize against US militarism, particularly the military recruitment of indigenous peoples to support US imperial wars. If we try to end US colonial practices at home, but support US empire by joining the military, we are strengthening the state's ability to carry out genocidal policies against people of color here and all over the world.

. . . These approaches might help us to develop resistance strategies that do not inadvertently keep the system in place for all of us, and keep all of us accountable. In all of these cases, we would check our aspirations against the aspirations of other communities to ensure that our model of liberation does not become the model of oppression for others.

These practices require us to be more vigilant in how we may have internalized some of these logics in our own organizing practice. For instance, much racial justice organizing

within the United States has rested on a civil rights framework that fights for equality under the law. An assumption behind this organizing is that the United States is a democracy with some flaws, but is otherwise admirable. Despite the fact that it rendered slaves three-fifths of a person, the US Constitution is presented as the model document from which to build a flourishing democracy. However, as Luana Ross notes, it has never been against US law to commit genocide against indigenous peoples—in fact, genocide *is* the law of the country. The United States could not exist without it. In the United States, democracy is actually the alibi for genocide—it is the practice that covers up United States colonial control over indigenous lands.

Our organizing can also reflect anti-Black racism. Recently, with the outgrowth of "multiculturalism" there have been calls to "go beyond the black/white binary" and include other communities of color in our analysis, as presented in the third scenario. There are a number of flaws with this analysis. First, it replaces an analysis of white supremacy with a politics of multicultural representation; if we just *include* more people, then our practice will be less racist. Not true. This model does not address the nuanced structure of white supremacy, such as through these distinct logics of slavery, genocide, and Orientalism. Second, it obscures the centrality of the slavery logic in the system of white supremacy, which is *based on a black/white binary*. The black/white binary is not the *only* binary which characterizes white supremacy, but it is still a central one that we cannot "go beyond" in our racial justice organizing efforts.

If we do not look at how the logic of slaveability inflects our society and our thinking, it will be evident in our work as well. For example, other communities of color often appropriate the cultural work and organizing strategies of African American civil rights or Black Power movements without corresponding assumptions that we should also be in solidarity with Black communities. We assume that this work is the common "property" of all oppressed groups, and we can appropriate it without being accountable.

. . .

. . . Simply saying we need to move beyond the black/white binary (or perhaps, the "black/non-black" binary) in US racism obfuscates the racializing logic of slavery, and prevents us from seeing that this binary constitutes Blackness as the bottom of a color hierarchy. However, this is not the *only* binary that fundamentally constitutes white supremacy. There is also an indigenous/settler binary, where Native genocide is central to the logic of white supremacy and other non-indigenous people of color also form "a subsidiary" role. We also face another Orientalist logic that fundamentally constitutes Asians, Arabs, and Latino/as as foreign threats, requiring the United States to be at permanent war with these peoples. In this construction, Black and Native peoples play subsidiary roles.

Clearly the black/white binary is central to racial and political thought and practice in the United States, and any understanding of white supremacy must take it into consideration. However, if we look at only this binary, we may misread the dynamics of white supremacy in different contexts. . . . [C]ritical race theorist Cheryl Harris's analysis of whiteness as property reveals this weakness. In *Critical Race Theory*, Harris contends that whites have a property interest in the preservation of whiteness, and seek to deprive those who are "tainted" by Black or Indian blood from these same white property interests. Harris simply assumes that the positions of African Americans and American Indians are the same, failing to consider US policies of forced assimilation and forced whiteness on American Indians. These policies have become so entrenched that when Native peoples make political claims, they have been accused of being white. When Andrew Jackson removed the Cherokee along the Trail of Tears, he argued that those who did not want removal were really white. In contemporary times, when I was a non-violent witness for the Chippewa spearfishers in the late 1980s, one of the more frequent slurs whites hurled when the Chippewa attempted to exercise their treaty-protected right to fish was that they had white parents, or they were really white.

Status differences between Blacks and Natives are informed by the different economic positions African Americans and American Indians have in US society. African Americans have been traditionally valued for their labor, hence it is in the interest of the dominant society to have as many people marked "Black," as possible, thereby maintaining a cheap labor pool; by contrast, American Indians have been valued for the land base they occupy, so it is in the interest of dominant society to have as few people marked "Indian" as possible, facilitating access to Native lands. "Whiteness" operates differently under a logic of genocide than it does from a logic of slavery.

Another failure of US-based people of color in organizing is that we often fall back on a "US-centrism," believing that what is happening "over there" is less important than what is happening here. We fail to see how the United States maintains the system of oppression here precisely by tying our allegiances to the interests of US empire "over there."

HETEROPATRIARCHY AND WHITE SUPREMACY

Heteropatriarchy is the building block of US empire. In fact, it is the building block of the nation-state form of governance. . . . Christian Right activist and founder of Prison Fellowship Charles Colson makes the connection between homosexuality and the nation-state in his analysis of the war on terror, explaining that one of the causes of terrorism is same-sex marriage:

> Marriage is the traditional building block of human society, intended both to unite couples and bring children into the world . . . There is a natural moral order for the family . . . the family, led by a married mother and father, is the best available structure for both child-rearing and cultural health. Marriage is not a private institution designed solely for the individual gratification of its participants. If we fail to enact a Federal Marriage Amendment, we can expect not just more family breakdown, but also more criminals behind bars and more chaos in our streets.

Colson is linking the well-being of US empire to the well-being of the heteropatriarchal family. He continues:

> When radical Islamists see American women abusing Muslim men, as they did in the Abu Ghraib prison, and when they see news coverage of same-sex couples being "married" in US towns, we make this kind of freedom abhorrent—the kind they see as a blot on Allah's creation. We must preserve traditional marriage in order to protect the United States from those who would use our depravity to destroy us.

As Ann Burlein argues in *Lift High the Cross*, it may be a mistake to argue that the goal of Christian Right politics is to create a theocracy in the United States. Rather, Christian Right politics work through the private family (which is coded as white, patriarchal, and middle class) to create a "Christian America." She notes that the investment in the private family makes it difficult for people to invest in more public forms of social connection. In addition, investment in the suburban private family serves to mask the public disinvestment in urban areas that makes the suburban lifestyle possible. The social decay in urban areas that results from this disinvestment is then construed as the result of deviance from the Christian family ideal rather than as the result of political and economic forces. As former head of the Christian Coalition, Ralph Reed, states: "The only true solution to crime is to restore the family" (Reed, 1990). . . .

C
O
N
T
E
X
T

As I have argued elsewhere, in order to colonize peoples whose societies are not based on social hierarchy, colonizers must first naturalize hierarchy through instituting patriarchy. In turn, patriarchy rests on a gender binary system in which only two genders exist, one dominating the other. . . . Just as the patriarchs rule the family, the elites of the nation-state rule their citizens. Any liberation struggle that does not challenge heteronormativity cannot substantially challenge colonialism or white supremacy. . . . [S]uch struggles will maintain colonialism based on a politics of secondary marginalization where the most elite class of these groups will further their aspirations on the backs of those most marginalized within the community.

. . . [N]ational liberation politics become less vulnerable to being coopted by the Right when we base them on a model of liberation that fundamentally challenges right-wing conceptions of the nation. We need a model based on community relationships and on mutual respect.

CONCLUSION

Women of color–centered organizing points to the centrality of gender politics within antiracist, anticolonial struggles. Unfortunately, in our efforts to organize against white, Christian America, racial justice struggles often articulate an equally heteropatriarchal racial nationalism. This model of organizing either hopes to assimilate into white America, or to replicate it within an equally hierarchical and oppressive racial nationalism in which the elites of the community rule everyone else. Such struggles often call on the importance of preserving the "Black family" or the "Native family" as the bulwark of this nationalist project, the family being conceived of in capitalist and heteropatriarchal terms. The response is often increased homophobia, with lesbian and gay community members construed as "threats" to the family. . . . Perhaps, instead, we can reconstitute alternative ways of living together in which "families" are not seen as islands on their own. . . .

13

La conciencia de la mestiza

Towards a New Consciousness

Gloria Anzaldúa

Por la mujer de mi raza
bablará el espíritu.

José Vasconcelos, Mexican philosopher, envisaged *una raza mestiza, una mezcla de razas afines, una raza de color—la primera raza síntesis del globo*. He called it a cosmic race, *la*

raza cósmica, a fifth race embracing the four major races of the world. Opposite to the theory of the pure Aryan, and to the policy of racial purity that white America practices, his theory is one of inclusivity. At the confluence of two or more genetic streams, with chromosomes constantly "crossing over," this mixture of races, rather than resulting in an inferior being, provides hybrid progeny, a mutable, more malleable species with a rich gene pool. From this racial, ideological, cultural and biological cross-pollinization, an "alien" consciousness is presently in the making—a new *mestiza* consciousness, *una conciencia de mujer*. It is a consciousness of the Borderlands.

UNA LUCHA DE FRONTERAS/A STRUGGLE OF BORDERS

> Because I, a *mestiza*,
> continually walk out of one culture
> and into another,
> because I am in all cultures at the same time,
> *alma entre dos mundos, tres, cuatro,*
> *me zumba la cabeza con lo contradictorio.*
> *Estoy norteada por todas las voces que me hablan*
> *simultáneamente.*

The ambivalence from the clash of voices results in mental and emotional states of perplexity. Internal strife results in insecurity and indecisiveness. The *mestiza*'s dual or multiple personality is plagued by psychic restlessness.

In a constant state of mental nepantilism, an Aztec word meaning torn between ways, *la mestiza* is a product of the transfer of the cultural and spiritual values of one group to another. Being tricultural, monolingual, bilingual, or multilingual, speaking a patois, and in a state of perpetual transition, the *mestiza* faces the dilemma of the mixed breed: which collectivity does the daughter of a darkskinned mother listen to?

El choque de un alma atrapado entre el mundo del espíritu y el mundo de la técnica a veces la deja entullada. Cradled in one culture, sandwiched between two cultures, straddling all three cultures and their value systems, *la mestiza* undergoes a struggle of flesh, a struggle of borders, an inner war. Like all people, we perceive the version of reality that our culture communicates. Like others having or living in more than one culture, we get multiple, often opposing messages. The coming together of two self-consistent but habitually incompatible frames of reference causes *un choque*, a cultural collision.

Within us and within *la cultura chicana*, commonly held beliefs of the white culture attack commonly held beliefs of the Mexican culture, and both attack commonly held beliefs of the indigenous culture. Subconsciously, we see an attack on ourselves and our beliefs as a threat and we attempt to block with a counterstance.

But it is not enough to stand on the opposite river bank, shouting questions, challenging patriarchal, white conventions. A counterstance locks one into a duel of oppressor and oppressed; locked in mortal combat, like the cop and the criminal, both are reduced to a common denominator of violence. The counterstance refutes the dominant culture's views and beliefs, and, for this, it is proudly defiant. All reaction is limited by, and dependent on, what it is reacting against. Because the counterstance stems from a problem with authority—outer as well as inner—it's a step towards liberation from cultural domination. But it is not a way of life. At some point, on our way to a new consciousness, we will have to leave the opposite bank, the split between the two mortal combatants somehow healed so that we are on both shores at once and, at once, see through serpent

CONTEXT

and eagle eyes. Or perhaps we will decide to disengage from the dominant culture, write it off altogether as a lost cause, and cross the border into a wholly new and separate territory. Or we might go another route. The possibilities are numerous once we decide to act and not react.

A TOLERANCE FOR AMBIGUITY

These numerous possibilities leave *la mestiza* floundering in uncharted seas. In perceiving conflicting information and points of view, she is subjected to a swamping of her psychological borders. She has discovered that she can't hold concepts or ideas in rigid boundaries. The borders and walls that are supposed to keep the undesirable ideas out are entrenched habits and patterns of behavior; these habits and patterns are the enemy within. Rigidity means death. Only by remaining flexible is she able to stretch the psyche horizontally and vertically. *La mestiza* constantly has to shift out of habitual formations; from convergent thinking, analytical reasoning that tends to use rationality to move toward a single goal (a Western mode), to divergent thinking, characterized by movement away from set patterns and goals and toward a more whole perspective, one that includes rather than excludes.

The new *mestiza* copes by developing a tolerance for contradictions, a tolerance for ambiguity. She learns to be an Indian in Mexican culture, to be Mexican from an Anglo point of view. She learns to juggle cultures. She has a plural personality, she operates in a pluralistic mode—nothing is thrust out, the good the bad and the ugly, nothing rejected, nothing abandoned. Not only does she sustain contradictions, she turns the ambivalence into something else.

She can be jarred out of ambivalence by an intense, and often painful, emotional event which inverts or resolves the ambivalence. I'm not sure exactly how. The work takes place underground—subconsciously. It is work that the soul performs. That focal point or fulcrum, that juncture where the *mestiza* stands, is where phenomena tend to collide. It is where the possibility of uniting all that is separate occurs. This assembly is not one where severed or separated pieces merely come together. Nor is it a balancing of opposing powers. In attempting to work out a synthesis, the self has added a third element which is greater than the sum of its severed parts. That third element is a new consciousness—a *mestiza* consciousness—and though it is a source of intense pain, its energy comes from continual creative motion that keeps breaking down the unitary aspect of each new paradigm.

En unas pocas centurias, the future will belong to the *mestiza*. Because the future depends on the breaking down of paradigms, it depends on the straddling of two or more cultures. By creating a new mythos—that is, a change in the way we perceive reality, the way we see ourselves, and the ways we behave—*la mestiza* creates a new consciousness.

The work of *mestiza* consciousness is to break down the subject-object duality that keeps her a prisoner and to show in the flesh and through the images in her work how duality is transcended. The answer to the problem between the white race and the colored, between males and females, lies in healing the split that originates in the very foundation of our lives, our culture, our languages, our thoughts. A massive uprooting of dualistic thinking in the individual and collective consciousness is the beginning of a long struggle, but one that could, in our best hopes, bring us to the end of rape, of violence, of war.

LA ENCRUCIJADA/THE CROSSROADS

> A chicken is being sacrificed
> at a crossroads, a simple mound of earth
> a mud shrine for *Eshu*,
> *Yoruba* god of indeterminacy,
> who blesses her choice of path.
> She begins her journey.

Su cuerpo es una bocacalle. La mestiza has gone from being the sacrificial goat to becoming the officiating priestess at the crossroads.

As a mestiza I have no country, my homeland cast me out; yet all countries are mine because I am every woman's sister or potential lover. (As a lesbian I have no race, my own people disclaim me; but I am all races because there is the queer of me in all races.) I am cultureless because, as a feminist, I challenge the collective cultural/religious male-derived beliefs of Indo-Hispanics and Anglos; yet I am cultured because I am participating in the creation of yet another culture, a new story to explain the world and our participation in it, a new value system with images and symbols that connect us to each other and to the planet. *Soy un amasamiento*, I am an act of kneading, of uniting and joining that not only has produced both a creature of darkness and a creature of light, but also a creature that questions the definitions of light and dark and gives them new meanings.

We are the people who leap in the dark, we are the people on the knees of the gods. In our very flesh, (r)evolution works out the clash of cultures. It makes us crazy constantly, but if the center holds, we've made some kind of evolutionary step forward. *Nuestra alma el trabajo*, the opus, the great alchemical work; spiritual *mestizaje*, a "morphogenesis," an inevitable unfolding. We have become the quickening serpent movement.

Indigenous like corn, like corn, the *mestiza* is a product of crossbreeding, designed for preservation under a variety of conditions. Like an ear of corn—a female seed-bearing organ—the *mestiza* is tenacious, tightly wrapped in the husks of her culture. Like kernels she clings to the cob; with thick stalks and strong brace roots, she holds tight to the earth— she will survive the crossroads.

Lavando y remojando el maíz en agua de cal, despojando el pellejo. Moliendo, mixteando, amasando, haciendo tortillas de masa. She steeps the corn in lime, it swells, softens. With stone roller on *metate*, she grinds the corn, then grinds again. She kneads and moulds the dough, pats the round balls into *tortillas*.

> We are the porous rock in the stone *metate*
> squatting on the ground.
> We are the rolling pin, *el maíz y agua*,
> *la masa harina. Somos el amasijo.*
> *Somos lo molido en el metate.*
> We are the *comal* sizzling hot,
> the hot *tortilla*, the hungry mouth.
> We are the coarse rock.
> We are the grinding motion,
> the mixed potion, *somos el molcajete.*
> We are the pestle, the *comino, ajo, pimienta,*
> We are the *chile colorado,*
> the green shoot that cracks the rock.
> We will abide.

. . .

C
O
N
T
E
X
T

SOMOS UNA GENTE

Hay tantísimas fronteras
que dividen a la gente,
pero por cada frontera
existe también un puente.

Gina Valdés

Divided Loyalties. Many women and men of color do not want to have any dealings with white people. It takes too much time and energy to explain to the downwardly mobile, white middle-class women that it's okay for us to want to own "possessions," never having had any nice furniture on our dirt floors or "luxuries" like washing machines. Many feel that whites should help their own people rid themselves of race hatred and fear first. I, for one, choose to use some of my energy to serve as mediator. I think we need to allow whites to be our allies. Through our literature, art, *corridos*, and folktales we must share our history with them so when they set up committees to help Big Mountain Navajos or the Chicano farmworkers or *los Nicaragüenses* they won't turn people away because of their racial fears and ignorances. They will come to see that they are not helping us but following our lead.

Individually, but also as a racial entity, we need to voice our needs. We need to say to white society: We need you to accept the fact that Chicanos are different, to acknowledge your rejection and negation of us. We need you to own the fact that you looked upon us as less than human, that you stole our lands, our personhood, our self-respect. We need you to make public restitution: to say that, to compensate for your own sense of defectiveness, you strive for power over us, you erase our history and our experience because it makes you feel guilty—you'd rather forget your brutish acts. To say you've split yourself from minority groups, that you disown us, that your dual consciousness splits off parts of yourself, transferring the "negative" parts onto us. (Where there is persecution of minorities, there is shadow projection. Where there is violence and war, there is repression of shadow.) To say that you are afraid of us, that to put distance between us, you wear the mask of contempt. Admit that Mexico is your double, that she exists in the shadow of this country, that we are irrevocably tied to her. Gringo, accept the doppelganger in your psyche. By taking back your collective shadow the intra-cultural split will heal. And finally, tell us what you need from us.

. . .

14

Patrolling Racial Borders

Discrimination Against Mixed Race People

Heather Dalmage

"Is she part Black?" asked the imposing woman ahead of us in line at the Dollar Store. "Yes," I responded, not wanting to continue this conversation in an impersonal and public

arena in front of my two-year-old daughter for whom the word race still meant, "last one to the porch is a rotten egg."

Raising her voice, the Black woman bent down toward my daughter's face and proclaimed, "We call that mulatto. Yes, indeed, you're a mulatto."

I felt strongly compelled to respond but was uncertain which piece should be addressed and how. Should I have begun to talk with this woman about the ugly origins of the term mulatto? Should I have addressed the dehumanizing and degrading aspects of categorizing other people (especially children)? I knew I was not going to let someone else impose the context of a race debate in front of my two-year-old. I left the store.

While such intrusions are not uncommon, more often they remain in the realm of the silent stare. A multiracial woman once said to me that being stared at was such a part of her existence that when it came time for her to perform in front of an audience she was very comfortable. Historically, in academic research and beyond, much emphasis has been placed on the ways multiracial people adjust to race in society. The assumption underlying much of the analysis is that race is a concrete, objective, and static phenomenon. I propose that if we want to more fully understand multiracial experiences we need to "flip the script" and analyze why racial categories have been created in particular ways and why people who identify themselves with a single racial category feel the need and right to intrude upon, pass judgement on, and discriminate against multiracial people and their families.

GROUP BOUNDARIES AND DISCRIMINATION

Race thinking developed in the U.S. around and through questions of citizenship and resource distribution. The history of U.S. immigration and citizenship reflects a system deeply embedded in the protection of White privilege and the denial of rights to people of color. Colonization, slavery, genocide of indigenous people, the Chinese Immigration Exclusion Acts of the 1800s, the Bracero Program, internment camps, Jim Crow laws, and numerous other legally sanctioned forms of discrimination have been used to define and defend Whiteness by creating clear distinctions between White people and all others. When the distinctions seemed threatened, anti-miscegenation laws—those that denied people the right to marry across race lines—were enforced through penalties that included imprisonment, enslavement, and death. The primary threat was not the marriage itself but rather the fact that in the U.S. marriage legitimizes the offspring. If multiracial children were deemed legitimate, then all laws based on the separation of "the races" would be delegitimized. After three centuries of anti-miscegenation laws, in 1967, buttressed by the strength of the Civil Rights Movement, the Supreme Court ruled that interracial marriages must be recognized in every state. Unfortunately, multiracial families still face discrimination, and the children of these marriages are still expected to claim only one race.

While the Civil Rights Movement paved the way for the legal acceptance of multiracial families, it also created a new set of struggles for these families. The Civil Rights Movement included various groups struggling for liberation and self-definition such as the Young Lords, the Chicano Movement, the Black Power Movement, the Asian American Movement, and the American Indian Movement. Through these struggles, groups of color that had previously been on the defensive against White supremacist abuses began to define themselves for themselves. This meant that the distinction between insider and outsider was defined from *within* each of these groups rather than predominantly imposed from the outside by Whites. However, the way lines were drawn caused many problems for those who found themselves on the borders of racial groups, particularly those who

were racially mixed. Moreover, the struggle for civil rights led to the passing of legislation meant to address and redress racism. The government needed a way to track compliance and by 1977 had agreed on four discrete racial categories; every U.S. citizen was required to check one. The census became a vehicle for protecting people of color against White supremacist abuse, *and* it strengthened the distinctions between racial categories. As a result, multiracial people, already discriminated against in a White supremacist society, became more susceptible to discrimination from all sides.

How "sides" are defined is a matter of history. Those people with whom we identify most closely, those with whom we share a history, a collective memory, and a collective way of knowing are generally considered our in-group, our side. For instance, a quick trip to the Gaza Strip makes the point clear. Stone-throwing Palestinians do not have a natural or inherent disdain for the Jews at whom they throw the stones. Likewise the tank-driving Israelis are not genetically driven to violence toward Palestinians. This particular conflict is driven by historical circumstances in which children are raised and through which they understand themselves and their world. The collective memories on each side are used to define the boundaries of in-groups. Often, as is the case in the Middle East, in-group cohesion is strengthened through the hatred of an out-group, those against whom in-group members define themselves. Moreover, each side knows itself in the negation of the other; for it is at the boundaries that identities are framed. In such a construction, little room exists for someone to be both Palestinian and Israeli.

The history of Whiteness and various forms of racism directed at groups of color has meant that in the U.S. being a member of one race—or one side—has immediately placed an individual as an out-group of the other. The greater the power imbalance between groups, the greater the emphasis on maintaining boundaries between sides. The boundaries are maintained on both the institutional and individual levels through various forms of discrimination. On an institutional level, discrimination occurs as an outcome of laws and the way society functions. For example, many children of color are denied equal access to education as a result of years of housing discrimination in a society in which a large portion of school funding is tied to property values through taxes. The segregated housing market ensures that children of color, particularly African Americans and Latinos, are disproportionately receiving an inferior education relative to White children. Discrimination and racism also play out between individuals. For instance, one student refuses to speak to another because she sat at the wrong lunchroom table. In this case, the discriminatory act is clear; the individual discriminator can be identified. Given that institutional mechanisms, from the housing market to the census, have functioned to keep lines between racial and ethnic groups clear and defined, multiracial children are facing unending demands to choose a side and stake a claim. In other words, demands are made that they adhere to the larger rules of race that guide U.S. racial thinking.

On all sides, border patrollers, or the race police, believe the color line is static and immutable, and thus they think they can distinguish between "us" and "them." Border patrollers claim that race is a simple concept, demand that others comply, and make their presence felt through various actions. The most common action, by far, is the stare. Other forms of border patrolling include probing and inappropriate questions. "What are you?" is one of the most common questions faced by multiracial people. Many times, however, people will not ask: instead they will begin to label a multiracial person. A friend of mine once told me that cab drivers assume she is whatever they are. Because border patrollers think they can determine "authentic" behaviors they also think they have the right to grant or withhold acceptance. Even when acceptance is not granted, individuals are expected to act in ways deemed appropriate; to do otherwise will provoke further patrolling.

All racial groups patrol the borders; thus, in addition to facing White racist abuse, multiracial people also face discrimination from their communities of color. Here I identify

five broad areas of everyday life in which multiracial children are patrolled and face discrimination and demands to comply with existing racial rules.

1. PATROLLING OF THE CHILD'S PHYSICALITY

All children tend to be conscious of appearance; however, not all children have to give conscious thought to the racial implications of their choice of hairstyle, make-up, weight and body shape, clothes, shoes, bags, and hats. Multiracial children do—they must because border patrollers on each side are watching and commenting. This form of discrimination can be very hurtful to multiracial children who must expend an inordinate amount of energy negotiating their appearance. For example, a Black-White multiracial woman I interviewed spoke of the devastation she felt as a child because her White mother did not learn to do "Black hair." As a result she faced relentless teasing from Black girls at school. Unfortunately, many parents, particularly White parents, do not understand the importance of hair and other physical markers to their child's ability to negotiate racial borders.

2. PATROLLING LINGUISTICS

Individuals who think that they can tell who is an "authentic" member of their race and who is not often listen intently to the use of language. Multiracial children are patrolled for their ability to "speak the language." For instance, a young multiracial student was granted acceptance by his Black peers only after he proved that he could play the dozens (or snaps, e.g., "Yo mama is so big . . ."). Once he could show that he understood the nuances of the language as it defines racial groups, then he was more accepted. Multiracial children are often bilingual; that is, they have the ability to comfortably converse as an insider with more than one racial group. Unfortunately, multiracial children who engage in bilingual practices are criticized as being wishy-washy and fake. Parents and teachers sometimes reinforce this idea by advising the child to "be yourself" thus implying that strong, certain, and clear-headed people speak only one way regardless of audience. In short, the message is that bilingualism is not acceptable and the child should choose a side. Such advice can be hurtful to a multiracial child for whom the ability to switch gears may be part of being her or himself.

3. PATROLLING INTERACTION WITH MEMBERS OF THE OUT-GROUP

Here the border patrollers demand a denial of all connections to, or affections for, the racial out-group. While this most often occurs around the issue of dating and friendship circles, multiracial children are even pressured, at times, to deny their parents and relatives. Most multiracial children have been in conversations in which White people are portrayed as universally evil. In these instances, if the child says, "But my father and my grandparents are White, and they are not evil," her loyalties will be called into question; she risks becoming an outsider. Moreover, multiracial children who appear White are assumed by Whites to be an insider and are often subjected to White racist conversation. Multiracial children who speak out in these situations sometimes face the racist compliment, "Oh, we don't think of you as Puerto Rican, you're different, we think of you as White." In this case, the child is devalued, and those Whites giving the "compliment" assume White to be something highly valued and that they have the right to bestow an identity on another human being. The children expend much energy deciding how to respond to the patrolling and discrimination.

4.   PATROLLING GEOGRAPHIES

Here, I am using geographies to address the physical spaces individuals occupy in their lives. Because of the segregation in society, racial groups are often geographically defined. Children have little control over where they live, and yet they are held responsible by border patrollers for a street address that might place them on the wrong side of the race line. In addition, other geographies are patrolled including what school a child attends, choice of classes, choice of lunchroom table, and how leisure time is spent. Multiracial children who might be comfortable sitting at several different (and racially defined) lunchroom tables may be reprimanded, "You are either one of us or you are not, you need to decide." A multiracial woman who attended high school in Manhattan recalled that White, Black, Latino, and Asian students each exited the school from different doors. Each day she left the school she was made aware that her choice of exit was being noted by others. In short, because all social spaces are raced, the spaces multiracial children occupy throughout the day carry messages to others about the child's loyalty to a particular side.

5.   PATROLLING OF CULTURAL CAPITAL

Cultural capital is the resources individuals can draw upon to give them status and credibility in society. Given racial divisions in society, cultural capital is used by all sides to determine who is a loyal and credible insider. The cultural capital important among children as they become aware of racial categories includes taste in music, television programs, sports, and magazines. A multiracial man who grew up in the Bronx reported that in high school he loved the music of Barry Manilow but that he always hid the tapes and listened to that music when he was alone. His enjoyment of that music marked him "too White," and his Latino friends would have shunned him. Another Black-White multiracial young man remembered the difficulty he had with his Black friends when he joined the high school hockey team. He was given the label "White boy" for playing.

All children face patrolling; however, multiracial children face racial border patrolling in addition to the usual demands children place on each other for conformity. Some children are given (or assigned to) one racial group by parents and teachers and expected to comply. Unfortunately, too often parents and teachers dismiss border patrolling by invoking "colorblind" language. The children are told to avoid labeling themselves and that they are part of the human race. In many cases, however, teachers and some parents just ignore race altogether. In the silence, the children are left to fend for themselves. Fortunately, most multiracial children do successfully negotiate border patrolling; however, if parents and teachers were more aware of the unique forms of discrimination these children face, they might be able to reduce the burden.

While all sides patrol and police the boundaries of their racial communities, the reason for and consequence of the patrolling vary. Everyone who has learned about race, U.S. style, looks for clues about how to racially categorize others. Some White people need to take this step before they feel comfortable interacting with new people. They may sense that the color line is shifting and fear losing their racial status. Thus, until they can categorize others, they feel vague and uneasy about their own racial status and identity. For people of color, the desire to make distinctions may concern a quest for allegiance and unity, a means to determine who is "us" and who is "them" politically, socially, and culturally. Individuals who comfortably claim one racial identity or think that race is something that can be observed or uncovered with enough clues may feel confusion, anger, skepticism, concern, pity, hostility, curiosity, or superiority when they meet someone who does not seem to fit neatly into a preset racial category. These feelings play out through the course of interaction, and a multiracial person, regardless of how he or she identifies, must contend with the response of these individuals. For instance, Kimberly, a multiracial woman living

in Manhattan, grew up being chastised by her parents and grandparents for not speaking "proper" English; in school Kimberly was taunted by Black students who insisted that she was trying to be White. As a person with racially ambiguous features, she receives many comments and stares from strangers. She is tired of hearing the same questions and comments and has also grown tired of defending herself:

> People come up to me and they'll say, "Do you get confused between being Black and White?" I say, "Well, yeah, you know, some mornings I wake up with this craving for fried chicken, and other mornings I just can't get the beat, I start dancing and can't get the beat." I want them to see how narrow-minded they're being. What do you think? One day I like fried chicken and the next I don't? It's not like that.

Kimberly points to the thinking that underlies the unique discrimination faced by multiracial people. If it is believed that race is inherent to an individual and that race is a way to group people into discrete categories, then it stands to reason that multiracial people must have separate races compartmentalized within them. Depending on the mix, multiracial people are assumed to have a genetically programmed way of being that can cause, at the extreme, an "internal war." Responding to people the way she does, Kimberly externalizes the problem of race and, at the same time, gives others the opportunity to think about race in a more sophisticated manner.

Given the history of race politics in the U.S., multiracial people have been largely ignored and more generally subsumed under communities of color for statistical and research purposes. Thus, until recently, multiracial people have not had a collective voice and have had to negotiate border patrolling individually. The explosion of writings since the early 1990s has begun the process of documenting and creating a voice for multiracial people and their families. While multiracial children have many more resources available today than they did a generation ago, they still face a society that assumes and demands that people comply with racial codes of conduct—codes that have historically denied the existence of multiracial people.

CONCLUSION

In this chapter I have addressed a brief history of and social context for the discrimination faced by multiracial people in the United States. I have identified those who discriminate against multiracial people as "border patrollers." While the majority of this chapter addresses the individual outcomes of this discrimination, it is important to note that institutional forms of discrimination against multiracials maintain the framework in which border patrolling takes place. For instance, in the United States we have a segregated housing market and thus segregated schools. Stable, racially-mixed areas are few and far between. Thus, multiracial children often find themselves in situations in which they are the "only one" or one of a few. If their families live in predominantly White areas, then they will be the child of color in a White environment. If they are in an area that is predominantly of color, depending upon their own background and the background of the neighborhood, they will be labeled as different. Patrolling takes place on an individual level, the level of daily experience, the level that children are most likely to name and articulate. However, the fact is that border patrolling is the outcome of a larger system of racial injustice and segregation. Parents and teachers should be aware of the unique forms of discrimination faced by multiracial children and the White supremacist system in which that discrimination flourishes.

C O N T E X T

15

Injustice for All

The Rise of the U.S. Immigration Policing Regime

National Network for Immigrant and Refugee Rights

INTRODUCTION

HURRICANE's 2009–2010 report, *Injustice for All: The Rise of the Immigration Policing Regime*, finds that the U.S. government has put into place a brutal system of immigration control and policing that criminalizes immigration status, normalizes the forcible separation of families, destabilizes communities and workplaces, and fuels widespread civil rights violations. This "immigration control policing regime" is also contributing to and tolerating an upsurge in racial discrimination and hate violence against immigrants and those perceived to be foreign born or "illegal."

Based on over 100 stories of abuse reported, collected and documented by volunteers, staff and members of NNIRR's initiative, HURRICANE: The Human Rights Immigrant Community Action Network, *Injustice for All* shows how a new dimension of immigration control, ICE-police collaboration and border security, are hurting communities from the rural areas of New Mexico and North Carolina to New York City and the suburbs of Chicago.

. . .

Over the last ten years, the U.S. has built a policing regime that uses immigration status to segregate people, thereby scapegoating people of color in a new way for the worsening fiscal crisis. Public officials and corporations collaborate to cut and/or privatize public services, including using for-profit private prisons to incarcerate people for immigration charges, destroying civil and labor rights. Immigration status is also being used to deny Indigenous people their right to identity, land and community.

The results are ominous. Congress and the Obama Administration have institutionalized this immigration policing, intensifying criminalization through immigration-police collaboration and other policies and programs. The U.S. has expanded workplace immigration policing, enhancing employer sanctions through the E-verify program to detect and force "unauthorized" workers out of certain kinds of work. In fiscal year 2010, ICE reported more than 2,200 audits, up from 1,400 in 2009, issuing 240 fines totaling $6.9 million, up from 52 fines totaling about $1 million in 2009. And the prospects that Congress or the Obama Administration will reverse policies or restrain policing are unlikely, as dozens of states, local, and county governments and federal agencies are considering similar policies and legislation, egged on by a reactionary nativist movement. Since 2000, some 107 towns, cities and counties have passed anti-immigrant ordinances affecting access to services, housing and employment.

THE RISE OF AN IMMIGRATION POLICING REGIME

In 2003, the majority of U.S. immigration service and policing responsibilities were transferred from the former Immigration and Naturalization Service to the then newly-formed Department of Homeland Security (DHS). In the wake of the September 11th terrorist attacks, the U.S. created the DHS as an umbrella agency that directly incorporated immigration affairs with national security policies. DHS also launched Operation Endgame, a 10-year strategic detention and deportation plan designed to build the capacity to "remove all removable aliens." (11.1 million undocumented immigrants are currently estimated to reside in the United States.)

Operation Endgame represents a significant turning point in U.S. immigration policy. Endgame has built a new "immigration policing regime" that attempts to connect the dots between disparate issues—including immigration, citizenship, the "war on terror," border control, national security, crime, law enforcement, and the economy—all under the guise of "protecting the homeland." This approach to immigration control and enforcement consists of four pillars:

Relentless criminalization of immigration status and the use of incarceration through U.S. laws, policies, measures and practices—weakening and even eliminating constitutional rights, particularly due process rights, and labor protections for noncitizens.

Persistent linking of immigration to the politics of national security and engaging in policing tactics that rely upon racial, ethnic/nationality and religious profiling.

Escalating militarization of immigration control and border communities; reinforcing policies and strategies that deliberately "funnel" migrants, forcing them to cross through the most dangerous segments of the U.S.-Mexico border and compromise the rights and safety of border residents.

Scapegoating immigrants for the economic crisis and leveraging anti-immigrant sentiment to push federal, state, county and local laws and policies that cut and/or eliminate public services, and roll back civil rights, environmental, labor and other social protections. These policies contribute to corporate profit-making and are integral to "free" trade and other economic development programs that displace communities and force individuals around the world into involuntary migration.

. . .

In reports from California, Arizona, New Mexico, Illinois, North Carolina, and New York, different forms of immigration-police collaboration are impacting communities, youth, women, workers, Indigenous people and people of color. Immigration policing is taking different forms along the border (local police and the Border Patrol, for example) than in the interior (driver's license and DUI checkpoints) but the impacts are just as devastating. Immigration-police collaboration creates more problems in all communities:

- Police collusion with ICE undermines community safety. Residents will not report crimes and fires if they fear detection and deportation.
- Women are less likely to report domestic violence if they or their partners have immigration status. Batterers are also more likely to threaten their partners with turning them over to ICE to stop them from reporting an abusive relationship.
- Equally troubling, local law enforcement is not trained in immigration law and requires substantial amounts of time and money to reach a satisfactory level of expertise. As a result, local police departments, already strapped on resources and manpower, cut back other vital community services, affecting community safety.

- Police cooperation with ICE encourages racial profiling, already illegal, resulting in civil rights violations and abuses against immigrant and refugee communities. Even where police departments have worked to end racial profiling, such collaboration undermines the credibility of police departments to effectively serve all communities.

. . .

IMMIGRATION-POLICE COLLABORATION GOES VIRAL

In the past year, dozens of states and other local and county governments have been spurred to create copycat Arizona-style laws. And there is an undeniable economic angle to such immigration policing. For example, Arizona's SB1070 was developed by lawmakers in collaboration with corporations that build private jails to incarcerate immigrants; these companies stand to earn considerable profits from the growing trend of detaining immigrants for enforcement and deterrence. Indeed, some two-thirds of persons imprisoned for immigration charges are held in local jails. In southern California alone, DHS is set to pay almost $57 million to 13 jails.

Other state and local governments are also looking at ways to use the "illegal immigration problem" as a means to solve their fiscal crises. From Virginia to Oregon and Pennsylvania, ICE offers governments immigration jails as a job creation and revenue source strategy. ICE has approached different localities to build and, in some cases, run public-private immigrant jails, where investors will reap millions in profits and governments will boost their revenues. Localities also fear losing an ICE detention center; Etowah County in Alabama faces a ruinous fiscal crisis because ICE is planning to end its contract that pays the county $14,000 a day to jail immigrants. Additionally, SB1070 is costing Arizona huge losses in revenues.

. . .

RECORD YEAR OF REPRESSION

Fiscal year 2010 was a record year of repression: the U.S. government deported a total of 392,862 immigrant workers, students, women, and youth—many of whom were long-time residents of the United States. Beyond these individuals, untold numbers of family members were separated, children left hopeless, and neighborhoods and workplaces diminished by the absence of hardworking individuals who contributed significantly to the social, economic, and political fabric of our country.

2010 was also a record year for the detention of immigrants, subjected by ICE to inhumane treatment and conditions. Since 2003, at least 104 deaths have been documented of persons in ICE immigrant detention centers and jails.

ICE has some 32,000 jail beds exclusively for persons charged with immigration violations or in deportation proceedings. The DHS runs or contracts with some 350 public and private jails and prisons across the country to detain immigrants who have been arrested for status violations and are awaiting deportation. Many of these facilities are located in remote areas where there is little or no access to qualified, low-cost immigration legal service providers (there is no guaranteed right to counsel for immigrant detainees as in the criminal justice context). Moreover, the DHS frequently transfers immigrant detainees

to new facilities without providing notice to their attorneys or family members. There is little accountability for guaranteeing a prison's minimal conditions and basic human rights protections for detained immigrants, including access to medical treatment, recreation, and the freedom to worship. The DHS also uses semi-secret court proceedings to judge, try, and summarily deport immigrants accused of minor immigration offenses, in gross violation of constitutional rights and due process.

Women, who make up over half of all migrants to the United States, have been particularly impacted by the new immigration policing regime. HURRICANE'S database is filled with documentation of abuses committed against immigrant women. (In most instances, women are HURRICANE'S principal monitors and reporters of rights abuses.)

In addition to the rights violations and abuses male migrants face, women in migration are subjected to sexual harassment, assault and rape during the arduous border-crossing journey, at work and in ICE detention. For example, ICE jailed over 10,000 immigrant women in 2008; after routine testing, 965 of the women (nearly 10%), tested pregnant; many of these women reported being raped during the border crossing.

In deportation proceedings, ICE and the courts mete out severe punishment and treatment to women who are mothers and workers, especially, if they are undocumented and Indigenous. In some areas, various U.S. public agencies have taken away and placed into adoption the children of undocumented and Indigenous women. HURRICANE also received reports of immigration jail guards sexually assaulting women detained at the Hutto detention facility.

. . .

Another alarming example of impact of the current immigration policing regime is the growing human rights crisis at the U.S.-Mexico border. In 2010, a record number of migrants died in the border crossing: the remains of 253 migrants were recovered in Arizona border alone. (See Coalición de Derechos Humanos report in *Injustice for All*.) Human rights groups that work on the border to uphold the rights of migrants report that for every migrant dead recovered in the border at least ten others are believed to have disappeared. An average of two migrant deaths are recorded every day; border groups estimate that from 5,000 to 8,000 migrant deaths have occurred since this border control strategy was implemented in 1994.

. . .

RECOMMENDATIONS

The *2009–2010 HURRICANE Report* urges the U.S. government to undertake a major shift in immigration policies, to address the patterns of human and civil rights violations, harm and traumatization of immigrants and their communities, and to provide access to the adjustment of immigration status, a process long held at bay by a lack of political will and action at the federal level. Without such a shift, millions of men, women and children residing in this country will continue to face lives of fear, uncertainty and economic insecurity.

There are significant steps that the Obama Administration can authorize, including:

- The restoration of due process rights and other Constitutional protections, including an expansion of access to the courts;
- The suspension of detentions and deportations, other enforcement operations and high profile raids; undertake a high-level investigation and hearings with impacted communities;

- An end to the policy and practice of jailing persons solely for immigration status offenses, except in cases where there is a high risk to public safety;
- The prohibition of ICE and local, county, state and federal law enforcement from using all forms of racial, ethnic/nationality and religious profiling;
- A thorough investigation of complaints of abuses in public and private corporate detention centers and jails housing immigrants; a moratorium on the expansion of detention centers and privately run prisons;
- An end to all inter-agency and immigration-police collaboration programs;
- Prohibit local, county, and state governments from legislating immigration enforcement, such as Arizona's SB1070;
- The roll back and end to the militarization of immigration control and border communities; end Operation Stonegarden, a federal program for police collaboration with Border Patrol, and Operation Streamline that violates due process, making unauthorized entry a felony with automatic sentencing.

We are disturbed by the lack of congressional action to enact fair immigration policies, and we call on our elected officials in the House and Senate to:

- Hold field hearings with members of interior and border communities to document the impacts and abuses caused by U.S. immigration enforcement and border security policies, measures and practices;
- Repeal employer sanctions and stop all E-Verify programs; protect and expand the labor rights of all workers, native and foreign-born; and increase Department of Labor inspectors;
- Repeal the 287(g), "Secure Communities" initiatives;
- Provide and expand options to legal migration, including access to legal permanent residency and citizenship;
- Institute routine programs, including legalization, to adjust the immigration status and provide "green cards" to immigrants, to ensure civil and labor rights, keep families together and reinforce healthy communities.

Finally, we call upon the Administration and members of Congress:

- To address the root causes of displacement and involuntary migration, by promoting and implementing fair trade and sustainable community development policies;
- To help lead a nationwide condemnation of racial intolerance and xenophobia in keeping with our country's legal and moral commitment to equality for all.

We further urge the United States to respect and uphold international human and labor rights standards, including the ratification and implementation of the U.N. International Convention for the Protection of the Rights of All Migrant Workers and Members of Their Families and the U.N. Declaration on the Rights of Indigenous People.

. . .

NEW AFRICANS IN OLD AMERICA

Nunu Kidane

Following New York, California has the highest number of immigrants from Africa. Estimated conservatively at 145,453 (American Community Survey 2006–08), the African immigrant community is one of the most undercounted.

PAN's recent mobilization activities for the 2010 Census exposed the complexities involved in counting African community members that are unlike any other. African immigrants organize themselves largely along their national or ethnic identities (as opposed to the assumed continental "African") and therefore remain in clusters of small groups, fragmented and excluded from traditional mainstream institutions.

PAN estimates that the actual size of the African community is at least three times this number. After Los Angeles, the Bay Area in particular is home to a high number of African immigrants. A recent study had an estimate of African immigrants in the Bay Area at 2% of the population; no doubt this figure will increase significantly over the coming years.

CLIMATE OF FEAR AND "TRIPLE JEOPARDY"

For the growing population of immigrants from Africa, the recent anti-immigrant raids and attacks have had unexpected impacts, both direct and indirect. Whether or not directly targeted by enforcement agencies, the climate of fear has permeated every association without exception. Prevailing assumptions about African immigrants is that they largely "blend" into existing African American communities and, on the basis of skin color at least, are less likely to be targeted by immigration law enforcement. This is considered, ironically, as one of the few instances where there's a positive factor on being Black in America.

The facts, however, are that African immigrants face the double threat of being Black and immigrant. They are twice as likely to be racially profiled, first on the basis of their skin color and additionally on their status as immigrants. Then, an added factor of *"triple jeopardy"* comes into play for the large numbers of African immigrants who are also Muslim.

. . .

The recent immigration raids in homes and workplaces largely exposed in the Spanish-speaking and other Latin American-origin communities set off a wave of fear in the African immigrant community. Less known and less visible, the sense of fear that reverberated across African immigrant communities left them with no access to information or resources. Consequently, new Africans whose status may be questionable are less likely to be engaged in civic activism or join in community organizing for fear of "not returning home." Individuals have expressed being paralyzed with the fear of being picked up by ICE while out on a casual errand, and separated from their children or families.

RACIAL AND RELIGIOUS PROFILING

Still, the most common experience of negative encounters with police is of African men who report being constantly stopped for "driving while Black." Incidents of being stopped (usually for no reason or weak reasons) have been mentioned on more occasions than can be counted. Many are professionals who work in corporate offices and commute long distances and are likely to experience this multiple times. This fits the standard practice of racial profiling commonly experienced by African American men. The new African

immigrant, however, does not have the advantage of contextualizing the experience in the history of race and racism in this country. Many express a sense of feeling targeted, frustrated and at odds with what they consider to be violations of principles of fairness, which they expect from this country.

Additionally, once police stop and question them, their foreign accents identify them as immigrants, leaving them vulnerable to detention if they are unable to prove their "legal" status.

Other shared stories include Somali women in the Santa Clara County, where the largest concentration of Somali communities resides in the San Francisco Bay Area. Highly visible in their traditional veils, the women express a sense of fear in the way they are regarded daily. They are asked to present documents of their status when registering their children at schools or receiving treatments in hospital/clinic.

. . .

Nunu Kidane is the coordinator for Priority Africa Network (PAN), an Africa-promoting/ African immigrant community mobilizing grassroots organization based in the San Francisco Bay Area.

SOUTH ASIAN WORKERS ORGANIZE FOR THEIR RIGHTS
AGAINST ABUSIVE EMPLOYERS IN NEW YORK

Ayesha Mahmooda

The South Asian community has the second largest number of undocumented people in New York City after Latinos. At DRUM—Desis Rising Up & Moving, South Asian retail, restaurant, construction, and domestic workers along with taxi drivers are organizing to end abuses they face every day and win better working conditions for all immigrant workers. . . . The worker leaders build alliances with Latino worker centers, labor unions, the NY State Department of Labor's new Wage Watch program, and attorneys who file wage claims.

Through a series of meetings, surveys and community research, DRUM'S worker members identified common issues in local industries and reported the following abuses:

- Working long hours without overtime pay;
- Substandard low wages, violating minimum wage protections;
- Employer mistreatment of workers, including unsafe worksite conditions, undermining their health and safety; and
- Employers and owners blacklisting workers who speak out in the industries.

. . .

FATIMA'S STORY

At an early morning DRUM Worker Committee meeting, a Bangladeshi retail store worker named Fatima (not her real name) spoke out about the exploitative conditions at the Jackson Heights clothing stores where she worked. She described how the bosses paid low wages or no back wages, made them work long hours, and harassed them constantly. The store owners instilled fear in the workers, making it hard for her and her co-workers to

speak up who were afraid of losing their jobs. She spoke about how difficult it felt for her and her co-workers to stand up for their rights because they are undocumented women.

One day in December 2009, Fatima's boss ordered her to get supplies from his other store across the street. As he rushed her out the door, he began to yell at her to hurry up as she crossed the busy street. Scared and pressured, Fatima got hit by an oncoming car and was thrown 15 feet away. She lay on the cold sidewalk in severe pain, unable to move her shoulder. With the help of some bystanders, Fatima managed to walk back to her store to call 911 for an ambulance and to file a police report. But her boss immediately threatened her as well as all her co-workers in the store, saying that if they called 911, he would get in trouble for having undocumented workers and they would get deported. He also threatened to fire anyone who tried to call 911. After some bystanders and customers persuaded the boss, he allowed Fatima to call a cab and go to the hospital.

At the hospital, doctors told Fatima that she would need surgery to get her shoulder working properly again. Since Fatima had no insurance to pay for the surgery, the hospital advised her to file a police report against the driver and receive some money to pay for her medical expenses.

The next day at work, Fatima's employer threatened to fire her again if she reported the incident to police. She went to the local police station anyway; police told her she could not file a report without the license plate number of the vehicle that hit her, which she did not have.

. . .

The following day she went to the police station again to ask for a report, but police again told her that they could not do anything without the license plate number. When she asked again if they could look at the security cameras near the area where she was hit, they rudely refused, telling her that she should go back to her country if she did not like it.

. . .

Later that same day, the boss fired Fatima. She was never able to file the police report and never received the surgery. Unfortunately, thousands of undocumented immigrant workers in Jackson Heights and New York City face similar abuses and exploitation by their employers coupled with active neglect by law enforcement who fail to protect their rights.

Fatima became a leader and founding member of DRUM Workers' Committee and has reached out to dozens of other workers in similar situations. . . .

16

Finding My Eye-dentity

Olivia Chung

I watched the spoken-word group I Was Born With Two Tongues perform and was inspired by their style of reflecting on personal experiences. This piece flowed from my desire for self-expression and hopes of challenging other Asian American girls to question their definition of beauty. I am a second-generation Korean American, born and raised in a loving family in Silver Spring, Maryland. Currently, I'm a sophomore at the University of Pennsylvania,

pursuing interests in activism, writing, and hip-hop. My ultimate goal is to keep it real and selflessly live for the Lord.

Olivia, you wanna get *sang ka pul*?

I'm driving my mother to work, when she randomly brings up the eyelid question. The question that almost every Korean monoeyelidded girl has had to face in her life. The question that could change the future of my naturally noncreased eyelids, making them crease with the cut of a cosmetic surgeon's knife.

You know your aunt? She used to have beany eyes just like you! She used to put on white and black eyeliner every morning to make them look BIG. Then she went to Korea and got the surgery done. Now look! She looks so much better! Don't you want it done? I would do it . . .

I think this is about the 346,983,476th time she has brought this topic up. Using the exact same words. You would look so much more prettier with bigger eyes! she says. *You know, because they look kind of squinty and on top of that you have an underbite, so you look really mean . . .* She explains while narrowing her eyes and jutting out her jaw in emphasis of her point.

A couple of years ago, I would have taken her suggestion seriously. I remember reading a section of *Seventeen* magazine, where the once-did-funky-makeup-for-100-anorexic-white-girls-on-runways beauty expert revealed the secret to applying eye makeup. As a desperate preteen girl seeking beauty advice, I remember it perfectly. Put dark shadow right over the eyelashes, light powder all over, medium shadow over the edge of the crease of your eyelid. That's where I always tripped up. Crease? Umm . . . excuse me? These so-called beauty experts never gave me enough expertise to figure out how to put makeup on my face without looking like a character in a kabuki play. I tried to follow the beauty experts' advice. But I decided it wasn't working when people asked me if I had gotten a black eye.

My friends suggested training my eyelids to fold with tape. *My mother did that and now she has a real crease, one of my friends told me.* I, however, never learned the magic behind that, and always felt too embarrassed to ask. Another friend once excitedly showed me how she had bought a bottle of make-your-own-eye-crease glue from Korea. I let her try it on me too. I could barely open my eyes, thanks to the fierce stinging sensation resulting from the glue that got on my eyeball. And when I finally did take a quick glimpse of myself in the mirror, I saw a stranger with uneven eyelids.

The first time I remember being insulted was when I was little. . . .

In kindergarten, I believe. Oh, it was classic. A little blond kid pulled the edges of his eyes out, yelling, *Ching chong chinaman!* I, being new to this game, could only make a weak comeback. *I'm not Chinese. . . . I'm KOREAN.* I remember feeling a confused hurt, realizing that I looked different and not understanding why being different was bad.

Couldn't we all just get along? I had learned that God loves people as they are, as different as they are. I learned that He looks at the heart, and that it really doesn't matter how a person looks. I think my belief in this, combined with my fear of a sharp object cutting the skin above my eye, kept me away from the *sang ka pul* surgery. Yet, I continued to receive comments on my "chinky" eyes, and I always emerged from these situations feeling confused and angry . . . without ever really knowing why. Why couldn't I be accepted with my so-called chinky eyes? Why in the world were they even called "chinky" eyes? If they meant to insult Chinese, all the Chinese people I knew had huge eyes. With the crease.

As I grew older, the childish "ching chong"s came with less frequency. Still, the magazines continue to give me unhelpful directions on how to apply makeup. Still, I witness my own friends getting the surgery done in an effort to be "more beautiful." Still, my mother continuously confronts me with the dreaded eyelid question. *You wanna get* sang ka pul? I

always answer her with an *are-you-crazy?* but simple *no.* All the things I wish I could have told her come flowing on this page with my pen. . . .

Umma, my mother, don't you see that my noncreased eyes are beautiful? Asian eyes are beautiful. Your eyes are beautiful. My eyes are beautiful. Asian is beautiful. After all these years of wanting to open up my eyes with tape and glue and surgery, I have opened up my eyes to a different definition of beauty. A broader definition of beauty, one that embraces differences and includes every girl, who can hold her head up, *sang ka pul*-less and chinky-eyed, because being *Asian is beautiful.*

17

Identification Pleas

Eric Gansworth

So it's the summer of 2002, . . . in the town of Del Rio, Texas, perhaps one of the last places on earth I thought I would be engaged in an identity crisis. . . . I am here with a friend, Donnie, who has a piece of land in this small border town. . . . He asks me if I want to cross the border into Acuña, as it is right there. Though the temperature is over a hundred degrees, we walk across the bridge above the Rio Grande into Mexico. On the exact border, large metal pegs mar the full surface of the pavement, gleam in the heat, and announce the change of country in full-size versions of that dotted line one sees on maps.

Here, trucks pull up, from the United States' end of the bridge, and stop, right on the dotted line. Other trucks meet them on the Mexican side. The drivers descend from their cabs and carry large boxes from the cargo areas of the United States trucks to those of the Mexican trucks. The border guards sit disinterested, watch this transaction under the bright sun, so I take a cue from them that this activity is nothing worth noting, and move on.

. . .

While it was an unpleasantly hot walk across, I see little justification for a bus to make the trip, and again Donnie clarifies that sometimes it is less of a hassle for Mexicans to cross the border if they use the bus instead of walking the bridge.

We leave Mexico a few minutes later, on the bridge's north-bound sidewalk, again stepping on the hot metal pegs, delineating one place from another. Below us, the Rio Grande seems more like the Rio Average, a muddy stream surrounded by dense growth of cane, and above the sidewalk overlooking the river, heavy-gauge steel mesh curves inward on sturdy beams nearly encircling us overhead. This architectural feature is designed to dissuade jumpers from making the five-story leap into the river or thick brush below. Donnie mentions that people have made the attempt and that random surveillance cameras are mounted in the cane—all of this to keep people from entering the United States in inappropriate fashion. . . .

We arrive at the [immigration] office and are both relieved that it is air-conditioned. Donnie shows his license to the officer, who waves him on, and I reach into my pocket, pull out my wallet, and wonder how many minutes it will take for Donnie's truck cab to cool down.

Opening the fold, I am momentarily confused by the version of my face staring back at me from the plastic card in the easiest access slot. I am almost ten years younger, wearing

enormous late-eighties glasses, my hair is long, wavy, and pulled back, and behind me the lush foliage of a reservation road fills the rest of the image. It is my tribal identification card, documenting my name, birth date, clan, tribe, reservation address, blood quantum, and the signature of the man on the reservation who officiates on such matters, next to my own signature. Mine is a little more complicated than some, but not unfathomably so. I am a member of the Onondaga Nation, ... The back of the card lists several agreements with the United States, asserting the sovereignty of the Haudenosaunee, the league of six nations to which both the Onondaga and Tuscarora nations belong, known in the United States as "the Iroquois."

The card itself is not confusing to me, of course, but it usually rests in my wallet behind a document I tend to need much more frequently: my driver's license. My license is nowhere to be found within the wallet, and then I suddenly can see the card in my mind, can picture its exact location, and thus can confirm it is not on my body. . . .

Since September 2001, . . . the most consistent change has been nearly relentless requests for my identification from airport personnel. To make things easier on myself and on those asking, I have gotten a "flight wallet" the size of an airline ticket, and in this I keep my boarding pass, frequent flyer card, and, yes, while I am traveling, my driver's license. The flight wallet, at the moment I approach the immigration officer, sits approximately a hundred yards away, in Donnie's truck, across the road, but more important, across the border.

"Identification?" the officer asks, and I hand him my Native American Identification Card. He looks at it, tosses it down, and looks at me, smirking. "Now," he says, ...

"Now," he repeats, snapping the card on his desk this time, perhaps for emphasis, as if he had gotten an ace in a game of solitaire, "do you have any real ID?"

I am what you might call ethnically ambiguous in appearance. Over the years the odd looks, vague frowns, and unasked questions have become the routine. It has been kind of interesting, existing as a walking, breathing Rorschach test for others' perceptions and stereotype templates.

I have been mistaken for Italian, Armenian, Middle Eastern, Hawaiian, Russian, Polish, German, Portuguese, and Jewish, but I am most often wrongly assumed to be Latino. The first time it happened was in a men's room at a concert, when a drunken patron at the next urinal insisted I was a member of Los Lobos, the band whose set had finished about a half hour before. . . . The less glamorous mistake with my ethnicity happens nearly every time I am in the Southwest. This stands to reason, as Mexicans are Indians across the border, in essence, and we are the same in that we had very different, unique cultures before colonialism came along and divided us up with those stainless steel rivets in the bridge.

I was born and raised on a reservation in western New York State, a small place, home to fewer than two thousand people. Many of those people claim full-blood status, though some are blond, some have blue eyes. . . . My complexion is slightly dark, and deepens easily in the summer, so that by the end of June, even with minimal exposure, I usually sport what used to be called "a savage tan." My eyes are dark brown as well, and my hair appears to be black most of the year, but by late summer dark red highlights have burned into it. My body also reveals other telltale signs that prevent me from claiming full-blood status. I have genetic qualities that allow me to grow a beard and a mustache, and I have chosen to cultivate those traits.

. . . My hair was long a fair amount of my childhood and through adolescence—though not the long, straight Lakota hair all Indians are *supposed* to have. It seems many eastern Indians have a rougher textured hair, and mine falls into this category. No matter how much I might brush my hair out every morning, invariably I looked less like any Indians in Edward Curtis photographs and more like Jerry Garcia from the Grateful Dead, ...

On the reservation, as in many other places, hair is a political statement. I learned this reality early. One of my brothers, Lee, . . . began growing his hair long in the late

1960s, before he burned his draft card but after our oldest brother had been shipped out to Vietnam. Lee was suspended from high school a number of times for having his hair too long, until one time my mother grew tired of his forced removals, took him to school herself, grabbed an idle white kid in the hallway whose hair was longer than my brother's, and dragged them both into the office to confront the principal with this discrepancy. My brother was reinstated, but one of his instructors insisted he had missed too much time in his suspensions to graduate, so he went to summer school, but he did it in long hair and graduated in August.

He is not the first member of my family to have an educational institution concern itself with his hair. In the early part of the twentieth century, the Dawes Act was in full swing, and my grandfather's parents were persuaded by government agents to allow their son the great privilege of attending one of the Indian boarding schools. They claimed that he would have a much better chance of surviving in the world if he could learn a trade in the broader culture. He learned to play a western instrument, the piccolo, I believe, and eventually remembered nothing about water drums but was well versed in snare and bass. . . .

Through college I had kept my hair in various stages of long, but it always looked wild, ... In graduate school I got rid of it all and kept a reasonably short style through that period, until I graduated and got past my first set of job interviews. As I began teaching at the college a few miles from the reservation where I grew up, my hair was still fairly short, appropriate for the era, the early 1990s, but as soon as I signed the contract I let it grow back out, and in 1998 my braid was about a foot and a half long, when I decided to get rid of it.

. . .

Other, strangely resonant events occurred in the few months following that, and I finally decided that while I could not stop the perpetuation of this stereotype, I did not have to be a contributing member. Tying off both ends of my braid, I cut it off in 1999, reduced my hair to a flattop, and grew my mustache to join the goatee at the same time. The braid is in my top-right desk drawer, where I keep it to remind me of where I have been.

. . .

Here, at the border, I am suddenly in Los Lobos land again, and my tribal identification is not good enough. National identification papers, it seems, are good enough documentation for the United States from every other nation except those housed within its borders. Haudenosaunee law stipulates we are not citizens of the United States, regardless of any federal laws on Indian citizenship. I am still not sure what the full dynamics are here. Perhaps it is not that our ID cards are not legitimate enough, but instead that braidless and hairy, I am not legitimate enough for my ID. This officer, I see, stares at me, is certain my name is Pedro, Hector, Jesus, and as a result of this perception he wears his illegal alien Polaroid sunglasses. Regardless of what might or might not be in my pocket, he has decided it is all right to treat me with disdain because I have been forward enough to attempt crossing borders without swimming my way in, and am merely getting what I deserve.

. . .

My faculty ID card looks promising. It is contemporary and formal, professionally laminated, and even has a bar code on it . . . . I hand this over and the officer looks at it. He rapid-fires questions at me. Suddenly I am taking a pop quiz on the academic calendar where I teach—when were finals, when was graduation, when does the school year begin, how many courses do I teach, and then it comes: What in Acuña, Mexico could possibly interest a college professor from New York? This question is so odd, so full of his emptiness, that no answer I can give short of "cheap dentistry," "stuffed armadillos," or "controlled substances" would be satisfactory. Back to the wallet.

My driving license convictions card surfaces next. This has my New York State license number on it, and a spotless driving record, I might add, the entire convictions section

blank. The officer rejects this offer as well, observing it has no photograph. I suggest he can match the names from this to my other documents, and he merely raises his right eyebrow in a knowing way. . . .

Finally I remember that the attendants at the gym where I work out insist on picture ID, in addition to their own issued membership card, every time I enter. . . . We solved the dual ID show by photocopying my license and taping it to the gym card. I rifle back through the less-convincing documents in my wallet and find the card, my shoddily photocopied license taped to it, and I am in luck; the numbers are visible, and more important, they match the numbers on my convictions record. I feel like a lotto winner as we compare numbers, the officer and I, and he is satisfied enough to run them through his international-criminal-driver's-license database and see, indeed, that I do live in western New York, or at least that someone who looks remarkably like me does. He gathers my variety pack of ID cards, hands them to me, and tells me, reluctantly, that I am free to go.

My braid is seventeen hundred miles from where I am as I leave the air-conditioned building and head out into the West Texas sun, and the fact that I can now slide my license back into my wallet and become someone I am not—a citizen of New York State, and thus a citizen of the United States of America as well—is no great comfort.

18

The Arab Woman and I

Mona Fayad

I am haunted by a constant companion called The Arab Woman. When I shut myself alone in my home, she steps out of the television screen to taunt me. In the movies, she stares down at me just as I am starting to relax. As I settle in a coffee shop to read the newspaper, she springs out at me and tries to choke me. In the classroom, when I tell my students that I grew up in Syria, she materializes suddenly as the inevitable question comes up: "Did you wear a veil?" That is when she appears in all her glory: the Faceless Veiled Woman, silent, passive, helpless, in need of rescue by the west. But there's also that other version of her, exotic and seductive, that follows me in the form of the Belly Dancer.

As a construct invented by the west, this two-in-one Arab Woman is completely intractable. Her voice drowns mine. It is no use pointing out that in Syria, Arab school girls wear khaki uniforms and are required for school credit to work on urban improvement projects, planting trees and painting walls. Or that Syrian television is constantly running ads for women to join the army. As I try to assert my experience of being an Arab woman, the Arab Woman tries to make me write about *her*. For a brief moment, I give in.

My one personal encounter in Syria with a fully veilled woman happens during my third year at the University of Damascus. I take a bus home. (Yes, we do have buses in the Middle East. We did away with camels as a means of transportation five years ago.) A veiled woman climbs aboard, the only one on the bus. I pay her no attention until she rushes up and embraces me enthusiastically. "Mona, how wonderful to see you!"

I know the voice, but somehow I can't place it. Realizing my predicament, she raises the veil for a minute. It's Mona, a friend of mine from university that I haven't seen recently.

A bouncing, energetic person, she is very active socially. I have never seen her veiled. I ask if it's a recent decision.

"Not really. I come from a conservative neighborhood, so I prefer to wear the veil when I arrive there." She shrugs. "My family isn't very concerned, but I prefer to do it this way."

The old souk (market) in downtown Kuwait is one of my favorite places to go. The tradition of bargaining is still in practice. It's a sharp contrast to the cold, impersonal supermarkets that have now almost completely eradicated the social exchanges that have been a part of buying and selling in the Middle East for centuries. In this section of town, many women wear burqas or are completely veiled since they belong to an older genera-tion. Here the real haggling happens, and the high-pitched shouting of women dins the lower and more cracked voices of the men. "What a cheat," the woman announces to whoever is willing to listen. "Can you believe how much he's asking for this worthless piece of cloth?"

In another corner, two women selling men's underwear laugh good-naturedly as they target a young man whose embarrassment is apparent. "How *big* did you say you were?"

These are some veiled Arab women. Neither silent nor passive, they have a place within their culture, like women all across the world. But once again, The Arab Woman has intruded, preventing me from talking about myself, pushing me to feed you what you want to hear.

Part of the reason I obey her is that it's easier to be exotic. To talk about an ordinary Arab woman, one who wears pants or a plain dress or a suit and walks around looking like everyone else is uninteresting, to say the least. I feel pressured to produce something *special*, something different. I try to shut out The Arab Woman who is controlling my thoughts. She is asking me for facts, figures, ways of classifying women so they can be clearly placed in boxes and the doors can be shut on them once and for all. She wants order, a rational explanation, something easy to understand.

After much thinking, it occurs to me that it is you who veil the Arab woman, it is you who make her into a passive victim, it is you who silence her. Arab women get on with our lives. I try to get on with my life, but it is difficult to constantly confront what I am not.

I am not The Arab Woman. And, further, I cannot represent Arab women. Each Arab woman must represent herself, with the range of identities that include Syrian or Saudi Arabian, Berber or Copt, bedouin or society woman from Beirut, Druze or Alawite, vil-lager in the Upper Nile or Minister of Culture from Damascus. We're not an object that can be crushed together and concentrated for Western consumption in a box labelled: Organic Arab Woman.

There's no doubt within *me* that I'm an Arab woman. The problem is whether you will believe me.

19

My Tongue is Divided into Two

Quique Aviles

. . . As far back as I can remember, the promise of English was part of my life.

. . . In 1969, when I was four, my mother borrowed money from her mother to travel to the United States as a tourist. Her real intention was to stay in the States, get a good job, and offer her children a better life. She made a promise to bring us, her four children, one by one—starting with the oldest and ending with the youngest, which was me. . . .

> My tongue is divided into two
> by virtue, coincidence or heaven
> words jumping out of my mouth
> stepping on each other
> enjoying being a voice for the message
> expecting conclusions . . .

I've learned English in three different phases.

PHASE ONE: CURIOSITY AND WONDER

Having a mother who was in the United States meant that my brothers, my sister, and I got American gifts with words in English each time she came home. . . . I would sit with a dictionary and struggle to make out a few words so I could know more about my mother's new world.

In the mid-1970s, the Salvadoran Education Department brought "Televisión Educativa" to schools across the country. With it, came televised English classes . . . .

> my tongue is divided into two
> into heavy accent bits of confusion
> into miracles and accidents
> saying things that hurt the heart
> drowning in a language that lives, jumps, translates . . .

Like most kids anywhere in the world. American music and television were also my English teachers. . . . My family was only the second family in our whole town to own a television. . . . I would watch *Kojak, Mission Impossible*, and *Starsky and Hutch*—swallowing up English, aspiring to be cool, and knowing that my mother had my ticket on layaway.

In late 1978, I had a political awakening. My country was ruled by the military and their martial law against ideas. I was 13 years old and joined the student movement. We demanded books, chalk, better teachers, and cleaner bathrooms. In the revolutionary fervor of those days, the coolness of English was ruined by Marx and Lenin. The language that fed my wonder and curiosity was now, according to my comrades, the language of the enemy of Yankee Imperialism. It was no longer cool. The next thing I knew, I was on a plane to the United States to save me from the death squads.

> My tongue is divided by nature
> by our crazy desire to triumph and conquer
> this tongue is cut up into equal pieces
> one wants to curse and sing out loud
> the other one simply wants to ask for water . . .

PHASE TWO: FRUSTRATION AND NEED (HOW ENGLISH BECAME MY IMPERIAL LIBERATOR)

In the fall of 1980, I started 9th grade at Francis Junior High in Washington, D.C. Kids from Central America were coming into the school in droves every week. We were thrown into English as a Second language (ESL) classes where Mrs. Padrino taught us . . . to say, "Hello, how are you today? I am fine, thank you," in crisp English. On weekends, I went to rallies and protests—ESL classes for leftists. There, I got to repeat "No draft, no war/US out of El Salvador!" . . . .

By this time, I was beginning to understand that English was not just one language. At school, I became friends with Pichi, a chubby white Puerto Rican who . . . spoke three languages: Puerto Rican Spanish (which I barely understood), formal English (which I was beginning to understand), and Black English (which I now understood I needed to learn in order to survive). Pichi became my real ESL teacher:

> tongue
> English of the funny sounds
> tongue
> funny sounds in English
> tongue
> sounds funny in English
> tongue
> in funny English sounds

It was Pichi who gave me a copy of *Puerto Rican Obituary*, a poetry book by Pedro Pietri, one of the first and most influential of the Nuyorican poets of the 1970s. I had been writing poetry since I was ten years old, mainly rhyming, cheesy love poems. This book changed my life. . . . It introduced me to the possibility of words as a weapon. I started mixing my anger, my Spanish, and my limited English into poetry. . . . But English began to feel good. I began to feel that it was something I could use as revenge.

When it was time for me to start high school, I decided to audition for the Theater Department at the Duke Ellington School of the Arts. With my angry, broken English, I made an impression and got in. My first year was very hard. I was the only Latino in the whole school of more than 400 students. Rosemary Walsh, my acting teacher, would tell me, "You're a good actor, but I can't understand what the fuck you're saying. We're gonna work on you." . . . My second year at Ellington, I was assigned to speech classes. We studied phonetics and the anatomy of our sound-making factory: the mouth, the throat, the vocal chords, and the diaphram. These classes consisted of repetitive speech exercises, such as:

"Theophilus thistle, the unsuccessful thistle sifter, while sifting a sieve of unsifted thistles thrusts three thousand thistles through the thick of his thumb . . ." "Unique New York, Unique New York, Unique New York . . ."

. . .

So, here I was, thinking that I was making so much progress with my English, I could move to New York or L.A. and make it big.

> my tongue is divided into two
> a border patrol runs through the middle
> frisking words

asking for proper identification
checking for pronunciation . . .

By my senior year I had become a punk rocker, a combat-boot wearing rebel. I realized that there were no parts for me in traditional theater, that if I wanted to be an actor, I would have to write my own parts. With that realization, I began a deeper, artistic relationship with the English language. My new teachers became Nikki Giovanni, June Jordan, Lucille Clifton, and Alice Walker—black writers who were using language to say that we are beautiful, that we deserve things. I began to write monologues for characters that came from my life. As I began to develop my own voice, English became my imperial liberator.

PHASE THREE: SUBTLETY AND PAYBACK

I am still learning English. *El inglés.* . . .

Since the mid-1980s I have been writing and performing one-person shows that weave together poetry and monologues in English. Latinos often ask me, "Why don't you do more in Spanish?" I often respond, "Because you all don't pay my rent." But the real answer is: payback. I use English to challenge English speakers to question their assumptions about us Latinos, about each other, and, in these xenophobic times, about immigrants in general. I use it to poke, prod, question, and make people feel uncomfortable. I always read my poems from a music stand (I have very few of them memorized), and whenever I leave my house for a gig, carrying my music stand to the car, I always feel that I am carrying my *machete*. Words are my weapon.

They are also the way I build alliances. I have learned that building trust with someone who is different from you in this country is all about mastering their own version of the English language. Most of my work in D.C. has been with black kids. I go into classrooms and use theater improvisation as a tool for encouraging kids to write about their lives. Most kids want to do improvs about drugs and guns, the thug life. I challenge them by asking, "Does your momma love you? Do you smile? Do you laugh? Are there tender moments in your life?" For the majority of kids, the answer is yes. So I challenge them to create skits about those soft and tender moments and then to write poetry about it. I challenge them not to fulfill society's expectations of poor kids by being drug dealers and thugs. And I always tell them, "Ain't nobody gonna sing our song, so we might as well sing it ourselves."

For me, learning English has been about learning to sing my own song.

my tongue is divided into two
my tongue is divided into two
I like my tongue
it says what feels right
I like my tongue
it says what feels right

20

The Emperor's New Clothes

Patricia J. Williams

My son used to attend a small nursery school. Over the course of one year, three different teachers in his school assured me that he was color-blind. Resigned to this diagnosis, I took my son to an ophthalmologist who tested him and pronounced his vision perfect. I could not figure out what was going on until I began to listen carefully to what he was saying about color.

As it turned out, my son did not misidentify color. He resisted identifying color at all. "I don't know," he would say when asked what color the grass was; or, most peculiarly, "It makes no difference." This latter remark, this assertion of the greenness of grass making no difference, was such a precociously cynical retort, that I began to suspect some social complication in which he was somehow invested.

The long and the short of it is that the well-meaning teachers at his predominantly white school had valiantly and repeatedly assured their charges that color makes no difference. "It doesn't matter," they told the children, "whether you're black or white or red or green or blue." Yet upon further investigation, the very reason that the teachers had felt it necessary to impart this lesson in the first place was that it *did* matter, and in predictably cruel ways: some of the children had been fighting about whether black people could play "good guys."

My son's anxious response was redefined by his teachers as physical deficiency. This anxiety redefined as deficiency suggests to me that it may be illustrative of the way in which the liberal ideal of color-blindness is too often confounded. That is to say, the very notion of blindness about color constitutes an ideological confusion at best, and denial at its very worst. I recognize, certainly, that the teachers were inspired by a desire to make whole a division in the ranks. But much is overlooked in the move to undo that which clearly and unfortunately matters just by labeling it that which "makes no difference." The dismissiveness, however unintentional, leaves those in my son's position pulled between the clarity of their own experience and the often alienating terms in which they must seek social acceptance.

There's a lot of that in the world right now: someone has just announced in no uncertain terms that he or she hates you because you're dark, let's say, or Catholic or a woman or the wrong height, and the panicked authority figures try to patch things up by reassuring you that race or gender or stature or your heartfelt religion doesn't matter; means nothing in the calculation of your humanity; is the most insignificant little puddle of beans in the world.

While I do want to underscore that I embrace color-blindness as a legitimate hope for the future, I worry that we tend to enshrine the notion with a kind of utopianism whose naïveté will ensure its elusiveness. In the material world ranging from playgrounds to politics, our ideals perhaps need more thoughtful, albeit more complicated, guardianship. By this I mean something more than the "I think therefore it is" school of idealism. "I don't think about color, therefore your problems don't exist." If only it were so easy.

But if indeed it's not that easy then the application of such quick fixes becomes not just a shortcut but a short-circuiting of the process of resolution. In the example of my son's experience at school, the collective aversion to confronting the social tensions he

faced resulted in their being pathologized as his individual physical limitation. This is a phenomenon that happens all too frequently to children of color in a variety of contexts. In both the United States and the United Kingdom, the disproportionate numbers of black children who end up in special education or who are written off as failures attest to the degree to which this is a profound source of social anxiety.

In addition, the failure to deal straightforwardly with the pervasive practices of exclusion that infect even the very young allowed my son's white schoolmates to indulge in the false luxury of a prematurely imagined community. By this I mean that we can all be lulled rather too easily into a self-congratulatory stance of preached universalism—"We are the world! We are the children!" was the evocative, full-throated harmony of a few years ago. Yet nowhere has that been invoked more passionately than in the face of tidal waves of dissension, and even as "the" children learn that "we" children are not like "those," the benighted creatures on the other side of the pale.

This tension between material conditions and what one is cultured to see or not see— the dilemma of the emperor's new clothes, we might call it—is a tension faced by any society driven by bitter histories of imposed hierarchy. I don't mean to suggest that we need always go about feeling guilty or responsible or perpetually burdened by original sin or notions of political correctness. I do wish, however, to counsel against the facile innocence of those three notorious monkeys, Hear No Evil, See No Evil, and Speak No Evil. Theirs is a purity achieved through ignorance. Ours must be a world in which we know each other better.

To put it another way, it is a dangerous if comprehensible temptation to imagine inclusiveness by imagining away any obstacles. It is in this way that the moral high ground of good intentions knows its limits. We must be careful not to allow our intentions to verge into outright projection by substituting a fantasy of global seamlessness that is blinding rather than just color-blind.

This is a dilemma—being colored, so to speak, in a world of normative whiteness, whiteness being defined as the absence of color. The drive to conform our surroundings to whatever we know as "normal" is a powerful force—convention in many ways is more powerful than reason, and customs in some instances are more powerful than law. While surely most customs and conventions encode the insights of ancient wisdom, the habits of racial thought in Western society just as surely encapsulate some of the greatest mistakes in human history. So how do we rethink this most troubled of divisions, the fault line in our body politic, the fault line in ourselves? The ability to remain true to *one* self, it seems to me, must begin with the ethical project of considering how we can align a sense of ourselves with a sense of the world. This is the essence of integrity, is it not, never having to split into a well-maintained "front" and a closely guarded "inside."

Creating community, in other words, involves this most difficult work of negotiating real divisions, of considering boundaries before we go crashing through, and of pondering our differences before we can ever agree on the terms of our sameness. For the discounted vision of the emperor's new clothes (or a little boy's color) is already the description of corrupted community.

Perhaps one reason that conversations about race are so often doomed to frustration is that the notion of whiteness as "race" is almost never implicated. One of the more difficult legacies of slavery and of colonialism is the degree to which racism's tenacious hold is manifested not merely in the divided demographics of neighborhood or education or class but also in the process of what media expert John Fiske calls the "exnomination" of whiteness as racial identity. Whiteness is unnamed, suppressed, beyond the realm of race. Exnomination permits whites to entertain the notion that race lives "over there" on the other side of the tracks, in black bodies and inner-city neighborhoods, in a dark netherworld where whites are not involved.

At this level, the creation of a sense of community is a lifelong negotiation of endless subtlety. One morning when my son was three, I took him to his preschool. He ran straight to a pile of Lego and proceeded to work. I crossed the room and put his lunchbox in the refrigerator, where I encountered a little girl sitting at a table, beating a mound of clay into submission with a plastic rolling pin. "I see a Mommy," she said to me cheerfully. "That must mean that your little boy is here somewhere, too." "Yes, he's here," I answered, thinking how sweetly precocious she was. "There, he's over by the Lego."

She strained to see around the bookcases. "Oh yes," she said. "Now I see that black face of his."

I walked away without responding, enraged—how can one be so enraged at an innocent child—yet not knowing what to say just then, rushing to get the jaggedly dangerous broken glass of my emotions out of the room.

I remember being three years old so well. Three was the age when I learned that I was black, the colored kid, monkeychild, different. What made me so angry and wordless in this encounter forty years later was the realization that none of the little white children who taught me to see my blackness as a mark probably ever learned to see themselves as white. In our culture, whiteness is rarely marked in the indicative there! there! sense of my bracketed blackness. And the majoritarian privilege of never noticing themselves was the beginning of an imbalance from which so much, so much else flowed.

But that is hard to talk about, even now, this insight acquired before I had the words to sort it out. Yet it is imperative to think about this phenomenon of closeting race, which I believe is a good deal more widespread than these small examples. In a sense, race matters are resented and repressed in much the same way as matters of sex and scandal: the subject is considered a rude and transgressive one in mixed company, a matter whose observation is sometimes inevitable, but about which, once seen, little should be heard nonetheless. Race thus tends to be treated as though it were an especially delicate category of social infirmity—so-called—like extreme obesity or disfigurement.

Every parent knows a little of this dynamic, if in other contexts: "Why doesn't that lady have any teeth?" comes the child's piping voice. "Why doesn't that gentleman have any hair?" And "Why is that little boy so black?" *Sssshhhh!* comes the anxious parental remonstrance. The poor thing can't help it. We must all pretend that nothing's wrong.

And thus we are coached upon pain of punishment not to see a thing.

Now, to be sure, the parent faces an ethical dilemma in that moment of childish vision unrestrained by social nicety. On the one hand, we rush to place a limit on what can be said to strangers and what must be withheld for fear of imposition or of hurting someone's feelings. As members of a broad society, we respect one another by learning not to inflict every last intimate, prying curiosity we may harbor upon everyone we meet.

That said, there remains the problem of how or whether we ever answer the question, and that is the dimension of this dynamic that is considerably more troubling.

"Why is that man wearing no clothes?" pipes the childish voice once more. And the parent panics at the complication of trying to explain. The naked man may be a nudist or a psychotic or perhaps the emperor of the realm, but the silencing that is passed from parent to child is not only about the teaching of restraint; it is calculated to circumnavigate the question as though it had never been asked. "*Stop asking such silly questions.*"

A wall begins to grow around the forbidden gaze; for we all know, and children best of all, when someone wants to change the subject, forever. And so the child is left to the monstrous creativity of ignorance and wild imagination.

Again, I do believe that this unfortunate negotiation of social difference has much in common with discussions about race. Race is treated as though it were some sort of genetic leprosy or a biological train wreck. Those who privilege themselves as Un-raced—usually but not always those who are white—are always anxiously maintaining that it doesn't

matter, even as they are quite busy feeling pity, no less, and thankful to God for their great good luck in having been spared so intolerable an affliction.

Meanwhile, those marked as Having Race are ground down by the pendular stresses of having to explain what it feels like to be You—why are you black, why are you black, why are you black, over and over again; or, alternatively, placed in a kind of conversational quarantine of muteness in which any mention of racial circumstance reduces all sides to tears, fears, fisticuffs, and other paroxysms of unseemly anguish.

This sad, habitual paralysis in the face of the foreign and the anxiety-producing. It is as though we are all skating across a pond that is not quite thoroughly frozen. Two centuries ago, or perhaps only a few decades ago, the lake was solidly frozen, and if for those skating across the surface things seemed much more secure, it was a much more dismal lot for those whose fates were frozen at the bottom of the pond. Over time, the weather of race relations has warmed somewhat, and a few of those at the bottom have found their way to the surface; we no longer hold our breath, and we have even learned to skate. The noisy, racial chasm still yawns darkly beneath us all, but we few brave souls glide gingerly above, upon a skim of hope, our bodies made light with denial, the black pond so dangerously and thinly iced with the conviction that talking about it will only make things worse.

And so the racial divide is exacerbated further by a welter of little lies that propel us foolishly around the edges of our most demanding social stresses: Black people are a happy people and if they would just stop complaining so much, they would see how happy they are. Black people who say they're unhappy are leftist agitators whose time would be better spent looking for a real job. White people are victims. Poor Bangladeshis are poor because they want to be. Poor white people are poor because rich Indians stole all the jobs under the ruse of affirmative action. There is no racism in the marketplace—"each according to his merit" goes the cant, even as the EEOC has a backlog of 70,000 cases by the most conservative estimates; even as top executives funnel the jobs to school chums and their next of kin, or chief executives at major corporations are captured on tape destroying subpoenaed records of ongoing discriminatory practices. Immigrants are taking over the whole world, but race makes no difference. If sixty percent of young black men are unemployed in the industrialized world, well, let them watch Oprah. If some people are determined to be homeless, well then let them have it, if homelessness is what they like so much . . .

Triage is a word I hear bandied about a lot these days. I have heard it used by many of my friends who are economists; they used it to convey an urgency of limited resources. If there's not enough to go around, then those with the least should be written off first because it will take more to save them anyway. And we don't have more.

This word *triage* originally cropped up in the context of the medical profession. It is a term borrowed from overtaxed hospitals in theaters of war. On body-strewn battlefields, doctors would divide the survivors into three groups. The third, in the worst condition, might be left to die because bandages were better spent wrapped around those more likely to survive.

In the context of today's ghettos, inner cities, and those places doomed to be called the Third World, I hear the word *triage*.

I worry about this image that casts aside so many so easily. It envisions poor and dying populations as separate, distant, severable. I worry that perhaps we have mischosen our metaphors.

I fear triage; I fear that one cannot cut off a third of the world without some awful, life-threatening bleeding in the rest of the body politic. The Malthusian nightmare has never been a simple matter, I think, of letting someone else go hungry, or of letting someone else die. It is a matter of amputation—that's the metaphor I'd rather use. And one can't cut off one's leg and pretend it never belonged.

It is as though we are employing, in our economic analysis of distributive justice, the images of the very earliest days of medical experimentation. *Oh, well, let's see now . . . The soul abides in the liver . . . Therefore we can chop off that troublesome, heretical head and no one will be the less holy for it . . .*

Maybe. But quite a few martyrs have been made that way.

Anthropologist Michael Taussig has written about the phenomenon of public secrets. He writes of a ritual in Tierra del Fuego in which the men come out of the men's hut wearing masks. The women hail them by singing "Here come the spirits!" On some level, everyone must know that these are not spirits but husbands and brothers and fathers and sons, but so powerful is the ritual to the sense of community that it is upon pain of death that the women fail to greet them as spirits.

In our culture, I think that the power of race resembles just such a public secret. I understand the civic ritual that requires us to say in the face of all our differences, We are all one, we are the world. I understand the need for the publicly reiterated faith in public ideals as binding and sustaining community. Such beliefs are the very foundation of institutional legitimacy and no society can hold itself together without them. Yet such binding force comes from a citizenry willing to suspend disbelief for the sake of honoring the spiritual power of our appointed ideals. And where suspicion, cynicism, and betrayal have eaten away at a community to the degree that the folk parading from the men's hut look like just a bunch of muggers wearing masks—or badges, as the case may be—then hailing the spirit will sound like a hollow incantation, empty theater, the weary habit of the dispossessed.

. . .

Such is the legacy of racism in the modern world. Perhaps it is less and less fashionable these days to consider too explicitly the kinds of costs that slavery and colonialism exacted, even as those historical disruptions have continued to scar contemporary social arrangements with the transcendent urgency of their hand-me-down grief.

I realize therefore that it might be considered impertinent to keep raising the ghost of slavery's triangle trade and waving it around; there is a pronounced preference in polite society for just letting bygones be bygones. And I concede that a more optimistic enterprise might be to begin any contemporary analysis of race with the Civil Rights Movement in the United States, or the Notting Hill riots in the United Kingdom. Beginning at those points is a way of focusing one's view and confining one's reference to the legitimately inspiring ideals that coalesced those movements: the aims of color-blindness, the equality of all people, and the possibility of peaceful coexistence.

Yet if that well-chosen temporal slice allows us to be optimistic about the possibility of progress, there are nonetheless limitations to such a frame. First, it is the conceptual prehistory of those movements that explains the toll of racism and its lingering effects. There can be no adequate explanation without reference to it. Second, the diasporic complexity of today's social problems requires an analysis that moves those ideals of the social movements of the 1960s and 1970s beyond themselves, into the present, into the future—to a more complex, practical grappling with such phenomena as the hybridizing of racial stereotypes with the fundamentalisms of gender, class, ethnicity, religion. Third, the problem of race is overlaid with crises in environmental and resource management that have triggered unparalleled migrations from rural to urban locations within national boundaries, and that have impassioned debates about immigration across national boundaries. Finally, not a few aspects of our New Age global economics, much like the commercial profiteering of colonialisms past, threaten to displace not just the very laws to which we persistently make such grand appeal but the nation-state itself. I believe that a genuine, long-term optimism about the future of race relations depends on a thorough excavation of the same.

A memory slips into my mind. I was riding the train from New York to Washington, D.C., some years ago on my way to some lawyers' conference or other; I was accompanied by two

black colleagues. An hour into the trip, the train stopped in the city of Philadelphia. A young white woman got on whom my colleagues knew. She was also a lawyer, headed to the same conference. She joined us, sitting among us in a double row of seats that faced each other. A little while later, the conductor came along. The new woman held up her ticket, but the conductor did not seem to see her. He saw four of us seated and only three ticket stubs.

"One of you hasn't paid," he said, staring at me, then at each of my two black friends. I remember pointing to the white woman, and someone else said, "Over there." But the conductor was resolute.

"Which one of you hasn't paid?" he asked again. Two of us kept saying, "Our receipts, see?" and the white woman, speaking *very* clearly said, "Here. I am trying to give you my ticket."

The conductor was scowling. He still did not hear. "I am not moving till one of you pays up."

It was the longest time before the conductor stopped staring in all the wrong directions. It was the longest time before he heard the new woman, pressing her ticket upon him, her voice reaching him finally as though from a great distance, passing through light-years of understanding as if from another universe. The realization that finally lit his face was like the dawning of a great surprise.

How precisely does the issue of color remain so powerfully determinative of everything from life circumstance to manner of death, in a world that is, by and large, officially "colorblind"? What metaphors mask the hierarchies that make racial domination frequently seem so "natural," so invisible, indeed so attractive? How does racism continue to evolve, post-slavery and post-equality legislation, across such geographic, temporal, and political distance?

No, I am not saying that this is the worst of times. But neither will I concede that this is the best of all possible worlds. And what a *good* thing, is it not, to try to imagine how much better we could be . . .

"I had a dream," said my son the other morning. Then he paused. "No," he said, "it was more of a miracle. Do you know what a miracle is?" "Tell me," I said, thunderstruck, and breathless with maternal awe.

"A miracle is when you have a dream and you open your eyes in it. It's when you wake up and your dream is all around you."

It was a pretty good definition, I thought. And even though my son's little miracle had something to do with pirates meeting dinosaurs, I do think that to a very great extent we dream our worlds into being. For better or worse, our customs and laws, our culture and society are sustained by the myths we embrace, the stories we recirculate to explain what we behold. I believe that racism's hardy persistence and immense adaptability are sustained by a habit of human imagination, deflective rhetoric, and hidden license. I believe no less that an optimistic course might be charted, if only we could imagine it. What a world it would be if we could all wake up and see all of ourselves reflected in the world, not merely in a territorial sense but with a kind of nonexclusive entitlement that grants not so much possession as investment. A peculiarly anachronistic notion of investment, I suppose, at once both ancient and futuristic. An investment that envisions each of us in each other.

21

Waking Up White

What It Means to Accept Your Legacy, for Better and Worse

Jan Arminio

The realization that I am white actually came only after the birth of my children. Though I recognized since I was young that I had white skin, it was not until recently that I saw my whiteness went beyond my skin. It was a part of my identity—an identity that was socially constructed in part, but my identity nonetheless. It was, it is, who I am.

During high school, college, and early adulthood, I was what could be called a well-intentioned, color-blind white person who believed she treated everyone the same. Though I never yelled racial epithets at anyone, never wrote racial slurs on walls or doors, I did laugh at racist jokes, I never reached out to international students or students of color, and I perpetuated notions of heterosexism. While I was in college, I attended my sister's commencement. The speaker was from a sister institution in Korea. I distinctly remember making fun of her with my friends (who, of course, were all white). We laughed at her accent, her robe, and likely the shape of her eyes, although it truly pains me now to think back on it. I also remember during my first year in college, several African American students lived across the hall. My friends and I said hello to them, but I never invited them to our rooms, never knocked on their door, and never made any attempt to get to know them. I had a number of classes with an African American student who was from a large city. I always wondered why he came to "my" rural institution far from his home, but I never bothered to ask him.

To make a long, unfortunate story short, I did little to improve the world but instead helped to make it an unwelcoming, uncomfortable, and unfriendly place for some. Why? Looking back on this behavior, I can see that it accentuated my membership in my group of friends and my status in society. I can also see I was acting out behavior modeled by others around me. Seeking out social connections that were committed to social justice was foreign. I was simply incapable at that stage in my life of recognizing the hypocrisy of my actions in a country supposedly established on the principle of equality.

But after I graduated, things—and I—began to change. The two most significant changes were that I had children and started in a doctoral program in college student personnel. I credit my children and my doctoral work with helping me to wake up and see who I am and the role I must play as a white person in society.

One of my first memories of this awakening is when my four-year-old son asked me a question that a lot of young children ask when they first learn the terms *white* and *black* to describe people. "Why do we call white people white, when we really are not?" he asked. "We are pink people. We are not white like the clouds on a sunny day. And black people aren't really black, they are brown." I did not know quite how to respond, but I did realize at that instant that someone or a group of someones had chosen to use the words *white* and *black*, thereby emphasizing the contrast. My son had planted a seed that, to grow into genuine understanding, needed accurate information about people, the differences among them, and a critical examination of myself. Through my doctoral work I was able to nurture that understanding. I came to understand who those someones were who came up with the concept of race. They were philosophers, writers, scientists—predominantly

white—who developed these categories to serve their own purposes. I came to see that race is not a biological fact but an arbitrary social construction. Still, this fact didn't diminish its social significance. Race, regardless of how it came to be, is a burden of our society.

Another important turning point came at a diversity workshop I was asked to participate in for my doctoral work. I received a handout entitled "White Racial Identity." As soon as I read it, the knowledge hit me that I was a part of this thing called the "white race." I experienced this realization as a jolt in my gut. I had a racial identity. But what did this mean? Why did I not realize this before? What were the implications?

I decided to use the work on my doctoral dissertation to try to better understand my own race and ancestry, my own white identity, and its relationship to the oppression of people of color by conversing with white students about how they made meaning of being white. I bought a transcribing machine to help me in this work. Shortly after that, my children and I were experimenting with my new machine, listening to our voices on the tape recorder. My sons asked if I would pretend that I was interviewing them. I agreed and asked a question that I had prepared to ask my dissertation participants: "What does it mean for you to be white?" Both looked astonished and were speechless. So to warm them up to the topic, I asked, "What is it like being a boy?" They answered quite quickly that boys didn't have to wear pink and play with stupid dolls. Clearly, they had better toys. I then returned to my original question, "What does it mean to be white?" My seven-year-old slowly stated, "It's easier to be lucky if you're white." I was astounded by his ability to capture the subtlety of racism: it's easier to be at the right place at the right time, to have things go your way.

All whites must wake up. This means acknowledging who we were as a group, questioning whether this is still a part of who we are as individuals, and deciding who we want to become. Finding out who we were as a people includes an accurate history of white atrocities and white benevolence rather than the PG-rated version that is more commonplace. The truth demonstrates the best and worst of me that is possible. Knowing who I am means knowing the undesirable tendencies that I must consciously avoid while increasing benevolent behavior. I believe acknowledging my heritage and acquainting myself with my ancestors enhances my ability to accomplish that.

My children have taught me that becoming a just white person means caring for the education of all children. Justness is not about being first in line but, rather, having a place at the table. All of us should be about the task of ensuring that everyone has a place at the table of good education, good housing, safe cities, good medical care, and good jobs. Each of us must ask: What have I done today to accomplish this? Do I reach out to others to better understand differences, or do I cling to the comfort of similarities? Do I accurately view my attitudes and behaviors as both oppressor and oppressed? Do I connect with my experiences of being oppressed in order to work to eliminate those experiences for others or solely to ensure that they will not happen to me? Can I recognize and stop oppressive acts to guarantee that children I bring into this world, live with in my community, and encounter on my campus will not pass on a legacy of oppression?

As my children grow older, the pervasiveness of racism threatens their wisdom. I begin to see other attitudes and behaviors intruding into their lives. My children now seem less able to recognize injustice and condemn it. They seem more willing to blame victims for injustice. I wonder how their painful experiences of being called "faggot" on the school bus have influenced them. Is it leading them to realize that it's less painful to be the perpetrator than the victim? Will their previous sense of justice also become a victim of oppression? The insight my children offered me years ago I must now offer them. I must help them wake up before it's too late for them and other children so they might experience a more just future.

22

Women, Race, and Racism

A Dialogue in Black and White

Andrea Ayvazian and Beverly Daniel Tatum

Beverly Daniel Tatum: . . .

Jean Baker Miller has written eloquently about the constructive power of relational connections and the potentially destructive force of relational disconnections and violations. This theme of connections, disconnections, and violations is certainly central to our thinking about how we can connect across racial lines. What happens when our experience is validated by another in a mutually empathic relationship? We feel a strong sense of connection. But when we have experiences that are not validated, for example, when I as a black woman encounter racism and I am unable to talk about that experience with white colleagues, I may feel a sense of disconnection from them. Or should I choose to share those experiences and in fact find them invalidated by my colleagues, I may question my own perceptions. Without validation from others, I may choose to deny my own perceptions in order to avoid the isolation that comes from disconnection. Repeatedly separating myself from my own experience in order to stay in relationship with others ultimately results in a psychological state of violation. Negotiating the choices involved in maintaining connections across racial lines is a central focus of our dialogue . . . .

Andrea Ayvazian: . . . Beverly and I are venturing into new territory by offering an analysis of our own relationship as a case study of women connecting across racial lines. We want to speak very personally . . . [I]n traveling and doing speaking with Beverly, white women often stop me in hallways and restrooms and at the coffee machine and say, "You two seem so close. How did you create that bond?" . . . We are going to focus on the following three areas, which we call the critical junctures in our relationship: how the relationship was established, the theme of mutuality in our relationship, and difficult periods we have faced. A thread that is also woven into our talk is what we call "common differences," areas where there is sameness between us, where we have similar feelings, viewpoints, even experiences, and yet these similarities are expressed in different ways in our lives. We will close by talking about our friendship as a work in progress. . . .

CRITICAL JUNCTURES

Ayvazian: . . .

In many ways, my kinship with Beverly is *very* easy. Deep affection and admiration flows between us and the friendship is strong, nourishing, and treasured. However, it is also fair to say that nowadays any adult relationship that crosses racial lines is "not easy." If the friends are conscious of the social, political, and economic realities in this country today, their "kinship," . . . will inevitably have times that are "not easy." And we have faced those times.

. . . Beverly and I do not live in the same neighborhood, although we live in the same town, and we do not work in the same place. Our children do not attend the same schools. We were brought together by an agency that does antiracism education, paired up as a biracial team to do some antiracism training at a college in the Boston area. We were brought together initially on a professional basis and immediately had the experience of preparing to work together as a team. . . . Beverly and I call that first professional collaboration, during which our relationship was formed, our "trial by fire." The group of college students with whom we were working proved to be a very challenging group. . . . Yet, this adversarial experience actually pulled us together as a twosome. Going into what turned out to be a hostile environment forced us to really scrutinize the material that we were presenting to the group.

Consequently, Beverly and I had the experience of talking very deeply about painful issues around race and racism very early in our professional/personal relationship. We had potentially difficult conversations analyzing racial inequity because we had to scrutinize the material we were presenting to this challenging group. These conversations in the first days of our relationship, we have discovered, are of the sort that biracial friendships sometimes avoid for months or years. Looking back on it now, we believe that this process was a bonding experience.

We also found that our rides to and from Boston were opportunities to talk not only about our work but about our personal lives. We discovered some common ground as women, as mothers, and as professionals in our community. Early on, Beverly was very helpful to me as I was going through a difficult period with my then 1-year-old son. We forged close personal ties through what was initially a professional connection.

Tatum: . . . As Andrea has told you, we don't live in the same neighborhood, our children don't go to the same school, and we don't worship in the same places; our lives are separate in many ways. Even though we frequently work together and certainly spend leisure time together now that our friendship has developed, our paths would not likely have crossed in other ways. Given the reality of social segregation, work does provide one of the few places where women of color and white women may come together across racial lines. So, it is not an accident that it was our work together that laid the groundwork for a friendship to develop.

. . . [O]ne of the things that has been very important is that at the beginning of our relationship there was an examination of our values as they related to the work that we did. We were forced to talk at a deeper level—not the superficial chitchat that you might engage with someone over the coffee machine—regarding what we thought about a very significant issue, in this case race relations in the United States. The mutuality that evolved in that relationship was very much in keeping with what Jean Baker Miller calls the "five good things." When a relationship is in fact mutually reinforcing, it gives you a feeling of increased zest, a sense of empowerment, greater self-knowledge, increased self-worth, and—most important in the context of a friendship—a desire for more connection (Miller, 1988). . . .

But as in all relationships, conflict arises. There certainly has been some conflict in our relationship, which we want to talk about, too, because it is also an important part of how one negotiates relationships that are going to be genuinely mutual. The most significant conflict, a real test of mutuality in our relationship, occurred when Andrea and I were conducting a workshop in St. Louis about 3 years ago. At that time, we were facilitating a workshop with a group of clergy on racism and, as we often do, we made reference to other "isms," including heterosexism. This topic . . . triggered a rather heated discussion about homosexuality in which a range of religious viewpoints were expressed. As we struggled to deal with this issue . . . Andrea and I became aware of the fact that we had differing strategies for interacting with our participants on this issue. While we were

able to deal with that difference productively in the context of the workshop, as we were processing the event on the flight home we had a conversation that led to a real test of the mutuality in our relationship.

As background information for this incident, . . . I had just joined a church, which was a very important and significant step in my personal life, and as we talked about the controversy that had arisen in our workshop, we talked about the positions that our own religious communities had regarding homosexuality and heterosexism in the church. I am a member of a Presbyterian church. At this writing, that denomination is in the midst of a struggle around whether or not to ordain gay men and lesbian women. Andrea is a Quaker and belongs to a Meeting that is openly gay affirming and sanctions and supports same-sex commitment ceremonies. So our two worship communities have very different positions.

Andrea said to me that she didn't understand how I could be a part of a religious community that was exclusionary in the way that the Presbyterian church currently is, and in fact suggested that I should find another church. When she first said it, I was taken aback by the comment but had some trouble figuring out exactly what it was about it that bothered me. In fact, I shared her concern about the heterosexism in my denomination and in my local church. I have raised, and continue to raise, questions about this issue with my pastor and with fellow parishioners. On the other hand, my local congregation is a relatively progressive, predominantly black, Afrocentric congregation that is very affirming of my racial and spiritual identity . . . . I experienced Andrea's suggestion that I should leave this congregation as an affront. . . .

It occurred to me that there was really a lot of white privilege in her statement. As a black woman living in a predominantly white community, there are not many opportunities for me or my children to be part of a community where our African American heritage is explicitly affirmed. Consequently our Sunday worship experience in a congregation that defines itself as "unashamedly black and unapologetically Christian" is extremely valuable to me. I did feel that her statement that I should withdraw from this community was a statement of her white privilege. In fact, she was taking for granted the many churches or worship communities that she can choose from because almost all of them are predominantly white and will affirm her racial identity. . . . Her statement to me was a failure to recognize that privilege.

I felt that I had to say something to her about this. At the same time, I hesitated because this relationship was important to me and I did not want to alienate our friendship. Yet, it was a real juncture in terms of this issue of connections, disconnections and violations, because I could feel myself disconnecting. . . . In order for us to be able to maintain the growth and development of our relationship, certainly being able to talk about my spiritual journey and my worship community was an important point of connection that I needed to be able to maintain. I decided to share my perspective with Andrea, and I am happy to report that she responded in a very validating way. She simply listened to what I had to say and then said, "You're right."

Ayvazian: I want to speak to this because a potentially serious "disconnection" threatened our relationship—a relationship that had developed strong bonds, one that had become mutually important. When Beverly raised her feelings and concerns with me, two things went through my mind—two things that I knew she and I had said specifically to white people many times in the past! One was that when a person of color tells you something you have said or done is racist or reveals your inattention to white privilege, take a deep breath and begin by assuming she/he is correct until proven otherwise. The other point is that as white people strive to be strong white allies, we do not have to hold ourselves to a standard of perfection. It is impossible, given our socialization, our background, the struggle, the sensitivity, and the pain surrounding these issues, that we can be perfect white allies. I try to remember that I am not called to be perfect. I am called to be faithful and

N
E
X
T

S
T
E
P
S

N
E
X
T

S
T
E
P
S

consistent on these issues. Beverly was exactly right. . . . I tried to follow the very advice that I had given to others. . . . That was an important juncture: a disconnection threatened, but we managed to talk it through.

There was another time that a disconnection threatened but was overcome by both of us being aware of what was going on in the relationship. This happened around the time of the Rodney King beating and the Simi Valley verdict in which the four Los Angeles police officers were acquitted. . . . In our shock and grief following the Simi Valley verdict, we essentially separated for a period of time and turned to different communities for comfort and support. Bev talked about her reactions to the events primarily with other African Americans. . . . In my own state of pain, shock, and anger, I found myself talking to two white men who I specifically called and met with, two men who identify as white allies. Meeting with them was the appropriate place for me to take my grief and do some healing and action planning in order to move forward.

. . .

Following the Simi Valley verdict it was appropriate for Beverly and me to separate for a while and immerse ourselves in our own groups to work on these issues. . . . This is an important point because white people can feel a loss, and even a sense of personal rejection, when this happens. . . . Beverly and I see these as normal, necessary, and even predictable after racial trauma. The bridges that have been built may be perfectly strong, but there still may be a need to separate for a time.

Tatum: I want to add just a few comments to what Andrea has said. In fact, the weekend when the events following the Simi Valley verdict were unfolding, I was at a small women's conference, a gathering of about 20 women, to which I had been invited. The only person I knew in the group was the woman who had invited me, and I was the only woman of color there. As we were arriving, everyone was very much aware of the riots that were unfolding in Los Angeles following the acquittal, and what struck me was the reluctance among the group to talk in any serious way about what was going on in Los Angeles. A few people expressed a need to talk about what was happening and what it meant for the country and for their own particular communities, but generally speaking the majority of the participants seemed to disregard these events as someone else's problem, not of concern to us as a group. I felt very alienated by that response, I have to say. Perhaps because I was with white women I didn't know, it did not feel like a safe place for me to completely engage. I was quite concerned about what was happening in communities of color in Los Angeles and in other parts of the country in response to this verdict. Yet I felt that my concern, a part of who I was, a part of my own perspective as an African American woman, could not be safely brought to this meeting. I certainly experienced that as very disconnecting, and in fact I went home early from the conference and declined the invitation to attend the following year.

Ayvazian: . . . White people often say to me, "It sounds like you two work together on issues of racism and talk about them very openly in your friendship, but are you, Andrea, always in the position of learner?" Beverly and I want to take a moment to remind all of us that each individual has multiple social identities. We feel this point is important because there are ways that Beverly and I are, in some areas of systematic oppression, both in the dominant category. We both receive the privilege or advantage, and we support each other in being strong allies. I am not always in the position of being dominant, and Beverly is not always in the position of being targeted. In the area of race inequity and racism—in that form of systematic oppression—I am clearly dominant. I receive the privilege, the unearned advantage and benefit of being white, and Beverly is targeted.

But there are other areas where Beverly and I are both targeted and areas where we are both dominant. We're both targeted as women, and we're both dominant as Christians, as heterosexuals, as able-bodied, as middle class. We felt it was useful to remember that as

women we both feel targeted in groups of men where we are negotiating around money, for example. We are both disadvantaged systematically in a society that overvalues male attributes and characteristics. . . . The fact that we are both practicing Christians and women of faith and identify very strongly and publicly in that way means we are both dominant. We are not Jewish or Muslim. We are both able-bodied, both heterosexual, both middle-class women, and we offer each other support in remembering that we have a responsibility to interrupt anti-Semitism, to interrupt homophobia and heterosexism, to interrupt classism, and so on. . . .

   . . .

COMMON DIFFERENCES

Ayvanzian: . . .

   We are two mothers with school-age children who have many similarities but who have made some different choices, we believe, because of our racial difference. In particular, we have made different choices about the schooling for our sons and the environments we feel they need in order to thrive. My son is in a public school in our town and fits in well in his kindergarten class and in his school. During a parent–teacher conference this past spring, his teacher said to me, "Andrea, your son is just like a thousand other rambunctious, big-for-his-age 6-year-old boys that I have had in my teaching career." And I thought to myself, "I'm sure he is. I'm sure he doesn't stand out in very many ways. He's like a thousand other children that this woman has had in her long career of teaching kindergarten." In our predominantly white community, the same could not be said about Beverly's sons. . . .

   Tatum: . . . Like many of the black families I interviewed and wrote about in my book, *Assimilation Blues: Black Families in a White Community* (Tatum, 1987), I have worried about how my children will be responded to by what has been to date an entirely white teaching staff (with the exception of an occasional student teacher of color). Though it may only be an illusion, I believe I have been able to exercise more control over my children's classroom experiences as a result of enrolling them in private schools. There have been times when I have felt that racial issues were present in both peer and teacher interactions, and both my husband and I have been actively involved in negotiating those issues with the school and our children.

   The task of raising young African American children, especially boys, in contemporary society is not an easy one. My children are also big for their ages, but unlike for white boys for whom physical maturity is often a social advantage, being black and big for your age places you at some psychological risk: 7-year-old black boys may be thought of as cute; 14-year-old black boys are often perceived as dangerous. The larger you are, the sooner you must learn to deal with other people's negative stereotypes, and you may not yet be cognitively and emotionally mature enough to do so effectively. The smallness of their private school environment, where I can easily make myself known as a parent and where my children may be seen as individuals rather than representatives of a racial group, may offer some small margin of protection for them. They will need all the margin they can get. Though I am a product of public schools myself and I support quality public education, I have not regretted our decision to send our children to private schools.

   . . .

NEXT STEPS

CHOOSING THE MARGIN

The last point that we want to talk about as another example of common differences is what Beverly and I have come to call from "margin to center" or from "center to margin." Both of us have been influenced by the works of bell hooks, particularly *Feminist Theory: From Margin to Center* (1984), and Audre Lorde's work, *Sister Outsider.* . . . Beverly and I have remarkably similar political views. We share very similar progressive politics, but again in this area of common differences we have expressed our personal politics in different ways. . . . As a white, middle-class, heterosexual, able-bodied person, I receive considerable privilege in society. (I'm in so many dominant groups.) I start at the center where social, political, and economic power rests. Consequently, bell hooks's book, *Feminist Theory: From Margin to Center*, speaks to me, but in the reverse. I recognize that I start at the center and I feel called to move to the margin.

As I move to the margin, I try to take other progressive people, specifically in my case well-intentioned white people, with me into more progressive politics, living a more progressive agenda, choosing the margin. To accomplish this, I have made decisions like choosing, since 1981, to be a war tax resister, which means I don't pay a portion of my federal income tax every April; I make a public protest, objecting to the priorities reflected in the military portion of our federal budget and our ongoing preparation for and involvement in war. Also in my journey from center to margin, my life partner (who is male) and I have chosen not to sanctify our union and our love of each other in a formal wedding. Instead we had a ceremony of commitment that could be replicated exactly for same-sex couples. We made this decision so that we can advocate as allies to gay, lesbian, and bisexuals as a couple that has chosen in one small way not to accept heterosexual privilege. Because I start with so much privilege—so clearly at the center—these are two ways that I can move to the margin, stir up good trouble, and invite other people like me to question their politics and live their commitments to the principles they hold dear. . . . There are ways that because of my privilege I've had the luxury to step out of the center, to do what is unexpected and in some ways unacceptable. But I have not during the last 5 years suggested that Beverly make the same choices. . . . I recognize that my daily life is more advantaged and more comfortable than hers because of my color. Consequently, I do not advocate that she should choose war tax resistance. She expresses her political convictions in other ways. The same is true around formal marriage and same-sex unions. It has not been an issue for me and it has not been a source of disconnection for us that Beverly has made different choices for her behavior as a strong ally to gay men and lesbians. Her allied behavior is evident in other ways. . . .

Tatum: As Andrea said, this idea, from margin to center, has been important and I'd like to refer to a reading that I found very helpful from Letty M. Russell's book, *Church in the Round: Feminist Interpretation of the Church* (1993). She refers to the work of Audre Lorde and bell hooks, and uses this idea to make the following point. She says, "We make choices about moving from margin toward center or from center toward margin according to where we find ourselves in relation to the center of power and resources and the cultural and linguistic dominance in any particular social structure. Our connection to the margin is always related to where we are standing in regard to social privilege, and from that particular position we have at least three choices, not to choose, to choose the center, or to choose the margins" (p. 192).

As Russell points out, our first choice is not to choose. If we make this choice, if we choose not to choose, we are essentially saying that those of us who are marginalized by gender, race, sexual orientation, class, or disability have the possibility of doing nothing. But, as she says, in so doing we internalize the oppression. I think that if we consider

not choosing, if we think about internalizing our oppression and allowing ourselves to be defined as marginal, then we have in effect been psychologically violated. . . . because it forces us to disconnect from our own experience, to try to ignore and not name the particular alienation that we are exposed to in our society.

Our second choice . . . is to choose the center. She says, "those on the margin choosing the center do so by emulating the oppressors and doing everything to pass or to be like those who are dominant and be accepted by them" (p. 192). Whenever we make this choice we are choosing disconnection in the sense that we are saying, "Yes I want to be in relationship with you. If I have to deny certain aspects of my experience to do so, then I will. I will disconnect from that part of my experience in order to maintain my connection with you." . . .

Our third choice is for the margin. Here Russell says, "Those on the margin claim the margin by working in solidarity with others from the margin as they move toward the center. They seek a transformed society of justice where they will be empowered to share the center and no one will need to be marginalized" (p. 193). As I reflect on this choice, it seems to me this is the choice of connection. This is the choice of saying, "I will be connected to those who are able to acknowledge and affirm my experience in the world, who are able to stand on the margin with me." . . . Society can be transformed by those on the margin only if we "choose" the margin. Otherwise we collude in our own oppression and the oppression of others.

I choose to stand on the margin as someone who is defined by society as marginal in terms of my race and in terms of my gender. I also recognize that there are places where I am in the center and need to choose the margin because, as Andrea has already pointed out, there are places where I am dominant. But the primary point here is that those of us on the margin—or in the center—claim the margin by working in solidarity with others from the margin as they move toward the center. It is in this context that I can warmly embrace Andrea as my friend, as someone who has chosen to stand on the margin with me. . . .

Ayvazian: . . . We have forged a relationship that is not based on the false goal of color blindness. We recognize the differences in our life experiences and the difference that race makes in a relationship, and we have built a sturdy bridge across that divide.

In closing I want to share with you two lines of a Pat Parker poem called "For the White Person Who Wants to Know How to Be My Friend." The first two lines are as follows: "The first thing you do is forget that I'm black. Second, you must never forget that I'm black." Do I forget that Beverly is black? Sure I do. She is a dear friend with whom I spend time. Love, admiration, and affection flow between us. . . . But do I really forget that Beverly is black? Yes and no. . . . That is who she is in the world, and yes it is forgotten, and no it is not actually ever forgotten. But in the end, I have discovered that the issue . . . for me is, how I have come to understand social, political, and economic power and my unearned advantage and privilege as a white woman in a racist society. . . . It is my understanding of my own whiteness, not my response to her blackness, that allows me to interact with Beverly in a way that continues to foster mutuality, connection, and trust.

. . . Beverly calls us "partners in justice": shoulder to shoulder we move toward our goal. . . .

NEXT STEPS

23

FLEXing Cross-cultural Communication

Carmelita (Rosie) Castañeda

Multicultural competence is a phrase that acknowledges the ability of a person to communicate effectively across cultural boundaries with sensitivity to the cultural differences and preferences involved on both sides of those boundaries. Achieving multicultural competency challenges an individual to know his or her own culture and the cultures of others and to employ that knowledge by engaging people of other cultures in mutually gainful communication. Learning multicultural competency and sustaining its practice in our demographically changing society is imperative in order for people to live, communicate, and remain connected to one another.

Multicultural competence incorporates knowledge and skills that enable people to engage in culturally responsive ways of interacting and functioning in the world (Romney, 2002). It further incorporates the capacity for self-awareness and the ability to model this behavior to others. Cultural responsiveness is determined by many factors, including, but not limited to, people, cultures, situational contexts, environments, and school and work settings (Cheesebro, O'Conner, and Rios, 2006). All these factors impact the ability to communicate with one another from a culturally competent stance.

Writing on cross-cultural communication skills, Clyde W. Ford submits that causing an "us-versus-them" schism by reacting defensively to the speaker's emotional message is counterproductive (1994). However, when we step back from an interaction and reflect on its path, we can change the style of our understanding and response by listening to the speaker's message. Ford advises us to call the following approaches into service as we communicate cross-culturally: "build mutual understanding . . . bridge differences rather than insist on similarity of views . . . seek agreement through synthesis . . . [and] hold the parties you communicate with in the highest positive regard" (1994, 54). Such culturally responsive communication requires stepping back, depersonalizing the emotional content of the interchange, refraining from becoming defensive, and listening to the message by allowing people to express their thoughts freely, whether in a loud or soft voice, in anger or in frustration. It requires, perhaps most importantly, a willingness on the part of the listener to engage in this form of communication.

Accessing the level of cross-communication that authors such as Ford (1994) and Cheesebro, O'Conner, and Rios (2006) describe is a benchmark trait of multiculturally competent people. They are able to recognize that a person's own way of thinking and behaving is not the only way. Because they recognize that there are multiple paths to achieving goals, they are able to think and behave flexibly. Moreover, the sense that our universe is a place inhabited by multiplicity and diversity encourages in multiculturally competent people the ability to be comfortable with differences in others.

The FLEX model below was adapted from a training program developed by M. Arsenault, R. Castañeda and T. Williams (2001) that was used in the Office of Training and Development at the University of Massachusetts Amherst. This model offers suggestions for developing multicultural competence:

Foster interconnectedness
- Understand your own values, beliefs and practices

- Explore commonalities
- Assume the positive
- Recognize humanity

Listen and communicate

- Understand one's frame of reference
- Paraphrase ideas through describing; avoid judgment
- State ideas clearly and constructively

Encourage respect

- Treat others as they would like to be treated
- Consider working with people on their terms
- Preserve dignity

eXplore differences

- Ask questions
- Approach people, ideas, behaviors and actions with curiosity
- Approach ambiguity

This FLEX model provides an introductory tool and constant referent for understanding and practicing multicultural competency.

CONCLUSION

This FLEX model provides more than the upbeat thought processes promoted via its compact phrases. Behind each phrase crouches its behavior-affecting antithesis. For example, if we do not foster interconnectedness and listen and communicate, how can we arrive at an understanding of people of other cultures' values, beliefs, and practices? If we do not encourage respect and explore differences between cultures, how are we to rid our behavior of the anger-invoking insensitivities of communication that distance us from people of other cultures? Utilizing the genuinely effective communication filters, as well as the opportunity for thoughtful introspection and relearned behavior, offered in this FLEX model promotes access to multicultural competency. This tool may spark a motivation to frame words to those from other cultures in ways that engender mutual benefit. When we accomplish that, we inhabit the realm of multiculturally competent communicators.

NEXT STEPS

24

The Personal is Political

Richard (Chip) Smith

Being involved in the struggle against white supremacy is, first, a personal decision. But how to connect one's everyday activities to the large-scale plan of action proposed in this book is not always clear. Doing so is essential, however, to building a movement—person by person, in a widening circle of activity and commitment.

Here are ten ways people can jump into things right where they are—wherever that might be—and, if already involved, how they can deepen that engagement:

1. **Become aware of privilege and internalized oppression.** Peggy McIntosh has a well-regarded exercise, "White Privilege: Unpacking the Invisible Knapsack," which helps European Americans understand how they are privileged by being white. McIntosh points out that people can be aware that others are worse off than they are; but these same people remain unaware—and the culture keeps them unaware—of how this situation translates into their benefiting from privileges themselves.

   "White privilege is like an invisible weightless knapsack of special provisions, maps, passports, codebooks, visas, clothes, tools and blank checks," comments McIntosh. She asks people to take stock of what they have in their own personal knapsacks and offers more than 25 examples—such as, "I can arrange to protect my children most of the time from people who might not like them," or "I am never asked to speak for all the people of my racial group." McIntosh notes that some items everyone in a decent society should be entitled to—things like "the expectation that neighbors will be decent to you, or that your race will not count against you in court." Other privileges confer power, like "My skin color [is] an asset for any move I . . . want to make," or white people are "morally neutral, normative, and average, and also ideal, so that when we work to benefit others, this is seen as work which will allow 'them' to be more like 'us.'"

   A similar exercise can be conducted by men, non-working class people, and heterosexuals to get at the specifics of male, class and hetero privileges. Coming from the opposite side, popular education methods developed by the Brazilian educator Paolo Freire, such as *Pedagogy of the Oppressed*, can help oppressed people gain insights into the social system where they live. Anger at oppressive conditions—which may be deeply internalized or bubbling near the surface—can turn into positive energy to transform society. Regardless of color or nationality, the common objective of these exercises is clarity—an awareness of social reality as it is and one's place in it. Without this kind of clarity, people's attempts to bring about change will likely remain unfocused and only occasionally effective.

2. **Build intentional relationships based on equality . . . .**

   A key element for these relationships to be beneficial for everyone is that they be based on equality. The burden here is on those with privilege to be primarily in a learning mode—being willing to examine the reality of their privilege together with others in the relationship. Ultimately the goal is to turn privilege—be it in education, social access, or material wealth—to everyone's advantage by making it available for use by the social justice movement.

   . . .

   Privilege also affects relationships through the deeply internalized feelings of confidence that people with privilege have—and which other very competent people sometimes lack. Important to building up this sense of confidence is the actual experience of struggle—fighting back, taking leadership—as well as coming to understand the historical and social roots of powerlessness.

3. **Study and discuss the history of peoples of color, as well as of white working class people. . . .** Developing personal relationships is essential; but there is also an obligation to learn other folks' history—and to do it on one's own time, so to speak, and not expect to be spoon-fed by friends.

   All these considerations apply to questions of class and gender as well. One goal . . . has been to approach these varied aspects of people in an intersectional way. . . . The movement is only beginning to create a common history of struggle

that people of all nationalities can identify with. Learning each other's histories, and drawing on all our varied experiences, is essential to creating a collective memory appropriate to the emerging society the movement hopes to build.

4. **Question, talk about, and challenge the evidence of white supremacy all around us.** Simply putting into words an observation or a question can help people see more clearly what is going on—the composition of a meeting, people's body language, or who is interrupting whom. Questions are good because they leave the answer open and allow folks to respond freely. At the same time, when someone asks a question back, there is the opportunity to "tell it like it is"—or at least as it appears to you—simply and directly.

Resistance or non-cooperation are options when other people voice a snide comment about a certain part of town, a put-down of a particular class of people, or a color-coded joke. Ted Allen suggested one way to respond in this situation: "Oh, you must think I'm white?" Another is to point to a personal relationship with the targeted group—"Just so you know, my wife is a Chinese immigrant." And however one responds, the goal can be more than just silencing the speaker. Most desirable is being able to turn the conversation into a straightforward discussion of race and its role in society. Tim Wise gives an example from a conversation in a bar, when working to defeat David Duke in his campaign for governor of Louisiana in 1991, and concludes: "There are ways to talk to people" even truly tough cases, and make some headway, break down some defenses, get people to at least begin to question the things they have always taken for granted precisely because they have *never been challenged before* by anyone who looked like them." Finally Noel Ignatiev calls for people to become "race traitors":

. . .

In this spirit, one can be proactive by crossing the color line to hear a speaker, attend a holiday celebration, volunteer one's time, go to church, or take part in a discussion. At the same time, it is important to be sensitive about spaces that people of color reserve for themselves—but not jumping to such a conclusion based on little or no information. Discovering what is possible, and what is not, can feel a little risky, but being willing to step out of one's comfort zone is necessary to break down the social barriers that divide people. Still, the invasion and domination of other people's spaces is a real concern—and verges over into the larger issues of gentrification of neighborhoods and cultural appropriation.

Finally, the direct rejection of privilege can make sense at appropriate times—usually combined with organizing others to do the same. Examples include 1) a group of workers who turn down a raise aimed at undercutting their support for a union contract; or 2) the officers in the Civil War movie *Glory* refusing their pay until black soldiers received the same wages as the white soldiers.

5. **Take a good look at your home.** Paul Kivel, in *Uprooting Racism*, notes that people's homes are their most intimate spaces and they reflect who we are. One useful exercise is to look around and see what our home tell us about ourselves. The pictures on the walls, the books or magazines lying around—or their absence; the sound of conversations, TV shows, or music; the traffic in and out of children, friends, or activists; the smells of food, coffee or farmland—all these aspects of people's homes say something about who we are. There is no pre-judgment implied here, because homes depend in part on how much money folks have, their ages, and whether they live in the city, the suburbs, or the country. The point is, however, that if people profess to be against white supremacy, yet everything in their home reflects a white culture, then there is a disconnect. At the same time, there can be a downside here, too, in collecting—or appropriating as commodities—others' cultures. Consciously altering

N
E
X
T

S
T
E
P
S

the home environment, however, can reflect movement in a new direction—and can reinforce efforts to be consistent in one's values and to identify with a shared history of struggle. As Kivel notes, engaging children in this project can make it a learning experience for the next generation, too.

6. **Challenge white supremacy (sexism, homophobia) in family life.** A lot of emotional energy goes into maintaining the structure of relationships in a family. Raising questions about the internal culture—the humor, the assumptions about peoples of other races, or who does what tasks around the house—can stir up people's defenses. The challenge is to find ways to address these topics while still maintaining a connection with folks. For white people who become anti-racist activists—and in doing so break with their families to varying degrees—facing up to this responsibility is often difficult.

    Two women from the South who broke with the white supremacist environment in which they grew up make this point. Mab Segrest, in *Memoirs of a Race Traitor*, tells how she came to accept her obligation to her family at the urging of African American mentors in North Carolina. Anne Braden, in *The Wall Between*, reflects on her own struggles with family members and the slow, almost imperceptible changes she saw in her father's attitudes over decades of loving struggle. Neither woman regrets her rejection of the dominant Southern ways and their values; and each sees her personal transformation as a necessary and liberating step forward. At the same time, by reengaging with their families, both women were able to understand better the social sources of their parents' prejudices—and, in doing so, come to accept their folks' humanity, while continuing to hold up a mirror to offensive words and practices. Just as the family has a powerful ability to shape and contain a person; so too, once free from its negative influences, one can bring that same power to bear to reshape the family culture. The lessons learned in this most intimate struggle—and the sense of personal wholeness achieved—can radiate outward in relationships with friends, coworkers, and other activists.

7. **Take an inventory of activism in the community.** It can be helpful to look around to see who the grassroots activists are in the community—and then plug into what is going on. By being supportive, putting in the time, and establishing ties on the basis of joint work, people can learn the skills needed to bring about change. Building relationships with folks from different oppressed nationalities helps foster understanding and unity. And if of European descent, orienting oneself in this way helps ground a person's activism—providing a base from which to reach out and organize other white people.

    If the community is homogeneous—as is the case with many white people, who overall tend to live in segregated communities—the basic approach can still be the same: seek out those who are active in a progressive way and then link up with them. The problem, however, is that when organizations are racially isolated—as in white suburbia or small-town rural areas—they can drift in directions that end up setting people against other grassroots folks. Efforts to improve suburban schools can pit people against the needs of oppressed nationality children in a nearby city. Or the children of immigrant farmworkers can be viewed as a drain on the state's education resources, rather than the asset they actually are to the community. For white organizers who do not have oppressed nationality people to orient themselves to, the challenge to stay ideologically grounded increases. Under such conditions, seeking out activists and movements of color—even if at some distance from where an person lives—can be important to keeping one's bearings.

8. **Be intentional about building a base for activism at the workplace.** For most people who want to be active, it has to be right where they happen to be at that moment

in their lives. For others, especially students or youth who are not already tied to a job or a community, there can be an element of freedom to shape where they spend their working life. One possibility is to select a workplace based on its potential as an organizing site—by considering the make-up of the workforce, its history of struggle, and the degree to which the workers share connections to a particular town or neighborhood. Then, rather than getting a job, say, as a union staffperson—where the relationships with workers are less direct—one can hire on as a rank-and-file worker for the long haul. On this basis of equality with others, an organizer can then build ties with coworkers over time in a way that fits with the strategic front against white supremacy . . . .

9. **Examine other aspects of life to see if changes would favor increased activism.**

- **Where you live:** perhaps a house or apartment in a different community would enable the building of intentional relationships and a social base for activism.
- **The church, synagogue, sangha, or other religious institution you might attend:** possibilities for increased social engagement might flow from proposing a project or, where necessary, by making a change to a different gathering.
- **The amount of TV watched:** maybe a different pattern of activity would free up some time for activism, for a progressive book club, or for a class at the local community college.
- **One's physical condition:** working out, a basketball league, karate or other activity can help keep a person physically fit and more prepared to take on the challenges of an activist's life. Also, the older a person gets, the more important such activity is so that one can bring all the accumulated wisdom of a lifetime to bear for social change.
- **Where and with whom one socializes:** one of the most segregated spaces in the United States—along with people's religious activities—is where folks relax and enjoy leisure activities. Perhaps other options are available—new places to visit, or new friends to go out with or have over.
- **Learning a new language:** with the increase of immigrants of color in the United States, learning a second language like Spanish, Tagalog, or Haitian Creole is nearly a necessity for anyone who wants to be effective in opposing white supremacy.

Generally, the idea is to look at all the ways one might free up time and develop the ability to be more intentionally engaged with others. Having an overarching political perspective is important, too, since it can help a person see the link between everyday activities and the long-term goal of social transformation. The challenge is for people to take responsibility for their lives, be aware of how they spend their time, and make the best use of whatever freedom—or privilege—they may have.

10. **Finally, what if people are just too busy or overwhelmed by trying to hold everything together?** What if they feel they can't change anything, that they will never be effective as a change agent, or that everyone out there is already doing about what they can anyway? The key here is probably not to "do" anything, but just to be open—to people's history, to really seeing what is going on in one's life, to new relationships, and to new kinds of conversation. This society being the way it is, just about everything a person does is tied in somehow with color, class, and gender. A starting point is to keep one's eyes and ears open—along with one's heart and mind—and see what happens.

NEXT STEPS

SECTION 3

CLASSISM

Introduction

Maurianne Adams

COMING TO CLASSISM AWARENESS DURING THE 2007–2012 ECONOMIC RECESSION

Once upon a time, not very long ago, people didn't feel comfortable talking about classism or thinking about their own specific class location. Not any more. Ever since the financial bubble burst in 2007, the ongoing recession has destroyed the economic fabric of entire nations, threatened the stability of the Eurozone and the Middle East, and thrown millions of U.S. families into a downward spiral of job loss, home foreclosure, and personal bankruptcy.[1] Some 5.1 million Americans were laid off in the first year of the recession—that is, 8.5 percent of the national workforce—with up to 10 percent unemployment in several states and 18 percent unemployment among recently discharged military veterans. The recovery of the last few years has been described as slow, sluggish, stagnant, scarcely noticeable to middle-class, impoverished, jobless, or underemployed Americans.[2]

The depth and duration of this recession have focused public attention onto the glaring inequities in wealth and income that were already apparent, if less visible, in the preceding decades, as the cumulation of many long-term factors: industrial and then service jobs moved offshore, tax policies favoring financial instruments and investments over professional income and wage labor, and a stagnation or decline in hourly wages. These growing class inequities had for many years been disguised by the fact that families had more participants in the workforce (women largely) and ready access to credit. But with the collapse of global financial markets in 2007, and the dramatic loss of family wealth based on inflated home and mortgage values, the median net worth of U.S. families dropped precipitously to $70,000 in 2008, a 28 percent loss from pre-recession levels. The 2011 Census Bureau reported 46.2 million Americans were below the poverty line (including 16.4 million children), and poor Americans became poorer—deep poverty rose 44.3 percent, the highest poverty level in 36 years, with about one in eight Americans and one in four children dependent on aid.[3]

The overall recession did not affect all Americans equally. Despite huge losses for banks "too large to fail," the actual wealth concentrated at the top of the U.S. economy continued its upward progression. From 1983 to 2009, 82 percent of wealth gains went to the top 5 percent of the U.S. population, and the top 1 percent, who already had been earning 8 percent of all U.S. income in 1979, by 2007 had increased their share to 23 percent (Collins, 2012). As the United States inched out of deep recession by 2010, the top 1 percent had captured 93 percent of income gains and 21 percent of all 2010 U.S. income. These dramatic disparities in wealth and income, accelerated by the recession, need to be understood in the context of longer-term economic patterns, including job loss and wage decline as labor became "outsourced" and huge profits accrued to the high end of the economic spectrum through manipulation of global financial markets. These disparities result in the advantages and disadvantages based on social and economic class that this section describes as class*ism*.

The two factors that before the recession had obscured enormous economic gaps based on class differences—namely, more family members in the workforce, and ready access to credit cards, high-interest loans, and equity on home ownership—were stripped away by the two major forces driving the recent economic meltdown. These recessionary forces included, first, the loss of credit for families whose standard of living had been based on borrowing rather than wage growth, and second, the collapse of overheated financial markets based on monetized mortgage-backed securities.[4] Thus black and Latino households, for whom home equity had been a major source of wealth, were disproportionately harmed by the collapse of the housing market—53 percent and 66 percent losses in wealth for black and Latino families respectively, compared to the 16 percent loss for white families. Many black and Latino homes had been located in California, Florida, Nevada, and Arizona, states hardest hit by the housing crisis.

GLOBAL ECONOMIC CONTEXT: MARKETS AND LABOR

The collapse of financial markets and soaring private debt after 2008 have shaken everyone from Main Street(s) to Wall Street(s) in a global context where "Wall Street" also refers to financial networks linking New York and Los Angeles to London, Paris, Frankfurt, Tokyo, and Shanghai. To understand the international scope and local consequences of global financial interdependency requires us to trace the entanglements of global capital (finance, ownership, and trade) with global resources (cheap labor and raw materials). Several specific examples will be obvious, such as the U.S. dependency on oil markets that have also supported inequities throughout the Middle East, or the outsourcing of clothing manufacture to low-wage workers in South Korea and China to maintain a price-advantage within U.S. markets, or the geo-economics by which heroin from poppies grown in Peru and Afghanistan gets refined in local drug labs and transported by murderously competing drug cartels who control trade routes across national borders to reach the drug markets in the United States and elsewhere.

REVERBERATIONS OF CLASS AND CLASSISM IN THE UNITED STATES

Economic uncertainties on Wall Street reverberate immediately on Main Street, as anyone knows who is or cares about someone facing home foreclosure, personal bankruptcy, or unemployment, unable to get a car loan or a line of credit or afford greater debt to cover college costs. The news, whether through blogs, TV, or newspapers, provides unending economic shockers—Ponzi schemes (Bernie Madoff and others), exposés of financial influence on the political sector,

business and banking regulatory failures, and insider trading. The recent 2012 election campaign included debates over tax policy such as whether to preserve tax loopholes and lower rates for corporate profits, capital gains, and dividends combined with the comparably higher payroll tax rates for most wage-earning Americans, or whether to enact "the Buffett Rule" that asks wealthy Americans to pay "their fair share."

It is not surprising that the consequences of this recession have brought issues of class inequity and class location, for so long considered to be impolite or taboo, out into the open. By now, almost everyone has heard the Occupy Wall Street slogan "We are the 99%," described in selection 39, "How Occupy Wall Street Changes Everything." Popular movements such as Occupy Wall Street and the Tea Party (although at opposite ends of the political spectrum) have transformed our political culture to reflect the current economic disparities and class-based issues. It is no longer considered subversive to point out the glaring class difference, or to identify super PAC contributors who provide unlimited financial resources to candidates or incumbents for public office, or to contrast the different consequences for bank bailouts and personal bankruptcies, or holding executive bonus contracts sacrosanct while union contracts and worker health benefits and pensions are stripped.

There are many reasons why it has for so long been so difficult and uncomfortable to publicly acknowledge the role of social economic class and class*ism* in the United States. One reason is our belief in *meritocracy* (that hard work and talent will be rewarded). Another reason is our conflation of the U.S. *democratic political system*, based on the premise of political equality, with the U.S. *capitalist economic system*, based on the premise of equality of economic opportunity. The democratic myth that every child can grow up to be President has been conflated with the capitalist myth that every child can become rich through hard work and talent. *Democracy* has characterized the United States from its beginnings, although limited at its inception to the white, male, propertied, land-owning colonial elite. Democracy is a *political* system, characterized by basic freedoms and a representative (not an egalitarian) system of governance. Struggle, sometimes violent, has attended each new broadening of representative democracy—to include African Americans, women, Native Americans, and through changes in the meanings that attach to "whiteness" that determined citizenship based on race for Asian and Arab immigrants (Haney López, 1996).

Democracy, the U.S. political system, is not the same as *capitalism*, the U.S. economic system that is characterized by the private ownership of capital (land, buildings, factories, and the labor of others) in which owners benefit from the labor or productivity of workers and machinery. Early- and mid-nineteenth-century capitalist expansion rationalized the seizure and management of farmland and mines through the displacement of Native Americans, the enslavement of a largely African workforce, the peonage of Chinese workers, and the wage exploitation of several generations of immigrants from Europe, Asia, and the Americas (Steinberg, 1989; Takaki, 1993; Zinn, 2001). Thus, open and knowledgeable discussion of contemporary class differences and economic inequality is stifled in part by the loss of historical knowledge due to the conflation of capitalism with democracy.

Generations of U.S. citizens have felt confident that they and their children as well as all other citizens and their children (regardless of class, race, or national origins) would have equal economic opportunity—a confidence undercut by the realities of inequality based on class, race, and national origins. But now, even this cornerstone of the American Dream, however naïve it may have seemed, is under assault. Scholarly studies confirm the experience of many Americans, regardless of race, class, gender, or national origins, that the United States has less economic mobility than comparable nations; that 62 percent of the children of families located in the top fifth based on their income stay within the top two-fifths, while 65 percent of children raised in the bottom fifth stay in the bottom two-fifths—so that the unalterable significance of U.S. family status and class position has resulted in a country that is *less* equal and *less* mobile than comparable countries (DeParle, 2012). Contemporary scholarship as well as the historical record makes it

difficult if not impossible to argue that poverty can be overcome by merit and hard work (that is, the Horatio Alger myth of pulling oneself up by one's bootstraps—as if everyone had boots, let alone boots with straps), or that the poor and unemployed are to blame for their condition.

SOCIAL AND PSYCHOLOGICAL DIMENSIONS OF CLASS MYTHS AND STATUS

Many people who are privileged as well as those disadvantaged by class find it difficult to acknowledge their internalized denials of their own class location. This denial is based in part on the widely held belief that the United States was created by (white) European migrants who built a classless society that threw off the shackles of class-distinctions from the "Old World." (This belief, not surprisingly, is not so widely shared by communities of color in the United States, whose primary experience includes recurrent instances of race- and class-based disadvantage.) The denial of class is also based in part on a widespread belief in meritocracy and its reverse, the shaming and blaming of those who are economically unsuccessful, and whose failure to thrive is mistakenly thought to be their own fault.

It is not difficult to see how the belief in meritocracy—that it was hard work alone that enabled generations of European immigrants to become middle- and professional-class Americans—has become ingrained in the U.S. national identity. The belief in meritocracy celebrates as earned the success achieved by European colonists, settlers, and immigrants who had advantages based on economic, racial, linguistic, educational, and/or cultural assets relative to enslaved or marginalized communities of color without these advantages. This belief in meritocracy thus obscures the racial disadvantage (resulting in long-term intergenerational economic deprivations) for Native American nations confined on reservations, African American descendents of slaves and debt peonage, and Mexican American and Asian victims of wage inequity and unfair labor practices. To this record of cultural, political, linguistic, and racialized disadvantage, we add the economic, social, and cultural challenges experienced by people with disabilities, or youth and elders marginalized on the two ends of the "ageism and adultism" spectrum.

ECONOMIC, SOCIAL, AND CULTURAL DIMENSIONS OF CLASS: WEALTH AND INCOME, SOCIAL, AND CULTURAL-INTELLECTUAL CAPITAL

Wealth consists of what one owns (cars, stocks or securities, homes) minus what one owes (credit card or school debt, home mortgages). Despite the simplicity of this equation, it is confusing to keep track of the various indicators of class location, which include but are not limited to wealth, and are complicated by the social, intellectual, political, and economic networks into which class privilege provides ready access. For example, the stereotyped superiority of "old money" to "new money" suggests that class privilege based on a fortunate intergenerational accumulation of wealth is preferable to "self-made millionaires," and calls attention to established upper-class status (as distinct from "newcomers") based upon long family traditions of elite education, international travel, private clubs, political and corporate leadership, membership on corporate or non-profit Boards of Directors, and domestic servants at multiple homes and vacation houses.

The indicators of class privilege often include *wealth* based on long-term investments rather than the uncertainties of *wages* based on skill or labor (this includes the vagaries of high-paid sports or celebrity wages). But the privileges based on class are not solely economic. They can include social and intellectual "capital" that may no longer be accompanied by considerable

wealth, as in the case of families who have lost their money over several generations but may not have lost their social and intellectual connections, and can thus claim ongoing social or intellectual capital.

To help provide consistency as well as clarity in discussing the various dimensions of class and class*ism* in the selections that follow, we propose Leondar-Wright and Yeskel's definition of *class* as "a relative social ranking based on income, wealth, education, status, and power" and their definition of *classism* as "The institutional, cultural, and individual set of practices and beliefs that assign differential value to people according to their socioeconomic class; and an economic system that creates excessive inequality and causes basic human needs to go unmet" (Leondar-Wright and Yeskel, 2007, p. 314 and Appendix C; see also Fiske and Markus, 2012; Lareau and Conley, 2008).

The distinctive institutional, cultural, and individual practices and beliefs related to class privilege are important to notice. By *economic capital*, we generally refer to wealth enhanced by income. *Social capital* refers to social resources such as elite education, health care, political connections, legal and financial advisors, and "concierge" health services. *Social capital* also includes valuable personal networks that ensure and enhance professional mobility, corporate profits, and political advantage. *Intellectual and cultural capital* refer to the knowledge, language, and self-presentation needed to leverage major social institutions—such as education, the law, the political system, the health-care system. This includes "who one knows" in order to access these resources for personal and family benefit. Indicators of intellectual and cultural capital include accent and speech that convey sophistication and education (as distinct from regional or ethnic-based accent or speech), an understated but expensive wardrobe, a "good" neighbor-hood address, tasteful home furnishings.

The interconnections of economic, social, intellectual, and cultural forms of capital, and the ballooning problems for families posed by student debt are two highlights of this section, of special interest to today's students for whom the likelihood of escalating debt endangers their investment in a baccalaureate degree. The soaring costs of higher education in the context of cuts to public-funded loans or grants have resulted in the accumulation of more than $1 trillion in student debt as of 2012, with 94 percent of all students in debt, up from 45 percent in 1993, debt-totals averaging $23,300 per student but running as high as $100,000.[5] This debt burden needs to be coupled with the current youth unemployment figures (16.3 percent) noted earlier to grasp the human tragedy facing this current generation of college graduates and indebted dropouts, hobbled by unprecedented levels of personal debt and aggressively pursued by student-loan debt collectors—for example, the number of student complaints filed against collection agencies has grown by 45 percent.

READING SELECTIONS IN THIS SECTION

The selections in this section will call into question the master-narrative still taught in most K-12 schools, which claims an inevitable, step-wise upward-mobility by (white) immigrants into the middle and upper classes. This master-narrative largely ignores the parallel counter-narratives of class-revolt and violent suppression which characterize the larger story of labor organizing and union resistance to inadequate wages, child labor, unpaid overtime, unsafe working conditions—by white working-poor indentured servants in the early colonies and later by immigrants who worked the mines and the railroads, often Irish and Italian and Eastern European (Loewen, 1995; Takaki, 1993; Zinn, 2001). The 2012 political season has revived attacks on public sector labor unions and blamed teachers' unions for the problems of poverty and racial segregation in public education. Most students have not been taught about the achievements of the union movement that gave the United States its two-day weekends, 40-hour work weeks, employment

benefits, and outlawed child labor (with the exception of contemporary sex trafficking and labor peonage). Because this important history cannot be adequately reflected in this section, we ask that you draw on the resources for further study about these counter-narratives suggested in the citations as well as the section website.

The reading selections in this section reflect the main issues outlined in this introduction, although it is difficult to track the incredibly rapid pace of economic change, with attendant changes in class location, at the present moment. The conceptual frameworks presented in Section 1 will help readers understand the class dynamics described in this section. For example, it is important to have read about the role of identity and socialization in maintaining class inequalities (Section 1, selections 1–3, and 6) and to understand ways in which different social identities intersect or the ways in which different "levels of oppression" (individual, institutional, societal) interact as they play out in the "five faces of oppression" and lead to questions about who is responsible for justice (Section 1, selections 4, 6, and 7). Thus, the conceptual frameworks presented in Section 1 will help readers make sense of the selections in this and in the other sections.

The first nine selections in this section present Contexts for understanding the role of social institutions in maintaining and reproducing class-based inequality. In selection 25, "Class in America," Mantsios punctures the myth of classlessness (or its variant, that everyone is middle class) with portraits that dramatize differences of class status and opportunity in the United States, juxtaposing upper- and middle-class opportunities with working-poor constraints. In selection 26, Collins and Yeskel portray the consequences of these disparities, such as the loss of health insurance, rising personal and family debt, job loss or reduction to part-time or underpaid work—disparities that have become only more devastating during the current recession. They use graphic visual representations to convey the top/bottom differences in the ownership of wealth in the United States.

Whereas the first two selections personalize the dramatic differences in class location, Oliver and Shapiro (selection 27) show the historical and intergenerational basis for black/white wealth inequality that is an ongoing legacy of U.S. law and policy. They describe historical moments in which federal policies structured black poverty on the one hand, and white opportunity on the other—for example, the availability of the 1950s GI Bill education grants and Fair Housing Administration suburban housing loans along racial lines, with intergenerational consequences for home ownership and home equity that extend to the present day. While the emphasis in this selection is on white/black racial disparities in wealth, this kind of historical exploration offers a template for identifying the obstacles that restrict the economic and social mobility of other U.S. communities of color that are described elsewhere in this section (for example, selection 33 by Rakesh Kochhar, Richard Fry, and Paul Taylor for the Pew Research Center, selection 34 by Romero, and selection 36 by Saint).

"What's Debt Got to Do with It," "The Near-Trillion-Dollar Student Loan Bubble," and "The Debt Trap" (selections 28, 30, and 38) present portraits and consequences of the present-day personal debt overload on individuals and families. "What's Debt Got to Do with It" looks at the poverty debt market in which high-interest, debt-generating businesses provide a $5 billion-a-year industry for international chain financial services through the deceptive practices and lush profits of so-called "easy credit" pawnshops, rent-to-own stores, and credit-card vendors. It shows how these poverty-exploiting storefronts advertise "refund anticipation loans," E-Z credit and check-cashing services, all the while piling on fees and interest rates that are profitable only to the banks and chains that operate them.

The ease of access to elite higher educational institutions for well-to-do "legacy" applicants (selection 29) and the debt burden on economically strapped college students (selection 30) is a theme that resonates for an increasing number of American families, at a time when access to higher education has become increasingly "classed," as costs sky-rocket (122 percent increase in public tuition from 1986 to 2007), as states decrease their subsidies for public higher education, as federal Pell grants are cut, and as funding for higher education becomes loan-based, leaving

college graduates with huge debts at a time of rising unemployment and underemployment. The financial struggles experienced by college students from middle- as well as low-income families are compounded in the case of students with disabilities (selection 31) who often come from families with low incomes—37 percent, as compared to 20 percent non-disabled peers. Further, students with disabilities struggle with costs for needed professional services—counselors, physical therapists, assistive devices, personal assistants, and a host of other expenses not covered by funding sources.

Some of the Context readings (selections 27, 31–33) highlight the mutually reinforcing negative effects of disability, sexism, and racism intersecting with class and exacerbating its personal destructiveness. "Trafficking in Persons Report 2011" (selection 32) documents contemporary instances of forced labor, sex trafficking, domestic servitude, and child labor, with personalized vignettes that intersect gender, age, migrant status, and class. It sketches vivid examples in the context of global industrial, agricultural, service, and sex markets, while suggesting some regulations and policies that can and should be enforced to stop such trafficking in persons.

Five selections in Voices speak from contexts of privileged as well as disadvantaged class positions compounded by racism and sexism. In selection 34, African-diaspora and migrant women of color in domestic service tell in their own words their experiences of exploitation, humiliation, and powerlessness. They vividly describe domestic isolation, devalued and gendered household labor, race-based and class-based insult. In selection 35, bell hooks works against stereotype to recount the complex race/class hierarchies of her remembered rural Southern small-town childhood, where class deeply complicated the expected differences based on race. She remembers how poor Whites clung to their racial advantage and power over Blacks, and also how Whites with class privilege scorned Whites without. In different ways, the selection told by "Saint" (selection 36) also works against stereotype, by depicting an inner-city black childhood in which personal and gang hierarchies are based on gendered as well as racialized violence and fear—but also on the giving and receiving of mutual respect.

By way of contrast, selection 37, "Classified: How To Stop Hiding Your Privilege and Use It For Social Change," presents snapshots of privilege and wealth based on family advantage, white privilege, cultural capital, social networks, and family legacies derived from a U.S. legacy of land theft, slavery, and exploitation—as well as hard work, monetary investment, education, and good luck. In contrast, selection 38, "The Debt Trap," presents a white woman's downward spiral out of marginal middle-class status because of her ballooning credit card and mortgage debt, accelerated by her illness and medical debt in the absence of health insurance.

There are clear implications throughout this section for positive social change. Different forms of class exploitation and abuse require remedies at different economic and institutional levels—such as protective legislation (minimum wage, overtime, health and safety, mandatory education); new protections for workers in agribusinesses or in domestic servitude; and judicial enforcement of anti-trafficking and anti-peonage laws to safeguard vulnerable migrant workers. In response to every example of exploitation and abuse described in these selections, there are also clear steps that can be taken toward legal or institutional remedy, and toward greater equity and empowerment. On the personal level, "Classified: How to Stop Hiding Your Privilege and Use It For Social Change" (selection 37) suggests some first steps that can be taken by individuals.

The Next Steps selections in this section focus on political, community, and classroom efforts to correct injustice and create greater educational equity. The emphasis in this section on cross-class coalition building points to the importance of class awareness, especially among middle-class people who have thought about their class position and who feel ready to coordinate their efforts with less-privileged organizing partners.

The first selection, "How Occupy Wall Street Changes Everything" (selection 39) lives up to its title. Selection 40 quotes personal examples of the everyday classism that makes it difficult for people with privilege to work effectively in cross-class organizations and coalitions (such as the

Occupy Wall Street movements). In this vein, selection 41 challenges readers to figure out their own examples of internalized class privilege.

Selection 42 places participants in difficult advocacy roles, by asking them to come up with a plan to reconcile competing demands at the fictional "Sunnyvale Nursing Home" for higher wages. Students are invited to make the case for CEOs, doctors, nurses, aides, kitchen workers, security guards, janitors, and gardeners, whose wage claims compete with arguments for subsidies to fixed- and low-income patients or elderly on nursing home waiting lists. Having presented the arguments and advocated for these different roles and positions, participants must then become decision-makers—noting that in a unionized workplace, everyone would vote, but that in a non-union workplace, these would be CEO decisions. This selection illustrates the possibilities for interactive classroom simulations and discussions, since the "participants" described in the activity would presumably be classroom students or workshop colleagues.

Additional Next Steps dealing with classism intersecting with other social justice issues can be found in other sections of this book, such as selection 110 which describes ways to ease the transition to college for students without cultural capital. The catastrophic debt triggered by lack of health insurance (selection 38) is addressed by the National Latina Institute for Reproductive Health's "Statement on Healthcare for All" (selection 72). The final section on "Working for Social Justice: Visions and Strategies for Change" has several selections with direct relevance to classism— "What Can We Do?", "Social Struggle," "Unite and Rebel! Challenges and Strategies in Building Alliances," and "Top Youth Activism Victories of 2009" (selections 130, 134, 136, and 137).

INTERSECTIONS OF CLASS WITH OTHER FORMS OF PRIVILEGE AND DISADVANTAGE

It is obvious that every person experiences either privilege or disadvantage on the basis of class position as shaped and complicated by race and racism, gender and sexism, ability or disability and ableism, youth or elder status, ageism or adultism, religion and religious oppression, sexuality and gender identity and expression. Although class is a visible thread that connects all the multiple forms of oppression, it is possible for upper-class people of color, or gay, lesbian, queer, or transgender identity, to experience racism or heterosexism or transgender oppression unmediated by their class status. Tracing the thread of class privilege or disadvantage highlights the intersections of class position with other privileged or disadvantaged identities. Thus, the ways in which class is shaped by and intersects with other social identities are noted throughout this volume, in readings that illustrate the links between economic, social, and intellectual-cultural capital (or its lack) to the feminization of poverty and to the special vulnerabilities of women, children, migrants of color, the disabled, youth, and elders. For example, the connections between classism and racism are clearly delineated in selections 12, 13, and 17; with religious oppression in selections 53–55; with sexism in selections 73 and 76; with ableism in selections 102–110. We encourage readers to use the Table of Intersections to locate these and other specific reading selections that connect classism with other social justice topics.

One dimension of class—it might be seen as a dimension of social capital—has to do with the powerful role of the medical profession and medical technologies in shaping current understandings and experience of transgender people, of people with disabilities, and of youth and elders. Selection 100 shows the impact of professional medical terminology and technologies on the choices available to transgender people. Selections 98 and 110 extend the analysis of economic, social, and intellectual-cultural capital to the construction of disability and the economic, social, cultural challenges experienced by people with disabilities. Selections 115–116, 119, and 122 illustrate multiple interconnections between class, ageism and adultism, and racism.

All selections in this section on classism raise questions, challenges, and possibilities for change, that go well beyond the limits of any one section of this book. We urge all

readers—instructors and students—to turn to the website for further references and resources, for related discussion questions and classroom activities, and for consideration of some of the challenges and opportunities that could emerge from discussion of the readings in this and other sections.

See Companion Website for Additional Resources and Material

Notes

1 Sources include A. Hacker (February 23, 2012), We're more unequal than you think, *The New York Review*, pp. 34–36; G. Morgenson and J. Rosner (2012), *Reckless Endangerment: How Outsized Ambition, Greed, and Corruption Led to Economic Armageddon* (Time Books/Holt); R. J. Schiller (2008), *The Subprime Solution: How Today's Global Financial Crisis Happened, and What To Do About It* (Princeton University Press); R. D. Wolff (2010), *Capitalism Hits the Fan: The Global Economic Meltdown and What To Do About It* (Olive Branch Press).

2 Sources include L. Alvarez (November 18, 2008), New veterans hit hard by economic crisis, *The New York Times* (www.nytimes.com/2008/11/18/us); S. Armour (April 16, 2009), Foreclosures take a big jump, *USA Today*; T. S. Bernard and J. Anderson (November 16, 2008), Bankruptcies by consumers climb sharply, *The New York Times*; M. Lewis and D. Einhorn (January 4, 2009), The end of the financial world as we know it, *The New York Times*.

3 Sources include Pew (February 9, 2012), *Young, Underemployed and Optimistic*, p. 1 (Pew, 2011, 13); S. Tavernise (September 13, 2011), Soaring poverty casts spotlight on "lost decade," *The New York Times*; J. Deparle and S. Tavernise (September 15, 2011), Poor are still getting poorer, but downturn's punch varies, census data shows, *The New York Times*.

4 Sources include Collins (2012); P. Krugman (2009), *The Return of Depression Economics and the Crisis of 2008* (Norton); K. Phillips (2008), *Bad Money: Reckless Finance, Failed Politics, and the Global Crisis of American Capitalism* (Viking); E. Porter (March 21, 2012), Inequality undermines democracy, *The New York Times*; R. Reich (2007), *Supercapitalism: The Transformation of Business, Democracy, and Everyday Life* (Vintage).

5 Sources include A. Martin and A. Lehren (May 13, 2012), A generation hobbled by debt, *The New York Times*; PBS Need to Know (February 10, 2012) *The Student Debt Dilemma* and *Anya Kamenetz on the "Debt Generation*," www.pbs.org/wnet/need-to-know/video/

References

Collins, C. (2012). *99 to 1: How Wealth Inequality is Wrecking the World and What We Can Do About It*. San Francisco: Berrett-Koehler.

DeParle, J. (January 5, 2012). Harder for Americans to rise from economy's lower rungs. *The New York Times*.

Fiske, S., Markus, H. R. (eds). (2012). *Facing Social Class: How Societal Rank Influences Interaction*. New York: Russell Sage Foundation.

Haney López, I. F. (1996). *White by Law: The Legal Construction of Race*. New York: New York University Press.

Lareau, A., Conley, D. (eds). (2008). *Social Class: How Does It Work?* New York: Russell Sage Foundation.

Leondar-Wright, B., Yeskel, F. (2007). Classism curriculum design. In M. Adams, L. A. Bell, P. Griffin (eds), *Teaching for Diversity and Social Justice* (2nd edition, pp. 308–333). New York, Routledge. Appendix C on CD. (See section website for these materials.)

Loewen, J. W. (1995). The land of opportunity. In *Lies My Teacher Told Me: Everything Your American History Textbook Got Wrong* (pp. 200–213). New York: Simon & Schuster.

Steinberg, S. (1989). *The Ethnic Myth: Race, Ethnicity, and Class in America* (updated edition). Boston: Beacon Press.

Takaki, R. (1993). *A Different Mirror: A History of Multicultural America*. Boston: Little, Brown, & Co.

Zinn, H. (2001). *A People's History of the United States* (revised and updated edition). New York: Harper & Row.

25

Class in America—2006

Gregory Mantsios

People in the United States don't like to talk about class. Or so it would seem. We don't speak about class privileges, or class oppression, or the class nature of society. . . . For the most part, avoidance of class-laden vocabulary crosses class boundaries. There are few among the poor who speak of themselves as lower class; instead, they refer to their race, ethnic group, or geographic location. Workers are more likely to identify with their employer, industry, or occupational group than with other workers, or with the working class.

Neither are those at the other end of the economic spectrum likely to use the word "class." In her study of thirty-eight wealthy and socially prominent women, Susan Ostrander asked participants if they considered themselves members of the upper class. One participant responded, "I hate to use the word 'class.' We are responsible, fortunate people, old families, the people who have something." Another said, "I hate [the term] upper class. It is so non-upper class to use it. I just call it 'all of us,' those who are wellborn."

. . .

There are, however, two notable exceptions to this phenomenon. First, it is acceptable in the United States to talk about "the middle class." Interestingly enough, such references appear to be acceptable precisely because they mute class differences. References to the middle class by politicians, for example, are designed to encompass and attract the broadest possible constituency. Not only do references to the middle class gloss over differences, but these references also avoid any suggestion of conflict or injustice.

This leads us to the second exception to the class-avoidance phenomenon. We are, on occasion, presented with glimpses of the upper class and the lower class (the language used is "the wealthy" and "the poor"). In the media, these presentations are designed to satisfy some real or imagined voyeuristic need of "the ordinary person." . . .

We are left with one of two possibilities: either talking about class and recognizing class distinctions are not relevant to U.S. society, or we mistakenly hold a set of beliefs that obscure the reality of class differences and their impact on people's lives. Let us look at four common, albeit contradictory, beliefs about the United States.

Myth 1: The United States is fundamentally a classless society. Class distinctions are largely irrelevant today, and whatever differences do exist in economic standing, they are—for the most part—insignificant. Rich or poor, we are all equal in the eyes of the law, and such basic needs as health care and education are provided to all regardless of economic standing.

Myth 2: We are, essentially, a middle-class nation. Despite some variations in economic status, most Americans have achieved relative affluence in what is widely recognized as a consumer society.

Myth 3: We are all getting richer. The American public as a whole is steadily moving up the economic ladder, and each generation propels itself to greater economic well-being. Despite some fluctuations, the U.S. position in the global economy has brought previously unknown prosperity to most, if not all, Americans.

Myth 4: Everyone has an equal chance to succeed. Success in the United States requires no more than hard work, sacrifice, and perseverance: "In America, anyone can become a millionaire; it's just a matter of being in the right place at the right time."

In trying to assess the legitimacy of these beliefs, we want to ask several important questions. Are there significant class differences among Americans? If these differences do exist, are they getting bigger or smaller, and do these differences have a significant impact on the way we live? Finally, does everyone in the United States really have an equal opportunity to succeed?

THE ECONOMIC SPECTRUM

Let's begin by looking at difference. An examination of available data reveals that variations in economic well-being are, in fact, immense. Consider the following:

- The wealthiest 1 percent of the American population holds 34 percent of the total national wealth. That is, they own over one-third of all the consumer durables (such as houses, cars, and stereos) and financial assets (such as stocks, bonds, property, and savings accounts). The richest 20 percent of Americans hold nearly 85 percent of the total household wealth in the country.
- Approximately 183,000 Americans, or approximately three-quarters of 1 percent of the adult population, earn more than $1 million **annually**. There are nearly 400 billionaires in the U.S. today, more than three dozen of them worth more than $10 billion each. It would take the average American (earning $35,672 and spending absolutely nothing at all) a total of 28,033 years (or approximately 400 lifetimes) to earn just $1 billion.

Affluence and prosperity are clearly alive and well in certain segments of the U.S. population. However, this abundance is in contrast to the poverty and despair that is also prevalent in the United States. At the other end of the spectrum:

- Approximately 13 percent of the American population—that is, nearly one of every eight people in this country—live below the official poverty line (calculated in 2004 at $9,645 for an individual and $19,307 for a family of four). An estimated 3.5 million people—of whom nearly 1.4 million are children—experience homelessness in any given year.
- Approximately one out of every five children (4.4 million) in the United States under the age of six lives in poverty.

The contrast between rich and poor is sharp, and with nearly one-third of the American population living at one extreme or the other, it is difficult to argue that we live in a classless society. Big-payoff reality shows, celebrity salaries, and multi-million dollar lotteries notwithstanding, evidence suggests that the level of inequality in the United States is getting higher. Census data show the gap between the rich and the poor to be the widest since the government began collecting information in 1947 and that this gap is continuing to grow. In 2004 alone, the average real income of 99 percent of the U.S. population grew

by little more than 1 percent, while . . . the richest 1 percent saw their income rise by 12 percent in the same year.

Nor is such a gap between rich and poor representative of the rest of the industrialized world. In fact, the United States has by far the most unequal distribution of household income. The income gap between rich and poor in the United States (measured as the percentage of total income held by the wealthiest 20 percent of the population versus the poorest 20 percent) is approximately 12 to 1, one of the highest ratios in the industrialized world. The ratio in Japan and Germany, by contrast, is 4 to 1.

Reality 1: There are enormous differences in the economic standing of American citizens. A sizable proportion of the U.S. population occupies opposite ends of the economic spectrum. In the middle range of the economic spectrum:

- Sixty percent of the American population holds less than 6 percent of the nation's wealth.
- While the real income of the top 1 percent of U.S. families skyrocketed by more than 180 percent between 1979 and 2000, the income of the middle fifth of the population grew only slightly (12.4 percent over that same 21-year period) and its share of income (15 percent of the total compared to 48 percent of the total for the wealthiest fifth) actually declined during this period.
- Regressive changes in governmental tax policies and the weakening of labor unions over the last quarter century have led to a significant rise in the level of inequality between the rich and the middle class. Between 1979 and 2000, the gap in household income between the top fifth and middle fifth of the population rose by 31 percent. During the economic boom of the 1990s, the top fifth of the nation's population saw their share of net worth increase (from 59 to 63 percent) while four out of five Americans saw their share of net worth decline. . . .

The level of inequality is sometimes difficult to comprehend fully by looking at dollar figures and percentages. To help his students visualize the distribution of income, the well-known economist Paul Samuelson asked them to picture an income pyramid made of children's blocks, with each layer of blocks representing $1,000. If we were to construct Samuelson's pyramid today, the peak of the pyramid would be much higher than the Eiffel Tower, yet almost all of us would be within six feet of the ground. . . .

Reality 2: The middle class in the United States holds a very small share of the nation's wealth and that share is declining steadily. The gap between rich and poor and between rich and the middle class is larger than it has ever been.

AMERICAN LIFE-STYLES

At last count, nearly 37 million Americans across the nation lived in unrelenting poverty. Yet, as political scientist Michael Harrington once commented, "America has the best dressed poverty the world has ever known." Clothing disguises much of the poverty in the United States, and this may explain, in part, its middle-class image. With increased mass marketing of "designer" clothing and with shifts in the nation's economy from blue-collar (and often better-paying) manufacturing jobs to white-collar and pink-collar jobs in the service sector, it is becoming increasingly difficult to distinguish class differences based on appearance.

Beneath the surface, there is another reality. Let's look at some "typical" and not-so-typical life-styles.

Name: **Harold S. Browning**

Father: manufacturer, industrialist

Mother: prominent social figure in the community

Principal child-rearer: governess

Primary education: an exclusive private school on Manhattan's Upper East Side. . . .

Supplemental tutoring: tutors in French and mathematics

Summer camp: sleep-away camp in northern Connecticut

Secondary education: a prestigious preparatory school in Westchester County

Supplemental education: private SAT tutor. After-school activities: private riding lessons. *Ambition:* "to take over my father's business." *High-school graduation gift:* BMW

Family activities: theater, recitals, museums, summer vacations in Europe, occasional winter trips to the Caribbean.

Higher education: an Ivy League liberal arts college in Massachusetts. *Major:* economics and political science. *After-class activities:* debating club, college newspaper, swim team. *Ambition:* "to become a leader in business"

First full-time job (age 23): assistant manager of operations, Browning Tool and Die, Inc. (family enterprise)

Subsequent employment: 3 years—executive assistant to the president, Browning Tool and Die; responsibilities included: purchasing (materials and equipment), personnel, and distribution networks. 4 years—advertising manager, Lackheed Manufacturing (home appliances). 3 years—director of marketing and sales, Comerex, Inc. (business machines)

Present employment (age 38): executive vice president, SmithBond and Co. (digital instruments). *Typical daily activities:* review financial reports and computer printouts, dictate memoranda, lunch with clients, initiate conference calls, meet with assistants, plan business trips, meet with associates. *Transportation to and from work:* chauffeured company limousine. *Annual salary:* $324,000. *Ambition:* "to become chief executive officer of the firm, or one like it, within the next five to ten years"

Present residence: eighteenth-floor condominium on Manhattan's Upper West Side, eleven rooms, including five spacious bedrooms and terrace overlooking river. . . .

Second residence: farm in northwestern Connecticut, used for weekend retreats and for horse breeding (investment/hobby). . . .

Harold Browning was born into a world of nurses, maids, and governesses. His world today is one of airplanes and limousines, five-star restaurants, and luxurious living accommodations. The life and life-style of Harold Browning is in sharp contrast to that of Bob Farrell.

Name: **Bob Farrell**

Father: machinist

Mother: retail clerk

Principal child-rearer: mother and sitter

Primary education: a medium-size public school in Queens, New York, characterized by large class size, outmoded physical facilities, and an educational philosophy emphasizing basic skills and student discipline. . . .

Supplemental tutoring: none

Summer camp: YMCA day camp. . . .

Secondary education: large regional high school in Queens. . . .

Supplemental education: SAT prep course offered by national chain. *After-school activities:* basketball and handball in school park. *Ambition:* "to make it through college." *High-school graduation gift:* $500 savings bond

Family activities: family gatherings around television set, softball, an occasional trip to the movie theater, summer Sundays at the public beach

SPHERES OF POWER AND OPPRESSION

When we look at society and try to determine what it is that keeps most people down—what holds them back from realizing their potential as healthy, creative, productive individuals—we find institutional forces that are largely beyond individual control. Class domination is one of these forces. People do not choose to be poor or working class; instead, they are limited and confined by the opportunities afforded or denied them by a social and economic system. . . . Class divisions arise from the differences between those who own and control corporate enterprise and those who do not.

Racial and gender domination are other forces that hold people down. Although there are significant differences in the way capitalism, racism, and sexism affect our lives, there are also a multitude of parallels. And although class, race, and gender act independently of each other, they are at the same time very much interrelated.

On the one hand, issues of race and gender cut across class lines. Women experience the effects of sexism whether they are well-paid professionals or poorly paid clerks. As women, they are not only subjected to catcalls and stereotyping, but face discrimination and are denied opportunities and privileges that men have. Similarly, a wealthy black man faces racial oppression, is subjected to racial slurs, and is denied opportunities because of his color. . . .

Chances of Being Poor in America					
White Male/ Female	White Female Head[1]	Hispanic Male/ Female	Hispanic Female Head[1]	Black Male/ Female	Black Female Head[1]
1 in 10	1 in 5	1 in 5	1 in 3	1 in 4	1 in 3

1 Persons in families with female householder, no husband present.

Reality 7: Racism and sexism significantly compound the effects of class in society.

None of this makes for a very pretty picture of our country. Despite what we like to think about ourselves as a nation, the truth is that opportunity for success and life itself are highly circumscribed by our race, our gender, and the class we are born into. As individuals, we feel hurt and anger when someone is treating us unfairly; yet as a society we tolerate unconscionable injustice. A more just society will require a radical redistribution of wealth and power. We can start by reversing the current trends that further polarize us as a people and adapt policies and practices that narrow the gaps in income, wealth, and privilege.

26

The Dangerous Consequences of Growing Inequality

Chuck Collins, Felice Yeskel, with United for a Fair Economy and Class Action

. . .

PRESSURES FACING OUR HOUSEHOLDS

Let's start by looking at the impact of the changing economy close to home. There are new pressures and some alarming trends facing a growing number of households in this country. . . .

The decline of leisure time and the breakdown of civil society. One powerful consequence of growing inequality is an erosion in the amount of free time that families have. As individuals and families struggle to stay afloat and remain secure in the changing economy, they are spending more hours at work.

Falling wages in the 1970s and early 1980s were masked by the entry of a second wage earner in many households—usually a woman—into the workforce. Families now have to work longer hours to make up for falling wages. At the same time, temporary and part-time workers generally do not have paid vacations, and their numbers in the workforce are growing. The number of overall hours worked, per household, has increased since 1972. The number of hours worked per person each year has increased 4 percent, from 1,905 in 1980 to 1,966 in 2001. . . .

Technological advances in the workplace, instead of increasing the amount of free time, are having the opposite effect. Productivity has been steadily increasing, but these gains have not translated into higher wages or increased free time. Blue-collar and service workers have experienced a veritable "speed-up" in the workplace as employers squeeze productivity gains into increased profits. Not only are people working longer hours, but in many cases the tempo and scope of their jobs have become more harried and stressful.

. . .

This loss of leisure time has a direct impact on the quality of people's lives. As people have less free time, they have less time available to care for children and elders, less time to be involved in schools and education, and less time to volunteer to help others. This dramatically increases stress, particularly on women, whose unpaid labor is largely performed in this non-monetary "caring economy." Stress leads to increased illness and the unraveling of communities, the breakdown in voluntary mutual-aid systems, and the fragmentation and isolation of people. It leads to "latchkey" children and a lack of support for the next generation, with serious consequences. . . .

Fewer households with health insurance. . . . Between 2000 and 2004, the cost of health care coverage grew by 35.9 percent, while average earnings only grew 12.4 percent. Over the same period, the number of households paying more than one-quarter of their earnings on health care rose by 23 percent, from 11.6 million to 14.3 million. Over 45 million

people in the nation lack health insurance, up from 31 million a decade ago. This makes the United States the only industrialized nation that views health care as a privilege, not a basic human right.

Having a job does not guarantee health insurance. The percentage of Americans under the age of 65 covered through employer-sponsored health insurance declined from 70.4 percent in 1999 to 63 percent in 2003. Among low-income Americans, the share of those with employer-sponsored health insurance fell from 40.3 in 1999 to 35.0 percent in 2002. Twenty-four million of those without insurance are employed, 17 percent of whom are in the temporary or contingent workforce. In 2003, 83 percent of part-time employees had no access to health care benefits through their employers.

. . . Thirty-four percent of the nation's 37.4 million Hispanic people have no health insurance, compared to 22 percent of blacks and 12 percent of non-Hispanic whites.

Rising personal debt. Another way families continue to make up for falling wages in order to maintain (or in some cases attain) a certain standard of living is by going deeper into debt. Approximately 60 percent of all American households carry credit card balances, unable to pay their full month bill. In 2004, the credit card industry claimed that the average household consumer debt was approximately $9,000. Yet, when the roughly 40 percent of households that pay their balances each month were taken out of the equation, average household consumer debt was closer to $13,000 and late payments are at a five-year high. Total credit card debt increased from $243 billion in 1990 to $735 billion in 2004. Some of this is rooted in consumerism, but a central reason for growing debt lies in declining or stagnant wages. People are now using credit cards for things like food and medicine—items previously paid for with cash. One downside of growing personal indebtedness is the increasing number of personal bankruptcies, which are now at an all-time high. In 2003, 1.6 million individuals filed for personal bankruptcy, up from 1.4 million in 2002 and almost triple the 661,000 who filed in 1990.

Declining personal savings. The flip side of greater debt is less savings. The savings rate is the percentage of annual income that is actually saved each year. Since 1980, the savings rate has generally fallen. The United States has the lowest savings rate of any industrialized country. In 2003, the U.S. savings rate was 1.4 percent, down from 4.5 percent in 1997 and 10.8 percent in 1984. In contrast, the savings rate in 2003 in Japan was 7 percent and in Germany it was 10.8 percent.

. . . [T]he main reason for the lower savings rate is linked to the rising cost of health care and the increase in other involuntary costs such as day care and bank-service fees.

Diminishing retirement security. Those employees lucky enough to have pensions have ones that are less secure. The percentage of workers in the private labor force in monthly pension plans (where companies bear the risk of falling markets) has declined from 38 percent in 1980 to 25 percent in 1998. These are called "defined-benefit plans," which are better for workers because they are federally insured and provide a guaranteed monthly pension amount. More workers now have "defined-contribution plans," like 401(k) plans, in which the benefit amount depends on how well the underlying investments perform. This growth in private 401(k) pension plans has failed to broaden overall pension coverage. In fact, there is more inequality in 401(k) plans than in defined-benefit plans, as they tend to be held by higher-income workers. The decline in both savings and guaranteed pensions are two concrete indicators of growing insecurity.

Retirement planners suggest that Social Security should be only one leg of the three-legged stool of retirement security. Personal savings and an employer-funded pension fund are the other two legs. But as personal savings plummet and fewer and fewer workers have pension funds, the prospects for a large percentage of people retiring into poverty grows. Worse yet, people will never be able to stop working, even as they go into their seventies.

Growing number of temporary jobs. The greatest percentage of new jobs in the workforce are filled by temporary and part-time workers. Currently about 30 percent of the

workforce is what is called "contingent," including temporary, part-time, contract, and day laborers. Some of these workers are voluntarily part-time. But a growing number are involuntarily part-time, often holding two to three jobs to pay their bills. According to the Bureau of Labor Statistics, two-thirds of contingent workers would like traditional permanent jobs. . . . The "temping of America" is part of a larger economic restructuring that is changing the nature of work and contributing to economic inequality.

The growing number of temporary and part-time jobs is a depressing trend for many younger people entering the workforce after high school or college. Only 11 percent of female and 15 percent of male full-time temporary workers have health insurance provided through their employer. In fact, fewer than 30 percent of all contingent workers have health insurance, and only 11 percent have pensions.

Higher education, higher reach. The cost of going to college has risen, while government support to ensure access to higher education has failed to keep pace. Going to college is more of a privilege than it was twenty years ago. Federal college loans have now replaced college grants, rising from 41.4 percent of student financing in 1982 to 58.9 percent in 2001. Student debt between 1991 and 1997 totaled $140 billion—more than the total combined student borrowing for the 1960s, 1970s, and 1980s. Student debt has dramatically increased from an average of $8,200 per student in 1991 to $18,900 in 2003. Many students will still be paying off college loans in their mid-thirties.

The rising cost of college affects who gets to go to college. The country's poorest families are increasingly underrepresented in higher education, particularly at four-year schools. Only 20 percent of all community college students nationally come from families with annual income under $25,000, only 11 percent at public four-year colleges, and just 8 percent at private four-year colleges. In 1995, 83.4 percent of high school students in the top fifth of income-earning households went to college, compared to 56.1 percent of students in the middle three quintiles and 41.3 percent in the bottom quintile. As of 2001, 29 percent of whites had completed four years of college compared to 17 percent of blacks and 11 percent of Hispanics. Higher education is becoming much more class-segregated than it was a decade ago.

. . .

WHAT IS WEALTH AND WHY IS IT IMPORTANT

Income and wages are one index of how prosperity is distributed; the ownership of wealth is another. If income is the stream of money that comes into our lives each year, wealth is our reservoir. From our income stream, we take our bucket and pull out our housing costs, food expenses, and health care costs. At the end of the year, any left over goes into our reservoir, becoming accumulated wealth.

Wealth comprises assets (all the stuff you own) minus liabilities (what you owe). This remainder is called "net worth." If you own a car worth $4,000, but you owe $5,000 in car loans, you are in the red. . . .

Wealth for working-class people is usually in the form of savings, consumer goods like cars, and, if they are fortunate, equity in a home. As people move up the economic ladder, wealth takes the form of greater savings and home value—but also includes second homes, recreational equipment (like boats), shares in corporations (called securities or stocks), bonds, and commercial real estate. It may also include luxury items like high-priced artwork, racehorses, jewelry, and antiques.

Wealth is important because it is what people have to fall back on and pass on to their children. Yet today, about one out of six households in the United States has zero or negative wealth. This means they literally have no financial reserves to fall back on in times

of trouble, or, in fact, they owe more than they own. The percentage of households with zero or negative net worth has increased in the last thirty years, from 15.5 percent in 1983 to 17.6 percent in 2001. When factoring in race, the figures increase significantly. The percentage of African American households with zero or negative net worth is disturbingly high, at 30.9 percent or roughly one in three black households.

. . .

It is in the area of wealth and asset accumulation that the legacy of racial discrimination has left its most profound mark. While black and Latino *incomes* have begun to catch up to white earnings, black and Latino *wealth* continues to lag dramatically behind that of white households. Since wealth accumulates over generations, discrimination has taken its toll on wealth accumulation for people of color. Blacks were prohibited from building wealth by slavery and prohibitions against owning property after the Civil War. Bank lending practices have also discriminated against black and Latino households and kept them from home ownership, business development, and other asset-building measures.

In 2001, the median black household had a net worth of just $19,000 (including home equity), compared with $121,000 for whites. Blacks had 16 percent of the median wealth of whites, up from 5 percent in 1989. At this rate, it will take until 2099 to reach parity in median wealth. Blacks were 13 percent of the U.S. population in 2001 but owned 3 percent of the assets. There is obviously a high correlation between income and wealth. Most assetless households are in the bottom fifth of the income ladder. There are people deep in debt all up and down the income spectrum, but in most cases, we can assume that assetlessness correlates with lower income.

THE CONCENTRATION OF WEALTH

In the last twenty years, the overall wealth pie has grown, but virtually all the new growth in wealth has gone to the richest 1 percent of the population.

In 1976, the wealthiest 1 percent of the population owned 20 percent of all the private wealth. The top 10 percent of the population owned about 50 percent of all private wealth. By 2001, the richest 1 percent's share had increased to over 33 percent of all household financial wealth, increasing the top 20 percent's share to 84.4 percent. The top 1 percent of households now has more wealth than the entire bottom 95 percent. As of 2001, to join the top 1 percent club you need at least $5.8 million in net worth.

Financial wealth (net worth minus net equity in owner-occupied housing) is even more concentrated. The top 1 percent of households has nearly half of all stock (44.9 percent) and 39.7 percent of all financial wealth. This is compared to the bottom 90 percent of households, which owns 20.2 percent of all financial wealth.

Between 1962 and 2001, the relative share of wealth owned by the bottom 90 percent of the population declined from 33.1 percent to 28.5 percent. What does this loss of wealth actually mean? It means less savings, growing personal debt, less retirement security, and fewer households having access to home ownership. It means fewer financial reserves to fall back on in the event of a setback or job loss.

THE WEALTH-HOLDERS

. . .

There are three ways in which the very wealthy accumulate money: through slow accumulation over their lifetimes by starting a business and saving; through cornering a critical element of the market and controlling it; or through inheritance.

U.S. Private Wealth in Perspective

Each chair
= 10% of U.S. wealth

Each person
= 10% of U.S. population

2001
10% owns 70%
of all wealth

90% owns 30%
of all wealth

Top 10%: Seven Chairs   Bottom 90%: Three Chairs

John Lapham

Figure 26.1 Ten Musical Chairs. Source: Arthur B. Kennickel, "A Rolling Tide: Changes in the Distribution of Wealth in the U.S. 1989–2001," Jerome Levy Economics Institute, November 2003.

Most press coverage goes to describing the self-made millionaires, the Horatio Algers of the modern day. In Thomas Stanley and William Danko's best-selling book, *The Millionaire Next Door*, the profile of America's 3.5 million millionaires is not the stereotype of the high-roller with five fancy sports cars and several mansions in desirable zip codes. According to Stanley and Danko, the typical millionaire is white, over fifty-five years old, has a net worth of between $1 and 10 million, and lives in the same house he bought thirty years ago. The most common sources of wealth: small-business ownership and steadily rising home value. . . .

CONTEXT

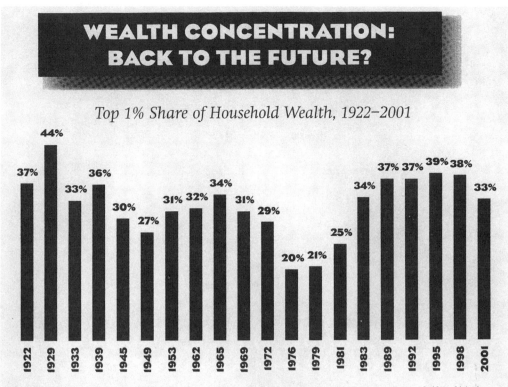

WEALTH CONCENTRATION: BACK TO THE FUTURE?

Top 1% Share of Household Wealth, 1922–2001

Sources: 1922–81: Edward N. Wolff, *Top Heavy* (The New Press: 1996). 1983–2001: Edward N. Wolff, "Changes in Household Wealth in the 1980s and 1990s in the U.S.," Jerome Levy Economics Institute, May 2004.

What if workers had been paid for productivity gains?

Between 1973 and 1998, productivity increased 33 percent. What if hourly wages grew at the same rate? What if workers shared in the 1990s productivity gains they helped to create? The average hourly wage in 1998 would have been $18.10, rather than $12.77.[29] That's the difference of $5.33 an hour—more than $11,000 for a full-time, year-round worker. The 30 cents workers gained in their hourly wages between 1997 and 1998 pales by comparison. The cumulative wages lost since 1973 will never be recovered—much less their lost investment potential. This is money working families could have saved, invested, or spent on consumer items rather than going into debt. This is money that could have stimulated markets in low- and moderate-income communities rather than benefiting absentee shareholders who take their investments anywhere on the planet in search of the highest return.

Figure 26.2 Wealth Concentration: Back to the Future?

But there are many other factors, including timing, luck, and white privilege that are less acknowledged in America's mythology of success. Starting a business in the rapidly expanding economy of the 1950s and 1960s was a very different story than starting a business in today's more competitive global economy. Prior to the 1970s, many domestic small

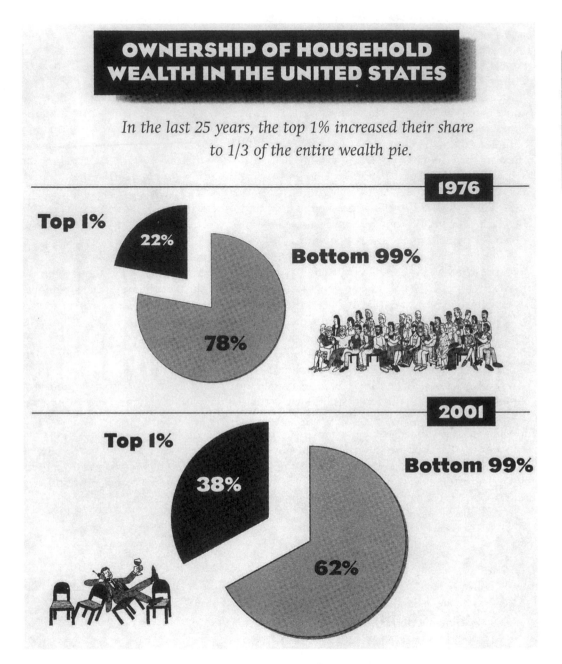

Figure 26.3 Ownership of Household Wealth in the United States. Sources: For 1976: Edward N. Wolff, unpublished data. For 2001: Arthur B. Kennickel, "A Rolling Tide: Changes in the Distribution of Wealth in the U.S. 1989–2001," Jerome Levy Economics Institute, November 2003.

businesses were protected from the full brunt of competition from international producers and national conglomerates. Imagine trying to start a locally owned hardware store or pharmacy today in the same marketplace with Home Depot, Costco, and CVS. Access to credit for the purchase of assets, whether a home in an appreciating neighborhood or a start-up small business, remains a function of education, skill, personal connections, and—despite government antidiscrimination policies—race.

Many of the largest fortunes—those in excess of $10 million—are tied to cornering a part of the market that everyone needs. Indeed, many of the great robber barons of the late 1800s (the Rockefellers, the Carnegies, etc.) dominated some market (usually in natural resources like timber, oil, coal, and steel), or developed a monopoly on a much-needed public service like railroads.

Today, fortunes are made in information-age technology. Bill Gates and Paul Allen, the founders of Microsoft, are good examples. A growing number of the new fortunes on the Forbes 400 annual listing of the richest Americans are built on computers and information technology. Like the railroad barons of the late 1800s, Gates and Allen developed advances in products—computer operating systems and software—that have become central to our lives. Between 1996 and 1999, Bill Gates's personal wealth went from $18 billion to over $85 billion dollars. Thanks to changes in the market and his aggressive charitable giving ($28 billion donated to the Gates Foundation and other charities), Gates's net worth in 2004 was $48 billion, but his personal wealth still exceeds the combined wealth of the bottom 45 percent of the U.S. population.

In spite of the success stories of small entrepreneurs and "dot-com millionaires," the most sure-fire way to get rich remains to be born into a wealthy family. A substantial amount of wealth is passed on from one generation to the next through inheritance. Economist Lester Thurow estimates that between 50 and 70 percent of all wealth is inherited. A 1997 study found that of the 400 individuals and families on the 1997 Forbes 400 list, 42 percent inherited their way onto the list, another 6 percent inherited wealth in excess of $50 million, and another 7 percent started life with at least $1 million. Overall, more than 50 percent started life with at least $1 million. . . .

While it still is possible for a few to make the "rags to riches" transition, it is important to question the underlying belief and value system that dangles this fantasy before our eyes. This national obsession is so compelling that we are willing to accept large-scale poverty in exchange for the prospect of a few lucky folks hitting the big time. We can't possibly *all* invent the next mousetrap or computer operating system. We can't *all* win the lottery. A few folks cornering the market (or hitting the daily number) depends on many others failing. Unfortunately, the classist belief systems we are indoctrinated by are powerful. We are trained to identify up the class spectrum and fantasize about getting there.

27

Race, Wealth, and Equality

Melvin L. Oliver and Thomas M. Shapiro

Over a hundred years after the end of slavery, more than thirty years after the passage of major civil rights legislation, and following a concerted but prematurely curtailed War on Poverty, we harvest today a mixed legacy of racial progress. We celebrate the advancement of many blacks to middle-class status. . . . An official end to "de jure" housing segregation has even opened the door to neighborhoods and suburban residences previously off-limits to black residents. Nonetheless, many blacks have fallen by the wayside in their march toward economic equality. A growing number have not been able to take advantage of the

opportunities now open to some. They suffer from educational deficiencies that make finding a foothold in an emerging technological economy near to impossible. Unable to move from deteriorated inner-city and older suburban communities, they entrust their children to school systems that are rarely able to provide them with the educational foundation they need to take the first steps up a racially skewed economic ladder. Trapped in communities of despair, they face increasing economic and social isolation from both their middle-class counterparts and white Americans.

. . .

Disparities in wealth between blacks and whites are not the product of haphazard events, inborn traits, isolated incidents, or solely contemporary individual accomplishments. Rather, wealth inequality has been structured over many generations through the same systemic barriers that have hampered blacks throughout their history in American society: slavery, Jim Crow, so-called de jure discrimination, and institutionalized racism. How these factors have affected the ability of blacks to accumulate wealth, however, has often been ignored or incompletely sketched. By briefly recalling three scenarios in American history that produced structured inequalities, we illustrate the significance of these barriers and their role in creating the wealth gap between blacks and whites.

RECONSTRUCTION: FROM SLAVERY TO FREEDOM WITHOUT A MATERIAL BASE

. . .

The close of the Civil War transformed four million former slaves from chattel to freedmen. Emerging from a legacy of two and a half centuries of legalized oppression, the new freedmen entered Southern society with little or no material assets. . . . The slave's often-cited demand of "forty acres and a mule" fueled great anticipation of a new beginning based on land ownership and a transfer of skills developed under slavery into the new economy of the South. Whereas slave muscle and skills had cleared the wilderness and made the land productive and profitable for plantation owners, the new vision saw the freedmen's hard work and skill generating income and resources for the former slaves themselves. W. E. B. Du Bois, in his *Black Reconstruction in America*, called this prospect America's chance to be a modern democracy.

Initially it appeared that massive land redistribution from the Confederates to the freedmen would indeed become a reality. . . . Real access to land for the freedman had to await the passage of the Southern Homestead Act in 1866, which provided a legal basis and mechanism to promote black landownership. In this legislation public land already designated in the 1862 Homestead Act, which applied only to non-Confederate whites but not blacks, was now opened up to settlement by former slaves in the tradition of homesteading that had helped settle the West. . . .

This social and economic transformation never occurred. . . . First, instead of disqualifying former Confederate supporters as the previous act had done, the 1866 legislation allowed all persons who applied for land to swear that they had not taken up arms against the Union or given aid and comfort to the enemies. This opened the door to massive white applications for land. One estimate suggests that over three-quarters (77.1 percent) of the land applicants under the act were white. In addition, much of the land was poor swampland and it was difficult for black or white applicants to meet the necessary homesteading requirements because they could not make a decent living off the land. What is more important, blacks had to face the extra burden of racial prejudice and discrimination along with the charging of illegal fees, expressly discriminatory court challenges and court decisions, and land speculators. . . .

THE SUBURBANIZATION OF AMERICA: THE MAKING OF THE GHETTO

. . .

The suburbanization of America was principally financed and encouraged by actions of the federal government, which supported suburban growth from the 1930s through the 1960s by way of taxation, transportation, and housing policy. . . . As a consequence, employment opportunities steadily rose in the suburban rings of the nation's major metropolitan areas. In addition, transportation policy encouraged freeway construction and subsidized cheap fuel and mass-produced automobiles. These factors made living on the outer edges of cities both affordable and relatively convenient. However, the most important government policies encouraging and subsidizing suburbanization focused on housing. In particular, the incentives that government programs gave for the acquisition of single-family detached housing spurred both the development and financing of the tract home, which became the hallmark of suburban living. While these governmental policies collectively enabled over thirty-five million families between 1933 and 1978 to participate in homeowner equity accumulation, they also had the adverse effect of constraining black Americans' residential opportunities to central-city ghettos of major U.S. metropolitan communities and denying them access to one of the most successful generators of wealth in American history—the suburban tract home.

This story begins with the government's initial entry into home financing. . . . Charged with the task of determining the "useful or productive life of housing" they considered to finance, government agents methodically included in their procedures the evaluation of the racial composition or potential racial composition of the community. Communities that were changing racially or were already black were deemed undesirable and placed in the lowest category. The categories, assigned various colors on a map ranging from green for the most desirable, which included new, all-white housing that was always in demand, to red, which included already racially mixed or all-black, old, and undesirable areas, subsequently were used by Federal Housing Authority (FHA) loan officers who made loans on the basis of these designations.

Established in 1934, the FHA aimed to bolster the economy and increase employment by aiding the ailing construction industry. The FHA ushered in the modern mortgage system that enabled people to buy homes on small down payments and at reasonable interest rates, with lengthy repayment periods and full loan amortization. The FHA's success was remarkable: housing starts jumped from 332,000 in 1936 to 619,000 in 1941. . . .

This growth in access to housing was confined, however, for the most part to suburban areas. The administrative dictates outlined in the original act, while containing no anti-urban bias, functioned in practice to the neglect of central cities. Three reasons can be cited: first, a bias toward the financing of single-family detached homes over multifamily projects favored open areas outside of the central city that had yet to be developed over congested central-city areas; second, a bias toward new purchases over repair of existing homes prompted people to move out of the city rather than upgrade or improve their existing residences; and third, the continued use of the "unbiased professional estimate" that made older homes and communities in which blacks or undesirables were located less likely to receive approval for loans encouraged purchases in communities where race was not an issue.

. . . [T]he FHA . . . provided more precise guidance to its appraisers in its *Underwriting Manual*. The most basic sentiment underlying the FHA's concern was its fear that property values would decline if a rigid black and white segregation was not maintained. The *Underwriting Manual* openly stated that "if a neighborhood is to retain stability, it is necessary that properties shall continue to be occupied by the same social and racial classes" and

further recommended that "subdivision regulations and suitable restrictive covenants" are the best way to ensure such neighborhood stability. The FHA's recommended use of restrictive covenants continued until 1949, when, responding to the Supreme Court's outlawing of such covenants in 1948 (*Shelly v. Kraemer*), it announced that "as of February 15, 1950, it would not insure mortgages on real estate subject to covenants."

. . .

The FHA's actions have had a lasting impact on the wealth portfolios of black Americans. Locked out of the greatest mass-based opportunity for wealth accumulation in American history, African Americans who desired and were able to afford home ownership found themselves consigned to central-city communities where their investments were affected by the "self-fulfilling prophecies" of the FHA appraisers: cut off from sources of new investment their homes and communities deteriorated and lost value in comparison to those homes and communities that FHA appraisers deemed desirable. One infamous housing development of the period—Levittown—provides a classic illustration of the way blacks missed out on this asset-accumulating opportunity. Levittown was built on a mass scale, and housing there was eminently affordable, thanks to the FHA's and VHA's accessible financing, yet as late as 1960 "not a single one of the Long Island Levittown's 82,000 residents was black."

CONTEMPORARY INSTITUTIONAL RACISM: ACCESS
TO MORTGAGE MONEY AND REDLINING

. . .

In May of 1988 the issue of banking discrimination and redlining exploded onto the front pages of the *Atlanta Journal and Constitution*. This Pulitzer Prize-winning series, "The Color of Money," described the wide disparity in mortgage-lending practices in black and white neighborhoods of Atlanta, finding black applicants rejected at a greater rate than whites, even when economic situations were comparable. . . .

A 1991 Federal Reserve study of 6.4 million home mortgage applications by race and income confirmed suspicions of bias in lending by reporting a widespread and systemic pattern of institutional discrimination in the nation's banking system. This study disclosed that commercial banks rejected black applicants twice as often as whites nationwide. In some cities, like Boston, Philadelphia, Chicago, and Minneapolis, it reported a more pronounced pattern of minority loan rejections, with blacks being rejected three times more often than whites.

The argument that financial considerations—not discrimination—are the reason minorities get fewer loans appears to be totally refuted by the Federal Reserve study. The poorest white applicant, according to this report, was more likely to get a mortgage loan approved than a black in the highest income bracket. In Boston, for example, blacks in the highest income levels faced loan rejections three times more often than whites. . . .

The problem goes beyond redlining. Not only were banks reluctant to lend in minority communities, but the Federal Reserve study indicates that discrimination follows blacks no matter where they want to live and no matter how much they earn. A 1993 *Washington Post* series highlighted banks' reluctance to lend even in the wealthiest black neighborhoods. . . .

These findings gave credence to the allegations of housing and community activists that banks have been strip-mining minority neighborhoods of housing equity through unscrupulous backdoor loans for home repairs. Homes bought during the 1960s and 1970s in low-income areas had acquired some equity but were also in need of repair. Mainstream

banks refused to approve such loans at "normal" rates, but finance companies made loans that, according to activists, preyed on minority communities by charging exorbitant, pawn-shop-style interest rates with unfavorable conditions. Rates of 34 percent and huge balloon payments were not uncommon. . . .

In Boston more than one-half of the families who relied on these kinds of high-interest loans lost their homes through foreclosure. One study charted every loan between 1984 and mid-1991 made by two high-interest lenders. Families lost their homes or were facing foreclosure in over three-quarters of the cases. Only 55 of the 406 families still possessed their homes and did not face foreclosure. The study also showed that the maps of redlined areas and high-interest loans overlapped.

. . .

Even briefly recalled, the three historical moments evoked in the pages above illustrate the powerful dynamics generating structured inequality in America. Several common threads link the three scenarios. First, whether it be a question of homesteading, subur-banization, or redlining, we have seen how governmental, institutional, and private-sector discrimination enhances the ability of different segments of the population to accumulate and build on their wealth assets and resources, thereby raising their standard of living and securing a better future for themselves and their children. The use of land grants and mass low-priced sales of government lands created massive and unparalleled opportunities for Americans in the nineteenth century to secure title to land in the westward expansion. Likewise, government backing of millions of low-interest loans to returning soldiers and low-income families enabled American cities to suburbanize and their inhabitants to see tremendous home value growth after World War II. Quite clearly, black Americans for the most part were unable to secure the same degree of benefits from these government programs as whites were. Indeed, in many of these programs the government made explicit efforts to exclude blacks from participating in them, or to limit their participation in ways that deeply affected their ability to gain the maximum benefits. . . .

Second, disparities in access to housing created differential opportunities for blacks and whites to take advantage of new and more lucrative opportunities to secure the good life. White families who were able to secure title to land in the nineteenth century were much more likely to finance education for their children, provide resources for their own or their children's self-employment, or secure their political rights through political lobbies and the electoral process. Blocked from low-interest government-backed loans, redlined out by financial institutions, or barred from home ownership by banks, black families have been denied the benefits of housing inflation and the subsequent vast increase in home equity assets. Black Americans who failed to secure this economic base were much less likely to be able to provide educational access for their children, secure the necessary financial resources for self-employment, or participate effectively in the political process.

. . .

RACIAL INEQUALITY IN CONTEXT

. . .

The most visible advances for blacks since the 1960s have taken place in the political arena. As a result of the civil rights movement, the percentage of Southern blacks registered to vote rose dramatically. The number of black elected officials increased and the black vote became a crucial and courted electoral block. Yet, in 1993, blacks still accounted for less than 2 percent of all elected officials. . . .

Since the 1960s blacks have also made gains in education. By the late 1980s the propor-tion of blacks and whites graduating from high school was about equal, reversing the late-1950s black disadvantage of two to one. The percentage of blacks and whites attending college in 1977 was virtually identical, again reversing a tremendous black disadvantage. Since 1976, however, black college enrollments and completion rates have declined, threatening to wipe out the gains of the 1960s and 1970s. The trends in the political and education areas indicate qualified improvements for blacks.

Full equality, however, is still far from being achieved. Alongside the evidence of advancement in some areas and the concerted political mobilization for civil rights, the past two decades also saw an economic degeneration for millions of blacks, and this consti-tutes the crux of a troubling dilemma. Poor education, high joblessness, low incomes, and the subsequent hardships of poverty, family and community instability, and welfare depen-dency plague many African Americans. Most evident is the continuing large economic gap between blacks and whites. Median income figures show blacks earning only about 55 percent of the amount made by whites. The greatest economic gains for blacks occurred in the 1940s and 1960s. Since the early 1970s, the economic status of blacks compared to that of whites has, on average, stagnated or deteriorated. Black unemployment rates are more than twice those of whites. Black youths also have more than twice the jobless rate as white youths. Nearly one out of three blacks lives in poverty, compared with fewer than one in ten whites. Residential segregation remains a persistent problem today, with blacks being more likely than whites with similar incomes to live in overcrowded and substandard housing. Nearly one in four blacks remains outside private health insurance or Medicaid coverage. Infant mortality rates have dropped steadily since 1940 for all Americans, but the odds of dying shortly after birth are consistently twice as high for blacks as for whites. Close to half (43 percent) of all black children officially lived in poor households in 1986. A majority of black children live in families that include their mother but not their father. . . . A recent major accounting of race relations summarized it like this: "the status of black America today can be characterized as a glass that is half full—if measured by progress since 1939—or a glass that is half empty—if measured by the persisting disparities between black and white Americans."

. . .

DWINDLING ECONOMIC GROWTH AND RISING INEQUALITY

The standard of living of American households is in serious trouble. For two decades the United States has been evolving into an increasingly unequal society. After improving steadily since World War II, the real (adjusted-for-inflation) weekly wage of the average American worker peaked in 1973. During the twenty-seven-year postwar boom the aver-age worker's wages outpaced inflation every year by 2.5 to 3 percent. The standard of living of most Americans improved greatly, as many people bought cars, homes, appli-ances, televisions, and other big-ticket consumer goods for the first time. The link between growth and mobility was readily apparent. Between the end of World War II and the early to mid-1970s, the economy created a steady stream of jobs that permitted workers and their families to escape poverty and become part of a growing and vibrant middle class. The economy could absorb millions of new workers and a growing part of the population found middle-class life within reach. . . .

Since 1973, however, a far bleaker story has unfolded. Real wages have been falling or stagnating for most families. The 1986 average wage in the United States bought nearly 14 percent less than it had thirteen years earlier. Also beginning in the mid-1970s, after a long

period of movement toward greater equality and stability, the distribution of annual wages and salaries became increasingly unequal. . . .

These changes have profoundly affected blacks. Plant closings and deindustrialization more often occur in industries employing large concentrations of blacks, such as the steel, rubber, and automobile sectors. Black men, especially young black men, are more likely than whites to lose their jobs as a result of economic restructuring. One study of dein-dustrialization in the Great Lakes region found that black male production workers were hardest hit by the industrial slump of the early 1980s. From 1979 to 1984 one-half of black males in durable-goods manufacturing in five Great Lakes cities lost their jobs.

. . .

The underlying weakness of the economy in the 1990s is increasingly apparent. Debt and global competition pose enormous challenges to stable economic growth and vitality. The larger economic context for the analysis of contemporary race relations is dominated by slow or stagnant growth, deindustrialization, a two-tiered job and earning structure, cuts in the social programs that assist those at the bottom, budget deficits, increasing economic inequality, a reconcentration of wealth, a growing gap in incomes between whites and blacks, and a much-diminished American Dream, however one wishes to define or gauge it.

. . .

WHY STUDY WEALTH?

. . .

Although related, income and wealth have different meanings. *Wealth* is the total extent, at a given moment, of an individual's accumulated assets and access to resources, and it refers to the net value of assets (e.g., ownership of stocks, money in the bank, real estate, business ownership, etc.) less debt held at one time. Wealth is anything of economic value bought, sold, stocked for future disposition, or invested to bring an economic return. *Income* refers to a flow of dollars (salaries, wages, and payments periodically received as returns from an occupation, investment, or government transfer, etc.) over a set period, typically one year.

. . .

Most people use income for day-to-day necessities. Substantial wealth, by contrast, often brings income, power, and independence. Significant wealth relieves individuals from dependence on others for an income, freeing them from the authority structures associated with occupational differentiation that constitute an important aspect of the stratification system in the United States. If money derived from wealth is used to purchase significant ownership of the means of production, it can bring authority to the holder of such wealth. Substantial wealth is important also because it is directly transferable from generation to generation, thus assuring that position and opportunity remain in the same families' hands.

Command over resources inevitably anchors a conception of life chances. While resources theoretically imply both income and wealth, the reality for most families is that income supplies the necessities of life, while wealth represents a kind of "surplus" resource available for improving life chances, providing further opportunities, securing prestige, passing status along to one's family, and influencing the political process.

In view of the limitations of relying on income as well as the significance of wealth, a consideration of racially marked wealth disparities should importantly complement exist-ing income data. An investigation of wealth will also help us formulate a more detailed picture of racial differences in well-being. Most studies of economic well-being focus solely on income, but if wealth differences are even greater than those of income, then these

studies will seriously underestimate racial inequality, and policies that seek to narrow differences will fail to close the gap.

28

What's Debt Got to Do with It?

Brett Williams

. . .

"THEY WILL GLADLY TAKE A CHECK"

. . . America's Cash Express . . . is a plain, grim storefront, staffed by one woman behind ceiling-high Plexiglas, offering pagers for $80, laser tear gas for $10, and myriad one-stop financial services. Customers can apply for a telephone calling card or a secured credit card for a $25 processing fee and a $300 deposit (to be charged against) in First Deposit National Bank in New Hampshire. The annual fee is $35 and the annual percentage rate is 19.8 percent. You can wire a moneygram to pay a bill (for 10 percent of the total and a 10 percent discount on Greyhound) or "wire money in minutes worldwide" through an American Express moneygram. (In some places American Express charges as much as 24 percent of the amount wired.)

You can file a tax return and receive a refund anticipation loan ("After all . . . it's *your* money!" beams the promotional material). If you want ACE to prepare your return, that costs about $30. You can pay gas, water, telephone, and electric bills; play the lottery ("We've got your ticket!"); and purchase money orders with the cash you receive when you cash your payroll, government, insurance, or tax refund check. Some call these outlets "welfare banks" because of their heavy traffic in public assistance checks, and sometimes the government sends checks and food stamps directly there.

. . . For the most routine checks, the outlet charges 2 percent of the total, but this varies quite a bit depending on the amount and type of the check and whether or not you have ID. It can cost as much as 6 percent to cash a payroll check and 12 percent to cash a personal one. The most outrageous, expensive, and quasi-legal transactions are called "payday loans," advances secured by a postdated personal check. These loans can charge interest from 20 to 35 percent of the amount advanced; a typical transaction would offer the customer $200 for a $260 check. . . .

Despite the shame, expense, and tedium of the process, many residents of this neighborhood conduct all their bankless business at places like America's Cash Express. Citizens in poor urban neighborhoods find it increasingly difficult to get to a bank. Even if there is a local bank, residents often cannot afford its minimum balance requirements, fees for checks, or high bounced-check penalties. They may not have enough money in their account at the end of the month to cash a paycheck to pay their bills. They may need immediate cash to deliver to the phone company in person. Some residents do not have

the major credit card that is to serve as a second major ID; some cannot manage a bank's restricted hours. Some cannot open checking or saving accounts because of even minor problems with their credit or immigration histories. . . .

Using check-cashing outlets further impoverishes and disenfranchises residents, leaving them with no records or proof of payment, no ongoing relationship to build up a credit history, and in greater personal danger from carrying cash (itself in jeopardy from fire, theft, or loss). From where they stand, residents may find it hard to connect the storefronts to the larger financial system or to the injustices they endure. . . . Atlanta snack-food sales-man Ronald Hayes . . . makes a weekly visit to cash his $400 paycheck and buy a money order to pay a bill per week. The total cost to Hayes is $15 a week. . . . He fails to recognize that he is probably paying ten times more than a bank would charge. Even if some poor residents recognize the cost, others bow to hand-to-mouth demands for immediacy, safety, or convenience. One homeless man, coping successfully with the dangers of carrying cash, purchases a money order made out to himself each month, cashes it repeatedly at a 2 per-cent rate, and then buys another money order to carry the balance. He carries his money more safely, but at a huge cost. Hudson interviewed two men in Manassas, Virginia, who paid $270 to cash a $4,500 insurance check because they didn't have time to wait for the check to clear. At the Eagle Outlet, where they cashed their check, owner Victor Daigle claimed that his customers "would rather pay a little bit more to us and have their conve-nience. They go to McDonald's because they want their hamburger right now. . . . They can come to us and get their money right now."

. . .

"THAT'S WHY THEY'RE MY CUSTOMERS"

Another, more venerable fringe bank is the pawnshop, a familiar sight in cities for many years. . . . These have proliferated in Washington, D.C., and throughout the nation, doub-ling during the 1980s to number 10,091 in 1994 and certainly many more today. They have changed in other ways as well, to become centralized and chain-operated, backed by upscale marketing, ruthless acquisitions, and persistent pressure on local governments to raise usury rates. Like check-cashing outlets, they displace small businesses, family-owned pawnshops, and local chains, offering young residents of urban neighborhoods downscale, minimum-wage, no-benefits financial services jobs.

For example, Cash America, founded in 1983, operates hundreds of shops. One of five chains to be publicly traded, it boasts NYSE: PWN (for "pawn") as its symbol, turns lush profits for investors, and has tried to upgrade the pawnshop image as it eyes markets all over the world. If you multiply its monthly rate by twelve, its average annual percentage rate (APR) hovers at around 200 percent, not unusual in an industry that often charges 240 percent, and it recorded $5 million in net income from lending activities in the last quarter of 2000, up 17 percent from the year before. In Washington, D.C., Famous Pawn has been enormously successful by gobbling up mom-and-pop stores including pawn shops in poor neighborhoods.

. . . The store is stuffed with former collateral for these expensive secured loans: from gold chains, wedding bands, and watches to baseball cards, leather jackets, computers, VCRs, television sets, compact discs, cameras, pianos, guitars, saxophones, power tools, and lawnmowers. . . .

Customers pawn these items for 10 percent interest each month, a relatively low rate set by Maryland and the District. A borrower would receive $100 for a pawned item and redeem it in thirty days for $110. One customer complains: "They don't give you nothin'

for it. But when they sell it, that's when they mark it up." If a customer is unable to redeem it after thirty days, the shop will keep it on hold for as long as he or she can pay each month's interest. Often, pawnshops' profits lie in nurturing these long-term relationships with borrowers, who come in to pay their "dues" on the first of each month but eventually give up and let their treasures go. Their misfortune allows Famous Pawn to bulge out of its space, overflowing with pawns, featuring a long line of borrowers every day, and swallowing its neighboring establishments. Secondary buyers cruise through periodically, buying up items in bulk and boosting profits in the retail side of the business, long less profitable than the interest-collecting side.

. . .

[T]he vast majority of borrowers are poor, with incomes between $9,000 and $17,000 a year, according to fringe-bank researcher John Caskey. They are young, in and out of work, and disproportionately of color. Cash America's *Annual Report* describes them this way: "The cash-only individual makes up the backbone of America. He's [*sic*] the hard-working next door neighbor, the guy at the corner service station, or the lady who works as a checker at the local supermarket." Caskey quotes Jack Daugherty of Cash America to somewhat different effect: "I could take my customers and put them on a bus and drive them down to a bank and the bank would laugh at them. That's why they're my customers."

"AND YOU DON'T NEED CREDIT TO GET IT"

. . .

By redefining what they are doing as "renting," rent-to-own stores have emerged to evade usury laws that limit the interest paid by people who buy appliances and furniture on credit. Profits in this $3.7 billion-a-year business stem from astounding markups, as customers often pay five times what they would for retail. By the mid-1990s rent-to-own stores had tripled in number, so that by 1994 there were some seventy-five hundred rent-to-own outlets nationwide. Like check-cashing outlets and pawnshops, they increasingly come in corporate chain sizes.

The Rent-A-Center chain boasts twelve hundred stores, a large share of this market. But another patriotic chain, RentAmerica, dominates the Washington, D.C., area. Mostly located in two poorer suburbs (including Jenkins's) and southeast D.C., RentAmerica is a temple to consumption. To walk in is to discover a lush cornucopia of household consumer goods: florid bedroom furniture; leather couches; brightly colored, blaring television sets; giant, gleaming refrigerators; and shimmering gold jewelry. The store offers impoverished customers a shot at the postwar American dream.

But the American-flag sign that soars from the parking lot, the giddy interior, the slick brochures, and the "convenience" (or urgency?) of instant purchases and free delivery belie RentAmerica's harsh and greedy terms. . . . The terms explain that the baby-bear TV requires seventy-eight weekly payments of $9.99, or $779.22 (plus tax); the twenty-seven-inch TV costs seventy-eight weekly payments of $15.99, or $1,247.22 (plus tax); and the thirty-two-inch TV will not be yours until you have paid in full: 104 weekly payments of $24.99, or $2,598.96 (plus tax). Retail prices are much lower. RentAmerica has the good sense *not* to mention either the alleged or actual prices for gold jewelry, refrigerators, freezers, the "bedroom suite," or the "living-room group." The brochure recommends: "Ask for Details!"

. . .

To understand their excesses, it might be helpful to contrast rent-to-own terms and interest rates to the consumer credit available to residents of wealthier neighborhoods, who

can receive a 10 percent discount on a purchase up to $300 at Woodward and Lothrop, for example, just by applying for a store card—though if they do not pay on time and in full, they owe 21 percent interest. Or at CompUSA, a computer store in the Maryland/Virginia suburbs, approved customers can charge a computer and pay no interest for six months; they pay accumulated interest, however, if they do not pay in full at that time. Seeing RentAmerica helps put these admittedly harsh, austere, and misleading terms into perspective.

A FESTIVAL OF DEBT

. . .

Poor neighborhoods in Washington, D.C., are plagued by finance companies peddling loans, to consolidate debt or to make home repairs, to people who are financially desperate or credit starved. These firms target minority, fixed- or low-income, low-wage, and Social Security-dependent households who often hold substantial equity in their homes as their sole resource. Not surprisingly, the finance companies charge high interest: from 36 to 50 percent. They tack on worthless, expensive "credit insurance." They offer shoddy work and pursue ruthless, haranguing collection policies. Sometimes they refinance these loans several times, piling on fees along the way: prepayment penalty fees, more credit insurance, and loan origination fees. They front for some of the country's largest financial institutions: NationsBank (after it acquired ChryslerFirst), Ford Financial Services (whose Associated Services division may keep it afloat), Chemical Bank, ITT, Fleet Financial Services, BankAmerica (through its Security Pacific division), General Motors, General Electric, Westinghouse, and Citicorp. These large lenders front money through lines of credit to finance companies, then buy up and bundle the loans and sell them on Wall Street via secondary securities markets. The customer may be left with shoddy repair work, a huge debt, the threat of foreclosure, and nobody to hold responsible.

. . .

While the poor have developed many creative strategies to provide the essentials of life, such as doubling up, working under the table, managing collective living, and negotiating ongoing exchanges with friends and kin, they are increasingly vulnerable in the current economic climate. When intergenerational network flows, employment, and government assistance fail them, when relatives can no longer provide small loans between checks or the exchange of food stamps for cash, poor people develop strategies to work the fringe banking system: pawning televisions and VCRs when between checks, redeeming them when they can; cashing their checks at America's Cash Express; paying their bills with money orders and moneygrams they purchase at ACE; using the poor person's telephone, the pager; and "renting" their grossly overpriced furniture and appliances for as long as they can.

. . . The same developers who refused to maintain or build low-cost urban housing have gone bust on overpriced condominiums, unnecessary office space, and underutilized shopping centers in the suburbs. The same lenders who disinvested in cities, jobs, workers, and infrastructure squandered their money on junk bonds and takeovers. Now they're back, extending credit to fringe banks for loans of last resort and thus passing on high-cost debt to the poor.

29

At the Elite Colleges

Peter Schmidt

C
O
N
T
E
X
T

Autumn and a new academic year are upon us, which means that selective colleges are engaged in the annual ritual of singing the praises of their new freshman classes. Surf the websites of such institutions and you will find press releases boasting that they have increased their black and Hispanic enrollments, admitted bumper crops of National Merit scholars or became the destination of choice for hordes of high school valedictorians. Many are bragging about the large share of applicants they rejected, as a way of conveying to the world just how popular and selective they are.

What they almost never say is that many of the applicants who were rejected were far more qualified than those accepted. Moreover, contrary to popular belief, it was not the black and Hispanic beneficiaries of affirmative action, but the rich white kids with cash and connections who elbowed most of the worthier applicants aside.

Researchers with access to closely guarded college admissions data have found that, on the whole, about 15 percent of freshmen enrolled at America's highly selective colleges are white teens who failed to meet their institutions' minimum admissions standards. Five years ago, two researchers working for the Educational Testing Service, Anthony Carnevale and Stephen Rose, took the academic profiles of students admitted into 146 colleges in the top two tiers of Barron's college guide and matched them up against the institutions' advertised requirements in terms of high school grade point average, SAT or ACT scores, letters of recommendation, and records of involvement in extracurricular activities. White students who failed to make the grade on all counts were nearly twice as prevalent on such campuses as black and Hispanic students who received an admissions break based on their ethnicity or race.

Who are these mediocre white students getting into institutions such as Harvard, Wellesley, Notre Dame, Duke, and the University of Virginia? A sizable number are recruited athletes who, research has shown, will perform worse on average than other students with similar academic profiles, mainly as a result of the demands their coaches will place on them. A larger share, however, are students who gained admission through their ties to people the institution wanted to keep happy, with alumni, donors, faculty members, administrators, and politicians topping the list.

Applicants who stood no chance of gaining admission without connections are only the most blatant beneficiaries of such admissions preferences. Except perhaps at the very summit of the applicant pile—that lofty place occupied by young people too brilliant for anyone in their right mind to turn down—colleges routinely favor those who have connections over those who don't. While some applicants gain admission by legitimately beating out their peers, many others get into exclusive colleges the same way people get into trendy night clubs, by knowing the management or flashing cash at the person manning the velvet rope.

Leaders at many selective colleges say they have no choice but to instruct their admissions offices to reward those who financially support their institutions, because keeping donors happy is the only way they can keep the place afloat. They also say that the money they take in through such admissions preferences helps them provide financial aid to students in need. But many of the colleges granting such preferences are already well-financed, with

huge endowments. And, in many cases, little of the money they take in goes toward serving the less-advantaged.

A few years ago, *The Chronicle of Higher Education* looked at colleges with more than $500 million in their endowments and found that most served disproportionately few students from families with incomes low enough to qualify for federal Pell Grants. A separate study of flagship state universities conducted by the Education Trust found that those universities' enrollments of Pell Grant recipients had been shrinking, even as the number of students qualifying for such grants had gone up. Just 40 percent of the financial aid money being distributed by public colleges is going to students with documented financial need. Most such money is being used to offer merit-based scholarships or tuition discounts to potential recruits who can enhance a college's reputation, or appear likely to cover the rest of their tuition tab and to donate down the road.

Given such trends, is it any wonder that young people from the wealthiest fourth of society are about 25 times as likely as those from the bottom fourth to enroll in a selective college, or that, over the past two decades, the middle class has been steadily getting squeezed out of such institutions by those with more money?

A degree from a selective college can open many doors for a talented young person from a humble background. But rather than promoting social mobility, our nation's selective colleges appear to be thwarting it, by turning away applicants who have excelled given their circumstances and offering second chances to wealthy and connected young people who have squandered many of the advantages life has offered them.

When social mobility goes away, at least two dangerous things can happen. The privileged class that produces most of our nation's leaders can become complacent enough to foster mediocrity, and less-fortunate segments of our society can become resigned to the notion that hard work will not get them anywhere.

. . .

30

Is the Near-Trillion-Dollar Student Loan Bubble About to Pop?

Sarah Jaffe

. . .

Tarah Toney worked two full-time jobs to put herself through college, at McMurry University in Abilene, Texas, and still has $75,000 in debt. She graduated in six years with a Bachelor's in English and wanted to go on to teach high school.

"Right about the time I graduated, Texas severely cut funding to our education system—thanks, Perry—and school districts across the state stopped hiring and started firing. It became abundantly clear that there was no job for me in the Texas public school system," she told me. "After two months of job searching I got a temporary position in a real estate office."

She continued, "In August my post-graduation grace period was up and all of the payments on my student loans amount to $500/month. Adding that expense to my monthly

bills puts me at $2,100 per month. If I don't make my payments they will revoke my real estate license, which I need in order to do my job."

Max Parker (not his real name) enrolled at Texas A&M in College Station, Texas to get a BA in economics and a BS in physics. His freshman year was great—his parents had saved some money to help pay the bills, and after that he was able to get "more generous" student loans. He took a job to help cover the fees and bills that his student loans wouldn't cover, and worked about 35 hours a week during his sophomore year while taking 15 hours of classes—but found that his grades dropped with his workload. . . . He adjusted his course load, but in the spring of his junior year, a family emergency led him to withdraw midway through the semester, taking incompletes in his courses.

"I am 25 years old now, and shacking up in my parents' guest bedroom," he told me. "I have successfully made four payments on my student loans in the past three and a half years. I have over $48,000 dollars of student loan debt, and absolutely nothing to show for it. No degrees. No certificates. No qualifications. I have continued my education to the best of my ability since leaving A&M, but always at community colleges and always paying for everything out of pocket. As you can imagine, since I'm not 'qualified' for a decent paying job, my savings for school piles up very slowly, and then disappears when August and January roll around. I haven't been back to school in about a year now, and I currently work at Subway, making sandwiches. I don't make my loan payments."

He's about to join the military because he sees it as his only option. "I am depressed at the idea of signing my life away for four years so I can fight someone else's wars. I am angry beyond belief that it's come to this" he said.

Kate Sternwood (not her real name) was recently laid off from a job at a nonprofit organization where she was making $55,000 a year. She has $40,000 in debt from the University of Massachusetts. "When I called my repayment program to tell them I was losing my job, they told me my payment would go from $400 a month to $384 a month because making $55K a year I already qualified for the 'hardship' rate."

The agency in question is Van Ru, a collection agency that takes loans from the Dept. of Education if they go into default. Sternwood said they can't even tell her what the rate will be when she's paid enough to get out of default because they don't know which bank will end up with her loans.

. . .

The story is the same around the country. The economy is stagnant, the job market terrible, and graduates who used to believe their degrees would lead to good jobs are struggling. Meanwhile, the unforgiving student loan system continues to penalize them for their inability to pay.

THE BUBBLE

Since the beginning of the recession, most types of credit have gone down. The only exception to that rule has been student loans.

A recent piece in the Atlantic noted that student debt has grown by 511 percent since 1999. At that time, only $90 billion in student loans were outstanding—by the second quarter of 2011, that balance was up to $550 billion, according to the New York Fed. And the Department of Education estimates that outstanding loans total closer to $805 billion—and that number will pass $1 trillion soon.

As student loans rise, so has delinquency. Phil Izzo at the *Wall Street Journal* reported that 11.2 percent of student loans were more than 90 days past due and that rate was

steadily going up. "Only credit cards had a higher rate of delinquency—12.2 percent—but those numbers have been on a steady decline for the past four quarters," he noted.

It shouldn't be surprising to anyone that student loan defaults are going up as young workers especially are struggling in the current economy. Izzo reported, "Workers between 20 and 24 years old have a 14.6 percent unemployment rate, compared to the national average of 9.1 percent recorded in July. That comes even as the share of 20- to 24-year-olds who are working or looking for a job is at the lowest level since the 1970s, before women entered the labor force en masse."

In his *Huffington Post* blog, Michigan Democratic Representative Hansen Clarke noted, "This year, the average borrower graduating from a four-year college left school with roughly $24,000 of student debt, despite the grim statistic that—according to a Rutgers University study – only 56 percent of 2010 graduates were able to find work following completion of their studies."

. . .

How did student loans go from "good debt" that could be expected to pay off—Pew found that an adult with a bachelor's degree earns about $650,000 more during their career than a typical high school graduate—to a bubble that threatens the economy?

According to the National Center for Education Statistics, college enrollment skyrocketed 38 percent, from 14.8 million to 20.4 million, between 1999 and 2009. (The previous decade it had only gone up 9 percent.) This should be a good thing—except it was not accompanied by measures to make tuition affordable for working families who wanted to send their kids to school. Combined with the decline in the type of union manufacturing jobs that used to allow workers to be comfortably middle-class without a college degree, we've wound up with working-class families taking on debt to send their kids to college, which they are told will help those kids make more money.

. . .

As student loans are relatively easy to come by, both from the government and from private lenders increasingly getting into the game, universities have been able to keep hiking tuition without seeing a drop in enrollment. Students are still advised that student debt is "good debt," as noted above, and that they will be able to pay it off—but the costs are rising far more rapidly than average incomes.

The *Philadelphia Inquirer* reported that Temple University has raised tuition every year since 1995—it's gone up 9.9 percent for in-state students. At the University of Pennsylvania (an Ivy League private university—Temple is the state school) tuition went up 3.9 percent to $42,098 a year. "Throw in a dormitory bed, meals and books, and the price reaches $57,360," wrote *Inquirer* reporter Jeff Gammage.

. . .

All of these factors have combined to send student loan debt into the stratosphere. . . . [S]tudent debt has far outplaced the growth of all other household debt over the past 10 years—including increasing twice as fast as housing debt. . . . [T]he same banks that broke the economy by creating that housing bubble are responsible for the student debt crisis—as well as the federal government, which issues student loans.

. . .

Student loans are not really comparable to housing loans, though: if you default on your student loans, there's nothing to repossess. Instead, you'll face a drop in your credit rating, and constant pressure from . . . collection agencies. . . . They can garnish your wages, and even if you declare bankruptcy, your student loans don't go away. . . . [M]iss a payment, and your interest rate goes up, creating a punitive spiral of debt there's no way to escape from.

Even if mass default isn't likely to happen the same way mortgage defaults did, . . . the cost of college and debt is already slowing the economy. . . . [A]ll the money going into

colleges and the pockets of lenders in the form of interest is being funneled away from other places it could be spent.

. . .

THE SOLUTIONS

. . . [J]ust last year in his State of the Union, President Obama proclaimed, "No one should go broke because they chose to go to college." He called for student loans to be forgiven after 20 years—10 for those who go into public service—and a $10,000 tax credit for families paying for a four-year college.

But that's not a solution for people like Parker, who was unable to finish school because of the cost, or Toney, who wanted to go into public service but saw that door shut in her face with state budget cuts. They're in debt now, not in 20 years, and $10,000 doesn't begin to cover their debt. . . . As tuition goes up thousands of dollars a year, a $10,000 tax credit looks pretty measly—and the chances of getting even that through the current Congress are slim to none.

The *Philadelphia Inquirer* reported that New Jersey's state legislature has a bill under consideration that would ban state colleges from raising tuition more than 2 percent a year. Keeping tuition down is certainly part of the solution—tuition growing faster than wages is a recipe for defaults as students struggle to pay back their loans. In addition, just as housing prices going way up wound up pricing many people out of home-buying, increases in tuition will price students out of an education—particularly if the benefits of that education become less clear, as jobs remain hard to come by.

. . .

An idea that's been getting a lot of traction lately—including an online petition pushed by MoveOn member Robert Applebaum that has 320,000 signatures as of this writing—is student loan forgiveness as economic stimulus.

Rep. Hansen Clarke introduced a resolution in Congress, co-sponsored by 12 other members, that includes student loan forgiveness in its suggestions for bringing down the U.S.'s "true debt burden."

In his Huffington Post blog, Clarke wrote:

> Congress is now completely focused on reducing debt. This would be a positive development, if not for one detail: it's focused on the wrong kind of debt.
>
> With over a quarter of all American homeowners "underwater"—owing more on their homes than their homes are worth—and total student loans slated to exceed $1 trillion this year, it is household debt, not government debt, that is constraining spending, undermining confidence, and precluding sustainable long-term growth.

Clarke is right. For years, credit was a substitute for real wage growth in the U.S. And now as that debt burden has grown unsustainable, working families are barely able to keep up with payments, let alone spend enough to get the economy back on its feet. And student debt, as we've shown, is on the least sustainable trajectory of all.

. . .

Student debt forgiveness would put $400 a month back into Sternwood's pockets. . . . Even just forgiving the government loans would probably allow Parker to finish his degree instead of going to war.

Of course the resolution is unlikely to pass Speaker John Boehner's Congress, and even if it does, it's just a resolution. But the instant popularity of Applebaum's petition shows

something: Americans realize that student debt at the current levels is completely untenable, and something must be done soon.

Republicans love to talk about the debt we're leaving our children with. But saddling them with record levels of student debt and no jobs with which to earn money to pay it back hurts young people much, much more than government budget deficits.

. . .

31

Students with Disabilities

Financial Aid Policy Issues

Thomas R. Wolanin

About nine percent of all undergraduate students in the United States reported having a disability in 2000. This amounts to approximately 1.3 million students. . . . Students with disabilities generally have lower incomes than their peers without disabilities. Thirty-seven percent of students with disabilities in high school came from families with household incomes below $25,000, compared to only 20% of their peers. At the college level, students from the lowest-income quartile have the highest rate of disability, especially independent students. . . .

Low-income students with disabilities, like other low-income students, need financial assistance in order to afford the costs of higher education. However, being disproportionately low-income, students with disabilities have an even greater need for financial assistance than other students. Thus, the financial barriers to higher education opportunities faced by students from low-income families are also even more widespread for students with disabilities . . . .

HAVING A DISABILITY IS EXPENSIVE

In addition to the problems faced by all low-income students, students with disabilities from low-income families face particular financial barriers to higher education not faced by other students. To meet their special needs, persons with disabilities often receive services from a variety of professionals. These may include counselors, doctors, psychologists, and therapists of all kinds, who must be visited in their respective offices, clinics, and hospitals. For persons with disabilities, insurance payments and support from public and private agencies rarely cover the entire cost of the treatments and services they receive. The difference is made up out-of-pocket.

Having a disability also involves incidental costs such as special foods to meet dietary restrictions, cab fares to the doctor, wheelchair maintenance, dog food and veterinary bills for a guide dog, over-the-counter medications, and higher utility bills from running computers and assistive devices. . . . For a low-income student with a disability, in theory at

least, all of these additional costs of having a disability can be met through student financial aid sources. . . . Unfortunately, the system does not live up to its ideals, and faces difficulties in practice. . . . Students with disabilities must document to the financial aid administrator the expenses related to their disabilities that are not provided for by another source. This requires self-confidence and self-advocacy skills that often have not been well developed in students with disabilities. These students must undertake the difficult and complex task of cataloging and documenting all of the expenses related to their disabilities and reducing that amount by support received from elsewhere, such as Vocational Rehabilitation (VR). This is a formidable challenge that would test the skills of anyone and is sometimes unreasonable for students with disabilities.

. . .

Currently, fully meeting the needs of students with disabilities would require diverting resources from other low-income students. This would not be a just or desirable result. The most important policy change required to meet the financial needs of low-income students with disabilities is to expand the amount of financial aid available for all low-income students. Otherwise, the process becomes a matter of rationing and redistributing limited financial aid dollars among various groups of financially needy students, including those with disabilities.

HAVING A DISABILITY IS TIME CONSUMING

Generally, students with disabilities in higher education can attain the same academic levels as their peers without disabilities; however, students with disabilities cannot do it as quickly. Students with disabilities may have conditions that slow them down in general. For example, it takes longer to walk from point A to point B when one's energy and stamina are sapped by chronic illness. A person in a wheelchair or with cerebral palsy needs more time to bathe, dress, shop, and accomplish other self-care tasks. Students with disabilities have multiple demands on their time for the treatments and services required to meet their needs apart from their studies. Trips to doctors, therapists, counselors, and administrators take time. It also takes time to acquire, set up, learn how to use, and maintain auxiliary learning aids such as electronic readers or videotext displays. Software bugs and computer crashes are not just inconveniences for a student with a disability, who must have electronic aids to study—these technical glitches bring a halt to learning.

Further, students with disabilities often take longer to perform academic tasks. Many disabilities, particularly learning disabilities, increase the time needed to process information, which is the central task of most academic work. A student with dyslexia needs more time to read and understand a given amount of written text compared with a student without this disability. The speed at which an aide reads text to a blind student is slower than the reading speed of sighted students. Listening to a lecture over again on tape takes longer than reviewing notes taken in the classroom.

. . .

Given the time demands faced by students with disabilities, it follows that the time to degree completion for students with disabilities is longer than for their peers without disabilities. . . . The longer time that students with disabilities need to complete their studies increases their costs of higher education. Their forgone income is greater than that of their peers without disabilities. Most importantly, even if students with disabilities are taking a reduced or part-time course load, they still have to live full time. They face additional years of room and board costs, semester fees, and the extra costs associated with their disability to make the same academic progress that their peers without disabilities make in a shorter

time. They may also be charged more per credit hour or per course if they are taking less than the standard full-time course load.

. . .

In sum, low-income students with disabilities generally have a greater need for financial aid than their peers without disabilities. But, they face additional obstacles in assembling the package of resources to pay for college. A larger burden is placed on students with disabilities who may have less capacity to bear it.

. . .

32

Trafficking in Persons Report 2011

U.S. Department of State

WHAT IS TRAFFICKING IN PERSONS?

Over the past 15 years, "trafficking in persons" or "human trafficking" have been used as umbrella terms for activities involved when one person obtains or holds another person in compelled service. The Trafficking Victims Protection Act (TVPA) describes this compelled service using a number of different terms: involuntary servitude, slavery, debt bondage, and forced labor.

. . .

Major forms of human trafficking include:

FORCED LABOR

Also known as involuntary servitude, forced labor may result when unscrupulous employers exploit workers made more vulnerable by high rates of unemployment, poverty, crime, discrimination, corruption, political conflict, or cultural acceptance of the practice. Immigrants are particularly vulnerable, but individuals also may be forced into labor in their own countries. Female victims of forced or bonded labor, especially women and girls in domestic servitude, are often sexually exploited as well.

SEX TRAFFICKING

When an adult is coerced, forced, or deceived into prostitution—or maintained in prostitution through coercion—that person is a victim of trafficking. All of those involved in

recruiting, transporting, harboring, receiving, or obtaining the person for that purpose have committed a trafficking crime. Sex trafficking also can occur within debt bondage, as women and girls are forced to continue in prostitution through the use of unlawful "debt" purportedly incurred through their transportation, recruitment, or even their crude "sale"—which exploiters insist they must pay off before they can be free. It is critical to understand that a person's initial consent to participate in prostitution is not legally determinative: if they are thereafter held in service through psychological manipulation or physical force, they are trafficking victims and should receive benefits outlined in the Palermo Protocol and applicable domestic laws.

BONDED LABOR

One form of force or coercion is the use of a bond, or debt. Often referred to as "bonded labor" or "debt bondage," the practice has long been prohibited under U.S. law by the term peonage. . . . Workers around the world fall victim to debt bondage when traffickers or recruiters unlawfully exploit an initial debt the worker assumed as part of the terms of employment. Workers also may inherit debt in more traditional systems of bonded labor. In South Asia, for example, it is estimated that there are millions of trafficking victims working to pay off their ancestors' debts.

DEBT BONDAGE AMONG MIGRANT LABORERS

Abuses of contracts and hazardous conditions of employment for migrant laborers do not necessarily constitute human trafficking. However, the imposition of illegal costs and debts on these laborers in the source country, often with the support of labor agencies and employers in the destination country, can contribute to a situation of debt bondage. This is the case even when the worker's status in the country is tied to the employer in the context of employment-based temporary work programs.

INVOLUNTARY DOMESTIC SERVITUDE

A unique form of forced labor is the involuntary servitude of domestic workers, whose workplaces are informal, connected to their off-duty living quarters, and not often shared with other workers. Such an environment, which often socially isolates domestic workers, is conducive to nonconsensual exploitation since authorities cannot inspect private property as easily as they can inspect formal workplaces. Investigators and service providers report many cases of untreated illnesses and, tragically, widespread sexual abuse, which in some cases may be symptoms of a situation of involuntary servitude.

FORCED CHILD LABOR

Most international organizations and national laws recognize children may legally engage in certain forms of work. There is a growing consensus, however, that the worst forms of

child labor, including bonded and forced labor of children, should be eradicated. A child can be a victim of human trafficking regardless of the location of that nonconsensual exploitation. Indicators of possible forced labor of a child include situations in which the child appears to be in the custody of a non-family member who has the child perform work that financially benefits someone outside the child's family and does not offer the child the option of leaving.

Anti-trafficking responses should supplement, not replace, traditional actions against child labor, such as remediation and education. When children are enslaved, however, their abusers should not escape criminal punishment by virtue of long-standing administrative responses to child labor practices.

CHILD SOLDIERS

Child soldiering is a manifestation of human trafficking when it involves the unlawful recruitment or use of children—through force, fraud, or coercion—as combatants or for labor or sexual exploitation by armed forces. Perpetrators may be government forces, paramilitary organizations, or rebel groups. Many children are forcibly abducted to be used as combatants. Others are unlawfully made to work as porters, cooks, guards, servants, messengers, or spies. Young girls can be forced to marry or have sex with male combatants. Both male and female child soldiers are often sexually abused and are at high risk of contracting sexually transmitted diseases.

CHILD SEX TRAFFICKING

According to UNICEF, as many as two million children are subjected to prostitution in the global commercial sex trade. International covenants and protocols obligate criminalization of the commercial sexual exploitation of children. The use of children in the commercial sex trade is prohibited under both the Palermo Protocol and U.S. law as well as by legislation in countries around the world. There can be no exceptions and no cultural or socioeconomic rationalizations preventing the rescue of children from sexual servitude. Sex trafficking has devastating consequences for minors, including long-lasting physical and psychological trauma, disease (including HIV/AIDS), drug addiction, unwanted pregnancy, malnutrition, social ostracism, and possible death.

. . .

VICTIMS' STORIES

U.S.A.

Alissa, 16, met an older man at a convenience store in Dallas and after a few dates accepted his invitation to move in with him. But soon Alissa's new boyfriend convinced

her to be an escort for him, accompanying men on dates and having sex with them for money. He took her to an area known for street prostitution and forced her to hand over all of her earnings. He made Alissa get a tattoo of his nicknames, branding her as his property, and he posted prostitution advertisements with her picture on an Internet site. He rented hotel rooms around Dallas and forced Alissa to have sex with men who responded to the ads. The man, who kept an assault rifle in the closet of his apartment, threatened Alissa and physically assaulted her on multiple occasions. The man later pled guilty to trafficking Alissa.

. . .

HONDURAS-U.S.A.

Maira was 15 when two well-dressed men driving a nice car approached her and two friends in a small Honduran village. They told the girls they were businessmen and offered to take them to the United States to work in a textile factory. Maira thought it was the perfect opportunity to help her single mother, who struggled to support seven children.

But upon arriving in Houston, the girls were held captive, beaten, raped, and forced to work in cantinas that doubled as brothels. Men would come to the cantina and choose a beer and a girl, sometimes as young as 12. They would pay for the beer and sit with the girl while she drank it. If they wanted to have sex with the girl, they would take her to the back and pay cash for a mattress, paper towels, and spermicide. The captors beat the girls daily if they did not make enough money.

After six years, Maira was able to escape the cantina and return to her mother with the help of a kind American family. Her two friends remain missing.

. . .

PHILIPPINES-U.S.A.

Maria came to the United States with some 50 other Filipino nationals who were promised housing, transportation, and lucrative jobs at country clubs and hotels under the guest worker program. Like the others, Maria dutifully paid the substantial recruitment fees to come to the United States. But when she arrived, she found that there was no employment secured for her. She did not work for weeks, but the recruiters seized her passport and prohibited her from leaving their house. She and other workers slept side-by-side on the floors of the kitchen, garage, and dining room. They were fed primarily chicken feet and innards. When the workers complained, the recruiters threatened to call the police or immigration services to arrest and deport them. A federal grand jury indicted the two defendants for conspiracy to hold the workers in a condition of forced labor.

. . .

INDIA-U.S.A.

Ravi was among hundreds of workers lured to the United States from India by an oil rig construction company operating in the Gulf Coast. Lacking skilled welders and pipefitters to help rebuild after Hurricane Katrina struck the area in 2005, the company brought Ravi and others from India on [work permit] visas, promising them permanent visas and residency. But, the promises were false. Instead, Ravi was forced to live with 23 other men in a small room with no privacy and two toilets. The camp was lined with barbed wire and

security guards, so no one on the outside knew Ravi's whereabouts. The company charged so much for food and a bunk bed that Ravi was unable to send any money home or repay the money he borrowed for his travel expenses to the United States. When the workers began organizing to protest their working conditions, the company began arbitrary firings and private deportations of the protest leaders. Those who remained filed a class action lawsuit and applied for TVPA immigration services.

. . .

MOVING TOWARDS A DECADE OF DELIVERY – PREVENTION

The demand for cheap goods, services, labor, and sex opens opportunities for the exploitation of vulnerable populations. And it is on this demand that human trafficking thrives. People are bought and sold as commodities within and across borders to satisfy demand from buyers. Poverty, unemployment, lack of opportunity, social upheaval, and political instability facilitate traffickers' ability to recruit victims, but they do not in themselves cause trafficking. The economic reality is that human trafficking is driven by profits. If nobody paid for sex, sex trafficking would not exist. If nobody paid for goods produced with any amount of slavery, forced labor in manufacturing would be a thing of the past. Increasingly, anti-trafficking actors are looking to combat modern slavery from the demand side rather than focusing on arrests and prosecutions (the supply side) alone.

. . .

Governments can go a long way toward tackling demand. They can, for example, require that government contractors and subcontractors ensure that employees are not hired or recruited through fraudulent means or the use of excessive fees. Such policies would increase transparency and make it more difficult for unscrupulous labor brokers to use debt bondage as a means of providing cheap labor for government contracts. This is particularly important for third-country nationals, who are often imported for large construction projects and who are more susceptible to exploitation due to distance and isolation, language barriers, and dependence on the employer for visas or work permits, among other factors. Public-private partnerships that create transparency in supply chains can have a significant impact on demand reduction, helping to make freedom the business of both governments and the private sector.

Governments can attack demand for commercial sex by establishing "zero tolerance" policies for government employees and contractors who participate in trafficking or procure commercial sex acts. Such policies should make clear that contracting and subcontracting companies are responsible for notifying employees of the prohibited behavior, and they should provide penalties for violations as severe as termination of the contract and/or debarment from future government contracting. This gives companies, many of whom stand to lose multimillion dollar contracts if penalized, a major incentive to ensure that their employees and subcontractors are in no way contributing to the demand that contributes to sex trafficking.

. . .

WATCH WHAT YOU EAT: SLAVERY AND FOOD

The dusty images of slaves working on plantations line bookshelves and museum walls, but the demand for cheap goods in a globalized economy sustains slavery today in fields

and farms. Transcontinental slavery and the Triangle Trade drove the bygone mercantile empires of Europe and the Americas. But the International Labour Organization (ILO) estimates 60 percent of child labor worldwide is in agriculture, and agricultural products comprise the largest category of items on the List of Goods Produced by Child Labor or Forced Labor published by the U.S. Department of Labor (DOL).

From the cocoa farms of West Africa to the cotton fields of Uzbekistan to the tomato fields of the United States, this modern form of slavery remains common in the agricultural industry and is marked by techniques that are anything but modern. According to DOL, there may be more forced child laborers in farming than in manufacturing. In some countries, particularly in South Asia, families of farmers continue to inherit the debts of their ancestors that, in many cases, have been passed down for generations. And slavery reportedly extends into the oceans, with forced labor rampant in the commercial fishing industries in some regions.

Businesses and governments both have important roles to play in eradicating slavery in supply chains. In this age of increasingly aware customers, companies will have to be more thorough in tracing their raw materials and monitoring their supply chains. Governments must be more diligent in enforcing existing laws and regulations. With the passage of new laws, raw material traceability is shifting from a voluntary best practice into a legal obligation. Companies in all industries are facing growing pressure to understand the conditions under which their raw materials were attained.

PROMULGATING BUSINESS STANDARDS

In today's globalized economy, there are often complex intersections between legal business operations and illegal human trafficking. Increasingly, the private sector is acknowledging its role in eradicating human trafficking, both in preventative measures to ensure that corporations are not fueling demand for forced labor and in proactive initiatives to alleviate or ameliorate such abuses. There is also growing public interest to know where and how goods and foods are produced, manufactured, processed, and distributed. Consumers, activists, and investors are urging companies to sign and implement ethical codes of conduct.

Businesses play a crucial role in ensuring that forced labor does not contribute to the products we buy. Given the complexity of today's supply chains, however, the most effective solutions for ending forced labor will come from collaboration among governments, corporations, civil society, and consumers. Some recent examples of multi-stakeholder approaches to addressing slavery in supply chains have shown great promise.

. . .

The California Transparency in Supply Chains Act of 2010 requires retail sellers and manufacturers in California to publicly disclose their efforts to eradicate slavery and human trafficking throughout their direct supply chains. The legislation applies to retailers and manufacturers with more than $100 million in annual worldwide gross receipts. It affects more than 3,000 companies doing business in California. These companies represent approximately 87 percent of economic activity in the state, which has the eighth largest economy in the world. Beginning in January 2012, companies affected by the act will have to post on their websites what policies they have in place to ensure that their supply chains are free of slavery and human trafficking. These policies can include evaluating and addressing the risk of human trafficking, auditing suppliers, and training employees and management on human trafficking and slavery. The text of the California law can be found at http://go.usa.gov/D8n.

PEOPLE ARE NOT COLLATERAL

One of the most common assumptions about "average" trafficking victims is that they come from the poorest, most isolated communities. Studies of populations in countries of origin for transnational and internal trafficking have shown that the incidence of trafficking is highest among those who have become empowered enough to aspire to a better life but have few good options for fulfilling those aspirations. They have attended a girls' school and now realize they are overeducated for the few options in their villages. They have seen someone return home with money to provide for their families. They have watched a television show that depicts the excitement of city life, or they simply have enough courage to try and make a better life for themselves, if only they knew where to start.

That's where the traffickers come in. Exploiting the information gap, they offer to make that connection—to a good job, a better life, a transportation option. They prey on their victims' innate hope and ability to conceive of some opportunity for a better life. They exploit their victims' trust and confidence in their own ability to succeed. They find people who have nothing and coerce them into using their lives and freedom as collateral to guarantee a better future. While broad-based economic initiatives cannot automatically be construed as anti-trafficking prevention activities, governments must recognize the inequality of access to capital when considering efforts to reduce vulnerability to modern slavery. Migrant workers should not need to incur debt from labor brokers to secure jobs overseas. Instead, governments could provide small-scale loans to cover travel costs and protect workers' rights while they are abroad. Entire villages should not be trapped in bonded labor because of debts inherited from previous generations. Instead, governments could provide legal alternatives for credit and enforce decades-old laws banning generational debt bondage.

Modern history has proven that microcredit and microfinance can improve the status of women, promote better nutrition, increase access to healthcare and education, and broaden communities' access to credit. When combined with targeted anti-trafficking programming, microfinance initiatives can act as liberators, providing opportunities without risk and rehabilitation with a money-backed future. And micro-lending is not the only solution—putting traffickers in prison and distributing their ill-gotten gains to their victims is the ultimate debt forgiveness program.

SENDING AND RECEIVING: THE CHALLENGE OF LABOR IN A GLOBAL SOCIETY

Migrants are vulnerable to modern slavery. Women travel with dreams of better lives and jobs as waitresses or maids, only to be enslaved in prostitution or domestic servitude. Workers are trapped in debt bondage—in myriad ways, as a result of the costs of migration, such as recruitment fees. And it is not just illegal migration; the 2011 reporting year saw cases around the world where the victims traveled to their destination country through legal means, only to be enslaved after arrival.

. . .

While migration is an important tool for economic development from the individual level to the national level, there is an urgent need to strengthen international cooperation and standards to manage labor migration. According to the IOM, most countries in the world—and not just in the developing world—lack the capacity to manage effectively the international mobility of people today. The increased flows and the dramatic growth of a profit-minded recruitment industry that operates across borders mean that today's

migrants are vulnerable to a wide range of abuses, including situations of forced labor and sex trafficking.

International migration is relatively unregulated. At best, it is dominated by a handful of bilateral agreements—with varying degrees of implementations—and nonbinding bilateral memoranda of understanding or regional arrangements. At worst, it is controlled by unscrupulous private recruiters whose deceit and surcharges can quickly place migrants in debt bondage.

Even when policies are in place to allow for legal labor migration, governments must act to ensure the protection of migrants throughout the process. Where there are government-to-government agreements (increasingly common between sending and destination countries), they do not diminish the need for worker protections in "sponsorship" or "guestworker" programs. Much needs to be done to prevent migrant laborers from subsequent exploitation under these programs. The high level of documented exploitation of low-skilled workers—particularly domestic workers—throughout the Middle East, for example, is proof of this vulnerability.

. . .

The 2011 reporting period showed a disturbing trend: cases in which domestic servant guestworkers who had suffered sexual abuse in the home were then turned over by their bosses to third parties for prostitution, unable to seek help because of restrictive guestworker laws and the debts that they owed.

These abuses are possible because the normal employer-employee relationship is skewed by the financial pressure of recruiting fees that are out of balance with the services rendered or that represent much of the money the migrants would earn if everything went perfectly. Sometimes, the most effective threats by employers who want to keep foreign employees fearful and working are threats not to allow them to work. Because guestworkers are often restricted from obtaining outside employment, being banned from the workplace does not represent freedom but can be, in itself, the coercion that the Palermo Protocol seeks to preclude. For example, when workers attempt to claim the salary they've earned or even just to get enough food to live, employers often threaten to confine them to a dormitory, where they will be unable to seek outside employment and forced to watch their debt mount.

. . .

Continued identification of trafficking victims among migrant populations underlines the need for a strong international framework to manage labor migration. Migration governance must focus on facilitating humane and orderly migration policies for the benefit of all. This must be done at the national, regional, and international levels, as suggested by the ILO's Multilateral Framework on Labor Migration. Without an adequate framework, the exploitation and abuse of migrant workers will become increasingly dire as labor migration continues to grow.

. . .

UNITED STATES OF AMERICA (TIER 1)

The United States is a source, transit, and destination country for men, women, and children subjected to forced labor, debt bondage, document servitude, and sex trafficking. Trafficking occurs for commercial sexual exploitation in street prostitution, massage parlors, and brothels, and for labor in domestic service, agriculture, manufacturing, janitorial services, hotel services, hospitality industries, construction, health and elder care, and strip club dancing. Vulnerabilities are increasingly found in visa programs for legally documented

students and temporary workers who typically fill labor needs in the hospitality, landscaping, construction, food service, and agricultural industries. . . . U.S. citizen victims, both adults and children, are predominantly found in sex trafficking; U.S. citizen child victims are often runaways, troubled, and homeless youth. Foreign victims are more often found in labor trafficking than sex trafficking. In 2010, the number of female foreign victims of labor trafficking served through victim services programs increased compared with 2009. The top countries of origin for foreign victims in FY 2010 were Thailand, India, Mexico, Philippines, Haiti, Honduras, El Salvador, and the Dominican Republic.

. . .

Recommendations for the United States: Improve data collection on human trafficking cases at the federal, state and local levels; continue federal partnerships with state and local law enforcement agencies to encourage training, protocols, and dedicated and incentivized personnel at the state and local level; train field reporting collectors to recognize and report on human trafficking; mandate training in the detection of human trafficking for Department of Labor and Equal Employment Opportunity Commission investigators; increase the incorporation of anti-trafficking efforts into existing structures such as labor, child protection, education, housing, victim services, immigration courts, runaway/homeless youth, and juvenile justice programs; provide victim identification training for immigration detention and removal officers and conduct screening in immigration detention centers; increase funding for victim services, including legal services; offer comprehensive services to identified, eligible victims regardless of type of immigration relief sought, if any; increase training for consular officers to reduce vulnerabilities in visa programs; examine guestworker programs to reduce vulnerabilities; conduct briefings for domestic workers of foreign diplomats to ensure that they know their rights; improve oversight and enforcement of employment-based visas to forestall vulnerability and abuse; increase cooperation between the private and public sectors to encourage business practices that rid supply chains of human trafficking; and expand anti-trafficking outreach, services, and training in the insular areas.

. . .

33

Wealth Gaps Rise to Record Highs Between Whites, Blacks, Hispanics: Twenty-to-One

Rakesh Kochhar, Richard Fry, and Paul Taylor
for the Pew Research Center

The median wealth of white households is 20 times that of black households and 18 times that of Hispanic households, according to a Pew Research Center analysis of newly available government data from 2009.

These lopsided wealth ratios are the largest since the government began publishing such data a quarter century ago and roughly twice the size of the ratios that had prevailed between these three groups for the two decades prior to the Great Recession that ended in 2009.

The Pew Research analysis finds that, in percentage terms, the bursting of the housing market bubble in 2006 and the recession that followed from late 2007 to mid-2009 took

a far greater toll on the wealth of minorities than whites. From 2005 to 2009, inflation-adjusted median wealth fell by 66% among Hispanic households and 53% among black households, compared with just 16% among white households.

As a result of these declines, the typical black household had just $5,677 in wealth (assets minus debts) in 2009; the typical Hispanic household had $6,325 in wealth; and the typical white household had $113,149.

Moreover, about a third of black (35%) and Hispanic (31%) households had zero or negative net worth in 2009, compared with 15% of white households. In 2005, the comparable shares had been 29% for blacks, 23% for Hispanics and 11% for whites.

Hispanics and blacks are the nation's two largest minority groups, making up 16% and 12% of the U.S. population respectively.

. . .

Plummeting house values were the principal cause of the recent erosion in household wealth among all groups, with Hispanics hit hardest by the meltdown in the housing market.

From 2005 to 2009, the median level of home equity held by Hispanic homeowners declined by half—from $99,983 to $49,145—while the homeownership rate among Hispanics was also falling, from 51% to 47%. A geographic analysis suggests the reason: A disproportionate share of Hispanics live in California, Florida, Nevada and Arizona, which were in the vanguard of the housing real estate market bubble of the 1990s and early 2000s but that have since been among the states experiencing the steepest declines in housing values.

. . .

White and black homeowners also saw the median value of their home equity decline during this period, but not by as much as Hispanics. Among white homeowners, the decline was from $115,364 in 2005 to $95,000 in 2009. Among black homeowners, it was from $76,910 in 2005 to $59,000 in 2009. There was little or no change during this period in the homeownership rate for whites and blacks; it fell from 47% to 46% among blacks and was unchanged at 74% among whites.

. . .

Household wealth is the accumulated sum of assets (houses, cars, savings and checking accounts, stocks and mutual funds, retirement accounts, etc.) minus the sum of debt (mortgages, auto loans, credit card debt, etc.). It is different from household income, which measures the annual inflow of wages, interest, profits and other sources of earning. Wealth gaps between whites, blacks and Hispanics have always been much greater than income gaps.

The 2005 to 2009 time frame allows for a before-and-after look at the impact of the Great Recession. However, those dates do not align perfectly with the downturn, which ran from December 2007 to June 2009, according to the National Bureau of Economic Research.

In 2005, both the stock and housing markets were still rising. Thus, had the base year for these measurements of wealth been closer to the top of these markets in 2006 or 2007, the recorded declines are likely to have been even steeper.

Moreover, since the official end of the recession in mid-2009, the housing market in the U.S. has remained in a slump while the stock market has recaptured much of the value it lost from 2007 to 2009. Given that a much higher share of whites than blacks or Hispanics own stocks—as well as mutual funds and 401(k) or individual retirement accounts (IRAs)—the stock market rebound since 2009 is likely to have benefited white households more than minority households.

Other key findings from the report:

Hispanics: The net worth of Hispanic households decreased from $18,359 in 2005 to $6,325 in 2009. The percentage drop—66%—was the largest among all groups. Hispanics derived nearly two-thirds of their net worth in 2005 from home equity and are more

likely to reside in areas where the housing meltdown was concentrated. Thus, the housing downturn had a deep impact on them. Their net worth also diminished because of a 42% rise in median levels of debt they carried in the form of unsecured liabilities (credit card debt, education loans, etc.).

Blacks: The net worth of black households fell from $12,124 in 2005 to $5,677 in 2009, a decline of 53%. Like Hispanics, black households drew a large share (59%) of their net worth from home equity in 2005. Thus, the housing downturn had a strong impact on their net worth. Blacks also took on more unsecured debt during the economic downturn, with the median level rising by 27%.

Whites: The drop in the wealth of white households was modest in comparison, falling 16% from $134,992 in 2005 to $113,149 in 2009. White households were also affected by the housing crisis. But home equity accounts for relatively less of their total net worth (44% in 2005), and that served to lessen the impact of the housing bust. Median levels of unsecured debt among whites rose by 32%.

Asians: In 2005 median Asian household wealth had been greater than the median for white households, but by 2009 Asians lost their place at the top of the wealth hierarchy. Their net worth fell from $168,103 in 2005 to $78,066 in 2009, a drop of 54%. Like Hispanics, they are geographically concentrated in places such as California that were hit hard by the housing market meltdown. The arrival of new Asian immigrants since 2004 also contributed significantly to the estimated decline in the overall wealth of this racial group. Absent the immigrants who arrived during this period, the median wealth of Asian households is estimated to have dropped 31% from 2005 to 2009. Asians account for about 5% of the U.S. population.

. . .

Wealth Disparities within Racial and Ethnic Groups: During the period under study, wealth disparities increased not only between racial and ethnic groups, they also rose within each group. Even though the wealthiest 10% of households within each group suffered a loss in wealth from 2005 to 2009, their share of their group's overall wealth rose during this period. The increase was the greatest among Hispanics, with the top 10% boosting their share of all Hispanic household wealth from 56% in 2005 to 72% in 2009. Among whites, the share of wealth owned by the top 10% rose from 46% in 2005 to 51% in 2009. These trends indicate that those in the top 10% of the wealth ladder were relatively less impacted by the economic downturn than those in the remaining 90%.

. . .

34

Bonds of Sisterhood—Bonds of Oppression

Mary Romero

. . .

Domestic service reveals the contradiction in a feminism that pushed for women's involvement outside the home, yet failed to make men take responsibility for household

labor. Employed middle- and upper-middle class women escaped the double day syndrome by hiring poor women of color to perform housework and child care, and this was characterized as progress. Some feminists defined domestic service as progressive because traditional women's work moved into the labor market and became paid work. However, this definition neglects the inescapable fact that when women hire other women at low wages to do housework, both employees and employers remain women. As employers, women continued to accept responsibility for housework even if they supervised domestics who performed the actual labor. . . .

Although the system of gender domination places the burden of housework on women, middle-class women have financial resources to escape the drudgery of housework by paying someone else to do her work. . . . Thus, middle-class American women aim to "liberate" themselves by exploiting women of color—particularly immigrants—in the underground economy, for long hours at relatively low wages, with no benefits.

. . .

PHYSICAL LABOR

On the surface, the idea of hiring another person to perform the housewife's physical labor appears fairly straightforward. However, it is complicated by the fact that employers hire persons to replace labor at once considered demeaning and closely identified with family roles of mothers and wives. As employers, housewives decide what aspects of their physical labor they no longer want to perform, and in doing so they determine the employee's work. The needs fulfilled through domestics' physical labor structure the work: thus some employers choose to include tasks that they feel are demeaning, others add new tasks and methods of housekeeping that they themselves never engage in, and still others are more interested in having their status affirmed and enhanced than in having their floors scrubbed. . . . The list of physical labor reported by household workers included housecleaning, laundry, sewing, gardening, babysitting, and cooking. . . .

In their efforts to escape the diffuse duties of their housewife roles, employers do not acknowledge work boundaries. Even when the worker's tasks were agreed upon in a verbal contract, employees frequently reported that employers requested additional duties. For instance, household workers commonly complained that employers did not differentiate between housework and child care. In her interviews with women hired to do child care in New York City, Kathy Dobie found that "many of the women are hired as nannies and then asked if they wouldn't mind straightening up a bit. They are asked if they wouldn't clean, then shop, then do the laundry, then, etc." One child care worker told Dobie:

> I give her coffee. I take care of Stephen. I do the laundry. I go out and do the shopping. I buy her birth control tablets. I couldn't believe that. . . . Even the light bulbs in the ceiling, I change. Even her panties, I pick them up when she drops them on the floor.

. . . One of the most common experiences reported by women of color in reference to different standards was the request to scrub floors on their hands and knees rather than simply mopping. Maggie Holmes summed up the feelings of most women of color: "They [white women employers] don't get on their knees, but they don't think nothin' about askin' a black woman." . . .

EMOTIONAL LABOR

. . . Domestics are hired not only for their physical labor but to do emotional labor. . . . One clue to the importance emotional labor has for the employer can be found in accounts showing the lack of concern over the *amount* of housework completed. . . .

> When I went there they told me, "We're not paying you to scrub floors, but paying you just to take care of the woman, be a companion-like"; but I would do it all. If she was sick, I would stay nights. In the summer *we* would rent a summer cottage and I went there for five years with her.

> . . .

One Chicana I interviewed explained why she continued working for a seventy-eight-year-old employer who lived a long distance from her, regardless of the low wages: "I guess you can say she needs companionship. I feel sorry for her, you know, she is one of my farthest ones [employers]. I go once a month to her house. I like to go early so I can sit and talk to her."

Domestics almost invariably found themselves counseling and consoling their employers. Mrs. Okamura described the following work situation to Glenn:

> I'd been working for a lady for two hours a week for a long time, but she didn't even give me a chance to work. Upon my arrival, she kept talking and going on and on. For me, housework was much easier because even though I didn't understand English well, I still had to say, "Is that so?" "no" and "yes." . . . They just wanted to complain about their son or their son's wife.

> . . .

Gift-giving is domestic workers' almost universal experience and stands as the most obvious symbol of employers' maternalism. Structurally, gift-giving occupies an important place within the underground economy, whereby working-class women are often given presents by middle-class employers in lieu of higher wages and benefits. Chicanas reported that Christmas gifts to them or their children were more common than annual raises. Unlike gift-giving in other work settings, gifts frequently replace higher wages, raises, or other benefits. The following quote from a domestic describes conditions under which the gift occurs: "I'm trying to show you they would do something nice for you when they really felt you needed it. But they wouldn't pay you nothing but these menial wages. Nobody else paid more, and nobody wanted to break the standard." . . .

Employers in domestic service commonly redefine as gifts items that would have gone to the Salvation Army or the trash. Glenn found that old clothes and other discarded items were the most common gifts given to Japanese American domestics. I found a similar case among Chicana domestics. Judith Warner and Helen Henderson reported that sixty percent of the 200 Mexican immigrant women surveyed in Laredo received used clothes from their employers. This practice of giving old clothes within a work setting is unique to domestic service. It is almost inconceivable that the same woman would consider offering her old linen jacket to her secretary.

> . . .

PURCHASING STATUS BY HIRING A WOMAN OF COLOR

. . .

Taking an innovative research tack of analyzing family photographs, [one researcher] observed the importance of race and ethnicity in affirming employers' class and racial status in their communities. In her analysis of employers' family albums, she observed that "an attractive, well-dressed black domestic signified the family's membership in 'the better class' in the community." In subsequent interviews with domestics, [she] asked about their inclusion in the employers' family portraits. These African American women confirmed that "whites 'liked to dress blacks up' and sought to show that they had 'good-looking servants.'"

The physical appearances of household workers can be further manipulated to function as visible signs of the hierarchical status distinguishing domestics from employers. . . . White uniforms are used to distinguish the maid from families and friends, particularly when employers fear that others might mistake the reason for her presence. . . . "The maid puts on a uniform when there's company"; otherwise she is allowed to wear jeans. Most private household workers report that employers request a uniform to be worn on particular occasions, such as serving a special dinner or party or when accompanying the family on vacation. Mrs. Nishi expressed her opinion of the employer's request to Glenn: "I had to dress up in the maid's outfit when they had dinner parties. It was all part of it about how phoney these people were that I worked for." . . .

PURCHASING DEFERENCE

Confirmation of the employer's status is not always accomplished by the mere physical presence of women of color or white uniforms; it frequently requires daily practices of deferential behavior that continually affirm and enhance the domestic's inferiority. . . .

> She [employer] would make me feel like I was nothing or like I was doing this [domestic service] because I was so poor or because I was a Mexican. One day she said that Mexican people are all very poor. They weren't educated. And that did it! I dropped what I was doing. I left it there and I said, "here take this and shove it. I don't have to take this abuse from you or from anybody. I'm Mexican, yes, but I'm proud of what I am and I'm working." I says, "Everybody has a job and I have this as my job and if you felt this way, you didn't have to hire me." . . .

Another common and almost universal practice was to address domestics by their first names and employers by their last names. Employer Elinor Birney revealed the significance of the practice to Susan Tucker when she expressed her concern over her daughter's refusal to follow the custom: "The servant calls the woman Mary and Mary calls the servant by her name. Now, I think your employer-employee relationship sometimes could get very sticky if you don't have some separation." West Indian domestics reported that employers in New York used their first names but expected to be addressed formally. Laurino remarked on the irony of the practice because a domestic was in the position of knowing "the personal details of the employer's life, yet will most likely address her as Miss or Mrs.—and in return, she'll be called by her first name."

. . .

Several Chicana domestics similarly reported that employers refused to pronounce their names correctly and eventually Anglicized them. On the basis of the stereotype that all Mexican women are named Maria, white employers in the Southwest frequently refer to all Latina domestics as "Maria."

. . .

Deferential behavior is also constructed through eating arrangements. Rarely did domestics eat in the dining room or in the presence of mistresses' husbands. Mrs. Garcia remembered an employer who told her: "If you brought your lunch you wait out in your car or in the patio or out in the street or where ever." West Indians in New York City employed as live-in workers faced the archetypal situation of the domestic eating alone in the kitchen. As one woman described, "I couldn't eat with them at the table. . . . I have to eat after they finish eating. . . . And then I eat in the kitchen." Aware of the status hierarchy produced from acts of deference, the woman quoted above also commented that "there are people who do that because they want us to know that we are not equal." Another West Indian woman described the purpose of deferential eating arrangements as a way to create symbols of her inferiority: "The first day I got there [the employer] took out a fork and a plate and told me that this was mine to always use. They gave me the impression that I wasn't clean enough."

. . .

Household-labor negotiations frequently occur within the underground economy; they involve few government regulations. Consequently, employers have enormous leeway to determine the working conditions by setting wages, establishing job descriptions, and determining the work structure. . . . Employers decide whether to give raises, and they usually decide whether social security or benefits are obtained. Domestics have little influence over working conditions outside the choice to accept a job or to quit. Given the power that employers exert over working conditions, domestics—more than other workers—feel dependent on and at the mercy of their employers. Since the majority of household workers are not unionized, the struggle to improve working conditions remains an individual struggle.

. . .

The system of gifts and obligations in domestic service tends to shape the personalism in the employee-employer relationship into a strategy of oppression. Redefining work obligations as family or friendship obligations assures employers access to both the emotional and the physical labor of their employees. Personalism camouflages work conditions which become distorted and unintelligible within the context of the interpersonal relationships between domestics and employers. Employers' refusal to relate to domestics' concerns as workers' rights distorts the real conditions of their interaction.

JUST LIKE ONE OF THE FAMILY

Alice Childress testified to the way that personal relationships distort working conditions in her essay on the family analogy in *Like One of the Family: Conversations From a Domestic's Life*. The domestic's view of the employer's attempt to redefine her as "one of the family" rather than as a domestic was presented in an exchange between the two. Mildred, the domestic, overheard the employer tell a friend:

> "We just love her! She's *like* one of the family and she *just adores* our little Carol! We don't know *what* we'd do without her! We don't think of her as a servant!"

Mildred responded later to the employer's characterization by listing the ways her interaction with the family distinguished her as a nonmember, an outsider with inferior status.

> The family eats in the dining room and I eat in the kitchen. Your mama borrows your lace table cloth for her company and your son entertains his friends in your parlor, your daughter takes her afternoon nap on the living room couch and the puppy sleeps on your satin spread . . . and whenever your husband gets tired of something you are talkin' about he says, "Oh, for Pete's sake, forget it. . . ." So you can see I am not *just* like the family.
>
>   . . .

Although the phrase "one of the family" represents "the epitome of the personalized employer-employee association," domestics' use of the family analogy points to aspects of the emotional labor that some workers are willing to accept and those that they reject. On the one hand, this analogy suggests that domestics are engaged in the emotional labor involved in nurturing and caring; on the other hand, it suggests that domestics are treated with respect and are not forced into doing the emotional labor required to create deference.

    . . .

THE BUSINESSLIKE RELATIONSHIP

. . .

Establishing and maintaining a businesslike relationship is difficult in many respects. Virtually all contemporary jobs are structured to include breaks. However, regular morning and afternoon breaks are aspects of work culture absent from domestic service. . . .

> One of the biggest problems with household work is that the employers work you too hard. They want you to do everything in one day. They aren't sensitive to you even taking a half hour lunch break.

Structuring breaks and time off is a particularly serious problem for live-in domestics because the hours, tasks and obligations of the job are constantly redefined. Furthermore, live-in workers even find it difficult to guarantee their days off. . . .

> Thursday was my day off. But every Thursday morning, she would get up as she did every other morning and give me something to do. And usually she would say you can leave after you do so and so. Well, often by the time I finished the task, or giving the children lunch it was usually after 2 o'clock and I had no real day off.
>
>   . . .

Like other employers who hire workers in the underground economy, middle-class housewives seldom structure a regular routine for raises. The Chicanas who were interviewed in Denver rarely found employers who offered raises annually or on any regular basis. Domestics generally feel that domestic service is like any other type of job and that employers should thus understand that raises are part of hiring workers. . . .

In their accounts of requesting raises, some domestics expressed a need to force employers to recognize that domestic service is "real work." . . .

> So one day I say to her, I say, "Miz Brown," I said, "things is high now." I say, "And what you pay for meat and bread," I say, "that's what I have to pay, too." I say, "I been working here for a long time." I say, "I'd like a raise."
>
>   . . .

Wages are the tip of the iceberg. Benefits assumed in other working environments: overtime, vacation, sick pay, a health care plan, and any procedures for redress of grievances, are rarely if ever found in domestic service. At the same time, negative sanctions against employees are common, domestics report that employers expect breakage costs to be borne by the workers. Consider the following account by one of the Chicanas whom I interviewed. After waxing the kitchen floor, Mrs. Tafoya left an open can of floor wax on the dining room table. While she was upstairs vacuuming, her employer opened the sliding doors next to the dining room table to let a breeze in. The curtains flew up, tipped the can, and spilled floor wax onto the table. Mrs. Tafoya was held financially responsible for half of the cost of the repair. . . .

DISCUSSION

Descriptive accounts offered by women of color challenge many perceptions about the function of domestic service in American society today. Even though employers state that they hire domestics to escape the drudgery of housework and to gain freedom to engage in other activities, descriptions of working conditions reveal a more complex set of needs. Interviews with employers and employees alike indicate that domestic service still performs important functions in enhancing the status of middle-class housewives and their families. Moreover, the analysis of the structure of paid housework reveals that the work includes both physical and emotional labor, much of it as shadow work and unpaid labor.

The daily rituals and practices of domestic service reproduce the systems of gender, class, and race domination. All of the gender-specific aspects of unpaid housework—identified in the housewife experience—are also present in domestic service. Even though domestics are paid workers, they do not escape the sexism attached to housework but rather carry the burden for their middle-class women employers. The never-ending job described by housewives is transferred to workers employed by women who treat domestic service as an opportunity to "hire a wife." Employers frequently disregard the contractual or informal labor arrangement made with employees, constantly increasing the work load and incorporating more of their own homemaking duties and obligations. Household workers are faced with tasks that both exceed their job descriptions and are as emotionally and physically burdensome as those completed by housewives. The most common violation of the original labor agreement is the practice of adding child care to general housecleaning instead of keeping the two jobs separate.

. . .

Paid housework that is structured to replicate the unpaid domestic work of the housewife includes practices affirming women's inferiority. The sexist division of labor that exists in employers' homes, assigning mothers and wives the duty of waiting on and serving their husbands and children, is passed on to the domestics. Middle-class women employers who expect women household workers to "pick up" after their husbands and children reproduce the demeaning and sexist aspects of housework. Rejection of such sexist practices is reflected throughout the service sector when workers refuse to "pick up" after others by saying, "I am not your mother." In the same vein, domestics resist practices that structure paid housework to affirm sexist cultural values by requiring the employer to confront her children and husband about leaving their clothes and wet towels on the floor, leaving dishes and glasses throughout the house, and not throwing trash into the garbage. However, many women employers simply perpetuate the sexist division of labor by passing on the most devalued work in their lives to another woman—generally a woman of color. Thus, white middle-class women escape the stigma of "women's work" by laying the burden on working-class women of color.

. . .

VOICES

35

White Poverty

The Politics of Invisibility

bell hooks

In the southern world of racial apartheid I grew up in, no racialized class division was as intense or as fraught with bitter conflict as the one between poor whites and black folks. All black people knew that white skin gave any southern "cracker or peckerwood" (ethnic slurs reserved for the white poor) more power and privilege than even the wealthiest of black folks. However, these slurs were not the product of black vernacular slang, they were the terms white folks with class privilege invented to separate themselves from what they called poor "white trash." On the surface, at least, it made the lives of racist poor white people better to have a group they could lord it over, and the only group they could lord it over were black people. Assailed and assaulted by privileged white folks, they transferred their rage and class hatred onto the bodies of black people.

Unlike the stereotypes projected by the dominant culture about poor black folks, class stereotypes claimed poor whites were supposedly easily spotted by skin ailments, bad dental hygiene, and hair texture. All these things are affected by diet. While poor southern black folks often had no money, they usually had homegrown food to eat. Poor whites often suffered from malnutrition. Living under racial apartheid, black children learned to fear poor whites more than other whites simply because they were known to express their racism by cruel and brutal acts of violence. And even when white folks with class privilege condemned this violence, they could never openly oppose it, for to do so they would have had to take the word of black folks over those of white folks, thus being disloyal to white supremacy. A white person of privilege opposing violence against blacks perpetuated by poor whites might easily ruin their reputation and risk being seen as a "nigger lover."

When I was a small child we lived in the hills without neighbors nearby. Our closest neighbors were "white trash," as distinct from poor whites. White trash were different because they flaunted their poverty, reveled in it, and were not ashamed. Poor whites, like poor blacks, were committed to trying to find work and lay claim to respectability—they were law abiding and patriotic. White trash saw themselves as above the law and as a consequence they were dangerous. White trash were folks who, as our neighbors were fond of saying, "did not give a good goddamn." They were not afraid to take the Lord's name in vain. Most poor white folks did not want to live anywhere near black folks. White trash lived anywhere. . . .

Our "hillbilly white trash" neighbors lived by their own codes and rules. We did not call them names, because we knew the pain of slurs. Mama made it clear that they were people just like us and were to be shown respect. While they did not bother us and we did not bother them, we feared them. I never felt that they feared us. They were always encouraging us to come over, to play and party with them. To most respectable black people, poor whites and white trash were the lowest of the low. Even when they were nice, black folks felt it was important to keep a distance. I remember being whipped for being overly friendly with poor white neighbors. At that time I did not understand, nor did our parents make it clear, that if anything had happened to us in their homes, as black folks we would just have been seen as in the wrong; that was the nature of Jim Crow justice. While

V
O
I
C
E
S

we were encouraged to keep a distance from all white children no matter their class, it was clear that black people pitied and often felt contempt toward the white poor.

Desegregation led to the closing of all black schools. Busing took us out of our all-black neighborhoods into worlds of whiteness we did not know. It was in high school that I first began to understand class separation between whites. Poor white kids kept to themselves. And many of their well-to-do white peers would rather be seen talking to a black person than speaking to the white poor, or worse, to white trash. There was no danger that the black person they were talking to would want to come and hang out at their home or go to a movie. Racial lines were not crossed outside school. There could be no expectation of a reciprocal friendship. A privileged white person might confuse the issue if they showed attention to an underprivileged white peer. Class boundaries had to remain intact so that no one got the wrong idea. Between black and white there was no chance of a wrong idea: the two simply did not meet or mix.

Since some folks saw mama's family as backwoods, as black hillbillies, she was always quick to punish any act of aggression on our part toward an underdog group. We were not allowed to ridicule poor whites—not even if they were taunting us. When we began to ride the bus across town to the white school, it was a shock to my sensibilities to interact with black children who were scornful of the misfortune of others. . . .

To this day I have sad memories of the way Wilma, the white girl who was in my class, was treated by aggressive black children on the bus. Their daily taunts reminded her that she was poor white trash, the lowest of the low, that she smelled bad, that she wore the same dress day after day. In loud mean talk they warned her not to sit next to them. She often stood when there was an empty seat. A big girl with dark hair and unusually fair skin, she endured all the taunts with a knowing smirk. When she was pushed too far she fought back. She knew that with the exception of her ten minutes on that predominately black bus, white power ruled the day. And no matter how poor she was, she would always be white.

. . .

The white poor make up the vast majority of the poor in this society. Whereas mass migration of poor blacks from southern states to northern cities created a huge urban poor population, the white poor continue to live in isolated rural and suburban areas. Now and then they live hidden in the midst of white affluence. From their invention to the present day, the world of trailer park homes has been the territory of the white poor. While marking class boundaries, trailer park communities do not carry the stigma of degradation and deprivation commonly associated with the "ghetto"—a term first used to identify poor white urban immigrant communities. Indeed, in the not so distant past the psychological and economic self-esteem of the white working class and the white poor has been significantly bolstered by the class politics of white supremacy. Currently, we are witnessing a resurgence of white supremacist thinking among disenfranchised classes of white people. These extremist groups respond to misinformation circulated by privileged whites that suggests that black people are getting ahead financially because of government policies like affirmative action, and they are taught to blame black folks for their plight.

While anti-black racism has intensified among whites of all classes in recent years as part of civil rights backlash, overall the white underprivileged are . . . far more likely to see immigrants as the group taking needed jobs. Their racism toward non-white immigrants who are perceived to be taking jobs by virtue of their willingness to work for less mirrors that of black workers who blame immigrants. More and more the white and black poor recognize that ruling class greed ensures their continued exploitation and oppression.

. .

More and more Americans of all colors are entering the ranks of the poor. And that includes white Americans. The evidence is in the numbers. In the essay "Trash-O-Nomics," Doug Henwood states what should be obvious but often is not: "Of course, the average

white person is better off than the average non-white person, those of Asian origin excepted, and black people are disproportionally poor. But that sort of formula hides as much as it reveals: most officially poor people are white, and these days, a white household should consider itself lucky if its income is only stagnant rather than in outright decline." It serves white supremacist capitalist patriarchal ruling class interests to mask this reality. Hence, the almost invisibility of the white poor in mass media.

Today, most folks who comment on class acknowledge that poverty is seen as having a black face, but they rarely point to the fact that this representation has been created and sustained by mass media. Concurrently, reports using statistics that show a huge percentage of black folks in the ranks of the poor compared to a small percentage of whites make it seem that blacks are the majority group in the ranks of the poor. Rarely do these reports emphasize that these percentages are based on population size. The reality they mask is that blacks are a small percentage of the population. While black folks disproportionate to our numbers are among the poor, the vast majority of the poor continue to be white. The hidden face of poverty in the United States is the untold stories of millions of poor white people.

Better to have poor and working-class white folks believe white supremacy is still giving them a meaningful edge than to broadcast the reality that the poor of any race no longer have an edge in this society, or that downsizing daily drags previously economically sound white households into the ranks of the poor. . . . Undue media focus on poor nonwhites deflects attention away from the reality of white poverty.

. . .

No doubt ruling class groups will succeed in new efforts to divide and conquer, but the white poor will no longer direct its class rage solely at black people, for the white poor is divided within its ranks. Just as there are many poor whites who are racist, there are a substantial group of poor whites who refuse to buy into white supremacist politics, who understand the economic forces that are crippling the American working class. Progressive white poor and working-class people understand the dynamics of capitalism. All over the United States class unrest is mounting. . . .

Ending welfare will mean that more white women than ever before in our nation's history will enter the ranks of the underclass. Like their black counterparts, many of them will be young. Workfare programs, which pay subsistence wages without the backdrop of free housing, will not enhance their lives. As the future "poorest of the poor" they are far less likely to be duped into believing their enemies are other economically disadvantaged groups than their predecessors. . . .

Given that today's culture is one where the white and black working class and poor have more to say to one another, there is a context for building solidarity that did not exist in the past. That solidarity cannot be expressed solely through shared critique of the privileged. It must be rooted in a politics of resistance that is fundamentally anti-racist, one that recognizes that the experiences of underprivileged white folks are as important as those of people of color. The class segregation that historically divided the white poor from their more privileged counterparts did not exist in predominately black communities. And while generations of white families have historically remained poor, a host of black folks pulled themselves out of poverty into privilege. In solidarity these folks have historically been strong advocates for the black poor even though that too is changing. More often than not they did not encourage solidarity with the white poor because of persistent anti-black racism. Now they must become advocates for the white and black poor, overcoming their anti-white prejudices. Concurrently, the black and white poor must do the work of building solidarity by learning more about one another, about what brings them together and what tears them apart. We need to hear more from all of us who have bridged the gap between white and black poor and working-class experience.

V
O
I
C
E
S

V
O
I
C
E
S

When I left the segregated world of my poor and working-class home environment to attend privileged-class schools, I found I often had more in common with white students who shared a similar class background than with privileged class black students who had no experience of what it might mean to lack the funds to do anything they wanted to do. No matter our color, students from poor and working-class backgrounds had common experiences history had not taught us how to sufficiently name or theoretically articulate. While it was definitely easier for folks from poor white backgrounds to assimilate visually, we all experienced estrangement from our class origin as well as the fear of losing touch with the worlds we had most intimately known. The bonds we forged in solidarity were and are not documented. There is no record of our conversations or how these solidarities shaped our future politics. Many of us used this bonding through class across the boundary of race as a groundwork for a politics of solidarity that has stood the test of time.

While racism remains an integral fact of our culture, it too has changed. Xenophobia more so than racial hatred often characterizes where white citizens stand on race. The utterly segregated black neighborhoods of my upbringing are no more. The white poor in need of shelter move into places where once no white face was ever seen. This contact does not mean an absence of racism. But it does mean that the criteria and the expression of racism has changed. It also means that there is more of a concrete basis for positive interaction between poor black and white folks. When I walk in these communities created by class division, I see grown white and black folks refusing to interact with each other even as I see more interaction than in the past. And I see white and black children freely crossing the boundaries of race to meet at that class juncture which brings them together in a common landscape they call home.

These bonds may mean little given the fact that there are so many more race-segregated white working-class and poor communities. Even in the places where white and black do not meet, there are more diverse opinions about class and race. Nothing is as simple as it was in the past when the needs of the white poor were pitted against the needs of the black poor. Today, poverty is both gendered and racialized. It is impossible to truly understand class in the United States today without understanding the politics of race and gender. Ultimately, more than any previous movement for social justice, the struggle to end poverty could easily become the civil rights issue with the broadest appeal—uniting groups that have never before taken a stand together to support their common hope of living in a more democratic and just world—a world where basic necessities of life are available to everyone, to each according to their need.

36

Why Can't Everybody Fear Me like That?

Saint

All right, my name is Saint. I was born in Brooklyn, Crown Heights. Grew up with my mother and my father my brother my grandfather. All of us lived in the same house for years. I had a pretty good childhood. No problems no stress, basically got everything I want.

I lived in Crown Heights until I was like maybe four or five years old. I can't remember that much because I was young. I used to enjoy it over there because even until now in the same building where we was at, probably still got like eight cousins over there. I've got a lot of family in that same building, in like three different apartments. Ours was like the fourth. It was fun because there's not too many places where you could be five years old and be able to run through a whole building without your parents chasing you 'cause they know there's nothing but your whole family in the building.

. . .

When we moved from there we ended up on Martense on East Flatbush with another set of family, with my mother's uncles and aunts. And it was like the whole building was family because my uncle owned the building. That was my first real house, in Flatbush. It was a nice two-family house with a basement. Me and my brother and my mother and my grandfather had rooms on the top floor. And downstairs was the kitchen the living room, basement. We rented the basement out to some close friends of the family.

My mother and my father used to work for years until recently. My father used to work night shifts and my mother used to work morning shifts. So, one of them was always home because both of them had to work. It was a nice house in a pretty good neighborhood. We had to move out of there because of certain things that I did and police kept coming back and forth to the house and that embarrassed my parents.

. . .

Our block was known for shootouts and a lot of gang activity and stuff like that. So my mother ain't want us outside, so we just had to stay in the house; that's why she moved. She would tell us, "All right, well y'all can't go outside." And as kids, you know we'll always be like, "Aw, we want to go outside." I was about seven, my brother was like nine. We was old enough to realize that yeah, everyday when we sit in our apartment there's always gunshots. Shots probably came through our window before. So we would be mad, but she would never give us a reason like, "Well, people getting shot outside." But we basically knew, we look at it and be like, "All right, we know what time it is."

. . .

It was me, my brother, my mother and my aunt. We was all watching *Leroy The Last Dragon* and we just heard mad gun shots, the gunshots sounded like they were coming from real close. So my mother just told everybody automatically, "Just get on the floor," because we were already used to it. So everybody just got on the floor, we stayed there, and it was like, we're so used to it that I was still watching the movie. I'm on the floor laying down with my head down and all that, and I'm just watching the movie. The gunshots went on for about five or ten minutes. It just kept going and going.

So after a while the movie is done, so I get up and I go and look out the window and I see mad police. So when we go downstairs, there was this drug dealer guy that used to live in the basement right next door to our building. And he was a cool guy because back then, a dollar used to be a lot of money. He used to give kids on the block twenties, like, "Go buy ice cream and keep the change, bring me back a dollar water or something and keep the change for y'all." So all the kids on the block used to love him. A fat Puerto Rican guy named Joe. So we came outside, police just told us that they found him in the basement dead with a lot of drugs on the table. He was down there by himself and people came to rob him. He killed like two of them, but it was like five people and some of them killed him and they said it was a trail of blood leading out. So he must've shot like three or four of them, but he killed two of them down there in the basement and he got killed. And I ain't never forget that because he used to give us money and all that. He was a pretty cool guy; he used to look out for all the young kids on the block. Take us whenever we ran out of money to the arcade. He always used to pass through, look for anybody from the block,

and say, "Y'all good? Aight, here, five dollars, go ahead spend it all on video games." So I always remember him even until now.

Once you hear gunshots, and you're in your house, always get on the floor because you don't want a bullet to come through your window and hit you. It happens like that all the time in the hood. So you just start to learn wherever you at, you hear bullets, duck. At least if you in the streets duck. In your house, get on the floor. You can't run because if you run, you might run into a bullet or get hit in your back. That's why it's always good to just get low because it might not be for you.

. . .

Then I went to Walt Whitman Junior High School in Brooklyn; that's in Flatbush too. And that's when everything basically started going downhill. That's when I started smoking weed. I always noticed girls in school, but that's when I really started, because everybody in high school and junior high had a girlfriend. I started cutting school to go by my girlfriend's house and chill. We had hooky parties and stuff like that. That was like '97, '98.

Around them times that's when the gang thing was going on real hard. I kind of stayed away from it a little bit even though we had like our own little crew from our neighborhood that we all stuck up for each other. But we still was getting pressure from other gangs. But we wasn't having it because it was known in the neighborhood, our gang, our hood and the other hood from the other side be the two hoods that we would war. So it don't matter, we war with each other and we war with anyone else. So it was like that for a while. Then I started getting into more fights, because after being around so much of the older people in my neighborhood, it was like a lot of times you see people doing violent things. You like, "Oh that's real violent, but I won't do it." After seeing the same thing every day, you see a kid get stabbed every day, see a kid get shot every day, it's just another part of life. It's nothing for me to do it, so I started getting more violent. I started stabbing people, fighting people for no reason, jumping people.

. . .

The guys that stood up for me were the rough guys from the hood. We looked up to them. "Yeah when I grow up, I want to be like him." Because in the hood it's all about a fear and a respect thing, because once you fear somebody, like really and truly, you respect them. You might fear them, but when I see you fear them, I'll respect them like, "Damn why can't everybody fear me like that?" You could see somebody just walk up to a group of kids about to go in the corner store and just take everybody money. Like damn, I'm walking around with two dollars. This kid came out his crib with nothing, left his house with nothing. And he got fifteen, twenty dollars on him right now. They had all the girls. You know, of course, the girls wanna be with the thugs. So they had all the girls. The rest of the kids—even the thug kids from our hood hung out with the thug kids from them other hoods because like they say, birds of a feather flock together. So they got the perfect crew. Ain't nobody stepping to they crew 'cause everybody in that crew is gangsta. All of us little homies were like, damn, we wanna be like them. They got money and fresh sneakers all the time.

. . .

So I wanted to be just like that. Like when I was younger—the same way when I used to look at the older guys and be like, "Word, I'm gonna grow up and be just like them." Even though you're older, a lot of people think you don't wanna be like nobody. But, really and truly, when you look deep down inside, you're like, "Yeah, I do want to be like him. I want to have the same type of respect he had." So I joined the Crips, thinking that I'm gonna get the same type of respect he had. But I ain't know the type of work that he had to put in to get that respect. I ain't really know what he did to get that respect. I just thought maybe he fought, bust his gun once or twice. Then, when I start hearing stories about what he been through, how he put it down in the hood, then I'm like, "Oh he went through a lot to get the respect that you get." So that's when I'm like, "You know what? I'm gonna go through

a lot to get this respect too, because I wanna be just like him." You can't be rolling with a gangsta all day and you a punk. Then they gonna look at you like you a funny-ass n____. How you rolling with this G'ed up n____ and he's a punk ass n____? That's when n____s goin' go up to the G like, "Stop rolling with him, he's soft." So basically, you gotta pull your own weight too, even though you're in a gang and ya'll fight for each other, you got to pull your own weight. So I joined the Crips right after that. Got jumped in. After that you gotta go get high and y'all family, basically.

. . .

My mother, she don't know too much about the gang thing, but she know I'm affiliated. She said that I've been lying to her, 'cause if I tell her, "Yeah, well Mom, I'm Crip," that's gonna stress her out too much. But she already know, basically she's not a stupid woman, she know that I'm gang related. So, it hurts her, she cries, she's like, "You always in and out of jail, you my youngest son, you my baby boy. When you ain't had the GED—you got kicked out of school, you still getting locked up, you went and left the house already, I don't know how you getting money, you twenty years old, you went from a Honda, now you driving a Lexus." My mother's like, "I know you doing something in the streets that's not good." So that hurts her. My mother's a God-fearing woman, go to church every week and all that, so every time I speak to her she like, "You know I pray for you every night." I tell her, "Same thing Ma, you know I pray for you too every night, and I'm good in here, Mom, you ain't gotta worry about nothing." But you know it hurts her a lot, I ain't gonna lie. That's the—the main thing about this, this bid right here that hurts me, is knowing that I hurt my mother so much. I could do this time, it's nothing for me, I've been through this, but just to think about what my mother go through, that hurts me. Sometimes that makes me want to cry, but—you do the crime you gotta do the time, so I never cry, I sit here and do what I gotta do, you feel me? I know—I know it's not easy for my mother. As hard as it is for me, it's probably thirty times harder for my mother, to tell you the truth. Nobody gonna be feeling as much as my mother, as much as my family. But I know my mother feels it the most.

. . .

37

Classified

How To Stop Hiding Your Privilege and Use It for Social Change

Karen Pittelman and Resource Generation

Jaimie: "My parents came from working and middle class families. My dad became a professor of finance and over the course of my life he's steadily been making more money. By the time I was in college my parents had made money on investments and started a business selling study guides for people taking the Chartered Financial Analyst exam. When I was 26 my folks sold the business for many millions of dollars.

There's different ways to look at how they made this money. One is to look at how it had to do with the skin privilege my parents had—I mean my dad's family is Irish and German and my mom's family is Russian Jewish. So the way whiteness has worked and how they've been allowed to be white is part of why my parents had access to a greater range of opportunities.

Another way to look at it is they were really hard-working and they set out to make a lot of money. I have a lot of respect for the work that they did and the way they went from working their way through college to being multi-millionaires.

Then there's another analysis that asks, what were they actually doing? Investing. My dad's analysis about investing is, 'that's the way the free market works.' But there's also the idea that you're loaning money to companies that are raping the earth, destroying people's homelands and paying money to special interest lobby groups that destroy democracy even in our own country.

I feel like what my parents valued was financial security because they wanted to take care of their family, and I don't think that's a bad motivation at all. But I do think that it's sad to see the other kinds of values that get left behind. Having financial security is one way to take care of people, but having community and having a spiritual tradition are also ways to take care of people."

Laurel: "I have an ancestor who was named Edward F. Beale. He's my great great great uncle (or something.) He was the President of the Bureau of Indian Affairs out in California and he was responsible for putting a number of Indians on reservations. He then made millions of dollars off of land back in the 1850s. What I get from that is that he was making millions off of stolen land from Native Americans.

What I would love to do in my family is be able to trace all the different lines of where the money came from. I'd love to gather with other people with wealth and be able to tell our stories with a lot of analysis and make a case for reparations; to be able to really articulate to other people with wealth the ways in which—really literally—the wealth was stolen. To look at how labor was stolen from Chinese people and African American people and how this land was stolen from Native Americans. If we're talking about it from a white wealthy point of view, it might be less threatening to other white wealthy people because we're owning it rather than accusing from the outside.

My mother and my aunt keep saying stuff like, 'He wasn't such a bad guy, Edward F. Beale.' But I guess what I keep trying to articulate—both for them and for myself—is the difference between the institutional and personal. That, for instance, Edward F. Beale was part of a genocidal movement which he profited from, and within that he was an individual person who had relationships and feelings and was blind to what was going on, just like all of us at certain times. The institutional piece doesn't cancel out the personal piece. And the personal doesn't cancel out the institutional."

Noy: "The story of my parents' wealth is not all just about their individual will—so much else played into it. My dad was very poor, but he was extremely fortunate because he got an education at a Wat (a Thai Buddhist temple). He then passed the exams to get into Chulalongkorn, which is like the Harvard of Thailand. That's where he met my mother. My mother's side of the family owned some land, so they were better-off. My parents both became doctors.

They decided to move to the United States in 1971 in part because of all the political turmoil—it was an extremely tumultuous period in Southeast Asian history, and tensions between students and the Thai military were rising. It was only because the U.S. had changed its immigration laws in the 1960s that they were able to go—before that Asian immigration was extremely restricted. It was also easier for them because they were doctors and the law gave preference to professionals, scientists and artists.

My parents set up their own practice and they worked like crazy, so I hardly saw them. Then my dad started getting into the stock market, reading all these books and doing investments. That was how they built up a fairly significant amount of money.

With immigrant families, when one person makes it you get everyone else holding on to you. You get this money and then you are expected to support everyone—filial piety and all. I think it can get a little crazy with the power and the pressure of being in that privileged position. At the same time, there was a real starvation mentality, especially coming from my dad. I remember cutting napkins in half to save money and having really cheap clothes. I think my dad felt like if you act like you have a lot of money then you aren't really Thai anymore."

Katrina: "My father inherited from his father and that money came from a few generations back when his family owned coal mills in western Pennsylvania. But what I'll really inherit will be from money that he earned in his own life as a lawyer.

Then on my mom's side I won't be inheriting money via her branch of the family, but I will be inheriting—similar to on my dad's side—a kind of social elite status and upper class attitude that comes in a pretty direct line from my mom's mom's branch of the family being descended from slave traders. That was back seven generations ago in Rhode Island. At that time, not the guy who I'm descended from, but his sons and their sons, a few of them made a huge fortune in the slave trade. I'm not in a direct line from those huge fortunes, most of which were spent within a few generations. So technically speaking I haven't inherited money directly from the slave trade. However, I have definitely inherited social class status. I think it's important to name that and notice that whether it's the slave trade or any other major financial success in business—even if the money disappears—people typically marry into other families with money. So for us, this 'normal' sense of old-money New England entitlement really settled in.

The process of naming my privilege and the slave trade history has been liberating in the sense that when it was a subconscious thing, the guilt was really strong. It's been a gradual process of saying, 'Okay, since I'm not inherently a bad person, and my people are really good-hearted people nowadays, then I can start to look at this more objectively,' and saying, 'well, this was what the history was and it was totally fucked up and now what am I going to do about it?'"

38

The Debt Trap

Given a Shovel, Americans Dig Deeper into Debt

Gretchen Morgenson

The collection agencies call at least 20 times a day. For a little quiet, Diane McLeod stashes her phone in the dishwasher.

But right up until she hit the wall financially, Ms. McLeod was a dream customer for lenders. She juggled not one but two mortgages, both with interest rates that rose over time, and a car loan and high-cost credit card debt. Separated and living with her 20-year-old

son, she worked two jobs so she could afford her small, two-bedroom ranch house in suburban Philadelphia, the Kia she drove to work, and the handbags and knickknacks she liked. Then last year, back-to-back medical emergencies helped push her over the edge. She could no longer afford either her home payments or her credit card bills. Then she lost her job. Now her home is in foreclosure and her credit profile in ruins.

. . .

Years of spending more than they earn have left a record number of Americans like Ms. McLeod standing at the financial precipice. They have amassed a mountain of debt that grows ever bigger because of high interest rates and fees. While the circumstances surrounding these downfalls vary, one element is identical: the lucrative lending practices of America's merchants of debt have led millions of Americans—young and old, native and immigrant, affluent and poor—to the brink. More and more, Americans can identify with miners of old: in debt to the company store with little chance of paying up.

It is not just individuals but the entire economy that is now suffering. Practices that produced record profits for many banks have shaken the nation's financial system to its foundation. As a growing number of Americans default, banks are recording hundreds of billions in losses, devastating their shareholders.

. . .

But behind the big increase in consumer debt is a major shift in the way lenders approach their business. In earlier years, actually being repaid by borrowers was crucial to lenders. Now, because so much consumer debt is packaged into securities and sold to investors, repayment of the loans takes on less importance to those lenders than the fees and charges generated when loans are made.

Lenders have found new ways to squeeze more profit from borrowers. Though prevailing interest rates have fallen to the low single digits in recent years, for example, the rates that credit card issuers routinely charge even borrowers with good credit records have risen, to 19.1 percent last year from 17.7 percent in 2005—a difference that adds billions of dollars in interest charges annually to credit card bills. Average late fees rose to $35 in 2007 from less than $13 in 1994, and fees charged when customers exceed their credit limits more than doubled to $26 a month from $11, according to CardWeb, an online publisher of information on payment and credit cards. Mortgage lenders similarly added or raised fees associated with borrowing to buy a home—like $75 e-mail charges, $100 document preparation costs and $70 courier fees—bringing the average to $700 a mortgage, according to the *Department of Housing and Urban Development*. These "junk fees" have risen 50 percent in recent years . . . .

Lenders have been eager to expand their reach. They have honed sophisticated marketing tactics, gathering personal financial data to tailor their pitches. They have spent hundreds of millions of dollars on advertising campaigns that make debt sound desirable and risk-free. The ads are aimed at people who urgently need loans to pay for health care and other necessities.

. . .

Tallying what the lenders have made off Ms. McLeod over the years is revealing. In 2007, when she earned $48,000 before taxes, she was charged more than $20,000 in interest on her various loans. Her first mortgage, originated by the EquiFirst Corporation, charged her $14,136 a year, and her second, held by CitiFinancial, added $4,000. Capital One, a credit card company that charged her 28 percent interest on her balances, billed $1,400 in annual interest. GE Money Bank levied 27 percent on the $1,500 or so that Ms. McLeod owed on an account she had with a local jewelry store, adding more than $400. Olde City Mortgage, the company that arranged one of Ms. McLeod's loans, made $6,000 on a single refinancing, and EquiFirst received $890 in a loan origination fee.

. . .

But with so many borrowers in trouble, some bankruptcy experts and regulators are beginning to focus on the responsibilities of lenders, like requiring them to make loans only if they are suitable to the borrowers applying for them. The *Federal Reserve Board*, for instance, recently put into effect rules barring a lender from making a loan without regard to the borrower's ability to repay it.

. . .

BORROWING TO SHOP

For decades, America's shift from thrift could be summed up in this familiar phrase: When the going gets tough, the tough go shopping. Whether for a car, home, vacation or college degree, the nation's lenders stood ready to assist. Companies offered first and second mortgages and home equity lines, marketed credit cards for teenagers and helped college students to amass upward of $100,000 in debt by graduation. Every age group up to the elderly was the target of sophisticated ad campaigns and direct mail programs. "Live Richly" was a Citibank message. "Life Takes *Visa*," proclaims the nation's largest credit card issuer.

. . .

Mortgage lenders took to cold-calling homeowners to persuade them to refinance. Done to reduce borrowers' monthly payments, serial refinancings allowed lenders to charge thousands of dollars in loan processing fees, including appraisals, credit checks, title searches and document preparation fees.

Not surprisingly, such practices generated dazzling profits for the nation's financial companies. And since 2005, when the bankruptcy law was changed, the credit card industry has increased its earnings 25 percent, according to a new study by Michael Simkovic, a former James M. Olin fellow in Law and Economics at Harvard Law School.

. . .

Among the most profitable companies were Ms. McLeod's creditors. For Capital One, which charges her 28 percent interest on her credit card, net interest income, after provisions for loan losses, has risen a compounded 25 percent a year since 2002. GE Money Bank, which levied a 27 percent rate on Ms. McLeod's debt and is part of the GE Capital Corporation, generated profits of $4.3 billion in 2007, more than double the $2.1 billion it earned in 2003.

. . .

A RISING TIDE OF BILLS

Just two generations ago, America was a nation of mostly thrifty people living within their means, even setting money aside for unforeseen expenses. [As of 2008], Americans carry $2.56 trillion in consumer debt, up 22 percent since 2000 alone, according to the Federal Reserve Board. The average household's credit card debt is $8,565, up almost 15 percent from 2000. College debt has more than doubled since 1995. The average student emerges from college carrying $20,000 in educational debt. Household debt, including mortgages and credit cards, represents 19 percent of household assets, according to the Fed, compared with 13 percent in 1980.

V
O
I
C
E
S

Even as this debt was mounting, incomes stagnated for many Americans. As a result, the percentage of disposable income that consumers must set aside to service their debt—a figure that includes monthly credit card payments, car loans, mortgage interest and principal—has risen to 14.5 percent from 11 percent just 15 years ago. By contrast, the nation's savings rate, which exceeded 8 percent of disposable income in 1968, stood at 0.4 percent at the end of the first quarter of this year, according to the Bureau of Economic Analysis.

More ominous, as Americans have dug themselves deeper into debt, the value of their assets has started to fall. Mortgage debt stood at $10.5 trillion at the end of last year, more than double the $4.8 trillion just seven years earlier, but home prices that were rising to support increasing levels of debt, like home equity lines of credit, are now dropping. The combination of increased debt, falling asset prices and stagnant incomes does not threaten just imprudent borrowers. The entire economy has become vulnerable to the spending slowdown that results when consumers like Ms. McLeod hit the wall.

THAT FIRST CREDIT CARD

Growing up in Philadelphia, Diane McLeod never knew financial hardship, she said. Her father owned six pizza shops and her mother was a homemaker. "There was always money for everything, whether it was bills or food shopping or a spur-of-the-moment vacation," Ms. McLeod recalled. "If they worried about money, they never let us know." Hers was a pay-as-you-go family, she said. Although money was not discussed much around the dinner table, credit card debt was not a part of her parents' financial plan, and sometimes personal purchases were put off.

When Ms. McLeod married at 18, she and her husband carried no credit cards. She stayed at home after her son was born, but when she was 27 her husband died. She remarried a few years later and continued as a homemaker until her son turned 13. Between her husband's job laying carpets and her own, money was not exactly tight.

In the mid-'90s, Ms. McLeod got several credit cards. When the marriage began to founder, she said, she shopped to make herself feel better. Earning a livable wage at *Verizon* Yellow Pages, Ms. McLeod finally decided to leave her marriage and buy a home of her own in February 2003. The cost was $135,000, and her mortgage required no down payment because her credit history was good. "I was very proud of myself when I bought the house," Ms. McLeod explained. "I thought I would live here till I died." Adding to her burden, however, was about $25,000 in credit card debt she had brought from her marriage. Because her husband did not have a regular salary, all the cards were in her name.

After she had been in the house for a year, a friend who was a mortgage broker suggested she consolidate her debts into a new home loan. The property had appreciated by about $30,000, and once again she put no money down for the loan. "It was amazing how easy it was," she recalled. "But that's a trap, and I didn't know it then."

Naturally, the refinance had costs. There was an $8,000 penalty to pay off the previous mortgage early as well as roughly $1,500 in closing costs on the new loan. To cover these fees, Ms. McLeod dipped into her retirement account. Only later did she realize that she had to pay an early-withdrawal penalty of $3,000 to the *Internal Revenue Service*. Short on cash, she put it on a credit card.

Soon she had racked up another $19,000 in credit card debt. But because her home had appreciated, she once again refinanced her mortgage. Although she was making $50,000 a year working two jobs, her income was not enough to support the new $165,000 loan. She

asked her son to join her on the loan application; with his income, the numbers worked. "Boy, would I regret that," she said. The decision would drive a wedge between mother and son and damage his credit profile as well.

Almost immediately after she refinanced, in late 2005, the department store where she worked her second job, as a jewelry saleswoman at night and on weekends, cut back her hours. She quit altogether, and her son moved out of the house, where he had been helping with the rent, to live with a girlfriend. Ms. McLeod was on her own and paying $1,500 a month on her mortgage. Because the house had been recently appraised at $228,000, she said, she felt sure she could refinance again if she needed to pay off her credit card. "You felt like you had a way out," she said.

But as happens with many debt-laden Americans, an unexpected illness helped push Ms. McLeod over the edge. In January 2006, her doctor told her she needed a hysterectomy. She had health care coverage, but she could no longer work at a second job. She made matters worse during her recovery, while watching home shopping channels. "Eight weeks in bed by yourself is very dangerous when you have a TV and credit card," Ms. McLeod said. "QVC was my friend."

Later that year, Ms. McLeod realized she was in trouble, squeezed by her mortgage and credit card payments, her $350 monthly car bill, rising energy prices and a stagnant salary. She started to sell knickknacks, handbags, clothing and other items on eBay to help cover her heating and food bills. She stopped paying her credit cards so that she could afford her mortgage.

A year ago she was back in the hospital, this time with a burst appendix. Her condition worsened, and she lost the use of one kidney. She spent 19 days in the hospital and six weeks recuperating. Her prescription-drug costs added to her expenses, and by September she could no longer pay her mortgage.

When her father died in early January, she was devastated. About a month later, on Feb. 14, Ms. McLeod was suspended and soon afterward fired from Verizon. Toting up her financial obligations, Ms. McLeod said she owed $237,000 on her home mortgage. Of that, sheriff's costs are $4,350, and "other" fees related to the foreclosure come to $3,000. A house of similar size down the street from Ms. McLeod sold for $153,000 in January. Her credit card debt totals around $34,000, she said. Each month the late fees and over-limit penalties add to her debt. Ms. McLeod said she would probably file for bankruptcy.

Patricia A. Hasson, president of the Credit Counseling Service of Delaware Valley, said Ms. McLeod would probably wind up having to repay 40 percent to 60 percent of her credit card debt. The owner of her mortgages could come after her for the difference between what she owes on her loan and what her house ultimately sells for. The first mortgage was sold to investors; Citigroup declined to say whether it held onto the second mortgage or sold it to investors.

A sheriff's auction of her home on June 12 received no bidders, Ms. McLeod said. The bank will soon evict her. "Oh, I definitely have regrets," Ms. McLeod said. "I regret not dealing with my emotions instead of just shopping. And I regret involving my son in all this because that has affected him and his finances and his self-esteem."

Ms. McLeod says she hopes to be living in an apartment she can afford soon and to get back to paying her bills on time. She does not want another credit card, she said. But even though her credit profile is ruined, she still receives come-ons. Recently an envelope arrived offering a "pre-qualified" Salute Visa Gold card issued by Urban Bank Trust. "We think you deserve more credit!" it said in bold type.

A spokeswoman at Urban Bank said the Salute Visa is part of a program "designed to provide access to credit for folks who would not otherwise qualify for credit." The Salute Visa offered Ms. McLeod a $300 credit line. But a closer look at the fine print showed that $150 of that would go, as annual fees, to Urban Bank.

V
O
I
C
E
S

39

How Occupy Wall Street Changes Everything

Sarah van Gelder

. . .

Something happened in September 2011 so unexpected that no politician or pundit saw it coming.

Inspired by the Arab Spring and uprisings in Europe, sparked by a challenge from *Adbusters* magazine to show up at Wall Street on September 17 and "bring a tent," and encouraged by veteran New York activists, a few thousand people gathered in the financial district of New York City. At the end of the day, some of them set up camp in Zuccotti Park and started what became a national—and now international—movement.

The Occupy movement, as it has come to be called, named the source of the crises of our time: Wall Street banks, big corporations, and others among the 1% are claiming the world's wealth for themselves at the expense of the 99% and having their way with our governments. This is a truth that political insiders and the media had avoided, even while the assets of the top 1% reached levels not seen since the 1920s. But now that this genie is out of the bottle, it can't easily be put back in.

Without offices, paid staff, or a bank account, Occupy Wall Street quickly spread beyond New York. People gathered in Boston, Chicago, Los Angeles, Portland, Atlanta, San Diego, and hundreds of other cities around the United States and claimed the right of *we the people* to create a world that works for the 99%. In a matter of weeks, the occupations and protests had spread worldwide, to over 1,500 cities, from Madrid to Cape Town and from Buenos Aires to Hong Kong, involving hundreds of thousands of people.

The Occupy Wall Street movement is not just demanding change. It is also transforming how we, the 99%, see ourselves. The shame many of us felt when we couldn't find a job, pay down our debts, or keep our home is being replaced by a political awakening. Millions now recognize that we are not to blame for a weak economy, for a subprime mortgage meltdown, or for a tax system that favors the wealthy but bankrupts the government. The 99% are coming to see that we are collateral damage in an all-out effort by the super-rich to get even richer.

. . .

By naming the issue, the movement has changed the political discourse. No longer can the interests of the 99% be ignored. The movement has unleashed the political power of millions and issued an open invitation to everyone to be part of creating a new world.

Historians may look back at September 2011 as the time when the 99% awoke, named our crisis, and faced the reality that none of our leaders are going to solve it. This is the moment when we realized we would have to act for ourselves.

THE TRUTH IS OUT: THE SYSTEM IS RIGGED IN FAVOR OF THE WEALTHY

One of the signs at the Occupy Seattle protest reads: "Dear 1%. We were asleep. Now we've woken up. Signed, the 99%."

This sign captures the feeling of many in the Occupy movement. We are seeing our ways of life, our aspirations, and our security slip away—not because we have been lazy or

undisciplined, or lacked intelligence and motivation, but because the wealthiest among us have rigged the system to enhance their own power and wealth at the expense of everyone else.

. . .

The government actively facilitates this concentration of wealth through tax breaks for corporations and the wealthy, and bailouts for giant banks and corporations. These entities also benefit from mining rights, logging rights, airwave rights, and countless other licenses to use common assets for private profit. Corporations shift the costs of environmental damage to the public and pocket the profits. Taxpayers bear the risk of global financial speculation while the payoffs go to those most effective at gaming the system. Instead of investing profits to provide jobs and produce needed goods and services, the 1% put their wealth into mergers, acquisitions, and more speculation.

The list of government interventions on behalf of the 1% goes on and on: Tax breaks favor the wealthy, global trade agreements encourage offshoring jobs, agricultural subsidies favor agribusiness over family farms, corporate media get sanctioned monopolies while independent media gets squeezed.

. . .

This lopsided division of wealth corrupts government. Few among the 99% now believe government works for their benefit—and for good reason. With the 1% commanding an army of lobbyists and doling out money from multimillion-dollar campaign war chests, government has become a source of protection and subsidies for Wall Street. No wonder there isn't enough money left over for education, repairing roads and bridges, taking care of veterans and retirees, much less for the critical transition we need to make to a clean energy future.

The system is broken in so many ways that it's dizzying to try to name them all. This is part of the reason why the Occupy movement hasn't created a list of demands. The problem is everywhere and looks different from every point of view. The one thing the protesters all seem to agree on is that the middle-class way of life is moving out of reach. Talk to people at any of the Occupy sites and you'll hear stories of people who play by the rules, work long hours, study hard, and then find only low-wage jobs, often without health care coverage or prospects for a secure future.

And many can find no job at all. In the United States, twenty-five million people are unemployed, underemployed or have given up looking for work. Forty-five percent of those without jobs have been unemployed for more than twenty-seven weeks. Some employers won't hire anyone who is currently unemployed. Meanwhile, the cost of health care, education, rent, food, and energy continues to rise; the only thing that's falling is the value of homes and retirement funds.

Behind these statistics are real people. Since the Occupy movement began, some who identify themselves as part of the 99% have been posting their stories at wearethe99percent. tumblr.com. Here's one: "I am a lucky one. I have enough money to eat three of four weeks of the month. I have been paying student loans for fifteen years and still no dent. My husband lost his job . . . Last year I took a 10 percent pay cut to 'do my share' and keep layoffs at bay. I lost my house. I went bankrupt. I still am paying over one thousand dollars in student loans for myself and my husband and that is just interest. We will not have children. How could we when we can't even feed ourselves? I am the 99%."

Another personal story, by a sixty-year-old, reads, "Got laid off. Moved two thousand miles for new job. Pays 40 percent less than old job. Sold home at a loss. Filed Chapter Eleven. Owe IRS fifty thousand dollars. Fifteen thousand dollar per year debt for son's tuition at state university. Seventy-five percent of retirement funds shifted to the 1%! I am the 99%!"

The Web site contains thousands of stories like these.

N
E
X
T

S
T
E
P
S

Now that we know we are not alone, we are less likely to blame ourselves when things are hard. And now that we are seeing the ways the system is rigged against us, we can join with others to demand changes that will allow everyone to thrive.

. . .

Hundreds of thousands have participated in the protests and occupations, millions support the occupations, and tens of millions more support their key issues. Polls show that jobs continues to be the issue that most concerns us, yet the national dialogue has been dominated by obsession with debt. While just 27 percent of Americans responding to an October 2011 *Time Magazine* poll held a favorable view of the Tea Party, for example, 54 percent held a favorable view of the Occupy Wall Street movement. Of those familiar with the protests, large majorities share their concerns: 86 percent agreed that Wall Street and lobbyists have too much power in Washington, DC, 68 percent thought the rich should pay more taxes, and 79 percent believe the gap between rich and poor has grown too large.

The movement has been criticized for its diversity of people and grievances, but in that diversity lies its strength. Among the 99% are recent graduates and veterans who can't find work, elderly who fear losing their pensions, the long-term unemployed, the homeless, peace activists, people with a day job in a corporate office who show up after work, members of the military, and off-duty police. Those involved cannot be pigeonholed. They are as diverse as the people of this country and this world.

The movement has also been criticized for its failure to issue a list of demands. In fact, it is easy to see what the movement is demanding: quite simply, a world that works for the 99%. The hand-lettered protest signs show the range of concerns: excessive student debt; banks that took taxpayer bailouts, then refused to help homeowners stay in their homes; cuts in government funding for essential services; Federal Reserve policies; the lack of jobs.

A list of specific demands would make it easier to manage, criticize, co-opt, and divide the movement. Instead, Occupy Wall Street is setting its own agenda on its own terms and developing consensus statements at its own pace. It's doing this in spaces that it controls—some in parks and other public spaces, others in union halls, libraries, churches, and community centers. On the Internet, the movement issues statements and calls to action through Twitter, Facebook, and its own Web sites. From the start it was clear that the movement would not rely on a mainstream media corrupted by corporate interests.

The Occupy Wall Street movement does not treat power as something to request—something that others can either grant or withhold. *We the people* are the sovereigns under the Constitution. The Occupy Wall Street movement has become a space where a multitude of leaders are learning to work together, think independently, and define the world we want to live in.

Those leaders will be stirring things up for years to come.

. . .

WHAT NEXT?

The organizers of the September 17 occupation say they weren't planning for an occupation that would go on week after week. It just hadn't occurred to them. And no one can say where things will go from here. Harsh weather could drive people away. Other hazards could undercut the movement. Police violence could frighten away would-be protesters, or it could galvanize the movement, as did the pepper spraying of unarmed women in Manhattan and police violence against occupiers in Oakland.

. . .

But the movement has important strengths that add to its resilience. It is radically decentralized, so a disaster at any one occupation will not bring down the others; in fact, the others can take action in support. There is no single leader who could be co-opted or assassinated. Instead, leadership is broadly shared, and leadership skills are being taught and learned constantly.

. . .

New support is flowing in, some from unexpected sources. A group of Marine veterans has formed OccupyMARINES, which will work to recruit police and members of other branches of the military to support the occupations, and to nonviolently protect protesters from police assaults. The Marines also plan to help the occupations sustain themselves through cold weather. The group was inspired by a viral video showing Marine Sergeant Shamar Thomas dressing down the police for brutalizing protesters. "There is no honor in this," he shouted at the police. The wounding of Marine veteran Scott Olsen, who at twenty-four years old had already served two tours in Iraq, has further fired up fellow Marines. Olsen was critically injured by a police-fired projectile in an Oakland police action against occupiers.

Police, though often shown cracking down on occupations, have also expressed sympathy with the movement. In Albany, New York, state and city police declined to follow orders from the mayor to arrest and remove peaceful protesters. "We don't have those resources, and these people were not causing trouble," an official with the state patrol told the *Times Union* newspaper.

Will there come a time when there is no one willing to enforce orders to evict members of the 99% from occupation encampments—or from their homes, for that matter? And if popular support grows, will elected officials look to ally themselves with the movement, rather than suppress it? The fact that these are even questions shows how radically things have changed since a few hundred people occupied Zuccotti Park on September 17, 2011.

Whatever happens next, Occupy Wall Street has already accomplished something that changes everything. It has fundamentally altered the national conversation.

. . .

Now that millions recognize the injustice resulting from the power of Wall Street and giant corporations, that issue will not go away. The central question now is this: Will we build a society to benefit everyone? Or just the 1%?

N
E
X
T

S
T
E
P
S

10 WAYS THE OCCUPY MOVEMENT CHANGES EVERYTHING

Sarah Van Gelder, David Korten, and Steve Piersanin

Many question whether this movement can really make a difference. The truth is that it is already changing everything. Here's how.

1. **It names the source of the crisis.**
   The problems of the 99% are caused by Wall Street greed, perverse financial incentives, and a corporate take-over of the political system.
2. **It provides a vision of the world we want.**
   We can create a world that works for everyone, not just the wealthiest 1%.
3. **It sets a new standard for public debate.**
   Those advocating policies and proposals must now demonstrate that their ideas will benefit the 99%. Serving only the 1% is no longer sufficient.
4. **It presents a new narrative.**

The solution is no longer to starve government, but to free society and government from corporate dominance.

5. **It creates a big tent.**
We, the 99%, are made up of people of all ages, races, occupations, and political beliefs, and we are learning to work together with respect.

6. **It offers everyone a chance to create change.**
No one is in charge. Anyone can get involved and make things happen.

7. **It is a movement, not a list of demands.**
The call for transformative structural change, not temporary fixes and single-issue reforms, is the movement's sustaining power.

8. **It combines the local and the global.**
People are setting their own local agendas, tactics, and aims. But we also share solidarity, communication, and vision at the global level.

9. **It offers an ethic and practice of deep democracy and community.**
Patient decision-making translates into wisdom and common commitment when every voice is heard. Occupy sites are communities where anyone can discuss grievances, hopes, and dreams in an atmosphere of mutual support.

10. **We have reclaimed our power.**
Instead of looking to politicians and leaders to bring about change, we can see now that the power rests with us. Instead of being victims of the forces upending our lives, we are claiming our sovereign right to remake the world.

40

"Classism From Our Mouths" and "Tips From Working-Class Activists"

Betsy Leondar-Wright

We've all learned classist prejudices, and none of us has completely eradicated them from our minds.

. . .

And we all make mistakes. There's not a middle-class person alive who hasn't said dumb, insensitive things that step on working-class toes. Hiding our classist mistakes or defending ourselves ("I didn't mean it that way") doesn't do any good. The only thing to do is to 'fess up, apologize, laugh at ourselves, and commit to learning how do better in the future.

As we talk, working-class people notice how oblivious or how aware of class issues we seem, and make decisions about how much to collaborate with us based on those evaluations, among other factors. The goal of reducing the classism in our speech is not to keep ourselves out of trouble by avoiding angering working-class people, and it's not to reach some kind of perfect non-classist purity. The goal is to make ourselves more trustworthy and to alienate working-class people less so that we can work together for economic justice and other common goals.

TOP THESE!: A FEW CLASSIST THINGS I'VE SAID
(IF I CAN ADMIT MINE, YOU CAN ADMIT YOURS)

- I came back from college and bumped into a working-class guy I'd known in high school. I asked what he was doing. "Bagging groceries at the supermarket." I said, "Oh, is it interesting?" He just looked at me like I was an idiot.
- In college, I was going door-to-door in the dorms signing people up for an Oxfam fast in which we would all skip eating for a day and donate the money for famine relief. One guy said, "No, this isn't for me; I'm working my way through college. This is for people whose parents pay their tuition." I told him, "No, this is for everyone!" I wouldn't take no for an answer. He actually opened a drawer and showed me those little packages of peanut butter crackers he was eating for meals, and still I badgered him to contribute.
- My friend with an Associates degree said, "I am *so* tired of teaching dental hygiene." I said, "Well, why don't you try teaching something else?" She looked at me like I was clueless and said, "Because I don't know anything else."

WHAT'S THE MOST CLASSIST THING YOU'VE HEARD AN ACTIVIST SAY?

Five interviewees' answers to this question – and mine:

Recently I was facilitating a discussion for an organization that was trying to decide how much severance pay to give a staff person leaving because the organization couldn't afford to keep them full-time. Someone said, "Let's give them a huge party and show them we love them, and they'll remember that a lot longer than any money we give them."

—Paul Kivel

Most of the Homeowners Associations wanted in an icky way to "color up" with racial diversity. They were happy to have people of color at the table as long as they were in the minority and didn't get to make any decisions. At one meeting, this one white homeowner was complaining about "why Latinos won't come to our meetings" and she suggested that maybe people should bring their maids! It was too gross!

—Roxana Tynan

Find the Invisible Working-Class People in These Statements

- Women still have to choose between career success and children.
- I bought some land in Vail and built my dream house.
- Everybody got burned in the stock market crash.
- I run an institute at the university.
- When I was a girl, every family had a cook.

—blw

There was a fund-raising event that cost $50 and I heard comments about how "anyone can afford that."

—Pam McMichael

Several times I've heard social welfare professionals say about poor mothers, "We have to speak for them because they can't speak for themselves."

—Theresa Funiciello

There was one guy I worked with, he thought he was the smartest organizer, and he would say things to me like "Can you turn out 500 people for this meeting and then we'll go and do the negotiations for them?" He thought of working-class people as props and their voices as sound bites.

I've heard people patronize, tokenize, and fetishize, like "Let's hear from the welfare recipient now! Isn't she smart?"

—Gilda Haas

A new friend said, "My neighbor wanted to put up a 15-foot fence that would block my view. He's real redneck low-life trailer trash." I told her I was offended by that, and we had a big argument that lasted all day.

—blw

. . .

In many organizations I've been part of, decision-making is hard. Middle-class people with more education are just faster and more articulate. Others are silenced because they can't keep up with the style of arguing.

—Barbara Willer

. . .

HANG IN

Low-income folks believe that middle-class folks won't stick around. When the going gets tough, they'll leave. It's a vicious cycle: it happens so much that there's no trust, so middle-class people wonder why they should stick around if they're not trusted. The key is to stick with it even if pushed away. You'll be tested. Like when [civil rights pioneer] Septima Clark sent me as a white person to a black church meeting, and I came back saying they didn't want me there. She asked "What did you expect? Now, next time you go . . ." She kept sending me back to that group until I had built trust.

I really value middle-class activists when they're willing to stick it through hard times—and I say that coming out of an area where doing this work meant Klan harassment and threats.

—Linda Stout

. . .

SUPPORT WORKING-CLASS ISSUES

. . .

Want to be an ally? Honor boycotts, buy union, use union printers, don't cross picket lines, pay a living wage, and give family leave and good benefits.

—Felice Yeskel

In the 1980s in my city, the Nuclear Freeze campaign put a referendum on the ballot, and 60 percent of the voters supported a freeze on nuclear weapons. Then Jobs with Peace proposed a followup referendum calling for more jobs through peace conversion, which had the potential for even more public and labor support. But most of the Freeze people just faded away, uninterested.

I was asked to speak at a statewide Freeze convention, and I made a strong pitch for reaching out to labor and working-class people. Afterwards, in the hallway, a number of working-class people came up to me and said it made a big difference to them; they hadn't had the nerve to raise it themselves.

Sometimes peace activists kind of raise their noses, as if it's more pure to be against war for idealistic reasons, as if it's a bit tawdry to be concerned with jobs and self-interest.

—George Lakey

USE YOUR PRIVILEGE

If you have privilege, have a conversation with low-income leaders about how you could use it strategically. If you have a country house, maybe we could have a retreat there. It's not just your money, it's who you know, what you know, how you talk.

We were organizing a conference on homelessness, and members of our group who were homeless were going to speak. There was a woman who had a lot of classism. She said, "How are you going to find homeless people to ask to speak? Would they know enough? How could you find homeless people who can talk well enough?" I was going to debate someone on the Governor's Council, and she said, "Do you know how to debate? Do you know enough information to debate? Would you be able to keep up with him?" I asked my owning-class coworker to talk with her, and she persuaded her. Now this woman points out classism when it happens. That's the fastest turn-around I've seen. My coworker was able because of her similar background to explain how things sounded. It was a strategic use of privilege.

—Lisa Richards

People with more privilege need to figure out how to equalize things, which doesn't mean to empty out their bank accounts. But it's the responsibility of activists to be generous and to figure out how to support things they care about materially if they possibly can.

—Barbara Smith

NEXT STEPS

I resent people who try to pass as someone like me. I met an upper-middle-class woman who said, "I'm on welfare so I can be a full-time activist with youth." That's not what welfare's there for. I hate it when people hide their privilege and don't acknowledge it.

—Rachel Rybaczuk

If grassroots people have attitudes of racism or antiimmigrant prejudice, a negative approach isn't productive. Nobody likes to be told they are wrong, especially by a more privileged person. Instead, ask questions and help someone learn. Hold fast to principles, but let go of ideology. Equity is a principle, but "only one way to get there" is ideology.

—Barbara Willer

LET GO OF CONTROL

I've seen this pattern over and over. A cross-class alliance is formed to deal with a problem. A group with resources offers to sponsor it. They staff it, they control the funding, they control the information . . . . Next thing you know, we have our own class divide internally. We build power just to give it away, without knowing it's been given away until it's gone.

—Sam Grant

I helped start a community development corporation that created affordable housing. The board was all professionals, and all of us in the houses were neighborhood people. There was so much tension over decision-making and who had the control. We argued over what color paint to use. The middle-class folks didn't get the concerns about power and why the working-class folks were so frustrated. We had no language for it, because everyone was white, so weren't we all the same?

—Barbara Willer

RECOGNIZE WORKING-CLASS PEOPLE'S CONSTRAINTS

I remember going to a national women's group conference. They wanted low-income people and people of color there, so we said sure, Piedmont Peace Project would bring a group of folks in. First, they didn't do a sliding scale, which was shocking enough. But the worst thing was, we came with kids in tow, and we got there and there was no childcare. We had to turn around and go home. We were so used to providing childcare, we assumed there would be childcare.

Some groups have meetings in the middle of the day, and then wonder why no working people come. Ridiculous! We used to plan meetings taking people's work hours into consideration. In farm communities, we'd meet after dark. With millwork-ers, we'd have meetings in shifts, one in the morning and one at 6 P.M. You've got to know your constituency.

—Linda Stout

41

Deep Thoughts About Class Privilege

Karen Pittelman and Resource Generation

CLASS PRIVILEGE AFFECTS OUR FINANCIAL FUTURE

A job interview is only one of many situations where class privilege affects our financial future. Every time we walk into a bank for a loan, into a real estate broker's office for a home, even into an important meeting at work, being a young person with wealth gives us an unspoken advantage.

Another advantage comes from the fact that class privilege can place us in some very powerful networks. Networks are one of the main ways people find out about things like jobs, housing and business opportunities. Class privilege gives us access to exclusive formal associations like alumni groups and prestigious clubs, as well as informal webs of influential neighbors, family and friends.

These connections don't just tell us about possible opportunities, they can also help us act on them. When someone "in the know" puts in a good word for us, it transforms us from an anonymous name into a friendly face—and that can often make all the difference.

THIS DOESN'T MEAN WE DON'T WORK HARD

Thinking about the impact of class privilege on our lives can be unsettling, especially if we grew up wealthy and don't have any other class experience to compare it to. We want to say that our successes happen because we deserve them—because we worked hard, because we studied and sacrificed, because we were committed to our goals. We want to say that maybe we had that privilege, but we chose not to use it, that we didn't need it, that we could make it on our own merits.

The problem is that privilege isn't something that can be turned on or off. While money can be laid aside unused, privilege is deeply embedded in our lives. It's a part of the experiences that make us who we are, that shape how we see the world and the way the world sees us. Class privilege even becomes a part of our bodies, from straight teeth to a "firm" handshake.

Acknowledging how class privilege impacts our lives doesn't have to mean abandoning pride in ourselves. Our hard work is still hard work. Our fabulousness is still fabulous. It just means that, as young people with wealth, the story of where we are and how we got there is more complicated than a list of our merits. There's a lot more there to uncover.

DEEP THOUGHTS ABOUT CLASS PRIVILEGE

Here are some seriously heavy questions about the impact of class privilege in our lives. Woo hoo! Yeah!

Okay, maybe that's a little overzealous. It'd probably be much more fun to watch *MacGyver* reruns and eat Funyuns. But even though it isn't easy, understanding our privilege has the potential to change our lives and our relationships in some amazing ways. Plus, the more we understand, the better we'll be at using our privilege for social change. . . . And, obviously, depending on your background and what's up for you right now in your life, some of these questions will be more or less relevant. Feel free to skip anything that doesn't pertain . . .

BIG DECISIONS

- Think about a big decision you've made recently. Were there ways that having class privilege factored into that decision?
- Has having class privilege ever affected the way you've been able to cope with a difficult or painful time in your life? How so?
- What's one of the biggest risks you've taken—or wish you could have taken—in your life? Were there resources of your own or family resources that you could have fallen back on if it didn't work out? Did that affect your choice to take the risk?

WORK AND SCHOOL

- Has having class privilege affected your education? How so? Has it had an effect on your choices about schools? About what to study?
- Has having class privilege had an effect on your decisions about work? Has it had an impact on your salary, income or level of prestige associated with your work?

WHERE YOU LIVE

- Has having class privilege played a role in your housing decisions? Has it affected where you've lived in the past? Where you live now? The way other people involved, like brokers, realtors and landlords, treated you? Whether you rent or own? If you own, did it impact the way you paid for your home?

DISCRIMINATION

- Are there ways that class privilege *hasn't* made any difference for you in dealing with discrimination? How so?
- Are there ways that class privilege *has* made a difference for you in dealing with discrimination? How so?
- How have your experiences with discrimination impacted the way you understand class privilege?

OTHER KINDS OF PRIVILEGE

- Do you have other kinds of privilege in addition to class privilege? How does that affect the way you look at your experiences with class privilege?
- Has there ever been a time when having privilege made it harder to hear what someone was trying to say to you?

NEXT STEPS

1. polite
2. great smile
3. reliable
4. high GPA
5. confident
6. impressive résumé
7. great references
8. well spoken
9. impressive degree
10. well-rounded
11. energetic
12. looks put-together

NEXT STEPS

If you grew up with wealth . . .

- Were there ways that class privilege had an impact on your daily life? How so?
- Did having class privilege ever affect the way people treated you? How?
- Did having class privilege affect the way you saw your own potential and your role in the world? How?

If wealth is a more recent thing in your life . . .

- Are there ways that having class privilege has changed your daily life?
- Are there ways that having class privilege has changed the way people treat you?
- Has having class privilege affected your sense of what's possible in your life and your hopes for the future? How so?

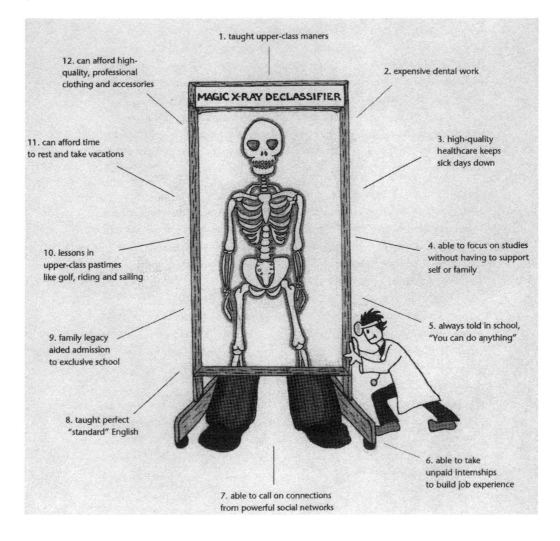

The following labels appear around the illustration:

1. taught upper-class maners
2. expensive dental work
3. high-quality healthcare keeps sick days down
4. able to focus on studies without having to support self or family
5. always told in school, "You can do anything"
6. able to take unpaid internships to build job experience
7. able to call on connections from powerful social networks
8. taught perfect "standard" English
9. family legacy aided admission to exclusive school
10. lessons in upper-class pastimes like golf, riding and sailing
11. can afford time to rest and take vacations
12. can afford high-quality, professional clothing and accessories

MAGIC X-RAY DECLASSIFIER

SOCIAL SITUATIONS

- Have you ever been in a situation where you knew the "right" way to act because of your class privilege? Or the "right" way to speak? Or where you got a joke or a reference to something that you understood because you had class privilege?

FINANCIAL STATUS

- Does having class privilege affect your current income and expenses? Do you have loans? Car payments? Mortgage payments? Do you have a financial safety net or family resources you can fall back on?
- Does having class privilege affect the way you are treated at the bank? How?

HEALTH

- Does having class privilege impact the kind of healthcare you receive? The quality of your doctors? Dental work? Therapy?

NEXT STEPS

- If you've had to deal with a major illness or injury, either your own or a family member's, did having class privilege have an impact on your choices about treatments and options?

LEGAL SYSTEM

- If you've had to deal with the police or the legal system, did having class privilege affect your options and the outcome of the experience? How?

In boarding school, I remember being told, "You guys are the cream of the cream. The education you are receiving here is preparing you to be leaders in the world." I realized that the other young people in my class weren't necessarily that special. They were nice, but they weren't so great. It just made me wonder why these people get to be the leaders. Why do I get to be the leader? There's no real reason for that. It's the luck of the draw.

—Christian

42

Distributing Income

You Be the Judge

Tamara Sober Giecek with United for a Fair Economy

N
E
X
T

S
T
E
P
S

OBJECTIVES

- Experience the realistic decision making process of determining who should have an increase or decrease in income.
- Explore how most decisions are made in the business world regarding increases and decreases in income.

CONCEPTS AND KEY TERMS

- distribution of income
- how businesses often decide to distribute income
- the merits of belonging to a union

INSTRUCTIONAL TIME

- 55 minutes

PREPARATION

- Five chocolate bars ("$100 Grand" bars if available).
- Seven sets of five sticky notes marked $100,000. Mark one of the seven sets with "B" on the bottom of each $100,000 bill. Hand these to the Bosses when you are handing out the $100,000 sticky note bills.
- Seven 8.5"×11" placards, each displaying one of the job titles in the chart shown below. Put strings through each sign so students can hang them over their necks.
- The following chart made into poster size, and hung at the front of the classroom.

Bosses	$400,000/year
Doctors	$100,000/year
Nurses	$30,000/year
Kitchen Workers and Nurses' Aides	$11,000/year
Gardeners/Security Guards/Janitors	$15–18,000/year
Patients	fixed income, social security
Low-income Elderly on Waiting List	$10,000/year

- Place the profiles below onto seven separate index cards.

You are the **Bosses:** the management of Sunnyvale and of the nursing home chain that owns Sunnyvale.

Possible Arguments:
- Managers here make less money than at other nursing homes. At another chain, managers make $200,000 to $700,000!
- Because of this, turnover is high. There have been three financial managers in five years!
- We deserve a raise! We only received a $5,000 raise last year. We cut costs by reducing the number of nurses and gardeners last year. We should be rewarded for this cost cutting.
- With just three of the $100,000 bills, all five of the top managers could make as much as we would at other nursing homes.

You are the **Doctors** at Sunnyvale.

Possible Arguments:
- If we went into private practice, we'd all make $200,000 a year or more—double the measly amount we make here.
- The patients we treat are getting older and sicker, so our work is getting more complicated.
- We have the longest training and the most advanced skills of anyone here. We deserve to get the biggest raise. Two of the five $100,000 should go to us.

You are the **Nurses** at Sunnyvale.

Possible Arguments:
- There are fewer nurses taking care of more patients than last year. We are working harder and so should get paid more—but we only received a $400 raise last year! For some of us, our rent went up more than that!
- It's ridiculous that we go to four years of specialized school and our pay ceiling is $40,000. It's because most of us are women!
- Just two of the five $100,000 bills would give us raises we think would be fair.

You are the **Janitors, Security Guards, and Gardeners** at Sunnyvale.

Possible Arguments:
*   Our work is dirty and sometimes dangerous. We have to work outside in all weather. Two gardeners now do all the work that four gardeners used to do.
*   We can hardly support our families on this pay. We can't save money or buy health insurance, or send our kids to college.
*   Some of us have worked here since Sunnyvale started 15 years ago, and we've hardly gotten any raises in all that time!
*   With two of the $100,000 bills, we could get health insurance and a raise to a living wage.

You are the **Kitchen Workers and Nurses' Aides** at Sunnyvale.

Possible Arguments:
*   We can't support our families on the pay here. Many of us don't have cars, phones or health insurance.
*   We think it's because we're all women, mostly women of color or recent immigrants, that we're paid less than anyone else here.
*   We are the ones who actually care for the patients.
*   Our work is dirty and difficult. We change diapers and bathe patients. We stay an average of only five months because we are continually looking elsewhere for higher pay. This high turnover is bad for the patients, who see new faces constantly.
*   With two of the $100,000 bills, we could get raises to a wage where we could meet our expenses and pay our monthly bills. With a third one, we could have health insurance.

You are the **Patients** at Sunnyvale.
Possible Arguments:
*   The fees for our nursing home are so high that they harm our families. The fees take their money that they need for other things.
*   Some nursing homes charge less and have nice facilities that we don't have, like a swimming pool, and activities every day instead of every other day.
*   With just two of the $100,000 bills, we could get a cut in the fees we pay AND some new and improved facilities and activities.

You are the **Low-income Elderly People on a Waiting List** to get into one of the 10 government subsidized* slots at Sunnyvale.

Possible Arguments:
*   We really need a nursing home. We can't live at home any more, because we can't feed or dress ourselves and we need daily medical care. It might be many months before a Medicaid (subsidized*) slot opens up.
*   On our incomes of $10,000 or so, how could we afford the regular $30,000 a year price for Sunnyvale?
*   Our families can't afford it either.
*   Sunnyvale should spend three of the $100,000 bills subsidizing slots for us, so we can move in now.

* Subsidize: to grant public aid (money) to an individual or a private enterprise (corporation) for public benefits.

CONDUCTING THE LESSON

INCOME DISTRIBUTION ROLE PLAY

1. Tell the class, "We have been talking about how American workers are losing ground. We will now look at "why" this happens by conducting a role-play based on a real life situation where we will look at the fairness in the distribution of incomes."

N
E
X
T

S
T
E
P
S

2. Announce: "Sunnyvale Nursing Home has an extra $500,000. We are going to decide who should get this extra money. These five candy bars represent five $100,000 bills, and at the end of the role-play I will divide the candy up the way the money is allocated in the role-play. Each of you get five $100,000 bills to vote on who you think should get the money. There are seven different groups at Sunnyvale Nursing home, so I need seven volunteers (to sit in the middle of the circle or at the front of the room). You will be given teams and you will be the spokesperson for your team."

3. Divide the rest of the students evenly among the seven volunteers and ask them to sit together as seven separate teams. Give each team's spokesperson their bills (give marked bills to the bosses), index cards, and signs (to hang around their necks).

4. Announce: "Your job is to persuade the other groups that your group should get some of the money. Read and discuss your card with your group, then decide where you think the five $100,000 bills should go. Each spokesperson (and members of their group) will have a turn to state their opinion. You can propose something different than what is on the card; these are just suggestions."

5. After seven people speak in turn, conduct discussion as time allows, then conduct a "vote" by asking the spokesperson from each group to place the $100,000 bills on the chart at the front of the room, allocating the funds as they feel they should be distributed.

6. Announce the tallies of how everyone voted. Then hand out the candy bars according to the bosses' vote (marked on the back of their $100,000 bills). See if people object or offer to share, then hold a discussion. Make the point that in a unionized work-place, workers would be represented in this discussion; at a worker coop, everyone would have a vote; at non-union workplaces, the bosses would decide behind closed doors.

See Chapters 11 and 12 in *Teaching for Diversity and Social Justice* for corresponding teaching materials.

SECTION 4

RELIGIOUS OPPRESSION

Introduction

Maurianne Adams and Khyati Y. Joshi[1]

Ask anyone what the United States stands for and most people would place freedom of religion high on the list. Most school children learn that the United States is a beacon of freedom, a place where everyone freely practices their own religion. Freedom of religion is one of the most enduring and powerful founding narratives about the United States. A second and equally powerful foundational narrative is that the U.S. Constitution separates religion and government, and protects religious practice from interference. These deeply held but largely unexamined foundational narratives obscure a less visible history of the influence of Protestant Christianity on the development of law, politics, and social institutions of the United States. Deconstructing these two foundational narratives and understanding their mythic status is an essential first step toward understanding the historical role of Christian privilege and the religious oppression of non-Christian faith traditions, both of which are central concepts in this section.

This section provides readings that explore Contexts for the ways in which dominant (predominantly Protestant) Christianity in the United States maintained, justified, and continues to reproduce the subordination of Buddhism (and Buddhists), Hinduism (and Hindus), Judaism (and Jews), Islam (and Muslims), Santería (and Santeríans), Sikhism (and Sikhs), Wiccan (and Wiccans) as well as non-mainstream Christian sects and their practitioners, as well as non-believers, through institutional practices such as health care, schooling, and public safety. Readings in Voices illustrate the constraints forged by hegemonic Christianity on the religious practices, personal safety, harassment, modes of dress, and the everyday lives of different religious minorities. Reading selections in Next Steps provide examples of coalition and alliance between marginalized religious communities, and ways in which school communities can teach about religious difference to foster respectful, knowledgeable, and pluralistic classroom learning communities.

CONCEPTUAL APPROACH TO RELIGIOUS OPPRESSION

Deconstructing the mythic standing of the two core national narratives noted above involves the exploration of the historical roots of religious and national U.S. identity. It also focuses attention on the influence of hegemonic Christianity on shaping governmental and legal policy, and on

social institutions such as schools. This section presents numerous examples of how Christianity has been used to maintain cultural and political domination over non-Christian religious practices.

We introduce the concept of *religious oppression* in order to focus attention on the social structures, federal and local policies, and cultural practices that maintain *religious hegemony* through "the everyday practices of a well-intentioned liberal society" (Young, selection 5). Readings throughout this section will describe many of the "five faces of oppression" of Christian privilege (Blumenfeld, selection 45) and the individual, institutional, and societal-cultural levels of oppression (Joshi, selection 46) that have been normalized by (mainly) Protestant U.S. Christianity, as exemplified by the efforts to erase Native American Indian religious traditions through federally supported missions, forced residential schooling, and military and legal encroachments, as well as genocidal slaughters (Echo-Hawk, selection 50; Grinde, selection 51). Our section title thus draws upon an understanding of oppression as "structural" and "systemic" (Bell, Hardiman, Jackson, and Griffin, selection 4) that operates through society's "unquestioned norms, habits, and symbols," its "normal processes of everyday life," its "assumptions underlying institutional rules and the collective consequences of following those rules" (Young, selection 5).

The terms *Christian hegemony* and *Christian privilege* are critical in deconstructing these two core national myths—that all U.S. Americans enjoy freedom of religion and that the Constitution requires the separation of religion from policy and supports free religious practice. The term *Christian hegemony* captures the pervasive cultural role of *normative Christianity* in everyday life within U.S. schools, neighborhoods, and workplaces. *Hegemony* is a term used to convey unconscious reproduction of dominant group norms, values, beliefs, cultural forms carried on as part of everyday life. *Christian hegemony* refers to a society's unacknowledged adherence to a dominant religious worldview that in the United States publicly affirms Christian observances, holy days, and sacred spaces, at the expense of the non-Christian and within a culture that normalizes Christian values as intrinsic to an explicitly U.S.-American identity. Christian norms are termed *hegemonic* in that their maintenance depends not on any special effort, but on conducting "business as usual." Examples of hegemonic Christianity include school and workplace holidays keyed to the Christian calendar, political references to the Christian Bible, a weekend that supports Christian worship, and the difficulty of refusing Christian proselytizing (see selections 44–46, 56–59). *Christian privilege* refers to the view that Christian beliefs, language, and practices do not require any special effort to be recognized, since they are embedded within U.S. American culture. For example, Christian worship can be practiced in ways that are considered "normal" and without fear of harassment (Schlosser, selection 44).

CORE MYTH 1: FREEDOM OF RELIGION FOR ALL

The founding narrative that dramatizes freedom of religion in the United States derives from the early history of Pilgrims and Puritans who fled sectarian religious persecution in England and established a religious haven for themselves and their co-religionists. Religious freedom in the Massachusetts colony meant a place to practice *their* religion without fear or persecution, but where non-Puritan practice was forbidden and religious heresy rooted out—Puritans hanged four Quakers to make the point. Puritanism was in effect the first of many ethnocentric and parochial "immigrant faiths" planted on U.S. soil in opposition to the Native American religious traditions already practiced in areas colonized by the Puritans, and also in conflict with the Spanish and French Roman Catholic outposts and missions earlier established throughout the Americas. In reality, the colonial period in the Americas was complex, with Quakers, Anabaptists, Catholics, Jews (and some Muslims) and others also in search of religious refuge and in economic as well as religious conflict with each other. The mutual ill will and religious competition among different Protestant Christian faith traditions, for example, led the people of New Netherland to "cleanse" their colony of Lutherans and Quakers, and to try to do the same with Jews. At one time, Protestants drove Catholics out of New England to settle in what today is Maryland.

The predominantly Protestant Christian ethos of contemporary U.S. life is rooted in the colonial religious competition over homogeneous religious identity, community control, wealth, and land. This ethos dictated the rules of political life in the colonies (mandatory Church attendance, tax-supported religious institutions) and the assumption of Christian superiority over the oral religious traditions of Native Americans or enslaved Africans, and, later, over Buddhist, Hindu, Jewish, and Muslim religious traditions. Similarly, hostility (sometimes violent) was directed against non-Protestant religions such as the Church of Jesus Christ of Latter-Day Saints (the Mormons), the Seventh-Day Adventists, and the Jehovah's Witnesses, each of them critical of Protestant orthodoxy and denominational organization, and resistant to the Protestant hegemony established by state or federal authorities. Likewise, cultural hostility toward and discrimination against atheists is deeply rooted in this dominant Protestant historical tradition, and continues in the present era. To make these points, the historical framework by Lippy (selection 43) examines the conflicting religious traditions that characterize the United States as a "Christian nation or pluralistic culture" (see section website for further resources).

CORE MYTH 2: "SEPARATION OF CHURCH AND STATE"

The second myth in need of deconstruction is the belief that the U.S. Constitution requires the separation of church (religion) and state (government). The language about separation is based not in the text of the Constitution (whose only reference to religion is "there shall be no religious test for public office") but in the religion clauses of the First Amendment to the U.S. Constitution (1791). There, the First Amendment stipulates that "Congress shall make no law respecting an establishment of religion, or prohibiting the free exercise thereof" and provides, in effect, a religious mutual assurance pact, agreed upon by the major competing Protestant denominations in the original thirteen colonies, to prevent any one of them from becoming a federally established religion subsidized by federal taxes (although established state churches were funded by state taxes until the mid-nineteenth century).

The first part of the religion clause of the First Amendment, known as the *Establishment Clause* ("Congress shall make no law respecting an establishment of religion"), prohibits the federal government from supporting any single religion or religious denomination or sect and is generally known as the *separation of church and state.* The phrase "separation of church and state" is not derived from the Constitution but appears in an 1802 letter by Thomas Jefferson to a Baptist congregation in Connecticut, responding to their worries by assuring them that the Constitution would provide "a wall of separation between Church and State."

The second part of the First Amendment guarantee, known as the *Free Exercise Clause* ("Congress shall make no law . . . prohibiting the free exercise thereof"), has been subject to numerous Supreme Court interpretations, whose net effect has been to support free religious practice claims brought by Christian groups, but to restrict free religious practice on the part of some non-Christian groups, especially Native Americans (described in selections 49 and 50).

These important First Amendment protections do not mean that religion should be entirely absent from public life. Rather, they prevent the federal government from legislating for or against any specific religion. While successful in preventing the political establishment of an officially mandated religion (such as existed in the early colonies), the founders were less successful in preventing cultural hegemonic religion, as Jefferson's Christian-centric word "church" in the phrase "church and state" illustrates. Similarly, the pervasive cultural assumptions that are rooted in *Christian hegemony* are evident in the state and federal court interpretations directed against non-Christian plaintiffs in cases of free religious practice. For example, courts did not find credible the free religious practice constitutional claims made in the courts by members of marginalized faiths (Eck, selection 49), or efforts by Native American Indians to practice religious rituals in their sacred sites (Echo-Hawk, selection 50). (See the Section 4 website for examples of First

Amendment litigation that illustrate these limitations in the application of constitutional protection to marginalized religious practice.)

INTERSECTIONS OF RACE AND RELIGION: THE RACIALIZATION OF U.S. RELIGIONS

During colonial times, the *Christian white* landowners justified their violence against Native Americans along with their maintenance of African race-based slavery, on the basis of Christian superiority (Native Americans and Africans were considered infidels and heathen) as well as on the emergent ideology of white racial superiority. So-called "settler" appropriations of Native American lands, and justifications for the brutality and profits of slavery, set in motion an interwoven white *racial* and Christian *religious* national identity that advantaged free, white Christian men as citizens in the new republic. Throughout U.S. history *Christian*, *English*, *free*, and *white* have been juxtaposed to form mutually supporting advantages based on the co-construction of religion, race, and national origins (Fredrickson, 2002; Goldschmidt and McAlister, 2004; Takaki, 1993). Devout colonists saw Divine purpose behind epidemics of malaria and influenza that wiped out Native populations and enabled colonists to appropriate entire Native villages and surrounding farmlands (Loewen, 1995; Mann, 2005). The ensuing tribal displacements and cultural genocide were justified by belief in the inevitable victory of Christianity over heathens, and Western civilization over primitive savagery. In later periods of U.S. history, Christian texts rationalized race-based segregation between white and black congregations within the same Protestant denominations (Baptists, Methodists, Pentecostals) and maintained exclusion and exploitation of Buddhists, Hindus, Muslims, and Sikhs viewed as the threatening and racial/religious "Other." Religious profiling, the presumption that religious "others" are terrorists, and the resistance by Christian neighbors to mosques, temples, and *gurdwaras* are detailed in selections by Eck (selection 49) and Williams (selection 52), and in the Voices selections (selections 54 and 55).

Centuries before the period of European exploration, colonization, and slave trade, European Christian society had traditionally restricted the living conditions of Jews, having pushed Muslims out of its Spanish and East European borders. Jews throughout Christian Europe had been demonized, vilified, expelled, or segregated in ghettos, mainly on religious grounds, although by the eighteenth and nineteenth centuries, as notions of racial superiority or inferiority became part of the culture, Jews in Europe were racialized according to the "pseudo-scientific" view that they constituted an essentially inferior and impure "race" of "Semites." Originally outcast from Christian European society because they did not accept Christ and were blamed for the Crucifixion, Jews had been forcibly converted and absorbed into Christian culture if they were willing to become Christians. However, anti-Judaism morphed into racialized anti-semitism, when even the converted Jews came to be seen as "intrinsically and organically evil" (Fredrickson, 2002, p. 19), resulting in Jewish expulsions, massacres, and genocide. This essentialized view of inferiority based on racism, and compounded by religion, traveled with European Christian migrants to the "New World" as a template for the racialization of other non-Christian religious groups.

Modern anti-semitism is heir to this centuries-old conflation of religion with racial difference as a way of isolating and delegitimizing the Jew as "Other" (Hilberg, Gilbert, and Kaye/Kantrowitz, selections 47, 48, and 54; further resources on the section website). The Christian domination over the religious "other" can also be seen in European colonizing projects in Africa, Asia, and the Americas. European colonialism was a worldwide enterprise in which Christian missions to the "natives" were often the advance guard for colonization, economic exploitation, and the spread of white Christianity to the uncultured heathen masses. These religious "others" were increasingly seen through a miasma of entangled religious and racial meanings that justified European domination over peoples whose religions were seen through racial filters (Buddhists,

Hindus, African and Asian Muslims, animist religious traditions). In the United States, the extension of *racialization* to Native American Indians, African Blacks, Asians, and Arabs living within white-dominated U.S.-America continues to exacerbate the exclusion of those communities who identify themselves primarily as *religious* and do not maintain a primary self-identity on the basis of race (for example, Native American religions, Muslims, Hindus, and Sikhs).

In the contemporary United States, the racialization of religion conflates religions such as Islam, Hinduism, and Sikhism—assumed to be practiced soley by brown peoples—with their presumed ethnic/racial identities (Arab or South Asian), so that phenotypic stereotypes are linked to religious practices (Joshi, 2006). Thus, *brown skin* has come to connote Muslim, conflating Arabs, South Asians, and Latinos/as into the same identity. Singh (2003) comments on the blatant racism in the powerful two-word linkage of "Muslim terrorists" and compares that to "the complete dearth of depictions of the perpetrators of the Oklahoma City Federal Building bombing, abortion clinic bombers, and various white Militia groups, as 'Christian terrorists'" (pp. 88–89). In Europe and the United States, Jews have historically been racialized as non-White, or not-quite-White (selections 47, 48, and 54). The conflation of religious marginalization with ethnocentrism and racism is apparent in selections 46, 47, 49–55, and 57–58, which illustrate various ways that religious oppression is experienced as independent from yet also connected with racism.

NATIVISM AND ANTI-IMMIGRATION

In the early 1800s, it is estimated that over half the U.S. population and 85 percent of Protestants were evangelical (Emerson and Smith, 2000), and that the total number of immigrants was low (143,000 in 1820s), European, and White. Given these early demographics, the linkage between Protestantism and a white American national identity is not surprising. Beginning in the 1840s and continuing into the early twentieth century, European and Asian immigration challenged this homogeneous and racialized, mainly Protestant assumption of U.S.-American national identity. Catholics fled the Irish potato famine of the 1840s, Italian Catholics and Eastern European Jews escaped European revolutions, poverty, and pogroms, and Chinese and Punjabi laborers sought employment. By 1920, more than a third of the total population of 105 million Americans included immigrant families (36 million), the majority of them Roman Catholic, Greek Orthodox, and Jewish, with smaller numbers of Buddhists and Sikhs (Daniels, 2002)—all of them outside Protestantism and considered ethnically or racially inferior (Chinese, Irish, Italians, Japanese, Slavs, Jews, Poles, Greek).

These immigrant religious outsiders poked large holes in the already-stretched fabric of Protestant U.S.-American national identity. The demographic challenge posed by waves of immigrants to a U.S. identity based on religion (Protestantism), culture (Western European heritage) and race (Whiteness) led to a violent xenophobic backlash, anti-immigration policies, and an insurgence of nativist sentiment. The first wave of U.S.-American "nativism" refers to the anti-immigrant backlash from Protestant U.S.-born "Americans" whose ancestry was northern European and whose virulent anti-Catholicism was aimed largely at Irish and German Catholics (1830s–1850s). A second wave of nativism was more generally anti-Asian, and led politically to a series of restrictive immigration laws—the Chinese Exclusion Act of 1882 and the Immigration Act of 1917 (known as the "Barred Zone" Act). The nativist backlash culminated with the Johnson–Reed Immigration Act of 1924, which set a cap on immigrants entering the United States at 2 percent of the total of any nation's residents in the United States reported in the 1890 census, thus severely limiting Catholic and Jewish immigration. In both the 1917 Asian Barred Zone Act and the 1924 Johnson–Reed Act, while religion was not mentioned in the text of the legislation, a byproduct of limiting immigration from southern and eastern Europe along with most of Asia meant the exclusion of non-Protestant faiths. These immigration restrictions, which later restricted refugees such as the Jews fleeing Nazi Europe, for the most part, stayed in place until the Immigration Act of 1965.

After World War II, the barriers were slowly dismantled for white Ashkenazi Jews and for white Catholics (Italians and Irish), but not for black or brown Catholics or Protestants (African Americans, Puerto Ricans, Chicanos/as and Mexican Americans, South or Central Americans) (see resources on the website). This was a period during which most Jews and Catholics "became" White (were accorded a White ethnic/racial assignment by the dominant white Protestant majority) or at least "almost" if "not always quite" White (Brodkin Sachs, 1998; Guglielmo, 2003; Ignatiev, 1995; Roediger, 1991). This example highlights the fact that "race" itself is not a biological reality, but, rather, is socially constructed dependent on time and place.

The 1952 McCarran–Walter Act and then the Immigration and Naturalization Act of 1965 re-opened the door to immigration and permanently altered the racial, ethnic, and religious make-up of the United States. By 2000, immigrant and second-generation Americans numbered nearly 55 million people, more than 32.5 million of them immigrants. One result of the 1965 Immigration Act has been the unification of immigrant families and the growing Hindu, Muslim, and Sikh religious, cultural, and ethnic communities in the United States (Eck, selection 49; Joshi, selection 46; Ahmad and Zawam, selection 55). The recent national debates over immigration, such as Arizona's SB 1070 bill that the governor signed into law in 2010, are also race based. For example, SB 1070 mandates police officers to stop and question people about their immigration status if they suspect they may be in this country illegally; criminalizes undocumented workers who do not possess an "alien registration document"; allows U.S. citizens to file suits against government agencies that do not enforce the law; and criminalizes employers who transport or hire undocumented workers.

INTERSECTIONS WITH OTHER FORMS OF OPPRESSION

The contemporary conflation of terrorism with Islam makes it especially urgent to disentangle the *religious* dimensions of current domestic and global conflicts and hostilities, from dimensions that are political, ideological, or cultural. We need to understand how religious motives and justi-fications can inflame cultural, ethnic, racial, and class antagonisms. This point has been captured in the aphorism, "It is not so much that religion has become politicized, but that politics have been religionized" (Juergensmeyer, 2004, p. 2). Religion interacts in important ways with ethni-city, class, gender, sexuality, and nationalism, and these interacting dimensions of social identity need to be understood in their complex interrelations instead of as either/or forced choices that misinterpret one at the expense of the other.

The complex interrelationship of religion with political, ideological, and cultural forces is impor-tant to understand if we are to make sense of current-day conflicts. Religious difference suffuses some of today's most intractable global, regional, ethnic, national, and domestic conflicts, which generate intense partisanship and sectarian solidarity. For example, Christians v. Muslims in the Balkans, Jews v. Muslims in the Middle East, Hindus v. Muslims in South Asia, Sunni Muslims v. Shiite Muslims in the Middle East, and Catholics v. Protestants until recently in Northern Ireland illustrate this "co-constitutive relationship" (Goldschmidt and McAlister, 2004). Religion links with the other social categories considered elsewhere in this volume—religion *and* race *and* ethnic-ity *and* economic class—*and* nationalism, this last a phenomenon that has had severe conse-quences for the religiously identified "other" and national "outsider" (Marty and Appleby, 1997). For example, several reading selections examine the oppression of Native American Indians in the United States as a complex and cumulative interaction of religion (Christian v. heathen), race (White v. Red), culture (civilized v. barbarian), and economic competition over land (Echo-Hawk, selection 50; Grinde, selection 51). Selections by Eck (selection 49), Joshi (selection 46), Williams (selection 52), and Semple (selection 53) similarly braid religion—Muslim, Hindu, Sikh, Buddhist, Catholic—with race and ethnicity (South Asian Indian, Japanese, Somali, Latino/a). The history of global anti-semitism involves a similarly complex and cumulative braiding of religious hatred, economic resentment, and racial stereotyping (see resources on section website). Religion and sexuality is also discussed within the "Heterosexism" section of this volume.

Contemporary manifestations of Christian hegemony interacting with cultural and political ideology can be seen in divisive instances of "religionized" domestic U.S. politics. They include bitter disputes over competing end-of-life and beginning-of-life issues (such as euthanasia and stem cell research), competing rights such as "the right to decide" v. "the right to life," the authority of local school boards to substitute creationism or intelligent design for evolution in science curricula. Religionized policy issues further include whether to expand the definition of "marriage" to include same-sex couples or whether to codify marriage as constituting a union only between one man and one woman; whether to restrict sexuality education within the schools to basic biology and "abstinence only" or to provide accurate and age-appropriate sexuality education. Other policy issues whose politics interact with religion include the question of whether religious hospitals, charities, foster homes, and adoption agencies should receive federal funding based on legal requirements that employee health care coverage includes contraceptive and other reproductive health choices options. "Religionized" issues also include legal and Constitutional struggles to extend or prohibit marriage for same-sex couples, controversies concerning school prayer, religious displays at Christmas or Easter, the use of tax-funded vouchers for private religious schools, and the funding of faith-based initiatives as a substitute for increased public services. The "Heterosexism" section includes an important example (selection 82).

STEPS AND CHALLENGES IN ACHIEVING A RELIGIOUS PLURALISM

It is important to also understand Christianity's dramatic historical and contemporary role in contesting oppression and fostering coalitions that have created lasting social change. Examples include the historical role of Protestant churches in the anti-slavery and Abolition movements and in the Civil Rights movement (resources on the section website). Christian Liberation Theology has contributed to social justice movements around the world, such as in the Americas and South Africa. In addition, some U.S. Catholic women are attempting to change the church from within by working to increase their initiative in providing service and working toward justice.

For oppressed communities, religion has been a source of community strength and empowerment in times of political crisis. Williams (selection 52) describes the importance of Buddhist solidarity during Japanese internment, and Bernards (selection 59) traces her inspiration from Jewish tradition to build coalitions across communities in religious conflict to foster cooperation and change. Other examples of organized resistance to oppression and maintenance of group solidarity, such as the Black Church, and the role of Hindu temples, Sikh *gurdwaras*, and Muslim mosques to support religious, ethnic, and linguistic-identified communities, can be followed on the website for this section.

Only by questioning the pervasive assumption that freedom of religious practice has already been achieved can the specific role of *religion* in American social and cultural life become clear. While many think we live in a religiously pluralistic democracy, it should be clear we have a long way to go in achieving that goal. Present-day immigration is increasing U.S. religious diversity and facilitating the growth of Latino/a and Asian Catholic and evangelical congregations whose identity and forms of worship are firmly rooted in their ethnic communities of origin (see section website for citations and for current population statistics for different religious groups).

The challenges have already been noted in this section introduction. The opportunities must be noted as well. There are at least two openings in our society that might enable us to strengthen religious pluralism and freedom of religious practice—in our schools and through interfaith organizations.

We started this section with common myths perpetuated by the U.S. educational system. The educational arena is a perfect location for advancing religious pluralism by teaching about religions. Another myth that is perpetuated today is that religion cannot be taught and discussed in schools. This myth needs to be dismantled.

Beginning in the late 1800s into the 1900s, schools incorporated Protestant Christianity into their curriculum, with daily Protestant Bible readings and texts such as the *New England Primer*. As the public school movement expanded nationally, it collided with religiously diverse immigrant communities who objected to the requirements of Protestant prayer and moral guidance. Prayer in public schools was challenged, and in the educational arena became a legal battleground over religion and public schools, culminating with two major Supreme Court decisions (*Engel v. Vitale*, 370 U.S. 421 [1962] and *Abington Township School District v. Schempp*, 374 U.S. 203 [1963]). These key Supreme Court cases derive from religious objections to Protestant prayer and scriptural reading in public schools. To broaden this discussion, selection 56 describes an eleventh grader's objection to school prayer based on her religious convictions as an atheist—and the assaults she experienced within her local community.

The Supreme Court decisions cited above encourage teaching about religion as an important part of schooling. They draw a firm distinction between "teaching religion," which violates the separation of church and state, and "teaching *about* religion," which is constitutionally allowable and educationally desirable. "It might well be said that one's education is not complete without a study of comparative religions or the history of religion and its relationship to the advancement of civilization . . . [when] presented objectively as part of a secular program of education" (*School District of Abington Township, Pennsylvania, et al. v. Schempp et al.*, 1963). Selection 58 provides an overview of some of the many ways that learning about religion can be incorporated into the P-12 curriculum. The section website presents examples of effective K-12 programs that teach *about* religions, with the goal of increasing understanding of all faiths.

There is also an important tradition of interreligious dialogue and understanding created by people motivated by diverse faith and religious traditions to work for social change. Historical examples date back to the Abolitionist Movement, worker and Liberation Theology movements, settlement and social reform movements, and the Civil Rights movement. Today, peace activists and interfaith communities work at the local level to provide support for the needs of different faith communities, and members of religious and spiritual communities join forces to safeguard the local and the global environment. Minority religious advocacy organizations work to protect the religious and civil rights of their community members and assist one another (see selection 59 and section website for examples, references, and resources).

See Companion Website for Additional Resources and Material

Note

1. We ask that those who cite this work always acknowledge by name both the authors listed rather than either only citing the first author or using "et al." to indicate coauthors. Both collaborated on the conceptualization, development, and writing of this section.

References

Brodkin Sachs, K. (1998). *How Jews Became White Folks and What That Says About Race in America*. New Brunswick: Rutgers University Press.

Daniels, R. (2002). *Coming to America: A History of Immigration and Ethnicity in American Life* (2nd edition). Princeton, NJ: HarperPerennial.

Emerson, M. O., Smith, C. (2000). *Divided by Faith: Evangelical Religion and the Problem of Race in America*. Oxford: Oxford University Press.

Fredrickson, G. M. (2002). *Racism: A Short History*. Princeton, NJ: Princeton University Press.

Goldschmidt, H., McAlister, E. A. (2004). *Race, Nation, and Religion in the Americas*. Oxford ; New York: Oxford University Press.

Guglielmo, T. A. (2003). *White on Arrival : Italians, Race, Color, and Power in Chicago, 1890–1945*. New York: Oxford University Press.

Ignatiev, N. (1995). *How the Irish Became White*. New York: Routledge.

Joshi, K. Y. (2006). The racialization of religion in the United States. *Equity and Excellence in Education*, 39 (3), 211–226.

Juergensmeyer, M. (November 1, 2004). *Religious Terror and the Secular State* (Global & International Studies Program. Paper 22). Retrieved September 4, 2006, from http://repositories.edlib.org/gis/22

Loewen, J. W. (1995). *Lies My Teacher Told Me: Everything Your American History Textbook Got Wrong*. New York: New Press: distributed by Norton.

Mann, C. C. (2005). *1491: New Revelations of the Americas Before Columbus* (1st ed.). New York: Knopf.

Marty, M. E., Appleby, R. S. (eds) (1997). *Religion, Ethnicity, and Self-identity: Nations in Turmoil.* Hanover, NH: University Press of New England.

Roediger, D. R. (1991). *The Wages of Whiteness: Race and the Making of the American Working Class*. London; New York: Verso.

Singh, J. (2003). The racialization of minoritized religious identity: Constructing sacred sites at the intersection of white and Christian supremacy. In J. N. Iwamura, P. Spickard (eds), *Revealing the Sacred in Asian and Pacific America* (pp. 87–106). New York: Routledge.

Takaki, R. (1993). *A Different Mirror: A History of Multicultural America*. Boston: Little, Brown and Company.

43

Christian Nation or Pluralistic Culture

Religion in American Life

Charles H. Lippy

. . .

EUROPEANS PLANT CHRISTIANITY IN NORTH AMERICA

. . . Most . . . [colonists] who came from England brought with them a religious conscious-ness shaped by Protestant Christianity. In southern areas like Virginia, although there were some variations of belief, colonial arrangements included legal establishment of the Church of England. Establishment meant that Church of England parishes and the few clergy serv-ing them were supported by public tax money and that all who lived there would in theory be expected to be part of a parish.

. . .

Before the end of the seventeenth century, however, political changes in Britain man-dated in the colonies a broader toleration of variant forms of Protestantism, so long as they did not disrupt public order and peace. Roman Catholics, however, were still not formally recognized, although they had carved a presence for themselves when Maryland was established. . . .

EARLY SIGNS OF DIVERSITY

Even so, patterns of immigration generated a far greater diversity in many parts of the English colonies than was recognized by public policy. From the arrival of the first slave ships in Virginia in 1619, an African tribal substratum made most southern Christian life diverse, since many congregations in time became biracial. White Christians were at first reluctant to share their religion with the slaves, fearing that conversion would automatically bring freedom from the bonds of slavery. When more sustained efforts were made to preach Christianity to African Americans from the middle of the eighteenth century on, the result was a vibrant fusion of African ways with evangelical Protestantism. . . . In addition, some of the first slaves were Muslims, although the conditions of slavery made it impossible for Muslim practice to last very long among the African population.

Ethnicity also contributed to other manifestations of diversity. The Dutch who had originally settled in New York (New Netherlands) brought with them their Calvinistic Reformed faith; even after the English took control, they remained a strong presence. To what became New Jersey, clusters of Scandinavian immigrants brought their Lutheran religion with them. Various communities of German immigrants who came to Pennsylvania carried a variety of religious labels, most still within the orbit of Protestant Christianity. And almost from the inception of the colonies came Jewish immigrants, who remained on the margins of colonial religious life but established synagogues and communities in places such as Charleston, South Carolina; Savannah, Georgia; New York; and Newport, Rhode Island. . . .

English control did not extend to all areas of North America that eventually became part of the United States. The presence of Spanish settlements in areas from Florida through Texas and the Southwest to California adds another layer to the tale of diversity. The last of the Spanish missions, the one in San Francisco, was founded in 1776, the same year that the English colonies proclaimed their independence from Britain. In addition, a Catholicism reflecting the French experience flourished in areas along the Gulf of Mexico from Mobile to New Orleans and along the southern Mississippi River. When these areas became part of the United States, they intensified the story of diversity because of the long history of both Spanish and French Catholicism that had supported adjoining colonial empires.

COMMON THEMES

Presbyterians and Methodists, Lutherans and Dutch Reformed, Congregationalist Puritans and Baptists—all were part of the larger Protestant heritage that had marked European Christianity since the Reformation of the sixteenth century. . . . Even the arrival of thousands of Roman Catholics from Ireland in the 1830s and 1840s did not diminish that influence, for Protestant folk were also the ones who ran the developing businesses and industries and usually the ones elected or appointed to political office. This Protestant Christian character became deeply etched into American culture more subtly as public education began to develop in the 1830s. . . . Hence, even though there were other groups present—Irish Catholics, German Catholics, Jews, and more—this broad evangelical Protestantism influenced every sector of common life, reinforcing the image of the United States as a Christian nation.

The decades between the close of the Civil War and the outbreak of World War I, when immigration from Europe reached its peak, brought challenges to that hegemony. Most of the millions who arrived on American shores in those decades came not from Protestant

or even Catholic areas of Northern and Western Europe, but from Southern, Central, and Eastern Europe. The majority were not Protestants, but Roman Catholics, Eastern Orthodox Christians, and Jews. Many Catholic parishes established parochial or parish schools, in part because Protestant assumptions pervaded the public school curriculum and instruction. But some of those in positions of social, economic, and political power recoiled not only at the religious orientation of these immigrants but also at their cultural and ethnic folkways. Calls to Americanize the immigrants, however, were also most often quite clearly calls to Protestantize them, to force them into the dominant religious style and therefore perpetuate the image of the United States as a (Protestant) Christian nation.

. . .

Nonetheless, Protestants from the mainline denominations continued to exert an influence in the business and political affairs of the nation that was increasingly out of proportion to their numbers in the whole population. Hence, after World War I, when Congress enacted the first laws restricting immigration overall, there had already been earlier legislation affecting primarily Chinese and Japanese immigration to California and other areas of the West. The new quotas assured that the bulk of those allowed to enter the United States each year would give at least tacit assent to Protestant Christian belief and thus preserve the image of the U.S. as a Christian nation. . . .

RELIGIOUS FREEDOM AND THE SEPARATION OF CHURCH AND STATE

. . .

In the context of the early Republic, one reason for refraining from having a nationally established religion was pragmatic. If most citizens of the new United States identified with one of the numerous Christian bodies, primarily Protestant ones, no one denomination or sect could count a majority as adherents, much less as members. Already Baptists, Methodists, Presbyterians, Quakers, Lutherans of many ethnic varieties, Episcopalians, and a host of others had learned to live in relative peace and harmony. This diversity, which some later would celebrate as a kind of pluralism, meant that it would be unfair—undemo-cratic—to single out one group to receive governmental support. Another assumption undergirded this nod to diversity—namely, a conviction that regardless of label, all such groups inculcated the same values and morals that made their followers good citizens. . . .

[T]he danger in having government endorse a particular belief system, no matter how worthy it was, or in giving official status to any one religious group or tradition, no matter how pervasive its influence, was the potential tyranny such a belief or group could exert over others. If a religious community could call on the coercive power of the state to force conformity to its beliefs and practices, it lost its legitimacy. . . .

Even before ratification of the Bill of Rights, the state of Virginia had adopted a statute providing for near-total religious freedom. Inspired by Thomas Jefferson, the Virginia stat-ute became something of a model for other states, since the Constitution restricted only the Congress from establishing a religion. . . . The phrase with which later generations are familiar, *separation of church and state*, is not strictly speaking part of the constitutional or legal heritage of the nation. Rather, it comes from a letter written in 1802 by Thomas Jefferson, while president, to a group of Connecticut Baptists in which he referred to a "wall of separation between church and state." . . .

This legal arrangement did mean that the United States became a nation where extraor-dinary religious experimentation and diversity prevailed just beneath the surface, even if a broadly evangelical Protestantism centered around a few denominations dominated public life. In the 1830s in upstate New York, for example, Joseph Smith reported having a vision

that led to the founding of the Latter-Day Saints, better known as the Mormons. . . . The Saints represent what some historians regard as the first genuinely "new" religion to emerge in the American context. . . . In the 1830s as well, the Shakers, although planted on North American soil by their founder Ann Lee and a handful of adherents just before the American Revolution, also reached their peak. About 6,000 men and women were leading the simple, celibate life in hopes of salvation in nearly two dozen different communities, several of them in upstate New York and New England. . . .

By the end of the nineteenth century, many other groups had emerged, some reflecting the religious styles of the continuing streams of immigrants and others arising from ideas offered by dynamic speakers and writers. Among the better-known immigrant communities are the Amish and their religious cousins, the Mennonites, who sought to live their version of a simple life without involvement in a larger society that they saw as hopelessly corrupted by modernity. . . . These few examples demonstrate some of the diversity and pluralism beginning to color American religious life, a diversity and pluralism made possible in part because of the legal arrangements embedded in the First Amendment. Other factors aided this religious experimentation. The seemingly vast amount of land available in the expanding nation literally meant that there was room for various religious teachers and groups to go about their business without really interrupting or interfering with the lives of those around them. . . .

DIVERSITY, RELIGIOUS FREEDOM, AND THE COURTS

At the same time, some religious groups seemed to many Americans, primarily those identified with Protestant denominations, to push the limits of freedom too far. After all, they were minority groups on the margins of the larger religious culture. If their beliefs and practices were too far out of step with the majority, should they not be restrained or curtailed before they undermined the dominant religious style? In one sense, the basic issues were how much diversity free exercise allowed before it became dangerous and how much control government should wield to protect a presumed majority before it became tyrannical.

. . .

Laws protecting Sabbath observance go back to the colonial period. Among the earliest was a provision in Virginia, part of "Dale's Laws" issued in 1610, that not only required attendance at Christian worship but also prohibited "any gaming" in public or private on Sunday. As the Jewish population of the United States grew, those identified with Orthodox Judaism, with its emphasis on strict observance of the Sabbath from sundown Friday until sundown Saturday, found laws favoring Sunday as the Sabbath discriminatory. However, because the numbers of Jews were small and the Jewish population fairly scattered, there were few challenges to the status quo.

Sunday laws also affected Seventh-Day Adventists, who, as their name indicates, hold to the Hebrew practice of keeping the Sabbath, the seventh day or Saturday, as sacred. Most Christian groups, whether Protestant, Catholic, or Orthodox, that represented the majority of Americans believed that the Christian practice or keeping Sunday, the first day, as a sacred and holy day superseded seventh-day sabbath observance. Well into the twentieth century, many states and local communities legally restricted what kinds of work could be done on Sunday, whether and what goods and products could be sold, and access to certain recreational activities. Popularly known as "blue laws," such regulations aroused little concern when the overwhelming majority of citizens in a town or area accepted the Christian practice for themselves. . . .

The most familiar cases wrestled with whether practices sanctioned by law resulted in a *de facto* establishment of religion, particularly in areas affecting education in public schools. Some of the earliest concerned children who were Jehovah's Witnesses. On religious grounds, Witnesses refuse to salute the flag, insisting that reciting the Pledge of Allegiance places a blasphemous loyalty to the state before their allegiance to God. Most cases brought by Witnesses came decades before the recent controversy over whether the phrase *under God* that was inserted into the Pledge of Allegiance by Congress in 1954 represented unconstitutional support for religion. Until the rights of the Witnesses received legal protection, episodes in several communities resulted in children who were Witnesses being expelled from school and their parents being prosecuted. . . .

As noted above, when public education began to become the norm in the United States in the nineteenth century, a majority of students came from families with ties to mainline Protestant denominations, and curriculum materials often reflected the beliefs and practices of those groups. Christian holidays, such as Christmas and Holy Week before Easter, were times when classes were suspended; Jewish holy days did not as a rule receive such preferential treatment, although Jewish children were not penalized for absences on religious holidays. In some school districts school facilities were used, primarily by Protestant groups, for religious instruction, occasionally held during the regular class day. In 1948, in *McCollum v. Board of Education*, the Supreme Court ruled against using school facilities and class time for instruction in a particular faith tradition, even when participation was voluntary.

. . .

The greatest controversy, however, has revolved around Bible reading and prayer in the public schools and whether such activities represent a tacit establishment or favoring of a particular religious tradition. In local communities there have been other cases, most notably those that challenged prayers at athletic events, such as those included in pregame ceremonies at football games or commencement exercises. . . .

In the early twenty-first century, debates continued over what separation of church and state involved and how to assure the free exercise of religion. Some echoed earlier themes, such as a case involving whether Santeria was a religion and therefore its ritual of sacrificing chickens a protected religious practice. Others touched on dimensions of how religion and education might legally be linked, such as whether states or communities could provide vouchers that citizens could use to defray the cost of parochial or church-sponsored education. Yet others focused on whether creationism was a science and should be included in biology textbooks if theories of evolution were also presented.

In retrospect, it seems that early cases concerned how to protect the rights of religious minorities, but some had come to believe that later cases imposed minority rule on the majority. Regardless, the array of legal cases concerning religion suggested that a deep and abiding diversity marked American life, even if in an earlier epoch a broadly based evangelical Protestantism had exercised dominant influence.

. . .

THE NEW FACES OF PLURALISM

Changes in immigration laws in 1965 have resulted in a dramatic increase in immigrants from both Latin America and Asia, and with them has come a burgeoning interest in the religions indigenous to those areas and fresh awareness of the links between ethnicity and religious style. In the last decade of the twentieth century, the greatest proportional growth in immigration from Latin America, the Near East, and Asia came in the Sun Belt. . . .

In most urban areas across the nation, Roman Catholic parishes have added services in Spanish, recognizing that Hispanic Catholicism brings a rich blend of traditions to Catholic life, many reflecting the cultures of Central and South America. . . . Some Protestant denominations have launched special ministries to Spanish-speaking Americans, while many Pentecostal congregations, like their Roman Catholic counterparts, now provide services and programs designed to reflect the spirituality and concerns of Hispanic followers. Theologically, Hispanic Americans—both Protestant and Catholic—tend to be more traditional and conservative in their thinking, even as their practice reveals considerable syncretism in its expression. Even within the Christian tradition, it has become impossible to look at Anglo-American styles as normative.

Immigration from Asia swelled the ranks of Hindus, Buddhists, and Muslims in the United States. American interest in Asian religious cultures has a long history. In the nineteenth century, Transcendentalist writers such as Ralph Waldo Emerson were drawn to Asian religious philosophy, while thousands devoured reports of seemingly exotic religious practices in Asia through letters from missionaries published in scores of popular religious magazines. But, except for a relatively small number of immigrants from China and Japan on the West Coast, few Americans had first-hand experience with these religions; even fewer were inclined to practice them.

. . .

The 1960s also witnessed a spate of Asian religious figures who sought to gain American converts, particularly from among those who were disenchanted with traditional American religious life and who saw the dominant religious institutions as mired in racism and torn apart over government policy in Vietnam. . . . While some forms of Buddhism, such as that promoted by the Dalai Lama, and some popular forms of Hinduism, like Krishna Consciousness, have attracted primarily American devotees, the majority of American Buddhists, Hindus, and Muslims come from families who are doing what Americans have done for centuries—practicing the religion that the first generation of immigrants brought with them, albeit adapting it to the American context. What is changing the face of pluralism in the first decade of the twenty-first century is the steadily growing presence of immigrants for whom these traditions represent the heritages they bring with them when they come to the United States. . . .

Estimates suggest that the United States was home to only 30,000 Buddhists in 1900, but to two million a century later; to a mere 1,000 Hindus in 1900, but 950,000 at century's end; to just 10,000 Muslims in 1900, but perhaps—and the estimates vary widely here—between two and one-half to four million a century later, not counting those affiliated with the Nation of Islam (U.S. Census Bureau, 2000). The Hindu tradition has never been inclined to proselytize; in other cultural contexts, Buddhists and Muslims have been more active in seeking converts. However, in the U.S. context, there is relatively little association among the various immigrant Buddhist communities and the centers that cater primarily to American converts to the various strands of Buddhism. American Muslims report that they are reticent to proselytize because popular perception links Muslims to international terrorism. Those Americans who have converted to Islam are more likely to be persons of African descent; they join a small but growing number of African immigrants who are also Muslim.

The growth of these groups signals the pluralism that marks American religious life and the impossibility of regarding a single tradition as normative or perhaps even culturally dominant in the twenty-first century.

. . .

44

Christian Privilege

Breaking a Sacred Taboo

Lewis Z. Schlosser

. . .

A BEGINNING LIST OF CHRISTIAN PRIVILEGES

1. I can be sure to hear music on the radio and watch specials on television that celebrate the holidays of my religion.
2. I can be sure that my holy day (Sunday) is taken into account when states pass laws (e.g., the sale of liquor) and when retail stores decide their hours (e.g., on Saturdays, they are open about 12 hours; on Sundays, they are closed or open for only a few hours).
3. I can assume that I will not have to work or go to school on my significant religious holidays.
4. I can be financially successful and not have people attribute that to the greed of my religious group.
5. I can be sure that when told about the history of civilization, I am shown people of my religion who made it what it is.

. . .

6. I can worry about religious privilege without being seen as self-interested or self-seeking.
7. I can be sure that when my children make holiday crafts, they will bring home artistic symbols of the Christian religion (e.g., Easter bunny, Christmas tree).
8. I am never asked to speak for all the people of my religious group.
9. I can, if I wish, arrange to be in the company of people of my religion most of the time.
10. I can do well in a challenging situation without being called a "credit to my religion" or being singled out as being different from other members of my religious group.

. . .

11. I can be sure that my children will be given curricular materials that testify to the existence and importance of the Christian religion.

. . .

12. I can have a "Jesus is Lord" bumper sticker or Icthus (Christian fish) on my car and not worry about someone vandalizing my car because of it.
13. I can buy foods (e.g., in grocery store, at restaurants) that fall within the scope of the rules of my religious group.
14. I can travel and be sure to find a comparable place of worship when away from my home community.

. . .

15. I can be sure when I hear someone in the media talking about g-d that they are talking about my (the Christian) g-d.
. . .
16. I can be sure that people are knowledgeable about the holidays in my religion and will greet me with the appropriate holiday greeting (e.g., Merry Christmas).
17. I can remain oblivious to the language and customs of other religious groups without feeling any penalty for such a lack of interest and/or knowledge.
18. I can display a Christmas tree and/or hang holly leaves in my home without worrying about my home being vandalized because of my religious identification.
. . .

45

Christian Privilege and the Promotion of "Secular" and Not-So "Secular" Mainline Christianity in Public Schooling and in the Larger Society

Warren J. Blumenfeld

. . .

THE "FACES" OF [RELIGIOUS] OPPRESSION

Many overt forms of oppression are obvious when a dominant religious group tyrannizes a subordinated group, as in the mass slaughter of Jews and other stigmatized minorities in Nazi Germany, and the merciless killing of Jews and Muslims during the Christian "Crusades." Other forms of religious oppression are not as apparent, especially to members of dominant groups. Oppression in its fullest sense also refers to structural/systemic constraints imposed on groups even within constitutional democracies, and "[i]ts causes are embedded in unquestioned norms, habits, and symbols, in the assumptions underlying institutional rules and the collective consequences of following those rules." Young places these forms of oppression and privilege under five overarching categories or "faces" of powerlessness, exploitation, marginalization, cultural imperialism, and violence. The following sections adapt Young's taxonomy to investigate the concept of Christian privilege and religious oppression in the United States [see selection 5 in this volume].

POWERLESSNESS

Subordinated groups have less access to social power than members of dominant groups to engage in the decision-making processes that affect the course of their lives or that name the terms of their existence. "[T]he powerless are situated so that they must take orders and rarely have the right to give them . . . and they rarely command respect" [see selection 5 in this volume].

Historical foundations of religious powerlessness in the colonial period. The spiritual beliefs and identity that were foundational to the Native peoples originally inhabiting the vast territories now known as the United States were violently confronted with the advent of Christian European expansionism to North America. The Pilgrims, for example, who left England for Massachusetts in 1620 believed that they were a divinely chosen people, and soon established "a biblical commonwealth" considered superior to "heathen," "infidel" Native peoples. Massachusetts Puritans crafted their own form of Christianity in which "the church and the state were to support and protect each other."

Over the decades after the Puritans first landed on the shores of North America, other Christian, primarily Protestant "settlers" from Europe included Presbyterians, Methodists, Lutherans, Dutch Reformed, Congregationalist Puritans, and Baptists. In their attempts to assure religious freedom for themselves, under the leadership of William Penn, Quakers founded the colony of Pennsylvania, and Roman Catholics founded Maryland in the 1640s. In the following decades, however, Protestants established political power in Maryland, and in 1704, Protestant legislators passed anti-Catholic legislation unequivocally titled "An Act to Prevent the Growth of Popery within This Province" banishing Jesuits from the territory.

The pattern of Protestant domination and powerless subordinated religious groups continued from the colonial period throughout U.S. history. As recently as the middle-20th century, shortly after the U.S.'s entry into World War II, the government, in a mass relocation effort, interned over 112,000 Japanese Americans, many of them Buddhist, in concentration camps located far from their homes. Many of these incarcerated Japanese were U.S. citizens, born and living in this country for years. Officials used government policy to confiscate the homes, stores, and other property of the politically powerless Japanese Buddhists and to suspend their rights.

EXPLOITATION

Young views the "face" of exploitation as "a steady process of the transfer of the results of the labor of one social group to benefit another" . . . .

Religious justifications for exploitation. In colonial America, as private farms grew larger and farmers needed more cheap laborers to cultivate the land and tend the crops, many white landowners turned increasingly to the slave trade for their labor. Race and religion were intertwined as justifications for slavery in the Americas where "heathen" black Africans were stolen from their homelands and forced into slavery for the remainder of their lives. They were carried by slave ships, some of which were named the "Jesus," the "Grace of God," the "Angel," the "Liberty," and the "Justice," many with Christian ministers on board to help oversee the passage. In fact, Protestant churches offered scriptural justifications for slavery.

Conflicts between biblical justifications for slavery and biblical arguments for abolition split many Protestant congregations. The issue of slavery became a lightning rod in the 1840s among members of The Baptist General Convention, to organize a separate Southern Baptist Convention on a pro-slavery plank. One-hundred and fifty years later, the Southern Baptist Convention officially apologized to African Americans for its support and collusion with the institution of slavery, and also apologized for its rejection of civil rights initiatives of the 1950s and 1960s.

The expansion of the republic and movement west was in part justified by "Manifest Destiny": the belief that God intended the U.S. to extend its holdings and power across North America over native Indian tribes from east to west. The doctrine of "Manifest Destiny" also assumed Anglo-Saxon superiority. "This continent," a congressman declared, "was intended by Providence as a vast theatre on which to work out the grand experiment of Republican government, under the auspices of the Anglo-Saxon race."

During the early years of the new republic, with its increasing population and desire for land, political leaders, such as George Washington and Thomas Jefferson, advocated that Indian lands be obtained through treaties and purchase. President Jefferson in 1803 wrote a letter to then Tennessee political leader, Andrew Jackson, advising him to convince Indians to sell their "useless" forests to the U.S. government and become farmers. Jefferson and other government leaders overlooked the fact that this style of individualized farming was contrary to Indian communitarian spiritual/cultural traditions.

MARGINALIZATION

Marginalization is the "face" of oppression whereby entire categories of people—in the following examples, non-Protestant Christians—are restricted from meaningful involvement in the social life of the community and nation, and thus subjected to acute economic deprivation and even annihilation. Young defines *marginals* as "people the system of labor cannot or will not use" [see selection 5 in this volume].

Marginalization in the schools and society. The media constitute a major societal and institutional means of transmitting religious norms and beliefs, while maintaining the marginalization of the "other." Beaman describes the marginalization of new religious movements, "cults," Muslims, and indigenous Native peoples (2003, 315):

> New religious movements attract media attention for apocalyptic views and actions, and remain "cults" in public discourse. Muslims are the subject of biased media reports that seem to result in attacks on mosques and anti-Muslim sentiment. Aboriginals, for whom daily life and the physical world are inseparable from spirituality, are constructed as "problematic" because of their demands for equality and restitution.

Schools are another institutional means by which social norms are maintained and reproduced. Norms of Christian privilege and marginalization of members of other faith communities and non-believers in the schools are conveyed by curricular materials (curricular *hegemony*), which focus upon heroes, holidays, traditions, accomplishments, and importance of a European-heritage, Christian experience. Students who are Hindu, Muslim, Sikh, Jewish, and of other faiths, and non-believers, for example, see few, if any, people who look like them, who believe as they believe, or who adhere to the cultural expressions that they adhere to introduced and discussed in their classroom lessons.

In addition, the school calendar is organized to meet the needs of Christian faith communities, while marginalizing others. Examples include Jewish students who are compelled to request an excuse from school to attend religious services for their "High Holy Days" on and between Rosh Hashanah and Yom Kipper, which usually fall during the beginning of the academic year. In addition, Jehovah's Witnesses, who do not celebrate holidays—religious or otherwise—must also seek permission to be excused from the observance of holidays in school. (Jehovah's Witnesses, while a Christian denomination, are often marginalized within Christianity, and not accorded the same degree of Christian privilege as members of other so-called "mainstream" Christian faith communities.)

Muslim students, faculty, and staff often are not accorded the opportunity to have a safe prayer space on campus to perform the *salat* (prayer), as required by the Five Pillars of Islam. A case in point involved a 17-year-old high school junior in Ohio who was barred by school administrators from praying in an empty classroom at lunch and before and after class hours. Though a 1963 U.S. Supreme Court case ruled unconstitutional any *mandatory* prayers or Bible readings at public schools, subsequent rulings declared the constitutionality of many forms of personal religious expression on school campuses. In this case, the Council on American-Islamic Relations (CAIR) stepped in on the student's behalf, and convinced the school district to reverse its policy.

CULTURAL IMPERIALISM

Young states that "[c]ultural imperialism involves the universalization of a dominant group's experiences and culture, and its establishment as the norm" [see selection 5 in this volume].

Christian cultural imperialism and privilege. The manifestations of Christian privilege as cultural imperialism are numerous. First, the federal and school calendars are scheduled around Christian holidays and celebrations. In fact, the Christian holiday of Christmas has been declared a *national* holiday in which most businesses and government offices are closed and services suspended.

Society marks time through a Christian lens. Even the language we use in reference to the mainstream calendar reflects Christian assumptions. Not long ago we heard and read of the coming of the "21ˢᵗ Century," and the dawning of "*The* new millennium." Let us not forget, however, that the year 2000 is calculated with reference to the birth of Jesus, and it is, therefore, the beginning of the next *Christian* millennium. In fact, the dictionary definition of "millennium" notes "the thousand years mentioned in Revelation 20 during which holiness is to prevail and Christ is to reign on earth." This fact is apparent when someone mentions the date followed by "in the year of our Lord, Jesus Christ." The century markers B.C. (before Christ) and A.D. (*anno Domini*) are clearly Christian in origin. Therefore, the year 2000 is *one* important milepost, though, for many religious traditions, it also marks a heightening of their invisibility. Even recent attempts to decenter Christian hegemony in the marking of time by replacing B.C. with B.C.E. (before the common era) and A.D. with C.E. (common era), do not in actuality affect the marking of time before and after a "common" (Christian) era.

The workweek is structured to allow Christians the opportunity to worship on Sundays without conflicting with their Monday to Friday work schedules. For most of our history, state and local "Blue Laws" restrict sales, business operations, recreational activities, and governmental services on Sunday, the Sabbath for most Christian denominations. "Blue Laws" date back to colonial times when Sunday church attendance was mandatory. In 1816, a Jewish man named Abraham Wolf was convicted in Pennsylvania of the "crime" of "having done and performed worldly employment on the Lord's day" (Sunday). He appealed his sentence but lost.

In the schools, children or their parents or caretakers of other faiths must take responsibility to request accommodations from school officials either to be excused from ongoing school activities or to be absent to practice their religious traditions. For example, a Muslim elementary school student in central Iowa requested permission to attend the school library or to remain in her classroom for the duration of her lunch period during the Muslim holy month of Ramadan in which it was her practice to fast from sunrise to sunset. The school, however, had a *written* policy mandating that students must be present in the cafeteria during their lunch breaks. After repeated discussions with the school principal, the mother of the student convinced him to allow her daughter to go to an alternate space during the month of Ramadan while the student's classmates were at lunch.

Other examples of Christian cultural imperialism are numerous: the promotion of music, especially Christmas, by radio stations, and Christmas specials played on TV throughout November and December each year; Christmas decorations (often hung at taxpayer expense) in the public square throughout the United States; and the widespread availability of Christian holiday decorations, greeting cards, food, and other items during Christian (and Easter) holiday seasons.

Further examples of Christian cultural imperialism include the phrase "under God" in the Pledge of Allegiance or "In God We Trust" on U.S. currency and *Annuit Coeptis* (He [God] (or Providence) has favored our undertakings) on the Great Seal of the United States and printed on the back of the one-dollar bill, or the teaching of "Intelligent Design."

The phrase "under God" was added to the school Pledge of Allegiance in 1954 during the Cold War in reaction to what many saw as a godless Soviet Union attempting to impose its economic and political system throughout the world. The phrase "In God We Trust" was added to U.S. coins during the American Civil War by Abraham Lincoln, and to paper currency in the 1950s during the Cold War.

Deculturalization and schooling of native peoples. In an attempt to add further dimensions and elaborations of Young's concept of cultural imperialism, I employ Spring's discussions of "cultural genocide" defined as "the attempt to destroy other cultures" through forced acquiescence and assimilation to majority rule and Christian cultural and religious standards. This cultural genocide works through the process of "deculturalization," which Joel Spring (2004) describes as an educational process that destroys a people's culture and replaces it with a new culture.

An example of "cultural genocide" and "deculturalization" can be seen in the case of Christian European American domination over Native American Indians, whom European Americans viewed as "uncivilized," "godless heathens," "barbarians," and "devil worshipers."

White Christian European Americans deculturalized indigenous peoples through many means: confiscation of land, forced relocation, undermining of their languages, cultures, and identities, forced conversion to Christianity, and forced removal of Native children to Christian day schools and off-reservation boarding schools far away from their people.

The first of many off-reservation Indian boarding schools was established in Carlisle, Pennsylvania in 1879 and run primarily by white Christian teachers, administered by Richard Pratt, a former cavalry commander in the Indian Territories. At the school, Indian children were stripped of their culture: the males' hair was cut short, they were forced to wear Western-style clothing, they were prohibited from conversing in their native languages and English was compulsory, all their cultural and spiritual symbols were destroyed, and Christianity was imposed.

"Civilizing" Indians became a euphemism for Christian conversion. Christian missionaries throughout the United States worked vigorously to convert Indians. A mid-19th century missionary wrote: "As tribes and nationals the Indians must perish and live only as men, [and should] fall in with Christian civilization that is destined to cover the earth."

VIOLENCE

A number of groups live with the constant fear of random and unprovoked systematic violence directed against them simply on account of their social identities. The intent of this xenophobic (fear and hatred of anyone or anything seeming "foreign") violence is to harm, humiliate, and destroy the "other."

During colonial times, religious dissension was violently repressed. For example, the Pilgrims "warned out of town" a Sephardic Jewish merchant, and banished Quaker missionaries. Later, as Quakers kept coming, the Puritans enacted harsher penalties, for example, cutting off their ears, or using hot irons to bore holes through their tongues. Then between 1659 to 1661, Puritans executed four Quakers on the gallows on Boston Common.

Recent examples of religious violence. Violence against Muslims, Sikhs, Hindus, and Jews has escalated in the United States since September 11, 2001. The Council on American Islamic Relations (CAIR), an American Muslim civil and human rights organization, in their 2005 annual report listed a total of 1,522 civil rights violations against American Muslims, 114 of which were violent hate crimes. This was a 49% increase in total incidents from just one year before. The report included incidents of violence, as well as harassment and discriminatory treatment, including "unreasonable arrests, detentions, searches/seizures, and detentions." The CAIR report included an incident in which a Muslim woman wearing

a *hijab* (the garment many Muslim women wear in public) was taking her baby for a walk in a stroller, and a man driving a truck nearly ran them over. The woman cried out that, "You almost killed my baby!," and the man responded, "It wouldn't have been a big loss."

Nearly one-quarter of all reported civil rights violations against American Muslims involve unwarranted arrests and searches. Law enforcement agencies routinely "profile" Muslims of apparent Middle Eastern heritage in airports or simply while driving in their cars for interrogation and invasive and aggressive searches. In addition, governmental agencies, such as the IRS and FBI, continue to enter individuals' homes and mosques and make unreasonable arrests and detentions. Anti-Muslim hate crimes also occur on college and university campuses across the United States.

Sikhs have been the targets of increasing numbers of hate crimes as well. Since 2002, the Sikh Coalition organization listed 62 hate crimes directed against Sikh citizens of the United States. Many of the attacks committed against Sikhs are classified under the category of "personal attacks" or assaults as well as vandalism and arson. One incident involved a Sikh student at the University of North Carolina who was assaulted by three local teenagers. National attention focused on the severe beating of Rajinder Singh Shalsa in New York City, and the fatal shooting of Sikh gas station owner Balbir Singh Sodhi in Mesa, Arizona. It is widely assumed that Sikhs are targeted because they wear turbans, which the public imagination equates with terrorism.

Hindus have likewise been targeted. In June 2003, for example, Saurabh Bhalerao, a 24-year-old Indian graduate student studying in Massachusetts, was robbed, burned with cigarettes, beaten, stuffed in a truck, and twice stabbed before his assailants dumped him along the road. The attackers allegedly misidentified this Hindu student for a Muslim because during the assault, the perpetrators yelled at him, "Go back to Iraq."

Each year the Anti-Defamation League, a Jewish social advocacy organization, documents incidents of anti-Jewish hate crimes. They reported over 1,500 such incidents in 2004 alone, including verbal and physical assault, harassment, vandalism, property damage, and other acts of hate. These included the burning of a Holocaust museum in Indiana, and the spray-painting of swastikas and epithets on the walls and driveway of a Jewish community center near Phoenix, Arizona. This latter incident occurred on my campus, Iowa State University, in 2005. Among the swastikas, the vandals also spray-painted anti-Muslim, racist, misogynist, and homophobic epithets.

"MULTI-FACETED" PRIVILEGE AND OPPRESSION: IMMIGRATION BATTLES

The history of the 19th-century anti-immigration battles illustrates the intersections and interactions among Young's five faces of powerlessness, exploitation, marginalization, cultural imperialism, and violence, by which non-Christian religious status interacted with subordinated racial(ized) status. Throughout the 19th and into the 20th centuries, nativist exclusionist movements gained momentum within the United States. "Nativist" refers to an anti-immigrant ideology by U.S.-born, European-heritage Protestants, directed especially against non-Protestants such as Italian or Irish Catholics, Eastern European Jews, Asian Hindus, Muslims, Sikhs, and Buddhists. In some cases, non-white, non-Protestant ethnic and religious groups were *socially constructed* as lower "racial" forms by the mainline Protestant power structure as a justification for exclusion, exploitation, marginalization, cultural imperialism, and violence. Subsequently, religion was itself "racialized."

Strong "nativist" currents against Asian Muslim, Sikh, and Buddhist immigrants led the United States Congress to bar Chinese immigrants in 1882, and also made it illegal for Chinese to marry white or black Americans. The exclusionist sentiment regarding the Chinese held by many U.S. citizens was summarized by the editor of the newspaper in Butte, Montana: "The Chinaman's life is not our life, *his religion is not our religion.* . . . He

belongs not in Butte." The Immigration Act of 1917 further prohibited immigration from Asian countries from the "barred zone," including parts of China, India, Siam, Burma, Asiatic Russian, Polynesian Islands, and parts of Afghanistan.

This "nativist" anti-immigration fever culminated in 1924 with the National Origins Act, which set restrictive quotas of immigrants from *Eastern* and *Southern* Europe, that is, mainly on Catholics and Jews (the latter referred to as members of the so-called "Hebrew race"). The law, however, permitted large allocations of immigrants from Great Britain and Germany in order to "protect our values . . . [as] a Western Christian civilization." Jews were considered racial as well as religious undesirables by the 19th century scientific community as a lower "racial" type, with essential immutable biological characteristics—a trend that increased markedly into the early 20th century C.E. Once seen as largely a religious, ethnic, or political group, Jews were viewed by "nativists," who valued American racial and religious "purity," as a "mixed race" (a so-called "mongrel" or "bastard race"), a people who had crossed racial barriers by interbreeding with black Africans during the Jewish Diaspora.

These restrictions on immigration based on "national origins" were not lifted until The Immigration and Nationality Act of 1965. This legislation resulted in dramatic increases in immigration from both Asian and Latin American countries of many religious backgrounds including Islamic, Hindu, Buddhist, Jain, Sikh, Zoroastrian, varying forms of Catholicism, and African, and Afro-Caribbean religious traditions. The 1965 law allowed for 170,000 immigrants from the Eastern Hemisphere and 120,000 from the Western Hemisphere with 20,000 immigrants per Eastern Hemisphere country. Partly as a result of the removal of restrictions on immigration that were specifically race-based and implicitly religion-based reflecting between 1882 until the 1960s—an effort to create an U.S.-American culture that was Protestant as well as northern European—the United States today stands as the most religiously diverse country in the world. This diversity poses great challenges as well as opportunities.

46

Religious Oppression of Indian Americans in the Contemporary United States

Khyati Y. Joshi

In the United States, we have a Constitutionally guaranteed "freedom of religion," the right to choose and practice the faith we hold dear; the Constitution prohibits the state from sponsoring a religion and from restricting people's exercise of their religious beliefs. But having free choice is not the same as to have one's choice accepted and supported by the institutions and culture of one's country, rather than ignored, marginalized, exoticized or demonized. In this section, I discuss the concepts of religious oppression and Christian privilege and then apply them to the contemporary experiences of Indian American Hindus, Muslims and Sikhs. The dynamics of religious oppression and Christian privilege are complicated by the fact that these populations are religious minorities as well as members of visible racial and ethnic minority groups. While followers of these faiths have been present in the U.S. since the early 1800s, it was not until the passage of the Immigration Act of 1965 that the United States saw the arrival of substantial numbers of immigrant

families—families that established homes, built ethnoreligious communities, and sent their children into the U.S. school system in substantial numbers.

RELIGIOUS OPPRESSION

Religious discrimination is not a post 9/11 phenomenon. Indeed, it is not even a 21st century phenomenon, nor has it been limited to non-Christian faiths. The United States has a history of religious intolerance from its beginnings. Native Americans, Catholics, Quakers, Mennonites, and Eastern Orthodox Christians faced religious persecution in 17th, 18th and 19th century America. Here, I use the term *religious oppression* to refer to the historic and systemic pattern of domination and subordination of religious minorities at cultural, institutional, and interpersonal levels—and focus my attention here on the experiences of Hindus, Muslims, and Sikhs within the dominant U.S. Christian milieu. This subordination is a product of the unequal power relationships among religious groups within American society and is supported by the actions of individuals, and by institutional structures (*religious discrimination*), as well as by cultural norms (*religious prejudice*) and societal practices. Through religious oppression, Christianity is used to marginalize, exclude, and deny the members and institutions of non-Christian religious groups in society the privileges and access that accompany a Christian affiliation. Using the term *religious oppression* to refer to a social system operating at these three levels—individual, institutional, and cultural/societal—recognizes that the disadvantages of non-Christianity exist not merely at the one-on-one level but also at a societal and institutional level where individuals are socialized, punished, rewarded and guided in ways that maintain and perpetuate oppressive structures.

In the context of America's racial schema, religious oppression sets up a dichotomy between the privilege and normativity associated with Whiteness and Christianity, and the othering of dark skin and non-Christian-ness. For Indian American Hindus, Muslims and Sikhs, who are not white and not Christian, religious discrimination may be exacerbated by racial discrimination. This privileging and othering takes place at the overarching level of society and culture, where norms are perpetuated implicitly and explicitly. By comparison with these hegemonic (or assumed and everyday) norms, these non-Christian "other" religions come to be seen as evil, wrongful, deviant and/or sick. In the act of defining Hinduism, Islam and Sikhism as exotic and illegitimate, and thereby excluding them from society, American white Christians are able to represent themselves as good, normal, and righteous. Moreover, because systemic racialization of religion reinforces this pattern of religious exclusion and inferiority, that same discourse serves to reinforce the inclusion and superiority of white Christianity.

Societal norms are reproduced through written laws and policies as well as inscribed in the daily behaviors of the populace. Christian holidays—"holy days"—are endorsed institutionally through a calendar that serves the convenience and priorities of Christians, as in a Monday–Friday workweek and Sunday worship, or official days off for Christmas. Government sanction reinforces the dominant status of Christianity and the implied illegitimacy of other faiths. The mindset of rightness and privilege is manifested in the treatment of religious minorities by members of the majority—whether that treatment is meant to harm and threaten members of the target religion (as does the assumption that Muslims or Sikhs are terrorists), or "save" them (by Christian proselytizing). These attitudes and behaviors, whether conscious or not, maintain systemic religious oppression.

Let me be clear. I am not saying Christianity, as a faith or a belief system, is to be held accountable for religious oppression, or that all Christians consciously or purposely harbor prejudice toward non-Christians or approve of institutional religious discrimination. But I

am saying that Christianity and Christian identity in the U.S. functions as a tool of oppression in the largely unconscious privileging of Christians through a hegemonic culture and social system. The issue at hand here is not one of intention, but one of consequences, of noticing the effects on religious minorities of the many instances of marginalization and disadvantage, despite our pluralistic society.

In the case of Hindus, Muslims, and Sikhs, the phenomenon of religious oppression in the U.S. exists and is perpetuated by and through a specific combination of facts and acts, each building upon its precedent. These include: (1) in the sociocultural and historical context of the United States, Christians have the power to define normalcy; (2) because Christianity has been normalized, the belief systems of Hinduism, Islam, and Sikhism are misrepresented and/or discounted; (3) the normalization of Christianity within social institutions leads to harassment, discrimination, and other forms of unequal treatment towards non-Christians; (4) religious oppression justifies violence or the threat of violence.

1. CHRISTIAN GROUPS HAVE THE POWER TO DEFINE NORMALCY

To be nominally Christian requires no conscious thought or effort on the part of Christian Americans. "Business as usual" follows their schedule and reflects their theological understandings. Social norms and rituals, language, and institutional rules and rewards all presume the existence of a Christian sociopolitical history and sociocultural norms of dress, behavior, and worship. America's vocabulary of faith, practice, prayer, belief, sites of worship and religious history largely ignore the existence of other religions, some of which are older than Christianity (for example, Buddhism, Hinduism, Judaism, and Native American spiritual practices).

We can observe Christianity's normative nature at three levels of society: institutional, societal/cultural, and individual. At the institutional and societal levels, there are examples in federal and state law and policy. Clearly, the First Amendment requires that the state allow and accommodate individual religious practices, and forbids the government to show hostility toward any particular religion. While acknowledging that this is nominally true, we must look at which religion is accommodated and which religions are not. The United States Senate and House of Representatives each employ Chaplains whose salaries are paid for by all U.S. taxpayers; both are Christian. An image of Moses with the Ten Commandments, along with other "law-givers," is etched in stone on the wall of the Supreme Court of the United States of America. The vacation schedules of most public schools are structured around Christian holidays, particularly Christmas and Easter. "Spring Break," for example, often coincides with the week between Palm Sunday and Easter. Policies like these permit Christian children to accompany their parents to worship and participate in the festivities leading up to each holiday without missing school or having to make up work.

Christian hegemony at the cultural and societal level is maintained in American society via the exercise of Christian privilege. In the United States, Christian privilege, like white privilege, exists through the cultural power norms that are largely invisible and thus unquestioned. Some examples of the norms underlying Christian privilege are:

- WORSHIP. The idea that it is something that occurs in a church, led by a member of the clergy. Here, the church represents both a place outside the home to go and pray, and the idea that prayer, properly performed, is done in groups and led by a person imbued by an institution with special theological authority.
- IMAGES of God, derived from western (i.e., Christian) art and literature. This god is anthropomorphized in a particular manner: singular, male, white, often elderly, and usually bearded, with two arms and two legs.

- ARCHITECTURE. The norms for houses of worship in which, for example, a steeple is "normal" but a minaret is something foreign.
- PRAYER. The western image involves an act of worship performed in a seated or kneeling position, in silence, and with crossed hands.
- SACRED STORIES. In American society, Biblical stories, however fantastical, are treated as credible. . . . Stories based in the Christian tradition, such as the Virgin birth, are believed to be credible and true, whereas stories based in the Muslim tradition, such as Mohammed's midnight flight to heaven, or the Hindu tradition, such as Vishnu's periodic visitation upon earth in different incarnations, are not believed and considered to be incredible and fantastical.
- HOLIDAYS. State and federal holidays, including the position of the "weekend" on Saturday and Sunday, are structured around the Christian calendar.
- SAFETY. Most Christians are able to pray publicly and visibly in safety, without fear of violence or mockery. Also, Christian congregations can build their houses of worship without opposition from neighbors and local authorities.

Christian privilege benefits not only people who identify with Christianity or consider themselves "religious," but also those born Christian who are no longer observant. Christian privilege involves a legacy of public acceptance from which Christians benefit whether they want to or not, and whether they know it or not. It is an unearned perquisite of their identity as Christians. They can live their lives unaware of the daily exclusions, insults, and assaults endured by Hindus, Muslims, and Sikhs.

Contrariwise, non-Christians find themselves forced to explain their religions not in their own terms but by reference to a Christian vocabulary: "What is your church like? What is your Bible? When is your Christmas?" The conveniences of life as a Christian are lost to the Hindu who must leave work to observe a Hindu New Year, the Sikh who must cut his hair in order to join the military, or the Muslim student who must participate in gym class while fasting for Ramadan.

2. THE BELIEF SYSTEMS OF HINDUISM, ISLAM, AND SIKHISM, ALONG WITH THEIR RESPECTIVE HISTORIES AND CULTURES ARE DELEGITIMIZED, MISREPRESENTED AND/OR DISCOUNTED

By exacerbating the "otherness" of Indian American Hindus, Muslims, and Sikhs, the racialization of religion contributes to the delegitimization of these three faiths in a number of ways. First, in everyday interactions the Christian norm is applied, and Hinduism, Islam and Sikhism are compared to this norm. Second, differences, real or imagined, from the Christian norm are highlighted, such as the Christian posture of "prayer" (kneeling, with the fingers of both hands interlaced) compared to Muslim bowing eastward or to Hindu *aarti* (fire offering). In terms of belief, the power of the norm is found at the line between what the western mind views as "credible" and what it considers "incredible." Consider these three stories: A Jewish virgin gives birth to the child of God, after an angel visits her at night and tells her what to name the child. A prophet rides a flying horse to Heaven, accompanied by an angel. God comes to earth in the form of a dwarf and saves the world from a demon king. The first of these stories is the Biblical story of the Annunciation and the birth of Jesus to the Virgin Mary. What makes it more credible or "believable" an idea than Mohammed's midnight flight from Jerusalem, or Vishnu's periodic visitation of the Earth in different incarnations? Yet in the United States, it is. Biblical stories, however fantastical, are treated as fact, or at least as "faith." The beliefs of other religions are

viewed as silly (at best) or heretical (at worst); they are branded with the more dismissive terminology of "myth" or "superstition."

Christian norms are reinforced by the Christian majority who assume these norms, and also assume without question the illegitimacy of other different faith traditions by comparison. The perception of illegitimacy grows out of ignorance, contempt, and mischaracterization of Hinduism, Islam, and Sikhism by the mass media as well as social and political institutions and individuals. Its negative effect is felt most dramatically by children and adolescents from marginalized faith traditions, whose home belief systems are invalidated and even actively contested by educators, other adults, and peers, and whose invisibility is manifested in the absence of news coverage or the congratulatory public service announcements aired around Christmas, Easter, and other "recognized" holidays. Disrespect is shown by the co-option of holy images and prayers to sell candles, perfume, and other commercial goods.

3. HARASSMENT, DISCRIMINATION, AND OTHER FORMS OF DIFFERENTIAL TREATMENT ARE INSTITUTIONAL AND UNCHALLENGED

Another dimension of Christian privilege appears in the non-acceptance, disrespect, and invisibility of minority religious traditions, despite the Constitutional guarantee of the free exercise of religion. Christian privilege in this case involves both legal "freedom" (which is shared, at least in theory, by members of other religions) and social sanction, which is not available to marginalized faith traditions. As Christians are made to be confident, comfortable, and oblivious to their privilege because of the omnipresence of Christianity in the American culture and social system, other religious groups are made unsure, uncomfortable and alienated. Being Christian protects one from many kinds of hostility, distress, and violence, which—even when subtle—are part of daily experience for people of Hindu, Sikh, Muslim, and other non-western religious backgrounds. While society's endorsement may be tacit, and even invisible to the Christian eye, it's absence is conspicuous and visible to these religious minorities.

4. VIOLENCE AND THE THREAT OF VIOLENCE

Many South Asian and Arab Americans and other "double minorities"—non-White and non-Christian—experience verbal attacks and physical threats and attacks from people who are both White and Christian. Students in the K-12 school setting are threatened because of their religious identity (often signified by turban or hijab) and racialized phenotype. While hate crimes and threats of violence against these populations did in fact increase during the weeks and months after September 11, 2001, they were not confined to this "9/11 backlash" and in fact have occurred both before and since that time.

Indian American Hindus, Muslims and Sikhs are part of immigrant communities, and for these communities, although experiencing racism, the experience of religion is paramount. The communities are built on the edifice of religion, and while they also encounter racism, the experience of religious oppression is critical and must not be ignored. The impact of racial oppression takes on *religious* dimensions, arising from the belief in religion as something especially profound and "never changing." Religious oppression results in Indian American Sikhs, Muslims and Hindus identifying more closely with their home religion, magnifying religion's role in one's life and increasing the likelihood the individual will identify as "religious" and engage in worship, ritual, and religious study in adulthood.

47

Precedents

The Destruction of the European Jews

Raul Hilberg

. . .

Anti-Jewish policies and actions did not have their beginning in 1933. For many centuries, and in many countries, the Jews had been victims of destructive action. . . . The first anti-Jewish policy started in the fourth century after Christ in Rome. Early in the fourth century, during the reign of Constantine, the Christian Church gained power in Rome, and Christianity became the state religion. From this period, the state carried out Church policy. For the next twelve centuries, the Catholic Church prescribed the measures that were to be taken with respect to the Jews. Unlike the pre-Christian Romans, who claimed no monopoly on religion and faith, the Christian Church insisted on acceptance of Christian doctrine.

For an understanding of Christian policy toward Jewry, it is essential to realize that the Church pursued conversion not so much for the sake of aggrandizing its power (the Jews have always been few in number), but because of the conviction that it was the duty of true believers to save unbelievers from the doom of eternal hellfire. Zealousness in the pursuit of conversion was an indication of the depth of faith. The Christian religion was not one of many religions, but the true religion, the only one. Those who were not in its fold were either ignorant or in error. The Jews could not accept Christianity.

In the very early stages of the Christian faith, many Jews regarded Christians as members of a Jewish sect. The first Christians, after all, still observed the Jewish law. They had merely added a few nonessential practices, such as baptism, to their religious life. But their view was changed abruptly when Christ was elevated to Godhood. The Jews have only one God. This God is indivisible. He is a jealous God and admits of no other gods. He is not Christ, and Christ is not He. Christianity and Judaism have since been irreconcilable. An acceptance of Christianity has since signified an abandonment of Judaism.

In antiquity and in the Middle Ages, Jews did not abandon Judaism lightly. With patience and persistence the Church attempted *to convert* obstinate Jewry, and for twelve hundred years the theological argument was fought without interruption. The Jews were not convinced. Gradually the Church began to back its words with force. . . . Step by step, but with ever widening effect, the Church adopted "defensive" measures against its passive victims. Christians were "protected" from the "harmful" consequences of intercourse with Jews by rigid laws against intermarriage, by prohibitions of discussions about religious issues, by laws against domicile in common abodes. The Church "protected" its Christians from the "harmful" Jewish teachings by burning the Talmud and by barring Jews from public office.

. . .

Expulsion is the second anti-Jewish policy in history. In its origin, this policy presented itself only as an alternative—moreover, as an alternative that was left to the Jews. But long after the separation of church and state, long after the state had ceased to carry out church policy, expulsion and exclusion remained the goal of anti-Jewish activity.

. . .

The expulsion and exclusion policy was adopted by the Nazis and remained the goal of all anti-Jewish activity until 1941. That year marks a turning point in anti-Jewish history.

In 1941 the Nazis found themselves in the midst of a total war. Several million Jews were incarcerated in ghettos. Emigration was impossible. A last-minute project to ship the Jews to the African island of Madagascar had fallen through. The "Jewish problem" had to be "solved" in some other way. At this crucial time, the idea of a "territorial solution" emerged in Nazi minds. The "territorial solution," or "the final solution of the Jewish question in Europe," as it became known, envisaged the *death* of European Jewry. The European Jews were to be killed. This was the third anti-Jewish policy in history.

To summarize. Since the fourth century after Christ there have been three anti-Jewish policies: *conversion*, *expulsion*, and *annihilation*. The second appeared as an alternative to the first, and the third emerged as an alternative to the second.

The destruction of the European Jews between 1933 and 1945 appears to us now as an unprecedented event in history. Indeed, in its dimensions and total configuration, nothing like it had ever happened before. As a result of an organized undertaking, five million people were killed in the short space of a few years. The operation was over before anyone could grasp its enormity, let alone its implications for the future.

Table 47.1 Canonical and Nazi Anti-Jewish Measures

Canonical Law	Nazi Measure
Prohibition of intermarriage and of sexual intercourse between Christians and Jews, Synod of Elvira, 306	Law for the Protection of German Blood and Honor, September 15, 1935
Jews and Christians not permitted to eat together, Synod of Elvira, 306	Jews barred from dining cars (Transport Minister to Interior Minister, December 30, 1939)
Jews not allowed to hold public office, Synod of Clermont, 535 . . .	Law for the Re-establishment of the Professional Civil Service, April 7, 1933 . . .
Jews not permitted to show themselves in the streets during Passion Week, 3d Synod of Orléans, 538	Decree authorizing local authorities to bar Jews from the streets on certain days (i.e., Nazi holidays), December 3, 1938
Burning of the Talmud and other books, 12th Synod of Toledo, 681 . . .	Book burnings in Nazi Germany . . .
Jews obliged to pay taxes for support of the Church to the same extent as Christians, Synod of Gerona, 1078 . . .	The "Sozialausgleichsabgabe" which provided that Jews pay a special income tax in lieu of donations for Party purposes imposed on Nazis, December 24, 1940
Jews not permitted to be plaintiffs, or witnesses against Christians in the Courts, 3d Lateran Council, 1179, Canon 26 . . .	Proposal by the Party Chancellery that Jews not be permitted to institute civil suits, September 9, 1942 (Bormann to Justice Ministry, September 9, 1942) . . .
The marking of Jewish clothes with a badge, 4th Lateran Council, 1215, Canon 68 (Copied from the legislation by Caliph Omar II [634–644], who had decreed that Christians wear blue belts and Jews, yellow belts)	Decree of September 1, 1941 (Jews must [wear the] yellow star of David)
Construction of new synagogues prohibited, Council of Oxford, 1222	Destruction of synagogues in entire Reich, November 10, 1938 (Heydrich to Göring, November 11, 1938)
Christians not permitted to attend Jewish ceremonies, Synod of Vienna, 1267 . . .	Friendly relations with Jews prohibited, October 24, 1941 (Gestapo directive)
Compulsory ghettos, Synod of Breslau, 1267	[Compulsory ghettos] by order by Heydrich, September 21, 1939
Christians not permitted to sell or rent real estate to Jews, Synod of Ofen, 1279 . . .	Decree providing for compulsory sale of Jewish real estate, December 3, 1938 . . .
Jews not permitted to act as agents in the conclusion of contracts, especially marriage contracts, between Christians, Council of Basel, 1434, Sessio XIX	Decree of July 6, 1938, providing for liquidation of Jewish real estate agencies, brokerage agencies, and marriage agencies catering to non-Jews
Jews not permitted to obtain academic degrees, Council of Basel, 1434, Sessio XIX	Law against Overcrowding of German Schools and Universities, April 25, 1933

. . .

Yet, if we analyze this singularly massive upheaval, we discover that most of what happened in those twelve years had already happened before. The Nazi destruction process did not come out of a void; it was the culmination of a cyclical trend. One may observe the trend in the three successive goals of anti-Jewish administrators. The missionaries of Christianity had said in effect: *You have no right to live among us as Jews.* The secular rulers who followed had proclaimed: *You have no right to live among us.* The German Nazis at last decreed: *You have no right to live.*

These progressively more drastic goals brought in their wake a slow and steady growth of anti-Jewish action and anti-Jewish thinking. The process began with the attempt to drive the Jews into Christianity. The development was continued in order to force the victims into exile. It was finished when the Jews were driven to their deaths. The German Nazis, then, did not discard the past; they built upon it. . . .

The significance of the historical precedents will most easily be understood in the administrative sphere. The destruction of the Jews was an administrative process, and the annihilation of Jewry required the implementation of systematic administrative measures in successive steps. There are not many ways in which a modern society can, in short order, kill a large number of people living in its midst. This is an efficiency problem of the greatest dimensions, one which poses uncounted difficulties and innumerable obstacles. Yet, in reviewing the documentary record of the destruction of the Jews, one is almost immediately impressed with the fact that the German administration knew what it was doing. With an unfailing sense of direction and with an uncanny path-finding ability, the German bureaucracy found the shortest road to the final goal. . . . Necessity is said to be the mother of invention, but if precedents have already been formed, if a guide has already been constructed, invention is no longer a necessity. The German bureaucracy could draw upon such precedents and follow such a guide, for the German bureaucrats could dip into a vast reservoir of administrative experience, a reservoir that church and state had filled in fifteen hundred years of destructive activity.

In the course of its attempt to convert the Jews, the Catholic Church had taken many measures against the Jewish population. These measures were designed to "protect" the Christian community from Jewish teachings and, not incidentally, to weaken the Jews in their "obstinacy." It is characteristic that as soon as Christianity became the state religion of Rome, in the fourth century A.D., Jewish equality of citizenship was ended. "The Church and the Christian state, concilium decisions and imperial laws, henceforth worked hand in hand to persecute the Jews." Although most of these enactments did not cover all of Catholic Europe from the moment of their conception, they became precedents for the Nazi era. Table 47.1 compares the basic anti-Jewish measures of the Catholic Church and the modern counterparts enacted by the Nazi regime.

48

Maps—History of Anti-Semitism

Sir Martin Gilbert

The maps are shown on the following pages.

TWO THOUSAND YEARS OF JEWISH LIFE IN EUROPE

This map shows the age of the principal European Jewish communities in 1939. It was the Jewish communities shown here - their culture, their customs, and their deep local roots - which the Nazis sought utterly to destroy in the second world war.

North Sea

Baltic Sea

Adriatic Sea

Black Sea

0   miles   200
0   km   200

NORWAY
88 YEARS

ESTONIA
600 YEARS

LATVIA
400 YEARS

DENMARK
317 YEARS

LITHUANIA
600 YEARS

HOLLAND
800 YEARS

WHITE RUSSIA
550 YEARS

BELGIUM
700 YEARS

GERMANY
1,618 YEARS

POLAND
850 YEARS

UKRAINE
822 YEARS

LUXEMBOURG
653 YEARS

CZECHOSLOVAKIA
1,000 YEARS

CRIMEA
1,900 YEARS

FRANCE
1,936 YEARS

HUNGARY
1,900 YEARS

RUMANIA
1,800 YEARS

AUSTRIA
1,030 YEARS

YUGOSLAVIA
1,000 YEARS

ITALY
2,100 YEARS

GREECE
2,239 YEARS

Most of the Jewish communities of Europe had come into existence hundreds of years *before* the founding of the States of which they were to become a part. Others had subsequently been destroyed by expulsion and persecution in the middle ages - but had then been refounded a second, a third, and even a fourth time. The Jews of Germany had already been living continuously in different parts of Germany for more than 1,500 years when the German Empire was established in 1870, the year of German unity under Bismarck.

The age, by 1939, of the Jewish communities of Europe.

—·—· The European frontiers of 1937.

© Martin Gilbert 1978

C
O
N
T
E
X
T

SOME EARLY RECORDS OF JEWISH TOWN LIFE IN EUROPE BEFORE 1600

Jewish settlements throughout Europe flourished from Roman times. Early local records show different aspects of Jewish town life, from trade and prosperity to persecution and expulsion. This map gives 19 examples of contemporary records mentioning Jews *before* 1600. By 1937 there were more than 35,000 European towns and villages with Jewish communities. This map shows the European frontiers of that year. The Nazis made it one of their first aims to drive the Jews from their long-established homes, including from each of the towns shown here.

1561. Tallin. Jews, who had lived in the town for at least 200 years, expelled. They were not allowed to return until the town was annexed by Russia in 1710.

1489. Minsk. Jews obtain the lease of all customs dues

1173. Wroclawek. Local coins discovered with Hebrew inscriptions.

1367. Przemysl. Local records mention a Jewish community in the town.

1117. Jewish houses attacked during a local rebellion.

960 AD. Worms The local Jews send a letter to Palestine asking for verification of a rumour that the Messiah had come.

321 AD. An Imperial Decree mentions the Jewish citizens.

1074 Permission granted to the Jews to trade without having to pay customs dues.

1310. A Jewish scribe completes a fine illuminated manuscript.

576 AD. A local document records that the five hundred Jewish citizens in the town and neighbourhood were forced to chose between baptism and expulsion.

839 AD. Local records reveal a Jewish family owning land out-side the city walls, and being protected by special order of the Emperor Louis the Pious.

1229. Munich A Jew appears in court as a witness during a trial.

1188. Strasbourg. Jews flee the town to avoid persecution from the crusaders, but return soon afterwards.

388 AD. Bishop Ambrose comments on the destruction of the synagogue "by act of God". It was soon rebuilt.

1090. Prague. A Christian scribe mentions Jewish citizens.

1204. Vienna. The existence of a synagogue is recorded.

81 AD. A Greek inscription refers to the Jewish community, and to the liberation of a Jewish slave.

140 BC. A Greek inscription records the arrival of Jews from Egypt.

142 BC. Rhodes. A Roman decree announces the renewal of a pact of friendship between the Roman Senate and the Jewish nation.

Tallin

Minsk

Wroclawek

Kiev

Przemysl

Cologne

Brussels

Frankfurt

Worms

Prague

Strasbourg

Munich

Vienna

Clermont-Ferrand

Milan

Carcassonne

Adriatic Sea

Salonica

Black Sea

Kerch

Rhodes

© Martin Gilbert 1978

PERSECUTION, EXPULSION AND REFUGE, 1050 AD - 1650

In the six hundred years between 1050 AD and 1650 the Jews were frequently uprooted from their homes, and driven out of the lands in which they had lived and traded for many generations, even for centuries. This map shows some of the expulsions, and a few of the towns in which the Jews rebuilt their lives and livelihood. In these same towns, four hundred years later, their descendants were to be uprooted again, when the Nazis sought their total elimination from European life and culture

■ Some of the areas from which the Jews were expelled, often with great violence and cruelty, between 1050 AD and 1650

⊙ Some of the towns in which Jews found refuge from persecution; towns in which they were to grow and flourish, but from which, in the Nazi era, they were deported to death camps, or murdered in mass-execution sites

```
0    miles   150
0    km    200
```

© Martin Gilbert 1978

THE PERSECUTION OF THE JEWS OF GERMANY IN THE FIRST FIVE YEARS OF NAZI RULE 1933 - 1938

9 March 1933. First anti-Jewish riots in Berlin.
1 April 1933. All Jewish shops in Berlin boycotted.
10 May 1933. In Berlin the Nazis hold a public burning of books written by Jewish and other authors.
October 1933. All hospitals in Berlin declared "free" of Jewish doctors. These doctors could find no other hospital work.

30 January 1933. Hitler becomes the Chancellor of Germany. Many Jews arrested, ill-treated, and tortured.
15 September 1935. The Nuremberg Laws make the Jews second class citizens, and lead to their being driven from public and professional life.
9 November 1938. 191 synagogues set on fire throughout Germany. Over 2,000 Jews murdered in the camps.
15 November 1938. All German schools closed to German Jewish children.

North Sea

Baltic Sea

Esterwegen

Sachsenhausen

1933-1939. Of Germany's 525,000 Jews in 1933, over 280,000 emigrated or escaped by 1939.

Berlin
Columbia Haus

13 March 1933. All Jewish lawyers and judges expelled from the law courts.

Braunschweig

Buchenwald

THURINGIA

Breslau

Nuremberg

FRANCONIA

1933. The first Province to eliminate Jews from all official and professional positions.

13 March 1933. Jewish owned shops ransacked and destroyed.

Dachau

Munich

10 August 1938. The synagogue destroyed.

1935. 100,000 German children swear "eternal enmity" to the Jews.

9 June 1938. Synagogue destroyed.

—·— The borders of Germany, 1919 - 1937.

······· Other European borders.

From 1933, "Jews not wanted" signs were put up throughout Germany on shops, cafes, sports stadiums, and on roads leading into towns and villages. In some towns, all Jewish names were scratched off war memorials of the first world war. The savage anti-Jewish propaganda of the "Stürmer" magazine was in public display cases, and within six years, the 2,000 year old Jewish community was turned into a community of outlaws who could expect nothing but harassment and persecution.

Concentration camps set up on German soil by 1938.

Among the many indignities forced upon the Jews was a revival of the medieval practice of making all Jews wear a yellow "Star of David" on their clothing. ✡

© Martin Gilbert 1978

GERMAN OFFICIAL PLANS FOR THE "FINAL SOLUTION", 20 JANUARY 1942

The number of Jews mentioned at the **Wannsee Conference**, country by country and area by area, for eventual deportation, and subsequent death. More than 14 million people were thus marked out for death.

One of the macabre features of the numerical list of the Jews submitted to the Wannsee Conference was the fact that no figure was given for the Jews of Estonia, merely a brief note that Estonia was 'Free of Jews'. This was true; the 1,000 Estonian Jews who had come under German rule in October 1941 had all been murdered during the three months before the Wannsee Conference.

ESTONIA
"Free of Jews"

USSR
5 million

NORWAY
1,300

DENMARK
5,600

LATVIA
3,500

LITHUANIA
34,000

HOLLAND
160,800

BIALYSTOK DISTRICT
400,000

WHITE RUSSIA
446,484

BELGIUM
43,000

GERMANY
131,800
Berlin

Wannsee
Chelmno

FRANCE OCCUPIED ZONE
165,000

BOHEMIA AND MORAVIA
74,200

GENERAL GOVERNMᴺᵀ.
2,284,000

EASTERN TERRITORIES
420,000

88,000

UKRAINE
2,994,684

SLOVAKIA

AUSTRIA
43,700

HUNGARY
742,800

FRANCE UNOCCUPIED ZONE
700,000

10,000

CROATIA
40,000

SERBIA

RUMANIA
342,000

BULGARIA

ITALY
58,000

ALBANIA
200

48,000

O   miles   200
O   km   300

GREECE
69,600

In December 1941, a month *before* the Wannsee Conference, the first Nazi extermination camp had already come into operation, at Chelmno, responsible for the mass-murder of Jews, Gypsies, and Soviet prisoners-of-war. After passing through corridors marked 'To the showers' and 'To the doctor', the victims were forced into a large truck which was in fact a gas-chamber, where they were killed within a few minutes. By the end of 1944 more than 360,000 Jews had been murdered in Chelmno alone.

The Wannsee Conference also specified the number of Jews in *unconquered* countries for eventual destruction, including 330,000 from Britain, 18,000 from Switzerland, 6,000 from Spain and 4,000 from Ireland.

© Martin Gilbert 1978

THE CONCENTRATION CAMPS

Between 1939 and 1945, six million unarmed and innocent Jewish civilians - men, women, children and babies- were murdered in Nazi-controlled Europe, as part of a deliberate policy to destroy all traces of Jewish life and culture. As many as two million of these were killed in their own towns and villages, some confined in ghettoes where death by slow starvation was a deliberate Nazi policy, others taken to be shot at mass-murder sites near where they lived. The remaining four million Jews were forced from their homes and taken by train to distant concentration camps, where they were murdered by being worked to death, starved to death, beaten to death, shot, or gassed.

Among the hundreds of thousands of *non*-Jews sent by the Nazis to concentration camps were anti-Nazis, Jehovah's Witnesses, homosexuals, the mentally ill, and the chronically sick. In addition, more than 250,000 Gypsies were murdered, in a Nazi attempt to eliminate Gypsies as well as Jews from the map of Europe.

In many of the camps shown here so-called "medical" experiments were carried out, without anaesthetics, solely to satisfy the curiosity and sadism of the doctors. Hundreds of otherwise healthy "patients" were tortured and murdered during these experiments.

Auschwitz concentration camp in which more than 2 *million* people were murdered between 1941 and 1944, including Jews, Gypsies, and Soviet prisoners-of-war.

Camps set up solely for the murder of Jews.

Other camps in which Jews and non-Jews were put to forced labour, starved, tortured, and murdered in conditions of the worst imaginable cruelty. Most of these camps had "satellite" labour camps nearby.

© Martin Gilbert 1978

0   100 miles
0   100 km

North Sea

FRANCE

GERMANY

Neuengamme
Bergen-Belsen
Sachsenhausen
Mittelbau Dora
Buchenwald
Flossenberg
Natzweiler
Dachau
Mauthausen

AUSTRIA

Ravensbrück

Gross Rosen

Stutthof

Chelmno   Treblinka

POLAND

Sobibor

Auschwitz   Maidanek

Plaszow   Belzec

CZECHOSLOVAKIA

HUNGARY

RUMANIA

USSR

Baltic Sea

Vaivara

Klooga
ESTONIA

LATVIA

LITHUANIA

Gospič   Jasenovac

YUGOSLAVIA

Sajmište

Adriatic Sea

ITALY

CONTEXT

NON-JEWISH VICTIMS OF NAZI RULE

Twenty-six of many thousands of Nazi reprisal and murder actions against unarmed *non*-Jews, with the approximate number murdered in each massacre.

Countries in each of which more than a *million* non-Jewish civilians died as a result of deliberate Nazi brutality.

In all occupied lands, the Nazis carried out large-scale reprisals against completely innocent and unarmed civilians, whenever a single German soldier was killed by partisans, or even when German property was attacked. In mass-murder actions against non-Jews, they also massacred 4 *million* unarmed Soviet prisoners-of-war, 1 *million* Soviet civilians, more than 1 *million* Polish civilians, and 1½ *million* Yugoslav civilians. In May 1940, at two villages near Dunkirk, a total of 170 *disarmed* British prisoners-of-war were murdered in cold blood. In June 1944, at three villages near Caen, 70 *disarmed* Canadian prisoners-of-war were likewise murdered, by German S.S. troops.

U.S.S.R.

Burashevo 350

Jeglava 700

Mikulino 275

Baranowicze 1,000

Holland 7 March 1945 400

Prague 860

Zinyany 484

Gorodets 434

POLAND

Borow 300

Ala 1,758

North Sea

GERMANY

Dunkirk 170

English Channel

Caen 70

Lidice 250

CZECHOSLOVAKIA

Zamosc 200

Studenets 402

FRANCE

Brno 395

AUSTRIA

HUNGARY

RUMANIA

Oradour-sur-Glane 642

Belgrade 4,750

Kragujevac 7,253

Black Sea

YUGOSLAVIA

Kraljevo 1,700

BULGARIA

ITALY

Mediterranean Sea

Rome 335

Adriatic Sea

GREECE

Distomon 270

0   miles   200
0   km   150

Kalvrithia 50

Athens 200

Klissura 233

Kastelli 200

CRETE

In each of the actions shown here, unarmed men, women and children, almost all non-Jews, were chosen as the victims of Nazi hatred and vengeance. Many of those killed were beaten to death by blows of rifle butts, burned to death after petrol had been poured over them and ignited *while they were still alive,* or stripped naked and then shot. Those murdered at Klissura included 50 children under ten years of age. At Mikulino, all those killed were women patients in a mental hospital. In the Ardeatine caves in Rome, 253 Catholics and 70 Jews were murdered, among them many shopkeepers, students, lawyers and peddlers.

An estimated 32,000 German civilians were executed between 1933 and 1945 for so-called "political" offences. Those killed included Conservatives, Socialists, Communists, Catholics, Protestants, writers, journalists and teachers. All over Europe, non-Jews who were discovered sheltering Jews were also shot.

© Martin Gilbert 1978

THE DEPORTATION OF JEWS FROM HOLLAND, BELGIUM, FRANCE, ITALY AND GREECE

Driven from their homes and deprived of their possessions, more than four million of the six million Jews of Europe who were murdered by the Nazis were sent in cattle trucks to Nazi death camps in the east. Up to a thousand people were forced into each train, deprived of food or water, and shunted eastwards. Many died during the journey. On arrival at the death camps, the majority, weakened, sick and bewildered, were sent straight to the gas-chambers.

⊚ Some of the principal towns from which Jews were deported from the countries shown here.

卐 Some of the deportation centres, in which Jews were confined before deportation.

↗ Main deportation routes, mostly operating between July 1942 and August 1944.

卐 Death camps.

C O N T E X T

North Sea

Baltic Sea

HOLLAND

Amsterdam
BELGIUM
Brussels

Bergen - Belsen

Treblinka

CHANNEL ISLANDS

Sobibor

Auschwitz

Paris

LUXEMBOURG

F R A N C E

Mauthausen

Atlantic Ocean

Lyons

Turin

Bordeaux

Marseilles

Genoa

Florence

Pyrennees

Adriatic Sea

I T A L Y

Rome

Skopje

Salonica

CORFU

GREECE

Athens

KOS

RHODES

0   200 miles
0   100 km

This map shows some of the longest of the deportation journeys, from western Europe and the Balkans. As a result of the journeys shown here more than **320,000** Jews perished.

Mediterranean Sea

—·—·— European frontiers of 1937.

© Martin Gilbert 1978

CONTEXT

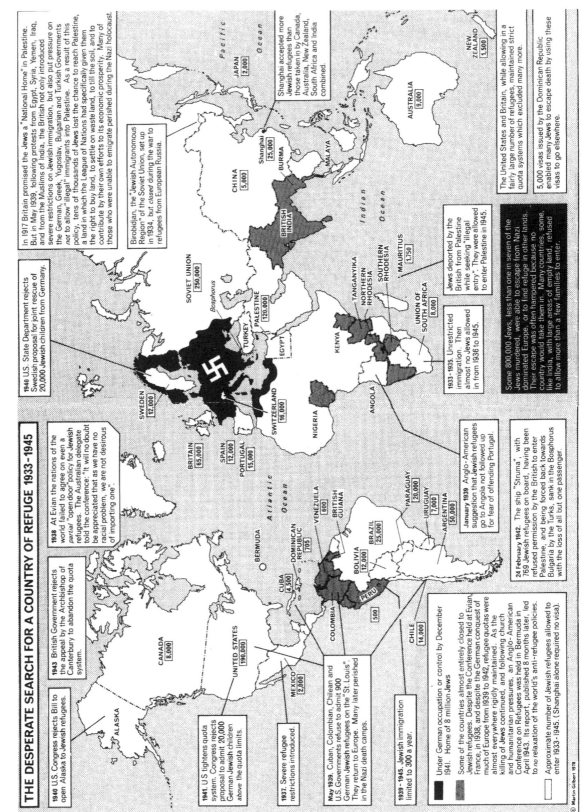

THE DESPERATE SEARCH FOR A COUNTRY OF REFUGE 1933–1945

In 1917 Britain promised the Jews a "National Home" in Palestine. But in May 1939, following protests from Egypt, Syria, Iraq, and from the Muslims of India, the British not only introduced severe restrictions on Jewish immigration, but also put pressure on the German, Greek, Yugoslav, Bulgarian and Turkish Governments *not* to allow "illegal" immigrants into Palestine. As a result of this policy, tens of thousands of Jews lost the chance to reach Palestine, a land in which the League of Nations had specifically given them the right to buy land, to settle on waste land, to till the soil, and to contribute by their own efforts to its economic prosperity. Many of those who were unable to emigrate perished during the Nazi holocaust.

Birobidjan, the "Jewish Autonomous Region" of the Soviet Union, set up in 1934, but *closed* during the war to refugees from European Russia.

1940 U.S. State Department rejects Swedish proposal for joint rescue of 20,000 Jewish children from Germany.

1943 British Government rejects the appeal by the Archbishop of Canterbury to abandon the quota system.

1938 At Evian the nations of the world failed to agree on even a *partial* "open door" policy for Jewish refugees. The Australian delegate told the conference: "It will no doubt be appreciated that as we have no racial problem, we are not desirous of importing one".

1940 U.S. Congress rejects Bill to open Alaska to Jewish refugees.

1941 US tightens quota system. Congress rejects proposal to admit 20,000 German Jewish children *above* the quota limits.

1937 Severe refugee restrictions introduced.

May 1939. Cuban, Colombian, Chilean and U.S. Governments refuse to admit 900 German Jewish refugees on the "St. Louis". They return to Europe. Many later perished in the Nazi death camps.

1939–1945. Jewish immigration limited to 300 a year.

Shanghai accepted more Jewish refugees than those taken in by Canada, Australia, New Zealand, South Africa and India combined.

The United States and Britain, while allowing in a fairly large number of refugees, maintained strict quota systems which excluded many more.

5,000 visas issued by the Dominican Republic enabled many Jews to escape death by using these visas to go elsewhere.

Jews deported by the British from Palestine while seeking "illegal entry". They were allowed to enter Palestine in 1945.

1933–1935. Unrestricted immigration. Then almost no Jews allowed in from 1936 to 1945.

Some 800,000 Jews, less than one in seven of the Jews murdered, were able to escape from Nazi dominated Europe, or to find refuge in other lands. Their escape was often hampered because no country would take them in. Many countries, some, like India, with large areas of empty land, refused to allow more than a few families to enter.

January 1939. Anglo–American suggestion that Jewish refugees go to Angola not followed up for fear of offending Portugal.

24 February 1942. The ship "Struma", with 769 Jewish refugees on board, having been refused permission by the British to enter Palestine, and being forced back towards Bulgaria by the Turks, sank in the Bosphorus with the loss of all but one passenger.

Some of the countries almost entirely closed to Jewish refugees. Despite the Conference held at Evian in France, in 1938, and despite the German conquest of much of Europe from 1939 to 1942, refugee quotas were almost everywhere rigidly maintained. As the killing of Jews continued, and following church and humanitarian pressures, an Anglo–American Conference on Refugees was held in Bermuda in April 1943. Its report, published 8 months later, led to *no* relaxation of the world's anti-refugee policies.

Under German occupation or control by December 1941. Home of 8 million Jews

Some of the countries almost entirely closed to Jewish refugees.

Approximate number of Jewish refugees allowed to enter 1933–1945. (Shanghai alone required no visa).

Pacific Ocean

Indian Ocean

Atlantic Ocean

Bosphorus

JAPAN 2,000

NEW ZEALAND 1,500

AUSTRALIA 9,000

CHINA 5,000

Shanghai 25,000

BURMA

MALAYA

BRITISH INDIA

SOVIET UNION 250,000

PALESTINE 120,000

TURKEY

EGYPT

SWEDEN 12,000

SWITZERLAND 16,000

BRITAIN 65,000

SPAIN 12,000

PORTUGAL 15,000

TANGANYIKA

NORTHERN RHODESIA

SOUTHERN RHODESIA

MAURITIUS 1,750

UNION OF SOUTH AFRICA 8,000

KENYA

ANGOLA

NIGERIA

CANADA 8,000

UNITED STATES 190,000

MEXICO 2,000

BERMUDA

CUBA 4,500

DOMINICAN REPUBLIC 705

COLOMBIA

VENEZUELA 600

BRITISH GUIANA

PARAGUAY 20,000

URUGUAY 7,000

ARGENTINA 50,000

BRAZIL 25,000

BOLIVIA 12,000

PERU

CHILE 14,000

500

ALASKA

© Martin Gilbert 1978

JEWISH REVOLTS 1942–1945

Despite the overwhelming military strength of the German forces, many Jews, while weakened by hunger and terrorised by Nazi brutality, nevertheless rose in revolt against their fate, not only in many of the Ghettoes in which they were forcibly confined, but even in the concentration camps themselves, snatching from the very gates of death the slender possibility of survival.

Ghettoes in which Jews rose up in revolt against the Germans, with dates. Many of those who revolted were able to escape to the woods, and to join Jewish, Polish or Soviet partisan groups.

Death camps in which the Jews revolted, with date of the revolt. In almost every instance, those who revolted were later caught and murdered.

This map shows twenty of the Ghettoes and five of the death camps in which Jews joined together and sought, often almost unarmed, to strike back at their tormentors. These twenty-five uprisings are among the most noble and courageous episodes not only of Jewish, but of world history.

CONTEXT

PONARY
19 MAY 1944

Vilna
1 SEPTEMBER 1943

River Neimen

Mir
9 AUGUST 1942

Nieswiesz
22 JULY 1942

Kuldichvo
25 MARCH 1943

Kletsk
21 JULY 1943

miles 50
km 80

Bialystok
16 AUGUST 1943

TREBLINKA
2 AUGUST 1943

Lakhva
3 SEPTEMBER 1942

River Vistula

Warsaw
19 APRIL 1943

CHELMNO
17 JANUARY 1945

Minsk Mazowiecki
10 JANUARY 1943

Krushin
17 DECEMBER 1942

SOBIBOR
14 OCTOBER 1943

River Bug

Lublin
3 NOVEMBER 1943

Lutsk
12 OCTOBER 1942

Chenstochov
25 OCTOBER 1943

Bedzin
3 AUGUST 1943

River Vistula

Tuchin
3 SEPTEMBER 1942

Brody
17 MAY 1943

Tarnow
1 SEPTEMBER 1943

Kremenetz
9 SEPTEMBER 1942

AUSCHWITZ
7 OCTOBER 1944

Lvov
1 JUNE 1943

River Dniester

CZECHOSLOVAKIA

Stryj
28 APRIL 1943

HUNGARY

© Martin Gilbert 1978

THE RIGHTEOUS AMONG THE NATIONS 1939 - 1945

One of the awards for Norway was a collective one for the members of the Norwegian Resistance movement, all of whom helped Jews to escape. The Danish awards include one which was made to the King in honour of the Danish nation.

—·—·— Frontiers of 1937

● Numbers of 'righteous gentiles' honoured up to 1990 by the State of Israel for having helped individual Jews to escape deportation and death between 1939 and 1945.

0   200 miles

0   300 km

NORWAY **3**

North Sea

SWEDEN **7**

LATVIA

LITHUANIA **13**

DENMARK

HOLLAND **10**

148

Baltic Sea

USSR **150**

3265

GREAT BRITAIN **9**

GERMANY **240**

2972 POLAND

Atlantic Ocean

BELGIUM **453**

92 CZECHOSLOVAKIA

68

AUSTRIA **145** HUNGARY

PORTUGAL

FRANCE **670**

135

74 YUGOSLAVIA

RUMANIA **36**

1

3 SPAIN

ITALY

BULGARIA **11**

GREECE **105**

1 TURKEY

Mediterranean Sea

On 19 August 1953 the Israeli Parliament passed a law making it the duty of the State of Israel to recognize the work done by non-Jews in saving Jewish lives during the war. An expression of honour was awarded in the name of the Jewish people, to every non-Jewish person or family who had risked their lives to save Jews. Evidence of such action has to come initially from one of those who was actually saved; the evidence is then examined by a committee of eighteen judges and experts.

At the national Holocaust memorial, known as "Yad Vashem", in Jerusalem, an "avenue of the righteous" was begun 1962, where each non-Jew who is honoured plants a tree, or has a tree planted in his or her name. This map shows the number of "righteous gentiles" honoured between 1962, when the first tree was planted, and 31 December 1990; the total number is 8611.

© Martin Gilbert 1978

THE JEWISH DEATH-TOLL
1939-1945

This map shows the number of Jews murdered in Nazi-dominated Europe between 1939 and 1945. All the figures are approximate, but most of them are probably *underestimates*. In all, more than **5,950,000** deaths are shown even with these minimum figures.

CONTEXT

NORWAY
868

North Sea

ESTONIA
1,000

FURTHEST ADVANCE OF THE GERMAN ARMY 1942

DENMARK
120

LATVIA

LITHUANIA

HOLLAND
106,000

Baltic Sea

BELGIUM
24,000

GERMANY
125,000

4,565,000

POLAND

WESTERN USSR

LUXEMBOURG
700

CZECHOSLOVAKIA
277,000

FRANCE
83,000

HUNGARY
300,000

RUMANIA
264,000

AUSTRIA
70,000

Adriatic Sea

YUGOSLAVIA
60,000

Black Sea

ITALY
7,500

GREECE
65,000

Mediterranean Sea

Approximate Jewish death-toll, country-by-country.

- ·-··- European frontiers of 1937.

© Martin Gilbert 1978

49

Working it Out

Diana Eck

One of the places we most commonly encounter religious difference in America today is the workplace. What religious attire may one wear? A cross? Yarmulke? Head scarf? Turban? Where and when is it appropriate to pray? What facilities do employers need to provide, and what policies do they need to implement? Religious difference is a question not just for theological schools and religious institutions but increasingly for businesses and corporations, offices and factories. These are the places where "we the people" most frequently meet, and how we manage our encounters here might be far more important than how we cope with imaginary encounters in the realm of theologies and beliefs.

The most common workplace issues have traditionally concerned working on the Sabbath, which is Saturday for Jews and Seventh-Day Adventists. Consider the case of a computer operator at a hospital in Fort Smith, Arkansas. Although he is a Seventh-Day Adventist and asked not to work on Saturdays, he was placed on call on Saturdays. When he refused to make himself available on his Sabbath, the hospital fired him. Title VII of the Civil Rights Act of 1964 prohibits discrimination on the basis of race, color, religion, national origin, or sex. In interpreting the act in relation to the religious practices of workers, the employer must try to make "reasonable accommodation" of religious practice, at least as long as it does not impose an "undue hardship" on the employer. In this case, the court ruled that the hospital was in violation of the Civil Rights Act. But just what constitutes "reasonable accommodation" and "undue hardship" is the thorny issue as each case comes forward.

In the past ten years the Equal Employment Opportunity Commission (EEOC), which considers workplace complaints that may violate the Civil Rights Act, has reported a 31 percent rise in complaints of religious discrimination in the workplace. This is not surprising given the number of new immigrants in the workforce and the range of questions their attire, their holidays, and their religious life bring to the workplace environment. We have already looked at the incivility and prejudice Muslim women wearing the *hijab* may encounter. But sometimes incivility slides up the scale toward discrimination. For example, in 1996 Rose Hamid, a twelve-year veteran flight attendant with U.S. Air, became increasingly serious about her faith in the wake of some health problems and made the decision to wear a head scarf. Her first day at work, she was ordered to take it off because it was not part of the uniform of a flight attendant, and when she refused she was put on unpaid leave. Rose filed a complaint with the Equal Employment Opportunity Commission. What is reasonable accommodation in Rose's case? Rose had modeled different ways in which the colors of her uniform would be duplicated in her scarf, and some would argue that reasonable accommodation would mean allowing some flexibility in the uniform as long as it was readily recognizable. But U.S. Air moved Rose to a job that did not require a uniform and hence put her out of public visibility. . . .

Hair and beards have also raised workplace issues. In 1987 a Sikh immigrant, Prabhjot Kohli, who had managed a pharmaceutical company in India before coming to the U.S., was turned down for a job at Domino's Pizza in Baltimore because of his religiously mandated beard. "Domino's wants clean-shaven people," he recalls being told, "and you've got a beard." In this case, wearing the baseball cap was not enough. For Domino's it was a business decision: people prefer to be served pizza by clean-shaven employees. The case

went to the Maryland Human Relations Commission and was resolved only after a twelve-year lawsuit. In January 2000 the pizza chain dropped its no-beard policy. In California, Manjit Singh Bhatia, a machinist, was removed from his job at Chevron company because new safety requirements mandated the shaving of facial hair. His beard might prevent him from having an airtight seal when he wore a respirator. Chevron moved him to a different job that did not require a respirator and promised to reinstall him as a machinist if a respirator were developed that he could safely use. For the courts, this was "reasonable accommodation."

Some Muslim men, though not all, choose to keep a neatly trimmed beard, considering it part of their customary religious observance. A discrimination case went to court in New Jersey where members of the Newark police force sued for the right to wear a beard for religious reasons. In a 1999 ruling (*Fraternal Order of Police v. City of Newark*) the U.S. Court of Appeals upheld the right of Muslim members of the Newark police force to wear beards on the job. As we have seen from the Sikh experience however, workplace decisions on beards have varied. And so too with Muslim men. A bus driver for a New York transit company can now wear a beard, but an employee of one of the major airlines cannot.

Prayer in the workplace is another issue that has gained complexity with the new immigration. A Christian group might gather at 7:15 to pray together before work. A Buddhist meditation group might spend part of its lunch hour in sitting practice. In the spring of 1998 I received a CAIR bulletin with information on three similar cases of workplace prayer accommodation in manufacturing plants around Nashville. Whirlpool Corporation reportedly had refused to allow Muslim employees to offer obligatory prayers on the job. One Muslim employee quit, and the others continued to perform their obligatory midday prayer secretly during bathroom breaks. When CAIR intervened, contacted the managers, and began a dialogue, together they envisioned a solution: the Muslim employees could perhaps customize their coffee breaks so that they could fit an Islamic prayer schedule. Today, Muslim organizations, including CAIR, are taking the initiative in providing the kind of information that might head off the endless round of discrimination cases. They have published a booklet called *An Employer's Guide to Islamic Religious Practices*, detailing what employers might need to know about the obligations of Muslim workers.

Employers today are encountering workplace issues most of us have never even thought about. For example, where do Muslim cab drivers who work the airport routes pray during the long days in line at the airport? In Minneapolis, at last word, they stand outside in a lot, according to Salina Khan of *USA Today*. She wrote, on June 25, 1999,

> Taxi driver Farhad Nezami rolls out his prayer rug, removes his shoes and raises his hands to begin the early afternoon prayer. Nezami's not worshipping in a mosque. He's standing in a lot near the Minneapolis-St. Paul International Airport that about 300 Muslim cab drivers turn into a makeshift prayer hall several times a day. They pray there in rain, snow and sleet because the Metropolitan Airports Commission has repeatedly denied their request for a room for four years.

The case is not clear-cut, and it probably falls more in the realm of civility than legality. But Denver handled a similar case differently. A hundred Muslim cab drivers there put the question to the Denver Airport authority and received a positive response. Jillian Lloyd of the *Christian Science Monitor* reported, "When the city of Denver moved a glass shelter to its international airport this winter, giving Muslim cabbies a warm place to pray to Allah, it did not merely show government goodwill toward a religious minority. The move highlighted the growing willingness of American employers to provide for their workers' religious needs."

At the federal level, the White House has addressed the complexity that our new religious texture has brought to the workplace. In 1997 it released *Guidelines on Religious Exercise and Religious Expression in the Federal Workplace*. They provide a pathway through some of the issues, generally following one principle: "Agencies shall not restrict personal religious expression by employees in the Federal workplace except where the employee's interest in expression is outweighed by the government's interest in the efficient provision of public services or where the expression intrudes upon the legitimate rights of other employees or creates the appearance, to a reasonable observer, of an official endorsement of religion." For example, employees can keep a Bible or Koran in their desk and read it during breaks. Employees can speak about religion with other employees, just as they may speak about sports or politics. Employees may display religious messages on items of clothing to the same extent as they are permitted to display other messages. A supervisor can post an announcement about an Easter musical service on a bulletin board or can invite co-workers to a daughter's bat mitzvah as long as there is no indication of expectation that the employee will attend. There is a veritable thicket of examples in this nine-page document. It is the first herald of a new day in the workplace.

. . .

49 (CONTINUED)

See You in Court

Diana Eck

The American Constitution guarantees that there will be "no establishment" of religion and that the "free exercise" of religion will be protected. As we have seen, these twin principles have guided church-state relations in the United States for the past two hundred years. But the issues have become increasingly complex in a multireligious America, where the church in question may now be the mosque, the Buddhist temple, the Hindu temple, or the Sikh gurdwara. Every religious tradition has its own questions. Can a Muslim schoolteacher wear her head covering on the job as a public school teacher? Can a Sikh student wear the *kirpan*, the symbolic knife required of all initiated Sikhs, to school, or a Sikh worker wear a turban on a hard-hat job, in apparent violation of safety regulations? Should a crèche be displayed in the Christmas season on public property? Can the sanctity of Native lands be protected from road building? Should the taking of peyote by Native Americans be protected as the free exercise of religion? Can a city council pass an ordinance prohibiting the sacrifice of animals by the adherents of the Santería faith?

These difficult questions make clear that one vital arena of America's new pluralism is the courts. Since about 1960, church-state issues in America have been increasingly on court agendas. Just as the "church" is not a single entity in multireligious America, the "state" is multiple too, with zoning boards, city councils, state governments, and the federal government. At all levels, courts hear disputes and offer interpretations of laws and regulations and the constitutional principles that undergird them.

The First Amendment principles of nonestablishment of religion and the free exercise of religion sometimes almost seem to be in tension: the free exercise of religion calling for the protection of religious groups, while the nonestablishment of religion prohibiting any such

special treatment. On the "no establishment" side, a landmark Supreme Court decision was made in the case of *Everson v. Board of Education* (1947) in which a school busing program in New Jersey was ruled to be accessible to students going to parochial schools. The Supreme Court's decision was clearly and narrowly defined: the busing program was a "generally available benefit" that should not be denied to children simply because their destination was a religious school. While the court has consistently ruled against state support of private religious schools, in this case, the benefit in question was not to the schools, but to the children. Justice Black wrote, "[T]he First Amendment requires the state to be neutral in its relations with groups of religious believers and non-believers; it does not require the state to be their adversary. State power is no more to be used so as to handicap religions than it is to favor them." The extended logic of this decision was that religious communities should have "equal access" to those benefits that are available to nonreligious communities. In other words, if a high school gymnasium in Bethesda, Maryland, can be used by the Girl Scouts or the Garden Club, its use cannot be denied to a Hindu temple community for its annual fall Diwali festival.

In "free exercise" cases, the *Sherbert v. Verner* decision in 1963 set a precedent that guided religious liberty cases for thirty years. In South Carolina, Adell Sherbert, a Seventh-Day Adventist, was fired from her job because she refused to accept a schedule requiring her to work on Saturday, her Sabbath, and was then refused state unemployment compensation. In her case, the Supreme Court articulated three questions to guide its decision: Has the religious freedom of a person been infringed or burdened by some government action? If so, is there a "compelling state interest" that would nonetheless justify the government action? Finally, is there any other way the government interest can be satisfied without restricting religious liberty? In sum, religious liberty is the rule; any exception to the rule can be justified only by a "compelling state interest." This form of reasoning came to be called the "balancing test"—balancing state interest against the religious freedom of the individual.

In the Sherbert case, the court ruled that there was no state interest compelling enough to warrant the burden placed upon Sherbert's religious freedom. Similarly, when an Amish community in Wisconsin insisted on withdrawing its children from public schools after the eighth grade and the State of Wisconsin insisted the children comply with compulsory education laws, the Supreme Court applied the three-pronged test and ruled that the religious freedom of the Amish outweighed the state's interest in four years' more compulsory education (*Wisconsin v. Yoder*, 1972).

Beginning in the 1980s, however, a series of Supreme Court rulings gradually weakened the force of the Sherbert balancing test and, in the view of many, weakened the constitutional guarantee of the free exercise of religion. These rulings began to raise disturbing questions about the religious rights of minorities. In the case of *Lyng v. The Northwest Indian Cemetery Protective Association* (1988), the issue was whether the Native Americans' right to preserve intact their sacred sites outweighed the government's right to build roads through Forest Service land. The Yurok, Karok, and Tolowa Indians argued that building a logging road through the land would have "devastating effects" on their religious ways. A lower court acted to prevent the Forest Service from building the road, but the Forest Service appealed to the Supreme Court. In this case, the Supreme Court supported the Forest Service, saying,

> Incidental effects of government programs which may make it more difficult to practice certain religions, but which have no tendency to coerce individuals into acting contrary to their religious beliefs [do not] require government to bring forward a compelling justification for its otherwise lawful actions. . . . However much we might wish that it were otherwise, government simply could not operate if it were required

to satisfy every citizen's religious needs and desires. . . . Whatever rights the Indians may have to the use of the area, however, those rights do not divest the government of its right to use what is, after all, its land.

Here, the balance tipped precipitously in favor of the government, whose policies, just incidentally, compromised Native religious practice.

For the Indians, one of the issues in this and other cases is whether the government recognizes the deeply held religious importance of preserving particular sacred sites undisturbed. A Hopi and Navajo case (*Wilson v. Block*, 1983) questioned whether a ski area could be built on a sacred mountain. The court ruled that the Forest Service had not infringed the religious rights of the Indians because it had not denied them access to the mountain. But the Navajo and Hopi argued that the mountain, the home of the Kachinas—divine messengers—would be desecrated by its commercial development. The court seemed to give little weight to the fact that the Native peoples considered the mountain to be inherently sacred, the very locus of the Divine, and not simply the place where they pray to the Divine. Here, the very nature of Native religious claims for the sanctity of the land seemed to be undermined, or perhaps not even understood, by the court's reasoning.

These and other cases led many to see an increasingly restrictive interpretation of the scope of religious freedom by the Supreme Court. In each case, the government did not have to demonstrate a "compelling interest" in order to restrict religious freedom. And in each case, the government did not have to alter its basic procedures to accommodate a specific religious claim. For example, an Abnaki Indian asked that his daughter, Little Bird of the Snow, be exempt from having to have a Social Security number in order to receive the benefits from the Aid to Families with Dependent Children program (*Bowen v. Roy*, 1986). The father insisted that to assign a number to his daughter would "rob her of her spirit" and interfere with her spiritual growth by making her a number, regulated by the federal government. The court ruled that the First Amendment could not be interpreted to require the government to alter its procedures in this way. Little Bird of the Snow would have to have a Social Security number.

Altering government procedures to accommodate various religious practices was also at stake in the case of *Goldman v. Weinberger* (1986). Dr. Goldman, an Orthodox Jewish psychiatrist serving in the U.S. Air Force, insisted on his right to wear his yarmulke on duty in the hospital, even though Air Force regulations prohibited a uniformed officer from wearing a head covering inside. The Air Force insisted that its code of military discipline requires that it not be continually making exceptions. The court said it would defer to the Air Force's judgment in this matter, which was to say: no yarmulkes.

Friday prayer for a Muslim prisoner was decided along similar lines in the case of *O'Lone v. Estate of Shabazz* (1987). Here, a Muslim prison inmate wanted to return from the work gang at noon for Friday prayers with other Muslims. He was turned down because officials insisted that it would require extra prison security at the work site and the gate in order to bring him back, and the court upheld the prison system's refusal to alter prison practices. In making this ruling, the court also said that a restrictive institution like the prison system had security needs and regulations that would necessarily mean that constitutional rights would not be as broad as those of ordinary citizens.

These increasingly restrictive interpretations of the guarantees of the First Amendment culminated in the controversial 1990 Supreme Court decision about peyote use. In this case (*Employment Division, Department of Human Resources of Oregon v. Smith*, 1990) two members of the Native American church ingested peyote, as is common in the ceremonial life of the church, and were subsequently fired from their jobs for "misconduct." The state of Oregon denied them unemployment compensation because they had been dismissed for the use of peyote, which was classified as an illegal drug. The Supreme Court

upheld Oregon's decision, arguing that the state had a "generally applicable" law against drug use. The law did not specifically target the Native American church or any other group, and carving out exceptions to such laws would be impracticable, according to the 5–4 majority of the court. Justice Antonin Scalia argued that to require the government to demonstrate a "compelling state interest" in enforcing generally applicable laws would be "courting anarchy."

The Smith decision thus reversed many years of court precedent, which presumed that religious freedom would be the rule, with any infringement requiring the demonstration of a compelling state interest. Many critics insisted that for the court to refuse to apply the balancing test to "generally applicable laws" would seriously damage the first-amendment protection of religious freedom. The Smith decision, critics argued, would be especially hard on minority religions, since generally applicable laws are passed by the majority. Freedom of religion, on the other hand is not subject to majority rule. The purpose of the Bill of Rights was precisely to limit the power of the majority in areas of fundamental rights, such as the freedom of conscience and speech.

The Santería Church of the Lukumi Babalu Aye in Hialeah, Florida, was a minority group in danger of losing its freedom of religious practice due to its unpopular and widely misunderstood practice of animal sacrifice. An estimated fifty thousand practitioners of the Afro-Caribbean Santería religion now live in South Florida, and their ceremonial life includes the sacrifice of chickens, pigeons, or other small animals to the *orisha*, their gods. The case that came to the Supreme Court (*Church of the Lukumi Babalu Aye v. City of Hialeah*, 1993) began in 1987 when Ernesto Pichardo, a priest of the Santería religion, purchased a building and a former used car lot to open a place of worship. The city council of Hialeah met to consider the matter, and many voices hostile to Santería were raised. The council passed three ordinances that effectively prohibited animal sacrifice within the city limits. As the city attorney explained, "This community will not tolerate religious practices which are abhorrent to its citizens."

Ernesto Pichardo and his community protested, insisting that the ordinances specifically targeted Santería, as they did not prohibit the killing of animals within city limits for secular reasons but only for religious ones and only, seemingly, for those of the Santería religion. Indeed, the ordinances specifically excluded Jewish kosher slaughter practices. Animals could be killed in butcher shops and restaurants but not in the religious context of Santería. Many quipped that the Church of Lukumi Babalu Aye was being persecuted for killing a few chickens with a prayer, while Frank Perdue and Colonel Sanders kill tens of thousands without one. The question before the Supreme Court was whether the three ordinances passed by the city council were constitutional or whether they violated the constitutional rights of the practitioners of Santería by specifically legislating against their religious practices. The judges unanimously struck down the ordinances, stating that they were not generally applicable laws at all but specifically aimed at the Santería religion. As Justice Anthony M. Kennedy wrote, "Although the practice of animal sacrifice may seem abhorrent to some, 'religious beliefs need not be acceptable, logical, consistent, or comprehensible to others in order to merit First Amendment protection.'"

The Santería case was an easy one, resting on the principle that "government may not enact laws that suppress religious belief or practice." However, many people, including Justice David Souter, were still disquieted about the merits and the precedent of the Smith decision. By this time, legislation called the Religious Freedom Restoration Act had been introduced in Congress precisely to restore the religious freedom many people in public life felt had been eroded with the Smith decision. This act, passed in 1995, stated simply, "The government cannot burden a person's free exercise of religion, even if the burden results from a rule of general applicability, unless the burden is essential to further a compelling governmental interest and is the least restrictive means of furthering that interest." In

effect, it reinstituted the balancing test of the Sherbert case, this time in law. The legislation was eventually ruled unconstitutional by the Supreme Court in 1997, in part because it was a legislative maneuver to reestablish a form of judicial reasoning. This, the court believed, was the prerogative of the judiciary.

Questions of religious freedom lie at the heart of some of America's most hotly contested cases. The courts are one site of the encounter and disputation that are endemic to America's new pluralism. They represent the difficult places where we the people do not seem to be able to resolve our differences on our own. Cases involving America's newer religious communities have gradually made their way into the court system and into case law. The willingness to take advantage of access to the courts is itself a signal of the Americanization process.

In California's Livingstone School District, for instance, the schools and the Sikh community arrived at a stand-off on the question of whether three young Khalsa-initiated students would be permitted to attend school wearing the symbolic *kirpan*, a ceremonial dagger that is one of the five sacred symbols of the Sikh faith and is worn by all initiated Sikhs. In 1994 classmates of an eleven-year-old Sikh youngster had spotted his *kirpan* when his shirt slid up on the playground and reported this to the teacher. From the standpoint of the school, policy prohibited carrying weapons, including knives, on the school premises. From the standpoint of the Sikh youngster and his two siblings, the *kirpan* was part of their religious life, a symbol of their historic willingness to stand up for justice, and being required to take it off amounted to an infringement of their religious freedom. The U.S. District court barred the three youngsters from wearing the *kirpan*, and their parents kept them home from school. But when the case came to the Ninth U.S. Circuit Court of Appeals, the court overturned the ruling and required the Livingstone School District to make "all reasonable efforts" to accommodate the religious beliefs and practices of the three Sikh youngsters. According to the ruling, as long as the *kirpans* are small, sewn in the sheath, and not a threat to the safety of other students, the Sikh students must be allowed to wear them to school. Here, the courts were an avenue for working out a genuine dilemma that schools had not before encountered.

In New Jersey the Indo-American Cultural Society also found the court system necessary in order to resolve a community dispute having to do with its annual festival of Navaratri, the "Nine Nights" of the Goddess, observed on a series of weekend nights on the grounds of the Raritan Convention Center in Edison. This fall festival attracted as many as twelve thousand celebrants, and though it was arguably well out of earshot of residential areas, a group of citizens tried to block the festival. A 1995 meeting with the Township Council of Edison revealed a level of overt prejudice that was shocking to the representatives of the Indo-American Cultural Society. The chair of the society wrote to the township council following the meeting,

> We wonder if there is any awareness in Edison of freedoms of assembly and religion. We are immigrants to a democracy that provided the model for the constitution India adopted less than fifty years ago. We wonder how the folk who inspired our struggle against colonialism can arbitrarily dismiss our rights.

The council passed an ordinance aimed at restricting the hours of the festival, permits for the festival were delayed, and the Indo-American Cultural Society responded by seeking an injunction against what it considered the township's unfair ordinance. Eventually, in July of 1996, a district judge upheld the rights of the Indo-American Cultural Society. But all this required the willingness of the Hindus to use the court system. Reflecting on the whole affair, Vivodh Z. J. Anand, a New Jersey human rights advocate, wrote,

As a New Jersey State Civil Rights Commissioner, I have, since my immigration in 1963 at the height of the American Civil Rights movement, personally struggled for equity. I can report that the courts seem to be the only venue available to resolve vexing communal conflicts. While advocacy groups for a wide spectrum of social issues exist, the onus of resolving issues of religious freedom and rights, and in this case the more complex conflation of religious and racial "otherness," seems to rest only on those who are wronged and whose rights have been compromised.

Anand went on to report that during the entire struggle of the Indian community in New Jersey not a single religious group or community leader reached out to support the Indo-American Cultural Society in its well-publicized case. "In our democracy there is a paucity of institutions to study, educate, arbitrate, and promote the credence of the religious 'other.' Yet for a democracy to flourish, it is imperative that both individuals and groups be enabled to recognize that their own stories may be found in the stories and lives of fellow citizens who may appear dissimilar to themselves."

50

Native American Religious Liberty

Five Hundred Years After Columbus

Walter R. Echo-Hawk

. . .

HISTORICAL SUPPRESSION OF NATIVE RELIGION

Christopher Columbus's baggage included Europe's long heritage of religious intolerance. In 1492 Spain—fresh from centuries of religious crusades against the infidels for possession of holy places in the Middle East— . . . the Spanish Inquisition was in full force and effect. The King expelled the Jews from Spain on August 2, and, on January 4, military unification as a Christian nation was achieved with the Moorish defeat, which led to the expulsion of the Moslems.

. . .

On 12 October 1492, Columbus wrote this about the native inhabitants he encountered on his arrival in the Western Hemisphere:

> They ought to be good servants and of good intelligence . . . . I believe that they would easily be made Christians because it seemed to me that they had no religion. Our Lord pleasing, I will carry off six of them at my departure to Your Highnesses, in order that they may learn to speak.

. . .

Old World attitudes of religious intolerance became ingrained in the United States government's Indian policies from the very inception of this nation. . . . A basic goal of federal Indian policy was to convert the "savage" Indians into Christian citizens and separate them from their traditional ways of life. President Jackson's Indian removal policy was justified in the name of converting and civilizing the Indians. During this removal period, Supreme Court decisions that upheld the government's taking of Indian lands and the reduction of tribal sovereignty from independent nation to "domestic dependent nation" status under discovery and conquest principles of international law referred to Indians as "heathen" savages.

Christian missionaries, hired as government Indian agents, were an integral part of federal Indian policy for over one hundred years. The government placed entire reservations and Indian nations under the administrative control of different denominations to convert the Indians and separate them from their traditions. A number of federal laws, still on the books today, authorize the secretary of the interior to give Indian lands to missionary religious groups for "religious or educational work among the Indians," 25 U.S.C. 348. In *Quick Bear v. Leupp*, 210 U.S. 50, 81–82 (1908), the Supreme Court upheld the use of federal funds to establish a Catholic school on the Rosebud Indian Reservation despite a claim that this government support of religion violated the Establishment Clause of the First Amendment.

. . .

Despite the government's goal to supplant tribal culture with Christianity, many Indians clung to their beliefs and practices even after they were confined on reservations. Chief Walking Buffalo's remarks show defiant native resistance to government-enforced proselytization:

> You whites assumed we were savages. You didn't understand our prayers. You didn't try to understand. When we sang our praises to the sun or moon or wind, you said we were worshipping idols. Without understanding, you condemned us as lost souls just because our form of worship was different than yours.
>
> We saw the Great Spirit's work in almost everything: sun, moon, trees, wind, and mountains. Sometimes we approached him through these things. Was that so bad? I think we have a true belief in the supreme being, a stronger faith than that of most of the whites who have called us pagans . . . . Indians living close to nature and nature's ruler are not living in darkness.

Consequently, in the 1890s, federal authorities became more belligerent toward Indian religion. In that decade, United States troops were called in to quell the Ghost Dance, a widely practiced tribal religion that impeded government assimilation policies. In 1890, more than one hundred Lakota Ghost Dance worshipers were massacred at Wounded Knee, South Dakota. In 1892, Pawnee Ghost Dance leaders were arrested in Oklahoma. In the same year, the BIA [Bureau of Indian Affairs] outlawed the Sun Dance religion and banned other ceremonies that were declared "Indian offenses" and made punishable by withholding of rations or thirty days' imprisonment. Facing the threat of military intervention, arrest, and starvation, many Indians stopped practicing the Ghost Dance and took other rituals underground.

Formal government rules suppressing tribal religions continued well into the 1900s. In 1904, the BIA promulgated regulations for its Court of Indian Offenses, including "offenses" that banned Indian religious leaders and ceremonies:

C
O
N
T
E
X
T

. . . The "sun dance," and all other similar dances and so-called religious ceremonies, shall be considered "Indian offenses," and any Indian found guilty of being a participant in any one or more of these offenses shall . . . be punished . . . .

The usual practices of so-called "medicine men" shall be considered "Indian offenses" . . . and whenever it shall be proven . . . he shall be adjudged guilty of an Indian offense, and upon conviction . . . shall be confined in the agency guardhouse . . . .

Even though this ban was lifted in 1934, serious government infringements on native religious freedom continued into the 1970s. Tribes witnessed governmental suppression of their religious practices in numerous ways: arrests of traditional Indians for possession of tribal sacred objects such as eagle feathers; criminal prosecutions for the religious use of peyote; denial of access to sacred sites located on federal lands; actual destruction of sacred sites; and interference with religious ceremonies at sacred sites. . . .

The treatment of native worship by the Supreme Court in the recent *Lyng* and *Smith* decisions, analyzed below, is especially troubling when considered in the context of the above history. Given the long history of government suppression of tribal religions, it is highly doubtful that these unique and irreplaceable indigenous religions can continue to survive without any American legal protection.

THE LYNG DECISION: NEED FOR FEDERAL SACRED SITES LEGISLATION

. . .

Worship at sacred sites is a basic attribute of religion itself. Since the inception of the major world religions, control over holy places in the Middle East has always been of deep international concern. Beginning around A.D. 1000, the Christian world engaged in a number of military/religious crusades, spanning several centuries, to wrest control of its holy places from the non-Christian world. Following the Crusades, Christian nations resorted to numerous treaties with countries in control of the Holy Land to preserve sacred sites and protect freedom of worship there. The Crimean War between France and Russia was fought over control of Christian holy places.

However, when most Americans think of holy places, they think only of well-known Middle Eastern sites familiar to the Judeo-Christian tradition, such as the Church of the Holy Sepulcher (Grave of Christ) and Basilica of the Nativity in Jerusalem and Bethlehem; Mecca; the Wailing Wall; or Mount Sinai. . . .

Traditional Native American religious sites—some of which rank among the most beautiful and breathtaking natural wonders left in America—serve a variety of important roles in tribal religion, which should be readily understandable to most people. However, in truly understanding and protecting Native American holy places, society may have to confront and modify basic values first implanted in this hemisphere by Columbus, because native sacred sites are natural, not man-made, sites. . . . It is undoubtedly difficult for a culture with an inherent fear of "wilderness" and a fundamental belief in the "religious domination" of humans over animals to envision that certain aspects of nature can be sacred. . . .

[H]owever, federal agencies such as the Forest Service and the National Park Service have repeatedly destroyed irreplaceable native sacred sites. The courts have consistently been unwilling to find any protections for Indians under the First Amendment or any statute. The struggle in the courts culminated in 1988, when the Supreme Court ruled

in *Lyng* that Indians stand outside the purview of the First Amendment entirely when it comes to protecting tribal religious areas on federal lands for worship purposes.

In *Lyng*, a sharply divided Court denied First Amendment protection to tribal worship at a sacred site in northern California that would admittedly be destroyed by a proposed Forest Service logging road. The frightening aspect of the Court's refusal to protect worship at this ancient holy area was that the Court withheld protection, knowing that "the threat to the efficacy of at least some religious practices is extremely grave." . . .

In short, government may destroy an entire Indian religion under *Lyng* with constitutional impunity, unless it also goes further and punishes the Indians or forces them to violate their religion. The Court reached this result by an unprecedented narrow construction of the Free Exercise Clause. It held that Free Exercise protections arise *only* in those rare instances when government *punishes* a person for practicing religion or *coerces* one into violating his religion. Because it is hard to imagine rare instances in which that will happen, the Court's narrow interpretation renders the Free Exercise Clause a virtual nullity. This crabbed reading of the Bill of Rights is one that should deeply concern all citizens who cherish religious freedom principles, because, under *Lyng*, United States law guarantees less religious freedom than most other democracies and some nondemocratic nations.

As to the Indians in *Lyng*, the Court disclaimed judicial responsibility to safeguard religious freedom from government infringement, stating that any protection for them "is for the legislatures and other institutions." Former Justice Brennan's dissent noted the "cruelly surreal result" produced by the majority decision:

> [G]overnmental action that will virtually destroy a religion is nevertheless deemed not to "burden" that religion.

. . .

As a result of *Lyng*, there are no legal safeguards for native worship at sacred sites under the United States Constitution and laws, laying bare a basic attribute of religion itself. This legal anomaly has frightening implications for remaining tribal religions struggling to survive. . . .

From a policy standpoint, no religious group should be stripped of First Amendment protections in a democratic society so that its ability to worship is made wholly dependent on administrative whim. This is especially true for unpopular or despised minority religious groups, such as American Indians, who have suffered a long history of government religious suppression.

The failure of American law to protect holy places illustrates a larger failure of law to incorporate indigenous needs into a legal system otherwise intended to protect all citizens. Certainly, if this country contained holy ground considered important to the Judeo-Christian tradition, American law and social policy would undoubtedly accord stringent protections. Because important Judeo-Christian sites are located in other nations, it is understandable that, as American law developed in the United States, it never addressed this aspect of religious freedom. Thus, when native religious practitioners—who are the only ones with religious ties to holy ground located in this country—petitioned the courts, they found that the law was ill equipped to protect their religious liberty. However, if the purpose of law is to fairly protect all fundamental interests of our diverse and pluralistic society, then it must someday address indigenous needs, so that all basic human rights are fairly and equally protected.

. . .

51

Taking the Indian Out of the Indian

U.S. Policies of Ethnocide through Education

Donald A. Grinde Jr.

As the genocidal policies to eliminate Native American populations in North America began to lose momentum at the end of the nineteenth century (the Native American population in the United States had been reduced to 500,000 by 1890), American Indians faced a new U.S. colonial policy that aimed to obliterate American Indian culture through education. This "civilizing" policy had three cornerstones: Christianization, education, and the instilling of private property (usually in that order). . . . These policies were erroneously based on the assumption that Native Americans had no educational structures, no sense of property, and an inferior brand of spirituality. In fact, Native Americans had educational systems long before 1492, with Native teachers and scholars imparting knowledge to children and adults on a day-to-day basis both before and after white contact. Elders as well as people knowledgeable about specific ideas and techniques instructed members of their societies about a broad range of topics including history, religion, arts and crafts, literature, geography, zoology, botany, medicine, law, political science, astronomy, soil science, and theater. Since American Indian models of instruction centered on oral tradition, Europeans often typified Native American education as "primitive," defective, or nonexistent. . . .

In the nineteenth century, white Americans took these assumptions one step further and declared that American Indians had no government, education, or spirituality. Although such observations of Native American cultures meant little to the soldiers who were sent to conquer Native peoples, these ideas and policies were important to the reformers, educators, and missionaries who wanted to convert Native peoples to the civilization of white Christian capitalism. . . .

In the late nineteenth century, the chief advocate for the "civilization" policy was Captain Richard Henry Pratt, a veteran of Indian wars and the Civil War. In 1879, Pratt petitioned the federal government for the army barracks at Carlisle, Pennsylvania, and turned it into an off-reservation boarding school for American Indian children. . . . By the early twentieth century, American Indian boarding schools could be grouped into four categories:

1 Agency reservation boarding schools established and conducted by the federal government. The schools were built, furnished, and funded by the U.S. government, and all employees were appointed by the commissioner of Indian affairs upon nomination by the Indian agent.
2 Reservation boarding schools established by religious groups under contract to educate at a specific per capita rate.
3 Independent reservation boarding schools established by the government but made independent of supervision by Indian agents because they were located too far from government agencies.
4 Mission reservation boarding schools established by religious associations with their own paid employees. . . .

In government boarding schools, posters were given to American Indian schoolchildren well into the twentieth century that exhorted white Christian values:

1 Let Jesus save you.
2 Come out of your blanket, cut your hair, and dress like a white man.
3 Have a Christian family with one wife for life.
   . . .
4 Go to church often and regularly.
5 Do not go to Indian dances or to medicine men.

   . . .

Thus, education was presented to American Indians as a value system to be substituted for their traditions and as a mechanism to destroy traditional Native American ways. American Indian students attending government boarding schools were immersed in a totally different culture; students' clothes, habits, and appearance changed. . . . Just like the white man's religion, the white man's education demanded a cleansing process. The option of adding the white man's learning to Native cultures was not allowed. Instead, the American Indian was required to rid himself of his traditional knowledge if he wished to acquire a civilized education. . . .

By the early twentieth century, this militant cultural war against American Indians began to change. In 1904, Pratt left Carlisle after publicly calling for the abolition of the Bureau of Indian Affairs. . . . Thus, this new educational philosophy offered some cultural preservation and respect but promised little in the way of equality for Native Americans. . . .

In conclusion, it was clear by the 1920s that coercive educational policies had not only failed but also actually continued the genocidal practices that marked the U.S. government's relationship with Native peoples from the outset. The overall American Indian population had dropped from about 500,000 in the 1880s to 250,000 in 1934 when these policies were formally abandoned under the Indian New Deal. The Indian New Deal was created and controlled by white academics who usurped the power of missionaries in the Bureau of Indian Affairs when Franklin D. Roosevelt became president in 1933. While these social scientists did not grant American Indian people much self-determination during and after Roosevelt's Indian New Deal, they did abandon the coercive aspects of the "civilization" policies, stating that Native Americans should have a choice between "assimilating" into the dominant society and retaining traditional ways. Throughout much of the last half of the twentieth century, the tensions in American Indian affairs have focused on more empowerment for Native communities. But there is still little power for American Indian nations when it comes to the allocation of their resources: ethnocide (the systematic destruction of a people's ways) was finally abandoned in the 1930s, but economic exploitation of Native American resources still continues largely unabated into the twenty-first century.

52

From Pearl Harbor to 9/11

Lessons from the Internment of Japanese American Buddhists

Duncan Ryûken Williams

Buddhist priests, classified by the Federal Bureau of Investigation (FBI) as potentially the most dangerous Japanese aliens, were among the first groups arrested by government officials following the bombing of Pearl Harbor on December 7, 1941. . . . Unlike Japanese American Christian priests and ministers, Buddhist priests were closely associated with Japan and thus with potentially subversive activity. . . . This perception that Buddhists (in contrast to Christians) were more Japanese than American was held not only by the FBI and the Wartime Relocation Authority (WRA) but also by the public at large, including some members of the Japanese American community. The history of Japanese American Buddhism during World War II, in fact, centers on this question of identity, both ethnic and religious.

. . .

The first Japanese Buddhist priests arrived in Hawaii and the U.S. mainland in the 1890s to minister to the first-generation issei. Most issei were Buddhists who had initially immigrated to Hawaii to work on plantations and to the mainland as contract laborers for railroad, lumber, mining, and cannery companies as well as on farms. In 1900, the Japanese immigrant population had risen to 24,326, most of them transient men. In 1930, however, the Japanese American population had grown to 138,834 and increasingly was composed of families with stable jobs and even small businesses. By the eve of the war, Buddhist temples functioned as both religious and community centers in all areas where Japanese Americans were concentrated, especially in California. . . . The FBI's decision to target Buddhist priests can be traced primarily to the conflation of Buddhism with state Shinto, which emphasized worship of the emperor as a deity and loyalty to the Japanese imperial empire. Not until the postwar period would Americans see Japanese Buddhism as a distinct tradition.

Newspaper editors and members of Congress accused all Japanese, including Japanese American children, of being loyal to the Japanese government and called for their removal from the West Coast. After their priests were taken away to "enemy alien" camps, the remaining members of Buddhist temples tried their best to continue religious services as well as community affairs. For example, the wives of priests and nonordained temple leaders took on duties that priests previously had performed exclusively.

By February 1942, the U.S. government set in motion the large-scale incarceration of the broader Japanese American community. On February 19, 1942, President Roosevelt issued Executive Order 9066, which ultimately led to the designation of restricted military zones on the West Coast and the subsequent removal of all persons of Japanese ancestry from those areas. In the ensuing months, the atmosphere in the community was one of anxiety, uncertainty, and fear. . . .

During this period of war hysteria, some Buddhists converted to Christianity, while others burned Japanese-language books and other personal Japanese cultural artifacts in an attempt to destroy, literally and symbolically, their Japaneseness while simultaneously demonstrating their Americanness. Mary Nagatomi, for example, remembers her parents

telling her to go to the wood stove used for the family bath to burn everything in the household with "Made in Japan" on it, including her favorite traditional Japanese doll set. The one item the family members could not bring themselves to burn was a set of Buddhist sutras, which the father buried after wrapping the scriptures in kimono cloth, placing them in a metal rice-cracker box, and using a backhoe to dig a hole for them on the family farm. These sacred texts remain buried somewhere in central California, a silent testimony to the enduring Buddhist identity of one family, testimony that could not be completely obliterated despite the seeming necessity of doing so.

. . .

Japanese American Buddhists faced a crisis of identity and faith as they endured a harsh journey to the internment camps and the realities of the desert heat, coupled with the knowledge that they were prisoners in their own land. Within the camps, surrounded by barbed wire and armed guards, arose the question of what it means to be simultaneously American and Buddhist. What is an American Buddhist?

Buddhist life in the camps revolved around the barrack "churches," which held religious services and education classes (in some cases in mess halls and recreation buildings), especially on Sundays. According to the Reverend Arthur Takemoto, a young man during the internment period, Buddhist teachings such as those on suffering and patience helped alleviate the pain and confusion that many residents faced: "Understanding the basic tenets of Buddhism orients people to understand the reality of life, that things don't go the way we want them to go. This becomes *dukkha*, suffering and pain. To be able to accept a situation as it is means we could tolerate it more."

. . .

In this way, Buddhism not only provided a spiritual refuge for internees but also served the social function of maintaining family and communal cohesion through ancestral and life-cycle rituals and traditional Japanese festivals and ceremonies.

While Buddhism was, in this sense, a repository of Japanese traditions, it was also forced to operate in the context of an Americanization program promoted by the WRA. This program was organized to assimilate the Japanese and allow them to demonstrate loyalty to the United States. According to the *Investigation of Un-American Propaganda Activities in the United States* (1943) prepared by the Subcommittee of the U.S. House of Representatives Special Committee on Un-American Activities, camp administrators should promote recreational activities such as baseball and basketball as well as encourage internees to join groups such as the Boy and Girl Scouts and the YMCA/YWCA. Being Buddhist obviously was not listed as a method of demonstrating loyalty, but Buddhist groups made their own attempts at Americanization.

In May 1944, the name of the largest Buddhist organization in the Topaz Camp was changed from the Buddhist Mission of North America (BMNA) to the Buddhist Churches of America (BCA) to give the organization a more Christian-sounding name. The camp experience, however, only accelerated an assimilation process that had already begun prior to the war. The swastika symbol, often used on Buddhist temple stationery or on temple equipment prior to the internment, disappeared and was replaced almost universally by the dharma wheel. . . . By singing *gathas* as hymns, including Dorothy Hunt's "Onward Buddhist Soldiers" . . . Buddhists within the camp created a new medium for Americanizing Buddhism. They did so, however, in a way that honored their Buddhist traditions while simultaneously demonstrating loyalty to the United States. The young members of the community, having studied the Buddhist "Junior Catechism," for example, used a Christian medium to maintain Buddhist identity. Many of these elements constitute what might be called the Protestantization of Buddhism. . . .

As Buddhists attempted to find a place in mainstream American society, the English-speaking nisei also worked to gain a place for American Buddhism in the public sphere.

They organized two closely related campaigns to remember the lives and sacrifices made by the many nisei servicemen who had served in the 100th/442nd in Europe or as translators and intelligence gatherers in the Pacific Theater's Military Intelligence Service. A war veteran and devout Buddhist, Tad Hirota, led a *B* for Buddhism campaign to have the army officially recognize Buddhists in the armed services by creating a *B* designation on dog tags. (During World War II, the military had only three official preferences: *P* for Protestant, *C* for Catholic, and *H* for Hebrew.) . . . After some deliberation, a compromise was reached in 1949 that designated *X* to be used on dog tags for anyone not of the existing three religious preferences. Furthermore, an additional dog tag could be supplied by the soldier's church or temple that would positively identify his religion. The National Young Buddhist Coordinating Council subsequently campaigned for a Buddhist symbol to be placed on the headstones of Buddhist veterans at national cemeteries. After petitions were sent to Secretary of Defense, Louis Johnson, the army agreed late in 1949 to inscribe the "Buddhist emblem" for American soldiers of the Buddhist faith. These two campaigns represent an important legacy of the camps, testing both Japanese American Buddhist loyalty to America and America's loyalty to its Buddhist citizens.

. . .

While the long history of the Japanese American Buddhist experience obviously holds lessons for more recent Asian American immigrant Buddhist groups, one wonders if the war and incarceration experience cannot also inform and illuminate the recent unfolding of a "new religious America," as Diana Eck puts it. In particular, one wonders whether the targeting and harassment of Muslim Americans, Arab Americans, and those who may look like those who were responsible for the 9/11 attacks (such as Sikhs and other south Asians) parallels the Japanese American experience following Pearl Harbor.

According to the Council on American-Islamic Relations, which was tracking anti-Muslim incidents long before 9/11, cases of discrimination and attacks have soared since that event. Ethnic and religious profiling at airports and workplaces as well as physical violence (including the shooting of Balbir Singh Sodhi, a Sikh gas station owner in Mesa, Arizona) recall the hate crimes and discrimination faced by Japanese Americans after Pearl Harbor. Just as Japanese American Buddhist temples were vandalized and ancient Buddhist symbols, such as the swastikas (manji) that hung at temple doors, were riddled with shotgun fire by angry white neighbors, one saw an angry mob of three hundred people chanting "U.S.A., U.S.A." and marching on a mosque in Bridgeview, Illinois, right after 9/11. Whether it was the vandalizing of a Muslim bookstore in Alexandria, Virginia, on September 12, or someone shooting into a Dallas-area mosque, the Islamic Center of Irving, Islamic symbols quickly became targets for those caught up in war hysteria. "Visible religion," whether in dress or looks, combined with ethnic profiling has once again proved to be a factor in how American religious pluralism and tolerance are defined.

Just as hundreds of Buddhist priests were picked up by the FBI and hysterical claims were made that Buddhist bells were going to send Morse code message to the Japanese navy, the post-9/11 period has seen its share of indiscriminate arrests of thousands of young Muslim "enemy aliens" as well as the targeting of Muslim charitable organizations accused of having terrorist links. Many have developed the same kind of loyalty strategies as Japanese Americans did following Pearl Harbor: calls by organizations such as the American Muslim Council to cooperate with the FBI and support the president or drives to donate blood for the victims of the World Trade Center. While the rush to conversion, a strategy followed by some Japanese American Buddhists, is not an option for many Muslims, not only Muslims but also Sikhs and Hindus have sought ways of demonstrating loyalty to America, such as flying American flags or toning down religious or ethnic differences.

. . .

In the sixty years since Pearl Harbor, America has changed dramatically for Japanese Americans. In a June 2000 White House ceremony, President Bill Clinton bestowed the military's highest award, the Medal of Honor, on twenty-two Asian American war veterans. Japanese American veterans of the 442nd Regimental Combat Unit and the 100th Battalion, such as Senator Daniel Inoue (D-Hawaii), were honored for their valor in war. This action clearly signaled that Japanese Americans are no longer seen as foreigners. . . . Japanese American and Buddhist occupation of such high-profile public positions demonstrates a significant shift in America's religious, social, and political life. . . .

While the camp experience appears to have accelerated these types of post-war assimilationist tendencies—wanting to belong and to appear loyal—a lingering suspicion of mass incarceration and the denial of civil liberties for Muslim Americans remains strong among Japanese Americans, especially after the FBI brought in five thousand men, primarily of Arab and south Asian descent, for questioning in the domestic "war on terror." Within two and a half weeks of 9/11, two *New York Times* articles, "War on Terrorism Stirs Memory of Internment" and "Recalling Internment and Saying 'Never Again,'" chronicled what many Japanese Americans felt was a special responsibility to guard against ethnic scapegoating. Proclaiming that "we need to do everything that we wish good Americans had done 59 years ago," the executive director of the San Francisco Japanese American Cultural and Community Center, Paul Osaki, was one of many community leaders speaking out against violence and discrimination against Muslim Americans. On September 19, Japanese American leaders coordinated an unprecedented gathering of ethnic and religious leaders, including those from the American-Arab Anti-Discrimination Committee, the American Muslim Council, and the Council on American-Islamic Relations, to meet at the National Japanese American Memorial in Washington, D.C., and call for law enforcement officers and others to adequately address hate violence against religious and ethnic minorities.

. . .

Many Japanese Americans took on the conflicted identity of being a Japanese American Buddhist in the crucible of war. One wonders if 9/11 will also turn out to be similarly significant for Muslim Americans as they struggle with Americanization and resistance to it in their ethnic and religious identity formation.

53

A Somali Influx Unsettles Latino Meatpackers

Kirk Semple

Grand Island, Neb.—Like many workers at the meatpacking plant here, Raul A. Garcia, a Mexican-American, has watched with some discomfort as hundreds of Somali immigrants have moved to town in the past couple of years, many of them to fill jobs once held by Latino workers taken away in *immigration* raids.

Mr. Garcia has been particularly troubled by the Somalis' demand that they be allowed special breaks for prayers that are obligatory for devout Muslims. The breaks, he said, would inconvenience everyone else. "The Latino is very humble," said Mr. Garcia, 73, who

has worked at the plant, owned by JBS U.S.A. Inc., since 1994. "But they are arrogant," he said of the Somali workers. "They act like the United States owes them."

Mr. Garcia was among more than 1,000 Latino and other workers who protested a decision last month by the plant's management to cut their work day—and their pay—by 15 minutes to give scores of Somali workers time for evening prayers. After several days of strikes and disruptions, the plant's management abandoned the plan. But the dispute peeled back a layer of civility in this southern Nebraska city of 47,000, revealing slow-burning racial and ethnic tensions that have been an unexpected aftermath of the enforcement raids at workplaces by federal immigration authorities.

Grand Island is among a half dozen or so cities where discord has arisen with the arrival of Somali workers, many of whom were recruited by employers from elsewhere in the United States after immigration raids sharply reduced their Latino work forces. The Somalis are by and large in this country legally as political refugees and therefore are not singled out by immigration authorities.

In some of these places, including Grand Island, this newest wave of immigrant workers has had the effect of unifying the other ethnic populations against the Somalis and has also diverted some of the longstanding hostility toward Latino immigrants among some native-born residents. "Every wave of immigrants has had to struggle to get assimilated," said Margaret Hornady, the mayor of Grand Island and a longtime resident of Nebraska. "Right now, it's so volatile."

The federal immigration crackdown has hit meat- and poultry-packing plants particularly hard, with more than 2,000 immigrant workers in at least nine places detained since 2006 in major raids, most on immigration violations. Struggling to fill the grueling low-wage jobs that attract few American workers, the plants have placed advertisements in immigrant newspapers and circulated fliers in immigrant neighborhoods.

Some companies, like Swift & Company, which owned the plant in Grand Island until being bought up by the Brazilian conglomerate JBS last year, have made a particular pitch for Somalis because of their legal status. Tens of thousands of Somali refugees fleeing civil war have settled in the United States since the 1990s, with the largest concentration in Minnesota. But the companies are learning that in trying to solve one problem they have created another.

Early last month, about 220 Somali Muslims walked off the job at a JBS meatpacking plant in Greeley, Colo., saying the company had prevented them from observing their prayer schedule. (More than 100 of the workers were later fired.) Days later, a poultry company in Minnesota agreed to allow Muslim workers prayer breaks and the right to refuse handling pork products, settling a lawsuit filed by nine Somali workers. In August, the management of a Tyson chicken plant in Shelbyville, Tenn., designated a Muslim holy day as a paid holiday, acceding to a demand by Somali workers. The plant had originally agreed to substitute the Muslim holy day for *Labor Day*, but reinstated Labor Day after a barrage of criticism from non-Muslims.

. . .

Nationwide, employment discrimination complaints by Muslim workers have more than doubled in the past decade, to 607 in the 2007 fiscal year, from 285 in the 1998 fiscal year, according to the federal *Equal Employment Opportunity Commission*, which has sent representatives to Grand Island to interview Somali workers. The Civil Rights Act of 1964 forbids employers to discriminate based on religion and says that employers must "reasonably accommodate" religious practices. But the act offers some exceptions, including instances when adjustments would cause "undue hardship" on the company's business interests.

The new tensions here extend well beyond the walls of the plant. Scratch beneath Grand Island's surface and there is resentment, discomfort and mistrust everywhere, some

residents say—between the white community and the various immigrant communities; between the older immigrant communities, like the Latinos, and the newer ones, namely the Somalis and the Sudanese, another refugee community that has grown here in recent years; and between the Somalis, who are largely Muslim, and the Sudanese, who are largely Christian.

In dozens of interviews here, white, Latino and other residents seemed mostly bewildered, if not downright suspicious, of the Somalis, very few of whom speak English. "I kind of admire all the effort they make to follow that religion, but sometimes you have to adapt to the workplace," said Fidencio Sandoval, a plant worker born in Mexico who has become an American citizen. "A new culture comes in with their demands and says, 'This is what we want.' This is kind of new for me."

. . .

For their part, the Somalis say they feel aggrieved and not particularly welcome. "A lot of people look at you weird—they judge you," said Abdisamad Jama, 22, a Somali who moved to Grand Island two years ago to work as an interpreter at the plant and now freelances. "Or sometimes they will say, 'Go back to your country.'"

Founded in the mid-19th century by German immigrants, Grand Island gradually became more diverse in the mid- and late-20th century with the arrival of Latino workers, mainly Mexicans. The Latinos came at first to work in the agricultural fields; later arrivals found employment in the meatpacking plant. Refugees from Laos and, in the past few years, Sudan followed, and many of them also found work in the plant, which is now the city's largest employer, with about 2,700 workers.

In December 2006, in an event that would deeply affect the city and alter its uneasy balance of ethnicities, immigration authorities raided the plant and took away more than 200 illegal Latino workers. Another 200 or so workers quit soon afterward. The raid was one of six sweeps by federal agents at plants owned by Swift, gutting the company of about 1,200 workers in one day and forcing the plants to slow their operations.

Many of the Somalis who eventually arrived to fill those jobs were practicing Muslims and their faith obliges them to pray at five fixed times every day. In Grand Island, the workers would grab prayer time whenever they could, during scheduled rest periods or on restroom breaks. But during the holy month of *Ramadan*, Muslims fast in daylight hours and break their fast in a ritualistic ceremony at sundown. A more formal accommodation of their needs was necessary, the Somali workers said.

Last year, the Somalis here demanded time off for the Ramadan ceremony. The company refused, saying it could not afford to let so many workers step away from the production line at one time. Dozens of Somalis quit, though they eventually returned to work. The situation repeated itself last month. Dennis Sydow, the plant's vice president and general manager, said a delegation of Somali workers approached him on Sept. 10 about allowing them to take their dinner break at 7:30 p.m., near sundown, rather than at the normal time of 8 to 8:30.

Mr. Sydow rejected the request, saying the production line would slow to a crawl and the Somalis' co-workers would unfairly have to take up the slack. The Somalis said their co-workers did not offer a lot of support. "Latinos were sometimes saying, 'Don't pray, don't pray,'" said Abdifatah Warsame, 21.

After the Somalis went out on strike on Sept. 15, the plant's management and the union brokered a deal the next day that would have shifted the dinner break to 7:45 p.m., close enough to sundown to satisfy the Somalis. Because of the plant's complex scheduling rules, the new dinner break would have also required an earlier end to the shift, potentially cutting the work day by 15 minutes.

In a counterprotest on Sept. 17, more than 1,000 Latino and Sudanese workers lined up alongside white workers in opposition to the concessions to the Somalis. . . . The union

and the plant management backed down, reverting to the original dinner schedule. More than 70 Somalis, including Mr. Warsame, stormed out of the plant and did not return; they either quit or were fired.

Since then, Ramadan has ended and work has returned to normal at the plant, but most everyone—management, the union and the employees—says the root causes of the disturbances have not been fully addressed. A sizeable Somali contingent remains employed at the factory—Somali leaders say the number is about 100; the union puts the figure at more than 300, making similar disruptions possible next year.

. . .

Xawa Ahmed, 48, a Somali, moved to Grand Island from Minnesota last month to help organize the Somali community. A big part of her work, Ms. Ahmed said, will be to help demystify the Somalis who remain. "We're trying to make people understand why we do these things, why we practice this religion, why we live in America," she said. "There's a lot of misunderstanding."

54

Jews in the U.S.

The Rising Costs of Whiteness

Melanie Kaye/Kantrowitz

BEFORE AMERICA NO ONE WAS WHITE

In 1990 I had returned to New York City to do antiracist work with other Jews, when a friend sent me an essay by James Baldwin. "No one was white before he/she came to America," Baldwin had written:

> It took generations, and a vast amount of coercion, before this became a white country. . . . It is probable that it is the Jewish community—or more accurately, perhaps, its remnants—that in America has paid the highest and most extraordinary price for becoming white. For the Jews came here from countries where they were not white, and they came here in part because they were not white, and incontestably—in the eyes of the Black American (and not only in those eyes) American Jews have opted to become white. . . .

Everything I think about Jews, whiteness, racism, and contemporary U.S. society begins with this passage. What does it mean: *Jews opted to become white*. Did we opt? Did it work? Was it an illusion? Could we have opted otherwise? Can we still?

Rachel Rubin, a college student who's been interning at Jews for Racial and Economic Justice, where I'm the director, casually mentions: when she was eight, a cross was burned on her lawn in Athens, Georgia. I remember the house I moved into Down East Maine in 1979. On the bedroom door someone had painted a swastika in what looked like blood.

I think about any cross-country drive I've ever taken, radio droning hymn after Christian hymn, 2000 miles of heartland.

On the other hand, I remember the last time I was stopped by cops. It was in San Francisco. I was getting a ride home after a conference on Jews and multiculturalism. In the car with me were two other white Jews. My heart flew into my throat, as always, but they took a quick look at the three of us and waved us on—*We're looking for a car like this, sorry.* I remember all the stories I've heard from friends, people of color, in which a quick look is not followed by a friendly wave and an apology. Some of these stories are about life and death.

Liberals and even progressives kneejerk to simplistic racial—black/white—terms, evade the continuing significance of race, and confound it with class. Race becomes an increasingly complex muddle. Growing numbers of bi- and multiracial children. *Hispanic*—not a racial identity, but a cultural/linguistic category conflating Spain with its former colonies. No one was *Asian* before they came to America, either; the term masks cultures diverse and polychromatic as anything Europe has to offer; yet *Asian American* has emerged as a critical and powerful identity. In the academy, obligatory nods to issues of race/class/gender result in language so specialized it's incomprehensible to most people, including those most pressured by these biases, and students tell me, "When Jews are mentioned in class, there's an awkward silence."

Where is *Jewish* in the race/class/gender grid? Does it belong? Is it irrelevant? Where do those crosses and swastikas fit in?

RACE OR RELIGION?

"Race or religion?" is how the question is usually posed, as though this doublet exhausts the possibilities. Christians—religiously observant or not—usually operate from the common self-definition of Christianity, a religion any individual can embrace through belief, detached from race, peoplehood, and culture.

But I have come to understand this detachment as false. Do white Christians feel kinship with African-American Christians? White slaveowners, for example, with their slaves? White Klansmen with their black neighbors? Do white Christians feel akin to Christians converted by colonialists all over the globe? Doesn't Christianity really, for most white Christians, imply *white*? And for those white Christians, does *white* really include *Jewish*? Think of the massive Christian evasion of a simple fact: Jesus Christ was not, was never, a Christian. He was a Jew. What did he look like, Jesus of Nazareth, 2000 years ago? Blond, blue-eyed?

Of course Jewish is not a race, for Jews come in all races. Though white-identified Jews may skirt the issue, Jews are a multiracial people. There are Ethiopian, Indian, Chinese Jews. And there are people of every race who choose Judaism, or were adopted or born into it from mixed parents. The dominant conception of Jewish—European, Yiddish-speaking—is in fact a subset. Ashkenazi. Estimated at 85–97 percent of Jews in the U.S. today, Ashkenazi Jews are those whose religious practice and diaspora path can be traced through Germany. The huge wave of Jewish immigration from Eastern Europe was Ashkenazi (as was the earlier, much smaller, highly assimilated community of German Jews, who looked with dread upon the arrival of—from their perspective—an impoverished, Yiddish-babbling, superstitious horde). Ashkenazi Jews also migrated to the far points of the globe—to South America, Australia, Africa, Asia. They may be very fair or very dark.

Sephardic Jews are those whose mother tongue is/was Ladino (Judeo-Español) and whose religious practice and diaspora path can be traced at some point through the Iberian

Peninsula (Spain and Portugal), where they flourished, unghettoized, contributing along with Muslims to Spanish culture, until the Inquisition (read: *torture*) forced conversion or expulsion from Spain of all non-Christians. Sephardim migrated to—and lived for generations and even centuries—in Holland, Germany, Italy, France, Greece, the Middle East, and the Americas. The first Jews in the New World were Sephardim: 1492 marks not only Columbus's voyage but also the expulsion of the Jews from Spain. Some Sephardim consider themselves the aristocrats of the Jews, and look with contempt upon the Ashkenazi history of ghettoization and persecution. They may also be quite fair or quite dark.

Mizrachi Jews are those who lived in the Arab world and Turkey (basically, what was once the Ottoman Empire), as minorities in Muslim rather than Christian culture. Their mother tongue often is/was Judeo-Arabic. *Mizrachi* means "Eastern," commonly translated as "Oriental," and is used by and about Israelis, often interchangeably with *Sephardim*. The Spanish Sephardim sometimes resent the blurring of distinctions between themselves and the Mizrachim, reacting with pride in their history and with Eurocentric bias against non-Europeans, referring to themselves as "true" or "pure" Sephardim. The confusion between the categories is only partly due to Ashkenazi ignorance/arrogance, lumping all non-Ashkenazi together. Partly, it's the result of Jewish history: some Jews never left the Middle East, and some returned after expulsion from Spain, including to Palestine. Some kept Ladino, some did not. I imagine there was intermarriage. Mizrachim, though they may also range from fair to dark, are usually defined as "people of color."

The point is, categories of white and color don't correspond neatly to Jewish reality. (What does correspond is Ashkenazi cultural hegemony—in the U.S., where they are dominant by numbers, and in Israel, where Sephardi/Mizrachi Jews make up about two-thirds of the Jewish population and strongly contest this hegemony.) Jewish wanderings have created a people whose experience eludes conventional categories of race, nationality, ethnicity, geography, language—even religion. Cataclysm and assimilation have depleted our store of common knowledge.

No, Jews are not a single race. Yet there is confusion here, and subtext. Confusion because we have so often been racialized, hated *as if* we were a race. Ethnic studies scholars have labored to document the process of racialization, the fact that race is not biological, but a sociohistorically specific phenomenon. Observing Jewish history, Nancy Ordover has noted, offers an opportunity to break down this process of racialization, because by leaving Europe, Jews changed our "race," even as our skin pigment remained the same.

> For the Jews came here from countries where they were not white, and they came here in part because they were not white. . . .

Confusion, too, because to say someone *looks Jewish* is to say something both absurd (Jews look a million different ways) and commonsense communicative.

When I was growing up in Flatbush, Brooklyn, every girl with a certain kind of nose—sometimes named explicitly as a Jewish nose, sometimes only as "too big"—wanted a nose job, and if her parents could pay for it, often she got one. I want to be graphic about the euphemism *nose job*. A nose job breaks the nose, bruises the face and eye area like a grotesque beating. It hurts. It takes weeks to heal.

What was wrong with the original nose, the Jewish one? Noses were discussed ardently in Flatbush, this or that friend looking forward to her day of transformation. My aunts lavished on me the following exquisite praise: *Look at her—a nose like a shiksa* (gentile woman). This hurt my feelings. Before I knew what a *shiksa* was, I knew I wasn't it, and, with that fabulous integrity of children, I wanted to look like who I was. But later I learned my nose's value, and would tell gentiles this story so they'd notice my nose.

V
O
I
C
E
S

A Jewish nose, I conclude, identifies its owner as a Jew. Nose jobs are performed so that a Jewish woman does not look like a Jew.

Tell me again Jewish is just a religion.

Yet Nazi racial definitions have an "only a religion" response. Even earlier, the lure of emancipation (in Europe) and assimilation (in the U.S.) led Jews to define Judaism as narrowly as possible, as religion only: "a Jew at home, a man in the streets," a private matter, taken care of behind closed doors, like bathing.

Judaism, the religion, does provide continuity and connection to Jews around the globe. There is something powerful even for atheists about entering a synagogue across the continent or the ocean, and hearing the familiar service.

But to be a Jew one need not follow religious practice; one need not believe in god—not even to become a rabbi (an element of Judaism of which I am especially fond). Religion is only one strand of being Jewish. It is ironic that it is precisely this century's depletion of Jews and of Jewish identity, with profound linguistic and cultural losses—continuing as Yiddish and Ladino speakers age and die—that makes imaginable a Jewishness that is *only a religion*—only now, when so much else has been lost. But to reduce *Jewishness* to *Judaism* is to forget the complex indivisible swirl of religion, culture, language, history that *was* Jewishness until, in the eighteenth century, Emancipation began to offer some Jews the possibility of escaping from a linguistically/culturally/economically isolated ghetto into the European "Enlightenment." To equate Jewishness with religion is to forget how even the contemporary, often attenuated version of this Jewish cultural swirl is passed down *in the family*, almost like genetic code.

Confusion and subtext. *Jewish* is often trivialized as something you choose, a preference, like tea over coffee. In contrast with visible racial identity, presumptions of choice—as with gayness—are seen as minimizing one's claim to attention, sympathy, and remedy. As a counter to bigotry, *I was born like this* strategically asserts a kind of victim-status, modeled on race, gender, and disability: If you can't help yourself, maybe you're entitled to some help from others. . . .

What happens if, instead, I assert my right to choose and not suffer for it. To say, *I choose*—my lesbianism and my Jewishness. Choose to come out, be visible, embrace both. I could live loveless or sexless or in the closet. I could have kept the name *Kaye*, and never once at Christmas—in response to the interminable "What are you doing for . . . ? Have you finished your shopping?"—answer, "I don't celebrate Christmas. I'm a Jew." I could lie about my lover's gender. I could wear skirts uncomfortably. I could bleach my hair again, as I did when I was fifteen. I could monitor my speech, weeding out the offensive accent, as I was taught at City College, along with all the other first and second generation immigrants' children in the four speech classes required for graduation, to teach us not to sound like ourselves. I could remain silent when queer or anti-Semitic jokes are told, or when someone says, "You know how *they* are." I could endure the pain in the gut, the hot shame. I could scrunch up much, much smaller.

In the U.S., *Christian*, like *white*, is an unmarked category in need of marking. Christianness, a majority, dominant culture, is not about religious practice and belief, any more than Jewishness is. As *racism* names the system that normalizes, honors, and rewards whiteness, we need a word for what normalizes, honors and rewards Christianity. Jews designate the assumption of Christianity-as-norm, the erasure of Jews, as *anti-Semitic*. In fact, the erasure and marginalization of non-Christians is not just denigrating to Jews. We need a catchier term than *Christian hegemony* to help make visible the cultural war against all non-Christians.

Christianism? Awkward, stark, and kind of crude—maybe a sign that something's being pushed; *sexism* once sounded stark and kind of crude. Such a term would help contextualize Jewish experience as an experience of marginality shared with other non-Christians.

Especially in this time of rising Christian fundamentalism, as school prayer attracts support from "moderates," this contextualization is critical for progressive Jews, compelling us to seek allies among Muslims and other religious minorities.

I also want to contextualize Jews in a theoretical framework outside the usual bipolar frame of black/white—to go beyond dualism; to distinguish race from class, and both from culture; to understand whiteness as the gleaming conferral of normality, success, even survival; to acknowledge who owns what, and in whose neighborhood; to witness how money does and does not "whiten."

> *For in the eyes of the Black American (and not only in those eyes) American Jews have opted to become white. . . .*

To begin to break out of a polarity that has no place for Jews, I survey the range of color in the United States. People of color, a unity sought and sometimes forged, include a vast diversity of culture and history, forms of oppression and persecution. Contemporary white supremacists hate them all, but define some as shrewd, evil, inscrutable, sexually exotic, and perverse, and others as intellectually inferior, immoral, bestial, violent, and sexually rapacious. If it is possible to generalize, we can say that the peoples defined as shrewd and evil tend to be better off economically—or at least *perceived* as better off economically—than those defined as inferior and violent, who tend to remain in large numbers stuck at the bottom of the economic ladder (and are assumed by the dominant culture to be stuck there), denied access to decent jobs and opportunities, systematically disadvantaged and excluded by the educational system.

In other words, among the creeping fearsome dark ones are, on the one hand, those who exploit, cheat, and hoard money they don't deserve, and, on the other, those (usually darker) who, not having money, threaten to rob and pillage hard-working tax-paying white Christians. In this construct, welfare fits as a form of robbery, the women's form; the men are busy mugging. Immigrant bashing—whether street violence or political movements like "English-only" and California's overwhelming passage of Proposition 187—becomes a "natural" response to "robbery."

It is easier now to see where Jews fit: we are so good with money. Our "darkness" may not show, and this ability to pass confers protection and a host of privileges. But we are the model money-grubbing money-hoarding scapegoats for an increasingly punitive economic system. Jews, Japanese, Koreans, Arabs, Indians, and Pakistanis—let's face it: *interlopers*—are blamed for economic disaster; for controlling the economy or making money on the backs of the poor; for raising the price of oil; for stealing or eliminating jobs by importing goods or exporting production.

At the same time, those defined as inferior and violent are blamed for urban crime and chaos, for drugs, for the skyrocketing costs and failures of social programs. This blame then justifies the oppression and impoverishment of those brought here in chains and the peoples indigenous to this continent. Add in the darker, poorer immigrants from Latin America and the Caribbean, and recent immigrants from China and Southeast Asia. Media codes like "inner-city crime" and "teen gangs" distort and condense a vast canvas of poverty, vulnerability, and exploitation into an echoing story of some young men's violent response to these conditions. Thus those who are significantly endangered come to be defined as inherently dangerous.

That is, one group is blamed for capitalism's crimes; the other for capitalism's fallout. Do I need to point out who escapes all blame?

When a community is scapegoated, members of that community are most conscious of how they feel humiliated, alienated, and endangered. But the other function of scapegoating is at least as pernicious. It is to protect the problem which scapegoats are drafted to

conceal: the vicious system of profit and exploitation, of plenty and scarcity existing side by side.

THE COST OF WHITENESS

Aryan ideology aside, Jews are often defined as white, though this wipes out the many Jews who are by anyone's definition people of color, and neglects the role of context: many Jews who look white in New York City look quite the opposite in the South and Midwest. Radicals often exclude the category *Jewish* from discussion, or subsume us into *white*, unless we are by *their* definition also people of color, in which case they subsume us as *people of color*.

The truth is, Jews complicate things. *Jewish* is both a distinct category and an overlapping one. Just as homophobia is distinct from sexism yet has everything to do with sexism, anti-Semitism in this country is distinct from racism yet has everything to do with racism. It's not that a Jew like myself should "count" as a person of color, though I think sometimes Jews do argue this because the alternative seems to be erasure. But that means we need another alternative. The problem is a polarization of white and color that excludes us. We need a more complex vision of the structure of racism, one that attends to the sick logic of white supremacists. We need a more complex understanding of the process of "whitening."

55

Oral History of Adam Fattah

Amna Ahmad

I used to wear a little charm around my neck that said *Allah* in Arabic, so naturally people in my school would identify me as Muslim. The Muslim population at my school is also definitely significant, so it's not very difficult to point us out.

. . .

I had a government teacher who used to talk about religion in my class. He used to speak about how all religions—though he focused mainly on talking about Judaism, Islam, and Christianity—can be considered very similar. He used to put the words "Judaism," "Islam," and "Christianity" on the board and write all the characteristics they had in common, such as prayer and the concept of fasting. He actually made sense in the way he approached the idea of likening one religion to another and definitely inspired an interest in me in the topic. . . .

While many of my teachers seem to approach the topic of Islam respectfully, as was the case with my government class teacher, the administration at my high school has made it inconvenient for me to practice my religion. Unfortunately they don't allow students a place to pray during school. Once I had actually gone to my guidance counselor to set up my schedule for the following term and asked her to switch my last period class, which was

V O I C E S

gym, with my lunch period so that I would have been able to leave school early enough to go to the mosque and pray. My guidance counselor simply would not allow that. As a result of her obvious indifference, I missed an entire term of going to the mosque on Fridays for Jummah prayer. I viewed myself as being at a huge disadvantage and was really upset about the situation. . . .

Sometimes, it seems as though Islamic practices are barely tolerable for administrators. Every so often I feel like I'm being penalized for putting religion before education. This year especially, I'm taking very difficult classes and to take off for three days because of the Eid is hard because I have to miss three days of very difficult work. I can usually only take off for one day of those three because otherwise I would miss more work than I could possibly make up. I often spend entire weekends just focusing on making up the work that I miss. That puts me very far behind. The Islamic holiday season becomes very stressful, and stress is something I really don't need in my life right now. Every time I have to take off for a Muslim holiday I end up having to explain to a teacher or fight with a teacher who argues, "There's no NYC Board of Ed law recognizing it as a holiday. You can't take off on Muslim holidays." . . .

Every so often, I feel as though it is more difficult to be the parent of a Muslim child than a Muslim student when dealing with the complications of the world of academia. A few years ago, my mother went to a parent-teacher conference for my brother, Muhamad. . . . I remember my mother's facial expression when she got home and I was immediately affected by the clear discontentment she expressed following the brief visit. My mother took the seat in front of Muhammad's math teacher when her turn had come. The math teacher was being very condescending and she looked down on my mother because she was wearing the veil, which is a key aspect of Islamic culture. She assumed right away that my mother didn't speak very good English. She spoke to her in language that was choppy, with a face that was uninviting to someone who was meeting her for the first time. With little concern for making a good first impression on a parent, she seemed to presume that my mother wasn't very well educated. When my mother started speaking to her after keeping silent for the first few minutes, it because clear to the teacher that she had been wrong. The math teacher was surprised by the fact that my mother was very well educated and spoke perfect English once she was given a chance. My mother has a bachelor's degree and two master's degrees. She herself is a teacher and was so affected by this feeling of being belittled by a stranger. She knew that she would never approach a parent in a way that communicates such degradation and disrespect. I don't think I would have thought the teacher's approach was motivated by prejudice had I not seen it in the red of my mother's eyes when she returned home to tell the story.

I would never have put too much consideration into connecting my Muslim identity with the more adverse experiences I have had in my life had I not seen it in the eyes of the woman who was prevented from attending school by immigrant parents who didn't know better; the woman who went back to college after raising three boys into maturity.

V
O
I
C
E
S

55 (CONTINUED)

Oral History of Hagar Omran

Hoda Zawam

I identify myself as an Arab American. That's what I am because I was born here. I'm an American, but I'm not like every other American. I spice up the average American by being an Arab American because I have merged both cultures together. It's just like adding rainbow sprinkles on vanilla ice cream.

I am Egyptian and so are both of my parents. Even though I was born and raised here, my parents really stick to Egyptian culture. We eat a lot of Egyptian food. We listen to Arabic music and are very family oriented. . . .

I started wearing the hijab when I was a 6th grader. It wasn't hard for me because it doesn't really matter how I look—I'm still the same person from the inside. . . . My friends were cool and they all wore hijab and they made hijab look good, fun, and easy. Hijab makes me feel proud and it makes me stand out because everyone knows that I'm Muslim. Hijab is not a burden on me, rather it's a pleasure.

I'm an 11th grader in high school. My school is nice and it's pretty cool. But it's not fair that our holidays are not considered government holidays and we don't get time off, just like the Christians get off for Christmas, and the Jews get off for Hanukah. Now that we're a big population in America and we are not a minority anymore, we should get our rights. Another problem is the absence of halal food in schools. So, I don't feel that Muslims are treated equally in this country. . . .

I will never forget the day after September 11th when I went back to school. All of my friends said, "It couldn't be you guys. You guys are really good." My friends reacted this way because they know me, my personality and my family.

But then it was different with strangers after September 11th. We got stereotyped, like when this one guy that came up to me and said, "You immigrant! Go back to your country. You freakin' Arab terrorist!" I was in shock. The first thing I said to him was, "This is my country. I was born and raised here. I'm not an immigrant and neither am I a terrorist!" He was stupefied that I was able to speak such good English and at the fact that I am an American. His reaction was a result of ignorance because he automatically assumed that if you're wearing the hijab that you're an immigrant and you can't speak English. I really don't understand why when one person does something wrong, the whole Muslim community and religion gets blamed for it.

I hate when people assume things about me and believe all the stereotypes that they hear. They believe stereotypes like all Arabs are terrorists and all the girls that wear the hijab are oppressed and forced to wear it. I think all these stereotypes are wrong and they come from ignorance. If you inform the public about these wrong assumptions they'll change their minds about the Muslim community on the whole. I think that Muslims are not depicted correctly here in America, especially through the media.

One story I experienced dealing with stereotypes was with one of my teachers who brought in a cartoon called "The Veil." He then asked the class, "What do you guys think about that?" All the responses were around the same line: oppression, suppression, no women's rights, Taliban, sexism, forced, and sympathy. Since I was the only hijabi in my class my teacher asked me, "What do you think about this cartoon?" I responded by explaining that what everyone thinks are stereotypes, and that none of it was true. I told

them how the veil is supposed to protect women, keep them modest, keep them focused, help them respect themselves and others, and keep them pure of heart and soul. Islam values women and it treats them as jewels to be protected. I explained to them that the hijab brings out your personality not your looks. Women are not supposed to be talked to because of their looks or how big their boobs are or their butt or something. It's supposed to be about your personality. When you wear the hijab, it's not like a guy is going to check you out, look you up and down. He's going to talk to you because of your personality, not the way you look. Hijab makes me proud that I'm Muslim and it makes me respect my own body, myself, and it also makes other people respect me.

So as you can see I'm not weird and bizarre, even if I'm not the norm. I am different and unique. I can do fun things like going to beaches, pools, ice skating, skiing, paintballing, biking, and rollerblading. And, I do swim, believe or not, with my hijab. I have fun because I am a normal human being like you are, but I can do it all while I'm fully covered. I also have a life, a family that loves me, a God that cares for me, and a God that I pray to five times a day. I mean what more can you want from life when you are loved, know where your right path is? I want to finish school, get a good education, and get a good career. I want to represent the Muslim community as intelligent, educated, and civilized. I want to take part in raising the standards of the Muslim Ummah and benefiting them.

56

Modesto-Area Atheists Speak Up, Seek Tolerance

Sue Nowicki

It's difficult at times being a person of faith, but it can be even harder to be an atheist, someone who believes there is no God.

. . .

According to a recent, large-scale Pew Forum report, 92 percent of U.S. residents believe in God or a universal spirit. The Pew report and 50 years of Gallup surveys found that atheism in the United States has remained stable over the years, coming in at about 4 percent of the population when lumped with agnostics, who believe it is impossible to know if God exists.

. . .

[I]t's clear that atheists are an overwhelming minority, and atheists say there are several misconceptions about their beliefs. Several strongly make the point that they are not satanists, immoral or dumb. Those who spoke . . . range in age from 20s to 60s and from business owners to blue-collar workers. They'd like faith groups, especially Christians, to be more tolerant of their views.

Here are excerpts of what they had to say:

. . .

Mary Brush, a Modesto resident and teacher, 53, traces her atheist roots to her childhood in a Catholic home. "I went to catechism classes, but I gave my mother so much grief, I didn't take confirmation in eighth grade. The nuns frightened me. They really made me afraid of dying. I thought I'd go to hell."

Biblical accounts added to her doubts. "The stories sounded a little too fantastical to me," she said. "It didn't seem to go with reality. Over the many years, I've had (religious) friends and have gone to church and tried to pray. It just didn't work for me. I'm more of a scientist at heart; science works for me."

. . .

Brush wants people of faith to know: "I'm a good person. Just because you don't have a belief in God doesn't mean you're not a good person. I'd like a little more tolerance."

. . .

Jason Gale, a 57-year-old business manager, said, "As a child, my mom was religious, so I kind of came along for the ride." But when he was 25, someone told him his religion "was a belief in magic. That caused me to start thinking about removing magical things from my thinking."

Gale fell into agnosticism for a while—"someone who says God can neither be proved or disproved"—but didn't like being a "fence-sitter." So he turned to atheism. "It is a belief; not something you can prove, but it seems to be better supported by empirical observations around you than religion," he said. "In religion, you need to have a leap of faith."

Gale said his wife is a Christian and returned to church about three years ago after a 20-year hiatus. He supports her, but admitted, "I knew she believed in God, but I never thought she'd become active."

. . .

He said he "backs way off" when others talk emotionally about their faith or his. But he wants people to know, 'I'm not an evil person because I'm a nonbeliever. I don't torture dogs and cats just because I don't believe in God."

And he gives this advice to believers: . . . "'Keep it on the positive side.' Help people, like the Peace Corps. Do what Jesus said, visit the sick and the people in prison. Do all the good works and stay away from weapons."

. . .

Susan Robinson, 50, said, "I always had the feeling from childhood that (religious) things I was told were not right."

As she matured, Robinson said she "kept looking for something to believe in. I explored other churches—Presbyterian, Mormon. I even started reading the Koran. I could never find a god I considered to be moral.

"Very often, there are different rules for God than for people. Like the flood—I'm sorry; I made a mistake. Let's wipe everyone out except for one family and start all over again. Or when Jesus was born, every child up to two years old was killed. That's a huge price for a savior."

For many years, she said, "I was afraid to tell people I was an atheist because of their reaction. I've read of a poll that says people view atheists less good than Muslims, including terrorists out there, and homosexuals. I read about things happening to people—losing friends, losing family members, losing marriages."

She's still cautious, but not as fearful. And she'd like to tell believers "not to be afraid of atheists. They're usually striving to make the world a better place. And please, please keep religion out of government. Any time God is put into government or someone wants to be treated like a god, it's really bad news for all the people."

. . .

Peggy Gardiner, 62 and a business owner, said her only childhood religious experience was when her grandparents took her to a small church in south Modesto.

"The Sunday school teacher told a Bible story and asked if there were any questions. I raised my hand and said, 'How did God get here?' I was about 5 or 6 years old. She said, 'God has always been here.' That pretty well settled it for me."

. . .

Despite her views, Gardiner doesn't make a scene around believers, she said. "I have a sister and a brother-in-law, and when we go out, they like to say a prayer before a meal. I have no problem with bowing my head with them. To be agnostic or atheist, you have to be pretty open-minded."

She'd like to tell people of faith "that while they all think they have the answer, it's not the only answer. . . . If people would spend as much time trying to improve the world as they do proselytizing, we'd probably have a better world."

. . .

Chris Muir is a 51-year-old Modestan who works as a part-time secretary.

"I grew up in a religious, Mormon household in a little farm town in southeast Idaho. It was pretty much an all-Mormon town."

When he was 8 years old, "I started having doubts. One of the things they said is that when you were baptized, you'd be receiving the gifts of the Holy Ghost. I believed it, but when I was baptized, I didn't feel any different. Then I started finding discrepancies that didn't fit. By the time I was 14, I'd pretty much decided this was baloney."

Over the years, he said, he's studied "the tenets of other religions. Being a skeptic, I find the flaws in those religions, too. Basically, religion appears to be what people want to believe. If it comforts them and helps them cope in life, I'm not going to try to dissuade them. It might be cruel to take (religion) away from them. It may be a false hope, but it's still hope."

He said he remains on good terms with his devout family but is "quite happy without having to give donations and tithes to maintain the church anymore."

And he does have his own beliefs. "I get asked a lot, 'Is there anything you do believe in?' I have to say yeah. I believe the world does exist as we see it."

. . .

56 (CONTINUED)

Student Faces Town's Wrath in Protest Against a Prayer

Abby Goodnough

CRANSTON, R.I.—She is 16, the daughter of a firefighter and a nurse, a self-proclaimed nerd who loves Harry Potter and Facebook. But Jessica Ahlquist is also an outspoken atheist who has incensed this heavily Roman Catholic city with a successful lawsuit to get a prayer removed from the wall of her high school auditorium, where it has hung for 49 years.

A federal judge ruled this month that the prayer's presence at Cranston High School West was unconstitutional, concluding that it violated the principle of government neutrality in religion. In the weeks since, residents have crowded school board meetings to demand an appeal, Jessica has received online threats and the police have escorted her at school, and Cranston, a dense city of 80,000 just south of Providence, has throbbed with raw emotion.

State Representative Peter G. Palumbo, a Democrat from Cranston, called Jessica "an evil little thing" on a popular talk radio show. Three separate florists refused to deliver her roses sent from a national atheist group.

. . .

The prayer, eight feet tall, is papered onto the wall in the Cranston West auditorium, near the stage. It has hung there since 1963, when a seventh grader wrote it as a sort of moral guide and that year's graduating class presented it as a gift. It was a year after a landmark Supreme Court ruling barring organized prayer in public schools.

"Our Heavenly Father," the prayer begins, "grant us each day the desire to do our best, to grow mentally and morally as well as physically, to be kind and helpful." It goes on for a few more lines before concluding with "Amen."

For Jessica, who was baptized in the Catholic Church but said she stopped believing in God at age 10, the prayer was an affront. "It seemed like it was saying, every time I saw it, 'You don't belong here,'" she said the other night during an interview at a Starbucks here.

Since the ruling, the prayer has been covered with a tarp. The school board has indicated it will announce a decision on an appeal next month.

A friend brought the prayer to Jessica's attention in 2010, when she was a high school freshman. She said nothing at first, but before long someone else—a parent who remained anonymous—filed a complaint with the American Civil Liberties Union. That led the Cranston school board to hold hearings on whether to remove the prayer, and Jessica spoke at all of them. She also started a Facebook page calling for the prayer's removal (it now has almost 4,000 members) and began researching Roger Williams, who founded Rhode Island as a haven for religious freedom.

Last March, at a rancorous meeting that Judge Ronald R. Lagueux of United States District Court in Providence described in his ruling as resembling "a religious revival," the school board voted 4–3 to keep the prayer. Some members said it was an important piece of the school's history; others said it reflected secular values they held dear.

The Rhode Island chapter of the A.C.L.U. then asked Jessica if she would serve as a plaintiff in a lawsuit; it was filed the next month.

. . .

Rhode Island is the nation's most Catholic state, and dust-ups over religion are not infrequent. Just last month, several hundred people protested at the Statehouse after Gov. Lincoln Chafee, an independent, lighted what he called a "holiday tree."

In Cranston, the police said they would investigate some of the threatening comments posted on Twitter against Jessica, some of which came from students at the high school. Pat McAssey, a senior who is president of the student council, said the threats were "completely inexcusable" but added that Jessica had upset some of her classmates by mocking religion online. "Their frustration kind of came from that," he said.

. . .

Brittany Lanni, who graduated from Cranston West in 2009, said that no one had ever been forced to recite the prayer and called Jessica "an idiot." "If you don't believe in that," she said, "take all the money out of your pocket, because every dollar bill says, 'In God We Trust.'"

Raymond Santilli, whose family owns one of the flower shops that refused to deliver to Jessica, said he declined for safety reasons, knowing the controversy around the case. People from around the world have called to support or attack his decision, which he said he stood by. But of Jessica, he said, "I've got a daughter, and I hope my daughter is as strong as she is, O.K.?"

Jessica said she had stopped believing in God when she was in elementary school and her mother fell ill for a time. "I had always been told that if you pray, God will always be

there when you need him," she said. "And it didn't happen for me, and I doubted it had happened for anybody else. So yeah, I think that was just like the last step, and after that I just really didn't believe any of it."

Does she empathize in any way with members of her community who want the prayer to stay? "I've never been asked this before," she said. A pause, and then: "It's almost like making a child get a shot even though they don't want to. It's for their own good. I feel like they might see it as a very negative thing right now, but I'm defending their Constitution, too."

57

Creating Identity-Safe Spaces on College Campuses for Muslim Students

Na'ilah Suad Nasir and Jasiyah Al-Amin

The current national political context has brought Islam (as both a practice and an identity) into the media forefront. The events of 9/11 and the resulting war in Iraq have sparked renewed interest in the religion of Islam and the life of Muslims. One only has to visit any chain bookstore to notice an explosion of books on Islam, terrorism, and Islamic extremists. Unfortunately, this attention has been largely negative, and Muslim communities across the nation are increasingly fearful of discrimination and even violence. This context has made the discussion that we undertake in this article of the issues faced by Muslim college students at once more difficult and more important.

In this brief commentary, we explore some issues that arise for Muslim students on college campuses, drawing on both our own personal experiences and discussions and interviews with Muslim students from a wide range of college campuses. . . .

We begin with the stories of two students from different backgrounds and with very different experiences on their respective campuses.

RASHID

Rashid is a tall, African-American young man with a ready smile and playful eyes, who carries himself with dignity and humility. In our interview he wore an indigo-blue African-style long dashiki and loose pants. He grew up in a medium-sized Northern California city in a family that has struggled through economic and other woes. He won a full basketball scholarship to a well-known institution in another (but still liberal) state. Like many students, college was his first experience living out of the state, and the transition, while exciting, was a bit unsettling. But he adjusted to his new environment well and enjoyed a central role on the basketball team and a good relationship with his coach and teammates. Although he was raised a Christian, he started reading about Islam his freshman year and

N E X T S T E P S

converted during his sophomore year. He describes this as the turning point in his life on campus.

Rashid's conversion shifted, first and foremost, his relationship with his coach, who was suspicious of Islam. He accused Rashid of becoming a black nationalist, of hating whites, and of being racist. After his junior year, he asked Rashid not to return to the team. Rashid then became active in the largely international Muslim student group on campus and declared Islamic studies as a second major. Here he encountered another obstacle—a non-Muslim Islamic-studies professor who was openly hostile to him and derogatory about Islam.

FATIMA

Fatima is a soft-spoken (almost shy) young woman, with a bit of hesitancy in her voice that lessens as she gets more passionate about her topic. At our interview she wore jeans and a college sweatshirt with a white scarf over her hair, pinned under her chin. Although her father is from Pakistan, Fatima grew up in the same state where she attends college, but in a different region. She says the Muslim community wasn't her first priority in choosing a college, although she knew it was important, partly because her oldest brother (who was already in college and active in the Muslim Student Association in another state when she was choosing a college) told her so.

Her experience as a Muslim on her liberal college campus has been a positive one. She reported no instances of prejudice, and she said she feels involved with both the Muslim community and the broader community on campus. About a month before we spoke with her, Fatima had made a decision, which for her was a step in the practice of her faith—to wear *hijab*. Her biggest problem on campus was finding a place to pray and make *wudu* (a special way of washing up for prayer). She expressed concern about how she is perceived and about stereotypes of "oppressed" foreign Muslim women.

These two stories illustrate some of the variation in Muslim students' experiences on college campuses, which have to do both with characteristics of the student (including class, race, gender, and types of support needed) and characteristics of the campuses and their surrounding communities (including how "liberal" the campus is, the presence of Islamic student groups on campus, and the existence and constitution of the Islamic studies faculty). However, there are also important convergences in their accounts. Below we consider several core issues that these stories illustrate (and that others' experiences corroborate).

THE BURDEN OF MANAGING A POTENTIALLY "RISKY" IDENTITY

All of the students we talked to described (in one way or another) the burden of constantly feeling that others were judging them in terms of negative stereotypes about Islam, such as "Muslim terrorist" or "oppressed Muslim woman." Interestingly, this fear has much more to do with a perception of potential threat than any actual acts of prejudice or discrimination. . . .

For the students we interviewed, this threat became particularly salient in moments of practicing Islam (such as praying while on campus), where they felt vulnerable and highly visible. Since Muslim students need to pray five times a day, they constantly have to search

out places to do so, such as an empty classroom. One student noted, "You have to find a place to pray, so you look like you are sneaking, then you find a room, and people are thinking, what is she doing in there?" This student revealed her anxiety that others may judge her as sneaky or strange.

. . .

AN IDENTITY-THREATENING ENVIRONMENT AND
LOWERED ACADEMIC ACHIEVEMENT

This anxiety about the stereotypes that the Muslim identity might trigger also affects students' academic performance. . . . While our sample was not systematic or representative, we did observe that students who reported more discrimination and contention tended to perform more poorly academically. For instance, while Fatima, a biology major, is in excellent academic standing, Rashid left his university several units short of graduating, returning several years later to complete his degree. Most students we talked to had not been actively denigrated, but they felt taxed by the need to constantly manage others' impressions of them. This identity-management process required energy and time that could have been devoted to their studies.

A hostile environment also made students want to distance themselves emotionally, and such distancing sometimes resulted in a disconnection not just from that particular campus community but from school in general. In some cases, Muslim students reported that the experience of prejudice (at worst) and lack of understanding (at best) on the part of their professors affected their academic performance more directly. For example, Rashid's contentious relationship with the Islamic-studies professor resulted in his refusal to do some of the readings for the course (because he felt that they misrepresented the Muslim experience) and contributed to his low grades in the several courses with that professor that he needed to take for his second major.

AN IDENTITY-SAFE ENVIRONMENT AND WELL-BEING

While academic performance is certainly an important effect of a welcoming campus environment, students' feelings of well-being are perhaps equally significant. That is, students should feel positive about life and grow as people during their college years. They should feel whole and healthy. Our conversations made it clear that students who found their university environment supportive of their practice of Islam, who felt that they were accepted as Muslims and as students and who didn't feel penalized or ostracized, were able to grow in the practice of their faith at their own pace and with full confidence.

For instance, two of the female students we interviewed (both of whom were raised Muslim) spoke of deciding during their college careers to begin wearing *hijab* on campus. They reported the relief and acceptance they felt at receiving compliments on how they looked with the scarf on from both Muslims and non-Muslims. The first day Fatima wore *hijab* on campus, one of her professors told her that she looked beautiful. This remark made her feel good about this step in her faith.

. . .

CONFLUENCE OF GENDER, RACE, RELIGION, AND CLASS

Our two stories illustrate another important point about negotiating Islam on college campuses: Islamic identity interacts with other identities to color both how a student is perceived by others and how he responds to such perceptions. It is significant that Rashid is Muslim, male, African-American, and physically imposing (he is tall and muscular), as he noted in our conversation with him. It may also be significant that he is a first-generation college student from a working-class family, since his resources for surviving college are fewer than those of more affluent or system-savvy students. We might note that the response of the basketball coach to his becoming Muslim was a largely racialized response—the coach objected to what he judged as a black-nationalist political philosophy and feared that Islam would make Rashid too radical regarding race and politics.

We see in Rashid's story that negative reactions to him were compounded by the fact that he belongs to multiple stigmatized groups. He not only has to negotiate being Muslim on a largely non-Muslim campus but also being African-American on a largely white campus, as well as a student athlete (which makes him highly visible and subject to scrutiny). He was explicitly told that he couldn't be both a black male athlete and a serious student activist, but that he had to choose between the two. Then, once his identity as a Muslim caused him to be released from the basketball team and he turned to his school work more seriously, he encountered resistance from others as he attempted to take up a "serious-student" identity.

In other work we have named these sets of identities "identity constellations" to capture the idea that people have not just one but multiple, sometimes conflicting, identities. The opportunity to reorganize these sets is more or less available in different contexts. Indeed in some environments, students are asked to choose among the various identities within these constellations, as Rashid's story shows. He (and other African-American students) talked about the feeling that they must decide whether to affiliate with the Muslim or the African-American campus community. A female student joked that before she began wearing *hijab*, the Muslims on campus didn't speak to her, but once she began covering, the African-American students stopped speaking to her. Such forced choices make students feel as though they have to privilege one aspect of their identities to the detriment of other equally important parts of themselves.

SMALL COMFORTS AND ACTS OF KINDNESS

Our final point is a brief one, but it is critically important. When we asked students about what made their experiences as Muslims positive, they invariably mentioned incidents that seemed to us quite trivial—for instance, professors who acknowledged Ramadan or who complimented them on wearing *hijab*. One student noted with great fondness the special dinner and breakfast packets the dining hall provided during Ramadan. These small acts of kindness were highly valued by students and made a huge difference to their sense that both they and the practice of their religion belonged on campus.

Other things that make campuses more identity-safe for Muslim students include:

- A strong, diverse, and supportive Muslim student group on campus;
- Professors who are knowledgeable about Islam and positive towards it (this especially includes the Islamic-studies professors, since this program is where students often go in order to learn about themselves and to feel connected and supported);

NEXT STEPS

- The presence of a broader student community that is accepting of Islam and its practices;
- Access to physical spaces that facilitate the practice of Islam without ridicule or judgment (for instance, having a private place to pray and wash up for prayer);
- Access to *halal* meals (foods that don't contain pork and for which meats are slaughtered in a particular way) and the accommodation of the special meal times (before sunrise and after sundown) during the month of Ramadan.

CONCLUDING THOUGHTS

While this article has focused on Muslim students, we'd like to conclude with a more global perspective on the important work of supporting all students' religious practices and identities (as well as other dimensions of difference) on college campuses. . . . The idea that it benefits the larger organization to encourage the development of individuals in their respective communities is reflected in the experience of the students whose stories appear here. . . .

58

Religious Diversity in Schools

Addressing the Issues

Catharine R. Whittaker, Spencer Salend, and Hala Elhoweris

As the following vignettes indicate, today's schools are made up of diverse groups of students including those from a variety of religious and spiritual backgrounds. The situations and persons depicted are fictional.

- Every year Yousef, a second language learner, looks forward to the prayer, family time, and feasting of Eid al-Fitr, following the month-long observance of Ramadan. But this year, his science midterm exam and another major assignment in his English class were scheduled on the Eid al-Fitr holiday.
- Ms. Taylor, a coteacher, had just been appointed as a member of her school's Diversity Committee. The school's population had become increasingly diverse, including students who are Catholic, Jewish, Hindu, Muslim, and Protestant. As part of its examination of the ways to represent all religions fairly and accurately in the curriculum and school programs, the committee was having a heated discussion about the celebration of holidays.
- Ms. Ramirez's inclusion class includes two students who are Jehovah's Witnesses, who must be excused from saying the Pledge of Allegiance. These students' families contacted Ms. Ramirez because they were concerned that others were questioning their children's patriotism, as they are the only ones in the class who do not say the pledge.

- Mr. George, a special education teacher, was shocked and disappointed by some of his students' insensitive behavior outside of his classroom. While supervising students in the hallways, he heard students making fun of Andrew, a student who wears a yarmulke, and making disparaging remarks about Bella, a student who wears a large cross.

Not all teachers are in agreement about how these beliefs and practices should be addressed. Students feel safe and are better able to learn when issues of diversity are handled with sensitivity. This article provides guidelines and strategies for helping educators and students understand, accept, and value religious and spiritual diversity.

UNDERSTANDING LEGAL MANDATES AND LEGISLATIVE POLICIES

Many educators are reluctant to address their students' religious diversity because they are unaware of the legal mandates and legislative policies regarding religious diversity and schools. The First Amendment, which contains the Establishment and Free Exercise clauses, addresses religion and the schools. The Establishment Clause requires that states remain neutral among religions and between religion and nonreligion. The Free Exercise Clause ensures that governmental agencies such as public schools do not restrict religious freedoms.

The Establishment and Free Exercise clauses have been interpreted by the courts in several important cases that address religious diversity in schools (see Table 58.1). Additional

Table 58.1 Legal interpretations regarding issues of education and religion

Legal interpretations	Supporting cases
Curriculum: Schools can teach about religion but cannot teach religion.	*Everson v. Board of Education* (1947); *Abington School District v. Schempp* (1963); *Epperson v. Arkansas* (1968)
Neutrality: Schools must maintain neutrality toward religious activity and cannot require, organize, endorse, encourage, or sanction student religious or antireligious behaviors (e.g., official prayers for students).	*Lee v. Weisman* (1992); *Good News Club v. Milford Central School* (2001)
Student rights: Students are permitted to engage in individual- and group-based religious acts as long as they are not disruptive. Students can present their beliefs about religion in their assignments and artwork and these products should be evaluated based on accepted academic standards and pedagogical concerns.	*Tinker v. Des Moines Independent School District* (1969); *Santa Fe Independent School District v. Doe* (2000); *Good News Club v. Milford Central Schools* (2001)
Schools can adopt policies concerning student dress. However, these policies cannot single out religious clothing in general, the garb associated with a specific religion, or the wearing and displaying of religious messages on clothing.	
Schools may excuse students from instructional activities that are viewed as objectionable by students and their families based on their religious beliefs or other conscientious grounds, although students generally do not have a federal right to be excused from lessons that may be inconsistent with their religious beliefs.	
Pledge of Allegiance: Schools cannot require students to say the Pledge of Allegiance if it violates their religious beliefs.	*West Virginia State Board of Education v. Barnette* (1943)
Holidays: Schools can teach about the religious aspects of holidays and celebrate secular aspects of holidays. However, schools cannot celebrate holidays as religious events and take actions to encourage or discourage observance by students.	*Engel v. Vitale* (1962); *Florey v. Sioux Falls School District* (1980)
Distribution of religious literature: Schools can regulate the time, place and manner of the distribution of religious literature by students as long they apply the same restrictions to the distribution of all non-school-related literature.	*Hedges v. Wauconda Community Unit School District* (1993); *Muller v. Jefferson Lighthouse School* (1996)
Equal access: If a school opens its facilities to "any noncurriculum related group," it must open its facilities to all student groups.	*Westside Community Board of Education v. Mergens* (1990)

information regarding these decisions is available from the U.S. Department of Education (www.ed.gov/policy/gen/guid/religionandschools/prayer_guidance.html) and the First Amendment Center (www.firstamendmentcenter.org/default.aspx).

INCORPORATING CONTENT ABOUT RELIGION INTO THE CURRICULUM

One of the best ways to teach about religious diversity is through the curriculum. Whereas many state standards include instruction about religion as part of social studies, literature, and fine arts curricula, the study of various religions can be incorporated into other subject areas as well. For instance, science, physical education, and health teachers can teach about the different religious dietary regulations. Math teachers can use the architecture of the various houses of worship as examples of geometrical designs.

STUDYING HOLIDAYS AND DISPLAYING RELIGIOUS/SEASONAL SYMBOLS

The study of religious holidays often can meet learning standards across the curriculum. However, when studying holidays and displaying religious or seasonal symbols, educators should make sure that they are used for a variety of groups, are employed as teaching aids and for academic purposes, and are temporary.

Initially, teachers should clearly identify the academic and social goals for including holidays in the educational program, determine which holidays will be studied, and plan how they will be presented appropriately. As part of these activities, teachers can include lessons that address the religious and social meaning of various holidays. Plans for students whose families do not want them to participate should be arranged.

One inclusive way to study holidays is to organize them across a range of religions and around common themes. Thus, Ms. Taylor and her school's Diversity Committee could suggest that the school use the theme of "light" to teach students about different religious holidays that are related to that theme such as Hanukkah (Jewish), Christmas (Christian), and Diwali. Other common themes for holiday celebrations might focus on the family, life cycle, liberation, cooperation, fasting, seasons, harvests, and planting. Teachers can use these themes to refer to holidays and schoolwide activities in an inclusive manner.

It also is essential that holidays be studied in nonstereotypical and factual ways so that none of the students' religious backgrounds and rituals are excluded, trivialized, or portrayed as exotic. Role-playing and other activities should be avoided as they may be interpreted as a means of stereotyping a group or violating or trivializing the sacred nature of rituals. Therefore, it is important for educators to research and solicit information from families and religious leaders to understand the authentic and different ways that religious groups celebrate holidays.

INVITING GUEST SPEAKERS

Guest speakers who represent a range of religious groups can be good resource when teaching about religious diversity. They can present information about their religious beliefs and practices and important historical or social issues, as long as they present information but

do not proselytize. For example, guest speakers can help students and teachers understand why students like Yousef celebrate Ramadan and what fasting means to them.

Initially, it is important to identify speakers of different religious beliefs and to determine whether to have several speakers at the same time. Potential guest speakers can be identified by contacting community-based religious organizations and students' families. In selecting guest speakers, teachers should meet with them in advance to determine if they are knowledgeable and can communicate with a younger audience.

Once speakers have been selected, teachers can prepare and discuss the goals of the presentation and possible topics to be covered. It is also important for teachers to share the legal guidelines for teaching about religion with guest speakers.

ADDRESSING ISSUES THAT AFFECT SCHOOL PERFORMANCE

Educators need to be aware of aspects of their student's religions that may affect their school performance and may require teachers to make respectful accommodations. Religious practices may dictate medical and dietary restrictions, clothing choices, rituals and observances, participation in school events, and absences during holidays. Teachers should also be sensitive to the scheduling of assignments and tests near religious holidays. For example, during some holidays, students like Yousef may be required to fast or pray during school hours, miss exams or school for extended periods of time, or have difficulty completing assignments. Similarly, some students like those in Ms. Ramirez's class my not be able to participate in certain school activities because of their religious beliefs. Therefore, teachers and schools need to establish flexible policies that accommodate students who need to

- fast or follow dietary restrictions as part of religious observances,
- observe religious rituals during the school day.
- wear clothing required by religious practice that does not pose a threat to others, and
- be absent or excused from school activities that are of a religious nature.

It also means that educators should avoid scheduling assignments and exams during or near a range of religious celebrations.

INVOLVING FAMILIES

Good collaboration and communication with students' families can strengthen the connection between school and home and help schools identify and address religious issues that affect student performance. Families can be an excellent resource for helping educators understand and address the religious and spiritual traditions that affect their children's attendance, participation in activities, diet, dress, learning, or behavior in school. Family members also can collaborate with educators to plan and implement strategies to teach students about their faith (e.g., celebrating holidays, identifying valuable resources and appropriate literature, serving as guest speakers, identifying possible guest speakers). Teachers can solicit this information from families by sending them a letter such as the one presented in Figure 58.1.

DEALING WITH INSENSITIVE AND INTOLERANT ACTS

Sometimes students will, intentionally or unintentionally, show disrespect toward another student's religious beliefs or practices. Responses to such acts of insensitivity and intolerance will vary depending upon the school's policies; the nature and setting of the act; and the history, age, and intent of the individuals involved. If the intent of the act was not to hurt others, teachers might want to deal with students privately or present the situation confidentially at a class meeting to discuss ways to avoid similar insensitive acts and to respond in a just and caring manner.

. . .

Dear Family Members:

I look forward to having your child in our class this year. I would like to address and be sensitive to your family's religious traditions. If you would like to share information about your family's religious beliefs and practices, I want you to know that I will respect you and your child's confidentiality. Please answer the following questions as they relate to your child's educational program and return it with your signature. If you have any questions, please contact me.

1. Please describe any ways in which your religious traditions affect your child's attendance, participation in activities, diet, dress, learning, or behavior in school.

2. We will be studying the religious traditions of various groups including special occasions. Please describe any religious traditions and special occasions that are important to your family, and identify possible resources (e.g., books, media, technology) our class could use in learning about your family's religious traditions and holidays.

3. We would like to represent all the religious traditions of the students in the classroom. Please indicate if you would be able to talk with the class about your family's traditions, or can provide me with the name, address and phone number of someone who could visit our class to talk about your family's traditions.

4. Please add any other comments or considerations you wish me to know.

Signature _____   Date _____

Figure 58.1 Sample letter to families

Unfortunately, educators also are likely to encounter students being intentionally intolerant of others, such as making disparaging remarks about sacred symbols, clothing, and jewelry. When this occurs, educators like Mr. George can act promptly and decisively to help their students learn that discriminatory and hurtful behaviors are unacceptable. Prompt, consistent, and firm responses to all acts of intolerance, harassment, and exclusion can minimize their negative effects and serve as a model for how students can react to them.

LEARNING MORE ABOUT FOSTERING RELIGIOUS TOLERANCE

Addressing religious diversity in schools is an aspect of educational policies and practices that is constantly changing, and new programs, strategies, litigation, and legislation regarding such issues are evolving. Educators can engage in a variety of professional development activities to learn more about fostering religious diversity.

. . .

59

Pioneers in Dialogue

Jews Building Bridges

Reena Bernards

At every family seder when I was young, along with my grandmother who made the gefilte fish and horseradish with her own hands, and my father at the head of the table in a big chair fluffed with pillows, there were always some Gentiles. I remember being surprised that a Lutheran minister could sing along in Hebrew, which he was required to learn in seminary. And I remember the five-year-old daughter of one minister who enthusiastically took a big bite out of a fresh piece of horseradish, only to turn beet red and gag when she learned what this bitter herb was all about. These were not ordinary Christians. They were ministers, priests, nuns, educators, and theologians who had dedicated themselves to understanding Jews. They came to our seder year after year because my father was one of the pioneers in Christian–Jewish dialogue.

In the 1960s *dialogue* meant Jews and Christians studying together to understand the differences and similarities of their beliefs. It meant explaining to Christians that, in the eyes of Jews, Christianity did not supersede Judaism and that the religion of the Jews remains a unique and philosophically distinct monotheistic faith. It meant exploring with Christians the religious roots of anti-Semitism, helping them reexamine their contemporary texts to remove references to Jews as killers of Jesus or doomed souls because of a lack of belief in Christ. For Jews such as my father, dialogue was a natural response to living as a minority in a Christian-dominated society. It was a way to make oneself understood, and to help create a safer environment for other Jews.

The historic course of Jewish involvement in cross-cultural dialogue changed dramatically after the Six-Day War in 1967. The day after the war began my father frantically tried to gather signatures from his Gentile friends for a newspaper ad in support of Israel, to no avail. He was particularly pained by the lack of support from Black leaders. Along with other rabbis he had marched in Selma, Alabama, during the civil rights battles and assumed that the Black-Jewish alliance was strong and in the interest of both communities.

By the late 1960s that alliance could no longer be taken for granted. The painful rift brought yet another phase of dialogue into Jewish life during the 1970s and 1980s, this time between Blacks and Jews seeking to establish an alliance based on a more in-depth understanding of each other. No longer could issues such as Israel, the Palestinians, South Africa, and, most important, the economic disparity between Jews and Blacks be avoided. Many Black-Jewish groups also moved to the personal level, as participants told and compared their stories of growing up as members of a minority community.

My own work in dialogue began well into this stage in the history of Jewish engagement in cross-cultural communication. I founded the Dialogue Project between American Jewish and Palestinian Women in 1989, after the outbreak of the Palestinian intifada. My goal was to build an understanding between mainstream women leaders from both communities. Although it now seems obvious, it wasn't until years later that I realized the connection between my work and my father's. Both come from a commitment to breaking Jews' historic isolation from other peoples. This isolation is certainly a result of anti-Semitism, and it serves to reinforce it.

My father and I came to the process of dialogue from very different directions. He was a leader in the Jewish community (as National Director of Inter-religious Cooperation for the Anti-Defamation League); I was a community organizer active in grassroots efforts to bring together low-income Whites and Blacks on issues of housing, neighborhood development, and community empowerment. I left community organizing to work for Middle East peace because it was an issue that deeply affected me personally. Before I knew it I was promoting dialogue as a means of bridging the tremendous ideological and political gaps between American Jews and Arabs, as earlier Jewish leaders in the United States had used dialogue to bridge gaps between American Jews and Christians.

THE ROLE OF DIALOGUE

This work in Arab-Jewish relations led me to consider the role of dialogue in our increasingly multiethnic society, and I began to teach the practice of cross-cultural dialogue to diverse groups of community leaders in the United States. Other communities, such as African Americans and Asian Americans, are using dialogue as a method of bridging understanding between communities that are often pitted against one another. One such group, the Afro-Asian Relations Counsel, was founded in Washington, D.C., after Korean grocery store owners came in conflict with their Black customers. They discovered that through intensive discussions they were able to separate the cultural issues from the political ones. Whereas they had previously seen the other community as committed to their downfall and in collusion with the racism they faced in the broader society, through the process of dialogue they were able to stop seeing the other as their enemy. Blacks came to understand that immigrant Koreans were able to succeed in opening businesses because they pool capital and help one another overcome economic obstacles. Koreans came to understand that their ways of showing respect to a stranger are seen as distancing and actually disrespectful in the more outwardly expressive African American community.

Such lessons are important, but they do not go far enough in their impact. In order for dialogue to affect significantly the nature of race relations in our country, it must lead to deeper alliances and actions. For example, one potential project that came out of an African-Asian dialogue suggested that Black and Korean college students do internships in the businesses in each other's community, leading to an exchange of skills and knowledge as well as a sense of joint purpose. A Black-Jewish dialogue group in Washington, D.C., decided to focus on the issue of gun control, holding weekly vigils outside the headquarters of the National Rifle Association as well as lobbying for local legislation.

The ultimate purpose of dialogue is to create new relationships that work to change society. While the process may seem slow to many activists, the underlying thrust is radical. By forging alliances among minority groups where differences have kept them apart, the dialogue process breaks down the ability of the ruling establishment to divide and conquer. If members of minority communities do not allow themselves to be polarized, stronger movements for change can emerge. The point is not to recreate the civil rights alliance as it was, but to come together with a new understanding and create new movements that are stronger and have a heightened awareness of the richness of diversity.

. . .

The purpose of dialogue is not to obliterate legitimate conflict between groups. Dialogue participants are often aware that the people to whom they are talking are their opponents in a political battle. Each side maintains its right to continue to wage the political fight at every level; participation in a dialogue is not a truce. Yet dialogue enables groups to search for new options and possibilities and to create win-win solutions that were not considered before.

NEXT STEPS

JEWISH PARTICIPATION IN DIALOGUE

In many ways dialogue comes naturally to Jews. Several years ago I attended a workshop for Jews, Christians, and Muslims in Louisiana, led by the renowned Rev. Scott Peck. The purpose was ambitious: to build community with each other. Each group responded differently to the task. The Christians spoke in soft, conciliatory tones. The Muslims were guarded as they rationally explained Islam to the group. The Jews jumped in and bared our chests. We spoke about our own personal dilemmas, argued with fellow Jews, revealed our psychological pain, and challenged the other groups on basic assumptions—all without stopping to catch our breath.

We were at home in that process: this is the water we swim in. Dialogue fits Jewish notions of how you make change in the world: you talk, you study, you discuss, you argue. The Talmud itself is the record of an internal dialogue between rabbis as they tried to figure out the controversial issues of their day. Perhaps, it is no surprise that Sigmund Freud, the father of psychotherapy, was a Jew. What could be more Jewish than having a dialogue with the different parts of yourself?

. . .

Yet I have also noticed that the comfort Jews have with dialogue can lead to some serious problems between ourselves and the other groups we wish to engage. First, we sometimes have a need to control the agenda and are often fearful of giving up this control to the will of the group. Perhaps this comes from our fear of being used, which we have in common with other oppressed groups. Our history makes us mistrustful of those who have not already shown their allegiances to us. But because we Jews are often the initiators of dialogue, we need to remember that for the effort to be successful we have to overcome our fears and allow the power and control to be shared.

Second, Jews are often more willing to talk than to take concrete political action. To many Jews sitting and talking until agreements are hammered out is a natural part of the dialogue process. We believe that our very survival depends on being understood. Our yardstick of success is often whether we think learning is taking place on both sides. In addition, while early Christian-Jewish dialogue was often motivated by Jewish concerns for our own safety, dialogue with African American or American Arab partners requires a commitment to their security needs as well. At this point in history they often feel more urgent about their political and economic situation than we do as Jews. We therefore need to note that, to others, "just talking" is often seen as useless and a dialogue is successful only if it leads to concrete political action.

Because of these different expectations and tendencies, it is important to carefully craft the dialogue experience. Every group should pay attention to the steps involved in creating a dialogue, and should build the experience according to the particular needs of their group. What follows are some suggestions.

SETTING UP A DIALOGUE

One important principle applies to all successful dialogues: *all sides must feel empowered by the process*. This means that they should feel that their needs are being considered in the development of the dialogue group. This principle needs to be followed in making decisions on such issues as sponsorship, leadership, place, participant list, development of the agenda, and funding.

There are many other issues to consider over the life of a dialogue group that relate to this sense of empowerment. Should the group be public or confidential, short-term or long-term, discussion-only or action-oriented? Answers to these questions often reveal the important differences between participating communities. Resolving them collectively could be the most important test of the success of a dialogue experience.

I like to talk of a *leadership partnership* as an important ingredient in dialogue. When I started the dialogue between American Jewish and Palestinian women, I put a great deal of energy into building a relationship with my counterpart in the Palestinian community, Najat Arafat Khelil, president of the Arab Women's Council. Najat and I have spent many hours together, building both our friendship and our work relationship. We have lived through political crises together, including the intifada and the Gulf War, working to understand each other's perspective. It hasn't always been easy, and there were times when we shouted at each other or went for days without talking. We always knew, however, that we would work through it because we have a deep commitment to each other and to the success of our group. I believe that this was the glue that held our project together. Najat and I modeled that it is possible to work through issues and to bridge the ideological, religious, and political gaps.

Due to the sensitive nature of the dialogue experience, it is important to use a consultatory leadership style in order to involve other people in the decision-making process. I recommend that early on leaders set up a steering committee with an equal number of members from the different communities. This committee can help decide all structural issues for the group, setting up the agenda for meetings and deciding on joint projects. . . .

All parties in the dialogue need to be involved in the fundraising efforts, even if the dollar amounts they are able to raise are different. Some groups make the mistake of allowing one community to raise the funds, with the understanding that the other community will take on other pieces of the work. This can lead to a power imbalance and a difference in the sense of ownership of the project. A more equitable solution is to engage each community in raising what it can in the manner that it is most accustomed. In addition, the two communities can meet together with foundation boards or donors, helping expand and share access to funding sources.

AGREEING ON GOALS AND EXPECTATIONS

There are five potential goals for a dialogue group:

1. *Building community and celebrating differences.* Members of an organization or community come together to learn about each other's culture. The sharing of music, dance, food, and life stories is used as a means of building a sense of camaraderie.
2. *Healing pain and building understanding.* Participants are given an opportunity to voice their unique feelings and perspectives on a given problem or experience. This kind of open dialogue can be used after a traumatic event occurs in a community, or as a means of hearing from diverse people within a common institution.
3. *Problem solving about areas of conflict.* A more in-depth discussion occurs to find new solutions to intercommunal conflicts. Participants move from seeing the problem as a conflict between them, to seeing it as a common dilemma, engaging in joint problem solving.
4. *Modeling a different relationship.* Community leaders make a conscious commitment to demonstrate to the broader community that a more positive type of relationship is

N
E
X
T

S
T
E
P
S

possible between members of their groups. They show by example that a relationship of mutual respect can lead to alternative ways of interacting.

5. *Action toward political change.* Dialogue participants embark on a joint political campaign, organizing their communities to change the conditions that lead to separation between groups. Groups sign a joint statement, hold press conferences, organize rallies, support candidates, and engage in other visible activities designed to build coalitions on issues where there is common ground.

The most important criterion for a successful dialogue is that the goals and expectations be clear from the beginning. It is legitimate to say that you just want to celebrate differences, and to accomplish those goals you organize a potluck dinner or a cultural event. It is also all right to build a dialogue around problem solving without going to the next stage of action, *as long as this is clear from the beginning.* But most leaders and community activists will want to be engaged in dialogue for the purpose of ultimately taking action. Be aware of differences in expectations that need to be acknowledged and managed along the way.

In addition, dialogue organizers need to be persistent and at the same time pay close attention to timing. Does your group want to attract publicity or remain confidential? Sometimes agreeing on stages of public exposure is helpful. For example, members may choose to first write or speak about a dialogue only within their own communities. As the project proceeds, the group can then decide to more fully go public. . . .

Using an experienced facilitation team will often enable a group to handle difficult conflicts more successfully. This special team can include members of each community (such as the organizers), who can understand what the participants are going through and detect any unexpressed emotions. You may also want to add a third member of the team from outside both communities who is able to provide support to both groups. In addition, the facilitation team can help the group reexamine its guidelines for dialogue. These guidelines should be periodically reviewed by the group, so that any necessary changes can be made. For example, a group may decide to add to its original guidelines that certain words not be used if they are found to be inflammatory to one of the parties. These suggestions help ensure safety even when the issues feel scary.

Another important ingredient for safety is to allow for separate caucuses. Caucusing means that there are times when the members of each community will go into separate meetings to check in with members of their own group. For example, if you as a Jewish participant have a strong reaction to what a member of the other group has said, before getting angry you can discuss your feelings with your fellow Jews, ask for their advice, and hear their perspectives. Then, if you decide to confront the issue in the dialogue, you will feel on stronger footing and will have had a chance to work out some of your own emotions first. . . .

EXPECTING CRISIS

Every dialogue group can expect to go through at least one major crisis. In fact, every dialogue meeting will have its own "mini-crisis"; that is the time when the group is experiencing some chaos as it faces unresolved issues. This is the nature of group interaction, but it is also endemic to the dialogue process. If you expect a crisis then you will not be overwhelmed when it happens, nor will you experience the crisis as a failure. Instead, the crisis becomes an opportunity for each group to go deeper and to further understand the nature of its relationship to others.

When the Dialogue Project was on its joint trip to the Middle East, our major crisis involved visiting Yad Vashem, the Holocaust memorial museum. We had agreed ahead of time that each community could show the other community its homeland in any way it chose. The Jewish women decided a visit to the museum should be on the agenda. Palestinians, however, were reluctant to go. They already knew about the Holocaust and felt that its memory had been used politically against their community despite the fact that they were not responsible for its occurrence. The tensions this caused the group were resolved only after a visit to a refugee camp in Gaza. The Palestinian women could see that the Jews were deeply affected by the visit, and they were moved by the Jewish women's recognition of their pain. They then told the Jewish women that they would go to Yad Vashem, because they understood the need to witness each community's pain together. In this case, the group came through this crisis stronger and more assured of everyone's commitment to peace.

THE LIMITS OF DIALOGUE

The process of dialogue has its critics. Jonathan Kuttab, a West Bank human rights lawyer who was one of the first Palestinians to meet with Israeli Jews after the 1967 war, speaks of the pitfalls of a "false dialogue." A false dialogue is one in which participants are more interested in getting along than in delving into the depths of the conflict. Kuttab warns that dialogue groups may abandon moral positions in the name of compromise. Because of the desire to succeed there may be a tendency to underplay political differences and to focus on more comfortable issues such as mutual stereotypes, which downplay the nature of the oppressive situation. Dialogue participants can be tempted to ignore the realities in their own societies as they attempt to build a bridge to the other side.

Kuttab claims that a key pitfall in dialogue is the assumption of a false symmetry between groups where there is actually a large power imbalance. The basic condition of oppressor and oppressed is ignored, and members of the group are subtly pressured into an acceptance of the status quo. In this sense participants in dialogue can be coopted or misused. Finally, Kuttab charges that dialogue should never be a substitute for action.

Yet Kuttab himself speaks of a dialogue in service of "peace, justice, and reconciliation." By setting up a process that empowers both sides, an honest and open exchange can occur. Potentially through the process of exploring the dynamics of conflict, each community and individual will find new sources of power to effect political change.

CONCLUSION

. . .

In a world where interethnic, interreligious, and intercommunal conflicts threaten global security, conflict resolution methods are needed more than ever. Here in the United States, as our country becomes more multicultural, building an understanding among groups is essential for our cohesion as a nation. The experience that Jews bring is a vital resource. The more we as Jews can hone our skills, improve in problem areas, and become conscious about what makes dialogue work, the more we will be able to make a valuable contribution to a multicultural society. Dialogue is the wave of the future.

N
E
X
T

S
T
E
P
S

SECTION 5

SEXISM

Introduction

Heather W. Hackman

Question: How do you manage to oppress over 50 percent of this society's population and not have a revolution on your hands? Answer: You make it seem "normal." So normal, in fact, that to question it would be akin to asking a fish about water. In the college classes I teach, students often illustrate this by denying examples of sexism and saying, "That's just the way it's always been." Even the most overt examples of sexism go unquestioned because these students have been completely immersed in the incessant narrative of sexism and know nothing else . . . "it's normal." Fortunately, however, once students do begin to see sexism in its various manifestations they want to know how on earth this is possible in a society that espouses "liberty and justice for all." This is an important question—how *did* we get to a place where economic inequality for women, violence against women, and the denial of women's basic rights over their own lives and bodies are still so commonplace and still so unquestioned?

In early 2012, as the election year continued to pick up steam, Melissa Harris-Perry of MSNBC asked a similar question: "Who would have thought in 2012 that contraception would be a matter of debate again?" (Harris-Perry, February 21, 2012). Who indeed. And yet, the use of women's legal rights, bodies, and overall role in society as a battleground for the 2012 political campaigns did just that. Were this the seventeenth century, the absolute control of women legally, economically, and physically in the name of politics and nation building would be commonplace and go unquestioned. Over the last century, however, women have steadily gained myriad rights regarding the control of their lives and bodies (e.g. *Roe v. Wade* in 1973), making the current encroachments on those rights more obviously problematic. Specifically, in the name of political expediency and the (re)assertion of male power, we are again seeing efforts to control women's legal rights (i.e. diluting national laws like the Violence Against Women Act), economic rights (popular demands that women leave the workplace so unemployed men can have their jobs), and bodies (decreasing contraception access for many women). Citing these examples and more, many observers described the tone regarding women in the 2012 election campaigns as single-mindedly regressive, and it was; not only in how it attacked women's rights, but in how it deeply wove class, race, and Christian hegemony into the efforts to do so. For example, the political lauding of the cult of (compulsory) motherhood and the assertion that to stay home and raise children is the highest and *only* calling a woman can have was not only sexist, but also deeply rooted in the class privilege of being able to afford to stay home, a racial history of white

supremacy and women's "purity," and the same religiously based heteronormative mindset that has now allowed thirty (and counting) states to mandate that marriage is only between a man and a woman. Thus, while the more things have certainly changed for the better for women in this country, the more they seek to stay the same by working to diminish women's rights and ultimately maintain sexism in this society.

Returning to my students' question then, exactly how can all this happen well over a decade into the twenty-first century; how does this system of oppression work? Most simply, oppression involves a dominant group (the group possessing societal power) exerting both ideological and structural control over a subordinate group (the group without societal power) in order to benefit the dominant group. Importantly, the dominant group does not have to be the numeric majority (as is the case with men in the United States since they make up only 48 percent of the population), but simply has to be in control of the most significant structures of power in the society. In the case of sexism, the ideological control comes through the creation and enforcement of socially constructed gender roles, while the structural control arises from the use of cultural and institutional power held by men to deny resources to and extract resources from women for the benefit of men. The symbiotic nature of these two forms of control then work together to create the dominant and subordinate statuses, assign meaning to them (through gender stereotypes and assumptions), and then use them to justify a system of gender inequality that benefits men. Over time, this system becomes omnipresent and naturalized, thus becoming self-maintaining and self-reinforced (hegemony). Comprehending how these two components operate is an essential step in being able to challenge sexism and is, therefore, the focus of this entire section.

IDEOLOGICAL CONTROL AND GENDER

Understanding how gender supports sexism requires the explanation of a few key concepts such as gender roles, gender socialization, and gender identity. Socially constructed *gender roles* are the rigid categories (and there are only two) that characterize what it means to be "feminine" and "masculine" in this society. They are clearly articulated, ruthlessly enforced, and inflexible in their expression. Men do not cry, women should always look beautiful (for men), men never ask for directions, women are "natural" caretakers, men are tough, women are emotional, men are studs, women are domestic, and so on. These roles are taught to us by a process of *gender socialization* (see Harro, selection 6) whereby the messages of what it means to be a man or woman are conveyed to us by every possible socializing structure in society—our families tell us how to behave, our schools tell us what we can achieve, and our media tells us what we need to look like. And because people who identify as women make up over half of the U.S. population, this socialization begins before birth to ensure the highest level of compliance from women, as well as men.

There are four characteristics of gender roles that ideologically support the overarching structures of sexism, heterosexism, and transgender oppression, and the intersections between them. The first is that while these gender roles are *social constructions* (something created by the dominant social identity group, i.e. men, and then repeatedly reinforced through socialization so they seem real), the story we are actually told in this society is that masculinity and femininity are *biological* instead of socially constructed, *natural* rather than cultural, *inherent* to being a man or a woman and not learned behaviors. Thus, even though there is no causal relationship between one's biology and one's gender identity, the instilling of these gender roles and rules in us from the moment we are born makes it *appear* as if there is, thereby implying that we are physiologically marked with these gender roles from birth and they cannot be changed. As a result, the sexist dynamics inherent in these socially constructed gender roles (e.g. women are

too emotional to be good leaders) are also labeled as "natural" and unchangeable, making any attempt to identify and challenge them almost impossible.

Fortunately, by shedding light on the social construction of gender, the feminist, LGB, transgender, and intersex communities have disproven the assumption that biology determines gender, thereby disentangling it from the notion that gender is "natural" (see website for further resources). For example, if gender roles were "natural," they would manifest similarly in societies all over the world, but a global analysis reveals a rather diverse understanding and expression of gender across societies (Nanda, 2000). Similarly, if these roles were set and unchangeable they would be consistent throughout history, and yet within U.S. history alone the notion of what it means to be a man or woman has changed over time due to political, economic, and social influences. As such, what is perceived as "real" regarding gender roles is actually a manifestation of certain rules and expectations put on all of us by the macro gendered power structure.

A second core characteristic of gender roles is that *they are based on heteronormativity*, which refers to the normalizing of heterosexuality and the pathologizing of being lesbian, gay, bisexual, or queer. In my classes I often conduct an exercise where we divide into groups and develop lists of what it means to "act like a 'man'" or "act like a 'lady.'" For the nineteen years I have been doing this exercise, every element of what it has meant to "act like a 'lady'" has been connected to the heterosexual male gaze. Looking pretty, acting feminine, knowing how to cook, wanting children, etc. are not at all problematic of and by themselves, but when analyzed through a lens of gender critique it is apparent that they are consistently tied to heterosexual relationships and the need for women to appeal to heterosexual men. The connection between heterosexuality and what it means to be a real woman implies that lesbians and bisexual women are not actually women, are a threat to these gender roles for their lack of compliance, and therefore should be met with contempt and even violence. Suzanne Pharr (1988) suggests that homophobia is a weapon of sexism precisely because of the relationship between gender role conformity and what Adrienne Rich (1986) termed "compulsory heterosexuality." The powerful connection between gender roles and homophobia is discussed by Blumenfeld in the next section (selection 77 and Introduction to Section 6).

A third important characteristic of gender roles is that masculine and feminine roles are *diametrically opposed*, as opposites in a binary, and *hierarchically positioned*, as superior or inferior. For every characteristic that students defined as "masculine," for example being tough and strong (superior), they defined "feminine" as the exact opposite, weak and docile (inferior). Looking even further, all human attributes labeled as feminine were found to be consistently devalued in this society and used to insult or harass men, thus speaking volumes about the true status of women in this society. As evidence, the two worst things a man can be called in this society is a "fag" (tied into the heteronormativity discussed above) and a "woman," and the worst thing a man can do is to act like a woman in any way. Of course, while most people transgress gender roles on a daily basis, the existence of these roles and the rules that shape them are well known by all as demonstrated by the fact that it never takes students more than ten minutes to generate multiple examples.

A fourth characteristic in the creation and maintenance of socially constructed gender roles is the use of violence to punish those who defy them. This violence can take innumerable forms but its purpose is single-minded: to make sure that no one deviates (too far) from their expected gender role performance. For cisgendered (see the introduction to the "Transgender Oppression" section for an explanation of this term) women, this violence can more obviously range from verbal harassment, to physical violence, to sexual assault, but it can also take slightly more subtle forms such as "ideal female beauty" (Jhally and Kilbourne, 2010), economic marginalization and poverty, and the constant pressure to "be a good girl." For cisgendered men the violence looks like bullying in our schools, ever-increasingly violent performances of masculinity in our media, and the ruthless policing of gender that men foist upon each other through verbal, emotional and physical taunts and confrontations in everyday life. While the impact of the violence is devastating

to this society socially, economically, and physically, it should be noted that the severity of the violence speaks volumes about the critical importance of the maintenance of these gender roles as the ideological foundation of sexism. Why else would there be such extreme enforcement of them? Clearly there is much at stake for the system of gender oppression in their furtherance, and thus the steady companion of these gender roles is the incessant use of violence individually, culturally, and institutionally to protect them.

Thankfully, *gender identity* can be thought of in ways that are more flexible than gender roles. *Gender identity* arises from an inner, self-reflective location and manifests as a person's more authentic gendered self as a woman, man, or transgendered person. While gender roles exist in relation to each other within a binary, gender identity exists along a continuum and has a range of expressions. The section on "Transgender Oppression" (Section 7) more thoroughly explains the concept of gender identity and its range of expressions, and is a critical companion section for fully understanding sexism in this society. Gender roles and identity are experienced by others through their "expression" or "presentation." A person's expression or presentation of a gender role is based on the dichotomous categories of what "man" and "woman" should look, act, and feel like, whereas the expression or presentation of a person's gender identity exists within a broader and more fluid expression that more accords with the complexity of gender. To present or express one's gender on the basis of accepted gender roles usually garners acceptance and approval from individuals and institutions. On the other hand, gender expression that does not conform to the dominant power structure's ideals, while being more true to the individual's felt sense of self, often results in disapproval, marginalization, and violence from the larger society.

STRUCTURAL CONTROL AND SEXISM

Understanding that socially constructed gender roles are not natural, are created as an extreme binary, and are violently enforced, let's discuss how that serves as the foundation of sexism. Simply put, all forms of oppression require a dichotomous relationship between dominant and subordinate groups because it is much easier to justify, and thus maintain, an unequal allocation of power and resources when two social identity groups (within the same axis of identity) are positioned as diametrically opposed to each other as possible (see selections 4 and 5). Therefore, these roles form the basis for the structure of oppression of women and girls, or *sexism*, in our society. In this reader's companion book, *Teaching for Diversity and Social Justice* (second edition), Botkin, Jones and Kachwaha define sexism as "a system of advantages that serves to privilege men, subordinate women, denigrate women-identified values and practices, enforce male dominance and control, and reinforce norms of masculinity that are dehumanizing and damaging to men" (2007, p. 174). Allan Johnson (selections 3 and 62) further advances our understanding of sexism by describing *patriarchy* as the system and ideology that supports the dominance of men and the oppression of women on all levels of society.

The bell hooks reading (selection 63) offers a different take on understanding sexism by explaining what *feminism* is. In the words of a favorite bumper sticker, "feminism is the radical notion that women are people." Contrary to popular backlash rhetoric, feminism is not about hating men, but it does unapologetically require an end to the domination of women by men. While feminism certainly has a range of theoretical underpinnings from liberal to Marxist to environmental, a common element among them is the need to dismantle the patriarchal power structures that serve to subordinate women and transgender folks and unfairly advantage men in every aspect of society. Because of the connections noted among sexism, heterosexism, and transgender oppression, feminism also seeks an end to gender binaries and heteronormative societal structures.

Upon the foundation of a gender binary and the exercising of patriarchal power on individual, cultural, and institutional levels, the day-to-day structural mechanisms used to keep sexism in place take many forms. For example, if gender roles state that women are to be "feminine" and look attractive to men, then the creation of limiting and dehumanizing notions of "ideal female beauty" for women is an effective tool for keeping women powerless, especially in the public domain. Caroline Heldman's article on body image (selection 65) aptly describes the societal impact of these fabricated images of beauty on women and how they conspire to disempower women economically, psychologically, and politically. The Chernik reading (selection 67) adds to this discussion by demonstrating the deadly effects of this imagery on women in the form of eating disorders and the illusory power that the cult of thinness (Nagy Hesse-Biber, 2007) creates in this society. Other mechanisms of sexism such as the wage gap discussed in Aaron Bernstein's piece (selection 66), violence against women discussed in the Katz article (selection 64), or the use of language as seen in both the Morgan and Kirk and Okazawa-Rey pieces (selections 68 and 69) should be understood as both products of sexism and tools used to maintain it in our society.

HISTORY AND INTERSECTIONALITY

Acquiring a basic understanding of the ideological and structural dynamics of sexism in society begs the question of what to do about it. In my teaching and training throughout the years, I have encountered many people who suggest that while sexism is wrong, it is just too pervasive and there is nothing we can do about it. I am sure there are a range of reasons for their thinking this, but one that warrants highlighting is the often complete lack of knowledge about the long history of women's (and some men's) organizing, resistance, and social change movements in this country. While complicated and often problematic, the history of the women's movements in the United States demonstrates powerful and effective ways to challenge both the manifestations of sexism and the foundations that give rise to it. From the first "women's rights convention" in Seneca Falls, NY, in 1848 to the presidential, congressional, and local elections of 2012, we have seen examples of women making history through their challenges to the limiting gender roles and power structures that marginalize them. At its best, this history demonstrates the need for a broad-based platform addressing women's rights, the power of consciousness-raising groups, the transformational power of claiming voice, and the necessity for cross-issue organizing. There were also a range of mistakes made along the way and in particular the first and second waves' inaccurate, simplifying assumptions concerning a single, uniform, universal woman's experience. In the first wave, while the agenda called for "women's rights," the needs of women of color, and poor and working-class women, were marginalized in favor of the eventual limited agenda of suffrage for white, middle-class women. In the second wave, these same groups as well as lesbians and bisexual women, women with disabilities, and women who were not Christian were also pushed to the side in favor of the white, middle-class agenda for "equal rights."

Due to space limitations, this section cannot discuss the many important lessons gleaned from these movements and the value of knowing this history (see section website for resources). It does, however, take these lessons seriously and highlights how we can actualize them in this current moment of fighting for women's rights—the "third wave." The Next Steps part of this section includes Ross Neely's explanation of why, as a cisgendered man, he believes all men have a personal investment in feminism and a responsibility to end sexism (selection 70). This selection, along with Jackson Katz's list of "ten things men can do to prevent gender violence" (Katz, 1999), illustrate the importance of men taking action to end sexism. It is crucial that men as well as women acknowledge that no form of oppression can be eradicated until the advantaged group can see how their core values are compromised by the existence of that oppression. These pieces are followed by Alice Walker (selection 71) where she addresses the impact of

internalized oppression. Her article calls this out in simple but powerful ways, and while it does not blame women for sexism, it does demand that women take responsibility for the internalization of negative messages and transform these debilitating ideas into sources of power.

As stated above, one of the most egregious mistakes of both waves of the women's movement was the racist lack of attention to the needs and voices of women of color. For example, while the brief statement from the National Latina Institute for Reproductive Health (selection 72) helps to counter the historic mistake of white feminists assuming that what works for white, middle-class women's health works for all women, it is but one small step in broadening the women's health agenda to truly include all women. Similarly, the Hurdis reading (selection 73) discusses the critical importance of including the voices of women of color in today's third-wave feminism, while the Russo and Spatz reading (selection 74) helps white women remember not to be seduced by the apparent political expediency of white privilege and class privilege to advance their own agenda at the expense of women of color and working-class women. Similarly, Winona LaDuke (selection 75) and Dr. Wangari Maathai (selection 76) both offer lasting insight into the overall mindset and framework necessary to end the oppression of women and create social change from the ground up all over the world.

All of the readings in this section are meant to show the real-life complexity of addressing the oppression of women and girls. More and more the discussion of what has traditionally been known as "sexism" has broadened and deepened into a complicated nexus of gender, race, class, and sexual orientation axes of identity compounded by the structurally oppressive realities of age and ability. This is not to say that the history of feminist thought is outdated or should be dismissed in any way, but to simply note that knowledge of sexism must be complicated, as it was by radical feminists of color, and then built upon even further by postmodern theory, trans theory, critical race theory, and of course social justice theory. Thus for there be an effective and sustained movement to end the sexism, there must be an understanding of how the issues in this section intersect with all other issues of oppression. To that end the reader should also explore selections from other sections in this book such as the U.S. Department of State, Romero and Morgenson selections (32, 34, and 38) located in the "Classism" section which discuss class and gender intersectionality, burdensome debt, and human (often women for sex) trafficking. In the section on racism, the Chung, Fayad, Castañeda, and Smith readings (selections 16, 18, 23, and 24) highlight the role of heteropatriarchy in the maintenance of racism, the connections between sexism and racism, and ways to cross-culturally communicate about issues of race. Similarly, in the section on ableism, the Colligan reading (selection 100) explains why the intersexed should not be "fixed" and is key to understanding that biological sex exists on a continuum and thus supports the deconstruction of the "essentialist" position regarding gender. And, of course, the readings of the "Heterosexism" and "Transgender Oppression" sections are vital in fully understanding the overlapping complexity and mutually reinforcing structures of oppression among these three forms of oppression.

SUMMARY

In conclusion, I would like to underscore that this section offers only a sampling of issues and ideas for readers to consider regarding the very complex and multifaceted issue of the oppression of women and girls in this society. As mentioned above, there is no single voice for "women's issues" and therefore I strongly encourage the use of the supplemental materials from the section website as well as the intersectional guide in the front of this book as tools to gain a more comprehensive view of sexism in the United States. On the website you will find additional book and article references, specific articles themselves (e.g. the oft-used "The 'Rape' of Mr. Smith"),

links to websites and to current sources of discussion and action, and activities that can be used in the classroom or training settings.

In moving forward with this information, I would like to emphasize the importance of taking action, however subtle it may be, to end the oppression of women and girls. In an era where for the first time a woman has made a viable run for the White House, increasing numbers of women are in professional positions of power, and women are more represented in college admissions than men, it is tempting to say that sexism is over and do nothing. Scratching beneath the surface of these changes, however, it is obvious that sexism and patriarchy are both still firmly intact. Therefore, *now* is the time for broad-based and consistent action on the part of all us to end sexism and transform our society into one where women and girls feel safe and free and able to exercise their humanity to its fullest.

See Companion Website for Additional Resources and Material

References

Botkin, S., Jones, J., Kachwaha, T. (2007). Sexism curriculum design. In M. Adams, L. A. Bell, P. Griffin (eds), *Teaching for Diversity and Social Justice* (2nd edition, pp. 173–194). New York: Routledge.

Harris-Perry, M. (February 21, 2012). *The Melissa Harris-Perry Show* [Television Broadcast]. New York, NY: MSNBC.

Jhally, S. (Director) and Kilbourne, J. (Co-Producer). (2010). *Killing Us Softly 4* [Film]. Northampton, MA: Media Education Foundation.

Katz, Jackson. (1999). Ten Things Men Can Do to Prevent Gender Violence. Retrieved from http://www.jacksonkatz.com/topten.html.

Nagy Hesse-Biber, S. (2007). *The Cult of Thinness*. New York: Oxford University Press.

Nanda, S. (2000). *Gender Diversity: Crosscultural Variations*. Long Grove, IL: Waveland Press.

Pharr, S. (1988). *Homophobia as a Weapon of Sexism*. Little Rock, AR: Chardon Press.

Rich, A. (1986). *Blood, Bread and Poetry: Selected Prose, 1979–1985*. New York: Norton.

60

"Night to His Day"

The Social Construction of Gender

Judith Lorber

Talking about gender for most people is the equivalent of fish talking about water. Gender is so much the routine ground of everyday activities that questioning its taken-for-granted assumptions and presuppositions is like thinking about whether the sun will come up. Gender is so pervasive that in our society we assume it is bred into our genes. Most people find it hard to believe that gender is constantly created and re-created out of human interaction, out of social life, and is the texture and order of that social life. Yet gender, like culture, is a human production that depends on everyone constantly "doing gender."

And everyone "does gender" without thinking about it. Today, on the subway, I saw a well-dressed man with a year-old child in a stroller. Yesterday, on a bus, I saw a man with

a tiny baby in a carrier on his chest. Seeing men taking care of small children in public is increasingly common—at least in New York City. But both men were quite obviously stared at—and smiled at, approvingly. Everyone was doing gender—the men who were changing the role of fathers and the other passengers, who were applauding them silently. But there was more gendering going on that probably fewer people noticed. The baby was wearing a white crocheted cap and white clothes. You couldn't tell if it was a boy or a girl. The child in the stroller was wearing a dark blue T-shirt and dark print pants. As they started to leave the train, the father put a Yankee baseball cap on the child's head. Ah, a boy, I thought. Then I noticed the gleam of tiny earrings in the child's ears, and as they got off, I saw the little flowered sneakers and lace-trimmed socks. Not a boy after all. Gender done.

Gender is such a familiar part of daily life that it usually takes a deliberate disruption of our expectations of how women and men are supposed to act to pay attention to how it is produced. Gender signs and signals are so ubiquitous that we usually fail to note them—unless they are missing or ambiguous. Then we are uncomfortable until we have success-fully placed the other person in a gender status; otherwise, we feel socially dislocated. . . .

For the individual, gender construction starts with assignment to a sex category on the basis of what the genitalia look like at birth. Then babies are dressed or adorned in a way that displays the category because parents don't want to be constantly asked whether their baby is a girl or a boy. A sex category becomes a gender status through naming, dress, and the use of other gender markers. Once a child's gender is evident, others treat those in one gender differently from those in the other, and the children respond to the different treatment by feeling different and behaving differently. As soon as they can talk, they start to refer to themselves as members of their gender. Sex doesn't come into play again until puberty, but by that time, sexual feelings and desires and practices have been shaped by gendered norms and expectations. Adolescent boys and girls approach and avoid each other in an elaborately scripted and gendered mating dance. Parenting is gendered, with different expectations for mothers and for fathers, and people of different genders work at different kinds of jobs. The work adults do as mothers and fathers and as low-level workers and high-level bosses, shapes women's and men's life experiences, and these experiences produce different feelings, consciousness, relationships, skills—ways of being that we call feminine or masculine. All of these processes constitute the social construction of gender.

Gendered roles change—today fathers are taking care of little children, girls and boys are wearing unisex clothing and getting the same education, women and men are working at the same jobs. Although many traditional social groups are quite strict about maintaining gender differences, in other social groups they seem to be blurring. Then why the one-year-old's earrings? Why is it still so important to mark a child as a girl or a boy, to make sure she is not taken for a boy or he for a girl? What would happen if they were? They would, quite literally, have changed places in their social world.

To explain why gendering is done from birth, constantly and by everyone, we have to look not only at the way individuals experience gender but at gender as a social institu-tion. As a social institution, gender is one of the major ways that human beings organize their lives. Human society depends on a predictable division of labor, a designated alloca-tion of scarce goods, assigned responsibility for children and others who cannot care for themselves, common values and their systematic transmission to new members, legitimate leadership, music, art, stories, games, and other symbolic productions. One way of choos-ing people for the different tasks of society is on the basis of their talents, motivations, and competence—their demonstrated achievements. The other way is on the basis of gender, race, ethnicity—ascribed membership in a category of people. . . .

Western society's values legitimate gendering by claiming that it all comes from physiol-ogy—female and male procreative differences. But gender and sex are not equivalent, and gender as a social construction does not flow automatically from genitalia and reproductive

organs, the main physiological differences of females and males. In the construction of ascribed social statuses, physiological differences such as sex, stage of development, color of skin, and size are crude markers. They are not the source of the social statuses of gender, age grade, and race. Social statuses are carefully constructed through prescribed processes of teaching, learning, emulation, and enforcement. Whatever genes, hormones, and biological evolution contribute to human social institutions is materially as well as qualitatively transformed by social practices. . . . Thus, . . . gender cannot be equated with biological and physiological differences between human females and males. The building blocks of gender are *socially constructed statuses.* . . .

FOR INDIVIDUALS, GENDER MEANS SAMENESS

Although the possible combinations of genitalia, body shapes, clothing, mannerisms, sexuality, and roles could produce infinite varieties in human beings, the social institution of gender depends on the production and maintenance of a limited number of gender statuses and of making the members of these statuses similar to each other. Individuals are born sexed but not gendered, and they have to be taught to be masculine or feminine. As Simone de Beauvoir said: "One is not born, but rather becomes, a woman . . . ; it is civilization as a whole that produces this creature . . . which is described as feminine."

. . .

Many cultures go beyond clothing, gestures, and demeanor in gendering children. They inscribe gender directly into bodies. . . . In Western societies, women augment their breast size with silicone and reconstruct their faces with cosmetic surgery to conform to cultural ideals of feminine beauty. Hanna Papanek notes that these practices reinforce the sense of superiority or inferiority in the adults who carry them out as well as in the children on whom they are done. . . .

Sandra Bem argues that because gender is a powerful "schema" that orders the cognitive world, one must wage a constant, active battle for a child not to fall into typical gendered attitudes and behavior. In 1972, *Ms. Magazine* published Lois Gould's fantasy of how to raise a child free of gender-typing. The experiment calls for hiding the child's anatomy from all eyes except the parents' and treating the child as neither a girl nor a boy. The child, called X, gets to do all the things boys *and* girls do. The experiment is so successful that all the children in X's class at school want to look and behave like X. At the end of the story, the creators of the experiment are asked what will happen when X grows up. The scientists' answer is that by then it will be quite clear what X is, implying that its hormones will kick in and it will be revealed as a female or male. That ambiguous, and somewhat contradictory, ending lets Gould off the hook; neither she nor we have any idea what someone brought up totally androgynously would be like sexually or socially as an adult. The hormonal input will not create gender or sexuality but will only establish secondary sex characteristics; breasts, beards, and menstruation alone do not produce social manhood or womanhood. Indeed, it is at puberty, when sex characteristics become evident, that most societies put pubescent children through their most important rites of passage, the rituals that officially mark them as fully gendered—that is, ready to marry and become adults.

Most parents create a gendered world for their newborn by naming, birth announcements, and dress. Children's relationships with same-gendered and different-gendered caretakers structure their self-identifications and personalities. Through cognitive development, children extract and apply to their own actions the appropriate behavior for those who belong in their own gender, as well as race, religion, ethnic group, and social class,

rejecting what is not appropriate. If their social categories are highly valued, they value themselves highly; if their social categories are low status, they lose self-esteem. Many feminist parents who want to raise androgynous children soon lose their children to the pull of gendered norms. My son attended a carefully nonsexist elementary school, which didn't even have girls' and boys' bathrooms. When he was seven or eight years old, I attended a class play about "squares" and "circles" and their need for each other and noticed that all the girl squares and circles wore makeup, but none of the boy squares and circles did. I asked the teacher about it after the play, and she said, "Bobby said he was not going to wear makeup, and he is a powerful child, so none of the boys would either." In a long discussion about conformity, my son confronted me with the question of who the conformists were, the boys who followed their leader or the girls who listened to the woman teacher. In actuality, they both were, because they both followed same-gender leaders and acted in gender-appropriate ways. (Actors may wear makeup, but real boys don't.)

For human beings there is no essential femaleness or maleness, femininity or masculinity, womanhood or manhood, but once gender is ascribed, the social order constructs and holds individuals to strongly gendered norms and expectations. Individuals may vary on many of the components of gender and may shift genders temporarily or permanently, but they must fit into the limited number of gender statuses their society recognizes. In the process, they re-create their society's version of women and men: "If we do gender appropriately, we simultaneously sustain, reproduce, and render legitimate the institutional arrangements. . . . If we fail to do gender appropriately, we as individuals—not the institutional arrangements—may be called to account (for our character, motives, and predispositions)" (West and Zimmerman 1987).

The gendered practices of everyday life reproduce a society's view of how women and men should act. Gendered social arrangements are justified by religion and cultural productions and backed by law, but the most powerful means of sustaining the moral hegemony of the dominant gender ideology is that the process is made invisible; any possible alternatives are virtually unthinkable.

FOR SOCIETY, GENDER MEANS DIFFERENCE

The pervasiveness of gender as a way of structuring social life demands that gender statuses be clearly differentiated. Varied talents, sexual preferences, identities, personalities, interests, and ways of interacting fragment the individual's bodily and social experiences. Nonetheless, these are organized in Western cultures into two and only two socially and legally recognized gender statuses, "man" and "woman." In the social construction of gender, it does not matter what men and women actually do; it does not even matter if they do exactly the same thing. The social institution of gender insists only that what they do is *perceived* as different.

If men and women are doing the same tasks, they are usually spatially segregated to maintain gender separation, and often the tasks are given different job titles as well, such as executive secretary and administrative assistant. If the differences between women and men begin to blur, society's "sameness taboo" goes into action. At a rock and roll dance at West Point in 1976, the year women were admitted to the prestigious military academy for the first time, the school's administrators "were reportedly perturbed by the sight of mirror-image couples dancing in short hair and dress gray trousers," and a rule was established that women cadets could dance at these events only if they wore skirts. Women recruits in the U.S. Marine Corps are required to wear makeup—at a minimum, lipstick and eye shadow—and they have to take classes in makeup, hair care, poise, and etiquette.

This feminization is part of a deliberate policy of making them clearly distinguishable from men Marines. Christine Williams quotes a twenty-five-year-old woman drill instructor as saying: "A lot of the recruits who come here don't wear makeup; they're tomboyish or athletic. A lot of them have the preconceived idea that going into the military means they can still be a tomboy. They don't realize that you are a *Woman* Marine" (1989).

If gender differences were genetic, physiological, or hormonal, gender bending and gender ambiguity would occur only in . . . [those] who are born with chromosomes and genitalia that are not clearly female or male. Since gender differences are socially constructed, all men and all women can enact the behavior of the other, because they know the other's social script: "'Man' and 'woman' are at once empty and overflowing categories. Empty because they have no ultimate, transcendental meaning. Overflowing because even when they appear to be fixed, they still contain within them alternative, denied, or suppressed definitions" (J.W. Scott 1988). Nonetheless, though individuals may be able to shift gender statuses, the gender boundaries have to hold, or the whole gendered social order will come crashing down.

. . .

GENDER AS PROCESS, STRATIFICATION, AND STRUCTURE

As a social institution, gender is a process of creating distinguishable social statuses for the assignment of rights and responsibilities. As part of a stratification system that ranks these statuses unequally, gender is a major building block in the social structures built on these unequal statuses.

As a *process*, gender creates the social differences that define "woman" and "man." In social interaction throughout their lives, individuals learn what is expected, see what is expected, act and react in expected ways, and thus simultaneously construct and maintain the gender order: "The very injunction to be a given gender takes place through discursive routes: to be a good mother, to be a heterosexually desirable object, to be a fit worker, in sum, to signify a multiplicity of guarantees in response to a variety of different demands all at once" (J. Butler 1990). Members of a social group neither make up gender as they go along nor exactly replicate in rote fashion what was done before. In almost every encounter, human beings produce gender, behaving in the ways they learned were appropriate for their gender status, or resisting or rebelling against these norms. Resistance and rebellion have altered gender norms, but so far they have rarely eroded the statuses.

Gendered patterns of interaction acquire additional layers of gendered sexuality, parenting, and work behaviors in childhood, adolescence, and adulthood. Gendered norms and expectations are enforced through informal sanctions of gender-inappropriate behavior by peers and by formal punishment or threat of punishment by those in authority should behavior deviate too far from socially imposed standards for women and men.

Everyday gendered interactions build gender into the family, the work process, and other organizations and institutions, which in turn reinforce gender expectations for individuals. Because gender is a process, there is room not only for modification and variation by individuals and small groups but also for institutionalized change.

As part of a *stratification* system, gender ranks men above women of the same race and class. Women and men could be different but equal. In practice, the process of creating difference depends to a great extent on differential evaluation. As Nancy Jay (1981) says: "That which is defined, separated out, isolated from all else is A and pure. Not-A is necessarily impure, a random catchall, to which nothing is external except A and the principle of order that separates it from Not-A." From the individual's point of view, whichever gender

is A, the other is Not-A; gender boundaries tell the individual who is like him or her and all the rest are unlike. From society's point of view, however, one gender is usually the touchstone, the normal, the dominant, and the other is different, deviant, and subordinate. In Western society, "man" is A, "wo-man" is Not-A. (Consider what a society would be like where woman was A and man Not-A.) . . . The dominant categories are the hegemonic ideals, taken so for granted as the way things should be that, . . . [t]he characteristics of these categories define the Other as that which lacks the valuable qualities the dominants exhibit.

. . .

Societies vary in the extent of the inequality in social status of their women and men members, but where there is inequality, the status "woman" (and its attendant behavior and role allocations) is usually held in lesser esteem than the status "man." Since gender is also intertwined with a society's other constructed statuses of differential evaluation—race, religion, occupation, class, country of origin, and so on—men and women members of the favored groups command more power, more prestige, and more property than the members of the disfavored groups. Within many social groups, however, men are advantaged over women. The more economic resources, such as education and job opportunities, are available to a group, the more they tend to be monopolized by men. In poorer groups that have few resources (such as working-class African Americans in the United States), women and men are more nearly equal, and the women may even outstrip the men in education and occupational status.

As a *structure*, gender divides work in the home and in economic production, legitimates those in authority, and organizes sexuality and emotional life. As primary parents, women significantly influence children's psychological development and emotional attachments, in the process reproducing gender. Emergent sexuality is shaped by heterosexual, homosexual, bisexual, and sadomasochistic patterns that are gendered—different for girls and boys, and for women and men—so that sexual statuses reflect gender statuses.

When gender is a major component of structured inequality, the devalued genders have less power, prestige, and economic rewards than the valued genders. In countries that discourage gender discrimination, many major roles are still gendered; women still do most of the domestic labor and child rearing, even while doing full-time paid work; women and men are segregated on the job and each does work considered "appropriate"; women's work is usually paid less than men's work. Men dominate the positions of authority and leadership in government, the military, and the law; cultural productions, religions, and sports reflect men's interests. . . .

Gender inequality—the devaluation of "women" and the social domination of "men"—has social functions and a social history. It is not the result of sex, procreation, physiology, anatomy, hormones, or genetic predispositions. It is produced and maintained by identifiable social processes and built into the general social structure and individual identities deliberately and purposefully. The social order as we know it in Western societies is organized around racial, ethnic, class, and gender inequality. I contend, therefore, that the continuing purpose of gender as a modern social institution is to construct women as a group to be the subordinates of men as a group. The life of everyone placed in the status "woman" is "night to his day—that has forever been the fantasy. Black to his white. Shut out of his system's space, she is the repressed that ensures the system's functioning."

. . .

There is no core or bedrock human nature below these endlessly looping processes of the social production of sex and gender, self and other, identity and psyche, each of which is a "complex cultural construction." *For humans, the social is the natural.* Therefore, "in its feminist senses, gender cannot mean simply the cultural appropriation of biological sexual difference. Sexual difference is itself a fundamental—and scientifically

contested—construction. Both 'sex' and 'gender' are woven of multiple, asymmetrical strands of difference, charged with multifaceted dramatic narratives of domination and struggle" (Haraway 1990).

61

Masculinity as Homophobia

Fear, Shame, and Silence in the Construction of Gender Identity

Michael S. Kimmel

We think of manhood as eternal, a timeless essence that resides deep in the heart of every man. We think of manhood as a thing, a quality that one either has or doesn't have. We think of manhood as innate, residing in the particular biological composition of the human male, the result of androgens or the possession of a penis. We think of manhood as a transcendent tangible property that each man must manifest in the world, the reward presented with great ceremony to a young novice by his elders for having successfully completed an arduous initiation ritual. . . .

I view masculinity as a constantly changing collection of meanings that we construct through our relationships with ourselves, with each other, and with our world. Manhood is neither static nor timeless; it is historical. Manhood is not the manifestation of an inner essence; it is socially constructed. Manhood does not bubble up to consciousness from our biological makeup; it is created in culture. Manhood means different things at different times to different people. We come to know what it means to be a man in our culture by setting our definitions in opposition to a set of "others"— racial minorities, sexual minorities, and, above all, women.

. . .

This idea that manhood is socially constructed and historically shifting should not be understood as a loss, that something is being taken away from men. In fact, it gives us something extraordinarily valuable—agency, the capacity to act. It gives us a sense of historical possibilities to replace the despondent resignation that invariably attends timeless, ahistorical essentialisms. Our behaviors are not simply "just human nature," because "boys will be boys." From the materials we find around us in our culture—other people, ideas, objects—we actively create our worlds, our identities. Men, both individually and collectively, can change.

MASCULINITY AS A HOMOSOCIAL ENACTMENT

Other men: We are under the constant careful scrutiny of other men. Other men watch us, rank us, grant our acceptance into the realm of manhood. Manhood is demonstrated for other men's approval. It is other men who evaluate the performance. Literary critic

David Leverenz argues that "ideologies of manhood have functioned primarily in relation to the gaze of male peers and male authority." Think of how men boast to one another of their accomplishments—from their latest sexual conquest to the size of the fish they caught—and how we constantly parade the markers of manhood—wealth, power, status, sexy women—in front of other men, desperate for their approval.

That men prove their manhood in the eyes of other men is both a consequence of sexism and one of its chief props. "Women have, in men's minds, such a low place on the social ladder of this country that it's useless to define yourself in terms of a woman," noted playwright David Mamet. "What men need is men's approval." Women become a kind of currency that men use to improve their ranking on the masculine social scale. (Even those moments of heroic conquest of women carry, I believe, a current of homosocial evaluation.) Masculinity is a *homosocial* enactment. We test ourselves, perform heroic feats, take enormous risks, all because we want other men to grant us our manhood.

Masculinity as a homosocial enactment is fraught with danger, with the risk of failure, and with intense relentless competition. "Every man you meet has a rating or an estimate of himself which he never loses or forgets," wrote Kenneth Wayne in his popular turn-of-the-century advice book. "A man has his own rating, and instantly he lays it alongside of the other man." Almost a century later, another man remarked to psychologist Sam Osherson that "[b]y the time you're an adult, it's easy to think you're always in competition with men, for the attention of women, in sports, at work."

MASCULINITY AS HOMOPHOBIA

. . .

Homophobia is a central organizing principle of our cultural definition of manhood. Homophobia is more than the irrational fear of gay men, more than the fear that we might be perceived as gay. "The word 'faggot' has nothing to do with homosexual experience or even with fears of homosexuals," writes David Leverenz. "It comes out of the depths of manhood: a label of ultimate contempt for anyone who seems sissy, untough, uncool." Homophobia is the fear that other men will unmask us, emasculate us, reveal to us and the world that we do not measure up, that we are not real men. We are afraid to let other men see that fear. Fear makes us ashamed, because the recognition of fear in ourselves is proof to ourselves that we are not as manly as we pretend, that we are, like the young man in a poem by Yeats, "one that ruffles in a manly pose for all his timid heart." Our fear is the fear of humiliation. We are ashamed to be afraid.

Shame leads to silence—the silences that keep other people believing that we actually approve of the things that are done to women, to minorities, to gays and lesbians in our culture. The frightened silence as we scurry past a woman being hassled by men on the street. That furtive silence when men make sexist or racist jokes in a bar. That clammy-handed silence when guys in the office make gay-bashing jokes. Our fears are the sources of our silences, and men's silence is what keeps the system running. This might help to explain why women often complain that their male friends or partners are often so understanding when they are alone and yet laugh at sexist jokes or even make those jokes themselves when they are out with a group.

The fear of being seen as a sissy dominates the cultural definitions of manhood. It starts so early. "Boys among boys are ashamed to be unmanly," wrote one educator in 1871. I have a standing bet with a friend that I can walk onto any playground in America where 6-year-old boys are happily playing and by asking one question, I can provoke a fight. That question is simple: "Who's a sissy around here?" Once posed, the challenge is made. One

of two things is likely to happen. One boy will accuse another of being a sissy, to which that boy will respond that he is not a sissy, that the first boy is. They may have to fight it out to see who's lying. Or a whole group of boys will surround one boy and all shout "He is! He is!" That boy will either burst into tears and run home crying, disgraced, or he will have to take on several boys at once, to prove that he's not a sissy. (And what will his father or older brothers tell him if he chooses to run home crying?) It will be some time before he regains any sense of self-respect.

Violence is often the single most evident marker of manhood. Rather it is the willingness to fight, the desire to fight. The origin of our expression that one has a chip on one's shoulder lies in the practice of an adolescent boy in the country or small town at the turn of the century, who would literally walk around with a chip of wood balanced on his shoulder—a signal of his readiness to fight with anyone who would take the initiative of knocking the chip off.

As adolescents, we learn that our peers are a kind of gender police, constantly threatening to unmask us as feminine, as sissies. One of the favorite tricks when I was an adolescent was to ask a boy to look at his fingernails. If he held his palm toward his face and curled his fingers back to see them, he passed the test. He'd looked at his nails "like a man." But if he held the back of his hand away from his face, and looked at his fingernails with arm outstretched, he was immediately ridiculed as a sissy.

As young men we are constantly riding those gender boundaries, checking the fences we have constructed on the perimeter, making sure that nothing even remotely feminine might show through. The possibilities of being unmasked are everywhere. Even the most seemingly insignificant thing can pose a threat or activate that haunting terror. On the day the students in my course "Sociology of Men and Masculinities" were scheduled to discuss homophobia and male-male friendships, one student provided a touching illustration. Noting that it was a beautiful day, the first day of spring after a brutal northeast winter, he decided to wear shorts to class. "I had this really nice pair of new Madras shorts," he commented. "But then I thought to myself, these shorts have lavender and pink in them. Today's class topic is homophobia. Maybe today is not the best day to wear these shorts."

Our efforts to maintain a manly front cover everything we do. What we wear. How we talk. How we walk. What we eat. Every mannerism, every movement contains a coded gender language. Think, for example, of how you would answer the question: How do you "know" if a man is homosexual? When I ask this question in classes or workshops, respondents invariably provide a pretty standard list of stereotypically effeminate behaviors. He walks a certain way, talks a certain way, acts a certain way. He's very emotional; he shows his feelings. One woman commented that she "knows" a man is gay if he really cares about her; another said she knows he's gay if he shows no interest in her, if he leaves her alone.

Now alter the question and imagine what heterosexual men do to make sure no one could possibly get the "wrong idea" about them. Responses typically refer to the original stereotypes, this time as a set of negative rules about behavior. Never dress that way. Never talk or walk that way. Never show your feelings or get emotional. Always be prepared to demonstrate sexual interest in women that you meet, so it is impossible for any woman to get the wrong idea about you. In this sense, homophobia, the fear of being perceived as gay, as not a real man, keeps men exaggerating all the traditional rules of masculinity, including sexual predation with women. Homophobia and sexism go hand in hand.

The stakes of perceived sissydom are enormous—sometimes matters of life and death. We take enormous risks to prove our manhood, exposing ourselves disproportionately to health risks, workplace hazards, and stress-related illnesses. Men commit suicide three times as often as women. . . .

In one survey, women and men were asked what they were most afraid of. Women responded that they were most afraid of being raped and murdered. Men responded that they were most afraid of being laughed at.

HOMOPHOBIA AS A CAUSE OF SEXISM, HETEROSEXISM, AND RACISM

Homophobia is intimately interwoven with both sexism and racism. The fear—sometimes conscious, sometimes not—that others might perceive us as homosexual propels men to enact all manner of exaggerated masculine behaviors and attitudes to make sure that no one could possibly get the wrong idea about us. One of the centerpieces of that exaggerated masculinity is putting women down, both by excluding them from the public sphere and by the quotidian put-downs in speech and behaviors that organize the daily life of the American man. Women and gay men become the "other" against which heterosexual men project their identities, against whom they stack the decks so as to compete in a situation in which they will always win, so that by suppressing them, men can stake a claim for their own manhood. Women threaten emasculation by representing the home, workplace, and familial responsibility, the negation of fun. Gay men have historically played the role of the consummate sissy in the American popular mind because homosexuality is seen as an inversion of normal gender development. There have been other "others." Through American history, various groups have represented the sissy, the non-men against whom American men played out their definitions of manhood, often with vicious results. In fact, these changing groups provide an interesting lesson in American historical development.

At the turn of the 19th century, it was Europeans and children who provided the contrast for American men. The "true American was vigorous, manly, and direct, not effete and corrupt like the supposed Europeans," writes Rupert Wilkinson. . . . By the middle of the century, black slaves had replaced the effete nobleman. Slaves were seen as dependent, helpless men, incapable of defending their women and children, and therefore less than manly. Native Americans were cast as foolish and naive children, so they could be infantilized as the "Red Children of the Great White Father" and therefore excluded from full manhood.

By the end of the century, new European immigrants were also added to the list of the unreal men, especially the Irish and Italians, who were seen as too passionate and emotionally volatile to remain controlled sturdy oaks, and Jews, who were seen as too bookishly effete and too physically puny to truly measure up. In the mid-20th century, it was also Asians—first the Japanese during the Second World War, and more recently, the Vietnamese during the Vietnam War—who have served as unmanly templates against which American men have hurled their gendered rage. Asian men were seen as small, soft, and effeminate—hardly men at all.

Such a list of "hyphenated" Americans . . . composes the majority of American men. So manhood is only possible for a distinct minority, and the definition has been constructed to prevent the others from achieving it. Interestingly, this emasculation of one's enemies has a flip side—and one that is equally gendered. These very groups that have historically been cast as less than manly were also, often simultaneously, cast as hypermasculine, as sexually aggressive, violent rapacious beasts, against whom "civilized" men must take a decisive stand and thereby rescue civilization. . . . But whether one saw these groups as effeminate sissies or as brutal uncivilized savages, the terms with which they were perceived were gendered. These groups become the "others," the screens against which traditional conceptions of manhood were developed.

Being seen as unmanly is a fear that propels American men to deny manhood to others, as a way of proving the unprovable—that one is fully manly. Masculinity becomes a defense

against the perceived threat of humiliation in the eyes of other men, enacted through a "sequence of postures"—things we might say, or do, or even think, that, if we thought carefully about them, would make us ashamed of ourselves. After all, how many of us have made homophobic or sexist remarks, or told racist jokes, or made lewd comments to women on the street? How many of us have translated those ideas and those words into actions, by physically attacking gay men, or forcing or cajoling a woman to have sex even though she didn't really want to because it was important to score?

POWER AND POWERLESSNESS IN THE LIVES OF MEN

I have argued that homophobia, men's fear of other men, is the animating condition of the dominant definition of masculinity in America, that the reigning definition of masculinity is a defensive effort to prevent being emasculated. In our efforts to suppress or overcome those fears, the dominant culture exacts a tremendous price from those deemed less than fully manly: women, gay men, nonnative-born men, men of color. This perspective may help clarify a paradox in men's lives, a paradox in which men have virtually all the power and yet do not feel powerful.

Manhood is equated with power—over women, over other men. Everywhere we look, we see the institutional expression of that power—in state and national legislatures, on the boards of directors of every major U.S. corporation or law firm, and in every school and hospital administration. Women have long understood this, and feminist women have spent the past three decades challenging both the public and the private expressions of men's power and acknowledging their fear of men. Feminism as a set of theories both explains women's fear of men and empowers women to confront it both publicly and privately. Feminist women have theorized that masculinity is about the drive for domination, the drive for power, for conquest.

This feminist definition of masculinity as the drive for power is theorized from women's point of view. It is how women experience masculinity. But it assumes a symmetry between the public and the private that does not conform to men's experiences. Feminists observe that women, as a group, do not hold power in our society. They also observe that individually, they, as women, do not feel powerful. They feel afraid, vulnerable. Their observation of the social reality and their individual experiences are therefore symmetrical. Feminism also observes that men, as a group, *are* in power. Thus, with the same symmetry, feminism has tended to assume that individually men must feel powerful.

This is why the feminist critique of masculinity often falls on deaf ears with men. When confronted with the analysis that men have all the power, many men react incredulously. "What do you mean, men have all the power?" they ask. "What are you talking about? My wife bosses me around. My kids boss me around. My boss bosses me around. I have no power at all! I'm completely powerless!"

Men's feelings are not the feelings of the powerful, but of those who see themselves as powerless. These are the feelings that come inevitably from the discontinuity between the social and the psychological, between the aggregate analysis that reveals how men are in power as a group and the psychological fact that they do not feel powerful as individuals. They are the feelings of men who were raised to believe themselves entitled to feel that power, but do not feel it. No wonder many men are frustrated and angry.

. . .

The dimension of power is now reinserted into men's experience not only as the product of individual experience but also as the product of relations with other men. In this sense, men's experience of powerlessness is *real*—the men actually feel it and certainly act

on it—but it is not *true*, that is, it does not accurately describe their condition. In contrast to women's lives, men's lives are structured around relationships of power and men's differential access to power, as well as the differential access to that power of men as a group. Our imperfect analysis of our own situation leads us to believe that we men need *more* power, rather than leading us to support feminists' efforts to rearrange power relationships along more equitable lines.

. . .

Why, then, do American men feel so powerless? Part of the answer is because we've constructed the rules of manhood so that only the tiniest fraction of men come to believe that they are the biggest of wheels, the sturdiest of oaks, the most virulent repudiators of femininity, the most daring and aggressive. We've managed to disempower the overwhelming majority of American men by other means—such as discriminating on the basis of race, class, ethnicity, age, or sexual preference.

. . .

Others still rehearse the politics of exclusion, as if by clearing away the playing field of secure gender identity of any that we deem less than manly—women, gay men, nonnative-born men, men of color—middle-class, straight, white men can reground their sense of themselves without those haunting fears and that deep shame that they are unmanly and will be exposed by other men. This is the manhood of racism, of sexism, of homophobia. It is the manhood that is so chronically insecure that it trembles at the idea of lifting the ban on gays in the military, that is so threatened by women in the workplace that women become the targets of sexual harassment, that is so deeply frightened of equality that it must ensure that the playing field of male competition remains stacked against all newcomers to the game.

Exclusion and escape have been the dominant methods American men have used to keep their fears of humiliation at bay. The fear of emasculation by other men, of being humiliated, of being seen as a sissy, is the leitmotif in my reading of the history of American manhood. Masculinity has become a relentless test by which we prove to other men, to women, and ultimately to ourselves, that we have successfully mastered the part. The restlessness that men feel today is nothing new in American history; we have been anxious and restless for almost two centuries. Neither exclusion nor escape has ever brought us the relief we've sought, and there is no reason to think that either will solve our problems now. Peace of mind, relief from gender struggle, will come only from a politics of inclusion, not exclusion, from standing up for equality and justice, and not by running away.

62

Patriarchy, the System

An It, Not a He, a Them, Or an Us

Allan G. Johnson

"When you say patriarchy," a man complained from the rear of the audience, "I know what you *really* mean—me!" A lot of people hear "men" whenever someone says "patriarchy," so that criticism of gender oppression is taken to mean that all men—each and every one

of them—are oppressive people. Not surprisingly, many men take it personally if someone merely mentions patriarchy or the oppression of women, bristling at what they often see as a way to make them feel guilty. And some women feel free to blame individual men for patriarchy simply because they're men. Some of the time, men feel defensive because they identify with patriarchy and its values and don't want to face the consequences these produce or the prospect of giving up male privilege. But defensiveness more often reflects a common confusion about the difference between patriarchy as a kind of society and the people who participate in it. If we're ever going to work toward real change, it's a confusion we'll have to clear up.

To do this, we have to realize that we're stuck in a model of social life that views everything as beginning and ending with individuals. Looking at things in this way, we tend to think that if evil exists in the world, it's only because there are evil people who have entered into an evil conspiracy. Racism exists, for example, simply because white people are racist bigots who hate members of racial and ethnic minorities and want to do them harm. There is gender oppression because men want and like to dominate women and act out hostility toward them. There is poverty and class oppression because people in the upper classes are greedy, heartless, and cruel. The flip side of this individualistic model of guilt and blame is that race, gender, and class oppression are actually not oppression at all, but merely the sum of individual failings on the part of blacks, women, and the poor, who lack the right stuff to compete successfully with whites, men, and others who know how to make something of themselves.

What this kind of thinking ignores is that we are all participating in something larger than ourselves or any collection of us. On some level, most people are familiar with the idea that social life involves us in something larger than ourselves, but few seem to know what to do with that idea. . . . How, for example, do we participate in patriarchy, and how does that link us to the consequences it produces? How is what we think of as "normal" life related to male dominance, women's oppression, and the hierarchical, control-obsessed world in which they, and our lives, are embedded?

Without asking such questions we can't understand gender fully and we avoid taking responsibility either for ourselves or for patriarchy. Instead, "the system" serves as a vague, unarticulated catch-all, a dumping ground for social problems, a scapegoat that can never be held to account and that, for all the power we think it has, can't talk back or actually *do* anything. . . .

If we see patriarchy as nothing more than men's and women's individual personalities, motivations, and behavior, for example, then it probably won't even occur to us to ask about larger contexts—such as institutions like the family, religion, and the economy—and how people's lives are shaped in relation to them. From this kind of individualistic perspective, we might ask why a particular man raped, harassed, or beat a woman. We wouldn't ask, however, what kind of society would promote persistent *patterns* of such behavior in everyday life, from wife-beating jokes to the routine inclusion of sexual coercion and violence in mainstream movies. . . .

If the goal is to change the world, this won't help us. We need to see and deal with the social roots that generate and nurture the social problems that are reflected in the behavior of individuals. We can't do this without realizing that we all participate in something larger than ourselves, something we didn't create but that we have the power to affect through the choices we make about *how* to participate.

That something larger is patriarchy, which is more than a collection of individuals (such as "men"). It is a system, which means it can't be reduced to the people who participate in it. . . .

[P]atriarchy [is] a kind of society that is more than a collection of women and men and can't be understood simply by understanding them. *We are not patriarchy*, no more than

people who believe in Allah *are* Islam or Canadians *are* Canada. Patriarchy is a kind of society organized around certain kinds of social relationships and ideas. As individuals, we participate in it. Paradoxically, our participation both shapes our lives and gives us the opportunity to be part of changing or perpetuating it. But *we are not it*, which means that patriarchy can exist without men having "oppressive personalities" or actively conspiring with one another to defend male privilege. To demonstrate that gender oppression exists, we don't have to show that men are villains, that women are good-hearted victims, that women don't participate in their own oppression, or that men never oppose it. If a society is oppressive, then people who grow up and live in it will tend to accept, identify with, and participate in it as "normal" and unremarkable life. That's the path of least resistance in any system. It's hard not to follow it, given how we depend on society and its rewards and punishments that hinge on going along with the status quo. When oppression is woven into the fabric of everyday life, we don't need to go out of our way to be overly oppressive in order for an oppressive system to produce oppressive consequences. As the saying goes, what evil requires is simply that ordinary people do nothing.

. . .

The crucial thing to understand about patriarchy or any other kind of social system is that it's something people participate in. It's an arrangement of shared understandings and relationships that connect people to one another and something larger than themselves. . . .

PATRIARCHY

The key to understanding any system is to identify its various parts and how they're arranged to form a whole. . . . Patriarchy's defining elements are its male-dominated, male-identified, and male-centered character, but this is just the beginning. At its core, patriarchy is a set of symbols and ideas that make up a culture embodied by everything from the content of everyday conversation to literature and film. Patriarchal culture includes ideas about the nature of things, including men, women, and humanity, with manhood and masculinity most closely associated with being human and womanhood and femininity relegated to the marginal position of "other." It's about how social life is and how it's supposed to be; about what's expected of people and about how they feel. It's about standards of feminine beauty and masculine toughness, images of feminine vulnerability and masculine protectiveness, of older men coupled with young women, of elderly women alone. It's about defining women and men as opposites, about the "naturalness" of male aggression, competition, and dominance and of female caring, cooperation, and subordination. It's about the valuing of masculinity and maleness and the devaluing of femininity and femaleness. It's about the primary importance of a husband's career and the secondary status of a wife's, about child care as a priority in women's lives and its secondary importance in men's. It's about the social acceptability of anger, rage, and toughness in men but not in women, and of caring, tenderness, and vulnerability in women but not in men.

Above all, patriarchal culture is about the core value of control and domination in almost every area of human existence. From the expression of emotion to economics to the natural environment, gaining and exercising control is a continuing goal of great importance. Because of this, the concept of power takes on a narrow definition in terms of "power over"—the ability to control others, events, resources, or oneself in spite of resistance—rather than alternatives such as the ability to cooperate with others, to give freely of oneself, or to feel and act in harmony with nature. To have power over and to be prepared to use it are defined culturally as good and desirable (and characteristically

"masculine"), and to lack such power or to be reluctant to use it is seen as weak if not contemptible (and characteristically "feminine").

. . .

Going deeper into patriarchal culture, we find a complex web of ideas that define reality and what's considered good and desirable. To see the world through patriarchal eyes is to believe that women and men are profoundly different in their basic natures, that hierarchy is the only alternative to chaos, and that men were made in the image of a masculine God with whom they enjoy a special relationship. It is to take as obvious the idea that there are two and only two distinct genders; that patriarchal heterosexuality is "natural" and same-sex attraction is not; that because men neither bear nor breast-feed children, they cannot feel a compelling bodily connection to them; that on some level every woman, whether heterosexual or lesbian, wants a "real man" who knows how to "take charge of things," including her; that females can't be trusted, especially when they're menstruating or accusing men of sexual misconduct. To embrace patriarchy is to believe that mothers should stay home and that fathers should work out of the home, regardless of men's and women's actual abilities or needs. It is to buy into the notion that women are weak and men are strong, that women and children need men to support and protect them, all in spite of the fact that in many ways men are not the physically stronger sex, that women perform a huge share of hard physical labor in many societies (often larger than men's), that women's physical endurance tends to be greater than men's over the long haul, that women tend to be more capable of enduring pain and emotional stress. And yet such evidence means little in the face of a patriarchal culture that dictates how things *ought* to be . . . .

To live in a patriarchal culture is to learn what's expected of us as men and women, the rules that regulate punishment and reward based on how we behave and appear. These rules range from laws that require men to fight in wars not of their own choosing to customary expectations that mothers will provide child care, or that when a woman shows sexual interest in a man or merely smiles or acts friendly, she gives up her right to say no and control her own body. And to live under patriarchy is to take into ourselves shared ways of feeling—the hostile contempt for femaleness that forms the core of misogyny and presumptions of male superiority, the ridicule men direct at other men who show signs of vulnerability or weakness, or the fear and insecurity that every woman must deal with when she exercises the right to move freely in the world, especially at night and by herself. Such ideas make up the symbolic sea we swim in and the air we breathe. They are the primary well from which springs how we think about ourselves, other people, and the world. As such, they provide a taken-for-granted everyday reality, the setting for our interactions with other people that continually fashion and refashion a shared sense of what the world is about and who we are in relation to it. This doesn't mean that the ideas underlying patriarchy determine what we think, feel, and do, but it does mean they define what we'll have to *deal with* as we participate in it.

The prominent place of misogyny in patriarchal culture, for example, doesn't mean that every man and woman consciously hates all things female. But it does mean that to the extent that we don't feel such hatred, it's *in spite of* paths of least resistance contained in our culture. Complete freedom from such feelings and judgments is all but impossible. It is certainly possible for heterosexual men to love women without mentally fragmenting them into breasts, buttocks, genitals, and other variously desirable parts. It is possible for women to feel good about their bodies, to not judge themselves as being too fat, to not abuse themselves to one degree or another in pursuit of impossible male-identified standards of beauty and sexual attractiveness. All of this is possible; but to live in patriarchy is to breathe in misogynist images of women as objectified sexual property valued primarily for their usefulness to men. This finds its way into everyone who grows up breathing and swimming in it, and once inside us it remains, however unaware of it we may be. So, when

we hear or express sexist jokes and other forms of misogyny we may not recognize it, and even if we do, say nothing rather than risk other people thinking we're "too sensitive" or, especially in the case of men, "not one of the guys." In either case, we are involved, if only by our silence.

The symbols and ideas that make up patriarchal culture are important to understand because they have such powerful effects on the structure of social life. By "structure," I mean the ways that gender privilege and oppression are organized through social relationships and unequal distributions of rewards, opportunities, and resources. This appears in countless patterns of everyday life in family and work, religion and politics, community and education. It is found in family divisions of labor that exempt fathers from most domestic work even when both parents work outside the home, and in the concentration of women in lower-level pink-collar jobs and male predominance almost everywhere else. It is in the unequal distribution of income and all that goes with it, from access to health care to the availability of leisure time. It is in patterns of male violence and harassment that can turn a simple walk in the park or a typical day at work or a lovers' quarrel into a life-threatening nightmare. More than anything, the structure of patriarchy is found in the unequal distribution of power that makes oppression possible, in patterns of male dominance in every facet of human life, from everyday conversation to global politics. By its nature, patriarchy puts issues of power, dominance, and control at the center of human existence, not only in relationships between men and women, but among men as they compete and struggle to gain status, maintain control, and protect themselves from what other men might do to them.

. . .

THE SYSTEM IN US IN THE SYSTEM

One of the most difficult things to accept about patriarchy is that we're involved in it, which means we're also involved in its consequences. This is especially hard for men who refuse to believe they benefit from women's oppression, because they can't see how this could happen without their being personally oppressive in their intentions, feelings, and behavior. For many men, being told they're *involved* in oppression can only mean they *are* oppressive.

A common defense against this is to attribute everything to "society" as something external and autonomous, with wants, needs, interests, and the power to control people by making them into one sort of person or another. . . .

Societies don't exist without people participating in them, which means that we can't understand patriarchy unless we also ask how people are connected to it and how this connection varies, depending on social characteristics such as race, gender, ethnicity, age, and class. . . .

From this perspective, *who* we and other people think we are has a lot to do with *where* we are in relation to social systems and all the positions that people occupy. We wouldn't exist as social beings if it weren't for our participation in one social system or another. It's hard to imagine just who we'd be and what our existence would consist of if we took away all of our connections to the symbols, ideas, and relationships that make up social systems. . . .

In this sense, like all social systems, patriarchy exists only through people's lives. Through this, patriarchy's various aspects are there for us to see over and over again. This has two important implications for how we understand patriarchy. First, to some extent people experience patriarchy as external to them; but this doesn't mean that it's

a distinct and separate thing, like a house in which we live. Instead, by participating in patriarchy we are *of* patriarchy and it is *of* us. Both exist *through* the other and neither can exist without the other. Second, patriarchy isn't static; it's an ongoing *process* that's continuously shaped and reshaped. Since the thing we're participating in is patriarchal, we tend to behave in ways that create a patriarchal world from one moment to the next. But we have some freedom to break the rules and construct everyday life in different ways, which means that the paths we choose to follow can do as much to change patriarchy as they can to perpetuate it.

We're involved in patriarchy and its consequences because we occupy social positions in it, which is all it takes. Since gender oppression is, by definition, a system of inequality organized around gender categories, we can no more avoid being involved in it than we can avoid being female or male. *All* men and *all* women are therefore involved in this oppressive system, and none us can control *whether* we participate, only *how*. . . .

Because privilege is conferred by social systems, people don't have to feel privileged in order to *be* privileged. When I do public presentations, for example, I usually come away feeling pretty good about what happened and, therefore, about myself. If anyone were to ask me to explain why things went so well, I'd probably mention my abilities, my years of experience in public speaking, the quality of my ideas, and so on, as well as the interest and contributions of the audience. The last thing that would occur to me, however, would be that my success was aided by my gender, that if I'd performed in exactly the same way but happened to be a woman, research shows quite clearly that I'd have been taken less seriously, been evaluated less positively, and attributed less of my success to my own efforts and ability. The difference between the two outcomes is a measure of my gender privilege, and there is little I can do to get rid of it, because its authority doesn't rest in me but in society itself, especially in cultural images of gender. The audience doesn't know it's conferring gender privilege on me, and I may not be aware that I'm receiving it. But the privilege is there, nonetheless, whether we intend or want it. That all this may feel "natural" and nonprivileged only deepens the system's hold on all who are involved in it.

Since we're born into patriarchy, and since participating in social life is what makes us who we are, we can't escape growing up sexist to some degree. This means that the question we have to ask ourselves isn't whether sexism is part of who we are, but how broadly and deeply it is ingrained in us, how it appears in our experience and behavior, and what we can do about it. No one wants to think of themselves as involved in social oppression, but being involved doesn't mean we're bad or to blame for oppression, for people can and do participate in systems that produce horrible, immoral consequences without being horrible and immoral people. None of us is responsible or to blame for the world we were born into or the inevitable way in which we took it into ourselves. But—and this "but" is crucial—the ongoing reconstruction of that society is shaped by how people like us choose to participate in it once we're here. We are involved; we are part of the problem; the question is whether we'll choose to also be part of the solution.

63

Feminism

A Movement to End Sexist Oppression

bell hooks

A central problem within feminist discourse has been our inability to either arrive at a consensus of opinion about what feminism is or accept definition(s) that could serve as points of unification. Without agreed upon definition(s), we lack a sound foundation on which to construct theory or engage in overall meaningful praxis. Expressing her frustrations with the absence of clear definitions in a recent essay, "Towards A Revolutionary Ethics," Carmen Vasquez comments:

> We can't even agree on what a "Feminist" is, never mind what she would believe in and how she defines the principles that constitute honor among us. In key with the American capitalist obsession for individualism and anything goes so long as it gets you what you want. Feminism in American has come to mean anything you like, honey. There are as many definitions of Feminism as there are feminists, some of my sisters say, with a chuckle. I don't think it's funny.

It is not funny. It indicates a growing disinterest in feminism as a radical political movement. It is a despairing gesture expressive of the belief that solidarity between women is not possible. It is a sign that the political naïveté which has traditionally characterized woman's lot in male-dominated culture abounds.

Most people in the United States think of feminism or the more commonly used term "women's lib" as a movement that aims to make women the social equals of men. This broad definition, popularized by the media and mainstream segments of the movement, raises problematic questions. Since men are not equals in white supremacist, capitalist, patriarchal class structure, which men do women want to be equal to? Do women share a common vision of what equality means? Implicit in this simplistic definition of women's liberation is a dismissal of race and class as factors that, in conjunction with sexism, determine the extent to which an individual will be discriminated against, exploited, or oppressed. Bourgeois white women interested in women's rights issues have been satisfied with simple definitions for obvious reasons. Rhetorically placing themselves in the same social category as oppressed women, they were not anxious to call attention to race and class privilege.

Women in lower class and poor groups, particularly those who are non-white, would not have defined women's liberation as women gaining social equality with men since they are continually reminded in their everyday lives that all women do not share a common social status. Concurrently, they know that many males in their social groups are exploited and oppressed. Knowing that men in their groups do not have social, political, and economic power, they would not deem it liberatory to share their social status. While they are aware that sexism enables men in their respective groups to have privileges denied them, they are more likely to see exaggerated expressions of male chauvinism among their peers as stemming from the male's sense of himself as powerless and ineffectual in relation to ruling male groups, rather than an expression of an overall privileged social status.

From the very onset of the women's liberation movement, these women were suspicious of feminism precisely because they recognized the limitations inherent in its definition. They recognized the possibility that feminism defined as social equality with men might easily become a movement that would primarily affect the social standing of white women in middle and upper class groups while affecting only in a very marginal way the social status of working class and poor women.

. . .

In a recent article in a San Francisco newspaper, "Sisters—Under the Skin," columnist Bob Greene commented on the aversion many women apparently have to the term feminism. Greene finds it curious that many women "who obviously believe in everything that proud feminists believe in dismiss the term "feminist" as something unpleasant; something with which they do not wish to be associated." Even though such women often acknowledge that they have benefited from feminist-generated reform measures which have improved the social status of specific groups of women, they do not wish to be seen as participants in feminist movement:

> There is no getting around it. After all this time, the term "feminist" makes many bright, ambitious, intelligent women embarrassed and uncomfortable. They simply don't want to be associated with it.
>
> It's as if it has an unpleasant connotation that they want no connection with. Chances are if you were to present them with every mainstream feminist belief, they would go along with the beliefs to the letter—and even if they consider themselves feminists, they hasten to say no.

Many women are reluctant to advocate feminism because they are uncertain about the meaning of the term. Other women from exploited and oppressed ethnic groups dismiss the term because they do not wish to be perceived as supporting a racist movement; feminism is often equated with white women's rights effort. Large numbers of women see feminism as synonymous with lesbianism; their homophobia leads them to reject association with any group identified as pro-lesbian. Some women fear the word "feminism" because they shun identification with any political movement, especially one perceived as radical. Of course there are women who do not wish to be associated with women's rights movement in any form so they reject and oppose feminist movement. Most women are more familiar with negative perspectives on "women's lib" than the positive significations of feminism. It is this term's positive political significance and power that we must now struggle to recover and maintain.

Currently feminism seems to be a term without any clear significance. The "anything goes" approach to the definition of the word has rendered it practically meaningless. What is meant by "anything goes" is usually that any woman who wants social equality with men regardless of her political perspective (she can be a conservative right-winger or a nationalist communist) can label herself feminist. Most attempts at defining feminism reflect the class nature of the movement. Definitions are usually liberal in origin and focus on the individual woman's right to freedom and self-determination. . . .

This definition of feminism is almost apolitical in tone; yet it is the type of definition many liberal women find appealing. It evokes a very romantic notion of personal freedom which is more acceptable than a definition that emphasizes radical political action.

. . . Feminism is a struggle to end sexist oppression. Therefore, it is necessarily a struggle to eradicate the ideology of domination that permeates Western culture on various levels as well as a commitment to reorganizing society so that the self-development of people can take precedence over imperialism, economic expansion, and material desires. Defined in this way, it is unlikely that women would join feminist movement simply because we

are biologically the same. A commitment to feminism so defined would demand that each individual participant acquire a critical political consciousness based on ideas and beliefs.

. . .

Feminism defined in political terms that stress collective as well as individual experience challenges women to enter a new domain—to leave behind the apolitical stance sexism decrees is our lot and develop political consciousness. . . . By repudiating the popular notion that the focus of feminist movement should be social equality of the sexes and emphasizing eradicating the cultural basis of group oppression, our own analysis would require an exploration of all aspects of women's political reality. This would mean that race and class oppression would be recognized as feminist issues with as much relevance as sexism.

When feminism is defined in such a way that it calls attention to the diversity of women's social and political reality, it centralizes the experiences of all women, especially the women whose social conditions have been least written about, studied, or changed by political movements. When we cease to focus on the simplistic stance "men are the enemy," we are compelled to examine systems of domination and our role in their maintenance and perpetuation. . . .

Feminism is the struggle to end sexist oppression. Its aim is not to benefit solely any specific group of women, any particular race or class of women. It does not privilege women over men. It has the power to transform in a meaningful way all our lives. . . .

Feminism as a movement to end sexist oppression directs our attention to systems of domination and the inter-relatedness of sex, race, and class oppression. Therefore, it compels us to centralize the experiences and the social predicaments of women who bear the brunt of sexist oppression as a way to understand the collective social status of women in the United States. Defining feminism as a movement to end sexist oppression is crucial for the development of theory because it is a starting point indicating the direction of exploration and analysis.

The foundation of future feminist struggle must be solidly based on a recognition of the need to eradicate the underlying cultural basis and causes of sexism and other forms of group oppression. Without challenging and changing these philosophical structures, no feminist reforms will have a long range impact. Consequently, it is now necessary for advocates of feminism to collectively acknowledge that our struggle cannot be defined as a movement to gain social equality with men; that terms like "liberal feminist" and "bourgeois feminist" represent contradictions that must be resolved so that feminism will not be continually co-opted to serve the opportunistic ends of special interest groups.

64

Violence against Women Is a Men's Issue

Jackson Katz

Most people think violence against women is a women's issue. And why wouldn't they? Just about every woman in this society thinks about it every day. If they are not getting harassed on the street, living in an abusive relationship, recovering from a rape, or in

therapy to deal with the sexual abuse they suffered as children, they are ordering their daily lives around the *threat* of men's violence.

But it is a mistake to call *men's* violence a *women's* issue. Take the subject of rape. Many people reflexively consider rape to be a women's issue. But let's take a closer look. What percentage of rape is committed by women? Is it 10 percent, 5 percent? No. *Less than 1 percent of rape is committed by women.* Let's state this another way: over 99 percent of rape is perpetrated by men. Whether the victims are female or male, men are overwhelmingly the perpetrators. But we call it a women's issue? Shouldn't that tell us something?

A major premise of . . . [my work] is that the long-running American tragedy of sexual and domestic violence—including rape, battering, sexual harassment, and the sexual exploitation of women and girls—is arguably more revealing about *men* than it is about women. Men, after all, are the ones committing the vast majority of the violence. Men are the ones doing most of the battering and almost all of the raping. Men are the ones paying the prostitutes (and killing them in video games), going to strip clubs, renting sexually degrading pornography, writing and performing misogynistic music.

When men's role in gender violence is discussed—in newspaper articles, sensational TV news coverage, or everyday conversation—the focus is typically on men as perpetrators or potential perpetrators. These days, you don't have to look far to see evidence of the pain and suffering these men cause. But it is rare to find any in-depth discussion about the culture that's producing these violent men. It's almost like the perpetrators are strange aliens who landed here from another planet. It is rarer still to hear thoughtful discussions about the ways that our culture defines "manhood," and how that definition might be linked to the endless string of stories about husbands killing wives, or groups of young men raping girls (and sometimes videotaping the rape) that we hear about on a regular basis.

Why isn't there more conversation about the underlying social factors that contribute to the pandemic of violence against women? Why aren't men's attitudes and behaviors toward women the focus of more critical scrutiny and coordinated action? These days, the 24/7 news cycle brings us a steady stream of gender-violence tragedies: serial killers on the loose, men abducting young girls, domestic-violence homicides, periodic sexual abuse scandals in powerful institutions like the Catholic Church and the Air Force Academy. You can barely turn on the news these days without coming across another gruesome sex crime—whether it's a group of boys gang-raping a girl in a middle school bathroom or a young pregnant woman who turns up missing, and whose husband emerges a few days later as the primary suspect.

Isn't it about time we had a national conversation about the male causes of this violence, instead of endlessly lingering on its consequences in the lives of women? Thanks to the battered women's and rape crisis movements in the U.S., it is no longer taboo to discuss women's experiences of sexual and domestic violence. This is a significant achievement. To an unprecedented extent, American women today expect to be supported—not condemned—when they disclose what men have done to them (unless the man is popular, wealthy, or well-connected, in which case all bets are off.)

This is all for the good. Victims of violence and abuse—whether they're women or men—should be heard and respected. Their needs come first. But let's not mistake concern for victims with the political will to change the conditions that led to their victimization in the first place. . . . It is one thing to focus on the "against women" part of the phrase; but someone's responsible for doing it, and (almost) everyone knows that it's overwhelmingly men. Why aren't people talking about this? Is it realistic to talk about preventing violence against women if no one even wants to say out loud who's responsible for it?

For the past two decades, I've been part of a growing movement of men, in North America and around the world, whose aim is to reduce violence against women by focusing on those aspects of male culture—especially male-peer culture—that provide active or tacit

support for some men's abusive behavior. This movement is racially and ethnically diverse, and it brings together men from both privileged and poor communities, and everyone in between. This is challenging work on many levels, and no one should expect rapid results. For example, there is no way to gloss over some of the race, class, and sexual orientation divisions between and among us men. It is also true that it takes time to change social norms that are so deeply rooted in structures of gender and power. Even so, there is room for optimism. We've had our successes: there are arguably more men today who are actively confronting violence against women than at any time in human history.

Make no mistake. Women blazed the trail that we are riding down. Men are in the position to do this work precisely because of the great leadership of women. The battered women's and rape crisis movements and their allies in local, state, and federal government have accomplished a phenomenal amount over the past generation. Public awareness about violence against women is at an all-time high. The level of services available today for female victims and survivors of men's violence is—while not yet adequate—nonetheless historically unprecedented.

. . .

[I propose] that we adopt a much more ambitious approach. If we are going to bring down dramatically the rates of violence against women—not just at the margins—we will need a far-reaching cultural revolution. At its heart, this revolution must be about changing the sexist social norms in male culture, from the elementary school playground to the common room in retirement communities—and every locker room, pool hall, and boardroom in between. For us to have any hope of achieving historic reductions in incidents of violence against women, at a minimum we will need to dream big and act boldly. It almost goes without saying that we will need the help of a lot more men—at all levels of power and influence—than are currently involved. Obviously we have our work cut out for us. As a measure of just how far we have to go, consider that in spite of the misogyny and sexist brutality all around us, millions of non-violent men today fail to see gender violence as their issue. "I'm a good guy," they will say. "This isn't my problem."

For years, women of every conceivable ethnic, racial, and religious background have been trying to get men around them—and men in power—to do more about violence against women. . . . On both a micro and a macro level, women in this era have successfully broken through the historical silence about violence against women and found their voice—here in the U.S. and around the world.

Yet even with all of these achievements, women continue to face an uphill struggle in trying to make meaningful inroads into male culture. Their goal has not been simply to get men to listen to women's stories and truly hear them—although that is a critical first step. The truly vexing challenge has been getting men to actually go out and *do* something about the problem, in the form of educating and organizing *other men* in numbers great enough to prompt a real cultural shift. Some activist women—even those who have had great faith in men as allies—have been beating their heads against the wall for a long time, and are frankly burned out on the effort. I know this because I have been working with many of these women for a long time. They are my colleagues and friends.

My work is dedicated to getting more men to take on the issue of violence against women, and thus to build on what women have achieved. The area that I focus on is not law enforcement or offender treatment, but the *prevention* of sexual and domestic violence and all their related social pathologies—including violence against children. To do this, I and other men here and around the world have been trying to get our fellow men to see that this problem is not just personal for a small number of men who happen to have been touched by the issue. We try to show them that it is personal for them, too. *For all of us.* We talk about men not only as perpetrators but as victims. We try to show them that

violence by men against each other—from simple assaults to gay-bashing—*is* linked to the same structures of gender and power that produce so much men's violence against women.

We also make it clear that these issues are not just personal, to be dealt with as private family matters. They are political as well, with repercussions that reverberate throughout our lives and communities in all sorts of meaningful and disturbing ways. For example, according to a 2003 report by the U.S. Conference of Mayors, domestic violence was a primary cause of homelessness in almost half of the twenty-five cities surveyed. And worldwide, sexual coercion and other abusive behavior by men plays an important role in the transmission of HIV/AIDS.

Nonetheless, convincing other men to make gender violence issues a priority is not an easy sell . . . [and, t]here is no point in being naïve about why women have had such a difficult time convincing men to make violence against women a men's issue. In spite of significant social change in recent decades, men continue to grow up with, and are socialized into, a deeply misogynistic, male-dominated culture, where violence against women—from the subtle to the homicidal—is disturbingly common. It's *normal*. And precisely because the mistreatment of women is such a pervasive characteristic of our patriarchal culture, most men, to a greater or lesser extent, have played a role in its perpetuation. This gives us a strong incentive to avert our eyes.

Women, of course, have also been socialized into this misogynistic culture. Some of them resist and fight back. In fact, women's ongoing resistance to their subordinate status is one of the most momentous developments in human civilization over the past two centuries. Just the same, plenty of women show little appetite for delving deeply into the cultural roots of sexist violence. It's much less daunting simply to blame "sick" individuals for the problem. You hear women explaining away men's bad behavior as the result of individual pathology all the time: "Oh, he just had a bad childhood," or "He's an angry drunk. The booze gets to him. He's never been able to handle it."

But regardless of how difficult it can be to show some women that violence against women is a social problem that runs deeper than the abusive behavior of individual men, it is still much easier to convince women that dramatic change is in their best interest than it is to convince men. In fact, many people would argue that, since men are the dominant sex and violence serves to reinforce this dominance, it is not in men's best interests to reduce violence against women, and that the very attempt to enlist a critical mass of men in this effort amounts to a fool's errand.

For those of us who reject this line of reasoning, the big question then is how do we reach men? We know we're not going to transform, overnight or over many decades, certain structures of male power and privilege that have developed over thousands of years. Nevertheless, how are we going to bring more men—many more men—into a conversation about sexism and violence against women? And how are we going to do this without turning them off, without berating them, without blaming them for centuries of sexist oppression? Moreover, how are we going to move beyond talk and get substantial numbers of men to partner *with* women in reducing men's violence, instead of working *against* them in some sort of fruitless and counterproductive gender struggle?

. . .

I understand the skepticism of women who for years have been frustrated by men's complacency about something as basic as a woman's right to live free from the threat of violence. But I am convinced that men who are active in gender-violence prevention today speak for a much larger number of men. I would not go so far as to say that a silent majority of men supports everything that gender-violence prevention activists stand for, but an awful lot of men privately cheer us on. I have long felt this way, but now there is a growing body of research—in social norms theory—that confirms it empirically.

Social norms theory begins with the premise that people often misperceive the extent to which their peers hold certain attitudes or participate in certain behaviors. In the absence of accurate knowledge, they are more likely to be influenced by what they *think* people think and do, rather than what they *actually* think and do. . . .

There have been a number of studies in the past several years that demonstrate that significant numbers of men are uncomfortable with the way some of their male peers talk about and treat women. But since few men in our society have dared to talk publicly about such matters, many men think they are the only ones who feel uncomfortable. Because they feel isolated and alone in their discomfort, they do not say anything. Their silence, in turn, simply reinforces the false perception that few men are uncomfortable with sexist attitudes and behaviors. It is a vicious cycle that keeps a lot of caring men silent.

I meet men all the time who thank me—or my fellow activists and colleagues—for publicly taking on the subject of men's violence. I frequently meet men who are receptive to the paradigm-shifting idea that men's violence against women has to be understood as a men's issue, as their issue. These men come from every demographic and geographic category. They include thousands of men who would not fit neatly into simplistic stereotypes about the kind of man who would be involved in "that touchy-feely stuff."

Still, it is an uphill fight. Truly lasting change is only going to happen as new generations of women come of age and demand equal treatment with men in every realm, and new generations of men work with them to reject the sexist attitudes and behaviors of their predecessors. This will take decades, and the outcome is hardly predetermined. But along with tens of thousands of activist women and men who continue to fight the good fight, I believe that it is possible to achieve something much closer to gender equality, and a dramatic reduction in the level of men's violence against women, both here and around the world. And there is a lot at stake. If sexism and violence against women do not subside considerably in the twenty-first century, it will not just be bad news for women. It will also say something truly ugly and tragic about the future of our species.

. . .

65

Out-of-Body Image

Caroline Heldman

On a typical day, you might see ads featuring a naked woman's body tempting viewers to buy an electronic organizer, partially exposed women's breasts being used to sell fishing line, or a woman's rear—wearing only a thong—being used to pitch a new running shoe. Meanwhile, on every newsstand, impossibly slim (and digitally airbrushed) cover "girls" adorn a slew of magazines. With each image, you're hit with a simple, subliminal message: Girls' and women's bodies are objects for others to visually consume.

If such images seem more ubiquitous than ever, it's because U.S. residents are now exposed to anywhere from 3,000 to 5,000 advertisements a day—up from 500 to 2,000 a day in the 1970s. The Internet accounts for much of this growth, and young people are particularly exposed to advertising: 70 percent of 15- to 34-year-olds use social networking technologies such as MySpace and Facebook, which allow advertisers to infiltrate previously private communication space.

Although mass media has always objectified women, it has become increasingly provocative. More and more, female bodies are shown as outright objects (think Rose McGowan's machine-gun leg in the recent horror movie *Grindhouse*), are literally broken into parts (the disembodied woman's torso in advertisements for TV's *The Sarah Connor Chronicles*) or are linked with sexualized violence (simulated crime scenes on *America's Next Top Model* featuring seemingly dead women).

A steady diet of exploitative, sexually provocative depictions of women feeds a poisonous trend in women's and girls' perceptions of their bodies, one that has recently been recognized by social scientists as self-objectification—viewing one's body as a sex object to be consumed by the male gaze. Like W. E. B. DuBois' famous description of the experience of black Americans, self-objectification is a state of "double consciousness . . . a sense of always looking at one's self through the eyes of others."

Women who self-objectify are desperate for outside validation of their appearance and present their bodies in ways that draw attention. A study I did of 71 randomly selected female students from a liberal arts college in Los Angeles, for example, found that 70 percent were medium or high self-objectifiers, meaning that they have internalized the male gaze and chronically monitor their physical appearance. Boys and men experience self-objectification as well, but at a much lower rate—probably because, unlike women, they rarely get the message that their bodies are the primary determination of their worth.

Researchers have learned a lot about self-objectification since the term was coined in 1997 by University of Michigan psychology professor Barbara Fredrickson and Colorado College psychology professor Tomi-Ann Roberts. Numerous studies since then have shown that girls and women who self-objectify are more prone to depression and low self-esteem and have less faith in their own capabilities; which can lead to diminished success in life. They are more likely to engage in "habitual body monitoring"—constantly thinking about how their bodies appear to the outside world—which puts them at higher risk for eating disorders such as anorexia and bulimia. And they are prone to embarrassment about bodily functions such as menstruation, as well as general feelings of disgust and shame about their bodies.

Self-objectification has also been repeatedly shown to sap cognitive functioning, because of all the attention devoted to body monitoring. For instance, a 1998 study asked two groups of women to take a math exam—one group in swimsuits, the other in sweaters. The swimsuit-wearers, distracted by body concerns, performed significantly worse than their peers in sweaters.

Several of my own surveys of college students indicate that this impaired concentration by self-objectifiers may hurt their academic performance. Those with low self-objectification reported an average GPA of 3.5, whereas those with high self-objectification reported a 3.1. While this gap may appear small, in graduate-school admissions it represents the difference between being competitive and being out of the running for the top schools.

Another worrisome effect of self-objectification is that it diminishes political efficacy—a person's belief that she can have an impact through the political process. In another survey of mine, 33 percent of high self-objectifiers felt low political efficacy, compared to 13 percent of low self-objectifiers. Since political efficacy leads to participation in politics, having less of it means that self-objectifiers may be less likely to vote or run for office.

The effects of self-objectification on young girls are of such growing concern that the American Psychological Association published an investigative report on it last year. The APA found that girls as young as 7 years old are exposed to clothing, toys, music, magazines and television programs that encourage them to be sexy or "hot"—teaching them to think of themselves as sex objects before their own sexual maturity. Even thong underwear is being sold in sizes for 7- to 10-year-olds. The consequence, wrote Kenyon College psychology professor Sarah Murnen in the journal *Sex Roles*, is that girls "are taught to view their

bodies as 'projects' that need work before they can attract others, whereas boys are likely to learn to view their bodies as tools to use to master the environment."

Fredrickson, along with Michigan communications professor Kristen Harrison (both work within the university's Institute for Research on Women and Gender), recently discovered that self-objectification actually impairs girls' motor skills. Their study of 202 girls, ages 10 to 17, found that self-objectification impeded girls' ability to throw a softball, even after differences in age and prior experience were factored out. Self-objectification forced girls to split their attention between how their bodies looked and what they wanted them to do, resulting in less forceful throws and worse aim.

One of the more stunning effects of self-objectification is its impact on sex. Nudity can cause great anxiety among self-objectifiers, who then become preoccupied with how their bodies look in sexual positions. One young woman I interviewed described sex as being an "out of body" experience during which she viewed herself through the eyes of her lover, and, sometimes, through the imaginary lens of a camera shooting a porn film. As a constant critic of her body, she couldn't focus on her own sexual pleasure.

Self-objectification can likely explain some other things that researchers are just starting to study. For instance, leading anti-sexist male activist and author Jackson Katz observes, "Many young women now engage in sex acts with men that prioritize the man's pleasure, with little or no expectation of reciprocity." Could this be another result of women seeing themselves as sexual objects, not agents?

Disturbingly, some girls and women celebrate their object status as a form of empowerment. This is evident in a booming industry of T-shirts for women that proclaim their object status, such as one on which "Fuck Foreplay" is written across a half-used tube of KY Jelly, suggesting that the wearer is ready for penetration at a moment's notice. (This shirt also propagates the notion that men do not enjoy foreplay.) Other shirts make light of rape, with words such as "Violate Me" or "No Means Eat Me Out First."

It would be encouraging if these choices reflected the sexual agency for women that feminists have fought so hard for, but they do not. The notion of objectification as empowering is illogical, since objects are acted upon, rather than taking action themselves. The real power in such arrangements lies with boys and men, who come to feel entitled to consume women as objects—first in media, then in real life.

At the root of this normalization of self-objectification may lie new consumer values in the U.S. Unlike the "producer citizen" of yesteryear—invoked in the 1960s by John F. Kennedy's request to "ask not what your country can do for you, ask what you can do for your country"—the more common "consumer citizen" of today asks what the country, and everyone else, can do for him or her. Consumer citizens increasingly think of relationships with others as transactions in which they receive something, making them more comfortable consuming other human beings, visually or otherwise.

Self-objectification isn't going anywhere anytime soon. So what can we do about it? First, we can recognize how our everyday actions feed the larger beast, and realize that we are not powerless. Mass media, the primary peddler of female bodies, can be assailed with millions of little consumer swords. We can boycott companies and engage in other forms of consumer activism, such as socially conscious investments and shareholder actions. We can also contact companies directly to voice our concerns (see *Ms.*' backpage No Comment section, for example) and refuse to patronize businesses that overtly depict women as sex objects.

An example of women's spending power, and the limits of our tolerance for objectification, can be found in the 12-percent dip in profits of clothing company Victoria's Secret this year—due, according to the company's CEO, to its image becoming "too sexy." Victoria's Secret was not the target of an organized boycott; rather, its increasingly risqué "bra and panty show" seems to have begun alienating women, who perhaps no longer want to simply be shown as highly sexualized window dressing.

Another strategy to counter one's own tendency to self-objectify is to make a point of buying products, watching programs and reading publications that promote more authentic women's empowerment. This can be difficult, of course, in a media climate in which companies are rarely wholeheartedly body-positive. For instance, Dove beauty products launched a much-lauded advertising campaign that used "real women" (i.e., not super-skinny ones) instead of models, but then Dove's parent company, Unilever, put out hypersexual ads for Axe men's body spray that showed the fragrance driving scantily clad women into orgiastic states.

Locating unadulterated television and film programming is also tough. Even Lifetime and Oxygen, TV networks created specifically for women, often portray us as weak victims or sex objects and present a narrow version of thin, white "beauty." Action films that promise strong female protagonists (think of the women of *X-Men*, or Lara Croft from *Tomb Raider*) usually deliver these characters in skintight clothes, serving the visual pleasure of men.

Feminist media criticism, at least, is plentiful. *Ms., Bitch* and others, along with publications for young girls such as *New Moon Magazine*, provide thoughtful analyses of media from various feminist perspectives. NOW's Love Your Body website (http://loveyourbody. nowfoundation.org) critiques offensive ads and praises body-positive ones. Blogs, both well-known and lesser-known, provide a platform for women and girls to vent about how the media depicts them. And there's some evidence that criticizing media helps defuse its effects: Murnen's study found that grade-school girls who had negative reactions to pictures of objectified women reported higher self-esteem.

A more radical, personal solution is to actively avoid media that compels us to self-objectify—which, unfortunately, is the vast majority of movies, television programs and women's magazines. My research with college-age women indicates that the less women consume media, the less they self-objectify, particularly if they avoid fashion magazines. By shutting out media, girls and women can create mental and emotional space for true self-exploration. What would our lives look like if we viewed our bodies as tools to master our environment, instead of projects to be constantly worked on? What if our sexual expressions were based on our own pleasure as opposed to a narrow, consumerist idea of male sexual pleasure? What would disappear from our lives if we stopped seeing ourselves as objects? Painful high heels? Body hatred? Constant dieting? Liposuction? Unreciprocated oral sex?

It's hard to know. Perhaps the most striking outcome of self-objectification is the difficulty women have in imagining identities and sexualities truly our own. In solidarity, we can start on this path, however confusing and difficult it may be.

66

Women's Pay

Why the Gap Remains a Chasm

Aaron Bernstein

During the heyday of the women's movement more than 30 years ago, "59¢ on the dollar" was an oft-heard rallying cry, referring to how little women earned compared with men.

Those concerns seem outdated today, when it's easy to find female doctors, lawyers, pop stars, even Presidential advisers. The progress toward equality in the workplace also shows up in government data on wages, which pegs women's average pay at 77% of men's compensation today.

But there's new evidence that women's advances may not be quite so robust after all. When you look at how much the typical woman actually earns over much of her career, the true figure is more like 44% of what the average man makes. That's the conclusion of a new study by Stephen J. Rose, an economist at Macro International Inc., a consulting firm, and Heidi I. Hartmann, President of the Institute for Women's Policy Research in Washington.

Why the big discrepancy? The Bureau of Labor Statistics (BLS) numbers, published every year, are accurate as far as they go. But they only measure the earnings of those who work full-time for an entire year. Only one-quarter of women, though, achieve this level of participation consistently throughout their working lives. So Rose and Hartmann looked at the pay of all men and women over 15 years, including those who worked part-time and dipped in and out of the labor force to care for children or elderly parents. This long-term perspective still shows an arc of progress: The 44%, based on average earnings between 1983 and 1998, jumped from 29% in the prior 15 years. But the more comprehensive view gives a less rosy picture of women's position in the work world.

Outright discrimination against women probably accounts for only about 10 percentage points of the pay gap, according to numerous studies. The bulk of the problem, then, lies with the conflicting needs and norms of society and employers. A majority of men and women still work in largely sex-segregated occupations, Rose and Hartmann's study shows, leaving many women stuck in lower-paying jobs such as cashiers and maids.

Family responsibilities, too, typically still fall more heavily on women, and neither society nor employers have found good ways to mesh those with job demands. Rose and Hartmann's data show that women can get equal treatment today—but mostly when they behave like traditional men and leave the primary family responsibilities at home. For the majority who can't or won't do that, the work world remains much less accommodating. Of course, many women choose to take time off or to work part-time to be with their children rather than stay on the job. Yet that choice itself is constrained by the widespread lack of day care and flexible job options, Hartmann argues. "The 44% gap we found shows that there are still tremendous differences in how the labor market treats men and women," she says.

Hartmann and Rose came to their results by examining long-term earnings trends. The 77% figure comes from the BLS's 2002 earnings survey and looks at how much full-time, year-round workers make in a given year. By contrast, Rose and Hartmann used a University of Michigan survey that has tracked a sample of randomly chosen people and their children since 1968. They looked at how much each person made between 1983 and 1998 in every year from age 26 to 59 (to exclude students and retirees).

One surprise was just how many women work most of their adult lives. Fully 96% of these prime-age women worked at least one of those 15 years, and they clocked an average of 12 years on the job. In other words, few women these days drop out altogether once they have kids.

But those few years out of the labor market carry a stiff penalty. More than half of all women spent at least a year out of the labor force, the study found, and they earned an average of $21,363 a year over the years they worked, after inflation adjustments, vs. nearly $30,000 for women who stuck with it for all 15 years. Indeed, anyone who drops out risks derailing their career and permanently slashing their pay. Just one year off cuts a woman's total earnings over 15 years by 32%, while two years slice it by 46% and three by 56%, according to Hartmann and Rose. The work world penalizes men nearly as much;

their average pay drops by 25% if they take off a year. Fewer than 8% of men did so, however. "Our economic system is still based on a family division of labor, and women pay the price," says Rose.

Women also take a big hit for going part-time. On average, they work a lot less than men: 1,498 hours a year, vs. 2,219 worked by the typical man. The fewer hours women work account for about half of the total pay gap between the sexes, Rose and Hartmann concluded. Some women have turned to self-employment as a way to fit work and family together. But they often must accept lower pay in the process. Brita Bergland, a Windsor (Vt.) resident, found it difficult to manage her sales job at a printing company while she also cared for her aging mother and her daughter. So she struck out on her own six years ago and has managed the work-life balance much better ever since. The cost: about a $15,000 cut in annual earnings, down from the $55,000 to $60,000 she made as an employee. "These are the choices women make because society doesn't help them to support children and parents," says Bergland, who's now 50.

And while many women have made great strides in some highly visible professions such as law and medicine, historical patterns of sex segregation remain strong across much of the economy. Overall, just 15% of women work in jobs typically held by men, such as engineer, stockbroker, and judge, while fewer than 8% of men hold female-dominated jobs such as nurse, teacher, or sales clerk. These findings were reiterated in a detailed BLS analysis released on June 2 that uses the 2000 Census to look at the jobs men and women hold.

Such a sex-segregated economy leaves women with some startling disadvantages. Overall, they earn less than men with the same education at all levels. Incredibly, male dropouts pulled down an average of $36,000 a year between 1983 and 1998, after inflation adjustments, while women with a bachelor's degree made $35,000. Women with a graduate degree averaged $42,000, but men got nearly $77,000.

The good news is that the pay gap continues to narrow no matter how it's measured. That's likely to continue; female college graduation rates surpass those of men, and they're catching up in grad school, too, so they're likely to gain from an economy that rewards skill. Women also should benefit from the ongoing shift to services, where they're more likely to work, and lose less than men from the decline of factory jobs.

Still, speedier progress probably won't happen without more employers making work sites family-friendly and revamping jobs to accommodate women and men as they seek to balance work and family demands. "The workplace needs to change to match the workforce," says Ellen Bravo, national director of 9 to 5, National Association of Working Women. Until that happens, a woman's labor will continue to be worth a fraction of a man's.

67

The Body Politic

Abra Fortune Chernik

My body possesses solidity and curve, like the ocean. My weight mingles with Earth's pull, drawing me onto the sand. I have not always sent waves into the world. I flew off once, for five years, and swirled madly like a cracking brown leaf in the salty autumn wind. I wafted, dried out, apathetic.

I had no weight in the world during my years of anorexia. Curled up inside my thinness, a refugee in a cocoon of hunger, I lost the capacity to care about myself or others. I starved my body and twitched in place as those around me danced in the energy of shared existence and progressed in their lives. When I graduated from college crowned with academic honors, professors praised my potential. I wanted only to vanish.

It took three months of hospitalization and two years of outpatient psychotherapy for me to learn to nourish myself and to live in a body that expresses strength and honesty in its shape. I accepted my right and my obligation to take up room with my figure, voice and spirit. I remembered how to tumble forward and touch the world that holds me. I chose the ocean as my guide.

Who disputes the ocean's fullness?

Growing up in New York City, I did not care about the feminist movement. Although I attended an all-girls high school, we read mostly male authors and studied the history of men. Embracing mainstream culture without question, I learned about womanhood from fashion magazines, Madison Avenue and Hollywood. I dismissed feminist alternatives as foreign and offensive, swathed as they were in stereotypes that threatened my adolescent need for conformity.

Puberty hit late; I did not complain. I enjoyed living in the lanky body of a tall child and insisted on the title of "girl." If anyone referred to me as a "young woman," I would cry out, horrified, "Do not call me the W word!" But at sixteen years old, I could no longer deny my fate. My stomach and breasts rounded. Curly black hair sprouted in the most embarrassing places. Hips swelled from a once-flat plane. Interpreting maturation as an unacceptable lapse into fleshiness, I resolved to eradicate the physical symptoms of my impending womanhood.

Magazine articles, television commercials, lunchroom conversation, gymnastics coaches and write-ups on models had saturated me with diet savvy. Once I decided to lose weight, I quickly turned expert. I dropped hot chocolate from my regular breakfast order at the Skyline Diner. I replaced lunches of peanut butter and Marshmallow Fluff sandwiches with small platters of cottage cheese and cantaloupe. I eliminated dinner altogether and blunted my appetite with Tab, Camel Lights, and Carefree bubble gum. When furious craving overwhelmed my resolve and I swallowed an extra something, I would flee to the nearest bathroom to purge my mistake.

Within three months, I had returned my body to its preadolescent proportions and had manipulated my monthly period into drying up. Over the next five years, I devoted my life to losing my weight. I came to resent the body in which I lived, the body that threatened to develop, the body whose hunger I despised but could not extinguish. If I neglected a workout or added a pound or ate a bite too many, I would stare in the mirror and drown myself in a tidal wave of criticism. Hatred of my body generalized to hatred of myself as a person, and self-referential labels such as "pig," "failure" and "glutton" allowed me to believe that I deserved punishment. My self-hatred became fuel for the self-mutilating behaviors of the eating disorder.

As my body shrank, so did my world. I starved away my power and vision, my energy and inclinations. Obsessed with dieting, I allowed relationships, passions and identity to wither. I pulled back from the world, off of the beach, out of the sand. The waves of my existence ceased to roll beyond the inside of my skin.

And society applauded my shrinking. Pound after pound the applause continued, like the pounding ocean outside the door of my beach house.

. . .

By the time I entered the hospital, a mess of protruding bones defined my body, and the bones of my emaciated life rattled me crazy. I carried a pillow around because it hurt to sit down, and I shivered with cold in sultry July. Clumps of brittle hair clogged the drain

when I showered, and blackened eyes appeared to sink into my head. My vision of reality wrinkled and my disposition turned mercurial as I slipped into starvation psychosis, a condition associated with severe malnutrition. People told me that I resembled a concentration camp prisoner, a chemotherapy patient, a famine victim or a fashion model.

In the hospital I examined my eating disorder under the lenses of various therapies. I dissected my childhood, my family structure, my intimate relationships, my belief systems. I participated in experiential therapies of movement, art and psychodrama. I learned to use words instead of eating patterns to communicate my feelings. And still I refused to gain more than a minimal amount of weight.

I felt powerful as an anorexic. Controlling my body yielded an illusion of control over my life; I received incessant praise for my figure despite my sickly mien, and my frailty manipulated family and friends into protecting me from conflict. I had reduced my world to a plate of steamed carrots, and over this tiny kingdom I proudly crowned myself queen.

. . .

I spent my remaining month in the hospital supplementing psychotherapy with an independent examination of eating disorders from a social and political point of view. I needed to understand why society would reward my starvation and encourage my vanishing. In the bathroom, a mirror on the open door behind me reflected my backside in a mirror over the sink. Vertebrae poked at my skin, ribs hung like wings over chiseled hip bones, the two sides of my buttocks did not touch. I had not seen this view of myself before.

In writing, I recorded instances in which my eating disorder had tangled the progress of my life and thwarted my relationships. I filled three and a half Mead marble notebooks. Five years' worth of: *I wouldn't sit with Daddy when he was alone in the hospital because I needed to go jogging; I told Derek not to visit me because I couldn't throw up when he was there; I almost failed my comprehensive exams because I was so hungry; I spent my year at Oxford with my head in the toilet bowl; I wouldn't eat the dinner my friends cooked me for my nineteenth birthday because I knew they had used oil in the recipe; I told my family not to come to my college graduation because I didn't want to miss a day at the gym or have to eat a restaurant meal.* And on and on for hundreds of pages.

This honest account of my life dissolved the illusion of anorexic power. I saw myself naked in the truth of my pain, my loneliness, my obsessions, my craziness, my selfishness, my defeat. I also recognized the social and political implications of consuming myself with the trivialities of calories and weight. At college, I had watched as classmates involved themselves in extracurricular clubs, volunteer work, politics and applications for jobs and graduate schools. Obsessed with exercising and exhausted by starvation. I did not even consider joining in such pursuits. Despite my love of writing and painting and literature, despite ranking at the top of my class, I wanted only to teach aerobics. Despite my adolescent days as a loud-mouthed, rambunctious class leader, I had grown into a silent, hungry young woman.

And society preferred me this way: hungry, fragile, crazy. *Winner! Healthy! Fantastic!* I began reading feminist literature to further understand the disempowerment of women in our culture. I digested the connection between a nation of starving, self-obsessed women and the continued success of the patriarchy. I also cultivated an awareness of alternative models of womanhood. In the stillness of the hospital library, new voices in my life rose from printed pages to echo my rage and provide the conception of my feminist consciousness.

I had been willing to accept self-sabotage, but now I refused to sacrifice myself to a society that profited from my pain. I finally understood that my eating disorder symbolized more than "personal psychodynamic trauma." Gazing in the mirror at my emaciated body, I observed a woman held up by her culture as the physical ideal because she was starving, self-obsessed and powerless, a woman called beautiful because she threatened no one except herself. Despite my intelligence, my education, and my supposed Manhattan

sophistication, I had believed all of the lies; I had almost given my life in order to achieve the sickly impotence that this culture aggressively links with female happiness, love and success. And everything I had to offer to the world, every tumbling wave, every thought and every passion, nearly died inside me.

As long as society resists female power, fashion will call healthy women physically flawed. As long as society accepts the physical, sexual and economic abuse of women, popular culture will prefer women who resemble little girls. Sitting in the hospital the summer after my college graduation, I grasped the absurdity of a nation of adult women dying to grow small.

Armed with this insight, I loosened the grip of the starvation disease on my body. I determined to recreate myself based on an image of a woman warrior. I remembered my ocean, and I took my first bite.

Gaining weight and getting my head out of the toilet bowl was the most political act I have ever committed.

. . .

Eating disorders affect us all on both a personal and a political level. The majority of my peers—including my feminist peers—still measure their beauty against anorexic ideals. Even among feminists, body hatred and chronic dieting continue to consume lives. Friends of anorexics beg them to please start eating; then these friends go home and continue their own diets. Who can deny that the millions of young women caught in the net of disordered eating will frustrate the potential of the next wave of feminism?

. . .

As young feminists, we must place unconditional acceptance of our bodies at the top of our political agenda. We must claim our bodies as our own to love and honor in their infinite shapes and sizes. Fat, thin, soft, hard, puckered, smooth, our bodies are our homes. By nourishing our bodies, we care for and love ourselves on the most basic level. When we deny ourselves physical food, we go hungry emotionally, psychologically, spiritually and politically. We must challenge ourselves to eat and digest, and allow society to call us too big. We will understand their message to mean too powerful.

Time goes by quickly. One day we will blink and open our eyes as old women. If we spend all our energy keeping our bodies small, what will we have to show for our lives when we reach the end? I hope we have more than a group of fashionably skinny figures.

68

Connect

A Web of Words

Robin Morgan

• Threat • Shout • Bellow • Hit • Slap • Smack • Strike • Beat • Bash • Batter • Pummel • Punch • Slash • Stamp • Pound • Maul • Hammer • Bludgeon • Fist • Belt • Knife • Gun • Punish • Control • Mutilate • *Blood* • Ambulance • Sorry • Drunk • Welt • Swollen • Scar • *Lies* • Made Me Do It • Deserved It • Her Own Fault • Taught a Lesson

• *Shame* • Neighbors • Secret • Whimper • *Fear* • Skulk • Shuffle • Wince • Tremble • Shudder • Shake • Cower • Cringe • Flinch • Crawl • Listen • Wait • Whisper • Bruise • Bandage • *Guilt* • Bumped into a Door • He Didn't Mean • Shatter • Wound • Fracture • Rupture • Harassment • Provoked It • Stalking • Invited It • Restraining Order • Funeral • *Scream* • Stranger Rape • Acquaintance Rape • Date Rape • Marital Rape • Child Rape • Asked for It • Wanted It • *Entitlement* • Masculine • *Selflessness* • Feminine • Disgust • Bitch • Cunt • Slit • 'Ho • Witch • Hag • Illiteracy • Purdah • Suttee • Clitoridectomy • Infibulation • Stoning • *Terror* • Burka • Chador • Forced Shrouding • Pornography • Forced Exposure • Sex Traffick • *Hunger* • Child Bride • Kidnapped Bride • Mail-order Bride • Bride Burnings • Harem • Forced Marriage • Child Marriage • Slavery • *Humiliation* • Tears • Begging • Prostitution • *Poverty* • Hooker • Pimp • John • Brothel • *Loneliness* • Hemorrhage • *Lovelessness* • Dread • *Exhaustion* • Hide • Run • Where • Duty • Family • Minister • Priest • Rabbi • Mullah • Trapped • *Again* • Stupid • Ugly • Fat • Old • Face-lift • Backstreet Abortion • Maternal Mortality • Female Infanticide • Suicide • *No* • Femicide • Gynocide • Genocide • Silence • *No* • Weep • Howl • *Blood* • Gasp • Wail • Grief • Mourning • Secrets • Lies • Propaganda • Torture • Waterboard • Electrodes • Lash • Cane • Whip • Burn • *Starve* • Boy Next Door • Serial Killer • Gang • Sect • Nation • Empire • Molotov Cocktail • IED • Patriot Missile • Peacekeeper Missile • "Big Boy" A-bomb • "Nuclear Hardness" • "Deep Penetration Capacity Bomb" • "Potent Kill Capability" • "Rigid, Hardened Silo" • "Erector Launchers" • "Thrust Ratios" • "Soft Targets" • Toy Gun • Toy Tank • Toy Missile • *No* • How • *Planet* • *Why* • Madness • *Rage* • Shrill • Strident • *Yes* • Crazy • *Hope* • Bread • Shelter • You *Too?* • Recognition • *Truth* • Strength • Dignity • Yes • *Transformation* • Human • *Together* • Yes •

69

He Works, She Works, But What Different Impressions They Make

Gwyn Kirk and Margo Okazawa-Rey

Have you ever found yourself up against the old double standard at work? Then you know how annoying it can be and how alone you can feel. Supervisors and coworkers still judge us by old stereotypes that say women are emotional, disorganized, and inefficient. Here are some of the most glaring examples of the typical office double standard.

The family picture is on HIS desk: Ah, a solid, responsible family man

The family picture is on HER desk: Hmm, her family will come before her career

HIS desk is cluttered: He's obviously a hard worker and busy man

HER desk is cluttered: She's obviously a disorganized scatterbrain

HE'S talking with coworkers: He must be discussing the latest deal

SHE'S talking with coworkers: She must be gossiping

HE'S not at his desk: He must be at a meeting

SHE'S not at her desk: She must be in the ladies' room

HE'S having lunch with the boss: He's on his way up	SHE'S having lunch with the boss: They must be having an affair
HE'S getting married. He'll get more settled	SHE'S getting married: She'll get pregnant and leave
HE'S having a baby: He'll need a raise	SHE'S having a baby: She'll cost the company money in maternity benefits
HE'S leaving for a better job: HE recognizes a good opportunity	SHE'S leaving for a better job: Women are undependable
HE'S aggressive	SHE'S pushy
HE'S careful	SHE'S picky
HE loses his temper	SHE'S bitchy
HE'S depressed	SHE'S moody
HE follows through	SHE doesn't know when to quit
HE'S firm	SHE'S stubborn
HE makes wise judgments	SHE reveals her prejudices
HE is a man of the world	SHE'S been around
HE isn't afraid to say what he thinks	SHE'S opinionated
HE exercises authority	SHE'S tyrannical
HE'S discreet	SHE'S secretive
HE'S a stern taskmaster	SHE'S difficult to work for

N E X T   S T E P S

70

Promises Made

Ross Neely

When I was ten years old, I was out with my mother when she was suddenly targeted with a barrage of sexist words and violent gestures by a group of men outside a grocery store. Afterward, as *she* was comforting *me*, my mother—who always took care of everyone else, who had been surrounded by gender violence her entire life—turned and studied me with eyes I'd never seen and said: *Are you going to grow up to hate women like every other man?* Everything in my body froze, but I knew on some cellular level that I never wanted to be those men. I promised: *No, mom. I won't. I won't.*

When I was eleven, I already hated my body. I was too soft. I needed to be harder. I needed to turn my curves into straight lines and my smooths into sharps. Secretly, I wrote poetry and stories, and loved to sing. Outwardly, I played sports like football and tried to "pass" and be the "tough" guy I was expected to be. A year later, after some older boys beat me up to make sure I knew who was most "masculine" in my new neighborhood, I renewed my promise: *I will not do this to anyone else. I will not become these men.*

But I did. The messages I received as a child about what it means to "be a man," and the rewards and punishments for "succeeding" or "failing" to perform the tough, confident, stoic, in-control masculinity I was taught, had taken their toll. When upset, I more quickly raised my voice with my mother than my father. My football coaches taunted us with the worst

insult of all, "playing like a girl," and I responded with more aggression and toughness. I hung out at fraternity houses where gender violence was constantly reproduced and did very little to interrupt it. I dropped off my girlfriend at her poorly-lit house late at night and didn't think to wait to make sure she got inside safely before driving away. My life was, and still is, shaped by white, cisgender (gender identity and expression are congruent with the dominant expectations of my birth-assigned sex), hetero-perceived male privilege that I rarely have to think about, but which is nonetheless ever-present.

Fortunately, I was introduced to women's studies, gender studies and queer studies, and got connected with people from all gender identities who were taking action and leading the way to gender liberation. It is from their work and through their example that I slowly began to understand that genderism (gender oppression rooted in socially constructed categories of woman/man and femininity/masculinity, with power held by men/masculinity) is not just about the *interpersonal* violence of a few bad perpetrators, but more significantly about the access (or lack thereof) to the *institutional power* attached to these pervasive gender categories. In this way, I came to see that the personal is truly political and that every action I take as a cisgender man either reinforces or challenges the systems of gender oppression all around me. The lesson for me at the time: understanding and ending genderism is my responsibility.

Genderism and male supremacy shape men's relationships with women and gender-nonconforming folks every day: the words we choose, how we position our bodies, the roles we take on, and our objectifying male gaze all make public spaces unwelcome or threatening to women. This is literally life and death—intimate partner violence is a leading cause of death for women 15–44, two million women a year are injured because of violence, a sexual assault occurs every two minutes, and one out of three women will be sexually assaulted in her lifetime. Genderism also shapes men's relationships with other men through the subtle and explicit ways we feel coerced to constantly prove our masculinities to each other: the way I straighten my shoulders and lower my voice when I speak with cisgender men, the ways I've been afraid to tell my male friends and family that I love them, and the way I'm supposed to always project power and dominance. This side of genderism is why a two-year-old boy was recently murdered by his father for crying "too much like a girl," and it's why a seven-year-old boy had his arm broken because he wanted to be a cheerleader.

Organizing to understand, dismantle and transform the systems of male supremacy and the culture of gender violence we all live in has historically been constructed as "women's work." And while I absolutely believe that women and trans* (gender identity and/or expression are incongruent with the dominant expectations of birth-assigned sex) folks must lead and guide this work, leaving it here gives cisgender men an easy out and removes us from our responsibility to work for gender liberation. I identify as an aspiring ally to feminist, gender, and trans* justice movements—"aspiring" because I don't get to decide if I'm being an authentic ally, the women and trans* folks I am in community with do. But being an ally cannot mean that I am working to paternalistically "save" others with my cis-masculine power. As I have learned from women and trans* activists, educators, organizers and scholars, I must work in honest solidarity (not charity) with gender justice movements, become aware of how I'm positioned within systems of power (gender, sexuality, race, class, dis/ability), and then use my privileged access to power in coalition with women and trans* folks to create change and liberate all of us from the poison of patriarchy.

Using what I have learned from trans-feminism, I know that while cisgender men certainly do not experience gender oppression, we are definitely dehumanized and harmed by it. All the stories that have been beaten into us about how to be men are simultaneously privileging and poisoning us, and beg the question why are we accepting this dehumanizing, violent, restrictive, brutal story about what we should do and who we should be?

Guided by the voices of feminist and trans* liberation movements, why don't we write a different story—a new collective story about what cisgender men can be. At its best this new narrative of what it means to "be a man" would be one where true strength lies in being

N
E
X
T

S
T
E
P
S

vulnerable and in not always being in control or at the center. In this story, cisgender men are working daily to end genderism by pushing back on gender socialization, speaking up about gender oppression, and using our privilege to interrupt, agitate and create change. Importantly, this work is not just in public moments (where we get disproportionate amounts of praise for doing gender justice work), but in the quiet, private moments when no one is watching like speaking up when my male friend is using sexism to complain about his college professor, calling out a masculine friend who is objectifying his feminine partner, drawing attention to moments when men talk over women at staff meetings, and asking how my femme-identified partner feels, really feels, about the way I am treating her.

It is time (well past time, actually) to write a new story where cisgender men are constant and committed allies in ending gender oppression, and in the process are able to come back to our true selves and reclaim our true humanity. Over twenty years ago I made a promise to my mother, and though it's been a circuitous path and I've faltered many times, I will spend the rest of my life rewriting the story of what it means to "be a man," and by doing so work to honor that promise.

Note on the text: Trans* is used here as an umbrella term for people transgressing binary gender norms, and/or people assigned one gender at birth who now identify as another gender; this may or may not include a diverse range of gender experiences and self-determined identities such as transgender, transsexual, trans woman, trans man, two spirit, intersex, genderqueer, and many more.

NEXT STEPS

71

To Stop the Violence against Woman

Alice Walker

WOMAN

TO STOP THE VIOLENCE
AGAINST
WOMAN
WOMAN
MUST STOP THE VIOLENCE
AGAINST
HERSELF.

WE CAN BEGIN TO DO THIS
NOW, NOW THAT WE SEE
A SKY
AND NOT A ROCK
A STICK
OR A FIST
ABOVE ALL
OUR HEADS.

WOMAN

TO STOP THE VIOLENCE
AGAINST WOMAN,
STOP THE VIOLENCE
THAT YOU
PERPETUATE
AGAINST
YOUR OWN
SISTER
WHO IS
A WOMAN, YOUR OWN
DAUGHTER
WHO IS
A WOMAN,
YOUR OWN
DAUGHTER-IN-LAW
WHO IS
A WOMAN,
YOUR OWN
MOTHER
WHO IS
A WOMAN.

WOMAN

TO STOP THE VIOLENCE
AGAINST WOMAN,
STOP THE VIOLENCE
THAT LIVES
IN OPPOSITION
TO YOUR LIFE,
DEEP IN YOUR
OWN TERRORIZED AND
UNCHERISHED
HEART.

WOMAN

REMEMBER WHO WE ARE:
NOT "GUYS"
BUT
THE MOTHER
OF ALL
LIVING.
WE CREATE OUT OF OUR OWN BLOOD
AND MILK
THE CREATURES
WHO OPPRESS
US;
WHETHER THEY ARE MEN
OR
OURSELVES.

NEXT STEPS

WOMAN

AWAKE!
ARISE!
STAND UP!

WOMAN

TO STOP THE VIOLENCE
AGAINST
WOMAN,
GET UP
ON YOUR PERFECTLY
UNBOUND
FEET!
WE HAVE LOST THE EARTH
LIVING ON OUR KNEES.

72

National Latina Institute for Reproductive Health (NLIRH) Statement on Healthcare for All

National Latina Institute for Reproductive Health

The National Latina Institute for Reproductive Health (NLIRH) supports healthcare reform that will move our current system toward one that will improve the health, and well-being of all Latinas, their families and communities. NLIRH embraces a human rights approach to health care, ensuring that all health services are accessible, available, affordable, and of good quality for everyone. These services should be provided on an equitable basis, free from discrimination or coercion. Healthcare reform can take many paths, and it is important that the needs of all Latinas, including immigrant women, women of color and low-income women, are front and center.

NLIRH supports a system that includes all people, regardless of income, immigration status, or any other limiting factor. The current healthcare system leaves many Latinas falling through the cracks; 38% of Latinas are uninsured, the highest rate amongst all groups of women. Some Latinas may have an income too high to qualify for Medicaid, yet too low to afford private insurance. Many Latinas who would qualify based on income are not eligible. Among the ineligible are undocumented Latinas and legal permanent residents who have been in the United States for less than five years. This lack of access to healthcare contributes heavily to the health disparities that Latinas face, in turn affecting many other aspects of Latinas' quality of life.

It is important that such a system includes a full and comprehensive range of services, including coverage for family planning, abortions, prenatal care and preventive services.

Currently Latinas—especially low-income, uninsured and immigrant Latinas—face numerous obstacles to obtaining these services, including cost and lack of access. Under the Hyde Amendment, no federal funds can be used for abortion services, meaning that many women on Medicaid are unable to access a full range of options when facing an unintended pregnancy, and may turn to unsafe terminations if they do not wish to carry the pregnancy to term. This and other obstacles create a disproportionate burden of morbidity and mortality on Latinas.

Moreover, NLIRH supports a system that is not only inclusive of all people and offers a comprehensive range of services, but is also one that emphasizes culturally competent and linguistically appropriate services. Comprehensive care is meaningless unless it is provided in a language with which patients are comfortable and accompanied by physicians and other clinicians that understand the needs of Latinas, immigrant women, and low-income women. Unless Latinas feel free of judgment, coercion and discrimination at our doctors' offices, health disparities will continue regardless of availability and access. Supporting health care reform that incorporates a human rights framework would ensure a holistic approach to the care needed for all Latinas to advance *salud, dignidad y justicia*!

73

Heartbroken

Women of Color Feminism and the Third Wave

Rebecca Hurdis

This essay isn't just about an adopted, woman of color feminist; rather, it is a story about how I came to believe that I was worthy of all of these identities. It isn't just a story about feminism or solely about adoption. It is an exploration of where the mind stops and the heart follows. . . . The struggle is not to find one place where I can exist, but to find it within myself to exist in all of these places, uncompromisingly. To live a life of multiplicity is as difficult as it is to write about it.

. . .

Growing up in a transracial adopted family, I was often confused by the images of the "normal, nuclear families." We didn't look like any other family I saw. I couldn't comprehend how I could love my family, feel accepted by them and believe that I belonged to them as much as my phenotypically white brothers. Yet every time I looked in the mirror, my reflection haunted me, because the face that stared back was not the same color as my family's. This awareness was reinforced by the sometimes brutal questions of others. I constantly had to explain that I really was my brother's sister. He was not my husband but truly my brother. I was not the foreign exchange student that just never left. Embarrassed by the attention, I tried to ignore the differences. I took the negativity and dissociation I felt and began to internalize the feelings. I fooled myself into thinking and acting the role of a "good little Asian saved from her fallen country and brought to the land of salvation."

I began to believe the messages about being an Asian girl and about being adopted. This compliance was one of the only ways I learned to gain acceptance and validation as a child. I realized that my identity was being created *for* me not *by* me.

. . .

When I would talk to my friends about it, they wouldn't and couldn't understand. I was told that I was making too big a deal out of being Asian and besides I *was* just like everyone else. They thought that I just worried too much. My friends went so far as to convince me by telling me that "I wasn't really Asian, I was white." But the truth couldn't be denied, just as the color of my skin couldn't either. . . .

I came across feminism as a first-year student at Ohio State University. I was extremely depressed at the time. Everything—my created identity, the world of whiteness that I knew, the denial of my race—that I had worked so hard at repressing and ignoring throughout my life was finally surfacing and emerging. I no longer had the validation of whiteness to protect my false identity. The world that I had understood was changing, and I was confronted with defining myself without the associations of my family and friends. I was forced to step outside of my white world, shedding my blinders to find that I wasn't white and that I had never really been so. The only illusion was the one that I had created for myself, the one that had found acceptance. But I was beginning to realize the cost of this facade.

. . .

My first women's studies course focused on the history of the women's movement, the social context and the contemporary issues facing feminism today. We looked at issues ranging from violence to sexual orientation to women-centered spirituality to representation in music and film to body image. I began to recognize my extensive history of sexual, mental and physical abuse with boyfriends, and I started to comprehend the cycle of abuse and forgiveness. I was able to begin to stop blaming myself and shift the responsibility back to those who had inflicted the abuse. Initially I had disconnected the abuse from racism, even though it was heavily intertwined and simultaneous. It was just too large for me to understand, and it was still too early for me to grapple with race. I still was thinking that I just needed to become the "right" kind of Asian American and then everything would make sense.

I know that for a lot of women of color, feminism is perceived as being a white woman's movement that has little space or acknowledgment for women of color. I understand how that is true, but back then this class became a catalyst for change and healing. It was a major turning point in my life, where I was able to break my silence and find empowerment within myself and for myself. Women's studies offered me a place where there was validation and reason. I was uncovering and understanding how my own internalization was tied to ideologies of racism and sexism. Although the analysis of racism was somewhat limited in these courses, it served as a lead for future interests. Women's studies and feminism was a steppingstone toward striving for a holistic understanding of myself.

. . .

But I left college feeling as though there was something missing to this feminism. Professors would talk about Black feminism or women of color feminism, but merely as another mark on their feminist timeline. Little time was dedicated to really examining the intersection of race and gender. Back home I went to my local new-age store (which also doubled as the feminist bookstore) and stumbled on *This Bridge Called My Back: Writings by Radical Women of Color* (edited by Cherré Moraga and Gloria Anzaldúa). It was the first time I had found a book that had the words "women of color" as part of the title. It was as if I had found the pot of gold at the end of the feminist rainbow. Even though I didn't find myself completely represented in the book, specifically because none of the

contributors had been an adopted child, I did find my thoughts, anger and pain represented through the eloquent voices of other women of color. Their writings incorporated race and sexuality.

Reading this anthology, I realized I was entitled to feeling something other than apologetic. I could be angry. I could be aggressive. I could be the opposite of this little china doll that everyone expected me to be. Given my background, this book was life-changing. It represented one of the first moments where I could claim something that was mine; something different from my parents, my friends, my community; something other than whiteness. I remember sitting at the town beach on a hot and humid August day, flipping through the book, my mind exploding and expanding. As I sat there frantically reading, I recall looking up at the sun, closing my eyes and thanking the goddess that I had found this work. Through this discovery I had found that I was not alone. Not only was I feminist, but I was a woman of color feminist.

What makes my relationship to women of color feminism different from most other women of color is how and why I entered the conversation. I began looking at race through gender, where most have the reverse experience. This idea of entry point is crucial. I call myself a woman of color before I call myself an Asian American. It reflects how I have come to see myself and how I understand my own identity. The term "women of color" seems broadly inviting and inclusive while "Asian American" feels rigid and exclusive. Women of color feminism took me from being a victim to being a warrior.

I am now in an ethnic studies graduate program trying to explore if women of color are within feminism's third wave, and if so, where. I began this project as an undergraduate but I had hit a wall. It was difficult locating voices that represented generation X or third wave women of color feminism. Not much had been written, as our voices were just beginning to emerge. I found women of color feminists in alternative places such as zines, anthologies, magazines and pop culture. I felt frustrated that our voices were deemed not "accredited" enough to be represented in the mainstream.

I held a certain expectation for Jennifer Baumgardner and Amy Richard's book, *Manifesta: Young Women, Feminism, and the Future*. This book markets itself as being *the* text for the third wave of feminism, and I had high hopes that it would address issues of race, gender and class sexuality. Instead, I found the specific history of white (privileged) women. . . .

I found it astounding that there is no extensive discussion of women of color feminism. This indicates that Baumgardner and Richards feel as though this is a separate issue, a different kind of feminism. It is as if their work is the master narrative of feminism, with women of color feminism as an appendage. I had hoped that they would have considered such books as *This Bridge Called My Back* and Audre Lorde's *Sister Outsider* as ground-breaking, as they are deemed by most generation X women of color. These books were life-changing to me not only because their critiques have historical value, but also because what these writers were saying in the 1980s was still relevant in the 1990s. *Manifesta* is successful in creating momentum for young white women's activism through the attempt to move feminism out of academia and back into a social and political movement. But the book's greatest contribution was that it raised a need for creating a lineage for women of color feminism.

. . .

What is it about the word "feminism" that has encouraged women of color to stand apart from it? Feminism has been indoctrinated into the academy through the discipline of women's studies. It has moved out of the social and political spaces from where it emerged. Women's studies have collapsed the diversity that was part of the feminist movement into a discipline that has become a homogeneous generality. For women in the third wave then,

NEXT STEPS

one needs to have the academic training of women's studies to be an "accredited feminist." Once race is added to the complexity, many women of color feel as though the compromise or negotiation is just too high a price to pay to be called a feminist. Women of color's participation in women's studies and feminism still causes splintering in our identities.

Many women believe that there is a certain required persona to be a feminist. In the ethnic studies course "Women of Color in the U.S." at Berkeley, for example, students expressed feeling that they didn't have enough knowledge or background to be able to call themselves feminists. The students' comments reflect how many women of color find difficulty in accessing feminism. Often the response is that "feminism is a white woman's thing." Whiteness in feminism comes to represent privilege, power and opportunity. It rarely positions women of color as being as legitimate as the identities of white women. Women's studies has been accurately accused of treating race as a secondary oppression through offering courses about race that are separate from the central curriculum, while ethnic studies feels more comfortable as a place to discuss race and gender. But even in ethnic studies, women's experiences and histories still remain on the margins. Like women's studies, they too have had problems integrating gender into the analysis of race.

. . .

Although I am a self-proclaimed woman of color feminist, I struggle with being an "authentic" woman of color feminist. Even though I realize it is self-defeating, I worry that other women of color will look at my feminism and judge it as being socialized whiteness and an effect of adoption. The roots of my feminism are connected to my adopted mother, although I am uncertain whether she would identify as a feminist. She was a woman who wouldn't let us watch the *Flintstones* or the *Jetsons* because of their negative portrayal of women, yet she unquestionably had dinner on the table every night for her husband, sons and daughter. Most important, she raised me to believe I could be whoever I wanted to be and in that a strong woman. If feminism has been bestowed onto me from my adopted mother, then I choose not to look at it as another indicator of whiteness or of being whitewashed. Rather, I see it as a gift that has shown me not the limitations of mainstream feminism but the possibilities of women of color feminism. People sometimes question my attachment to feminism. Despite the criticisms, it has served as a compass that navigates me away from paralysis into limitless potential.

. . .

Women of color feminism has currently been reduced to a general abstraction that has flattened out difference and diversity, causing tension between women of color. Instead of collectively forming alliances against whiteness, women of color now challenge the opposing identities that exist under the umbrella term "women of color." It raises questions about entitlement and authenticity. It tries to suppress the heterogeneous composition of women of color feminism by trying to create a unifying term. Yet the differences of class, racialization and sexuality have arisen and persisted, challenging assumptions that all women of color are in solidarity with each other. We all come with backgrounds and histories that differ from one another and despite knowing this, we still maintain this ideal and creation of the authentic "women of color." The one that is the right class, the right race, the right sexuality. We must refuse being reduced to an abstraction. We must address the conflicts that have begun to fester paralysis instead of fostering change. But that also means that we need to revitalize women of color feminism so that those actions can begin to take place.

It is crucial to explore and expose the problems of women of color feminism, but we also need to be weary of what we are willing to sacrifice. I think a new, third space is being created in women of color feminism. Those of us who are not easily recognized and acknowledged as women of color are coming to feminism as a place to discuss the implications of invisibility. We are pushing, expanding and exploding ideologies of multiplicity

NEXT STEPS

and intersectionality. We come as transracial adoptees, women of mixed race, bisexuals, refugees and hundreds of other combinations. For us, women of color feminism continues to be a living theory and a way to survive.

74

Stop the False Race/Gender Divide

A Call to Action

Ann Russo and Melissa Spatz

Where do feminists stand on issues of race and racism? The 2007–2008 democratic primary struggle between Hillary Clinton and Barack Obama brought out significant divides among feminists around gender and race. A small constituency of feminists garnered national attention by arguing that sexism trumped racism and that gender, not race, was the most enduring inequality. They argued that feminists must support Hillary Clinton because she is a woman who faced misogyny in her presidential campaign. Mainstream media took these ideas as if they represented most feminists and used them to fan the flames of a race/gender divide, harkening back to the divisive politics around suffrage in the late 19th and early 20th century. In the summer of 2008, we wrote this statement addressed primarily to white progressive and feminist activists to refuse such divisive and racist rhetoric and commit to coalitional feminist politics.

WE REFUSE . . .

We refuse a feminism that assumes that "women" are a homogeneous group. Women identify along a spectrum of identities, and gender is not always the most prominent one. Multiple systems of oppression and privilege, including racism, white supremacy, class hierarchy, religious intolerance, xenophobia, anti-immigrant policies, heterosexism, ableism and ageism shape women's lives and experiences.

We refuse a feminism that pits sexism against racism, that claims that sexism is more entrenched than racism, and that the existence of sexism means that racism no longer exists. Sexism, racism, and other forms of oppression are interconnected. The misogynist spectacle against Hillary Clinton is tied to her white, middle-class heterosexuality, and differs from attacks on women who are not. We are dismayed that when media pundits frame Michelle Obama as an angry black woman, or as unpatriotic, or suggest that she should be the target of a "lynching party," there has been no similar outcry by white feminists.

We refuse a feminism that claims to speak for all women, while denying and minimizing the ongoing legacy of white supremacy and racism in this country. This legacy includes the ways that women's movements are embedded in white supremacist structures, ideas, and practices. We refuse to participate in organizations that demand allegiance to women

NEXT STEPS

without accountability for privilege and complicity in racism, class exploitation, homophobia, transphobia, imperialism, ableism, ageism, etc.

We refuse a feminism that marginalizes and undermines young women's voices and perspectives. We reject the adultism of older activists who dismiss the views of young women as naïve, unrealistic, sexist, and based in sexual fantasy. We reject the presumption that if younger women do not agree with older women, it is because they are less radical.

We refuse a feminism that mobilizes white folks by cultivating solidarity on the basis of whiteness. We reject any attempt to play divide and conquer by cultivating the racism of white middle class professional women and white working class women and men against people of color. We reject the reframing of racism as "racial resentment."

We refuse a feminism that blames people of color for focusing attention on racism as if that focus was the cause of sexism and misogyny. We refuse this zero sum game politics, and we refuse to undermine efforts to dismantle white supremacy in order to bolster attention to sexism. We reject attempts by some white feminists to silence people of color and to cultivate white racist bonding with claims of "reverse racism."

We refuse a feminism that confuses a campaign with a movement. We reject the idea that as feminists, we must agree on a candidate. We must engage all candidates around their positions on issues and use campaigns as opportunities to push candidates to address our issues and visions for social change.

AND WE COMMIT . . .

We commit to consistently challenge ourselves to be self-reflective. We do not claim to have all of the answers. We are firmly committed to building our awareness of, and accountability for, our own participation in systems of power and privilege.

We commit to critically engaging our communities about this historic moment in U.S. feminism and progressive politics. We will take an active role in creating community dialogues and town hall forums that re-center feminist and women's activism based in coalitional politics.

We commit to holding all politicians accountable for their politics, rather than their identities. We believe that identity does matter in terms of who is represented in the government, and yet, we believe that candidates must be evaluated based on their commitments and actions.

We commit to challenging misogyny, racism and other forms of oppression in media coverage. We will challenge all discourses that make women of color invisible, by assuming that gender = white women, and race = men of color. We will disrupt the media's promotion of divisions between gender-based and race-based agendas, between racial and ethnic groups, and between political movements.

We commit to speaking publicly against white supremacy as it operates in our movement and in the upcoming election. It is the responsibility of progressive white women and feminists to consistently dialogue, challenge, disrupt, and transform white supremacist thinking, ideas, and practices.

We commit to challenging feminist media activists and organizations to use an anti-oppression approach. We commit to look at interconnected forms of oppression in media coverage, and we challenge other activists to do the same. We call on NOW's "Media Hall of Shame" to include all forms of oppression shaping women's representations, including racism, white supremacy, heterosexism, ableism, classism, adultism, xenophobia.

We commit to creating intergenerational dialogues between women of all ages. Older women need to check adultism. It is important to learn from young women, particularly young women of color and those facing multiple oppressions, who do not enter the social justice movement with a race versus gender versus sexuality divide. All of us, old and young, must create intergenerational dialogues that honor our different knowledge, experiences, and frames of reference.

We commit to building a broad-based movement for social justice by working in solidarity across differences. We commit to being accountable for our own privilege and complicity in systems of oppression. This accountability is a necessary starting point to creating collaborations, coalitions, and alliances across identities and issues.

75

Grassroots

Introduction

Winona LaDuke

I have spent my entire adult life as what you might call a political activist. I have testified at hearings, demonstrated at countless protests, and been involved in litigation. I've worked in a number of Native communities across the continent, and founded the White Earth Land Recovery Project (WELRP) on my home reservation. With our work here, we've been able to recover more than seventeen hundred acres of our land and create a land trust, while we work toward recovery of more of our own birthright. We also continue to work to protect our wild rice from genetic modification and ecosystems from contamination by pesticides, and to stop clear cuts of the forest. From inside my own house, we roast fair-trade and organic coffee. I have written books about the environment, run for vice president twice (as Ralph Nader's Green Party running mate in 1996 and 2000), and been arrested because I don't think that a thousand-year-old tree should become a phone book.

The perception of me, or of any well-known activist, is probably far from reality. Activists, the thinking goes, must be organized, focused, always working on the next strategy. My real life, the one in which I conduct all of my activism, is, of course, messy. If you came over, you might find my five children, ages four to sixteen, three dogs, fifteen horses, a few cats, several interns from around the country, and many friends who double as coworkers helping with WELRP's work. The 2000 veep campaign was conducted with me breastfeeding my newborn son before and after each stump speech and during many an interview. I still coordinate the sustainable food projects central to the White Earth Land

NEXT STEPS

Recovery Project literally from my kitchen table at the same time as I figure out meals for my kids, take coffee orders for Muskrat coffee company, and pop in videos for my youngest to watch on TV. I talk to Native community leaders from across the country as I cook meals and clean up (sort of an endless job). I write books at the same table where I make rawhide ornaments for sale as part of WELRP and help with maple syruping in the spring season, and my house is filled with labels that spell out the Ojibwe words for "bed," "book," "cupboard," and "table" as part of my ongoing commitment to indigenous language and culture preservation. My activism is simply in my life—it has to be, or it couldn't get done.

My own life as an identified activist has made me wonder at the term itself. What separates simple "responsibility" in life—motherhood, for example—from the fine line that one crosses to become an "activist"? I have been surprised and moved by encountering so many other mothers in my years as an activist: mothers in Chiapas breastfeeding their babies like anyone else, but who mask their faces as they speak with me because they can't afford to have their identifies known; Mohawk and Ojibwe mothers who face down General Motors and Potlach Corporation, knowing that if they don't, their kids won't ever know clean water, and generations ahead will have contaminated breast milk.

I have developed longstanding friendships with women who are engaged in struggles of responsibility—for their land, their own community health, and the water their children drink. Are these women feminists? That depends on who defines the term. Many of these women, including myself, are committed to the process of self-determination and believe in our inherent rights, as bestowed by the Creator, to live with dignity, peace, clean air and water, and our duty to pass on this legacy to our children and the generations to follow.

At the United Nations Conference on the Status of Women in Beijing, China, in 1995, I asked women from small countries around the world why they came all this way to participate in what was, in essence, a meeting. "I came because the World Bank is here," explained Victoria Tauli-Corpuz, an Igarok woman from the Philippines whose village is targeted for a Word Bank-funded dam. "I believe that those people at the World Bank and the IMF, those who make the decisions which will transform my life, should see my face." That sentiment applies whether you are an Igarok woman from the Philippines or Sherry Honkala from the Kensington Welfare Rights Union, challenging federal budget cuts to aid for dependent families or tending to the needs of homeless families. The message of self-determining women is the same for all people: *We want control over our lives, and we will challenge those who impose laws on our bodies, our communities, and our future.*

I believe that women move to activism out of sheer necessity. As a group, we are not of privilege—budget cuts devastated our household, the military wreaks havoc on our bodies and our homelands. The National Priorities Project reports that $152.6 billion spent on military aid in 2003 could have provided Head Start for an additional 20,211,205 children, health coverage for an additional 89,780,249 children, affordable housing vouchers for an additional 22,894,974 families, or salaries for 2,673,864 new elementary school teachers. Feminist activism, then, doesn't begin or end with my uterus: this is about my whole body, my life, and the lives of my children. We are women who redefine "Women's Issues," and say all issues are women's issues. I say: *We are the mothers of our nations, and anything that concerns our nations is of concern to us as women.* Those choices and necessities move us to speak out and to be active.

I happen to come from a line of these women who speak out, and I continue this work—our work. Women's work. My grandmother Helen Peskin, a Jewish woman from the Ukraine, recently passed into the Spirit World. Her early years were formed by the reality of war, first the Cossacks who overran her village and then the Nazis. With her life came a sheer determination to not be a victim, to speak for peace, to make a better life, and to demand dignity. Of her ninety years on this earth a good forty were spent as

a seamstress: a purse maker, a member of the Pocket Book Makers Union in the garment district in New York, a folk dancer, and a peace activist. *A woman's work is about economic justice, and about quality of life.* My mother, Betty LaDuke, made her own path as a muralist and art professor, one of the first women on the faculty of her college, and like other women, she had to do it better than any man around because it took that much to get recognized. She has done this work in a way that celebrates life, and celebrates the work of other women. And she has done this work by linking with women in Eritrea, Nigeria, and Peru. *A women's work is about creating and celebrating life.* Our parents' struggles become our own, in our own time. We can't escape from that history, nor can we escape from our time in it.

In the lives of women in my family, it was never about just our own selves, it was about the collective dignity and *everyone's* health and rights. This is counter, in many ways, to Americanism. Americanism teaches individualism. My family, and indeed movements for social transformation, are not about anything as limited as the better job or the better advantage for the individual woman. Even the tragic deaths of three of my closest friends, activists all, are lessons in the urgency of change on a broader scale. Marsha Gomez, a gifted artist, was killed by her own son, who lacked the psychiatric medical attention he so desperately needed; Nilak Butler passed from ovarian cancer because she did not have adequate health coverage; and Ingrid Washinawatok El-Issa was assassinated by the FARC, Revolutionary Armed Forces of Colombia, with a gun and a bullet that came from my tax dollars in the second most highly financed recipient of U.S. military aid in the world.

The compelling reason behind activism is that our most personal lives—even the intimacy of death—are actually embroidered in the reality of public policy, foreign policy, military aid, and economics. Each day, then, I, like the women in my family before me, and like so many other women in the world, recommit to continue this struggle for life, and to celebrate its beauty in the process. That struggle and that celebration are who we are as women, as we take responsibility for our destinies.

. . .

76

Unbowed

A Memoir

Wangari Maathai

On the morning of October 8, 2004, I was on my way from Nairobi to my parliamentary constituency, Tetu, for a meeting when my cell phone rang. I moved closer to the window of the van I was traveling in so I could hear better amid the static and the bumps on the road. It was the Norwegian ambassador, asking me to keep the line clear for a phone call from Oslo. After some time, it came. It was Ole Danbolt Mjos, chair of the Norwegian Nobel Committee. His gentle voice came through clearly. "Is this Wangari Maathai?" he inquired.

N
E
X
T

S
T
E
P
S

While I receive calls from all over the world, I may not catch the name of the caller or recognize their voice until the reason for the call has been explained. So I paid attention to the caller for the message. "Yes," I said drawing the phone closer to my ear. He gave me the news. It left me speechless.

. . .

It was clear now why the Norwegian ambassador had called. "I am being informed that I have won the Nobel Peace Prize," I announced to myself and those around me in the car with a smile as I pulled the cell phone away from my ear and reconnected with my fellow passengers. They knew it was not a joke because happiness was written all over my face. But at the same time, tears streamed from my eyes and onto my cheeks as I turned to them. They, too, were by now smiling broadly, some cheering loudly and hugging me as if to both comfort and congratulate me, letting my tears fall on their warm shoulders and hiding my face from some of my staff, whom they felt shouldn't see me cry. But these were tears of great joy at an extraordinary moment!

I thought of the long journey to this time and place. My mind went back and forth over all the difficult years and great effort when I often felt I was involved in a lonely, futile struggle. I didn't know that so many people were listening and that such a moment would come. Meanwhile, the car rambled on to Nyeri's Outspan Hotel, where I often take a break before continuing to my rural Tetu constituency.

. . .

The news spread quickly throughout the hotel and among the guests. The manager and his senior staff were quick to come out to congratulate me. Then the enterprising manager responded to a request to provide a tree seedling and a shovel so that I could celebrate the best way I know how: by planting a tree.

A member of the hotel staff quickly dug a hole as a small crowd of onlookers and journalists gathered to witness and record the planting of a Nandi flame tree. Surrounded by the local and international press, the hotel guests, and workers, I prepared to plant this hardy tree seedling along the edge of the green yard, overlooking the imposing Mt. Kenya to the distant north. I kneeled down, put my hands in the red soil, warm from the sun, settled the tree seedling in the ground. They handed me a bucket of clean water and I watered the tree.

I faced Mt. Kenya, the source of inspiration for me throughout my life, as well as for generations of people before me. I reflected on how appropriate it was that I should be at this place at this time and celebrating the historic news facing this mountain. The mountain is known to be rather shy, the summit often cloaked by a veil of clouds. It was hidden that day. Although around me the sun was bright and strong, the mountain was hiding. As I searched for her with my eyes and heart, I recalled the many times I have worried whether she will survive the harm we are doing to her. As I continued to search for her, I believed that the mountain was celebrating with me: The Nobel Committee had also heard the voice of nature, and in a very special way. As I gazed at her, I felt that the mountain too was probably weeping with joy, and hiding her tears behind a veil of white clouds. At that moment I felt I stood on sacred ground.

Trees have been an essential part of my life and have provided me with many lessons. Trees are living symbols of peace and hope. A tree has roots in the soil yet reaches to the sky. It tells us that in order to aspire we need to be grounded, and that no matter how high we go it is from our roots that we draw sustenance. It is a reminder to all of us who have had success that we cannot forget where we came from. It signifies that no matter how powerful we become in government or how many awards we receive, our power and strength and our ability to reach our goals depend on the people, those whose work remains unseen, who are the soil out of which we grow, the shoulders on which we stand.

The Nobel Peace Prize has presented me with extraordinary opportunities to travel, both home and abroad . . . to celebrate, encourage, and empower the huge constituency that felt honored by the prize: the environmental movement, those who work on women's and gender issues, human rights advocates, those advocating for good governance, and peace movements. There continues to be lot of interest among government leaders, academic institutions, development agencies, the corporate sector, and the media.

This interest was partly due to the connection the Norwegian Nobel Committee made between peace, sustainable management of resources, and good governance. This was the first time such a linkage had been forged by the Nobel Committee and it was the first time that the committee had decided to recognize its importance by awarding the Nobel Peace Prize to somebody who had worked in these areas for over three decades. As we had said for many years, humanity needs to rethink peace and security and work toward cultures of peace by governing itself more democratically, respecting the rule of law and human rights, deliberately and consciously promoting justice and equity, and managing resources more responsibly and accountably—not only for the present but also for the future generations.

In trying to explain this linkage, I was inspired by a traditional African stool that has three legs and a basin to sit on. To me, the three legs represent three critical pillars of just and stable societies. The first leg stands for democratic space, where rights are respected, whether they are human rights, women's rights, children's rights, or environmental rights. The second represents sustainable and equitable management of resources. And the third stands for cultures of peace that are deliberately cultivated within communities and nations. The basin, or seat, represents society and its prospects for development. Unless all three legs are in place, supporting the seat, no society can thrive. Neither can its citizens develop their skills and creativity. When one leg is missing, the seat is unstable; when two legs are missing, it is impossible to keep any state alive; and when no legs are available, the state is as good as a failed state. No development can take place in such a state either. Instead, conflict ensues.

These issues of good governance, respect for human rights, equity, and peace are of particular concern in Africa—a continent that is so rich in resources and yet has been so ravaged by war. The big question is, Who will access the resources? Who will be excluded? Can the minority have a say, even if the majority have their way?

. . .

As women and men continue this work of clothing this naked Earth, we are in the company of many others throughout the world who care deeply for this blue planet. We have nowhere else to go. Those of us who witness the degraded state of the environment and the suffering that comes with it cannot afford to be complacent. We continue to be restless. If we really carry the burden, we are driven to action. We cannot tire or give up. We owe it to the present and future generations of all species to rise up and walk!

N
E
X
T

S
T
E
P
S

See Chapter 9 in *Teaching for Diversity and Social Justice* for corresponding teaching materials.

SECTION 6

HETEROSEXISM

Introduction

Warren J. Blumenfeld

Oppression directed against all females, lesbians, gay males, bisexuals, pansexuals,[1] asexuals,[2] transgender people, and intersexuals[3] goes by many names and has a number of subdivisions and definitions. What connects them is the socially constructed and socially enforced binary systems that divide people along strictly demarcated boundaries and borders into either/or categories related to societal norms of self-presentation. The socially constructed notions of "sex," "gender," and "sexuality" are organized and maintained upon oppositional binary frames with their attendant meanings, social roles, values, stereotypes, and behavioral and attitudinal imperatives, expressions, and expectations. These features serve to maintain power and privilege for those who accord with these norms, while marginalizing and disempowering groups and individuals who violate them. This structure is established and enforced on the societal, institutional, and individual/interpersonal levels (Hardiman and Jackson, 1997). The most extreme and overt forms of oppression are directed against those who most challenge, confound, or contest these binary frames.

This section should be read in the context of the preceding section on sexism and the following section on transgender oppression. These three sections, taken together, present a comprehensive view of the ways in which societal privileges and disadvantages follow socially constructed understandings of the roles and expressions that attach to sex, gender, and sexuality. This section's website provides further resources to explore and understand these three interrelated yet distinctive components of sex, gender, and sexuality.

HETEROSEXISM DEFINED

I define *heterosexism* as the overarching system of advantages bestowed on heterosexuals based on the institutionalization of heterosexual norms or standards and founded on the ideology that all people are or should be heterosexual, which privileges heterosexuals and heterosexuality, while excluding the needs, concerns, cultures, and life experiences of lesbians, gay males, bisexuals, pansexuals, and asexuals. We live in a paradoxical society in which loving sameness makes

you different while loving difference makes you the same. Often overt, though at times subtle, heterosexism is oppression by neglect, omission, erasure, and distortion. A related concept is *heteronormativity* (Warner, 1991) and *compulsory heterosexuality* (Rich, 1986), which emphasize the normalization and privileging of heterosexuality on the personal/interpersonal, institutional, and societal levels.

Examples of heterosexism include parents who automatically expect their children to marry a person of another sex; media portrayals of only heterosexuals in positive and satisfying relationships; teachers presuming that all of their students and their students' parents are heterosexual, and teaching only about the contributions of heterosexuals. Heterosexism also takes the form of pity toward lesbians, gay males, bisexuals, pansexuals, and asexuals as unfortunate human beings who "can't help being the way they are."

Heterosexism's more active and at times visible component, called *homophobia*, is oppression by intent, purpose, and design. Derived from the Greek terms *homos*, meaning "same," and *phobikos*, meaning "having a fear of and/or an aversion toward," *homophobia* was coined by George Weinberg (1972). Other terms include: *homosexphobia*, *homonegativism*, *lesbian-* and *gay-hatred* or *-hating*. *Homophobia* refers to the fear and hatred of those who love and are attracted affectionally, emotionally, romantically, and sexually to some members of the same sex. Homophobia includes prejudice, discrimination, harassment, and acts of violence brought on by that fear and hatred. Other related concepts include *lesbophobia* or *lesbiphobia*, which can be defined as the fear, hatred, discrimination, and acts of violence stemming from this fear and hatred against women who love women, and *biphobia*, which is fear, hatred, and oppression directed against bisexuals and pansexuals: people who reject the sex/gender binary, and who find that gender and sex are irrelevant in influencing whether they will be sexually, emotionally, and romantically attracted to others—therefore, they are attracted to people regardless of their gender and sex.

Heterosexism is a more inclusive and expansive term than terms based on a "phobia" meaning a fear that is "irrational" or "unreasonable." This section takes the view that some fears and hatreds (and forms of prejudice) are *taught* as a normalized process of socialization and thus exist within the realm of *learned* responses. Therefore, for purposes of discussion throughout this book and this section, though we sometimes use the terms "homophobia" and "biphobia," we are also employing the term "heterosexism" in its expanded and inclusive form.

OPPRESSION AND LIBERATION FRAMEWORKS

The histories of homosexuality, bisexuality, and gender non-conformity are filled with incredible pain and enormous pride, of overwhelming repression and victorious rejoicing, of stifling invisibility and dazzling illumination. Throughout the ages, dominant groups have labeled minoritized sexual and gender people using many terms: from "sinners," "sick," and "criminal," to having a "preference," "orientation," "identity," and even being given "a gift from God." Though same-sex attraction and sexuality and gender non-conformity has probably always existed in human and most non-human species, the concept of "homosexuality," "bisexuality," "transgenderism," "heterosexuality," and "gender conformity," in fact, sexual and gender identities in general and the construction of identities and sense of community based on these identities is a relatively modern concept. It is only within the last 160 or so years that there has been an organized and sustained political effort to protect the rights of people with same-sex and both-sex attractions, and those who cross traditional constructions of gender identities and expression.

RELIGIOUS ENDORSEMENTS FOR HETEROSEXUALITY

Many people cite religious texts to support the social norms of heterosexuality, even though there is no monolithic theological endorsement for heterosexuality, and even though these religious texts contain many internal contradictions. Instead, religious scholars and various faith traditions and denominations within those traditions interpret religious textual passages related to same-sex sexuality, same-sex relationships, and transgressive expressions of gender very differently (see section website for further resources on this issue).

Though many religious denominations throughout the years have worked vigorously to end oppression toward a number of groups, including those who transgress heterosexual norms, religious textual passages have been referenced throughout the ages to justify and rationalize the practices that marginalize, harass, deny rights, persecute, oppress, and even kill entire groups of people based on non-conforming sexual, gender, and other social identities. During various historical periods, people within different faith traditions have applied specific religious texts to establish and maintain hierarchical positions of power, domination, and privilege over individuals and groups targeted by these texts. For example, individuals, organizations, and entire nations have quoted specific textual passages to justify the construction and maintenance of the institution of slavery, the persecution and murder of Jews, male domination over and denial of rights of women, adult domination and persecution of young people, and demonization, marginalization, denial of rights, and extreme forms of oppression against minoritized sexualities and gender non-conformity, considering them anywhere from being creations of the Devil, to sinners and immoral, to being the embodiment of evil in the world, which, left unchecked, would result in the destruction of peoples and nations.

History has shown a symbiotic relationship between religious teachings concerning homosexuality, bisexuality, and gender non-conformity, and the secular, legal, and political policies against homosexuality, bisexuality, and gender non-conformity. Religious, philosophical, social, and political attitudes set the groundwork for restrictive laws enacted toward the latter stages of imperial Roman civilization; Roman law was used as a basis for Medieval Canon Law (the law of the Catholic Church); Canon Law along with Roman law has been used as the cornerstone for punitive civil laws of the nineteenth and twentieth centuries and into the present day. Laws doling out punishments, such as denial of marriage and child custody benefits, restrictions on engaging in military service, constraints in gaining employment, housing, insurance, health benefits, and public accommodations, flogging, banishment, bodily mutilation, incarceration, and death of the accused have existed at various times in most countries. When we come to the contemporary United States, we must ask whether a society, founded on the guiding principle of the separation of religion and government, has the right to formulate and pass legislation based on religious tenets, which are not accepted by all—a question of great significance given the continuing religious sanctions supporting heterosexuality.

"MEDICAL MODEL" SUPPORTS FOR HETEROSEXUALITY

One important rationale for heterosexuality and gender conformity is based upon the biological and psychological pathologizing of sexual and gender transgressive people. From the so-called "Eugenics Movement" of the mid-nineteenth century through the twentieth century CE and beyond, medical and psychological professions have often proposed and addressed, in starkly medical language, the alleged "deficiencies" of, for example, gay, lesbian, bisexual, and transgender people, as well as peoples of color, people who are differently-abled, youth, and elders.

Some members of the scientific community view people attracted to their own sex and to both males and females as constituting distinct biological or "racial" types—those who could be distinguished from "normal" people through anatomical markers. Rather than considering homosexuality and bisexuality merely as emotional and physical attractions along a broad spectrum of emotional and sexual possibilities, some sectors of the medical and psychological communities employ terms to continue to pathologize people with same-sex and both-sex attractions, and those who cross traditional constructions of gender identities and expression. This has resulted in lesbians, gay males, bisexuals, and those who transgress normative gender expression (often against their will) being hospitalized, committed to mental institutions, jailed, lobotomized, electroshocked, castrated, sterilized, and undergoing "aversion therapy," "reparative therapy," "Christian counseling," and genetic counseling.

By deploying the "medical model" to investigate and pathologize the "other," heteronormativity is perceived as unremarkable or "normal," an unquestioned, hegemonic norm against which all others are judged. Heterosexual norms justify and explain away the otherwise unacceptable persecution and oppression of non-conforming sexual identity groups, while avoiding addressing issues of domination, privilege, subordination, and marginalization. This "medicalization" of homosexuality and bisexuality only serves to strengthen oppression and heterosexual privilege through its relative invisibility. Given this invisibility, issues of oppression and privilege are neither analyzed nor scrutinized, neither interrogated nor confronted.

We take the position that any problems with homosexuality and bisexuality are not with the sexual identity per se, not with who we are, but rather with the ways we are socially constructed and treated. Rather than projecting ourselves through the "medical model" as deficient, defective, diseased, disabled, criminal, inadequate, immature, functionally limited, troubled, many of us chose to project homosexuality and bisexuality though the "wellness model." This approach fosters a positive social identity with a strong sense of culture and community, and envisions lesbian, gay, and bisexual experiences as those of differences in the spectrum of human intimacy, relationships, emotions, and sexuality, and differences to be supported, cherished, and nurtured.

SOCIAL JUSTICE MODEL OF LIBERATION

Since the early to mid-nineteenth century CE, a linear history of homosexuality and bisexuality, predominately in the West, begins with the formation of a homosexual "identity" and a sense of community brought about by the growth of industrialization, competitive capitalism and wage labor, and the rise of modern science, which provided people with more social and personal options outside the home (D'Emilio, 1983). Since then, many individuals and organizations have rejected the medical and religious rationales of homosexuality and bisexuality, while embracing a social justice model, which investigates and attempts to address the ways in which social structures promote and maintain issues of domination and subordination.

A brief chronology of the movements toward societal liberation in this arena follows. Throughout this history, young people have been on the front lines serving as energetic and inspirational pioneering change agents and integral to the development and success of progressive movement for social justice. The "Homosexual Emancipation Movement" began in Germany in the 1860s when Karl Heinrich Ulrichs, a lawyer from Hanover, wrote on the topic of same-sex love. Karoly Maria Benkert (also known as Karl Maria Kertbeny) coined the terms "homosexual" and "heterosexual" in 1869 in an attempt to convince the religious, legal, and scientific communities that same-sex attractions, though not the norm, were widespread and therefore should not be legally penalized. Literary tradition in England in the nineteenth century CE celebrated same-sex relationships. The

first homosexual rights group in the United States, formed in 1924 in Chicago, was called the Society for Human Rights. It was founded by Henry Gerber, a German U.S.-American who had been influenced by the emancipation movement in Germany. The "Homophile Movement" in the United States began with such groups as the Mattachine Society and Daughters of Bilitis (see section website for resources describing this history). Many historians and activists place the beginning of the modern movement for lesbian, gay, bisexual, and transgender equality at the Stonewall Inn, a small bar frequented by young people including trans people, lesbians, bisexuals, gay males, street people, students, and others, located in New York City's Greenwich Village. In the early morning of June 28, 1969, when New York City police officers conducted a routine raid on the bar, the occupants fought back with bottles, rocks, bricks, trash cans, and parking meters used as battering rams.

In reality, even before these historic events at the Stonewall Inn, a little-known action preceded the Stonewall Inn demonstrations by nearly three years, and should more likely be considered as the founding event for the modern LGBT movement. In August 1966, at Gene Compton's Cafeteria, in what is known as the Tenderloin District in San Francisco, trans people and gay sex workers joined in fighting police harassment and oppression. Police, conducting one of their numerous raids, entered Compton's and began physically harassing the clientele. This time, however, people fought back by hurling coffee at the officers and heaving cups, dishes, and trays around the cafeteria. Police retreated outside as customers smashed windows. Over the course of the next night, people gathered to picket the cafeteria, which refused to allow trans people back inside.

Out of the actions at Gene Compton's Cafeteria and the Stonewall Inn, people, primarily young, formed a number of groups, for example, the Gay Liberation Front, Gay Activists Alliance, Radicalesbians, and others. The Christopher Street Liberation Day Umbrella Committee formed in New York City to plan activities and a march on Sunday, June 28, 1970, up Sixth Avenue. From that first march grew others throughout the world. June each year is now reserved for local "Gay, Lesbian, Bisexual, and Transgender Pride" events.

Bisexuals, who had since the beginning been alongside gay, lesbian, and transgender activists, began to organize for the rights of bisexuals in the mid to late 1970s. For a number of reasons, neither the gay and lesbian rights movements nor mainstream political movements initially responded to the needs of bisexuals. At first, bisexual women organized themselves in same-sex groups for support and consciousness-raising; bisexual men later followed this example.

By 1972, parents and friends were organizing support groups for themselves and their loved ones. Today, a national network of local chapters of the organization Parents, Families, and Friends of Lesbians and Gays (or P-FLAG) offers support and is on the front lines in helping to defeat heterosexism.

Founded to fight governmental and societal inaction, in 1986, the intergenerational direct-action group ACT UP (AIDS Coalition to Unleash Power) formed in New York City. A network of local chapters quickly grew in over 120 cities throughout the world under the theme "Silence = Death" beneath an inverted pink triangle. In addition, the youth-oriented group Queer Nation formed in 1990 with independent chapters soon appearing in local communities around the country. Chanting, "We're here. We're queer. We're fabulous. Get used to it," Queer Nation members stressed "queer visibility" and an end to heterosexual privilege and heterosexism.

And on the cutting edge in the movement for equality and pride are transgender people who are coming out of another closet in large numbers, and are making the links in our understanding of transgender oppression (also referred to as cissexism, genderism, or binarism), heterosexism, and sexism (see Section 7). Young people are "coming out of the closet" with pride earlier than ever before, and organizing school and community-based groups (such as Gay/Straight Alliances) in middle schools and high schools, colleges, and communities throughout the country and the world. A growing number of LGBT people are raising children, proving that love is

what it takes to make a family. Some activists are pushing for the right for same-sex couples to marry on a state and on a national level, while others successfully defeated the ban, the so-called "Don't Ask, Don't Tell" policy, which until 2011 prevented LGBT[4] service members from serving openly in the U.S. military. Others are working tirelessly to eliminate the harassment, bullying, and violence directed against anyone who appears "different" that continue to plague our schools and society, and to end the bullying- and larger societal-related suicides, which harms and literally kills so many each year.

Originally meaning "different" or "outside the norm," the term "queer" has often been used as a derogatory term. Some lesbian, gay, bisexual, and transgender people, however, have turned the term around by using it in an inclusive way and as a term of empowerment. First, young people adopted the term as a non-label to deconstruct sexual and gender categories as a form of resistance. It is used now at times to denote a person who is not heterosexual or not gender-normative. Following the lead of young people, what has come to be referred to as "Queer Theory" and "Queer Studies," with such notable writers as Michel Foucault, Judith Butler, and Eve Kosovsky Sedgwick, among many others, is now having enormous impact on college and university campuses as a bona fide academic discipline (see website for further resources).

READING SELECTIONS IN THIS SECTION

This section begins with a number of essays conveying key historical and social contexts of heterosexism. Warren J. Blumenfeld's "How Homophobia Hurts Everyone" (selection 77) provides a conceptual framework by discussing what homophobia is and how it affects everyone regardless of their actual or perceived sexual identity. "The InterSEXion: A Vision for a Queer Progressive Agenda" (selection 78), by Deepali Gokhale, cuts to the core of heterosexism by looking at the economic systems that support oppression. Devon W. Carbado's essay, "Privilege" (selection 79), provides an expanded and nuanced investigation of the concept of dominant group privilege. Pat Griffin, in "Sport: Where Men Are Men and Women Are Trespassers" (selection 80), addresses issues of heterosexism and, specifically, anti-female oppression in organized sports.

To begin the Voices part, in "Real Men and Pink Suits" (selection 81), Charles M. Blow uses recent public violence-inspiring statements from media commentators as a "teachable moment" to advance the dialogue in challenging the notion of a narrowly defined definition of "masculinity." Anna Quindlen's "The Loving Decision" (selection 82) connects the cause for the legalization of marriage for same-sex couples with past battles for interracial marriage. Daniel E. Solís y Martínez, in "*Mestiza/o* Gender: Notes towards a Transformative Masculinity" (selection 83), crosses cultural, gender, and sexuality borders to negotiate a personal vision of identity.

In the Next Steps part, Nancy J. Evans and Jaime Washington, in "Becoming An Ally: A New Examination" (selection 84), provide both a theoretical and practical foundation on the ways in which heterosexually identified people can become allies to lesbian, gay, bisexual, and transgender people. President Barack Obama took a historic move on May 9, 2012 in an interview with ABC TV "Good Morning America" host, Robin Roberts, when he "came out" for marriage equality asserting that "Same-sex couples should be able to get married." Prior to his announcement, Secretary of State Hillary Clinton gave a moving and historic address to the United Nations in Geneva, Switzerland, December 2011 on International Human Rights Day, in which she declared that LGBT rights are human rights. We conclude the "Heterosexism" section with her stirring speech (selection 85).

This section represents heterosexism from multiple perspectives, emphasizing the more overt forms of this type of oppression. Other selections that convey the joyful and day-to-day lived experiences and illustrate the diverse and multifaceted historical and cultural aspects of LGB people appear among the Further Resources section on the heterosexism section website.

See Companion Website for Additional Resources and Material

Notes

1 People who reject the sex/gender binary, and who find that gender and sex are irrelevant in influencing whether they will be sexually, emotionally, and romantically attracted to others. Therefore, they are attracted to people regardless of their gender and sex.
2 Also referred to as "non-sexuality," comprising approximately 1 percent of the population, includes people who are not attracted to other people or are not interested in sex. This definition differs from people who may be sexually attracted to others but choose not to engage in sexuality, and choose to be celibate.
3 A percentage of the population (approximately 1 in 4,000) is born with male and female sexual organs to various degrees, or indeterminate genitalia. They are neither male nor female, but, rather, comprise another birth sex. So, in actuality, there are more than two sexes.
4 Though the military still restricts trans people from participating in the military.

References

D'Emilio, J. (1983). Capitalism and gay identity. In A. Snitow, C. Stansell, S. Thompson (eds), *Powers of Desire: The Politics of Sexuality* (pp. 100–113). New York: Monthly Review Press.

Hardiman, R., Jackson, B. (1997). Conceptual foundations for social justice courses. In M. Adams, L. A. Bell, P. Griffin (eds), *Teaching for Diversity and Social Justice* (pp. 16–29). New York: Routledge.

Rich, A. C. (1986). Compulsory heterosexuality and lesbian existence. In *Blood, Bread, and Poetry: Selected Prose, 1979–1985*. New York: Norton.

Warner, M. (1991). Introduction: Fear of a queer planet. *Social Text* 9 (4 [29]), 3–17.

Weinberg, G. (1972). *Society and the Healthy Homosexual*. New York: St. Martin's Press.

77

How Homophobia Hurts Everyone

Warren J. Blumenfeld

It is often said that, in the midst of misfortune, something unexpectedly valuable arises, and this has indeed been my experience. While traveling alone through Scandinavia one summer, I began to lose the vision in both my eyes. When I reached Denmark. I went to a hospital for an evaluation, and, after a number of tests, a physician notified me that my retinas had detached, probably because of a congenital defect. She advised immediate surgery to prevent further deterioration, and I was admitted to the Community Hospital in Copenhagen.

The next day, my sister, Susan, flew to Copenhagen to be with me for what turned out to be nearly two months.

That summer in this distant northern land, fearing the permanent loss of my vision, I lay in a narrow hospital bed longing for friends and relatives back home. But as Susan sat with me day after day, giving her love, her courage, her humor (and spectacular Danish pastries), something remarkable happened. Amid the bells of a distant church tolling away the passing hours, Susan and I genuinely got to know one another for the first time.

Although we inhabited the same house for over seventeen years, there was always some unspoken tension between us, some wall keeping us apart. Having only eighteen months separating us in age, we attended the same schools and had similar peer groups. For the first few years of our lives, we seemed to get along fine. We had a few friends in common, and we usually found time to play together most days. Our closeness, however, was soon to come to an end.

By the time I reached the age of seven or eight, I was increasingly becoming the target of harassment and attack by my peers, who perceived me as someone who was different. Names like *queer, sissy, little girl*, and *fag* were thrown at me like the large red ball the children hurled on the school yard in dodge ball games. During subsequent years, the situation only got worse. I tried to avoid other children and increasingly kept to myself. Susan and I grew apart. Only when we were both in our early twenties, about the time I went to Denmark, were we beginning to rediscover one another and to share the details of our lives.

While in college, I began to sort out how I had suffered as a gay male under the force of homophobia, but until my hospitalization I had very little idea how it had also affected Susan growing up as my heterosexually oriented younger sister. Smart, attractive, outgoing, she appeared to have, at least from my vantage point, plenty of friends and seemed to fit in. In Denmark, however, she confided to me that, throughout our school years, she was continually teased for having a "faggot" brother. On one occasion, she recalled some of the older boys laughing at her, asking if she were "like her brother." When she witnessed other students harassing me, peer pressure, coupled with her own fear of becoming a target, compelled her to distance herself from me by adding her voice to the chorus of insults. I felt betrayed, and at the time despised her for it.

Our time together in my hospital room permitted us the needed chance to define the basis of our past estrangement. Through the tears, the apologies, the rage at having been raised in an oppressive environment, and the regrets over losing so much precious time, we began the process of healing our relationship. As it turned out, my vision was not the only thing restored to me that summer.

This essay represents the growth of a seed planted in my mind back in Denmark. It centers around one primary premise: within each of the numerous forms of oppression, members of the target group (sometimes called "minority") are oppressed while on some level members of the dominant or agent group are hurt. Although the effects of oppression differ qualitatively for specific target and agent groups, in the end everyone loses.

Most of us hold simultaneous membership in a number of groups based, for example, on our personal and physical characteristics, on our abilities and class backgrounds, and on our cultural, racial, or religious identifications. We may find ourselves both in groups targeted for oppression and in those dominant groups granted relatively higher degrees of power and prestige. By examining how we are disadvantaged as well as looking at the privileges we have, we can develop empathy for individuals different from ourselves and create a basis for alliances.

This essay, therefore, is really about alliances: support for the maintenance and strengthening of alliances where they currently exist and assistance in forging new ones where none has existed before—specifically, alliances between and among lesbians, gay males, bisexuals, transgender people, and heterosexuals.

HOW ARE LGBT PEOPLE OPPRESSED BY HOMOPHOBIA?

Lesbians, gay males, bisexuals, and transgender (LGBT) people are among the most despised groups in the United States today. Perhaps paradoxically, for many in our society,

love of sameness (i.e., *homo*-sexuality) makes people different, whereas love of difference (i.e., *hetero*-sexuality) makes people the same.

Much has been written about the ways homophobia in many Western cultures targets LGBT people, ranging from negative beliefs about these groups (which may or may not be expressed), to exclusion, denial of civil and legal protections, and, in some cases, overt acts of violence. Negative attitudes internalized by members of these groups often damage the spirit and stifle emotional growth.

Homophobia operates on four distinct but interrelated levels: the *personal*, the *interpersonal*, the *institutional*, and the *cultural* (also called the collective or societal).

Personal homophobia refers to a personal belief system (a prejudice) that LGBT people either deserve to be pitied as unfortunate beings who are powerless to control their desires or should be hated, that they are psychologically disturbed, genetically defective, unfortunate misfits, that their existence contradicts the "laws" of nature, that they are spiritually immoral, infected pariahs, disgusting—to put it quite simply, that they are generally inferior to heterosexuals.

Interpersonal homophobia is manifest when a personal bias or prejudice affects relations among individuals, transforming prejudice into its active component—discrimination. Examples of interpersonal homophobia are name calling or "joke" telling intended to insult or defame individuals or groups; verbal and physical harassment and intimidation as well as more extreme forms of violence; the withholding of support, rejection, or abandonment by friends and other peers, coworkers, and family members; refusal of landlords to rent apartments, shop owners to provide services, insurance companies to extend coverage, and employers to hire on the basis of actual or perceived sexual identity. And the list goes on.

A study by the National Gay and Lesbian Task Force (NGLTF) found that more than 90 percent of the respondents had experienced some form of victimization based on their sexual identity and that over 33 percent had been threatened directly with violence. Approximately one-third of the respondents were assaulted verbally, while more than one in fifteen were physically abused by members of their own families.

Reports of violence directed against lesbians, gay males, bisexuals, and transgender people have increased each year since the NGLTF has been keeping records, and such incidents are only the tip of the iceberg. By no means are they isolated to certain locales; rather, they are widespread, occurring throughout the country.

In 2009, the United States Congress passed the Matthew Shepard and James Byrd Jr. Hate Crimes Prevention Act, which for the first time made it a federal crime to assault or attack a person based on sexual orientation or gender identity.

Institutional homophobia refers to the ways in which governments, businesses, and educational, religious, and professional organizations systematically discriminate on the basis of sexual identity. Sometimes laws, codes, or policies actually enforce such discrimination. Few institutions have policies supportive of LGBT people, and many actively work against not only those groups but also heterosexuals who support them.

Consider, for example, the "Briggs" Initiative in the late 1970s: had it passed, it would have required the dismissal of California teachers who support gay, lesbian, and bisexual rights regardless of those teachers' actual sexual identification. The U.S. military had a long-standing policy excluding lesbians, gays, and bisexuals from service. In most instances, rights gained through marriage, including spousal benefits and child custody considerations, do not extend to LGBT people. Homosexual acts were outlawed in a number of states until 2003. And although a number of municipalities and some states have extended equal protection in the areas of employment, housing, insurance, credit, and public accommodations, no such statute exists on the national level.

Although agreement concerning same-sex relationships and sexuality does not exist across the various religious communities, and while some denominations are rethinking

their negative stands on homosexuality and bisexuality, others preach against such behaviors, and as a matter of policy exclude people from many aspects of religious life simply on the basis of sexual identity.

Until 1973, established psychiatric associations considered homosexuality a disordered condition. People were often institutionalized against their will, made to undergo dangerous and humiliating "aversion therapy," and even, at times, lobotomized to alter their sexual desires. Same-sex partners and friends are often still denied access to loved ones in hospital intensive-care units because of hospital policy allowing only blood relatives or a legal spouse visitation rights.

Today, although a number of practitioners within both the psychiatric and the medical professions hold genuinely enlightened attitudes regarding the realities of homosexuality, bisexuality, and transgenderism, some, unfortunately, remain entrenched in their negative perceptions of same-sex attractions and gender expression, and these perceptions often affect the manner in which they respond to their clients.

Cultural homophobia (sometimes called *collective* or *societal* homophobia) refers to the social norms or codes of behavior that, although not expressly written into law or policy, nonetheless work within a society to legitimize oppression. It results in attempts either to exclude images of lesbians, gays, bisexuals, and transgender people from the media or from history or to represent these groups in negative stereotypical terms. The theologian James S. Tinney suggests seven overlapping categories by which cultural homophobia is manifested.

1, 2 *Conspiracy to silence* and *denial of culture*. These first two categories are closely aligned. Although not expressly written into law, societies informally attempt to prevent large numbers of individuals of a particular minority (or target) group from congregating in any one place (e.g., in bars and other social centers), deny them space to hold social or political functions, deny them access to materials, attempt to restrict representation in any given educational institution or employment in any business, and inhibit frank, open, and honest discussion of topics of interest to or concerning these groups.

3 *Denial of popular strength*. Many studies have found that a significant percentage of the population experiences same-sex desires, and that these individuals often define their identity in terms of these desires. The cultural assumption exists, however, that one is heterosexual until "proven guilty." According to Tinney, "Society refuses to believe how many blacks there are in this country 'passing' for white and how many lesbians and gays [and bisexuals] there are out there passing as heterosexuals" (Tinney, 1983, 5).

4 *Fear of overvisibility*. A form of homophobia is manifested each time LGBT people are told that they should not define themselves in terms of their sexuality or gender identity or when they are accused of being "blatant" by expressing signs of affection in public, behaviors that heterosexual couples routinely take for granted. They are given the message that there is something inherently wrong with same-sex desire and that individuals so inclined should keep such desire well hidden and to themselves.

5 *Creation of defined public spaces*. Society tends to force disenfranchised individuals and groups into ghettos, where there is little possibility of integration into the general life of the community. Neighborhoods, business establishments, and even professions are thus set aside for LGBT people as they are for other target groups. Individuals enter these areas hoping to find temporary respite from the outside world's homophobia.

6 *Denial of self-labeling*. Epithets and other derogatory labels are directed at every target group. LGBT people have chosen terms of self-definition (e.g., gay, lesbian, bisexual, transgender, for example) to portray the positive aspects of their lives and loves more adequately. Recently, increasing numbers of lesbians, gays, bisexuals, and

transgender people have reappropriated such terms as *queer, faggot*, and *dyke* in order to transform these venomous symbols of hurt and bigotry into tools of empowerment.

7 *Negative symbolism* (stereotyping). Stereotyping groups of people is used as a means of control and a further hindrance to understanding and to meaningful social change. Stereotypes about LGBT people abound, ranging from their alleged predatory appetites, to their physical appearance, to the possible "causes" of their desires.

In addition to Tinney's categories of cultural homophobia, psychologist Dorothy Riddle suggests that the concepts of *tolerance* and *acceptance* should also be included: tolerance because it can, in actuality, be a mask for an underlying fear or even hatred (one is tolerant, e.g., of a baby crying on an airplane while simultaneously wishing it would stop or go away), and acceptance because it assumes that there is indeed something to accept.

HOW HOMOPHOBIA HURTS EVERYONE

It cannot be denied that homophobia, like other forms of oppression, serves the dominant group by establishing and maintaining power and mastery over those who are marginalized or disenfranchised. Individuals maintain oppressive behaviors to gain certain rewards or to avoid punishment, to protect their self-esteem against psychological doubts or conflicts, to enhance their value systems, or to categorize others in an attempt to comprehend a complex world. By excluding entire groups of people, those in positions of power obtain economic, political, ideological, and other privileges. In many ways, though, oppression, in this instance homophobia, ultimately limits heterosexuals.

Homophobia inhibits the ability of heterosexuals to form close, intimate relationships with members of their own sex.

Young people often form close same-sex attachments during their childhood years. But once they reach a certain age (usually around the time of puberty), their elders encourage them to distance themselves from these friends, with the implication that if they do not, their sexuality will be called into question. This means—especially for males—no more sleeping over at each other's houses, no more sharing intimate secrets, no more spending as much time together. Ultimately, this situation tends to hinder the ability of heterosexual adults to get as close to a same-sex friend as they once did when they were very young.

Homophobia locks all people into rigid gender-based roles that inhibit creativity and self-expression.

Much has been written about gender roles and how they constrain both females and males. In Western culture, concepts of masculinity and femininity promote the domination of males over females and reinforce the identification of maleness with power. Males are encouraged to be independent, competitive, goal oriented, and unemotional, to value physical courage and toughness. Females, on the other hand, are taught to be nurturing, emotional, sensitive, expressive, to be caretakers of others while disregarding their own needs.

Gender roles maintain the sexist structure of society, and homophobia reinforces those roles—for example, by casting such epithets as *faggot, dyke*, and *homo* at people who step outside designated gender roles. This pervasive social conditioning based on anatomical sex effectively generates great disparities between males and females. For evidence of this inequality one need only look at the preponderance of men over women in upper management positions and other positions of prestige, or at the fact that women still do not earn

equal pay for equal work. There is also evidence, in a classic 1935 anthropological study of three cultures by Margaret Mead, that there is an increased incidence of violence against women in male-dominated societies.

Homophobic conditioning (and indeed all forms of oppression) compromises the integrity of heterosexual people by pressuring them into treating others badly, which are actions contrary to their basic humanity.

By way of analogy. Frederick Douglass, the famous nineteenth-century abolitionist who escaped slavery, described what he called "the dehumanizing effects" of slavery not on slaves alone, but also on white slave owners, whose position to slavery corrupted their humanity. Describing his experiences with Mrs. Sophia Auld, mistress of the Baltimore household in which Douglass lived and worked during the 1820s, Douglass wrote,

> My new mistress proved to be a woman of the kindest heart and finest feelings. But, alas, this kind heart had but a short time to remain such. The fatal poison of irresponsible power was already in her hands, and soon commenced its infernal work. Slavery soon proved its ability to divest her of (her) heavenly qualities. Under its influence, the tender heart became stone, and the lamblike disposition gave way to one of tigerlike fierceness.
>
> (Douglass 1845, 77–78)

Homophobia can be used to stigmatize, silence, and, on occasion, target people who are perceived or defined by others as gay, lesbian, or bisexual but who are in actuality heterosexual.

For more than two millennia in the West, antihomosexual laws and decrees have been enacted by religious denominations and governments carrying punishments ranging from ridicule to death of the "accused." These decrees have been used to justify harsh treatment of those discovered or believed to have engaged in same-sex activity. But what is often forgotten or overlooked is the fact that these same laws have, on occasion, been used by individuals and governments to silence opponents, regardless of whether they have engaged in same-sex activity.

In 1871, Paragraph 175 of the German Penal Code banned homosexuality. It was later used by the Nazi regime to incarcerate and ultimately to send great numbers of men suspected of being homosexual to their death, and was also at times employed to incarcerate Catholic clergy, many of whom were heterosexual, as well as non-Catholic heterosexuals who opposed state authority. In addition, "sodomy" laws remained on the books until 2003 in many states in the U.S. Although designed chiefly to harass persons engaging in same-sex activity, they have also been used to prosecute heterosexuals.

The Lambda Legal Defense and Education Fund—a New York-based gay, lesbian, bisexual, and transgender-oriented legal organization—defended a twenty-six-year-old heterosexual man who was denied health insurance because he was unmarried, living in New York City with a male roommate, and therefore presumed to be gay and stereotypically assumed to be at increased risk for HIV/AIDS. Heterosexual male hairdressers and female gym teachers and other heterosexuals working in professions widely perceived to be "gay," along with single people living in red-lined "gay" zip codes, are also vulnerable to victimization by similar homophobia-based discrimination.

Violent "queer-bashing" is not infrequently directed against heterosexuals who are also perceived to be gay or lesbian. The clear implication here is that all people are at risk for attack, irrespective of their actual sexual identity, so long as any group remains the target of violent hate-motivated assaults.

Homophobia generally restricts communication with a significant portion of the population and, more specifically, limits family relationships.

No matter how they are constituted, families will continue to produce lesbian, gay, bisexual, and transgender offspring. The political and theocratic Right argues loudly that homosexuality poses a direct threat to "traditional family values." In actuality, however, it is homophobia that strains family relationships by restricting communication among family members, loosening the very ties that bind. Children, fearing negative reactions from parents, hold back important information about their lives. Parents, often not wanting to hear about their child's sexual or gender identity, never truly get to know their children. Even when parents and children reside in the same house, secret upon secret adds up to polite estrangement and sometimes to a total break.

When LGBT people finally do "come out" to their relatives and friends, the heterosexual relatives and friends sometime go into a "closet" as their homophobia and/or that of those around them leads them to withhold the truth from friends and neighbors. Indeed, family members sometimes become targets of stigmatization when the truth about an LGBT relative becomes known. In any case, the emotional toll can be great.

Homophobia ultimately undermines the process of parenting in all families. It harms not only those in the more obvious cases where there are LGBT children, or LGBT parents, but it also imposes great impediments to "mainstream" heterosexual families with heterosexual children.

Societal homophobia prevents some lesbian, gay, bisexual, and transgender people from developing an authentic self-identity, and adds to the pressure to marry, which in turn places undue stress and oftentimes trauma on themselves as well as their heterosexual spouses and their children.

The suppression of information about the gay, lesbian, bisexual, and transgender experience reinforces the heterosexist assumption that everyone is or should be heterosexual and should conform to standard conceptualizations of gender expression. This assumption, coupled with the frequently very real penalties for not conforming to heterosexual norms, has pressured many people either to hide their true sexual and/or gender identity or has restricted their self-realization. Some have married in an attempt to "fit in" or "pass," or in hopes of "being cured" of their same-sex attractions and/or their gender expressions.

Homophobia is one cause of premature sexual involvement that increases the chances of teen pregnancy and the spread of sexually transmitted diseases (STDs).

Young people, of all sexual identities, are often pressured to become *heterosexually* active to prove to themselves and others that they are "normal." If homophobia were reduced in the schools and society at large, in all likelihood, fewer young people would act out *heterosexually* during adolescence.

Homophobia combined with sexphobia (fear and revulsion of sex) results in the elimination of any discussion of the lives and sexuality of sexual minorities as part of school-based sex education, keeping vital information from all students. Such a lack of information can kill people in the age of AIDS.

Some religious and community leaders, educators, and parents actively work to prevent honest and nonjudgmental information concerning homosexuality, bisexuality, and transgenderism—indeed, sexuality and gender in general—from reaching young people. Students of all sexual and gender identities need this information to make informed decisions about their sexual activity. Without it, they are placed at greater risk for unwanted pregnancy, STDs, and HIV infection.

Homophobia (along with racism, sexism, classism, sexphobia, and others) inhibits a unified and effective governmental and societal response to AIDS.

It can be reasonably argued that if the majority of people with AIDS had initially been middle-class, white, suburban heterosexual males, rather than gay and bisexual men, people of color, working-class people, sex workers (prostitutes), and drug users, then governmental and societal institutions would have mobilized immediately to defeat the epidemic.

Because of the lack of wide-scale early attention, AIDS has spread to pandemic proportions. The government and society, at least initially, did not make a true commitment to education, research, and treatment. Funding remained insufficient for as many years as AIDS retained its erroneous reputation of a disease of outcast sexual and social minorities. The result was, and in some sectors continues to be, that many heterosexuals have a false sense that they will not be affected, and take no precautions.

Homophobia prevents heterosexuals from accepting the benefits and gifts offered by the lesbian, gay, bisexual, and transgendered communities: theoretical insights, spiritual visions and options, contributions in the arts and culture, to education, to religion, to family life, indeed to all facets of society.

In cultures where homophobia is present, there have been active attempts to falsify historical accounts of same-sex love—through censorship, deletion, half-truths, and altering pronouns signifying gender—making accurate reconstruction extremely difficult. This effectively distorts society's collective memory (i.e., history), clouding our sense of identity as individuals and as social beings. Everyone loses from this suppression of the truth.

John Boswell cites an example of this censorship in a manuscript of *The Art of Love* by the Roman author Ovid. A phrase that originally read, "A boy's love appealed to me less" (*Hoc est quod pueri tanger amore minus*) was altered by a Medieval moralist to read, "A boy's love appealed to me not at all" (*Hoc est quod pueri tanger amore nihil*), and an editor's note that appeared in the margin informed the reader. "Thus you may be sure that Ovid was not a sodomite" (*Ex hoc nota quod Ovidius nonfreit Sodomita*).

Boswell also cites a Renaissance example of homophobic censorship in which Michelangelo's grand-nephew changed the sex of the subject of his uncle's sonnets to make them more acceptable to the public.

Closer to our time, government-sponsored censorship of art deemed "homoerotic" by the National Endowment for the Arts ultimately restricted creativity and freedom of expression of the entire artistic community.

In addition, traditional religious teachings on homosexuality keep lesbians, gays, bisexuals, and transgender people from entering religious life or from being true to themselves. These teachings also inhibit the ability of many congregations to value and celebrate human diversity and, most importantly, impedes spiritual growth.

Homophobia saps energy from more constructive endeavors.

Like all forms of oppression, homophobia inhibits our ability to understand the nature and scope of truly serious and far-reaching social problems (e.g., poverty, illiteracy, war, disease, environmental decay, crime, and drug addiction). Oppression results in the scapegoating and distancing of people from one another, diminishing our capacity to address these problems and thereby degrading the quality of life for all of us. By reducing the various forms of oppression, we quite literally make our society more socially efficient, increasing our ability to find solutions to the social and ecological challenges that threaten our collective future.

Homophobia inhibits appreciation of other types of diversity, making it unsafe for everyone because each person has unique traits not considered mainstream or dominant. Therefore, we are all diminished when any one of us is demeaned.

As Reverend Martin Niemoeller wrote during World War II,

> In Germany they came first for the Communists, and I didn't speak up because I wasn't a Communist. Then they came for the Jews, and I didn't speak up because I wasn't a Jew. Then they came for the trade unionists, and I didn't speak up because I wasn't a trade unionist. Then they came for the Catholics, and I didn't speak up because I was a Protestant. Then they came for me, and by that time no one was left to speak up.
>
> (in Bartlett, 1980, 824)

The meaning is quite clear. When any particular group of people is scapegoated, it is ultimately everyone's concern. For today, gay, lesbian, bisexual, and transgender people are targeted. Tomorrow, they may come for you. Therefore, it is in everyone's self-interest to work actively to dismantle all the many forms of oppression, including homophobia.

CONCLUSION

In truth, homophobia is pervasive throughout the society and each of us, irrespective of sexual or gender identity, is at risk of its harmful effects. Within the schools, homophobia compromises the entire educational environment. Though homophobia did not originate with us and we are not to blame, we are all responsible for its elimination and, therefore, all can gain by a closer examination of the issues.

Lesbians, bisexuals, gay males, and transgender people have been, and continue to be, on the front lines in fighting against homophobia, and standing by our sides are supportive heterosexual allies—people who have worked and continue to work through their own homophobic conditioning, who are secure with their own sexual identities, who have joined us and have not cared when others called their sexuality into question.

We are *all* born into a great pollution called homophobia (one among many forms of oppression) that falls upon us like acid rain. For some people, spirits are tarnished to the core; others are marred on the surface, but no one is completely protected. Yet neither are we to blame. We had no control over the formulation of this pollution, nor did we direct it to pour down upon us. On the other hand, we all have a responsibility, indeed an opportunity, to join together to construct protective shelters from the corrosive effect of oppression while working to clean up the homophobic environment in which we live. Once sufficient steps are taken to reduce this pollution, we will all breathe a lot easier.

References

Bartlett, J. (1980). *Bartlett's Familiar Quotations.* Boston: Little, Brown and Company.

Douglass, F. (1982 [1845]). *Narrative of the Life of Frederick Douglass, an American Slave, Written by Himself.* H. A. Baker, Jr. (ed.). New York: Penguin.

Tinney, J. S. (1983). "Interconnections." *Interracial Books for Children Bulletin* 14(3–4),4–6.

78

The interSEXion

A Vision for a Queer Progressive Agenda

Deepali Gokhale

This vision is based on the fact that the queer community is a microcosm of humanity, intersecting through the common experiences of the oppression of gender identity and sexual identity, the observation that oppression is rooted in greed and perpetuated by the fear of scarcity, the assertion that no oppression can end without removing the systems that perpetuate it, the recognition that oppression and exploitation are the bases on which current power structures and economies rely, and the observation that because queer liberation requires the end of all forms of oppression and exploitation, the liberation of queer people can be seen as the key to the liberation of humanity itself.

THE ROOT OF QUEER OPPRESSION

Heterosexism is the belief that there are only two genders, and that a sexual relationship between a man and a woman is compulsory for full acceptance into society. It would seem that the root of queer oppression is heterosexism, and so queer folks should work against heterosexism. In order to get into any sort of depth in this work, we would need to know why heterosexism exists in the first place, and we would find that the reason for heterosexism is because it enforces patriarchy, which could lead us to join forces with the women's movement and oppose patriarchy. That venture would expose the fact that the reason patriarchy needs enforcement is because it is essential to capitalism, and that capitalism at its essence relies on greed. Therefore, the root of queer oppression, and in fact, the root of all systemic oppression as it exists in the world today, is unbridled greed.

Capitalism is based in greed, and as it exists today, cannot exist without exploiting labor. One person cannot make a disproportionately large share of profits unless somewhere in the process, another person is making a disproportionately small one. The most basic example of this is in the patriarchal nuclear family, where the man makes profits at the expense of a woman's (and children's) free labor. The people who most benefit from this unbridled greed are the ones who came up with capitalism to begin with: wealthy white men. This is true worldwide; every oppression that is in place exists to ultimately support white male power, and the United States is the clear leader and greatest benefactor of this system.

The main tools used to make an oppressive system work are a defined norm, economic power, and violence. In her book entitled *Homophobia: A Weapon of Sexism*, Suzanne Pharr explains it this way:

> To understand the connection among the oppressions, we must examine their common elements. The first is a defined norm, a standard of rightness and often righteousness wherein all others are judged in relation to it. This norm must be backed up

with institutional power, economic power, and both institutional and individual violence . . . . In the United States, that norm is male, white, heterosexual, Christian, temporarily able-bodied, youthful, and has access to wealth and resources . . . .

In order for these institutions to be controlled by a single group of people, there must be economic power . . . . Once economic control is in the hands of the few, all others can be controlled through limiting access to resources, limiting mobility, limiting employment options. People are pitted against one another through the perpetuation of the myth of scarcity which suggests that our resources are limited and blames the poor for using up too much of what little there is to go around . . . . The maintenance of societal and individual power and control requires the use of violence and the threat of violence. Institutional violence is sanctioned through the criminal justice system and the threat of the military—for quelling individual or group uprisings.

(1988, 53–56)

The patriarchal nuclear family, living in a single-family house in the suburbs, serves as the building block for capitalism. As the arbitrarily defined norm, it provides the perfect conditions for the oppression of women. Since men earn wage labor, they can easily control women's access to resources, and can easily accuse women of "spending too much" of "their" hard-earned money. By isolating women from each other, the nuclear family provides a safe haven for men to be violent towards women and thus enforce their power.

In relation to institutional power, the isolated nuclear family unit makes it easy for mass media to be the only source of information citizens receive, since people are no longer talking to their neighbors, and ideally, by isolating the male in the household as the only breadwinner, the nuclear family can easily be moved around for the convenience of those who need wage labor. Because each family needs a house, a car, and their own household items, the nuclear family also promotes the wasteful unending consumerism and environmental exploitation required for "economic progress." Irrespective of whether the nuclear family is actually the "norm," as long as this belief is widespread, other types of families can be judged by whether they conform to that structure.

Everyone strives to conform to the nuclear family model, and a false sense of pride and righteousness is evident in those who "make it." That many poor people, people of color, and immigrants do not fit into that kind of family is considered "their fault," and not the result of those in power limiting access to the resources it takes to sustain a nuclear family. When this shame and blame is internalized, those who don't fit the norm fight amongst themselves about why another oppressed group is the "problem with society."

It is not just gender oppression that keeps capitalism in place. It requires the exploitation of the labor of anyone outside the "norm": the white, wealthy, young, temporarily-abled, English-speaking Christian American male citizen. Racism exists to exploit the work of people of color, sexism exists to exploit women's work, xenophobia exists to exploit the "third world," and ageism/ableism devalues those who are assumed "less productive." Many of us experience more than one of these oppressions. In addition to the myth of the nuclear family, patriotism, the illusion of a meritocracy, and religious oppression are the tools used to brainwash one group to look down on another and trust that the system is working for the "believers." The illusion of scarcity and fear of our neighbors keeps us isolated from and fighting with each other. Divide and conquer is the rule. Meanwhile, those in power continue to reap the rewards.

A VISION FOR LIBERATION: THE INTER*SEX*ION

It is because the queer community categorically rejects this setup, simply by being who we are, that we are such a threat to those in power. When they call gay marriage a threat to human civilization as we know it, they are referring to the fact that gender oppression in the form of heterosexism is the weapon that keeps them in power, and if those gender "norms" weren't considered essential, there would be no way to enforce that oppression. It is precisely because we live outside the basic unit of the very nuclear family structure that would otherwise permit capitalism to continue unchallenged, and because our community experiences not only queer oppression but all oppressions, that we are most capable of creating an alternative culture outside of the culture of exploitation, resolving it for ourselves so that it can be expanded for those outside of our community.

A defining characteristic of the queer community is that within it is reflected all of the oppressions and privileges in our surrounding geography, and that these oppressions and privileges play out in similar proportions and methods. It is the intersection of every oppression and privilege, and the wholeness of the queer community is its power. There is no better place to understand the intersection of oppressions and figure out how to achieve liberation for all forms of life. Because we are an intersection based on gender identity and sexual identity, we can call ourselves the "interSEXion."

We can start by building a real sense of wholeness within the queer community. While our oppressors would like us to remain separate and at odds with each other, we can use our queer oppression to bind us into making connections and understanding the nature of oppression itself. We can begin by socializing with each other. We can each individually learn about our own oppressions so that we know what we need. We can also learn about our privileges, and use them to end the oppression of others. We can end racism, classism, sexism, and any other oppression within our community. We can create a safety net for ourselves so that we are not reliant on the systems of oppression used against us for our basic needs. We can pass the values of liberation that we create from one generation to the next, without the sense of ownership that is inherited with blood relations, and instead allowing each generation to use its own experience and creativity in the struggle. In this way, we will keep intact within our community what is being used to divide and conquer us elsewhere.

Once we have this safer community, non-reliant on the systems of oppression that keep us divided, we can break the systems of oppression for everyone else. We can use our wholeness as an advantage outside the queer community. As whole people with multiple identities, we can use our non-queer identities as bridges to other oppressed communities. Although it may be true that any oppressed community can build bridges, the queer community is particularly fortunate to have representatives from the actual communities surrounding it. Because the queer identity can many times be made invisible, queer people can have access to those communities in ways that no other oppressed community can.

Currently, the progressive community seems to operate in isolated spaces, divided by our issues and oppressions, with no one group to bind it together. We could use our wholeness and reflection of our geography to ensure our policy would most likely be beneficial for all progressive communities around us, and we can be the glue that binds it together and moves it forward. In many cases, we are leading those "other" progressive movements anyway.

The queer community could have a central "policy group" that would be informed by and be informative to any number of affinity groups. The responsibility of the policy group would be to take in the information from the affinity groups, get resources and create infrastructure to support the groups, and to create an overall policy/strategy/direction for

achieving our goal of ending exploitation and oppression. This policy group would be accountable not only to the affinity groups, but also to individuals in the community, and we can hold community forums to keep a dialogue going with those individuals who may not belong to any group.

Our affinity groups could organize by whatever affinity they chose (geography, race, ethnicity, religion, class, gender, sexuality, age, campaign, cause, . . .), they could be groups that already exist (like AIDS Survival Project, ZAMI, Trikone Atlanta), and they could dissolve if/when they were no longer necessary, like if they were organized around a campaign. The groups could provide safe spaces for people to talk about particular oppressions or issues. People could belong to as many affinity groups as they wanted. The goals for each group for now could be: figuring out the most important issues for a particular affinity group, building a coalition to support the group, and figuring out a proactive strategy to address the group's issues in order to inform the policy group.

If the affinity groups and the queer community make up an "inner circle" around our interSEXion, our allies could form a second circle around the first. Issue or campaign-based affinity groups can access our allies to form coalitions when needed. Our allies would benefit because through the interSEXion, we could be the quickest connection between allies that would form a coalition. Our allies could create connections even further outside our intersection, and reach people who would never associate themselves with a queer agenda, but would work on a particular issue or campaign through our allies.

Positioning our queer community as the interSEXion would not only ensure that we remain at the center of our own liberation, but it would also require us to leave no one behind. Being the interSEXion implies our community's wholeness, and it requires us to be no less than a full human rights movement. It requires us to honor and celebrate the wholeness of each individual in it, and restricts some of us from achieving our goal of liberation unless everyone in our community is free from oppression. It requires us to identify which parts of our community are underrepresented and to nurture those who are most wounded. It means we cannot even start towards a path of liberation until we are on equal footing within our own community. It requires us to walk our talk and liberate ourselves in order to liberate the world around us, and it is the reason why our interSEXion may be the key to the end of exploitation.

Reference

Pharr, S. (1988). *Homophobia: A Weapon of Sexism*. Little Rock: Chardon Press.

79

Privilege

Devon W. Carbado

. . . This essay is part of a larger intellectual project to encourage a shift in—or at least a broadening of—our conceptualization of discrimination. My aim is to expand our notion of what it means to be a perpetrator of discrimination. Typically, we define a

perpetrator of discrimination as someone who acts intentionally to bring about some discriminatory result. This is a narrow and politically palatable conception; it applies to very few of us. In this essay I suggest that those of us who unquestionably accept the racial, gender, and heterosexual privileges we have—those of us who fail to acknowledge our victimless status with respect to racism, sexism, and homophobia—are also perpetrators of discrimination.

Informing this privileged-centered understanding of discrimination is the notion that taking identity privileges for granted helps to legitimize problematic assumptions about identity and entitlement, assumptions that make it difficult for us to challenge the starting points of many of our most controversial conversations about equality. We simply assume, for example, that men should be able to fight for their country (the question is whether women should be entitled to this privilege); that heterosexuals should be able to get married (the question is whether the privilege should be extended to gays and lesbians); that white men should be able to compete for all the slots in a university's entering class (the question is whether people of color should be entitled to the privilege of "preferential treatment").

While a privileged-centered conception of discrimination usefully reveals the bi-directional effects of discrimination—namely, that discrimination allocates both burdens and benefits—the conception may prove entirely too much. After all, all of us enjoy some degree of privilege. Are all of us perpetrators of discrimination? The answer may depend on what we do with, and to, the privileges we have. Each of us makes personal and private choices with our privileges that entrench a variety of social practices, institutional arrangements, and laws that disadvantage other(ed) people.

For example, many of us get married and/or attend weddings, while lesbian and gay marriages are, in most parts of the United States (and the world), not legally recognized. Others of us have racially monolithic social encounters, live in de facto white only (or predominantly white) neighborhoods, or send our kids to white only (or predominantly white) schools. Still others of us have "straight only" associations—that is, our friends are all heterosexuals and our children's friends all have mommies and daddies. These choices are not just personal; they are political. And their cumulative effect is to entrench the very social practices—racism, sexism, classism, and homophobia—we profess to abhor.

In other words, there is a link between identity privileges, and our negotiation of them, on the one hand, and discrimination, on the other. Our identities are reflective and constitutive of systems of oppression. Racism requires white privilege. Sexism requires male privilege. Homophobia requires heterosexual privilege. The very intelligibility of our identities is their association, or lack thereof, with privilege. This creates an obligation on the part of those of us with privileged identities to expose and to challenge them.

Significantly, this obligation exists not only as a matter of morality and responsibility. The obligation exists for a pragmatic reason as well. We cannot change the macro-effects of discrimination without ameliorating the power effects of our identities. Nor can our political commitments have traction unless we apply them to the seemingly "just personal" privileged aspects of our lives. Resistance to identity privileges may be futile, we cannot know for sure. However, to the extent that we do nothing, this much is clear: we perpetuate the systems of discrimination out of which our identities are forged.

But precisely what constitutes an identity privilege? Further, how do we identify them? And, finally, what acts are necessary to deprivilege our identities and to disrupt their association with power? These questions drive this essay. . . .

HETEROSEXUAL PRIVILEGES

Like maleness, heterosexuality should be critically examined. Like maleness, heterosexuality operates as an identity norm, the "what is" or "what is supposed to be" of sexuality. This is illustrated, for example, by the nature versus nurture debate. The question about the cause of sexuality is almost always formulated in terms of whether homosexuality is or is not biologically determined rather than whether sexual orientation, which includes heterosexuality, is or is not biologically determined. Scientists are searching for a gay, not a heterosexual or sexual orientation, gene. Like female identity, then, homosexuality signifies "difference"—more specifically, sexual identity distinctiveness. The normativity of heterosexuality requires that homosexuality be specified, pointed out. Heterosexuality is always already presumed.

Heterosexuals should challenge the normativity and normalization of heterosexuality. They should challenge the heterosexual presumption. But heterosexuals might be reluctant to do so to the extent that they perceive such challenges to call into question their (hetero)sexual orientation. As Lee Edelman observes in a related context, there "is a deeply rooted concern on the part of . . . heterosexual males about the possible meanings of [men subverting gender roles]" (1990, 50). According to Edelman, heterosexual men consider certain gender role inversions to be potentially dangerous because they portend not only a "[male] feminization that would destabilize or question gender" but also a "feminization that would challenge one's (hetero)sexuality" (1990, 50). Edelman's observations suggest that straight men may want to preserve what I am calling the "heterosexual presumption." Their investment in this presumption is less a function of what heterosexuality signifies in a positive sense and more a function of what it signifies in the negative—*not* being homosexual.

And there are racial dimensions to male investment in heterosexuality. For example, straight black male strategies to avoid homosexual suspicion could relate to the racial aspects of male privileges: heterosexual privilege is one of the few privileges that some black men have. These black men may want to take comfort in the fact that whatever else is going on in their lives, they are not, finally, "sissies," "punks," "faggots." By this I do not mean to suggest that black male heterosexuality has the normative standing of white male heterosexuality. It does not. Straight black men continue to be perceived as heterosexually deviant (overly sexual; potential rapists) and heterosexually irresponsible (jobless fathers of children out of wedlock). Still, black male heterosexuality is closer to white male heterosexual normalcy and normativity than is black gay sexuality. Consequently, some straight (or closeted) black men will want to avoid the "black gay [male] . . . triple negation" to which Marlon Riggs refers in the following quote: "Because of my sexuality I cannot be Black. A strong, proud, 'Afrocentric' black man is resolutely heterosexual, not even bisexual. . . . Hence I remain a sissy, punk, faggot. I cannot be a black gay man because, by the tenets of black macho, a black gay man is a triple negation" (1999, 307) . . .

Keith Boykin, former director of the Black Gay and Lesbian Leadership Forum, maintains that "heterosexual sexual orientation has become so ingrained in our social custom, so destigmatized of our fears about sex, that we often fail to make any connection between heterosexuality and sex" (1997). Boykin is only half right. The socially constructed normalcy of heterosexuality is not due solely to the desexualization of heterosexuality in mainstream political and popular culture. It is due also to the sexualization of heterosexuality as normative and to the gender-norm presumptions about heterosexuality—that it is the normal way sexually to express one's gender.

Moreover, it is not simply that homosexuality is sexed that motivates or stimulates homophobic fears about gay and lesbian relationships. These fears also relate to the fact

that homosexuality is stigmatized and is perceived to be an abnormal way sexually to express one's gender. The disparate social meanings that attach to gay and lesbian identities on the one hand and straight identities on the other make individual acts of heterosexual signification a cause for concern.

Recently, I participated in a workshop where one of the presenters "came out" as a heterosexual in the context of giving his talk. This sexual identity disclosure engendered a certain amount of whispering in the back row. Up until that moment, I think many people had assumed the presenter was gay. After all, he was sitting on a panel discussing sexual orientation and had participated in the Gay and Lesbian section of the American Association of Law Schools. There were three other heterosexuals on the panel, but everyone knew they were not gay because everyone *knew* them; they had all been in teaching for a while, two were very senior, and everyone knew of their spouses or partners. Everyone also knew that there was a lesbian on the panel. She, too, had been in teaching for some time and had been out for many years. Apparently, few of the workshop participants knew very much about the presenter who "came out." Because "there is a widespread assumption in both gay and straight communities that any man who says something supportive about issues of concern to lesbian or gay communities must be gay himself," there was, at the very least, a question about his sexuality. Whatever his intentions were for "coming out," whatever his motivations, his assertion of heterosexuality removed the question. . . .

I became sensitized to the politics of heterosexuals "coming out" in the context of reading about James Baldwin. Try to find a piece written about Baldwin and count the number of lines before the author comes out as heterosexual. Usually, it is not more than a couple of paragraphs, so the game ends fast. The following introduction from a 1994 essay about Baldwin is one example of what I am talking about: "The last time I saw James Baldwin was late autumn of 1985, when my wife and I attended a sumptuous book party" (Forrest 1994, 267). In this case, the game ends immediately. Independent of any question of intentionality on the author's part, the mention of the wife functions as an identity signifier to subtextually "out" his heterosexuality. We *read* "wife," we *think* heterosexual. My point here is not to suggest that the essay's overall tone is heterosexually defensive; I simply find it suspicious when heterosexuals speak of their spouses so quickly (in this case the very first sentence of the essay) when a subject (a topic or a personality—here, James Baldwin) implicates homosexuality. . . . The author engages in what I call "the politics of the 3Ds"—disassociation, disidentification, and differentiation. The author is "different" from Baldwin (the author sleeps with women), and this difference, based as it is on sexual identity, compels the author to disassociate himself from and disidentify with that which makes Baldwin "different" (Baldwin sleeps with men).

Heterosexual significations need not always reflect the politics of the 3Ds. In other words, the possibility exists for heterosexuals to point out their heterosexuality without reauthenticating heterosexuality. Consider, for example, the heterosexual privilege list that I give below. While each item on the list explicitly names—outs—heterosexuality, in none of the items does heterosexuality remain unproblematically normative.

As a prelude to the list, I should be clear that the list is incomplete. Nor do the privileges reflected in it represent the experiences of all heterosexuals. As Bruce Ryder observes: "Male heterosexual privilege has different effects on men of, for example, different races and classes. . . . In our society, the dominant or 'hegemonic' form of masculinity to which other masculinities are subordinated is white, middleclass, and heterosexual. This means that the heterosexual privilege of, say, straight black men takes a very different shape in their lives than it does for straight white men" (1991, 292). My goal in presenting this list, then, is not to represent every heterosexual man. Instead, the purpose is to intervene in the normalization of heterosexual privileges. With this intervention, I hope to challenge the

pervasive tendency of heterosexuals to see homophobia as something that puts others at a disadvantage and not something that actually advantages them.

HETEROSEXUAL PRIVILEGES: A LIST

1. Whether on television or in the movies, (white) heterosexuality is always affirmed as healthy and/or normal (black heterosexuality and family arrangements are still, to some degree, perceived to be deviant).
2. Without making a special effort, heterosexuals are surrounded by other heterosexuals every day.
3. A husband and wife can comfortably express affection in any social setting, even a predominantly gay one.
4. The children of a heterosexual couple will not have to explain why their parents have different genders—that is, why they have a mummy and a daddy.
5. (White) heterosexuals are not blamed for creating and spreading the AIDS virus (though Africans—as a collective group—are blamed).
6. Heterosexuals do not have to worry about people trying to "cure" their sexual orientation (though black people have to worry about people trying to "cure" black "racial pathologies").
7. Black heterosexual males did not have to worry about whether they would be accepted at the Million Man March.
8. Rarely, if ever, will a doctor, on learning that her patient is heterosexual, inquire as to whether the patient has ever taken an AIDS test and if so, how recently.
9. Medical service will never be denied to heterosexuals because they are heterosexuals (though medical services may not be recommended to black people because they are black).
10. Friends of heterosexuals generally do not refer to heterosexuals as their "straight friends" (though nonblack people often to refer to black people as their "black friends").
11. A heterosexual couple can enter a restaurant on their anniversary and be fairly confident that staff and fellow diners will warmly congratulate them if an announcement is made (though the extent of the congratulation and the nature of the welcome might depend on the racial identities of the couple).
12. White heterosexuals do not have to worry about whether a fictional film villain who is heterosexual will reflect negatively on their heterosexuality (though blacks may always have to worry about their racial representation in films).
13. Heterosexuals are entitled to legal recognition of their marriages throughout the United States and the world.
14. Within the black community, black male heterosexuality does not engender comments like "what a waste," "there goes another good black man," or "if they're not in jail, they're faggots."
15. Heterosexuals can take jobs with most companies without worrying about whether their spouses will be included in the benefits package.
16. Child molestation by heterosexuals does not confirm the deviance of heterosexuality (though if the alleged molester is black, the alleged molestation becomes evidence of the deviance of black [hetero]sexuality).
17. Black rap artists do not make songs suggesting that heterosexuals should be shot or beaten up because they are heterosexuals.
18. Black male heterosexuality does not undermine a black heterosexual male's ability to be a role model for black boys.

19. Heterosexuals can join the military without concealing their sexual identity.
20. Children will be taught in school, explicitly or implicitly, about the naturalness of heterosexuality (they will also be taught to internalize the notion of white normativity).
21. Conversations on black liberation will always include concerns about heterosexual men.
22. Heterosexuals can adopt children without being perceived as selfish and without anyone questioning their motives.
23. Heterosexuals are not denied custody or visitation rights of their children because they are heterosexuals.
24. Heterosexual men are welcomed as leaders of Boy Scout troops.
25. Heterosexuals can visit their parents and family as who they are, and take their spouses, partners, or dates with them to family functions.
26. Heterosexuals can talk matter-of-factly about their relationships with their partners without people commenting that they are "flaunting" their sexuality.
27. A black heterosexual couple would be welcomed as members of any black church.
28. Heterosexual couples do not have to worry about whether kissing each other in public or holding hands in public will render them vulnerable to violence.
29. Heterosexuals do not have to struggle with "coming out" or worry about being "outed."
30. The parents of heterosexuals do not love them "in spite of" their sexual orientation, and parents do not blame themselves for their children's heterosexuality.
31. Heterosexuality is affirmed in most religious traditions.
32. Heterosexuals can introduce their spouses to colleagues and not worry about whether the decision will have a detrimental impact on their careers.
33. A black heterosexual male does not have to choose between being black and being heterosexual.
34. Heterosexuals can prominently display their spouses' photographs at work without causing office gossip or hostility.
35. (White) heterosexuals do not have to worry about "positively" representing heterosexuality.
36. Few will take pity on a heterosexual on hearing that she is straight, or feel the need to say, "That's okay" (though it is not uncommon for a black person to hear, "It's okay that you're black" or "We don't care that you're black" or "When we look at you, we don't see a black person").
37. (Male) heterosexuality is not considered to be symptomatic of the "pathology" of the black family.
38. Heterosexuality is never mistaken as the only aspect of one's lifestyle, but is perceived instead as merely one more component of one's personal identity.
39. (White) heterosexuals do not have to worry over the impact their sexuality will have personally on their children's lives, particularly as it relates to their social lives (though black families of all identity configurations do have to worry about how race and racism will affect their children's well-being).
40. Heterosexuals do not have to worry about being "bashed" after leaving a social event with other heterosexuals (though black people of all sexual orientations do have to worry about being "racially bashed" on any given day).
41. Every day is (white) "Heterosexual Pride Day."

CONCLUSION: RESISTING PRIVILEGES

I have argued that one of the ways to contest gender and sexual orientation hierarchy is for heterosexual men to detail their social experiences on the privileged side of gender and sexual orientation. In advancing this argument, I do not mean to suggest that the role of these men is to legitimize "untrustworthy" and "self-interested" victim-centered accounts of discrimination. There is a tendency on the part of dominant groups (e.g., males and heterosexuals) to discount the experiences of subordinate groups (e.g., straight women, lesbians, and gays) unless those experiences are authenticated or legitimized by a member of the dominant group. For example, it is one thing for me, a black man, to say I experienced discrimination in a particular social setting; it is quite another for my white male colleague to say he witnessed that discrimination. My telling of the story is suspect because I am black (racially interested). My white colleague's telling of the story is not suspect because he is white (racially disinterested). The racial transparency of whiteness—its "perspectivelessness"—renders my colleague's account "objective." . . .

Assuming that the identification/listing of privileges methodology I have described avoids the problem of authentication, one still might wonder whether the project is sufficiently radical to dismantle gender and sexual orientation hierarchies. Certainly the lists I have presented do not go far enough. They represent the very early stages in a more complicated process to end gender and sexual orientation discrimination.

The lists, nevertheless, are politically valuable. . . .

None of this is to say that awareness and acknowledgement of privilege is enough. Resistance is needed as well. But how does one resist? And what counts as resistance? With respect to marriage, for example, does resistance to heterosexual privilege require heterosexuals to refrain from getting married and/or attending weddings? It might mean both of those things. At the very least, resistance to identity privilege would seem to require "critical acquiescence": criticizing, if not rejecting, aspects of our life that are directly linked to our privilege. A heterosexual who gets married and/or attends weddings but who also openly challenges the idea that marriage is a heterosexual entitlement is engaging in critical acquiescence.

In the end, critical acquiescence might not go far enough. It might even be a cop out. Still, it is a useful and politically manageable place to begin.

References

Boykin, K. (1997). *One More River to Cross: Black and Gay in America*. New York: Doubleday.
Edelman, L. (1990). "Redeeming the Phallus: Wallace Stevens, Frank Lentricchia, and the Politics of (Hetero)sexuality." In J. A. Boone and M. Cadden (eds.), *Engendering Men: The Question of Male Feminist Criticism*. New York: Routledge.
Forrest, L. (1994). "Evidences of Jimmy Baldwin." In L. Forrest (ed.), *Relocations of the Spirit*. Emeryville, CA: Asphodel Press/Moyer Ball.
Riggs, M. T. (1999). "Black Macho Revisited: Reflections of a SNAP! Queen." In D. W. Carbado (ed.), *Black Men on Race, Gender, and Sexuality: A Critical Reader*. New York: New York University Press.
Ryder, B. (1991). "Straight Talk: Male Heterosexual Privilege." *Queen's Law Journal*, 16, 287–303.

80

Sport

Where Men Are Men and Women Are Trespassers

Pat Griffin

. . . Sport is more than games. As an institution, sport serves important social functions in supporting conventional social values. In particular, sport is a training ground where boys learn what it means to be men. Masculinity does not come naturally; it must be carefully taught. Specific rewards and punishments provide clear messages about acceptable and unacceptable behavior for boys. Boys who show an interest in "girl" activities, such as playing with dolls, dancing, or cooking, are teased by peers. Young boys learn at an early age that participation in athletics is an important, if not required, part of developing a masculine identity and gaining acceptance among peers.

Every Saturday morning in the fall little boys stagger up and down fields under the weight of full football drag, imitating the swagger and ritual they see in their professional sports heroes. Many fathers worry if their sons do not exhibit an interest in sports. They teach their sons to throw, catch, swing bats, shoot hoops. Adults comment on the size of young boys by predicting in which sports they will excel. Participation on school athletic teams, especially the big four (football, basketball, baseball, and ice hockey) ensure popularity and prestige among classmates and in the larger community. Young boys idolize professional and college team-sport athletes and coaches because of their physical size, strength, toughness, and competitiveness. Young boys and adult men wear caps, T-shirts, and jackets with their favorite professional or collegiate team mascot and colors.

Men's athletic events, especially the big four team sports, draw huge numbers of spectators. Men of all colors and social classes study team statistics and participate in intense postcontest analyses of strategy and performance. Cities spend millions of dollars building sports arenas with tax subsidies to woo men's professional teams to town or prevent them from moving to another city. The athletic equipment and clothing industries are multibillion-dollar enterprises that depend on the large number of boys and men who buy their increasingly sophisticated and specialized products.

The importance of sport in socializing men into traditional masculine gender roles also defines the sport experience for women. Because sport is identified with men and masculinity, women in sport become trespassers on male territory, and their access is limited or blocked entirely. Despite huge increases in women's sport participation, there is still tremendous resistance to an equitable distribution of resources between men's and women's athletics. *USA Today* reported that on the 25th anniversary of the passage of Title IX, the federal law prohibiting sex discrimination in education, 80 percent of college and university athletic programs in the United States are still not in compliance with the law.

Sometimes resistance to women's sport participation is more personal. In the spring of 1997 Melissa Raglin, 12, was the starting catcher for a Boca Raton Babe Ruth baseball team. During a game the plate umpire asked Melissa if she was wearing a protective cup. Melissa removed her helmet and catcher's mask and told him she was a girl. However, the Babe Ruth rules state that all players (assumed to be male) must wear a cup to protect their genitals. When Melissa, who had been playing in the Babe Ruth league for over two seasons, refused to comply with the rule, she was prohibited from playing catcher.

C
O
N
T
E
X
T

She was allowed to play again only when she ordered a special cup designed for women, even though most doctors agree that there is no medical reason why a girl should wear a protective cup. This example shows the absurd lengths to which some men will go to try to humiliate a young girl to make sure she knows that she is trespassing on male turf. Male league officials' insistence that Melissa wear a cup, even at the risk of ridicule in news stories, demonstrates the seriousness and importance of protecting sport from female encroachment.

Women's presence in sport as serious participants dilutes the importance and exclusivity of sport as a training ground for learning about and accepting traditional male gender roles and the privileges that their adoption confers on (white, heterosexual) men. As a result, women's sport performance is trivialized and marginalized as an inferior version of the "real thing." These arguments ignore the overlap in sport performances among men and women in all sports and the growing interest among young girls in sport participation.

Sexism as a system of male privilege and female subordination is based on the acceptance of particular definitions of gender (what constitutes a man or a woman) and gender roles (what qualities, talents, and characteristics women and men are supposed to have). Women's serious participation in sport brings into question the "natural" and mutually exclusive nature of gender and gender roles. If women in sport can be tough minded, competitive, and muscular too, then sport loses its special place in the development of masculinity for men. If women can so easily develop these so-called masculine qualities, then what are the meanings of femininity and masculinity? What does it mean to be a man or a woman? These challenges threaten an acceptance of the traditional gender order in which men are privileged and women are subordinate. Thus, they account for much of the strong resistance to gender equity in sport and the need to marginalize and control the growth of women's athletics.

THE POWER OF THE LESBIAN LABEL

One of the most effective means of controlling women in sport is to challenge the femininity and heterosexuality of women athletes. When a woman is called "masculine," "unfeminine," or "dyke," she knows she has crossed a gender boundary or challenged male privilege. In this way, homophobia serves as glue that holds traditional gender role expectations in place. Because most women are afraid to be called lesbian or to have their femininity called into question, their sport experience can be controlled by using the lesbian label to intimidate them. The purpose of calling a woman a lesbian is to limit her sport experience and make her feel defensive about her athleticism.

Though lesbians are the direct targets of these insinuations, antilesbian bias affects the experience of all women. Using the lesbian label to discourage the bonding that occurs among women in athletics is an effective way to keep women from discovering their own power. Consequently, stigmatizing lesbian identity serves the interests of those who want to maintain the imbalance of opportunity and power in athletics based on gender. As long as women's sports are associated with lesbians and lesbians are stigmatized as sexual and social deviants, the lesbian label serves an important social-control function in sport, ensuring that only men have access to the benefits of sport participation and the physical and psychological empowerment available in sport.

The preservation of athletics as a male-only activity is essential in maintaining a gender order in which men and women adopt separate and unequal gender roles. The interconnections of sexism, homophobia, and heterosexism are powerful forces that ensure that male privilege and dominance endure.

SPORT AND THE MAINTENANCE OF MASCULINITY

Sport for men serves five social functions that ensure that the gender order supporting presumed male superiority and female subordination is maintained. These functions are (1) defining and reinforcing traditional conceptions of masculinity, (2) providing an acceptable and safe context for male bonding and intimacy, (3) reinforcing male privilege and female subordination, (4) establishing status among other males, and (5) reinforcing heterosexuality.

DEFINING AND REINFORCING TRADITIONAL CONCEPTIONS OF MASCULINITY

Team sports in particular teach boys masculinity skills. They learn to be competitive and tough. They learn to deny feelings of compassion or other feelings that coaches teach them to associate with weakness. Boys learn to value physical strength and size, aggressiveness, and a will to dominate. Young boys learn to accept the necessity of establishing hierarchical relationships among competitors and teammates based on athletic performance. None of these qualities or values are innate, but young boys learn that they are essential and natural components of a masculine identity. Boys who are perceived to be weak or soft or who do not have an interest in developing these traditional masculine qualities are shunned, harassed, and ridiculed by peers. Adult men who were labeled "sissy" in elementary school or "faggot" and "pussy" in later grades can tell painful stories of abuse that attest to the intensity of this socialization process.

Much of this harassment takes place on athletic teams and in physical education classes. Male coaches and physical educators are important teachers of masculinity. Lessons learned on the athletic field reinforce the importance of learning to "be a man." "Proving one's manhood," facing challenge "like a man," and dominating opponents represent a hard strength and stoicism especially prized in team sports.

Not all men in sport can easily meet the standards of masculinity set in athletics. Gay men, men of color, and poor and working-class men represent what Connell calls *competing masculinities*. Their experiences of masculinity are mediated by their race, sexual identity, and class status. Because their social group memberships deviate from the white, heterosexual, and middle-class norm, these men have less access to privilege even though they might excel in sport. A gay male athlete must hide his identity. An African-American male athlete is stereotyped by racist expectations and disadvantaged by institutional racism. These competing masculinities also enable these men to create a different approach to the development of masculinity, as in the ironic stance of the gay male athlete described by Pronger.

PROVIDING A CONTEXT FOR ACCEPTABLE AND SAFE MALE BONDING AND INTIMACY

Athletics is one of the few social contexts in which men can openly express physical affection and love for other men. Team members spend an enormous amount of time together during the course of a season, practicing and competing, traveling to games, spending nights in hotels, and socializing. The emotional intensity of competition and sharing the highs and lows of winning and losing encourage strong bonds among teammates. . . .

In addition to this emotional bond, athletics involves physical intimacy as well. Participating in team sports in particular requires physical contact with both teammates and opponents. In addition, athletes spend a lot of time together in hotel rooms, locker rooms, showers, and whirlpool baths—all places that suggest a high degree of physical closeness or nudity. During victory celebrations men can, without fear of ridicule, hug and kiss each other. Men can also

cry without shame about losing a big game. Fanny slaps and chest bumps are commonplace in men's athletics, especially in team sports. It is not a coincidence that expressions of male-to-male physical affection and love are acceptable in few other contexts. In athletics men can admire other men's bodies and their physical accomplishments openly without arousing suspicions about their heterosexuality. The bond among male teammates is an important lesson in male solidarity around their masculine identities. . . .

REINFORCING MALE PRIVILEGE AND FEMALE INFERIORITY

Defining masculinity is as much about rejecting so-called feminine qualities as it is about embracing so-called masculine ones. Male coaches send strong messages about women and about the need for men to avoid being like women when they compare a poor performance by a male athlete to that of a girl (for example, throwing like a girl). Many coaches know they can inspire male athletes to perform better by calling them demeaning names intended for women (pussies) or hybrids like wussy (wimp and pussy). Being called a woman, compared to a woman, or—the worst insult—being beaten by a woman in any sport contest provokes anger and shame in many men and boys. . . .

As Mariah Burton Nelson points out in her insightful book *The Stronger Women Get, The More Men Love Football*, many men need to establish the "fact" that no matter what gains women make in sport, they could never play football. They believe that football is the epitome of athletic excellence and legitimacy. In New Jersey a female member of a high school football team was physically assaulted by her male teammates who were trying to dissuade her from playing. Elizabeth Balsley was punched, hit with blocking dummies, and spat upon as she walked toward the practice field. Three of her male teammates were charged with assault, suspended from classes for two to four days, and barred from playing in one football game. . . . As this incident illustrates, young women who dare to challenge the notion that football is too tough for women must be taught a lesson.

This need to establish male superiority extends beyond comparing the performance merits of male and female athletes. Studies of talk in men's locker rooms describe consistent patterns of antiwoman and antigay interactions. Many men talk about women as sexual possessions or receptacles, not as equals or even as human beings. In this climate male athletes learn to despise qualities within themselves that they perceive to be feminine and to accept female inferiority in sport as fact. They develop a sense of entitlement and superiority in relationship to women on and off the athletic field. . . .

A study by Crosset, Benedict, and McDonald indicates that there is a higher incidence of violence against women by male athletes than by other men on college campuses. Athletic team participation in gang rapes or the development of a scoring system to rank sexual conquests are disturbing examples of how bonding among male athletes based on contempt for women can lead to antisocial criminal behaviors. . . .

ESTABLISHING STATUS AMONG OTHER MALES

Sport is the single most important element of the peer-status system for U.S. adolescent males. Moreover, athletics is a rehearsal for the status many white, middle-class boys hope to achieve later through work, education, and economic accumulation. Poor, working-class men of all colors often view success as a professional athlete as the only route, no matter how unrealistic, to economic success and social status. As a result, athletics takes on a special status in the culture of boys and young men. Messner describes how boys learn that acceptance by and status with peers, fathers, and coaches is achieved by winning in sports. According to Messner, boys learn that just participating in sports is not enough. To achieve the kind of attention and connections they seek, it is necessary to be better than other boys,

to beat them in sports. In high school and college, male athletes, particularly team-sport athletes, are often treated as high-status members of the community by peers, teachers, and other community members. As such, they often receive special treatment and recognition not given to other boys. . . . Being judged acceptable in this public sport-performance hierarchy is an important ritual in establishing self-worth among boys and young men. Sport for boys is serious business, and girls have no place in it.

REINFORCING HETEROSEXUALITY

For many people the male team-sports hero is the epitome of masculinity: strong, tough, handsome, competitive, dating or married to the most desirable woman. An accepted perquisite of professional athletic fame for men is a rich and varied sex life with many willing young female groupies. Many people believe that the terms *gay man* and *athlete* used together are an oxymoron. A gay male athlete violates both the image of male athletes as strong, virile, and heterosexual and the image of gay men as swishy and effeminate. Just as it is important to keep women out of sport or marginalized in sport, it is essential to keep gay men in sport invisible. If gay men can be strong, tough, competitive, and part of a male bonding experience in the locker room with straight men, how can straight men confidently differentiate themselves from gay men? Just as young men in athletics learn that women are inferior, they also learn that gay men are contemptible. Being called a "faggot" or "pansy" is an insult of the highest order to one's sense of masculinity. The incidence of antigay talk in locker rooms and the participation of male athletes in gay bashing reflect this attitude.

Maintaining the myths that all male athletes are heterosexual and that sexual attraction among male athletes does not occur allow men to enjoy the physical and emotional intimacy of the athletic team experience. They do not need to worry that teammates might think they are gay. These myths also protect male athletes from confronting the possibility that someone else in that locker room might be gay. Many heterosexual men are extremely uncomfortable with the possibility of being the object of another man's sexual interest. By displaying contempt for gays through antigay name-calling, jokes, harassment, or violence, men reassure themselves and teammates that everyone in the locker room is heterosexual in an intimate all-male context. If this illusion is threatened by the presence of openly gay men, the complex feelings of love and intimacy, physical contact, and communal nudity could not be enjoyed without fear and suspicion. The fear of being perceived as gay or being the object of gay sexual desire is a powerful social control that keeps men in athletics safely within the bounds of traditional masculinity.

This need to believe that there are no gay men present in the locker room or on the playing field makes the male athletic environment extremely hostile for openly gay athletes and coaches. . . . A closeted gay athlete can participate without suspicion, as long as he is willing to keep his identity a secret. Being an athlete is so consistent with traditional masculine and heterosexual expectations for men that gay athletes can pass if they are willing to. While women athletes must constantly prove their heterosexuality, most people assume that male athletes are heterosexual unless they provide evidence that they are not. . . .

Defenders of a sexist and heterosexist status quo are right to fear the potential that sport has for the empowerment of women. Sport can be a catalyst for empowering women to become the center of their own experience, whether demanding equal access to resources; making connections among sexism, racism, and heterosexism; developing and reveling in their own strength and physical competence; or falling in love with a teammate. When women take sport participation seriously, it is, as Mariah Burton Nelson asserts, a feminist activity: "All of us collectively, are a threat—not to men exactly, but to male privilege and to masculinity as defined through manly sport." . . .

81

Real Men and Pink Suits

Charles M. Blow

New York Times, February 10, 2012

Twitter claims another casualty.

This week, Roland Martin, a bombastic cultural and political commentator was suspended by CNN from his role as a political analyst on the network for Twitter messages published during the Super Bowl.

One message read: "If a dude at your Super Bowl party is hyped about David Beckham's H&M underwear ad, smack the ish out of him! #superbowl." Another read: "Who the hell was that New England Patriot they just showed in a head to toe pink suit? Oh, he needs a visit from #teamwhipdatass."

The Gay and Lesbian Alliance Against Defamation said the messages advocated "violence against gay people" and asked CNN to fire Martin. CNN called the messages "regrettable and offensive" and suspended him "for the time being." Martin issued an apology in which he said that he was just "joking about smacking someone."

There is vigorous debate online about what Martin meant, about GLAAD's reaction, and about CNN's policy on who gets suspended or fired and for what kinds of statements.

Martin and GLAAD have signaled, over Twitter, that they plan to meet and discuss the matter. Maybe something positive will emerge from that.

But whether it does or not, I don't want to let this incident pass without using it as a "teachable moment" for us all about the dangerous way in which we define manhood and masculinity. At the very least, Martin's comments are corrosive on this front.

I follow Martin on Twitter. I know that he likes to joke and tease. I have even joked with him. So I can believe that, in his mind, he may have thought that these were just harmless jokes in which the violence was fictional and funny.

But in the real world—where bullying and violence against gays and lesbians, or even those assumed to be so, is all too real—"jokes" like his hold no humor. There are too many bruised ribs and black eyes and buried bodies for the targets of this violence to just lighten up and laugh.

We all have to understand that effects can operate independent of intent, that subconscious biases can move counter to conscious egalitarianism, and that malice need not be present within the individual to fuel the maliciousness of the society at large.

(This is not to say that Martin has been egalitarian on this front. In fact, a widely cited 2006 post on his Web site suggests otherwise. In it, he criticized the Rev. Al Sharpton for appealing to black churches "to become more accepting and embracing of homosexuality." Martin wrote that gays and lesbians "are engaged, in the eyes of the church, in sinful behavior." Furthermore, he said, "My wife, an ordained Baptist minister for 20 years, has counseled many men and women to walk away from the gay lifestyle, and to live a chaste life." And he compared homosexuals to adulterers, disobedient children, alcoholics and thieves.)

Words have power. And power recklessly exerted has consequences. It's not about being politically correct. It's about being sensitive to the plight of those being singled out. We can't ask the people taking the punches to also take the jokes.

And it's about understanding that masculinity is wide enough and deep enough for all of us to fit in it. But society in general, and male culture in particular, is constantly working to render it narrow and shallow. We have shaved the idea of manhood down to an unrealistic definition that few can fit in it with the whole of who they are, not without severe constriction or self-denial.

The man that we mythologize in the backs of our minds is a cultural concoction, an unattainable ideal, a perfect specimen of muscles and fearlessness and daring. Square-jawed and well-rounded. Potent and passionate. Sensitive but not sentimental. And, above all else, unwaveringly heterosexual and without even a hint of softness.

A vast majority of men will never be able to be all these things all the time, but they shouldn't be made to feel less than a man because of it.

And this narrowed manhood ideal has a truly damaging effect on boys.

In *Boy Culture: An Encyclopedia*, which was published in 2010, the editors point out: "Boys are men in training. As such, most strive to enact and replicate hegemonic masculinity so that they achieve status among male peers, and pre-emptively guard against accusations or perceptions that their masculinity is deficient." The editors went on to quote a 2001 study in which a boy who does not measure up to dominant prescriptions of masculinity is "likely to be punished by his peers in ways which seek to strip him of his mantle of masculinity."

In fact, a 2005 report entitled "From Teasing to Torment: School Climate in America," which was commissioned by the Gay, Lesbian and Straight Education Network, found that a third of all teens said that they are often bullied, called names or harassed at their school because they are, or people think that they are, gay, lesbian or bisexual.

We have created this culture, and we can undo it.

Start with this fact: The truest measure of a man, indeed of a person, is not whom he lies down with but what he stands up for. If we must be judged, let it be in this way. And when we fall short, as we sometimes will, because humanity is fallible, let us greet each other with compassion and encouragement rather than ridicule and resentment.

Whatever was in Martin's heart, what was in his Twitter messages wasn't helpful. They may not lead directly to intimidation or violence, but they may add to a stream of negativity that feeds a culture in which intimidation and violence by some twisted minds is all too real. I don't believe that Martin wanted that.

Let's show the whole of mankind that men can indeed be kind, even to other men who dare to wear pink suits.

82

The Loving Decision

Anna Quindlen

Same-sex marriage was beaten back at the ballot box. Now here's a history lesson on why victory is inevitable in the long run.

One of my favorite Supreme Court cases is *Loving v. Virginia*, and not just because it has a name that would delight any novelist. It's because it reminds me, when I'm downhearted,

of the truth of the sentiment at the end of *Angels in America*, Tony Kushner's brilliant play: "The world only spins forward."

Here are the facts of the case, and if they leave you breathless with disbelief and rage it only proves Kushner's point, and mine: Mildred Jeter and Richard Loving got married in Washington, D.C. They went home to Virginia, there to be rousted out of their bed one night by police and charged with a felony. The felony was that Mildred was black and Richard was white and they were therefore guilty of miscegenation, which is a $10 word for bigotry. Virginia, like a number of other states, considered cross-racial matrimony a crime at the time. It turned out that it wasn't just the state that hated the idea of black people marrying white people. God was onboard, too, according to the trial judge, who wrote, "The fact that He separated the races shows that he did not intend for the races to mix." But the Supreme Court, which eventually heard the case, passed over the Almighty for the Constitution, which luckily has an equal-protection clause. "Marriage is one of the basic civil rights of man," the unanimous opinion striking down the couple's conviction said, "fundamental to our very existence and survival." That was in 1967.

Fast-forward to Election Day 2008, and a flurry of state ballot propositions to outlaw gay marriage, all of which were successful. This is the latest wedge issue of the good-old-days crowd, supplanting abortion and immigration. They really put their backs into it this time around, galvanized by court decisions in three states ruling that it is discriminatory not to extend the right to marry to gay men and lesbians.

The most high-profile of those rulings, and the most high-profile ballot proposal, came in California. A state court gave its imprimatur to same-sex marriage in June [2008]; the electorate reversed that decision on Nov. 4 with the passage of Proposition 8, which defines marriage as only between a man and a woman. The opponents of gay marriage will tell you that the people have spoken. It's truer to say that money talks. The Mormons donated millions to the anti effort; the Knights of Columbus did, too. Like the judge who ruled in the *Loving* case, they said they were doing God's bidding. When I was a small child I always used to picture God on a cloud, with a beard. Now I picture God saying, "Why does all the worst stuff get done in my name?"

Just informationally, this is how things are going to go from here on in: two steps forward, one step back. Courts will continue to rule in some jurisdictions that there is no good reason to forbid same-sex couples from marrying. Legislatures in two states, New York and New Jersey, could pass a measure guaranteeing the right to matrimony to all, and both states have governors who have said they would sign such legislation.

Opponents will scream that the issue should be put to the people, as it was in Arizona, Florida and California. (Arkansas had a different sort of measure, forbidding unmarried couples from adopting or serving as foster parents. This will undoubtedly have the effect of leaving more kids without stable homes. For shame.) Of course if the issue in *Loving* had been put to the people, there is no doubt that many would have been delighted to make racial intermarriage a crime. That's why God invented courts.

The world only spins forward.

"I think the day will come when the lesbian and gay community will have its own *Loving v. Virginia*," says David Buckel, the Marriage Project director for Lambda Legal.

Yes, and then the past will seem as preposterous and mean-spirited as the events leading up to the *Loving* decision do today. After all, this is about one of the most powerful forces for good on earth, the determination of two human beings to tether their lives forever. The pitch of the opposition this year spoke to how far we have already come—the states in which civil unions and domestic partnerships are recognized, the families in which gay partners are welcome and beloved.

The antis argued that churches could be forced to perform same-sex unions, when any divorced Roman Catholic can tell you that the clergy refuse to officiate whenever

V
O
I
C
E
S

they see fit. They argued that the purpose of same-sex marriage was the indoctrination of children, a popular talking point that has no basis in reality. As Ellen DeGeneres, who was married several months ago to the lovely Portia de Rossi (great dress, girl), said about being shaped by the orientation of those around you, "I was raised by two heterosexuals. I was surrounded by heterosexuals. Just everywhere I looked: heterosexuals. They did not influence me." As for the notion that allowing gay men and lesbians to marry will destroy conventional marriage, I have found heterosexuals perfectly willing to do that themselves.

The last word here goes to an authority on battling connubial bigotry. On the anniversary of the *Loving* decision last year, the bride wore tolerance. Mildred Loving, mother and grandmother, who once had cops burst into her bedroom because she was sleeping with her own husband, was quoted in a rare public statement saying she believed all Americans, "no matter their race, no matter their sex, no matter their sexual orientation, should have that same freedom to marry." She concluded, "That's what *Loving*, and loving, are all about."

83

Mestiza/o Gender

Notes towards a Transformative Masculinity

Daniel E. Solís y Martínez

... On December 9, 1531, on the sacred hill of Tepeyacac, just outside the recently-conquered city of Tenochitlan, an indigenous man who is now known only as Juan Diego combined the traditional Mexica goddess Tonantzín with the Spaniards' Virgin Mary to create the Virgin of Guadalupe. Juan Diego, a recent convert to Catholicism, was visited on Tepeyacac by an unusually brown-skinned Virgin Mary. This seemingly indigenous Virgin Mary told Juan Diego to visit the Spanish Bishop in Mexico City and to ask him to build a church dedicated to her at Tepeyacac. Juan Diego did as she asked; but the Bishop refused to believe the lowly *indigena* (indigenous person) Juan Diego and demanded proof of this miraculous apparition of the Mother of God. Juan Diego returned to the sacred hill in search of proof and found the Virgin Mary waiting for him. The Virgin Mary instructed him to ascend to the mountaintop of Tepeyacac where he would find a bounty of beautiful flowers miraculously growing out of season that would serve as his proof. Juan Diego gathered the flowers into his cloak and then descended the holy mountain to return to the disbelieving Bishop.

Once again, Juan Diego repeated the Virgin Mary's request for the construction of a church at Tepeyacac. The Bishop again demanded proof. Juan Diego simply replied by unfurling his cloak and dropping the flowers at the feet of the Bishop, immediately filling the room with a tremendous fragrance. It was at that moment that the Bishop saw the divine imprint of the brown-skinned Virgin Mary on Juan Diego's cloak. Being humbled by both the choice of the indigenous Juan Diego as the Virgin Mary's messenger and the brown skin of the Virgin herself, the Bishop agreed to build the church at Tepeyacac.

The acceptance of the brown-skinned Virgin Mary on Juan Diego's cloak by the Spanish Bishop was the beginning of the officially-sanctioned cult of the Virgin of Guadalupe in the Americas. Within the racially-mixed form of the Virgin of Guadalupe, indigenous people like Juan Diego were able to merge their traditional religions with the Catholicism imposed

on them by the colonizing Spanish, so as to produce a truly new form of cultural and religious expression. Given their inability to directly confront the more powerful Spanish, the indigenous peoples of Mexico and Central America used the Virgin of Guadalupe to create within the dominance of the Spanish a space of their own. Utilizing the legitimization that the Spanish Catholic Church conferred on the Virgin of Guadalupe, *indigenas* such as Juan Diego forged religious customs that were neither Catholic nor the traditional practices of the Mexica, but that mixed elements from both. The birth of the brown-skinned Virgin of Guadalupe was a powerful event that signaled the beginning, first in Mexico and Central America and then in the United States, of a process of cultural mixing that has given rise to new ethnic and national identities.

The story of Juan Diego, with its unequal marriage of conflicted ideas and practices in the face of powerful forces, is a compelling metaphor for my own life as a Latino gay man attempting to create a way of being queer that is ethical, freeing and true to myself. Like Juan Diego's merging of the repressed indigenous goddess Tonantzín into the ascendant European Virgin Mary, I endeavor to create my own gayness through a blending of two distinct systems of homosexuality: that which my parents brought with them from El Salvador and that which I grew into in the United States. Growing up, my queerness was contained by my family within the traditional homosexuality of El Salvador. In that system, homosexuality is a matter of gender difference that is expressed by both sexual behavior and deviant gender practices. In El Salvador and much of Latin America, homosexual men and boys like me are seen not as women or men but instead occupy an ambiguous place in between. Under this particular system of homosexuality, my parents raised me quite differently from my brothers: I am the only one who was taught by my mother and grandmother how to cook, clean, sew, and even now am responsible for organizing family events such as birthdays, holidays and dinners. As a child, I was allowed to socialize with girls and women, all without my gayness being explicitly named. Within my home, my budding gayness was silently accepted and integrated into the larger fabric of my family so long as it did not threaten the heterosexual status quo. . . .

Throughout Latin America and in El Salvador, homosexuality is understood primarily as a matter of gender. Homosexual behavior—particularly the act of penetration—determines to a large degree whether one is or isn't a man. *Maricónes, culeros*, and *putos* are all words that name the non-maleness of the homosexual in the traditional Latin American conceptualization of homosexuality. Mexican anthropologist Héctor Carrillo describes the traditional operation of this gender-sexuality system in Mexico as creating men through non-men. . . . Carrillo notes the distinction between, ". . . masculine men were *hombres* or *machos*," and ". . . their counterparts were the effeminate men, the *maricones*, who were perceived as having forfeited their manhood altogether" (Carrillo 2003, 352). Carrillo further explains that *maricones* served to legitimize the masculinity of the *hombres*. As such, normative masculinity in the Latin American context was not possible without *maricones*. . . .

In the traditional understanding of homosexuality in Latin America, homosexual male-bodied individuals are not men at all. Instead, they are seen as another type of gender category altogether, existing in a shifting location between women's femininity and men's bodies. Carrillo's observations of Mexican homosexuality hold true for much of Latin America. In fact, many names for male homosexuals throughout Latin America speak to this in-between gendered status. In most of its Latin American articulations, homosexuality is a matter of gender, not sexual identity.

This in-between homosexual gender is centered on the matter of penetration: he who is penetrated is a homosexual. By being the receptive partner in anal intercourse, Latin American *homosexuales* give up their claim to masculinity. Instead they enter into a gender space that borrows and claims much from femininity but that is decidedly different from woman-ness. This articulation of homosexuality as a different gender, which essentializes it into a biological trait, creates spaces for Latin American *homosexuales* within Latin

American societies and families. These spaces are often created not by the overt presence of homophobic discourses, but instead by their silent operation. Queer Puerto Rican sociologist Manolo Guzmán describes "... this absence of speech [as] no longer talking about things like marriage, represents a suspension of the assumption of heterosexuality" (Guzmán 2006, 88). It is in those spaces of absent speech in which Latin American homosexuality rests. My own parents' response to my budding gender deviance and homosexuality was shaped by this system of homosexual gender. My family's acceptance of my queer impulses was predicated on its safe containment in the traditional queer gender space of the Latin American family structure. So long as my homosexuality was not explicitly named it did not threaten the traditional supremacy of my father over our family. . . .

My childhood experiences in the vast stretches of Los Angeles were defined by a constant shift between two separate worlds firmly divided by a border made up of language, class, and race. The Salvadoreño culture of my home and neighborhood in the eastern San Fernando Valley was an island in the surrounding sea of Americanness. Moving from the Spanish of my family to the English of my teachers and school forced me from an early age to be constantly aware of the need to shift my way of being depending on where I was. Who I was depended on where I was, who I was with and what language I was speaking. Like many budding homo boys, the need to constantly move back and forth between worlds made me a talented performer from an early age. I quickly became a skilled border-crosser.

At the very core of my role switching was a fundamental clash between the migrant gender-sexuality worldview of my family and the "native" system of the United States. My parents were locked in a battle—internally and externally—to craft a family that was the best of the values and cultural forms they had been raised with, but that at the same time recognized the sheer reality that they were not in El Salvador anymore. This battle was never explicitly named by my parents as the source of their discomfort with my brothers' and my own rapid Americanization, but it quietly informed every action they took. . . . My parents' struggle was centered in our home. Patriarchy was the central axis around which my parents constructed our family. My father worked an inhuman amount of hours as a machine-shop operator to support my family, but his salary was simply not enough to make ends meet. In the rapidly de-industrializing Los Angeles of the 1980s, machine-shop work was on the decline. My father's lack of an American education and legal status exacerbated the dwindling supply of work, resulting in a continuous cycle of migration from one job to the next. This instability finally forced my father to allow my mother's entrance into the working world. Like my grandmother and aunt, she too became a domestic worker for the rich and white of the West San Fernando Valley.

The emergence of my mother as our family's co-supporter led to fierce fights for dominance and power within our home. Quite simply, my mother's departure from her traditional role as homemaker undermined my father's masculinity. The assault on my father's manhood was twofold. Since he couldn't fully provide for all of our family's financial needs, he was failing at his manly obligations. This was compounded by the loss of mental and physical control over my mother. It was perhaps the loss of total control over my mother that most undermined my father's masculine power. With work, my mother gained independence as she learned how to drive and for the first time had money of her own to spend. Implicit in my father's frustration was the fear that her daily sojourns to the outside world would corrupt my mother and render her unfit as both mother and wife. My father's fears would explode in dramatic and often violent outbursts aimed particularly at my mother, but also at my brothers and me. These poverty-driven gendered struggles set the stage for the emergence of my queerness within my family.

As is the case for many homo boys, from an early age my mother was my world. The bond between us was one of sameness; in my mind I was just like her. My mother is fond of reminding me of how as a baby she alone had the power to stop my tears. To this day, she is still one of the few people that can get me to shut up. Given the close affinity between my

mother and me, when my parents would fight I would stand at her side ready to battle my father, and often my older brother as well. It wouldn't matter who was wrong or right, but simply that my mother was threatened. Since I saw my mother as not only my role model but as the source from which I had sprung, when she was threatened I was threatened.

Often the fights between my parents were about the bond of affinity between my mother and me. My father accused her of spoiling me, which in our working class home had strong undertones of feminization and emasculation. In claiming that my mother was spoiling me, my father was really saying that she was turning me into a non-boy. His accusations were further complicated by his patronizing of my older brother as his Chosen Son. Subtly undermining my mother's authority over him, my father drew my older brother into his orbit as an ally. As time wore on, those battle lines became entrenched gender lines dividing us into two opposing camps: my father and older brother as the men and my mother and I as the women. It was in those moments of anger, of a family divided along lines of what I can only call queer genders that my own unique place in my family began to emerge.

My queer gender developed out of those fights within my family. While never openly named by either of my parents, they had tacitly agreed that I was to be raised differently from my clearly male-gendered brothers. I was to be the *culerito*. As a child, I was the son taught to cook, clean, listen and nurture. At the never-ending string of quinceañeras, birthday parties, and baptismal celebrations, I was always with the women. I would sit among my mother, grandmother, aunt, godmother, and a host of their friends, listening to them gossip about one another, or lovingly (yet critically) pick at their husbands, their sons, and their daughters. Meanwhile, my brothers would play with other boy-children. My inclusion in these circles of women was never questioned, at least while I was present. If whispered conversations of concern about my affiliation with women happened between my mother and her women friends, I was not aware. . . .

The relative acceptance of my family was matched by the unease I felt towards the world "*out there.*" I don't really remember an exact moment when I became conscious of the fact that my love for girl-child toys and women superheroes was a *private* matter—a matter of the home and family. Somehow I just understood that it was not okay for me to take my dolls out of the home. Whenever I played with the other children in my apartment complex, I never mentioned that my favorite G.I. JOE was Scarlett, the red haired counter-terrorist vixen of the team, and I certainly never dared to bring her out with me to play. Like my constant transitions from English and Spanish between school and home, I also switched my gender performance from home to the outside. The queer child I was inside my home butched it up whenever I crossed the threshold of our door. . . .

My family's tolerance of my gayness was markedly different from the clearly defined homosexuality of the United States that I found first on the playgrounds and in the class-rooms of my elementary school, and later on in the queer identity groups I joined as a teenager. The homosexuality I found outside of my family was one of a clearly defined gayness that was accessed through personal identification. In what I call the American system of homosexuality, a person was gay either because they called themselves gay or because others labeled them that way. As I grew older, I discovered communities of queer people in the United States built around a shared sense of identity and personal experience. At the core of these communities was the idea of "coming out"—or publicly naming one's queerness to others. This explicitly named gayness was quite different from the unnamed ambiguous position I held within my family. After I came out, my position in my family changed as I sought to force them to accept American gayness as the basis for how they understood me and my queerness. My efforts led to great conflicts between myself and most of my family members. As I grew increasingly isolated from my family, I realized that American gayness with its emphasis on the individual wasn't sufficient for me or my particular situation. I began to seek a way to construct an empowering queerness that challenged heterosexism but that also didn't isolate me from the people I love so much.

Constructing my queerness solely out of either Latin American homosexuality or American gayness presents great obstacles to the type of queerness I want to embody. Like Juan Diego, my options are seemingly limited. Do I choose the gendered homosexuality I grew up with in my family or the individualistic gayness of the country I was born in? Given the overwhelming power of both types of homosexuality to resist challenges to their oppressive elements, I find myself moving within and between both systems to create the queerness I seek. . . .

At the core of both my journey and this essay is a creative process of reclamation. Rather than simply giving up on both of these homosexualities, I seek to work within them by taking elements from both and combining them together in a new way that can challenge the oppressive components within each. Queer theorist José Esteban Muñoz, in studying the oppositional and creative use of mainstream heterosexual and queer cultures by queer performance artists of color, has articulated a process similar to the one I wish to engage in. Muñoz calls this process disidentification. He describes this as,

> . . . the third mode of dealing with dominant ideology, one that neither opts to assimilate within such a structure nor strictly opposes it; rather, disidentification is a strategy that works on and against dominant ideology . . . this "working on and against" is a strategy that tries to transform a cultural logic from within, always laboring to enact permanent structural change while at the same time valuing the importance of local or everyday struggles of resistance.

(1999, 11–12)

Moving beyond the binary idea that in the face of oppressive forces one can either purely resist or assimilate, Muñoz instead sees disidentification as a means to creatively engage with structures of injustice. Disidentification allows marginalized individuals to take the tools of oppression used against them and use them in new ways that alter their meaning so as to challenge the very oppression from which they are drawn. Muñoz values disidentification because it presents a means to escape the binary of assimilation and counteridentification which both serve to reinforce the dominance of oppressive systems. It is what Muñoz calls "working on and against" that makes disidentification a powerful means of altering the harmful elements of both Latin American homosexuality and American gayness.

I utilize disidentification to blend the two forms of homosexuality so as to construct a third path of queerness that can escape the limitations of both. Through disidentification, I can work against the totalizing power of Latin American homosexuality to trap queers in the gender system of man/woman. A third queerness can also work against a gayness in the United States that is increasingly becoming nothing more than a colorful and non-threatening alternative to heterosexuality. As gayness in the United States becomes more mainstream, it is not only leaving unchallenged dominant ideals of consumerism as citizenship, but in fact it is using those same ideals as the definition of social justice for queers. Since both forms of homosexuality are limiting and perpetuate violent forms of oppression, I must create a queerness through my daily practices that draws from the most transformative in both while challenging the most repressive in each. . . .

With the *mestiza/o gender* I am creating, my queerness moves beyond a matter of sexual identity and becomes an encompassing gender location. I embrace the ambiguous position of the Latin American *puto* and realize that pursuing masculinity is not only futile but it is harmful both to me and others. The *mestiza/o* politics of ambiguity show me that to be a gay man in a unified and stable sense isn't possible. The acts of exclusion that are required in creating a stable identity of gay masculinity, through the *mestiza/o* lens, are exposed as immoral and highly suspect. By buying into the binary gender system, queer men support the oppression of women, transpeople, and other gender deviants. The space that Latin

American homosexuals occupy in the gender system can provide queer men with a means to construct identities that alter patriarchy and create coalitions of change with others. The gendered basis of Latin American homosexuality, however, must be tempered by the protection of the individual that American gayness so heavily emphasizes. By ensuring that individuals are allowed to develop and creatively construct their own identities, the gendered articulation of homosexuality in Latin America can become truly emancipatory. This *mestiza/o* combination is what I seek to create by living it everyday.

I recognize the potential dangers of engaging in the selective extraction and mixing of elements from diverse cultures, but I believe that the need for new forms of homosexualities justifies taking those risks. A politics of *mestizaje* can produce an impure queerness that is less about how each individual identifies, but instead focuses on how individuals relate to one another in the pursuit of justice. Claiming common cause with others, that is building a coalitional community of change, is an uneven process that must center not on the identities people wear and own, but instead on the act of relating. Who we relate to and how we relate to them is what should define us as queer. Thinking about queerness as a set of relations moves it from the realm of individual sexual identity towards a way of being. This shift sets queerness in the realm of gender, an all-encompassing script that defines who and what we are. *Mestizaje* opens up the category of gender, which is rightfully seen as a limiting force, into a means to structure the conflicting mixture of privilege and oppression that defines many queer men's masculinities. . . . Like the race mixing that *mestiza/o* has traditionally referred to, I am interested in creating a gayness that is a mixture—imperfect, always in process of becoming, yet resisting with all of its might. It is towards that end, that I write these notes, themselves imperfect and in process of articulation. . . .

References

Carrillo, H. (2003). "Neither Machos nor Maricones: Masculinity and Emerging Male Homosexual Identities in Mexico." In M. C. Gutmann (ed.), *Changing Men and Masculinities in Latin America.* Durham, NC: Duke University Press.

Guzmán, M. (2006). *Gay Hegemony/Latino Homosexualities.* New York: Routledge.

Muñoz, J. E. (1999). *Disidentifications: Queers of Color and the Performance of Politics.* Minneapolis: University of Minnesota Press.

84

Becoming an Ally

A New Examination

Nancy J. Evans and Jamie Washington

What does it mean to be an ally? Students in a graduate program that prepares student affairs professionals in higher education responded to this question with the following reflections:

- Being an ally is being supportive of other people who are different than you. . . . This support should be flexible and elastic so that it does not define a person but rather the person defines the needed support. (gay male)
- Being an ally is being open to learning. It is essential to be open to admitting your ignorance in order to grow. Being an ally also requires a commitment. . . . Being an ally requires an examination of our own privilege. In order to be an ally we have to be able to recognize how our privilege might play a role in the oppression of the very group/identity we want to be an ally to. Being an ally is using your powers for good. (lesbian)
- Being an ally is being aware of your own identities, advocating for the rights of others, supporting a cause, and challenging the oppression that particular populations face. It can mean lending a supportive hand to a peer. Being an ally is recognizing the inequality and inequity that exists in society, persistence, learning and teaching. (heterosexual woman)
- Being an ally is listening to other views and ideas without judgment; putting yourself in someone else's shoes; respecting people for who they are; advocating for resources, respect, equal treatment, laws; challenging your previous personal beliefs and ideas; working with underrepresented populations to better understand them and their unique needs; wanting to learn how to help, even in the little things; using non-discriminating language; [it is] important to the campus climate and overall student development; [it is] difficult and can have backlash. [An ally] must be committed and ready. (heterosexual male)
- An ally looks different to everyone. Sometimes an ally is a listening ear and a shoulder to cry on. Sometimes an ally is a fighter, fighting the powers to see justice done. (heterosexual woman)
- Being an ally is confusion, hard, being yelled at, learning, acceptance, fighting to change, and learning you don't have to be right. . . . An ally can be the scapegoat in the room. Being an ally is knowing that you have privilege and oppressions and you can use both. Sometimes it is being called out and trying to realize you can learn from that. Learning when you can tell a story and learning when you can't explain no matter what and to just shut up. (questioning woman)

As these students suggest, being an ally is a difficult and complex role that can take on many meanings and require a wide variety of actions, many of which are challenging. What it means to be an ally often depends on who one asks and the particular situation and context in which one is involved. In this essay, we examine various definitions of *ally*, explore factors associated with becoming an ally of LGBT individuals, including the importance of recognizing heterosexual privilege, motivations for becoming an ally, the practice of advocacy, what an ally should know, and positive and negative consequences of advocacy. This essay is a revised and updated version of a chapter that appeared in the book, *Beyond Tolerance: Gays, Lesbians and Bisexuals on Campus.*

DEFINITIONS

As most writers and scholars in the area of oppression and multicultural education will concur, our language is imperfect and inherently "ism"-laden or oppressive. Therefore, clarifying the meaning of the term, "ally," is important. According to *Webster's New World Dictionary of the American Language*, an ally is "someone joined with another for a common purpose." This definition serves as a starting point for developing a working definition of *ally* as this term relates to issues of oppression. In our earlier work, we

defined ally as "a person who is a member of the 'dominant' or 'majority' group who works to end oppression in his or her personal and professional life through support of, and as an advocate with and for, the oppressed population." More recently, Broido defined allies as "members of dominant social groups (e.g., men, Whites, heterosexuals) who are working to end the system of oppression that gives them greater privilege and power based on their social group membership" (2000). While similar to our earlier definition, Broido highlighted that allies must work at the systemic level, as well as the individual level, and more clearly defined what it means to be a member of a dominant group in terms of access to privilege and power.

Both definitions stress that although an oppressed person can certainly be a supporter and advocate for his or her own group, the impact and effect of such activity are different for the dominant group, and are often more powerful when the supporter is not a member of the oppressed population. Understanding this notion is an important first step toward becoming an ally for any "targeted" or oppressed group. Members of the LGBT community will sometimes argue that they can be allies for other members of the community, since "the community" is an umbrella group that includes many different subgroups, e.g., lesbians, gay males, bisexuals, transgendered individuals, and other populations that might choose to identify with the LGBT community (pansexual, questioning, etc.). We certainly acknowledge that with regard to dimensions of identity *other than* sexual identity, members of oppressed groups can be allies to other oppressed groups. For example, a gay man can be an ally to a lesbian woman with regard to *gender* oppression. With regard to *sexual* identity, however, both are oppressed. Given the definitions noted above, only heterosexual individuals can serve as allies of lesbian, gay, and bisexual people.

HETEROSEXUAL PRIVILEGE

The individual who decides to undertake the ally role must recognize and understand the power and privileges that one receives, accepts, and experiences as a heterosexual person. According to Johnson, who drew on the work of Peggy McIntosh, "privilege exists when one group has something of value that is denied to others simply because of the groups they belong to, rather than because of anything they've done or failed to do" (2006, 21). McIntosh noted that privilege comes in two forms: "unearned advantages and conferred dominance," with the former being things of value freely given to members of one group but arbitrarily denied to another group, and the latter referring to power given to one group over another. Developing awareness of one's privilege is often the most painful part of the process of becoming an ally.

Some of the powers and privileges heterosexuals generally have that gay and lesbian, and in some cases bisexual and transgender, persons do *not* have include:

- Family memberships to health clubs, pools, and other recreational facilities
- The right to legalized marriage
- The ability to purchase property as a couple
- The option to file joint income tax returns
- The ability to adopt children as a couple
- Health insurance for one's life partner
- The right to make decisions on health-related issues as they relate to one's life partner
- The assumption that one is psychologically healthy

NEXT STEPS

In addition to such tangible privileges of the heterosexual population, there are a great many other, not so tangible, privileges. One important intangible privilege is living one's life without fear that people will find out that who one falls in love with, dreams about, or makes love to is someone of the same sex or that they were not always the gender with which they now identify. These fears affect the lives of gay, lesbian, bisexual, and transgender persons from the day they first begin to have "those funny feelings" until the day they die. Although many LGBT persons overcome these fears and turn the fear into a positive component of their lives, they have still been affected, and those wounds, even after healed, can be easily reopened.

Coming to terms with the very fact that "as a heterosexual I do not experience the world in the same way as LGBT people do" is an important step in becoming an ally. This awareness begins to move the heterosexual from being a caring, liberal person who feels that we are all created equal and should be treated as such, toward being an ally who begins to realize that although equality and equity are goals that have not yet been achieved, they can have a role in helping to make these goals realities.

Mohr introduced a model of heterosexual identity development, a process that he saw as related to the development of LGBT-affirmative attitudes. This model focuses on the development of awareness of heterosexual privilege. Mohr suggested that four "working models of sexual orientation" exist. Similar to Helms's contact status of white racial identity development in which individuals see themselves as color-blind, in the first working model proposed by Mohr, *democratic heterosexuality*, heterosexuals "tend to view people of all sexual orientations as essentially the same" (2002, 540–541). Individuals using this model rarely think about sexual identity issues and consider them unimportant. *Compulsory heterosexuality*, the second working model, is underscored by a belief that heterosexuality is the only acceptable form of sexual identity and that individuals who identify as LGBT are sick, perverted, and deserve to be oppressed. Individuals who base their beliefs on the third working model, *politicized heterosexuality*, recognize the privilege associated with heterosexuality and experience the emotions of guilt, sadness, and shame noted earlier that come with this awareness. They may also idealize LGBT people rather than seeing them as individuals who lead complex lives that are not solely centered around their sexual and gender identities. In the fourth working model, *integrative heterosexuality*, individuals are cognizant of the system of oppression that exists related to gender and sexual identity and the ways in which this system affects all people, regardless of their specific identity.

When heterosexual persons first learn that their lesbian, gay, bisexual, or transgender friends are truly mistreated on the basis of sexual or gender identity, they often feel anger toward heterosexuals and guilt toward themselves for being members of the same group. This process can only happen, however, if individuals have progressed at least to Mohr's third working model, when persons have an understanding of sexual and gender identity and do not see it as grounds for discrimination, violence, or abuse. These feeling do not occur when the person still believes that lesbian, gay, bisexual, or transgender persons are sick sinners who either need to have a good sexual relationship with a person of the other sex or see a psychologist or a spiritual leader so that they can be cured. Such persons, who might be classified as being in Mohr's second working model, are not yet ready to start down the ally road.

MOTIVATIONS FOR BECOMING AN ADVOCATE

What motivates heterosexuals to become LGBT rights advocates? There are certainly more popular and less controversial causes with which one can become involved. Goodman

NEXT STEPS

noted that support of social justice in general is related to empathy, moral and spiritual values, and self-interest. Since involvement in LGBT rights advocacy is often deemed a moral issue, moral development theory suggests some possible underlying reasons for such activity. Lawrence Kohlberg hypothesized that moral reasoning develops through three levels: preconventional, conventional, and postconventional. At the preconventional level, moral decisions are based on what is good for the individual. Persons functioning at this level may choose to be involved in gay rights issues to protect their own interests or to get something out of such involvement (e.g., if this issue is particularly important to a supervisor whose approval is sought). At the conventional level, Kohlberg indicated that decisions are made that conform to the norms of one's group or society. Individuals at this level may work for LGBT rights if they wish to support friends who are gay, lesbian, bisexual, or transgender or to uphold an existing institutional policy of nondiscrimination. Kohlberg's third level of reasoning involves decision making based on principles of justice. At this level the individual takes an active role to create policies that assure that all people are treated fairly and becomes involved in LGBT rights advocacy because it is the right thing to do.

While Kohlberg focused on justice as the basis of moral decision making, Carol Gilligan used the principle of care as the basis of her model of moral reasoning. Her three levels of reasoning are (1) taking care of oneself, (2) taking care of others, and (3) supporting positions that take into consideration the impact *both* on self and others. Using this model, individuals at the first level become advocates to make themselves look good to others or to protect themselves from criticism for not getting involved. At the second level, individuals reason that they should "take care of" LGBT people. The final perspective leads individuals to believe that equality and respect for differences create a better world for everyone, and that these are worthwhile goals.

One could argue that the latter position in each scheme is the enlightened perspective that any advocate needs to espouse. We should, however, be aware that not every person is functioning at a postconventional level of moral reasoning, and that arguments designed to encourage people to commit themselves to LGBT rights advocacy need to be targeted to the level that the individual can understand and accept. Kohlberg indicated that active involvement in addressing moral issues is an important factor in facilitating moral development along his stages. We can, therefore, expect that as people become involved in LGBT rights issues, their levels of reasoning may move toward a postconventional level.

In some ways paralleling our analysis of the moral reasoning that may be involved in advocacy, Edwards introduced a conceptual model of ally identity development. He suggested that self-interest, altruism, and a desire for social justice can all motivate potential allies. *Aspiring allies for self-interest* would take action when an LGBT person they care about is in danger of being hurt. They act on behalf of specific individuals to stop specific actions that are harmful or discriminatory and do not understand or care about the larger system of oppression that affects LGBT people as a group. Edwards noted that aspiring allies for self-interest often thrive on the feelings of power that come with "rescuing" their friend and being seen as a hero, thus perpetuating the system of oppression that creates the problem in the first place.

Edwards suggested that as individuals become aware of the privilege they experience, they can become motivated to be allies to assuage the guilt they feel. While *aspiring allies for altruism* would see the issues that confront LGBT individuals as a group, they would be likely to place the blame for oppression on other heterosexual individuals rather than seeing that they also benefit from an oppressive system. They would be likely to exhibit a paternalistic attitude as they seek to come to the aid of the oppressed LGBT population and, consciously or unconsciously, expect recognition and praise for the work they do on behalf of this group.

NEXT STEPS

The final type of allies that Edwards discussed is *allies for social justice*. These allies "work *with* those from the oppressed group in collaboration and partnership to end the system of oppression" (2006, 51). They would be aware that acting to end oppression of LGBT people in the end benefits heterosexuals as well. Thus, their goal in working to address the issue of oppression would be to achieve a just society rather than to gain recognition for their efforts.

Edwards acknowledged that individuals may experience each of these motivations for ally work depending on the specific situation in which they find themselves. He also stated that "the Ally for Social Justice status is an aspirational identity one must continuously work towards" (53). He argued that understanding each motivation can lead to the development of more consistent and effective ally behaviors.

ADVOCACY IN ACTION

Advocacy can take a number of different forms and target various audiences. Heterosexual supporters may focus some of their energy toward LGBT individuals themselves. At other times the target may be other heterosexuals, and often strategies developed for college and university campuses are focused on the campus community as a whole.

Advocacy with LGBT people involves acceptance, support, and inclusiveness. Examples of acceptance include listening in a nonjudgmental way and valuing the unique qualities of each individual. Support includes such behaviors as championing the hiring of LGBT staff; providing an atmosphere in which LGBT issues can be discussed in training or programming; or attending events sponsored by LGBT student organizations. Inclusiveness involves activities such as the use of nonexclusionary language; publications, fliers, and handbooks that take into account sexual and gender identity differences; and sensitivity to the possibility that not everyone in a student organization or work setting is heterosexual.

Being an advocate among other heterosexuals is often challenging. Such a position involves modeling advocacy, support, and confronting inappropriate behavior. In this context, heterosexual supporters model nonheterosexist behaviors such as being equally physical with men and women, avoiding joking or teasing someone for nontraditional gender behaviors, and avoiding making a point of being heterosexual. Allies are spokespersons for addressing LGBT issues proactively in program and policy development. Confronting such behaviors as heterosexist joke telling; the exclusion of LGBT people either intentionally or by using language that assumes heterosexuality; discriminatory hiring practices; or the evaluation of staff based on factors related to their sexual or gender identities is also part of the role of the advocate.

Advocacy in the institution involves making sure that issues facing LGBT students and staff are acknowledged and addressed. This goal is accomplished by developing and promoting educational efforts that raise the awareness level and increase the sensitivity of heterosexual students, staff, and faculty on campus. Such activities include inviting speakers to address topics relevant to the LGBT community; developing panel discussions on issues related to sexual and gender identities; including LGBT issues as a topic in resident advisor training programs; promoting plays and movies featuring LGBT themes; and advocating for curricular inclusion across the academic disciplines focusing on LGBT-related issues and themes.

Encouraging LGBT student and staff organizations is also part of institutional advocacy. Such groups need to have access to the same campus resources, funding, and sponsorship as other student and staff organizations. Developing and supporting pro-LGBT policies are also necessary aspects of advocacy. Anti-harassment policies, anti-discriminatory hiring

policies, and provisions for gay and lesbian couples to live together in campus housing are arenas that deserve attention.

STEPS TOWARD BECOMING AN ALLY

When dealing with issues of oppression, there are four basic levels of ally involvement. The following examples relate specifically to being an ally to LGBT persons.

- *Awareness* is the first level. It is important to become more aware of who you are and how you are different from and similar to LGBT people. Such awareness can be gained through conversations with LGBT individuals, attending awareness-building workshops, reading about LGBT life, and self-examination.
- *Knowledge/education* is the second level. You must begin to acquire knowledge about sexual and gender identities and the experiences of LGBT people. This step includes learning about laws, policies, and practices and how they affect LGBT people, in addition to educating yourself about LGBT culture and the norms of this community. Contacting local and national LGBT organizations for information can be very helpful.
- *Skills* make up the third level. This area is the one in which people often fall short because of fear, or lack of resources or supports. You must develop skills in communicating the knowledge that you have learned. These skills can be acquired by attending workshops, role-playing certain situations with friends, developing support connections, or practicing interventions or awareness raising in safe settings—for example, a restaurant or hotel out of your hometown.
- *Action* is the last, but most important, level and is the most frightening step. There are many challenges and liabilities for heterosexuals in taking actions to end the oppression of LGBT people. Some are addressed later in this essay in our discussion of factors that discourage advocacy. Nonetheless, action is, without doubt, the only way that we can effect change in the society as a whole; for if we keep our awareness, knowledge, and skill to ourselves, we deprive the rest of the world of what we have learned, thus keeping them from having the fullest possible life.

In addition to the four levels of ally involvement, there are six additional points to keep in mind:

1. Defining yourself as an ally is somewhat presumptuous. Whether your actions would qualify as those of an ally can best be determined by members of the LGBT population. Certainly, a person can advocate for equity and social justice for LGBT people without the permission of the LGBT community but declaring oneself to be an ally and demanding recognition as such can be off-putting to many LGBT people. Referring again to Edwards's model, such behavior seems more indicative of someone who is motivated by self-interest or altruism rather than by social justice.
2. Have a good understanding of sexual and gender identities and be aware of and comfortable with your own. If you are a person who chooses not to identify with a particular sexual or gender identity, be comfortable with that decision, but recognize that others, particularly LGBT people, may see your stance as a cop-out.
3. Talk with LGBT people and read about the coming-out process. This is a process and experience that is unique to this oppressed group. Few other populations of oppressed persons need to disclose so much to family and close friends in the same way. Because of its uniqueness, this process brings challenges that are often not understood.

NEXT STEPS

4. As any other oppressed group, the LGBT population gets the same messages about homosexuality, bisexuality, and gender expression as everyone else. As such, there is a great deal of internalized heterosexism, homophobia, and transgender oppression. There are LGBT people who believe that what they do in bed is nobody's business, and that being an "out" lesbian, gay, bisexual, or transgender person to them would mean forcing their sexual practices on the general society, something they feel should not be done. It is, therefore, very important not only to be supportive, recognizing that you do not share the same level of personal risk as a lesbian, gay, bisexual, or transgender person, but also to challenge some of the internalized oppressive notions, thus helping to develop a different, more positive, perspective.

5. As with most oppressed groups, there is diversity within the LGBT community. Heterosexism is an area of oppression that cuts across, but is not limited to, race, ethnicity, gender, class, religion, culture, age, and level of physical or mental ability. For all of these categories, there are different challenges. Certainly, LGBT individuals as members of these diverse populations share some common joys and concerns; however, issues often manifest themselves in very different ways in different groups, thus calling for different strategies and interventions.

6. It is difficult to enter into a discussion about heterosexism and homophobia without the topic of AIDS/HIV infection arising. Knowing at least basic information about the illness is necessary for two reasons: (1) to address myths and misinformation related to AIDS and the LGBT community, and (2) to be supportive of the members of the community affected by this disease. Although we recognize that AIDS is a health issue that has and will continue to affect our entire world, the persons who live in the most fear of this disease and have lost the most members of their community are LGBT individuals. Accepting that reality helps an ally to understand the intense emotions that surround this issue within the community.

These six points and the previously discussed levels of ally involvement provide some guidelines for becoming an effective ally. Although we recognize that these concepts seem fairly reasonable, there are some real challenges or factors that can discourage a potential ally from taking these steps.

N
E
X
T

S
T
E
P
S

FACTORS THAT DISCOURAGE ADVOCACY

Involvement in LGBT rights advocacy can be a scary and unpopular activity. Individuals who wish to take on such a role must be aware of and reconcile themselves to several potentially unpleasant outcomes. Some of these problems involve reactions from other heterosexuals, and some come from members of the LGBT community.

An assumption often is automatically made within the heterosexual community that anyone supporting LGBT rights is automatically gay, lesbian, bisexual, or transgender. Although such an identity is not negative, such labeling can create problems, especially for unmarried heterosexuals who might wish to become involved in a heterosexual romantic relationship. Heterosexuals also often experience derisive comments from other heterosexuals concerning involvement in a cause that is viewed as unimportant, unacceptable, or unpopular. Friends and colleagues who are uncomfortable with the topic may become alienated from the heterosexual supporter of LGBT rights, or may noticeably distance themselves from the individual. Difficulty may arise in social situations if the heterosexual ally is seen in the company of LGBT individuals. Discrimination, either overt or subtle, may also result from getting involved in controversial causes. Such discrimination may

take the form of poor evaluations, failure to be appointed to important committees, or encouragement to seek a position at a school "more supportive of your ideas."

The LGBT community may also have trouble accepting the heterosexual ally. Often an assumption is made that such persons are really gay, lesbian, bisexual, or transgender but not yet accepting of their identity. Subtle or not-so-subtle pressure is placed on such people to come out or at least to consider the possibility of a nonheterosexual identity.

The LGBT community is one that has its own language and culture. Heterosexual supporters can feel out of place and awkward in settings populated exclusively or mainly by gay males, lesbians, bisexuals, and transgender people. LGBT people may be exclusionary in their conversations and activities, leaving the heterosexual ally out of the picture.

Since most LGBT people have had mainly negative experiences with heterosexuals in the past, the motives of heterosexuals involved in LGBT rights activities are often questioned. These experiences make it difficult for LGBT people to accept that individuals will involve themselves in a controversial and unpopular cause just because it is "right." Many LGBT individuals also believe that persons who are not members of their community cannot truly understand the issues they face and should therefore leave it to LGBT people to educate and advocate for their own rights. They can become angry and resentful of heterosexuals' involvement in programs, spaces, and activities they believe should be exclusively theirs.

THE BENEFITS OF BEING AN ALLY

Although the factors that discourage individuals from being an ally are very real, there are many benefits of being an ally, including:

1. You open yourself up to the possibility of close relationships with an additional percentage of the world.
2. You become less locked into sex-role stereotypes.
3. You increase your ability to have close and loving relationships with same-sex friends.
4. You have opportunities to learn from, teach, and have an impact on a population with whom you might not otherwise interact.
5. You may be the reason a family member, coworker, or community member finally decides that life is worth something and that dependence on chemicals or other substances might not be the answer.
6. You may make the difference in the lives of adolescents who hear you confront anti-LGBT epithets that make them feel as if they want to drop out of junior high, high school, or college. As a result of your action, they will know they have a friend to turn to.
7. Lastly, you can get invited to some of the most fun parties, have some of the best foods, play some of the best sports, have some of the best intellectual discussions, and experience some of the best music in the world, because everyone knows that LGBT people are good at all these things.

Although the last factor is meant as a joke, there is a great deal of truth concerning the positive experiences to which persons open themselves when they allow themselves to be a part of and include another segment of the population in their world. Imagine what it could be like to have had such close friends as Tennessee Williams, Cole Porter, Bessie Smith, Walt Whitman, Gertrude Stein, Alice Walker, James Baldwin, Virginia Woolf, Joan of Arc (trans). Imagine the world without their contributions. It is possible for gay, lesbian,

NEXT STEPS

bisexual, and transgender people, as well as heterosexuals, to make a difference in the way the world is, but we must start by realizing equity in our humanness and life experiences.

References

Broido, E. M. (2000) "The Development of Social Justice Allies during College: A Phenomenological Investigation." *Journal of College Student Development*, 41, 3–18.

Edwards, K. E. (2006). "Aspiring Social Justice Ally Identity Development: A Conceptual Model". *NASPA Journal*, 43 (2), 39–60.

Johnson, A. G. (2006). *Privilege, Power, and Difference* (second edition). Boston: McGraw-Hill.

Mohr, J. J. (2002). "Heterosexual Identity and the Heterosexual Therapist: An Identity Perspective on Sexual Orientation Dynamics in Psychotherapy." *Counseling Psychologist*, 30, 532–566.

85

United Nations Address on Global LGBT Rights

Hillary Clinton

NEXT STEPS

Good evening, and let me express my deep honor and pleasure at being here. . . . This weekend, we will celebrate Human Rights Day, the anniversary of one of the great accomplishments of the last century.

Beginning in 1947, delegates from six continents devoted themselves to drafting a declaration that would enshrine the fundamental rights and freedoms of people everywhere. In the aftermath of World War II, many nations pressed for a statement of this kind to help ensure that we would prevent future atrocities and protect the inherent humanity and dignity of all people. . . .

At three o'clock in the morning on December 10th, 1948, after nearly two years of drafting and one last long night of debate, the president of the UN General Assembly called for a vote on the final text. Forty-eight nations voted in favor; eight abstained; none dissented. And the Universal Declaration of Human Rights was adopted. It proclaims a simple, powerful idea: All human beings are born free and equal in dignity and rights. And with the declaration, it was made clear that rights are not conferred by government; they are the birthright of all people. It does not matter what country we live in, who our leaders are, or even who we are. Because we are human, we therefore have rights. And because we have rights, governments are bound to protect them.

In the 63 years since the declaration was adopted, many nations have made great progress in making human rights a human reality. Step by step, barriers that once prevented people from enjoying the full measure of liberty, the full experience of dignity, and the full benefits of humanity have fallen away. In many places, racist laws have been repealed, legal and social practices that relegated women to second-class status have been abolished, the ability of religious minorities to practice their faith freely has been secured. . . .

Now, there is still, as you all know, much more to be done to secure that commitment, that reality, and progress for all people. Today, I want to talk about the work we have left to do to protect one group of people whose human rights are still denied in too many parts of the world today. In many ways, they are an invisible minority. They are arrested, beaten,

terrorized, even executed. Many are treated with contempt and violence by their fellow citizens while authorities empowered to protect them look the other way or, too often, even join in the abuse. They are denied opportunities to work and learn, driven from their homes and countries, and forced to suppress or deny who they are to protect themselves from harm.

I am talking about gay, lesbian, bisexual, and transgender people, human beings born free and given bestowed equality and dignity, who have a right to claim that, which is now one of the remaining human rights challenges of our time. I speak about this subject knowing that my own country's record on human rights for gay people is far from perfect. Until 2003, it was still a crime in parts of our country. Many LGBT Americans have endured violence and harassment in their own lives, and for some, including many young people, bullying and exclusion are daily experiences. So we, like all nations, have more work to do to protect human rights at home.

Now, raising this issue, I know, is sensitive for many people and that the obstacles standing in the way of protecting the human rights of LGBT people rest on deeply held personal, political, cultural, and religious beliefs. So I come here before you with respect, understanding, and humility. Even though progress on this front is not easy, we cannot delay acting. So in that spirit, I want to talk about the difficult and important issues we must address together to reach a global consensus that recognizes the human rights of LGBT citizens everywhere.

The first issue goes to the heart of the matter. Some have suggested that gay rights and human rights are separate and distinct; but, in fact, they are one and the same. Now, of course, 60 years ago, the governments that drafted and passed the Universal Declaration of Human Rights were not thinking about how it applied to the LGBT community. They also weren't thinking about how it applied to indigenous people or children or people with disabilities or other marginalized groups. Yet in the past 60 years, we have come to recognize that members of these groups are entitled to the full measure of dignity and rights, because, like all people, they share a common humanity.

This recognition did not occur all at once. It evolved over time. And as it did, we understood that we were honoring rights that people always had, rather than creating new or special rights for them. Like being a woman, like being a racial, religious, tribal, or ethnic minority, being LGBT does not make you less human. And that is why gay rights are human rights, and human rights are gay rights.

It is a violation of human rights when people are beaten or killed because of their sexual orientation, or because they do not conform to cultural norms about how men and women should look or behave. It is a violation of human rights when governments declare it illegal to be gay, or allow those who harm gay people to go unpunished. It is a violation of human rights when lesbian or transgender . . . women are subjected to so-called corrective rape, or forcibly subjected to hormone treatments, or when people are murdered after public calls for violence toward gays, or when they are forced to flee their nations and seek asylum in other lands to save their lives. And it is a violation of human rights when life-saving care is withheld from people because they are gay, or equal access to justice is denied to people because they are gay, or public spaces are out of bounds to people because they are gay. No matter what we look like, where we come from, or who we are, we are all equally entitled to our human rights and dignity.

The second issue is a question of whether homosexuality arises from a particular part of the world. Some seem to believe it is a Western phenomenon, and therefore people outside the West have grounds to reject it. Well, in reality, gay people are born into and belong to every society in the world. They are all ages, all races, all faiths; they are doctors and teachers, farmers and bankers, soldiers and athletes; and whether we know it, or whether we acknowledge it, they are our family, our friends, and our neighbors.

NEXT STEPS

Being gay is not a Western invention; it is a human reality. And protecting the human rights of all people, gay or straight, is not something that only Western governments do. South Africa's constitution, written in the aftermath of Apartheid, protects the equality of all citizens, including gay people. In Colombia and Argentina, the rights of gays are also legally protected. In Nepal, the Supreme Court has ruled that equal rights apply to LGBT citizens. The Government of Mongolia has committed to pursue new legislation that will tackle anti-gay discrimination.

Now, some worry that protecting the human rights of the LGBT community is a luxury that only wealthy nations can afford. But in fact, in all countries, there are costs to not protecting these rights, in both gay and straight lives lost to disease and violence, and the silencing of voices and views that would strengthen communities, in ideas never pursued by entrepreneurs who happen to be gay. Costs are incurred whenever any group is treated as lesser or the other, whether they are women, racial, or religious minorities, or the LGBT. Former President Mogae of Botswana pointed out recently that for as long as LGBT people are kept in the shadows, there cannot be an effective public health program to tackle HIV and AIDS. Well, that holds true for other challenges as well.

The third, and perhaps most challenging, issue arises when people cite religious or cultural values as a reason to violate or not to protect the human rights of LGBT citizens. This is not unlike the justification offered for violent practices towards women like honor killings, widow burning, or female genital mutilation. Some people still defend those practices as part of a cultural tradition. But violence toward women isn't cultural; it's criminal. Likewise with slavery, what was once justified as sanctioned by God is now properly reviled as an unconscionable violation of human rights.

In each of these cases, we came to learn that no practice or tradition trumps the human rights that belong to all of us. And this holds true for inflicting violence on LGBT people, criminalizing their status or behavior, expelling them from their families and communities, or tacitly or explicitly accepting their killing.

Of course, it bears noting that rarely are cultural and religious traditions and teachings actually in conflict with the protection of human rights. Indeed, our religion and our culture are sources of compassion and inspiration toward our fellow human beings. It was not only those who've justified slavery who leaned on religion, it was also those who sought to abolish it. And let us keep in mind that our commitments to protect the freedom of religion and to defend the dignity of LGBT people emanate from a common source. For many of us, religious belief and practice is a vital source of meaning and identity, and fundamental to who we are as people. And likewise, for most of us, the bonds of love and family that we forge are also vital sources of meaning and identity. And caring for others is an expression of what it means to be fully human. It is because the human experience is universal that human rights are universal and cut across all religions and cultures.

The fourth issue is what history teaches us about how we make progress towards rights for all. Progress starts with honest discussion. Now, there are some who say and believe that all gay people are pedophiles, that homosexuality is a disease that can be caught or cured, or that gays recruit others to become gay. Well, these notions are simply not true. They are also unlikely to disappear if those who promote or accept them are dismissed out of hand rather than invited to share their fears and concerns. No one has ever abandoned a belief because he was forced to do so.

Universal human rights include freedom of expression and freedom of belief, even if our words or beliefs denigrate the humanity of others. Yet, while we are each free to believe whatever we choose, we cannot do whatever we choose, not in a world where we protect the human rights of all.

Reaching understanding of these issues takes more than speech. It does take a conversation. In fact, it takes a constellation of conversations in places big and small. And it takes

a willingness to see stark differences in belief as a reason to begin the conversation, not to avoid it.

But progress comes from changes in laws. In many places, including my own country, legal protections have preceded, not followed, broader recognition of rights. Laws have a teaching effect. Laws that discriminate validate other kinds of discrimination. Laws that require equal protections reinforce the moral imperative of equality. And practically speaking, it is often the case that laws must change before fears about change dissipate.

Many in my country thought that President Truman was making a grave error when he ordered the racial desegregation of our military. They argued that it would undermine unit cohesion. And it wasn't until he went ahead and did it that we saw how it strengthened our social fabric in ways even the supporters of the policy could not foresee. Likewise, some worried in my country that the repeal of "Don't Ask, Don't Tell" would have a negative effect on our armed forces. Now, the Marine Corps Commandant, who was one of the strongest voices against the repeal, says that his concerns were unfounded and that the Marines have embraced the change.

Finally, progress comes from being willing to walk a mile in someone else's shoes. We need to ask ourselves, "How would it feel if it were a crime to love the person I love? How would it feel to be discriminated against for something about myself that I cannot change?" This challenge applies to all of us as we reflect upon deeply held beliefs, as we work to embrace tolerance and respect for the dignity of all persons, and as we engage humbly with those with whom we disagree in the hope of creating greater understanding.

A fifth and final question is how we do our part to bring the world to embrace human rights for all people including LGBT people. Yes, LGBT people must help lead this effort, as so many of you are. Their knowledge and experiences are invaluable and their courage inspirational. We know the names of brave LGBT activists who have literally given their lives for this cause, and there are many more whose names we will never know. But often those who are denied rights are least empowered to bring about the changes they seek. Acting alone, minorities can never achieve the majorities necessary for political change.

So when any part of humanity is sidelined, the rest of us cannot sit on the sidelines. Every time a barrier to progress has fallen, it has taken a cooperative effort from those on both sides of the barrier. In the fight for women's rights, the support of men remains crucial. The fight for racial equality has relied on contributions from people of all races. Combating Islamaphobia or anti-Semitism is a task for people of all faiths. And the same is true with this struggle for equality.

Conversely, when we see denials and abuses of human rights and fail to act, that sends the message to those deniers and abusers that they won't suffer any consequences for their actions, and so they carry on. But when we do act, we send a powerful moral message. Right here in Geneva, the international community acted this year to strengthen a global consensus around the human rights of LGBT people. At the Human Rights Council in March, 85 countries from all regions supported a statement calling for an end to criminalization and violence against people because of their sexual orientation and gender identity.

At the following session of the Council in June, South Africa took the lead on a resolution about violence against LGBT people. The delegation from South Africa spoke eloquently about their own experience and struggle for human equality and its indivisibility. When the measure passed, it became the first-ever UN resolution recognizing the human rights of gay people worldwide. In the Organization of American States this year, the Inter-American Commission on Human Rights created a unit on the rights of LGBT people, a step toward what we hope will be the creation of a special rapporteur.

Now, we must go further and work here and in every region of the world to galvanize more support for the human rights of the LGBT community. To the leaders of those countries where people are jailed, beaten, or executed for being gay, I ask you to consider this:

NEXT STEPS

Leadership, by definition, means being out in front of your people when it is called for. It means standing up for the dignity of all your citizens and persuading your people to do the same. It also means ensuring that all citizens are treated as equals under your laws, because let me be clear—I am not saying that gay people can't or don't commit crimes. They can and they do, just like straight people. And when they do, they should be held accountable, but it should never be a crime to be gay.

And to people of all nations, I say supporting human rights is your responsibility too. The lives of gay people are shaped not only by laws, but by the treatment they receive every day from their families, from their neighbors. Eleanor Roosevelt, who did so much to advance human rights worldwide, said that these rights begin in the small places close to home—the streets where people live, the schools they attend, the factories, farms, and offices where they work. These places are your domain. The actions you take, the ideals that you advocate, can determine whether human rights flourish where you are.

And finally, to LGBT men and women worldwide, let me say this: Wherever you live and whatever the circumstances of your life, whether you are connected to a network of support or feel isolated and vulnerable, please know that you are not alone. People around the globe are working hard to support you and to bring an end to the injustices and dangers you face. That is certainly true for my country. And you have an ally in the United States of America and you have millions of friends among the American people. . . .

The women and men who advocate for human rights for the LGBT community in hostile places, some of whom are here today with us, are brave and dedicated, and deserve all the help we can give them. We know the road ahead will not be easy. A great deal of work lies before us. But many of us have seen firsthand how quickly change can come. In our lifetimes, attitudes toward gay people in many places have been transformed. Many people, including myself, have experienced a deepening of our own convictions on this topic over the years, as we have devoted more thought to it, engaged in dialogues and debates, and established personal and professional relationships with people who are gay. . . .

There is a phrase that people in the United States invoke when urging others to support human rights: "Be on the right side of history." The story of the United States is the story of a nation that has repeatedly grappled with intolerance and inequality. We fought a brutal civil war over slavery. People from coast to coast joined in campaigns to recognize the rights of women, indigenous peoples, racial minorities, children, people with disabilities, immigrants, workers, and on and on. And the march toward equality and justice has continued. Those who advocate for expanding the circle of human rights were and are on the right side of history, and history honors them. Those who tried to constrict human rights were wrong, and history reflects that as well.

. . . [A]ll persons are created free and equal in dignity and rights. We are called once more to make real the words of the Universal Declaration. Let us answer that call. Let us be on the right side of history, for our people, our nations, and future generations, whose lives will be shaped by the work we do today. I come before you with great hope and confidence that no matter how long the road ahead, we will travel it successfully together. Thank you very much.

NEXT STEPS

See Chapter 10 in *Teaching for Diversity and Social Justice* for corresponding teaching materials.

SECTION 7

TRANSGENDER OPPRESSION

Introduction

Chase Catalano and Davey Shlasko[1]

Since the late 1990s, transgender issues have gradually come into increasing public awareness in academia, law, and popular culture. The past few years have seen a handful of new academic publications that are able to go beyond explorations of transgender identity or queer/gender theory, and focus on specific venues where transgender oppression plays out.[2] These new resources mean that students and scholars (and sometimes activists) have data and analysis to draw on and build from, no longer limited to narratives, memoirs, and anthologies of personal stories to piece together how systems of oppression manifest in trans lives and experiences.

At the same time, a number of legislative and policy victories have the potential for positive impact on many trans people's lives. For example, in 2011 the states of Nevada, Connecticut, and Massachusetts all passed laws banning discrimination on the basis of gender identity and expression, bringing the total number of states with such protections up to sixteen (National Gay and Lesbian Task Force [NGLTF], 2012). We can feel hopeful when we consider that in sixteen states, the District of Columbia, and some smaller jurisdictions, it is illegal to discriminate against trans people in housing, employment, and in some cases public accommodations. However, in total, this means that only 44 percent of the U.S. population lives in areas covered by these laws (NGLTF, 2011). The media coverage of such changes, along with flurries of stories about celebrity or celebrated trans people such as Chaz Bono, Thomas Beatty (a trans man who gave birth to a baby in 2008), and Jenna Talackova (a trans woman who was disqualified from the Miss Universe competition based on her trans status), may make it appear that trans issues are now "mainstream." Yet trans communities still face tremendous obstacles, and contemporary examples of oppression against trans individuals and communities are widespread.

Violence and discrimination against transgender people are still of pandemic proportions. Although gender identity and expression are now included in federal hate crimes legislation,[3] federal law enforcement does not yet track or report crimes based on gender identity and expression, as they do with hate crimes based on federally protected classes, such as race, religion, and sex (FBI, 2009, 2011). For this reason it is very difficult to state with any certainty the number of bias-motivated crimes against transgender and gender non-conforming people. However, members of the trans community try to keep track of publicized incidents, and memorialize each year at the Transgender Day of Remembrance on November 20 transgender and gender non-conforming people who have been murdered. According to these community groups' estimates, at least 221

people were murdered in anti-transgender hate crimes worldwide between November 2010 and November 2011, including at least nine in the U.S. Compared to the previous years' counts of 179 and 162, this seems to show a rising trend in reported murders of trans people (Transgender Europe, 2011). These counts of confirmed cases are definitely a drastic undercount, since they only include people whose transgender identities were known and since police departments in most jurisdictions have no obligation and indeed no way to report these murders as hate crimes.

Because non-discrimination laws do not protect most transgender people in the United States, we may be denied housing, employment, and public benefits with little if any legal recourse. The first national survey of trans people's experiences with discrimination resulted in a release in 2011, by the National Center for Transgender Equality and National Gay and Lesbian Task Force, which showed that 63 percent of transgender survey respondents had experienced "a serious act of discrimination," such as being fired, evicted, or assaulted due to their gender identity or expression (Grant, Mottet, Tanis, Harrison, Herman, and Keisling, 2011). Respondents were nearly twice as likely as the general population to have attained a four-year college degree, yet nearly four times as likely to be earning less than $10,000 a year, indicating severe and pervasive employment discrimination. Nearly one fifth of respondents had been homeless at some point, and the same proportion report having been denied health care based on their gender identity or expression (Grant, Mottet, Tanis, Harrison, Herman, and Keisling, 2011). For many trans people, the ability to update their name and gender on identification documents such as a drivers license or passport can offer some protection from discrimination and harassment; unfortunately there are many barriers to making these updates, and this report found only 21 percent of respondents who have transitioned gender have been able to update all relevant ID and records. People of Color and lower-income people were even less likely to have updated their documents (Grant, Mottet, Tanis, Harrison, Herman, and Keisling, 2011). Trans people also are arrested and imprisoned disproportionately to the general population, due both to economic marginalization and to stereotyping by police officers, and once in prison they are extremely vulnerable to sexual assault, medical neglect, and other abuses (Sylvia Rivera Law Project, 2007). All these challenges take their toll: the report indicates that over 40 percent of trans people have attempted suicide (Grant, Mottet, Tanis, Harrison, Herman, and Keisling, 2011).

The reality represented by these discouraging statistics leads us to identify the oppression of transgender people as a problem worthy of study and action within a multi-issue social justice liberation movement.

DEFINITIONS

Transgender oppression (sometimes referred to as cissexism, genderism, or binarism) is closely related to sexism and to heterosexism, and there are also important differences (see Griffin, 2007, on the section website). In order to distinguish them, we need to define some terminology. Many people understand gender to be synonymous with sex, referring to the categories of male and female. In fact, *sex* and *gender* are not the same thing, and both are more complicated than a male/female binary. In this section (as in the preceding two sections on sexism and heterosexism), we use *sex* to describe biological factors, such as chromosomes, genitals, and hormone levels that are used to categorize people as male or female at birth and throughout their lives. In reality, more possibilities exist; many people have some aspect of their biology that would challenge simple categorization of their body as male or female (Fausto-Sterling, 2000; Kessler, 2002). Individuals whose physical bodies are not easily categorized as male or female are called *intersex*.[4]

Gender refers to a wide range of social/cultural meanings that are ascribed to sex categories. We like to think of gender as composed of both *gender identity* and *gender expression*. *Gender identity* refers to a person's internal self-concept with regard to gender categories like man, woman, transgender, genderqueer, and many others. *Gender expression* refers to behaviors,

such as attire, demeanor, and language, through which we intentionally or unintentionally communicate gender. As Hackman describes (in the introduction to the section on sexism), *gender roles* are specific sets of expectations for gender expression, which characterize what men and women are "supposed to" be in a particular society. The dominant assumption is that an individual's sex, gender identity, and gender expression always line up—for example, that all female-bodied people identify as women and express themselves through femininity—and further that there are two and only two sexes, and two and only two genders (where identity and expression are conflated). This faulty assumption, often referred to as the *sex/gender binary*, is the foundation of our analysis of transgender oppression.

It is also common to confuse gender identity and expression with *sexual orientation* (i.e., the gender/s one is emotionally, romantically, or sexually attracted to), and, thus, to confuse transgender oppression with heterosexism. In fact, one's gender identity and expression is not necessarily related to one's sexual orientation. Transgender people, like all people, have a variety of sexual orientations including heterosexual, gay, lesbian, pansexual, and queer.[5] For further discussion of gender, sexuality, and terminology, we refer readers to the sections on heterosexism and sexism, as well as to Pat Griffin's discussion included on this section's website.

Based on these definitions, we use the term *transgender* broadly to describe people whose gender identity and/or gender expression do not match societal expectations (Catalano, McCarthy, and Shlasko, 2007) and for whom this fact is central to their identity and/or important in determining their life circumstances. Transgender is also a term of self-identity that is claimed by some, but not all, people who fit in our broad definition. People who fall under the transgender umbrella may or may not identify as transgender, and may also identify with others terms such as male-to-female (MtF), butch, female-to-male (FtM), genderqueer, femme, androgynous, two-spirit, and others.

The ability to name and define one's own identity and experiences is a vital element of empowerment for marginalized peoples. Terms of self-identity are important tools that help people to survive with, in, and/or in resistance to the gender binary. At the same time, we use transgender as a broad descriptor so that we can discuss social phenomena that affect people in this category, across many variations in how people understand and describe themselves. Responsible study of transgender issues requires constant reflection about the language we use. In particular we urge readers to consider whether any term you might come across is being used by trans people to identify themselves, or by professionals in public health, social services, law or academia to describe a group of people whose relationship to that term may be fraught (see e.g. Valentine, 2007).

We define *transgender oppression* as the system of oppression that targets and marginalizes people who are transgender in the broadest sense. The system privileges non-transgender people, also called *cisgender*[6] people, whose gender identity and expression conform with relative ease to societal expectations. Like other forms of oppression, transgender oppression is harmful and limiting to everyone, including those who occupy a privileged position. It has particular impact on those who transition from living entirely or primarily in one of the two socially sanctioned genders (man or woman) to living entirely or primarily in the other, or who live between or outside these categories. Often, this is the group that people are referring to when they say transgender. Although we use transgender more broadly, many of the phenomena we focus on as examples of transgender oppression are particularly evident for this group.

Because many people view gender as a presumed-natural binary, those of us whose experience does not match this assumption are often viewed as unnatural. The medical system reinforces this view, especially with regard to those of us who choose to change our bodies, in the *Diagnostic and Statistical Manual V*, which classifies the desire to change the sex of one's body (through hormones, surgeries, or other options) as evidence of a mental illness called gender identity disorder. This diagnosis forms the basis of the current "*medical model*" of transgender identity, which positions transgender identity as an illness with biomedical transition as the cure, thereby establishing medical authority to "diagnose" gender identity and to supervise gender transition.[7]

One central assumption of the medical model is that all trans people experience extreme distress about being trans. This can lead well-meaning allies to feel pity or sympathy for transgender people. Some trans people do experience internal struggles about their gender, and many trans people also find joy and pride in our gender identity and expression. The medical model ignores positive aspects of trans experience.

It is difficult to overestimate the historical and current impact of the medical model on transgender lives, communities, and movements because much of how we understand transgender has been shaped by the medical model. Transgender people inevitably end up having to navigate the medical system's assumptions about us, whether because we choose to participate in the system in order to seek medical transition or because medical providers pass judgment on our non-conformity and create barriers to accessing even basic primary health care. Dean Spade's piece in this section (selection 88) addresses some of the complexities of trans communities' relationships to the medical model.

Like all forms of oppression, transgender oppression can be internalized. At the most basic level, *internalized transgender oppression* is internalization of the sex/gender binary. The binary asserts that only two categories of people exist: masculine, man-identified males, and feminine, woman-identified females. For some trans people, the internalization of this belief system may lead us to doubt whether we can be a "real" man or "real" woman, or even whether we are "real" at all. For others, the internalization of the gender binary may lead us to enact hyper-femininity or hyper-masculinity in attempts to "prove" our identity.

Another aspect of internalized transgender oppression is internalization of the medical model. Many trans people disagree with some aspects of the medical model and prefer to see trans identity not as pathology but rather as a natural expression of human variation. Yet the influence of the medical model is so pervasive that we may accidentally accept some of its assumptions even if we do not believe in them (such as the assumption that all trans people experience a certain kind of discomfort in their bodies).

When we are able to come together as a community, we can mitigate some of the brutal effects of internalized oppression and create space for trans people to have more agency in defining and making choices about our lives. The recent emergence of numerous trans memoirs, biographies, and documentaries, as well as trans advocacy organizations around the world are further examples of resistance by trans people who refuse to buy into the messages of shame and isolation. We hope more will be published about the complexities of internalized transgender oppression and the ways in which individuals and communities are working toward liberation.

SEXISM, HETEROSEXISM, AND TRANSGENDER OPPRESSION

There are various ways to understand the relationships among sexism, heterosexism, and transgender oppression. The way we think of it is that these three systems, along with the oppression of intersex people, are conceptually distinct but overlapping systems. They have in common an overarching system of norms and expectations related to bodies, gender, sexuality, and family relationships that dictate which identities are considered normal, which are deviant, and in some cases which identities are acknowledged to exist at all.

In addition, there are many specific manifestations of oppression that play out similarly. For example, lesbian, gay, and bisexual (LGB) and transgender people may be labeled as mentally ill when we are not and may be discouraged from interacting with children because of irrational fears that we will influence the children to become LGB or T. Both women and trans people are often targeted for sexual assault and are encouraged to entrust our bodies to doctors while dissociating from our own knowledge of what our bodies need and want. In addition, sexism, heterosexism, and transgender oppression often occur in tandem. When a gay man with a feminine gender expression is targeted for violence based on his femininity, gender non-conformity,

and presumed sexual orientation, all three systems are at play. With the constant evolution of terminology and philosophy around transgender issues, we look forward to seeing the new ways we will conceive and describe these relationships.

The history of trans communities and movements has often been intertwined with LGB activism and with feminism. Many LGB organizations now include transgender issues in their mission and extend the acronym to LGBT. The inclusion of transgender within LGB movements and organizations acknowledges the historical connections of the communities and has created space for the concerns of trans people to be addressed as part of broader LGBT liberation efforts. However, it is not always a natural fit, and often these organizations struggle with how to enact their intention of being trans-inclusive. The lumping in of T with LGB has also reinforced confusion about the meaning of transgender, which many people misunderstand as being a sexual orientation.

In some ways, transgender liberation movements should be a natural fit with feminist movements, since they share a fundamental goal of eliminating oppression based on gender. However, ideological conflicts between trans and non-trans feminists have surfaced on many fronts.[8] In order to work together to overcome the overlapping systems that target all women (whether or not they are trans) and all trans people (whether or not they are women), trans and feminist movements need to seek a mutually beneficial definition of feminism that would "dismantle the structures that prop up gender as a system of oppression, but [. . .] without passing moral judgment on people who feel the need to change their birth-assigned gender" (Stryker, 2008, p. 3).

Even with the tension around trans issues in feminist and LGBT movements, trans people have always been part of LGBT and feminist organizing. Trans people's participation in these and other social movements has been omitted from many accounts, sometimes out of carelessness and sometimes out of intentional reframing of the historical facts (Namaste, 2000; Nestle, Howell, and Wilchins, 2002; Stryker, 2008), leading to widespread ignorance about trans people's history and, indeed, our very existence.

By setting aside space for discussion about transgender oppression, we acknowledge and honor the experiences of those who transgress the gender binary. We hope readers will use this section to add complexity to, rather than supersede or distract from, conversations about other forms of oppression with which it intersects. This section represents only a fragment of the innovative thinking on transgender issues that has been published, which is in turn only a tiny fragment of the brilliant wisdom and scholarship that resides unpublished in transgender communities. We hope that this section will encourage readers to seek out more information and to find your own voices about this issue.

INTRODUCTION TO THE READINGS

The pieces in this section provide a basic framework for understanding the context, acknowledging some voices, and exploring next steps about transgender experience and transgender oppression. Our focus is on contemporary transgender communities in the United States. In selecting pieces, we considered what resources would be most relevant and appealing to people who are thinking about transgender issues for the first time.

We also wanted to emphasize the interconnections among transgender oppression and other forms of oppression, especially racism and classism. One of the criticisms we often hear when attempting to include transgender issues in college curricula or student life programming is that the transgender movement is a white, upper-class movement and, thus, transgender oppression is a white, upper-class problem. Indeed it is true that much—though certainly not all—of transgender theorizing that has been published is from a perspective of race and class privilege. That should not be surprising, since most published academic theory on many topics tends to come from that perspective. In fact, gender transgression exists in all cultures, and transgender communities in the United States are as diverse racially as the nation as a whole. As far as

socioeconomic class, the economic survey data cited above suggests that transgender people are disproportionately likely to become working class and poor, even if they were raised with class privilege. We have attempted to include readings that speak to the diversity of trans experiences, and to the complex interplay among systems of oppression as they impact trans lives.

Joanne Meyerowitz's excerpt from her book *How Sex Changed: A History of Transsexuality in the United States* (selection 86) outlines the historical evolution of transgender identities and definitions in the United States, using the iconic 1950s case of Christine Jorgensen to show how science has affected this evolution. Susan Stryker's piece (selection 87) outlines the Compton Cafeteria Riots of the 1960s, an early example of transgender social justice activism in U.S. history. Dean Spade (selection 88) describes some of the complexities of and problems with the medical model, including how class and gender non-conformity can limit access to medical care. Julia Serano (selection 89) discusses the rejection of trans women's issues from the feminist movement and explores some links between misogyny and transgender oppression. Finally, Ware (selection 90) describes how trans youth, and specifically trans youth of color, are impacted within the prison industrial complex.

For our Voices part, in "Passing Realities," Allie Lie (selection 91) gives a compelling account of her daily experience, including her desire to be recognized and her complex relationships with family and strangers. Jamison Green's "Look! No, Don't!" (selection 92) discusses his experience of passing and invisibility after medical transition.

In Next Steps, Taylor's "Cisgender Privilege" (selection 93) parallels Peggy McIntosh's classic article on white privilege to outline examples of how cisgender people benefit from their relatively privileged position in the system of transgender oppression. "Calling All Restroom Revolutionaries" (selection 94) reports on an organization of college students who advocate for inclusive restrooms, which benefit not only trans students but also people with disabilities and parents of young children.

FURTHER RESOURCES

This section provides an introduction to transgender history, voices, and issues and the system of transgender oppression. There is far more that could and should be explored about the range of gender transgression in the United States and globally, both historically and currently, and the variety of ways in which trans-ness has been understood by gender transgressors and those who have observed and studied their transgression. Even though this section is U.S.-focused, there are conversations going on around the world about transgender issues in culture, law, and policy. We encourage readers who would like a more international perspective, as well as many further U.S.-related resources, to go to the section website.

See Companion Website for Additional Resources and Material

Notes

1 We ask that those who cite this work always acknowledge by name both the authors listed rather than either only citing the first author or using "et al." to indicate coauthors. Both collaborated equally in the conceptualization, development, and writing of this chapter.

2 See the following examples: Beemyn and Rankin's (2011) *The Lives of Transgender People*; Spade's (2011) *Normal Life: Administrative Violence, Critical Trans Politics, and the Limits of Law*; Stanley and Smith's edited volume (2011) *Captive Genders: Trans Embodiment and the Prison Industrial Complex*; and Valentine's (2007) *Imagining Transgender: An Ethnography of a Category*. These stand out, among others.

3 Many advocates for trans rights do not support hate crimes legislation because they argue it does not actually reduce violence and only punishes poor people of color who are already most vulnerable to criminal prosecution and imprisonment (see Spade, 2011).

4 For more information on intersex issues, we refer readers to the Accord Alliance (www.accordalliance.org/), and to Sumi Colligan's piece in the ableism section of this anthology (selection 100).

5 Some transgender people also identify as bisexual, but many trans people reject this category because the word itself reinforces the gender binary, and instead use pansexual or queer.

6 *Cisgender* means non-trans, from the etymology *cis* meaning "on the same side," as *trans* means "across" or "crossing."

7 Revisions from the previous edition of the DSM (DSM IV-TR) incorporated some changes for which trans activists had been advocating for many years. At the same time, trans groups still find many shortcomings in the DSM's approach (e.g. De Cuypere, Knudson and Bockting, 2011).

8 For more discussion on transgender inclusion in feminist movements, see Califia (2003); Prosser (1998); Raymond (1979); Stone (1991); Stryker (2008)

References

Beemyn, G., Rankin, S. (2011). *The Lives of Transgender People*. New York, NY: Columbia University Press.

Califia, P. (2003). *Sex Changes: Transgender Politics* (2nd edition). San Francisco, CA: Cleis Press.

Catalano, C., McCarthy, L., Shlasko, D. (2007). Transgender oppression curriculum design. In M. Adams, L. A. Bell, P. Griffin (eds), *Teaching for Diversity and Social Justice* (2nd edition). New York: Routledge.

De Cuypere, G., Knudson, G., Bockting, W. (2011). Second response of the World Professional Association for Transgender Health to the proposed revision of the diagnosis of gender dysphoria for DSM 5, *International Journal of Transgenderism*, 13 (2), 51–53

Fausto-Sterling, A. (2000). *Sexing the Body: Gender Politics and the Construction of Sexuality*. New York: Basic Books.

Federal Bureau of Investigation (2009). *Matthew Shepard/James Byrd, Jr., Hate Crimes Prevention Act of 2009*. Retrieved from http://www.fbi.gov/about-us/investigate/civilrights/hate_crimes/shepard-byrd-act-brochure

Federal Bureau of Investigation (2011, November). *Hate Crime Statistics, 2010*. Retrieved from http://www.fbi.gov/about-us/cjis/ucr/hate-crime/2010/resources/hate-crime-2010-methodology

Grant, J. M., Mottet, L. M., Tanis, J., Harrison, J., Herman, J. L., Keisling, M. (2011). *Injustice at Every Turn: A Report of the National Transgender Discrimination Survey*. Washington: National Center for Transgender Equality and National Gay and Lesbian Task Force.

Griffin, P. (2007). Overview: Sexism, heterosexism, and transgender oppression. In M. Adams, L. A. Bell, P. Griffin (eds), *Teaching for Diversity and Social Justice* (2nd edition, pp. 167–172). New York: Routledge.

Kessler, S. J. (2002). *Lessons from the Intersexed*. New Brunswick, NJ: Rutgers University Press.

Meyerowitz, J. (2002). *How Sex Changed: A History of Transsexuality in the United States*. Cambridge, MA: Harvard University Press.

Namaste, V. K. (2000). *Invisible Lives: The Erasure of Transsexual and Transgendered People*. Chicago: University of Chicago Press.

National Gay and Lesbian Task Force (2011). *Jurisdictions with Explicitly Transgender-Inclusive Nondiscrimination Laws*. Retrieved May 5, 2012, from http://thetaskforce.org/reports_and_research/all_jurisdictions_w_pop_10_11.pdf

National Gay and Lesbian Task Force (2012). *State Non-Discrimination Laws in the U.S.* Retrieved from http://www.thetaskforce.org/downloads/reports/issue_maps/non_discrimination_1_12_color.pdf

Nestle, J., Howell, C., Wilchins, R. (eds). (2002). *Genderqueer: Voices From Beyond the Sexual Binary*. Los Angeles: Alyson Books.

Prosser, J. (1998). *Second Skins: The Body Narratives of Transsexuality*. New York: Columbia University Press.

Raymond, J. (1979). The *Transsexual Empire: The Making of the She-Male*. London: The Women's Press.

Spade, D. (2011). *Normal Life: Administrative Violence, Critical Trans Politics, and the Limits of Law*. Brooklyn, NY: South End Press.

Stanley, E. A., Smith, N. (eds). (2011). *Captive Genders: Trans Embodiment and the Prison Industrial Complex*. Oakland, CA: AK Press.

Stone, S. (1991). The empire strikes back: A posttranssexual manifesto. In J. Epstein, K. Strauss (eds), *In Body Guards: The Cultural Politics of Gender Ambiguity* (pp. 280–304). New York: Routledge.

Stryker, S. (2008). *Transgender History*. Berkeley, CA: Seal Press.

Sylvia Rivera Law Project (2007). *"It's war in here": A Report on the Treatment of Transgender and Intersex People in New York State Men's Prisons*. Retrieved April 26, 2009, from http://srlp.org/files/warinhere.pdf

Transgender Europe (2011). *Transgender Europe's Trans Murder Monitoring Project Reveals 221 Killings of Trans People in the Last 12 Months*. http://www.transrespect-transphobia.org/en_US/tvt-project/tmm-results/tdor2011.htm

Valentine, D. (2007). *Imagining Transgender: An Ethnography of a Category*. Durham, NC: Duke.

86

Introduction—How Sex Changed

A History of Transsexuality in the United States

Joanne Meyerowitz

On December 1, 1952, the *New York Daily News* announced the "sex change" surgery of Christine Jorgensen. The front-page headline read: "Ex-GI Becomes Blonde Beauty: Operations Transform Bronx Youth," and the story told how Jorgensen had traveled to Denmark for "a rare and complicated treatment." For years, Jorgensen, born and reared as a boy, had struggled with what she later described as an ineffable, inexorable, and increasingly unbearable yearning to live her life as a woman. In 1950 she sailed to Europe in search of a doctor who would alter her bodily sex. Within months she found an endocrinologist who agreed to administer hormones if she would in return cooperate with his research. Over the next two years she took massive doses of estrogen and underwent two major surgeries to transform her genitals. At the end of 1952 the *New York Daily News* transformed her obscure personal triumph into mass media sensation.

. . .

Jorgensen was more than a media sensation, a stage act, or a cult figure. Her story opened debate on the visibility and mutability of sex. It raised questions that resonated with force in the 1950s and engage us still today. How do we determine who is male and who is female, and why do we care? Can humans actually change sex? Is sex less apparent than it seems? As a narrative of boundary transgression, the Jorgensen story fascinated readers and elicited their surprise, and as an unusual variant on a familiar tale of striving and success, it inspired them. It opened possibilities for those who questioned their own sex and offered an exoticized travelogue for armchair tourists who had never imagined that one could take a journey across the sex divide. In the post-World War II era, with heightened concerns about science and sex, the Jorgensen story compelled some readers to spell out their own versions of the boundaries of sex, and it convinced others to reconsider the categories they thought they already knew. In response, American doctors and scientists began to explore the process of defining sex.

. . .

At the start of the twenty-first century, we routinely distinguish sex, gender, and sexuality, but we cannot, it seems, seal off the borders. Scientists, their popularizers, and their critics still debate whether sex-linked genes or prenatal sex hormones or specific sites of the brain determine the behaviors associated with masculinity and femininity and with hetero- and homosexuality. In much of the popular culture, sex still seems to dictate particular forms of gender, which in turn dictates particular forms of sexuality. In this default logic, a female is naturally and normally a feminine person who desires men; a male is naturally and normally a masculine person who desires women. All other permutations of sex, gender, and sexuality still appear, if they appear at all, as pathologically anomalous or socially strange. . . . [T]he categories of sex, gender, and sexuality—now analytically distinct—remain insistently intertwined in American science and culture.

Jorgensen was not the first transsexual, nor was the publicity accorded her the first media coverage of sex-change surgery. Cross-gender identification, the sense of being the other sex, and the desire to live as the other sex all existed in various forms in earlier

C
O
N
T
E
X
T

centuries and other cultures. The historical record includes countless examples of males who dressed or lived as women and females who dressed or lived as men. Transsexuality, the quest to transform the bodily characteristics of sex via hormones and surgery, originated in the early twentieth century. By the 1910s European scientists had begun to publicize their attempts to transform the sex of animals, and by the 1920s a few doctors, mostly in Germany, had agreed to alter the bodies of a few patients who longed to change their sex.

. . .

The sex-change experiments in Europe reached the United States through the popular culture. From the 1930s on, American newspapers and magazines—and later radio, television, and film—broadcast stories on sex change. . . .

Only after World War II did American doctors and scientists seriously address the issue of sex change. . . . From the start, the doctors and scientists fought among themselves about the explanatory powers of biology and psychology, the use and abuse of medical technology, and the merits of sex-change operations.

In the point and counterpoint of debate, the doctors and scientists gradually shifted their focus from concepts of biological sex to concepts of what they came to call gender. When they tried to explain the desire to change sex, they less often referred to conditions of mixed bodily sex and more frequently wrote of "psychological sex," and later "gender identity," a sense of the sexed self that was both separate from the sex of the body and, some claimed, harder to change than the body itself. The sex of the body, they now asserted, had multiple components—hormones, chromosomes, genitals, and more—some of which could be altered. A few of them began to emphasize the immutability of adult gender identity and to acknowledge the despair of those patients who wanted the sex of their bodies to match their unshakable sense of self. This new understanding of gender was forged and refined in the discourse on transsexuality. With it, more American doctors gradually began to endorse and perform "sex reassignment surgery."

From the doctors' and scientists' point of view, medical examinations and psychological tests could determine a person's sex and verify a person's gender identity. From the point of view of their patients, sex and gender were usually matters of self-knowledge. They had studied themselves, and sometimes they had also read widely in the medical literature. Like the doctors, many of them distinguished between the sex of the visible body and the firm sense of sex that came from an inner sense of self. They had determined for themselves what they were and what they wanted to become. After Christine Jorgensen made the news, hundreds of them approached doctors in order to convince them to recommend or perform surgery. But they ran into constant conflicts with doctors who insisted on their own authority to define sex and gender, diagnose the condition, and recommend the treatment.

. . . After Jorgensen made the news, American doctors and scientists took up the taxonomic process of sorting out a tangled thicket of varied conditions of sex, gender, and sexuality. On the ground, those who identified as transsexuals, transvestites, lesbians, and gay men sorted themselves out in a parallel social process. Amidst a multiplicity of variations, some of them came to define their conditions not only in contradistinction to the mainstream norm—the heterosexual masculine male or heterosexual feminine female—but also with regard to others on the margins. In everyday life, especially in the cities, they gravitated toward each other, schooled each other in the customs and language of particular subcultures, and developed their own vernacular that delineated finer gradations of gender variance than the language used by doctors.

In the 1960s the complicated process of redefining sex took place within a culture increasingly preoccupied by a "sexual revolution," by more liberal attitudes toward individual choice, and by revitalized human rights movements that insisted on social change in the name of justice. In this climate the doctors and scientists who studied transsexuality

began to organize programs, clinics, conferences, and associations to promote study of and treatment for transsexuals, and self-identified transsexuals began to organize to demand their own rights.

. . .

[T]he birth of a new identity evolved socially and politically into the birth of a new minority. Self-identified transsexuals distinguished themselves from other "deviants" and saw themselves as members of a distinct social group. In the late 1960s and early 1970s a few transsexuals began to challenge the doctors' authority and to reject the medical model that cast them primarily as patients. They observed and sometimes joined the 1960s movements for civil rights, feminism, and gay liberation, and they began to organize collectively and demand the right to quality medical care and also the right to live, free from harassment, with whatever presentation of gender they chose to express. By the century's end the push for transsexual rights had blossomed into a vocal social movement with local, national, and international organizations and with a new scholarship that sought again to clarify the contested meanings of sex.

. . .

As this thumbnail sketch suggests, the history of transsexuality engages a number of key trends of the twentieth century. It demonstrates the growing authority of science and medicine, and it points to the impact of sensational journalism. It illustrates the rise of a new concept of the modern self that placed a heightened value on self-expression, self-improvement, and self-transformation. It highlights the proliferation of sexual identities, and it offers a new angle of vision into the breakdown of traditional norms of gender. In the 1970s and 1980s the women's and gay liberation movements eclipsed transsexuality as the sites of public debate over sex, gender, and sexuality. But the history of transsexuality had already laid the definitional groundwork and helps explain the peculiar configuration that sex, gender, and sexuality had already assumed in American popular culture, medicine, and law.

. . .

87

Transgender Liberation

Susan Stryker

. . .

THE COMPTON'S CAFETERIA RIOT OF 1966

By the middle of the 1960s life in the United States was being transformed by several large-scale social movements. . . . The most militant phase of the transgender movement for social change, from 1966 to 1969, was part of this massive social upheaval.

The 1966 Compton's Cafeteria Riot in San Francisco's seedy Tenderloin neighborhood was similar to earlier incidents at Cooper's [in Los Angeles in 1959] and Dewey's [in Philadelphia in 1965]. For the first time, however, direct action in the streets by transgender people resulted in lasting institutional change. One weekend night in August—the precise date is unknown—Compton's, a twenty-four-hour cafeteria at the corner of Turk and Taylor streets, was buzzing with its usual late-night crowd of drag queens, hustlers, slummers, cruisers, runaway teens, and down-and-out neighborhood regulars. The restaurant's management became annoyed by a noisy young crowd of queens at one table who seemed be spending a lot of time without spending a lot of money, and it called in the police to roust them—as it had been doing with increasing frequency throughout the summer. A surly police officer, accustomed to manhandling Compton's clientele with impunity, grabbed the arm of one of the queens and tried to drag her away. She unexpectedly threw her coffee in his face, however, and a melee erupted: Plates, trays, cups, and silverware flew through the air at the startled police officers, who ran outside and called for backup. Compton's customers turned over the tables and smashed the plateglass windows and then poured out of the restaurant and into the streets. The paddy wagons arrived, and street fighting broke out in Compton's vicinity, all around the corner of Turk and Taylor. Drag queens beat the police with their heavy purses and kicked them with their high-heeled shoes. A police car was vandalized, a newspaper stand was burned to the ground, and—in the words of the best available source on what happened that night, a retrospective account by gay liberation activist Reverend Raymond Broshears, published in the program of San Francisco's first Gay Pride march in 1972—"general havoc was raised in the Tenderloin." The small restaurant had been packed when the fighting broke out, so the riot probably involved fifty or sixty patrons, plus police officers and any neighborhood residents or late-night passersby who jumped into the fray.

CONTEXTUALIZING COMPTON'S

Although the exact date of the riot remains a mystery . . . its underlying causes are reasonably clear. Understanding why the riot happened where and when it did reveals a great deal about the issues that have historically motivated the transgender social justice struggle and helps us understand similar dynamics at work today.

The location of the riot was by no means random. San Francisco's downtown Tenderloin neighborhood had been a sex-work district since the early 1900s. . . .

Much of the so-called vice trade in the neighborhood was supported by nonresidents of one sort or another. . . . But the neighborhood's resident population tended to be those who could least afford to live elsewhere, or who were prevented from doing so: released convicts and parolees, old-timers on small pensions, recent immigrants, pimps, prostitutes, drug addicts, alcoholics—and transgender women.

Housing and employment discrimination against transgender people are still legal in most places in the United States, and this discrimination was even more common in the past than it is now. In the 1960s, more so than today, a person who looked transgendered would be less likely to be rented to and would have a great deal of trouble finding work. As a result, a great many transgender women lived in the Tenderloin in cheap residential hotels, many of them along Turk Street near Compton's. To meet their basic survival needs they often worked as prostitutes or as maids in the hotels and bars where their friends sold sex. While most people who participated in the Tenderloin's illicit economy of sex, drugs, and after-hours entertainment were free to come and go, the neighborhood functioned as more of an involuntary containment zone for transgender women. Police actually helped

concentrate a population of transgender women in the Tenderloin by directing them to go there when they were picked up in other parts of the city.

The police could be especially vicious to "street queens," whom they considered bottom-of-the-barrel sex workers, and who were the least able to complain about mistreatment. Transgender women working the streets were often arrested on suspicion of prostitution even if they were just going to the corner store or talking with friends; they might be driven around in squad cars for hours, forced to perform oral sex, strip-searched, or, after arriving at the jail, humiliated in front of other prisoners. Transgender women in jail often would have their heads forcibly shaved, or if they resisted, be placed in solitary confinement in "the hole." And because they were legally men (with male genitalia in spite of their social lives as women, and often in spite of having breasts and no facial hair) they would be placed in the men's jail, where their femininity made them especially vulnerable to sexual assault, rape, and murder.

This chronically bad situation became even worse in the mid-1960s, when U.S. involvement in the war in Vietnam escalated. Wartime is typically a time of heightened surveillance of commercial sexual activity in cities where large numbers of troops are being mobilized for deployment. . . . There were wartime crackdowns on prostitution in San Francisco during the Spanish-American War in the Philippines in the 1890s, during World War II in the 1940s, and during the Korean conflict in the 1950s. Among the hardest-hit establishments in San Francisco during the crackdown associated with the 1964–66 escalation of U.S. troops in Vietnam were the gay and drag bars, which even then catered to the "Don't ask, don't tell" military crowd.

Yet another factor that changed an already grim situation from bad to worse for transgender women in the Tenderloin was the effect of urban renewal and redevelopment. Their increasingly serious plight was directly related to very broad-scale social and economic changes. . . .

In response to the massive social dislocations of urban renewal and redevelopment. Tenderloin residents launched a grassroots campaign for economic justice in 1965. . . . Their immediate goal was to establish needed social services by qualifying the neighborhood for federal antipoverty funding. . . . The Tenderloin organizers not only had to document economic need in their neighborhood; they also had to persuade poor communities of color that adding an additional antipoverty target zone predominately populated by white people would be the right thing to do, even if that meant the already existing zones got a smaller slice of a fixed amount of money. Compounding matters even further, most of the white people were queer, and most of the people of color were straight. The eventual establishment of the Central City Anti-Poverty Program thus represented a singular accomplishment in the history of U.S. progressive politics: the first successful multiracial gay/straight alliance for economic justice.

Tenderloin activists involved in the antipoverty organizing campaign were striving to create conditions in which people could truly participate in structuring the society they lived in instead of just reacting to changes created by others. One unexpected consequence of neighborhood mobilization was the formation of Vanguard, an organization made up mostly of young gay hustlers and transgender people. Vanguard, which formed in the summer of 1966, is the earliest known queer youth organization in the United States. . . .

Vanguard described itself as "an organization of, by, and for the kids on the streets." Its goals were to promote a sense of self-worth among its members, to offer mutual support and companionship, to bring youth issues to the attention of older people, and to assert its presence in the neighborhood. One of the group's early flyers urged people to think past racial divisions and focus instead on shared living conditions: "You've heard about Black Power and White Power," the flyer said, before telling its readers to "get ready for Street Power." . . . Vanguard's first major political action . . . was to confront the management of

Compton's Cafeteria over its poor treatment of transgender women. Compton's Cafeteria functioned as a chill-out lounge for the whole neighborhood; for young people who often had no homes, families, or legal employment, who were marginalized by their gender or sexuality, it provided an especially vital resource.

Vanguard held its meetings at Compton's, and during the course of the summer of 1966, tensions there had been on the rise. As the restaurant's customers increasingly claimed its turf as their own, the management asserted its property rights and business interests more and more strongly. It instituted a "service charge" for each customer to make up for income lost to tables of young people "camping out" and not buying any food, but it applied the charge in a discriminatory manner. It hired security guards to harass the street kids and shoo them outside, particularly the transgender youth. And with greater and greater frequency, it called the cops. In July, Vanguard worked with ministers from Glide [Glide Memorial United Methodist Church] and with older members of San Francisco's homophile organizations to set up a picket line protesting the mistreatment of its members, much as the customers and gay activists in Philadelphia had done at Dewey's. In San Francisco, however, the restaurant's management turned a deaf ear to the complaints. Soon after the picket failed to produce any results, frustration boiled over into militant resistance.

. . .

Looking back, it's easy to see how the Compton's Cafeteria riot in 1966 was related to very large-scale political, social, and economic developments and was not just an isolated little incident unrelated to other things that were going on in the world. The circumstances that created the conditions for the riot in the first place continue to be relevant in the transgender movement today: discriminatory policing practices in minority communities, harmful urban land-use policies, the unsettling domestic consequences of U.S. foreign wars, access to healthcare, civil rights activism aiming to expand individual liberties and social tolerance on matters of sexuality and gender, and political coalition building around the structural injustices that affect many different communities. The violent resistance to the oppression of transgender people at Compton's Cafeteria did not solve the problems that transgender people in the Tenderloin faced daily. It did, however, create a space in which it became possible for the city of San Francisco to begin relating differently to its transgender citizens—to begin treating them, in fact, as citizens with legitimate needs instead of simply as a problem to get rid of. That shift in awareness was a crucial step for the contemporary transgender social justice movement—the beginning of a new relationship to state power and social legitimacy. It would not have happened the way that it did without direct action in the streets on the part of transgender women who were fighting for their own survival.

. . .

88

Mutilating Gender

Dean Spade

. . .

This essay examines the relationship between individuals seeking sex reassignment surgery (SRS) and the medical establishments with which they must contend in order to fulfill their goals. . . .

Throughout this essay, I draw on my own experience of attempting to find low-cost or free counseling in order to begin the process of getting a double mastectomy. The choice to use personal narrative in this piece comes from a belief that just such a combination of theoretical work about the relationships of trans people to medical establishments and gender norms and the experience of trans people is too rarely found. Riki Anne Wilchins describes how trans experience has been used by psychiatrists, cultural feminists, anthropologists, and sociologists "travel[ling] through our lives and problems like tourists . . . [p]icnicking on our identities . . . select[ing] the tastiest tidbits with which to illustrate a theory or push a book." In most writing about trans people, our gender performance is put under a microscope to prove theories or build "expertise" while the gender performances of the authors remain unexamined and naturalized. I want to avoid even the appearance of participation in such a tradition, just as I want to use my own experience to illustrate how the requirements for diagnosis and treatment play out on individual bodies. The recent proliferation of academic and activist work on trans issues has created the impression in many people (mostly non-trans) that problems with access to services for trans people are being alleviated, and that the education of many specialists who provide services to trans people has made available sensitive therapeutic environments for trans people living in large metropolitan areas who can avail themselves of such services. My unsuccessful year-long quest for basic low-cost respectful counseling services in Los Angeles, which included seeking services at the Los Angeles Gender Center, the Los Angeles Gay and Lesbian Services Center, and Children's Hospital Los Angeles is a testament to the problems that still remain. This failure suggests the larger problems with the production of the "transsexual" in medical practice, and with the diagnostic and treatment criteria that made it impossible for the professionals from whom I sought care to respectfully engage my request for gender-related body alteration.

I hope that the use of my experience in this paper will provide a grounding illustration of the regulatory effects of the current diagnosis-treatment scheme for GID and resist the traditional framing of transsexual experience which posits trans people as victims or villains, insane or fascinating. Instead, I hope to be part of a project already taken up by Riki Anne Wilchins, Kate Bornstein, Leslie Feinberg, and many others which opens a position for trans people as self-critical, feminist, intellectual subjects of knowledge rather than simply case studies.

I. GOVERNANCE: PASSING AS A TRANSSEXUAL

Here's what I'm after: a surgically constructed male-appearing chest, no hormones (for now—maybe forever), no first-name change, any pronouns (except "it") are okay, although when it comes to gendered generics I happen to really like "Uncle" better than "Aunt," and definitely "Mr. Spade." Hausman writes, "transsexuals must seek and obtain medical treatment in order to be recognized as transsexuals. Their subject position depends upon a necessary relation to the medical establishment and its discourses." I've quickly learned that the converse is also true, in order to obtain the medical intervention I am seeking, I need to prove my membership in the category "transsexual"—prove that I have GID—to the proper authorities. Unfortunately, stating my true objectives is not convincing them.

. . .

II. THE TRANSSEXUAL CHILDHOOD

"When did you first know you were different?" the counselor at the L.A. Free Clinic asked. "Well," I said, "I knew I was poor and on welfare, and that was different from lots of kids at school, and I had a single mom, which was really uncommon there, and we weren't Christian, which is terribly noticeable in the South. Then later I knew I was a foster child, and in high school, I knew I was a feminist and that caused me all kinds of trouble, so I guess I always knew I was different." His facial expression tells me this isn't what he wanted to hear, but why should I engage this idea that my gender performance has been my most important difference in my life? It hasn't, and I can't separate it from the class, race, and parentage variables through which it was mediated. Does this mean I'm not real enough for surgery?

I've worked hard to not engage the gay childhood narrative—I never talk about tomboy-ish behavior as an antecedent to my lesbian identity, I don't tell stories about cross-dressing or crushes on girls, and I intentionally fuck with the assumption of it by telling people how I used to be straight and have sex with boys like any sweet trashy rural girl and some of it was fun. I see these narratives as strategic, and I've always rejected the strategy that adopts some theory of innate sexuality and forecloses the possibility that anyone, gender-troubled childhood or not, could transgress sexual and gender norms at any time. I don't want to participate in an idea that only some people have to engage a struggle of learning gender norms in childhood either. So now, faced with these questions, how do I decide whether to look back on my life through the tranny childhood lens, tell the stories about being a boy for Halloween, not playing with dolls: What is the cost of participation in this selective recitation? What is the cost of not participating?

Symptoms of GID in the Diagnostic and Statistical Manual (DSM-IV) describe at length the symptom of childhood participation in stereotypically gender inappropriate behavior. Boys with GID "particularly enjoy playing house, drawing pictures of beautiful girls and princesses, and watching television or videos of their favorite female characters. . . . They avoid rough-and-tumble play and competitive sports and have little interest in cars and trucks." Girls with GID do not want to wear dresses, "prefer boys' clothing and short hair," are interested in "contact sports, [and] rough-and-tumble play." Despite the disclaimer in the diagnosis description that this is not to be confused with normal gender non-conformity found in tomboys and sissies, no real line is drawn between "normal" gender non-conformity and gender non-conformity which constitutes GID. The effect is two-fold. First, normative childhood gender is produced—normal kids do the opposite of what kids with GID are doing. Non-GID kids can be expected to: play with children of the own sex, play with gender appropriate toys (trucks for boys, dolls for girls), enjoy fictional characters of their own sex (girls, specifically, might have GID if they like Batman or Superman), play gender appropriate characters in games of "house," etc. Secondly, a regulatory mechanism is put into place. Because gender nonconformity is established as a basis for illness, parents now have a "mill of speech," speculation and diagnosis to feed their children's gender through should it cross the line. As Foucault describes, the invention of a category of deviation, the description of the "ill" behavior that need be resisted or cured, creates not a prohibitive silence about such behavior but an opportunity for increased surveillance and speculation, what he would call "informal-governance."

The Diagnostic Criteria for Gender Identity Disorder names, as a general category of symptom, "[a] strong and persistent cross-gender identification (not merely a desire for any perceived cultural advantages of being the other sex)." This criterion suggests the possibility of a gender categorization not read through the cultural gender hierarchy. This requires an imagination of a child wanting to be a gender different from the one assigned to hir without having that desire stem from a cultural understanding of gender difference defined by the "advantaging" of certain gender behavior and identities over others. To use an

C O N T E X T

C
O
N
T
E
X
T

illustrative example from the description of childhood GID symptoms, if a child assigned "female" wants to wear pants and hates dresses, and has been told that this is inappropriate for girls, is that decision free from a recognition of cultural advantages associated with gender? Since a diagnosis of GID does not require a child to state the desire to change genders, and the primary indicators are gender inappropriate tastes and behaviors, how can this be separated from cultural understandings of what constitutes gender difference and gender appropriateness? If we start from an understanding that gender behavior is learned, and that children are not born with some innate sense that girls should wear dresses and boys shouldn't like Barbie or anything pink, then how can a desire to transgress an assigned gender category be read outside of cultural meaning? Such a standard does, as Billings and Urban argue, privatize and depoliticize gender role distress. It creates a fictional transsexual who just knows in hir gut what man is and what woman is, and knows that sie is trapped in the wrong body. It produces a naturalized, innate gender difference outside power, a fictional binary that does not privilege one term.

The diagnostic criteria for GID produces a fiction of natural gender, in which normal, non-transsexual people grow up with minimal to no gender trouble or exploration, do not crossdress as children, do not play with the wrong-gendered kids, and do not like the wrong kinds of toys or characters. This story isn't believable, but because medicine produces it not through a description of the norm, but through a generalized account of the transgression, and instructs the doctor/parent/teacher to focus on the transgressive behavior, it establishes a surveillance and regulation effective for keeping both non-transsexuals and transsexuals in adherence to their roles. In order to get authorization for body alteration, this childhood must be produced, and the GID diagnosis accepted, maintaining an idea of two discrete gender categories that normally contain everyone but occasionally are wrongly assigned, requiring correction to reestablish the norm.

It's always been fun to reject the gay childhood story, to tell people I "chose" lesbianism, or to over articulate a straight childhood narrative to suggest that lesbianism could happen to anyone. But not engaging a trans childhood narrative is terrifying—what if it means I'm not "real"? Even though I don't believe in real, it matters if other people see me as real—if not I'm a mutilator, an imitator, and worst of all, I can't access surgery.

Transsexual writer Claudine Griggs' book takes for granted that transsexuality is an illness, an unfortunate predicament, something fortunate, normal people don't have to go through. . . .

This is precisely the approach I want to avoid as I reject the narrative of a gender troubled childhood. My project would be to promote sex reassignment, gender alteration, temporary gender adventure, and the mutilation of gender categories, via surgery, hormones, clothing, political lobbying, civil disobedience, or any other means available. But that political commitment itself, if revealed to the gatekeepers of my surgery, disqualifies me. One therapist said to me, "You're really intellectualizing this, we need to get to the root of why you feel you should get your breasts removed, how long have you felt this way?" Does realness reside in the length of time a desire exists? Are women who seek breast enhancement required to answer these questions? Am I supposed to be able to separate my political convictions about gender, my knowledge of the violence of gender rigidity that has been a part of my life and the lives of everyone I care about, from my real "feelings" about what it means to occupy my gendered body? How could I begin to think about my chest without thinking about cultural advantage?

III. CHOOSING PERSPECTIVE: PASSING "FULL-TIME"

From what I've gathered in my various counseling sessions, in order to be deemed real I need to want to pass as male all the time, and not feel ambivalent about this. I need to be

willing to make the commitment to "full-time" maleness, or they can't be sure that I won't regret my surgery. The fact that I don't want to change my first name, that I haven't sought out the use of the pronoun "he," that I don't think that "lesbian" is the wrong word for me, or, worse yet, that I recognize that the use of any word for myself—lesbian, transperson, transgender butch, boy, mister, FTM fag, butch—has always been/will always be strategic is my undoing in their eyes. They are waiting for a better justification of my desire for surgery—something less intellectual, more real.

I'm supposed to be wholly joyous when I get called "sir" or "boy." How could I ever have such an uncomplicated relationship to that moment? Each time I'm sirred I know both that my look is doing what I want it to do, and that the reason people can assign male gender to me easily is because they don't believe women have short hair, and because, as Garber has asserted, the existence of maleness as the generic means that fewer visual clues of maleness are required to achieve male gender attribution. This "therapeutic" process demands of me that I toss out all my feminist misgivings about the ways that gender rigidity informs people's perception of me.

. . .

Perhaps the most overt requirement for transsexual diagnosis is the ability to inhabit and perform "successfully" the new gender category. Through my own interactions with medical professionals, accounts of other trans people, and medical scholarship on transsexuality, I have gathered that the favored indication of such "success" seems to be the gender attribution of non-trans people. Because the ability to be perceived by non-trans people as a non-trans person is valorized, normative expressions of gender within a singular category are mandated.

. . .

IV. MAYBE I'M NOT A TRANSSEXUAL

The counselor at the L.A. Free Clinic decided I wasn't transsexual during the first (and only) session. When I told him what I wanted, and how I was starting counseling because I was trying to get some letter that I could give to a surgeon so that they would alter my chest, he said, "You should just go get breast reduction." Of course, he didn't know that most cosmetic surgeons won't reduce breasts below a C-cup (I wouldn't even qualify for reduction), and that breast reduction is a different procedure than the construction of a male-looking chest. I also suppose that he wasn't thinking about what happens to gender deviants when they end up in the hands of medical professionals who don't have experience with trans people.

> *Some surgeons have strong reactions to transsexual patients, and often, if the surgery is done in a teaching hospital, the surgeon turns out to be a resident or staff member who is offended by the procedure. "In one case, with which I am familiar," writes a doctor, "the patient's massive scars were probably the result of the surgeon's unconscious sadism and wish to scar the patient for 'going against nature.'"*

To this counselor, my failure to conform to the transsexuality he was expecting required my immediate expulsion from that world of meaning at any cost. My desire couldn't be for SRS because I wasn't a transsexual, so it must be for cosmetic surgery, something normal people get.

All my attempts at counseling, and all those experiences of being eyed suspiciously when I suggested that I was trans, or told outright I was not by non-trans counselors, made me

expect that I would get a similar reception from trans people in activist or support contexts. This has not been the case. I've found that in trans contexts, a much broader conception of trans experience exists. The trans people I've met have, shockingly, believed what I say about my gender. Some have a self-narrative resembling the medical model of transsexuality, some do not. However, the people I've met share with me what my counselors do not: a commitment to gender self-determination and respect for all expressions of gender. Certainly not all trans people would identify with this principle, but I think it makes better sense as a basis for identity than the ability to pass "full-time" or the amount of cross-dressing one did as a child. Wilchins posits an idea of identity as "an effect of political activism instead of a cause." I see this notion reflected in trans activism, writing, and discussion, despite its absence in the medical institutions through which trans people must negotiate our identities.

Feinberg writes:

> Once I figured out that "transgendered" was someone who transcended traditional stereotypes of "man" and "woman," I saw that I was such a person. I then began a quest for finding words that described myself, and discovered that while psychiatric jargon dominated the discourse, there were many other words, both older and newer, that addressed these issues. While I accepted the label of "transsexual" in order to obtain access to the hormones and chest surgery necessary to manifest my spirit in the material world, I have always had a profound disagreement with the definition of transsexualism as a psychiatric condition and transsexuals as disordered people.

V. TELLING STORIES: STRATEGIC DEPLOYMENT OF THE TRANSSEXUAL NARRATIVE

. . .

After attending only three discussion group meetings with other trans people, I am struck by the naiveté with which I approached the search for counseling to get my surgery-authorizing letters. No one at these groups seems to see therapy as the place where they voice their doubts about their transition, where they wrestle with the political implications of their changes, where they speak about fears of losing membership in various communities or in their families. No one trusts the doctors as the place to work things out. When I mention the places I've gone for help, places that are supposed to support queer and trans people, everyone nods knowingly, having heard countless stories like mine about these very places before. Some have suggestions of therapists who are better, but none cost less than $50/hr. Mostly, though, people suggest different ways to get around the requirements. I get names of surgeons who do not always ask for the letters. Someone suggests that since I won't be on hormones, I can go in and pretend I'm a woman with a history of breast cancer in my family and that I want a double mastectomy to prevent it. I have these great, sad, conversations with these people who know all about what it means to lie and cheat their way through the medical roadblocks to get the opportunity to occupy their bodies in the way they want. I understand, now, that the place that is safe to talk about this is in here, with other people who understand the slipperiness of gender and the politics of transition, and who believe me without question when I say what I think I am and how that needs to look.

. . .

VII. CONCLUSION

Personal narrative is always strategically employed. It is always mediated through cultural understandings, through ideology. It is always a function of selective memory and narration. Have I learned that I should lie to obtain surgery, as others have before me? Does that lesson require an acceptance that cannot successfully advocate on behalf of a different approach to my desire for transformation?

An examination of how medicine governs gender variant bodies through the regulation of body alteration by means of the invention of the illness of transsexuality brings up the question of whether illness is the appropriate interpretive model for gender variance. The benefits of such an understanding for trans people are noteworthy. As long as SRS remains a treatment for an illness, the possibility of Medicaid coverage for it remains viable. Similarly, courts examining the question of what qualified a transsexual to have legal membership in the new gender category have relied heavily on the medical model of transsexuality when they have decided favorably for transsexuals. A model premised on a disability- or disease-based understanding of deviant behavior is believed by many to be the best strategy for achieving tolerance by norm-adherent people for those not adhering to norms. Such arguments are present in the realm of illicit drug use and in the quest for biological origins of homosexuality just as they are in the portrayal of transsexuality as an illness or disability.

However, it is vital that the costs of such an approach also be considered. First, the medical approach to gender variance, and the creation of transsexuality, has resulted in a governance of trans bodies that restricts our ability to make gender transitions which do not yield membership in a normative gender role. The self-determination of trans people in crafting our gender expression is compromised by the rigidity of the diagnostic and treatment criteria. At the same time, this criteria and the version of transsexuality that it posits produce and reify a fiction of normal, healthy gender that works as a regulatory measure for the gender expression of all people. To adopt the medical understanding of transsexuality is to agree that SRS is the unfortunate treatment of an unfortunate condition, to accept that gender norm adherence is fortunate and healthy, and to undermine the threat to a dichotomous gender system which trans experience can pose. The reification of the violence of compulsory gender norm adherence, and the submission of trans bodies to a norm-producing medical discipline, is too high a price for a small hope of conditional tolerance.

89

Trans Woman Manifesto

Julia Serano

This manifesto calls for the end of the scapegoating, deriding, and dehumanizing of trans women everywhere. For the purposes of this manifesto, *trans woman* is defined as any person who was assigned a male sex at birth, but who identifies as and/or lives as a woman. No qualifications should be placed on the term "trans woman" based on a person's ability to "pass" as female, her hormone levels, or the state of her genitals—after all, it is

downright sexist to reduce any woman (trans or otherwise) down to her mere body parts or to require her to live up to certain societally dictated ideals regarding appearance.

Perhaps no sexual minority is more maligned or misunderstood than trans women. As a group, we have been systematically pathologized by the medical and psychological establishment, sensationalized and ridiculed by the media, marginalized by mainstream lesbian and gay organizations, dismissed by certain segments of the feminist community, and, in too many instances, been made the victims of violence at the hands of men who feel that we somehow threaten their masculinity and heterosexuality. Rather than being given the opportunity to speak for ourselves on the very issues that affect our own lives, trans women are instead treated more like research subjects: Others place us under their microscopes, dissect our lives, and assign motivations and desires to us that validate their own theories and agendas regarding gender and sexuality.

Trans women are so ridiculed and despised because we are uniquely positioned at the intersection of multiple binary gender-based forms of prejudice: transphobia, cissexism, and misogyny.

Transphobia is an irrational fear of, aversion to, or discrimination against people whose gendered identities, appearances, or behaviors deviate from societal norms. In much the same way that homophobic people are often driven by their own repressed homosexual tendencies, transphobia is first and foremost an expression of one's own insecurity about having to live up to cultural gender ideals. The fact that transphobia is so rampant in our society reflects the reality that we place an extraordinary amount of pressure on individuals to conform to all of the expectations, restrictions, assumptions, and privileges associated with the sex they were assigned at birth.

While all transgender people experience transphobia, transsexuals additionally experience a related (albeit distinct) form of prejudice: *cissexism*, which is the belief that transsexuals' identified genders are inferior to, or less authentic than, those of *cissexuals* (i.e., people who are not transsexual and who have only ever experienced their subconscious and physical sexes as being aligned). The most common expression of cissexism occurs when people attempt to deny the transsexual the basic privileges that are associated with the trans person's self-identified gender. Common examples include purposeful misuse of pronouns or insisting that the trans person use a different public restroom. The justification for this denial is generally founded on the assumption that the trans person's gender is not authentic because it does not correlate with the sex they were assigned at birth. In making this assumption, cissexists attempt to create an artificial hierarchy. By insisting that the trans person's gender is "fake," they attempt to validate their own gender as "real" or "natural." This sort of thinking is extraordinarily naive, as it denies a basic truth: We make assumptions every day about other people's genders without ever seeing their birth certificates, their chromosomes, their genitals, their reproductive systems, their childhood socialization, or their legal sex. There is no such thing as a "real" gender—there is only the gender we experience ourselves as and the gender we perceive others to be.

While often different in practice, cissexism, transphobia, and homophobia are all rooted in *oppositional sexism*, which is the belief that female and male are rigid, mutually exclusive categories, each possessing a unique and nonoverlapping set of attributes, aptitudes, abilities, and desires. Oppositional sexists attempt to punish or dismiss those of us who fall outside of gender or sexual norms because our existence threatens the idea that women and men are "opposite" sexes. . . .

In addition to the rigid, mutually exclusive gender categories established by oppositional sexism, the other requirement for maintaining a male-centered gender hierarchy is to enforce *traditional sexism*—the belief that maleness and masculinity are superior to femaleness and femininity. Traditional and oppositional sexism work hand in hand to ensure that those who are masculine have power over those who are feminine, and that

only those born male will be seen as authentically masculine. For the purposes of this manifesto, the word *misogyny* will be used to describe this tendency to dismiss and deride femaleness and femininity.

Just as all transgender people experience transphobia and cissexism to differing extents (depending on how often, obvious, or out we are as transgender), we experience misogyny to differing extents too. This is most evident in the fact that, while there are many different types of transgender people, our society tends to single out trans women and others on the male-to-female (MTF) spectrum for attention and ridicule. This is not merely because we transgress binary gender norms per se, but because we, by necessity, embrace our own femaleness and femininity. Indeed, more often than not it is our expressions of femininity and our desire to be female that become sensationalized, sexualized, and trivialized by others. While trans people on the female-to-male (FTM) spectrum face discrimination for breaking gender norms (i.e., oppositional sexism), their expressions of maleness or masculinity themselves are not targeted for ridicule—to do so would require one to question masculinity itself.

When a trans person is ridiculed or dismissed not merely for failing to live up to gender norms, but for their expressions of femaleness or femininity, they become the victims of a specific form of discrimination: *trans-misogyny*. When the majority of jokes made at the expense of trans people center on "men wearing dresses" or "men who want their penises cut off," that is not transphobia—it is trans-misogyny. When the majority of violence and sexual assaults committed against trans people is directed at trans women, that is not transphobia—it is trans-misogyny. When it's okay for women to wear "men's" clothing, but when men who wear "women's" clothing can be diagnosed with the psychological disorder transvestic fetishism, that is not transphobia—it is trans-misogyny. When women's or lesbian organizations and events open their doors to trans men but not trans women, that is not transphobia—it is trans-misogyny.

In a male-centered gender hierarchy, where it is assumed that men are better than women and that masculinity is superior to femininity, there is no greater perceived threat than the existence of trans women, who despite being born male and inheriting male privilege "choose" to be female instead. By embracing our own femaleness and femininity, we, in a sense, cast a shadow of doubt over the supposed supremacy of maleness and masculinity. In order to lessen the threat we pose to the male-centered gender hierarchy, our culture (primarily via the media) uses every tactic in its arsenal of traditional sexism to dismiss us:

1 The media hyperfeminizes us by accompanying stories about trans women with pictures of us putting on makeup, dresses, and high-heeled shoes in an attempt to highlight the supposed "frivolous" nature of our femaleness, or by portraying trans women as having derogatory feminine-associated character traits such as being weak, confused, passive, or mousy.

2 The media hypersexualizes us by creating the impression that most trans women are sex workers or sexual deceivers, and by asserting that we transition for primarily sexual reasons (e.g., to prey on innocent straight men or to fulfill some kind of bizarre sex fantasy). Such depictions not only belittle trans women's motives for transitioning, but implicitly suggest that women as a whole have no worth beyond their ability to be sexualized.

3 The media objectifies our bodies by sensationalizing sex reassignment surgery and openly discussing our "man-made vaginas" without any of the discretion that normally accompanies discussions about genitals. Further, those of us who have not had surgery are constantly being reduced to our body parts, whether by the creators of tranny porn who overemphasize and exaggerate our penises (thus distorting trans women into "she-males" and "chicks with dicks") or by other people who have been

so brainwashed by phallocentricism that they believe that the mere presence of a penis can trump the femaleness of our identities, our personalities, and the rest of our bodies.

Because anti-trans discrimination is steeped in traditional sexism, it is not simply enough for trans activists to challenge binary gender norms (i.e., oppositional sexism)—we must also challenge the idea that femininity is inferior to masculinity and that femaleness is inferior to maleness. In other words, by necessity, trans activism must be at its core a feminist movement.

. . .

It is no longer enough for feminism to fight solely for the rights of those born female. That strategy has furthered the prospects of many women over the years, but now it bumps up against a glass ceiling that is partly of its own making. Though the movement worked hard to encourage women to enter previously male-dominated areas of life, many feminists have been ambivalent at best, and resistant at worst, to the idea of men expressing or exhibiting feminine traits and moving into certain traditionally female realms. And while we credit previous feminist movements for helping to create a society where most sensible people would agree with the statement "women and men are equals," we lament the fact that we remain light-years away from being able to say that most people believe that femininity is masculinity's equal.

. . .

But it is not enough for us to empower femaleness and femininity. We must also stop pretending that there are essential differences between women and men. This begins with the acknowledgment that there are exceptions to every gender rule and stereotype, and this simply stated fact disproves all gender theories that purport that female and male are mutually exclusive categories. We must move away from pretending that women and men are "opposite" sexes, because when we buy into that myth it establishes a dangerous precedent. For if men are big, then women must be small; and if men are strong then women must be weak. And if being butch is to make yourself rock-solid, then being femme becomes allowing yourself to be malleable; and if being a man means taking control of your own situation, then being a woman becomes living up to other people's expectations. When we buy into the idea that female and male are "opposites," it becomes impossible for us to empower women without either ridiculing men or pulling the rug out from under ourselves.

It is only when we move away from the idea that there are "opposite" sexes, and let go of the culturally derived values that are assigned to expressions of femininity and masculinity, that we may finally approach gender equity. By challenging both oppositional and traditional sexism simultaneously, we can make the world safe for those of us who are queer, those of us who are feminine, and those of us who are female, thus empowering people of all sexualities and genders.

90

The Impact of Juvenile Court on Queer and Trans/Gender-Non-Conforming Youth

Wesley Ware

. . .

Working with queer and trans/gender-non-conforming youth in the Deep South, I hear stories of state and personal violence from a wide range of people. There was the 16-year-old, black self-identified "stud" in detention after her mom referred her to family court for bringing girls to the house. Then there was the incarcerated white 16-year-old trans youth from a rural town of 642, whose access to transgender healthcare resided in the hands of one juvenile judge. I was told of a black trans-feminine youth in New Orleans who was threatened with contempt for wearing feminine clothing to her court hearing. There was also the 12-year-old boy, perceived to be gay by his mother, who was brought into judge's chambers without his attorney and questioned about being gay before he was sentenced for contempt after being found "ungovernable." There was the public defender who refused to represent his gay client because the lawyer believed him to be "sick" and in need of the "services" offered by prison. And there was the black lesbian arrested over and over again for any crime where witnesses described the perpetrator as an African American "boyish-looking" girl. Nowhere is the literal regulation and policing of gender and sexuality, particularly of low-income queer and trans youth of color, so apparent than in juvenile courts and in the juvenile justice system in the South.

Understanding how the juvenile justice system operates and impacts queer and trans/gender-non-conforming youth requires a critical look at the history of youth rights and the inception of juvenile court. During the Industrial Revolution (1800–1840s), poor youth worked in factories, received no public education and were often arrested for the crime of poverty. These youth, some as young as 7 years old, were incarcerated with adults and placed in prisons until they were 21. Inspired by the belief that young people who committed crimes could be rehabilitated and shocked by the horrific treatment of white children in adult prisons, the juvenile justice system was developed. This new system was based on *parens patriae*, the idea that the role of the system was to place youth in the state's custody when their parents were unable to care for them. Later, in 1899, the first juvenile court was established, designed to "cure" children and provide treatments for them rather than sentences. Still rooted in a Puritan ideology, white young women were often sent to institutions "to protect them from sexual immorality."

Black children, however, who were viewed as incapable of rehabilitation, continued to be sent to adult prisons or were sent to racially segregated institutions. In Louisiana, black youth were sent to work the fields at Angola State Penitentiary, a former slave plantation, until 1948 when the State Industrial School for Colored Youth opened. The facilities were not desegregated until the United States District Court ordered desegregation of juvenile facilities in 1969. More recently, the goal of juvenile justice reform has been to keep youth in their homes and in their communities whenever possible while providing appropriate treatment services to youth and their families.

However, with the juvenile justice system's intent to provide "treatment" to young people, many queer/trans youth inherit the ideology that they are "wrong" or in need of "curing," as evidenced by their stories. As sexual and gender transgressions have been

deemed both illegal and pathological, queer and trans youth, who are some of the most vulnerable to "treatments," are not only subjected to incarceration but also to harassment by staff, conversion therapy, and physical violence. . . .

Worse than just providing damaging outcomes for youth once they are incarcerated, this rehabilitative system funnels queer and trans/gender-non-conforming youth into the front doors of the system. Non-accepting parents and guardians can refer their children to family court for arbitrary and subjective behaviors, such as being "ungovernable." Police can bring youth in for status offenses, offenses for which adults cannot be charged, which often become contributing factors to the criminalization of youth. Charges can range from truancy to curfew violations to running away from home. Like in the adult criminal justice system, queer and trans youth can be profiled by the police and brought in for survival crimes like prostitution or theft. Youth may be referred for self-defense arising from conflict with hostile family members or public displays of affection in schools that selectively enforce policies only against queer and trans youth.

. . .

Further aggravated by the public's fear of youth sexuality and our desire to control young people and their bodies, juvenile court presents a unique opportunity to destroy the lives of queer and trans/gender-non-conforming youth. The agenda of juvenile court then, for queer and trans youth at least, often becomes to "rehabilitate" youth into fitting heteronormative and gender-typical molds. Guised under the "best interest of the child," the goal often becomes to "protect" the child—or perhaps society—from gender-variant or non-heterosexual behavior.

While not as explicit as the sumptuary laws (laws requiring people to wear at least three items of gender-appropriate clothing) or sodomy laws of the past that led to the Compton's Riots and Stonewall Rebellion, the policing of sexuality and state regulation of gender has continued to exist in practice—perhaps nowhere more than in juvenile courts. In many ways, the system still mirrors the adult criminal justice system, whose roots can be traced to slavery, the commodification of bodies as free labor, institutionalized racism, and state regulation of low-income people of color, immigrants, and anyone deemed otherwise "deviant" or a threat to the political norm. Combined with the Puritan beliefs that helped spark the creation of juvenile courts, it becomes clear that, borrowing the words of Audre Lorde, queer and trans youth of color "were never meant to survive."

. . .

Once locked up, queer and trans youth experience the same horrors that their adult counterparts in the system do, but magnified by a system designed to control, regulate, and pathologize their very existence. In Louisiana's youth prisons, queer and trans youth have been subjected to "sexual-identity confusion counseling," accused of using "gender identity issues" to detract from their rehabilitation, and disciplined for expressing any gender-non-conforming behaviors or actions. Youth are put on lock-down for having hair that is too long or wearing state-issued clothing that is too tight. They are instructed how to walk, talk, and act in their dorms and are prohibited from communicating with other queer youth lest they become too "flamboyant" and cause a disturbance. They are excessively punished for consensual same-sex behavior and spend much of their time in protective custody or in isolation cells. In meetings with representatives from the Juvenile Justice Project of Louisiana, directors of youth jails have referred to non-heterosexual identities as "symptoms" and have conflated youth adjudicated for sex offenses with youth who are queer. In addition, when advocates asked what the biggest problem was at a youth prison in Baker, Louisiana, guards replied, "the lesbians."

. . .

While protections afforded to youth in the juvenile justice system like a greater right to confidentiality are extremely important for youth, they can also be another strike against

queer and trans youth seeking to access resources or support networks while inside. Like queer and trans adults in the criminal justice system who have difficulty receiving information that "promotes homosexuality," youth are unable to access affirming information during a particularly formative time in their lives, which can already be plagued with confusion and questioning. The right to confidentiality for youth in prison can result in their being prohibited from communicating with pen pals or seeking services from community organizations. Other rights are afforded to adults but not to minors, such as accessing legal counsel to challenge the conditions of their confinement. Youth under 18 must rely on their guardians to assist with filing a civil complaint, despite the fact that many queer and trans youth have had difficulty with their families prior to their incarceration—and that those family members may have contributed to their entering into the system in the first place. This barrier also holds true for transgender youth who are minors and seeking healthcare or hormones. . . .

Meanwhile, as state institutions are placing queer and trans/gender-non-conforming youth behind bars and effectively silencing their voices, prominent gay activists are fighting for inclusion in the very systems that criminalize youth of color (such as increased sentencing for hate crimes) under the banner of "we're just like everybody else." A far stray from the radicalism of the early gay rights movement, mainstream "gay issues" have become focused on the right to marry and "don't ask, don't tell" policies in the military, despite the fact that queer youth of color have consistently ranked these at the bottom of their list of priorities of issues that impact their lives. Likewise, the public "face of gay" as white, middle-class men has become a further detriment to queer and trans youth in prison. . . . [J]uvenile justice stakeholders . . . assume that any concern for these youth to be coming from white advocates who believe that queer and trans youth have been funneled into a system made for "poor black children;" in other words, into a system that is "OK for some children, but not for others." We must be clear about why we do this work—it is not because *some* children belong locked away at night and others do not—it is because *no* child should be behind bars.

Further, the data tells us that queer and trans youth in detention are equally distributed across race and ethnicity, and comprise 15 percent of youth in detention centers. So far, the data has been consistent among youth in different regions in the United States, including the rural South. Since queer and trans youth are overrepresented in nearly all popular feeders into the juvenile justice system—homelessness, difficulty in school, substance abuse, and difficulty with mental health—the same societal ills, which disproportionately affect youth of color—it should not be surprising that they may be overrepresented in youth prisons and jails as well.

Since incarcerated youth have so few opportunities to speak out, it is critically important for individuals and organizations doing this work to keep a political analysis of the failings of the system at the forefront of the work—particularly the inherent racial disparities in the system—while highlighting the voices of those youth who are most affected and providing vehicles through which they can share their stories.

Despite the targeting and subsequent silencing of queer and trans/gender-non-conforming youth in youth prisons and jails across Louisiana, young people have developed creative acts of resistance and mechanisms for self-preservation and survival. By failing to recognize the ways that young people demonstrate their own agency and affirm each other, we risk perpetuating the idea of vulnerable youth with little agency; victims rather than survivors and active resisters of a brutal system.

. . .

Although prohibited from even speaking publicly with other queer youth in prison, queer and trans youth have formed community across three youth prisons in the state, whispered through fences, and passed messages through sympathetic staff. They have made

matching bracelets and necklaces for one another, gotten each other's initials tattooed on their bodies, and written letters to each other's mothers. They have supported each other by alerting advocates when one of them was on lock-down or in trouble and unable to call.

Trans-feminine youth have gone to lockdown instead of cutting their hair and used their bed sheets to design curtains for their cells once they got there. They have smuggled in Kool-Aid to dye their hair, secretly shaved their legs, colored their fingernails with markers, and used crayons for eye shadow. When a lawyer asked her trans-masculine client to dress more "feminine" for court, knowing that the judge was increasingly hostile toward gender-non-conforming youth, her client drew the line at the skirt, fearlessly and proudly demanding that she receive her sentence in baggy pants instead.

Queer and trans/gender-non-conforming youth have made us question the very purpose of the juvenile justice system and holding them behind bars in jails and prisons made for kids. By listening to their voices it becomes apparent that until we dismantle state systems designed to criminalize and police young people and variant expressions of gender and sexuality, none of us will be free. . . .

91

Passing Realities

Allie Lie

CAMBRIDGE—SUMMER 1998

We leave the café on Massachusetts Avenue, my young sons, "J" and "A," and I. It's seasonably hot and humid. I wear flip-flops, khaki shorts, a sleeveless T-shirt, and a wide-brimmed straw hat. I am not "presenting." I've promised the boys I won't embarrass them. (Children are defenseless against attacks aimed at nonconformity. Adults—their mother, for instance—just have to deal with it.)

As we cross Mass Ave., we come to a small park-cum-island in the middle of the intersection. Two men sit on one of the benches, and their small dog, tethered to a red nylon leash, sits beneath the bench. A, my oldest, who has a fondness for animals that way surpasses any he'd have for humans, goes up and asks if he can pet the dog. J and I have walked past them and are on the other side of the park. I hear the man saying, "Sure"—I see him nod in my direction—"but you'd better ask your mother first."

After work she stops at a grocery store a block from her apartment. She has been here many times, both *en femme* and not. Today, as with every working day, she is *en femme*. She goes to the freezer section, pulls out a frozen yogurt and takes it up to the checkout counter. The middle-aged man behind the counter is not particularly friendly. No one who works at the store is. Once she pays for the yogurt, she asks the checkout man where she can find a plastic spoon. He gestures over his shoulder with a thumb, "Over there . . . pal."

She finds the spoons, then walks over to one of the luncheon tables in the front of the store and sits. She begins slowly eating the yogurt, carving out small, hard-frozen spoonfuls from the top layer, working around the edges first. She holds the spoon upside down, puts

it in her mouth, and sucks on it meditatively. As she does this, she overhears the sotto voce reprimand of the store manager behind her. Words like harassment, trouble, careful . . .

I am with the boys again, this time buying ice cream. The line at the counter has unwound itself into an amorphous crowd. No one seems to know who's next or who's helping whom. Someone has been summoned from the back of the store. A man appears and begins scanning the crowd. Our eyes meet. "Ma'am, what would you like?" J and A and I squeeze up to the counter. J takes my hand. "Dad, he called you . . ." "Shush, I know."

I order two vanilla cones for J and myself. As usual, A takes more time deciding. J gets his cone, then I get mine. The cashier motions to A (who wears his hair long because he's terrified of change and, despite his adolescent male misogyny, appears enviably androgynous). "What kind of cone would she like?" A looks at the floor.

"He'll have a sugar cone, please."

At a different grocery store . . .
"I'd like to write a check. How much over the amount can I write it for?"
Shrug. "Do you have a card?" "Yes."
Shrug again. "Fifty . . .?"
She writes the check and hands it to the cashier. The cash register jams—seems not to like what it's been told. The cashier looks at her apologetically, then summons help. A manager appears.

"Her total came to——." "And she wrote a check?" "Yes. But he wrote it for $30 over the amount." "Does he have a card?" "Yes, she does." "Well, she can only write it for 25 over the amount . . ." "That's no problem," she says. "I'll just write another check."

The cashier is again apologetic. "Do you mind?" "No," she says. "Not at all."

I am in the men's room of a restaurant. I have just washed my hands and looked in the mirror. This mirror is particularly unforgiving—thus I trust it. I am seldom happy with what I see. Reflective surfaces are to be avoided at all costs. The disparity between what I want to see and what actually greets me is too great. What I want to see: someone who could be Michelle Pfeiffer's female second cousin. What I see: longish, thinning hair; age lines (a.k.a. nasal labial folds); the faint, plucked remnants of beard; the wrong cheeks; the wrong lips. At times like this I think the course my life has taken is evidence of a delusional personality. I'm reminded of Nabokov's *Despair*, the story of a man who imagines that a stranger who looks not even remotely like him is his virtual twin.

This is why I am surprised when I turn to leave the restroom and see another man entering, noticing me, halting, then looking back to double-check the sign on the door.

CAMBRIDGE—LATE FALL 1998

She leaves the elevator at the sixth floor and heads for the door marked "The Ass. of Tedium, Drudgery, and Objectified Labor." She is here for a job interview—a job she already knows she doesn't want, but after three months of uncompensated unemployment, a job that she needs like nobody's business. She is dressed in her only polyester power suit, in burgundy with matching jacket and skirt. She opens the door and walks to the receptionist's desk. "I'm here to see Mrs. Z." "Take a seat, she'll be right with you."

She's had to pee for the last half hour. "Excuse me, may I please use the restroom first?"

The receptionist takes a key from her desk drawer and hands it to her. "Down at the end of the hall." She thanks the receptionist, exits the office and hurries to the room marked "W." She tries the lock. The door doesn't budge. She tries again. Still no success. The key

ring is attached to a plastic badge. She turns the badge over and reads the words written in black indelible marking pen: "Men's Room."

CAMBRIDGE—WINTER 1998–99

E and I have been separated for more than six months now. We'd been through couples counseling eight months before the separation. Eight months slogging through the muck of my midlife journey back and forth across the gender boundaries; eight months of soul searching (for both of us); dredging up all our fears, our needs; establishing who we are and what we are about. I volunteered everything I knew about myself and about the *condition* mental health practitioners choose to call *gender identity disorder*. I offered texts, testimonials, contacts for spouse and significant other support groups. She heard, but chose not to listen. The work failed. It was finally determined that (1) I couldn't live unless I established permanent residence in the land of the feminine, and (2) she couldn't live with me if I did.

Shortly after our separation, I transitioned to three-quarter time living as Allie. Very shortly after that I was fired from my job. I assured E that I'd continue to support her and the boys in any way I could; I borrowed money from my family and engaged in exhausting legal battles for unemployment benefits and for financial damages as the result of my unlawful firing. Through all this I remained committed to my newly found state of mental health, determined that I could face anything as Allie. I was also amply aware of the irony that, as hormones inexorably reduced Robert's potency, shrinking his gonads to the size of unripe May apples, Allie had more *balls* than Robert ever did.

Soon there were many people who knew me only as Allie, people who had never seen the vestiges of my past. The boys were introduced to her: J actually liked her; A would take some time. E, whenever we met, appeared as if she'd seen a ghost.

So now E and I are standing in her kitchen (formerly known as "ours"). We are discussing logistics: She will be going through a routine exam at a local hospital—nothing serious, but it will leave her groggy and in need of transportation home. Would I mind picking her up from the hospital? No, of course not. I want to do anything to help. Good. E wants to say something else . . . What . . . ? When you pick me up . . . ? Yes . . . ? Will you be wearing women's clothes?

The snow leaves only a small path on the sidewalk. I am heading back to my apartment after visiting the boys. I'm wearing clogs and a big wool hat but still not technically "presenting." I'm right behind a family of out-of-town parents and their college-age kids. The father is holding up the rear of the caravan. He senses me walking up behind him. The caravan is moving slowly, a herd of contented cows. The father turns to look at me, smiles, then moves to the side of the walkway. He yells to the others in front of him, "Wait, let this woman pass."

WESTERN PENNSYLVANIA—CIRCA WINTER 1961:
ONE PASSING RETROGRADE FANTASY

"My daughter would like to play basketball."
"Sorry, the team isn't coed."
"Excuse me?"
"No girls. Only boys."

"My daughter is a boy."

A look of confusion . . .

"Go ahead, dear, show the man your penis."

"Well, ah . . . yes . . . But he can't play looking the way he does."

"How do you mean?"

"His hair. The pigtails. He can't play like that."

"Why not?"

"It'll affect his playing."

"Go ahead, dear, show the man . . ."

She dribbles the basketball a few times, then shoots from mid court. The ball whooshes through the net.

"That's fine . . . but . . . she still looks like a girl."

"Well, naturally . . . . He *is* a girl."

92

Look! No, Don't! The Invisibility Dilemma for Transsexual Men

Jamison Green

. . .

Walking down the street in San Francisco or New York City, Boston, Atlanta, Portland, Seattle, London, Paris, Rome, no one seems to take any special interest in me. I am just another man, invisible, no one special. I remember what it was first like to feel that anonymity as testosterone gradually obliterated the androgyny that for most of my life made others uncomfortable in my presence. It was a great relief . . .

Now . . . people are quite comfortable with my male presentation. My psyche seems to fit nicely into male packaging: I feel better; people around me are less confused, and so am I. So why tell anyone about my past? Why not just live the life of a normal man? Perhaps I could if I were a normal man, but I am not. I am a man, and I am a man who lived for 40 years in a female body. But I was not a woman. I am not a woman who became a man. I am not a woman who lives as a man. I am not, nor was I ever a woman, though I lived in a female body, and certainly tried, whenever I felt up to it, to be a woman. But it was never in me to be a woman. Likewise, I am not a man in the same sense as my younger brother is a man, having been treated as such all his life. I was treated as other than a man most of the time, as a man part of the time, and as a woman only rarely. Certainly I was treated as a little girl when I was young, but even then people occasionally assumed I was a little boy. I always felt like something "other." Can I be just a man now, or must I always be "other"?

. . .

Seeking acceptance within the system of "normal" and denying our transsexual status is an acquiescence to the prevailing binary gender paradigm that will never let us fit in, and will never accept us as equal members of society. Our transsexual status will always be used to threaten and shame us. We will always wear a scarlet T that marks us for treatment as a pretender, as other, as not normal, as trans. But wearing that T proudly—owning the label and carrying it with dignity—can twist that paradigm and free us from our subordinate

prison. By using our own bodies and experience as references for our standards, rather than the bodies and experience of non-transsexuals (and non-transgendered people), we can grant our own legitimacy, as have all other groups that have been oppressed because of personal characteristics.

Transgendered people who choose transsexual treatment, who allow themselves to be medicalized, depend on a system of approval that grants them access to treatment. That approval may be seen as relieving them of their responsibility—or guilt—for being outside the norm. They then become either the justification for the treatment by embodying the successful application of "normal" standards; or they become the victims of the treatment when they realize they are still very different in form and substance from non-transsexual people, and they still suffer from the oppression they wished to escape by looking to doctors to make them "normal." By standing up and claiming our identity as men (or women) who are also transpeople, by asserting that our different bodies are just as normal for us as anyone else's is for them, by insisting that our right to modify our bodies and shape our own identities is as inalienable as our right to choose our religion (though not nearly as inexpensive or painless), we claim our humanity and our right to be treated equally under law and within the purviews of morality and culture.

. . .

Look! No, don't! Transsexual men are men. Transsexual men are men who have lived in female bodies. Transsexual men may appear feminine, androgynous or masculine. Any man may appear feminine, androgynous, or masculine. Look! What makes a man a man? His penis? His beard? His receding hairline? His lack of breasts? His sense of himself as a man? Some men have no beard, some have no penis, some never lose their hair, some have breasts. All have a sense of themselves as men.

. . . Look! No, don't! What is true, what is false? What is a "real" man?

I am real; I am an authentic and reliable man. I am also a transsexual man. I am a man who lived for 40 years in the body of a woman, so I have had access to knowledge that most men do not have. Invisibility has been a major issue in my life. Throughout my childhood and young adulthood I—my identity—was, for the most part, invisible. I was always defined by others, categorized either by my lack of femininity, or by my female body, or by the disquieting combination of both. The opportunity to escape the punishing inadequacy imposed on me by self-styled adjudicators of sex role performance was one I could not ignore. I simply will not accept a similar judgement of my masculinity. And I have yet to meet someone who could look me in the face, who could spend any time at all in conversation with me, who would deny my masculinity now the way they would dismiss it before as "just a phase" or "inappropriate behaviour for a girl."

. . . One of the most difficult things for me to reconcile about my own transition was my movement out of a place in lesbian culture and into a white heterosexual embodiment. Let me emphasize: Not all transsexual men have lesbian histories, and not all transsexual men are heterosexual. Nonetheless, my personal politics are quite closely aligned with queer culture, so I am again a different sort of heterosexual man. I am not afraid of homosexuality, though I do not practice it. Many gendered and heterosexist social constructs collapse like cardboard sea-walls against the ocean of my transsexual reality.

. . .

Look! No, don't! It all comes down to attitude. If you accept me—if you can acknowledge that I am a man, even a transsexual man—then you can accept that life has variation, life is rich, you don't control it, you experience it. You can still analyse concepts, you can still have opinions, you can even disagree with me. And if you don't accept me, well, then you don't. But as you go through life categorizing and qualifying, judging and evaluating, remember that there are human beings on the other end of the stick you're shaking, and they might have ideas and feelings and experiences that are different from your own. Maybe they look different from you, maybe they are tall women with large hands, maybe they are men who

have given birth to their own children, maybe the categories you've delineated won't work in all cases. Look! No, don't! Transsexual men want to disappear because we are tired of being forced into categories, because we are beyond defending ourselves.

Look! No, don't! Transsexual men are entering the dialogue from more perspectives, more angles, than were ever theorized as being possible for them. Maybe if we are ignored we will go away. Maybe if we are continually not permitted to speak, not allowed to define ourselves, not given any corner of the platform from which to present our realities, then we will disappear and refrain from further complicating all the neat, orderly theories about gender and sex. Maybe if no one looks at us we will be safe.

At first I thought my transition was about not being looked at any longer, about my relief from scrutiny; now I know it is about scrutiny itself, about self-examination, and about losing my own fear of being looked at, not because I can disappear, but because I am able to claim my unique difference at last. What good is safety if the price is shame and fear of discovery? So, go ahead: Look!

93

Cisgender Privilege

On the Privileges of Performing Normative Gender

Evin Taylor

N
E
X
T

S
T
E
P
S

The latin prefix "cis," loosely translated, means "on this side," while the prefix "trans" is generally understood to mean "change, crossing, or beyond." Cisgender people are those whose gender identity, role, or expression is considered to match their assigned gender by societal standards. Transgender people are individuals who change, cross, or live beyond gender.

Privilege is the "cultural currency" afforded to a person or group of persons who are recognized as possessing a desired social or political characteristic. Privilege is the stability society affords us when we don't rock the boat.

Gendered privilege is the collective advantages that are accepted, most often unknowingly, by those who are not positioned in opposition to the dominant ideology of the gender binary. Simply put: A person who is able to live in a life and/or body that is easily recognized as being either man/male or woman/female generally needs to spend less energy to be understood by others. The energy one need not expend to explain their gender identity and/or expression to others is gendered privilege.

The following questionnaire was inspired by Peggy McIntosh's article "Unpacking the Invisible White Knapsack" (1988). This questionnaire is intended to inspire some insight into the privileges of those who are, for the most part, considered to be performing normative gender. It is certainly not an exhaustive list, nor can it be generalized to people in every social position. Gendered privilege is experienced differently depending on the situation and the individual people involved. Readers of this article are encouraged to adapt the questions to suit their own positioning and to come up with questions that can be added to the list.

1. Can you be guaranteed to find a public bathroom that is safe and equipped for you to use?
2. Can you be sure to find a picture of someone whose gender expression resembles yours somewhere on a magazine rack?
3. Can you be reasonably sure whether to check the M or F box on a form?
4. Can you be reasonably sure that your choice of checked box on such forms will not subject you to legal prosecution of fraud or misrepresentation of identity?
5. Are you able to assume that your genitals conform relatively closely to portrayals of "normal" bodies?
6. Can you expect to find a doctor willing to provide you with urgent medical care?
7. Are you able to make a decision to be a parent without being told that you are confused about your gender?
8. Can you be confident that your health care providers will not ask to see your genitals when treating you for a sore throat?
9. Can you be confident that your health care providers will provide treatment for your health concerns without assuming that you chose to be ill?
10. Can you obtain a passport and travel without government employees asking explicit questions regarding your genitals?
11. Do people often act as if they are doing you a favor by using the appropriate pronouns for your gender?
12. Can you undress in a public changing room without risk of being assaulted or reported?
13. Are you able to discuss your childhood without disguising your gender?
14. Can you provide government identification without risking ridicule for your name or legal sex status?
15. Do you need to prove your gender before others will refer to you with your chosen name and pronouns?
16. Can you wear a socially acceptable bathing suit?
17. Does the government require proof of the state of your genitals in order to change information on your personal identification?
18. Are incidental parts of your identity defined as a mental illness?
19. Can you reasonably expect to be sexual with your consenting partner of choice without being told you have a mental illness?
20. Do other people consider your lifestyle a mental illness?
21. How many mental illnesses can be put into total remission through medical surgeries?
22. Can you expect that your gender identity will not be used against you when applying for employment?
23. Do your sexual preferences cause people to assume that your gender identity is mistaken?
24. Can you expect to be reasonably eligible to adopt children if you should choose to?
25. Do people assume that they know everything about you because they saw an investigative news episode about plastic surgery?
26. On most days, can you expect to interact with someone of a gender similar to your own?
27. Can you expect to find a landlord willing to rent to someone of your gender?
28. Do teachings about your national and cultural history acknowledge the existence of people of your gender identity?
29. Can you be sure that your children will not be harassed at school because of your gender?
30. Can you be sure that school teachers will not try to convince your children that their understanding of their family members' bodies is incorrect?
31. Are you able to use your voice and speak in public without risk of being ridiculed?

32. Can you discuss feminism with others without the appearance of your genitals being called into question?
33. Can you freely use checks, credit cards, or government-issued ID in a grocery store without being accused of using stolen finances?
34. Can you wait at a bus stop at noon without passers-by assuming that you are working in the survival sex trade?
35. If you are asked for proof-of-age in order to purchase tobacco or alcohol, can you be reasonably sure that the cashier is trying to prove your age, not your gender?
36. Can you be reasonably sure that, when dating someone new, they will be interested in getting to know your personality over and above your medical history?
37. Can you smile at a young child without their parents scorning or explaining you to the child?
38. Can you be sure that your gender identity doesn't automatically label you as an outsider, an anomaly, abnormal, or something to be feared?
39. Can you argue for gender equality without your right or motivation to do so being questioned?
40. Does the state of your genitals cause you to fear violence if they are discovered?
41. Are your height, weight, muscle mass, or hair follicles used as "proof" that your gender identity is mistaken?
42. Are your height, weight, muscle mass, or hair follicles consistently pointed out as being incongruent with your gender?
43. Are your basic healthcare needs minimized by others who contrast them in priority with lifesaving surgeries?
44. Can you find a religious community that will not exclude you based upon your genital or hormonal structures?
45. If you are having a difficult time making new friends, can you generally be sure that it is not because of your gender identity?
46. Can you choose whether or not to think of your gender as a political or social construct?
47. When you tell people your name, do they ask you what your "real" name is?
48. Can you consider social, political, or professional advancements without having to consider whether or not your gender identity will be called into question as being appropriate for advancement?
49. Do people assume that they have a right to hear, and therefore ask, about your intimate medical history or future?
50. Can you find gendered privilege in other places?

94

Calling All Restroom Revolutionaries!

Simone Chess, Alison Kafer, Jessi Quizar, and Mattie Udora Richardson

Everyone needs to use bathrooms, but only some of us have to enter into complicated political and architectural negotiations in order to use them. The fact is, bathrooms are

N
E
X
T

S
T
E
P
S

easier to access for some of us than for others, and the people who never think about where and how they can pee have a lot of control over how using restrooms feels for the rest of us. What do we need from bathrooms? What elements are necessary to make a bathroom functional for everyone? To make it safe? To make it a private and respectful space? Whose bodies are excluded from the typical restroom? More important, what kind of bodies are assumed in the design of these bathrooms? Who has the privilege (we call it pee-privilege) of never needing to think about these issues, of always knowing that any given bathroom will meet one's needs? Everyone needs to use the bathroom. But not all of us can.

And that's where People in Search of Safe and Accessible Restrooms (PISSAR) comes in. PISSAR, a coalition of UC-Santa Barbara undergrads, grad students, staff, and community members, recognizes that bathrooms are not always accessible for people with disabilities, or safe for people who transgress gender norms. PISSAR was formed at the 2003 University of California Student of Color Conference, held at UC-Santa Barbara. During the lunch break on the second day of the conference, meetings for the disability caucus and the transgender caucus were scheduled in adjacent rooms. When only a few people showed up for both meetings, we decided to hold a joint session. One of the members of the disability caucus mentioned plans to assess bathroom accessibility on the campus, wondering if there was a similar interest in mapping gender-neutral bathrooms. Everyone in the room suddenly began talking about the possibilities of a genderqueer/disability coalition, and PISSAR was born.

For those of us whose appearance or identity does not quite match the "man" or "woman" signs on the door, bathrooms can be the sites of violence and harassment, making it very difficult for us to use them safely or comfortably. Similarly, PISSAR acknowledges that, although most buildings are required by the Americans with Disabilities Act to provide accessible bathrooms, some restrooms are more compliant than others and accessible bathrooms can often be hard to find. PISSAR's mission, then, is threefold: 1) to raise awareness about what safe and accessible bathrooms are and why they are necessary; 2) to map and verify existing accessible and/or gender-neutral bathrooms on the campus; and 3) to advocate for additional bathrooms. We eventually hope to have both web-based and printed maps of all the bathrooms on campus, with each facility coded as to its accessibility and gender-safety. Beyond this initial campaign, PISSAR plans to advocate for the construction or conversion of additional safe and accessible bathrooms on campus. To that end, one of our long-term goals is to push for more gender-neutral bathrooms and showers in the dormitories, and to investigate the feasibility of multistall gender-neutral bathrooms across the campus as a whole.

As it turned out, we weren't the only restroom revolutionaries on campus. We soon joined forces with a student-run initiative to stock all campus tampon and pad machines, a group called, appropriately enough, Aunt Flo and the Plug Patrol. Aunt Flo's goal is to use funds garnered from the sale of tampons and pads in campus bathroom dispensers (blood money, if you will) to support student organizations in a time of tremendous budget cuts. We liked their no-euphemism approach to the bathroom and the body and joined their effort to make the campus not only a safer and more accessible place to pee but also to bleed. We also expanded our focus to include issues of childcare, inspired in part by one of our members' experiences as a young mom on campus. PISSAR decided to examine whether campus bathrooms featured changing tables, a move that increased our intersectional analysis of bathroom access and politics.

By specifically including the work of Aunt Flo and concerns about childcare access, PISSAR challenges many of the assumptions that are made about genderqueer and disabled bodies. Why shouldn't every gender-neutral restroom have a tampon/pad machine? Putting tampon/pad machines only in women's rooms, and mounting them high on the wall, restricts the right to menstruate conveniently to those with certain bodies. It suggests

that the right to tampons and pads is reserved for people who use gender-specific women's rooms and can reach a lever hanging five feet from the ground. This practice reinscribes ideas about disabled bodies being somehow dysfunctional and asexual (as in, "People in wheelchairs get their periods too?") and perpetuates the idea that genderqueer folks are inherently unbodied (as in, "Only real women need tampons, and you don't look like a real woman").

. . .

From the information garnered in the PISSAR patrols, we are in the process of making a map that will assess the safety and accessibility of all the bathrooms on campus. The map is vital to our project because it offers genderqueer and disabled people a survey of all the restrooms on campus so that they can find what they need without the stigma and frustration of telling a possibly uninformed administrator the details of their peeing needs. For people who have never had to think about bathrooms, the map's detailed information suggests the ways in which our everyday bathrooms are restrictive and dangerous. Thus the map also functions as a consciousness-raising tool, educating users about the need for safe and accessible restrooms.

PISSAR patrols aren't simply about getting information. They're also a way to keep our bodies involved in our project. PISSAR is, after all, a project about bodies: about bodily needs, about the size and shape of our bodies, and about our bodily presentation. The very nature of our bathroom needs necessitates this attention to the body. So it makes sense that when we tried to theorize about what a safe, respectful restroom might look like, we realized we needed to meet in the bathroom. Because the bathroom is our site, and the body in search of a bathroom is our motivation, we recognized early on the need to be concerned with body and theory together. PISSAR's work is an attempt at embodying theory, at theorizing from the body.

. . .

Our concern with body/theory is also evident in our insistence that bathroom accessibility is an important issue for a lot of different people. Everyone should be able to find a bathroom that conforms to the needs of their body. Everyone should be able to use a restroom without being accused of being in the "wrong" place. Everyone should have access to tampon dispensers and facilities for changing diapers, regardless of gender or ability. Homeless folks should have access to clean restrooms free of harassment. Bathroom activism is, from the outset, a multi-identity endeavor. It has the potential to bring together feminists, transfolks, people with disabilities, single parents, and a variety of other people whose bathroom needs frequently go unmet. It creates a much needed space for those of us whose identities are more complicated than can be encompassed in a single-issue movement. Viewed in this light, restroom activism is an ideal platform from which to launch broader coalition work. In PISSAR, we tend to think about "queerness" as encompassing more than just sexual orientation; it includes queer bodies, queer politics, and queer coalitions.

NEXT STEPS

See Chapter 14 in *Teaching for Diversity and Social Justice* for corresponding teaching materials.

SECTION 8

ABLEISM

Introduction

Carmelita (Rosie) Castañeda, Larissa E. Hopkins, and Madeline L. Peters[1]

WHAT IS A DISABILITY?

The Americans with Disabilities Act (ADA, 1990, amended 2008) considers a person to have a disability if she or he has a significant impairment that interferes with a major life activity, such as walking, seeing, hearing, learning, speaking, breathing, standing, lifting, or caring for one's self. The ADA covers both physical and mental impairments, such as mental retardation, orthopedic, hearing, visual, speech, or language impairments, emotional disabilities, learning disabilities, autism, traumatic brain injury, attention deficit disorder, depression, mental illnesses (such as bipolar disorder or schizophrenia), environmental illnesses, and chronic illnesses, such as diabetes, HIV/AIDS, cancer, and epilepsy. Disabilities are wide-ranging and impact the lives of many people worldwide. Approximately 10 percent of the world's population or 650 million people live with a disability and constitute the world's largest minority (United Nations Enable, n.d.). We must, however, understand the broadest sense of the word disability by expanding beyond the image of someone in a wheelchair or a person with a visual or hearing impairment in order to recognize that disability is a vast category; a category that includes an infinite number of possible experiences and realities that may or may not be visible to others.

ABLEISM AND DISABILITY OPPRESSION

Ableism or disability oppression is a term used to describe the all-encompassing system of discrimination and exclusion of people living with disabilities. Similar to other forms of oppression discussed in this book, ableism functions on individual, institutional, and cultural levels to advantage people who are temporarily able-bodied and disadvantage people with disabilities (Griffin, Peters, and Smith, 2007; see selection 4). We use the term *temporarily able-bodied* to raise consciousness that people who do not have disabilities may become disabled by illness, the process of growing older, accidents, and war, for example. Disability oppression also addresses how we as a society value "productivity" (Wendell, 1996). Economic productivity is a highly

valued standard in the United States, and this emphasis contributes to our undervaluing other social and material contributions while perpetuating socially constructed ideas about disability, dependence, and independence.

HISTORICAL TREATMENT OF PEOPLE WITH DISABILITIES

Historically, disability was perceived through a religious lens and considered an unchangeable condition that resulted from sin (Covey, 1998). In Western societies infants with disabilities were dropped off balconies to their death; children with disabilities were abandoned and left to live on the streets where they had no choice but to beg for food and money to survive (Wood, 1998). The term *handicapped* emerged in England from people with disabilities who used their cap in hand on street corners to plead for money. Many people with disabilities were placed in jails or asylums where they endured inhumane treatment. By the early eighteenth century, people with disabilities were seen as freaks, monsters, and less than human. In Europe and the United States, curiosity about people with severe disabilities made "freak shows" a very popular form of entertainment. Paradoxically, "freak shows" became one of the few viable ways for people with disabilities to earn a living (Vogtan, 1988).

In Western societies, as scientific and medical fields became more powerful, their guidelines began to shape the ways in which disability was perceived and understood. Early Western medical textbooks classified people with disabilities as genetically defective. The medicalization of disability fostered the belief that people with disabilities needed to be monitored and controlled by licensed physicians and medical specialists with authoritarian powers. The medical goal was to "cure" the disability, get rid of a deformity, fix the body, and/or numb the existing pain of the person who was described as the patient. This thinking and methodology resulted in solutions that were invasive usually by surgery or drugs, and which required submission from the person with a disability. The view that disabilities are deficiencies that require medical treatment and repair remains pervasive today.

During the 1880s and 1890s, people with "mental retardation," as well as people who spoke English as a second language, were considered disabled or defective in the United States. For example, "medical imbecility" was attributed to people with mental retardation, as well as to paupers, prostitutes, immigrants, and others unable to express themselves in English (Longmore and Umanski, 2001). The power of the early-nineteenth-century Eugenics movement spurred policies to segregate and sterilize people considered to be hopelessly unredeemable because of their disabilities. "Eugenics" as a movement was coined in 1883 in England by Sir Francis Galton, a cousin of Charles Darwin. *Eugenics* is derived from the Greek word meaning "well born" or "of good origins or breeding," and it became the "science" of supposedly improving qualities of a so-called "race" by controlling human breeding. Eugenics at its most extreme became the "scientific" rationale for Germany's genocidal policies during World War II in which thousands of people with mental or physical disabilities (Gallagher, 1995) (as well as members of supposed "lower races," for example Jews, Poles, and other groups, such as homosexuals) were shot, gassed, or left to starve to death.

Veterans returning with disabilities from World War II spurred medical fields to focus on rehabilitation and the development of devices to help soldiers return to work and live productive lives, rather than be restricted to hospitals or asylums. Although a new focus on rehabilitation emerged, many people with disabilities continued to be segregated and treated as patients who needed supervision and care from others who "knew best." In the 1960s and 1970s, a social movement among people with disabilities and allies began to emerge, leading to the Independent Living Movement. On the heels of other civil rights and justice movements, disability activists organized and powerfully fought for their civil rights. This struggle resulted in the passage of Section 504 of the Rehabilitation Act of 1973, the Education for all Handicapped Children Act (PL 94-142) of 1975, Americans with Disabilities Act (ADA) 1990, Individuals with Disabilities Education Act (IDEA) 1990, 1997, and Individuals with Disabilities Education Improvement Act (IDEIA) 2004, all significant feats protecting the rights of people with disabilities.

On September 25, 2008, the ADA was amended, thereby expanding the definition of disability. The new regulation better defines the term "substantially limits" and expands the definition of "major life activities." For example, learning, reading, concentrating, thinking, communicating, and working are now recognized as major life activities. Also added to the law are major bodily functions, such as functions of the immune system. The amended ADA further states that conditions that are episodic or in remission may be labeled as disabilities when the active impairment can substantially limit a major life activity.

CURRENT ISSUES IN DISABILITY DISCOURSE

Many of the current issues presented here have been ongoing issues for years, but they have not received the amount of attention or debate that we are presently seeing. These issues include, but are not limited to, attention deficit hyperactivity disorder (ADHD) diagnosis and treatment for children and adults; traumatic brain injury (TBI) and post-traumatic stress disorder (PTSD) diagnosis and treatment for our veterans of war; and the disproportionality of students of color placed in special education programs. Newer developments include the controversial elimination of Asperger's syndrome from the *Diagnostic and Statistical Manual of Mental Disorders* (DSM; APA, 1994) and the inclusion of students with intellectual disabilities at some institutions of higher education.

Present debates relate to whether ADHD is a socially constructed disorder or a valid neurobiological disorder and whether youth are being overdiagnosed and unnecessarily medicated. While there is overwhelming scientific evidence to support that ADHD is a valid neurobiological disorder (National Institute of Health, 2002), research examining the possibility of overdiagnosis and overprescription of drug therapies presents inconclusive and conflicting information. The DSM outlines specific criteria for diagnosing ADHD, which includes a constellation of symptoms, such as inattentiveness, impulsivity, and hyperactivity with evidence of a clinically significant impairment in social, educational, or occupational performance. While there are set criteria for diagnosing ADHD, the consistency or lack of consistency across psychologists, psychiatrists, and other licensed clinicians is raising concern.

Discussions regarding PTSD and TBI are being brought to our attention as significant numbers of veterans of war have returned with PTSD and mild-to-severe TBIs. During World War I, veterans returning from war were diagnosed with "shell shock" including uncontrollable shaking, reoccurring nightmares, and imagined re-enactments of the horrific events. Today, these symptoms along with others are categorized as PTSD. Well over 1.5 million service personnel were deployed to Iraq and Afghanistan beginning in 2002 (Karney, Ramchand, Osilla, Calderone, and Burns, 2008), and PTSD is currently one of the enduring and invisible effects of the war. Veterans with PTSD are among the unnoticeably wounded. Veterans' hospitals and medical facilities around the nation are encountering staggering number of veterans who are not always able to get the full treatment they need to navigate the changed world. With a single trauma, PTSD generally lasts from three to five years (Kessler, Sonnega, Bromet, Hughes, and Nelson, 1995), although many experience multiple traumas in life, and a typical person with PTSD may experience symptoms that last more than twenty years (Breslau, Kessler, Chilcoat, Schultz, Davis, and Andreski, 1998; Kessler, 2000).

Related to the invisible and distressing consequences of war is traumatic brian injury (TBI). TBIs can result from any type of injury to the brain that causes it to swell, such as artillery fire, car crashes, explosions, and any non-war-related incidents, such as sports incidents. The manifestations of TBI include impaired cognition, sensory processing, communication, and mental health, and/or personality changes (National Institute of Neurological Disorders and Stroke, 2009). Although the incidence of TBI among veterans is on the rise, actual statistics are still unknown.

Another pressing issue within disability discourse brings our attention to the overrepresentation of students of color in special education. Since the 1960s, racial bias, cross-cultural misunderstanding, assessment bias, and teacher referral processes have contributed to the

overrepresentation of racial and ethnic minorities in special education (Dunn, 1968; Ford and Moore, III, 2004; Harry and Klingner, 2006, 2007; Losen and Orfield, 2002; Skiba, Simmons, Ritter, Raush, Cuadradod, Chung, 2008). In 2002, Donovan and Cross reported that African American students in particular are over two times more likely than white students to be labeled as mentally retarded. Recent research also points out that English language learners are similarly being disproportionately placed in special education programs (Harry and Klingner, 2006; Shepherd, Linn, and Brown, 2005). According to the U.S. Department of Education, in the late 1990s, only 25.5 percent of students with disabilities graduated with a standard diploma (U.S. Department of Education, 2000). Rendering a solution to this significant issue requires education reform that will minimally include overhauling educational processes and organizational structures, and stressing effective teacher preparation and professional development in multicultural education.

An additional matter in the arena of disability issues is that of autism and Asperger's syndrome. Autism and autism spectrum disorders (ASD) are complex developmental disabilities characterized by difficulties communicating and interacting with others and by restricted and repetitive thoughts and behaviors. Asperger's syndrome (AS), a mild form of autism, is described by symptoms such as repetitive routines or rituals, little or no eye contact, peculiarities in speech and language, difficulties interacting socially with peers, problems with non-verbal communication, and unusual facial expressions or postures. Colleges have seen an increase in the number of students with autism spectrum disorders and Asperger's syndrome and as such administrators and faculty are engaging in conversations about how to better support the social and academic success of this population. Meanwhile, the forthcoming American Psychiatric Association's DSM-V will eliminate Asperger's syndrome and instead include revised criterion for diagnosing autism spectrum disorders. This decision is causing a great stir, especially for many with Asperger's syndrome who express having developed a sense of pride, support, and community in relationship to their Asperger's diagnosis.

Another important topic receiving greater attention is the steadily growing number of students with intellectual disabilities attending programs at institutions of higher education. Intellectual disabilities are defined by significant limitations in intellectual and cognitive functioning and in adaptive behaviors required for everyday functioning. While students with intellectual disabilities have been historically excluded from higher education, college programs are providing an opportunity for such students to continue their academics, to socialize, to build career and technical skills, and to prepare for gainful employment. To date there are 110 officially registered college programs for students with intellectual disabilities across 28 states (CTC, 2012).

UNIVERSAL ARCHITECTURAL AND INSTRUCTIONAL DESIGN

Advocates for people with disabilities have called for an adaptation of architectural design, as well as instructional changes to curriculum and pedagogy, which will allow access for all people (Pliner and Johnson in selection 97). Universal Architectural Design (UAD) incorporates ramps, Braille signage, wider hallways and doorways, lower/adjustable desks and fixtures, and easy access door openers. The same principle of access for everyone is applied in Universal Instructional Design (UID). Both UAD and UID benefit all people with and without disabilities.

GLOBAL ISSUES

The global population of people with disabilities is growing because of aging, ethnic and sectarian violence, war, poverty, and the contamination of the environment (Harrison, 2004). It is estimated that there are 600 million people with disabilities in today's world. Many countries are passing

laws that recognize the rights of people with disabilities. Great Britain and Austria adopted the Disability Discrimination Act of 1995, while countries such as South Africa, Malawi, Uganda, the Philippines, Finland, Brazil, Austria, and Germany have adopted statutes that prohibit discrimination against people with disabilities (Harrison, 2004).

ABLEISM INTERSECTIONS

The complex social identities people occupy and the social context we live in largely shape how people with disabilities are treated and how one's disability is personally experienced. As people with disabilities represent various races, classes, genders, sexual orientations, ages, and religious backgrounds, people often simultaneously experience intersections with racism, classism, heterosexism, ageism, transgender oppression, religious oppression, and sexism.

The intersection between one's disability and classism is a glaringly important example of how the issues may be intertwined. People with disabilities, particularly low-income and people of color, face many barriers as the costs of health care, assistive technology, and digital hearing aids (to name a few) are often unattainable. This results in some receiving inadequate health care, limited employment opportunities, and significant learning disadvantages while attending school. On the contrary, people with disabilities who are born into families with greater financial means gain significant access to expensive medical treatment and diagnostic testing, assistive technology, personal care attendants, and other necessary resources.

Likewise, the intersection between disability and sexism further demonstrates how our complex identities and societal manifestations of oppression are overlapping. Unlike the current attention focusing on veterans returning from war with PTSD, there continues to be little consideration given to the reality that one out of nine women is diagnosed with PTSD symptoms, most often as a result of experiencing rape, sexual assault, domestic abuse, and/or violence (emedicinehealth.com, 2009). Sexual assault, for example, has wide-reaching effects on women, including an impact on physical and mental health, functionality, issues regarding basic needs, and difficulty reading social cues. With PTSD, a raised hand, a half-open door, a pointed object, or phraseology in a conversation can unconsciously set in motion intense reactions and the re-creation of the original traumatic incident. The continued cultural and institutional silencing of women being disproportionately and violently targeted perpetuates a cycle of abuse against women that is significantly tied to numbers of women being diagnosed with particular disabilities.

READINGS IN THIS SECTION

In this section, we have attempted to create a better understanding of the complexities of disability by including a representation of issues, ideas, and experiences of people with disabilities across multiple social identities. The section in no way represents every aspect of disability history, reform, treatment, and social, educational, or international issues and experiences. Rather, we present an overview of the issues that individuals, instructors, students, and others can refer to in their search for greater understanding and strategies regarding disabilities.

The articles in this section are as varied as the issues regarding disability. We begin our section with Willie Bryan's overview of the disability rights movement (selection 95) as a way of contextualizing the historical issues that were faced and the types of efforts that were led by people with disabilities. Another article that highlights historical developments is Janet Cerney's (selection 96) recounting of historical figures, events, and cultural shifts that have strongly shaped deaf education.

Focusing on global issues, we have included two articles that address war and a third on neocolonialism and disabilities. David Grossman's piece (selection 101) shares stunningly

important information about the effects of war on the human body and the significant number of soldiers who become psychiatric casualties. Miguel Cyr (in selection 104 by Edward D. Murphy), an Iraqi veteran, gives a personal account of his struggles with post-traumatic stress disorder, how this invisible disability has impacted relationships with friends and relatives, and his ability to maintain steady employment. Cyr also discusses the difficulty of living with a psychological disorder because of the significant stigma attached to such disorders. On another global front, Nirmala Erevelles's article (selection 102) gives us more insight into how transnational capitalism and (neo)colonial institutions and policies have influenced the social construction of disability in Third World contexts and have particularly impacted the lives of Third World women.

Discussions on disability and hate crimes are often omitted by the media, and Lennard Davis (selection 99) draws our attention to this omission. Davis uses the lack of news coverage of a hate crime in which the murdered victim, James Byrd, is described only by his race, ignoring the fact that he was also a person with a disability. Davis asks that we deconstruct hierarchies of oppression by acknowledging intersections and the multiple identities that are targeted by oppression. Further, drawing upon intersections, Sumi Colligan's article (selection 100) explores the parallels between the cultural representations and everyday struggles of intersexed persons and people with disabilities with a particular focus on the medicalization of intersexed/disabled bodies and the construction of asexuality.

The personal narratives included in this section provide a glimpse into the many ways that people with disabilities, who live across multiple social identities, experience issues of oppression and liberation. Eli Clare's personal narrative (selection 103) about society's dehumanizing actions and reactions toward people with disabilities elicits the urgent need for better role models, heroes, and allies. As a genderqueer person with a physical disability, Clare describes the common use of demeaning language and belittling stares that play a significant role in the perpetuation of ableism and transgender oppression. In another personal account (selection 105), Jess Watsky describes both the relief and struggle of understanding her diagnosis of Asperger's syndrome in the article, "On the Spectrum, Looking Out." After learning how to navigate the world of academia and other life situations, Watsky shares that the very medical reference she's used to understand her life and make great strides is being eliminated from the DSM-V. Watsky's compelling story sheds light on how this change might have an enormous impact on her life and her ability to access suitable accommodations.

Another account of a child growing up with a disability is provided by Ashley and Deborah's story (selection 106) in "How to Curse in Sign Language." The article describes a mother and daughter's struggle for educational rights in the public school system, and acceptance with a religious institution and society in general. Jason Kingsley (selection 107) reflects on what he would tell parents and doctors about being born with Down syndrome. He reminds them not to set limitations on people with Down syndrome and their ability to learn, and to have relationships and participate in all kinds of life activities. In "In the LD Bubble," Lynn Pelkey (selection 108) shares her elementary and secondary public school experience in special education classrooms for students with learning disabilities. Her narrative describes her feelings of isolation and the hurtful effects this had on her self-esteem and her connection to her peers. Her message is one of overcoming institutionalized ableism and making progress in the college context.

The final part offers multiple ways to address the prejudice and discrimination toward people with disabilities on the individual, cultural, and institutional levels. Thomas Hehir (selection 109) opens this part by offering four suggestions to address ableist practices. Hehir asserts that we must challenge ableist assumptions in education that contribute to lower levels of success in educational pursuits and gainful employment. Also included in this section is an article by Heather Oesterreich and Michelle Knight (selection 110) that examines how the intersections of race, class, language, and disability inform the responsibilities of special educators to help students with disabilities. The overrepresentation of working-class students of African, Latino/a, and Native American heritages in special education have been a long-standing part of special education reform. Oesterreich and Knight provide "teacher tips" to educators in order to increase

the social and cultural capital of students with disabilities to support their prospective college-going and vocational identities. The authors are proponents of Universal Instructional Design, including use of assistive technology to meet the needs of particular students. Susan Pliner and Julia Johnson's article (selection 97) outlines the core principles and concepts of Universal Instructional Design necessary for achieving accessibility and inclusion in institutions of higher education. Critical for understanding how social conditions affect disability, Susan Wendell's article (selection 98) explores the physical, social, and cultural environments that cause disability.

Cheryl Howland and Eva Gibavic's article (selection 111) presents a learning disability identity development model that incorporates a discussion of several influential variables from dual diagnosis to support systems. Overall, this model helps individuals come to a greater understanding of the complex stages people with learning disabilities might encounter. Also included are additional influences of other identity development models, such as gender, race, and moral identity development. In "Creating a Fragrance-Free Zone" (selection 112), the Invisible Disabilities Advocate alerts us to the growing environmental illness identified as multiple chemical sensitivity. This article provides concrete practices that can be incorporated individually and institutionally to create safe and comfortable environments for all people. Finally, Madeline L. Peters, Carmelita (Rosie) Castañeda, Larissa E. Hopkins, and Aquila McCants (selection 113) provide examples of beliefs and practices that are ableist on individual, cultural, and institutional levels, followed by the actions people can take to eliminate these discriminatory practices and act as unified allies. For additional information on disabilities please refer to our section website.

See Companion Website for Additional Resources and Material

Note

1 We ask that those who cite this work always acknowledge by name both of the authors listed rather than only citing the first author or using "et al." to indicate coauthors. Both collaborated equitably on the conceptualization, development, and writing of this section.

References

Americans with Disabilities Act of 1990 (ADA), PL 101–336 (July 26, 1990). Title 42, U.S.C. §§ 12101 et seq: U.S. Statutes at Large. 104, 327–78.

American Psychiatric Association (1994). *Diagnostic and Statistical Manual of Mental Disorders (DSM-IV)*. Washington, DC: American Psychiatric Association.

Breslau, N., Kessler, R. C., Chilcoat, H. D., Schultz, L. R., Davis, G. C., Andreski, P. (1998). Trauma and post-tramatic stress disorder on the community. The 1996 Detroit Area Survey of Trauma. *Archives of General Psychiatry* 55, 626–632.

College Transition Connection (CTC) (2012). Retrieved from http://collegetransitionconnection.org.

Covey, H. (1998). *Social Perceptions of People with Disabilities in History*. Springfield, IL: Charles Thomas.

Donovan, S. Cross, C. (2002). *Minority Students in Special and Gifted Education*. Washington, DC: National Academy Press.

Dunn, L. M. (1968). Special education for the mildly retarded: Is much of it justifiable? *Exceptional Children* 35, 5–32.

emedicinehealth.com (2009). *Post Traumatic Stress Disorder*. Retrieved May 1, 2009, from http://www.emedicinehealth.com/post-traumatic_stress_disorder_ptsd/article_em.htm

Ford, D. Y., Moore III, James L. (2004). Creating culturally responsive gifted education classrooms: Understanding "culture" is the first step. *Gifted Child Today*, 27 (4), 34–39.

Gallagher, H. (1995). *By Trust Betrayed: Patients, Physicians, and the License to Kill in the Third Reich*. Arlington, VA: Vandamere.

Griffin, P., Peters, M. L., Smith, R. M. (2007). Ableism curriculum design. In M. Adams, L. A. Bell, P. Griffin (eds), *Teaching for Diversity and Social Justice* (2nd edition, pp. 335–358). New York: Routledge.

Harrison, O. (2004). As disability is emerging globally, so is advocacy for full participation for people with disabilities. *Access New England* 9 (1), 1. Retrieved June 25, 2006, from http://www.adaptenv.org/newsletter/pdf/Access_Fall_2004.pdf

Harry, B., Klingner, J. (2006). *Why Are So Many Minority Students in Special Education. Understanding Race and Disability in Schools*. New York: Teachers College Press.

Harry, B., Klingner, J.(2007). Discarding the deficit model. *Educational Leadership,* 64 (5).

Karney, B., Ramchand, R., Osilla, K., Caldarone, L., Burns, R. (2008). *Predicting the Immediate and Long-Term Consequences of Post-Traumatic Stress Disorder, Depression, and Traumatic Brain Injury in Veterans of Operation Enduring Freedom and Operation Iraqi Freedom*. Santa Monica, CA: RAND Center for Military Health Policy Research.

Kessler, R. C. (2000). Posttraumatic stress disorder: The burden to the individual and to society. *Journal of Clinical Psychiatry* 61 (Suppl. 5), 4–12.

Kessler, R. C., Sonnega, A., Bromet, E., Hughes, M., Nelson, C. B. (1995). Posttraumatic stress disorder in the National Comorbidity Survey. *Archives of General Psychiatry* 52, 1048–1060.

Longmore, P., Umanski, L. (eds). (2001). *The New Disability History: American Perspectives*. New York: New York University Press.

Losen, D., Orfield, G. (2002). *Racial Inequity in Special Education.* Cambridge, MA; Harvard Education Press

National Institute of Health (2002). *Attention Deficit/Hyperactivity Disorders: Are Children Being Over Medicated?*" Retrieved from http://www.nimh.nih.gov/health/publications/attention-deficit-hyperactivity-disorder/what-is-attention-deficit-hyperactivity-disorder.shtml

National Institute of Neurological Disorders and Stroke (2009). Retrieved May 1, 2009, from http://www.ninds.nih.gov

Shepherd, T., Linn, D., Brown, R. (2005). The disproportionate representation of English language learners for special education services along the border. *Journal of Social and Ecological Boundaries,* 1 (1), 104–116.

Skiba, R. J., Simmons, A. B., Ritter, S., Raush, M. K., Cuadradod, J., Chung, C. G. (2008). Achieving equity in special education: history status and current challenges. *Exceptional Children*, 74 (3), 264–288.

United Nations Enable: Development in human rights for all (n.d.). *Fact Sheets on People with Disability*. Retrieved April 15, 2012 from http://www.un.org/disabilities/default.asp?id=18

United States Department of Education (2000). *The Longitudinal Evaluation of School Change and Performance in Title I Schools: Final Report*. Washington, DC: Planning and Evaluation Service, United States Department of Education.

Vogtan, R. (1988). *Freak Show: Presenting Human Oddities for Amusement and Profit*. Chicago: University of Chicago Press.

Wendell, S. (1996). The social construction of disability. In *The Rejected Body: Feminist Philosophical Reflections* (pp. 36–56). New York: Routledge.

Wood, I. M. and Associates. (Producer). (1998). *A Little History Worth Knowing: Disability Down Through the Ages* [DVD]. Available from Program Development Associates, 32 Court Street, 21st Floor, Brooklyn, NY 11201.

95

Struggle for Freedom

Disability Rights Movements

Willie V. Bryan

. . .

LACK OF CONCERN

Since World War II, there has been an increasing emphasis on human and civil rights in the United States. Minorities and women have spoken out on their own behalf attempting to gain the privileges, freedoms, and rights guaranteed for all Americans by the Constitution.

While legal and social ground has been won and lost throughout the years, many minorities and women now enjoy a somewhat more equal existence in the United States than some fifty years ago. Still, the battle for equality is far from victorious. While other groups continue their struggle, individuals with disabilities have joined forces to end discrimination in their lives and claim a life of equality in the United States.

The Civil Rights Movement of the sixties resulted in legislation designed to bar discrimination based on sex, race, and national origin; however, prohibition of discrimination based on physical and/or mental disabilities was not included. As Thomas D. Schneid reminds us, a bill introduced in Congress in 1971 to amend Title VI of the Civil Rights Act of 1964 to prohibit discrimination based on physical or mental disability died in committee. Similarly, in 1972, another bill introduced in Congress, this time to amend Title VII of the Civil Rights Act to bar discrimination in employment based upon physical or mental disabilities, also died in committee. This may be seen as somewhat of a barometer of the level of concern lawmakers and many other nondisabled Americans had with regard to the civil rights of persons with disabilities.

Perhaps the lack of concern demonstrated by these actions of Congress is more of a reflection of ignorance of the needs and capabilities of persons with disabilities rather than a blatant desire to deny the civil rights of a group of people. At the time, the thought was that employers should not be forced to hire persons who could not adequately perform the required tasks. Persons with disabilities and their friends certainly were not advocating employment of nonqualified persons; they were simply asking that employers be required to look beyond a person's limitation to see abilities and attempt to match them with the required job. Employers also had a number of misconceptions with regard to employing persons with disabilities, such as they would not be able to secure insurance for the person and the company's insurance premiums would increase. Another major misconception was the belief that persons with disabilities were unsafe employees. This erroneous belief was held despite safety records indicating that persons with disabilities had fewer accidents than nondisabled employees. Many employers were aware that by making modifications to the work site and/or its environment, a significant number of jobs could be made accessible to persons with disabilities; however, these same employers harbored the belief that making these accommodations would be too expensive. Again, this belief was held even though the DuPont Company had demonstrated that many changes to a work site could be done inexpensively.

These and other misconceptions were firmly held by employers because persons with disabilities and their advocates did not vigorously dispute them. The lack of opposition to discrimination against persons with disabilities with respect to employment allowed long-held stereotypes and prejudices to continue unchallenged. Activism would be necessary to dramatize the extent of the lack of concern for the rights of persons with disabilities and cause action to be taken to correct the neglect that had become an accepted method of treatment of persons with disabilities.

MINORITY STATUS

The political wheels of American progress appear to turn best when pressure is applied. For example, protests by minorities, particularly African Americans, led to the Civil Rights Act of 1964. Similarly, women's organizations engaged in various activities that placed pressure on state and federal government leaders to enact legislation that required equality of rights for women. One may assume that in a free and open democracy which most of us enjoy in America, there would be available on an equal basis to all citizens, the right to vote, to live wherever one can afford, the right to eat wherever one desires, and the right to be educated at the maximum level of one's abilities. However, it was precisely the denial of

these basic rights, rights upon which this country was founded, rights for which thousands of Americans have paid the supreme price, that led multitudes of Americans into the streets to practice civil disobedience, until these and other basic rights were granted.

In the process of securing these rights, the minority groups learned that their minority status was not shameful. In fact, they learned that they were a very important cog in the wheel of American life and by withholding their labor and being selective as to how and where they spent their hard earned money, they could considerably slow down the democratic wheel of progress. These groups also learned that by networking they added strength to their demands.

Until recently, persons with disabilities were not widely considered a minority group. In fact, it was not until the Rehabilitation Act of 1973 that they were considered a "class" of people. Persons with disabilities are members of other groups of people, they are male or female, and they have an ethnic identity; their rights and privileges are associated with whatever cultural and/or gender group they belong. It is ironic that with regard to human rights their disabilities were secondary to their cultural and/or gender identity, but with regard to their rights as citizens, their disabilities were primary, overshadowing gender and/or cultural identity. Since disability groups were not considered a culture at the time, the person with a disability was viewed as a "disabled member of another class." To be more specific, they were considered to be a disabled female or a disabled American Indian female. Hopefully, the point has been made. It is in part because of this dual and sometimes triple classification that the disability label was not considered a class unto itself.

Another reason for the lack of class status is that there are large numbers of disabilities and each one is considered a separate condition within its own group identity. For example, there are persons who have disabilities resulting from polio, arthritis, visual impairments, hearing impairments, lupus, mental illness, mental retardation, amputations, and paralysis, to mention only a few. In most cases, there was and continues to be associations or foundations which are considered the official representative for all who have a particular condition. This has the effect of segregating disabilities into distinct disease groups, thus causing each disabling condition to stand alone and not be part of a larger whole. This internal segregation combined with society's segregation of persons with disabilities has been devastating to efforts of persons with disabilities to unite and demand their constitutional rights.

Although it would not be until the passage of the Rehabilitation Act of 1973 that persons with disabilities would obtain the classification of minority status and be officially viewed as a class of people, several years before the passage of the act they began to think of themselves as a minority. And more importantly, they began to view their life conditions as having been deprived of their basic human rights similar to other minority groups. They also began to think of themselves as being oppressed and disenfranchised. With this realization, they began to unite and to speak openly about the manner in which they were being excluded from full participation in society's activities. Thinking of themselves as oppressed minorities, they also thought of the manner in which other minority groups had placed their agenda before the American people; thus a "grassroots disability rights movement" began which has resulted in the passage of the ADA in 1990.

GRASSROOTS MOVEMENT

. . .

Despite the concern exhibited by charitable organizations and Congress, the one aspect often missing was the involvement of persons with disabilities. For example, much of the legislation prior to the Rehabilitation Act of 1973 had been developed with little, if any,

input from persons with disabilities. Charitable organizations established telethons to raise funds for research and/or provide services without giving much thought to the negative images being projected. This was "business as usual" or stated another way, it was the continuation of the paternalistic attitude that has existed in America for many decades. Perhaps without meaning harm to persons with disabilities, nondisabled persons have treated them as though they are incapable of determining and expressing how they would like to live their lives. Regardless of how well-intended the motivation of a nonoppressed person there are some things he/she will either overlook or not understand with regard to the effects of being oppressed. Therefore it is imperative that those effected must be involved in determining the best methods for eliminating the problems created by oppression.

There are undoubtedly many reasons why it took persons with disabilities approximately two centuries before they organized and began to speak out on their own behalf. With "sit-ins," marches, and attempts to integrate previously segregated southern schools, the fifties served as the "staging" years of the Civil Rights movement; then in the sixties the final "assault" years were launched which culminated in victory with the passage of the Civil Rights Act of 1964. Similarly for the Disability Rights Movement, the sixties served as the "staging" years with emphasis on consumerism, self-help, and demedication demands as well as demands for self-care rights and deinstitutionalism. Perhaps then the seventies can be considered the "watershed" years of the movement. The sixties was the decade when persons with disabilities began to view themselves as oppressed minorities and demanded their constitutional rights. Similar to the Civil Rights Movement which culminated in the Civil Rights Act of 1964, the Disability Rights Movement led to what has been called the Civil Rights Act for persons with disabilities: The American's With Disabilities Act of 1990.

. . .

Activism: . . . In the early seventies, rehabilitation leaders backed by disability rights groups began to push for changes in the legislation to advocate a broader nonvocational role for rehabilitation programs. In 1972, such legislation was passed by Congress and Verville informs us that President Nixon vetoed the legislation because it "strayed too far from the essential vocational objective of the program."

This Act had provisions for Independent Living Centers. It would take six more years before this important concept would become a reality. The veto of the 1972 Rehabilitation Act is a classic example of not involving those most effected. Perhaps the veto served a useful purpose in that it became an issue around which the grassroots movement could unite. While attempting to get the Independent Living Centers provisions included in future legislation, the disability rights organizations gained considerable experience in politics, coalition building, and lobbying, as well as the act of compromising, thus gaining the respect of lawmakers and the admiration of millions of persons both with and without disabilities.

In the interim, additional legislation was passed with provisions to issue directives that persons with disabilities were not to be discriminated against nor treated as second-class citizens. One such piece of legislation was the Rehabilitation Act of 1973. Included in this legislation was Section 504 which forbade any United States institution that received federal financial assistance in the amount of $2,500 or more and all federal and state agencies from discriminating against persons with disabilities in employment. . . .

INDEPENDENT LIVING MOVEMENT

. . .

The quest for independence by most Americans does not occur by accident, but is a quality that is taught and reinforced to every American youth, both by formal teaching

and by example. American history is replete with both fictional and factual persons accomplishing or attempting to accomplish extraordinary deeds to establish or maintain their independence.

Independence is therefore highly valued in American society; it is considered an essential building block in constructing and maintaining a democracy. Freedom, to an extent, is reliant upon its citizens having the independence to build better lives for themselves and in the process of accomplishing their dreams, they lift freedom and democracy to new levels. Conversely, being dependent is devalued in American society and those that are considered so are often assigned lower positions on the social totem pole. To many, the word "dependent" denotes lack of initiative, laziness, and a burden upon society. Although public and private social welfare agencies and organizations including hospitals, clinics, and rehabilitation centers, to mention a few, have been developed to assist persons who by virtue of illness, accident, or birth defects must rely upon assistive services, the recipients are often viewed in a negative light and at best given sympathy instead of empathy and understanding.

Illness or disability often places the individual, and sometimes the family, in a state of dependency. For some it is a permanent situation, but for the majority it is temporary. The degree to which a person becomes dependent is obviously affected by several things, not the least of which are attitudes. [A]ttitudes of family, friends, medical and rehabilitation personnel as well as employers have an impact on the level of dependency of the person with a disability.

Given the value placed on independence by American society, no one should be amazed that persons with disabilities began to recognize and resent the limited role society drafted for them. They correctly perceived that society equated disability with dependency. They also recognized that this perception created a very low ceiling and an almost insurmountable wall around their abilities to function and achieve.

    . . .

In the early seventies, persons with disabilities began to realize that to be truly free they must take and maintain control of their lives. This train of thought resulted in the development of Independent Living Centers (ILCs). Dejong provides a brief history of the genesis of Independent Living Centers as he reveals that a small group of persons with disabilities at the University of Illinois and at the University of California at Berkeley moved out of their residential hospital setting into the community and organized their own system for delivery of survival services. The centers established by these students became the blueprint by which future centers would be established. As might be expected, since the inception of these centers, the scope of services has expanded. Even so, the idea of persons with disabilities taking greater control of their lives remains the same. Perhaps Dejong best summarizes the independent living philosophy when he said the dignity of risk is what the independent movement is all about. Without the possibility of failure, a person with a disability is said to lack true independence and the mark of one's humanity: the right to choose for good or evil.

When one considers that the independent living movement was initiated by persons with disabilities, many of whom were persons with severe disabilities such as spinal cord injuries, it became quite apparent that these individuals exhibited courage of the highest magnitude. Although prior to the movement they lived in conditions that made them almost totally dependent upon others, it was however a safe environment; therefore, moving from this safe environment to face the many uncertainties created by a society with many barriers and obstacles certainly qualifies the founding members as pioneers.

    . . . Laurie also contributes to our understanding of the goal of independent living centers with these comments:

Independent living is freedom of choice, to live where and how one chooses and can afford. It is living alone or with a roommate of one's choice. It is deciding one's own pattern of life: scheduling food, entertaining, vices, virtues, leisure and friends. It is freedom to take risks and freedom to make mistakes.

Frieden and Cole define the independent living concept as control over one's life based on the choice of acceptable options that minimize reliance on others in making decisions and in performing everyday activities. This may include managing one's affairs, participating in day-to-day life in the community, fulfilling a range of social roles, and making decisions that lead to self-determination and the minimizing of physical or psychological dependence upon others.

Frieden, Richards, Cole, and Bailey tell us that the independent living movement was based on the premise that with reasonable support services, adults with disabilities could manage their own affairs, and participate as full members of the community in all respects. They continue by speaking to the philosophy of the movement as full participation in community life and point out that the movement also was an advocate for a set of services that would meet the long-term support needs of citizens with disabilities. . . .

MORE THAN WORK

Work is so much a central part of most Americans' lives that it, in part, defines who we are. It is common for Americans to describe someone by identifying their occupation. For example, we may identify someone as Mary Smith the attorney, or John Smith the teacher. Work has been the defining feature in American lives for many years. The Puritan work ethic is a standard by which Americans often judge each other. While we no longer subscribe to the theory of hard work for all, we most certainly subscribe to the idea of work for all. Work provides us with economic power to purchase goods and services which in part by virtue of the amount and types of goods we accumulate determines our social standing in America. Social condemnation is the reward for those that are able to work but do not. Work not only is a means by which we develop, maintain or improve our societal standing in American society, it also is patriotic. In a capitalist society, it is through the production of products that our nation develops its standing in the world as compared to other nations.

Obviously, work has many important meanings to Americans and American society. Considering the position work holds in American life, it is easy to understand why virtually all rehabilitation legislation prior to the 1972 Rehabilitation Act emphasized "vocational rehabilitation." In fact, when we speak of rehabilitating a person with a disability we think the ultimate goal of the rehabilitation process is to make the person ready for a job. There is one thing wrong with this approach: what about the person who is unable to work because of the severity or perhaps type of disability? Unless they and/or their families have sufficient financial resources, they have to rely upon sympathy and charity of others as well as some social welfare assistance from the federal government. Because of the social stigma of not working and receiving charity, these persons' independence, self-dignity, and ability to participate as full American citizens are in jeopardy.

Perhaps these reasons, as well as others, caused the disability rights movement leaders to lobby Congress to deemphasize "vocational" in the Rehabilitation Act of 1972. It is unfortunate that the Nixon Administration did not comprehend what persons with disabilities were saying as they lobbied for removal of "vocational" from the rehabilitation act. In part, what they were saying, and perhaps today we are just beginning to hear, is that a person's

worth, self-respect, and dignity should not be measured by employment and moreover measured by whether employed in a job, especially if that person is unable to work. The leaders were wise to note that no person with a disability would be totally free until all persons with disabilities had opportunities to more fully participate in American life. Again it was this type of thinking that led them to push for Independent Living Centers, and the abolishment of the segregation of persons with disabilities so they could not only become more involved in American society, but also make decisions that would affect the quality of their lives. In short, they recognized that to be free, life for a person with a disability meant more than being able to work.

. . .

96

Historical and Cultural Influences in Deaf Education

Janet Cerney

HISTORICAL AND CULTURAL CONTEXT IN THE EDUCATION OF DEAF STUDENTS

Conceptualizing the issues surrounding the education of deaf students involves understanding the historical context of deaf education, the political platforms that have developed, and the current forces that are impacting deaf education today. The subject of deaf education is highly charged both emotionally and politically. The answers are neither perfect nor simple.

For centuries the education of deaf children has been polarized into two main camps, the manualists (those who sign) and the oralists (those who rely on speech and speech-reading). A third camp has more recently been added—supporters of cued speech (those who use a sound-based visual communication system). But the clash between manualists and oralists reaches deep into history and deep into the emotions and experiences of those who have been educated under their slogans. So that we can gain sensitivity toward the plight of deaf students and not repeat the mistakes of our past, it seems important that educators, parents, and administrators understand the history behind the controversy and recognize the juncture between feelings and facts.

A GLIMPSE INTO HISTORY

On April 15, 1817, a motley group of twelve deaf students entered the Connecticut Asylum for the Education and Instruction of Deaf and Dumb Persons. They ranged in age from 12 to 51 years old. Some students were from prominent New England families, while others came from the unrestrained and spirited deaf community at Martha's Vineyard. Their

walk through the open doors signified the beginning of formal deaf education in America, a history that has sparked one of the most radical and controversial educational wars of all time.

This bold beginning to American deaf education was laid by the friendship and camaraderie of two men: Thomas Hopkins Gallaudet, a hearing minister, and his chosen counterpart Laurent Clerc, a deaf Frenchman. It was through their joined effort that the school thrived. Culturally, the school was deaf friendly, embracing the visual language of its students. . . .

The prompt and spectacular success of the Connecticut Asylum brought enthusiasm to the burgeoning field of deaf education. By 1820, plans to educate deaf Americans were being made around the country. As new residential schools for the deaf began to spring up, many deaf students discovered language and a new cultural family after living for years in communicative isolation within hearing communities. Within the walls of these schools, the older deaf children would pass down to younger generations of children the cultural attribute that made deaf Americans a distinct subculture within America—sign language.

This early academic culture was marked by a prevalent respect for deaf people as teachers and school leaders. Hearing administrators tended to approach the students from a loving but paternalistic viewpoint, consistent with other educational institutions of that time. Sign language flourished, and the brightest deaf students were later recruited as teachers. By 1858, deaf teachers accounted for a full 40.8% of the total teaching force in schools for the deaf.

. . .

Frederick Knapp also attempted inclusion in 1877, when he admitted deaf pupils to his private school in Baltimore. However, his perspective was far more condescending, as he believed that "the more deaf students socialized with hearing students, the less they would notice their defect." In Knapp's school, hearing children were forbidden to sign to deaf children, in an attempt to keep them from reminding deaf students of their affliction. If a hearing or deaf child were caught signing, he or she was forced to wear gloves to signify "punishment and stupidity."

Although American Sign Language enjoyed widespread support through the first half of the nineteenth century, by mid-century, a new method of teaching deaf children, oralism, began to emerge. This method emphasized lipreading and speech and prohibited the use of signs. It gained international support during a meeting of administrators and teachers in Milan, Italy, in 1880. Though this deaf educators' conference drew participants from France, Italy, America, and various other European countries, it was dominated by the oral teachers from France and Italy. The American delegation included Thomas Hopkins Gallaudet's two sons, Edward Miner Gallaudet (the president of Gallaudet College) and Thomas Gallaudet, who both spoke strongly in support of sign language. The oralist agenda dominated, though, and in the end a motion passed to pledge full support to this "method of articulation"—giving international approval to the idea that deaf children should be forced to communicate without signs. . . .

The highly vocal Alexander Graham Bell led the charge to abolish sign language, becoming the "most feared enemy of the American Deaf." He firmly believed that deaf people were "a defective race of human beings" and a "great calamity to the world." Ironically, both his mother and wife were deaf, and Bell himself was a fluent signer. In 1883, he presented a paper to the National Academy of Science in New Haven, Connecticut, "Upon the Formation of a Deaf Variety of the Human Race." His presentation supposed that since we can modify breeds of animals by careful selection, it should be possible similarly to modify the varieties of the human race. Based on his assumption that deaf marriages lead to deaf children, he found deaf residential schools, deaf community events, socializations,

and the hiring of deaf teachers disturbing and intolerable in nature because they could lead to intermarriage.

Initially, the residential schools were skeptical of Bell's efforts. Though many teachers, including Edward Miner Gallaudet, found value in teaching some speech techniques to hard of hearing students, they were mostly interested in teaching content to students through signs instead of wasting endless hours on speechreading drills. Bell and other oralists realized that in order to have a significant effect on these institutions, they would have to organize. Bell used his influence to enlist the National Education Association in his struggle against sign language. Ultimately, he was able to use their lobbying powers to win the hearts of politicians and public school teachers for the oralist movement. By 1920, despite deaf students' need to use signs to communicate and build a knowledge of the world, 80% of deaf students were educated without using any signs.

The effect on deaf education and the deaf community was devastating. The ban on sign language had a great impact on the deaf teachers, who had once been welcomed. As oralism spread, deaf teachers were removed from their positions, some without any compensation, and were quickly replaced by hearing teachers who did not know sign but were well versed on the drills of speech training. The ranks of deaf teachers shrank rapidly, as most administrators would not risk their positions by hiring a deaf teacher. By the time pure oralism was at its height, the number of deaf teachers had shrunk from 40% to only 14% of the total deaf education work force. This viable career option for deaf adults was removed, leaving them to search for less desirable work.

In enforcing the oralist teaching framework, children were subjected to sitting on their hands, having their hands tied behind their backs, and receiving other hideous forms of punishment to deter them from signing. Even now, our older deaf population remembers vividly the variety of punishments enacted for breaking the stringent rules of oralism.

. . .

The pendulum swing toward oralism also brought with it a movement of deaf students from residential schools to day schools and integrated classroom settings. The roots of this movement seem to have begun in Bell's strong conviction that deaf people should not associate with each other, for fear that this association would encourage deaf marriages and the continuation of deaf culture. Though vehemently opposed by most deaf people, many other people, including doctors, hearing parents, and their professional organizations, once again led the charge for a forced assimilation of the deaf student population. Perhaps the most serious threat came in the form of a seemingly well-meaning initiative, the Education for All Handicapped Children Act of 1975. This law mandated that all children should receive a "free, appropriate public education" in the "least restrictive environment." Many parents of disabled children welcomed the opportunity to have their children live at home and to enroll them in public schools. Regardless of its good intentions, the law strikes at the heart of the residential schools, where generations of deaf students have found their community, their language, and a shared culture. A related by-product of this law has been a shifting away of funds from the residential schools and shrinking enrollments. For some residential schools, it has meant a slow death, the painful closing of an institution that is dearly loved and valued.

Today, many deaf community members believe that "the dark world of oralism," in which educators tried to eliminate signing, has given way to an uncertain world of inclusion, where deaf children face "a different kind of isolation." The deaf community's insistence on its status as a unique and culturally viable minority group seems at odds with the educational system of assimilation. A language-rich learning environment, where deaf students have full access to direct communication with everyone in their environment, is not even remotely possible in most current integrated settings. Given this situation, what can be done to ensure that deaf students have full access to the educational system? Are

the cultural elements of the residential schools able to be adapted to the inclusion setting? What is a communicative, rich learning environment for deaf students, and how can one be nurtured and maintained? Is the essence of hearing/deaf peer relationships anemic in comparison to deaf/deaf relationships, or do they provide sufficient foundations on which to build solid friendships? How do the issues of isolation and alienation impact student learning? As we explore the answers to these questions, it is imperative that we listen to the stories of deaf students and the professionals who serve them. It is through their eyes that we can truly understand the complexity of issues that frustrate those children we serve.

CULTURAL COMPETENCY: SALIENT VALUES OF THE DEAF COMMUNITY

Imagine—deafness not as a defect, but as a source of connection! Imagine yourself deaf, growing up with a beautiful language, visual literature, humor, and theater. Imagine taking pride in your identity without any desire to become a member of the majority culture.

The critical juncture of communication and relationship building is culture. Many agree that educators can best serve deaf children by understanding the salient features of deaf culture in order to create culturally competent learning environments for deaf students. While it certainly seems true that a rudimentary understanding of the cultural heritage of deaf students would give educators greater insight into the world of being deaf, this knowledge should be coupled with inquiry into the level of ownership that deaf students hold to this heritage.

The salient values of deaf culture are tied to language, and the sites of cultural transmission, namely residential schools. In the deaf community, initial conversations usually begin by asking where you are from. A deaf person often responds by naming the residential school attended, rather than their hometown. Due to the fact that the majority of hearing parents do not learn to sign, depriving their child of meaningful family relationships, deaf friendships become extremely important to deaf people. Friendships from their residential school days often last a lifetime.

For deaf people, sign language is often an "embodiment of their personal and cultural identity." As with other languages, signed conversations have a certain etiquette that serves as both an exclusive and inclusive gate into the culture and community of deaf people. For new signers, this etiquette, or lack thereof, gives the person away. But as Edward Miner Gallaudet himself wrote, the greatest value of sign language to the deaf is to be found in "the facility it affords for free and unconstrained social intercourse"—which in fullness of expression is in "no respect inferior, and is in many respects superior, to articulated speech as a means of communicating ideas." "Speech and hearing thinking is negatively valued in deaf culture," while mastery of ASL and ASL storytelling are highly valued. It is sometimes assumed that ASL does not have literature, since it is not written down. However, there is a wealth of ASL literature—stories woven around themes of how deaf people see their own lives, their world within the deaf community, and the outside world, namely, the hearing community. Deaf literature often surfaces and flourishes at deaf events and informal gatherings—including vibrant ASL jokes, naming rituals, sign play, plays, fables, tall tales, stories, historical accounts, legends, anecdotes, poetry, and much more. Much of the literature of deaf culture is related directly, or indirectly to issues of power, control and domination between the hearing and deaf world.

. . .

Members of the deaf community highly value their deaf identity, as well as the collective value of deaf children. The shared experience of deafness generally overrides other dividing factors such as socioeconomic status or ethnicity. Fierce loyalty, hugs, and long goodbyes, are common markers of deaf culture, as is intermarriage. As many as 9 out of 10 deaf people marry other deaf in America. Deaf adults feel strongly about the need for deaf role models in the lives of deaf children and go out of their way to nurture these children with exposure to aspects of their culture. Deaf children who have had no exposure to deaf adults sometimes believe that they will grow up hearing, because they have never met a deaf adult. Many stories in deaf literature expand on this experience and serve as subtle reminders for the deaf adult population to be active in the lives of young deaf children. These cultural values that drive the deaf community are passed on from generation to generation as deaf children become deaf adults.

. . .

97

Historical, Theoretical, and Foundational Principles of Universal Instructional Design in Higher Education

Susan M. Pliner and Julia R. Johnson

To educate as the practice of freedom is a way of teaching that anyone can learn. . . . To teach in a manner that respects and cares for the souls of our students is essential if we are to provide the necessary conditions where learning can most deeply and intimately begin.

Although institutes of higher education serve an increasingly diverse student body, they have traditionally been resistant to change, especially in accommodating the needs of students marked as "minorities" because of race, class, ethnicity, gender, disability, religion, nationality, or sexual identification or orientation. After 150 years of status quo preservation, the creation of higher education environments that are accepting and supportive of students with diverse needs is a formidable task that requires a major cultural transformation. In order to create inclusive environments for diverse student populations, the system of higher education must be totally reconfigured, which will require shifts in our educational practices that range from how we admit students, to the curriculum we teach, to pedagogical practices, to career placement, and so forth. These changes not only are desirable from an ethic of inclusion, they also are necessary because our higher education institutions cannot operate in a cultural vacuum: Educational institutions must engage in the same inexorable challenges for inclusion that our total society is facing, that is, full integration and nothing less.

The concept of universality provides an important starting point for educational and social transformation. Activists such as Russell note the preliminary steps needed to achieve "universal social justice" and "the possibility for a common humanity . . . for human emancipation." One primary step toward full integration is accessibility or access to programs

and physical structures. Universal Instructional Design offers a range of options and strategies to achieve this first step of accessibility and inclusion.

. . .

CORE PRINCIPLES AND CONCEPTS OF UNIVERSAL INSTRUCTIONAL DESIGN

The goal of Universal Design for Learning (UDL) (Center for Applied Special Technology; CAST 2001) or Universal Instructional Design (UID) (Silver, Bourke, and Strehorn 1998) is to expand institutional teaching methodologies so that students with disabilities and all students with diverse learning needs have equal access to classroom teaching and learning. When classroom teaching practices are inclusive of diverse learning styles and needs from their inception, it is not necessary for students to rely as heavily on support systems that are secondary to primary instructional programs. Furthermore, the established bureaucracy that students must navigate in order to receive accommodations are alleviated by a UID approach. Aune and Kroeger note that "barrier-free environments that are naturally inclusive and that require minimal amounts of adaptation would alleviate much of the tension that results when 'disability interacts with institutions, systems, space and culture.'"

The development of UID as a concept draws from many different fields, but the term itself is borrowed directly from the architectural concept of Universal Design. Universal Design, introduced by Ronald Mace, is designed to make physical spaces accessible and usable by all people, including persons with physical disabilities. The Center for Universal Design at North Carolina State University defines Universal Design as "the design of products and environments to be usable by all people, to the greatest extent possible, without the need for adaptation or specialized design." The Center for Universal Design developed the following guiding principles for implementing Universal Design so that all persons would have access to physical space. These concepts include:(1) equitable use; (2) flexibility in use; (3) simple and intuitive use; (4) perceptible information; (5) tolerance for error; (6) low physical effort; and (7) size and space for approach and use. One commonly understood implementation of these principles is to provide ramps so that wheelchair users, as well as parents pushing strollers, can gain access to buildings (equitable use, flexibility in use, size and space for approach and use). Providing Braille lettering in elevators, the presence of electric door openers, accessible and marked parking, and bathroom stalls large enough to accommodate wheelchairs are additional examples with which most are familiar.

Universal Design in architecture is meant to accommodate the range of potential users in a physical environment. Similarly, Universal Instructional Design or Universal Design for Learning (UDL) accommodates a range of diverse learners in a learning environment. The principles of Universal Design have been applied to instruction, materials, and technology. CAST has led the field in applying UID to the use of technology in teaching and learning. CAST defines UDL as "a new paradigm for teaching, learning, and assessment, drawing on new brain research and new media technologies to respond to individual learner differences." This new paradigm requires a shift in thinking about how faculty design courses to include

alternatives to make it accessible and appropriate for individuals with different backgrounds, learning styles, abilities, and disabilities in widely varied learning contexts. The "universal" in universal design does not imply one optimal solution for everyone. Rather, it reflects an awareness of the unique nature of each learner and the need

to accommodate differences, creating learning experiences that suit the learner and maximize his or her ability to progress

CAST emphasizes the need for flexibility and encourages faculty to consider a framework for designing courses that provide for flexible means of representation, expression, and engagement.

At present, disability studies and education scholars who focus on issues of access have adapted the core principles of Universal Design in architecture to learning and instruction, resulting in the development of UID. The most current list is provided by Scott, Mc Guire, and Shaw, and includes nine primary principles for implementing UID:

1. Equitable use—making classroom material accessible to diverse learning needs and styles
2. Flexibility in use—the practice of using a variety of instructional methods
3. Simple and intuitive—teaching "in a straightforward and predictable manner"
4. Perceptible information—ensuring that course material is accessible to students regardless of their "sensory abilities"
5. Tolerance for error—building diversity of learning "pace and prerequisite skills" into course process
6. Low physical effort—designing instruction "to minimize . . . physical effort" so that students can attend to essential learning
7. Size and space for approach and use—engaging the classroom space in ways that address diverse student needs based on "body size, posture, mobility, and communication"
8. A community of learners—teaching and learning environment supports and encourages "interaction and communication among students and between students and faculty"
9. Instructional climate—all students are encouraged to meet "high expectations" as they are "welcomed" to participate in the course.

These principles highlight the need for a varied and flexible approach to teaching because no single method supports or challenges all students. Multiple methods and materials provide a sufficiently broad base that enables all students to learn. In our overview of the remaining articles in this volume, we explain how specific examples of UID principles can be implemented.

At its core, UID calls for equity and inclusiveness in education. UID engages faculty in thinking more broadly about the following: what they teach; why and how they teach it; and, why and how they assess student learning. UID calls for innovative teaching techniques and materials that are suitable for general use, and that are particularly helpful to students with identified or unidentified disabilities, students learning in a second (or third or fourth) language, or students who need additional academic support. Examples of such techniques include:

1. Routine placement of syllabi and reading lists on computer disks or the Web (so that text can be formatted by individual students according to needs)
2. Variable options for assignment and assessment of all students (multiple exam formats, flexibility in time and location, flexibility in presentation of ideas)
3. Provision of supplemental materials in multiple formats, such as oral lectures with overhead projection of "key point" outlines, study guides, or prepared notes.

Students do not have to be disabled to benefit from greater access to teaching materials. Furthermore, UID also allows faculty the freedom to be more flexible in achieving course goals and expectations. Too often, faculty assume that their methods of delivery are synonymous with the student's achievement of course goals. On the contrary, student learning goals are often more easily achieved when the possibilities of diverse learning styles and methods are explored.

The application of UID principles enables all students to have access to a greater range of teaching materials and this access to teaching materials, in turn, is one way to transform educational structures and create more equitable and socially just learning environments. Quite simply, UID is about social justice and transforming oppressive social relationships. As such, it is consistent with the missions of multicultural education and social justice education.

. . .

98

The Social Construction of Disability

Susan Wendell

. . .

I see disability as socially constructed in ways ranging from social conditions that straightforwardly create illnesses, injuries, and poor physical functioning, to subtle cultural factors that determine standards of normality and exclude those who do not meet them from full participation in their societies. I could not possibly discuss all the factors that enter into the social construction of disability here, and I feel sure that I am not aware of them all, but I will try to explain and illustrate the social construction of disability by discussing what I hope is a representative sample from a range of factors.

SOCIAL FACTORS THAT CONSTRUCT DISABILITY

First, it is easy to recognize that social conditions affect people's bodies by creating or failing to prevent sickness and injury. Although, since disability is relative to a person's physical, social, and cultural environment, none of the resulting physical conditions is necessarily disabling, many do in fact cause disability given the demands and lack of support in the environments of the people affected. In this direct sense of damaging people's bodies in ways that are disabling in their environments, much disability is created by the violence of invasions, wars, civil wars, and terrorism, which cause disabilities not only through direct injuries to combatants and noncombatants, but also through the spread of disease and the deprivations of basic needs that result from the chaos they create. In addition, although we more often hear about them when they cause death, violent crimes such as shootings, knifings, beatings, and rape all cause disabilities, so that a society's success or failure in protecting its citizens from injurious crimes has a significant effect on its rates of disability.

The availability and distribution of basic resources such as water, food, clothing, and shelter have major effects on disability, since much disabling physical damage results directly from malnutrition and indirectly from diseases that attack and do more lasting harm to the malnourished and those weakened by exposure. Disabling diseases are also contracted from contaminated water when clean water is not available. Here too, we usually learn more about the deaths caused by lack of basic resources than the (often life-long) disabilities of survivors.

Many other social factors can damage people's bodies in ways that are disabling in their environments, including (to mention just a few) tolerance of high-risk working conditions, abuse and neglect of children, low public safety standards, the degradation of the environment by contamination of air, water, and food, and the overwork, stress, and daily grinding deprivations of poverty. The social factors that can damage people's bodies almost always affect some groups in a society more than others because of racism, sexism, heterosexism, ageism, and advantages of class background, wealth, and education.

Medical care and practices, traditional and Western-scientific, play an important role in both preventing and creating disabling physical damage. . . . Lack of good prenatal care and dangerous or inadequate obstetrical practices cause disabilities in babies and in the women giving birth to them. Inoculations against diseases such as polio and measles prevent quite a lot of disability. Inadequate medical care of those who are already ill or injured results in unnecessary disablement. On the other hand, the rate of disability in a society increases with improved medical capacity to save the lives of people who are dangerously ill or injured in the absence of the capacity to prevent or cure all the physical damage they have incurred. Moreover, public health and sanitation measures that increase the average lifespan also increase the number of old people with disabilities in a society, since more people live long enough to become disabled.

The pace of life is a factor in the social construction of disability that particularly interests me, because it is usually taken for granted by non-disabled people, while many people with disabilities are acutely aware of how it marginalizes or threatens to marginalize us. I suspect that increases in the pace of life are important social causes of damage to people's bodies through rates of accident, drug and alcohol abuse, and illnesses that result from people's neglecting their needs for rest and good nutrition. But the pace of life also affects disability as a second form of social construction, the social construction of disability through expectations of performance.

When the pace of life in a society increases, there is a tendency for more people to become disabled, not only because of physically damaging consequences of efforts to go faster, but also because fewer people can meet expectations of "normal" performance; the physical (and mental) limitations of those who cannot meet the new pace become conspicuous and disabling, even though the same limitations were inconspicuous and irrelevant to full participation in the slower-paced society. Increases in the pace of life can be counterbalanced for some people by improvements in accessibility, such as better transportation and easier communication, but for those who must move or think slowly, and for those whose energy is severely limited, expectations of pace can make work, recreational, community, and social activities inaccessible.

. . .

Pace is a major aspect of expectations of performance; non-disabled people often take pace so much for granted that they feel and express impatience with the slower pace at which some people with disabilities need to operate, and accommodations of pace are often crucial to making an activity accessible to people with a wide range of physical and mental abilities. . . .

Much of the public world is also structured as though everyone were physically strong, as though all bodies were shaped the same, as though everyone could walk, hear, and see

well, as though everyone could work and play at a pace that is not compatible with any kind of illness or pain, as though no one were ever dizzy or incontinent or simply needed to sit or lie down. (For instance, where could you rest for a few minutes in a supermarket if you needed to?) Not only the architecture, but the entire physical and social organization of life tends to assume that we are either strong and healthy and able to do what the average young, non-disabled man can do or that we are completely unable to participate in public life.

A great deal of disability is caused by this physical structure and social organization of society. For instance, poor architectural planning creates physical obstacles for people who use wheelchairs, but also for people who can walk but cannot walk far or cannot climb stairs, for people who cannot open doors, and for people who can do all of these things but only at the cost of pain or an expenditure of energy they can ill afford. Some of the same architectural flaws cause problems for pregnant women, parents with strollers, and young children. This is no coincidence. Much architecture has been planned with a young adult, non-disabled male paradigm of humanity in mind. In addition, aspects of social organization that take for granted the social expectations of performance and productivity, such as inadequate public transportation (which I believe assumes that no one who is needed in the public world needs public transportation), communications systems that are inaccessible to people with visual or hearing impairments, and inflexible work arrangements that exclude part-time work or rest periods, create much disability.

When public and private worlds are split, women (and children) have often been relegated to the private, and so have the disabled, the sick, and the old. The public world is the world of strength, the positive (valued) body, performance and production, the non-disabled, and young adults. Weakness, illness, rest and recovery, pain, death, and the negative (devalued) body are private, generally hidden, and often neglected. Coming into the public world with illness, pain, or a devalued body, people encounter resistance to mixing the two worlds; the split is vividly revealed. Much of the experience of disability and illness goes underground, because there is no socially acceptable way of expressing it and having the physical and psychological experience acknowledged. Yet acknowledgement of this experience is exactly what is required for creating accessibility in the public world. The more a society regards disability as a private matter, and people with disabilities as belonging in the private sphere, the more disability it creates by failing to make the public sphere accessible to a wide range of people.

Disability is also socially constructed by the failure to give people the amount and kind of help they need to participate fully in all major aspects of life in the society, including making a significant contribution in the form of work. Two things are important to remember about the help that people with disabilities may need. One is that most industrialized societies give non-disabled people (in different degrees and kinds, depending on class, race, gender, and other factors) a lot of help in the form of education, training, social support, public communication and transportation facilities, public recreation, and other services. The help that non-disabled people receive tends to be taken for granted and not considered help but entitlement, because it is offered to citizens who fit the social paradigms, who by definition are not considered dependent on social help. It is only when people need a different kind or amount of help than that given to "paradigm" citizens that it is considered help at all, and they are considered socially dependent. Second, much, though not all, of the help that people with disabilities need is required because their bodies were damaged by social conditions, or because they cannot meet social expectations of performance, or because the narrowly-conceived physical structure and social organization of society have placed them at a disadvantage; in other words, it is needed to overcome problems that were created socially.

Thus disability is socially constructed through the failure or unwillingness to create ability among people who do not fit the physical and mental profile of "paradigm" citizens. Failures of social support for people with disabilities result in inadequate rehabilitation, unemployment, poverty, inadequate personal and medical care, poor communication services, inadequate training and education, poor protection from physical, sexual, and emotional abuse, minimal opportunities for social learning and interaction, and many other disabling situations that hurt people with disabilities and exclude them from participation in major aspects of life in their societies.

For example, Jongbloed and Crichton point out that, in Canada and the United States, the belief that social assistance benefits should be less than can be earned in the work force, in order to provide an incentive for people to find and keep employment, has contributed to poverty among people with disabilities. Although it was recognized in the 1950s that they should receive disability pensions, these were set, as were other forms of direct economic help, at socially minimal levels. Thus, even though unemployed people with disabilities have been viewed by both governments as surplus labour since at least the 1970s (because of persistently high general rates of unemployment), and efforts to increase their employment opportunities have been minimal, they are kept at poverty level incomes based on the "incentive" principle. Poverty is the single most disabling social circumstance for people with disabilities, since it means that they can barely afford the things that are necessities for non-disabled people, much less the personal care, medicines, and technological aids they may need to live decent lives outside institutions, or the training or education or transportation or clothing that might enable them to work or to participate more fully in public life.

Failure or unwillingness to provide help often takes the form of irrational rules governing insurance benefits and social assistance, long bureaucratic delays, and a pervasive attitude among those administering programs for people with disabilities that their "clients" are trying to get more than they deserve. . . .

I do not want to claim or imply that social factors alone cause all disability. I do want to claim that the social response to and treatment of biological difference constructs disability from biological reality, determining both the nature and the severity of disability. I recognize that many disabled people's relationships to their bodies involve elements of struggle that perhaps cannot be eliminated, perhaps not even mitigated, by social arrangements. But many of the struggles of people with disabilities, and much of what is disabling, are the consequences of having those physical conditions under social arrangements that could, but do not, either compensate for their physical conditions, or accommodate them so that they can participate fully, or support their struggles and integrate those struggles into the cultural concept of life as it is ordinarily lived.

CULTURAL CONSTRUCTION OF DISABILITY

Culture makes major contributions to disability. These contributions include not only the omission of experiences of disability from cultural representations of life in a society, but also the cultural stereotyping of people with disabilities, the selective stigmatization of physical and mental limitations and other differences (selective because not all limitations and differences are stigmatized, and different limitations and differences are stigmatized in different societies), the numerous cultural meanings attached to various kinds of disability and illness, and the exclusion of people with disabilities from the cultural meanings of activities they cannot perform or are expected not to perform.

The lack of realistic cultural representations of experiences of disability not only contributes to the "Otherness" of people with disabilities by encouraging the assumption that their lives are inconceivable to non-disabled people but also increases non-disabled people's fear of disability by suppressing knowledge of how people live with disabilities. Stereotypes of disabled people as dependent, morally depraved, superhumanly heroic, asexual, and/or pitiful are still the most common cultural portrayals of people with disabilities. Stereotypes repeatedly get in the way of full participation in work and social life. For example, Francine Arsenault, whose leg was damaged by childhood polio and later by gangrene, describes the following incident at her wedding:

> When I got married, one of my best friends came to the wedding with her parents. I had known her parents all the time I was growing up; we visited in each other's homes and I thought that they knew my situation quite well.
>
> But as the father went down the reception line and shook hands with my husband, he said, "You know, I used to think that Francine was intelligent, but to put herself on you as a burden like this shows that I was wrong all along."

Here the stereotype of a woman with a disability as a helpless, dependent burden blots out, in the friend's father's consciousness, both the reality that Francine simply has one damaged leg and the probability that her new husband wants her for her other qualities. Moreover, the man seems to take for granted that the new husband sees Francine in the same stereotyped way (or else he risks incomprehension or rejection), perhaps because he counts on the cultural assumptions about people with disabilities. I think both the stigma of physical "imperfection" (and possibly the additional stigma of having been damaged by disease) and the cultural meanings attached to the disability contribute to the power of the stereotype in situations like this. Physical "imperfection" is more likely to be thought to "spoil" a woman than a man by rendering her unattractive in a culture where her physical appearance is a large component of a woman's value; having a damaged leg probably evokes the metaphorical meanings of being "crippled," which include helplessness, dependency, and pitifulness. Stigma, stereotypes, and cultural meanings are all related and interactive in the cultural construction of disability. . . .

99

Go to the Margins of the Class

Disability and Hate Crimes

Lennard J. Davis

With great ceremony, the press reported the February 1999 conviction of white supremacist John William King for the kidnapping and murder of James Byrd, Jr., who had been chained to a truck in Jasper, Texas, dragged two miles, and dismembered. Likewise, the conviction of coconspirator Lawrence Russell Brewer in September 1999 seemed to imply that justice had been done. If justice in a broader sense is to be served, however, another

fact of the case deserves attention. Byrd was not only black and the victim of race hatred; he was also disabled. The press has noted this so casually that few people realize it; those who do, including myself, found out that Byrd was severely arthritic and subject to seizures. This information was ferreted out only after extensive searches of news reports.

Indeed, I myself was uncertain that Byrd was a person with disabilities. I recalled reading, on the day the crime was first reported, that a disabled African American had been brutally murdered. Since I was interested in disability, the article caught my eye. Yet when the story reappeared days, weeks, and months later, Byrd was simply referred to as African American. Almost all the news stories contained this simplification. Indeed, when I decided to write a piece on the subject for *The Nation*, I at first thought I might have made an error in thinking that Byrd was a person with disabilities. When I went to the library to look up the articles on microfilm, I found that the *New York Times* mentioned only twice, in the first two reports, that Byrd was a person with disabilities. Any newspaper story I checked tended to follow that pattern.

. . .

Initially, I wanted to write this story as an op-ed piece for the *New York Times*. An acquaintance who is on the editorial board of the paper read my initial article and responded in a somewhat condescending and negative way. He asked me if I seriously thought that race could be equated with disability, whether the history of lynching and slavery could be meaningfully equated with occasional violence against people with disabilities. The editors for both these progressive journals saw race as the primary category and disability as a poor third cousin of race. Their assumption was that violence toward a person of color with disabilities is primarily the result of the color and much less the result of the disability.

But disability is hardly a minor category. Approximately 16 percent of Americans have a disability and, as such, they comprise a significant minority group with an inordinately high rate of abuse. According to the Center for Women's Policy Studies, disabled women are raped and abused at a rate more than twice that of nondisabled women. The risk of physical assault, robbery, and rape, according to researcher Dick Sobsey, is at least four times as great for adults with disabilities as for the general population. In February 1999, for example, a mentally retarded man in Keansburg, New Jersey, was abducted by a group of young people who tortured, humiliated, and assaulted him. In March 1999, advocates for another mentally retarded man filed a lawsuit against a group of Nassau County, New York, police officers who beat him while he was in custody.

People with disabilities and deaf people report that they are routinely harassed verbally, physically, and sexually in public places. In private institutions or group homes, they are often the prime victims of violence and sexual abuse; in their own homes, they are subjected to sexual abuse, domestic violence, and incest, preyed upon by family members, family "friends," and "caretakers." So the question remains, why is American society largely unaware of or indifferent to the plight of people with disabilities? Is it because as an ableist society, we do not really believe that disability constitutes a serious category of oppression? Whenever race and disability come together, as in the King case, ethnicity tends to be considered so much the "stronger" category that disability disappears altogether.

As a society, we have long been confronted by the existence of discrimination against people of color. Students pour over the subject of race in their textbooks and read the work of multicultural writers in high school and college. Martin Luther King Day and Kwanzaa raise our consciousness, and the heroic tales of people like Rosa Parks inspire us.

But while we may acknowledge we are racist, we barely know we are ableist. Our schools, our textbooks, our media utterly ignore the history of disability; the dominant culture renders invisible the works of disabled and deaf poets, writers, and performance artists. The closest we have come to a national media engagement is the 1998 six-part NPR radio series *Beyond Affliction* and a few references to deafness in the TV series ER. Motion

pictures still largely romanticize or pathologize disability; there is not much else to make the experience of 16 percent of the population come alive realistically and politically.

Yet 72 percent of people with disabilities are unemployed, and their income is half the national average. Among working-age adults with disabilities, the poverty rate is three times that of those without impairments. One-third of all disabled children live in poverty; and despite the Americans with Disabilities Act, a judicial backlash has been under way ever since its passage in 1990. From 90 to 98 percent of discrimination cases brought under the ADA by people with disabilities have been lost in court. . . .

Anita Silvers notes this fact when she writes: "the courts tend to implement prohibitions against discrimination so as to favor paradigmatic members of the protected class. In doing so, they propel individuals whose experiences diverge from those of the class's prototypes, but who are equally at risk, to the class's margins." Thus when disability meets race, disability is propelled to the margins of the class.

From a legal perspective, one wants to make sure that members of a historically unprotected class receive proper justice and consideration under the law. Thus in America, women and minorities have been the focus of antidiscrimination law. There has been much cultural work done to make it acceptable at the end of the millennium for such groups to have public respect and sympathy. Countless novels, movies, and plays have accomplished this goal over the course of the twentieth century. It is unimaginable that a film could be made now that would present African Americans, Native Americans, or women as members of a deservedly subordinate, disenfranchised group. Thus the courts will, in the most obvious cases, uphold the right of members of such groups to redress wrongs in housing, employment, discrimination, and so on.

However, disability occupies a different place in the culture at this moment. Although considerable effort has been expended on the part of activists, legislators, and scholars, disability is still a largely ignored and marginalized area. Every week, films and television programs are made containing the most egregious stereotypes of people with disabilities, and hardly anyone notices. Legal decisions filled with ableist language and attitudes are handed down without anyone batting an eyelid. . . . Newspapers and magazines barely notice the existence of disability and largely use ableist language and metaphors in their articles. In other words, disability may be the last significant area of discrimination that has not yet been resolved, at least on the judicial, cultural, and ethical levels, in the twentieth and twenty-first centuries. . . .

So when it comes to violence against people with disabilities, several factors intervene. Although many states have statutes that describe disability in a list of categories that are protected under hate crime legislation, the actual enforcement of such policies may be muted by the intersectionality I have been describing. The Violent Crime Control and Law Enforcement Act of 1994 defines a hate crime as one "in which the defendant intentionally selects a victim, or in the case of a property crime, the property that is the object of the crime, because of the actual or perceived race, color, religion, national origin, ethnicity, gender, disability or sexual orientation of any person." . . .

Tellingly, though, a distinction is often made in this legislation. For example, previously under California's hate crime law, a murder committed because of the victim's race, color, religion, ancestry, or national origin could bring the death penalty or life in prison without parole. However, the maximum penalty for a murder based on gender, sexual orientation, or disability was twenty-five years to life in prison. A new bill signed in September 1999 increases the maximum in those latter categories to life in prison without parole. Federal efforts to prevent hate crimes, however, are now restricted to race, color, religion, and national origin.

Several U.S. senators have sponsored legislation to extend protections to gender, disability, and sexual orientation. But this idea ultimately did not pass into law and, even if

it had, hate crimes based on disability are unlikely to carry as stringent a penalty as crimes based on hate for race, color, religion, or national origin. . . .

But how do we determine, in any philosophical sense, that one kind of identity is more important than another? Historically, although the United States was founded on a separation of church and state, religion has been seen as a "holy" category certainly higher in status than, for example, one's sexual orientation; race, so embroiled in the nation's history, must be more important than something like disability; and so on—the arguments are based more on ad hoc judgments about the viciousness of different kinds of prejudice than on any principle one can articulate. This seems to be the same unreflective influence that gives priority to race over gender or disability in the intersectionality argument.

We can see this contradiction in another arena. The FBI is required to keep track of hate crimes. It has produced a report that found that of the 8,049 incidents of hate crime reported to police in 1997, 12 were motivated by bias based on disability; of these, 9 were based on the victim's physical condition and 3 were based on the victim's mental condition. These numbers seem shockingly low when compared to other studies such as Dick Sobsey's tabulations. Sobsey also notes that when a person with disabilities is a victim of crime, it tends to be a violent crime rather than a property crime.

. . .

Indeed, I am sure that when it comes time for the FBI to list the report on Byrd, they will file it under racial hate crime rather than a disability-related crime. Also, many of the crimes against people with disabilities will simply be seen as ordinary rather than hate crimes. So the rape or murder of a mentally ill resident of a sheltered facility will be seen as a rape or murder, not as one motivated by the status of the person involved. Indeed, one of the arguments used by opponents of hate crime legislation, particularly as it applies to gender or disability, is that crimes such as rapes will have to be investigated by the FBI, putting an undue burden on that organization. Since such crimes are daily occurrences, and since it could be argued that rape itself is a hate crime against women, the FBI will be taxed to the utmost in trying to detail all these acts of violence.

Intersectionality argues that individuals who fall into the intersection of two categories of oppression will, because of their membership in the weaker class, be sent to the margins of the stronger class. What these statistics suggest is that the category of disability, while a weak one to judges or legislators, is a powerful one to those who seek to victimize. Rather than minimizing an identity, victimizers are drawn to the double or triple categories of race, gender, and disability. Each of these categories enhances the opportunity for hate and the likelihood that the crime will go unnoticed, unreported, or disbelieved. For example, the Center for Women's Policy Studies reports that virtually half of the perpetrators of sexual abuse against women with disabilities gained access to their victims through disability services, and that caregivers commit at least 25 percent of all crimes against women with disabilities. In other words, the dependency of such women, compounded by their lower economic status, ethnicity, and diminished mobility or ability to communicate to authorities, is an enticement to victimizers.

. . .

The point here is that the general climate of ableism makes it comfortable for us to regard systematic violence against people with disabilities as accidental. Could one claim that the university's policy of negligence toward students with disabilities, especially after being forewarned, was a willed act of violence? The consciousness of the general public and the legal system would have to undergo a dramatic change for the truth of such a claim to be obvious.

Likewise, the definition of "hate" has to change as well. One of the reasons there is resistance to calling attacks against people with disabilities "hate" crimes is because the general ideology toward people with disabilities rules out hate as a viable emotion. In our

culture, it is permissible to "pity" or even "resent" people with disabilities. . . . Thus the idea that crimes against people with disabilities might be a result of "hate" seems to most people somehow wrong. Who would act violently toward a person using a wheelchair merely because that person could not walk? . . . someone cannot see a clearly posted sign, cannot walk up unblocked stairs, needs special assistance above what other "normal" citizens need[?] This kind of hatred is one that abhors the possibility that all bodies are not configured the same, that weakness and impairment are the legacy of a cult of perfection and able embodiment. When the law begins to catch on to this level of hatred, justice will be served.

. . .

100

Why the Intersexed Shouldn't Be Fixed

Insights from Queer Theory and Disability Studies

Sumi Colligan

The initiatives the Intersex Society of North America (ISNA) promoted to prevent "corrective" surgery for genitals not clearly identifiable as male or female have recently come to my attention. This discovery has stimulated my own reflections on the parallels between American cultural representations and the everyday struggles of the intersexed and those of people with disabilities. Both groups are subjected to anomalous classification, medical management, silencing, and shame; both groups titillate the projected, and often repressed, fantasies of outsiders; and both intersexed and disabled individuals and organizations are challenging the assumptions that underlie these negative images to reclaim their own impassioned, desirable, and desirous bodies. These activists seek to assert the value of their own presence in the world and to raise questions about a system of cultural ordering that renders them symbolically, if not literally, neutered or "fixed."

David Mitchell and Sharon Snyder point out that while there is an abundance of critical theory on the body, disability remains largely untheorized, often appearing as a natural backdrop for the exploration of already established social issues and themes. They explain: "Within this common critical methodology physical difference exemplifies the evidence of social deviance even as the constructed nature of physicality itself fades from view." Yet opportunities to explore the cultural construction of physicality and its intersections with race, class, gender, and sexuality are abundant, appearing both within the realms of popular and medical culture. These references are often quite explicit and should not require the sensitized lens of disability studies for quick detection. For example, apropos of disability and the trans and/or nebulously gendered, talk show host Jerry Springer is quoted as saying:

> When you think of all the things that could go wrong at birth or at least not be as they ought to be, from blindness to mental retardation to cystic fibrosis to, indeed, the entire litany of possible birth defects, why do we assume that the one thing that

can never be out of sync is our gender identity? And yet, while we are quick to heap our love and compassion and charity on any of these disabilities, if it has something to do with sex suddenly we don't want to hear about it. . . . And so with the same compassion that we are offering to those who are trying to fix other parts of their body that perhaps aren't working as they should, why not a word of understanding to those whose gender seems to be out of whack?

A number of issues here go unquestioned: Why are charity and compassion considered to be a desirable and automatic response to certain kinds of physical variation? Why is there an assumption that disability has nothing to do with sex? Why do genitals and gender identity have to match? Why is being fixed a moral imperative?

It is instructive to begin to explore these intersections and parallels by interrogating the meaning of *fixed*. The dictionary definition of the verb indicates "to set in order," "to repair," "to attach or fasten immovably"; even the noun, *fix*, is defined as "an embarrassing or uncomfortable position." Through the lens of *fixed*, I consider how and why Western cultures have come to disable the intersexed and neuter the disabled, subjecting them to similar disciplines of normalization. . . .

MEDICALIZING INTERSEXED/DISABLED BODIES: RETROFITTING AND REFORM

Michel Foucault has documented the forces that have converged in the last two centuries in Western Europe and the United States that contribute to the medical scrutiny of the flesh and its moral attributes. For example, in *The Birth of a Clinic*, Foucault describes processes by which the bodies of individuals undergoing medical treatment came to be viewed as discrete and docile entities whose hidden recesses contained the secrets to their ailments. Likewise, in *The History of Sexuality*, he addresses a range of professions (demography, pedagogy, medicine, and psychiatry among them) that emerged during this period to shape the contours of modernity. These fields used their professional powers to name, locate, regulate, punish, and remold individuals associated with aberrant corporealities. Foucault referred to these approaches as "bio-power," as they are "techniques that make possible a special alliance between specialized knowledge and institutionalized power in the state's management of life."

However, whereas Foucault draws out the implications of the deployment of these forms of power/knowledge to define and contain illness, madness, and sexuality, historian Henri-Jacques Stiker notes that disability is lacking from Foucault's analysis. I contend that such an analysis should be broadened to include the role that the development of statistics played in turning disability into deviance, a process that included upholding a statistical norm against which all else was rendered abnormal. Moreover, the analysis should consider the manner in which the growth of the rehabilitation industry was catalyzed by a drive to remove the "lack" and restore the disabled body to its "assumed, prior normal state." As we shall see, all these powers collided and collaborated to refashion, retrofit, and reform intersexed and disabled bodies to eradicate their "abnormalities" from our social presence and/or to render them invisible.

In Foucault's introduction to *Herculine Barbin: Being the Recently Discovered Diary of a Nineteenth Century French Hermaphrodite*, he states that by the mid-1800s, medical doctors had concluded that everyone had a "true" sex, which even when masked, could be discerned by the penetrating eye of science. This conviction was also corroborated by Alice Dreger, a researcher of French and British physicians between 1860 and 1915, who remarks that "the history of hermaphroditism is largely the history of struggles over the

'realities' of sex—the nature of 'true' sex, the proper role of the sexes, the question of what sex can, should, or must mean." The medical examination of hermaphrodites rested on the assumption of sexual dimorphism such that one's true sex could only be read as male or female. The sorting out of the sexes was conducted by navigating one's way through "genital geography," deciphering anatomical excesses and deficiencies, and distinguishing "veritable" from "pseudo vulvas." If anatomy alone wasn't quick to release its secrets, doctors would also seek clues in behaviors and aptitudes because of an assumed linear correlation between genitals and gendered attractions and performances (ergo, testicles and ovaries are us). Additionally, parents were interrogated for recollections of maternal impressions and "hereditary antecedents," physical indicators of past parental transgressions. Overall, if bodies and actions didn't conform to medical expectations and social conventions, they were forced to comply to nature's imagined calling by medical declaration and legal protocol.

In the past fifty years, surgery and hormonal therapy have become routine, technical solutions for individuals whose genitals are deemed medically problematic. That normative physicality is being constructed here should be readily apparent and is captured humorously by intersex ("intersex" is in common use now because it doesn't carry the mythical connotations of "hermaphrodite") writer Raphael Carter who defines ambiguous genitalia as "genitalia that refuse to declare their sex to doctors—no doubt on the principle that under interrogation by the enemy you should give only name, rank and serial number." This queering of medical authority serves to underscore the invasive consequences of accepted medical definitions and procedures. Intersex reporter Martha Coventry reveals that according to scientific standards, "girls, if they perceive themselves, or want to be perceived as fully 'feminine,' should have clitorises no longer than $3/8$ inch at birth. Boys, if they hope to grow up 'masculine,' should have penises that are about one inch in stretched length at birth. Girls should have vaginas fit for future intercourse, and boys should have urethra openings at the tip of the penis in order to be able to urinate standing up."

Of course, the irony here is that self-identity has nothing to do with this medical intervention because surgeons now generally perform these reconstructive feats on the intersexed in infancy. Biologist Anne Fausto-Sterling argues that the intersexed excite discomfort in medical professionals because "they possess the irritating ability to live sometimes as one sex and sometimes as the other, and they raise the specter of homosexuality." It is clear, then, that intersexed babies are being fixed, at least in part, as a form of rehabilitation that facilitates their bodily deployment into society according to heteronormative measures. In keeping with the body's truth, doctors, however, contend that their medical tampering is simply a means of restoring the infants to their naturally gendered state, denying the role that culture plays in enforcing this imperative.

In parallel fashion, in the last several centuries, people with disabilities have been subjected to pacification through the medical gaze's fixation on essentialized and internalized bodily truths and to reform through the disciplined practices of sheltered workshops, special education, and physical rehabilitation. The benevolence and charity that have been extended to these individuals rest on their willingness, through medical treatment, physical retraining, and mental acquiescence, to strive to achieve normative standards of bodily appearance and physical, linguistic, and cognitive use. By means of these institutional practices, "the disabled are to be 'raised up,' restored." Indeed, historian Stiker concludes: "rehabilitation marks the appearance of a culture that attempts to complete the act of identification, of making identical."

Alternatively, for those who can't be medically disappeared as with the intersexed, there remains the role of desexualized, childlike, dependents who are destined to institutionalization as they await the promise of cure. As historian Paul Longmore notes, these individuals are extended the benevolent hand of charity because, particularly in the United States, their images help reaffirm the virtue and moral fitness of its nondisabled citizens.

Stiker asserts that cure suggests removal and that rehabilitation suggests assimilation. Regardless of an emphasis on cure or rehabilitation, "compassion tends to be channeled into normalizing." And either way, intersexed and disabled persons, viewed as destabilizing physical, sexual, gendered, and classificatory presences, have clearly been the targets of coercive regimes of routinization which have nearly, but not so successfully, extinguished their bodily knowledge and their desires.

FIXING BODIES, EXTINGUISHING DESIRES: CONSTRUCTING ASEXUALITY

. . . Both intersexed and disabled bodies have been construed as threatening, with their imagined excesses and deficiencies. Consequently, these bodies have been stripped of their ability to pleasure and be pleasured through the mechanism of denial, the social erasure of sexuality. From this standpoint, both intersexed and disabled bodies are lurking in the social margins, fluctuating between the overly intrusive and the wispy. In this vein, James Porter notes:

> viewed in itself (an essentializing perspective—but that is part of the point), a disabled body seems somehow too much a body, too real, too corporeal: it is a body that, so to speak, stands in its own way. From another angle, which is no less reductive, a disabled body seems to be lacking something essential, something to make it identifiable and something to identify with; a body that is deficiently itself, not quite a body in the full sense of the word, not real enough.

And as Foucault has aptly demonstrated, societal regulatory regimes have been deployed not only to survey these excesses and deficiencies but to contain them as well.

Medicalization of the intersexed and disabled has profoundly shaped their cultural representations and interpersonal relationships, as well as their phenomenological experiences of and with their own bodies. Whereas historically, the intersexed conjured up erotic associations, more recently, repeated medical diagnosis and intervention and medical jargon bantered about in exclusionary or hushed tones have contributed to shrouding disabled/ intersexed bodies with an aura of taboo, secrecy, and shame. Overall, medical and cultural assumptions about sex being reserved for heterosexed, symmetrical, and genitally specific bodies tend to promote the expectation that sex and sexuality are privileges awarded to the "normate" only.

The rigid molding of bodies to conform to conventional standards and allowances clearly exacts a toll in conceiving of alternative means of desiring. For the intersexed, "to grow up in a world in which there is no name, at least no spoken name, for what you are" is frightening and confusing. Fear of rejection undermines sexual choices. For instance, Morgan Holmes, an intersexed bisexual, explains: "I learned then that my desire wasn't necessarily linked to my physical difference. However, even that knowledge could not assuage the fear that my lovers of whatever sex, but particularly female, would know I had a fake 'cunt' and would abandon me." In this way, the expectation that our bodies should be strictly products of nature and not culture (as if any human body occupies space outside of culture), awards sexual gratification and relationships to those whose bodies pass the test of normative authenticity.

The story of a person called Toby who was brought up as a girl, then lived as a boy, eventually adopted the label of neuter, and in 1987, endeavored to form a self-help group for others who similarly self-identified, further illustrates the psychic cost of growing up with a body that the surrounding culture denies is possible. "As Toby conceived it, the

group's purpose was to provide a forum for people who think of themselves as neuter and/ or asexual to make (nonsexual) connections with others." Toby's hope was that such a group would provide "'a setting free of pressure to define ourselves in terms of maleness or femaleness.'" While asexuality should be respected as a chosen identity and practice, the fact that abstinence is the only acceptable alternative in our society for the unmarried, disabled, or nonheteronormative leaves me wondering why neuter was the one option to fill the interspace. Is this yet one more instance of a presence concealed as an absence because Western binary categories disallow more creative possibilities?

What is perhaps most remarkable in the testimonies of intersex though, particularly those individuals whose bodies have escaped medical tampering, is the sense of content-edness with their own bodies. In the video ISNA produced, "Hermaphrodites Speak," Angela Moreno describes the delight she received from her large clitoris at the age of twelve before doctors insisted on performing a "clitoral reduction" as "time in the pleasure garden before the fall." She asserts that what has been most profoundly removed from the intersexed through medical intervention is a uniquely "hermaphroditic eroticism."

Unfortunately, the idea that our bodies harbor our deepest truths tends to obscure the part that our culture and its naturalizing agents play in imposing these so-called truths upon us. Instead we are cast in the role of deceivers if we don't wear our bodies on our sleeves, for we are said to deprive others of their ability to manage us, anchor us, and fix our meaning. Joshua Gamson suggests that on television talk shows, for example, "any dissonance between genital status and genital identity [is taken] as a sign of inauthenticity." Foucault would, in fact, argue that this compulsion to speak incessantly of our sexualities is a manifestation of modern surveillance techniques rather than an expression of our innermost thoughts. This point would indicate that, as much as discourse may attempt to contain the truth of our bodies, there will inevitably be discontinuities between the stories we tell and our bodies themselves. From this vantage point, there can never be a complete correlation between our genital status and our gender identities, no matter who we are. Moreover, David Halperin further complicates this issue of truth telling by stating that "coming out" has the advantage of "claiming back . . . a certain interpretive authority," but never effectively eliminates the "superior and knowing gaze" of the outside viewer.

On the other hand, those of us who have visible disabilities are often neutralized by external fixations that rob us of the opportunity to speak our own pleasures and desires. Part of the problem is that the larger society simply assumes that sexuality and disability are so antithetical to one another that there is no discussion to be had. Certain British disability theorists assert: "In modern Western societies, sexual agency (that is, potential or actual independent sexual activity) is considered the essential element of full adult personhood, replacing the role formerly taken by paid work: because disabled people are infantalized, and denied the status of active subjects, so consequently their sexuality is undermined." Eli Clare argues further that, because disabled bodies are equated so thoroughly with medical pathology, they are generally denied even the distorted and magnified sexuality attributed to many marginalized people.

The tendency to deny any recognition to the sexuality of people with disabilities also contributes to a blurring of their gender identification such that they share a gender ambi-guity not so dissimilar from the intersexed. Disability and queer writer Eli Clare explains: "The construction of gender depends not only on the male and female body, but also on the nondisabled body." This refusal to read disabled bodies correctly may even pose a problem for entry and acceptance into gay, lesbian, bisexual, and transgender subcultures as they, too, rely upon visible markers to signify group membership. Attention to the more culturally loaded, but misunderstood qualities of disabled bodies may cause "their less vis-ible identity to be neglected." More generally, visuality and visibility produce complex and contradictory effects for those whose bodies are deemed unnatural because the impulse to

stabilize our identities and to mold us into singular subjects is there regardless of the source of our visibility (i.e., by our appearance, our actions, and/or our words). The fact that all of us, in some way, participate in this dynamic suggests that these misreadings are powerful cultural scripts to resist and transform.

. . .

101

Mass Psychiatric Casualties

Dave Grossman

In every war in which American soldiers have fought in this [twentieth] century, the chances of becoming a psychiatric casualty—of being debilitated for some period of time as a consequence of the stresses of military life—were greater than the chances of being killed by enemy fire. The only exception was the Vietnam War, in which the chances were almost equal.
—Richard Gabriel, *No More Heroes*

Are the warriors of today any better than those who fought in the trenches of World War I? Are today's warriors tougher than those who landed on the beaches of Normandy or Iwo Jima in World War II? Are they better than the ones who fought their way out of the frozen Chosen or the Puson Perimeter in Korea? No. Today we are no better than those heroes. And we are no worse. We are the same warriors. We might be better equipped, better trained and better prepared, but we are the same basic, biological organisms as those who have gone before us.

Richard Gabriel, in his excellent book, *No More Heroes*, tells us that in the great battles of World War I, World War II and Korea, there were more men pulled off the front lines because of psychiatric wounds than were killed in combat. There was a study written on this phenomenon in World War II entitled "Lost Divisions," which concluded that American forces lost 504,000 men from psychiatric collapse. A number sufficient to man 50 combat divisions!

On any given day in World War II, thousands of psychiatric casualties were in camps close to the front lines. A procedure called "Immediacy, Expectancy, and Proximity" was applied, meaning they were kept in proximity of the front lines with a sense of immediacy and expectancy that they would go back into battle. Even with that in place, as well as the normal cycles where men rotated out of combat after a reasonable time, more soldiers were lost from psychiatric casualties than all of the physical casualties combined.

Very few people know about this. While everyone knows about the valiant dead, most people, even professional warriors, do not know about the greater number of individuals who were quietly taken out of the front lines because they were psychiatric casualties. This is another aspect of combat that has been hidden from us, and it is something we must understand.

Worst of all were those rare situations in which soldiers were trapped in continuous combat for 60 to 90 days. In those cases, 98 percent became psychiatric casualties. Fighting all day and all night for months on end is a twentieth century phenomenon. The Battle of Gettysburg in 1863 lasted three days, and they took the nights off. This has been the case throughout history. When the sun went down, the fighting stopped, and the men gathered around the campfire to debrief the day's fight.

It was not until the twentieth century, beginning with World War I, that battles went day and night, for weeks and months without end. This resulted in a huge increase in psychiatric casualties and it got vastly worse when soldiers were unable to rotate out of the battle. On the beaches of Normandy in World War II, for example, there were no rear lines, and for two months there was no way to escape the horror of continuous fighting, of continuous death. It was learned then that after 60 days and nights of constant combat, 98 percent of all soldiers became psychiatric casualties.

. . .

Consider the six-month-long Battle of Stalingrad, the decisive World War II Soviet victory that stopped the German southern advance and turned the tide of the war. Some Russian reports say that their veterans of that great battle died around age 40, while other Russian males not involved lived into their 60s and 70s. The difference? The war veterans had been exposed to continual stress 24 hours a day for six, long, grueling months.

To fully comprehend the intensity of mental stress from combat, we must keep other environmental stressors in mind, while at the same time understanding the body's physiological response as the sympathetic nervous system is mobilized. In addition, we must understand the impact of the parasympathetic nervous system's "backlash" that occurs as a result of overwhelming demands placed upon it.

If we agree that we are basically no different creatures than the warriors of World War I, World War II and Korea, then we must admit that the same thing could happen to us. . . .

102

Disability in the New World Order

Nirmala Erevelles

. . .

In this chapter, I speak from the critical vantage point of two theoretical perspectives: Third World feminism(s) and disability studies. By deploying the term Third World feminism(s), I am referring to the political constituency of women of African, Caribbean, Asian, and Latin American descent, as well as Native peoples of the United States who constitute an oppositional alliance against the sexist, racist, imperialist, neocolonial structures that shape our lives. When defining Disability Studies, I refer particularly to the social, political, and economic conditions within the category of "disability" which is constituted as "deviant" difference, and the ideological effects that such constructions of "disability" have on the reproduction of racial, gendered, and class oppression. At the same time, my discussion will address the actual conditions and experiences of Third World people's lives when mediated via the oppressive and often violent social relations of race, class, caste, gender, and disability.

The dialectical relationship between poverty and disability has been recognized for some time. Living with a disability adds to the risks of living in poverty, while at the same time, conditions of poverty increase the possibility of becoming disabled. In this essay, I will elaborate on this relationship between poverty and disability in Third World contexts—with a special focus on India—in the wake of sweeping economic reforms implemented by state governments in deference to structural adjustment policies (SAPs) which have been recommended by the World Bank and the IMF. . . .

ENGENDERING ECONOMIC REFORM: IMPLICATIONS FOR DISABILITY

Third World feminists have documented how the effects of (neo)colonial institutions and policies have transformed indigenous patriarchies and consolidated hegemonic middle-class cultures in metropolitan and colonized areas in support of oppressive patriarchal structures, albeit in new forms. This has been especially true in the context of the SAPs, where women and children have become the most vulnerable populations. Critics of the World Bank and the IMF have pointed out that SAPs were instituted to prioritize the efficient management of debt, rather than to transform the abject conditions of poverty in contexts where women and children represent the disproportionate percentage of the world's poor. Programs instituted by the World Bank and the IMF also supposedly sought to include women as active participants in wage labor markets to enable their emancipation from patriarchal oppression.

However, most of the labor activities offered to Third World women are for low-wage work, because these women are considered "cheap" and "pliable" labor in both factory production and the service industry. As a result, this new gendered labor shift has forced men out of jobs, and, as a result, poor Third World women are forced to balance wage labor along with subsistence and domestic production. Because of the sharp fall in the purchasing power of their incomes, Third World women, many of whom are single heads of households, are faced with the sole responsibility of meeting household reproduction costs. In the desperation for employment, poor women are forced to take jobs in the informal and other low-wage sectors while, at the same time, their unpaid labor escalates because they must stretch limited funds to cover the subsistence of their households. Additionally, their health is also affected because of reduced food consumption, stress, and domestic violence—experiences that affect fertility, infant mortality, and disabling conditions in both their children and themselves.

It is this economic context that sets the stage for the social construction of disability. According to Elwan, UNICEF's list of major causes of disability among children in Third World countries includes inadequate nutrition of mothers and children, vitamin deficiencies, abnormal prenatal or perinatal events, infectious diseases, accidents, and various other factors including environmental pollution and lack of adequate sanitation—all of which occur as a result of poverty conditions. Notwithstanding the World Bank's claims that the SAPs would eventually lead to a reduction in poverty, according to UNICEF, there has been a drop of 10% to 25% in average incomes, a 25% reduction in spending per capita on health, and a 50% reduction in spending per capita on education in the poorest countries in the world. Though officials argue that they advise sound macroeconomic policies and strategies that favor investment in basic human capital—primary health care and universal primary education—the implementation of the SAP's belie this claim. Abbasi points out that even though World Bank lending for health services has increased over the years, low-income countries are unable to meet and maintain health service costs and at the same time pay their debts, and have therefore begun to levy a small fee also called a "user charge"

to all clients using public health services. In already destitute communities, these user charges have resulted in a decline in access to health services with disastrous consequences to these populations. As a result, according to Andrew Creese, a health economist at the World Health Organization (WHO), increases in maternal mortality and the incidence of communicable diseases such as diphtheria and tuberculosis have been attributed to such policies.

India offers a good case study of these practices. Forced to implement the structural adjustment programs (SAPs) in the early 1990s to meet the deficit in its balance of payments, the Indian state was encouraged to liberalize its economy, which required that it perform three main functions: protect and sustain the functioning of markets; use all policy instruments available to entice foreign capital investment; and undertake certain minimal expenditures so as to ameliorate the excesses perpetrated by the market. The implementation of the SAPs has only exacerbated the relationship between poverty and disability in India. Thus, for example, nearly fifteen thousand children in India under the age of five go blind because of a vitamin A deficiency caused by malnutrition. Additionally, limited access to clean water supplies as well as overcrowding in inadequate and unsanitary living conditions are responsible for the spread of intestinal, infectious, and vector-carrying diseases that also contribute to the onset of disability.

Even health policies actively supported by the international organizations barely address the crux of the problem. For example, the Indian state's investment in "Health for All by 2000," based on the Alma Ata Declaration of 1978, fostered only two major programs—oral rehydration therapy and immunization—instead of providing general health care for everyone. While such programs produced good statistics that claimed a lower rate of infant mortality, malnutrition and morbidity rates increased. And in the current context, as SAPs have mandated the increased privatization of health care and user financed health services, the transfer of resources from its poor clients to the wealthy investors of health care is the main outcome.

Additionally, even the rehabilitation projects, such as community based rehabilitation (CBR) programs (which are actively supported by the World Bank and other international organizations, such as ActionAid), also have served to accentuate inequalities along the axes of gender, class, caste, and disability. The dominant representation of the philosophy of CBR has been to integrate disabled people into the social mainstream. In a context where the resources allocated to rehabilitation programs are low and where there is a shortage of trained personnel to provide these services, CBR has become one of the most cost-efficient means to save on mounting staff costs, waste of labor, and the low efficiency of services. Thus, in an attempt to ensure maximum cost-efficiency, policy makers assume that the primary support for these programs will come from the community, where parents and workers, supervised by health volunteers (a village rehabilitation worker, or VRW, and a multipurpose rehabilitation worker, or MRW), will provide more specialized services to disabled members of the community.

However, the very concept of inclusion becomes exploitative in such contexts. Like the health programs supported by SAPs, CBR only serves to transfer the costs of services to the community. Thus, for example, even one of its advocates, Maya Thomas, director of the disability division ActionAid International-India has admitted that "the trend of progressive impoverishment of rural dwellings and the growing abandonment of extended family systems leave little economic and manpower resources in families that continue to look after the needs of their disabled members." Further, in patriarchal contexts, the provision of rehabilitation services by the family predominantly implies the woman, and so this becomes another burden in the life of the rural housewife caught up in her struggle for day-to-day economic survival. At the same time, most of the rehabilitation aides, who are low down in the occupational hierarchy and who receive pitiably low wages, are once

again predominantly poor women from the community. Therefore, what has happened is that these state-initiated policies that have been celebrated for their cost-effectiveness are actually geared to "[mobilize] people's resources for government programs," where the additional costs of these services continue to be absorbed by both the paid and unpaid labor of women.

. . .

103

Gawking, Gaping, Staring

Eli Clare

Gawking, gaping, staring: I can't say when it first happened. When first a pair of eyes caught me, held me in their vice grip, tore skin from muscle, muscle from bone. Those eyes always shouted, "Freak, retard, cripple," demanding an answer for tremoring hands, a tomboy's bold and unsteady gait I never grew out of. It started young, anywhere I encountered humans. Gawking, gaping, staring seeped into my bones, became the marrow. I spent thirty years shutting it out, slamming the door.

The gawkers never get it right, but what I want to know is this: will you? When my smile finds you across the room, will you notice the odd angle of my wrists cocked and decide I am a pane of glass to glance right through? Or will you smile back?

Thirty years, and now I am looking for lovers and teachers who will hold all my complexities and contradictions gently, honestly, appreciatively. Looking for heroes and role models who will accompany me through the world. Looking for friends and allies who will counter the gawking, gaping, staring.

I come from peoples who have long histories of being on stage—freaks and drag queens, court jesters and scientific experiments. Sometimes we work for money and are proud. Other times we're just desperate. We've posed for anthropologists and cringed in front of doctors, jumped through hoops and answered the same questions over and over, performed the greatest spectacles and thumbed our noses at that shadow they call normal.

William Johnson—African American and cognitively disabled in the mid-1800s—worked the freak-show stage. He donned an ape costume and shaved his head, save for a tuft of hair at the very top, and became the monkey man, the missing link, the bridge between "brute" and "man." P. T. Barnum, showman extraordinaire and shaper of the institution of the freak show, named William's exhibit "What-Is-It?" People paid to gawk, and William died a well-off man. The folks who performed alongside William affectionately called him the "dean of freaks." Today that question—what is it?—still lingers, still haunts us, only now the gawkers get in for free.

Billy Tipton worked the jazz stage with his piano, saxophone, and comedy routines. Billy lived for fifty years as a female-bodied man. He married five times and adopted three sons. He turned down major, high-profile music gigs. He died of a bleeding ulcer rather than seeking out medical care. He was much admired by the men he played music with. This we know about Billy, but there is also much we don't know: how he thought of himself, his gender; what prompted him to make the move from woman to man; what

went through his head as he lay dying in his son's arms. But really, the questions I want to ask aren't about his gender but rather about his life as a musician. *Billy, what did your body feel like as your fingers raced into a familiar song, playing in front of great throngs of people?* The gawking started after his death as the headlines roared, "Jazz Musician Spent Life Concealing Fantastic Secret."

I listen to the histories and everywhere hear the words *cripple, queer, gimp, freak*: those words hurled at me, those words used with pride. When I walk through the world, the bashers see a fag, the dykes see a butch, and I myself don't have many words. I often leave it at genderqueer or transgender butch. The gawkers never get it right. They think I'm deaf or "mentally retarded." They think I'm a twenty-one-year-old guy or a middle-aged dyke. They can't make up their minds, start with sir, end with ma'am, waver in the middle. They think I am that pane of glass.

Cripples, queers, gimps, freaks: we are looking for lovers and teachers—teachers to stand with us against the gawking; lovers to reach beneath our clothing, beneath the words that attempt to name us, beneath our shame and armor, their eyes and hands helping return us to grace, beauty, passion. *He cradles my right hand against his body and says, "Your tremors feel so good." And says, "I can't get enough of your shaky touch." And says, "I love your cerebral palsy." This man who is my lover. Shame and disbelief flood my body, drowning his words. How do I begin to learn his lustful gaze?*

Believing him takes more than trust. I spent so many years shutting the staring out, slamming the door. Friends would ask, "Did you see that person gaping at you?" and I'd answer, "What person?" It's a great survival strategy but not very selective. In truth the door slammed hard, and I lost it all, all the appreciation, flirtation, solidarity that can be wrapped into a gaze. These days I practice gawking at the gawkers and flirting as hard as I know how. The first is an act of resistance; the second, an act of pride. I am looking for teachers.

If I had a time machine, I'd travel back to the freak show. Sneak in after hours, after all the folks who worked long days selling themselves as armless wonders and wild savages had stepped off their platforms, out of their geek pits, from behind their curtains. I'd walk among them—the fat women, the short-statured men commonly called dwarves and midgets, the folks without legs, the supposed half-men/half-women, the conjoined twins, the bearded women, the snake charmers and sword swallowers—as they took off their costumes, washed their faces, sat down to dinner. I'd gather their words, their laughter, their scorn at the customers—the rubes—who bought their trinkets and believed half their lies. I'd breathe their fierceness into me.

I am looking for teachers and heroes to show me the way toward new pride, new understanding, new strength, a bigger sense of self. Often it is history I turn to, history I grasp and mold in my search. I am not alone in this endeavor. I think of a kid we've come to know as Brandon Teena: twenty-one years old, living as a guy in rural Nebraska, revealed as female-bodied, raped, and murdered by so-called friends. In trans community, we've chosen him. Claimed him as an FTM (a female-to-male trans person) based on how his life makes sense to us without listening to his confusion. Named him Brandon Teena without paying attention to the dozen other names he used. We have made him hero, martyr, symbol of transphobic violence. I think again of Billy Tipton. In the lesbian community, many have taken Billy to be an emblem of the sexism in the jazz world of the mid-1900s. They shape his life as a man into a simple survival strategy that allowed him to play music. I myself read the life of William Johnson and find someone who turned a set of oppressive material and social conditions to his benefit and gained a measure of success and community. That reading strengthens me. But in truth William might have been a lonely, frightened man, coerced, bullied, trapped by freak-show owners and managers. We use and reshape history, and in the process it sometimes gets misshapen.

V
O
I
C
E
S

At the same time, we all need teachers and heroes: folks to say, "You're not alone. I too was here. This is what I did and what I learned. Maybe it'll help." My best heroes and teachers don't live on pedestals. They lead complex, messy lives, offering me reflections of myself and standing with me against the gawkers.

The gawkers who never get it right. They've turned away from me, laughed, thrown rocks, pointed their fingers, quoted Bible verses, called me immoral and depraved, tried to heal me, swamped me in pity. Their hatred snarls into me, and often I can't separate the homophobia from the ableism from the transphobia.

The gawkers never get it right, but what I want to know is this: will you? If I touch you with tremoring hands, will you wince away, thinking cripple, thinking ugly? Or will you unfold to my body, let my trembling shimmer beneath your skin?

These days, I practice overt resistance and unabashed pride, gawking at the gawkers and flirting as hard as I know how. The two go together. On the Castro, I check out the bears, those big burly men with full beards and open shirts. One of them catches my eyes. I hold his gaze for a single moment too long, watch as it slips down my body. He asks, "Are you a boy or a girl?" not taunting but curious. I don't answer. What could I possibly say? I walk away smiling, my skin warm.

In another world at another time, I would have grown up neither boy nor girl, but something entirely different. In English there are no good words, no easy words. All the language we have created—transgender, transsexual, drag queen, drag king, stone butch, high femme, nellie, fairy, bulldyke, he-she, FTM, MTF (a male-to-female trans person)— places us in relationship to masculine or feminine, between the two, combining the two, moving from one to the other. I'm hungry for an image to describe my gendered self, something more than the shadowland of neither man nor woman, more than a suspension bridge tethered between negatives. I want a solid ground with bedrock of its own, a language to take me to a brand new place neither masculine nor feminine, day nor night, mortise nor tenon. What could I possibly say to the bears cruising me at 3 P.M. as sunlight streams over concrete?

Without language to name myself. I am in particular need of role models. I think many of us are. Who do we shape our masculinities, our femininities, after? Who shows us how to be a drag queen, a butch, a trannyfag (a gay FTM) who used to be a straight married woman and now cruises the boys hot and heavy, a multigendered femme boy/girl who walks the dividing line? I keep looking for disabled men to nurture my queer masculinity, crip style. Looking for bodies a bit off-center, a bit off-balance. Looking for guys who walk with a tremble; speak with a slur; who use wheelchairs, crutches, ventilators, braces; whose disabilities shape, but don't contradict, their masculinities.

And in truth I am finding those role models. There is a freak-show photo: Hiram and Barney Davis offstage—small, wiry men, white, cognitively disabled, raised in Ohio. They wear goatees, hair falling past their shoulders. They look mildly and directly into the camera. Onstage, Hiram and Barney played "Waino and Plutano, the Wild Men of Borneo." They snapped, snarted, growled, shook their chains at the audience. People flocked to the "Wild Men," handing over good money to gape. I hope just once Hiram and Barney stopped mid-performance, up there on the sideshow platform, and stared back, turning their mild and direct gaze to the rubes, gawking at the gawkers.

It usually takes only one long glance at the gawkers—kids on their way home from school, old women with their grocery bags, young professionals dressed for work. Just once I want someone to tell me what they're staring at. My tremoring hands? My buzzed hair? My broad, off-center stance, shoulders well-muscled and lopsided? My slurred speech? Just once. But typically one long, steely glance, and they're gone. I am taking Hiram and Barney as my teachers.

The gawkers never get it right, and what I want to know is this: will you? When I walk through the world, will you simply scramble for the correct pronoun, failing whichever one you choose, he not all the way right, she not all the way wrong? Or will you imagine a river at dusk, its skin smooth and unbroken, sun no longer braided into sparkles? Cliff divers hurl their bodies from thirty, forty, fifty feet, bodies neither flying nor earth-bound, three somersaults and a half turn, entering the water free-fall without a ripple. Will you get it right?

I am looking for friends and allies, for communities where the staring, gaping, gawking finally turns to something else, something true to the bone. Places where strength gets to be softened and tempered, love honed and stretched. Where gender is known as more than a simple binary. Where we are encouraged to swish and swagger, limp and roll, and learn the language of pride. Places where our bodies begin to become home. Gawking, gaping, staring: I can't say when it first happened.

104

Post-Traumatic Stress Disorder Leaves Scars "on the Inside," Iraq Veteran Says

Edward D. Murphy

Miguel Cyr said it's understandable, but still frustrating, to see friends and family members struggle to comprehend the problems he faces in dealing with post-traumatic stress disorder.

"People say, 'There's nothing wrong with you. You have no scars,' but they're on the inside," said Cyr, who served a year in Iraq with a Maine Army National Guard engineering battalion.

Cyr, who lives in Minot, said he joined the National Guard as a way to pay for college, but his battalion was sent to Iraq for a year in early 2004. The unit was based in Mosul, he said, and was building a road to connect several cities in the area.

As he headed out to the work site in July 2004, Cyr said, his truck was rocked by the explosion of a roadside bomb. Cyr said he had no visible wounds, but doctors later determined he had suffered a brain injury similar to a mild concussion.

His unit was also under mortar attack almost daily, he said, and friends of his were injured in the attacks.

"I had constant anxiety" about attacks while in Iraq, he said, and meanwhile, friends and relatives in the United States were pushing him to stay in closer contact.

"I just felt like I wasn't doing enough—(people asked) why wasn't I writing more?" he said. "I didn't need more from people, I just wanted people to stop needing me so much."

That took its toll on relationships when he came home in March 2005, Cyr said. He broke up with his girlfriend, lost track of friends and felt disconnected from fellow students when he attempted to go to college.

"I was only 19, but I felt like I didn't fit anymore," he said, feeling "a constant sadness and depression."

Cyr said he started to have bad dreams, had difficulty keeping a job and has had trouble finding work for the past few years because employers seemed turned off that he's disabled from his military service.

He felt constantly on edge, spent too much money, drank too much and started smoking marijuana because it was the only thing that seemed to help him keep calm.

Cyr signed up for the Army Reserve but eventually resigned because he had trouble following assignments and didn't feel comfortable around his fellow soldiers. His officers, he said, urged him to get tested for PTSD. He was diagnosed by VA [Veterans Administration] doctors four years ago.

Cyr said he takes medication the VA doctors prescribed, including antidepressants and pills to help him sleep, and goes to psychiatric therapy sessions. The treatment helps, he said, especially when he feels the need to talk about an incident in Iraq that's been bothering him.

"I get so emotional, but I keep it to myself because I feel like I'd be depressing people," he said. "Veterans need someone to relate to without bothering their friends and family."

Cyr has since gotten married and now has two children. He says his wife is "a special person to put up with someone who has panic attacks, can't sleep at night, won't sleep in the bed and just has serious rage sometimes."

On a day-to-day basis, Cyr believes he's functioning better, but said he also realizes there's no "cure" for PTSD, just treatment and strategies for managing it better.

"Things are OK, but every day is really affected by it," he said. "Post-traumatic stress is invisible. It's an injury to your emotions and it's lifelong, forever lasting."

105

On the Spectrum, Looking Out

Jess Watsky

My world was changed for the better by a big, technical book, called *The Diagnostic and Statistical Manual of Mental Disorders*. Looking back, I never expected to be at odds with the very publication that opened my eyes to my mind's inner workings. When I was thirteen, flipping through the pages of my mother's copy of the DSM IV-TR, the name of one "mental disorder" stuck out like a sore thumb, enticing peals of laughter from me and my friends—*Asperger's Syndrome*. Though it shouldn't have been a surprise, coming from a child whose idea of fun with friends was to look through psychology diagnostic manuals, it was both a shock and a comfort to be diagnosed a year later from that very same section of the very same book.

Because "Asperger's" was described, my world was a little more transparent. It unveiled some of the intricacies in my own mind that had seemed unexplained. The clearly defined obsessions, ranging from a six-month flirt with marbles to a three-year binge on molecular gastronomy, now had a name—"repetitive interests and obsessions"—and my childhood propensity for big words and inability to comprehend idioms was no longer simply a foible of my past. Even if I didn't feel like Rain Man, I now had a name for the many quirks to my mannerisms that had plagued me for the last decade and a half. Needing to go to three

different grocery stores to make sure I hadn't missed any interesting foods was no longer the end result of anxiety, but a starting point, an issue I had the tools to confront and stop in its tracks before I ran my car out driving to other states in search of unique food.

I know this diagnosis has soothed people's fears as well as my own, and served as a jumping ground to plot their next move, just as it has certainly done for me. My Asperger's diagnosis helped me to learn about boundaries and conversational norms, allowed me to rethink my inner-arguments and has given me time to pause and think about what I say, rather than reverting to a repetitive monopoly of a conversation. Without the diagnosis, it felt as though I had been working with a consistently clever, yet idiosyncratic machine for many years without having even a manual or well-versed technician alongside to help me troubleshoot.

That's not to say that things were immediately easier for me. I still struggled in school, unable to foster interactions with peers. When I explained to many of them that I wasn't just strange and had, in fact, an inability to interact as they did, my confession was met with derision. It is a cruel twist of irony that a disorder centering on a social hindrance would don the incredibly clunky—but for me, helpful—moniker of "Asperger's Syndrome." But now, for its new edition, *The Diagnostic and Statistical Manual of Mental Disorders* plans to eliminate the diagnosis of Asperger's Syndrome as a stand-alone condition, and to merge it into the more generalized description of Autism Spectrum Disorder (ASD). This puts me at odds with the very publication that opened my eyes to my mind's inner workings. Although I have prospered through many hardships both socially and academically as a result of working with my Asperger's Syndrome, the new approach may mean that I may not fit the diagnostic criteria for ASD and will not be eligible for related health insurance coverage needs. In fact, in reviewing the proposed diagnostic standards for ASD, for all intents and purposes I fit only three of the four criteria necessary for a diagnosis. Certainly, that is sufficient evidence of a dysfunction, yet not enough (one must meet all four) to receive a diagnosis of ASD. In the eyes of the American Psychiatric Association, as of May 2013 I will cease to have Asperger's Syndrome or ASD.

With this change, thousands of successfully and well-functioning Asperger's-diagnosed adults, and many, many more undiagnosed children, will lose a diagnosis and a name to put to their unique, curious lives. In May of 2013, I am anxiously anticipating another life-changing event, because in that same month I will be graduating from college with a bachelor's degree in History. Although my mental abilities always foretold a future with college, I'm sure that if I hadn't been diagnosed with Asperger's Syndrome, I wouldn't have excelled so well and taught myself to fluently navigate the turbulent university atmosphere. I wouldn't be writing this, thinking about this, realizing my dreams without this key component of my brain.

The changes in the DSM-IV are only one variable in the complicated equation of what it means to have Asperger's Syndrome. The rest is up to society to read words like mine and listen to the people they interact with and understand them. Meet us at face value without forcing us to make eye contact or expect an immediate adherence to your social customs and understand that we are people with different wiring, but similar desires. It is not solely a dream of the Aspergian to want to live in a world where they are accepted and appreciated for their unique talents. People automatically perceive disabilities to be something automatically visible or detectable from their conceptions of "normal" people. It hurts to be told we blend seamlessly into the world, but that we are shunned because of how we work inside. Capture that feeling and meet us with compassion and know that reaching out to us is important. We are not emotionless robots, nor are we calculating sociopaths as some would believe. Nor should we be pigeonholed into relationships with other Aspergians solely because the rest of the world has overlooked us. We have just as much of a right to coexist in society as anyone else, and have the potential to change the

world in amazing ways. Regardless of formal status or legal terminology, there are still thousands of people in this world with Asperger's Syndrome, whose identities have been enhanced and helped with such a diagnosis, and we will not vanish simply because our name has gone away. We cannot disappear. We are people, too.

106

How to Curse in Sign Language

Ashley and Deborah

. . .

When I arrived at Starbucks, I saw Deborah, sitting alone, not drinking any coffee. She appeared to be in her midforties and was wearing tapered jeans and white shoes. She looked like a nurse who was exhausted after working the night shift. Raising a child like Ashley, I thought, she must feel fatigued all the time. She sat in her chair like someone who had been standing for years.

I sat down and introduced myself. There was no small talk. Deborah started right in with her story. She had grown up in a rural setting, in Virginia Beach, in a middle-class Catholic home. The household income was just enough to meet the family's needs. Deborah had a twin brother, and their extended family was large. Family gatherings often included more than seventy-five people, "nudging and talking over each other," she told me. "I loved it."

. . .

The problems continued even after the birth of their son, Chip. Finally, after months of drama and upheaval, Deborah—with the support of an Episcopal minister—filed for divorce, went to court, and eventually got custody of her son.

Ashley came into Deborah's life through an announcement posted at a local United Methodist church not long after she and her young son had moved to Richmond. Deborah was trying to rebuild her life. She was working in computers, a career she had set in motion when she was still a cop, and completed her bachelor's degree in computer science while working full-time. She was also taking an exercise class at the aforementioned church. One day, she arrived early, thirty minutes before her class began. To kill time, she stood around reading various postings on the church bulletin board. The tip of a yellow piece of paper, burled under the rest, caught her eye, and she uncovered an announcement from the United Methodist Family Services. This organization was holding an adoption information program for people who might consider "challenging" adoptions. She decided to attend the session just to "see what the group had to say."

. . .

After the meeting, Deborah signed up for a nine-week training session followed by what is known as a "home study." This training was a prerequisite for going any further in the adoption process. According to Deborah, "the leaders of the training didn't pull any punches and shared the very difficult things involved in the adoption of special-needs or older children." Many of these children would need lifelong care. Many would require advanced medical supervision at home. Many would have emotional problems. But after each session, Deborah "felt even more strongly about adoption as an option." Most people

who have gone through the adoption process consider the home study to be the most difficult. It requires the prospective parent to undergo multiple background checks, physical exams, and a financial audit; to obtain three letters of recommendation; to write an autobiography; and to submit to three unannounced home inspections by a social worker. Deborah passed the home study with an almost perfect score, and then, in her words, "the search began."

It lasted over a year and a half. Deborah was looking for a child with physical disabilities, not a child with emotional challenges. Here and there were children who could be a good match, but they always went to another family. "I began to wonder," Deborah said, "if I had read my 'leading' incorrectly." She was on the verge of giving up when she got a call from her social worker about Ashley. Deborah was one of two finalists vetted from a field of eighty-five. "Don't expect much," the social worker said. "Ashley looks different. She is not the cutest baby around."

Ashley had been born to an alcoholic, anorexic mother fourteen weeks prematurely. She weighed just over one and a half pounds, and her medical birth records state that she smelled of alcohol when she was delivered. A liver biopsy was performed right after her birth, and it showed that a tumor was present. She also had a "brain bleed." Even more threatening to Ashley's health was a rare condition she had, called Juvenile Xanthogranulomas, which cause tumors to form all over the body. These tumors, according to Deborah, "formed on Ashley's skin, under her skin, on her eyes and ears, on other vital organs, and on her brain."

Deborah and her social worker drove to Ashley's foster mother's apartment. Deborah was warned again about Ashley's condition. At that point, Ashley was about eighteen months old and had just been through surgery to have her first brain tumor removed. She was a "failure to thrive" baby, which meant she ate nothing and only drank a little milk. The apartment was nice enough, Deborah remembers, but had a hushed feeling.

After the introduction and pleasantries, the foster mother pointed to a crib. The three women walked over together, and Deborah peered down at the baby she was told was not quite normal. But that is not what she saw. "I thought she was beautiful," Deborah recalled. "Her left eye, because of glaucoma, was about twice the size of her right eye. And although that skewed the symmetry of her face, she had a smile that lit up the room! She was not the least bit intimidated by having three extra people in her small space and was quite friendly with everyone. She let everyone hold her, and as we all talked and cooed to her, she explored everyone's face with her hands."

Deborah walked away from the crib and pulled the social worker aside. "I love that baby," she said. "I would very much like her to be a part of my family." . . .

Ashley's early struggle for life was far from over. She had a second brain tumor removed just before she turned two years old. Soon, she also had her gallbladder removed because of a tumor, and there was another one forming between her ears and brain. Ashley also had a seizure disorder. On top of all that, she was deaf and blind. Most of us would have seen Ashley's life as either not worth living or pitiful. Deborah saw something different. Deborah saw her as nothing exceptional, as just a little baby.

. . .

After coffee, I followed Deborah to her house in the burbs. It was a typical suburban house with a slight difference. Out front was a large street sign that said *deaf-blind child area*. Once inside, Deborah gave me the obligatory tour, the dining room, the kids' rooms, and the kitchen, with its linoleum floor and faux wood cabinets. I noted that Deborah had a peaceful, quiet way about her when she wasn't talking about Ashley's struggles. Anger did not have a place in her world. Faith played a huge role in Deborah's life. As we walked through her house she told me that finding a church that was welcoming to Ashley had

been nearly impossible. The world—even churches, it seemed—shared my fear of people like Ashley and all of its subtle manifestations.

"When I have tried to take her into the service with me," Deborah said, "I am constantly asked to take her out because of the noises she makes and her overall restless nature. It is always the same old story—Ashley appears and acts different from others in the church. It really saddens me." This actually wasn't surprising. Most of the major religions of the world have a long history of associating disability with sin, evil, or the devil. The Church has often been one of the leading institutions to dehumanize people on the wrong side of normal.

. . .

Ashley had had terrible experiences at her regular public school. Referring to Ashley's school trouble, Deborah said, "You know, they are often afraid of Ashley, some of the kids and the teachers. They treat her sometimes as if she is contagious." I nodded my head, feeling ashamed for understanding their feelings. "They *stare*."

These gazes, according to Deborah, were some of the most painful things that she and her daughter endured together. "Surgeries or any medical procedures are things that hurt, but only for a short while," Deborah continued. "The pain of rejection, the pain of being thought of as somehow a 'broken' or inferior person, the pain of ridicule or derision doesn't go away." These experiences "were ten times as painful as her surgeries."

At the time of my visit, Ashley was attending a wonderful school called the Starling Child Care and Learning Complex. . . .

This institution was also committed to a policy of inclusion. As we walked through the halls, I saw many students with disabilities. Ashley was in a fully inclusive, mixed-age classroom. When Deborah and I arrived, the class was having lunch. "There is my little girl," Deborah said, pointing across the small kids' desks, her face illuminated with the first smile I saw all day. I followed the trajectory of Deborah's outstretched hand and saw a little girl who struck me as strong, not sickly at all. She had a body that looked at least twelve years old. "She's a good eater," Deborah said. "Isn't she beautiful?"

I didn't answer the question. Not because I disagreed with Deborah, but because I really had no way to make sense out of Ashley. I didn't see Ashley as a whole. It was as if all I could take in were parts of her. She was wearing a red dress, and her hair was short and black. Her right eye was smaller than its counterpart and was glassy and colorless. She walked around the lunch table like a spinning top that had lost its centrifugal force. She made strange noises, which ranged in pitch from a low hum to an ear-piercing scream. Ashley heard nothing but felt vibrations.

I hoped Deborah didn't notice, but I was staring at Ashley. Not a genial get-to-know-you kind of glance, but a deeply dehumanizing stare, the kind of look that Deborah had talked about earlier. This is the type of stare that people with physical disabilities are very familiar with. But I didn't know how to stop. I didn't know how to make sense out of Ashley. I am ashamed to write this, but a part of me wondered if Ashley and I belonged to the same species.

Ashley confronted me with my own deep prejudices about what it means to be a valuable human being. I didn't know if I could truly value a body that was so damaged. Ashley also challenged some of my ideas about intelligence. If Ashley couldn't hear, speak, or see, how could she learn? And if Ashley couldn't learn, was she a fully functioning member of the human race?

Unfortunately, my reaction to Ashley is not without historical precedent. The history of the deaf, blind, and the deaf/blind is a story of being seen as less than human. . . .

It was Aristotle's contention that, of all the senses, hearing contributed most to intelligence and knowledge. This led Aristotle to characterize deaf individuals as senseless and incapable of reason. Much of the early marginalization of the deaf had to do with religious

mythology. The ability to speak was considered a gift from the breath of God. Without speech, the deaf were denied moral status. Even during the Enlightenment, a period defined by questioning religious beliefs, the deaf were denied full humanity. . . .

As we waited for Ashley, Deborah talked about how her daughter was treated. "My experience has been that people will try to avoid that which they do not understand. So many people look at Ashley, see the physical differences in her, and assume that everything else about her is different, *and inferior*. What they don't see is the warmth and compassion inside her, her ability to forgive and forget all the slights from other people, her drive to experience everything she possibly can, her love of nature, and her gentleness around babies and young children."

. . .

At this point in our day, it was time for Ashley's language instruction, a mix of American Sign Language (ASL), touch sign, and speech therapy. Later, I asked Deborah about sign language and about whether Ashley's blindness prevented her from using it. Deborah reminded me that while Ashley has no vision at all in her left eye, the vision in her right eye is 20/2000. This means she can focus at about one to two inches from her face. Deborah elaborated: "She does her signing directly in front of her body, and if she perceives the person to whom she is signing is not paying attention, she will gently put her hands on both sides of their face and move their face to look at her."

Ashley's language instructor came right up to me and introduced herself. "I'm Theresa," she said as she shook my hand. Theresa was in her late thirties and was a large, joyful woman. She seemed like a natural educator, and had a son with a learning disability who struggled with learning to read and write.

"I think that helps me when I work with Ashley," she said. "You know, a struggle with language is a struggle with language whether you're deaf-blind or not. "Theresa then turned her attention to her student, signing something to Ashley who signed back. But because I don't know ASL, I had no idea what was being communicated. "I asked her if she was ready to work," Theresa translated. "What did she say?" I asked. "What would any kid say? No, of course," Theresa reported.

I spent the next twenty minutes watching Theresa, trying to understand what she could see, but I could not. Deborah pointed out that the first thing Theresa did when she saw Ashley was smile. I didn't smile when I first saw Ashley, thinking that Ashley couldn't see my expression. Deborah laughed when I mentioned this to her. "To Ashley, your body can't lie." Ashley could feel a smile even if she couldn't see it. After Theresa smiled at Ashley, she touched her on her arm and then got down close to Ashley's stronger eye. She spoke and signed, "Good afternoon." Then she asked, "How are you?"

Theresa was vigilant about letting Ashley know what was going on in her environment. She signed and told Ashley what was on the floor, what chairs had been moved, what time the bell would ring. According to Deborah, this is essential. "One of the biggest potential sources for stress and frustration for Ashley is not being aware of something, especially something that would impact her. She needs access to the environment."

. . .

But like many deaf children, Ashley has had, at best, limited access to signing class-rooms. When Ashley started school at the age of two and a half, she was in a classroom led by a teacher who signed with the other signing children. According to Deborah, after one year the school district abolished all signing classes and reassigned the teachers to classes for children with cochlear implants, which are a huge issue in the deaf community. The National Institutes of Health describes a cochlear implant as "a small electronic device that can help to provide a sense of sound to a person who is profoundly deaf or severely hard-of-hearing. The implant consists of an external portion that sits behind the ear and a second portion that is surgically placed under the skin." Many in the deaf community

believe, however, that cochlear implants are a nefarious form of cultural genocide for the deaf. The essence of deaf culture is its language—sign language. Implants threaten to suck the life out of ASL.

Teachers are now told to emphasize speech and not to sign. Lipreading was also actively discouraged or prevented. "Classroom teachers were instructed to cover their mouths when they spoke so the children would not be able to read their lips," Deborah said. "The entire emphasis was on getting the children to adjust to their implants and learn to 'hear' and speak." Children without implants, which are initially painful and not always effective, were moved into segregated classrooms with children who had a myriad of other disabilities. Without signing support, according to Deborah, "the education of those children like Ashley suffered greatly. Many formative years were lost, and I'm not sure they will ever be made up."

. . .

What is the cost of teaching speech versus developing Ashley's mind and communication skills through ASL? Research is unequivocal: Deaf and deaf-blind children who acquire signing early have the best educational outcomes. Without signing, education becomes limited. "The school would like to pigeonhole Ashley as incapable of doing academic work," Deborah said, "Rather, they do things like learning to cook, community trips, and learning to clean up." A policy of emphasizing speech for these children is really a policy of forced assimilation of a unique minority group.

"It has been my experience," said Deborah, "that the school staff expects the children to change and is determined to help 'fix' them. The sad thing in my mind is that these children are not 'broken' and do not need fixing." . . .

Before the end of the language lesson Deborah tapped my shoulder and pointed to Ashley. "Do you see that?" she asked me. I didn't know what she was talking about, so I just shrugged my shoulders. "She's laughing. Take a close look."

I looked to the other side of the room. I watched Ashley's face, not her awkward gait or her colorless eye, but her whole face. Her face looked like a Picasso, a face held together with its own inherently savage beauty. Deborah was right; Ashley was laughing. And so was Theresa. I looked back at Deborah, and she was laughing too. Everyone was in on the joke except me. "What's so funny," I asked. "Oh nothing," Deborah said. I pressed her again. "Well, I don't want you to think less of Ashley, but Ashley just cursed us all out in sign language," said her mother. "She has a problem with that; we're working on it." . . .

I ended my day with Deborah and Ashley back at their home. The plan was to have dinner with the family: Ashley; her brother, Chip; and Deborah. Deborah had invited me to dinner at the beginning of the day, when we sat talking at Starbucks, and I had lied, saying I had somewhere I needed to be. But now I wouldn't have missed a dinner with this family for the world. Deborah and I had some time to kill before the rest of the family got home. So before dinner we sat around and talked about Ashley's experiences, the power of language, and the importance of inclusion. When we got onto the latter topic, Deborah told me a story that she had already shared with me over e-mail and in a phone conversation. In fact, she had already shared this story with me during our day together. It was as if this story was somehow the essence of her and Ashley's struggle.

It was the Christmas season, December 2002. That night, Deborah and the kids piled into their car and headed to the elementary school for the big holiday show. Ashley had been given a part. This was huge. Ashley was educated in a fully segregated special educational room, but on this night she would be on the stage with the rest of the kids. She was given a tiny baby rattle that she was supposed to shake at various times during the performance with the prompting of her aide. That's all the teachers thought she was capable of, but Deborah went along with the plan. At least Ashley would be on the stage.

Deborah and Chip sat in the makeshift auditorium, on steel-blue chairs. She had her camera in hand, just like all the other parents. When the lights went out, Ashley walked on the stage with the rest of the kids. She wobbled a little, but she found her spot. These things matter, Deborah thought. These small moments of inclusion. Sure, it's just a first-grade holiday program. But if Ashley can't be here, what's next? Who gets to draw these lines, and where would they stop? No, this night, this act of inclusion mattered, Deborah thought. She poised her camera and sat on the edge of her seat.

Then it happened. Before the program began, Ashley was placed three feet to the side of the group. Her aide stood next to her, holding her hand. The aide did not know touch sign or American Sign Language, Ashley's primary forms of communication. The only way Ashley would have to communicate would be to grip the aide's hand harder.

The first song was "Frosty the Snowman." Ashley waited for her cue, a slight touch on the hand, to shake the rattle. As the kids sang, she swayed. The aide seemed nervous, but when the time for Ashley's part came, she shook the rattle with force. Deborah was filled with a sense of pride. When the first song was over, there were more songs to come, but not for Ashley. The aide led her off the stage. Deborah wondered why. What was going on? Why was she leaving? Ashley was supposed to stay on stage for the whole night. That had been the plan all along, but someone didn't want Ashley on the stage for the whole performance. As they escorted Ashley off the stage and out of the auditorium, a parent in a fancy coat stopped the aide and, looking right past Ashley, said, "Good job." To the aide.

. . .

Ashley lived in a world without sight or sound, but she had heightened senses of smell, of taste, of touch. As Deborah explained to me, "If Ashley doesn't recognize a particular food on her plate, she smells it first. If she is looking for new clothes, she runs her hands down the fabric first to see if it is something that feels like she wants it to feel." We should not underestimate the power of touch. The philosopher Jean-Jacques Rousseau believed that touch was the essence of an ethical life; touch defined our humanity.

. . .

Before I said my good-byes I asked Deborah if she had anything she could give me to help me remember our day. She left the room and came back holding a photograph of Ashley sitting on the beach. "I just love this picture," she said as she handed it to me. "This is my beautiful little girl. Feeling everything."

That picture was taken in the late summer of 2002 at Virginia Beach. It was a few days before school started. Deborah, who had fond memories of the beach, had saved a little money for a vacation. She got her family a hotel room right on the ocean, so the kids could see the sun rise. On the last day of their holiday, they went out on the beach at sunset. Deborah's twin brother, a photographer, was there. Ashley had been to other bodies of water before—lakes, rivers—but she had never been to the ocean. She stepped onto the sand, wobbled a little, as everyone does on the beach, and started walking toward the ocean. But fifty feet or so from the water, she stopped and put her hands out. Other kids were running around in the sand, whining about the cold, asking to go home and eat ice cream, but not Ashley. She stood there in a world of vibration and taste and touch, "relishing every sensory experience."

After a while, Ashley walked up to the line where the ocean meets the sand and sat down. The reaching palms of the surf touched the tips of her toes and she lifted her hands to feel the wind and salt spray. She sat like that for five minutes on the edge of the world, the sea, a shifting line, its edges never anywhere for long. Ashley pressed her hands out like she was feeling someone's face. When a wave washed up on shore, the spray lifted off the water and the ocean came to her toes and then her shins. She laughed in a pitch somewhere between a scream and a song.

107

What I'd Tell That Doctor

Jason Kingsley

I am Jason Kingsley. I am now almost twenty-nine years old. Ten years ago I wrote an article for *Count Us In: Growing Up with Down Syndrome*, a book that Mitchell Levitz and I wrote. That article is about a confrontation I would have had with the obstetrician—if I had met him—about what he said years ago to my parents when I was born.

What I would say to the obstetrician is the same as what I would say to the parents of any newborn child who is born with a disability and who is born with Down syndrome.

The things I said ten years ago are true now and even more so.

When I wrote that article, I was still in school. But now I am on my own. I live in a house with two other roommates. We have very little supervision. We do our own cooking; we do our own shopping and cleaning. We do take public transportation. And above all else, our house is accessible to the community and to our work.

All three of us work in the community. I happen to work in the White Plains (New York) Public Library. My roommate Raymond works at PETCO, a pet store, and has been there for six years. And Yaniv works at an Armonk (New York) law firm.

In conclusion, I hope you will look at this article that I wrote ten years ago. Then get *Count Us In: Growing Up with Down Syndrome* and read the whole thing. You will find it very essential, inspiring, and helpful.

Here is my article:

When I was born, the obstetrician said that I cannot learn, never see my mom and dad and never learn anything and send me to an institution. Which I think it was wrong.

Today we were talking about if I could see my obstetrician and talk to him, here are things I would say . . .

I would say, "People with disabilities *can learn*!"

Then I would tell the obstetrician how smart I am. Like learning new languages, going to other foreign nations, going to teen groups and teen parties, going to cast parties, becoming independent, being . . . a lighting board operator, an actor, the backstage crew. I would talk about history, math, English, algebra, business math, global studies. One thing I forgot to tell the obstetrician is I plan to get a academic diploma when I pass my RCTs . . .

I performed in "The Fall Guy" and even wrote this book! He never imagined how I could write a book! I will send him a copy . . . so he'll know.

I will tell him that I play the violin, that I make relationships with other people, I make oil paintings, I play the piano, I can sing, I am competing in sports, in the drama group, that I have many friends, and I have a full life.

So I want the obstetrician will never say that to any parent to have a baby with a disability any more. If you send a baby with a disability to an institution, the baby will miss all the opportunities to grow and to learn . . . and also to receive a diploma. The baby will miss relationships and love and independent living skills. Give a baby with a disability a chance to grow a full life. To experience a half-full glass instead of the half-empty glass. And think of your abilities not your disability.

108

In the LD Bubble

Lynn Pelkey

. . .

As much as I want to find the perfect words to express what it is like to be dyslexic, I cannot. I can no more make you understand what it is like to be dyslexic than you can make me understand what it is like not to be. I can only guess and imagine. For years, I have looked out, wanting to be normal, to shed the skin that limits me, that holds me back. All the while, others have looked upon me, as well. There were those who have pitied me and those who have just given up on me, those who stood by, supporting me and believing in me, and those who looked at me as if I were an exhibit at the zoo. But, in general, people have shown a desire to understand what dyslexia is and how to teach those afflicted with it. Each side, it seems, longs to understand the other.

My dyslexia is like a bubble. I am enclosed in an invisible sheath that allows me to come excitingly close to being "normal" but never completely there. It is flexible yet confining. I can move within it but never outside of it. You cannot see it, but I can feel it. It has thick walls that are impossible to break free from. Sometimes, I hardly know it is there at all, and other times I have felt as if it were suffocating me, killing me.

I invite you into my world for two reasons. One is the hope that you will gain some insight, understanding, compassion, or even strength. I also write for myself in the hope that this process will help me to love myself for who I am and all that I can be. For, you see, I believe I was taught to hate myself.

"Dyslexia" is a label and only a label, but it carries so much negative weight. Had I been described as "gifted and talented," this, too, would have meant dealing with a label, but a positive one. Why must LD categories be classified around negative attributes? Can we not focus on strengths or positive attributes? As a child, my foundation for hating myself grew out of my much noted shortcomings and a lack of any abilities deemed positive.

I cannot remember my infancy, but I doubt very much that I hated myself then. My memories of my early years of childhood are happy. I was loved, and I felt loved. It was during my elementary school years that I started to feel different from the other children. It was discovered that reading and writing were difficult for me. I began some special programs designed to assist in my learning process. On the playground, in gym and art classes, or playing games, I was the same as any other child, but academically I could not achieve what other children could. As academics took on a more important role in my daily life, being with my playmates became less than pleasurable. We were no longer equal. At times, I was physically separated from my classmates. During these times, I was brought to the "special" room where I would receive help with my school work in hopes of bringing me "up to my class level." No one ever said this to me directly; it was what I overheard: "She is not doing as well as the other children," "She is having difficulty," "Scoring low," "Not trying," "Lazy." I knew the latter two were not true, but they certainly did not make me feel good about myself. It was in these ways that I became *less than*.

. . .

At first, the gap between me and my classmates was small. However, it was not long before I was ashamed of myself. I would compare myself to those around me. My performance was always less, the lowest, the bottom of the class. As the years passed, the gap

grew, and the shame turned to deep-rooted self-hate. The gap, the shame, and the self-hate were not just my doing. Others, too, perceived me as "less than," and they taught me to accept their perceptions. Other students did not have any trouble telling me what was wrong with me, "Stupid," "Mental," "Idiot." I had to go to the "Retard Room" for a lot of my classes. This classroom was different from all the other classrooms. The doors were metal, and they had a long, thin window, which made it difficult to see in or out of the room. This had some advantages, because once you were inside, people in the hallways could not see you. The trick was getting into the room. I would usually hang out across the hall, by the entrance to the library, until after the second bell, waiting for a chance when the coast was clear. Then, quick as a dart, I would run into the room. In an arc printed across the top of the door in big black letters was "Remedial Reading." RR. The Retard Room.

The normal class had neat little rows of wooden-topped desks with metal blue legs facing the front of the classroom. The teacher's desk and the blackboard looked back at them. Above the blackboards were rolled up maps of far-off places that would snap up like the shades in my bedroom. The rooms were quiet in color. I always wanted to be in one of those rooms.

The RR was different. We had one large room about the size of two normal rectangular tables. Our tables did not face the front of the room but were randomly placed throughout the room. Our blackboard was on wheels, and it was mostly used as a partition to separate us from each other. We did not have any maps; I guess they felt there was not a need to teach us that kind of stuff because we wouldn't need it for the types of lives that we would lead. It was during a humiliating episode with my cousin that I learned that Massachusetts was a state and not a country. The RR was cheerfully decorated, the bulletin boards were covered with construction paper in bright and happy colors. The decorations and colors would change to correspond with the seasons. The curtain that divided the room had been embroidered with a sort of spring scene. It was all very cute, like kindergarten. This room only fortified my feelings that I was dumb. Something was very wrong. All the other kids my age were growing up, but I was still in kindergarten. I felt humiliated going in and out of that room.

. . .

During junior high, I did have a few regular classes such as science, art, and gym, but the rest of my time was spent in the Retard Room. I do not recall exactly the first day that I entered the remedial reading room at the junior high school, but I do remember an assortment of feelings associated with being there: fear, anxiety, uncertainty, and many more. I did not have one positive feeling about going into that room. Just me and the guys. What a group! Maybe about ten of us, ranging in types and degrees of disabilities. One girl (me) and the rest boys. That's right, I was the only girl in the whole school that was stupid, and it remained that way until I graduated.

. . .

Being LD must be similar to how some gay people feel. You spend so much time and energy trying to hide who you really are. You are ashamed of what you are, and at times you long to be like others, but you are who you are, and so you lead this double life. Some know you as LD, and others know you as one of them, but you are not one of them. You are just pretending. You hate yourself for being LD, and you hate yourself for being a fake. And in the end, who are you? It is all very confusing. All the while you really just want to be you, without any fears. We LDs live a life of deceit—pretending to be like others—and shame—not wanting to be who we are.

My self-efficacy, my belief about my competence, fell into the category of failure-accepting. I expected to fail, so I set no goals, believing my ability was set (I had none). Thus, I learned helplessness. Everything was black and white, with no grey areas. There

was good and evil, positive and negative, and, of course, smart and dumb. As I grew, I started to believe the negative stereotypes associated with my academic abilities. I was stupid! I couldn't do it! I accepted these stereotypes and let them define me. I erased myself. I hid who I was out of shame. I also had a growing fear of the unknown. What was really wrong with me? There had to be a reason and an explanation for why I was the way I was. Would it get worse as I got older? Was this it? Was I retarded? I was not sure that I wanted the answers to these questions. Eventually, I turned my back on academics.

. . .

Not long ago, it became very clear to me that I would have to come face-to-face with my feelings about being stupid if I was going to find peace within myself. Four years ago, my mother encouraged me to go with her to an open house at a local community college, the same college that I had flunked out of ten years earlier. I agreed to go, but I had no intention to sign up. I went just to satisfy her, to say that I went. I started to talk to a woman about my diagnosis, and she guaranteed me that if I wanted to learn, they could and would teach me. The next thing I knew, I was agreeing to give college another try. I can still remember sitting in class the first day and thinking to myself, "How long are you going to carry on this charade?" I was certain that I would last only about a week or two. But, I kept hanging in there. I was facing the monsters of my past. I was no longer going to be held back. I had to admit what I was. I heard myself saying out loud to my professors that I had dyslexia. It's not that it all came easy to me, because it didn't. Saying it made it very real. All the promises that were made to me on that open house day didn't quite pan out. I was supposed to have my books on tape, have extra time to do assignments, and be given untimed tests. This all sounded good, but it took a lot of work and persistence to get the things that I needed. I really learned to become an advocate for myself. I no longer fell into the role of helplessness; I knew that if I did, I wouldn't make it. As the semester went on, I realized that I wanted this. Not only did I want to succeed, but I wanted to be one of the best. I had a goal.

No longer were my classrooms "special." They were real. I was with real students. At first, I did not say anything, because I was sure that they must be so much smarter than me. After all, this was college, someplace I thought I would never be. As time passed, I realized that I wasn't the dummy in the class. The professor would ask a question, I would have an answer in my head, and most of the time someone would say what I was thinking. I wasn't so different after all. In time, I began to ask questions or respond to those asked. And I was learning, right along with the normal students. The gap that was once about the size of the Grand Canyon was beginning to close. I couldn't believe it when my fellow students asked me for help. This sounds very childish, but it was an experience that I had missed out on as a child, and it was a wonderful feeling. I was not worthless, and my opinion mattered. My success at that college was a milestone for me. Not only did I graduate with an Associate's Degree, but I did so with honors.

My success at the community college gave me the strength to believe in myself enough to continue my education. So here I am, a junior at a four-year college with a goal. Being LD has become less important to me. There are arrangements that I make due to my disability so that I am able to learn, but no one is giving me the answers. I certainly don't get a free ride. I don't have a tattoo on my forehead saying that I am dyslexic, but I don't hide it either.

In junior high school, being LD was a big part of my life. At that time, the universe revolved around me. I was my biggest concern. I was self-centered. My world consisted of very little, and so being LD was a big part of who I was. But as I became older, I grew out of the self-centered mode and into a more complex way of being. As my life evolved, being LD became a smaller piece of the whole.

Above all, I thank my parents for their unconditional love and support. I am fortunate to have had parents who emphasized my attributes rather than my shortcomings. They always saw in me what others could not, and they taught me to love myself for what I could do. It is from their encouragement that I found the strength to face my fears and become who I am. While my disability will last my lifetime, it no longer has to limit me.

I now strive to see myself as my parents see me.

109

Toward Ending Ableism in Education

Thomas Hehir

There is much that educators, parents, and advocates can do toward ending ableism in education. As is the case with racism and sexism, progress toward equity is dependent first and foremost on the acknowledgment that ableism exists in schools. The examples given here have centered around three disability groups: the deaf, the blind and visually impaired, and the learning disabled. However, I believe that deconstructing dominant educational practices applied to other disability groups can yield similar results. Ableist assumptions and practices are deeply embedded in schooling. Further, the absence of discussion and dearth of scholarly inquiry within mainstream educational circles concerning the effects of ableism is stunning.

Though the lack of attention to ableism in schooling is unfortunate, activists within the disability community have long recognized its impact. Therefore, as more adults with disabilities take on more powerful roles in society and seek to influence schooling, the attention to these issues will hopefully increase. In addition to this political force, the lack of acceptable educational outcomes for large numbers of children with disabilities in an era of standards-based reform should force a reexamination of current practices. Fortunately, there is a foundation in both research and practice upon which to build a better future. Schools can take action now. I offer the following suggestions:

Include disability as part of schools' overall diversity efforts. Schools are increasingly recognizing the need to explicitly address diversity issues as the country becomes more racially and ethnically diverse. Some schools are expanding diversity efforts to include disability. Recently, a local high school student with Down's syndrome, whom I had met at a school assembly devoted to issues of disability rights, addressed one of my classes. She stated, "There are all kinds of kids at my school: Black kids, Puerto Rican kids, gay and lesbian kids. Meagan uses a wheel chair. Matt's deaf, and I have Down's syndrome. It's all diversity." Her high school has done a great job of including disabled kids and has incorporated discussions about disability in its efforts to address diversity issues. Adults with disabilities address student groups and disability is presented in a natural way. Students learn about people with disabilities who have achieved great things as well as those who live ordinary lives. People with disabilities are not presented in a patronizing or stereotypical manner. Deaf people are not "hearing challenged" nor are people with mental retardation "very special." Ableism is not the norm; disability is dealt with in a

straightforward manner. In schools like this, students with disabilities learn about their disabilities and learn how to be self-advocates.

Encourage disabled students to develop and use skills and modes of expression that are most effective and efficient for them. This article has sought to demonstrate that the strong preference within society, reflected in school practice, to have disabled students perform in the same way that nondisabled children perform can ultimately be handicapping for some students. This is not to say that it is not desirable for disabled kids to be able to perform in the way nondisabled kids perform. For instance, deaf students who can read lips have a competitive advantage in a hearing world. However, assuming that most deaf children can develop elaborate language through oral methods has been proven false, and employing these methods without allowing for the natural development of language almost assures poor language development. What may appear to be a paradox to some is that a deaf child who has well-developed language through learning ASL from birth may actually have a higher likelihood of reading lips because he simply has a larger vocabulary. The problem is not, therefore, in the natural desire of parents and educators to have children be able to perform in a typical manner, but rather the missed educational opportunities many disabled kids experience because of a lack of regard for what are often disability-specific modes of learning and expression.

. . .

Move away from the current obsession with placement toward an obsession with results. The movement to include greater numbers of students with disabilities, particularly those with significant cognitive disabilities, in regular education classes has had a profound effect on the education of students with disabilities. Over the past decade, more and more students with disabilities are educated for more of the day in regular education classrooms.

The inclusion movement in education has supported the overall disability movement's goal of promoting societal integration, using integration in schooling as a means to achieve this result. In 1977, disability activists took over federal offices in San Francisco for twenty-five days, demanding that regulations for implementing Section 504 of the Rehabilitation Act, the first federal act to broadly ban discrimination based on disability, be released. Of particular concern to the protesters were leaked draft regulations that provided for separate segregated education for disabled students. Judy Heumann, one of these protesters, stated, "We will accept no more segregation." The final rules were revised to encourage integration in schooling, and the newly passed PL 94–142 (later renamed IDEA) incorporated the current requirement that children be educated in the least restrictive environment (i.e., in regular classes as much as is appropriate for the child).

The strong legal preference for placement in regular classes, coupled with the political movement of disability activists and parents, has resulted in significant positive change for students with disabilities, who are moving on to jobs and accessing higher education at unprecedented levels. Virtually every school has had to confront the issue of inclusion as parents seek integration for their children with disabilities. However, like all change movements, inclusion has encountered opposition. Some opposition has reflected deeply held negative attitudes toward people with disabilities similar to that experienced by Joe and Penny Ford when he sought enrollment in first grade. I can recall a principal challenging me in a large public meeting concerning our efforts to promote inclusion in Chicago: "You don't really mean kids who drool in regular classes?" The reaction against the integration of students with significant disabilities into regular schools and classrooms has been so strong that TASH, an advocacy group promoting integration, adopted the slogan, "All means all," which reflects the group's efforts to clarify its goal to promote integration for students with significant disabilities.

Another source of criticism has come from within the disability community. Deaf advocates have expressed concerns over the lack of language development and communication

NEXT STEPS

access many deaf children experience in regular classes. Supported by some of the research cited above, advocates for the learning disabled have questioned the ability of regular education classrooms to provide the intensive help these students need for skill development. These criticisms receive support from research. The NLTS documented that many students integrated into regular education classrooms did not receive much in the way of accommodation or support, and that many who were integrated into regular classes failed, thus increasing their likelihood of dropping out. The issue is so controversial within the community that virtually every disability group has developed a position. A review of websites reveals, for example, TASH's strong support for full inclusion and deep reservation on the part of the Learning Disabilities Association of America (see http://tash.org and www.ldanatl.org).

The controversy over inclusion within the disability community is ultimately dysfunctional and allows those who would limit the rights of students with disabilities to use this as a wedge issue. Fortunately, the community united during the reauthorization of IDEA in 1997 to help prevent a weakening of the act. However, threats to IDEA's fundamental protections remain. In 2001, Congress considered amendments to the Elementary and Secondary Education Act that would enable schools to fully exclude some students with disabilities. In order to fight these regressive provisions, the community must be united.

I believe the lens of ableism provides a useful perspective through which the inclusion issue can be resolved within the disability community. First, there needs to be a recognition that education plays a central role in the integration of disabled people in all aspects of society both by giving children the education they need to compete and by demonstrating to nondisabled children that disability is a natural aspect of life. Central to this role is the need for students with disabilities to have access to the same curriculum provided to nondisabled children. Further, education plays a vital role in building communities in which disabled children should be included. Therefore, for most children with disabilities, integration into regular classes with appropriate accommodations and support should be the norm.

However, the lens of ableism should lead to the recognition that for some students certain disability-related skills might need attention outside the regular classroom. Learning Braille or ASL or how to use a communication device are typically not in the curriculum and might be more efficiently taught outside the mainstream classroom. The dyslexic high school student who needs intensive help in reading may feel deeply self-conscious if such instruction is conducted in front of his nondisabled friends. The 19-year-old student with a significant cognitive disability may need to spend a good deal of time learning to take public transportation, a skill that will ultimately increase her ability to integrate into the community as an adult. Nondisabled students do not spend time in school learning this skill because they learn this easily on their own. The nature of mental retardation is such that this type of learning does not typically happen incidentally; it must be taught over time and within the context in which the skill will be used. Uniting around the goal of societal integration and recognizing that the difference inherent in disability is a positive one that at times gives rise to disability-specific educational needs may help advocates move away from the fight over placement to one that focuses on educational results.

Promote high standards, not high stakes. An important point to reiterate here is that the most damaging ableist assumption is the belief that disabled people are incapable. Therefore, the movement to include students with disabilities in standards-based reforms holds promise. However, high-stakes testing that prevents students from being promoted or from receiving a diploma based on performance on standardized tests is problematic, given the concerns previously cited about basic access to the curricula and those surrounding the construct validity of the tests. In a very real sense, some students with disabilities will have to become nondisabled in order to be promoted or graduate. This is ableism

in the extreme. Thus, a promising movement, standards-based reform, may ultimately reinforce current inequities if performance on high-stakes tests becomes the only means by which disabled students can demonstrate what they know and are able to do. As such, disability advocates should oppose high-stakes testing. It is important to note that disabled students are not the only group for whom high-stakes testing is being questioned. Other groups that have been poorly served by our educational systems, such as children from high-poverty backgrounds and children with limited English proficiency, may be equally harmed by these policies.

. . .

110

Facilitating Transitions to College for Students with Disabilities from Culturally and Linguistically Diverse Backgrounds

Heather A. Oesterreich and Michelle G. Knight

The overrepresentation of working-class African American, Latino/Latina, and Native American students in special education has been well documented and the implications that are raised for identification and intake of students with disabilities has been the focus of special education reform for many years. Even as schools have worked to change how students are identified for special education, special educators continue to see a disproportionate number of working-class African American, Latino/Latina, and Native American students in their caseloads. Disproportionate representation is not a problem because something is inherently wrong with special education; however, placement in special education is linked to a number of negative issues including poor graduation rates, high drop-out rates, and limited access to postsecondary education opportunities. Specifically, the overrepresentation of working-class culturally and linguistically diverse students with disabilities in special education is coupled with an underrepresentation in college attendance. Recent research suggests that disability in combination with other characteristics (e.g., race and class) has a much more powerful effect on educational attainment than any one of these characteristics alone. This article examines how the intersection of race, class, and disability informs the responsibilities of special educators. A diverse set of practices needs to be used with working-class African American, Latino/Latina, and Native American students with disabilities to increase their social and cultural capital and support their prospective college-going identities.

THE LAY OF THE LANDS

Increasing opportunities for educational access to college for underserved populations, including students who are first-generation, working-class, and underrepresented culturally

and linguistically diverse students labeled with a disability, is a priority of K–16 educational systems. Frequently, however, the hectic pace and large caseloads for special education teachers require them to focus on the immediacy of high school completion for their students. Recently, demographic shifts in the college freshman population highlight the growing numbers of students with disabilities entering college. In 2000, 6% of full-time, first-time freshmen who were enrolled in 4-year public and private institutions had disabilities. Although this statistic represents an increase of postsecondary students reporting a disability, it obscures the link between the race and class of students with disabilities in high school and their transition to college. The increase in students with disabilities who attend college is most notable in students labeled with a learning disability (LD). They have increased from 16.1% to 40.4% of college students with disabilities in the past 12 years. Notably, this increase represents a Caucasian, upper-middle class increase in postsecondary attendance and attainment.

This race and class divide leads to a differentiation in the academic college preparation that many affluent, Caucasian students with LD receive, as opposed to that provided to poor, culturally and linguistically diverse students. These students often are labeled with more stigmatizing disabilities within special education. They also are underrepresented as a result of their disability in college preparation courses, including advanced placement courses. In addition, they cannot afford and do not have access to private tutoring and other out-of-school services (e.g., SAT preparation). These discrepancies in access to quality education limit culturally and linguistically diverse students' acquisition of social and cultural capital to assist them in developing college-going identities.

BUILDING SOCIAL AND CULTURAL CAPITAL FOR COLLEGE

Students' social and cultural capital creates differences in college-going identities. Social capital for students with disabilities in relation to college includes the availability of information-sharing networks about college. Cultural capital is the value placed on obtaining a college education and the information available about acquiring one. Special educators' ability to influence working-class African American, Latino/Latina, and Native American students with disabilities' college-going identities and their subsequent success in college is directly related to nurturing social and cultural capital in relation to college. This includes addressing social and economic stratification that exists in society in relation to race, class, and disability; understanding the law; and facilitating the selection of a college with resources and demographics that match students' social, economic, and emotional needs.

ADDRESSING SOCIAL AND ECONOMIC STRATIFICATION

In a society where inequities in college access still reflect racism, classism, and ableism, it is useful to assist students in understanding the economic and social stratification that affects college admittance and completion. Helping students to understand that their life possibility may be situated in structures of oppression while at the same time helping them to challenge the belief of society that they are deficient, disinterested, with confused priorities, and responsible for their own failure to enter college provides youth with disabilities a place to understand the lives that they are living. With facilitation by the special education teacher, students can not only critique social structures but can also be encouraged to become active agents in fighting the social structures by viewing themselves as college material.

UNDERSTANDING THE LAW

Special education teachers must provide the cultural capital about the differences in services provided in K–12 and postsecondary schools. Under Section 504 of the Rehabilitation Act of 1973 and the Americans With Disabilities Act (ADA) of 1990, at the postsecondary level, students must self-identify with the ADA office on a college campus. In addition, they are responsible for the documentation verifying their need for accommodation, making specific requests for accommodations, and meeting the same academic requirements of all other students. This differs dramatically from the K–12 setting, where it is the responsibility of the institution to reach out and identify students in need of special education, pay for the documentation to evaluate these students, and provide specialized programming. If special education teachers do not work with students, particularly working-class, African American, Latino/Latina, and Native American students with disabilities, who are more likely to be first-generation college students, in identifying these fundamental differences between postsecondary and K–12 services, the transition between the two systems can leave students frustrated and isolated without the accommodations that they require to meet the academic standards of postsecondary education.

Becoming advocates. In this legal context, students must advocate in relation to their disabilities. Special education teachers need to work with students to be able to name their disability, understand the nature of their learning difficulties, and know strategies that allow them to negotiate their learning difficulties. Students who learn early on how to state their accommodation needs in functional, real-world terms will be able to help postsecondary institutions effectively accommodate their needs.

College visits. In addition to teaching students about the shift in laws between K–12 and postsecondary institutions, when dealing with first-generation college students, part of fortifying their social and cultural capital lies in the necessity and structure of on-campus visits. These visits must include planned meetings at the ADA office and a presentation by the personnel there to create a sense of accessibility.

Community connections. Providing mentors, role models, community leaders, and speakers to motivate students can raise their social capital and sense of advocacy in making the shift between disability laws. Specifically, these adults should reflect the race, class, and disability status of the students. They can help working-class, culturally and linguistically diverse students with disabilities realize that their college attendance is part of a larger community pattern and that they have been preceded by earlier college graduates and will be followed by others following their example.

Addressing economic limitations. Although connecting to campuses and people is important for working-class culturally and linguistically diverse students with disabilities, the economic realities associated with college tuition, student fees, and cost of living are only compounded by economic burdens implicit within the necessary documentation of a disability. Section 504 of the Rehabilitation Act of 1973 and the ADA Act of 1990 places the burden on the student to provide and pay for appropriate testing and evaluation to document disability. Each postsecondary institution has specific requirements for what constitutes viable documentation, but the minimum standards require the certified qualifications of the evaluator, the types of testing, and other background documents that must be provided. In addition, the evaluation must have been conducted within the last 3 to 5 years. This type of testing can cost from $300 to $3,500.

To help defray the costs of the burden of proof of disability, special education teachers should ensure that their working-class students graduate with a complete, up-to-date battery of tests verifying their disabilities so that these tests can be used by the students in their freshman year of college—and perhaps beyond—as verification of the necessity to them of services from the ADA on campus.

NEXT STEPS

Table 110.1 Teacher Tips for Increasing Social and Cultural Capital for Post-Secondary Education

Social and Cultural Capital	Questions to Ask	Teacher Tips
Admissions requirements		
These include requirements such as GPA scores, short essays, and minimum standardized test scores that depend on the institution. Students with disabilities may have nontraditional testing materials as well as documentation that could be essential when they apply	Does the school have a separate admission policy for students with disabilities? Do admission requirements include the recognition of certificates of attendance, GEDs, or high school diplomas? Can other documentation be included to support the student beyond academic achievement?	Review the admissions requirements of the institution(s) with the student Create checklists of admission requirements and follow through with the students to make sure they are taking the right steps to meet those requirements Assist students with applications and study sessions for required admissions tests
Cost		
Tuition costs can be daunting to students and their families. Financial aid is often available for students, but aid alone does not always cover all the costs especially the "hidden" costs of books, living expenses, and accommodations and extra educational supports	Are the cost and opportunities for financial aid consistent with the need of the student? What forms are required for financial aid? How far in advance do students need to start applying for financial aid? Do they have specific disability assistance? Are grants available explicitly for students with disabilities?	Create spreadsheets that compare costs of tuition as well as "hidden" costs that will be important to consider (i.e., additional testing materials to document their disabilities, tutoring, technology, transportation needs) Host a family Free Application for Federal Student Aid (FAFSA) night to assist students and their families with forms. Information for the FAFSA is available at http://www.fafsa.ed.gov Assist students with research of specific financial aid resources for students with disabilities, available in Creating Options: Financial Aid for Individuals with Disabilities at http://www.heath.gwu.edu
Demographics		
Demographics include race/ethnicity, language, gender, and disabilities of the full-time, part-time, nontraditional students, faculty, and staff that create the higher institution environment	What is the representation of students and faculty/staff who are African American, Latino/Latina, or Native American on the campus? How many students and faculty/staff with disabilities does the college serve? Are their academic/social groups in any of these areas? Are there institutionally supported mentor programs in these areas?	Create math assignments in which students chart the racial and disability demographics of institutions they are interested in attending Have students develop an interview protocol to ask students with disabilities about their experiences and any advice they might offer Contact the admissions offices for student/faculty/staff names for students to interview. The interviews can be conducted via phone, Internet (i.e., e-mail, instant messaging), or in person

Social and Cultural Capital	Questions to Ask	Teacher Tips
Disability office/resources		
Institutions of higher education have offices for student services for students with disabilities, but often students are unfamiliar with these offices and the specific services they provide. This is a particularly important resource because these offices represent advocates for the students and their rights	Do they offer the services (e.g., books on tape, text-to-speech software) that the student requires and is familiar with? What other academic support systems are available? Is there a free writing center on campus or a study skills course offered? What about accessible and free tutoring labs?	Assist students with naming their disabilities, knowing specific tests that are required to verify disabilities, and having lists of accommodations
		Use books such as *Peterson's Colleges With Programs for Students With Learning Disabilities or Attention Deficit Disorders* to help students research schools that match their needs
		Compile a specific contact list with e-mails and phone numbers of individuals in the student services office
Location		
Students with disabilities should consider the campus that will best suit them and their specific needs when looking at institutions of higher education	Do students need to live at home to defer costs? Is being close to their family for gatherings a necessity for the student? Does the stimulation of a city or the confines of a small town better appeal to the student?	Coordinate students interested in visiting the same schools together or in small groups for support and to cut on costs of transportation
		Assist students in critically analyzing the pros and cons of campuses for their specific needs
Size		
One size does not fit all in education. Most students coming from the secondary education setting can be thrown off by the 300-person lecture halls they may experience in higher education. Students with disabilities need to know how their classes will be able to accommodate their specific needs regarding attention, identity, and participation in the classroom environment	How large is the university? What is the average class size? What types of interactions with faculty are promoted institutionally? What is the standard format/size of general education courses? What is the student-to-teacher ratio in the college in which the student will be studying? Do the classes get smaller, population-wise, as the course of study continues?	Arrange for students to shadow a freshman on a college campus to experience different types of courses
		Acknowledge and discuss with students that some classes may be in a format with which they are not familiar and help them plan accommodations such as tutoring, extra time on tests, and making regular visits to the professor's office

SELECTING A COLLEGE

Selecting a college to apply to and attend is important for any student, but it takes on added significance for working-class, African American, Latino/Latina, or Native American students with a disability. Several resources exist to assist teachers, counselors, students, and families in the college selection process, and much has been written about college selection for low-income, culturally and linguistically diverse youth. Rarely, however, is the information combined. Table 110.1 includes questions and strategies that special education teachers should use to help their working-class, culturally and linguistically diverse students with disabilities research their decisions for postsecondary attendance.

SUMMARY

A critical challenge facing special educators over time has been the overrepresentation of working-class African American, Latino/Latina, and Native American students in their programs. Although much has been done to curtail this overrepresentation, educators have a long way to go now in terms of making sure that those students who are currently overrepresented in special education have the social and cultural capital to envision possibilities for themselves beyond high school. Special educators can be at the forefront of bridging the racial, economic, and ability gaps in college admittance, retention, and graduation by engaging in professional practices that confront the discrimination and bias that may have placed many of those students in special education classrooms. Their intentionality and attention to thinking and promoting college in the future of their students can change the landscape of postsecondary attainment for working-class African American, Latino/Latina, and Native American students with disabilities.

NEXT STEPS

111

Learning Disability Identity Development and Social Construct

A Two-Tiered Approach

Cheryl L. Howland and Eva Gibavic

INTRODUCTION: THE LD WALL

Most of the time people with a learning disability (LD) look, act and perform like everyone else. However, when they encounter an experience that puts them face to face with their

disability it is very much like hitting a wall at full speed. The LD wall is usually invisible to everyone else, yet when a person with a learning disability hits this "wall" s/he can have a powerful and painful reaction.

So here we have a student with LD having just hit the LD wall. Our student is unable to perform as required, and s/he is also having a reaction to the impact. In addition, all around him/her are family, teachers, and friends who did *not* hit this wall and who cannot perceive that there is a wall. These non-learning-disabled individuals often cannot see or understand that our student is severely impacted by his/her experience and, while our student may have a real desire and need to perform in the prescribed manner, s/he cannot.

In the moment when individuals face their hidden disability, having been impacted by their learning disability "wall," they have to deal with the following: 1. They cannot perform in the prescribed manner. 2. They are hurting from the impact. 3. Their experience is denied and questioned by well meaning parents, peers, teachers and others who do not understand. 4. They MUST perform somehow. 5. If you were that person, how would you react?

RESISTANCE TO ASSISTANCE

Why do some students with learning disabilities resist when teachers and other professionals try to help them? Why are some willing and eager for accommodations one day and reluctant the next? What is at the core of their refusals? Why do some teachers still see some students with learning disabilities as "willful non-learners"?

These questions are ones that are often raised in our consulting work by college students, parents, grade school teachers, college professors, and disability advocates. Even with the best of intentions and most current knowledge, teachers and parents can become frustrated with a student's resistance. Even with the best of intentions, students can feel that there is a failure on the part of many helpers to "get it," to truly walk in their LD shoes. This can lead to a functional collapse in the teaching/learning contract and an inability to positively address the issues faced by people with learning disabilities.

THE HOWLAND/GIBAVIC MODEL OF IDENTITY DEVELOPMENT
IN PERSONS WITH LEARNING DISABILITIES

The kernel of our identity development model was formed by the basic premise that neurodevelopmental differences plus life circumstances impact our sense of who we are, in other words, our identity. Who we become in life begins with our inherent makeup and evolves and changes over our life as a result of our experiences. Our goal was to propose a model that would assist helpers, learners, parents and teachers understand the developmental processes that can impact individuals with a learning disability. As these experiences are multi-faceted, we propose a complex, two-tiered model of identity development. The model is based in the stage theory of development, well grounded in the works of Erikson, Vgotsky, Kohlberg and Gilligan, and Jackson and Hardiman.

At the time we began our work, an extensive literature search revealed no models of identity development for individuals with learning disabilities, but as our work continued two models were published at the University of Massachusetts by Rodis and Pliner. While very helpful, we found the models to be limited in their respective abilities to address the complex yet powerful effects of social influences, the widely varying impacts of different

NEXT STEPS

types of learning disabilities, and the ongoing life challenges that routinely occur when the expectations of self and others collide with an individual's learning disabilities. These ongoing collisions with the "LD wall," which can result in grief, relief, and resistance periodically over the course of a lifetime, is central to the recycling and re-adjusting of individual identity. In essence, while adjustment and integration can occur with each run-in with the wall, there is typically another "wall" around the corner. The "walls" associated with learning disabilities present themselves through life's various experiences as does a continuation of identity integration. For a model to provide assistance in understanding the experience of an individual with a learning disability, it needs to have a level of complexity, complexity that is not typically explicit in identity development models. Our two-tiered model speaks to these considerations.

TIER ONE: INFLUENTIAL VARIABLES: SOCIAL SYSTEMS AND TIMING

Support Systems: How a person receives and perceives support from their family, community, and teachers represents perhaps the most significant variable in the development of a positive sense of identity related to a learning disability. Children who receive positive support from their family, school and surrounding community develop a positive self-identity more often than a child who is perceived as deficient and or defective by their family, peers, educators and culture. Families and school structures with less knowledge, resources, and social support can contribute to a negative identity development by labeling and stereotyping the child as stupid or lazy or ill-behaved.

Timing: The timing of when a person becomes aware that they have a learning disability and the particular life stage they are in can have a significant impact on the development of their self-identity. Some children in elementary school receive a sufficient amount of remediation and support so that as they grow up they see their LD as only a small part of their learning portfolio. Conversely, children with poor school services and a lack of support can experience the shame of having an LD that shapes their entire school experience. Children who receive their diagnosis in high school have spent a significant part of their learning experience without an understanding of their learning needs. This can result in an inaccurate series of labels and poor self-beliefs. Individuals who receive diagnosis in college or in later adult years may have developed a number of compensation techniques that have assisted them in living and learning while lacking remediation and accommodation and may have developed a significant and largely inaccurate belief system and defensiveness about their learning. This can often be seen as strong negative resistance to help from helping professionals when it may be a positive coping skill developed by the individual struggling to maintain positive self-worth.

Social Receptivity/Acceptance: In 1994 and 1999, the Emily Hall Tremaine Foundation funded two Roper Starch national opinion surveys looking at the social perception of individuals with learning disabilities. The results of these surveys showed that an "alarming 48% of parents think that in the long run being labeled as learning disabled causes children and adults more trouble than if they struggle privately with their learning problems." Some individuals such as Tri-athlete Bruce Jenner (dyslexia) are spared this stigma due to success in other areas, such as sports.

Dual Diagnosis: Having another diagnosis in addition to a learning disability is not unusual for people with learning disabilities. Co-morbidity rates are high, with many people struggling with emotional/behavioral difficulties, ADHD, as well as mental health and other medical issues. The interplay among these multiple diagnoses can complicate and intensify the self-identity process.

N E X T   S T E P S

Cause of the Disability: While most often the cause of a learning disability is unclear, if the cause of a specific learning disability can be ascertained it can be a powerful variable in terms of self-understanding.

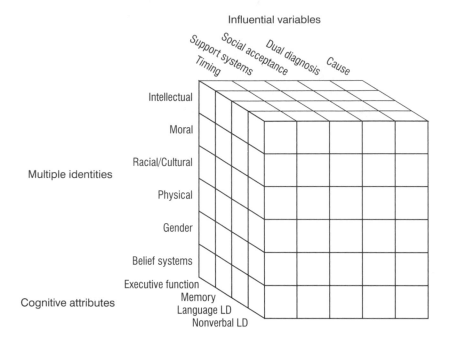

Figure 111.1 Influential variables, multiple identities and cognitive attributes

Multiple Identity Development

Multiple Intelligences: Gardner's theory of Multiple Intelligences posits the existence of eight different forms of intelligence: linguistic, logical mathematical, musical, visual spatial, interpersonal, intrapersonal, natural, and bodily kinesthetic. People with learning disabilities struggle to understand and experience the development of their gifts as positive identities ("I succeed") that are separate from their disability identities ("I struggle"). Those who are able to see themselves from multiple capability perspectives are better able to integrate disability identities than those who are not.

Moral Identity Development: Identity development theory is founded upon theories of moral reasoning and development. Most recognize that children begin with a self-centered approach to the world and, through experiences, develop into beings that interrelate to others in an interdependent, socially-conscious manner. The stages of moral development can influence passage through the stages of learning disability identity development and affect how an individual will respond to his/her learning issues.

Racial/Cultural Identity: In societies where one racial group is unfairly advantaged, people from marginalized cultures and races are impacted by racial oppression, which further influences their racial/cultural identity development. As a student of color struggles to achieve a positive self-identity, the addition of a learning disability and the concurrent stereotyping can further complicate integration, growth, and resolution of one's identity. The interplay between racism and ableism can be seen in the much higher percentages of students of color who are being placed in special education classes (Harry and Klingner 2006).

Gender Identity: Gender oppression continues to be a significant factor influencing how individuals are treated in our society and plays a role in learning disability assessment and

intellectual expectations. Boys are diagnosed with an LD more often than are girls. It has been suggested that this is . . . [because boys tend to act out in the classroom more than girls and, as a result, are subjected to more disciplinary action.]

Physical Identity: Physical identity can be experienced positively for some and negatively for others. Peers, as mentioned above, may give an outstanding athlete respect that s/he does not receive academically. Physical attractiveness may have a socially positive effect, whereas individuals with physical challenges or medical co-morbidities may experience negative social reinforcement.

Belief Systems: Individual beliefs can have a profound influence on learning disability identity development and integration. For example, a student of ours was told by a teacher in middle school that individuals with dyslexia have limited brain space and that perhaps her brain was full. She approached all of her learning challenges from that foundation of belief and perspective. The belief acted as a powerful disincentive to achievement.

Cognitive Attributes

Learning Disabilities: Learning disabilities are defined in various ways, but for simplicity in this model we have chosen to delineate four areas, those involved with the auditory/language area, the nonverbal/visual-perceptual area, memory issues and those related to organizational/executive functioning.

Auditory/Language Processing: Included in this would be central auditory processing, receptive and expressive language, including syntax and word retrieval, written language, and phonologically based dyslexia. Also under this broad category we recognize that some math disabilities are verbally based, having to do with math vocabulary and syntax specific to mathematical reasoning.

Nonverbal/Visual-Spatial Processing: Nonverbal communication is believed to represent 60% of all human communication. Individuals who struggle with nonverbal communication fail to accurately perceive and/or express those many and varied nonverbal signals which most of us take for granted. When this happens, they are often socially isolated due to poor social skills development. In addition these people can struggle academically with nonverbal forms of analysis, synthesis and reasoning.

Memory Difficulties: Students who struggle with various memory issues can have their learning impacted by short and long term deficits in verbal, auditory, visual, and/or working memory. Working memory allows the individual to hold the various parts of a problem actively in mind or "on-line."

Executive Functioning: The executive realm involves the ability to initiate tasks, focus and sustain attention for the task, inhibit behaviors unrelated to the task and inhibit preponderant responses, as well as develop appropriate strategies and shift strategies as required to complete the task.

TIER TWO: STAGES OF IDENTITY DEVELOPMENT

Tier Two of our model addresses the following Stages of Identity Development: Problem with the Wrong Name, Diagnosis, Grief and/or Relief, Resistance and/or Alienation, Passing, Redefinition, and Ongoing Resolution Process.

Problem with the Wrong Name: In this stage, the individual and the family has an understanding that there is something different, perhaps something wrong in the learning process, whether it be a problem with behavior, a slower reading rate, an inability to comprehend reading material, and/or difficulty in mathematics, but there is no actual diagnosis. This lack of clarity can often lead to mislabeling, with individuals being called "dumb," "stupid," "lazy," "slacker," or "willful non-learner."

Diagnosis: With diagnosis of a learning disability, a greater understanding of the individual's learning strengths and weaknesses is developed. The individual, if a child, may or may not be told about the diagnosis and what it means. Many college students come to school with a poor understanding of their learning strengths and struggles.

Grief and/or Relief: Diagnosis typically brings change. These changes may be seen by the individual as positive, leading to a sense of relief, such as an individual who appreciates specialized help. There can also be a sense of grief. Grief may come in the recognition of one's differences and/or due to changes that may be seen as unwanted and negative. A great deal depends on the reaction of the individual's family and teachers, and the nature of the changes.

Resistance and/or Alienation: In this stage, the individual may resent the learning disability itself, resent the consequences of the label, and/or resent the remediation that s/he has received due to the LD. This often co-occurs with the "Passing" stage: the individual may be resistant in classes, while at the same time trying to pass socially.

Passing: The individual downplays the LD, denying it when possible and trying to be like peers. This is a very common stage/place for a student to be in because our society does not easily accept differences and who really wants the disability label?

Redefinition: The individual realizes that passing and resistance doesn't make the LD go away and doesn't make life easier. This re-evaluation may result from some sort of crisis or may grow out of recognition of the value of the individual's strengths as well as different learning needs.

Ongoing Resolution Process: This stage is perhaps the most important to understand. This stage offers the understanding that the whole model is not static, but rather an ever changing launching point as an individual goes through life. It is here that the above-mentioned influences, variables and the actual disability take on a fluidity that forces a person living with a learning disability to re-cycle through an ongoing process.

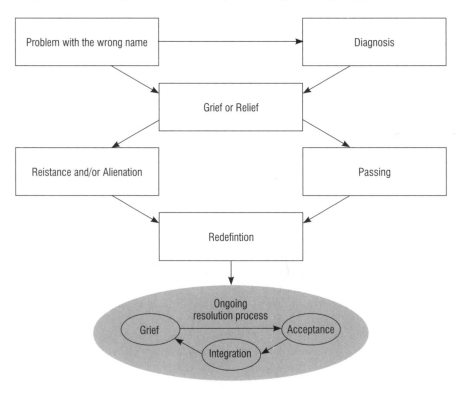

Figure 111.2 Stages

N
E
X
T

S
T
E
P
S

USING THE MODEL

Using these components, including stages and the factors, should guide us to a better understanding of an individual and, therefore, how best to address a variety of issues, including personal, educational and clinical.

CASE STUDY

"David" was a student diagnosed with a significant language-based learning/reading disability with some indication of ADD but with a solid IQ. In the past, he had refused to register with Disability Services. He was seeking readmission to school after failing out two previous times. The admitting Dean required David to sign a contract agreeing to register with Disability Services, meet with me weekly, and achieve a solid 2.0 or better for the semester.

For our first meeting, he was angry, defensive, and independent-minded. He held little hope that anyone including me could or would help him. He came from a working class background where he was the first person in his family to attend college. He'd received little or no help for his disability in high school and (he told me later) expected me to be just another adult who was a harsh judge of his motivation and performance.

David was stuck in the "resistance and alienation" stage of learning disability development and was only willing to attempt school out of love and respect for his mother who was ill. He wanted very much to please her and she had asked him for one Christmas present—a "C" average. He was particularly angry with one professor who had failed him several times and who was unwilling to budge on his grade. Most professionals and adults in David's life saw his struggle as a failure of his character. His anger and resistance reinforced their misunderstanding of David and what he truly wanted and felt about his situation.

In order for us to be helpful to David, we had to allow him to be safe in his resistance and alienation while simultaneously encouraging the part of him that wanted to succeed. Additionally, we had to really help him succeed academically. He was assigned to an Academic Assistant who would work jointly with both of us to help him develop learning strategies that worked for him. We set him up with a schedule that respected his need for physical fun and relaxation but that also made study time more automatic and routine. He met with us every week and soon his resistance faded in the face of his burgeoning academic success. He did not, however, wish anyone including his roommate to know that he was meeting with us and protected his privacy fiercely. He had moved from resistance and alienation to passing. Over the course of our two-year relationship David moved in and out of resistance and alienation, passing, and into the ongoing resolution process. He would sometimes hit his "LD wall" and find himself angry and resistant all over again. But we were able to show that while his learning disability and the frustration associated with it was likely a permanent part of his life, he could and would develop coping skills that would allow him to live a good and successful life. David was able to give his mother her Christmas present that year and for two more Christmases afterward. Most importantly, he took our help and understanding and made it his own. He graduated with a 3.2 GPA.

The Howland/Gibavic model of LD Identity Development allows for a greater understanding of the nature and complex struggles associated with developing a positive LD self-identity, while providing a template that shows the way for individuals and professionals alike to relate and work positively and effectively with themselves and others with learning disabilities.

112

Creating a Fragrance-Free Zone

A Friendlier Atmosphere for People Living with Environmental Illness

Invisible Disabilities Advocate

Did you know there is a growing number of people who can become ill from simply running an errand in a store, going to work or attending a gathering? Simple tasks that most of us take for granted can cause this group to have mild to severe medical reactions. Even their own homes and work environments can lash out at them.

Why is this happening? "Approximately 12.6% of the population suffers from multiple chemical sensitivity (MCS), a condition in which they experience reactions from exposure to low concentrations of common chemicals . . ."

MCS (also known as Environmental Illness or Toxic Injury) is " . . . marked by *multiple symptoms* in *multiple organ systems* (usually the neurological, immune, respiratory, skin, 'GI,' and/or musculoskeletal) that recur chronically in response to *multiple chemical exposures*. MCS Symptoms commonly include difficulty breathing, sleeping and/or concentrating, memory loss, migraines, nausea, abdominal pain, chronic fatigue, aching joints and muscles, and irritated eyes, nose, ears, throat and/or skin. In addition, some with MCS show impaired balance and increased sensitivity not just to odors but also to loud noises, bright lights, touch, extremes of heat and cold, and electromagnetic fields."

The numbers of Americans battling MCS seem to be rising quickly. Most with MCS tell a story of once being healthy and not effected by fragrances. "MCS usually starts with either an acute or chronic toxic exposure, after which this initial sensitivity broadens to include many other chemicals and common irritants . . ." Many experts have found that once a person becomes reactive to a chemical or toxin, their intolerance is rarely reversible.

Furthermore, "In 1998, it was estimated that 26.3 million Americans have been diagnosed with asthma." Asthma is a serious respiratory disorder that can constrict and cause swelling of the airways. "The Institute of Medicine placed fragrance in the same category as second hand smoke in triggering asthma in adults and school age children." What's more, "Up to 72% of asthmatics report their asthma is triggered by fragrance. Asthmatics and others that are negatively impacted by fragrance often have difficulties working, obtaining medical care, and going about activities of daily living because of others' use of scented products."

For those living with asthma and/or MCS, just going to work, a meeting or an activity may expose them to chemicals that could make them ill. These reactions can be very serious and have changed the lives of millions. Because they have to avoid public situations and even having people in their own homes, they can also experience isolation, loneliness, lose their jobs and may even become homebound.

N
E
X
T

S
T
E
P
S

WHAT CHEMICALS?

Most of us are aware that such things as pollution and car exhaust fumes are not good for us. We even realize that sometimes a work environment, like a lab or factory can be hazardous. However, most do not even think twice when entering a building, automobile or even a home that may contain new paint, car smell, carpet or mold, glue, stain, vinyl upholstery, plastic, rubber, smoke, household cleaners, etc.

Moreover, the culprits most of us will never even give a thought to being bothersome are our sweet smelling perfumes, colognes and fragranced products. But aren't these made from natural ingredients like flowers and herbs? Actually, "Perfume formulations changed sometime around the late 70s and early 80s. Today, they are approximately 95–100% synthetic (man-made)." Even seemingly harmless fragrances in our favorite soap, deodorant, lotion, powder, candles, air freshener and laundry products can cause reactions for many.

For the average person, short term exposures to these environmental, everyday household products and perfumes may only seem "bothersome" on occasion. Nevertheless, many people claim they never believed they had an issue until they suddenly or gradually developed their sensitivity or intolerance after normal use of these items.

Author Connie Pitts explained why, "Perfumes, colognes, and many other *scented* products contain an abundance of harmful chemicals, many of which are listed on the EPA's Hazardous Waste List. They also include numerous carcinogenic chemicals, neurotoxins, respiratory irritants, solvents, aldehydes, hundreds of untested and unregulated petrochemicals, phthalates (which can act as hormone disrupters), narcotics, and much more."

WHAT CAN WE DO?

Because many with asthma, MCS and immune disorders risk becoming ill when they go to work, to run errands, to a doctor's office or when attending a gathering, we can all do our part to help.

1) For our own well-being and for the sake of others, we can discontinue the use of products containing VOCs, synthetic fragrances and harmful chemicals.
2) Make meetings and events Fragrance-Free for all to enjoy. This can be done simply by posting this information along with the notices for the event in bulletins, emails, websites and flyers.
3) Office or building management can ask the cleaning crew to start using natural cleaning products like baking soda, vinegar, hydrogen peroxide or environmentally safe products. Moreover, they should not use "air fresheners" in the building or bathrooms. Instead, exhaust fans and air purifiers can do the job.
4) Office or building management can create a list of people who are sensitive to chemicals and fragrances. They would then call people on the list when someone paints the walls, shampoos the carpet, replaces the carpet, gets new furniture or uses glues, insecticides, stains, polishes, etc. In addition, signs should be placed on the doors to notify all employees and customers of the use of these products.
5) Before visiting someone in their home or inviting them to ours, we should ask those living with asthma, chronic illness, immune issues, MCS and/or allergies what fragrances, lotions, soaps, deodorants, candles, air fresheners, detergents, cleaning products, etc. they can and cannot tolerate.
6) For added protection, a Fragrance-Free Zone can be implemented.

CREATING A FRAGRANCE-FREE ZONE

A Fragrance-Free Zone is a smoke, fragrance and chemical free area, designed for those who report mild to serious reactions to these items. Adding a Fragrance-Free Zone can help many in our community work and frequent your establishment in comfort.

At first glance, we may think there are not enough people who struggle with these issues to justify the hassle of providing a Fragrance-Free Zone. However, for every 100 people in America, there is an average of 10 with asthma, 20 with an autoimmune disorder and/or 12.5 with MCS.

Here are basically 3 types of Fragrance-Free Zones that can be implemented in the office or store:

Fragrance-Free Zone #1: Building, Office or Store Policy. Establish a policy of no perfumes or fragrances worn by employees inside the building. In addition, the use of non-toxic cleaning supplies, natural pesticides, etc. can be included. This concept is becoming more and more popular among businesses, doctor's offices and churches, because it makes it possible for many to work in or visit your building. Many medical facilities and religious organizations are also asking patients and congregations not to wear fragrances.

Fragrance-Free Zone #2: Separate Room in Workplace. This is a separate room or floor of a building for employees that provides extra protection from fragrances, as well as paints, glues, formaldehyde, mold, smoke and chemical cleaners. It is sealed off with walls, a door to a direct entrance and exit. It also contains a Fragrance-Free bathroom and a break-room (if space permits).

Fragrance-Free Zone #3: Section in Office. This is a simple and quick way to set up a section in the office. Designate several rows of desks just for those with chemical sensitivities. You can post signs to signify that this section is a perfume, cologne, fragrance and smoke free zone. Put this section in an area where they can have easy access to an outside entrance and away from high traffic areas.

Please note that just creating a "section" within a room is not always a viable answer. Perfumes and fragrances can permeate the air and waft through the area, as well as linger in the hallway, lobby and bathrooms. "Scented products are volatile substances and get into the air quickly. Once in the air, containment to a defined space is impossible. Further, scented products are designed to diffuse into the air and linger."

Finally, "According to the AARDA, approximately 50 million Americans [or] 20 percent of the population . . . suffer from some 80 autoimmune diseases." Thus, for the benefit of all around us, particularly those with immune disorders, when we are sick with a cold or a virus, maybe we should consider staying home. After all, we could infect several more people, who in turn infect several more people—causing them to miss work, activities and maybe even be hospitalized. Consequently, even when we are just "coming down with" a virus or we are "getting over" something, we can still be contagious. If we cannot stay home from work, we should at least steer clear of other people, especially those with immune issues.

Thank you for your cooperation in providing a safer environment, so that millions of people can live better lives, with fewer boundaries! Without everyone's help, going to work or entering a building can put many at risk of having mild to severe reactions that may last several hours or even several weeks. With it, many can live their lives with less risk of exposure.

NEXT STEPS

113

Recognizing Ableist Beliefs and Practices and Taking Action as an Ally

Madeline L. Peters, Carmelita (Rosie) Castañeda,
Larissa E. Hopkins, and Aquila McCants

Ableism is a pervasive form of oppression that tends to be minimally examined and understood by mainstream society. From a young age we learn powerful messages about groups of people, especially those who are perceived to be different than us. These consistent messages are translated into strongly rooted beliefs, stereotypes, and behaviors directed towards other human beings. Our internalization of negative thoughts and subsequent actions has systematically, generation-by-generation, supported the dehumanization and denigration of people with disabilities.

It is vitally important that we begin to question the historical and contemporary patterns and practices that reproduce the discrimination and exclusion of people with intellectual, emotional, and physical disabilities. Challenging ableism truly requires that we recognize how this oppression is manifested on the individual, institutional, and cultural levels of engagement. It is with this recognition that we will be able to replace our harmful language and behaviors with empowering words and actions, and our marginalizing institutional practices with supportive and inclusive practices. By reevaluating our perceptions and stereotypical responses, we can learn to build respectful, dynamic and fulfilling relationships with people living with disabilities. A significant factor necessary for challenging manifestations of oppression is the formation of allies.

An ally is typically a member of advantaged social groups who uses their social power to take a stand against social injustice directed at targeted groups. For example, White people who speak out against racism, men who speak out against sexism, and heterosexual people who challenge heterosexism and homophobia. An ally works to be an agent of social change rather than an agent of oppression. While there are many important characteristics of an effective ally, there are a few that we would like to highlight. We believe an ally takes responsibility for learning about his/her own and targeted group heritage, culture and experience, and how oppression works in everyday life. Allies listen to and respect the perspectives and experiences of targeted group members. They acknowledge unearned privileges and work to eliminate or change privileges into rights that targeted group members also enjoy. Allies recognize that unlearning oppressive beliefs and actions is a lifelong process, and welcome each learning opportunity. They are willing to take risks, try new behaviors, and act in spite of their own fear and resistance from other advantaged group members. Allies believe they can make a difference by acting and speaking out against social injustice.

The chart below is designed to provide people with information needed in becoming a stronger, more supportive, and aware ally to people living with disabilities. The left side of the chart organizes perceptions, language, and behaviors about the limiting factors at three levels of engagement: individual, institutional, and societal/cultural levels. The right side of the chart responds to the limiting factors by providing people with examples of supportive ally behaviors and actions. The need for each of us to act as an ally by fostering supportive practices is imperative for the well-being of all people.

Recognizing Ableist Beliefs and Practices and Taking Action as an Ally

Limiting Factors for People with Disabilities	Supportive Practices for People with Disabilities
Individual	
Denying people with disabilities equal opportunities and seeing him/her as second class citizens. Behaving as if people with disabilities are invisible, a nuisance, disgusting, and should be institutionalized	Recognize the full potential and humanity of people with disabilities in relationships, employment, and cultural, political, social and physical activities in our multicultural world
Assuming that people with disabilities are unaware and unable to make decisions regarding their daily needs. Limiting and/or interfering with their ability to make their own decisions	Accept that a person is more than their disability. They are complex human beings with the ability to make decisions about their daily needs with varying degrees of success and failure like the rest of the population
Not acknowledging people with disabilities: i.e., ignoring, not speaking to, avoiding eye contact, and behaving as if people with disabilities do not exist	Be aware of your body language and avoid staring at people with disabilities. Refrain from talking about the person with a disability in front of them. Establish eye contact and speak directly to the person with a disability
Imposing "help" thereby taking control away from the person: i.e., grabbing the arm of a person who is blind to assist them across the street without asking	Ask the person with a disability if they need assistance, allowing them to have control of the situation. Stay within the boundaries of the stated request for assistance
Not treating people with disabilities as you would treat others: i.e., being afraid to give feedback or advice to person with a disability by being overly concerned about how the person will react to criticism	State ideas and concerns clearly and constructively. Recognize that constructive feedback is meant to help a person grow and learn
Establishing lower expectations for people with disabilities: i.e., a teacher setting lower standards for a student who is deaf or a teacher who inflates the grade of a person with a disability not based on the person's ability but based on the teacher's pity	Lowered expectations are demeaning and a disservice to the person with a disability and only reflect ableist assumptions. Recognize that inflating grades does not benefit people with disabilities. Understand that accommodations can be put in place to allow students to successfully participate and excel in the classroom
Not encouraging people with disabilities to take risks	Encourage people with disabilities to reach their full potential. Encouragement includes praise when one has met a goal and an inquiry about the next goal to be set, suggesting that higher goals are attainable
Discounting the opinions of people with disabilities, except on issues of disabilities	Seek the opinions of people with disabilities for their perspectives on any issue. They may have valuable opinions and may have experience on a breadth of issues
Institutional	
Employing people with disabilities in low-paying occupations or guiding people with disabilities to solely work in jobs geared towards disability services and/or other related specialized fields: i.e., instilling in people with disabilities that the only work available to them is menial tasks	Recognize that people with disabilities can perform essential functions of various jobs. People with disabilities can and do work in every field of employment, from entertainment, science, and technology to philosophy and mathematics, and have strong qualities and attributes like other employees and deserve to earn a livable wage
Assuming all people with disabilities require the same services thereby establishing a uniform system of accommodations	Recognize and provide services on a case by case basis, because all disabilities are manifested differently in each individual
Placing people with disabilities in segregated environments i.e. all students with special needs' classes are held in the basement of the school. Holding segregated events for people with disabilities without the goal and practice of inclusive integration or making all activities accessible	Schedule all activities with accessibility in mind: i.e., space should be wheelchair accessible, bathrooms should be conveniently located; be conscientious of how lighting impacts individuals with disabilities; advocate for a chemically free/fragrance free environment. Mainstream people with disabilities so that they are afforded similar social, cultural and academic experiences. Make inclusive integration the norm (i.e., use multiple teaching methods, make sure all handouts are also printed in Braille and/or on MP3 auditory format; verbally describe all visual aids; welcome sign language interpretation; and provide frequent breaks)

NEXT STEPS

Recognizing Ableist Beliefs and Practices and Taking Action as an Ally

Limiting Factors for People with Disabilities	Supportive Practices for People with Disabilities
Depictions of people with disabilities in mainstream media as different, grotesque, evil, villains, monsters, an alien: i.e., Beauty and the Beast, The Hunchback of Notre Dame, and The Hulk	Recognize that the media has used people with disabilities to incite fear of difference. Be acquainted with positive portrayals of people with disabilities in the media, such as "My Left Foot," etc. Seek out media that portrays people with disabilities as human beings who are living their everyday lives
Maintaining a "hidden" and/or separate set of policies that require people with disabilities to jump through additional hoops in order to prove they need a particular type of service/accommodation	Institutions need to implement policies that are inclusive of the needs of all people with consideration to the individual needs of people with disabilities. Separate is not equal

Cultural

Assuming that the lives of people with disabilities (i.e., daily living, relationships, choices, passions, emotions, work and lack of work, housing, education, abilities, and civic rights) revolve solely around their disability/ies	Assume that the lives of people with disabilities are full, diverse and complex. People with disabilities make daily decisions, have plans for the future, and enjoy relationships, work and leisure. They also have passions, hobbies, families and friends. The disability is not the essence of who they are in the world
Assuming that people with disabilities do not want a career and prefer to live off of government assistance	Government assistance has never been more than subsistence living. Most people with or without a disability would rather make a meaningful contribution to society than be subject to the stigma of being "lazy" and receiving "a handout." Although many are entitled to disability assistance, they also are searching (despite barriers) to find something more meaningful in their lives, such as good employment, decent shelter, and stimulating recreation
Using limiting language or language with negative connotations to describe people with disabilities: i.e., associating them with terms such as "sick," "bad," "disabled," "broken," "mental," "scary," "stupid," and "sped." For example, "Sam is in Sped, where all the stupid children are"	Recognize that language is a reflection of how people see one another. Use words that locate people with disabilities in a positive and nondestructive manner. Refer to people with disabilities as people first. For example, "Sam is in room 224"
A belief system that people with the same disabilities are the same or share the same experience, not taking their individuality into account	Understand that all people with disabilities are individuals and all individuals have unique qualities. Some wheelchair users are able to walk brief distances, some individuals who are legally blind may be able to see and experience certain sights, and people with learning disabilities may have an Intelligence Quotient in the gifted-to-genius range
Societal belief that people with disabilities are helpless and/or unable to accomplish daily living tasks, thus taking individual power away from the person: i.e., in a restaurant the wait staff asking friends to order for a person with a disability	To think of people as helpless is yet another way of disempowering a group or an individual. All individuals and groups with disabilities lead their daily lives with the same dreams and aspirations as everyone else. There may be accommodations to help them meet their daily goals, but they are not helpless. Helplessness is a learned behavior that can be countered by empowering people to advocate for and do things for themselves as much as is possible
During certain holiday seasons, the gathering of families, the cluttering of aisles, the overcrowded nature of shopping centers, and the added daily responsibilities may result in one's disability becoming more prominent: i.e., increase anxiety, depression, and post traumatic stress syndrome (PTSD)	The holiday seasons are important times to raise one's awareness of the needs of people with disabilities. It is important to be aware of accessibility in your home, and in public spaces, and to be attentive to those who may be left alone. Be supportive and reassuring of the individual's situations
Society's standards of beauty leave people with disabilities invisible: i.e., popular magazines, catalogs, and advertisements do not feature photographs of people with visible disabilities	Society's standards of beauty need to be inclusive of all people from diverse backgrounds, and thus need to include people with disabilities. Recognize that traditional standards of beauty have limited our society's perception of beauty. Standards of beauty are based on the eye of the beholder. Recognize that people with disabilities are beautiful

See Chapter 15 in *Teaching for Diversity and Social Justice* for corresponding teaching materials.

SECTION 9

AGEISM AND ADULTISM

Introduction

Keri DeJong and Barbara J. Love[1]

This section, on ageism and adultism, is concerned with the oppression of young people and elders as age-based social identity groups, and the ways in which access to participation in society and the establishment of relationships of domination and subordination are organized on the basis of age (Hardiman, Jackson, and Griffin, 2007). Chronological age is a physical reality. What is deemed appropriate for people of any age group is societally constructed. The roles, behaviors, and expectations that society has deemed appropriate for any given age groups vary across societies and within societies across time, corresponding to the economic and technological developments within that society.

Some social relationships, such as the caretaking of the very young and of elders, are rooted in physical and biological realities. Decisions about power, voice, and decision making connected to young people and elders are determined by societal expectations and structures rather than biological differences. For example, high-school students have played an important part in organizing and participating in political campaigns but are not permitted to vote until they are eighteen years old. Elders are often subjected to layoffs and may struggle to find employment due to stereotypes about elders even though they are fully capable of meeting the expectations of employers. Young people and elders are socially constructed identities with attendant stereotypes and misinformation that impact their ability to exercise power, be listened to and acknowledged, and make decisions that will be supported by the dominant society. Our discussion of ageism and adultism as issues of social justice acknowledges that, like all other forms of oppression, the oppression of young people and elders exists independent of our ability to observe and acknowledge it.

One strategy to increase our capacity to observe the disempowerment and lack of respect accorded to young people is to examine societal rules and regulations targeted specifically toward young people. Youth escort laws provide one contemporary example. Like sundown laws of the old South requiring black people to get out of town before dark, youth escort laws require young people to be accompanied by an adult over the age of twenty-one or to depart malls before 7 p.m. These laws regulate the presence of members of the subordinate group to suit the needs and preferences of members of the dominant group. These laws determine when and under what circumstances youth, the target group, can be in the presence of adults, the dominant group, reinforcing and highlighting adult power and the powerlessness of youth. Rooted in

the adage of a not-so-long-gone era, "children are to be seen and not heard," youth escort laws reflect absolute adult power over young people along with societal attitudes of disdain and lack of respect. Another easily observed example takes place daily in schools where young people spend a large portion of their time. Young people in schools must request and receive adult permission to go to the bathroom though they are legally approved to drive, work, and even take care of other young people. Young people may be stopped, detained, and punished by any adult in the school if they decide to go to the bathroom without explicit adult permission. Beginning at a very early age, young people learn that they must submit to adult authority.

Societal prohibitions against and contempt for growing older are equally pernicious. The advertisements and news lines that are displayed regularly urging us to fight back against aging is an indicator of the negative societal attitude toward growing old. Predatory lending practices and the disproportionate targeting of elders for reverse equity and other mortgage schemes designed to prey on elders with fixed incomes results in elders being forced from their homes, often with devastating results (references to examples and resources are on our section website). Mandatory retirement age, scandalous nursing home conditions, coupled with the prevalence of stereotypes and disparaging humor, all signal loss of power and mistreatment of people who are old in current society.

DEFINITIONS AND MANIFESTATIONS OF AGEISM AND ADULTISM

One of the first writers on ageism, Robert Butler (1975, p. 12) defines ageism as "A process of systematic stereotyping of and discrimination against people because they are old. . . . Old people are categorized as senile, rigid in thought and manner, old fashioned in morality and skills" (p. 35). To Butler's definition, we add a social justice framework that examines the loss of power, voice, and limited access to participation in society from a basis of equity. We define adultism as the systematic subordination of younger people, as a targeted group, who have relatively little opportunity to exercise social power in the United States through restricted access to the goods, services, and privileges of society and are denied access to participation in the economic and political life of the society. This subordination of young people and elders is sup-ported by the actions of individuals, cultural norms, attitudes and values, and the institutional structures and practices of society. Adult supremacy is maintained by a network of laws, rules, policies, procedures, and organizational norms that consistently deny youth access to power, privilege, and opportunity and ensure the continued targeted status of people that are young. Young people and elders are affected by the legal, societal, and institutional norms and practices that marginalize and exclude them and give adults the power to act on and for young people and elders without their agreement. Thus, while elders may be revered for their presumed wisdom, they are nevertheless legally excluded from the workplace. While young people may be appreci-ated for their vigor, energy, and enthusiasm, their participation is likewise restricted.

While adultism and ageism are both forms of oppression sharing the identity marker of age, we distinguish between the two, specifically naming *adultism* as the oppression of young people by adults and elders, and *ageism* as the oppression of elders by youth and adults (Love and Phillips, 2007). Some writers use the term "ageism" to refer interchangeably to the oppression of elders and young people. Rather than using the same term to refer to both types of oppression, we find it important to distinguish between the two given the distinctive ways in which these two age-related forms of oppression play out in everyday life.

Our focus in this section is limited to illustrating the ways in which the mistreatment of young people and elders meets our theoretical framework for understanding oppression and providing examples of everyday manifestations of the oppression of young people and elders—that is, examples that are normalized by the culture, rather than dramatic or horrific. The litany of critical

issues in the everyday lives of young people and elders illustrate the long-term consequences of the loss and/or absences of power among members of these two groups. Our focus is on creating a framework for understanding how these experiences illustrate not only mistreatment but oppression as well.

The elements of oppression described in the section on conceptual frameworks (selections 4 and 5) are underlying conceptual tools for the analysis of the experience of both young people and elders. For example, it is useful to think about the way schools have become more like prisons. The presence of metal detectors, police or security guards in classrooms, and building design that emphasizes surveillance indicate that society has accepted a view of young people as a criminal threat. Similarly, in an effort to ensure that they continue to receive the income of elder residents, nursing homes have been charged with illegally forcing elders to remain in the institution rather than choosing where they wish to live. A federal lawsuit filed on behalf of 8,500 institutionalized Floridians claims that nursing homes pressured politicians to pass legislation making it more difficult for elders to qualify for community care (AOL News, 2008). These examples illustrate powerlessness, which Young describes as an element of oppression (selection 5).

Recognition of the oppression of young people and elders is hampered by the normalization of mistreatment, which renders it invisible. A variety of laws and institutional arrangements make age the sole criteria for determining when an individual can leave school, drive a car, drink alcohol, get married, or join the armed services. Mandatory retirement ages and age-based health-care allocations clearly indicate the denial of power and privilege on the basis of age. Similar to the suggestion of a former Harvard University president that biological difference accounted for the limited participation of women in math and science, there will be those who assume that biological and developmental differences justify the differential treatment of young people and elders. As the scientific community was quick to condemn the assertions of that university president, our goal is to increase the consciousness about the oppression of young people and elders so that objection to this oppression can be as clear and unequivocal (Bombardieri, 2005).

INTERNALIZED AGEISM AND ADULTISM

The designation of young people and elders as social identities is so widespread that people of every culture, language, religion, and nationality are sure that their ways of responding to these identities are rooted in the rationality of laws, policies, and principles dictated by biology. Across many societies, people are sure that the control of members of these two groups, by those with more power, more resources, more strength, and more size, is justified by that size, strength, power, and possession of those resources. The assumption of the rightness of those with more power and more resources to make decisions about the lives of those with less power and fewer resources is shared not only by those of the dominant group but by those of the target group as well. Both young people and elders have internalized the belief that decisions regarding their lives are appropriately made by members of the dominant group (middle-aged adults). Bonnichsen (2003) contends,

> Very few young people actually feel solidarity with young people as a group . . . [Many young people] spend their entire childhood identifying with the perspective of adults . . . [and] feel that . . . other young people . . . actually deserve to be treated with disrespect. . . . [Youth employ a variety of strategies] to dissociate themselves from other young people, trying to shed the negative status of childhood. (p. 2)

Young people are encouraged and rewarded for practicing adultism toward other young people. Similar to the internalized racism that causes some black people to provide greater respect and

deference to other black people who look and act more like white people, young people some-times accord respect on an age-based scale and act out the oppression on anyone younger, weaker, with fewer resources, and smaller than themselves. They learn quickly (from their own experience) the prevailing conditions under which humans can behave in an oppressive way toward other humans.

The stereotypes, prejudices, and forms of discrimination against elders, discussed by Butler (selection 117), are practiced not only by middle-aged adults and younger people; they are also practiced and reinforced by elders with each other. "I'm having a senior moment," is a common expression among elders who have accepted the idea that forgetfulness is a condition of aging. This enforcement of the oppression of elders by elders constitutes internalized ageism. The depression sometimes associated with isolation, feeling unwanted, and fear of senility can be a manifestation of internalized ageism. Elders internalize ageism as they internalize feelings of loss of value, being a bother, worthlessness, feeling that they are unworthy of the caretaking of others, and living with the fear of one day being unable to take care of themselves. For both young people and elders, it is the acceptance of these negative stereotypes about themselves that makes it difficult to name their mistreatment as a form of oppression and to effectively organize to change it.

As in the case of elders, the internalization of the oppression by young people has many negative and dysfunctional consequences. One consequence is the enforcement of adultism by young people on other young people. A second major consequence of internalizing adultism is that young people learn the roles of target and agent of oppression to be played out in other manifestations of oppression (racism, sexism, classism, and the like). In this way, adultism inter-sects with all other forms of oppression in its preparation of young people for the roles required to secure their participation in the maintenance of systems of oppression (Love, 2010). Young people are taught to perform the role of subordinant[2] and concomitantly learn to desire the role of dominant. Concern about learning appropriate behavior in order to be safe is often the guise under which this socialization takes place. Young people (as subordinants) are taught that adults (as dominants) are entitled to speak for them and to make decisions for them. In turn, they learn not to trust their own thinking, decisions, or feelings. The internalization of the idea that dominants know best what is appropriate for subordinants and are entitled to make decisions for them is replayed in every other manifestation of oppression where young people will eventually be required to play the role of dominant (Freire, 1994).

INTERCONNECTION BETWEEN AGEISM, ADULTISM, AND OTHER FORMS OF OPPRESSION

Other forms of oppression converge with ageism and adultism to produce differential results for members of particular intersecting social identity groups. The interaction between age-based oppression and racism, for instance, means that elders of color are more likely to have lower income than white elders, and that young people of color are more likely to attend underfunded schools with limited curricular offerings, police in the hallways, and metal detectors at the door. Youth of color are less likely to complete high school or college, are more likely to be placed in foster-care settings, and are five to ten times more likely to be imprisoned than white youth who display the same patterns of behavior (Fulbright-Anderson, Lawrence, Sutton, Susi, and Kubisch, 2005). A recent study by Stanford psychologists examining how race affects juvenile sentencing reveals that racism intersects with adultism as adults who simply *imagine* youth offenders to be black develop policies that result in harsher treatment of all young people (Donald, 2012). African American youth, and in some cases Latino/a youth, receive fewer primary care, mental health, and asthma services than white youth even when family income and health insurance are taken

into account. Schools spend, on average, nearly $9,000 less per pupil on youth of color than on white youth.

Ageism intersects with classism and sexism to produce differences in the distribution of retirement resources for the elderly. Women of all ethnic groups live longer than men and generally have fewer economic or health-care resources than men in their old age. Women, poor and working-class people, and people of color often have lower paying jobs resulting in limited discretionary funds and lower contributions to Social Security. In old age, women of color and poor and working-class women have fewer Social Security benefits, and are less likely to have pensions from discretionary funds that were invested for retirement (O'Rand, cited by Calasanti and Slevin, 2001). Ageism intersects with heterosexism so that same-sex partners cannot collect survivor benefits that are restricted to "spouses."

When a boy plays dress-up with his sisters and is ridiculed or told that his behavior is inappropriate, messages of adultism, sexism, heterosexism, and transgender oppression are conveyed simultaneously. Because the boy in this example could potentially experience name-calling, social isolation, or even violence for dressing, acting like, or simply aligning himself with girls, he is forced to perform a prescribed version of masculinity that clearly distinguishes his gender apart from that of his sisters and simultaneously conveys the ideas that it is shameful to be or act "like a girl." Ridicule and shame are often used to teach the role of dominant and subordinate to young people and is justified to be "for their own good." In their efforts to keep young people safe from potential violence, adults' "that's-just-the-way-it-is" attitude conveys a sense of powerlessness to youth who, as other forms of oppression are experienced, are thereby trained to accept them without questioning, challenging, or fighting back.

Infantilization functions on both the micro and macro levels. Infantilization employs the characteristics ascribed to youth to justify the consolidation of power into the hands of the dominant group. Speaking to elders, people with disabilities and people of color in the same tone that adults use to speak to babies and pets is an example of infantilization and leads to both individual and systematic confusion about appropriate interactions with and support for members of these groups. Describing native peoples (Americans, Africans, Australians, and other native peoples) as childlike was the rhetoric used to justify colonial acquisition of their land and resources, removal of power from their government and society, and exercise of cultural and physical genocide. The rhetoric of "developing nations and economies" conveys the image of youth "becoming," justifying the actions of imperial powers which dictate and prescribe how "developing" nations should orient their economic and political policies. Similarly, colonized and formerly colonized populations are seen as dependent, justifying their treatment as inferior (infantile/underdeveloped) and in need of the intervention of imperial (adult/developed) powers (DeJong, 2012).

GLOBAL DIFFERENCES IN THE TREATMENT OF YOUNG PEOPLE AND ELDERS

The treatment of young people and old people varies from one society to another, and within different cultural groups in a given society. For instance, research shows differences between Western and non-Western and between post-industrial and less-industrialized societies in the treatment of both young people and elders (Rogoff, 2003, p. 9). While the focus in this section is on the experience of young people and elders in U.S. society, it is important to recognize the variations among and within cultural and socioeconomic groups globally as well as within the United States.

Different treatment does not connote oppression or the lack of oppression. In many societies, for instance, elders are revered based on the assumption that with age comes increased wisdom. At the same time, there is an assumption in many of those same cultures that age brings inevitable senility and decline. We recognize that both the revering of elders and youth and the

oppression of elders and youth can exist within the same racial/cultural/familial context. Our research shows that this simultaneous revering and enforcement of oppression occurs across societies in Africa, Asia, South and Central America, as well as Europe and North America. In addition, it is not limited to rural, urban, industrialized, agrarian, or post-technological contexts.

LIBERATION: ELIMINATING AGEISM AND ADULTISM AND THE TRANSFORMATION OF SOCIETY

Age-based identities are shared by all humans, across race, gender, class, nationality, sexuality, language, religion, ability, culture, ethnicity, or any other identity, whether target or agent. Their specific meanings will differ in various cultures. Every single human is or has been young. Every human who lives long enough will become an elder. Age-based oppression affects all humans, and so it is in the interest of all humans to work for the elimination of ageism and adultism. Our purpose in seeking a deeper understanding of oppression is to facilitate liberation, that is, the transformation of society through the elimination of age-based oppression. Here and there, we witness bits and parts of models and theory that contribute to our unfolding vision of a liberatory society.

Contemporary Western society has evolved a particular way of thinking about young people and elders that is rooted in structures of domination and subordination. A social justice perspective requires us to envision and develop responses that enable more equitable participation of elders and young people in society. For example, some organizations have young people on their boards of directors who are central to making decisions about the organization with their adult colleagues. Groups like the Gray Panthers, whose membership is comprised of elders, are working to challenge ageist attitudes and put pressure on legislative bodies to create policies that protect elders from abuse and support views of elders as productive and important members of a multi-generational, diverse society (Woolf, 2005). Challenging adultist attitudes about young people's role in decision making can increase the likelihood that young people's needs and perspectives are represented. Challenging ageist attitudes about elders' roles as participants in political and economic life can increase the likelihood that elders' needs and perspectives are represented.

In many parts of the world, young people, elders, and their allies are engaged in research and model building that result in societal transformation and lead to the creation of a liberatory society. They are developing relationships, organizations, programs, and policies that enable young people and elders to participate in society from a position of equity. As we broaden our understanding of these manifestations of oppression and work toward the elimination of ageism and adultism, young people and elders can increasingly anticipate living empowered lives with complete dignity and respect. This is a benefit for every single human.

THE SELECTIONS

The selections in the Context part address definitions of ageism and adultism, and individual, institutional, societal, and cultural manifestations of ageism and adultism. Robert Butler's article (selection 117) defines ageism on the basis of attitudes, stereotypes, and behavior patterns that embody the mistreatment and oppression of elders and a discussion of institutional manifestations of ageism. John Bell's article (selection 114) defines adultism and describes common occurrences of adultism. His discussion provides a method for examining individual behavior to determine the extent to which it perpetuates adultism. Sheets (selection 118) discusses the experiences of elders with disabilities, while the selection on "Black Elderly" (selection 119) describes

specific difficulties encountered by elders who are black. Looking at adultism on an institutional level, Dohrn (selection 115) and Durkin (selection 116) discuss the ways young people are criminalized in contemporary society.

The selections in Voices, by Huber (selection 120), Larabee, (selection 121) and Curry (selection 122), describe young people and elders' experience of ageism and adultism. We note that it was challenging to find descriptions of the experience of adultism written by young people, as was locating the voices of elders; most descriptions of the experiences of young people and elders that we found were, more often than not, written by middle-aged adults. We think that this reflects the reality of the oppression and the internalization of powerlessness (we include some recent resources on the section website).

The selections in Next Steps offer strategies to eliminate ageism and adultism and to move toward liberation. It includes specific suggestions for what allies can do. Jenny Sazama with Boston Area Youth (selection 124) describes strategies to learn about adultism, interrupt adultism, and support the empowerment of young people. Kazu Haga (selection 123) describes a program developed by young people to take charge of the environment of their school. They provide suggestions to stimulate thinking about both individual and systemic and institutional changes that can help in the elimination of adultism. Gullette (selection 125) examines contemporary cultural assumptions that support ageism and encourages the development of coalitions to interrupt and defeat what the author describes as "new ageism." Markee (selection 126) provides a helpful discussion of specific things that allies of elders can do. We include Marge Larabee's "Elder Liberation Draft Policy Statement" (selection 121) because it provides a good model for examining the oppression of elders from a position of empowerment and with a view toward liberation. In addition to a description of conditions for elders, this statement discusses both how elders can work on ending internalized oppression, what they can do to promote their own liberation, as well as what allies can do to support elders to have good lives.

See Companion Website for Additional Resources and Material

Notes

1 We ask that those who cite this work always acknowledge by name both the authors listed rather than either only citing the first author or using "et al." to indicate coauthors. Both collaborated equally in the conceptualization, development, and writing of this chapter.
2 We prefer the spelling *subordinant* because it parallels the term used to refer to dominants. We do not use the term *dominate* to refer to those in the dominant role. The use of the term *subordinate*, which is a modifying adjective, seems to contribute to the reduction and objectification of members of the group to which this term is applied.

References

AOL News (September 20, 2008). *For Some, Nursing Homes Are a Prison*. Retrieved April 8, 2009, from http://www.tilrc.org/assests/news/0908comm20.html

Bombardieri, M. (January 17, 2005). Summers' remarks on women draw fire. *The Boston Globe*. Retrieved April 8, 2009, from http://www.boston.com/news/local/articles/2005/01/17/summers_remarks_on_women_draw_fire/

Bonnichsen, S. (2003). *Objections to Calling Adultism an Oppression*. Retrieved December 13, 2008 from http://www.youthlib.com/notepad/archives/2003/12/objections_to_c.html

Butler, R. N. (1975). *Why Survive? Being Old in America*. New York: Harper and Row.

Calasanti, T. M., Slevin, K. F. (2001). *Gender, Social Inequalities and Ageing*. Walnut Creek, CA: AltaMira Press.

DeJong, K. (2012). *On Being and Becoming: An Exploitation of Young People's Perspectives on Status and Power in Childhood*. Unpublished manuscript. Amherst, MA: University of Massachusetts.

Donald, B. (2012). *Stanford Psychologists Examine How Race Affects Juvenile Sentencing*. Retrieved May 30, 2012 from http://news.stanford.edu/news/2012/may/race-juvenile-offenders-052412.html

Freire, P. (1994). *Pedagogy of the Oppressed.* New York: Continuum.

Fulbright-Anderson, K., Lawrence, K., Sutton, S., Susi, G., Kubisch, A. (2005). *Structural Racism and Youth Development: Issues, Challenges, and Implications.* Aspen Institute Roundtable on Community Change. Washington, DC: Aspen Institute.

Hardiman, R., Jackson, B., Griffin, P. (2007). Conceptual foundations for social justice education. In M. Adams, L. A. Bell, P. Griffin (eds), *Teaching for Diversity and Social Justice* (2nd edition). New York: Routledge.

Love, B. J. (2010). Developing a liberatory consciousness. In M. Adams, W. J. Blumenfeld, R. Castañeda, H. Hackman, M. Peters, X. Zúñiga (eds), *Readings for Diversity and Social Justice* (2nd edition, pp. 599–603). Routledge: New York.

Love, B. J., Phillips, K. J. (2007). Ageism and adultism curriculum design. In M. Adams, L. A. Bell, P. Griffin (eds), *Teaching for Diversity and Social Justice* (2nd edition). New York: Routledge.

Rogoff, B. (2003). *The Cultural Nature of Human Development.* New York: Oxford University Press.

Woolf, L. (2005). *An In-depth Look at Ageism.* Retrieved June 20, 2006, from http://www.webster.edu/~woolflm/ageism.html

Citation for this section introduction

DeJong, K., Love, B. (2013). Ageism & adultism introduction. In M. Adams, W. J. Blumenfeld, R. Castañeda, H. Hackman, M. Peters, X. Zúñiga (eds) *Readings for Diversity and Social Justice* (3rd edition). Routledge: New York.

114

Understanding Adultism

A Key to Developing Positive Youth-Adult Relationships

John Bell

Most of us are youth workers because we care about young people. Personally we want to both be effective and have good relationships with young people. . . .

To be successful in our work with young people, we must understand a particular condition of youth: that young people are often mistreated and disrespected simply because they are young. The word *adultism* refers to behaviors and attitudes based on the assumption that adults are better than young people, and entitled to act upon young people without their agreement. This mistreatment is reinforced by social institutions, laws, customs, and attitudes.

. . . [E]xcept for prisoners and a few other institutionalized groups, young people are more controlled than any other group in society. . . . [M]ost young people are told what to eat, what to wear, when to go to bed, when they can talk, that they will go to school, which friends are okay, and when they are to be in the house. . . . [T]he opinions of most young people are not valued; they are punished at the will or whim of adults; their emotions are considered "immature." In addition, adults reserve the right to punish, threaten, hit, take away "privileges," and ostracize young people when such actions are deemed to be instrumental in controlling or disciplining them.

If this were a description of the way a group of adults was treated, we would all agree that their oppression was almost total. However, for the most part, the adult world considers

this treatment of young people as acceptable because we were treated in much the same way, and internalized the idea that "that's the way you treat kids." . . .

THE HEART OF IT

. . .

Adults have enormous importance in the lives of almost every young person. This fact may make it difficult to understand what I am calling *adultism*. Not everything the adult world does in relation to young people is *adultist*. It is certainly true that children and young people need love, guidance, rules, discipline, teaching, role modeling, nurturance, protection. Childhood and adolescence are a steady series of developmental stages, each of which has a different set of needs, issues, and difficulties. For example, a three year old needs a different amount of sleep than a 15 year old; or, what works to physically restrain a seven year old will not work with an 18 year old; or, how you explain conception and birth to an inquisitive toddler will be quite different from how you explain these to a sexually active teenager.

Differing cultural, ethnic, gender, class, or religious approaches to these developmental stages can further complicate the identification of *adultism*. For example, what is considered "weak" in one gender, may be considered "strong" in another; or, belching may be considered rude in one culture and an expression of appreciation in another; or, childhood sex play may be condoned in one culture and condemned in another.

The point is that no one act or policy or custom or belief is in itself necessarily *adultist*. Something can be labeled *adultist* if it involves a *consistent* pattern of disrespect and mistreatment that has any or all of the following affects on young people:

- an undermining of self-confidence and self-esteem;
- an increasing sense of worthlessness;
- an increasing feeling of powerlessness;
- a consistent experience of not being taken seriously;
- a diminishing ability to function well in the world;
- a growing negative self-concept;
- increasing destructive acting out;
- increasing self-destructive acting "in" (getting sick frequently, developing health conditions, attempting suicide, depression, etc.);
- feeling unloved or unwanted.

Certainly these serious conditions do not entirely stem from *adultism*. Other factors like sexism, racism, poverty, physical or mental disability, and so on, may also contribute to these results. But systematic disrespect and mistreatment over years simply because of being young are major sources of trouble.

EVIDENCE THAT ADULTISM EXISTS

Other "isms" like racism and sexism are well established and accepted as realities. They each have a huge body of literature and research documenting the effects and history of the oppression. There are novels, movies, media presentations, political organizations, and social movements devoted to illuminating and or eliminating the existence of the "ism."

The concept of *adultism*, the systematic mistreatment and disrespect of young people, is relatively new and has not been widely accepted as a reality. There is certainly much research and literature on children and youth, but very little that concludes that young people are an oppressed group in our society, with parallels to other such groups. Part of my effort in this article is to draw forth enough examples, primarily from the United States, to point to the reality of *adultism*.

COMMON STATEMENTS

Consider how the following comments are essentially disrespectful. What are the assumptions behind each of them? Do you remember having heard any of these as a younger person?

- "You're so smart for fifteen!"
- "When are you going to grow up?"
- "Don't touch that, you'll break it!"
- "As long as you are in my house, you'll do it!
- "You're being childish."
- "You're so stupid (or clumsy, inconsiderate, etc.)!"
- "Go to your room!"
- "Don't ever yell at your mother like that!" (yelling)
- "She doesn't understand anything." (about a baby)
- "You are too old for that!" or "You're not old enough!"
- "Oh, it's only puppy love."
- "What do you know? You haven't experienced anything!"
- "It's just a stage. You'll outgrow it."

COMMON OCCURRENCES

PHYSICAL AND SEXUAL ABUSE

There are numerous examples of disrespect toward young people. Of course, there is the obvious oppressive treatment: physical and sexual abuse of young people. Official reports of child abuse reached 2.7 million in 1993.

OTHER PUNISHMENT AND THREATS

There is also a whole range of nonphysical punishments or threats: being routinely criticized, yelled at, invalidated, insulted, intimidated, or made to feel guilty with the effect of undermining a child's self-respect; being arbitrarily or unfairly "grounded" or denied "privileges." If young people protest against their mistreatment, they are often subjected to more punishment.

DENIED CONTROL

Young people are denied control and often even influence over most of the decisions that affect their bodies, their space, and their possessions. For example, most adults seem to think they can pick up little children or kiss them or pull their cheeks or touch their hair

without asking or without its being mutual. Adults can often be seen grabbing things out of children's hands without asking.

VERBAL INTERACTIONS

Most young people know that in a disagreement with an adult, their word will not be taken over the adult's. Most adults talk down to children, as if children could not understand them. Adults often talk about a young person with the young person present as if he or she were not there. Many adults give young people orders to do things or lay down rules with no explanation. Adults, in general, do not really listen to young people, do not take the concerns of a young person as seriously as they would an adult's, and have a hard time hearing the thinking of young people as worthy of adult respect, let alone on a par with the quality of adult thinking. Yet young people are expected to listen to adults all the time.

COMMUNITY INCIDENTS

Adolescent young people are frequently followed by security guards in stores, passed over by clerks who serve adults in line behind them, chased from parks or gathering places for no good reason by police, assumed by passing adults to "be up to no good." The media often promote negative images and stereotypes of them, especially of urban youth and black youth.

SCHOOL EXAMPLES

Schools subject students to incredible control through the use of hall passes, detention, suspension, expulsion, and other penalties. Any community certainly needs rules to live by, but the rules in most school communities are *imposed* on young people and enforced by the adult staff.

Consider these examples:

- Teachers sometimes yell at students with impunity, but students are disciplined if they yell back at teachers.
- Young people are sometimes punished unfairly because adults feel frustrated.
- Students are forced to accept their "grades" that, over time, cause students to eventually internalize a lifelong view of themselves as "smart" or "average" or "dumb"—with profound impact on many aspects of their lives. However, students do not get to officially "grade" teachers. If a student receives an "F," it is assumed the student failed, not the teacher.
- Young people have no real power in the important decisions that affect their lives in school.

SOCIETAL ADULTISM

LAWS

There is a different set of laws for young people. They do not have the same rights as adults. Of course, some laws specifically protect young people from mistreatment but other laws unduly restrict the life and freedom of young people. Curfew ordinances that exist in many communities apply to young people but not to adults. In divorce cases, until

a recent landmark custody case, young people were not even permitted to have a voice in deciding which parent, if either, they wished to live with.

CHILD DEVELOPMENT LITERATURE AND EDUCATION

An institutional example of *adultism* can be found in the literature of child development, which is full of misinformation and unfounded claims about young people that severely underestimates what young people are capable of. For example, in one classic textbook used by many students of child development, *The Magic Years* by Selma Freiberg, the author states that the only reason an infant before six months of age cries is because of physical pain. An infant has no emotional pain before this age, she says, because "an infant's intelligence has not yet developed the cognitive apparatus that gives rise to emotional responses." Many parents, including myself, in observing their own infants closely, know that this is not true. Yet, young child development professionals, often without children, are taught a distorted view of infant functioning as if it were gospel.

THE EFFECT OF CULTURAL PRACTICES: AN INTERESTING EXAMPLE

Generations of young people in western culture have grown up with their development limited by vast cultural biases that consistently underestimate human potential or misunderstand human development. For example, Joseph Chilton Pierce, in his *Crack in the Cosmic Egg*, found that in certain Ugandan cultures, infants reach the milestones of sitting, walking, and talking in half the time it takes for children in the United States. This seems to challenge accepted western norms. Researchers hypothesized two reasons for such seemingly accelerated development:

- From the moment of birth until well into the toddler stage, infants spend most of their time strapped skin to skin next to their mothers. From this vantage point the infants intimately experience the rhythms of body movement and speech, the cues in the environment that their mothers paid attention to, and constant tactile closeness.
- When not being carried, infants and toddlers were given loving massages for long periods every day by their mothers and other women in the community.

Researchers concluded that the combinations of these two practices stimulate complex neurological, motor, and hormonal systems of the infants to speed sitting, walking, and talking compared to what is considered "normal" in the West. The mere existence of such huge differences in the rate of development raises large questions about our assumptions about what is normal.

(The interesting back end of the Ugandan example is that at age five, after this extremely intimate early childhood experience, the children go through a rite of passage that includes being sent alone into the forest for several days, then being forced to leave their mother's home and sent to live with another relative. This shock appears to arrest the earlier rapid development, and maturation slows way down.)

GENERAL ADULT ATTITUDES

Many of us have heard older people say to us or other young people something like, "Growing up is giving up. You'd better get used to it." It is the accumulation of disappointments, losses, smashed dreams, unaccepted love, and other such painful experiences that

lead adults to say things like that. This crippling attitude is gradually forced upon young people. It is like a contagion, a virus about aging.

INSTITUTIONAL EXAMPLES

Young people in this country are forced to go to school for 12 years, whether school is an effective learning environment for them or not. They are forced by law and by parents (with the exception of those who exercise the demanding option of home schooling). If their spirit, energy, or learning style does not dovetail with the prevailing teacher, school, or educational philosophy, they begin to "fail," have "special needs," are "tracked," and may eventually be labeled as a "dropout." Throughout the 12 years, students have no voice, no power, no decision-making avenues to make significant changes. A critique of our educational system is beyond the scope of this article. Suffice it to say here that while society's motivation of providing education for all its young people is laudable, the school system as an institution perpetuates *adultism*.

Another institutional example is the absence of socially responsible, productive, and connected roles for young people in most societies. Certainly in the United States, young people find few jobs, no real policy-making roles, no positions of political power, and no high expectations of young people's contributions to society.

On the other hand, the youth market is exploited for profit as the manufacturing and entertainment industries manipulate styles, fads, popularity, and all other aspects of mass culture.

A MIRROR

A handy mirror for reflecting what may be *adultist* behavior is to ask oneself questions like the following:

- "Would I treat an adult this way?"
- "Would I talk to an adult in this tone of voice?"
- "Would I grab this out of an adult's hand?"
- "Would I make this decision for an adult?"
- "Would I have this expectation for an adult?"
- "Would I limit an adult's behavior this way?"
- "Would I listen to an adult friend's problem in this same way?"

Sometimes the answer may be "no" for good reason, depending on the circumstance. For example, I insist that my six year old son hold my hand when crossing the street, but not my 18 year old daughter. However, many times there is no justifiable reason for treating a younger person differently except habit and attitude. If your "no" sounds a little hollow, it might be worth re-examining your reasons for doing it.

THE EMOTIONAL LEGACY

I hope this short list of examples begins to put our work with young people in a larger context. Most of the examples I used have been reported to me by young people. They

consistently report that the main message they get from the adult world is that they are not as important as adults; they do not feel that they are taken seriously; they have little or no power.

They say that the emotional legacy of years of this kind of treatment is a heavy load, which can include any or all of the following: anger, feelings of powerlessness, insecurity, depression, lack of self-confidence, lack of self-respect, hopelessness, feeling unloved and unwanted.

What are some possible results of such feelings on their behavior, especially as they get into adolescence and early adulthood?

- Some act "out" by bullying, being prone to violence, rebelling against the "norm," leaving home early, and so on.
- Some act "in" by becoming self-destructive: suicide, alcohol and drug abuse, depression, etc.
- Some gain a sense of belonging or safety by joining a gang, a clique, a club, teams
- Some isolate themselves, being lonely, not asking for help, not having any close relationships, not trusting.

Again, *adultism* is not the only source of such behaviors, but it surely plays a major role.

A LINK TO OTHER FORMS OF OPPRESSION

There is another important reason for understanding and challenging *adultism*. The various ways we were disrespected and mistreated have, over time, robbed us of huge amounts of our human power, access to our feelings, confidence in our thinking and ability to act, and enjoyment of living. The pain we experience as young people helps condition us to play one of two roles as we get older: to accept further mistreatment as women, as people of color, as workers, etc., or to flip to the other side of the relationship and act in oppressive ways toward others who are in relatively less powerful positions than ours.

A simple illustration might help make this clear. Picture this: a sixth grader is humiliated by the teacher in front of the class for not doing the math problem at the board correctly. The recess bell rings. He is fuming. He feels disrespected. He goes outside and picks on someone to get his feelings out. Whom does he pick on? Someone smaller and often someone younger. And so it goes: the 6th grader picks on the 5th grader. The 5th grader turns and knocks down the 3rd grader. The 3rd grader hits the 1st grader. The 1st grader goes home and picks on his little sister. The little sister turns and kicks the cat.

We can observe among a group of children the mistreatment being passed down among them. It is being passed down the line of physical power, bigger to smaller, and often older to younger.

The significance of this early experience becomes clearer when it is generalized to other forms of the abuse of power. Men, for example, who were routinely beaten as little boys, grow up to be wife beaters. This is a clinical truism. Similarly, white people, disrespected as children, turn the same attitude, embellished with misinformation, on people of color.

This is one of the pervasive and lasting effects of the mistreatment of young people. Bullies have been bullied. Abusers have been abused. People who have been put down put others down. If a person had not been disrespected and mistreated over and over again as a child and young person, that person would not willingly accept being treated that way as he got older, nor would he willingly heap disrespect on others.

Adultism, racism, sexism, and other "isms" all reinforce each other. The particular ways young people are treated or mistreated are inseparable from their class, gender, or ethnic

background. However, the phenomena of being disrespected simply because of being young holds true across diverse backgrounds.

. . .

115

"Look Out, Kid, It's Something You Did"

The Criminalization of Children

Bernadine Dohrn

A seismic change has taken place. Youngsters are to be feared. Our worst enemy is among us. Children must be punished, held accountable, expelled. We have developed zero-tolerance for children.

The tragedy at Columbine further escalated the decade-long process of criminalizing the behavior of children, recasting an additional icon to accompany the fearful, racially coded language describing *some* youth in trouble with the law as "superpredators." The newly sensationalized school shootings of 1997–1999 involved suburban or small-town religious White boys with guns, killing their fellow students, spawning a White, upper-middle-class discourse of violent youth based on alienation and isolation. School shootings have become a trope—an inspiration for politicians, funding streams, educational pandemonium, and law enforcement expansion. Yet perhaps more significantly, beneath the rarely occurring but dominant focus on youth homicides, normal youth behavior and misbehavior became further criminalized, all in the name of safety. Children bore the brunt of the national soul-searching into the conditions of childhood in America at the end of the twentieth century.

No one can ignore the shocking fact that in the decade of 1985–1994, 25,000 children were murdered in the United States. In fact, there is the equivalent of a Columbine virtually every day in America. The proliferation of lethal handguns in the possession of children that resulted in children killing children (83% of victims aged 12–18 were killed by handguns); the syndication of youth gangs into illegal-drug cartels; the flourishing of youth violence reported on local TV news stations; the resulting public fear and pandering of politicians and law enforcement officials; and the popularization of youth demonization by noted academics—these are the tangled elements that reinforce and strengthen one another, spiraling into an overlapping system of causes and consequences and qualitative changes in how society perceives, and even thinks about, its adolescents.

Today, behaviors that were once punished or sanctioned by the school vice-principal, family members, a neighbor, or a coach are more likely to lead to an adolescent being arrested, referred to juvenile or criminal court, formally adjudicated, incarcerated in a detention center, waived or transferred to adult criminal court for trial, sentenced under mandatory sentencing guidelines, and incarcerated with adults. The increase in discretion ceded to prosecutors and police has transformed the decision of what to charge for a given offense: Yesterday's battery may be inflated into assault, simple assault into aggravated assault, a schoolyard fight into multiple felony charges. The arrest of multiple juvenile defendants for each incident further escalates youth crime statistics.

This massive shift toward criminalizing youngsters is evident in the increasing numbers of court cases, detained and incarcerated youth in overcrowded facilities, and legislative crackdowns on juvenile crime. In the past decade, the number of formally processed delinquency cases increased 78%.

Within this climate, a less visible, less sensational shift has quietly been executed. This change profoundly impacts millions of children, their classmates and families, and our common future.

This decade of relentless reconditioning of how citizens think about children—on the part of law enforcement, legislators, professionals, academics, the media, and frightened neighborhood residents—has shifted the paradigm. Through the catalyst of changes in criminal and juvenile law, much of adolescent behavior has been criminalized and youngsters themselves demonized. Casting children as frightening makes full use of racial, ethnic, and gender stereotyping, resulting in both disproportionate impact as well as generalizations impacting all youth. This transformation in how we think about ourselves thinking about children has taken an incalculable toll on adults and children alike. The daily discourse about children has shifted from innocence to guilt, from possibility to punishment, from protection to fear. This sinister criminalization of childhood now permeates basic life: the schools, the parks and neighborhoods, child protection, and health care.

In the 1990s, fiscal priorities shifted from education, child protection, and scholarships to prison construction, law enforcement growth, and expanded mechanisms for the social control and exile of sectors of youth. Correctional spending nationally now exceeds $40 billion per year, to pay for a 500% rise in the prison population since 1972. In two short decades, budgets for prisons grew twice as fast as for education; prison spending increased 823% between 1988 and 1995, while education expenditures grew only 374%. More sobering, the vast majority of the states now spend at least one and a half times as much on prisons as they do on education.

In the past decade, New York State spent more than $700 million on prisons, while slashing the state and city college budgets by $600 million, with one result being that the number of people of color enrolled in New York's state colleges and universities is substantially lower than the number currently incarcerated there. Not only are more children currently seeing the inside of prison walls rather than classrooms, there is a new movement to place more, and younger, children into the adult criminal system.

One hundred years ago in Chicago, the world's first juvenile court for children was premised on the removal of children from adult jails and adult poorhouses. At the centennial of the juvenile court, children are being reincarcerated with adults, tried as adults in adult criminal court, and subject to imputation of adult *mens rea* with mandatory-sentencing statutes that reject rehabilitation as a goal.

. . .

CRIMINALIZING YOUTH BEHAVIORS

A major consequence of the tidal wave of fear, violence, and terror associated with children has been adult legislative and policy decisions to criminalize vast sectors of youth behavior. In part, this tendency is fueled by an organized drive on the part of certain political forces to "get tough on youth violence"; in part the changes have resulted from an accumulation of legislative reactions to a particular sensationalized case, the hackneyed mantra to "do something."

The sum total of a decade's *legal* responses is the transformation of the social landscape that children inhabit. Schools have become military fortresses. Hanging out becomes

illegal. Fewer systems want to work with adolescents in need. Youngsters who have themselves been neglected or abused by adults pose too many challenges and have too many problems to be addressed. Health care and mental health services are rarely organized for adolescents. Schools want to get rid of the troublemakers and the kids who bring down the test scores. Minor offenses are no longer dealt with by retail stores, school disciplinarians, parents, or youth workers, but rather the police are called, arrests are made, petitions are filed.

Six of seven juvenile arrests are for a nonviolent offense. Of the 2.7 million arrests of young people under 18 years of age, property offenses (particularly larceny/theft), drug offenses, disorderly conduct, runaways, curfew and loitering, and liquor law violations account for the vast majority of the arrests. Ironically, if all male children aged 10–18 were incarcerated until their 25th birthday, eliminating youth crime tomorrow, there would still be 90% of violent crime: the adult offenders. The intense focus on a youth crime epidemic thus is a social choice rather than a strategic response to the facts about crime and public safety.

The criminalizing of adolescent behavior takes place in multiple ways. Major social institutions for youth have constricted eligibility and eased methods for expulsion. Schools, child welfare systems, probation, and health services have all made it easier to violate, terminate, exclude, and expel youngsters. Where these youth go for survival, help, socialization development, care, and attention is unclear. One door that always remains open is the gateway to juvenile and criminal justice. Overcrowded juvenile correctional institutions, deficient youth facilities, and disproportionate minority confinement are among the consequences.

POLICING THE SCHOOLS

> I would there were no age between ten and three- and twenty, or that youth would sleep out the rest; for there is nothing in the between but getting wenches with child, wronging the ancientry, stealing, fighting.
> —Shakespeare, *The Winter's Tale*, act III, scene III. ll. 61–66

Schools have become a major feeder of children into juvenile and adult criminal courts; simultaneously, schools themselves are becoming more prisonlike. Closed campuses, locker searches, contraband, interrogations and informers, heavily armed tactical police patrols, uniforms (M. M. Harrigan, personal communication, 1998)—these are elements of public and even private high school life today. It is paradoxical but fundamental that a handful of high-profile school shootings masks a broader and deeper criminalization of school life, accompanied by the policing of schools, which has transformed public schools across America into a principal referral source for juvenile-justice prosecution.

Two policies contribute to this dramatic new role for schools: first, the increased policing of schools, leading to a significant increase in school-based arrests and the simultaneous abdication of educators; and second, the substantial increase in school exclusions, including suspensions/expulsions of students, propelled initially by the legislative green light that mandated "zero-tolerance" policies for gun possession as a condition of federal funding. That limited definition of zero-tolerance rapidly exploded, in practice, to include misdeeds of all sorts, both in school and outside of school. Rather than insisting on the teaching potential in adolescent misbehavior for both the miscreant and the other students, rather than seizing the "teachable moment," rather than keeping an educational perspective on sanctioning and social accountability, principals and teachers—admittedly under pressure from frightened parents—have ceded their authority to law enforcement personnel, particularly to police and prosecutors, and willingly participated in excluding troublemakers,

difficult kids, disabled youth, and children in trouble from the very education that is their primary hope. These so-called zero-tolerance and security policies were escalating before the high-profile school shootings of 1997–98 and the 1999 Columbine High School tragedy. Since then, the policies, the dollars, and the hardware for policing and militarizing schools have mushroomed, and the trend is likely to continue into the next decade.

School-Based Arrests. How grave is the school crime problem? In 1997, there were more than 180,000 school fights leading to arrests, almost 120,000 thefts in schools leading to arrests, nearly 110,000 incidents of school vandalism leading to arrests, and fewer than 20,000 violent crimes. Serious violent crime is extremely rare within schools and constitutes a small percentage of the total amount of school offending. Ninety percent of principals surveyed reported no major serious, violent crime in their schools. In fact, victim self-reports indicate that actual school crime numbers have not changed significantly during the past 20 years.

The first three categories (some 400,000 arrests) are noteworthy. Most school crime is theft, some 62%. School-based incidents such as fighting, theft, and vandalism have traditionally been handled within a school disciplinary system. Forty years ago, an offender would be sent to the office of the vice-principal, a parent might be called, detention hall (remaining for an hour after school) might be mandated, a letter of apology might be required. It would have been difficult to imagine police being called, arrests and handcuffs employed, court filings and incarceration being options.

In today's Chicago public schools, and increasingly in suburban and rural school districts, police are routinely employed by schools. Some schools employ police officers in their teacher salary lines, and encourage police in uniforms, armed, tactical-unit police, and plainclothes police to patrol their schools. Police officers may make half again their salary by moonlighting with the public schools outside their regular duty hours. School-assigned police may be evaluated based on their numbers of arrests. Police may be under no obligation to consult with the school principal about how to respond to a particular youth's misbehavior or to a particular incident. In certain locations, police fail to inform principals or school officials that a student has been arrested during school hours, on school grounds. One authority has replaced another.

At Paul Robeson High School in Chicago, for example, local police precinct data indicate that 158 students were arrested at Robeson in 1996–97. The breakdown of those arrest charges, from a major urban high school, is revealing: 61 arrests for pager possession, 21 for disorderly conduct, 14 for mob action, 16 for (nonfirearms) weapon possession. In 1998, after the school adopted a strategy of small-school reform—breaking the massive high school into smaller units where no youth slips through the cracks—arrests plummeted to 28, 22 of those for pager violations!

Massive locker searches began in 1994–95 in Chicago schools, resulting in numerous student arrests during a single day's lockdown: 40 students at Westinghouse High School, 46 at Kenwood High School, 50 at Roosevelt High School, and 57 at Lincoln High School. In each case, the substantial majority of teens were charged with possession of beepers. Possession of pagers appears to be an offense that is both a status offense (for which adults would not be arrested) and an expansion of drug laws by labeling pagers as "drug paraphernalia" or contraband: transforming a technological convenience into a crime. School-based arrests for possession of pagers is a classic example of the criminalization of youth.

Additional school-based arrests include offense charges such as disorderly conduct or mob action, discretionary decisions that could be based on incidents involving significant disruptions or merely minor occurrences. Decisions to call a shouting match, a no-harm tussle, or locker graffiti a crime, to arrest rather than see a teachable moment, to prosecute rather than resolve disputes—these practices are turning schools into policed territory. Researchers suggest that the expectation of school crime in fact creates it.

This pattern of accelerating school incidents into delinquency offenses or criminal acts further heightens disproportionate minority arrests and confinement in juvenile justice. To date, it is the large, public, urban high schools that have become sites of substantial police presence, that are under pressure to control youth misbehavior, and that are without influential parents with resources to buffer their children from the juvenile justice system. Since Jonesboro and Littleton, suburban and rural high schools are also becoming fortresses, and arrests and mandatory expulsions are escalating. This bleeding of urban responses into middle-class life has its own dynamic and momentum, focusing more, perhaps, on drugs, tobacco, dress, and behavior toward authority, with more private institutionalization of youth as a consequence.

The increasing regimentation of school time results in few breaks, little time for lunch, less physical education, an attrition of music, art, and humanities classes, and closed campuses in high schools. Closed campuses result from neighborhood residents' and parents' complaints about the mobile presence of children during the school day. Teachers monitor student lunch periods and move their own lunch time to the end of the day, shortening the school day. In fact, schools are increasingly simulating prisons, as if preparing their students for a likely future: locked in, regimented, searched, uniformed, pressured to become informers, and observed with suspicion.

Search and seizure of student lockers, backpacks, and persons is legitimized. A culture of informing on fellow students is encouraged and mandated by school officials, without exploration of ethical considerations and conflicting values involved. The blurring of school discipline and delinquency accelerates.

When school sanctioning is handed over to law enforcement *in the first instance* for the vast majority of minor school infractions, not only do the offender and the victim fail to learn from the incident, and not only is the consequence more likely to be crushing rather than illuminating, but the entire community fails to take hold of the problem as a school-community matter.

The failure to place serious reliance on peer juries, teen courts, or community-justice alternatives and to rely instead on armed police for school safety has startling and profound consequences. It is an abdication of adult responsibility and engagement with youngsters. It creates a juvenile delinquency record for vast numbers of youth who might otherwise not be in trouble with the law. Having any delinquency or criminal record has increasing consequences for scholarships, higher education, job eligibility, and escalated sanctions if there is a subsequent police investigation or arrest.

School Exclusion: Suspensions and Expulsions. Suspensions and expulsions from schools have simultaneously exploded as a new national trend, exemplified by the struggle over the expulsion of six Decatur, Illinois, high school students and their subsequent arrest. Fueled by federal legislation in 1994 mandating a one-year "exclusion" for possession of a firearm on school property (Gun Free Schools Act, 1994), new legislation was passed in every state within a 5-month period to maintain federal-funding eligibility. One year later, the Safe School Act (1994) revised and expanded the prohibition to "dangerous weapon" rather than "firearm"; and "dangerous weapon" was defined, in the amended language, as "a weapon, device, instrument, material, or substance, animate or inanimate, that is used for, *or is readily capable of,* causing death or serious bodily injury." This opened the door for a stampede—and for wide discretionary expansion of the new exclusion policy by school personnel that is applied disproportionately to African American and Latino students. In Decatur, for example, 82% of all expulsions of students for over 3 years involved African American youth, although they constitute only 46% of school enrollment. These youth are frequently left with dubious alternative education, leading to dropping out or incarceration, or with no educational resources or supports.

In Massachusetts, for example, the number of school expulsions or exclusions under state law rose to more than 1,500 in 1996–97, with a disproportionate racial impact. Statewide, although African American students made up 8.4% of the school population, in 1996–97 they suffered 23% of the expulsions; Latinos, who were 10% of the school population, constituted 33.8% of the expelled students. This pattern is doubly troubling in states such as Massachusetts where there is no mandatory alternative education. Further, it is rare to find students with legal representation at the administrative expulsion hearings. In Chicago, approximately 20 hearings per day are scheduled on expulsion of Chicago public school students. All but a handful of students are expelled, according to the law students who sit as administrative hearing officers.

This synergistic relationship of police and principals goes further in Chicago, where law permits schools to suspend or expel students who have been charged or convicted of violating the law, even when the alleged delinquent or criminal behavior did not occur on school property or during school hours. These laws and regulations presume that principals will find out about non-school-based felony arrests and convictions of students from their closer relationship with police and prosecutors. This embrace is codified in a series of laws recently passed by the Illinois legislature that facilitate even greater exchange of information between law enforcement personnel, schools, and child welfare personnel.

The Illinois School Records Act (105 ILCS 10/6, 1999) permits state's attorneys and police officers unrestricted access to student records and further requires the school to make law enforcement requests part of the child's permanent record; other provisions (705 ILCS 405/5–325) require school officials to provide to the State's Attorney, upon request, information or a written report relating to the alleged commission of an offense; and Illinois Public Aid Code (305 ILCS 5.11–9, 1999) permits law enforcement access to certain public aid records without subpoena or notice requirements. The U.S. House of Representatives seeks to offer incentives to states to accommodate even greater exchange of information between schools and law enforcement by including in a proposed juvenile justice bill a provision that gives states additional funds if they make juvenile records available to schools (Juvenile Justice and Delinquency Prevention Act, 1999).

This wholesale relaxation of confidentiality protections for youth, protections that were a fundamental principle of the original Juvenile Court Act founders in Chicago in 1899, has further increased the incidence of suspensions/expulsions and of school-based arrests. Schools are routinely notified of a student's non-school-site arrests, probation, or detention. The knowledge that a student is in trouble or is a troublemaker may be a factor in a student being more intensely scrutinized or being seen as a "bad kid."

It is worth noting that the school front door, as well as the exit door, has been transformed. School principals and administrators have wider discretion to refuse to enroll a student, even a public school student who resides in the appropriate district. This constricted eligibility for school registration is evident to those working with special education students, youth being released from juvenile detention or corrections, or youngsters in crisis who may manifest behavior problems. School enrollment and registration, once assumed to be a right, has become an arena of vast discretion and terrain for further educational exclusion.

Jane Addams and the other Hull House women, a century ago, were proponents of compulsory education, the abolition of child labor, and the creation of a separate court for children. These innovations were interrelated, for the primary goal was education and opportunity for children, not the exploitation of hazardous labor or incarceration with adults in prisons or adult poorhouses. Grace Abbott and her colleagues continued to document school attendance for decades as a bellwether for the well-being of children. What irony that 100 years after the establishment of the world's first juvenile court, schools and

courts have again partnered, but this time to exclude, arrest, expel, and suspend children *from* school and to punish, prosecute, and imprison them in the criminal justice system.

. . .

Loitering, Curfew, and Association Offenses. Local municipalities, frequently authorized by state legislatures, have rushed to enact new curfew ordinances, some 1,000 since 1990. Curfew laws, directed at youth to prevent youth crime in the late evening, fail to address the peak juvenile crime times, between 2 P.M. and 5 P.M. during the school year. Gang offending is similarly concentrated in mid to late afternoon.

In 1992, the Chicago City Council enacted the Gang Congregation Ordinance, which prohibits criminal street gang members from loitering with one another or with others in any public place (*City of Chicago v. Morales*, 1999). The ordinance created a criminal offense punishable by a fine of up to $500, imprisonment for not more than 6 months, and a requirement to perform up to 120 hours of community service. During the 3 years of its enforcement, police made more than 42,000 arrests and issued more than 89,000 dispersal orders. The ordinance was overturned by an appellate court, the Illinois Supreme Court, and the U.S. Supreme Court as unconstitutionally vague and failing to provide notice to the public about what conduct was illegal.

Curfew ordinances are notorious for being subject to racial and ethnic disparities in enforcement. Furthermore, arrests of girls for curfew violations increased by 155.2% between 1987 and 1996. Curfew violations have vastly widened the net of criminal involvement for youth, particularly youth of color and young women.

YOUNG WOMEN IN JUVENILE JUSTICE

Each year, girls account for one in four arrests of youth in America, yet their presence in the juvenile justice system remains largely invisible. Young women have traditionally been arrested and incarcerated in large numbers for status offenses: arrests and prosecutions of young women declined after the JJDP of 1974 mandate to deinstitutionalize and divert youth charged with status offenses into programs providing alternatives to legal adjudication. But the past decade of criminalizing youth has resulted in increasing arrests of girls, once again, for status offenses or other minor violations of law.

Fully one quarter of all female delinquency arrests are for status offenses (as compared with less than 10% for boys), while another quarter of girls arrested are charged with larceny theft (basically, shoplifting)! Girls arrested for running away from home increased by 20.7%, and as noted above, curfew arrests of girls mushroomed an astonishing 155.2%. Although media reports suggest that girls, as well as male delinquents, have become violent predators, the facts again belie this characterization of violence.

Arrests of girls for violent crime index offenses during the decade 1987–1996 did skyrocket, up 118.1%. Female delinquency charges for "other assault" increased 142.6% in the same period. Assault charges can range from conduct involving simple verbal aggression and threats, to minor school conflicts, nonserious disputes, and harmless fights; increasingly girls have been arrested for simple assault. Analysis suggests that much of the "tyranny of small numbers" (this phrase is attributed to Barry Krisberg, 1994) results from relabeling or bootstrapping—the practice by police, prosecutors, or judges that transforms a nondelinquency, noncriminal offense into an offense subject to incarceration. Girls, for example, are more likely to be arrested for noninjury assaults or as bystanders or companions to males involved in fighting. Virtually every person-to-person offense among girls in the Maryland juvenile justice system (97.9%) involved assault, and half of those were a fight with a family member, generally a parent. This form of escalated charging is most pronounced against African American girls.

Legislative erosion and organized opposition to the JJDP mandate against incarcerating children charged with status offenses has taken multiple forms, resulting in greater reincarceration of young women. In 1980, the definition of status offender in the federal law was amended to exclude children "who violated a court order." Girls in foster care placements or group homes, for example, who run away, can be classified as delinquents and incarcerated, rather than characterized as status offenders who could be diverted away from court adjudication into specified programs for youth. This subversion of the original intent and purpose of JJDP falls most heavily on female delinquents, where the gender double standard results in judges sentencing girls to detention for contempt citations (violations of court orders) in far greater numbers than boys—apparently attempting to control and contain young women to protect them from themselves, in a manner that would not occur with young men. The 4.3% likelihood of incarceration for girls in juvenile justice accelerates to 29.9% when they are held in contempt.

One consequence of the combination of traditional and contemporary juvenile justice pressures on young women is a racial, two-track system of justice, where White girls are institutionalized in private facilities and young women of color are detained in public facilities.

The numbers of girls held in private institutions has dramatically increased; 62% of incarcerated girls are being held in private facilities, and 85% of those are detained for "nondelinquent" offenses (such as violations of court orders, or status offenses). The number of young women detained in public detention facilities has remained steady. Translated bluntly, this means that White girls are recommended for "treatment" whereas African American and Latina girls are detained.

Pending federal legislation would encourage the uses of contempt violations as a path to detention and once again would permit the holding of children in adult jails. It is girls, frequently held in rural and small-town jails for minor infractions, who become most subject to violent abuse and suicide in such confinement.

Women have become the fastest growing sector of people in prison in the past decade; similarly, detentions of girls increased 23% between 1989 and 1993. Girls remain in detention longer awaiting placement in private facilities or correctional institutions and are generally disliked by those working in the overwhelmingly male system of juvenile justice. The failure to take into account past or current physical or sexual abuse and the lack of appropriate gender and cultural programming to address the needs of young women delinquents is pervasive.

Transgressions by girls have historically been treated differently from male misbehavior. It is profoundly disturbing that the combined invisibility and double standard paternalism/harshness against young females result in increasing loss of freedom for young women and inequality of response in programming. The women of Hull House would be dismayed and enraged by this backtracking on fundamental justice for children.

. . .

CHILDREN IN ADULT CRIMINAL COURTS

Crucial questions are going unasked as children are increasingly appearing in adult criminal courts. Criminal courts operate on guilty pleas, and informed, competent decisions to plead guilty may not be possible for many children. Adult courts fail to acknowledge the youth of the child, to take into account the child's age, developmental capacity, or experience when assessing culpability. Adult courts impose adult sentences, which differ from delinquency sentences in two critical ways: they are determinate, and they are significantly longer. Determinate sentences result in extended incarceration of children, beyond a time when they may be rehabilitated. Longer sentences mean that a child will ultimately be

incarcerated in an adult prison, where they may be subject to physical abuse, suicide, and an education from adult offenders, rather than rehabilitation for a future productive life. Youth sent to the adult criminal system are essentially cut off from educational and counseling programs, from juvenile probation officers, and from appropriate medical and mental health services. Sending children to prison encourages more sophisticated criminal behavior. There is ample evidence that children respond better to positive prevention programs than they do to punitive legislative measures.

THE EROSION OF CIVIC RESPONSIBILITY FOR CHILDREN

Addressing the needs of both public safety and positive youth development requires an active and participating public. If the only popular cry is for short-term fixes—"get them out of the neighborhood," "lock them up and throw away the key," and "something must be done"—society will continue on its current course of escalating punishment for children and increasing adult abdication of responsibility. If schools are not for learning from mistakes, if child welfare is not for protecting children who have been harmed, if health systems are not geared to healing youth—further reliance on exclusion, punishment, and prison becomes the likely option. Tens of thousands of productive adults who passed through the juvenile justice system in their youth are witness to the healing and redemptive effect of getting a second chance: the program, the judge, the probation officer who made a difference and allowed them to turn their life around.

The real adult problem is masked by our social focus on the "youth problem." In scapegoating kids, we reveal that as a society, we don't like adolescents very much. Youth, being the intelligent people they are, are vividly aware of the angry popular and policy backlash directed against them. They are keenly alert to issues of fairness (which are at the heart of justice); they observe the adult world around them with a laserlike ability to identify hypocrisy. They see that their voices, their opinions, and their interests are largely ignored, as are their rights as future citizens.

The use of the law to enforce a legal-educational-political system that harms the aspirations and best intentions of youth cannot be good for society. Holding children accountable for protracted social failures reeks of expediency and runs counter to developing international human rights standards for children around the world. Adult citizens are engaged in the social neglect and abuse of children, both in public fiscal policy and in the absence of the commitment of our own precious time and imagination.

Criminalizing youth behaviors, policing schools, punishing children by depriving them of an education, constricting social protections for abused and neglected youth, and subjecting youth to law enforcement as a "social service"—these trends smack of social injustice, racial inequity, dehumanization, and fear-filled demonization of youngsters, who are our prospective hope. At stake here is the civic will to invest in our common future by seeing other people's children as our own.

116

Police Make Life Hell for Youth of Color

Kathy Durkin

Going to the grocery store, visiting a friend and walking home from work or school are all ordinary, everyday occurrences. But not so for hundreds of thousands of people, mostly from African-American and Latin@ communities, who are stopped, questioned, asked for their I.D., searched and often arrested here in New York—and around the country. It happens to many youth and even to children.

At a time when more white people appear to be rejecting racism at the polls, racial profiling by police departments and other state agencies is on the rise. It is systemic and deeply entrenched in the "criminal justice system" nationwide.

Statistics given in new studies and reports starkly bear this out. But the statistics cannot convey the intimidation, anxiety and anger that so many people, especially Black and Latin@ youth, must live with on a daily basis, nor the effect this can have throughout their lives on them and their families.

In the first quarter of this year, New York City police, by their own report, stopped, questioned and/or searched 145,098 people, more than half of them African Americans. At this alarming rate, a record 600,000 people will be stopped this year.

In the last two years, nearly 1 million New Yorkers were harassed by police in this manner—90 percent of them people of color. That's 1,300 a day. And it's legally allowed.

These operations, just in the past two years, have put more than 1 million innocent people, mostly African-American and Latin@, into the huge police database; they are subject to future criminal investigations merely by their inclusion there.

The New York Civil Liberties Union (NYCLU) is challenging the legality of these potentially discriminatory practices and demanding information on the database kept by the NYPD—which the department refuses to turn over. It contains personal information on everyone stopped by police, though the vast majority—90 percent—have not been charged with any crimes.

The NYCLU is also demanding full disclosure from the NYPD about police shootings in this city. The full story of this horror is not known. In addition to the terrible, tragic and totally unjustified killings of unarmed individuals like Sean Bell, Amadou Diallo, Ousmane Zongo and Patrick Dorismund, countless other people of color have been shot. Yet the NYPD refuses to reveal what proportion of those shot over the last 10 years have been members of oppressed nationalities. In the two years prior to that, it was 90 percent (nyclu.org).

Another aspect of the NYPD's racial profiling scheme is the campaign of terror targeting youth for possessing miniscule amounts of marijuana. This, too, usually happens in communities of color, even though social studies show a higher rate of marijuana use among white youth (nyclu.org). In 2007 alone, police arrested more than 100 people per day, or 39,700 in total, for this so-called crime.

The NYCLU has just issued a report entitled, "The Marijuana Arrest Crusade in New York City: Racial Bias in Police Policy 1997–2007," by Prof. Harry G. Levin and Deborah Peterson Small. It describes the NYPD's campaign against oppressed youth. Of the nearly 400,000 people arrested in that 10-year period, 205,000 were African Americans and 122,000 were Latin@s. This represented a tenfold increase over the previous 10-year period.

Since decriminalization in 1977, the possession of a small amount of marijuana has not constituted a "crime" in New York City—as long as it is not shown in public. Possession since then has been merely a "violation," such as speeding and other traffic infractions.

However, the police frequently stop Black and Latin@ youth and then arrest them on the charge of misdemeanor possession—when, most of the time, this is not the case. High school students are kept in jail overnight until they go to court. Then they are pressured into a plea bargain, usually with an overworked, court-appointed attorney representing them.

In a city where police can gun down a young man like Sean Bell just hours before his wedding and get off with not even a slap on the wrist, youth stopped by cops never know what might happen to them.

These youth are then labeled with criminal records, which will follow them for the rest of their lives and can create future obstacles for them in higher education, employment and housing. They're also driven into the "criminal justice" system—their fingerprints and photographs go into the NYPD database—when they've done nothing wrong.

It is well known that there is serious drug abuse in many high-pressure professions in this city, yet the police don't occupy financial centers or carry out random searches in wealthy neighborhoods.

Rafael Mutis, coordinator of 7 Neighborhood Action Partnership Network, which works to repeal the draconian New York State Rockefeller drug laws, explains that "drug use" has become a pretext for stop-and-frisk searches in low-income neighborhoods. "They don't go after people on Wall Street," he said, "where there's a daily snowstorm" of cocaine use (highbridgehorizon.com).

It is no coincidence that police repression has increased even as billionaire Mayor Michael Bloomberg and his Wall Street cronies are trying to make New York City a haven for the super-rich, and the real-estate tycoons are gentrifying working-class neighborhoods as fast as they can. "Law-enforcement" agencies are helping them out by stepping up the intimidation of low-income and oppressed people to suppress opposition and try to drive them further out of the city.

All people need to show solidarity with the oppressed communities, especially the youth, in this struggle against police repression.

117

Ageism

Another Form of Bigotry

Robert N. Butler

Just as racism and sexism are based on ethnicity and gender, ageism is a form of systematic stereotyping and discrimination against people simply because they are old. As a group,

older people are categorized as rigid in thought and manner, old-fashioned in morality and skills. They are boring, stingy, cranky, demanding, avaricious, bossy, ugly, dirty, and useless.

An ageist younger generation sees older people as different from itself; it subtly ceases to identify with its elders as human beings. Old men become geezers, old goats, gaffers, fogies, coots, gerries, fossils, and codgers, and old women are gophers and geese. A crone, hag, or witch is a withered old woman.

Ageism takes shape in stereotypes and myths, outright disdain and dislike, sarcasm and scorn, subtle avoidance, and discriminatory practices in housing, employment, pension arrangements, health care, and other services. Older persons are subject to physical, emotional, social, sexual, and financial abuse. They are the focus of prejudice regarding their capacity for work and sexual intimacy, which Freud described as the two most important human activities. Taking away the validation of work or purposeful activities and demeaning the capacity for love are surely the most profound forms of age prejudice.

Historically, older persons have been venerated in most societies and cultures *in word*, although not always in deed. In fact, to be old or disabled was always a liability for practical reasons. Nomadic groups from North Africa to Alaska abandoned their old when the welfare of the entire tribe or group was at stake.

The term *ageism*, which I introduced in 1968, is now part of the English language. It is identical to any other prejudice in its consequences. The older person feels ignored or is not taken seriously and is patronized. Anthropologist Barbara Myerhoff speaks about "death by invisibility" when she describes an older woman who, "unseen," was "accidentally" killed by a bicyclist.

This invisibility extends to emergencies, such as the tragic case of September 11, 2001, in New York City. Animal activists evacuated dogs and cats within twenty-four hours after the World Trade Center was attacked, while disabled or older persons were abandoned in their apartments for up to seven days before ad hoc medical teams arrived to rescue them. Older persons were also invisible in the devastation caused by Hurricane Katrina in New Orleans.

Reminiscent of the great social scientist George Mead's concept of the "looking glass self," older persons may turn ageist prejudice inward, absorbing, accepting, and identifying with the discrimination. Some examples:

- Simone De Beauvoir, author of *The Coming of Age*, described her disgust at growing old, although she wrote lovingly of her own mother's aging in *A Very Easy Death*.
- Comedian George Burns noted the unfortunate tendency of old people to conform to their stereotype—what he called the old person's "act"—by learning to shuffle about and decondition in a kind of identification and collaboration with the ageist society that demeans them.
- Yale psychologist Becca R. Levy reports that constant bombardment of negative stereotypes increases blood pressure. *Ageism can make an older person sick.*

Advertisements and greeting cards depict older persons as forgetful, dependent, child-like, and—perhaps the ultimate insult in our society—sexless. Conversely, older people who continue to have sexual desires are dirty old men and ridiculous old women.

Wrinkles, crow's feet, liver spots, and dull skin are disparaged in our youth-dominated culture and exploited by the cosmetics industry and plastic surgeons. Women who have relied upon their appearance for self-definition and men and women who have depended upon a youthful appearance in their work are up against overwhelming odds. The clock does not stop. When does one cease to be beautiful and start on the journey to being

over-the-hill? How many women past fifty can look like model Lauren Hutton or Susan Sarandon? How many men and women can overcome disability with elegance and style?

A study conducted by the American Academy of Facial, Plastic and Reconstructive Surgery revealed that baby boomers have received nearly a quarter of a million face-lifts and other cosmetic surgeries. Most of these patients were over fifty. The Associated Press has quoted Karen Seccombe, a University of Florida sociologist, who said, "The thought of saggy breasts, hair loss or wrinkles doesn't sit well with people who have grown up emphasizing fitness and youth."

The film and television industries help to perpetuate ageism.

- Less than 2 percent of prime-time television characters are sixty-five or older, although this group is 12.7 percent of the population.
- 11 percent of male characters between fifty and sixty-four are categorized as old versus 22 percent of female characters.
- 75 percent of male characters sixty-five and older are characterized as old versus 83 percent of female characters of the same age.
- Only one-third of older characters are women.
- Middle-aged and older white males have joined women and minorities on the sidelines, as white men under forty get most of the jobs writing for television and film. Employment and earning prospects for older writers have declined relative to those for younger writers.
- According to one study, approximately 70 percent of older men and more than 80 percent of older women seen on television are portrayed disrespectfully, treated with little if any courtesy, and often looked at as "bad."
- Although Americans who are forty and over are 42 percent of the American population, more than twice as many roles are cast with actors who are under forty.

But there is some good news, too. By the 1990s, soap operas such as *The Guiding Light* were presenting older characters having more love affairs and not just worrying about their children. In 1994 *New York Magazine* put Paul Newman on the cover, calling him "The Sexiest (70 year old) Man Alive," and *More* magazine offered women over forty an alternative to those that cater to women in their twenties. Older models began to make their appearance in general women's magazines, too. One widely circulated magazine advertisement in 1994 described "Betty Mettler, age 101, Noxzema user since 1925."

OUR CULTURE'S FEAR OF GROWING OLD

As Tolstoy noted, *"Old age is the most unexpected of all the things that happen to a man."*

The underlying basis of ageism is the dread and fear of growing older, becoming ill and dependent, and approaching death. People are afraid, and that leads to profound ambivalence. The young dread aging, and the old envy youth. Behind ageism is corrosive narcissism, the inability to accept our fate, for indeed we are all in love with our youthful selves, as is reflected in the yearning behind the expression "salad days."

Although undoubtedly universal, ageism in the United States is probably fueled by the worship of youth in a still-young country dominated by the myth of the unending frontier. In 1965, the Who, a British rock group, sang, "I hope I die before I get old," while in America "you never say die." Hollywood veils older actresses with gauzy lens filters. Moreover, age carries less authority.

The powerful imagery of the birth and adoration of the infant Jesus, and the journey of the Magi to see the Christ child, describes a birth of hope. How this contrasts with the final years of life! Children are seen as the future; older people, the past. Grimm's fairy tales depict gnarled and evil old women cursing innocent and beautiful youths with spells and afflictions.

Denial is a close cousin of ageism; in effect, it eliminates aging from consciousness.

One of the striking facts of human life is the intensity with which people avoid aging. Narcissistic preoccupation with our own aging and demise and perhaps, according to Freud, the inability of the unconscious to accept death make it difficult for society as a whole to deal with the challenges of aging. Note our gallows humor at birthdays, the money we spend on cosmetic surgery, and the popularity of anti-aging medicine. This was not always the case. In Europe in generations past, young men in high positions wore wigs they had powdered white in an attempt to appear older and, by implication, wiser. Today, men flock to cosmetic surgeons and colorists to preserve the illusion of youth.

. . .

ELDER ABUSE

Elder abuse is a widespread phenomenon that affects older adults who live in rich and poor nations alike. In the United States alone it is believed that as many as 1.2 million older adults are physically abused or neglected each year. Elder abuse takes many forms, including physical, emotional, financial, and sexual abuse—often by family members. It may involve neglect, such as the failure to provide food, shelter, clothing, medical care, and personal hygiene, as well as narcotic overmedication.

In 2004, UN Secretary General Kofi Annan released a report on the abuse of older persons that mentioned practices such as the ostracism of older women, which occurs in some societies when they are used as scapegoats for natural disasters, epidemics, or other catastrophes. The report stated: "Women have been ostracized, tortured, maimed or even killed if they failed to flee the community."

The World Health Organization (WHO) reported that 36 percent of nursing home staff in the U.S. reported having witnessed at least one incident of physical abuse of an older patient in the previous year, and 10 percent admitted having committed at least one act of physical abuse themselves. This represents sexism as well as ageism, for about 75 percent of nursing home residents are women. Other statistics are equally alarming:

- 1 million to 3 million Americans sixty-five and older have been injured, exploited, or otherwise mistreated by someone on whom they depend for care or protection.
- Estimates of the frequency of elder abuse range from 2 percent to 10 percent.
- Only one out of six incidents of elder abuse, neglect, exploitation, and self-neglect is brought to the attention of authorities.
- Only twenty-one states report that they maintain an elder abuse registry/database on perpetrators of substantiated cases, and less than half of states maintain a central abuse registry.
- It is estimated that each year 5 million older Americans are victims of financial exploitation, but only 4 percent of cases are reported. Many of these cases involve the unauthorized use of older person's assets and the transferring of power of attorney for an older person's assets without written consent.
- Of the nearly $1 billion National Institute on Aging budget, only $1.7 million goes to NIA elder abuse and neglect research funding.

AGEISM IN HEALTH-CARE SETTINGS

Ageism can be invoked by aesthetic revulsion. Especially when weakened by disease, older persons can be disheveled, unwashed, and appear ugly and decaying. Some older persons "let themselves go" and unwittingly add fuel to the fire. Sphincters loosen, depositing stains and smells. Ear and nose hairs grow more quickly in older bodies, as does the cartilage, causing the nose and ears to enlarge. Some profound and common disorders of old age—mobility problems, dementia, and incontinence—are unattractive and provoke a negative response.

When older men or women are malodorous, scabrous, or disturbing in dress and language, they can scare, disgust, and discomfort younger people. Such older persons become untouchable. (Touch is powerful and therapeutic. Some older persons living alone have not been touched for years.)

Medical schools unwittingly promote the virus of ageism. Fresh out of college, young students are confronted with aging and death and their own personal anxieties about both. They are left to their own devices to insulate themselves from anxiety and pain about disease, disability, disfigurement, and dying. A cadaver that requires dissection is usually the first older person medical students encounter, and they are not ordinarily provided with effective group or individual counseling, either at the time of dissection or later, upon the death of their first patient.

Defense mechanisms like gallows humor, cynicism, denial, the invention of negative language, and facetiousness are common. Long hours in medical training lead to angry exhaustion and feelings of being "put upon."

It was in medical school that I first become conscious of the medical profession's prejudice toward age. For the first time I heard such insulting epithets as "crock," which was used to describe middle-aged women and older patients who were labeled hypochondriacal because they had no apparent organic basis for their complaints, as well as having many symptoms, and "GOMER" (Get Out of My Emergency Room).

The hidden curriculum in medical schools undermines student's idealism and can compromise their education. For example, in some studies up to 35 percent of doctors erroneously consider an increase in blood pressure to be a normal process of aging. In physical diagnosis courses, medical students meet older people who are stripped of their individuality and seen as archives or museums of pathology, rather than as human beings. Men and women in their eighties are particularly valuable in these sessions because they often have a plethora of symptoms and conditions about which the student must learn.

In addition, few medical school graduates will practice geriatrics, and practicing physicians often do not invest the same amount of time dealing with older patients. Medicare expenditures per capita steadily decline as people grow older. In fact, a UCLA study reported that, as people enter their forties, physicians spend less time with them per encounter. Logically, it should be the reverse since medical problems tend to increase as we grow older, and the ramifications are sobering. Sixty percent of adults over sixty-five do not receive recommended preventive services, and 40 percent do not receive vaccines for flu and pneumonia. They receive even less preventive care for high blood pressure and cholesterol.

Some doctors question why they should even bother treating certain problems of the aged; after all, the patients are old. Is it worth treating them? Their problems are irreversible, unexciting, and unprofitable. Their lives are over.

Between 1955 and 1966, Morris Rocklin, a volunteer in the NIMH Human Aging Study, was studied until he turned 101 years of age. Rocklin complained about his painful right knee to his physician, who said, "What do you expect at your age?" To this typical

statement by a physician, Rocklin replied indignantly, "So why doesn't my left leg hurt?" The symmetry of the human body offers a good test of the realities of medical ageism. Rocklin's oft-quoted response has been used by many geriatricians to educate medical students on the topic of ageism.

NURSING HOMES: AGEIST SCANDAL

Nursing homes are licensed by the states and must meet federal standards to participate in Medicaid or Medicare. About 95 percent of the nation's sixteen thousand nursing homes (which house 1.5 million men and women) participate in those programs. According to a government study conducted in 2002, nine of ten nursing homes in the United States lack adequate staff, and nurse's aides provide 90 percent of the care. In most nursing homes, the report said, a patient needs an average of 4.1 hours of care each day—2.8 hours from nurse's aides and 1.3 hours from registered nurses or licensed practical nurses.

In 2000, over 91 percent of nursing homes had nurse aide staffing levels that fell below the thresholds identified as minimally necessary to provide the needed care. In response, the Department of Health and Human Services concluded that "it is not currently feasible" for the federal government to require that homes achieve a minimum ratio of nursing staff to patients. Nursing homes would have to hire 77,000 to 137,000 registered nurses, 22,000 to 27,000 licensed practical nurses, and 181,000 to 310,000 nurse's aides. This would take $7.6 billion a year, an 8 percent increase over current spending. The solution given by the Bush administration was to encourage nursing homes to adopt better management techniques so nurse's aides can achieve high productivity and, ultimately, to rely on market forces.

AGE-BASED HEALTH-CARE RATIONING

Medical ageism is prevalent in preventive tests for cancer and treatment of a variety of illnesses, some of them life-threatening. For example:

- Only 10 percent of people sixty-five and over receive appropriate screening tests for bone density, colorectal and prostate cancer, and glaucoma. This despite the fact that the average age of colorectal cancer patients is seventy, that more than 70 percent of prostate cancer is diagnosed in men over sixty-five, and that people over sixty are six times more likely to suffer from glaucoma.
- Chemotherapy is underused in the treatment of breast cancer patients over sixty-five, even though for many of these patients it may improve survival.
- In a cost-cutting effort to reduce supposedly unnecessary medical tests in 1998, the American Cancer Society and government health agencies determined that if an older woman had no abnormalities in a Pap smear for three years in a row, she could be tested less often. Yet over 25 percent of cases of cervical cancer occur in women over sixty-five!
- The pelvic examination is often deferred because many doctors, especially men, do not like to do it. (In both men and women, the rectal examination may meet a similar fate.)
- Although deaths due to ischemic heart disease disproportionately affect persons over sixty-five (85 percent in the United States and 87 percent in France), few national

comparisons focus on older people. For example, WHO's MONICA Project—the important international longitudinal study that monitors cross-national trends in cardiovascular disease—focuses on death before sixty-five.

- A patient under the age of seventy-five who is admitted with a heart attack is six times more likely to receive blood clot-dissolving drugs such as streptokinase than a patient over seventy-five, even though data indicate the value of streptokinase in improving the chances for survival of older patients.
- Advanced surgery for Parkinson's disease is less available to older persons.

Unless older people are knowledgeable or have strong advocates, even the more affluent members of our society experience age-determined limits in medical care. Parenthetically, when malpractice suits are won, older persons usually receive lower monetary awards.

. . .

118

Aging with Disabilities

Ageism and More

Debra J. Sheets

People who are old and who also have disabilities—a growing proportion of the population—find themselves in "double jeopardy" of experiencing prejudice and discrimination, which often leads to difficulty gaining access to needed healthcare and social services. . . .

With older Americans living longer and healthier lives, recent trends suggest that disability is declining and possibly becoming less severe. Still, the combination of large numbers of baby boomers and the increased prevalence of disability accompanying age means that the size of the population with disability will grow rapidly in the next decade. Currently, 32 million people (12.5 percent) living in our communities have a sensory, mental, physical, or other disability that impairs their ability to take care of themselves; more than one in three (38 percent) is age 65 or older. Self-care disability affects 6.7 million people; adults age 65 and older constitute nearly one-half (3.1 million) of this group.

While population aging has received considerable attention, the aging of the "disability population" has gone largely without comment. In the past, people with disabilities often did not survive even into middle age because of complications related to their disability. Now, for the first time in history, an estimated one of every 100 older Americans is aging with a long-term disability such as spinal cord injury, cerebral palsy, multiple sclerosis, post-polio, and intellectual or developmental disabilities. Fifty years ago, the average life expectancy of an individual with spinal cord injury was less than three years after the accident occurred. Today 40 percent of all survivors of such injury are 45 years of age and older, and more than one-half of the estimated 600,000 to one million polio survivors are now age 55 and older. Approximately 526,000 Americans age 60 or older are aging with intellectual or developmental disabilities. Other groups aging with disability include 200,000 people with spinal cord injuries and 600,000 with cerebral palsy.

. . . Many of those with long-term disabilities are experiencing unanticipated health problems (e.g., fatigue, pain) and functional declines (e.g., muscle weakness, mobility limitations) as they reach midlife. These secondary health conditions are related to the effects of aging superimposed on the primary disability. The conditions have been described as "premature aging" because they occur about fifteen to twenty years earlier than would be the case with normal aging. A related problem is that people aging with disabilities may face early and forced retirement as they become physically unable to continue working. In such cases, they often have not had time to plan for how they will address typical retirement issues such as housing, health insurance, transportation, income, and caregiving. Yet they remain too young to qualify for the age-based service system as they shift out of the disability service system, with its strong vocational focus. The resulting gap in services poses a threat to independence and quality of life for people aging with disability.

. . .

TOWARD A SHARED AGENDA TO COMBAT PREJUDICE

The aging and disability service systems have historically developed in parallel but separate tracks, particularly because of different funding sources, despite often overlapping concerns about issues such as affordable housing, public transportation, access to healthcare, long-term-care needs, and economic stability. In the early 1980s, aging and disability advocates began discussing the need to work together to pursue a unified policy agenda that would reflect shared concerns about these issues. In the 1990s several modest attempts to develop a unified agenda were undertaken but to little effect. Efforts between the aging and disability service systems ultimately stalled over disagreements that reflected differences in philosophical perspectives, the definition of problems, and what counted as a solution.

. . .

Recently, economic and political pressures have prompted about two-thirds of all states to consolidate and integrate aging and disability services into a single agency serving both groups—older adults and people with disabilities. Regardless, some advocates remain pessimistic about overcoming the difficulties that keep the aging and disability systems from meaningful collaboration around a shared agenda. However, others are more optimistic and point to a number of state- and local-level initiatives that involve cross-network collaborations and may reflect a coalescing around issues that include improving consumer choice and the quality of longterm care. How this will play out remains to be seen, but there are some promising forces furthering efforts to bring the two service spheres together.

Improvements in the service systems will do much to counter the effects of ageism on older people aging with disabilities. Advocacy efforts by these two groups working together must counter prejudice against elders and those with disability by providing those aging with disability opportunities to maintain their competence, image, and sense of worth within our society. Agencies must replace problem-based approaches with a strengths-based paradigm that focuses on ensuring inclusion and participation in the broader society. In addition, both systems must endorse the self-determination of people aging with disability by adopting a shared focus on consumer choice and the empowerment of individuals to reach their potential. Neither age nor disability should be viewed as a special concern; they should be recognized as issues that are in the interests of our society as a whole.

. . .

119

Black Elderly

Center on Aging Studies, University of Missouri—Kansas City

- *In 1985 approximately 14% of the population, 65 and over, were people of color.* By 2020, 21% are projected to be people of color, and by 2050 this percent is anticipated to increase to 33%. These numbers translate into increasing numbers of black elderly adults in our society. However, despite growing numbers of black elderly adults, most of the programs and services provided to elders of color continue to be based on research and perceptions regarding the majority population. The result is a general lack of ethnic- and culture-specific knowledge.

- *Approximately 33% of black elderly live in poverty.* Black elderly males experience a decline in their longevity. Many black elderly regard themselves as "unretired-retired," since they generally continue to work after retirement. Black elderly retirement is frequently related to subsequent physical or mental disability. Black elderly females who have declining health are frequently sole heads of households, and thus responsible for children or grandchildren. Black elderly underutilize public health services and tend to use emergency room services. Many do not have a regular personal physician, and generally experience problems in accessing all health care systems. In rural areas, nearly one-half of black elderly live at or below the poverty level.

- *Black male elders generally have less personal post-retirement resources and are more dependent on Social Security and Supplemental Security Income.* More than twice as many black males as white males, over the age of 65, are divorced or separated. It is always important to remember that there is cultural diversity within each ethnic group, including differences in values, traditions, educational levels, socioeconomic status, and lifestyles.

  . . .

- *Due to life-long patterns of socioeconomic disadvantages (e.g., income, education, access to health care, etc.), and prejudicial treatment, many black elderly don't respond well to service providers of a different race.* In some cases, the elder person may demonstrate a complete lack of trust in the medical and/or mental health system. This can potentially result in fewer attempts to procure care, and low compliance with prescribed interventions. Blacks tend to be institutionalized for mental health reasons more often than whites; their admission to psychiatric institutions are also less likely to be voluntary. In addition, racial and ethnic minorities tend to receive less mental health treatment and are more likely to receive lower quality treatment.

- *Health conditions:* More than half of black elderly in America are in poor health. They also tend to experience higher rates of multiple chronic illnesses than the rest of the population. Hypertension, obesity, and diabetes, in particular, surface as three major diseases which are often found to be related to each other. Left untreated, any one of these diseases can progress into more severe health complications such as stroke, blindness, loss of an extremity, impaired mobility, kidney failure, or heart disease. These three diseases are often associated with a lifetime of poor dietary habits, limited exercise, behavioral responses to discrimination, socioeconomic factors (such as persistent poverty), and poor coping or problem-solving skills—some of which may include the use of sugar, food, alcohol, or drugs, in excess, as a means of minimizing

emotional pain and escaping the harsh realities of life. In turn, decreased self-image, self-worth, feelings of helplessness, hopelessness, and frustration often accompany these conditions. Another possible problem is noncompliance with medication instructions and schedules. This problem is often the result of fixed incomes which may not always cover ongoing medication costs. . . .

- *Cancer is found to be a critical problem for black elderly Americans.* For example, as compared to white Americans, black Americans experience significantly higher rates of several types of cancer, with death rates three times higher for esophageal cancer and twice the mortality rate from stomach cancer. In addition, the death rate from lung cancer is 45% higher in black males compared to white males. Black females are also two to three times more likely to die from cervical or uterine cancer than white females.

- *Concerning dementia, research has shown that black females may be at increased risk of multi-infarct dementia due to a higher incidence of obesity and hypertension.* The potential for black males to experience alcoholic dementia before age 50 is also increased due to early age onset of drinking and heavier patterns of consumption. Although the frequency of dementing illness is at least as frequent in the black American community as it is in the general population, black elderly may have lower rates of the Alzheimer's type of dementia. Because of a lack of resources, inefficient doctor-patient relationship, and/or lack of research data applicable to dementias in the black elderly, there is an above-average potential for misdiagnoses.

- *For black Americans, in particular, family is of primary importance.* Family networks provide the main source of needed assistance later in life for many black elderly. In fact, when black elderly live with their children, the possibility of them being institutionalized for disabilities decreases. In general, black elderly do not participate in social or recreational activities that are outside the realm of their individual cultural traditions, backgrounds, or experiences. However, they tend to utilize a more diverse pool of helpers, including both extended family and friends. This network, and its influence, must, in turn, be respected and utilized by outside caregivers and service providers. Increased spirituality, faith in God, and increased participation in religious activities and institutions can also play an important role in providing support for black elderly. Religious beliefs provide a resource for coping with the unexpected or losses (which naturally increase with age). The church may also serve as a focal point of supportive networks for emotional and material aid.

- *Developing a caregiving relationship:* For someone outside the family to establish and develop a caregiving relationship with a black elder may require special attention and sensitivity to the elder's unique ethnic and cultural experience, history, and family relationships. At a minimum, the service provider must make efforts toward building a trusting relationship—remembering that non-responsiveness or resistance on the part of the elder may represent a means of evaluating providers and their ability to work with the elder effectively. A big step in the right direction is achieved if the provider can meet elders where they are—which means helping the elder determine what will work best, rather than what the provider believes will be best for the elder.

120

Regardless of What You Were Taught to Believe

There Is Nothing Wrong with You: For Teens

Cheri Huber

. . .

CH: What do you wish adults understood about people your age?

B: I think they understand, because they were our age and they wanted to do exactly what we want to do. But for some reason they don't want us to do what they did. Even though their lives turned out fine, even though they have perfectly fine lives, they don't want us to follow them.

CH: So, do you feel like you know what happened with your parents, and they just won't cop to it?

Q: Sure. They say, "I did that but you shouldn't do it because it's bad. Even though I did it, you shouldn't do it. You should learn from my experience."

T: But we don't want to learn from someone else's experience. We want to have our own experience and learn from that. What happened to them doesn't mean anything to me. I want to find out for myself.

F: They think because they did something we're going to do it, too.

CH: So, adults keep bringing up the same stuff over and over and maybe you wouldn't even be thinking about it if they didn't keep bringing it up.

F: They keep accusing us of planning things that we're not even thinking about.

S: Sometimes they tell us too much. My parents have told me stuff I didn't want to hear like about where and when I was conceived and things they did when they were young. It's weird.

. . .

B: They don't let you talk back. Their idea of a conversation is interrogation. They say something and you try to say something back and they don't want to hear it. They say, "We want to talk to you about this." But they don't want you to say anything to them about it.

V: They won't let you question them and they won't explain their reasons. They won't ever tell you why.

CH: So do you often find yourself in a place of not understanding why they're doing what they're doing or demanding what they're demanding?

Group: YES!

CH: So what you're saying is that adults, even though they say they want to talk to you, aren't interested in having a conversation. Adults don't realize what conversation is. There isn't much of the one person says something then the other person replies.

V: Yeah, they want to preach.

G: They think a conversation revolves around their opinion and nothing else.

CH: And they're assuming you understand a lot of things you really don't understand?

Group: Yeah.

V: Like when my mom wants to talk to me, she never wants to talk to me on a personal level. She calls me out of my room and asks me "who ate the peanut butter?" And she

yells at me like it's my fault. I did eat the peanut butter. I'm the one in the house who likes peanut butter. She always yells at me when she talks to me. It's always like whatever it is is my fault. I never know if she's accusing me of something or if that's just the way she talks to me. But when I want to talk to her about something important she's, like, okay, whatever. But when it's not serious and she wants to talk to me, she gets mad. I can't remember the last actual conversation I had with my mom.

CH: Is that what it feels like, that you're really different from your parents?

Group: Not really.

T: I'm apparently just like my mom. We all turn into our parents and its horrible!

. . .

CH: So, what do you want to tell adults? What should adults know?

—LISTEN. Basically that's it. It would be really nice if people listened to you when you have something to say.

—We need support, some praise, some acknowledgment of the good stuff we do.

—Be open to the stuff that's important to us even if its not important to them—not necessarily condone it, but don't say don't do it. Like wanting to be with our friends all the time. My parents may think it's a waste of time, but it's what I want to do and it beats sitting around the house on my butt. So, ok, you think it's a waste of time, but it's what I want to do, so don't give me a hard time about it.

—Don't worry so much about who we hang out with. They just assume that if you're with certain people you're going to be just like those people. They think we have no will power, if someone suggests something or offers us something, we're going to go along with it automatically. They don't see us as individuals, they see us as who we're with.

—We have good morals, we can make good choices.

—We don't mean any harm. We just want to have fun. We're trying to learn new things.

—Trust us. Talk to us. Get to know us. And trust us.

—You want us to act like adults, treat us with the same respect you give to adults.

—If you want us to respect you, respect us.

CH: In other words, if the teaching is going to be successful, parents have to model what they want you to be.

—Teachers too. The best teachers I've had are the ones who treated us as actual people. I listened to them and excelled in their classes. But the teachers who hate us, the ones who are there for the summers off, I was exactly the opposite. We will be what adults expect us to be.

—You can't just tell us no. Give us a reason. We don't see what you see. We don't understand. You need to explain things to us.

—Don't say, "Because I'm the parent." If you don't have a good reason, if you can't explain it to me, I'm not going to do what you want.

—Adults want to know why. We have to give reasons. Give us the respect you want from us and explain to us your reasons. Tell us why we should do what you want us to do.

—"Because I said so," is not good enough. It makes me *have* to do the opposite!

—Adults have had a lot of experience we haven't had. Give us the benefit of that experience by explaining what they're thinking, how they see things.

—Give us all the information we need and support us in making a decision.

—Get to know who we are as individuals and support us.

—Don't constantly refer to the past and hold the past against us.

—We're not all alike. We're similar, but we are individuals.

—Support but don't push.

—We're not always going to be children.

—We have a lot of emotions inside. Sometimes we don't know what's best for us.

—We're not as bad as you think. You were our age once. Give us a break.

—Respect and support our relationships instead of just being freaked out about whether we're having sex.

—We're people, too.

—Going to your room and closing the door is normal!

—It doesn't matter what you see or hear on the outside, it's what's inside that counts.

—All teenagers want to have fun. Don't hold us back. Don't live your life through ours.

—We need privacy and we need attention.

. . .

121

Elder Liberation Draft Policy Statement

Marge Larabee

INTRODUCTION

Everyone is a particular age. Age is universal. One's age is a factor in the life of every person in every country, in every culture. We also deal with change and oppression at any age. However, age is of special importance to elders. We have lived long. In dealing with age oppression in our own lives, we elders also support each person of whatever age, especially young people, whatever country, whatever culture, to move outside the ageist oppression. Elders can be allies for successful aging at any age.

Like people of any age, we elders are: zestful, intelligent, fun-loving, powerful, creative, flexible, sexy human beings. We focus, in present time, on the steps we are now taking and will take in the short-term to accomplish our long range goals. We have a future.

. . .

We expect to be seen as unique individuals whose accomplishments and thinking are accepted on their own merit. Whether we choose traditional roles, and/or to "contemplate, reflect and guide," our actions are as valuable as production in the workplace. Any role we select rationally is appropriate for us.

In the world today there are increasing numbers of elders, more and more of whom continue to function as alert human beings as they chronologically reach eighty-five and older. We are a powerful political force. We plan on taking charge of our own activities and policies.

We have a vision and perspective on history and the way things can and should be now.

We have coped with much change and can apply what we have learned from those experiences.

We have gained better knowledge about how to keep ourselves well and functioning.

We are alive and lively and ready to break all stereotypes.

We will take time to spell out our oppression only to make clear what we need to do to liberate ourselves and others effectively and completely. Our focus will be on present time reality.

CHANGING SOCIAL PERSPECTIVES ON AGING AND AGEISM

When our society was based on agriculture, old age and experience were obvious assets for the group's survival. We turned to older persons for their wisdom and insights. These were relevant and essential. Landowners and others with economic and political power were often old people. Reverence for old age was based, in large part, on this reality. In most societies there is a strong correlation between the economic situation and the status of elders.

Dating from industrialization, western society has given old age a bad name. Rapidly evolving technologies have lessened the value of the knowledge and experience of older adults. In general, older persons have been considered obsolete. Older persons are seen as limiting the opportunities of newly trained young people and are expected to retire. The older people's skills, general wisdom and knowhow, gained from years of experience, are lost.

Knowledge and experience of age is changing. There is an increasing gap between chronological age and biological (functioning) age. A person can live seventy chronological years and still function as a forty year old. Yet many parts of our society, especially the work place, treat the elder stereotypically, in terms of the chronological seventy years, instead of the functioning age of forty years.

Society has lagged in addressing both the changing needs of elders who are functioning well, living longer, living healthier lives, and those caught in mental and physical patterns. The latter would benefit from a perception of them as persons *with* problems instead of *as* "problems."

A "youth" culture predominates at the expense of appreciating older adults' values and contributions. Myths and stereotypes about older persons are widespread. Elders are pictured as uninvolved, dependent, non-contributing. The growing numbers of individuals who contradict these stereotypes are considered the "exception" and "remarkable" instead of representative of what old age can really be like.

. . .

[A]geism is the invalidation and discrimination against older persons because of old age, or factors accompanying age, that have little to do with the person's worth, intelligence, or capabilities.

The resulting incorrect attitudes toward the older person are played out in our society. They condition people to think and act in terms of stereotypes and prejudice. The individual elder is affected by these social and cultural attitudes and values and internalizes them. We not only suffer from the external oppression but from the oppressive ideas and stereotypes that become internalized.

. . .

It is ageism whenever older persons are victimized, ignored or segregated, are flattered by being told they are different from other older persons, are not encouraged to take complete pride in themselves and live their lives fully.

. . . [A]geism, like other oppressions, supports the basic oppression of economic inequality and injustice (classism) by setting up antagonisms between different groups to keep them from acting together against injustice. This "divide and conquer" tactic has existed in each class society, from slavery through feudalism, and now under capitalism.

. . .

RETIREMENT

The institutionalized promotion of "retirement" goes along with the emphasis on young people. Industry moves older workers out of the labor force to make room for younger workers. "Retirement" was invented to enforce this replacement. Retirement is justified as necessary for our economy to function profitably. Retirement pits young against old in competition for security and esteem in an economy of (professed) scarcity. Incessant, insidious repetition fosters attitudes that elders have little to offer and can no longer participate in significant work and that any attempt to do so will limit the opportunities for younger people (similar arguments are made to discourage bringing women, people of color, or immigrants into the work force).

Older workers are encouraged to see retirement as a "reward" for years of effort. Retirement years are supposed to be "Golden Years." The facts are different: for many people, retirement is a time of enforced idleness, isolation, loss of self-esteem, and living on a dwindling or absent income.

Gradually, the convention that older persons cannot keep up the pace has been established. It is now widely believed that they cannot be productive, contributing members of society.

V
O
I
C
E
S

LIVING SITUATIONS

In the past it wasn't unusual for elders to live in an extended family in which they were known and had a place, and to which they contributed their wisdom and experience.

Today urbanization and increased geographic mobility have been factors in the breakdown of the extended family unit. As a result elders in nuclear families or alternative living situations experience increased invisibility and isolation.

Eighty-percent of the care of old people is provided by an informal network of family and friends, mostly women. This usually means wives, daughters and daughters-in-law. Many of these women are themselves elders, and they avoid institutionalizing their loved ones at great cost.

We need to examine the difficult role of caregiver. We need to find ways to offer a variety of services that will give help and support to this role.

HEALTH CARE

Limitation, deterioration and decline have erroneously been attributed solely to old age. Such decline may accompany old age, but it is actually separate and often reversible. The medical profession is slow to adopt a restoring or preventive approach to elders' health care. Because elders' health problems are often discussed as due to old age they are looked at as a questionable place to put time, money and resource. The disease process, the aging process and chronological aging must be viewed separately. When something goes wrong physically we cannot *assume* it's because of age.

RESEARCH ON ELDERS

Research on elders tends to be biased by ageist assumptions. Some studies focus on healthy people, others on sick people. No studies have been done of elders who systematically discharge and re-evaluate. As a result, the research findings have been limited or biased, or both. They have not given us a true picture of the wide range of ways in which elders age.

OLD AGE OPPRESSION AND OTHER OPPRESSIONS

The oppression of ageism intersects with and intensifies other oppressions. Sexism and old-ageism merge blatantly around the artificial standards of beauty for women and the value of women based on their reproductive functions. Older men suffer from stereotypical expectations of work performance and maintaining an ideal virility.

Elders also face intensified classism, racism, and homophobia.

INTERNALIZED . . . AGEISM

What does . . . ageism look like from the inside?

- As elders we often devalue our own work.
- We often feel and act inadequate. We act competitive and aggressive or else we withdraw.
- We sometimes criticize each other, settle for less, and have difficulty rejoicing in our achievements.
- We may feel intense irritation toward other elders and try to separate ourselves from them.
- We act as though we believe the stereotypes and forget how brave, smart and good-looking we are.
- We are flattered to be thought younger; we long to be youthful.
- We are grateful to be "included" by younger people.
- We give up on our future and our dreams.
- We don't feel we have much to say.
- We confuse growing older, aging and ill health.
- In some cases, we deny that old-ageism is real.

HOW WE INTERNALIZE . . . AGEISM

Denying old age leads to ignoring, overlooking, minimizing old age oppression. We think to ourselves: "It isn't really a very important oppression." The reality is that old-ageism is important to everybody and affects everybody, throughout their lives.

When young, we internalize stereotypes of disabled, old, sick and dying people. When we think of "old" we call to mind images of an old aunt, grandfather or neighbor we once knew. If they were sick, disabled or dying, these early memories remain as internalized stereotypes of "old." Then we have the same feeling responses to "old" now as we did

then (either positive or negative). These feeling responses, in turn, affect how we see the changes in our own bodies.

. . .

MOVING OUT OF THE OPPRESSION

Begin to act. Create good directions and commitments for yourself. Build support groups around you. Put your plans into action.

STEPS

- Elders and non-elders need to have confident, high expectations of elders. Recognize that we are always learning, growing, and developing, that we have not completed our lives, our contributions, our accomplishments. See elders as able to make changes, to live through many more beginnings. Remember that there are feelings, griefs, fears to be worked through at any age. It is incorrect to assume that elders' distresses are more intractable because we have lived longer.
- Elders, let's do what's important in our lives, live whatever way we need to live, and not neglect this because we are older.
- Let's live a "no limits" life, be increasingly mindful that we are in charge of ourselves physically and emotionally. Let's take as a basic assumption that a person with no distress would age slowly, if at all.
- Remember that we are our own best allies.
    . . .
- Enlist the support of non-elders as allies; develop a long list and call on them frequently. Other age groups, especially young persons, have challenges in common with elders.
- Find ways to celebrate and call attention to successful aging. Delight in and make festive every birthday. Take it as an opportunity to share what is good and positive about aging.
- Take initiative and leadership to challenge . . . ageism.
- In whatever group you are a part of, find ways to honor and show respect for older persons, call forth their abilities and talents, and interrupt any ageist practices and behaviors.
- Make yourself available as a speaker on liberation from . . . ageism.
- Develop and take responsibility for a personal health plan.
- When something goes wrong physically, don't assume it's because of age.
- Confront . . . fears about aging, sickness and death.
    . . .
- Enrich your life and theirs by sharing it with people of several different generations.
    . . .
- Know the laws pertaining to older persons and lobby to establish non-ageist policies on employment, housing, health care, etc.
- Focus on friendships with older persons across race, gender, class differences.
- Encourage all older persons to be fully proud of themselves, including being proud of their age.

VOICES

- Work cooperatively to rid ourselves of all oppressions, including old-ageism. None of us is free until we all are free.
- Develop your own strategies for ending old-ageism, and share them!
- Organize with other elders to take leadership for our liberation and the liberation of all other sections of the population. We can lead everything, and from such a position our interests can receive the attention and emphasis they deserve.
- Form alliances with all other oppressed groups, . . . to support each others' programs. To offer alliances to other liberation groups and request their support is to multiply our effectiveness and our confidence immediately.

. . .

122

People of Color Over Fifty

Dottie Curry

Aging has less stigma in communities of color. There is more respect for age and experience. A lot of the respect for elders is left over from our traditional cultures.

Though grandparents and other older adults are respected and loved within their families, they suffer more from the inhuman treatment of society towards elder citizens than members of the dominant culture. Because of the tradition of segregation and reduced access to opportunities, older people of color are less likely to have good health care, adequate housing and good nutrition. Consequently older people have a lower quality of life and a shortened life span.

Because of the poverty and violence in inner cities, older women in our communities are often taking care of grandchildren or other young people left by the death of the young people's parents. The extended family concept is a good one, but there is very rarely enough money to take care of these children properly. A lot of times the older people are on public assistance for the elderly while at the same time receiving aid for dependent children.

. . . Most of the time, just as with every other issue with people of color, the aging issue is buried under the issues connected with racism, so if there is some difficulty, old-ageism is not looked at. We need for other elders to step outside their fear and encourage older people of color to . . . work on this very important issue. We need younger people to act as our allies and . . . [talk with us about] our internalized oppression (the internalized racism and the internalized ageism).

We need for people . . . to understand that the problems facing all people, and especially people of color, are multiplied when we become elders. This is especially true in such cities as Austin, Texas and Atlanta, Georgia, where the median age is twenty-five. Since people of color have been traditionally denied some jobs (they are currently phasing people over forty out of certain jobs), the employment situation for people of color over fifty is pretty grim.

Older people of color have a lot to offer: we are an asset to any group. Our contribution to the history of this country is immense. We need a chance to share this with the . . . world.

123

Chicago's Peace Warriors

Kazu Haga

A group of students from Chicago's North Lawndale College Preparatory High were in the middle of a weeklong summer training to become Peace Warriors—peer nonviolence leaders. Suddenly, a sophomore named Alicia got a text message alerting her that one of her close friends was just involved in a shooting and was in critical condition at the hospital.

A conversation about the violence in Chicago followed. At one point in the discussion, Tiffany Childress, science teacher and civic engagement director at the school, told the students: "This level of violence is not normal. I've seen wealthy neighborhoods in Chicago where young people getting shot is not part of the daily reality. Even in this neighborhood, 50 years ago we did not have this level of violence."

The reactions came quickly.

"What!?"

"Really!?"

"How do you know that? You weren't around 50 years ago!"

The students were surprised, confused, resistant. The violence in their communities has become so normalized that they literally could not believe that this does not happen everywhere, that this is not how it has always been. It was a chilling reminder of the need to inspire hope, to give youth a vision of peace.

North Lawndale, a charter school located in gang territory on the west side of Chicago, is working hard to provide that vision. In 2009, Chicago witnessed 458 murders—more than the number of U.S. soldiers killed in Iraq or Afghanistan. Many of those killings involved teenagers. Yet, that same year, the rate of violence at the school dropped 70 percent.

Childress was at the heart of the change. "Several years ago there was a culture of violence that surrounded our school, and it was spiraling out of control," she began. "We needed to do something to get a hold of it."

That year, she had a conversation with a woman about Kingian Nonviolence at a birthday party. She was immediately interested and attended a presentation shortly thereafter. Kingian Nonviolence, she learned, is a training curriculum developed out of the teachings of Dr. Martin Luther King Jr. by two of his close allies, Bernard Lafayette Jr. and David Jehnsen. Used in schools, prisons, and communities around the world, it provides a framework to understand conflict and violence, and teaches communities a way to build peace.

King believed that nonviolence is not a passive, but a proactive force that can defeat violence and injustice. It is not about teaching people to turn the other cheek, but about teaching people how to confront the forces of violence and injustice in their lives and create a real, lasting peace. It is, as King put it, "the antidote to violence."

Childress saw right away how this curriculum could offer a new way to deal with conflict and violence in her school. "I was blown away by the material after the first day," she said.

With the support of school president John Horan, Childress facilitated a two-day workshop for the faculty as part of their professional development and organized a five-day training for a group of student leaders chosen by the teachers at the school. These were the first North Lawndale Peace Warriors, students who would lead their peers in creating a culture of peace in their school. "The kids are the most well equipped and knowledgeable source for figuring out how to make their schools peaceful," Childress said. "They know

their peers, they know what would make good incentives, they know who's ready to jump off, so you have to make them an authority so they can have ownership of the process."

The summer Peace Warrior training, which is now an annual event, includes a study of the principles and steps of Kingian Nonviolence . . ., the history of the Civil Rights Movement, and role plays dealing with conflict.

For example, one role play last summer involved a scenario in the school cafeteria: two boys getting into a conflict over a girl. A couple is sitting together. When the boy gets up to go get a drink, another boy comes and takes his seat next to the girl. When the first boy comes back, an argument begins to escalate. Just at the point where the conflict begins to boil over, the trainers had the actors pause.

Senior Kingian Nonviolence trainer Jonathan Lewis asked the students: "What are some nonviolent responses that the students could have taken that would have resulted in a different outcome?"

The ideas came quickly. "What if the first boy pulls up another chair and introduces himself to the second boy?" one young man suggested. The students realized that if they took a minute, they could think of dozens of ways to handle situations that easily escalate.

Lewis said: "One of the most important tenets of Kingian Nonviolence is to suspend your first judgment. Maybe the second boy meant no harm, and maybe the two kids would end up being great friends. Yet, in our society, we are always taught to distrust people. Having students think through possible nonviolent responses to conflict makes them realize that they already understand how to de-escalate conflict. They just need to get creative and they need to practice."

For Leticia, a 16-year-old trainee, a key learning was the first of the six steps of Kingian Nonviolence, information gathering: "Most times, we take action before we even realize what the problem is. Whether it's a school-wide thing or a problem between two kids, we need to gather information and understand what's really behind the problem before we act.

"I hope to stand up. We have problems in our school like gang violence and cyber bullying. It's time for people to take action. We often complain about things, but we never talk about the situation and come up with a plan. I want to be the person who stands up and takes action, because it's time."

**N
E
X
T

S
T
E
P
S**

CREATING A SCHOOL-WIDE SOLUTION

The initial trainings provided a common framework for students and staff to understand the conflicts in their school, a common vision to build toward, and a common language. "Once we had that," Horan said, "it was all about figuring out how to constantly reinforce this throughout our school. We have to teach the skills of building peace, just like we teach for the SATs [Standardized Achievement Tests]."

"We made a commitment to create peace in our school instead of just paying lip service to it," Childress explained. "Schools set academic goals each year, and we wanted to set peacemaking goals. Who sets goals for peace? But we have to dare to dream big, and we have to set measurable goals. We set goals like having 90 percent of our school days earning an 'A' in peace, that 100 percent of our faculty and 25 percent of our students will be introduced to this philosophy."

Students and faculty drew up posters of the six principles and plastered them over the campus, embedding the language into their vocabulary. The Peace Warriors wrote and created PSAs [Public Service Announcements] that were played over the school PA [Public Announcement] system. Each year during freshmen orientation, Childress and the Peace

Warriors introduce the philosophy and their school's commitment to peace to the incoming class. Part of the funds allocated to substitute teachers has been diverted to an in-school suspension teacher who teaches the philosophy as part of the "Learning to Rise" program. The entire faculty is trained every other year, and a Peace Committee composed of Peace Warriors and faculty provides mini-lessons on different aspects of the philosophy to the entire student body every week during assembly.

From the beginning, the school tracked data associated with measuring peace. Not only how many fights they had but also what time of day it happened, what areas on campus, the ages of the offenders.

"We learned a ton from tracking that data," Horan explained. "It helped us to figure out not only how successful we were, but also when, where, and how to deploy our staff."

The school also began tracking "Days of Peace" with a large public calendar marking off each day and offering student incentives for consecutive days with no fights. The incentives, which included dress-down days, a DJ in the cafeteria, a peace dance, and a community peace march and barbecue, helped to change the culture of the school.

The Days of Peace campaign was an idea that grew out of joint meetings between the student Peace Warriors and faculty. "It was so important to have the youth's voices present from the beginning," said Childress. "We would have never come up with some of these incentives ourselves. The students and faculty are both responsible for creating the culture and community at our school, so the solutions to our problems have to be figured out collectively. The incentives made peace cool and desirable in the school. The students took ownership of their community and began keeping the peace themselves."

Childress noted that the community peace march and barbecue were especially important, because the culture of peace they are creating needs to extend beyond the school. "The barbecue showed the larger public about the work we were putting in at our school, and allowed for more engagement from parents and the community at large. We started with the school, but we need to involve the community, to involve the parents if we are going to have sustained success."

It hasn't all been easy. As the school began to introduce Kingian Nonviolence, some community members saw it as nothing more than a band-aid solution to society's larger problems. It's one thing to teach students about the importance of investing in peace while on campus. But once they leave the school, they end up back in the violence of the larger society. The students have come to respect the school and its goals enough that there are few fights on campus. But plenty of violence happens just off campus, where the students interact with the larger community.

"Our school is located in gang territory," explained Childress. "Ninety-eight percent of our students are on free or reduced lunch. Many of our students come from families with multiple generations of gang involvement. Too many of them have lost family and friends to the streets."

Students living under crisis, perhaps receiving text messages during class that a family member or close friend has been shot, perhaps living in homes without proper heating or where they have not eaten a full meal in days, are often too damaged to hear the message about peace and nonviolence.

"At the end of the day, we are just a school," added Childress. "That's why we created my position of civic engagement director. We are organizing our students to meet with their aldermen, educating them about how power works. But after the geometry and the biology and the social studies, we're lucky if we are able to do one civic project a month."

Despite all the limitations, Dwayne, who is now a senior and has been a Peace Warrior for three years, believes the training brought about a personal transformation as a step in the school-wide transformation: "I wasn't always nonviolent, and I'd messed up in the past. It was a struggle for me at first, but I know that this is the only way we are going to make permanent change."

NEXT STEPS

Rasheed, who graduated last year, has hopes that the school program will have a broader effect. The Peace Warriors, he said, "promote peace in our school and outside of the school, to form a better community, which we call the beloved community. We show people that Kingian Nonviolence is a way of life that can better our lives and society as a whole."

INVESTING IN YOUTH, NOT SECURITY GUARDS

It isn't only students who need to change. For youth to have hope in the future, the adults need to have faith in them. Schools, and society in general, often set low expectations of our youth, especially those coming from low-income neighborhoods.

"Many teachers don't believe that students can live differently. They think that having metal detectors and police officers in the hallways is normal and acceptable," said Childress. "Having higher expectations of our youth and believing in them is the first step in reversing the school-to-prison pipeline."

Horan agreed: "A lot of adults believe that kids aren't capable of pulling this off. And that idea plays itself out racially and economically. It's a justice issue. If we think that kids who go to nice suburban schools can live without metal detectors, why can't our kids?

"When you believe that kids *can* pull it off, you can turn off the metal detectors and security guards. Having eight security guards costs you around $400,000, and security guards don't teach peace. They teach kids to hate security guards. What if you could teach peace with the money you saved?"

North Lawndale did just that. With the savings made from not having metal detectors and security guards, the school created a new program called Phoenix Rising, which sends students to various summer leadership, wilderness, and academic programs around the country.

"The beloved community is possible," Horan added. "It's just a matter of adults believing in our kids and adjusting the resources accordingly. It will ultimately save the school money, and will teach kids skills that will serve them a lifetime. Treating them like prisoners only teaches them that we don't believe in them, and that we expect them to screw up.

"Our inability to be peaceful in our school has larger social implications. Our failure to understand peace is a form of enslavement. We have to invest in peace."

RESTORATIVE JUSTICE

To truly invest in peace, the school realized it needed to develop restorative justice practices to deal with the conflicts that did arise. The nonviolence training taught them the negative impact that punitive forms of punishment—from suspensions to calling in law enforcement—can have on students and on the community.

Punishment can cause emotional harm. A punitive process that does not honor the voice of the "perpetrator" can lead that person to feel that an injustice was done to them. That pain can lead them to focus on anger toward the system handing down the punishment instead of taking ownership for their actions.

If North Lawndale was going to break the school-to-prison pipeline, they needed alternative strategies to deal with conflict. They needed to find strategies to hold perpetrators of violence truly accountable without further isolating, labeling, and

criminalizing them—strategies to enable them to right the wrong and restore the broken relationship.

"We raised funds to have 35 or 40 youth trained as peer jurors for a restorative justice conferencing process," explained Childress. "Now, when a fight breaks out, instead of being suspended for a day, they have to talk about what happened with a group of their peers. They then decide together what the consequences should be, and figure out an outcome that works for all parties."

One peer jury conference resulted in the two "offending" youth agreeing to walk around the school with large posters advocating peace. It was a form of punishment, but it was something all parties agreed to as an alternative to suspension. In the end, the two youth turned it into a positive experience, getting other youth to sign the posters and committing themselves further to peace.

As Howard Zehr wrote in *The Little Book of Restorative Justice*, "Restorative justice is a process to involve, to the extent possible, those who have a stake in a specific offense and to collectively identify and address harms, needs, and obligations, in order to heal and put things as right as possible." It allows people to hold *themselves* accountable, while at the same time teaching them a set of values and principles for dealing with conflict in the future.

"At the end of the day, we have to have high expectations for our kids, have faith that they can resolve conflict in a humane way. We have standards for academics, how do we not have them for humanity?" asked Childress.

INVESTING IN PEACE

According to Horan, without a school-wide commitment to building peace, their success would not have happened.

Childress agreed: "My administration trusted me and gave me free rein, which I think is often the biggest obstacle for teachers trying a new, alternative strategy."

And although "teaching peace" may not seem to fit within a typical school's curriculum, Dr. King believed that this was one of the critical roles of education: "The most dangerous criminal may be the man gifted with great reason and no morals."

In an effort to create peace, society often invests in violence prevention strategies, mistaking the two as the same. We can invest more in metal detectors, policing in schools, and even lock up every single young person in Chicago, and we would theoretically "prevent" a lot of violence. But that does not mean we are creating peace. Violence prevention is not enough. We must invest in peace creation. We have to teach people, young people in particular, the skills necessary to create peace in their lives and in their communities.

As Rasheed explained: "Nonviolence gave us the skills to act. And no matter how much violence there is in the world, nonviolence is much, much stronger. The universe is on the side of justice."

NEXT STEPS

124

Allies to Young People

Tips and Guidelines on How to Assist Young People to Organize

Jenny Sazama with help from teens in Boston

. . .

THINGS YOU CAN DO TO ASSIST YOUNG PEOPLE

Go to their space and their turf.

- Young people are so often asked to be a part of the adult world.
- Young people feel more empowered and groups build faster if work can be done on their terms and in a space where they feel comfortable.
- This is especially important when there are class and race differences. The unawareness of the "dominant" group is unintentional but strong. Safety needs to be built thoughtfully and carefully.

Build one-on-one relationships.

- This is a good way to get started in figuring out how to be an ally to young people. Choose one or two young people that you are interested in spending special time with. These may be young people that you notice are particularly sharp, or that you think would be good at bringing people together. There are things you are going to be able to accomplish one-on-one that are harder to do in a group.

Form an informal young people's advisory board for yourself.

- Get feedback from them. This will give you information about how to improve your work with young people continually. It will be an amazing growing experience for you, it will bring you closer to them, and it will help them feel that their thinking matters.

. . .

Assist young people to rely on each other and to take themselves and each other seriously.

- Adults cannot completely empower young people. They will not be truly powerful until they can rely on each other, trust each others' thinking and help each other. It's tempting to have the group center around us as adults, but our ultimate goal is for things to run well without us.

- Thoughtfully but firmly interrupt competition and put-downs. Society has told young people that they are not yet full humans and that their thinking is not valuable. They internalize these messages and then take them out on each other.
- Do group feedback. Ask people to give specific positive as well as growth/improvement information to another member of the group, including you. They will learn the most from each other.

Expect to make lots of phone calls and personal contact.

- Because young people are so often told by society that they are not important, adult allies need to make lots of phone calls to personally remind people that meetings are important and that they are wanted.
- They may not call you back. Don't take it personally. Keep calling. Assume you are wanted.
- Remember that in most situations, young people are not taken seriously, and they are told that their struggles don't matter. When you call, you are talking to someone who probably doesn't feel valuable, and thus doesn't remember that the work that she does is valuable. You need to keep reminding her how important she is.

Don't cancel meetings or events.

- It's okay if only a few people show up for things you have planned. Go ahead with them anyway. If you can even get two or three people to get closer to each other or work together on a project, you've come that much closer to the goals of your group.
- Young people have a lot of inconsistency in their lives. It means a lot to them if you can show them that you will follow through with what you say.

. . .

Young people should be a central part of any organization, movement, church group, etc.

- It's necessary for the total health of any movement or organization for young people to be a central part of all facets of the organization. It's great to have a young person chair a youth committee, but also have her chair the outreach committee, or be in charge of the budget. If young people do not have the skills to take on these roles then train them. A young person's perspective is invaluable.
- Make sure that young people are general members to committees and boards, not just occasional representatives.
- Token representation is not helpful in the long term.

In meetings, ask young people to talk first. Never believe that they don't know.

- You may have to ask them to express their ideas at least ten times and you may have to ask in ten different ways.
- They may say they don't know or don't have an opinion. This is what we have all been told as young people many times before.
- They do have thoughts on almost any situation if given enough information, time to think and the expectation that of course they can think.

NEXT STEPS

Ask young people what *they* think should be done in all situations.

- Discuss the goals of the group and how events reflect these goals, but resist the temptation to sway the group in the direction you think it should go.

Insist that young people are represented at every meeting, especially where young people are being discussed.

- It works better if there are at least two young people present.
- Meet with them ahead of time. Get them to share their thinking with you about the meeting topic. Remind them how important their thinking is and encourage them to speak during the meeting.

. . .

Get young people leading quickly.

- It's great for us as adults to begin facilitating and leading meetings. The faster we can turn it over to young people, however, the faster it will grow.

. . .

Appreciate yourself for the many important ways that you have been and continue to be a committed ally to young people.

125

Taking a Stand Against Ageism at All Ages

A Powerful Coalition

Margaret M. Gullette

New ageism is the term I use to describe the current American view of aging-past-youth. Whatever your age, you are likely to be affected by the new ageism—in your job, in your sexual life, in your sense of identity, in your intergenerational relations.

The new ageism has gotten so out of hand that it is culminating in the current Republican war against Social Security, Medicare and Medicaid. The first two are the most beloved and necessary government programs in the history of the Republic. And the third, Medicaid, ought to be another.

Virtually all Americans will eventually need Medicaid if we run out of money and need to be in a nursing home. This looks likelier for many of the so-called "Boomers"—especially the long-lived female Boomers—who lost savings in the ongoing Great Recession, had their pensions and unions taken away or lost their jobs and health insurance.

A person who is over 40 and has been laid off may well be a victim of *middle* ageism, which is discrimination against people over 40. People are suing their employers for midlife job discrimination in greater numbers than ever before; men in their 50s, women 10 years younger. Getting rid of midlife workers is a trend that has been worsening for 30 years, as I describe in my book, *Agewise*.

People under 40 are also immersed in what I call the American "culture of decline"— through the descriptions of later life in the media, if in no other way. Older people rarely appear in movies and never in ads for cool products—nothing but the young, the fit and the air-brushed. Why not airbrush older models?

Much worse: You listen to the radio and hear self-proclaimed "experts" tell about the horrors of longevity—how awful physical aging-into-old age will be personally, or how we on the cusp of retirement will break the bank by needing too much Medicare and Social Security. Some commentators even say that people should choose to die instead. (I call this the duty-to-die campaign.) Younger people overhear this, and it skews their expectations of the future and disheartens them. It alienates them from people older than they and from the selves they will one day become.

PUSHING BACK TERROR AND DENIAL

At the same time, some of us are told that "60 is the new 40" and that "the Boomers will change everything to their liking." These are the twin narratives of age terror and age denial. Parts of these narratives are out-and-out silly, but too much is malevolent.

Even what is positive and true can be true only of individuals or a class of people with access to health care, and the ability to meet other basic needs, rather than of everyone over a certain age. One thing is certain: In nothing, do people differ more than in their aging. In short, it makes more sense to fear ageism, not aging.

The war against people over 50 changes everything for the worse. In my state, Massachusetts, my Democratic governor wants to raise the age of retirement for public employees. Unionized "Boomers" in government service are told they are too costly. Uninsured people from 55 to 64 die at a higher rate than any other age group of uninsured. Raising the age of Medicare eligibility would be disastrous. None of this is to *my* liking.

There is, however, a backlash against the cuts aimed at Social Security, Medicare and Medicaid. I think anger is building. And justified anger can lead to activism.

The possibility exists of a nationwide coalition forming in order to try to save all the safety nets: WIC *(Women, Infants and Children)*, Social Security, Medicare, public health— and this coalition includes all of those concerned for the vulnerable. It would add together feminists, union people, AARP (the nonpartisan group formerly known as American Association of Retired People), OWL *(Older Women's League)*, so-called Boomers and Xers, who are alleged to be enemies in a *contrived war*, and people in cohorts not yet named by marketeers, plus people younger than 45 and older than 65.

If that coalition became not only powerful but self-conscious, it would have to declare itself "anti-ageist" in order to show how politically important the no-longer-so-young are. This coalition is concerned with social justice and the right to life in the broadest sense.

In the U.S. such a coalition could then be accompanied, I think, by a revolution in representation, meaning that some in the media would have to look at what topics they ignore and how they treat the issues they choose to cover.

NEXT STEPS

FINDING STRENGTH

For example, in Hurricane Katrina, 64 percent of the dead in New Orleans were over 65, although they were only 12 percent of the population, suggesting that older people were ignored in disaster planning. Most in the media did not notice age or ageism. Prior to a disaster, there have to be decisions about "who comes first and who comes last." . . .

Old, frail and disabled people seem to be the collective target of a new eugenics rhetoric. The "duty-to-die campaign" implies that such people are likely to be a "burden," unworthy of resources. If you are not active, engaged, productive, autonomous, close to the ideal healthy (middle-class) "youthful" person, you should somehow bow out. How? Are we expected to commit suicide? This dismissal can even be explicitly age-graded: older people on dialysis may fall into this useless category, especially if they have some cognitive impairment, but not people on dialysis under 65. If some in our society are unafraid to say such things, I fear for the rest of us. Triage involves split-second decisions, and bias is quickest on the draw. In emergencies the would-be rescuers and society at large have to put the neediest first if humanly possible.

There is an ongoing debate in age studies about whether women and men age differently, and I think they do. Women are aged by culture younger than men. I worry about how forced retirement will undermine my own cohort of working women, because they are like men in one new way: they have gotten a lot of satisfaction out of work and earning. And midlife job discrimination is wearing many people down, whether they know this is a collective problem or not.

But because of the women's movement and feminism, women have at least one big advantage—access to a more generous body of knowledge and a more progressive set of attitudes about growing past youth. Feminists in particular are the first to get the point of my book: to beware of ageism, not aging. More women seem to be liking "natural" looks and finding value in their accumulating experience. They read *Ourselves Growing Older*. They enjoy female company, which is going to be very important in late life.

American women are also turning against plastic surgery. The number of procedures reached a peak in 2004 (at 11,855,000), and has dropped every year since. *In 2010 the total was down* to 9,336,000—a decrease of over 20 percent. But when a *New York Times's blogger* did the annual story, she didn't try to find the trend line; instead she used only the surgical association's latest one-year data and a lead about a rise in one particular surgery (breast enhancement). Much depends on the media.

Journalists and scholars need to be more cautious about using releases or publicity from the uglification industries (surgeons, pharmaceutical companies, fashion magazines, even youth-focused health and fitness magazines) and the dysfunction industries (those selling aids to people supposedly declining from great youth sex). They get rich by peddling anxiety about our deficits. *New evidence* from novels, scholarly studies, and memoirs comes out from time to time suggesting that *sex can actually improve* across the life course. But any good news only gets whispered around because those industries are blaring our defects all the time.

The new longevity, along with Alzheimer's terror, coinciding with Republican deficit hysteria—this historical conjuncture is alarming. If our society can't make anti-ageism and anti-middle ageism into an activist mission, the consequences for American society are disastrous, even lethal. . . . Change will take not only resisting stereotypes but challenging the current dismal politics of midlife employment and old age.

NEXT STEPS

126

What Allies of Elders Can Do

Patricia Markee

It feels like you can ignore ageism until you reach the age when it affects you, but in truth it affects you now. It has affected you ever since you were born. It will affect you much more deeply as you grow older, especially if you keep putting it off, denying reality: your age and the treatment you receive.

Although you must acknowledge this oppression now, you may not have to devote much time to it. You can simply select an elder to support. Remember that what we current elders don't figure out is going to land squarely on your shoulders to figure out (if you're lucky enough to become an elder). Supporting an elder against the oppression is an investment in your own future.

In addition to the above, we ask that our allies:

- Assume that we are potentially brilliant. Do not believe any stupid, slow, or bumbly pattern. These are the effects of distress, not aging.
- Assume that we have long, productive futures. Many elders over sixty-five do not have to work and have more discretionary time to be productive. We are not ready to die nor are we waiting to die. I have seen movies in which the old are expected to be the ones to sacrifice their lives. This colludes with the belief that we no longer have anything to contribute.
- Assume that we have not given up on life. Remember that we have seen several generations of young people pass through their teens, twenties, and thirties, and we have noticed that some things last and some things don't. We may not be interested in everything that comes along not because we are intellectually stagnant or afraid, but, because we may have chosen to place our energy into fewer but more lasting things.
- Assume that we are sexually attractive and that we have in front of us many more years of being sexual.
- Assume that everyone can learn from much of our experience; invite us to share our thinking . . . . Don't give up on us at the first sign of distress. Let's break the cycle of abandonment now.
- Assume that memory loss and physical and mental deterioration may be accumulated distress or ill health, not the process of aging.
  . . .
- Don't assume that you know anything about our physical capacities. We may have trouble sitting in a chair, or we may be able to play basketball.
  . . .
- Interrupt others when they assume we're just being critical. We have a right to speak up for our rights without being dismissed.
- Use the same criteria for us to become leaders as you do for others. Expect us to become leaders, in spite of our individual distress. Don't give up on us at the first sign of distress. . . . It's nice if we're "very alive for a fifty-year-old," spontaneous, can have fun, can tap dance at seventy-eight, or are learning to do cart-wheels. But we are more than a vehicle for contradicting your fears [about aging].

N
E
X
T

S
T
E
P
S

- When we have become effective leaders, remember that we are not the all-loving, all-knowing parent you always wanted. We are human beings like you, struggling to figure out our lives. We may have had the time to figure out a few more things, but we are not gods.

  . . .

- Judy Malinowski has discovered that one's assumptions about elders can best be uncovered by asking the questions, "What surprised you about old people?" Asking the question, "What don't you like about old people?" seems to produce only the response, "I love old people," as in "I love children, Afro-Americans, disabled people, etc."
- Pick an elder leader who is not being supported and support her or him. This is simply an investment in your own aging and you may learn a great deal. Besides, . . . it is the role of leaders from the non-target group; it is the role of white leaders to support people of color leaders; it is the role of owning-class and middle-class leadership to support working-class leadership; and it is the role of younger leaders to support elder leaders.

N
E
X
T

S
T
E
P
S

SECTION 10

WORKING FOR SOCIAL JUSTICE
VISIONS AND STRATEGIES
FOR CHANGE

Introduction

Ximena Zúñiga

It takes courage to interrogate yourself. It takes courage to look at the mirror and see past your reflection to who you really are when you take off the mask, when you're not performing the same old routines and social roles. It takes courage to ask—how did I become so well adjusted to injustice?

—Cornel West, *Hope on a Tightrope* (2008)

Change means growth, and growth can be painful. But we sharpen self-definition by exposing the self in work and struggle together with those whom we define as different from ourselves, although sharing the same goals.

—Audre Lorde, *Sister Outsider* (1984)

As a democratic relationship, dialogue is the opportunity available to me to open up to the thinking of others, and thereby not wither away in isolation.

—Paulo Freire, *Pedagogy of Hope* (1994)

We believe social justice is both a process and a goal. The goal of social justice is full and equal participation of all groups in a society that is mutually shaped to meet their needs. Social justice includes a vision of society in which the distribution of resources is equitable and all members are physically and psychologically secure . . . The process for attaining the goal of social justice, we believe, should also be democratic and participatory, inclusive and affirming of human agency and capacities for working collaboratively to create change.

—Lee Anne Bell, *Teaching for Diversity and Social Justice* (2007)

INTRODUCTION

Throughout this volume we have articulated the view that developing awareness and knowledge about the systemic and interlocking qualities of social oppression is a critical step toward envisioning and working toward social justice. Our awareness and knowledge of these issues, as well as the way our identities are implicated in these issues, together shape our vision of what a more socially just world might look like, and motivate us to work toward realizing our vision of social justice. That is why so much of this book focuses on describing and analyzing systems of privilege and oppression from different perspectives, how they manifest themselves, and how they impact people's lives. However, learning about social injustices can be overwhelming, especially if we don't believe there is anything we can do to change them. Both inside and outside of the classroom, we need to find hope and to acquire practical tools for creating change. Otherwise, our awareness and knowledge may simply become "a prescription for despair" (Tatum, 1992, p. 24).

In this concluding section, we invite our readers to consider a vision for social justice and liberation that values critical consciousness, participation, connectedness, passion, bridge building across divides through dialogue and action, and alliances and coalitions for change, as pathways to individual and collective empowerment, equity, safety, and security for all social groups in society (Bell, 2007; Zúñiga, Nagda, Chesler, and Cytron-Walker, 2007). Such a vision requires an understanding of how various forms of privilege and oppression are connected at the psychological, interpersonal, intergroup, structural/institutional, and global levels.

As individuals, we may not be able to take actions against these injustices at all of these levels, but we can begin by learning about how we and others may participate in or be affected by injustices, such as adultism and ageism, ethno-religious oppression, racism, heterosexism, ableism, and so on, and by trying to change specific manifestations of oppression in our own spheres of influence (e.g. within ourselves and in our interpersonal relationships with family, friends, and co-workers). In so doing, we learn more about how dynamics of exclusion, privilege, and oppression come into play in our personal and community lives, how different individuals and groups are affected similarly and differently by these dynamics, and how these issues connect to larger national and global issues and systems. At the same time, we learn more about ourselves and develop the analytical, relational, and organizational skills needed to create change. As the words quoted at the head of this section from Audre Lorde remind us, working for change can be painful, it can also be liberating as our individual actions may lead us to change hearts and minds, foster new connections across differences, and forge meaningful ways of engaging with others and developing stronger ally relations. These kinds of actions provide us with tools to work within organizations and communities and to build stronger coalitions to work for social justice and help us to develop passion and a commitment for justice.

One set of tools for creating change includes our own growing awareness, knowledge, commitments, passions, and skills. These are necessary but not sufficient steps to challenge injustice and transform our schools, communities and the workplace. Collective action is needed to promote change beyond the personal level. The forging of pathways for personal and collective action, empowerment, and liberation calls for envisioning new possibilities, as well as understanding how change happens. For instance, we can envision new possibilities by educating ourselves and challenging injustice, as illustrated by several of the selections introduced earlier in this book (Katz, selection 64; Chess, Kafer, Quizar, and Richardson, selection 94; Hehir, selection 109); becoming an ally (Evans and Washington, selection 84; Peters, Castañeda, Hopkins, and McCants, selection 113; Sazama, selection 124); engaging in dialogue across differences (Ayvazian and Tatum, selection 22); or by joining organizations and creating coalitions to create change (Smith, selection 24; van Gelder, selection 39; Leondar-Wright, selection 40).

Although change may begin with a new critical awareness of inequality, dialogue across differences, participation in local, national, and global social movements, and coalitional efforts to create change at school, work, or in the community will expand our spheres of influence and contribute to wider systemic change (see Harro, selection 131 in this section). But working in coalition and collaborating across differences is not easy. It takes personal effort to "get ready" (as Harro describes it, in selection 131), by reading, talking, and learning with and from people from all walks of life—young and old, urban and rural, privileged and disadvantaged—who have resisted and created change individually or in conjunction with others. This is important because, as Freire (1994), Lorde (1984) and West (2008) explain in the passages quoted as headnotes to this section, we need to find the courage to question and engage in dialogue, not only with ourselves but with each other, to confirm that our visions for a more inclusive and just democracy are genuinely shared by the peoples we are working with. Social action needs to be informed by a shared and collective vision, inspiration, courage, love, and hope. Hence, our individual *and* collective visions of a more just society are what will sustain us and move us to take collaborative action against social injustice.

In closing, it is important to acknowledge that individual and collective actions are powerful forces that inspire and move people and groups to transform society and actively contribute to the development of visions, knowledge, networks, organizations, and tools for creating and sustaining change over the long haul. This is partly why so many of the selections included in this section are from activist writers who have been engaged in civil rights movements, labor movements, feminist movements, lesbian, gay, bisexual, and queer social movements, disability rights movements, and, more recently, in women of color and youth organizing and immigration rights and anti-globalization movements. It is also important to recognize the strengths and limitations of our current visions. For instance, twentieth-century activists focused primarily on class, race/ethnicity, gender, sexuality, or intersecting issues, while emerging social movements of the twenty-first century are grappling more with new issues and intersections, such as immigration, environmental, globalization, interfaith, and transgender and queer issues, religious oppression, and children's and youth rights. We do not know what the primary concerns of emerging and future activists in the coming decades will be, but we do know that they will bring new perspectives, new insights, and new tools for social change. We need both the wisdom and experience of older activists and the ideas and energy of young and emerging activists to create change. Together, we can build a world that is inclusive, democratic, and committed to human liberation and social justice.

READINGS IN THIS SECTION

The authors in our Contexts part outline conceptual frameworks for developing a vision for diversity and social justice and describe methods and practices that support the development of critical consciousness and actions and practices for social justice. In the first selection, Suzanne Pharr (selection 127) reminds us that "a truly democratic society is always in the process of redefining itself" and that struggles for liberation are an essential part of that process. She suggests that liberation requires transforming all forms of discrimination and barriers that keep large portions of the population from attaining economic and social justice, from participating fully in decisions affecting their lives, and from having the rights and responsibilities of living in a free society. In Pharr's view, being aware of the historical and social context of oppression and its manifestations at the cultural, institutional, and personal level is not sufficient. We need to have the ideological commitment to work for social justice and the willingness to engage with our hearts, build and honor relationships across differences, hear other perspectives, lend support

where there is pain and loss, develop individual and institutional integrity, and redefine and share power in our daily lives.

In the second selection, Barbara J. Love extends Freire's (1973) concept of liberatory consciousness for envisioning and creating change (selection 128). Love identifies four critical elements for developing such consciousness: awareness, analysis, action, and accountability/ally-ship. In her view, the development of liberatory consciousness is a crucial step because it enables us to live our lives "in oppressive systems and institutions with awareness and intentionality, rather than on the basis of the socialization to which we have been subjected." It also enables us to remain hopeful, connected through ally relationships, and not give up to despair.

In the third selection, Patricia Hill Collins (selection 129) proposes that those who wish to engage in social justice actions with people different from themselves need to learn how to transcend barriers created by their own experiences with race, class, and gender oppression to build the types of coalitions essential for social change. Collins identifies three major challenges: recognizing that differing experiences with oppression create problems in relationships; learning how to build relationships and coalitions around common causes with people of different races, genders, and socioeconomic statuses; and developing the capacity for empathy for the experiences of individuals and groups different from ourselves. Probably one of the biggest challenges for people who want to work for social justice is knowing where to begin to take responsibility for changing the systems that produce privilege and oppression. Allan G. Johnson (selection 130) identifies several approaches to help us think about "how to make ourselves part of the solution" as we transform ourselves, our schools, our workplaces, and our communities and urges us to "make noise, be seen," because systems of oppression feed on silence. He also provides many examples of actions we can take and asks us to "dare to make people feel uncomfortable, beginning with yourself"—that is, to question ourselves and others, even if it is personally challenging or risky, and to "actively promote change in systems that are organized around privilege," beginning in our own spheres of influence.

The process of becoming evermore aware and confident in one's ability to make a difference involves a life-long process of education, commitment, and empowerment. As Bobbie Harro suggests in "The Cycle of Liberation" (selection 131), this process requires education and building relationships with people "like you" and "different from you" to work for a more socially just future. Reading personal narratives and listening to personal stories from people actively involved in creating change is one of the ways we can begin to break the silence and learn from each other. The Voices section features two authors who have devoted their lives to promoting social justice for all people in distinct but connected areas. Cornel West (selection 132), an African American scholar and civil rights activist, writes about the need to muster the courage to work against the grain, think critically about how history is told to us, and to stand up against injustice. Gloria E. Anzaldúa (selection 133), a visionary Chicana/woman of color feminist, *maestra*/scholar activist, discusses the concept of "allies," and what it takes "to help each other heal," using her own experiences as a Chicana, *mestiza*, Mexican, lesbian, activist, poet and writer. She argues that when doing alliance work—bridge work, boundary work—talk about who you are and where you come from, even at the risk of being challenged or being betrayed.

The selections in the concluding section, Next Steps, offer varied approaches, methods, and strategies that people working alone or together can use to organize, build alliances, dialogue across differences, and take actions toward building a more just society. Chip Smith (selection 134) outlines a thought-provoking approach to organizing for social justice, starting with the premise that the systemic character of oppression becomes clearer as groups and organizations gain experience, resources, and influence. Drawing from his experience working against racism, sexism, and classism, Smith recommends merging social movements for national liberation, working-class power, and ending patriarchy. He proposes an approach that centers in self-determination, equity, and international solidarity. For instance, he invites organizers to "start where people are," develop critical understanding of complex issues, draw from social theory

and embrace social justice values, increase ties among organizations, and build progressive social change organizations. In the next selection, Ximena Zúñiga (selection 135) describes the methodology of Intergroup Dialogue, which is increasingly used in higher education, K-12 schools, and communities to bring people from different social identity groups together to examine controversial issues with the goal of consciousness-raising, bridging of differences and conflicts, and envisioning ways of creating greater equity and justice (Zúñiga, Nagda, Chesler, and Cytron-Walker, 2007). These sustained dialogues enable participants to engage in facilitated conversations and critical reflection about controversial topics across race/ethnicity, gender, sexuality, class, and other group differences and explore individual and collective ways of taking action in one's spheres of influence. Such an approach can increase ties among members' different social groups and facilitate coalitional efforts on campus.

From a social movement perspective, Elizabeth (Betita) Martínez (selection 136) underscores the importance of anticipating the challenges embedded in building alliances and the value of learning from our different and conflictual stories. Drawing from her women of color organizing experiences, she calls attention to what similar and different experiences of racism mean for different groups of women of color and how important it is to "act with integrity, speak with honesty, and reject any fear of our differences and conflicts." We conclude this section with an inspirational selection by the editors of WireTap (selection 137) on youth activism. This report from the trenches is a powerful reminder that young people, and people from all walks of life, are actively involved in social struggle and building alliances to fight the poor living conditions in youth detention centers, gender violence in schools, immigration reform for undocumented students, carbon emission levels, the persistent drop-out crisis in public high schools, and the tracking practices in public education that limit students' college choices. These efforts are both inspirational and educational. As César Chávez, leader of the United Farm Workers Union, remarked a long time ago, *Sí se puede, yes, we can*!

See Companion Website for Additional Resources and Material

References

Bell, L. A. (2007). Theoretical foundations for social justice education. In M. Adams, L. A. Bell, P. Griffin (eds), *Teaching for Diversity and Social Justice* (2nd edition, pp. 1–14). New York, NY: Routledge.

Freire, P. (1973). *Education for Critical Consciousness*. New York: Continuum.

Freire, P. (1994). *Pedagogy of Hope*. New York: Continuum.

Lorde, A. (1984). *Sister Outsider.* Freedom, CA: Crossing Press.

Tatum, B. D. (1992). Talking about race, learning about racism: The application of racial identity development theory in the classroom. *Harvard Educational Review* 62 (1), 1–24.

West, C. (2008). *Hope on a Tightrope*. Carlsbad, CA: Smiley Books, Hay House.

Zúñiga, X., Nagda, B. A., Chesler, M., Cytron-Walker, A. (2007). *Intergroup Dialogue in High Education: Meaningful Learning About Social Justice*. ASHE-ERIC Higher Education Report Volume 32, Number 4. San Francisco, CA: Jossey-Bass.

127

Reflections on Liberation

Suzanne Pharr

Liberation politics: seeking social and economic justice for all people; supporting inclusion, autonomy, choice, wholeness; building and honoring relationships; developing individual and institutional integrity, responsibility and accountability; redefining and sharing power.

These political times call for renewed dialogue about and commitment to the politics of liberation. Because a truly democratic society is always in the process of redefining itself, its evolution is fueled by struggles for liberation on the part of everyone wishing to participate in the development of the institutions and policies that govern our lives. Liberation requires a struggle against discrimination based on race, class, gender, sexual identity, ableism and age—those barriers which keep large portions of the population from having access to economic and social justice, from being able to participate fully in the decisions affecting our lives, from having a full share of both the rights and responsibilities of living in a free society.

. . .

This is the challenge for all of us. The work of liberation politics is to change hearts and minds, develop empathy with and sympathy for other people, and help each other discover how we are inextricably linked together for our common good and our survival on this planet.

Like power, liberation cannot be given; it must be created. Liberation politics requires

- helping individuals to fulfill their greatest potential by providing truthful information along with the tools and skills for using it, supporting their autonomy and self-government, and connecting them to life in community with others;
- fostering both individual freedom and mutual responsibility for others;
- recognizing that freedom demands people always be able to make their own choices about their lives;
- creating a politic of shared power rather than power-over;
- learning the non-violent skills of compromise and mediation in the sometimes difficult collective lives of family and community—in organizations, the workplace, and governing bodies;
- developing integrity in relationships through understanding that the same communal values—generosity and fairness, responsibility and freedom, forgiveness and atonement—must be maintained not just in personal relationships but in the workplace, social groups, and governing bodies;
- treating everyone as a valued whole person, not as someone to be used or controlled;
- maintaining civility in our relationships and being accountable for our behavior;
- seeing cultural differences as life-enhancing, as expanding possibilities;
- placing a broad definition of human rights at the center of our values: ensuring that every person has food, shelter, clothing, safety, education, health care, and a livable income.

. . .

We are seeking ways to bring people together to work on common causes across differences. If, indeed, all oppressions are connected, then it follows that the targets of this oppression are connected as well as their solution. This interconnection leads us to the idea of collaborative efforts to create democratic values, discourse and institutions.

We believe that we will succeed when we collectively create a vision that in practice offers a way of life so attractive that people will not be able to resist it. As progressive people across this country we are working to create a multi-issue, multi-racial and multicultural liberation movement; we are trying to redefine our work and bring more integrity to it; we are engaged in developing a clearer, more compelling vision, building stronger relationships among justice-seeking people, and including more people in the process of creating a democracy that works for all of us.

. . .

TRANSFORMATIONAL ORGANIZING AND BUILDING COMMUNITY

For whatever reasons, progressive people have not always talked a great deal about the strong moral convictions underlying why we do this work of social justice: *it is because we believe every person counts, has human dignity, and deserves respect, equality and justice.* This morality is the basis for our vision, and when we do our best vision-based organizing (as opposed to response-based or expediency-based), all our work flows from this basic belief.

Ours is a noble history. Because progressive people believe in the inclusion of everyone in the cause of justice and equality, we have struggled for civil rights for people of color, for women, for people with disabilities, and now for lesbians and gay men. We have worked to save the environment, to provide women autonomy and choice concerning our bodies, to end unjust wars, to end homelessness, hunger, and poverty, to create safe workplaces, decent wages and fair labor practices, to honor treaty rights, to eliminate HIV and improve health care, to eliminate biased crime and violence against women and children. We share broad principles of inclusion, fairness, and justice. We must not forget what provides the fire for our work, what connects us in the struggle for freedom and equality.

We are living in a time in which people are crying out for something to believe in, for a moral sense, for purpose, for answers that will bring some calm to the chaos they feel in their lives. As progressive people, we have not always offered up our vision of the world, our activities for justice, as a moral vision. When we have, as during the Civil Rights Movement, people working together for a common good have felt whole.

I believe it is our moral imperative to help each other make connections, to show how everyone is interrelated and belongs in community, or as it is currently expressed, "We all came on different ships but we're in the same boat now." It is at our peril if we do work that increases alienation and robs meaning from life. Today's expressions of violence, hatred, and bigotry are directly related to the level of alienation and disconnection felt by people. For our very survival, we must develop a sense of common humanity.

It may be that our most important political work is figuring out how to make the full human connection, how to engage our hearts as well as our minds, how to heal the injuries we have suffered, how to do organizing that transforms people as well as institutions. With these as goals, we need to re-think our strategies and tactics.

We have to think about our vision of change. Are we involved in a struggle for power that requires forces and resources on each side and a confrontational show-down in which only one side wins? If we are in a shoot-out, then the progressive side has already lost, for certainly there are more resources on the Right at this moment. In other cases where we

can organize the most resources, such as the 1992 "No on 9" campaign in Oregon, what is the nature and permanency of the win? The anti-gay and lesbian constitutional amendment was defeated, but in general, people did not have a sense of ecstatic victory. I think there were two primary reasons: 1) the Right immediately announced its intention to take the fight to local rural communities and to build a string of victories in areas where it had developed support—indicating that this is indeed a long struggle for the hearts and souls of Oregonians; and 2) the campaign did not facilitate the building of lasting relationships, of communities, of progressive institutions—because it did not see itself as part of a movement. At the end, I believe people felt a war-like atmosphere had been created, but that the language and tactics of war had failed them. In the months that followed the election victory, people seemed fatigued, wary, often dispirited and in retreat. Rather than being transformed into new politics and relationships by their experience, they seemed battered by it.

Transformational Organizing. There is something to be learned when victory feels like defeat. Somehow, people did not emerge from the Oregon experience with a sense of vitality, of wholeness, of connection. Justice-seeking people must call into question our methods of organizing. Often we have thought that effective organizing is simply being able to move people as a group, sometimes through manipulation, to act in a particular way to achieve a goal. Too often the end has justified the means, and we have failed to follow Ghandi's belief that every step toward liberation must have liberation embedded within it. By concentrating on moving people to action, we have often failed to hear the voice of their spirit, their need for connection and wholeness—not for someday after the goal has been gained, but in the very process of gaining it.

I am not arguing that we should give up direct action, civil disobedience, issue campaigns, political education, confrontation, membership and voter drives, etc. We need to do these things and much more. I am suggesting that we re-think the meaning of social change and learn how to include the long-term work of transforming people as we work for social justice. We must re-define "winning." Our social change has to be more than amassing resources and shifting power from the hands of one group to another; we must seek a true shift in consciousness, one that forges vision, goals, and strategies from belief, not just from expediency, and allows us to become a strong political force.

The definition of transformational politics is fairly simple: it is political work that changes the hearts and minds of people, supports personal and group growth in ways that create healthy, whole people, organizations, and communities, and is based on a vision of a society where people—across lines of race, gender, class and sexuality—are supported by institutions and communities to live their best lives.

Among many possibilities, I want to suggest one way to do transformational work: through building community that is based on our moral vision.

Building Community, Making Connections. Where do we build community? Should it be geographic, consisting of everyone who lives in the same neighborhood? Based on identity, such as one's racial identity, sexual identity? Organizational or work identity? Where are the places that community happens?

It seems to me that community can be created in a vast number of places and ways. What is more important is the *how* of building community. To get to the how, we first have to define what community is. Community is people in any configuration (geographic, identity, etc.) bonded together over time through common interest and concern, through responsibility and accountability to one another, and at its best, through commitment, friendship and love.

To live in authentic community requires a deeper level of caring and interaction than many of us currently exhibit in our drive for individualism and self-fulfillment. That is, it calls for living with communal values. And we face a daunting challenge here because we

all live in a culture that glorifies individualism. For example, what the Right calls "traditional family values" actually works against the often-quoted African proverb, "It takes a village to raise a child," which speaks to the communal value of the importance of every child in the life of the community, present and future. Such values point to very different solutions than those currently suggested for the problems of youth alienation, crime, and violence. Rather than increasing police forces and building more jails, with these shared values we would look toward more ways for the community as a whole to be responsible for and accountable to children. We would seek ways to support and nurture their lives. All of us would be teachers, parents and friends for every child.

Creating community requires seeing the whole, not just the parts, and understanding how they interrelate. However, the difficult part is learning how to honor the needs of the individual as well as those of the group, without denying the importance of either. It requires a balance between identity and freedom on the one hand and the collective good and public responsibility on the other. It requires ritual and celebration and collective ways to grieve and show anger; it requires a commitment to resolve conflict.

Most of all, it requires authenticity in relationships between and among whole people. This means that each of us has to be able to bring all of who we are to the relationship, neighbor to neighbor, friend to friend, worker to worker. Bringing all of who we are to community requires working across great differences in culture, in lifestyle, in belief. It demands that we look beyond our own lives to understand the lives of others. It demands that we interact with the lives of others. It requires understanding the connections among people's lives and then seeking comprehensive solutions to multi-issue, multifaceted problems. If we allow only certain parts of people to surface, and if we silence, reject or exclude basic pieces of their essential selves, then we begin designing systems of oppression. Community becomes based on power and non-consensual authority: those who have the most power and privilege dictate the community norms and their enforcement.

One of the goals of every political activity we engage in should be to move beyond superficial interactions to the building of relationships and community. Much of this work is simple, not difficult or complex; it merely requires redefining our values and how we spend our political time. For example, far too often I go to meetings, frequently held in sterile hotel conference rooms, where introductions are limited to people giving their names or, at best, what work they do. Building relationships—whether those of neighbor, friend, lover, work partner—requires that we ask *who are you*? In rural communities in the South and on American Indian reservations, people spend a lot of time talking about who their people are, how they are connected to people and place. Women activists in the housing projects in New Orleans get to know each other by telling their life lines, the major events that shaped them along the way. It is almost ritual for lesbians to get to know each other by telling their coming out stories—when and how they first experienced their lesbianism.

Building connection and relationship requires that we give it time, not just in meetings but in informal opportunities surrounding meetings, structured and unstructured. For instance, when I did political education on oppression issues within the battered women's movement, there was always a dramatic difference in the relationships that were built when we stayed in retreat centers or self-contained places away from distracting outside activities rather than in city hotels. So much of what happened in people's growth and understanding came from living, sleeping, and eating together in an atmosphere that encouraged interaction.

As a way to think about building community, we can ask ourselves these questions:

- In what settings with other people have I felt most whole? What is it that makes me feel known and accepted as who I am?

- What conditions make me most able to work well in partnership with other people? What makes me feel connected rather than alienated?
- What are communal values? What are the practices that support them?
- Where are the places where community is occurring? (For example, in care teams for people living with AIDS, in youth gangs, in certain churches or neighborhoods, in AA groups?) What are the characteristics of these communities?
- Who is being excluded from community? What barriers are there to participation?
- What are the qualities of an inclusive community as opposed to an exclusive community?
- What makes a community democratic?

Our communities are where our moral values are expressed. It is here that we are called upon to share our connection to others, our interdependence, our deepest belief in what it means to be part of the human condition, where people's lives touch one another, for good or for bad. It is here where the rhetoric of belief is forced into the reality of living. It is from this collection of people, holding within it smaller units called families, that we build and live democracy. Or, without care and nurturance, where we detach from one another and destroy our hope for survival.

POLITICAL INTEGRITY AND MULTI-ISSUE POLITICS

It is one thing for us to talk about liberation politics; it is of course another to live them. We lack political integrity when we demand liberation for one cause or one group of people and act out oppression or exploitation toward others. If we do not have an integrated analysis and a commitment to sharing power, it is easy to act out politics that simply reflect a hierarchy of domination.

In our social change organizations in particular we can find ourselves in this dangerous position: where we are demanding, for example, liberation from sexism but within the organization we act out racism, economic injustice, and homophobia. Each is reflected in who is allowed to lead, who makes the highest and lowest salaries, who is allowed to participate in the major decision-making, who decides how the resources are used. If the organization does not have a vision and a strategy that also include the elimination of racism, sexism, economic injustice, and homophobia (as well as oppressions relating to age, physical ability, etc.), then internal conflict is inevitable. People cannot single out just one oppression from their lives to bring to their work for liberation: they bring their whole selves.

Creating a multi-racial, multi-cultural, multi-issue vision of liberation is no easy task. It is much easier to stay within the framework of oppression where our women's organizations' leadership is primarily white, middle-class women, heterosexual or closeted lesbians; our civil rights organizations are male-dominated; our gay/lesbian/bi/transgender organizations are controlled by white gay men and/or white lesbians. And where the agendas for change reflect the values of those who dominate the leadership.

It is easier to talk about "diversity" than about shared power. Or to use a belief in identity politics to justify not including others in a vision for change. I do not believe in either diversity or identity politics as they are currently practiced.

First, diversity politics seem to focus on the necessity for having everyone (across gender, race, class, age, religion, physical ability) present and treated well in any given setting or organization. A core premise is that everyone is oppressed and all oppressions are equal. Since the publication of the report, "Workforce 2000," that predicted the U.S. workforce would be made up of 80% women and people of color by the year 2000, a veritable growth industry of "diversity consultants" has arisen to teach corporations how

to "manage" diversity. With integration and productivity as goals, they focus on issues of sensitivity and inclusion—a human relations approach—with acceptance and comfort as high priorities. Popular images of diversity politics show people holding hands around America, singing "We Are the World." People are generally reassured that they do not have to give up anything when they diversify their workplace. They simply have to include other people and become more sensitive to differences.

Because the history of oppression is one of excluding, of silencing, of rendering people invisible, I have great appreciation for the part of diversity work that concentrates on making sure everyone is included. However, our diversity work fails if it does not deal with the power dynamics of difference and go straight to the heart of shifting the balance of power among individuals and within institutions. A danger of diversity politics lies in the possibility that it may become a tool of oppression by creating the illusion of participation when in fact there is no shared power. Having a presence within an organization or institution means very little if one does not have the power of decision-making, an adequate share of the resources, and participation in the development of the workplan or agenda. We as oppressed people must demand much more than acceptance. Tolerance, sympathy and understanding are not enough, though they soften the impact of oppression by making people feel better in the face of it. Our job is not just to soften blows but to make change, fundamental and far-reaching.

Identity politics, on the other hand, rather than trying to include everyone, brings together people who share a single common identity such as sexual orientation, gender, or race. Generally, it focuses on the elimination of a single oppression, the one that is based on the common identity; e.g., homophobia/heterosexism, sexism, racism. However, this can be a limited, hierarchical approach, reducing people of multiple identities to a single identity. Which identity should a lesbian of color choose as a priority—gender, race or sexual identity? And does choosing one necessitate leaving the other two at home? What do we say to bisexual or biracial people? Do we tell them to choose? Our multiple identities allow us to develop a politic that is broad in scope because it is grounded in a wide range of experiences.

There are positive aspects of organizing along identity lines: clarity of single focus in tactics and strategies, self-examination and education apart from the dominant culture, development of solidarity and group bonding. Creating organizations based on identity allows us to have visibility and collective power, to advance concerns that otherwise would never be recognized because of our marginalization within the dominant society.

However, identity politics often suffers from the failure to acknowledge that the same multiplicity of oppressions, a similar imbalance of power, exists within identity groups as within the larger society. People who group together on the basis of their sexual identity still find within these groups sexism and racism that have to be dealt with—or if gathering on the basis of race, there is still sexism and homophobia to be confronted. Whole, not partial, people come to identity groups, carrying several identities. Some of liberation movements' major barriers to building a unified and cohesive strategy, I believe, come from our refusal to work directly on the oppressions—those fundamental issues of power—within our own groups. A successful liberation movement cannot be built on the effort to liberate only a few or only a piece of who we are.

Diversity and identity politics are responses to oppression. In confronting oppressions we must always remember that they mean more than people just not being nice to one another. They are systemic, based in institutions and in general society, where one group of people is allowed to exert power and control over members of another group, denying them fundamental rights. Also, we must remember that oppressions are interconnected, operating in similar ways, and that many people experience more than one oppression.

. . .

The question, as ever, is what to do? I do not believe that either a diversity or identity politics approach will work unless they are changed to incorporate a multi-issue analysis and strategy that combine the politics of inclusion with shared power. But, one might say, it will spread us too thin if we try to work on everyone's issue, and ours will fall by the wayside. In our external work (doing women's anti-violence work, working against police brutality in people of color communities, seeking government funding for AIDS research), we do not have to work on "everybody's issue"—we can be focused. But how can we achieve true social change unless we look at all within our constituency who are affected by our particular issue? People who have AIDS are of every race, class, age, gender, geographic location, but when research and services are sought, it is women, people of color, poor people, who are most overlooked. The HIV virus rages on because those in power think that the people who contract it are dispensable. Are we to be like them? To understand why police brutality is so much more extreme in people of color communities than in white, we have to understand also why, even within these communities, it is even greater against poor people of color, women who are prostitutes, and gay men and lesbians of color. To leave any group out leaves a hole for everyone's freedoms and rights to fall through. It becomes an issue of "acceptable" and "unacceptable" people, deserving and undeserving of rights, legitimate and illegitimate, deserving of recognition as fully human or dismissable as something less.

Identity politics offers a strong, vital place for bonding, for developing political analysis. With each other we struggle to understand our relationship to a world that says that we are no more than our identity, and simultaneously denies there is oppression based on race or gender or sexual identity. Our challenge is to learn how to use the experiences of our many identities to forge an inclusive social change politic. The question that faces us is how to do multi-issue coalition building from an identity base. The hope for a multi-racial, multi-issue movement rests in large part on the answer to this question.

Our linkages can create a movement, and our divisions can destroy us. Each point of linkage is our strongest defense and also holds the most possibility for long-lasting social change.

If our organizations are not committed internally to the inclusion and shared power of all those who share our issue, how can we with any integrity demand inclusion and shared power in society at large? If women, lesbians and gay men are treated as people undeserving of equality within civil rights organizations, how can those organizations demand equality? If women of color and poor women are marginalized in women's rights organizations, how can those organizations argue that women as a class should be moved into full participation in the mainstream? If lesbian and gay organizations are not feminist and anti-racist in all their practices, what hope is there for the elimination of homophobia and heterosexism in a racist, sexist society? It is an issue of integrity.

In the larger social change community our failure to connect issues prevents us from being able to do strong coalition and alliance work with one another. Most frequently, coalitions and alliances are created to meet crisis issues which threaten all of us. Made up of groups that experience injustice, they should have common ground. They most frequently fall apart, I believe, because of failure in relationships. As in all human relationships, it is difficult to solve the issue of the moment without a history of trust, common struggle, and reciprocity. Homophobia, for example, has kept us "quiet" and invisible in our anti-racist work; racism has kept us "quiet" in our lesbian and gay work. We need to be visible in our work on all fronts. Working shoulder to shoulder on each other's issues enables us to get to know each other's humanity, to understand the broad sweep of issues, to build trust and solidarity.

Our separateness, by identity and by issue, prevents the building of a progressive movement. When we grasp the value and interconnectedness of our liberation issues, then

we will at last be able to make true coalition and begin building a common agenda that eliminates oppression and brings forth a vision of diversity that shares both power and resources.

. . .

128

Developing a Liberatory Consciousness

Barbara J. Love

All members of society play a role in keeping a "dis-equal" system in place, whether the system works to their benefit or to their disadvantage. Through the socialization process, every member of society learns the attitudes, language, behaviors and skills that are necessary to function effectively in the existing society. This socialization prepares individuals to play roles of dominant or subordinant in systems of oppression.[1] For example, men are assigned the role of dominant and women are assigned the role of subordinant in the system of dis-equality based on gender. Whites are assigned to play the role of dominant and People of Color are assigned the role of subordinant in the system of dis-equality based on race. The socialization process of the society works to insure that each person learns what they need to know to behave in ways that contribute to the maintenance and perpetuation of the existing system, independent of their belief in its fairness or efficacy.

No single human can be charged with the creation of the oppressive systems in operation today. All humans now living have internalized the attitudes, understandings, and patterns of thoughts that allow them to function in and collaborate with these systems of oppression, whether they benefit from them or are placed at a disadvantage by them. The patterns of thought and behaviors that support and help to maintain racism, sexism, classism and other manifestations of oppression are not natural or inherent to any human. They are learned through this socialization process.

Many members of society, both those who benefit from oppression as well as those who are placed at disadvantage, want to work for social change to reduce inequity and bring about greater justice, yet continue to behave in ways that preserve and perpetuate the existing system. This happens because humans are products of their socialization and follow the habits of mind and thought that have been instilled in them. The institutions in which we live reward and reinforce behaviors that perpetuate existing systems and resist efforts toward change.

To be effective as a liberation worker—that is, one who is committed to changing systems and institutions characterized by oppression to create greater equity and social justice—a crucial step is the development of a liberatory consciousness. A liberatory consciousness enables humans to live their lives in oppressive systems and institutions with awareness and intentionality, rather than on the basis of the socialization to which they have been subjected. A liberatory consciousness enables humans to maintain an awareness of the dynamics of oppression characterizing society without giving in to despair and hopelessness about that condition, to maintain an awareness of the role played by each individual in the maintenance of the system without blaming them for the roles they play, and at

the same time practice intentionality about changing the systems of oppression. A liberatory consciousness enables humans to live "outside" the patterns of thought and behavior learned through the socialization process that helps to perpetuate oppressive systems.

ELEMENTS OF A LIBERATORY CONSCIOUSNESS

The process for developing a liberatory consciousness has been discussed by many educators working for social change and social justice. Paulo Freire, the Brazilian educator, described it as developing critical consciousness. Carter G. Woodson described it as changing the "miseducation of the Negro." Michael Albert's humanist vision and bell hooks's feminist critical consciousness are examples of other ways that a liberatory consciousness has been discussed.

Four elements in developing a liberatory consciousness are described here. They include awareness, analysis, acting, and accountability/ally-ship. The labeling of these four components in the development of a liberatory consciousness is meant to serve as reminders in our daily living that the development and practice of a liberatory consciousness is neither mysterious nor difficult, static nor fixed, or something that some people have and others do not. It is to be continually practiced event by event, each time we are faced with a situation in which oppression or internalized oppression is evident. These labels remind us that every human can acquire the skill to become a liberation worker.

Awareness, the first part of the task, includes practicing awareness or noticing what is happening. The second part includes analyzing what is happening from a stance of awareness along with the possibilities for action. The third part of the task includes deciding on the basis of that analysis what needs to be done, and seeing to it that the action is accomplished. The fourth part may be the most troublesome part for it requires that individuals accept accountability to self and community for the consequences of the action that has been taken or not taken.

With a liberatory consciousness, every person gets a chance to theorize about issues of equity and social justice, to analyze events related to equity and social justice, and to act in responsible ways to transform the society.

AWARENESS

The awareness component of a liberatory consciousness involves developing the capacity to notice, to give our attention to our daily lives, our language, our behaviors, and even our thoughts. It means making the decision to live our lives from a waking position. It means giving up the numbness and dullness with which we have been lulled into going through life. For some, facing life with awareness may at first seem painful. One student, in a class examining oppression, declared with dismay, "You have taken the fun out of going to the movies. Now I can't watch stupid movies and laugh anymore." This student had observed that even while watching "stupid movies" certain attitudes were being instilled in his consciousness. He noticed that some of these were attitudes and ideas that he would reject if he were consciously paying attention.

Living with awareness means noticing what happens in the world around you. If a salesperson reaches around you to serve the person in line behind you, a liberatory consciousness means taking notice of this act rather than ignoring it, pretending that it did not happen, or thinking it is of little consequence. If disparaging remarks about people of a different group are made in your presence, awareness requires taking note that an event

has occurred that effects the maintenance or elimination of oppression. It means noticing that the remark was made, and not pretending that the remark is harmless.

ANALYSIS

A liberatory consciousness requires every individual to not only notice what is going on in the world around her or him, but to think about it and theorize about it—that is, to get information and develop his or her own explanation for what is happening, why it is happening, and what needs to be done about it.

The analysis component of a liberatory consciousness includes the activity of thinking about what needs to be done in a given situation. Every human has the capacity to examine any situation in order to determine what seems to be true about that situation. Awareness coupled with analysis of that situation becomes the basis for determining whether change is required, and if it is, the nature of the change needed.

If what we observe to be true about a given situation seems consistent with our values of an equitable society, then the analysis will conclude that the situation is fine exactly as is. If, on the other hand, the observation leads to the conclusion that the situation is unjust, then a conclusion that the situation needs to be changed is reached.

Analysis will reveal a range of possible courses of action. Each possibility will be examined to determine what results are likely to be produced. Some possible activities will produce results that are consistent with our goals of justice and fairness while some will not. Analysis means considering the range of possible activities and the results that each of them is likely to produce.

ACTION

The action component of a liberatory consciousness proceeds from recognition that awareness and analysis alone are not enough. There can be no division between those who think and those who put thinking into action. The action component of a liberatory consciousness is based on the assumption that the participation of each of us in the liberation project provides the best possibility of gaining liberation for any of us.

The action component of a liberatory consciousness includes deciding what needs to be done, and then seeing to it that action is taken. Sometimes it means taking individual initiative to follow a course of action. Sometimes it means encouraging others to take action. Sometimes it means organizing and supporting other people to feel empowered to take the action that the situation requires. And sometimes, locating the resources that empower another person to act with agency is required. In still other cases, reminding others that they are right for the task, and that they know enough and are powerful enough to take on the challenge of seeing that the task is completed will be the action that is required. In any event, the liberatory consciousness requires each human to take some action in every situation when the opportunity to transform the society and move toward a more just world presents itself.

ACCOUNTABLE/ALLY-SHIP

The socialization to which we have been subjected results in our thinking and behaving in very role-specific ways. We have been socialized into roles of dominant and subordinant. One result is that our vision of possibilities for change is limited by our confinement in the roles to which we have been assigned. Many white people flounder in their efforts to extricate themselves from racist conditioning. They become stuck while working on racism because their socialization to the role of dominant provides very little opportunity

to understand what life might be like outside that role. A Person of Color will often have a perspective or "window of understanding" that is unavailable to a white person because of the latter's socialization into whiteness. Left alone in their struggle, some individual white people do eventually figure the difficulty out; many do not. When a Person of Color chooses to share her or his "window of understanding," the growth and development of a white person, away from racist conditioning, can be significantly enhanced and quickened.

Similarly, a Person of Color can become stuck in patterns of internalized racism and left alone to struggle. A white person can hold a perspective that is outside the socialization into racial subordination that, when shared, boosts the efforts of a Person of Color to eliminate patterns of internalized racism. The same holds true for men addressing sexism and for women addressing internalized sexism, as well as for "owning-class" people, those raised poor, and working-class people who are concerned with classism.

People raised on one end of patterns of gender, race, and class subordination or domination can provide a different perspective for people raised on the other end. At the same time, people within role groups can assist other members of their own role group to recognize and eliminate those patterns of thought and behavior that originate in internalized subordination or domination. For example, women, People of Color, those raised poor, and working-class people can help each other better understand the ways that our automatic responses help to perpetuate and maintain our own oppression.

The accountability element of a liberatory consciousness is concerned with how we understand and manage this opportunity and possibility for perspective sharing and allyship in liberation work. Individuals engaged in liberation work can have confidence that, left to their own struggles, others will eventually figure out what they need to know to disentangle thought and behavior patterns from the internalized oppression, either internalized domination or internalized subordination. But working in connection and collaboration with each other, across and within "role" groups, we can make progress in ways that are not apparent when working in isolation and in separate communities.

In our liberation work, many of us have taken the position that it is not the responsibility of members of the subordinant group to teach or help to educate members of the dominant group. This is a reasonable and essentially "righteous" position. Those people who bear the brunt of the oppression should not be required to also take responsibility for eliminating it. At the same time, it is self-evident that people in the subordinant group can take the lead in setting the world right. For one thing, if people in the dominant group had access to and were able to hold a perspective that allowed them to change systems and patterns of domination, they would have done so already. Members of the subordinant group can wait for members of the dominant group to recognize that their language or behavior is oppressive, or they can share their perspective in every place where it could make a difference, including in the lives of members of the dominant group. In the end, it is in their best interest to do so.

This does not mean that members of groups who have been socialized into roles of subordination should focus their attention outward on the dominant group, or that members of dominant groups should be focused on the subordinant group. It is to suggest that when the perspective of the other group can serve as the critical energy to move things forward, liberation will be hampered if we hold our thinking and perspectives back from each other. Concomitantly, it also suggests that individual members of dominant and subordinant groups offer their perspective to other members of their role group in the effort to move forward.

As liberation workers, it is axiomatic that we will make mistakes. Rather than self-condemnation or blame from others, it will be important to have the opportunity and the openness to hear an analysis from others that allows us to reevaluate problematic behaviors or positions. If a Black person notices another Black person acting out of internalized

racism, a liberatory consciousness requires considering the usefulness of sharing a viewpoint that enables that person to explore the implications of internalized racism for their behavior. While we do not take responsibility for another's thinking or behavior, accountability means that we support each other to learn more about the ways that the internalized domination and internalized subordination manifests itself in our lives, and agree with each other that we will act to interrupt it.

Accepting accountability to self and community for the consequences of actions taken or not taken can be an elusive concept for a people steeped in the ideology of individualism. Multiplicities of experiences and points of view contribute to problematizing the concept of accountability as well. None of us can claim for ourselves the right to tell another that her analysis is retrogressive. Recent discussions of "political correctness" can also prove troubling in the effort to grasp the idea of accountability and make it a workable concept.

There will be no easy answers here. The significance of a liberatory consciousness is that we will always question, explore, and interrogate ourselves about possibilities for supporting the efforts of others to come to grips with our conditioning into oppression, and give each other a hand in moving outside of our assigned roles. The accountability element of a liberatory consciousness requires us to develop new agreements regarding our interactions with each other. As a beginning, we get to decide the extent to which we will make ourselves available to interrupt language and behavior patterns that, in our best analysis, originate in an internalization of the ideology of domination and subordination.

SUMMARY

In the end, institutions and systems respond to the initiatives of individuals and groups of individuals. Systems do not perpetuate themselves: they are perpetuated by the actions of people who act automatically on the basis of their socialization. If we all acted on the basis of values and beliefs of our own choosing, systems and institutions would show greater flexibility and propensity for change. As it now stands, most of us act on the basis of values and beliefs instilled in us through the socialization process, designed to prepare us to act in ways that insure the perpetuation of existing systems of oppression.

The development of a liberatory consciousness would allow us the opportunity to reclaim choice in our values and attitudes and consequently, in our response patterns. It would enable us to move from an automatic response system grounded in our socialization, to the capacity to act on a range of responses based on our own awareness, analysis and decision making, and the opportunities we have to learn from our colleagues and others who are themselves embarked on a journey to liberation.

Note

1 I prefer the spelling *subordinant* because: (1) *subordinant* is a noun; *subordinate* is an adjective, modifying the noun; (2) *subordinant* parallels *dominant*, but *subordinate* describes what is done to the *subordinants*; (3) if we were to parallel *subordinate*, then we would need to write *dominate*; and (4) using the modifying adjective to refer to groups of people seems to further objectify and reduce.

129

Toward a New Vision

Race, Class, and Gender

Patricia Hill Collins

How can we transcend the barriers created by our experiences with race, class and gender oppression in order to build the types of coalitions essential for social change?

Reconceptualizing oppression and seeing the barriers created by race, class and gender as interlocking categories of analysis is a vital first step. But we must transcend these barriers by moving toward race, class and gender as categories of connection, by building relationships and coalitions that will bring about social change. What are some of the issues involved in doing this?

1. DIFFERENCES IN POWER AND PRIVILEGE

First, we must recognize that our differing experiences with oppression create problems in the relationships among us. Each of us lives within a system that vests us with varying levels of power and privilege. These differences in power, whether structured along axes of race, class, gender, age or sexual orientation, frame our relationships. African-American writer June Jordan describes her discomfort on a Caribbean vacation with Olive, the Black woman who cleaned her room:

> . . . even though both "Olive" and "I" live inside a conflict neither one of us created, and even though both of us therefore hurt inside that conflict, I may be one of the monsters she needs to eliminate from her universe and, in a sense, she may be one of the monsters in mine.

> (1985, 47)

Differences in power constrain our ability to connect with one another even when we think we are engaged in dialogue across differences. Let me give you an example. One year, the students in my course "Sociology of the Black Community" got into a heated discussion about the reasons for the upsurge of racial incidents on college campuses. Black students complained vehemently about the apathy and resistance they felt most White students expressed about examining their own racism. Mark, a White male student, found their comments particularly unsettling. After claiming that all the Black people he had ever known had expressed no such beliefs to him, he questioned how representative the viewpoints of his fellow students actually were. When pushed further, Mark revealed that he had participated in conversations over the years with the Black domestic worker employed by his family. Since she had never expressed such strong feelings about White racism, Mark was genuinely shocked by class discussions. Ask yourselves whether that domestic worker was in a position to speak freely. Would it have been wise for her to do so in a situation where the power between the two parties was so unequal?

C
O
N
T
E
X
T

In extreme cases, members of privileged groups can erase the very presence of the less privileged. When I first moved to Cincinnati, my family and I went on a picnic at a local park. Picnicking next to us was a family of White Appalachians. When I went to push my daughter on the swings, several of the children came over. They had missing, yellowed and broken teeth, they wore old clothing and their poverty was evident. I was shocked. Growing up in a large eastern city, I had never seen such awful poverty among Whites. The segregated neighborhoods in which I grew up made White poverty all but invisible. More importantly, the privileges attached to my newly acquired social class position allowed me to ignore and minimize the poverty among Whites that I did encounter. My reactions to those children made me realize how confining phrases such as "well, at least they're not Black" had become for me. In learning to grant human subjectivity to the Black victims of poverty, I had simultaneously learned to demand White victims of poverty. By applying categories of race to the objective conditions confronting me, I was quantifying and ranking oppressions and missing the very real suffering which, in fact, is the real issue.

One common pattern of relationships across differences in power is one that I label "voyeurism." From the perspective of the privileged, the lives of people of color, of the poor, and of women are interesting for their entertainment value. The privileged become voyeurs, passive onlookers who do not relate to the less powerful, but who are interested in seeing how the "different" live. Over the years, I have heard numerous African-American students complain about professors who never call on them except when a so-called Black issue is being discussed. The students' interest in discussing race or qualifications for doing so appear unimportant to the professor's efforts to use Black students' experiences as stories to make the material come alive for the White student audience. Asking Black students to perform on cue and provide a Black experience for their White classmates can be seen as voyeurism at its worst.

Members of subordinate groups do not willingly participate in such exchanges but often do so because members of dominant groups control the institutional and symbolic apparatuses of oppression. Racial/ethnic groups, women, and the poor have never had the luxury of being voyeurs of the lives of the privileged. Our ability to survive in hostile settings has hinged on our ability to learn intricate details about the behavior and world view of the powerful and adjust our behavior accordingly. I need only point to the difference in perception of those men and women in abusive relationships. Where men can view their girlfriends and wives as sex objects, helpmates and a collection of stereotyped categories of voyeurism—women must be attuned to every nuance of their partners' behavior. Are women "naturally" better in relating to people with more power than themselves, or have circumstances mandated that men and women develop different skills? Another pattern in relationships among people of unequal power concerns a different form of exploitation. In scholarly enterprises, relationships among students and teachers, among researchers and their subjects, and even among us as colleagues in teaching and scholarship can contain elements of academic colonialism. Years ago, a Black co-worker of mine in the Roxbury section of Boston described the academic colonialism he saw among the teachers and scholars in that African-American community:

> The people with notebooks from Harvard come around here and study us. They don't get to know us because they really don't want to and we don't want to let them. They see what they want to see, go back and write their books and get famous off of our problems.

Under academic colonialism, more powerful groups see their subordinates as people that they perceive as subordinate to them, not as entertainment as was the case in voyeurism, but as a resource to be benignly exploited for their own purposes.

The longstanding effort to "colorize" feminist theory by inserting the experiences of women of color represents at best, genuine efforts to reduce bias in women's studies. But at its worst colorization also contains elements of both voyeurism and academic colonialism. As a result of new technologies and perceived profitability, we can now watch black and white movie classics in color. While the tinted images we are offered may be more palatable to the modern viewer, we are still watching the same old movie that was offered to us before. Movie colorization adds little of substance—its contributions remain cosmetic. Similarly, women of color allegedly can teach White feminists nothing about feminism, but must confine ourselves to "colorizing" preexisting feminist theory. Rather than seeing women of color as fully human individuals, we are treated as the additive sum of our categories.

In the academy, patterns of relationships among those of unequal power such as voyeurism and academic colonialism foster reformist postures toward social change. While reformists may aim to make the movie more fun to watch by colorizing their scholarship and teaching via increased lip service to diversity, reformists typically insist on retaining their power to determine what is seen and by whom. In contrast, transformation involves rethinking these differences in power and privilege via dialogues among individuals from diverse groups.

Coming from a tradition where most relationships across difference are squarely rooted in relations of domination and subordination, we have much less experience relating to people as different but equal. The classroom is potentially one powerful and safe space where dialogues among individuals of unequal power relationships can occur. The relationship between Mark, the student in my class, and the domestic worker is typical of a whole series of relationships that people have when they relate across differences in power and privilege. The relationship among Mark and his classmates represents the power of the classroom to minimize those differences so that people of different levels of power can use race, class and gender as categories of analysis in order to generate meaningful dialogues. In this case, the classroom equalized racial difference so that Black students who normally felt silenced spoke out. White students like Mark, generally unaware of how they had been privileged by their whiteness, lost that privilege in the classroom and thus became open to genuine dialogue.

Reconceptualizing course syllabi represents a comparable process of determining which groups are privileged by our current research and pedagogical techniques and which groups are penalized. Reforming these existing techniques can be a critical first step in moving toward a transformed curriculum reflecting race, class and gender as interlocking categories of analysis. But while reform may be effective as a short term strategy, it is unlikely to bring about fundamental transformation in the long term. To me, social transformations, whether of college curricula or of the communities in which we live and work, require moving outside our areas of specialization and groups of interest in order to build coalitions across differences.

2. COALITIONS AROUND COMMON CAUSES

A second issue in building relationships and coalitions essential for social change concerns knowing the real reasons for coalition. Just what brings people together? One powerful catalyst fostering group solidarity is the presence of a common enemy. African-American, Hispanic, Asian-American, and women's studies all share the common intellectual heritage of challenging what passes for certified knowledge in the academy. But politically expedient relationships and coalitions like these are fragile because, as June Jordan points out:

It occurs to me that much organizational grief could be avoided if people understood that partnership in misery does not necessarily provide for partnership for change: When we get the monsters off our backs all of us may want to run in very different directions.

(1985, 47)

Sharing a common cause assists individuals and groups in maintaining relationships that transcend their differences. Building effective coalitions involves struggling to hear one another and developing empathy for each other's points of view. The coalitions that I have been involved in that lasted and that worked have been those where commitment to a specific issue mandated collaboration as the best strategy for addressing the issue at hand.

Several years ago, masters degree in hand, I chose to teach in an inner city, parochial school in danger of closing. The money was awful, the conditions were poor, but the need was great. In my job, I had to work with a range of individuals who, on the surface, had very little in common. We had White nuns, Black middle class graduate students, Blacks from the "community," some of whom had been incarcerated and/or were affiliated with a range of federal anti-poverty programs. Parents formed another part of this community, Harvard faculty another, and a few well-meaning White liberals from Colorado were sprinkled in for good measure.

As you might imagine, tension was high. Initially, our differences seemed insurmountable. But as time passed, we found a common bond that we each brought to the school. In spite of profound differences in our personal biographies, differences that in other settings would have hampered our ability to relate to one another, we found that we were all deeply committed to the education of Black children. By learning to value each other's commitment and by recognizing that we each had different skills that were essential to actualizing that commitment, we built an effective coalition around a common cause. Our school was successful, and the children we taught benefitted from the diversity we offered them.

I think that the process of curriculum transformation will require a process comparable to that of political organizing around common causes. None of us alone has a comprehensive vision of how race, class and gender operate as categories of analysis or how they might be used as categories of connection. Our personal biographies offer us partial views. Few of us can manage to study race, class and gender simultaneously. Instead, we each know more about some dimensions of this larger story and less about others. While we each may be committed to an inclusive, transformed curriculum, the task of building one is necessarily a collective effort. Just as the members of the school had special skills to offer to the task of building the school, we have areas of specialization and expertise, whether scholarly, theoretical, pedagogical or within areas of race, class or gender. We do not all have to do the same thing in the same way. Instead, we must support each other's efforts, realizing that they are all part of the larger enterprise of bringing about social change.

3. BUILDING EMPATHY

A third issue involved in building the types of relationships and coalitions essential for social change concerns the issue of individual accountability. Race, class and gender oppression form the structural backdrop against which we frame our relationship—these are the forces that encourage us to substitute voyeurism and academic colonialism for fully human relationships. But while we may not have created this situation, we are each responsible for

making individual, personal choices concerning which elements of race, class and gender oppression we will accept and which we will work to change.

One essential component of this accountability involves developing empathy for the experiences of individuals and groups different than ourselves. Empathy begins with taking an interest in the facts of other people's lives, both as individuals and as groups. If you care about me, you should want to know not only the details of my personal biography but a sense of how race, class and gender as categories of analysis created the institutional and symbolic backdrop for my personal biography. How can you hope to assess my character without knowing the details of the circumstances I face?

Moreover, by taking a theoretical stance that we have all been affected by race, class and gender as categories of analysis that have structured our treatment, we open up possibilities for using those same constructs as categories of connection in building empathy. For example, I have a good White woman friend with whom I share common interests and beliefs. But we know that our racial differences have provided us with different experiences. So we talk about them. We do not assume that because I am Black, race has only affected me and not her or that because I am a Black woman, race neutralizes the effect of gender in my life while accenting it in hers. We take those same categories of analysis that have created cleavages in our lives, in this case, categories of race and gender, and use them as categories of connection in building empathy for each other's experiences.

Finding common causes and building empathy is difficult, no matter which side of privilege we inhabit. Building empathy from the dominant side of privilege is difficult, simply because individuals from privileged backgrounds are not encouraged to do so. For example, in order for those of you who are White to develop empathy for the experiences of people of color, you must grapple with how your white skin has privileged you. This is difficult to do, because it not only entails the intellectual process of seeing how whiteness is elevated in institutions and symbols, but it also involves the often painful process of seeing how your whiteness has shaped your personal biography. Intellectual stances against the institutional and symbolic dimensions of racism are generally easier to maintain than sustained self-reflection about how racism has shaped all of our individual biographies. Were and are your fathers, uncles, and grandfathers really more capable than mine, or can their accomplishments be explained in part by the racism members of my family experienced? Did your mothers stand silently by and watch all this happen? More importantly, how have they passed on the benefits of their whiteness to you?

These are difficult questions, and I have tremendous respect for my colleagues and students who are trying to answer them. Since there is no compelling reason to examine the source and meaning of one's own privilege, I know that those who do so have freely chosen this stance. They are making conscious efforts to root out the piece of the oppressor planted within them. To me, they are entitled to the support of people of color in their efforts. Men who declare themselves feminists, members of the middle class who ally themselves with anti-poverty struggles, heterosexuals who support gays and lesbians, are all trying to grow, and their efforts place them far ahead of the majority who never think of engaging in such important struggles.

Building empathy from the subordinate side of privilege is also difficult, but for different reasons. Members of subordinate groups are understandably reluctant to abandon a basic mistrust of members of powerful groups because this basic mistrust has traditionally been central to their survival. As a Black woman, it would be foolish for me to assume that White women, or Black men, or White men or any other group with a history of exploiting African-American women have my best interests at heart. These groups enjoy varying amounts of privilege over me and therefore I must carefully watch them and be prepared for a relation of domination and subordination.

Like the privileged, members of subordinate groups must also work toward replacing judgments by category with new ways of thinking and acting. Refusing to do so stifles prospects for effective coalition and social change. Let me use another example from my own experiences. When I was an undergraduate, I had little time or patience for the theorizing of the privileged. My initial years at a private, elite institution were difficult, not because the coursework was challenging (it was, but that wasn't what distracted me) or because I had to work while my classmates lived on family allowances (I was used to work). The adjustment was difficult because I was surrounded by so many people who took their privilege for granted. Most of them felt entitled to their wealth. That astounded me.

I remember one incident of watching a White woman down the hall in my dormitory try to pick out which sweater to wear. The sweaters were piled up on her bed in all the colors of the rainbow, sweater after sweater. She asked my advice in a way that let me know that choosing a sweater was one of the most important decisions she had to make on a daily basis. Standing knee-deep in her sweaters, I realized how different our lives were. She did not have to worry about maintaining a solid academic average so that she could receive financial aid. Because she was in the majority, she was not treated as a representative of her race. She did not have to consider how her classroom comments or basic existence on campus contributed to the treatment her group would receive. Her allowance protected her from having to work, so she was free to spend her time studying, partying, or in her case, worrying about which sweater to wear. The degree of inequality in our lives and her unquestioned sense of entitlement concerning that inequality offended me. For a while, I categorized all affluent White women as being superficial, arrogant, overly concerned with material possessions, and part of my problem. But had I continued to classify people in this way, I would have missed out on making some very good friends whose discomfort with their inherited or acquired social class privileges pushed them to examine their position.

. . . As we go forth to the remaining activities of this workshop, and beyond this workshop, we might do well to consider Lorde's perspective:

> Each of us is called upon to take a stand. So in these days ahead, as we examine ourselves and each other, our works, our fears, our differences, our sisterhood and survivals, I urge you to tackle what is most difficult for us all, self-scrutiny of our complacencies, the idea that since each of us believes she is on the side of right, she need not examine her position.

(1985)

I urge you to examine your position.

References

Lorde, Audre. (1985). "Sisterhood and Survival." Keynote address, conference on the Black Woman Writer and the Diaspora, Michigan State University.
Jordan, June. (1985). *On Call: Political Essays.* Boston: South End Press.

130

What Can We Do?

Allan G. Johnson

. . .

The problem of privilege and oppression is deep and wide, and to work with it we have to be able to see it clearly so that we can talk about it in useful ways. To do that, we have to reclaim some difficult language that names what's going on, language that has been so misused and maligned that it generates more heat than light. We can't just stop using words like *racism, sexism, ableism*, and *privilege*, however, because these are tools that focus our awareness on the problem and all the forms it takes. Once we can see and talk about what's going on, we can analyze how it works as a system. We can identify points of leverage where change can begin.

. . .

For several centuries, capitalism has provided the economic context for privilege and oppression. As such, it has been and continues to be a powerful force, especially in relation to class, gender, and race. Its effects are both direct and indirect. Historically, it was the engine that drove the development of modern racism. In a less direct way, it creates conditions of scarcity that set the stage for competition, fear, and antagonism directed across differences of race, ethnicity, and gender. Through the class differences that it creates, it also shapes people's experience of privilege and the lack of it. This is an example of the matrix of domination (or matrix of privilege) through which the various forms of difference and privilege interact and shape one another.

. . .

Although disadvantaged groups take the brunt of the trouble, privileged groups are also affected by it, partly because misery visited on others comes back to haunt those who benefit from it, especially in the form of defensiveness and fear. But trouble also affects privileged groups directly by limiting and shaping the lives of people who have privilege. The trouble also affects entire social systems, from families to corporations and schools to communities, societies, and global political and economic systems.

The greatest barrier to change is that dominant groups . . . don't see the trouble as *their* trouble, which means they don't feel obliged to do something about it. This happens for a variety of reasons—because they don't know the trouble exists in the first place, because they don't *have* to see it as their trouble, because they see it as a personal rather than a systemic problem, because they're reluctant to give up privilege, because they feel angry and deprived and closed to the idea that they have privilege, because they're blinded by prejudice, because they're afraid of what will happen if they acknowledge the reality of privilege and oppression.

. . .

[To] think about the trouble as everyone's responsibility—everybody's "hook"—and nobody's fault . . . is especially useful for members of privileged groups who have a hard time seeing themselves in relation to privilege without feeling guilty. It's easy to fall into this trap because people tend to use an individualistic model of the world that reduces everything to individual intentions and goodness or badness. A powerful and liberating alternative comes from the fact that we're always participating in something larger than ourselves, social systems. To understand privilege and oppression, we have to look at what

we're participating in *and* how we participate . . . . This means we can be involved in a society's or organization's troubles without doing anything wrong and without being bad people.

Privilege is created and maintained through social systems that are dominated by, centered on, and identified with privileged groups. A racist society, for example, is white-dominated, white-centered, and white-identified. Since privilege is rooted primarily in systems—such as families, schools, and workplaces—change isn't simply a matter of changing people. The solution also has to include entire systems [that] . . . shape how people feel, think, and behave as individuals, how they see themselves and one another.

. . .

With this approach, we can begin to think about how to make ourselves part of the solution to the problem of privilege and oppression. . . .

It is in small and humble choices that privilege, oppression, and the movement toward something better actually happen.

. . . WHAT CAN WE DO?

. . .

ACKNOWLEDGE THAT PRIVILEGE AND OPPRESSION EXISTS

A key to the continued existence of every system of privilege is unawareness, because privilege contradicts so many basic human values that it invariably arouses opposition when people know about it. . . .

This is why most cultures of privilege mask the reality of oppression by denying its existence, trivializing it, calling it something else, blaming it on those most victimized by it, or diverting attention from it. Instead of treating oppression as a serious problem, we go to war or get embroiled in controversial "issues" such as capital gains tax cuts or "family values" or immigrant workers. There would be far more active opposition to white privilege, for example, if white people lived with an ongoing awareness of how it actually affects the everyday lives of those it oppresses as "not white." . . .

It's one thing to become aware and quite another to stay that way. The greatest challenge when we first become aware of a critical perspective on the world is simply to hang on to it. . . . In some ways, it's harder and more important to pay attention to systems of privilege than it is to people's behavior . . . . [F]or example, the structure of capitalism creates large social patterns of inequality, scarcity, and exploitation that have played and continue to play a major role in the perpetuation of various forms of privilege and oppression. It is probably wishful thinking to suppose we can end privilege without also changing a capitalist system of political economy that allows an elite to control the vast majority of wealth and income and leaves the rest of the population to fight over what's left. But such wishful thinking is, in fact, what we're encouraged to engage in most of the time—to cling to the idea that racism, for example, is just a problem with a few bad whites, rather than seeing how it is connected to a much larger matrix of privilege and oppression.

. . .

By itself, however, changing how we think won't be enough to solve the problem. Privilege will not simply go away as the result of a change in individual consciousness. Ultimately, we'll have to apply our understanding of how systems work to the job of changing systems themselves—economic, political, religious, educational, and familial. . . .

Maintaining a critical consciousness takes commitment and work. Awareness is something that either we maintain in the moment or we don't. And the only way to hang on to an awareness of privilege is to make that awareness an ongoing part of our lives.

PAY ATTENTION

Understanding how privilege and oppression operate and how you participate is where working for change begins. It's easy to have opinions, but it takes work to know what you're talking about. The simplest way to begin is to make reading about privilege part of your life. Unless you have the luxury of a personal teacher, you can't understand this issue without reading. Many people assume they already know what they need to know because it's part of everyday life. But they're usually wrong, because just as the last thing a fish would discover is water, the last thing people discover is society itself and something as pervasive as privilege.

We also have to be open to the idea that what we think we know is, if not wrong, so deeply shaped by systems of privilege that it misses most of the truth. This is why activists talk with one another and spend time reading one another's writing, because seeing things clearly is tricky. This is also why people who are critical of the status quo are so often self-critical as well—they know how complex and elusive the truth really is and what a challenge it is to work toward it. . . .

As you educate yourself, avoid reinventing the wheel. Many people have already done a lot of work that you can learn from. There's no way to get through it all, but you don't have to in order to develop a clear enough sense of how to act in meaningful and informed ways. . . . Men who feel there is no place for them in women's studies might start with books about patriarchy and gender inequality that are written by men. In the same way, whites can begin with writings on race privilege written by other whites. Sooner or later, however, dominant groups will need to turn to what people in subordinate groups have written, because they are the ones who have done most of the work of figuring out how privilege and oppression operate.

Reading is only the beginning. At some point you have to look at yourself and the world to see if you can identify what you're reading about. . . .

[T]aking responsibility means not waiting for others to tell you what to do, to point out what's going on, or to identify alternatives. If dominant groups are going to take their share of responsibility, it's up to them to listen, watch, ask, and listen again, to make it their business to find out for themselves. If they don't, they'll slide down the comfortable blindered path of privilege. And then they'll be *just* part of the problem and they *will* be blamed and they'll have it coming.

LEARN TO LISTEN

Attentive listening is especially difficult for members of dominant groups. If someone confronts you with your own behavior that supports privilege, . . . [d]on't tell them they're too sensitive or need a better sense of humor, and don't try to explain away what you did as something else than what they're telling you it was. Don't say you didn't mean it or that you were only kidding. Don't tell them what a champion of justice you are or how hurt you feel because of what they're telling you. Don't make jokes or try to be cute or charming, since only access to privilege can lead someone to believe these are acceptable responses to something as serious as privilege and oppression. Listen to what's being said. Take it seriously. Assume for the time being that it's true, because . . . it probably is. And then take responsibility to do something about it.

. . .

LITTLE RISKS: DO SOMETHING

. . .

When you *openly* change how you participate in a system, you do more than change your own behavior; you also change how the system happens. When you change how a system happens, you change the social environment that shapes other people's behavior, which, in turn, further changes how the system happens. And when you do that, you also help to change the consequences that come out of the dynamic relationship between systems and individuals, including patterns of privilege and oppression.

. . .

As you become more aware, questions will arise about what goes on at work, in the media, in families, in communities, in religious institutions, in government, on the street, and at school—in short, just about everywhere. The questions don't come all at once (for which we can be grateful), although they sometimes come in a rush that can feel overwhelming. If you remind yourself that it isn't up to you to do it all, however, you can see plenty of situations in which you can make a difference, sometimes in surprisingly simple ways. Consider the following possibilities.

Make noise, be seen. Stand up, volunteer, speak out, write letters, sign petitions, show up. Every oppressive system feeds on silence. Don't collude in it. Breaking the silence is especially important for dominant groups, because it undermines the assumption of solidarity that privilege depends on. If this feels too risky, practice being aware of how silence reflects your investment in solidarity with other dominant-group members. This can be a place to begin working on how you participate in making privilege and oppression happen: "Today I said nothing, colluded in silence, and this is how I benefited from it. Tomorrow I can try something different."

Find little ways to withdraw support from . . . [oppressive systems,] starting with yourself. It can be as simple as not laughing at a racist or heterosexist joke or saying you don't think it's funny, or writing a letter to your senator or representative or the editor of your newspaper, objecting to an instance of sexism in the media. When my local newspaper ran an article whose headline referred to sexual harassment as "earthy behavior," for example, I wrote a letter pointing out that harassment has nothing to do with being "earthy."

The key to withdrawing support is to interrupt the flow of business as usual. You can subvert the assumption that everyone's going along with the status quo by simply not going along. When you do this, you stop the flow, if only for a moment, but in that moment other people can notice and start to think and question. It's a perfect time to suggest the possibility of alternatives, such as humor that isn't at someone else's expense, or of ways to think about discrimination, harassment, and violence that do justice to the reality of what's going on and how it affects people.

. . .

Dare to make people feel uncomfortable, beginning with yourself. At the next local school board meeting, for example, you can ask why principals and other administrators are almost always white and male (unless your system is an exception that proves the rule), while the teachers they supervise and the lower-paid support staff are mostly women and people of color. Or look at the names and mascots used by local sports teams and see if they exploit the heritage and identity of Native Americans. If that's the case, ask principals and coaches and owners about it. Consider asking similar kinds of questions about privilege and difference in your place of worship, workplace, and local government.

It may seem that such actions don't amount to much, until you stop for a moment and feel your resistance to doing them—worrying, for example, about how easily you could make people uncomfortable, including yourself. If you take that resistance to action as a measure of power, then your potential to make a difference is plain to see. The potential

for people to feel uncomfortable is a measure of the power for change inherent in such simple acts of not going along with the status quo.

Some will say it isn't "nice" to make people uncomfortable, but systems of privilege do a lot more than make people feel uncomfortable, and there isn't anything "nice" about allowing that to continue. Besides, discomfort is an unavoidable part of any meaningful process of change. You can't grow without being willing to challenge your assumptions and take yourself to the edge of your competencies, where you're bound to feel uncomfortable. If you can't tolerate ambiguity, uncertainty, and discomfort, then you'll never get beneath superficial appearances or learn or change anything of much value, including yourself.

. . .

Openly choose and model alternative paths. [Identifying] . . . alternatives and [following] . . . them openly so that other people can see what we're doing . . . creates tension in a system, which moves toward resolution . . . . We don't have to convince anyone of anything. As Gandhi put it, the work begins with us trying to be the change we want to see happen in the world. If you think this has no effect, watch how people react to the slightest departures from established paths and how much effort they expend trying to ignore or explain away or challenge those who choose alternative paths.

Actively promote change in how systems are organized around privilege. The possibilities here are almost endless, because social life is complicated and privilege is everywhere. You can, for example,

Speak out for equality in the workplace.

Promote awareness and training around issues of privilege.

Support equal pay and promotion practices for everyone.

Oppose the devaluing of women, people of color, and people with disabilities, and the work they do, from dead-end jobs to glass ceilings.

Support the well-being of mothers, children, and people with disabilities, and defend their right to control their bodies and their lives.

Don't support businesses that are inaccessible to people with disabilities, and tell them why you don't.

Don't support businesses that engage in unfair labor practices, including union-busting. Support the formation of unions. Although the U.S. labor movement has a long history of racism, sexism, and ableism, unions are currently one of the few organized efforts dedicated to protecting workers from the excesses of capitalism.

Become aware of how class divisions operate in social systems, from workplaces to schools, and how this results in the oppression of blue- and white-collar workers. Find out, for example, if staff at your college or university are paid a living wage, and speak up if they aren't. There is a great silence in this country around issues of class, in part because the dominant cultural ideology presents the United States as a classless society. Break the silence.

Oppose the increasing concentration of wealth and power in the United States and the global economy. The lower, working, and lower-middle classes are the last to benefit from economic upturns and the first to suffer from economic downturns. Press politicians and candidates for public office to take a stand on issues of class, starting with the acknowledgment that they exist.

. . .

When you witness someone else taking a risk—speaking out, calling attention to privilege and oppression—don't wait until later to tell them in private you're glad they did. Waiting until you're alone makes it safer for you but does the other person little good. Support is most needed when the risk is being taken, not later on, so don't wait. Make your support as visible and public as the courageous behavior that you're supporting.

Support the right of women and men to love whomever they choose. Raise awareness of homophobia and heterosexism. For example, ask school officials and teachers about what's happening to gay and lesbian students in local schools. If they don't know, ask them to find out, since it's a safe bet these students are being harassed, suppressed, and oppressed by others at one of the most vulnerable stages of life. When sexual orientation is discussed, whether in the media or among friends, raise questions about its relation to male privilege. Remember that it isn't necessary to have answers to questions in order to ask them.

Pay attention to how different forms of oppression interact with one another. There has been a great deal of struggle within women's movements, for example, about the relationship between male privilege and privilege in other forms, especially those based on race, social class, and sexual orientation. . . .

One way out of this conflict is to realize that male privilege isn't problematic just because it emphasizes *male* dominance but because it values and promotes dominance and control as ends in themselves. In that sense, all forms of oppression draw support from common roots, and whatever we do that calls attention to those roots undermines *all* forms of privilege. If working against male privilege is seen simply as enabling some women to get a bigger piece of the pie, then some women probably will "succeed" at the expense of others who are disadvantaged by race, class, sexual orientation, and disability status. . . . [I]f we identify the core problem as *any* society organized around principles of domination and privilege, then changing *that* requires us to pay attention to all the forms of privilege those principles promote. Whether we begin with race or gender or disability or class or the capitalist system, if we name the problem correctly we'll wind up going in the same general direction.

Work with other people. This is one of the most important principles of participating in change. From expanding consciousness to taking risks, working with people who support what you're trying to do makes all the difference in the world. . . .

Make contact. Connect to other people engaged in the same work. Do whatever reminds you that you're not alone in this.

It is especially important to form alliances across difference, . . . for whites to listen to people of color, for example—and to give credence to what people say about their own experience. This isn't easy to do, of course, since members of dominant groups may not like what they hear about their privilege from those who are most damaged by it. It is difficult to hear anger and not take it personally, but that is what allies have to be willing to do. It's also difficult for members of privileged groups to realize how mistrusted they are by subordinate groups and to not take that personally as well. . . .

In many ways, the biggest challenge for members of privileged groups is to work with one another on issues of privilege rather than trying to help members of subordinate groups. . . . For members of privileged groups to become allies, they must recall Frederick Douglass's words that "power concedes nothing without a demand" and add their weight to that demand. When dominant groups work against privilege, they do more than add their voices. They also make it more difficult for other members of dominant groups to dismiss calls for change as simply the actions of "special interest groups" trying to better their position.

. . .

Don't keep it to yourself. A corollary of looking for company is not to restrict your focus to the tight little circle of your own life. . . . At some point, taking responsibility means acting in a larger context, even if that means letting just one other person know what you're doing. It makes sense to start with yourself, but it's equally important not to end with yourself.

A good way to convert personal change into something larger is to join an organization dedicated to changing the systems that produce privilege and oppression. . . .

If all this sounds overwhelming, remember again that you don't have to deal with everything. You don't have to set yourself the impossible task of transforming society or even yourself. All you can do is what you can *manage* to do, secure in the knowledge that you're making it easier for other people—now and in the future—to see and do what *they* can do. So, rather than defeat yourself before you start, think small, humble, and doable rather than large, heroic, and impossible. Don't paralyze yourself with impossible expectations. . . .

Don't let other people set the standard for you. Start where you are and work from there. Make lists of all the things you could actually imagine *doing*—from reading another book about privilege to suggesting policy changes at school or work to protesting against capitalism to raising questions about who cleans the bathroom at home—and rank them from the most risky to the least. Start with the least risky and set reasonable goals ("What small risk for change will I take *today?*"). As you get more experienced at taking risks, you can move up your list. You can commit yourself to whatever the next steps are for you, the tolerable risks, the contributions that offer some way—however small it might seem—to help balance the scales. As long as you do something, it counts.

In the end, taking responsibility doesn't have to involve guilt and blame, letting someone off the hook, or being on the hook yourself. It simply means acknowledging an obligation to make a contribution to finding a way out of the trouble we're all in and to finding constructive ways to act on that obligation. You don't have to do anything dramatic or earth-shaking to help change happen. As powerful as systems of privilege are, they cannot stand the strain of lots of people doing something about it, beginning with the simplest act of naming the system out loud.

131

The Cycle of Liberation

Bobbie Harro

As people come to a critical level of understanding of the nature of oppression and their roles in this systemic phenomenon, they seek new paths for creating social change and taking themselves toward empowerment or liberation. In my years as a social justice educator, it became increasingly clear that most socially conscious people truly want to "do something about" the injustices that they see and they recognize that simple, personal-level changes are not enough. They want to know how to make system-level change manageable and within their grasp, and they often become frustrated since so little has been written about the process of liberation.

As more students asked, "How do we make a dent in this thing that seems so big?" I began to think about how we might consciously transform the Cycle of Socialization. The cycle "teaches" us how to play our roles in oppression, and how to revere the existing systems that shape our thinking, leading us to blame uncontrollable forces, other people, or ourselves for the existence of oppression. If there is an identifiable pattern of events that repeats itself, becomes self-fulfilling, and leads us to a state of unconsciousness about issues of oppression, then there may be another identifiable pattern of events that leads us

toward liberation from that thinking. I began to read about and study efforts to eliminate oppression on a systemic level, and discovered that indeed, some paths were successful at actually creating the kind of lasting change that addressed the root causes of the oppression, and people's roles in it, while other paths were not. These paths were not always the same, and certainly were not linear, but they had in common the same cycle-like traits that characterized the socialization process that teaches us our roles in oppression. There were certain skills and processes, certain ways of thinking and acting in the world, certain seemingly necessary ingredients that were present in every successful liberation effort.

I am defining *liberation* as "critical transformation," in the language and thinking of Paulo Freire. By this I mean that one must "name the problem" in terms of *systemic* assumptions, structures, rules, or roles that are flawed. Significant social change cannot happen until we are thinking on a systemic level. Many people who want to overcome oppression do not start in the critical transforming stage, but as they proceed in their efforts, it becomes necessary for them to move to that level for success.

The following model describes patterns of events common to successful liberation efforts. Its purpose is to organize and name a process that may otherwise be elusive, with the goal of helping people to find their pathway to liberation. It could be characterized as a map of changing terrain where not everyone goes in the same direction or to the same destination or at the same speed, so it should be taken not as a "how to," but rather as a description of what has worked for some.

THE MODEL

The model described in this chapter combines theory, analysis, and practical experience. It describes a cyclical process that seems to occur in most successful social change efforts, leading to some degree of liberation from oppression for those involved, regardless of their roles. It is important to note that one can enter the cycle at any point, through slow evolution or a critical incident, and will repeat or recycle many times in the process. There is no specific beginning or end point, just as one is never "done" working to end oppression. Although there is not a specific sequence of events in the cycle, it is somewhat predictable that all of the levels (intrapersonal, interpersonal and systemic) will occur at some point.

WAKING UP

Often liberation begins when a person begins to experience herself differently in the world than s/he has in the past. It is marked by an intrapersonal change: a change in the core of someone about what s/he believes about her/himself. This may be the result of a critical incident or a long slow evolutionary process that shifts our worldviews. I refer to this phase as the *waking up* phase. We may experience some form of cognitive dissonance, where something that used to make sense to us (or that we never questioned), ceases to make sense. Perhaps a white mother adopts a child who is Puerto Rican and in dealing with her expectations for the child suddenly realizes that she has more deeply based racist attitudes than she thought she did. Perhaps a heterosexual woman who has a gay coworker recognizes that the longer she works with him, the more "ordinary" he becomes to her, and the more she gets angry when people make antigay remarks. Perhaps a welfare recipient begins to get angry that she is often treated with disrespect by service providers and the general public, and begins to see the disrespect as a pattern of how poorer people are treated in the United States. Any of these examples could mark the beginning of the Cycle of Liberation.

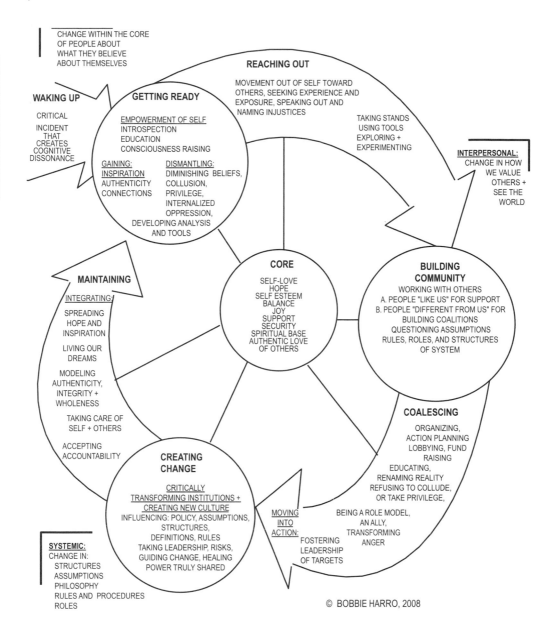

Figure 131.1 The Cycle of Liberation

GETTING READY

Once we know something, we can't *not* know it anymore. The process may not begin immediately, but odds are that it will begin at some point. Often the first part of the process involves a *getting ready* phase. This involves consciously dismantling and building aspects of ourselves and our worldviews based on our new perspectives. Processes that are central to this first part of liberation are introspection, education, and consciousness raising. We become introspective to identify which aspects of our beliefs, attitudes, and behaviors

need to be challenged. We tend to pay attention to and inventory thoughts, language, and actions to see if they are consistent with our newly recognized beliefs, or if they need to be dismantled. We may discover that we need to educate ourselves: read more, talk to people, bounce ideas and views around with others, begin listening to the news with new ears, seek expertise. We may begin to "make sense" of our experiences differently and seek out more chances to explore what we thought we knew, and how it compares to the reality. We may start exercising our questioning and challenging skills to expand our conscious understanding of the world.

This *getting ready* phase is composed of dismantling our wrong or diminishing beliefs (stereotypes, ignorance or misinformation), our discriminatory or privileged attitudes (superiority or inferiority), and behaviors that limit ourselves or others (collusion, oppressive language, or resignation). It also involves developing a consistency among what we believe, how we want to live our lives, and the way we actually do it. We move toward gaining authenticity and coherence between our worldview and how we live. We begin to see connections among all of the aspects of our lives and move toward integrity. Part of this phase also includes developing a coherent analysis of oppression and building a repertoire of skills and tools that will serve us throughout the rest of the process. We begin to take steps to empower ourselves.

The mother of the Puerto Rican child might decide to read about Puerto Rican history and cultures, talk to her Puerto Rican coworker, trace the origins of her assumptions and expectations about her child, or begin to catch herself when she makes excuses for her child's behavior. The heterosexual coworker may take a course on the gay rights movement, or pick up a copy of a gay newspaper, or ask her gay coworker to dinner. The woman on welfare may read a book on welfare rights, or start listening to the economic news, or start to keep a list of examples of "corporate welfare" totaling how much money goes from the federal government to large corporations when they are in financial trouble.

REACHING OUT

Almost inevitably, as we are getting ready, it becomes necessary for us to seek experiences outside ourselves in order to check our reality and to expose ourselves to a wider range of difference than we had before. We need to practice using our skills and tools with others, and experiment with expressing our new views, and speaking out when we disagree, instead of staying silent. This *reaching out* phase provides us with feedback about how our new worldviews will be met by others. We may get pressure from some to stop making waves, and accept the status quo (and this may arrest some people's progress for a while), and we may get encouragement and new friends as a result of taking a stand on something that we were quiet about before.

The adoptive mother may change social workers so she can talk to a Puerto Rican social worker about her child. She may suggest to her partner that they take a class in Spanish, or attend a local Puerto Rican festival. The heterosexual coworker may disclose in a conversation with friends that she supports the domestic partnership clause in their benefit package, or she may have a talk with her kids about not using the term *gay* to mean something bad. She may invite her gay coworker *and his partner* to dinner, or draw comparisons between her primary relationship and his. The woman on welfare may attend her first welfare rights meeting. She may object assertively when she is treated with disdain for using food stamps by the person behind her in the checkout line. She may decide to share her list of examples of corporate welfare with two friends also on welfare. All of these actions mark the transition from intrapersonal to interpersonal liberation.

BUILDING COMMUNITY

The interpersonal phase of the liberation process is marked by a change in how we value others and interact with them on a regular basis. It is the phase of *building community*, and consists of two steps: dialoguing with *people who are like us* for support (people who have the same social identities as we do, with regard to this issue of oppression), and dialoguing with *people who are different from us* for gaining understanding and building coalitions. This phase is characterized by the creation of an ongoing dialogue, where views are exchanged, people are listened to and valued, and we begin to view each others' points of view as making sense and having integrity, even if they are very different from our own.

In the first step, building community with people who are like us, we seek out people who may have similar experiences to our own, and talk with them to see how they have made sense of their experiences and what we can learn from them. This often begins happening informally, and even sometimes unconsciously: two mothers with adopted children meet in the pediatrician's waiting room and start comparing notes, or two neighbors who both receive welfare benefits talk in the laundry about their frustrations, or two friends going for a hike begin discussing "the gay people" who work with both of them. With increased knowledge and consciousness, these people might start looking for more organized forms of support discussions. These dialogues serve to prove to people that they are not alone in their situation, that there is a bigger "system" operating, that others have faced and are facing similar situations as our own, and that there are more strategies, ideas, and options than we had initially thought. We feel confirmed, and like we are part of a group that wants to change its role with regard to oppression.

A large part of this interpersonal step also involves dialoguing about how we see the "other" group (those with power if we are disempowered, or the disempowered if we possess power and/or privilege), and beginning to identify things that we may mutually have in common. We have moved out of stereotyping the "other" and have discovered those "others" who are more like us than different from us. We may begin to see that the "other" is no more to blame for the oppression than we are—that, in fact, we are both victims of a larger system that pushed us into roles. With this realization, a new level of analysis begins, and it becomes inevitable and necessary to expand our dialogue to include "others."

It's important to note that both privileged groups and targeted groups need to find this support step. We can't change *our* roles only; we must address changing the roles of *everyone* involved, as well as the assumptions and structures of the entire system, and we cannot do that alone. Coalitions are a necessity, and dialoguing across differences is the first step to building coalitions. We will never be able to focus on the real challenge—changing the system—until the barriers and boundaries that divide us are minimized. They will not be eliminated, but they can be significantly diminished in potency and clarified through the dialogue process.

This is not to say that creating dialogues about and across differences is easy. An integral part of this dialogue is exploring our differences, clarifying them, erasing assumptions, and replacing them with firsthand contact and good listening. That means that we must talk about our differences in a civil manner. It is useful, even desirable, to create together some guidelines for how our dialogues across differences will take place, and some principles to guide the process. These are best negotiated by all the parties who will participate.

Our mission is to question and challenge assumptions, structures and rules of the system of oppression, and to clarify our different needs, perceptions, strengths, resources, and skills in the process. Done well, these dialogues result in a deeper and richer repertoire of options and opportunities for changing the system. We are enhanced in many ways: our energy, our resources, our inspiration, our understanding, our compassion, our empathy, our humanness, and our motivation are all expanded in this process. We discover and are

sustained by inspirations that we have not met before. With these new springboards, we move into the coalescing phase.

COALESCING

Having minimized our barriers, joined with allies, and fortified our resolve, we are ready to move into action to interrupt the oppressive system. We may organize, plan actions, lobby, do fund raising, educate and motivate members of the uninvolved public. We coalesce and discover that we have more power as a coalition. This gives us encouragement and confidence. We may find ourselves taking more overt stands, expressing ourselves more assertively, rallying people to support us as we respond to overt oppression. We have begun to "see our reality" differently, and are naming ourselves differently. We are a "we" now, rather than adversaries. We are on the same side as those in our coalition, and that often surprises and confuses the system. We are refusing to "play our roles" and "stay in our places" as we had done before. We are refusing to collude in oppression, and to participate in self-fulfilling prophesies. We are refusing to accept privileges, and we are acting as role models and allies for others. We are interrupting the status quo, by speaking out calmly and with self-confidence. In this process, we have transformed our energy away from anger, frustration, guilt, and mistrust, and toward hope, shared power, trust, and optimism. We begin to see evidence that, working together, and organizing, we can make a difference. This doesn't mean that we will be successful at everything we try, but our likelihood of creating change is greatly enhanced.

CREATING CHANGE

The parameters of this phase of the cycle of liberation include using our critical analysis of the assumptions, structures, rules, and roles of the existing system of oppression, and our coalition power, to begin transforming the system. This means creating anew a culture that reflects our coalition's collective identity: new assumptions, new structures, new roles, and new rules consistent with a more socially just and equitable philosophy. It includes operating from a shifted worldview, where the values of a diverse and united community shape the system. It involves forming partnerships across differences to increase shared power. This manifests in influencing structure, policy, and management of organizations and systems of which we are a part. It involves taking leadership, taking risks, and guiding change. We must continue to heal from past differences by sharing power and by redefining power as collective power, power within, and power created through cooperation. In this phase, the very essence of the system is transformed, and nothing can remain the same after the transformation.

People experience this kind of transformation on a personal level, when, for example they or someone in their family is diagnosed with a terminal illness. Priorities shift, and what is important becomes totally different. With regard to oppression, some examples of critical transformation have occurred when psychiatric facilities began to appoint consumers to their boards of directors, or when community funding agencies began to be run by community constituents rather than elected officials. Critical transformation may take place when an organization decides to use only consensus decision making for all policy decisions, or to use a flat collaborative management structure rather than hierarchical.

Critical transformation in our examples might happen like this. The heterosexual coworker and the gay coworker might organize a human rights committee in their workplace; conduct dialogues among employees and a public awareness campaign; design a new domestic partners' benefits amendment and a new policy protecting gay, lesbian, bisexual, and transgendered people from discrimination in the workplace. The person receiving

welfare benefits might join a welfare rights coalition that lobbies local legislators, speak at a hearing in the state capital, and propose a referendum that for every dollar spent on "corporate welfare" in their state a dollar must also be spent on domestic welfare. The white mother of the Puerto Rican child might join a local Puerto Rican political action committee working to reform curriculum to include relevant Puerto Rican history, literature, famous people, and current events in her child's school. The committee might also be working to reform policies on bilingual education district-wide, so that her child can study and learn in both Spanish and English.

Efforts to critically transform systems are greatly enhanced by a wide range of resources, perspectives and creativity being brought to bear on a commonly defined problem. If good dialogue has taken place and the coalitions are as inclusive of every perspective as possible, systemic change becomes the logical outcome rather than an unlikely or unattainable goal. Making transformation happen is not, however, the last step. Creative new structures, assumptions, rules and roles must be maintained and nurtured.

MAINTAINING

In order to succeed, change needs to be strengthened, monitored, and integrated into the ritual of daily life. Just like anything new, it needs to be taken care of, learned about, "debugged," and modified as needed. It's rare if not impossible that new structures, assumptions, rules and roles are perfect or all-inclusive. It is imperative that a diverse group of "maintainers" work together to keep the change efforts aimed at their goals, and provided with resources. It's also necessary to celebrate successful change efforts. This process says to the larger world, "Look, this can work. You can change things by dialoguing and working together." It spreads hope and inspiration, and provides a model for others.

When a diverse group of people have worked to understand one another, and have created critical transformation together, we teach the lesson of hope and peace. It becomes increasingly possible that we can live our dream of equality and justice for all people. We become more human, more whole, more authentic, more integrated, and by living this way, we increase the likelihood that the human species will survive.

THE CORE OF THE CYCLE OF LIBERATION

At the core of the cycle of liberation is a set of qualities or states of being that hold it together. Some of these are present when people first begin the cycle, and they are nurtured, elaborated on, filled out, and matured as we proceed through the various phases. They exist and operate on both the individual and collective levels throughout the process of liberation. They are made stronger with each phase and with each human connection we make. Liberation is *the practice of love*. It is developing a sense of self that we can love, and learning to love others with their differences from us. Liberation is *finding balance* in our individual lives and in the agendas of our coalitions. Balance keeps us upright and oriented, moving toward our goals. Liberation is the *development of competence*, the ability to make something happen consistent with a goal. It is taking charge of our own destiny and creating the world we want to live in, together with all the others we need to survive. Liberation is the *belief that we can succeed*, a sense of confidence in ourselves and in our collective efforts. Liberation is *joy* at our collective efficacy and at surviving in a world that sometimes tries to kill us. Liberation is the knowledge that *we are not alone*. It is mutual support, encouragement, and trust that others will be there if we fall, and that we need to be there for others. Liberation is *commitment* to the effort of critical transformation, to the people in our community, to the goal of equity and justice, and to love. Liberation is *passion and compassion*, those strong and motivating feelings that we must live by our

hearts as well as our minds. Liberation is based in something far bigger than me as an individual, or us as a coalition, or our organization as a community, or any one nation, or any particular world. It's about that force that connects us all to one another as living beings, that force that is defined differently by every spiritual belief system but which binds us by the vision that there can be a better world and we can help to create it.

132

Courage

Cornel West

It takes courage to interrogate yourself.

It takes courage to look in the mirror and see past your reflection to who you really are when you take off the mask, when you're not performing the same old routines and social roles. It takes courage to ask—**how did I become so well-adjusted to injustice?**

It takes courage to cut against the grain and become nonconformist. It takes courage to wake up and stay awake instead of engaging in complacent slumber. It takes courage to shatter conformity and cowardice.

◆

The courage to love truth is one of the preconditions to thinking critically.

◆

Thinking for oneself is based on a particular kind of courage in which you hold truth, wisdom, and honesty in high esteem.

The reason you want to think for yourself is because you understand that people often are not telling you the truth. **When you place a high value on truth, you have to think for yourself.**

◆

If you're unwilling to muster the courage to think critically, then someone will do the thinking for you, offering doublethink and doubletalk relief. People will apply a certain kind of pressure to push you into complacency and maybe even cowardice. It's not long before you rationalize, *This isn't really me. I don't* really *think this way . . . but let's go!*

◆

As crucial and precious as the intellect is, it can become a refuge that hides and conceals emotional underdevelopment, and diminishes your ability to think critically.

What we need at this particular moment is to bring together those who are willing to muster the courage to think critically, look at the basic assumptions of public discourse, and **critique the way our history is told.**

◆

When ordinary people wake up, elites begin to tremble in their boots. They can't get away with their abuse. They can't get away with subjugation. They can't get away with exploitation. They can't get away with domination. **It takes courage for folk to stand up.**

♦

American democracy is great precisely because you have had courageous, compassionate citizens who were willing to sacrifice, to think critically, and connect with others to ensure that the Bill of Rights has had substance, that working people have had dignity, and that people of color have a status that ought to be affirmed. Think of the courage that went into that!

♦

February is a serious month because we start talking about Sojourner Truth, Harriet Tubman, Frederick Douglass, and Martin Luther King, Jr.

And we can't talk about these freedom fighters without acknowledging white brothers like Elijah Parish Lovejoy, an 1834 graduate of the Princeton Theological Seminary. He was shot down like a dog by a pro-slavery mob because of his part in the abolitionist movement, fighting for a free press, and affirming the Bill of Rights.

Lydia Maria Child was a white sister who in 1883 wrote *An Appeal in Favor of that Class of Americans called Africans*, in the same spirit as David Walker's *Great Appeal*.

Asian sisters like Grace Lee Boggs. Jewish brothers like Harry Magdoff. Well-to-do white brothers like Paul Sweezy. Brown sisters like Dolores Huerta. Brown brothers like César Chávez. Red brothers like Russell Means. We can go on and on. This is what makes a democratic tradition strong.

The democratic tradition says what? "Whosoever will, let them come."

♦

It's critical to understand your history, and then be true to oneself in such a way that one's connection to the suffering of others is an integral part of understanding yourself. This is a deep problem these days. To be great in our times too often means to have great material prosperity and no moral magnanimity at all.

♦

If you don't muster the courage to think critically about your situation, you'll end up living a life of conformity and complacency. You'll lose a very rich tradition that has been bequeathed to you by your foremothers and forefathers.

♦

In America, when we talk about a catastrophe, we talk about indigenous people. We talk about slavery. We talk about women coping with patriarchy and domestic violence. We talk about gay brothers and lesbian sisters being taught to hate themselves. We talk about workers crushed by the capitalist elite. **It is a view from the bottom up—through the lens of the cross.**

That view is too often a minority view within the Christian community because it requires too much love, too much courage. Who wants to pay the ultimate cost like Brother Medgar Evers? People are too scared. I understand that. I still love them. I affirm Medgar's courage because he dared to look at the world through the lens of the cross and paid the ultimate price.

Malcolm did it in the Islamic tradition. Martin certainly did it in his tradition. He bore his cross from age 26 until he was assassinated at 39. The American Empire is just so cross-averse.

America denies its night side until it breaks right through. There's no direct reference to slavery in the original U.S. Constitution. That's not just a slight gesture. That's lying.

You can't get away with that. You end up fighting a civil war over an institution not invoked in the Constitution. That's a level of denial that's incredibly deep. You think you're innocent, yet you've created the catastrophe right in your midst. You try to sanitize and sterilize it so expertly that you think the funk is not going to hunt you down. But it never works.

◆

It is unclear whether we're going to make it. I'm not an optimist at all. Brother Barack Obama says he has the audacity to hope. I say, "Well, what price are you willing to pay?"

It's no longer enough to be willing to die. **You have to be willing to live the truth.** Somehow, you have to be able to walk that tightrope.

◆

We have too much cynicism around here. It's too easy. There's too much pessimism. **Pessimism and optimism are the flip sides of the same coin.** We should reject the whole coin.

When you're optimistic, you can stand apart to see how things are going. But **when you're full of hope, you're in the midst of the muck.** You're working it out with love power and a commitment to justice. Your unshakable connection to the story and tradition that shaped you is what sustains you.

We have to expose the social breakdown that produces the conflict that separates human beings from hope and courage and discipline and risk-taking.

. . .

V O I C E S

133

Allies

Gloria E. Anzaldúa

Becoming allies means helping each other heal. It can be hard to expose yourself and your wounds to a stranger who could be an ally or an enemy. But if you and I were to do good alliance work together, be good allies to each other, I would have to expose my wounds to you and you would have to expose your wounds to me and then we could start from a place of openness. During our alliance work, doors will close and we'll have to open them up again. People who engage in alliances and are working toward certain goals want to keep their personal feelings out of it, but you can't. You have to work out your personal problems while you are working out the problems of this particular community or this particular culture.

When you are doing alliance work it is very important to say who you are. For example, I am a Chicana, Mexicana, dyke, whatever. I come from a *campesina* background but I have now put one foot into middle-classness. I belong to the *inteligencia*, the intelligence class, the artistic class as an artist, and I am speaking today to you as all these people, but primarily as a Chicana or as a dyke, etc. You must situate yourself and tell what your stance

is on particular things, so other allies know exactly where you are coming from. And they can later say, "Oh you say that you are talking from a working-class perspective but you have a house, you have a car, you have these privileges, you are a professor, or a salaried publisher, a privileged writer, etc." Allies might challenge some of your positions as a first step in finding out whether you are a real potential ally. Then you can get a sense of whether you can trust this person or not. And you go with your gut feeling. You go with how you feel, because sometimes they will say all the politically correct rhetoric, but you just know that they are trying to put one over on you.

I have edited three books, *This Bridge Called My Back*, *Haciendo Caras*, and *Signs: Theorizing Lesbian Experience*. In the first two books I consider anthologizing as my way of making alliances with women of color. In *Signs* it was more (or less) white women wanting to make alliances with lesbians of color. Many lesbians of color I asked to submit work didn't, because they didn't trust *Signs* because they know it to be elitist, esoteric and racist.

In the books that other people anthologize me in, some editors are very genuine and want to diversify their community. Then there are the anthologizers that call on me so that dykes of color will not call them and say, "You have one contributor of color and ninety white contributors, this is racist!" So they attempt to tokenize me, or they try to pull a fast one on their readers, by tokenizing in general. Some of my work is hard to assimilate and I consider assimilation in white culture like an amoeba trying to swallow me. But it is hard for them to assimilate me in that manner because of language and because of the way that I write. They can ignore some issues that I bring out, but because of my writing style, there are things they must confront. I don't write like a white person. I don't write like an academic or follow those rules. I break them.

If they can't assimilate my writing what they try and do is assimilate me, by tokenizing me. They bring me into their book, or into their conference, or into their alliance in a way that will acknowledge the easy stuff I raise, but ignore the more dangerous stuff. They try to do this to me all the time, so then I have to respond back, either on the phone or in a letter, and say, why? One anthology that asked for my work was called *Growing Up Latino*. Before I agreed to publish in it, I had this whole dialogue with one of the editors, and talked about naming the book Latino and not Chicano. I asked "How many Chicanos/Chicanas are in your book? How many are Latina and how do they identify themselves?" Once the magazine *New Chicano Writing* asked me to sit on their board. I called and voiced my objections to the editor before I agreed to join: I objected having Chican*o* writers but not Chican*a* in the title, and furthermore told them that the groundbreaking writing being done in the Chicano/Chicana community was by women. I also objected to their project only accepting work written in English. So the editor went home and thought about the issues and later called me and said, "I've changed the title of the magazine to New Chicana/Chicano writing, and people can write in Spanish, they can do bilingual, and they can do *Tex Mex*." Then I felt like the editor was open to me, and I agreed to be on their editorial board.

The biggest risk in forming alliances is betrayal. When you are betrayed you feel shitty. When I have been betrayed I have felt stupid, like why did I trust this person and allow this person to stab me in the back, it's all my fault, you know the victim syndrome. Betrayal, especially with Chicanas, betrayal is a big thing, because we were betrayed as women, as Indians, as a *minority* in this country, everything. We have been stabbed in the back by all of these various people. And betrayal makes you feel like less of a person, you feel shame, it reduces your self-esteem. It is politically deadening and dangerous, it's disempowering. When you lose your self-esteem you no longer trust yourself to make value judgments about other people, you lose confidence in yourself and your values. When a whole person is slowly destroyed, and this is what women of color are suffering from, their personhood is destroyed.

At first I felt really good belonging to the lesbian community, even though it was mostly white. It made me feel like where I had no home, I now had a new one. But after two or three or four years, I started looking at power, and who had power and who was trying to define for me what I was as a Chicana lesbian. I realized how my voice was silent and how my history was ignored and that drove me into looking at my roots, my queer roots in my own culture. I had to get a positive sense of being queer from my culture, not just from the white culture. Now I am in a place where I can look at both the white lesbian community and my own culture that is only beginning to have groups of lesbians organizing. *Ellas San Antonio* is a group of Chicana dykes, *Amigas y Que*, in Houston and Austin. But they were not in place when I was coming out. Chicana dyke organizations are just now coming into their power.

Now I look at my culture and white culture and the whole planet. I look at other nationalities and how they deal with their queer people, I'm getting a global perspective on being a queer person. And sometimes I feel very comfortable with a bunch of white dykes and other times I feel totally invisible, ignored. I feel that they only see the queer part of me. They don't see the Chicana part of me or the working class part of me. As long as I leave my class and culture outside the door when I enter a room full of white dykes I am okay, but if I bring in my race or class, then my role as educator starts.

I think that most white dykes really want a community that is diversified. And sometimes they want it so badly that they want to put everybody under this queer umbrella and say we are all in this together and we are all equal. But we are not equal. In their thirst and hunger for this diversity the issues of class and race are issues that they don't even want to examine, because they feel like they're divisive. So they are hungry for being politically correct and having women of color in their organizations, in their syllabi, and as performers, singers, writers and lovers. But a lot of times in order to bring us under the queer umbrella they will ignore or collapse the differences, not really deal with the issues. When it comes down to the numbers of who has power or *how many* dykes of color are getting in this anthology and how many don't—in terms of the real work, they fail. I mean the ideas are good, like the greater numbers/the greater strength kind of thing but they want us to leave our race and our class in the check room when we enter their space.

As a group, I think dykes are more progressively political than any other group because of feminism, and because of being (at least) doubly oppressed. Because they have been oppressed as dykes, I believe white lesbians are more apt to recognize the oppression of women of color. So they have a true wanting of multi-cultural groups. And there are always the false ones of course, there are always the ones that do want it to be white. But there is some honest motivation about wanting to be allies and in this they still have a lot of work to do. For example, one of the things they often don't contend with is the unconscious motivation of doing it out of guilt. But I am very hopeful and I think that I am one of the very few people. I think that most people of my age or younger have been burned out and disillusioned and feel like it's the pits right now. Much younger people than me have no hope, do not see alliances working, do not see white people reaching out or doing their work, and do not see the possibility of white people changing perspectives. Or allowing change to come into their lives, but I do.

134

Social Struggle

Richard (Chip) Smith

. . . As people connect with others actively engaged in struggle—and reach out to new forces in creative ways—the movement grows. Organizations gain experience, resources, and influence. The systematic character of oppression becomes clearer. Social forces join together, work through differences, learn how to challenge for political power and carry through social transformation.

. . . Here we want to suggest an approach to organizing that over time will have the greatest chance of bringing into being a strategic front against white supremacy and racism.

STAY CENTERED ON SELF-DETERMINATION, AFFIRMATIVE ACTION, AND INTERNATIONALISM

Self-determination focuses attention on the central demand for political power by . . . oppressed . . . peoples. Without the fundamental democratic right to political power . . . the system of white supremacy and the racist ideas it generates in people's minds will continue. The struggles to end patriarchy and capitalism also involve questions of power—in personal relations through to the organized power of the working class to reshape society, with leadership centered among the oppressed. . . .

Affirmative action in its broadest sense is simply another way to talk about ending privilege. It emphasizes the historic roots of race and gender privilege and calls for proactive policies to set matters straight—affirmative action on the job, in the home, in popular culture, in the criminal justice system, in politics and throughout society. By orienting to the struggles of people of color at any particular moment, white organizers can distinguish the specific form the struggle is taking at the moment—be it for reparations, Katrina reconstruction, or immigration rights; or for an end to right-to-work laws or male violence.

Internationalism is a third bedrock perspective, because of the imperialist role of the United States in the world. This standpoint allows people to see clearly the underlying forces driving an issue like immigration, for example, or the war in Iraq, the "War against Drugs" in Colombia, and the "War on Terror" generally. It helps one be mindful of the material benefits—and associated racial and national prejudices—that come from living in a superpower in the Global North. Armed with this awareness, one can then—as a simple act of solidarity and with no special recognition due—turn that privilege around and target U.S. imperialism from the inside. The prescription to "Think globally, act locally" is sound—but it can be broadened to "Think globally, act globally," as well. . . .

START WHERE PEOPLE ARE AT

"Starting where people are at" is a truism of organizing—but it has two aspects. The first is the obvious call to listen to what people say without prejudgment and without pushing

one's own views on others. In particular, for white people organizing among white workers, it means not leading with a rap on white privilege. The perspective of this book holds that white working class people are oppressed by capitalism. So the first step in organizing is to get a concrete feel for the ways people experience their lives and understand their situation. This listening aspect can help organizers appreciate both the problems people face and the ways they have to resolve them. Some individuals will be more active; others will be more passive—but observing all the while what is going on. And a few may be a source of issues themselves. By sorting out what the concerns are and who is dealing with them in what ways, an organizer can begin to get a sense of which folks to connect up with in a supportive way, and around which key issues.

The second aspect of this approach is less obvious. It comes down to being a true friend to folks you are working with. If the United States is white supremacist; if white folks are privileged simply by virtue of their skin color; and if this privilege has negative consequences for white people themselves, as well as for others—then there is an obligation to share this understanding and discuss it through with people. What makes the conversation possible is the underlying unity established by working together on issues of recognized importance. The overall learning process is two ways—but the main responsibility in connecting with people is the organizer's.

. . .

GO BROADER AND DEEPER

When engaging in struggle, the challenge often is to broaden the ranks of the forces fighting around an issue—take ending the war in Iraq, as one example. Two different approaches are possible for primarily white organizations in this situation: One amounts to activists' asking people of color to "come join our . . ." coalition, demonstration, or organization. As a way to entice a new constituency to take part in a demonstration, for example, the peace group might invite a speaker, include a slogan, or encourage an information table at their event. None of these steps is bad in itself, and the result can be a richer learning experience for the people who attend the demonstration. But the likelihood of large-scale participation by the new constituency is small at best.

A second approach is more long term in its outlook but carries with it the prospect of real unity of action in the future. Here the organizers identify issues of concern to the new constituency—perhaps by first bringing a speaker to the peace group's organizational meeting. The second step is then to offer organizational support to one or several groups within the new constituency that are active—say, around police violence, domestic abuse, or LGBTQ rights. By actually following through on the commitment of support, the original peace group develops new ties with people in the community, learns the kinds of pressures people are experiencing in their lives, and in the course of joint activity gains some first-hand understanding of people's attitudes toward the war. Over time, these relationships generate a new, richer common language of resistance to oppression at home, as well as to the war. The peace folks bring their people out to demonstrations against police abuse. And when the next peace demonstration comes along, new community forces may now decide to be part of the planning process—helping to shape the event in a way that resonates with their community. By actively linking up in this way, primarily white organizations can transform their outlook and put their relative privilege to work—through their personal connections and networks or fundraising skills—to oppose the concrete, material disadvantages being experienced by folks of color.

NEXT STEPS

DEVELOP CONSCIOUSNESS, THEORY, VALUES

People learn best from their own experience. People can hear all the arguments about why gay and lesbian folks are the same as everyone else and should enjoy the same rights. But until heterosexual folks meet and become friends with real human beings, the issue remains abstract. Personal relationships are critical—across the color line, among different oppressed nationality peoples, or with women in positions of leadership.

On becoming socially active, people are often open to new ideas as they search for ways to advance their issues. Engaging in struggle helps a person understand who holds power and what it takes to bring about a favorable result—what arguments work, in what settings, and with how many people mobilized to get the point across. No amount of discussion or study conveys a sense of popular power better than taking part in a campaign—win or lose. But people draw the clearest lessons through evaluating their collective experience together with others.

. . .

THE ROLE OF THEORY

. . . [T]heoretical work is essential to keep a movement on the path toward its goals, while adapting to changing circumstances.

Not paying attention to the deep structure of society and to long-term principles, by contrast, almost always leads people and organizations to conform to the system, even if they start out in militant opposition. . . . A community struggle around a school can turn into a platform for someone to run for city council—OK as far as it goes. But if that person's career becomes the goal instead of empowering the community, the campaign goes off track.

In general, campaigns can be summed up from three standpoints:

- What were the immediate benefits or losses from the struggle?
- To what extent did the broader popular movement gain strength?
- Were forces won to a deeper understanding of society, to the need for revolutionary organization, and to committing for the long haul?

A fourth criterion that overlaps the first two can be drawn out as well: Was there an advance in the battle for the minds of the broader public? Contesting the hegemony of ruling class ideas is critical to developing conditions where a mass movement can take hold and flourish.

By evaluating experience collectively along these dimensions, a movement deepens its theoretical understanding of the system and how to oppose it effectively. Also, individuals' summing up their personal experiences using these criteria can help people stay on course—by gaining insight into their strengths and weaknesses and clarifying how best to contribute to the struggle.

PHILOSOPHICAL OUTLOOK

Carrying the process of social activism and reflection more deeply can bring people to a philosophical outlook that embraces change and the power of ordinary people to transform the world. Seeing oneself in the flow of a constantly changing reality empowers people to relax into their role as change agents. Otherwise their activism can seem exceptional—passivity being the normal state—and required only by temporary difficulties in their lives. . . .

SOCIAL JUSTICE VALUES

The social justice movement embodies a set of values that can be brought to consciousness, validated, and taught to others. These values are secular in origin, emerging out of the concrete conditions of contemporary struggle. At the same time they overlap with the teachings of many religions, without requiring a specific accompanying belief system. Examples of such values are:

- *Solidarity:* realizing that "an injury to one is an injury to all"
- *Confidence in the power of ordinary people:* trusting grassroots people's ability to learn, struggle, and transform both the world and themselves
- *Openness and commitment to learning:* being skilled at listening, putting effort into study, and being willing to examine oneself and one's actions
- *Being active and useful:* being intentional about one's life; taking responsibility to understand the world and one's place in it, and to work to change things for the better
- *Courage:* being willing to take a stand and act on it—not only in relation to the dominant forces in society, but also in relation to one's family, friends, and comrades
- *Being all-sided:* striving to base judgments on the whole picture, while recognizing that all the information is usually not available
- *Commitment to shared effort:* rejecting privileges, and turning those that one must live with—like being white or male—to the advantage of the struggle
- *Being good at uniting:* seeing differences clearly while, at the same time, uniting wherever possible to broaden the movement and increase its impact
- *Reliability:* having one's words and actions be in accord with each other
- *Seeing clearly and acting appropriately:* being able to find one's bearings independently; making proper distinctions between who is a friend and who is not
- *Being principled, yet flexible:* knowing where one stands, while not being rigid
- *Valuing life:* having a sense of oneness with other people and the environment, and a commitment to their protection

. . .

Values should not be the exclusive property of the religious right, as they often seem to be today. The list above points to the powerful ethical system inherent in the revolutionary struggle to transform society. It also foreshadows the standards that are likely to guide behavior in the future—at least until people develop their moral outlook further under the new conditions of social liberation.

NURTURE THE STRATEGIC ALLIANCE WHERE YOU ARE

. . . While each movement has its own strategic configuration, priorities, and plan of action, the target is the same—a single, integral oppressive system that must be transformed . . . .

Being guided by such an awareness has implications for the way activists conduct their organizing work today. While engaging in a particular struggle, one can keep in mind the larger systemic reality of race, gender, and class oppression. By doing so, one can then look for intersections and ways to connect with other strategic forces. . . .

NEXT STEPS

INCREASE TIES AMONG ORGANIZATIONS

. . . [T]here is much to learn to enable people in groups to function effectively together. The points made there about managing differences while uniting to carry out work applies also to groups of organizations—in the form of coalitions, federations, and fronts. In order for one group to join in united action with another, both groups have to first exist—so the first responsibility is to the health of one's own organization. But once this aspect is taken care of, it is good to find ways to link up with others. Organizations together can magnify each other's impact, deepen understanding of the issues, and learn important lessons on how to keep decision-making power at the base.

The dominant culture works overtime to keep people fragmented—focused solely on their own personal and small group issues. Part of building a movement, and then a movement of movements, is learning how to keep all the many relationships among individuals and organizations working in a positive way—handling differences, allowing space for independence and initiative, and maximizing impact in a way that is flexible and adaptive to changing circumstances.

. . .

In this spirit, initiatives are underway in the United States to "refound the left"—efforts aimed at bringing conscious movement forces into a formation that can contest for power. For our purposes, however, it is the overall outlook activists have in their organizing work that we want to stress. As people engage in social struggles, they can keep in mind the need to bring everything together in an organizational form that can contest for political, economic, and social power. Overcoming white supremacy and racism requires 1) an uncountable number of individual actions every day, 2) a multitude of organizations struggling around the issues that grassroots people deal with daily in their lives, and 3) a wealth of experience flowing out of the specific conditions in every community across the country. It also requires a revolutionary organization—party, alliance, front, or federation—that can concentrate people's vast experience and put it back out to them in a way that keeps the movement growing, struggling, learning, and moving forward together.

Movement activists can strive to embody and represent this outlook in their own lives and organizing work. In doing so, each person becomes a center of initiative. And the old Buddhist saying, "the universe in a grain of sand," becomes "the social justice movement in each individual."

And just as each individual is an integral whole made up of many parts, so too the social justice movement is the same—not just a collection of oppositional trends, tendencies, and competing initiatives, but a movement foreshadowing a different world, a new way of living together.

. . .

135

Bridging Differences through Dialogue

Ximena Zúñiga

Building bridges between people from different social backgrounds becomes increasingly important as our society becomes more diverse and stratified. One way we can foster learning and understanding across differences is to bring college students together to talk and learn from each other, to find ways to comunicate, and to understand why it is not always easy to get along or to identify common ground. . . . This essay describes one promising approach for meeting this challenge, intergroup dialogue.

Intergroup dialogue is a face-to-face facilitated conversation between members of two or more social identity groups that strives to create new levels of understanding, relating, and action. The term social identity group refers to group affiliation based on a common status or history in society resulting from socially constructed group distinctions. Examples of groups that have participated in intergroup dialogues on college campuses include men and women; white people, biracial/multiracial people, and people of color; blacks, Latinos and Native Americans; lesbians, gay men, bisexual, and heterosexual people; people from working-, middle-, and upper-class socioeconomic backgrounds; and Christians, Muslims, and Jews. . . .

Intergroup dialogues encourage direct encounter and exchange about contentious issues, especially those associated with issues of social identity and social stratification. They invite students to actively explore the meanings of singular (as men or as women) or intersecting (as men of color or as white women) social identities and to examine the dynamics of privilege and oppression that shape relationships between social groups in our society. In addition, the dialogues build dispositions and skills for developing and maintaining relationships across differences and for taking action for equity and social justice.

. . .

Dialogue groups are co-led by trained facilitators who belong to the participating social identity groups. For example, a white student and a student of color would cofacilitate a cross-race dialogue. The programming strategies used to supervise and train dialogue facilitators vary across campuses. In some institutions, undergraduate students lead the groups after undergoing intensive training. In others, dialogue facilitators are professionals from counseling centers, student activities departments, human relations programs, or intergroup relations programs; or they are graduate students who have received specialized training in counseling, college student development, or social justice education as part of their programs of study. Regardless of the strategies used to train or supervise them, facilitators are expected to lead the dialogue process and to intervene when necessary. As discussed in a book chapter by Ruby Beale, Monita Thompson, and Mark Chesler entitled "Training Peer Facilitators for Intergroup Dialogue Leadership," efforts to prepare and support facilitators include the development of competencies in at least two areas: (1) knowledge and awareness about one's own and others' social identities and histories, and (2) small-group leadership skills, including the ability to lead difficult conversations and constructively explore conflicting needs or "hot" issues. A curricular guide and discussion questions to stimulate dialogue and reflection usually support the work of facilitators and student participants. . . .

NEXT STEPS

WHAT IS THE INTERGROUP DIALOGUE APPROACH?

The intergroup dialogue approach combines experiential learning and dialogic bridge-building methods with critical analysis of socially constructed group differences and the systems of stratification that give rise to intergroup conflicts and social injustice. It explores the causes and effects of group differences through a social justice lens and draws from multidisciplinary perspectives on social identity groups, systems of inequality, and inter-group relations. This approach starts with the proposition that meaningful dialogue and learning across race and other social group boundaries requires an educational practice that intentionally builds upon three interconnected pedagogical processes: sustained communication, critical social awareness, and bridge building. . . .

Sustained Communication. Sustained face-to-face conversations encourage listening and questioning across lines of difference, which in turn fosters mutual understanding of similar and conflicting needs and perspectives. Such communication must be continued over an extended period to allow for the development of reciprocal, active, and committed communication. Dialogic methods and techniques such as the ones described by Helen Fox in *When Race Breaks Out* and Stephen Brookfield and Stephen Preskill in *Discussion as a Way of Teaching: Tools and Techniques for Democratic Classrooms* are helpful to support the development of dispositions and skills that enable participants to listen attentively to each other, talk openly and honestly, appreciate different perspectives, and ask "dumb" or "politically incorrect" questions.

For example, modeling techniques that demonstrate "sensitive intercultural interaction" or methods such as "paired listening," "talking circles," "fishbowls," "circle of voices," and more can encourage authentic voicing, and listening from the very beginning of a dialogue group. As facilitators encourage participants to ask questions and probe deeper, participants begin to take more risks and challenge each other's views more directly. In a white-biracial—multiracial—people of color dialogue, for example, the facilitators may decide to show a short segment from a film by Frances Reid entitled *Skin Deep* to encourage conversation about contentious issues related to race and racism on campus. After a short "free-write" to allow for personal time for thinking and feeling, the facilitators may structure a listening circle to encourage everyone to participate, and then ask, "What about this video feels familiar or surprising to you?" After everyone has responded, the facilitators may invite students to acknowledge what they heard, raise questions, and make comments. For example, after viewing a film like *Skin Deep*, questions about related issues will likely emerge, such as "special-interest floors in the residence halls," "the school's new affirmative action policy," or "examples of white privilege on campus." As David Schoem and his associates note in *Intergroup Dialogue: Deliberative Democracy in School, College, Community and Workplace*, trust in this type of group process only grows and is tested as students feel more free and confident to probe issues, challenge themselves and others, express anger, offer support, and raise difficult or controversial questions.

Critical Social Awareness. Spotlighting the political realities that lead to group differences can stimulate thoughtful conversations across race and other social group boundaries. Dialogue participants must develop both a shared vocabulary and a way to pinpoint the origins and impacts of group differences at the personal, interpersonal, and systemic level. The intergroup dialogue process allows participants to recognize, question, and analyze prevailing beliefs and behaviors that maintain systems of stratification and perpetuate estranged and oppressive relations between groups.

Active learning methods, such as the ones described in a book chapter by Ellen Junn entitled "Experiential Approaches to Enhancing Cultural Awareness" and in the selections

in *Teaching for Diversity and Social Justice*, edited by Maurianne Adams, Lee Bell, and Pat Griffin, can gradually encourage intergroup dialogue participants to grapple with the differential impact of systems of privilege and oppression at the personal, community, and societal level. For instance, activities such as "privileged/targeted social identity time-line" or the "critical-incident exercise" take stock of students' experiences growing up as members of privileged (dominant status, more powerful) and targeted (subordinated status, less powerful) social groups. The "power shuffle" examines the impact of social group membership at the personal and community level. Simulation activities such as "star power" can help students recognize the impact of status differentials and power dynamics and make connections to everyday life. Through introspection, encounter, and critical analysis, active learning methods motivate students to become more aware of their own roles in interpersonal, group, and systemic conflicts. With the support of readings from various perspectives, students are encouraged to question their personal biases, to consider alternative perspectives toward a particular issue, and to situate each other's views and experiences in a larger social context.

An example of critical social awareness occurs in cross-race dialogues when the topic of "racial/ethnic separation and self-segregation" is explored. White students often perceive students of color as self-segregating on campus; yet to their surprise, students of color often see things the other way around. They think that white students are doing more of the self-segregation through their fraternities and sororities, intramural activities, study groups, living situations, and other campus activities. In the dialogue, the facilitators might challenge all students to consider what informs their perceptions of others' behaviors and encourage them to explore the interpersonal and institutional factors that may contribute to some of these dynamics. Facilitators ask questions, present relevant concepts or information, validate and acknowledge difficulties and challenges, question misinformation, and invite students to explore some of the reasons behind their perceptions. Such a discussion often sheds light on the extent to which the racial dynamics on campus create a hostile environment for students of color and contribute to their perceived need for "safe spaces." It also becomes apparent to white students that they actually are engaged in self-segregating behavior and that they need to take some responsibility for the campus climate.

Bridge Building. Critical and sustained conversation about issues of social identity and social stratification inevitably highlights conflicting perspectives across and within lines of difference. It also sheds light on the complex dynamics of connection and disconnection that result from estranged or oppressive relationships between members of social groups in the larger society. Such conflicts become valuable opportunities for students to engage in heart-to-heart conversations and discover together some of the underlying and multi-layered sources of tension and disconnection. The intergroup dialogue process begins to build bridges across differences when students can engage in difficult conversations, find value in each other's feelings or perspectives, establish areas of common concern, and be willing to work—separately or together—to counter some of the effects of social injustice.

For example, bridging may occur when a white male student acknowledges his own privileged status with increased self-awareness, openness, and sensitivity to the experience of others and is willing to take some responsibility for the racial climate on campus; or when a woman of color talks about how she experiences race and racism on campus, openly struggles to understand and appreciate some of the experiences of her white counterparts, and then explores ways of working with people from privileged groups to counter injustice.

The bridging process also engages participants in a journey that embraces new visions and possibilities for response. It offers support for exploring new ways of being, relating, and taking action with people across race and other group boundaries. As Patricia Hill Collins argues in "Toward a New Vision: Race, Class, and Gender as Categories of Analysis

NEXT STEPS

and Connection," transcending barriers requires that we recognize how our differing experiences with social oppression can compromise our relationships. When we develop empathy and accountability for the experiences of individuals and groups different from our own, everyone benefits. In the intergroup dialogues, these capacities are developed by cultivating a sense of co-responsibility and solidarity across and within lines of difference. Facilitators invite students to "walk the talk" in their personal, student, or work life and identify concrete ways of moving from dialogue to action outside the group. For instance, students may decide to take more courses focusing on racism or sexism, join an organization on campus that is dealing with some of the issues addressed in the dialogue, or become a resident assistant or a student leader to improve the racial or gender climate of their residence hall. By using educational and community practice methods such as the ones described by educators and community activists like John Anner in *Beyond Identity Politics* or http://www.thatway.org/dialogue, students can begin to identify possible actions and resources for working for change and coalition building. . . .

136

Unite and Rebel!

Challenges and Strategies in Building Alliances

Elizabeth (Betita) Martínez

Women of color have come together against violence—and expanded the very meaning of the term—as never before in US history. In their organizing, scholarship, and advocacy work, initiated at the first Color of Violence Conference in 2000, INCITE! Women of Color Against Violence demonstrates the electrifying capacity of women of color to organize against that common enemy across racial and ethnic lines. As we engage this mission more broadly and deeply, we learn more about both the strengths and challenges that confront us in working together toward unity.

Sharing experiences of violence, in one form or another, provides the foundation for alliance-building between women of color. But, as the late and beloved Gloria Anzaldúa said in her book *Making Face, Making Soul/Haciendo Caras*, "Shared oppression by itself does not override the forces that keep us apart." In fact, white supremacy encourages the forces that divide us. "Divide and Conquer" has been a major strategy for maintaining white supremacy for centuries.

We see intensified efforts at division today, as changing demographics promise that whites will be a minority in this country relatively soon. Divisive tactics feature emphasis on job competition between the native-born and immigrants. We also hear the counter-attack, accusing people of color of being "racist" toward each other or against whites. This tactic reminds us that we should understand racism to be an entire structure of power relations best called white supremacy. Communities of color rarely have structural power over each other (much less over white people) except in very limited situations such as on the job or in local political structures. At the same time, we can be prejudiced toward each

other and act in racist-like ways. This does not mean we have the power to be racists, but such prejudice, such actions can be a serious barrier to alliance-building.

White supremacy not only encourages subtle and not so subtle expressions of racist-type attitudes between women of different colors. It also encourages internalized racist attitudes toward oneself as an individual, and toward one's own group. This too can undermine alliance-building, by fomenting a narrow nationalism intended to restore necessary self-respect in ways that can backfire against long-range, collective goals.

ANTICIPATING CHALLENGES

Working in a group of women that combines different racial or national origins, we should assume problems will develop and strategize how to address them. It helps to think about those problems as rooted in differences of class, race, color (and other physical character-istics), as well as nationality, culture, sexuality, and age. Disability is also an issue; failure to recognize it can generate a sense of apartness, of isolation and indifference. All of these "differences" are linked to historical experience. All are interconnected and cannot be discussed in isolation from each other.

Before looking at each area of difference and its specifics, let's reaffirm our goals. First, we want to build our united strength so as to help transform this society into one of justice and peace for all. We are all in it together, and transforming this society would be a pre-cious achievement for us all. Is anything else more worthwhile?

Second, we should think in terms of building not only coalitions but also alliances. In a coalition, separate groups come together to address a common, usually immediate, single, problem or set of related problems. Coalitions are often necessary and even vital. They have potentially great immediate impact, and can pave the way for alliance-building.

Alliances should be broader in their focus, more profound, and more long-range, more lasting. The forces of white supremacy and imperialism are too strong for us to battle separately. Alliance can bring us together and give greater power to our resistant efforts over the years. Strong alliances make it possible for us to dream of someday seeing a global women of color movement to create a more just global society.

Finally, dealing with our differences and divisions cannot be left to casual concern or spontaneous resolution. It has to be one of our organizational priorities, a clear-cut part of program. That is the basic message of this article.

LEARNING OUR HERSTORIES

As we begin to examine the forces that obstruct alliance-building, we can see that ignorance and lack of understanding about our different communities greatly affect the influence of those forces. To combat the forces of division, we need to learn much more about the history of each community. Today, as Arab and Islamic people, as well as others of Middle Eastern/South Asian backgrounds have become the most recent, most visible victims of extreme racist oppression, we see yet another example of widespread ignorance. How much about the history and struggles of Arab, Islamic, Middle Eastern/South Asian com-munities is actually known by US-women of color not from these communities? How much is known about the long Palestinian struggle against US-supported Israeli expansion?

NEXT STEPS

For women of color all over the world, the most common and destructive experiences of violence have come from war. In modern times, at least, war has consistently left more women and children dead than soldiers. Here in the United States, we find that women of color have been subjected to racist violence in both similar and different ways. If we look at their different herstories, we find that war is not uncommon.

. . .

STRATEGIES FOR ALLIANCE BUILDING

The similarities and differences in historical experiences of racism mean that women of color have different collective memories of violence, and, therefore, they may relate differently to each other without always realizing it or knowing why. Dissimilar sources of pain may keep us focused on what separates rather than unites. For example, an African American may associate state violence with her color while a Mexican/Latina will associate it with her language or accent.

In addressing these and other challenges, each group of women of color could put together its own lists of do's and don't's based on real-life experiences; we each have different strategies to deal with the challenges, and to expand our strengths. Some will be very general and far-ranging, like the need to understand the different herstories and cultures of each racial group that have been discussed here. Yet, there are more specific rules and procedures centered on establishing mutual respect that can be drawn up.

For example, when a group of women goes to meet or work in a different setting from their own, be very aware of how the women in that unfamiliar setting do things: what are the spoken and unspoken rules, the protocols, the established values for human interchange. Don't be a know-it-all, but don't fail to share everything that might be helpful. Don't be in a hurry, too impatient to listen.

We also say, stick to dialogue. Don't give up, even if it becomes difficult. It's normal. There can be enormous resistance to speaking openly about one group's issues with another. And women are often especially afraid of hurting someone's feelings, stepping on toes, or sounding racist by bringing up feelings that might sound like stereotypes.

The Institute for MultiRacial Justice, whose mission is to help build alliances between peoples of color and combat conflicts, has experience with these barriers and inhibitions. One lesson has been the difficulty of having such dialogue in a large, public gathering. This was what happened at three forums with multicultural panelists in the late 1990s in the Bay Area. At the third session, the panelists included an African American journalist who came close to provoking real discussion when she described the feelings of some African Americans about bilingual education. She was not afraid of being provocative, which is often what we need most. But we often censor ourselves in public spaces. So the Institute tried smaller workshops as a way of facilitating dialogue. At one session, mixed-race participants expressed dissatisfaction with not having their own caucus like the race-specific people. This could be corrected.

What should we do, given the reluctance to speak openly? We must acknowledge our tendency toward silence around race and difference and work on solutions. Role-playing about some divisive issue can open people's eyes and generate discussion. Humor and a few provocative questions can loosen the grip of self-consciousness. It might help to set up a task force to undertake some specific project, like Black/Brown people working together to win more affordable housing.

Culture can also help generate communication and build bridges between different communities, as youth have shown with hip-hop, spoken word, and other forms of cultural expression. It can be a way for women to make fun of the differences or celebrate similarities,

as the Latina Theater Lab did together with young Asian women actresses a few years ago in San Francisco. Cultural expression can liberate our alliance-building energy and talents.

Building an alliance comes most easily when it emerges organically from a conflict situation. After the so-called "Rodney King riots" in Los Angeles, as clashes continued between African Americans and Koreans, church leaders from San Francisco's Black community invited their members to meet and talk about the conflict with Koreans and other Asian Americans. Again it was a large public meeting without a collective, in-depth analysis of problems. Still, I felt encouraged that the discussion happened at all.

Let me add one last comment about an elusive problem related to building cross-racial respect and solidarity. There is a kind of spiritual violence that women working together for social justice sometimes inflict on one another. Those with more standing, influence, and power within a group dynamic can unthinkingly do violence to the spirit of someone with less power in the group. To deprecate or humiliate a sister out of competitiveness, or out of habits of domination that sometimes accompany leadership skills and intelligence, is to do a harmful violence to her spirit.

This is an insidious kind of personal violence that must never be ignored, for when others say nothing, this second act of violence compounds the damage that's already been done. Silences can feed the cancer of unaddressed conflict, and this has destroyed more than one project, group, or organization. This is a matter of organizational integrity: we cannot righteously continue our struggle, any struggle, without facing it.

Women of color need to act with integrity, speak with honesty, and reject any fear of our differences and conflicts. To transform the goal of unity into a reason for denying conflict, as we sometimes do, is self-defeating. Today, as reactionary forces work to aggravate rather than diminish racism in this society, the times call for courage more than ever. Let us create a stubborn, imaginative, honest, powerful insurgency. Let us counter the enemy forces of divide and conquer with our strategy of unite and rebel!

137

Top Youth Activism Victories of 2009

WireTap

NEW BEGINNINGS FOR JUVENILE JUSTICE

The decades-long battle to close some of the nation's most decrepit youth prisons got a big boost in 2009.

On May 29, Washington, D.C. closed long-troubled Oak Hill Youth Center after years of reported scrutiny over rat-infested cells, abuse by guards and dismal educational programming.

The facility was replaced by New Beginnings Youth Center, a $46 million campus that eschews razor wire fencing and clunky cells for electronic entry cards, a library and a landscaped courtyard.

"[New Beginnings] is the anti-prison," Vincent N. Schiraldo, director of the Department of Youth Rehabilitation Services, told *The Washington Post* in May. "What we had before was a training school for them to become adult inmates. We want them to aspire to college, to be in a place that looks like you care about them."

In August, California state officials announced plans to close Herman G. Stark Youth Correctional Facility in Chino. A report released in 2007 concluded that the environment was so bad at the facility that youth were especially prone to violence or suicide.

The Community Justice Network for Youth (CJNY), a juvenile justice advocacy group based in California, warned that the Stark closure is bittersweet, adding that the state still intends to transform the facility into an adult prison.

. . .

RICHMOND, CALIF. STUDENTS LEARN FROM TRAGEDY

The horrific news of a 16-year-old girl who was allegedly gang-raped outside of her homecoming dance at Richmond High School in Northern California shocked millions. What made it even worse were reports that the attack was witnessed by over a dozen people who, over the course of two hours, allegedly took photos and joined the attack, but failed to intervene or call police.

In the weeks that followed, Richmond High students faced intense media scrutiny. The students, most of whom are working class and of color, were called "animals" and "monsters" by several outraged media observers.

Students acted quickly. With the help of campus-based organizations like Youth Together, a Bay Area education reform organization, hundreds of dedicated students and teachers mobilized candlelight vigils and financial support funds to help the victim recover.

. . .

Students and activists are also developing gender violence trainings to be added into the school's permanent curriculum. By the end of the training, organizers hope that students will examine how they perpetuate violence in their own lives, know how to respond to a bystander and become certified anti-violence trainers.

WISCONSIN STUDENTS DREAM BIG

While federal officials stalled on immigration reform this year, students in Wisconsin went full steam ahead when they successfully passed a state-based version of the DREAM Act.

According to immigration activists, each year thousands of undocumented students are barred from going to college because they don't qualify for state or federal financial aid. Student-led groups across the country have increased their efforts to pass the DREAM Act, a proposed piece of federal legislation that would provide undocumented students with a path toward legalization and qualify them for financial aid.

On June 29, Wisconsin became the 11th state in the nation to allow undocumented students to pay in-state tuition. Students organized with the support of immigrant advocacy groups Voces de la Frontera and Students United for Recognizing Immigrant Rights (SUFRIR).

. . .

N
E
X
T

S
T
E
P
S

It's estimated that between 400–650 undocumented students graduate each year from Wisconsin high schools.

WireTap reporter Antonio Daniel Ramirez, a former Milwaukee public school teacher, recalled that at the school where he taught, four of the class valedictorians in five years had been undocumented students.

GREEN JOBS, CLEAN ENERGY

In February, 12,000 young people descended on D.C. as part of the Power Shift '09 campaign—organized by the Energy Action Coalition—to push for a ban on coal, immediate action on climate legislation this year, investment in green jobs and a 40 percent carbon emissions reduction by 2020. Youth from all 50 states hammered their message home in some 370 meetings with Congressional members and staff.

Organizers have plenty of successes to tout. The stimulus package passed in February set aside $50 billion for the nation's energy economy, focusing mostly on renewable energy, including $5 billion to make homes more energy efficient. Another $500 million was specifically allocated for green jobs. The administration has pushed to eliminate Yucca Mountain nuclear waste storage, and in his address to the joint session of Congress, Obama asked members to deliver legislation to support caps on carbon pollution and investment in renewable energy.

MOVING VOTER REGISTRATION INTO THE 21ST CENTURY

The Bus Federation's affiliates in two states—the Oregon Bus Project and New Era Colorado—helped pass online voter registration bills, which moves the voter registration process in our country closer to the 21st century. These bills make voter registration easier by allowing anyone with a valid state ID the ability to register online and not deal with printing and mailing in the form, as is required in all but five states now. By pairing the voter registration database with state DMV [Department of Motor Vehicles] databases, county clerks can verify the signatures on file to prevent fraud. The whole system will reduce administrative costs in the long-term.

Jeff Mapes reported in *The Oregonian* that registering online has already become popular in Arizona and Washington, the first two states that adopted online registration—particularly among younger voters. In Washington last year, 25 percent of all new registrants signed up by internet.

The director of New Era Colorado, Steve Fenberg, says, "It took us two years to get the bill passed, but the second time we introduced it, it was broadly bipartisan—it passed unanimously in the Senate. I'd say the coolest part of the bill is that it was supported completely by a grassroots effort with no hired lobbyists and it was actually written and lobbied through by young interns of New Era."

STUDENTS WIN HIGHER EDUCATION STANDARDS

Tracking. It's a term used to describe the ugly practice in American public education of placing students in different academic settings based on ability. Score low on a standardized

NEXT STEPS

high school entrance test and a student might be given only remedial and non-rigorous classes, which ultimately can limit their college choices. Californians for Justice (CFJ), a grassroots statewide youth organizing non-profit working for educational and racial Justice in public schools, has been fighting for all students' rights to the A-G course sequence required for admittance at California State and University of California system colleges and universities.

In June 2009, CFJ scored a major victory in Oakland, Calif. when the Oakland Unified School District (OUSD) joined San Jose, Los Angeles and San Diego districts in making A-G courses the standard curriculum for all students.

"An A-G curriculum will allow more Oakland students to be eligible for university," says CFJ Communication Director Paul Tran. "It will lessen student tracking, which is often based on racial and ethnic stereotyping, and follows the will of Oakland parents and students who stated in many surveys that they were interested in attending college." Students played a lead role in achieving the new standards, which take effect in the fall of 2012.

According to CJF Executive Director Jeremy Lahoud, the "A-G for All" campaign involved student leaders from CFJ, Youth in Focus, Asian Immigrant Women Advocates (AIWA), Youth Together, and other youth organizations who worked with OUSD's Meaningful Student Engagement initiative and Education Trust-West to conduct action research on the issue of college access and readiness. Student leaders presented their findings and demands to the OUSD school board prior the board's vote on the A-G resolution.

In one crucial confrontation, Oakland High School senior Cecilia Lopez made her demands known when a skeptical retired teacher and school board meeting regular said A-G would fail. "We are an economically challenged urban community," Lopez said. "If you're saying that the classes are going to be too hard, that means you don't believe. We're not asking for more counselors, we're asking for a counseling system. If we have A-G, it's not whether we can do it or not, it's whether the adults are willing to support us." The school board agreed with Lopez and A-G passed. Now CFJ hopes to bring Fresno and other school districts in California on board.

Lahoud believes the A-G campaign victory in Oakland will build momentum for a statewide and national movement that demands that all students, especially low-income students of color, receive an education that fully prepares them for college, careers and civic participation. "All students deserve the right to choose their path after high school and deserve the curriculum, qualified teachers, supports and resources to get there," says Lahoud. "CFJ is part of a new national alliance, the Alliance for Educational Justice, that demands college and career preparation for all students, regardless of race, income or immigration status, and will be part of launching a national campaign in 2010 to ensure that this demand is part of the reauthorization of the Elementary and Secondary Education Act."

. . .

MEDIA ACTIVISTS PUSH BACK ON DROPOUT STATISTICS

A report by the Center for Labor Market Studies found that nearly 6.2 million students in the United States between the ages of 16 and 24 dropped out of high school in 2007, in what the study calls "a persistent high school dropout crisis." 27.5 percent of Latinos and one in five African Americans drop out in what even Congressm[a]n George Miller's (D-Calif.) Committee on Education and Labor describes as a crisis that threatens America's economic growth. Participants at New Haven, CT's Youth Rights Media (YRM) view these statistics as a call to action and an opportunity to explore hidden aspects of the dropout phenomenon.

YRM's latest documentary film, "Pushed," examines how students are discouraged from succeeding and sometimes forced to leave school after academic or disciplinary difficulties. Students deemed to be too much trouble for mainstream schools risk being "pushed out." An administrator interviewed in the documentary says that "push out" simply means "we've come up with official reasons to say [to a student], 'We don't want you.'"

In the documentary, young narrators ask probing questions about the local impact of the nation's largely invisible dropout crisis. Specifically, the video looks at how many New Haven students are really graduating from high school, and why others fall short of completing their diplomas. It examines where dropouts end up (largely in the criminal justice system) and makes a powerful economic argument for investing more in public education as opposed to pushing students into alternative schools and juvenile detention. The documentary presents perspectives from both young people and adults and succeeds in underscoring the need for more investment in education and youth training programs.

Youth Rights Media was initially founded in 2000 by Yale law students Homer Robinson, Gabriel Plotkin and undergrad Laura McCargar as the Juvenile Rights Advocacy Project, a student-run organization with the goal of shifting the dynamic between youth and police officers. They incorporated as YRM in 2002 and began producing documentaries like 2005's "Book 'Em: Undereducated, Overincarcerated," which explores the "school to prison pipeline" and 2007's "Help Wanted," which looks at youth employment opportunities.

. . .

L.A. COMMUNITY ACTIVIST JOINS OBAMA ADMINISTRATION

President Obama isn't the only grassroots community organizer to make it to the White House in 2009. He'll be joined in November by Los Angeles youth activist Alberto Retana . . . who spent the past 11 years working with the Community Coalition (CoCo), a non-profit social service and civic engagement organization based in South Central L.A. Retana joins the Obama administration as the new director of Community Outreach for the Department of Education. This is a major achievement for Retana and youth activists everywhere, illustrating that "people power" works.

According to CoCo Communications Director Jung Hee Choi, Retana joined the coalition in 1998 and served as youth director of the coalition's Youth Empowered thru Action program. He has been a strong advocate for African American and Latino unity and also led the fight to pass A-G curriculum standards for all students in L.A. public schools. Now at the Dept. of Ed he'll work with communities across the country to give them a voice in shaping federal education reform policy. Not bad for a man still in his 20s.

After being honored by CoCo at their annual staff dinner in October at the Biltmore Hotel in downtown L.A., where he was commended for his hard work and notable sense of humor, Retana set out touring schools with Secretary of Education Arne Duncan. Retana will help the Obama administration with its school turn-around projects in L.A. and other school districts.

Choi sees Retana's appointment as a validation of the Community Coalition's work. "We feel really proud that he comes out of our organization," she told WireTap by phone from her office in L.A. Choi says that Retana excels at both the "art and science" of organizing. Choi recalled how Retana inspired one young ardent female student organizer who challenged Retana's approach of allowing all youth to participate in his actions regardless of political knowledge or commitment. He eventually convinced her that activism is something that can be nurtured over time.

NEXT STEPS

Permission Acknowledgements and Citations

Ahmad, A. (2008). Oral history of Adam Fattah. In L. Cristillo (ed.), *This is Where I Need To Be: Oral Histories of Muslim Youth in NYC* (pp. 27–30). New York: Student Initiative Press/CPET, Teachers College, Columbia University. Reprinted with permission of the Student Initiative Press.

Anzaldúa, G. (1994). Allies. *Sinister Wisdom* (52), 47–52. Reprinted by permission of Anzaldúa Literary Trust.

Anzaldúa, G. (1999). *La Frontera: The New Mestiza* (2nd edition, pp. 99–120). San Francisco: Aunt Lute Books. Selections of "La Conciencia de la Mestiza: Towards a New Consciousness." From *Borderlands/La Frontera: The New Mestiza*. Copyright © 1987, 1999, 2007 by Gloria Anzaldúa. Reprinted by permission of Aunt Lute Books.

Arminio, J. (2000). Waking up white: What it means to accept your legacy, for better or worse. *About Campus* 5(1), 29–30. Reprinted with permission of John Wiley & Sons, Inc.

Ashley and Deborah. (2007). How to curse in sign language. In J. Mooney (ed.), *The Short Bus: A Journey Beyond Normal* (pp. 106–122). New York: Henry Holt. Adapted from pages 106–122 "How to curse in sign language" from *The Short Bus: A Journey Beyond Normal* by Jonathan Mooney. Copyright © 2007 by Jonathan Mooney. Reprinted by arrangement with Henry Holt and Company, LLC.

Aviles, Q. (2007). My tongue is divided into two. In R. Suarez, F. McCount, T. Miller (eds), *How I Learned English: 55 Accomplished Lessons in Language and Life* (pp. 175–181). Cambridge, MA: South End Press. By permission of the author.

Ayvazian, A., Tatum, B. D. (2004). Women, race and racism: A dialogue in black and white. In J. V. Jordan, M. Walker, L. M. Hartling (eds), *The Complexity of Connection* (pp. 147–163). New York: The Guilford Press. Reprinted with permission of the publisher.

Bell, J. (1995). *Understanding Adultism: A Key to Developing Positive Youth-Adult Relationships*. Available at http://www.freechild.org/bell.htm. Reprinted with permission of John Bell, Youth-Build USA.

Bell, L. A. (2007). Theoretical foundations for social justice education. In M. Adams, L. A. Bell, P. Griffin (eds), *Teaching for Diversity and Social Justice* (2nd edition, pp. 2–6). New York: Routledge. Permission to reprint granted by the editors.

Bernards, R. (2000). Pioneers in dialogue: Jews building bridges. In M. Adams, W. J. Blumenfeld, R. Castañeda, H. W. Hackman, M. L. Peters, X. Zúñiga (eds), *Readings for Diversity and Social Justice* (pp. 191–198). New York: Routledge. Reprinted with permission of the author

Bernstein, A. (2004, June 4). Women's pay: Why the gap remains a chasm. *Business Week* [on-line]. Reprinted by permission of the publisher.

Blow, C. (2012). Real Men and Pink Suits. *The New York Times* (November 2). © 2012 *The New York Times*. All rights reserved. Used by permission and protected by the Copyright Laws of the United States. The printing, copying, redistribution, or retransmission of this Content without express written permission is prohibited.

Blumenfeld, W. J. (1992). How homophobia hurts everyone. *Homophobia: How We All Pay the Price* (pp. 1–12). Boston: Beacon Press. Reprinted by permission of the author.

Blumenfeld, W. J. (2006). Christian privilege. *Equity & Excellence in Education* 39(3), 195–210. Taylor & Francis.

Bryan, W. V. (2006). Struggle for freedom: Disability rights movements. In W. Bryan (ed.), *In Search of Freedom: How Persons With Disabilities Have Been Disenfranchised from the Mainstream of American Society and How the Search for Freedom Continues* (pp. 31–50). Springfield, IL: Charles C. Thomas. From Willie V. Bryan, *In Search of Freedom*, 2nd edition, 2006. Courtesy of Charles C. Thomas Publisher, Ltd., Springfield, Illinois.

Butler, R. N. (2008). Ageism: Another form of bigotry. *The Longevity Revolution: The Benefits and Challenges of Living a Long Life* (pp. 40–59). New York: PublicAffairs. From *The Longevity Revolution: The Benefits and Challenges of Living a Long Life* by Robert N. Butler. All rights reserved. Copyright © 2008 by Robert N. Butler, M.D. Reprinted by permission of PublicAffairs, a member of Perseus Books Group.

Carbado, D. W. (2005). Privilege. In E. P. Johnson, M. G. Henderson (eds), *Black Queer Studies: A Critical Anthology* (pp. 190–206). Durham, NC: Duke University Press. Devon W. Carbado, "Privilege," in *Queer Black Studies*, pp. 190–191, 198–206. Copyright © 2005, Duke University Press. All rights reserved. Used by permission of the publisher.

Castañeda, C. (2008). *FLEXing Cross-Cultural Communication*. Unpublished manuscript. University of Wyoming. Reprinted by permission of the author.

Center on Aging Studies, University of Missouri-Kansas City and University of Missouri Extension. *Black Elderly*. http://cas.umkc.edu/casww/blackeld.htm. Printed with permission of the Center on Aging Studies, University of Missouri-Kansas City and University of Missouri Extension. http://cas.umkc.edu/casww/blackeld.htm.

Cerney, J. (2007). Historical and cultural influences in deaf education. In J. Cerney (ed.), *Deaf Education in America: Voices of Children from Inclusion Settings* (pp. 9–18). Washington, DC: Gallaudet University Press. From *Deaf Education in America: Voices of Children from Inclusion Settings*. Copyright © 2007 Janet Cerney. Reprinted by permission of Gallaudet University Press.

Chernik, A. F. (1995). The body politic. In B. Findlen (ed.), *Listen Up: Voices from the Next Feminist Generation* (pp. 103–111). Seattle, WA: Seal Press. From *Listen Up* by Barbara Findlen. Copyright © 1995, 2001 by Barbara Findlen. Reprinted by permission of Seal Press, a member of Perseus Books Group.

Chess, S., Kafer, A., Quizar, J., Richardson, M. U. (2008). Calling all restroom revolutionaries! In M. B. Sycamore (ed.), *That's Revolting! Queer Strategies for Resisting Assimilation* (pp. 216–229). Brooklyn: Soft Skull Press. Copyright © 2008 by Mattilda Bernstein Sycamore from *That's Revolting: Queer Strategies for Resisting Assimilation*. Reprinted by permission of Counterpoint.

Chung, O. (2001). Finding my eye-dentity. In V. Nam, A. Quil (eds), *YELL-Oh Girls! Emerging Voices Explore Culture, Identity, and Growing Up Asian American* (pp. 137–139). New York: Quill/HarperCollins. "Finding my eye-dentity" by O. Chung, pp. 137–139, from *YELL-Oh Girls!* by Vickie Nam. Copyright © 2001 by Vickie Nam. Reprinted by permission of HarperCollins Publishers.

Clare, E. (2003). Gawking, gaping, staring. In B. Guter, J. Killacky (eds), *Queer Crips: Disabled Gay Men and Their Stories* (pp. 211–215). New York: Harrington Park Press. Reprinted with permission of the publisher.

Colligan, S. (2004). Why the intersexed shouldn't be fixed: Insights from queer theory and disability studies. In B. Smith, B. Hutchinson (eds), *Gendering Disability* (pp. 45–58). New Brunswick, NJ: Rutgers University Press. Smith, Bonnie G., and Beth Hutchinson (eds), *Gendering Disability*. Copyright © 2004 by Rutgers, the State University. Reprinted by permission of Rutgers University Press.

Collins, C., Yeskel, F., United for a Fair Economy and Class Action (2005) Copyright © 2005 by Chuck Collins, Felice Yeskel, United for a Fair Economy and Class Action. Text and charts originally appeared in *Economic Apartheid in America* by Chuck Collins and Felice Yeskel with United for a Fair Economy and Class Action.

Collins, P. H. (1993). Toward a new vision: Race, class, and gender as categories of analysis and connection. *Race, Gender, and Class* 1(1), 36–45. Reprinted with permission of the publisher.

Curry, D. (1993). People of color over 50. *Older and Bolder* 5, 31. Copyright © 1993 Rational Island Publishers.

Dalmage, H. M. (2003). Patrolling racial borders: Discrimination against mixed race people. In M. P. Root and M. Kelley (eds), *Multiracial Child Resource Book: Living Complex Identities* (1st edition, pp.18–25). Seattle, WA: Mavin Foundation. Reprinted with permission.

Davis, L. J. (2000). Go to the margins of the class: Disability and hate crimes. In L. Francis, A. Silvers (eds), *Americans with Disabilities: Exploring Implications of the Law for Individuals and Institutions* (pp. 331–340). New York: Routledge.

Dohrn, B. (2000). "Look out kid, it's something you did": The criminalization of children. *The Public Assault on America's Children: Poverty, Violence, and Juvenile Injustice*. New York: Teachers College Press. Reprinted with permission of the publisher.

Durkin, K. (2008). *Police Make Life Hell for Youth of Color*. Available at http://www.workers.org/2008/us/police_OS22/print.php. Copyright © 2008 Workers World. Verbatim copying and

distribution of this entire article is permitted in any medium without royalty provided this notice is preserved.

Echo-Hawk, W. R. (1993). Native American religious liberty: Five hundred years after Columbus. *American Indian Culture & Research Journal* 17(3), 33–45. Reprinted from the *American Indian Culture and Research Journal*, volume 17, number 3, by permission of the American Indian Studies Center, UCLA. © 2008 Regents of the University of California.

Eck, D. (2001). *A New Religious America: How a "Christian Country" Has Become the World's Most Religiously Diverse Nation* (pp. 294–321). San Francisco: HarperSanFrancisco. Pages 297–300, 304—06, 316–20, 320–28 [3209 words], as specified, from *A New Religious America* by Diana L. Eck. Copyright © 2001 by Diana L. Eck. Reprinted by permission of HarperCollins Publishers.

Erevelles, N. (2006). Disability in the new world order. In INCITE! Women of Color against Violence (eds), *Color of Violence: The INCITE! Anthology* (pp. 25–31). Cambridge, MA: South End Press. Reprinted with permission of the publisher.

Evans, N. J., Washington, J. (2009). Becoming an ally: A new examination (updated version). Original (1991) in N. J. Evans, V. A. Wall (eds), *Beyond Tolerance: Gays, Lesbians, and Bisexuals on Campus* (pp.195–204). Alexandria, VA: American College Personnel Association. Reprinted with permission from the American College Personnel Association (ACPA), One Dupont Circle, NW at the Center for Higher Education, Washington, DC 20036.

Fayad, M. (1994) The Arab woman and I. In J. Kadi (ed.), *Food for Our Grandmothers: Writings by Arab American and Arab Canadian Feminists* (pp. 170–172). Cambridge, MA: South End Press. Reprinted with permission of the publisher.

Gansworth, E. (2003). Identification pleas. In M. Moore (ed.), *Genocide of the Mind* (pp. 269–279). New York: Thunder's Mouth Press/Nations Books. From *Genocide of the Mind* by MariJo Moore. Copyright © 2003 Amerinda. Reprinted by permission of Nation Books, a member of Perseus Books Group.

Giecek, T. S. with United for a Fair Economy. (2007). *Teaching Economics As If People Mattered: A High School Curriculum Guide to the New Economy*. Boston: United for a Fair Economy. Reprinted with permission of the publisher.

Gilbert, M. (2002). *The Routledge Atlas of the Holocaust* (3rd edition). New York: Routledge.

Gilbert, M. (2003). *The Routledge Atlas of Jewish History* (6th edition). New York: Routledge.

Gokhale, D. (2005). The InterSEXion: A vision for a queer progressive agenda. *InterSEXion*. Online journal: http://intersexion.org/?q=node/1. Reprinted with permission of INTERSEXION. ORG, an Online Queer Progressive Community. This essay was written by Deepali Gokhale, with valuable input from many conversations with members of the queer community in Atlanta, GA.

Goodnough, A. (2012). Student Faces Town's Wrath in Protest Against a Prayer. From *The New York Times* (January 27). © 2012 *The New York Times*. All rights reserved. Used by permission and protected by the Copyright Laws of the United States. The printing, copying, redistribution, or retransmission of this Content without express written permission is prohibited.

Green, J. (1996/1999). Look! No, don't! The invisibility dilemma for transsexual men. In K. More, S. Whittle (eds), *Reclaiming Genders: Transsexual Grammars at the Fin de Siècle* (pp. 117–131). New York: Cassell. By kind permission of Continuum International Publishing Group.

Griffin, P. (1998). Sport: Where men are men and women are trespassers. In *Strong Women, Deep Closets: Lesbians and Homophobia in Sport* (pp. 16–28). Champaign, IL: Human Kinetics. From P. Griffin, 1998, *Strong Women, Deep Closets: Lesbians and Homophobia in Sport* (Champaign, IL: Human Kinetics), 16–28.

Grinde, D. A., Jr. (2004). Taking the Indian out of the Indian: U.S. policies of ethnocide through education. *Wicazo SA Review* 19, 25–32. Reprinted by permission of the publisher, University of Minnesota Press. Copyright 2004 by the Association for American Indian Research.

Grossman, D., with Christensen, L. W. (1998). Mass psychiatric casualties. *On Combat: The Psychology and Physiology of Deadly Conflict in War and in Peace*. (pp. 11–13). Millstadt, IL: Warrior Science Group. Reprinted with permission of the author.

Gullette, Margaret, M. (2011). Taking a stand against ageism at all ages: A powerful coalition. In *On The Issues Magazine: The Progressive Women's Magazine*. Reprinted with permission.

Haga, K. (2012). *Chicago's peace warriors. Rethinking Schools: Stop the School to Prison Pipeline*, Winter 2011-2012, 26(2), 33–37. © Rethinking Schools. Reprinted with permission of the publisher.

Hardiman, R., Jackson, B., Griffin, P. (2007). Conceptual foundations. In M. Adams, L. A. Bell, P. Griffin (eds), *Teaching for Diversity and Social Justice* (2nd edition, pp. 2–6). New York: Routledge. Permission to reprint granted by the editors.

Harro, B. (2008). Updated version of The cycle of socialization (2000). In M. Adams, W. J. Blumenfeld, R. Castañeda, H. W. Hackman, M. L. Peters, X. Zúñiga (eds), *Readings for Diversity and Social Justice* (pp. 15–21). New York: Routledge. Printed by permission of the author.

Harro, B. (2008). Updated version of The cycle of liberation (2000). In M. Adams, W. J. Blumenfeld, R. Castañeda, H. W. Hackman, M. L. Peters, X. Zúñiga (eds), *Readings for Diversity and Social Justice* (pp. 463–469). New York: Routledge. Printed by permission of the author.

Hehir, T. (2002). Eliminating ableism. *Harvard Educational Review* 72(1), 1–32. Excerpted with permission from Thomas Hehir, "Eliminating ableism in education," *Harvard Educational Review*, Volume 72:1 (Pring 2002), pp. 1–32. Copyright © by the President and Fellows of Harvard College. All rights reserved. For more information, please visit www.harvardeducationalreview.org.

Heldman, C. (2008, Spring). Out-of-body image: self-objectification—seeing ourselves through others' eyes—impairs women's body image, mental health, motor skills and even sex lives. *Ms. Magazine*, pp. 52–55. Reprinted by permission of *Ms.* magazine, © 2008.

Hilberg, R. (1961/2003). *The Destruction of European Jews* (3rd edition, xi–8). New Haven, CT: Yale University Press. Copyright © 1961, 1985, 2003 by Raul Hilberg.

hooks, b. (1984). Feminism: A movement to end sexist oppression. *Feminist Theory: From Margin to Center* (pp. 17–31). Cambridge, MA: South End Press. Reprinted with permission of the publisher.

hooks, b. (2000). *Where We Stand: Class Matters*. New York: Routledge.

Howland, C. L., Gibavic, E. (n.d.). *Learning Disability Identity Development Model and Social Construct: A Two-Tiered Approach*. Unpublished manuscript. University of Massachusetts, Amherst, MA. Reprinted with permission of authors.

Huber, C. (2001). *Regardless of What You Were Taught to Believe . . . There is Nothing Wrong With You: For Teens*. Murphys, CA: Keep It Simple Books. Reprinted with permission of the publisher.

Hurdis, R. (2002). Heartbroken: Women of color feminism and the third wave. In D. Hernandez, B. Rehman (eds), *Colonize This!* (pp. 279–292). New York: Perseus Books. From *Colonize This!* by Daisy Hernández © 2002 by Daisy Hernández and Bushra Rehman. Reprinted by permission of Seal Press, a member of Perseus Books Group.

Invisible Disabilities Advocate. (2008). *Creating a Fragrance-Free Zone: A Friendlier Atmosphere for People Living With Environmental Illness*. http://www.invisibledisabilities.org/creatingafragrancefreezone. *Creating a Fragrance-Free Zone: A Friendlier Atmosphere for People Living with Environmental Illness*. (2008). The Cleaner Indoor Air Campaign (www.CleanerIndoorAir.org) – Launched by The Invisible Disabilities Advocate (www.InvisibleDisabilities.org). Pamphlet. *Creating a Fragrance-Free Zone: A Friendlier Atmosphere for People Living with Environmental Illness*. Copyright © 2008 The Invisible Disabilities Advocate: www.InvisibleDisabilities.org.

Jaffe, Sarah (Sept 28, 2011). *Is the Near-Trillion-Dollar Student Loan Bubble About to Pop?* Posted on AlterNet Sept 28, 2011. Reprinted with permission.

Johnson, A. G. (1997). Patriarchy. *The Gender Knot: Unraveling Our Patriarchal Legacy*. Philadelphia: Temple University Press. Material excerpted from "Patriarchy, the system: An it, not a he, a them, or an us" from *The Gender Knot: Unraveling Our Patriarchal Legacy* by Allan G. Johnson. Used by permission of Temple University Press. © 1997 by Allan G. Johnson. All Rights Reserved.

Johnson, A. G. (2006). What can we do? *Privilege, Power, and Difference* (2nd edition, pp. 17–40, 125–153). New York: McGraw Hill. Reprinted with permission of The McGraw-Hill Companies.

Joshi, K. Y. (2006). *New Roots in America's Sacred Ground* (pp. 118–144). New Brunswick, NJ: Rutgers University Press. Printed with permission of author and Rutgers University Press.

Katz, J. (1999). *Ten Things Men Can Do to Prevent Gender Violence*. Available at http://www.jacksonkatz.com/wmcd.html. Reprinted with permission of the author.

Katz, J. (2006). Violence against women is a men's issue. *The Macho Paradox* (pp. 5–18). Naperville, IL: Sourcebooks. Copyright © 2006 by Jackson Katz. Reprinted from the book *The Macho Paradox* with permission of its publisher, Sourcebooks.

Kaye/Kantrowitz, M. (1996). Jews in the U.S.: Rising costs of whiteness. In X. Thompson, X. Tyagi (eds), *Names We Call Home*. New York: Routledge.

Kimmel, M. S. (1994). Masculinity as homophobia: Fear, shame and silence in the construction of gender identity. In H. Brod, M. Kaufman (eds), *Theorizing Masculinities* (pp. 119–141). Thousand Oaks, CA: Sage. Reprinted with permission of the publisher.

Kingsley, J. (2004). What I'd tell that doctor. In S. Klein, J. Kemp (eds), *Reflections from a Different Journey: What Adults With Disabilities Wish All Parents Knew* (pp. 13–14). Blacklick, OH: McGraw-Hill Professional. Excerpt from "Who we are" in *Count On Us: Growing Up With Down Syndrome*, copyright © 1994 by Jason Kingsley and Mitchell Levitz, reprinted by permission of Houghton Mifflin Harcourt Publishing Company.

Kirk, G., Okazawa-Rey, M. (2001). Identities and social locations: Who am I? Who are my people? *Women's Lives: Multicultural Perspectives* (2nd edition, pp. 49–59). New York: McGraw Hill. Reprinted with permission of The McGraw-Hill Companies.

Kirk, G., Okazawa-Rey, M. (2001). He works, she works, but what different impressions they make. *Women's Lives: Multicultural Perspectives (2nd edition)*. New York: McGraw Hill. Reproduced with permission of The McGraw-Hill Companies.

LaDuke, W. (2005). Introduction. In J. Baumgardner, A. Richards (eds), *Grassroots* (pp. xi–xv). New York: Farrar, Straus, and Giroux. Introduction by Winona LaDuke from *Grassroots: A Field Guide to Feminist Activism* by Jennifer Baumgardner and Amy Richars. Introduction copyright © by Winona LaDuke. Reprinted by permission of Farrar, Straus and Giroux, LLC.

Larabee, M. (1993). Elder liberation draft policy statement. *Older and Bolder 5*, 19–24. Copyright © 1993 Rational Island Publishers. Reprinted with permission of the publisher.

Leondar-Wright, B. (2005). *Class Matters: Cross-Class Alliance Building for Middle-Class Activists*. Gabriola, BC [Canada]: New Society. Reprinted with permission of the publisher.

Lie, A. (2002). Passing realities. In J. Nestle, C. Howell, R. Wilchins (eds), *GenderQueer: Voices From Beyond the Sexual Binary* (pp. 166–170). Los Angeles: Alyson Books. Reprinted with permission of the publisher.

Lippy, C. H. (2005). Christian nation or pluralistic culture: Religion in American life. In J. A. Banks, C. A. M. Banks (eds), *Multicultural Education: Issues and Perspectives* (5th edition, pp. 110–131). New York: Wiley. Copyright © 2005 John Wiley. Reproduced with permission of John Wiley & Sons, Inc.

Lipsitz, G. (1998). *The Possessive Investment in Whiteness: From Identity to Politics* (pp. 1–23). Philadelphia: Temple University Press. Materials excerpted from "The possessive investment in whiteness" from *The Possessive Investment in Whiteness: From Identity to Politics* by George Lipsitz. Used by permission of Temple University Press. © 2006 by Temple University. All Rights Reserved.

Lorber, J. (1994). "Night to his day": The social construction of gender. *Paradoxes of Gender* (pp. 13–36). New Haven, CT: Yale University Press. Copyright © 1994 Yale University Press. Reprinted with permission of the publisher.

Love, B. J. (2000). Developing a liberatory consciousness. In M. Adams, W. J. Blumenfeld, R. Castañeda, H. W. Hackman, M. L. Peters, X. Zúñiga (eds), *Readings for Diversity and Social Justice* (pp. 470–474). New York: Routledge. Reprint permission granted by the editors.

Maathai, Wangari. From *Unbowed: A Memoir* by Wangari Muta Maathai, copyright © 2006 by Wangari Muta Maathai. Used by permission of Alfred A. Knopf, a division of Random House, Inc.

Mantsios, G. (2007). Class in America—2006. In P. Rothenberg (ed.), *Race, Class, and Gender in the United States: An Integrated Study* (7th edition, pp. 182–197). New York: Worth. Reprinted with permission of the author.

Markee, P. (1993). What allies of elders can do. *Older and Bolder 5*, 93–94. Copyright © 1993 Rational Island Publishers. Reprinted with permission of the publisher.

Martínez, E. (2006). Unite and rebel! Challenges and strategies in building alliances. In INCITE! Women of Color against Violence (eds), *Color of Violence: The INCITE! Anthology* (pp.191–195). Cambridge, MA: South End Press. Reprinted with permission of the publisher.

Meyerowitz, J. (2002). Introduction. *How Sex Changed: A History of Transsexuality in the United States* (pp. 1–9). Cambridge, MA: Harvard University Press. Reprinted by permission of the publisher from *How Sex Changed: A History of Transsexuality in the United States* by Joanne Meyerowitz, pp. 1–2, 4–9, Cambridge, Mass.: Harvard University Press, Copyright © 2002 by the President and Fellows of Harvard College.

Morgan, R. (2007). Connect: A web of words. In E. Ensler (ed.), *A Memory, a Monologue, a Rant and a Prayer* (pp. 119–120). New York: Villard. Reprinted by permission of the author.

Morgenson, G. (2008, July 20). The debt trap: Given a shovel, Americans dig deeper into debt. *The New York Times*. Available at: http://www.nytimes.com/2008/07/20/business/20debt.html?pagewanted=print. From *The New York Times*, July 20, 2008. © 2008 The New York Times. All rights reserved. Used by permission and protected by the Copyright Laws of the United

States. The printing, copying, redistribution, or retransmission of the material without express written permission is prohibited.

Murphy, E. D. (2011, Nov 27). *Post-traumatic Stress Disorder Leaves Scars on the Inside, Iraq Veteran Says*. McClatchy-Tribune Business News. © McClatchy-Tribune Information Services. All Rights Reserved. Reprinted with permission.

Nasir, N. S., Al-Amin, J. (2006). Creating identity-safe spaces on college campuses for Muslim students. *Change: The Magazine of Higher Learning*, March/April Special Issue, 23–27. Reprinted with permission of the Helen Dwight Reid Educational Foundation. Published by Heldref Publications, 1319 Eighteenth St., NW, Washington, DC 20036–1802. Copyright © 2006.

National Latina Institute for Reproductive Health. (2007). *National Statement on Healthcare For All*. Available at http://www.raisingwomensvoices.net/PDF-docs/JumpstartLinkFiles/2bNLIRHHe althcareforAllstatement-FINAL-2.20.08.pdf. Reprinted with permission of National Latina Institute for Reproductive Health.

National Network for Immigrant and Refugee Rights. (2010). *Injustice for All: The Rise of the U.S. Immigration Policing Regime* by the Human Rights Immigrant Community Action Network, an initiative of the National Network for Immigrant and Refugee Rights. Reprinted with permission.

Neely, Ross. Promises Made. Reprinted by permission of Ross Neely.

Nowicki, S. "Modesto-Area Atheists Speak Up, Seek Tolerance." *Modesto Bee* (Aug. 16, 2008). Reprinted with permission.

Oesterreich, H., Knight, M. (2008). Facilitating transitions to college for students with disabilities from culturally and linguistically diverse backgrounds. *Intervention in School and Clinic* 43(5), 300–304. Reprinted with permission of the publisher.

Oliver, M. L., Shapiro, T. M. (2006). Race, wealth, and equality. *Black Wealth/White Wealth: A New Perspective on Racial Inequality* (pp. 11–33). New York: Routledge.

Pelkey, L. (2001). In the LD bubble. In P. Rodis, A. Garrod, M. L. Boscardin (eds), *Learning Disabilities and Life Stories* (pp. 17–28). Boston: Allyn and Bacon. From Pano Rodis, Andre Garrod, and Mary Lynn Boscardin, *Learning Disabilities and Life Stories*, 1/e. Published by Allyn and Bacon/ Merrill Education, Boston, MA. Copyright © 2001 by Pearson Education. Reprinted by permission of the publisher.

Peters, M., Castañeda, C., Hopkins, L., McCants, A. (2008). *Recognizing Ableist Beliefs and Practices and Taking Action as an Ally*. Unpublished manuscript. University of Massachusetts, Amherst, MA. Printed by permission of the authors.

Pew Research Center: Social & Demographic Trends. (July 26, 2011) *Wealth Gaps Rise to Record Highs Between Whites, Blacks and Hispanics* (pp. 1–6). http://www.pewsocialtrends.org/2011/07/26/ wealth-gaps-rise-to-record-highs-between-whites-blacks-hispanics. Reprinted with permission.

Pharr, S. (1996). Reflections on liberation. *In the Time of the Right* (pp. 87–122). Little Rock, AR: Chardon Press. By permission of the author.

Pliner, S. M., Johnson, J. R. (2004). Historical, theoretical and foundational principles of universal instructional design in higher education. *Equity & Excellence in Education* 37(2), 105–113.

Pittelman, K., Resource Generation. *(2005)*. Classified: How To Stop Hiding Your Privilege and Use It For Social Change. Copyright by Karen Pittelman from *Classified*. Reprinted by permission of Counterpoint.

Pittelman, K., Resource Generation. *(2005)*. Deep Thoughts About Class Privilege. Copyright by Karen Pittelman from *Classified*. Reprinted by permission of Counterpoint.

Quindlen, A. (2008, November 24). The loving decision. *Newsweek* [On-line]. Reprinted by permission of International Creative Management, Inc. Copyright © 2008 by Anna Quindlen for *Newsweek*.

Romero, M. (1992). *Maid in the U.S.A*. New York: Routledge.

Roppolo, K. (2003). Symbolic racism, history and reality: The real problem with Indian mascots. In M. Moore (ed.), *The Genocide of the Mind* (pp. 187–198). New York: Thunder's Mouth Press/ Nations Books. From *Genocide of the Mind* by MariJo Moore. Copyright © 2003 Amerinda. Reprinted by permission of Nation Books, a member of Perseus Books Group.

Russo, A., Spatz, M. (n.d.). *Stop the False Race/Gender Divide: A Call to Action*. Unpublished manuscript. Reprinted by permission of the authors.

Saint. (2005). Why can't everybody fear me like that? In Teachers College's Student Press Initiative (eds), *Killing the Sky: Oral Histories from Horizon Academy, Rikers Island*. New York: Student Press Initiative. By permission of the Student Press Initiative.

Sazama, J. (1994). *Tips and Guidelines: For Allies to Young People*. Somerville, MA: Youth on Board. By permission of Youth on Board 58 Day Street Somerville, MA 02144 info@youthonboard.org (p) 617–741–1242 (f) 617–623–4359.

Schlosser, L. Z. (2003). Christian privilege: Breaking a sacred taboo. *Journal of Multicultural Counseling & Development* 31, 195–210. Reprinted from *Journal of Multicultural Counseling & Development* 31, 195–210. © 2003 The American Counseling Association. Reprinted with permission. No further reproduction authorized without written permission from the American Counseling Association.

Schmidt, P. (2007, September 28). At the elite colleges—dim white kids. *The Boston Globe*. © 2007 The Globe Newspaper Company.

Semple, K. (2008, October 16). A Somali influx unsettles Latino meatpackers. *The New York Times*, pp. A1, A21. From the New York Times, October 16, 2008. © 2008 The New York Times. All rights reserved. Used by permission and protected by the Copyright Laws of the United States. The printing, copying, redistribution, or retransmission of the material without express written permission is prohibited.

Serano, J. (2007). Trans woman manifesto. *Whipping Girl: A Transsexual Woman on Sexism and the Scapegoating of Femininity* (pp. 11–20). Emeryville, CA: Seal Press. From *Whipping Girl* by Julia Serano. Copyright © 2007 by Julia Serano. Reprinted by permission of Seal Press, a member of Perseus Books Group.

Sheets, D. J. (2005). Ageing with disabilities: Ageism and more. *Generations* 29(3), 37–41. Reprinted with permission from *Aging with Disabilities: Ageism and More*, volume 29, issue 3, pages 37–41. [Fall]. Copyright © 2005. American Society on Aging, San Francisco, California. www.asaging.org.

Smith, A. (2006). Heteropatriarchy and the three pillars of white supremacy: Rethinking women of color organizing. In INCITE! (eds), *The Color of Violence: The INCITE! Anthology* (pp. 66–73). Cambridge, MA: South End Press. Reprinted with permission of the publisher.

Smith, C. (2007). The personal is political. In *The Cost of Privilege* (pp. 374–382). Fayetteville, NC: Camino Press. Reprinted with permission of the author.

Smith, C. (2007). Social struggle. In *The Cost of Privilege* (pp. 393–402). Fayetteville, NC: Camino Press.

Solís y Martinez, D. E. (2008). Mestiza/o gender: Notes towards a transformative masculinity. In T. Hoppe (ed.), *Beyond Masculinity: Essays by Queer Men on Gender and Politics*. Available at http://www.beyondmasculinity.com/articles/martinez.php. Reprinted with permission of the author.

Spade, D. (2006). Mutilating gender. In S. Stryker, S. Whittle (eds), *The Transgender Studies Reader* (pp. 315–332). New York: Routledge/Taylor & Francis Group.

Stryker, S. (2008). Transgender liberation. *Transgender History* (pp. 59–75). Berkeley, CA: Seal Press/Perseus Books Group. From *Transgender History* by Susan Stryker. © 2008 Susan Stryker. Reprinted by permission of Seal Press, a member of Perseus Books Group.

Takaki, R. (1993). *A Different Mirror: A History of Multicultural America* (pp. 1–17). Boston: Little, Brown. From *A Different Mirror* by Ronald Takaki. Copyright © 1993 by Ronald Takaki. By Permission of Little, Brown & Company.

Tatum, B. D. (1997). *Why Are All the Black Kids Sitting Together in the Cafeteria? And Other Conversations About Race*. New York: Basic Books. From *Why Are All the Black Kids Sitting Together in the Cafeteria?* by Beverly Daniel Tatum. Copyright © 1997 Beverly Daniel Tatum, Ph.D. Reprinted by permission of Basic Books, a member of Perseus Books Group.

Taylor, E. (2010). *Cisgender Privilege: On the Privileges of Performing Normative Gender*. Seal Press. Copyright © 2010 Kate Bornstein. Reprinted by permission of Seal Press, a member of the Perseus Books Group.

van Gelder, Sarah. (2012). How Occupy Wall Street changes everything. In Sarah van Gelder and the editors of *YES! Magazine* (eds), *This Changes Everything: Occupy Wall Street and the 99% Movement* (pp. 1–13). San Francisco: BK: Berrett-Koehler Publishers. Reprinted with permission.

Walker, A. (2007). To stop the violence against women. In E. Ensler (ed.), *A Memory, a Monologue, a Rant and a Prayer* (pp. 173–175). New York: Villard. Reprinted with permission of The Wendy Weil Agency, Inc., First Published by Villard, © 2007 Alice Walker.

Ware, W. (2011). Rounding up the homosexuals: The impact of juvenile court on queer and trans/gender-non-conforming youth. In E. A. Stanley, N. Smith (eds), *Captive Genders: Trans Embodiment and the Prison Industrial Complex* (pp. 77–84). Oakland, CA: AK Press. Reprinted with permission.

Watsky, J. (2012) "On the Spectrum, Looking Out." Unpublished article. Reprinted by permission of the author.

Wendell, S. (1996). The social construction of disability. *The Rejected Body* (pp. 36–56). New York: Routledge.

West, Cornel. *Courage*. 1,034 word excerpt from *Hope on a Tightrope: Words and Wisdom* by Cornel West (SmileyBooks, 2009). Reprinted with permission of the publisher.

Whittaker, C, Salend, S., Elhoweris, H (2009). Religious diversity in schools: Addressing the issues. *Intervention in School and Clinic* 44(5). Copyright © 2009 SAGE Publications. Reprinted by Permission of SAGE Publications.

Williams, B. (2001). What's debt got to do with it? In J. Goode, J. Maskovsky (eds), *The New Poverty Studies: The Ethnography of Power, Politics, and Impoverished People in the United States* (pp. 79–101). New York: New York University Press. Reprinted with permission of the publisher.

Williams, D. R. (2006). From Pearl Harbor to 9/11: Lessons from the internment of Japanese American Buddhists. In S. Prothero (ed.), *A Nation of Religions: The Politics of Pluralism in Multireligious America* (pp. 63–78). Durham: University of North Carolina Press. From *A Nation of Religions: The Politics of Pluralism in Multireligious America* by Stephen Prothero. Copyright © 2006 by the University of North Carolina Press. Used by permission of the publisher. www.uncpress.unc.edu.

Williams, P. (1997). The emperor's new clothes. *Seeing a Color Blind Future: The Paradox of Race* (pp. 3–16). New York: Noonday Press, Farrar, Strauss & Giroux. "The emperor's new clothes" from *Seeing a Color Blind Future: The Paradox of Race* by Patricia J. Williams. Copyright © 1997 by Patricia J. Williams. Reprinted by permission of Farrar, Straus and Giroux, LLC. "The emperor's new clothes" from *Seeing a Color Blind Future: The Paradox of Race*, copyright © 1997 by Patricia J. Williams. Reprinted by permission of Brandt & Hochman Literary Agents, Inc.

WireTap, "Top Youth Activism Victories of 2009." Posted on December 23, 2009. Printed on December 28, 2009. © Wiretap Magazine.

Wolanin, T. R. (2005). Students with disabilities: Financial aid policy issues. *NASFFA Journal of Student Financial Aid* 35(1), 17–26. Reprinted with permission of the publisher.

Young, I. M. (1990). Five faces of oppression. *Justice and the Politics of Difference* (pp. 39–65). Princeton, NJ: Princeton University Press. Young, Iris M.; *Justice and the Politics of Difference*. © 1990 Princeton University Press. Reprinted by permission of Princeton University Press.

Young, Iris, M. (2011). *Responsibility for Justice*. Oxford: Oxford University Press. Reprinted with permission of Oxford University Press.

Zawam, Z. (2008). Oral history of Hagar Omran. In L. Cristillo (ed.), *This is Where I Need to Be: Oral Histories of Muslim Youth in NYC* (pp. 57–60). New York: Student Initiative Press/CPET, Teachers College, Columbia University.

Zúñiga, X. (2003). Bridging differences through intergroup dialogue. *About Campus* 7(6), 8–16. Reprinted with permission of John Wiley & Sons, Inc.

About the Editors

Maurianne Adams is Professor of Education Emerita, Social Justice Education Concentration, School of Education at the University of Massachusetts Amherst. She teaches graduate foundations of social justice courses and consults internationally on faculty leadership, student development, and program implementation for social justice education. She co-edited and (co)wrote chapters for *Teaching for Diversity and Social Justice* (second edition, 2007) and its companion volume *Readings for Diversity and Social Justice* (2000). She co-edited *Strangers and Neighbors: Relations Between Blacks and Jews in the United States* (1999), edited *Promoting Diversity in the College Classroom* (1992), and has published numerous chapters and articles on social justice educational theory and pedagogy. She is editor of *Equity & Excellence in Education.*

Warren J. Blumenfeld is Associate Professor in the School of Education at Iowa State University, specializing in multicultural education and queer studies. His books include *Warren's Words: Smart Commentary on Social Justice* (2012), *Homophobia: How We All Pay the Price* (1992), *Looking at Gay and Lesbian Life* (1993), *Butler Matters: Judith Butler's Impact on Feminist and Queer Studies* (2005), and *Investigating Christian Privilege and Religious Oppression in the United States* (2009). He coedited *Readings for Diversity and Social Justice* (2000, 2010, 2013).

Carmelita (Rosie) Castañeda is a professional educational consultant and trainer. She provides professional development seminars on topics of diversity and inclusion. She is author of *Teaching and Learning in Diverse Classrooms: Faculty Reflections on their Experiences and Pedagogical Practices of Teaching Diverse Students* (2002) and co-editor of *Readings for Diversity and Social Justice* (2000). She received the Latina leadership award, La Superación Latina (2007), given by Students for Campus and Community Chicana Awareness and La Radio Montañesa Voz de la Gente (KOCA) Bilingual Radio Station, Wyoming.

D. Chase J. Catalano is currently the Director of the LGBT Resource Center at Syracuse University and a doctoral candidate in the social justice education program at the University of Massachusetts Amherst. He is co-author of "Transgender Oppression Curriculum Design" for *Teaching for Diversity and Social Justice* (second edition, 2007). His research focuses on trans* men's experiences navigating and negotiating college, marginalized genders and sexualities and (trans) masculinity.

Keri DeJong is a doctoral student in social justice education, University of Massachusetts Amherst. She is an experienced intergroup dialogue facilitator, focusing on issues of race and ethnicity. She currently works in student affairs with young adults in higher education. Her doctoral research is focused on adultism, critical liberation theory, and intergroup dialogue.

Heather W. Hackman served as a tenured professor in the Department of Human Relations and Multicultural Education at St. Cloud State University for 12 years before resigning in 2012 in order to focus full time on her consulting firm (Hackman Consulting Group). While at St. Cloud State she taught courses on social justice and critical multicultural education, heterosexism and homophobia, race and racism in the U.S., and oppression and social change. She received her doctorate in Social Justice Education from the University of Massachusetts at Amherst in 2000 and now consults nationally on issues of deep diversity, equity, and social justice. A majority of her recent training work focuses on issues of racism and white privilege, gender oppression, heterosexism and homophobia, and classism. She has published in the area of social justice education theory and practice, racism in health care (with Stephen Nelson), and is currently working on two books, one addressing anti-racism professional development training for P-12 professionals and another examining racism through the lens of cellular wisdom. In 2009, she was awarded a Research Fellowship with the Great Place to Work Institute and has developed corporate training rubrics augmenting GPTWI's frameworks. She received the Professor of the Year Award four times while at St. Cloud State and is nationally known for her teaching and training. She has served on the board of Minnesota NAME as President, the board of Rainbow Families, numerous committees committed to multicultural and social justice work, and is currently an Advisory Board member for the White Privilege Conference.

Larissa E. Hopkins is the Assistant Director of Student Accessibility Services at Dartmouth College. She arranges academic adjustments and services for students with a wide range of disabilities, and serves as a disability specialist and consultant to students, faculty, staff, and administrative and academic offices. Larissa received her B.A. in Women's Studies and Education from Hamilton College and her M.Ed. in Social Justice Education from the University of Massachusetts Amherst, where she anticipates receiving her Ed.D. in the Fall of 2013. Her doctoral research focuses on the social and academic experiences of White low-income students at small elite liberal arts institutions.

Khyati Y. Joshi is Associate Professor in the Sammartino School of Education at Fairleigh Dickinson University in Teaneck, New Jersey. She is author of *New Roots in America's Sacred Ground: Religion, Race, and Ethnicity in Indian America* (2006), which received the National Association for Multicultural Education's Philip C. Chinn Book Award in 2007. She co-edited *Asian Americans and the New South* (2012) and *Understanding Religious Oppression and Christian Privilege* (2009), and co-wrote "Religious Oppression Curriculum Design" in *Teaching for Diversity and Social Justice* (second edition, 2007). She has presented her research at the White House, the Organization for Security and Cooperation in Europe, and at a host of scholarly and popular conferences in the United States and India, and has been an external advisor for two major Pew reports on Asian Americans. Dr. Joshi provides consultation and professional development for educational institutions on topics related to immigrants in schools, race in education, and religion and public schools.

Barbara J. Love is Professor of Education Emerita, Social Justice Education Concentration, School of Education at the University of Massachusetts Amherst. She co-edited and (co) wrote chapters for *Teaching for Diversity and Social Justice* (second edition, 2007) including the chapters "Ageism and Adultism Curriculum Design," "Racism and White Privilege Curriculum Design," and "Knowing Ourselves as Instructor." She has written chapters for the volume *Readings for Diversity and Social Justice*. She writes on issues of Black Liberation and Community Development and Social Justice and Transformation. She consults nationally and internationally with college faculty and administration, with school systems and with other organizations on issues of diversity, organizational and individual empowerment, and transformation. She has worked with organizations in North and South America, the Caribbean, Europe, the Middle East, and Africa.

Madeline L. Peters is the Director of Disability Services at the University of Massachusetts Amherst. She consults nationally on Accommodation Services. She co-wrote "Ableism Curriculum Design" for *Teaching for Diversity and Social Justice* (second edition, 2007), co-edited *Readings for Diversity and Social Justice* (2000), and as a disability advocate has won a national lawsuit for the disabled.

Davey Shlasko is a trainer and consultant who teaches skills for building just communities and organizations. Davey earned an M.Ed. in Social Justice Education and specializes in trans/gender issues, class/classism, and leadership training. Previous publications include "Queer (v.) Pedagogy" in *Equity & Excellence in Education* (2005), "Transgender Oppression Curriculum Design," with Chase Catalano and Linda McCarthy, in *Teaching for Diversity and Social Justice* (second edition, 2007), and the version of this chapter in the previous edition. Davey currently serves as Director of the Fellows Program in Public Affairs at Coro Center for Civic Leadership, Northern California as well as providing independent trainings.

Ximena Zúñiga is Associate Professor of Education, Social Justice Education Concentration, Department of Student Development, School of Education, University of Massachusetts Amherst. She specializes in philosophical and social foundations of social justice education, dialogues across differences, and action research methods. She is co-editor of *Multicultural Teaching in the University* (1993), *Readings for Diversity and Social Justice* (2000; 2010) and *Intergroup Dialogue in Higher Education: Meaningful Learning about Social Justice* (2007). She recently co-edited a special issue for the *Journal of Equity and Excellence in Education* on intergroup dialogues in k-12, higher education, and communities (February 2012) and has two co-authored books in press: *Dialogues across Difference: Practice, Theory and Research* (Russell Sage Foundation), and *Intergroup Dialogue: Engaging Difference, Social Identity and Social Justice* (Routledge). Recent articles and book chapters address racism, immigration, and globalization issues in anti-racist education and learning outcomes and engagement processes in diversity initiatives and intergroup dialogues in higher education. She also consults widely with faculty, student affairs, and community leaders on social justice education practices such as intergroup dialogues, intergroup leadership, and faculty development.